Praise for Ju

On *Arrows of the Sun*

"The tale is the kind of accomplished fantasy—featuring sound characterization, superior world-building, and more than competent prose—that has won Tarr a large audience." —*Booklist*

"With elegant prose, Tarr beautifully conveys splendid regal settings, realistic politics, convincing cultural details—and cultural clashes. Even when they wield awesome magic energies or manage empires, her appealing characters remain captivatingly human. This is a sweeping saga, spiced with exciting, unexpected plot twists." —*Publishers Weekly*

On *Spear of Heaven*

"This fifth book in Tarr's Avaryan Rising series boasts better writing and more penetrating observations than typical sword-and-sorcery fare." —*Publishers Weekly*

"Tarr leavens this tale of politics and magic with a strong dose of romantic—and sometimes humorous—intrigue, a combination for which she has a special talent." —*Library Journal*

"Tarr is consistently competent or better in all the essentials of fantasy saga construction—characterization, world-building, a system of magic, and, of course, prose . . . No reader who has followed this saga this far will want to miss a new installment. Fantasy collections, take note." —*Booklist*

On *White Mare's Daughter*

"*White Mare's Daughter* is a wonderful book, powerful and evocative. The characters come vividly alive, and the clash—and eventual melding—of the patriarchal nomadic and settled matriarchal agrarian cultures is fascinating."

—Roberta Gellis

"A great adventure, beautifully written!"—Diana Gabaldon

"Culture clashes, war, and goddess worship set the stage for Tarr's well-rounded and lively prehistoric epic . . . Tarr's skillful juxtaposition of two vastly different yet spiritually similar societies gives a sharp edge to this feminist epic."

—*Publishers Weekly*

On *Lord of the Two Lands*

"Judith Tarr's *Lord of the Two Lands* moves away from her previous medieval efforts to the story of Alexander the Great. This is Alexander seen from a viewpoint similar to that in Mary Renault's *The Persian Boy*—someone who joins his campaigns in mid-course. . . . Alexander is as compelling as ever as a central figure for a novel, and Tarr has done her research and writing as well as ever."

—*Chicago Sun-Times*

"Tarr spins an entertaining and often enlightening tale. . . . Her prose is lean and powerful, and she exerts admirable control over an impressive cast of characters."

—*The Washington Post Book World*

"Judith Tarr's *Lord of the Two Lands* is an exciting story of Alexander the Great and his move into Egypt, told through the eyes of Pharaoh Nectanebo's daughter, Meriamon. Tarr has portrayed, in a remarkably believable story, a rich sense of time and place. . . . I simply could not put it down until I had turned the last page."

—Jean M. Auel

"This is ONE OF THE BEST HISTORICAL FANTASIES of the last several years. It makes the character of Alexander the Great very much alive."

—Marion Zimmer Bradley

"The story of Alexander the Great has been pounded into dust, and I never thought to see it done fresh again, but Tarr's inspired choice of heroines has given her a whole new slant on material so familiar that the names of even minor figures fall on the ears with a thousand echoes."   —Cecelia Holland

AVARYAN RESPLENDENT

TOR BOOKS BY JUDITH TARR

Avaryan Rising
The Hall of the Mountain King
The Lady of Han-Gilen
A Fall of Princes

Avaryan Resplendent
Arrows of the Sun
Spear of Heaven
Tides of Darkness

The Hound and the Falcon
The Isle of Glass
The Golden Horn
The Hounds of God

Lord of the Two Lands

The Horse Goddess Books
Lady of Horses
White Mare's Daughter
Daughter of Lir
The Shepherd Kings

Historical Novels
Pillar of Fire
Throne of Isis
Queen of Swords
The Eagle's Daughter

JUDITH TARR

AVARYAN RESPLENDENT

A TOM DOHERTY ASSOCIATES BOOK
NEW YORK

AVARYAN RESPLENDENT

Copyright © 2003 by Judith Tarr

Arrows of the Sun copyright © 1993 by Judith Tarr
Spear of Heaven copyright © 1994 by Judith Tarr
Tides of Darkness copyright © 2002 by Judith Tarr

An Orb Edition
Published by Tom Doherty Associates, LLC
175 Fifth Avenue
New York, NY 10010

www.tor.com

Library of Congress Cataloging-in-Publication Data

Tarr, Judith.
    Avaryan resplendent / Judith Tarr.—1st Orb ed.
        p. cm.
    "A Tom Doherty Associates book"
    Contents: Arrows of the sun—Spear of heaven—Tides of darkness.
    ISBN 0-765-30902-5
    1. Avaryan (Imaginary place)—Fiction. 2. Fantasy fiction, American. I. Title.

PS3570.A655A938 2003
813'.54—dc22   2003056466

First Orb Edition: December 2003

Printed in the United States of America

0 9 8 7 6 5 4 3 2 1

CONTENTS

ARROWS OF THE SUN

To Susan Shwartz, for the idea,

and

To the regulars of GEnie's Science Fiction Round Table,
who preferred a finished novel to the usual social niceties

With special thanks to
Jeanne Zimmerman and Harry Turtledove

PART ONE

Endros Avaryan

ONE

HIS MAJESTY IS IN A RARE MOOD THIS MORNING."

His majesty, having flung back the shutters to let in the newborn sunlight, turned in the flood of it and laughed. "His majesty is his majesty this morning. What's rarer than that?"

Vanyi stretched in her tangle of pillows and coverlets. She was warm all through, and not with sunlight.

He was bathing in it, pouring it over him like water. Sun's child, that one, morning-born, bearing the Sun in his hand. It flamed there, gold born in the living flesh, mark and price of his lineage: *Ilu'Kasar*, brand of the god.

She, who would have welcomed more sleep, still found it in her to smile at the god's youngest child. "Oh, there are rarities, my lord, and there are rarities. But not every day sees a ten years' regency ended, or a throne taken that's sat empty so long."

He came out of the light, but it was on him still, limning with gold the arch of a cheekbone, the angle of a shoulder. "I should be terrified, I think," he said.

"Probably," said Vanyi. She sat up, drawing knees to chest and clasping them. She shivered. It was not the warmest of mornings, bare spring that it was, and the sun though bright was cool.

Warmth wound about her: coverlet, and Estarion's arms about that, and his white smile. "I had all my panic terrors yesterday. Today I'll be pure arrogance."

"Joy," said Vanyi. "Leave a little room for that."

He left more than a little: enough for both of them several times over.

She noticed before he did that they had a watcher. Green eyes blinked at them. Ivory fangs bared in a yawn.

"And a fair morning to you," said Vanyi, "milady ul-cat."

The great cat-body poured itself across their feet, rumbling with purr. Vanyi worked her toes into fur the color of shifting shadows, sleek and almost stiff without, soft as sleep within. Estarion ran a teasing finger down her ribs. She yelped and attacked him until he cried for mercy.

The next visitor announced herself more properly than the cat had. The page was young enough to look everywhere but where his master was. There was no telling if he blushed: he was a northerner, and dark as Lady Night. "My lord," he said. "Sire. The Empress Regent— The Lady — Your mother — She—"

"Let her come in," said Estarion before Vanyi could speak. She could have hit him. She scrambled at blankets, cursed the hair that knotted and tangled and got in the way, and added a choice word for young idiots of all-but-emperors who did not care who saw them naked in the morning.

He kissed her into fuming silence. Knowing—damn him—what his mother would see: her son making free of his favors with his lady of the moment.

"Not that," he said, drawing back, smoothing her hair. Reading her through all her shields and her magery, and hardly aware that he did it. "Never that, my love."

Vanyi let her gaze fall. Even when she was angry, his touch could make her body sing.

The empress found them almost decorous: Vanyi with the coverlet drawn to her chin, Estarion stretched across her feet with the cat. He raised himself on his elbow and smiled his sweetest smile. "Mother! I hadn't thought to see you here so early."

"Hardly early," said the empress. "The sun has been up for a long hour." But she smiled, and kissed him on forehead and cheeks with ceremony that was all love.

One could see, thought Vanyi, where Estarion had his darkness and his slimness, and much of his height. He did not have his mother's beauty. His face was pure Varyani: high-cheeked, hawk-nosed, neither ugly nor handsome but simply itself. He looked like his firstfather, people said, Mirain, who had called himself the son of the god: gone these fourscore years, and four emperors since, and Estarion the fifth of them, sixth in the line that sprang from the Sun. From Ganiman his father he had the thick curling hair of the western blood, and the family profile; and, through some alchemy of breeding, his eyes.

He was born to be stared at, but he hated to be stared at for that. When he was younger he had cultivated a concealment of flamboyance, made a fashion of hats and hoods, or worn garments so outrageously cut or colored that lookers-on forgot his single, and singular, oddity. He had grown out of that. But he still would not linger in front of a mirror, or happily remind himself that he was at least in part a westerner.

It might have been simpler if the rest of him had not seemed pure northern tribesman. But his eyes were Asanian, and worse than that: royal Asanian. Eyes of the Lion, they called them in the west. Pure and burning gold, seeming whiteless unless he opened them very wide; astonishing in that dusk-dark face.

He was not thinking of them now, regarding his mother with every evidence of content. But he said, "Do you mind terribly? That I'm taking your titles away?"

"I mind," she said, "that I am laying all the burdens on you, and you so young still."

He sat up sharply. The cat growled, startled. He soothed her with an absent hand. "I'm hardly a child any longer."

"You are a man," his mother agreed willingly, "and most well grown. And yet . . ."

"It's time," he said. His voice was steady.

"Time and past time," said the empress regent. "No; that office I lay down in all gladness. But I am still a mother, and to a mother her child is always and ever that, though he wear a beard of august silver, and hold empires under his sway."

Estarion's hand went to his chin. There was no silver in the stubble there, nor would be for a while yet, Vanyi reckoned.

The empress smiled and held out her hand. "Come, Starion. Your servants have been waiting this past hour and more."

He was up almost before she finished speaking, kissing her hand, casting himself upon the mercies of his bath-servants. The empress did not move to follow him. Vanyi, who had known better than to think herself forgotten, restrained herself from pulling the blanket over her head. She met the dark stare steadily. "Lady," she said.

"Priestess," said the empress. Her tone was cool.

"Are you sorry," Vanyi asked, "that virginity is no longer a requirement of priesthood?"

"Hardly," said the empress. "My son would object strenuously if you were sentenced to the sun-death."

"Ah," said Vanyi, "but would you?"

Her heart was beating hard. She had been Estarion's lover these past three seasons, and yet she had never exchanged more than brief courtesy with Estarion's mother. Vanyi knew what the court thought of her who had walked straight from the road of her priestess-Journey into the emperor's bed. What the empress thought, no one knew. Vanyi was mageborn and priestess of the Sun. The Lady Merian was a wisewoman of the north, priestess of the goddess who was the dark behind the sun, mistress of mages. Her soul was a blinding brilliance, her thoughts a shape of silence.

She said, "My son is very fond of you."

"I rather think he loves me," Vanyi said. There was a snap in it.

"He has a warm heart," said the empress. "And you were his first woman."

Vanyi's cheeks were burning. No doubt they blazed scarlet. It was all the color they ever had. Corpse-woman, people called her here, because she was as white as new milk, and they were all black or brown or ruddy bronze. Even the Asanians were, at worst, old ivory.

But Estarion loved her pallor; loved to cup his dark hand over her white breast, and marvel at the play of blue veins under the skin.

"Yes, he fancies that he loves you," the empress went on, gentle and cruel. "He knows he cannot marry you. You are a commoner, and an Islander at that."

"You tell me nothing I haven't long known," Vanyi said. "Why didn't you stop me when I first set eyes on him? I might have gone away then. I was appalled at myself: that I had such thoughts, and he so high."

"I trusted in your good sense," the empress said. Vanyi stared. The empress smiled. "You know what you are, and what you are not. You will not be empress: you are too thoroughly unsuitable. But you give yourself no airs; you claim no advantage, though he would give you the moons if you asked for them. You bear him no child, nor shall, while the bonds of the Journey seal your womb. And," she said, "you are very good for him."

Vanyi had nothing to say. The words had drained out of her.

"Remember," the empress said, "how his father died. How he had taken his son with him into Asanion after too long a sojourn in the east, for the heir to the throne must know all of the empire he would rule; and how, when he came to the city of kings, to Kundri'j Asan, his death was waiting for him. No clean death in battle, but poison in a cup, and malice wound about it, and sorcery sealed within it."

Vanyi knew. Estarion never spoke of it, but others did, round about; and she was a mage of the temple in his city. His father had died as he watched. He had known the poison for what it was. He found the mage who had wrought the poison, and mustered all his power of heart and soul and mind, and made of it a weapon, and killed the man who had killed his father. He lost his power for that, and nearly his mind. He was twelve years old. A child, but never a child after.

His power had come back, but slowly, and never in the measure that it had had. Of memory he had nothing, save that sometimes he dreamed, and woke screaming. And he would not go to Asanion, or speak of it save as he must, or grant more than cold courtesy to its people who came to pay him homage.

"Before you came," his mother said, "we had begun to fear for him. He had seemed to be recovered from the black days, in mind if not in magery; and then once more, as he became a man, the darkness closed in. Never a night passed but that he dreamed, and dreamed ill. He strove to hide it, to wall it with such power as was left to him. But we knew. We were in great dread for his sanity."

"He is perfectly sane," said Vanyi, more stiffly than she liked.

"He is," said the empress, unruffled. "We owe you a debt for that."

"But not enough to give us leave to marry."

"His empress must be bred to it," said the daughter of a mountain chieftain.

"And I was bred to the nets and the boats and the fish." Vanyi considered rage, but found it insufficient. "What, when he takes his proper bride, and I take my leave? What if the dreams come back? What will you do then?"

"We shall settle that when we come to it," the empress said. "No law forbids him a concubine, or a lover of choice apart from the woman who shares his throne."

"His empress might have something to say of that," said Vanyi.

"She may," the empress said. "She may not." She bent her head. It was almost a bow. "For this day and for the days until he takes his bride, you have my blessing. Prosper well, priestess of the Sun, Guardian of the Gates. Cherish my son."

"Always," said Vanyi. That much at least she could promise.

Time was in the north when the king came naked to his throne, and proved to his people that he was male and whole and fit to rule. Estarion might have liked that:

he had no shame of his body, and he loved to be outrageous. But the south was a staider place.

Estarion had not wanted excessive ceremony, and he would not suffer the tenfold robe of the western emperors. In the end he consented to be a southerner in trousers and embroidered coat, with his hair in the single plait of a priest, and no ornament but the heavy golden torque of his priesthood. The high soft boots and the trousers were white unblemished, and the coat was cloth of gold. Against it he was all the darker, his eyes all the more brilliantly gold. He did not, for once, try to hide them.

Vanyi, anonymous among the priests and the lesser nobles, watched as he passed in procession. He was aware of her: a ghost-hand lay brief against her cheek, a ghost-smile warmed her from within. Most of him was centered on the rite. For a moment she walked within him down the long aisle between the white pillars, from sun to shade and back to sun again, and before him, looming larger as he came closer to it, the simple chair set on its dais. The wall behind it burst and bloomed in gold, the rayed sun of his fathers, image and remembrance of the god. But he saw nothing of the gold, no more than he saw of the people who thronged the hall and filled the courts without. The throne was waiting.

He had never sat in it. He was too young and it too strong, his regents had thought, for the fragility of his mind. It was a simple thing, a chair carved of pale stone, neither silver nor grey but somewhere between. But there was mighty magic in it. It was carved of dawnstone, the stone that woke to the coming of the sun, and imbued with the power of his line.

It was glimmering, Vanyi thought. Faintly; difficult to see from so far, with so many bodies between. But it was more silver than grey.

He was closed to her now. For a moment she was empty, bereft; then she shook herself, bolstering the wards about her thoughts. Far behind them, deep and safe, she allowed herself to smile. A year yet, and four days: that long she had to wait until her Journey was done. Then the oath was ended. The bonds of her womb were loosed. And she would give him the gift she most longed to give: an heir of her body. Let another be empress if it would please his princes and his lady mother. Vanyi would bear his son.

The throne gleamed clearly now, a pure light that though pale was never cold, like the sky at the coming of the sun. She could not see Estarion's face. She knew that it was rapt, like the rest of him. Drawn toward it; bound to it.

He paused at the foot of the dais, with the high ones about him. The empress in royal white, tall and cold and beautiful. The chancellor of his empire, elegant southern prince with his startling bright hair. Priests of Sun and Shadow, god and goddess, torqued in gold and in black iron. The lords of his council in their manifold splendor, from bearded, kilted, glittering northerner to clean-shaven trousered southerner to robed and turbaned syndic of the Nine Cities. And one lone westerner in the fivefold robe of a prince, wearing an ambassador's fluted hat.

They surrounded their emperor, overwhelming him. Then he mounted above them. His mother followed, and his chancellor, a step behind, at right hand and left. On the last step he paused. They passed him and turned. They were of a height, northerner and southerner, dark woman and bronze-skinned man with his hair the color of new copper. They bowed to one another and held out each a hand.

Estarion laid his hands in theirs and let them draw him upward. He was taller than either, and for a moment he seemed very slight, almost frail.

He straightened. Vanyi saw his head come up, his shoulders go back. They were broad, those shoulders, for all the narrowness of the rest of him. He inclined his head to each of his regents. They bowed in return.

He turned. His face was a shadow against the sudden blaze of thronelight. His eyes were full of it.

Without great ceremony, but without haste, he sat. The thronelight blazed like the full sunrise. Vanyi staggered with the power and the glory of it—the great singing surge of exultation. Terrible, magical, awful thing: it knew its lord and servant. It took him to itself.

TWO

DRUMS BEAT, PULSE-BEAT. SLOW, SLOW, THEN SWIFTER, RISING UP AND UP TO a rattle of panic-terror.

The boy ran.

Sometimes as he ran he was himself: wind in his face, breath in his lungs, fire in his blood. Pain, sudden and sharp, as a branch caught his hair and tore it at the roots; or a stone turned underfoot and pierced the unprotected skin; or a thorn sank claw in his side.

Sometimes he was wholly outside of himself. A bird, maybe, in the dark of the trees, looking down at the pale naked thing running from it knew not what, leaving its panic-trail of flesh and blood and acrid human scent.

The law said, Run. The drums said, Run. Therefore he ran.

The mind paused. Saw wood, twilight dimness, sweat-streaming bloody self running from nothing at all, and said, *Why?*

It mastered the feet, slowed them, willed them to a standstill. The heart was harder, and the breath in starved lungs; those, it left to heal themselves. It brought its scattered selves together and bound them with its name.

"Korusan!"

No.

"Koru-Asan!"

Better.

He opened his eyes. The wood was gone, had never been, except in his mind, and in the rattle of the drums. They were silent now. He stood on stone, in walls of stone. Rough tunic rasped on skin as whole as skin could be, no mark that was not long since won, no scar that had not healed.

Cold metal touched his nape. He did not flinch, even inwardly.

"Strong," said the voice behind him, that had known his name. "And self-willed."

"Blood of the Lion," said the man who stood in front of him. The man had no face. None of them did, of all who stood about him: clad in black from crown to toe, not even a glitter of eyes through the swathing of veils. Korusan, whose face was bare for any to see, made of it a mask and schooled his eyes to stillness. They would always betray him, those eyes, unless he mastered them. He was named for them: Koru-Asan, Goldeneyes. Yellow eyes. Eyes of the Lion.

"Proud," said the one behind, the one who held the knife. "Haughty, if truth be told. And why? His blood is none of ours."

"It has its own distinction." Dry, that, from one who stood in the circle.

"And its own destruction." Cold and soft. Korusan stiffened at it. Infinitesimally; but here of all places, now of all times, there could be no concealment. "He will be dead before he is a man; and if he lives to get a son, what will that son be, as weakened as the blood has grown? Dead in infancy, or witless, or mad—if any are born at all of seed so sore enfeebled. Such is the Brood of the Lion."

"He will live long enough," said the dry voice. "He will do what he is born to do."

"Will he live so long?" the cold one inquired.

Run, said the law. And Korusan had run. Keep silent, it said. And he had kept silent. Running had won him nothing but pain. He said, "I will live as long as I must."

"You will be dead at twenty," said the cold one, the cruel one. "You fancy yourself strong enough now; and with magic and physic and training, so you are. But those have their limits. I see the darkness in you. Already it sinks claws in your bones."

"All men die," said Korusan steadily. "It is a gift, maybe, that I know what I shall die of, and when."

"Is it a gift, too, to hate those who willed this doom on you?"

He laughed. They started, those grim men in their circle, and that lightened his mood immeasurably. No one ever laughed in this rite, under this questioning. "They are dead who condemned my house to its death—man without woman and woman without man, lifelong, and never a child of any union but one; and that was their weakness, that they permitted her to live. Or maybe their cruelty. They would know that the sickness was in her, the blood-beast, the thing that goes down from father to son, from mother to daughter, and weakens and twists and kills. But—hate them? No," he said. "No. It was never their choice that she wed daughter to son and son to daughter, and they likewise, to preserve the line pure. If I hate anyone, it is that one. She was a fool, my ancestor. Far better had she done as her brother did, and wedded with barbarians."

"Then the Blood of the Lion would truly be lost," the dry voice said. Not so dry now; there was a whisper of passion in it.

"It is lost in any event," said Korusan. "My sisters are dead or idiots. I may die before I can sire sons. But before I die, I will have our blood-price. The blood of the Sun is more robust than mine, but it too resides in one man, and one man alone. And he has no son."

"That we know of," said the cold one.

"There is none." A new voice, that. It spoke with surety, from an unveiled face. Korusan regarded the man in grey who emerged from the circle. He was not afraid, though he saw the man's shadow, a woman in black, as barefaced as he, and as deadly keen of eye. Lightmage, darkmage.

He raised a brow. The lightmage met his stare blandly and said, "He has no son. No daughter, either."

"I hope," said Korusan, "that he refrains from women, then, until I hold his life in my hands." He smiled at the mages. "You will see to that."

They were affronted. He watched them remember who he was.

The knife shifted on his nape. He spun. The world ran slow, slow. Still, almost it failed to slow enough. He lost a lock of his hair, a drop of blood. He won the knife.

The one who had held it now held a length of uncut gold. Korusan grinned at him and finished what he had begun: set blade to the uncut mane of his youth and cut it away, lock by heavy lock, and stood up a man. The air was cold on his unprotected neck. His head was light. He ran fingers through cropped curls, tugging lightly at them, but never letting down his guard or his weapon.

"No," he said, "I am not of your blood. No bred warrior, I. I was bred to be your master. Bow then, Olenyas. Bow to your lord."

He did not think that he had appalled them. They knew what they had raised. But knowing in the head and knowing in the belly—there, he thought, was a distinction they had not made. There were no eyes to read, to uncover resentment or regret, or even fear, until the one whose knife he had won lowered the outer veil. And then—and this he had not looked for—the inner.

It was a younger face than he had suspected, and more like his own than he could have imagined, even knowing the women and the barefaced children. The Master of the Olenyai regarded him with eyes well-nigh as pure a gold as his, but white-bordered in simple human fashion, and no fear in them, nor overmuch

regret. Then they lowered, and he went down, down to the floor, in the full prostration. "You are my lord," he said, "and my emperor."

"I am not the emperor," said Korusan.

"Then there is none," the Master said. He rose. His eyes came up. That was permitted of Olenyai, to look in the face of royalty.

"I do not wish to be emperor," said Korusan. "I would be Olenyas."

"May you not be both?" the Master said.

Korusan was silent. He had spoken enough foolishness, and far beyond the limits of the rite. He reversed the knife in his hand and bowed as initiate to Master,
and returned the knife to its owner. The Master accepted it. Korusan drew a slow
breath. If it had been refused, then so likewise would he; and he would be emperor
without a throne and Olenyas without the veil, rejected and found unworthy.

The fine steel flashed toward him. He stood his ground even as it neared his
eyes. Even as it licked down, once, twice, and the pain came stinging. He kept his
eyes steady on the Master's face. Ninefold, the scars on that cheek: from cheekbone
to jaw, thinly parallel like the marks of claws. One for each rank of his ascent.

Korusan said, "I will not take second rank for my blood alone."

"Nor do you," said the Master. He wiped the knife clean of Korusan's blood and
sheathed it. "You could be swifter in defense."

"I was swifter than you."

The Master's hand was a blur, but Korusan caught it. The Master smiled. "Better," he said, then snapped free and slapped Korusan lightly on the unwounded
cheek. "That for your insolence. And this," he said, "for your wit." He set hands on
Korusan's shoulders and leaned forward, and set a kiss where his hand had stung.
"Now you are Olenyas. Be proud, but never too proud. Be strong, but never so
strong that you betray yourself. Be swift, but never as swift as your death. And take
the oath as your kinsmen have taught you."

Korusan knelt and laid his hands in the Master's, looking up into that face
which now he was entitled to see. He was aware of other faces, strange and yet
familiar, and eyes that he had known when all the rest was wrapped in darkness.
But for the moment he saw only the one, and the two that came up behind it, lightmage, darkmage, filling the Master's shadow. He shuddered a little inside himself.
Magic he knew, because he must know it. Magic he had, because it was bred in
him, like his eyes, like the death that would take him while lesser men were still no
more than boys. But he had no love for it.

"It is our custom," the Master said, "to give the oath and the protection, and to
seal them in bronze, and bind them about your neck."

"But for you," said the lightmage, "bronze is too little a thing, and a binding of
chain too feeble. You, we seal and bind with the Word, and with the Power that is
behind the Word."

Korusan felt it in his bones like the fire that had filled him in the wood. He
fought instinct that would have risen and swelled and thrust the magic away. He let

it crawl through him, though he shuddered at its touch. He hoped devoutly that his stomach would keep its proper place. It was never his most obedient servant; and he had not fed it since this rite began.

Preoccupied with keeping his belly quiet, he barely noticed the wrench and twist as the magic pulled free. He did see the lightmage sway, and the darkmage steady him. He heard the woman mutter, "Goddess! He is strong." And the man: "Hush! He hears us."

Then he knew that they had not spoken aloud, but as mages spoke, in the silence behind the words.

The lightmage met his gaze directly. "You are strong," he said, "but unschooled. Beware of arrogance. It will destroy you."

Korusan's lips stretched. It was not a smile. He spoke the words then as the Master bade him, words that meant everything and nothing after the touch of magic. The magic had sealed him to this rite; the magic, and the blood that ran down his scored cheek. The words were for his brothers, his Olenyai. To serve where he must serve, to command where he must command; to do battle for lord and land and kin; to show his face never but to his brothers, and to protect the secrets of his caste— *His* caste, he thought, half wry and half in pain. Only while it served him, and until his vengeance was won.

To protect, then, while he lived, and to defend to the death. He was warrior born, warrior bred if not to the blood. Their enemies were his enemies. He was all of their kin, as they were all of his. He took the robes and the veil, the knife and the swords. He sealed them with his blood.

Robed, veiled, armed, he danced. The circle opened itself for him and to him. He danced to the drums, and their beat now was swift, but that swiftness was joy. He drew his swords. They were steel, and they gleamed in lamplight and firelight. He spun. He leaped. He sang. *"Ohé! Ohé Olenyai!"*

Others sprang into the dance. Steel rang on steel. It was like a battle, it was like a willing woman. He whirled in its center. He was all of them, and all of himself. Korusan. Olenyas. Lion's cub. Warrior born, warrior raised, born to die young. Lord and weapon of his people. Arrow shot from the bow: an arrow in the Sun.

THREE

KINGSHIP. MAJESTY.

It was stronger than wine. Stronger than dreamsmoke. More dizzying even than the scent of Vanyi's hair, wonderful sea-sweet masses of it, and she wound in it, gleaming in moonlight and starlight and the nightlamp's flicker.

Estarion reined himself in. That was the throne, making him its own. The fire he carried in his right hand was shrunk to a sunlit warmth: painlessness after pain so long and so relentless that it shaped the world about it.

He turned his hand palm up in his lap. Without the price of pain the *Kasar* was a beautiful thing, beautiful and improbable and all perfectly the god's creation.

He closed his fingers carefully over the bright burning brand and looked up. His people waited for him. Eyes fixed on him, faces a blur of black, brown, bronze, gold, and one beloved white-bone glimmer. She was afraid for him. He gave her warmth and a promise.

His mother shifted all but invisibly, reminding; admonishing. He smiled at her. Grinned, she might have said, though he did try to damp it down. One grew accustomed to it, she had told him. But it was splendid, this first heady draught of empire.

He raised his branded hand. The silence, that had been absolute, shattered in one glorious wave of sound.

They paid him homage one by one, from the highest to the lowest. They wore the bright edge from his joy, but nothing could rob him of it.

Vanyi was not in the endless train of his people. When she came to the throne, it would be to sit beside him in it, empress to his emperor, mother of his heir. She was gone now about her duties: mage, priestess, guardian of the Gates between the worlds. Those would not wait for any man, even a man who was lord of the world.

They came without pause or diminution, to bow at his feet, to kiss his hands, to murmur the words that made them his people, and to hear him seal them with a word and a smile. His throat was raw. His face ached with smiling, his neck with bending to acknowledge bows or tribute. His backside, he decided, would do much better with a thicker cushion; and that almost betrayed him into laughter. The stout merchant in front of him received a smile that made him blink, dazzled, and the free-woman behind looked mildly smitten.

The one behind them, well out of proper order and walled in retinue, neither smiled nor appeared enraptured with Majesty incarnate. Estarion went cold.

There had been others of that ilk among the lords and princes. One could hardly avoid them. They were half of his empire, as his advisors never tired of reminding him. But he could not abide them. Oily yellow people with flat snake-eyes, bowing and groveling and thinking scorn at eastern barbarians. When he could read their thoughts at all. They thought slantwise, round corners; they made his head ache.

The Asanian lord bowed low. He wore the five robes of a prince, one atop the other, slender ivory feet bare as befit one who need walk only in palaces, straw-gold hair uncut and bound behind him with plaited gold. He bowed to the floor, prostrating himself, and his entourage went down with him, concerted as a dance.

Their minds were a babble of nonsense. They were warded, with magery in it. Not that the mage could be a priest of Avaryan, or Estarion would know it; nor could it be a mage of the old and broken Guild. No: it was but one half-hidden servant, grey man in a grey gown, with eyes as flat as coins.

Estarion set his teeth against the pain of that protection. Some small remnant of his power had come back since he lost it in the time he could not remember, when he had wielded it like a weapon, and killed the mage who killed his father; but it had come back flawed. Nothing could test his shields without his knowing it; and that knowledge was a stabbing pain.

He meant to say the words that set the prince free to rise. Pain locked his jaw upon them. Pain, and anger. How dare any mage, or any man, try his defenses here, where he was emperor? It smacked of contempt, if not of treason.

The moment stretched. The prince and his entourage lay on their faces, unmoving. The court began to shift uneasily.

"Estarion!" his mother hissed in his ear.

He recoiled from the sound of it, and from the rebuke that came as much from within as from without. "Get up," he said. Snapped. In High Court Asanian; but the inflections were all awry. He had addressed the prince of five robes as a minor eunuch of the Middle Court.

His lordship rose with grace they all learned in childhood. The others were less polished, or less composed. Their anger grated raw against his aching brain.

A prince could not declare death-insult against an emperor, but Estarion had made no friend in this one. The Asanian spoke the words of homage in precise, icy syllables, each inflection meticulously and lethally correct. His entourage did not echo him. That was insult less than mortal but more than minor.

The prince bowed again to the floor. This time he rose without Estarion's bidding, and bent his head a careful degree. Giving the emperor pardon. Forgiving a barbarian his ignorance.

As he began to back away down the long silent aisle, Estarion stopped him with a word. He stood stiff and still, and he did a terrible thing, a thing that no Asanian did to the emperor enthroned. He looked up into Estarion's face.

Estarion met the yellow eyes. They fit that face: old ivory, old gold, carved smooth and sleeked with scented oil. Their stare was bold beyond belief, as Asanians thought of it, and profoundly, wonderfully shocked.

Estarion smiled. "Am I what you expected?" he asked sweetly, in High Asanian that had remembered itself and given the man his proper rank.

The Asanian's gaze dropped, as did he, full on his face, all grace and dignity forgotten, and in him only fear. He had meant defiance, that was in every line of him, and contempt for the emperor who would not walk in the west and yet called himself lord of Asanion. He had forgotten, or chosen to forget, that there was Asanian blood in the barbarian, blood of the Lion, blood imperial.

He fled, there was no other word for it. Estarion sat back in his throne and set himself to be markedly gracious to the Islander who came forward shakily, almost creeping in the Asanian's wake.

Estarion stood in the middle of the robing-room and stretched. No servants beset him. He had locked them out, and bought a few moments' quiet.

There was wine on the table. He filled a cup, drank a heady draught. He ached, inside and out. Some of that was hunger. But he could not go to the feast until the servants, tyrants that they were, gave him leave. He must make an entrance, and so must enter last.

He circled the room, skirting the chests and the clothing-presses. His mood was odd, unsettled. The Asanian had taken the splendor out of it. The man had been testing him; and he had not done well. He had let himself be caught off guard. He had betrayed his weakness.

"I may be young," he said to the air, "but I am not stupid. Nor completely ignorant of my failings."

"Goddess forbid that you should be."

He whipped about. A locked door was small barrier to a mage, and his mother was one of rare power. Likewise the one who bulked behind her. Great tall northern barbarian in beard and braids and baubles—strangers never suspected the cultured delicacy of that mind, nor knew him for the great mage and scholar and priest that he was.

They were together more often than not, priestess of the dark and priest of the light. It was a jest in some quarters that they were like the old Guildmages, matched in their magic, darkmage and light. They had shared Estarion's regency, and shared his raising once his father was dead; they were not always of a mind, but they never failed to come to an accommodation, one way and another.

The Lady Merian settled herself in the room's one chair. She never looked less than queenly, but her eyes were tired. Estarion set a cup in her hand. She wrapped long fingers about it, gratefully maybe, but she did not drink the wine that was in it.

Avaryan's high priest in Endros betrayed no such hesitation. He drained his cup and set it down, and sighed.

Estarion looked at them both. Anger pricked. He was emperor, and these two not only invaded his solitude, they reduced him to a child.

"I cry your pardon," his mother said, reading him with maddening ease. "There is too much to say, and too little time to say it."

"Is it nothing that can wait until the morning?" Estarion demanded.

"I think not," said Lord Iburan. He was unwontedly quiet, almost grim, though his eyes on Estarion were gentle enough. Not angry, then. When Iburan was angry, mountains trembled.

Iburan laughed. "Do they? Come now, youngling, tuck in your thoughts. They're flapping like flags at a feast-day."

"Maybe I want them to." But Estarion shored up all his walls and slammed shut the gates and locked himself in the keep. Iburan winced. Estarion was briefly, nastily glad.

"Estarion," his mother said. Her tone was a warning.

He bit his tongue, then said it in spite of her. "Was it all a sham, then? Shall I be your puppet still, and you the empress regnant?"

Her eyes narrowed: the only sign she gave that he had struck the mark. "You will learn to rule yourself. Or so one may hope. You are young yet, and I have raised you ill, maybe; protected you too well, and shielded you from good as from harm."

"What, the good that's in Asanion?" Estarion met her stare. "It comes to that, doesn't it? I'm emperor of Asanion, too."

"So," she said. "You do remember it."

"I never forget."

"You never fail to regret it, either." She set down the untouched cup and pressed fingers to her brows. "Ah, child, I did ill and worse than ill to keep you here in Keruvarion. You should have gone long since to Asanion, and conquered your fear of it."

Estarion reared up. "I'm not afraid of the west!"

"No," she said too gently. "Only of the people in it, and the memories it may hold."

Estarion opened his mouth. No words came out. He shut it with great care.

"You cannot continue to shun Asanion," his mother said, "or to offend its lords and princes. We have spoken for you through the years of your youth. That now is over. You must speak in your own name, for your own honor."

"You must rule all of your empire," said Iburan, "not only the east or the north. The west should know you, and know you fair. And not as one who loathes all that it is."

"I do loathe it," said Estarion, breaking in on their antiphon. "I've seen it. I know it. I despise it."

"You remember nothing of it." Merian's voice was as calm as her eyes. "One fool passed all our guards and protections and destroyed your father. It could have been a northerner, or a man of the Hundred Realms. It could have been anyone at all."

Estarion's heart set hard and cold. "You never loved him, did you? He gave you a throne and an empire. He, himself, man and lover, was nothing to you."

Her hand was so swift, the blow so sharp, that he never saw it, or even felt it, till it was done. His own hand flew up. But he could not strike her, no matter the heat of his temper. So well at least she had reared him.

"Never," she said, soft and still. "Never say such a thing again."

Iburan's voice was deep and almost harsh, but there was calmness in it, and peace. "There now. Be still. You're on the raw edge, both of you."

"So we are," said Merian. Her voice for once had forsaken its sweetness, and its grace that set an empire in awe of her. "So we must continue to be. That one who faced you, Starion, came out of Asanion to defy us all, and not you alone. Keruvarion is yours by right and by choice. Asanion is a conquered kingdom. Thus it reckons itself. It chafes at the rule of barbarians and mongrels. My dear lord did ill when he took me to wife and refused the woman his council had chosen for him."

"An Asanian woman." Estarion shivered through the dregs of his temper. "Then I would never have been; or been far other than I am."

"Surely," said Merian, "and I could never have endured a rival. But Asanion took its revenge, takes it still, and forgets nothing. And never, never forgives."

"Then what's left to us?" Estarion said. "Civil war? Asanion chafes, it always has, but in the end it gives in. You saw how yonder princeling was, once I made him see what else I am."

"What you would rather not be." Iburan sounded tired. "He saw that, too. Be sure of it."

"What if he did? They're slaves born, all of them, even the princes. Once he knew that I have blood-right to his homage, he gave it. He'd have slit his own throat if I'd ordered him to."

"There," said Iburan more wearily than ever. "There you have it. Half of your empire is Asanian. Half of *you* is Asanian. And you know no more of the truth of yourself or your empire than a blindfish knows of the sun."

Estarion's head throbbed. "It is *not* half of me! It's a trickle in the tide that I am. No Asanian has tainted my blood since Hirel himself."

"'Tainted,'" said Merian. "Dear goddess help me. And you believe it."

"Is it false?" Estarion asked her.

She did not answer.

He swept his hand down his body. "Look at me. What do you see? Northerner, as pure as makes no matter. Except for this." His fingers clawed as if to rake his eyes; but he knotted them into fists. "If my father erred, then so did Varuyan before him, and Ganiman before that. None after Sarevadin endured an Asanian marriage. And she was married to Hirel Uverias, who was like no Asanian who ever was, or ever would be."

"No," said Iburan. "He was nothing remarkable, except that he loved a foreigner. And that, he always said, was a doom of his line."

"So it is," Estarion said slowly. He caught himself before he said something he would regret. He would not bring Vanyi into this, or soil her with its touch.

"Estarion," said Merian, "listen to me. The time is ill, but it will never be better; and you must know, and accept. When your father wedded me, he promised his council that his son would not repeat his error."

"It was an error to marry for love?"

"For him," said the empress mother, "and for his empire, it was. It killed him. You must not err as he erred. You must do what he failed to do. You must take a bride in the west."

"No," said Estarion flatly.

He could not say that he had not expected it. He had ears, and wits. He knew that his council did not approve of Vanyi. She was a commoner. Her father fished off the coast of Seiun Isle. She brought him no wealth or power, nor any dowry but herself.

But an Asanian. A yellow woman. Serpent-breed, to breed serpent-children.

His gorge rose. He would not do it. He could not.

"You will consider it," his mother said. "That much at least you will do."

"I have considered it," he said. "I refuse it."

"Have you ever even seen an Asanian woman?"

Estarion rounded on Iburan. "Why in nine hells—"

"How can you judge anything unseen and untested? Before your priestess came, you shuddered at Islanders and called them corpse-folk and fish-people, and reckoned them less than human."

"Islanders never killed my father," said Estarion.

"That's Asanian, you know. That obstinacy. That unwillingness ever to forgive."

Estarion laughed. It hurt. "You can't have both sides of it, foster-father. Either Asanians are sorely misunderstood, or all my vices are theirs, and none of my virtues."

"How can you know until you know them? You can't avoid them forever, no matter whom you choose for your empress. Asanion has had no emperor in its palace since your father died there. Soon or late, you'll have to face it and them."

"Are you telling me that I should ride west in the morning?"

"Hardly that," said Iburan, impervious to the weight of Estarion's irony. "You'll need a cycle or two at least to settle this half of the empire. But then, yes, I think you should begin a progress into the west. People are expecting it. They need to see you, to know what you are."

"As yonder princeling did?"

"Even so," said Iburan. "If you have nothing better to give them."

"God," said Estarion. "Goddess. That would be war."

"So shall it be, if you let him go back unchallenged to his people, and tell them what you did to him."

Estarion shut his aching eyes. It was no quieter in the dark. "I don't suppose one could apologize." The word caught in his throat.

"One could," said Iburan. "But he's only one man. What he did . . . he acted for a whole realm. That realm must see you. It must know that you belong to it as to the rest."

"My father took such counsel," Estarion said. "He died for it."

"He died because no one would believe that an emperor, a mage born, needed protection from magery in his own palace. He died because we were fools, Estarion."

"Yes," Estarion said. His throat was sour with bile. "You were fools. All of you. He too. I. Everyone." He swallowed hard. "I'll be a fool. I'll go. Damn you, fosterfather. I'll go."

"Soon?"

Estarion's head was splitting. No one was trying to get into it—it was not that kind of pain. This came from within. It made his sight blur, and made him say, "When Brightmoon comes back to the full. Four days—no. Three. I'll go into the west. I'll face my demons. I'll make myself remember. But I won't—I *won't*—bed an Asanian woman."

"That is as the god wills it," said the god's priest. There was no triumph in his voice. He was never one to gloat over victories, was Iburan of Endros.

FOUR

SILENCE RULED THE HEART OF AVARYAN'S TEMPLE IN ENDROS, silence so deep it seemed to drink the light, to transform the hiss of breath to a roar and the murmur of blood into thunder. No foot fell, no voice spoke. Even the air was still, wrapped in the temple's veils and bound with magery.

Vanyi kept vigil in her due turn, now praying to the omnipresence of the god, now casting nets of power on the seas that were the mageworld. Most often there were two to watch and to pray, but on this day of Estarion's enthronement, all mages who could were set to guard the palace and the emperor. He was more valuable by far than the Magegate that shimmered where wall should be. That might fail or close, but mages could restore it, however high the cost. If Estarion died, there would be no heir of the god on earth; and that would be beyond repairing.

Strange to think of him so, and to know what he had been in the morning, tousled laughing boy-man covering terror with exhilaration. Her power twitched, yearning toward him, but the magewall barred it. And she was forgetting her duty.

She traced the patterns of the dance, sang the song that sustained the Gate. Dance and song were part of her, had always been part of her. Even on the shores of Seiun, fingers raw from mending the nets, nostrils full of the stink of the fish, her feet had known the steps, her voice the notes. Mooncalf they had called her, and witch, and changeling, with her sea-eyes and her hair the color of moors in autumn. She knew the speech of the gulls, felt in her bones the sway of the tides.

That was far away now, long ago. She stood in this chamber as in a globe of glass, and even the pull of the moons was faint, overwhelmed in the roar and reach of the Gate. There was sea on the other side of it, tides that were no tide of this earth, waves heaving and falling on a shore that looked like dust of rubies, or like blood. As she watched, it blurred and shifted, and she looked into darkness full of stars; but stars that were eyes, great burning dragon-eyes staring into her own. Seeing her. Knowing her for what she was.

She gasped. A Word burst out of her, raw and barely shaped. The stars blinked, steadied. They were only stars.

A shudder racked her. The worlds changed: that was the way of Gates. Most were alien. Some were horrible, hells of ice or of fire, swarming with demons. None had ever left her as these stars had, crouched on her knees, heaving as if she had taken poison.

She scraped wits and power together. They were thin, threadbare, but they were enough to cast a net.

The seas were calm. Nothing swam there but what belonged in that place. Mages about their workings. Lesser folk dreaming, asleep or awake. Spirits of air and fire at their incalculable pursuits. No threat. Nothing to fathom that instant of horror.

She pulled in the net. Her heart had ceased its hammering. Her knees were steady again. The sweat dried on her body. She went down on her face before the Gate, and began the prayer of the sun's descent.

Estarion came to his chambers much earlier than Vanyi had expected. It would have been like him to leave the lords' feast and go down into the city and pass the night with his people, drinking their beer and singing their songs and showing them why they loved him. He never calculated that, or thought of it as politic. He liked them, that was all.

He had been in the city: the beer-scent came in before him. He was in plain city-walking clothes, his court robes long since laid away. She heard him calling goodnights to the battalion of his friends, and them chaffing him for turning lily maid while the night was young. "Maid!" someone cried. "And what's he got inside, then? Maybe he's got the right of it. Who's for a fine warm woman to while the night away?"

They roared at that. Estarion laughed and shut the door on them.

Vanyi looked up from the book she had been staring at for longer than she could reckon. Estarion was a shadow beyond the lamp's glimmer. She mustered a smile for him.

He moved into the light. There was no laughter in him, no sign that she could see of the face he had shown his friends. This was somber, almost grim.

"Troubles?" she asked him.

"No," he said. He gave himself the lie: snatched the rings from his ears, flung them at the wall. They clattered to the floor.

Carefully, precisely, she rolled the book shut and fastened the cords. "Disasters, then," she said.

He dropped his coat more gently than he had the rings. "When Brightmoon is full, I'm going to Asanion."

She stared at him.

"Surely someone told you?"

His tone was nasty. She ignored it. "I came direct from the temple. Everyone else was in the hall or elsewhere."

His long mouth twisted. She wanted to kiss it. He said, "I looked for you after your Gate-duty should have been over. I thought you would come to my banquet."

"I wanted to." She shivered. It was cold in the room, she told herself. She had dismissed the servants when they came to light the brazier, then forgotten it and them. "I was more tired than I thought. I slept a little." And waked to nightmares, and sought refuge in a book of which she remembered nothing, not even its name. "By the time I could have come, you were gone into the city."

He pulled his heavy plait over his shoulder and tugged at the bindings. They were stubborn. His brows knit.

She worked her fingers under his. They were stiff, quivering with tension. He let his hands fall, let her unwind the cords, loosen the braid. His hair was his great beauty, thick and curling yet soft and fine as silk, so black it gleamed blue. She filled her hands with it.

His body was taut. She kissed the point of his shoulder. He barely eased. "Why?" she asked. "Why exactly now?"

He told her all of it, words honed to a bitter edge. The Asanian, the test—he made little of it. Too little, maybe, but she was not ready to solve that riddle tonight. But his mother's command—

"I'll go west," he said through gritted teeth. "I'll face my demons. I'm no coward. But I won't—I *won't*—be stud bull to a herd of yellow women."

"It need only be one," Vanyi said. Her voice was steady. She was proud of that. "So. It's a long way to Kundri'j Asan. Long cycles of the moons. A year, maybe, at the pace of a royal progress."

"A year and three days?" His smile was thin. He kept count, too. "Not likely, my love. They'll have me over the border as fast as the court can travel, and into the Golden Land, marshaling parades of yellow women."

"Teaching Asanion that you are its emperor."

"It does need lessoning," he said. Breath gusted out of him. "God and goddess, Vanyi. I thought I was safe from this for years at least. There's empire enough here to keep any man occupied."

"Except that it's yours entirely, and always has been, and always will be. Keruvarion knows you, loves you. Asanion has never seen you."

"It saw plenty of me when I was younger. I do remember that much," he said, sharp, almost angry. "They marched me about like a prize calf. They dressed me in so many robes I could barely move, and perched me in a litter, and made me sit like an icon for people to gape at."

"You were a child then," Vanyi said. She did not know where the words were coming from. The earth, maybe. The cold thing that, a little while ago, had been her heart. Had the empress mother been trying to ease the blow this morning, telling her that she could never be empress? She worked the knots out of the emperor's shoulders and said to him, "They never knew you as a man. Now you'll show them. You'll teach them to love you as your easterners do, for the brightness that's in you."

"I'm as dull as an old stone," he said, with the soul burning so fierce in him that her mind's eyes were dazzled, and his eyes lambent gold, and gold burning in his hand. She felt the wash of it, the pain that would have sent any other man into whimpering retreat, but only sharpened his temper and made him rub his hand against his thigh.

She caught it, held it to her cheek. It was no more than humanly warm, stiff with the metal that was born in it, holy and impossible. All the heat burned within. "Oh, my lord," she said, and her eyes pricked with tears. "Oh, my dear lord. How can anyone keep from loving you?"

"You're besotted," he said. But a little of the tautness was gone. Not all, yet enough that he could lie down, and let her hold him, and be soothed into something resembling peace.

Dark. Stars. Eyes. Teeth that gleamed in the blackness. Maws opened wide, gaping to devour.

"Vanyi!"

She clutched at warm solidity. Estarion's voice thrummed out of it, deeper always than one expected, with a singer's purity. She clung as much to the voice as to the body, gulping air. He stroked the rigid line of her back. "Hush, love. Hush."

She pulled free. She was laughing, hiccoughing. "No! That's my part. You're the one with nightmares."

"Sometimes," he said, "one has to share." He was barely smiling. His eyes were as dark as lion-eyes could be, all pupil, and about it the thin rim of gold.

She burrowed into the warmth of him. The dream was fading in his brightness, the horror shrinking to insignificance. She had forgotten to eat after her vigil in the temple, that was all, and the oddity in the Gate had come back to haunt her empty stomach. No mage alive knew all the secrets of Gates. Maybe the Guild had, that in its prime had made them and used them and ruled them with fabled power.

The Guild was long since fallen. Vanyi was not supposed to regret that, or to wish that it had survived long enough to teach her what she yearned to know, of Gates, of magic, of the worlds beyond the world. But it was gone; only memory remained, embodied in the Gates.

Pride had laid it low. It had set empire against empire, Keruvarion against Asanion, striving to fell them both and set a puppet of its own making upon the doubled throne. But the puppet it had made had turned against it—and, wise cruelty, done nothing to destroy the Guild. Only let it be known what the Guild had done and intended, and offered a newer way to those who would be mages: the priesthood of god or goddess, and training in the temples of Sun or Dark. The Guild had withered, its twinned pairs of mages dead or lost. The robes that once had won such awe, lightmage grey and darkmage violet, were all faded, gone to the dim no-color of hedge-witches and hired sorcerers.

But the Gates endured. That one of them had gone briefly strange—it meant nothing. The priest who came to relieve Vanyi had said as much; and he was a mage and a master. She was initiate merely, priestess on Journey, mage in training. She was making nightmares of hunger and sleeplessness and a lover who might be taken from her.

Estarion did not know of this, nor would he. He had troubles enough. She attacked him suddenly with kisses. That made him laugh, reluctant at first, then more freely. Yes, she thought. Laughter drove away the dark. Laughter, and love; and that they had in plenty.

FIVE

THE CITY OF THE SUN lay in the arms of deep-running Suvien, where the river curved round a great prow of crag. To north and east the walls rose sheer. Southward they eased to a long level of windswept land and, half a day's journey down a smooth straight road, the white gates of its mother and its servant, Han-Gilen of the princes.

Westward was no wall but the river and the quays of ships and, black to its white beauty, that crag from which the city took its name, Endros Avaryan, Throne of the Sun. The sunrise bank teemed with men and beasts and boats. On the sunset side nothing walked, and no bird flew. The crag stood alone, dark against the sky, and on its crown a Tower. No window broke that wall, no gate marred its smoothness. Blind, eyeless, doorless, it clawed its way toward heaven.

Estarion stood atop the highest tower of his palace, on the northern promontory of his city, and glared across the river. He was nearly level with the summit of the black Tower, with the globe of crystal that, catching the sun, blazed blinding. But he was the Sun's heir: he could look unflinching on the face of his forefather. This, mere mage-wrought crystal, barely narrowed his eyes.

That whole Tower was a work of three mages conjoined, Sunborn king and Gileni empress and northern warrior, and they had wrought it in a night. "And why?" Estarion asked aloud. "Except to keep men off the crag, since any man who walked there must come down mad."

The cat Ulyai yawned vastly and stretched. She propped her forepaws on the parapet, leaning into Estarion. He wrapped an arm about her neck. "Have you ever seen a more useless braggart thing? Caves like lacework through that whole great rock, and tombs enough for a thousand years of kings, and he witches a Tower on top of it. And no way in or out, either, unless there's a Gate somewhere, or a key I haven't found."

Ulyai was not interested in the Tower across the river. There were ringdoves in the lower reaches of this lesser tower; she watched them with fierce intentness.

Estarion sighed. She would not care, either, that the Sunborn had left his bones there, and a story that he lacked the grace to die before he did it, but had himself ensorceled into sleep, because his empire was won, and there were no more battles to fight. He would rise again, the talespinners said, when the god called him back to his wars.

"It's only a story," Estarion said. "Or if it's true, it's so far away it doesn't matter. I'm all the Sun-blood there is, until I get myself an heir. I'm all the emperor this world will have." He shivered in the bright sunlight. "There's no Tower in Kundri'j Asan. He never came there, did the Sunborn. They stopped him before he marched so far. He was a madman, they say. I say he was saner than anyone else who came near him. He hated Asanion with all his heart."

"He was a fool," his mother said behind him.

He did not turn to face her. He had been aware of her coming, but he had chosen to take no notice. He had not spoken to her since the day of his enthronement, nor had she sought him out. A pleasant enough arrangement, he had been thinking.

"An emperor cannot hate the full half of his empire," she said. "Not and remain emperor."

"Is that what they hope for?" he asked, light, barely bitter. "That I'll hate them so much, I let them go of my own free will?"

"Maybe," she said.

His lips stretched back from his teeth. "Maybe I should do it, then. Give up Asanion. Leave it to rot in peace."

"It will hardly do that. More likely it will rise up and overwhelm the east, and rule us as it ruled us long ago, under an iron heel."

Estarion spun to face her. "Listen to yourself! Even you think of *us* and *them*. It's we in Keruvarion, they in Asanion. There's never been one empire. There never will be. Only irreconcilable opposites."

"If you think so," she said calmly, "you make it so. You have that power, Meruvan Estarion."

"I have too much power. Everyone has always said that. Too much power was never enough to save my father. Only to twist me and break me, and mend me awry." He laughed at her frown: laughter that tore his throat. "Yes, that's wallowing! I wallow extraordinarily well."

"You are too clever by half," his mother said. She was not smiling.

There was a silence. They had quarreled before—they could hardly help it: he had her temper, and that was as quick as her wits. But never for so long. Never for so much.

He would not be the one to end this. She asked of him what she had not had the strength to demand of herself. She could hardly fault him for seeing the flaw in it.

After a while she spoke, shaping the words carefully, as she did when she was holding anger at bay. "I am told that I am not to accompany you to Asanion. That I remain as regent in Keruvarion."

"There is a regent in Asanion," he said with equal care, but no more anger than she deserved.

"An Asanian," she said. "A great lord and prince, and loyal to the Blood of the Lion. But Asanian."

"Wasn't it you who said that I have to learn to face the rest of my empire?"

"The scars are deep. They will not heal in a day."

"Now you say it," he said.

"I have never failed to know it." She paused for breath, perhaps to nerve herself, perhaps simply to let him simmer. "Will you take me with you?"

"Do I have a choice?"

"Yes."

He looked at her. He loved her, he could hardly deny that. But love and hate were womb-kin. Someone had said that once, long ago. One of his ancestors, very likely. It was something they would understand. "So," he said, pitching his voice light, easy, purposely exasperating. "You would come, then? And hold my hand? And pimp for me in the harems of the Golden Empire?"

She did not answer that. "The Red Prince is wise, and the people love him. He would do well as regent in your absence."

"Hal is barely older than I am."

"And you are emperor."

He accorded her a swordsman's salute. "Well struck! And suppose he forgives me for leaving him behind—what then, Mother? Do you think I'm not to be trusted, where I'm going?"

"I think that you will need me. Even," she said, "if you hate me for it."

She stood as straight as ever, her face as still, its beauty unmarred. But she was fighting back tears. He felt them burning in his own eyes.

Tricks. She was a master of woman-sleights as of the wiles of courts. And she had magery: she wielded it on him, and no matter the cost to his aching head.

He was softening. Fool that he was. He knew what she was doing; knew what she would do if she rode with him, if she had leisure to work on him through the long leagues to Asanion.

Maybe he needed the challenge. And it was true enough: he would need her wits, and her skill in bending men's wills. Especially in Asanion, where deception was a game of princes, and murder their pastime.

"Come, then," he said, "and do as you please. What I do, in the end, I'll do because I will it. And for no other reason."

"Have you ever done otherwise?" she asked.

She would not lock stares. She was too canny for that. She set a kiss on his brow and left him there. The scent of her lingered for a long while after she was gone.

It was nearer nine days than three before the court could be ready for the long road into Asanion. Even at that, the chamberlains were beside themselves with the haste of it all.

"Talk to the sergeants," Estarion said to the chief of them. "They can move an army of twenty thousand inside of a day, and you can't move a court of twenty score in a tenday?"

Nuryan fluttered and squawked. Estarion did not trouble to listen. "I'm going," he said. "In the morning. Anyone who can ride, will ride. Anyone who is late, is late."

"Sire!" his chamberlain shrieked. "The baggage—the wagons—your wardrobe—"

Estarion said a word both brief and vulgar. It shocked Nuryan into silence. "I'll wear what I can carry. There are cloth merchants in Asanion, no? And tailors. And, I trust, jewelers and hatters and cobblers—"

"An emperor wears no shoes in his palace." Nuryan truly was distraught: he had interrupted his emperor.

"He rides, surely? And walks elsewhere?"

"No," said Nuryan, "sire. He never leaves his palace."

So Nuryan might think. Estarion was of another mind; but that was another battle. "He has to *get* to his palace," he said. "And so he shall. I ride in the morning. The court may follow as it will."

———

The emperor rode out on a fine bright morning, with the sun a dazzle in a flawless sky, and a brisk wind to set his banners flying. The slow and the litter-borne and the baggage would follow when they chose. These were the swift and the mounted. The emperor's guard in its full ranks, blazing in scarlet and gold; the empress' guard in gold and green; a battalion of high ones, lords and ladies both, and guards and grooms and servants; and a little company of priests and priestesses, bearing no emblem, affecting no great estate, but each marked by the torque at the throat and the plait down the back. Vanyi was with them, a white face amid the black and brown and gold.

Estarion rode at their head. His senel was a black of the Mad One's line, blue-eyed, dagger-horned, with a star on his forehead; young enough to be a little silly with all the tumult, but wise enough to keep his temper in hand. Umizan snorted at Ulyai who paced beside him, but not in fear: he had been foaled among the royal cats. She snarled amiably at him and paced just out of reach of the sharp cloven hoofs, queenly oblivious to the crowds that lined the road. All of Endros seemed to have streamed outside the walls to watch their emperor ride away.

Their cheering rolled over him. It was heartfelt, but there was darkness in it. They were losing him to the west. Not forever, that he had vowed to them, swearing it by the Tower on its crag. But the last emperor who had gone to Asanion had sworn that same vow; and he had come back, but never living.

His bones lay under the Tower. Estarion could see it beyond the city's white walls: black crag, black horns, crown of crystal that caught the sun's light. He saluted it, flinging up his burning hand. The sun, escaping a wisp of cloud, struck the crystal and blazed.

Estarion laughed at the glare of it. "Until I return," he said, "watch well, old bones. Look after my city."

"You take that one too lightly," said Iburan.

Estarion slanted a glance at the priest, who had ridden up through the line and matched his mare's pace to black Umizan's. He was not smiling. "There is a power there," he said, "that would make a god tremble."

"Isn't that a heresy?" asked Estarion, bowing to the crowd, dazzling them with his white smile, giving Umizan leave to dance and flag his tasseled tail.

Iburan said nothing. But neither did he leave Estarion's side.

The people followed them far out of the city, mounted and afoot, calling Estarion's name. At length even the most determined of them grew weary or felt the distance of their city and the sun's descent into the alien west. The last of them halted at the boundary-stone, the white pillar without adornment that marked the edge of Endros and the beginning of the Hundred Realms. It stood on a long hill cloven in two by the river, first outrider of the ridge-wall, and beyond it the land went up and up to a tree-clad height. It was nothing to the mountains of the north, but on that plain it stood high and haughty.

Estarion paused by the stone. "Go," he said to the rest. "I'll follow." Some hesitated, but he stared them down: even his mother. They rode on up the slope.

Umizan lowered his head to graze. Ulyai dropped down just beyond him and rolled in the sweet grass, singing a soft yowling song. Her mind was full of sunlight. No sadness there; no regret to be forsaking the city of her birth. All her kind remembered the free air and the wild places, even those born within Endros' walls: remembered it and yearned for it.

Estarion looked down upon his city. He could have cupped it in his two hands, as small as it seemed and as perfect, like a carving in ivory and gold.

He had left Endros often enough on journeys about his empire. But only in the east and the north. Never in the west. Never for so long or in such a mingling of anger and resentment, doubt and fear and piercing exhilaration.

Free. For however brief a time, for however unwelcome a purpose, he was free of those walls. It was terrifying, that freedom, and wonderful. That he went to a worse prison than he had escaped—it mattered, and yet after he was not sorry for it.

He touched heel to Umizan's side. The stallion snatched a last mouthful of grass and wheeled, turning away from the city and the plain. The Wall of Han-Gilen rose ahead of them, and the last of the escort riding slowly over the crest. Estarion wound fingers in the long mane. "Go," he said into the backturned ear. "Brother, go!"

SIX

Estarion's riding fell somewhere between an army's march and a royal progress: soldier-speed where land or weather allowed it, but long slow meanders through rough country, and pauses in this castle and that town and yonder temple. Once free of Endros he knew less urgency, or more patience. The pace was his to set, and he allowed his mood to set it, or Umizan's whim.

He rode in the swelling spring, up the long roll of Suvien with the Wall of Han-Gilen fading into mist behind him, through the hills and woods of Iban and Sarios, into the forest-ridings of Kurion. There the towns were fewer, the castles more frequent: crowning cliffs above the river, or warding islands in its center. Their lords were not always delighted to find the emperor at their gates of an evening, but he knew well enough how to talk them round. It was as simple as a word and a smile.

"The trouble with that," he said to Vanyi of a morning as they rode down yet another steep and twisting track, "is that once they have me, they don't want to let me go."

She had her hands full convincing her young idiot of a mare that she had come up this way; she could very well go down it. It was a while before Vanyi could answer. When she did, she was breathless and her face was flushed. Her words were calm enough for that. "Of course they want to keep you. You settle all their impossible cases, and physic their ailments with a touch, and bless their women and their cows."

"While my swarm of courtiers eats them straight into poverty."

"That's pride," she said. Her flush was fading; she pushed her hair out of her face, where it would fall no matter how she bound it, and smoothed the mane on her mare's sweating neck. Everyone else was waiting below, being patient and, in his mother's case, subtly disapproving. Vanyi took no more notice than he did. "They'll just expect the more from their vassals, or even from their equals, because they gave so much to you. Some will make a profit from it. You're a very useful guest, taking all in all."

He looked down at the mill and muddle of his escort, and the smaller party that belonged to the lord of the castle. That one looked ready to ride back up and discover what was keeping his majesty, but Iburan held him in what looked like easy conversation. Easy for Avaryan's high priest in Endros; excruciating, no doubt, for the lord of Inigal in Kurion.

Estarion rubbed his chin. One way and another he had been neglecting to keep it shaven. Laziness, his squire muttered. Good sense, he reckoned it. The stubble was ripening into a surprising luxuriance of beard. It itched now and then, but not enough to be a nuisance. Nuisance was cold water and cold razor on warm chin in the morning.

Vanyi liked to play with it. He grinned at her, touching the edge of her mind with a memory. She blushed gloriously and glared, but laughed through it. "I think," he said, "tonight, we'll make ourselves a camp. No towns a day's ride upriver of here, they tell me, and no castle past the meeting of the waters."

"But a great one there," she said, "and its lord waiting for you, like enough, if he's heard you're riding this way."

"So we'll summon him to be our guest under the moons. He'll reckon it a novelty."

"Not an insult?"

"Not with me to charm him out of it."

"Ah," she said, caressing him with the word. "You are incorrigible."

He kissed his burning palm and laid it on her cheek. "Bless you and all your lineage, my child."

She stiffened and went white, shocking him into stillness. "Don't," she said, strung tight. "*Don't* mock me so."

"Vanyi—" he began.

She shook herself so hard he heard the clack of her teeth. Her hair escaped the last of its plait and tumbled free, autumn-colored silk blowing in her eyes. She dug heels into her senel's sides. The mare grunted in surprise and shied, and nearly tumbled down the slope. Estarion gasped, snatched. Vanyi eluded him, scrambling mount and self together, half sliding, half running down the steep descent.

Once the road was level and the way clear in front of them, she found her voice again. It was tight, and it came close to trembling. "I'm not a cow," she said, "or a farmer's wife, for you to set a wishing on. I can't give you a child till my Journey is over. Don't make it hurt any more than it has to."

That was sharp, but just. Not that he would say so. He had his pride. He said instead, "Do you know, this is my Journey, too. I never had one before this."

"You have a dispensation," she said, with an edge still, but she was not refusing to speak to him. "And isn't it a life's Journey in itself, to be emperor?"

"Not without Asanion," he said.

Vanyi pondered that, gentling her senel as the mare objected to the slant of a shadow. Umizan snorted at her and lowered his horns. That was a mark of great disgust for a stallion to threaten a mare so, and she without horns to answer him. She laid her ears back at his presumption, but she settled somewhat.

"Yes," said Vanyi at length. "Yes, that's a Journey worthy of you, to go into the west and win it."

"If this were a proper Journey," Estarion said, "I'd be alone, or at most with one companion, and I'd go wherever the god led me."

"Isn't he leading you now?"

"No," said Estarion, but he paused. The road ran along the river through a colonnade of trees. Sun slanted through the branches, now dim, now dazzling. He gathered a handful of it as Umizan carried him through, holding it cupped in his palm. It was warm; it tingled. No one else, even a mage, could capture light as he did. He tasted it. It was heady, like wine. It tasted of evening and of the west, though it poured from a rising sun.

"You see," said Vanyi, who could read him like letters on a parchment.

He opened his fingers to let the light drain away. Umizan sidled, restless. Estarion gave him his head. He stretched from trot to canter to gallop, running ahead of them all down the long smooth track.

They camped a league short of the meeting of Suvien and Ilien, still on the sunrise side of Suvien. There was a ferry below Suvilien's fortress, or so the guides said, and boats enough to bring them all across. Here the river was both deep and wide, its banks high but less steep than they had been or would be, and a level of grass and trees stretching round a long bend.

"Eddy there," the guide said. He was a dour man, a forester in the service of the lord of Kurion, and in no apparent awe of the imperial majesty. "Round that bend she wraps her arms round an island, Suvien does, and up past that is the castle and the rivers' mating. There's good fishing in the quiet place. People come down from Suvilien with nets and poles, and bring catches up for milord's dinner. He's partial to fish, is milord."

"His majesty will dine on fish tonight," said Estarion's squire. Godri took his duties to heart. He did not approve of commoners who spoke too easily to his emperor.

The forester raised a brow at him. "Who's fishing for it, puppy? You?"

Godri drew himself up. He was a chieftain's son from the deep desert south of Varag Suvien, and the swirling scars that ornamented his cheeks were marks of one who had killed a man in battle. He was neither the eldest nor the chief of Estarion's squires; he had won his place in combat, though he would have been mortified to know that Estarion knew.

He looked like a court elegant, with his delicate hands and his slender grace. "We have servants," he said, "to do servants' work."

"Maybe I'll do it myself," said Estarion.

That silenced both of them. He laughed at their faces: matched astonishment and matched outrage. "My lord of Suvilien will be sharing our dinner tonight. See that he's received as his rank deserves."

"But—" said Godri.

"I am going fishing," said Estarion.

He escaped before they could marshal their resistance. There was camp to pitch, fire to build, mounts and baggage to see to. The lord of it all could slip away uncaught.

Vanyi's saddlebag yielded a hook and a coil of line, and a parcel wrapped in soft silk. She was with the priests, building wards about the camp. He touched the edge of her power, a bright singing thing like water in the sun. She was deep in the working, unaware of him save in her bones, where he was part of her. He set a smile where she could find it in the secret places of herself, and left the camp behind.

It was quiet round the bend of the river. Now and then the wind brought the sound of men's voices or the squeal of a senel. They comforted him, but they did not touch him. Escape was rare, solitude rarer yet. Even Ulyai was gone, hunting in the deep coverts. She would come back in the night, purring and replete, or she would appear in his shadow on the morning's ride, then ghost away again.

The air was colder here than in Endros. There summer would have begun after the long spring. Here it was spring still, the leaves young and green, and in hidden hollows a memory of snow. He paused to dip his hand in the river. It was snow-cold. He drank a little of it. Earth was in it, and snow, and something of the northern sky. That was the taste of Ilien that was born in the mountains of Ianon, first kingdom of the Sunborn, bastion of the world's edge.

He wandered along the bank. There was another bend farther up, where the river curved round one of its many promontories. High and forbidding as that was, the one beyond it, they said, was greater. Suvilien sat on that. Kurion's lord would be coming down from it even now, riding a boat on the river.

Estarion could see none of that from here. This arm of the river curved round a steep wooded islet, running aground on a spit of sand before a trickle of it freed itself to run back into the greater stream. It was more pool than river, its current faint, its water deep but almost clear.

Fish would gather here. He knew that from Vanyi's teaching. She had not taught him as much as she knew, and at that he had kept distracting her, but he had a little knowledge of finned folk's ways. He eyed the stretch of water and the dance of winged darters on its surface, and, keenly, the swirl and flash of scaled body as it struck for the kill.

One of the treasures from Vanyi's silken parcel was like enough to the darters to please his eye. He mated the line with the delicate weaving of thread and down and hidden, deadly hook. Foolishness, the forester would have decreed. So had Estarion once, and been proved false a dozen times over.

He cast the line with its lure as Vanyi had taught him. The breeze was fitful but strong enough to lift the false darter and tangle it in branches, where it would catch nothing but curses. The brush of his magery lifted it from certain capture and sent it winging out over the water, to settle among its mortal kin.

The fish took their time in coming to the lure. Estarion let them. The sun was warm, the air was sweet. No one came to trouble him, no squire bent on duty, no tribe of lordlings questing for mischief. He cast his line, he drew it in, he cast again. Some of the shadows beneath the water had begun to draw nearer, circling, closing for the strike.

"*There!*"

Estarion jumped nigh out of his skin. The lure sprang out of the water. Living silver arced after it, fell short, vanished with a scornful flick of tail.

He whipped about. "You thrice-begotten son of a leprous—"

It was not Godri, nor any of the hellions who rode with him. It was not any face he knew.

"You jump," the stranger said, "like a plainsbuck in rut."

Estarion's mouth was open. He shut it. "That was my dinner," he said. Calmly. All things considered.

"This?" The stranger drew in Estarion's line with cool and perfect insolence, and inspected the damp and draggled thing on the end of it. "Little enough meat on these bones."

"Were you born a fool," Estarion asked, "or did you study to become one?"

"Clearly you were born rude." The stranger cast the line long and low and level, as a darter flew. It barely brushed the surface of the water. Silver flashed. Line snapped taut. "There," said the stranger, but softly, almost tenderly. "There now."

Estarion stared at the fish flopping and gasping at his feet. Blank bliss had transmuted into blank rage, and thence into plain blankness.

The stranger was a woman, he realized with a small but penetrating shock. It was not obvious. She was whipcord-thin, dressed in ancient hunting leathers, hair plaited as simply as a priest's, although she wore no torque. Her nose was as fierce an arch as his own, her skin as velvet-dark, but her eyes were northern eyes, black in white, under brows as white as the flash of her teeth when she grinned at him. She was old:

and that too was not immediately obvious, for all the whiteness of her hair. Her skin was stretched taut over the haughty bones. She still had her teeth, and she carried herself like a young thing, with a light, arrogant grace that raised his hackles and set his pride to spitting.

She brought in another fish as quickly as the first, with ease that was like contempt. "You are a witch," he said.

"Oh, yes," said the stranger. "But here I'm a fisherman."

"Woman," Estarion said. His tone was nasty.

"You're jealous," she said. "Touchy, too. Here's enough for your dinner *and* mine. Where's your gratitude?"

"I'd have had my own dinner if you hadn't helped me out of it."

"And whose fault was that? This isn't milady's fishpond, where any idiot can drop a line in peace. There's a fair to middling army over yonder, and rakehells enough in it, and here are you, as if there was never a danger in the world."

"There isn't," he said.

"I walked right up to you. What if I'd been minded to stick a knife in you?"

"I'd have known if you were," he said. "Look here, whoever you are—if this is his lordship's personal pool, then tell him it's his dinner I'm fishing for, and would he mind not sending his servants to startle me out of nine years' growth?"

"You don't need that much," she said, measuring his length against her own. She was middling small for a woman in the north: he stood a head-height above her. She was anything but cowed. "And who says I'm anyone's servant?"

"You're from the castle, aren't you? You're not Lord Peridan, and you're not his mother, either, from anything I've heard."

"Oh," she said, rich with irony, "I certainly am not that delicate flower of womanhood. I came here from Suvilien, but I was never a bondsman there, nor anywhere on this wide earth. I'm no one's servant but my own."

"And the emperor's," Estarion said. It was a devil in him, a stab of wickedness. She did not know who he was, that was clear to see. He was not about to enlighten her.

"Not even the emperor's," she said. "He doesn't own the whole world, or even the most of it."

"What is there beyond the twofold empire? Wastes of sand or wastes of ice— fine prizes for a lord who has everything."

"The Realms of the Sun are great enough, but they're no more than a single continent on a single face of this wide and turning world. There's land beyond the desert, youngling, on the world's bottom, and land beyond the seas, both west and east."

"And you've seen it?"

She paused to hook another fish. He was interested in spite of himself; he hardly cared that she took her time in answering. "Some of it," she said at last, having freed the hook of its bright burden and cast again. "The seas are wide, and some few of the ships upon them are brave enough to sail out of sight of land. Or storm carries them, and they fetch up on isles no man of our race has ever seen."

"Are there people there? Or dragons?"

"People enough, who speak strange tongues, and reckon us gods for that we sail on ships out of the sea. Dragons? Nothing so dull or so common. Dragonels as big as hawks, yes. And fish with wings. And insects like jewels, and furred beasts that sing like birds."

"Stories," said Estarion.

"Certainly," she said. "But true enough for that."

"But if they were true," he said, "then wouldn't the Sunborn have conquered them?"

A shadow crossed her face, too brief almost to see. "If he had known of them, he would have tried."

"Someone will, you know. Eventually."

"Or one of them will conquer us."

"Not while I live," said Estarion, forgetting his pretense. But she did not seem to hear him. She was drawing in another fish, the largest yet and by far the most determined to escape. He lent a hand with the line. Together, hand over hand, they brought the catch to shore.

"We'll feed an army with this," the stranger said.

"Not the one yonder," said Estarion. "That would take a whole boatload. But milord of Suvilien will have a dainty for his dinner."

"He is a glutton," she said.

It was hardly polite to say so, even if she had not been a commoner. Estarion forbore to rebuke her. She would not have listened in any case, and he had other matters to settle. "Do you have a name?" he asked her.

"Do you?"

"Estarion," he said before he thought; and scowled. "You?"

She half shrugged, half smiled. "Many. Call me Sidani if you like."

Wanderer, that meant. And maybe, a little, *Exile*. It fit her well enough. "Sidani," he said, marking her with it.

"Estarion," she said, still halfsmiling. "I knew someone by that name once. His hair was as red as fire, and he had a temper to match. He married a priestess in Asanion. Fine scandal that was, too."

"That was the last Prince of Han-Gilen but three," Estarion said, "and he died young, and if you knew him, you must have known him in your cradle."

"Oh, I am terribly old," she said. "Are you named for him, maybe?"

"It's a common enough name in the south," he said. "You can't be as ancient as that."

"Why, youngling? Because you can't conceive of anything older than yourself?"

She wanted him to draw himself up haughtily and declare himself a man grown, he could well see, and then she could go on laughing at him. He said, "You'd have to be ninety at least, then, and you'd never be roving the roads. You'd have yourself a house somewhere, and a chair with cushions, and servants to run at your call."

"I had that," she said. "I wearied of it."

"But—"

She had stopped listening. She gutted the fish with a knife as lean and wickedly curved as a cat's claw, and strung them on a coil of the line, and presented them to him with a bow and a flourish. "Your dinner, my lord."

"And yours," he said. He did not know what demon possessed him, but he was not one to alter his word. "Come to camp with me. I can offer you a place by the fire, and all the dainties you can eat, and good company, too. Stories, even. Though maybe none as good as yours."

She frowned. She would refuse, he could taste it. He cast another lure. "You don't want Lord Peridan to eat all your hard-caught fish, do you?"

"That belly on legs." She spat just to leeward of Estarion's foot. "Very well then. I'll come. I hope you don't regret it."

So did Estarion. But if there had been evil in her, or any sorcery, he would have known; and his head was not aching even a little. Rather the opposite. He could not remember when he had felt as well as he did now. No pain, no ache of knotted muscles, no constant press and fret of rank and duty.

She cleaned her knife with a knot of grass and sheathed it at her belt. There was nothing feminine in the gesture, and everything female. He wondered how he could ever have failed to see that she was a woman.

"Well," she said in her deep sweet voice—nothing male in it, and nothing old, either. "Are you going to dawdle the day away?"

"Yes," he said, to take her aback; then he laughed. "Come then, lady and stranger. Try your wits on the emperor's men."

SEVEN

ESTARION'S RETURN WAS SOMEWHAT LESS CALAMITOUS THAN HE HAD FEARED. The camp was quiet; alarmingly so. Lord Peridan sat in the middle of it in a massive sulk. "The least," he was saying—growling—"the very least his majesty could do is to be present when his loyal vassal comes to attend him. Comes, it should be needless to say, at no little cost of time and inconvenience, not to mention the danger to his digestion, to dine at his rustic table, when the table in that lord's castle is renowned for its excellence, not to mention its comfort, and furthermore—"

Estarion swept a bow before him. It brought his peroration to a halt and began a new one. "And what, pray, are you? Who gave you leave—"

The man was a walking gullet, but he was a clever one. He heard the gasps. His eyes darted round the circle that had opened to admit Estarion. They settled on Estarion's face. The eyes, of course. Everyone always stopped at the eyes. "Sire," he said, as smooth as if the rest of it had been a litany of homage.

Estarion should not have spared a glance to see how the stranger was taking this revelation. She betrayed no flicker of surprise, and no repentance, either. The tilt of her brow almost pricked him to laughter.

He bit down hard on his tongue and schooled his face to blandness. "Lord Peridan," he said. "I trust your wait was pleasant. I bring a gift, as you see: a dainty for your dinner. Will you share it with me?"

Lord Peridan looked as if he had swallowed one of Estarion's fish, sidewise.

"Uncleaned," said Sidani's voice in Estarion's ear. He did not jump—in that much, training held. And how in the hells she knew what he was thinking—

No time now. He smiled at Suvilien's lord. "There, sir. Sit at your ease; Godri here will fetch you wine and whatever else you desire. And how is your lady? And your lady mother? Your sons are well, I trust? Your eldest son's son—a fine tall lad he must be, and ready soon to come out from among the women."

"In the autumn, sire," Lord Peridan said, warming perceptibly. Either he had forgotten his grievances, or he was choosing to play the game as Estarion led it. Estarion cared little which. This mountain of lard was his best defense against the storm that threatened in his mother's eyes, and perhaps worse, in Iburan's. He would keep it by him for as long as he could, and he would charm it into complacency, or he was no son of the Sun.

As he set himself to play the courtier, Sidani made herself a part of the camp. She did it with sublime simplicity: chose a fire, sat by it, began to tell one of her stories. He was aware of her, distant and yet close, as if she were a part of him; another thing to wonder at, but later, when there was time to spare for things that mattered. For now it was enough that she stayed.

"He has the gift," the stranger said. "No doubt of that."

Vanyi eyed her sidelong. The woman had come in with Estarion, walking in his shadow as if she had a right to be there. He never had got round to explaining her, nor had she seen fit to explain herself. She was simply there. People acted as if she belonged with them.

Idiots. Courtiers. If it walked with the emperor, it was his, and no one thought to question it.

Vanyi must have said it aloud. The stranger said, "What, like the royal cats? I like that, rather."

"What do you know of anything royal?"

"His thoughts exactly," the woman said. The fish had all gone to the great glutton of a lord, except one that came by Godri's hands, with his emperor's compliments couched in the elaborate phrases of the desert. She accepted it graciously, Vanyi granted her that, and she showed a mastery of phrase that left Godri blinking in awe. She did not, Vanyi noticed, include any of the many formulas of unworthiness. Nor did she try to decline the gift.

"And why should I?" she asked of Vanyi. "I caught it." She divided it neatly and laid half of it on Vanyi's plate. "Here, eat. It's as good as anything you'd catch at home."

"Fish of the sea is surpassingly fine," Vanyi said.

"But fish of the river is sweeter." The stranger disposed of hers with a cat's neatness and economy, and followed it with a noble quantity of lesser meats. In the middle of them she tilted her chin in the gesture that, where Vanyi was born, meant greeting, and said, "Sidani, they call me."

"Vanyi," said Vanyi. A mage guarded her name; but courtesy was older than magery, and deeper rooted.

This was not a mage. Vanyi was almost certain of that. Not a priestess, either. And yet she had an air of both. Maybe it was simply age, and arrogance that put Estarion's to shame. They were all like that in the north. They called southerners servile, and sneered at the grovelings of the west. Imperial majesty meant nothing to them except as they partook of it. They never forgot that the Sunborn was king of Ianon first, and Ianon was the heart of the north.

"I'm not Ianyn," Sidani said, "though my father was. I'm everything and nothing."

"You look Ianyn," Vanyi said. And stopped. "How do you do that?"

The dark eyes were as blankly innocent as a child's. "Do what, priestess?"

Read my mind, Vanyi said without words.

Nothing. No flicker of response. The mind before her was a clear pool, transparent to the bottom, and thoughts in it as quicksilver-elusive as fish. One, caught, was pleasure in the honeycake she ate. Another held nothing more or less terrible than Vanyi's own face, too white and sharp for beauty, but the stranger reckoned it splendid.

Vanyi did not like enigmas. Her body tensed to rise, to get away. Her mind held fast. This was danger. Not for herself, she never feared that, but for Estarion.

She looked harmless enough, an old wanderer woman taking the emperor's charity. He was free with it, as Vanyi well knew. A priestess on Journey had come once to his city, with nothing to distinguish her from any of a hundred like her, except a gift of magery, and that was hardly uncommon in that city of mages and priests. But he had seen her, and he had singled her out. He had chosen her for his beloved.

No threat of that here. This woman was long past any such thing. And if she was not, she would not want a youth as callow as Estarion.

The glint of her eye belied that. But she could not know what Vanyi was thinking. There was no power in her. Vanyi had a gift for such things. She knew.

"Who is that woman? Where did you find her?"

Estarion was easy to entrap. Vanyi simply followed him into his tent when that interminable feast was over, evicted his squire with a well-placed glare, and set herself to do the squire's duties. Estarion made no effort to resist her, but neither did he answer her. He said, "I hope my mother doesn't take it into her head to try the same thing. Seeing Lord Peridan settled for the night won't keep her occupied long."

Vanyi shook his hair out of its plait and reached for the comb. He sighed under her hands. "So," she said, "before her majesty comes to take her own piece of your hide: Who is that woman?"

"A wanderer," he said. "She tells stories. She caught the fish I fed to his lordship. She says she was in Suvilien before she came down to the river and found me."

"His lordship didn't act as if he'd seen her before."

"His lordship doesn't see anything beyond his next meal. How did such a glutton ever get hold of a castle as vital as Suvilien?"

"Most likely he inherited it. Why not ask Iburan? He'll know. And he'll be here on your mother's heels, you can be sure of it."

"Not if I can help it." He turned on the stool and clasped his arms about her. "Will you help me?"

She studied him. The new beard aged him, made him seem more a man, but from so close she could see the shape of the face beneath it, and that was still in great part a boy's.

"You trust too easily," she said. "What if the woman is an assassin? Remember the Exile who nearly destroyed the Sunborn in the womb, and came back when he was grown and tried to cast him down."

"There's no darkness in Sidani," said Estarion. "Maybe she is a little mad. Maybe more than a little. But she means me no harm."

Vanyi's arms locked about him, startling him into rigidity. "How do you know? How can you be certain? She's not what she seems, I know it. I feel it in my bones."

He eased slowly, though a remnant of tension lingered in the angle of his shoulders, the straightness of his back. "Maybe she isn't. She was a lord's bastard, I think. She has the air. What of it? She's neither mage nor sorceress. She interests me. I'd like to hear more of her stories."

"Child," said Vanyi tenderly. "Infant. Beloved idiot." His mouth tempted hers. She set a kiss in the corner of it. But she would not let him escape so easily. "I don't like her. Or," she said, "no. Not dislike, exactly. I don't think you were wise to bring her here."

"Maybe I wasn't," he said. "But when I did it, I felt that I'd done rightly—wise or unwise or whatever else it might have been. She won't hurt me. While I live, she'll never touch you but by your leave."

"She's no danger to me at all," Vanyi said. "That I'm sure of. Thank you, sweet child, for not suggesting that I'm jealous."

His eyes were wide with honest surprise. "Should you be?"

"She's beautiful in her way. And, as you say, interesting."

"She's *old*." He sounded all of ten years old himself. He was not too badly offended when she laughed, although he said, "She is. She says she's ninety at least."

"A hale seventy," Vanyi judged. "Sixty, more likely. Or less—the road is hard on aging bones. See? She tells stories. Keep her for that. But don't trust her, or anything she tells you."

"Not even if it's true?"

She hit him, but the blow turned to a caress. He would have made it more. She pulled away. In time, just, to appear decorous when his mother stepped into the tent, and in her shadow as always, the high priest of Avaryan in Endros, lightmage to her dark as the old tales said. But they were not twinned mages. Not in any way the Guild would have understood, though it might have understood that they were lovers. It was obvious to anyone with eyes to see.

Vanyi was expected to leave. That was the coward's part, and the prudent servant's. She was neither. She busied herself about the tent, keeping to the dimmer places, for the little good it did, and cursing his squire for the perfect order he kept.

"Oh, come," said Iburan at last, half weary, half amused. "Sit with us, priestess. We'll not be flaying him alive quite yet."

She felt the flush rise to her cheeks, and knew they saw it. Her chin came up. If it was defiant, then so be it. She set a stool by Estarion's right hand, and sat on it, and waited.

For a long while no one spoke. Estarion seemed content to rest his eyes on the lamp, letting it fill them, and him, with its little light.

Again it was Iburan who spoke, who said what had to be said. "Suppose we consider the matter disputed: that you left the camp unseen. That you took a truant's liberty, and nigh caused a scandal by your absence. Suppose it argued, and the matter settled as well as it ever may be, at no great profit to any of us."

"And no great disadvantage," Estarion said. "Are you telling me that I'm to be forbidden any more such escapades?"

"We can hardly forbid you," said Iburan. "You are the emperor."

Estarion laughed, brief and bitter. "When has that stopped you? No, I wasn't wise in what I did. I didn't mean to be wise. Maybe the god led me. Have you thought of that?"

"Certainly," said the god's priest. "And which god, my lord? He of the east, who is light and truth, or he of the west, who is darkness and the Lie?"

"Aren't they both, in the end, the same?"

"Not in their consequences."

"You may argue theology until the stars fall," the empress said, clear and cold, "but it changes nothing that is. Estarion, mere error we can forgive. Idiocy, never. What if you had been killed?"

Vanyi kept her eyes scrupulously on her feet. One of her boots needed mending. Tomorrow, if there was time. If tomorrow came.

She felt the heat that burned in her lover's body. Heat of the sun, and heat of temper banked, flaring to sudden brilliance. Yet he kept his voice low. "If I cannot walk alone in my own empire, by my own river, under my own sky, then god and goddess forbid that I call myself emperor." He drew a breath so sharp it must have cut. "This is Keruvarion, Mother. In Asanion, yes, I'll walk low and I'll walk soft, and I'll never walk unguarded. Here at least, while I walk in my own country, let me walk free."

"Very pretty," she said. "Very foolish. Is a border a wall and a warded fastness, that no assassin should pass it?"

"Not here," he said, lower yet, and fiercer. "Not in Keruvarion. I'm not an utter fool. I have an art or two here and there. I can guard myself."

"So your father said," said Merian.

Estarion started, then went still. Those were cruel words, Vanyi thought, but—yes—necessary.

He looked rather more angry than convinced. But he did not argue further, nor say much at all, until his mother was gone. And then he only said, low, as if to himself, "He never died in Keruvarion."

EIGHT

O H AYE," SAID SIDANI, "I SAILED THE SEAS WITH CHUBADAI. HE WAS NEVER quite the pirate that they say, but he took what he wanted, when he wanted it, and if he wasn't too careful about how he paid for it, well then, as often as he stole it outright, he rendered its value in gold thrice over."

"Stolen gold," someone said.

Someone else jeered at him. "I'll wager he magicked it out of the sea-salt, to deck his lady with."

"He never magicked any for me," Sidani said. That made them all laugh. The nearest yelped: she had a hard hand. "Puppy! I was none so ill to look at when I was young. Though I grant you, I'd lost the best of it by the time Chubadai set eyes on me. I was a whip-lean mad thing with an ear for the sea-spells, and so he took me on, and sailed the world around."

Vanyi listened in spite of herself. There was always a crowd where the wanderer was, pressing her for one of her wild tales or coaxing her into a song. She could sing with a voice that time had barely blunted, and she could play the harp that one of the lordlings had given her. God and goddess knew, *he* could barely play it; and for a wonder he knew it. He was in love with her. He made no secret of it. They were all twitting him for his ancient lady fair.

But never where the woman could hear. And never with conviction enough to suit Vanyi. The damnable creature was looking younger by the hour. On the ferry across Suvien, though the swirl and rush of water made the mages ill, all but Vanyi who was seaborn, Sidani stood in the bow with the wind in her hair, and she laughed as the great ungainly thing rocked and pitched under the weight of its cargo.

Estarion was delighted with her. She had claimed one of the remounts for herself, a mean-tempered gelding who knew too well the use of his stunted horns, and she rode him as if she were born to his back. They rode for long hours knee to knee, trading tales; or sat by the fire of an evening, arguing the ways of men and gods; or sang together, dark voice and light, and sometimes, by a trick of the wind, Vanyi could not tell which was which.

The nights were another matter. He was all Vanyi's then, so wholly that often she wanted to weep. She kept a brave face for him, and braver, the nearer they came to Asanion. "I'll never leave you," he said, "nor send you away, unless you ask to go. I swear it, my love. No matter what comes of this—I'll never be aught but yours."

"Hush," she said, and stopped his mouth with her hand. His beard was well grown in, rich and full; she had trimmed it that morning, smoothing its ragged edges. She tangled her fingers in the curls of it. "Don't swear to anything. Just let us have what we have now, for as long as we may have it."

"Always," he said.

Her throat locked. She flung herself on him as if he were a feast and she were starving.

He fell asleep unwontedly soon. This traveling tired him, for all that he denied it. And the last few nights had been short of sleep: all of them in towns along the edge of the great wood, and all much beset with petitions for him to grant, dignitaries for him to entertain, affairs for him to settle.

In a day or two they would enter Asanion. Tonight they guested in another of the numberless towns; but Saluyan was less importunate than the rest. Its people had let him go not long after sunset. Its priestess was compassionate. "Poor my lord," she said where Vanyi could hear, "you need sleep more than we need your sleeplessness. Rest, sire, and be comforted. We'll not trouble you till you wish to be troubled."

He would have argued with that, of course, but the priestess was adamant. He would sleep, and her people would let him be. Wise woman. Stubborn too, to resist Estarion.

Not that one would expect any less from Iburan's kinswoman. In her the northern blood ran thin, though it gave her height and breadth enough to tower over people here. She was a brown-gold woman, brown-gold skin, gold-brown hair, brown-gold eyes: Asanian blood, Asanian face, but enough of north and east that Estarion barely bridled at the sight of her. He warmed to her swiftly, even when she opposed his will: and that was a rarity.

They were still awake, Iburan and the priestess, cousin and cousin. The empress was with them. Vanyi was hardly tempted to join their company. Nor was she minded quite yet to sleep. Restlessness twitched in her, and something deep, like an ache, or a cramping in her middle. It had been vexing her off and on for a day or two. Travel-weariness; anxiety for Estarion and for herself; too much riding and too little walking and not enough plain stillness.

She kissed Estarion's brow. He murmured in his sleep, but did not wake. She left him softly, pulling on such clothes as came to hand, and crept barefoot out of the room they shared.

This was the priestess' house, the largest in this town and for leagues about. Vanyi had counted ten rooms besides the room they dined in. Still it was hardly large enough for an emperor's train. Most of Estarion's escort camped outside the town; only his Guard and his closest companions shared his lodging.

Sidani should not have been one of them, and yet she was. Vanyi found her in the temple, or rather at the entrance of it, leaning against the doorpost. As Vanyi approached she moved aside, somewhat to Vanyi's surprise. She had looked as immovable as one of the pillars.

Vanyi wanted to pray at this altar, to beg the god's protection for her lover and emperor. The wanting was as keen as a blade, twisting in her center. And yet she paused. The wanderer's face was a shadow in shadow, her mind a singing silence.

"Do you want to come in?" Vanyi asked her.

"Do you give me leave?" Sidani asked. Vanyi could hear no mockery in her, and yet surely that was what it was.

"Do you need it?"

"Maybe," the wanderer said. "I cursed the bright god long ago, and his dark sister too. They took from me all that I loved. They left me in ashes."

"They do that," said Vanyi. "They give, and they take away. Else they'd not be gods."

"Maybe we need no gods."

Vanyi was not unduly shocked. One learned on Journey: not everyone yielded easily to the gods' will.

Sidani moved forward into the light of the vigil-lamp, almost as if she had forgotten that she entered a temple. Her face was still a shadow, but her eyes were bright, fixed on Vanyi's face. "For once I don't appall you. Do you agree with me, then?"

"You know I don't."

Sidani looked down at her feet on the fine colored pavement, and up past Vanyi to the altar with its undying light. Her hand rose to her throat. Something, some trick of the lamplight, caught the thickening of scars. Old galls.

Slave's collar? There were no slaves under the sway of the Sun.

Vanyi touched her torque. No slaves. But priests enough, and the torque a cruel weight, rubbing raw the necks of those who bore it.

"Yes," said the wanderer. "I was a priestess of the Sun. No one else has seen, do you know that? Least of all your great one, your holy one, your mage and priest and master. He's blind to aught but light."

"You ran away," Vanyi said.

Sidani laughed, harsh as a gorecrow's cry. "Ran, and was not driven? Can you be so sure of that?"

"You're not one to do anything but what you choose for yourself."

"That's a flaw in me," Sidani said. "Yes, I ran. I flung my torque on the altar, cursed the day I took it, and declared myself dead and damned. They wouldn't help me, you see. They wouldn't lend me their power when my beloved was dying."

Vanyi shivered. "They can be cold, the Sun's priests. They'll do nothing for one the god has touched."

"So they said of him. But they always hated him. He wouldn't believe in them, you see, or bow to the god. Not even in the end, when the Light was in his face." Her own was stark, racked with memory. "Oh, he was a cold, cruel, godless, heartless monster of a man, and I loved him with all that I was. He was the half of me. But for him, I would never have been."

"Chubadai?"

Sidani's lips stretched back from her teeth. "That fat pirate? He never laid a hand on me. He knew I'd take it off if he tried."

"He died, your lover. And so you turned apostate." The words were cold on Vanyi's tongue, with a tang of bitterness. "I . . . don't know that I could do as much."

"Why should you? He'll live long, your lissome lad, if an assassin doesn't get him first. My beauty was born to die young. He didn't age too terribly before he went—that much grace the god gave him. He just . . . went. One moment all there for me, and a good hot quarrel we had going, too. The next, empty, drowned in Light."

"You *fought* on his deathbed?"

Sidani smiled. "It was splendid. He insisting to his last breath that there were no gods, and all the proof in front of him, and I ready to strangle him if I didn't kiss him to death first. It took him just then, like lightning from the core of him: seized him and consumed him. No long slow withering into dotage for my lord. He went up like a torch." Her smile died. "That was glorious. But the priests who refused to give him life when he took sick—them, I never forgave. Nor ever shall."

"I should rebuke you," Vanyi said, "if I were a proper priestess."

"You're proper enough." Sidani strode to the altar with the air of one who dares her greatest fear, and turned her face upward to the lamp that hung above it. "There," she said. "There, god and father. See what I think of you. Will you strike me now? You dragged out my life for years past counting, half a mind that I was, half a spirit, half a soul. Take me, damn you. Put an end to this endlessness."

Her grief was like a wind in that holy place, bleak and cold. It was older than Vanyi, and stronger, with power in it beyond magery. It left her empty of thought or will.

Perilous. Some small part of her knew it, fought it. The rest fell before it.

Pain. Her cheek stung. She looked into a face she knew and did not know, black eagle-face, eyes—

"Your eyes are wrong," she said.

They blinked. Sidani drew back. Both of them were on the floor, Vanyi lying, she kneeling, sitting on her heels. Her eyes were perfectly ordinary northern eyes, if sharper than most. Why Vanyi had wanted them to be yellow, she could not think. Fuddlement, no more. They all looked alike, these northerners, with their faces like birds of prey.

For the first time in a long while, she yearned for a face that was like her own. Brown, maybe, with wind and weather, but white under it, and eyes sea-colored, and hair neither straight nor curling but something of both. Sharp-chinned, long-nosed, Island-bred, and no great waveless shield of land between herself and it.

Her fingers clutched at unyielding floor. Her stomach heaved. Laughter choked her. All these days, months, years, and now of all times she succumbed to the land-sickness.

No wonder people said they wanted to die. It racked her: knotted her stomach, cramped her belly, doubled her up gasping.

A thin strong hand stroked her hair back from her sweating face. Arms lifted her. A voice spoke, cursing softly and with great inventiveness.

"Not," said Vanyi. "Not your fault."

"Only about half of it." Sidani held her as she struggled, with ease that froze her into stillness. "Stop that. This place is too strong for you, with what I woke in it. I'm taking you where you'll be safer."

"Don't need—don't want—"

Little good that did. Vanyi was going to be properly and catastrophically sick, and soon. She hoped she would not do it all over Sidani's coat.

These new eyes above her were as they should be, bright gold with astonishment in the dark face, and the temper that flared in it was oddly comforting. Arms somewhat stronger and much more welcome closed about her. Anger trembled in them. "What's wrong with her? What did you do to her?"

"Nothing," Vanyi said before Sidani could begin. "The sea. It's too far. My blood—my tides—"

They were flowing out of her. Relentless, as if the moons had set hooks in her belly and torn it apart. As if—

"No!"

Her courses were strong. They always had been. But this was stronger than anything she had known. There was more in it than the tide of the moons, more in her womb than vows and emptiness.

The bindings had failed. They had made a child together, she and Estarion— neither of them suspecting, neither of them dreaming that it could be possible.

And it died, this son, this daughter, it did not matter. The bindings, waking too late, closed in upon it. They killed it. Nothing that she did could stop it.

"What did you do to her?"

Estarion was much quieter this time. The anger was beaten out of him.

Neither of them had moved to fetch help. Sidani knew what to do: her hands were deft, catching the flood when it came, stanching it with cloths that she drew it seemed from air. One of her hands did not move as well as the other, he noticed with remote and bitter clarity. It was twisted somewhat, and its palm was scarred as if she had held it in a fire. Odd that he had not noticed before. Odd that he noticed now, or cared, when nothing should matter but Vanyi's life.

"I think," the woman said when Vanyi was quiet, more asleep than unconscious, "that you had somewhat more to do with this than I. Has she miscarried before?"

The word rang in his brain. "Mis—" He tossed his head. It would not come clear. "She can't! She's womb-bound. Spelled. She can't—"

"You forget what you are," Sidani said. "Did no one teach you to hold your seed until you were ready to beget your heir?"

He recoiled. "That's barbaric!"

Her laughter was weary beyond telling. Something in it struck him nearly to tears. "So. That much of Asanion is yours. Did your mother know what she was permitting? Or did she care?"

He could not think of that. Of what it would mean. That his mother knew, and had not prevented it.

"The goddess is a milder thing than she was when I was young," Sidani said, still in that tired voice, but without the terrible mirth. "But she's a cold one still, and heedless of life or light. I can't fault your mother, I suppose. She's but serving the power she's sworn to."

"My mother is not evil!"

"Of course not," said Sidani. "She's a good priestess and a strong empress. Your father chose her well." As if, thought Estarion, she had a right to judge. "But she did ill not to warn you that the Sun's seed is stronger than mages' bindings. That it could come to this."

He looked down at Vanyi. She seemed very small in the wide bed, very white and still. His heart twisted. "Oh, god and goddess. I could have killed her."

"Nonsense!" He jumped at the sharpness in Sidani's tone. "She's a good, strong wench—or she would be if your priests hadn't meddled with her cycles. Better for you both if she'd seen to it herself, and not trusted in someone else's bindings. Although," she added, musing, "even that might not have come to anything, you being what you are. *That* fire will burn in the void between the stars."

"What are you? How do you know so much?"

The bright black eyes slanted toward him and then away. There was nothing old in them at all, and nothing young. They were beyond age. "I tell stories. I live a few, maybe. Your grandfather got your father on a woman proven barren, proclaimed so by mages. He sowed his seed in the dry land, and it brought forth a bright fruit. She's no fallow field, this one, nor will be, now the gates are open."

Estarion's hands lowered of themselves to Vanyi's body, tracing the paths of life and magic. They ran clean and they ran straight, no knot of coiled spells beneath the heart. Blood had washed it away.

He began to shake. "Gods. Oh, gods. She'll be forsworn."

"Don't moan." Sidani gathered together bloodied sheets and cloths and made a bundle of them. "Someone will have to wash these."

"And explain them."

"Never explain," she said. "You are the emperor. That and no more is your explanation. But," she added, "if you insist, then your lady has had a particularly calamitous onset of her courses. They're never easy for her, are they?"

"No," said Estarion unwillingly. But, "Mages will know as soon as they see her."

"Let them. More fools they, for fancying that they could bridle Sun's blood."

He was not afraid of her, not exactly. But as he saw her standing there like a serving-woman with her armful of bloodied cloths, he knew suddenly and piercingly that she was more than he had imagined. Vanyi had seen it: blessed, damnable perception. She had not seen what was in her own body, not looking for it, not expecting it, and it had betrayed her.

"Go to sleep," said Sidani, dryly practical as any grandmother with a stubborn child. "She'll be sleeping for a while, and when she wakes she'll need you there, as strong as you can be. She wanted that baby too badly to be easy about losing it."

"But she didn't even know—"

The glance that raked him was burning cold. "Manchild," she said, "go to sleep."

And, like the infant that she reckoned him, he went. He sensed no sorcery in it. It simply was.

NINE

A son! A son for the Olenyai!"
The cry rang from the tower of their stronghold, riding the notes of a horn. So it always was when a son was born alive, unblemished, and spoken

for by the mages. Daughters were neither sung nor celebrated, although they suffered the same testing, the same speaking of mages, and the same hard fate if they
failed: death, and casting out for the birds to feed on.

"That's another one for Shajiz," Marid said, down below in the court of swords,
where he was alone but for his swordbrother. "What does that make now? Six?
Seven?"

"Five," said Korusan. He was honing his right-hand sword; he had barely
paused for the birthing-call.

Marid shrugged. "Then he's got two more coming. Remarkable. Do you remember when he was so behindhand in his duty that they were talking of forbidding
him the women altogether?"

Korusan ran the stone down the bright blade and up again. "So they were," he
said. His voice had no inflection.

Marid shot him a glance. Here where none could see them but Olenyai, he went
unveiled. The single scar on his cheek was as redly new and no doubt as itchy in its
mending as Korusan's: he rubbed it, fidgeting as he always did, for Marid was a
restless man. "Some come late to it, that's all."

Korusan's hand stopped. He thought of clasping the sharpened steel, for the
pleasure of the pain. "You have two sons," he said.

"So will you, when you get to it."

"I go to the women every night," said Korusan. "Every cycle of Brightmoon
they name themselves and the men who have gone to them, and the seed that has
sprouted in them. They often name me among the sowers. But never among the
harvest."

"You're very young," said Marid, who to be sure was a whole year the elder.

"I was doing a man's duty while you were still a flute-voiced child."

"And who was it that I heard last cycle, singing descant with the girls?"

Korusan's sword sang into its sheath. There had been a moment while he raised
it, when Marid's eyes had flickered, his hand twitched toward his own sheathed
blade. But he would not begin battle, if battle must be. Not against his swordbrother.

Korusan would have liked to be as certain of himself. Olenyai were loyal to their
lords and to one another. It was bred into them. But Korusan was not Olenyas—
not in the blood, and not in the soul.

"I think," said Korusan. "I fear . . ."

He could not say it, even to Marid, who was as close to him as any living thing
could be.

Nor would Marid set it in words for him. He was blind, was Marid, and deaf to
what he did not wish to hear. "Shajiz was one-and-twenty when his first son was
conceived; and he had been going to the women since he was twelve years old.
Early manhood isn't early fatherhood, brother."

"Early is all I have," said Korusan. But not loudly. Not for Marid to hear. He thrust himself to his feet. "Maybe it will be tonight."

Marid grinned, transparent in his relief. "Maybe it will. Luck to your sowing, Olenyas."

"Luck to your reaping," said Korusan, "Olenyas."

The woman was willing. She was beautiful, also, as they often were, and she was skilled in the high arts. She could receive as well as give pleasure. Her murmur of thanks seemed honest, her smile unfeigned when he paid her the compliment of asking, "May I come to you again?"

She lowered her eyes as was proper, and said, "My lord, you may." And then she said: "Tomorrow, if it pleases my lord."

His heart should have been light. The women of the Olenyai were given to choose whom they would see a second time, as it was given the men to choose whom they would visit once. He had pleased her, then, and well.

But he was in a bleak mood as he left the place of the women and entered the place of the men. Harems in the world without, he was told, were scented, close-walled places. This was walled, to be sure, but its scents were simple ones: clean flesh, clean garments, the pungency of herbs or the sweetness of a flower in a woman's hair. Olenyai knew well the arts of simplicity. It made them strong; it taught them to focus on what mattered.

Men leaving the women's quarters walked a path well trodden through the years, up a stair worn deep in the middle, along a passage hung with tapestries so old as to have lost all color and figure and faded to the muted brown-grey of the stone behind them. Then they turned, either up to their own place—whether chamber or barracks—or down to the training grounds and the gates.

Although it was late, well past the midnight bell, Korusan turned toward one of the gates. It was unguarded. No one in Asanion would enter the fortress of the Olenyai, even if he had won his way so far. To pass those walls was forbidden any not of the Order, or of the House of the Lion. The lands that lay about it were not wide as princely domains went, but they sufficed to feed and furbish the castle; and they were guarded as the gates were not, by men in black robes with hidden faces.

He slid the bolt easily, for it was kept well oiled, and stepped into the cool of the dark before dawn. It had rained in the early night, but now all the clouds were blown away. The moons were glorious: blood-red Greatmoon at the full, silver Brightmoon some days short of it, filling the sky with fire, overwhelming all but the brightest of the stars.

There was someone sitting near the gate on a heap of stone left over from the building and grown now into the earth it lay on. In the bright moonlight the robe was silver, but it would be grey in the sun; the hair was frosted white, but would be youthful gold where eyes saw daylight-clear.

Korusan knew this lightmage by sight. It was a woman, and often about the castle. He had not seen her alone before, without her darkmage shadow. Here she had shadows in plenty, but none lived and breathed. They were all born of the moons.

Her eyes glittered as she turned them toward him. He knew better than to think that she had not been aware of him from the moment he opened the gate, and likely before that.

"It is odd," he said, "to see a lightmage here, under the moons."

"But they are as bright almost as day," she said.

"Almost," said Korusan. Perhaps he should feel his presumption. Olenyai did not speak thus easily with mages, as if mages were folk like any other. But he was not born an Olenyas.

"We all must understand our opposites," the lightmage said, "or they may consume us."

"Have you consumed your opposite?" Korusan inquired.

She laughed, a silver sound, so alien to her rank and to this place that he started. "Oh, my darkmage! He is a daytime creature; the sun sets, and he falls asleep, and sleeps the night through. But I can never sleep when the moons are high. Do you hear them singing?"

"I am not a mage," said Korusan.

She took no offense at the flatness of his tone. "Of course you are not. But you have the gift. I saw you when you ran the dreamwood."

"All your ilk saw me," Korusan said. "I could wish to return the favor."

"You pay the price of princes," said the lightmage. She clasped her knees, looking all of his own age, if that, and smiled at him.

He could strike her, and she would have no defense.

Not of the body. But that was not what held his hand: not knowing that she had magic. He had a use for her. "Tell me somewhat," he said.

She raised moon-silvered brows and waited.

He wondered if she had tried to enter his mind. Mages did that. He had felt nothing, no crawling of the spine that would have warned him. "Tell me this, mage. Will I beget a son?"

Her brows rose higher. "Do you take me for a village witch, to tell your fortune for you?"

"Will I?" he pressed her, stepping closer. She neither recoiled nor betrayed alarm. Her magic would protect her, no doubt, and she was sure of it.

"Truly," she said, "I am not a soothsayer. Find you a market, prince, and ask there."

He stood over her. She was complacent still, but she had to lean back a little lest he topple her. "Look inside me. Tell me what all your kind know. Will there be another after me? Or am I the last?"

"Are you not young to fret over that?"

He struck her, flat-handed, on the cheek. She looked perfectly astonished. No one ever laid hand on a mage. No one dared.

"You are older than I," he said, "but which of us is the greater fool?"

"I could blast you with fire," she said, no rancor in it, nor threat, but simple certainty.

He laughed in her face. "So you could; and kill your magic with it. Yes, I know that secret of your trade. Who does not, after the plot that succeeded so well for your kind? You disposed of an emperor; you maimed his son. But you betrayed yourselves to those with wits to see."

"We betrayed nothing that belonged to us," she said, and now at last her voice had an edge of anger. "All who speak of that killing, speak of the fool who did it. No one knows who set him there, or who took his wits from him lest the priests discover the truth."

"No one," said Korusan, "but the Olenyai. And we are too valuable as we are. Tell me, mage. Tell the one whom you would make your emperor. Am I to be the last and only, and after me, nothing?"

"One will rule after you," she said.

"Indeed? And will that one be the Master of your Guild?"

She did not answer that.

"The blood has failed," he said. "Has it not? I remember, mage. When I was not quite yet a man, and one of my many fevers was fiercer than the rest, and you thought that I was unconscious, but I heard. You could save me, but you could not save my children who would be."

"Not I," she said. "That was not I."

"Are you not all one?" He stepped back, releasing her from his shadow. "It is true. I can beget no sons."

"You are young," she said, but faint, as if he had frightened her. "You cannot know . . ."

He wheeled. The moons spun. He flung himself through the gate. He did not care how he went, save that it was swift; or whom he trampled in going there.

When he stopped, it was not by choice of his own. He might have struck a wall, but there was only air, and a chamber lit with lamps—but none of them flickered as earthly fire would—and cold eyes regarding him from the cushions and coverlets of a bed.

The Master of mages slept alone, or liked to have it seem that he did. He slept decently in underrobe and outer robe, and warmed his sparse-haired crown with a cap. He looked like a merchant from the provinces, but that was a deception.

"You are violent this morning, my lord," he said. "Did our youngest girlchild offend your highness? Does your highness wish her heart on a salver?"

"If I assented, would you give it to me?"

The Guildmaster smiled. These mages were all as complacent as cats. "I would, my lord, if it would content you."

"Anything for the prince," said Korusan with a bitter twist. "Anything at all. Except an heir."

"I am sorry for that," the Guildmaster said.

Perhaps it was honest regret. "So it is true," Korusan said.

"Even had the fever not made sure of it, we would have held out little hope," said the Guildmaster. "You are a miracle in yourself, with all the aid that we have given you, to keep you living, to raise you to manhood. We would not look for another such chance."

Korusan was prepared for it. He had looked for no gentler truth, but it was no easier to face for that.

"Olenyai gain rank," he said, "for the number of sons they sire."

"Not only for that," said the Guildmaster, "and not even for that among the highest. Any beast can beget young. It needs a man to rule men."

"And what is a man but a father of sons?"

"I have no sons," the Guildmaster said. "No mage of my rank does, or can. We make that sacrifice when we choose this path."

Korusan was not shocked. That too he had known, from what he had heard or suspected. "But you are not a prince, mage. You will not be emperor. And emperors must beget heirs."

"Not all of them do," the mage said, "or have."

"What, then?" Korusan demanded as he had of the lightmage. "What comes after me?"

"Do you care?"

Korusan drew up short.

"Do you truly care?" the Guildmaster asked him. "You live to take revenge against the Sun's brood. Once they are gone and you are dead, what does it matter who calls himself lord of the world?"

"It matters," Korusan said, "if that lord is the lord of your Guild."

"Why? Might not a mage rule as well as any man?"

Korusan stood up against the mage's wall and tasted the savors of rage, impotence, raw grief. And hate, always hate, like blood and iron. "So that is what you intend. Why trouble with me, then? Why breed me, raise me, keep me alive? Why not simply face the Sun-worshippers direct, and fight an open war? Surely it would be less trouble. Even," he said, "for cowardice as mighty as yours."

The Master of the Guild was not to be pricked by such words, however bitter they might be. "Perhaps we prefer the symmetry of this conflict, Sun against Lion. Perhaps the gods demand it, or fate, or the turning of the worlds; and if we defy it or seek to alter it, we destroy ourselves with our enemies."

"Perhaps you are afraid to face the Sun and its priests, because they are strong, and they may defeat you."

"We are stronger," said the mage, "and we are older in our magic. But secrecy is our armor, that is true enough. And we owe the Lion a debt. It took us in when we were driven from the Sunborn's empire; it protected us when his heir would have blotted us from the earth. We repay in you, in raising you to the throne that is yours."

"A barren throne," said Korusan. "An empty victory."

"Do you believe that, Lion's cub? It will be your throne, your victory."

"And I your puppet."

"You are no man's puppet," said the Guildmaster.

"What if," said Korusan, "when I had won the victory, when I had my throne—what if I ordered all of you destroyed? What would you do then?"

"We would fight," the Guildmaster said. "We wager high, prince, and we wager long. We gamble on your clemency, as we gambled on your being born at all, or living to stand here now, and show yourself in truth the Lion's heir."

"Flattery," said Korusan. But the anger had gone out of him. He was cold within, and empty. Where another man had his little tribe of ancestors, he had a thousand years and more, an army of emperors. Where even the simplest man had hope of sons, he had nothing. Only emptiness and the line's ending.

"Perhaps it may console you," the Guildmaster said, "that your enemy has begotten a son, but the son is lost."

"And that too was your doing?"

"No," said the Guildmaster with all apparent calm. "His own priests did it for us, in womb-binding the woman who is his lover. Fools all. None bethought himself of what must come of working that spell on a Sunlord's leman."

Korusan's gorge rose. That his blood enemy should do what he could not do. That this fat merchant with his half-god's magic should gloat so over the death of a child.

He turned without speaking, without even the courtesy of a glance, and left as he had come, headlong. No wall barred him. Nothing stopped or slowed him but his own bones' weariness and the dawn breaking, and the rousing of the Olenyai to the morning's duties. His first duty was sword-practice. And though he ached within and without, he was glad of that grueling dance, glad of anything that bent his mind away from the dark.

TEN

VANYI HAD NO INTENTION OF FEIGNING ILLNESS, OR OF SUFFERING IT. SHE could ride. She had before when her courses racked her, numbed with a potion the priestesses brewed for just such troubles as this.

Estarion could not move her, even when he lost his temper. She turned her back on the blast of it and set about readying to depart.

The drug numbed her body. There was pain somewhere on the edge of things, but it was no part of her, no more than the memory of what had caused it: what had broken, and what had mended, before Avaryan's altar.

She had lost nothing that she had known she had. She had gained a thing beyond hope. She could bear a child now. She could give Estarion his heir.

Through drug and distance and grim endurance, her entrails clamped tight. Only Estarion's presence kept her erect. She reached blindly for she knew not what; stared at what her hand fell on. For a long moment she could not guess what it was, could not name it or imagine a use for it.

Her fingers clenched. She had not even known.

"Who took off my torque?" she asked. Her throat was tight, had been since she got up, not knowing itself unbound, no more than her womb until it gave up its burden.

"Sidani," Estarion answered. "She feared you'd choke."

"Damn her," said Vanyi. "*Damn* her."

He reached for her. She slid away. Her hands trembled as she lifted the torque. It was deadly heavy, and cold. It locked like jaws about her neck.

She looked up into Estarion's face. "She was a priestess, you know. Sidani. Or whatever her name was then. She turned apostate."

"She told you that?"

"Would I lie?"

He stiffened as if she had struck him. She should kiss him, or say something to comfort him. Mind and heart were empty, void of comfort. It had bled out of her in the long grim night.

She shouldered her saddlepacks. The world spun briefly. Estarion spun in it, too bleak for anger. She walked away from him.

"You may go," he said behind her, "but I am staying here."

She stopped. She refused to turn.

"I promised the priestess that I would sing the tenth-day rite with her. That is tomorrow. I'll not leave till that is done."

"And when did you promise that?"

"Does it matter?"

The doorpost swung toward her. She caught at it.

He was there, hovering. She did not want him to touch her. "Let me," she said, thick enough to choke on. "Let me be."

"Vanyi—"

"Let me be!"

He retreated, too startled for hurt. That would come later. She did not want to see it.

He had mercy. He left her alone.

"That was well done," said Iburan.

Vanyi burrowed deeper into her nest of blankets. How long it had been, whether it was morning or evening, she neither knew nor cared. People had come in at intervals. Some had left food or drink. Some had tried to speak to her. She had shut them out.

Iburan was not to be deterred by anything as simple as blankets or a magewall. His voice followed her wherever she escaped. "Yes, you did well, to drive away the one who could best have healed you."

"The one who caused my pain."

He heard her. "So. You blame him."

She erupted from her lair. "I blame myself. I should have known. I should have prevented—"

"You should," he said. "Therefore you punish him for your own failing."

"No," she said. She shivered, though the air was warm. "No. I—" The rest would not come. She cried out through it. "Don't you touch him. Don't you dare! He knew even less than I."

"Why would I touch him?"

"Time was," she said, "when you would have taken us both and bound us to altars of iron, and turned the burning glass on us, and called down the Sun to sear away the source of our sin."

"Those were older days, older laws. The Sunborn came to free us from them."

"The Sunborn's descendant is too free altogether."

"You yourself said he didn't know."

She blinked. Her eyes were full of tears. Iburan was a blur beyond them, a shadow and a gleam. "It shouldn't matter. Every turning of Brightmoon this comes to me, to every woman. Why I do want to weep and howl at the moons?"

"Because this time it took more than the moon's blood. It took the child you made, you and he together."

"No," she said. "The moon didn't take that. *You* took it, priest of the Sun. You and the magic you wove."

Not he, not for her. That had been a priestess in the Isles, raising the great rite over the god's new-made bride. But he knew what she meant. "We had no way of knowing that this would happen. This time, when we weave the bonds anew—"

"You will weave no bonds," she said.

"You will bear him no child while your Journey endures."

His voice was soft, but there was iron in it. She met it with iron as strong. "Nor shall I ever bear him one, if you have your way. His heir will be a yellow woman's son."

"Will you defy your vows?"

She sat stiff. Her body ached, but worse was the ache in her heart. "Are you binding me?"

"You said that I should not."

It was too much, this war of wills. Her belly cramped. To yield to it—to crumple with a cry—that would be a clever diversion, and he would fall to it. She would not do it. "At this moment," she said, struggling to say it steadily, "when I think of him, I love him with all that I am. And when I think of him touching me, I shudder in my soul. Something is wrong with me, my lord. Something broke when the binding went away. Aren't you glad?"

"Child," he said. "Oh, child."

His compassion did not make her want to weep. It made her want to kill him. "Don't pity me!"

"That, I never have." He seemed at last to recall that he was looming over her. He sat in the chair beside the bed, sighing as he did it, as if with weariness. Sleights and calculation. She hardened her heart against them.

His beard was braided with gold this morning, evening, whatever it was. He stroked it as he sat there, eyes turned away from her, fixed on something only he could see. He looked nothing like Estarion, except that he was so dark, and yet she could not get that other face out of her mind. Callow, beak-nosed, yellow-eyed face. She loved it, she hated it. She wanted to enfold herself in the memory of it. She wanted to efface it utterly.

"You hurt," said Iburan, so low it was like a mountain shifting. "You strike out at anything that approaches you. Time will heal you. Time, and the nearness of those who love you."

"Not his," she said. "You'll see to that, I'm sure. It's best for everyone. He has to make an Asanian marriage. I'm an intrusion, an inconvenience. You never planned for me or wanted me, or anyone like me. You were keeping him for his royal bride."

"He kept himself. Sun-blood are always so. They do not—cannot—love lightly."

"And no wonder," she said. Bitter laughter burst out of her. "Seed, you men call it? Arrows, the Sun-blood have. Nothing is proof against them."

Iburan did not laugh with her. "What will you do, then? Take yourself away?"

"Wouldn't it be best?"

"It would give him great pain."

"Brief pain. Assuaged, I'm sure, by a procession of lovely ladies. Royal ladies. Ladies fit to be his queen."

"Do you hold him so light?" Iburan asked her, as if he honestly wished to know.

She looked him in the face. "Sometimes, my lord, I wonder. I wasn't raised to be a Sunlord's bride. When I told my father I was going to the temple, he beat me. Loving me, you understand, and determined to save me from myself. I was to be a wife in Seiun town, marry one of the boys who hung about making eyes at me, breed his babies and mend his nets and weave his sails. The temple was for other people, priest-people, people bred to it. The witcheries that haunted me would go away, my father said, when I had a baby at the breast. So they'd done for my mother, and she a sea-eyed changeling too. The sea took her, I told him. Should I let it take me? So I went away, walking straight in spite of my bruises, and when I took the torque, he wouldn't speak to me. What he would say if he knew what I'd gone away to, I dread to think."

Iburan said nothing. Eloquent, she thought. Subtle.

"You can't understand," she said. "You're all lords and princes. You don't know what it's like not to know for certain who your grandfather's father was, or where he came from. You can't imagine the clench of hunger in a lean winter, or the stink of fish in the summer's heat. You've never gone barefoot because you had no shoes, or worn the same filthy shirt the year round because there was no cloth to make another. And you've never—never—been spat on for a witch, not for anything you'd done, but for that you looked like a changeling."

"Estarion has."

She caught her breath. "Estarion is the highest of all high princes. He's as far above me as the sun itself. And he doesn't know. He doesn't think. He thinks he loves me."

"He does."

"He's a fool," she said. "There. I said it. I'll go away now. I'll set him free."

"If you leave now," said Iburan, "he'll go after you. He does love you, child. With all his great heart."

The tears were threatening to come back. She willed them away. "So I'm to make him stop loving me. Is that it? Is that what you want me to do?"

"I doubt you could."

"Oh, it's easy," she said. "It's as easy as a slap in his face. He's never been denied anything, never had to do anything he didn't want to do. Even this journey to Asanion is his choosing, though he imagines that his mother forced him into it. He's always known he'd have to do it. He let her work her will on him."

"And you? What will you do to yourself?"

"Do I matter? Do I, my lord, when you consider the empire, and the man who is emperor of it?"

There, at last, a question Avaryan's high priest could not answer. She regarded him in something like pity. "You won't bind me, my lord. I'll bind myself. I can read the god's will as well as you. I can see that I'm not meant for the emperor."

"I can see," he said, "that you need rest, and healing for the soul as well as the body. The servant will bring you wine. You'll drink it: I'll mix in an herb I know of. It brings nothing more deadly than sleep."

"Maybe I have a drug of my own."

"That is too strong in you. It makes you say things you never mean. Lie down now, and grieve if you must. It will help you mend."

PART TWO

Kundri'j Asan

ELEVEN

ESTARION KNEW WHEN HE CROSSED THE BORDER INTO ASANION. IT WAS MORE than the softening of wild country into towns and tilled fields, forest tracks into roads, black or bronze faces into faces more truly gold and ivory. It was a thrumming in the blood, a quiver in the senses. Recognition—he did not want to call it that. Some part of him knew this earth, this air, this face of the world. It was not memory of his coming there half his life ago. It went deeper than that.

Half a day past the border, he stopped and dismounted and laid his hands on the earth. It was not so very different from the land he had left behind: rich black earth, fragrant with the rain that had fallen in the morning. It trembled under his touch. It knew him.

His companions were watching him as if they feared that he would break and run shrieking back to Keruvarion. He straightened. His right hand burned and throbbed. The earth that clung to it could not stain the gold in its palm.

He vaulted back into the saddle. "On," he said, snapping it off short.

The land knew him, welcomed him. But it lay crushed and flattened beneath the feet of the men who lived on it. There were no wild places. Even the woods were lords' possessions, their trees counted and reckoned for their worth, their beasts and birds preserved for the hunt or for their owners' pleasure. The rivers flowed in chains: locks and quays and bridges. The hills were tamed things, crowned with cities.

Worse still was the silence. People lined the ways to see him pass; came, it was evident, from many days' journey to look on their emperor. And when he was before them, they would not meet his eyes. They would not look at him at all, or cheer his passing, or speak when he spoke to them, but fell mute and bowed to the ground.

"All I see of them are their rumps," he said. "Their rumps, and the backs of their heads. How am I supposed to learn to know them?"

There would be no camps under the stars in the Golden Empire. On this, his first night in the west, he lodged with the lord of a town called Shon'ai. The man was endurable as Asanians went: old enough and secure enough not to be unduly touchy in his pride. Nor did he seem dismayed to be guesting the emperor himself.

"But he won't look me in the face," Estarion said. "What does he think I'll do to him if he does? Blast him with a glance?"

"It's their courtesy," Sidani said. What she was doing in the rooms he had been given, he did not know. She went where she would, did as she chose. Guards seemed to mean little to her, or princely privacy. She was adept at ignoring both.

Estarion was glad of her presence now: it gave him someone to storm at. Servants were no good for that. They cringed and fled. Godri was seeing that the seneldi were properly looked after. Vanyi was nowhere that Estarion could find, which was as well. She had been impossible since she lost the baby, would not open her mind to him, would not let him approach her, would accept nothing from him, no comfort, no anger, not even bleak endurance.

Sidani was the same as she always was. She sat in a chair like a throne, feet tucked up, hands folded in her lap, and watched him snarl and pace.

He came to a halt in front of her. He was breathing hard, somewhat to his surprise. The air was wrong here. Suffocating, even under the sky.

"You have a horror of closed spaces," she said. "You'll loathe Kundri'j Asan."

"What choice do I have?" he demanded.

She shrugged. "You could have been born a peasant's brat."

He dropped to the carpet at her feet. "No," he said. "I would have hated that, and wanted more. I wasn't made to be anything less than I am. Am I growing wise, do you think? Or simply arrogant?"

"You were born arrogant. Wisdom . . . you'll have it someday, if you live so long."

"Not now?"

"Now," she said, "you are a spoiled child. A dusty, dirty, sweaty one, who would profit from a bath."

She failed to make him angry, though she had made a noble effort. He bared his teeth at her. "I know why I keep you. To keep me humble."

"No man keeps me. I stay because I choose. To keep you humble."

He laughed. He did not get up at once, though a bath was a glorious temptation. "You keep me sane too, I think. Everyone else is so strange. Walking soft as cats, as if I'll go wild and tear them to pieces. Vanyi . . ." His throat tightened. "Vanyi shuns me. Because my body betrayed her."

"Not yours, youngling. She's not the mage she thought she was. She finds that hard to forgive in herself."

"Does she think I don't care? It was my baby, too."

"Did you want it as badly as she did?"

He could not answer that. He wanted an heir, yes. He had been bred and raised to want one. "It would be terribly impolitic, if my mother's to be believed. Then I wouldn't need an Asanian empress."

"That could be dealt with. There's the Sunborn's law, true, that the firstborn of the Sun's heir, whether son or daughter, is heir to the throne. But there's nothing in the law that the child's mother must be empress."

"It would be awkward if she weren't." He pulled himself to his feet. "They're waiting for me now. Hordes of them. Women of every size and shape, but only one color. I won't eat till I've passed them in review."

"It's not as bad as that," Sidani said.

"Do you want to wager on it?"

She said nothing. He took odd comfort in her disapproval. *She* did not want him to marry for cold politics. She cared nothing at all for such things.

"Only remember," she said. "They're people, not devils. Even if they do have yellow eyes."

He lowered his own. "I can't help it."

"Nonsense."

"They killed my father."

"A demented fool killed your father. Stop whining, child. He died, and that was an ill thing. You killed his murderer with magery, and that was a worse thing. It's none of it Asanion's fault."

"I don't need to listen to you," he said through gritted teeth. "I hear it from my mother, I hear it from Iburan, I hear it endlessly and forever, and it doesn't matter. Here, in my belly, I know what I know. Asanion will be the death of me."

"Poppycock," said Sidani. "You've stewed it in your innards till it's gone to bile, and not a drop of truth in it. You should have stayed here till you were whole again, or come back as soon as you could ride."

"How do you know what is truth and what is not?"

She smiled her terrible, sweet smile. "I've lived a little longer than you, child. There's nothing wrong with Asanion that a good scrubbing and a blast of fresh air won't mend."

"Maybe," he said, "I'll take the roof off the palace in Kundri'j. What will people say to that?"

"That you're stark mad. But they already know as much. You're Sun-blood."

She could drive him to the edge of rage, and back again to laughter. He bowed to her, all the way to the floor, and came up laughing, and went to his bath in better spirits than he could have imagined, his first night in Asanion.

The bath was none so ill. They wanted to shave him smooth, face and body, but he had been warned of that. The servants were men and boys, not women or eunuchs. Except one, maybe; he was beardless past the age one might expect. But he was the lightest-handed, and when the razors approached, he turned them aside before Estarion could do more than roll an eye at them. He even ventured a smile, which Estarion found himself returning.

When he was clean, bathed and oiled till he purred like Ulyai, they offered him garments. Not the ten robes of the imperial majesty, but a simple three, underrobe and inner robe and loose outer robe, all of them white, and the outermost embroidered with gold. It was not an insult, he judged, but a gesture toward his outland sensibilities. They fit him well, which was interesting. In the east he was middling tall; in the north a stripling. Here he rose to a towering height, even unshod as kings walked in their palaces.

Lord Miyaz's servants held up a mirror, a wonder of a thing, a shield of polished silver taller than Estarion by a full handspan. His face had grown no prettier since the last time he looked, though the beard lent it a degree of distinction. His eyes were a brighter gold than he remembered, bright as coins. Time was when he would have demanded a hat or a hood, to cast them in shadow.

Tonight he went bareheaded. The tallest servant bound his brows with a thin band of gold, confining his hair with no more than that, no plaits, no cords, no chains of gems.

He would never look Asanian, however they tried. Not with that face or that midnight skin. The robes made him seem even taller and narrower than he was. He was as exotic as a sunbird in a flock of finches.

He could hunch and creep and hope to pass unnoticed. Or he could stand straight, walk light and haughty, tilt his chin at its most rakish angle. Born arrogant, was he? Then let them see it, and think what thoughts they pleased.

The eunuch, who seemed to be the chief of servants, led him out of the baths and down a passage. He barely noticed its furnishings, if it had any. The air was full of mingled perfumes, amurmur with sweet voices.

He halted. "These are the women's quarters."

The eunuch regarded him without comprehension. He had spoken Gileni unthinking. He shifted to Asanian. "This is not the way to the place of feasting. Why are you leading me among the women?"

His guide bowed to the floor. "Majesty, forgive. The lady empress, she commanded—"

"So she would." Estarion lifted the boy—man—whatever he was—with hands that tried to be gentle. "Go on, then. Lead me where she bade you."

It was a hall of feasting after all, with tables laid, gleaming in the light of many lamps, and flowers banked about them, filling the air with their scents; but no food, no drink in the cups of gold and silver. And no sign of his mother. She was keeping herself out of it, then, or hiding behind an arras and a magewall, watching unseen. Wise lady. The feast stood arrayed before him, trembling or steady, white with terror or blushing scarlet with embarrassment, but every one gowned and jeweled till surely she could not move, and wrapped in veils to the eyes. Yellow eyes in plenty, but dark too, under brows of every color from dun to ivory.

No more than anyone else in this damnable country would they look into his face. But they darted glances. He caught a murmur: "How dark he is! And so tall. Can you imagine—"

The rest of it was drowned in a man's voice. "Sire," said the lord of Shon'ai, "for your majesty's pleasure, we have gathered a garden of flowers. Will you look on them? Will you taste their sweetness?"

Slow heat crawled up Estarion's face. He raised his chin a fraction. "I see a swathe of veils," he said, "and eyes too shy to look on me."

Lord Miyaz gestured sharply. The ladies glanced at one another. Slowly first one and then another raised a hand to her veil.

They were beautiful. He granted them that. Most were too smoothly plump for his taste, and some seemed barely out of childhood. Only one or two dared lift their eyes, and that only for a moment.

He walked down the line of them. They stood like troops on review, with the same air of mingled pride and panic. This was the battle they had been bred for, this war of beauty against beauty, lineage against lineage, and all triumph to the fairest.

He horrified them with his size, with his strangeness, with the rank he bore and the power he embodied. His head was aching. One of them at least was a mage. *Spy*, he thought. He could not muster the proper degree of wariness.

Even if he did not single out an empress, he was expected to choose one for his night's pleasure. That much of Asanian custom he knew.

His gorge rose. He came to the end of the line, turned. They watched him as birds would watch a cat: the same stunned fascination, the same willing acceptance of what must be. He was the predator and they were prey. So the world was made.

He mustered a smile. It was not, he hoped, too ghastly to look at. "My thanks," he said, "my lord and ladies. How can I choose any single lady from amid so much beauty? Will you dine with me, all of you, and enchant me with your company?"

The response was a little time in coming. He held his breath. If he had given insult, he would hear of it to infinity.

Then his lordship said, "The emperor is most kind, and most politic. Those men who wait without—"

"I'll go to them later," Estarion said quickly. "Bid them sit to their own dinner. When the wine comes round, I'll share it with them."

Thus providing himself with an escape. Lord Miyaz saw it, surely, but he bowed with every evidence of approval. "Wisely chosen, majesty." He smote his hands together. The eunuch bowed himself out. Miyaz remained, smiling, watchful, alert to the emperor's every need.

A prince's training had its uses. It taught a man to endure the excruciations of courtesy, to be charming when he would have preferred to turn and bolt. He spoke to every lady in that hall, however shy she was, however weary he grew of yellow faces, yellow eyes, yellow curls under silken veils. He put aside grimly his longing for a sweet dark face, or a sweet white one, sea-eyed, autumn-haired, and a body as supple as it was slender, and a voice that had never learned to giggle in chorus.

He left them smoothly enough, he hoped, to forget for a moment that he had chosen none of them for his bed or his bride. Their fathers and brothers and guardians were waiting for him, schooled to patience, and none quite bold enough to ask the question that burned in every mind. Frayed though he was about the edges, he had power left to charm them as he had their women.

Vanyi was not in the chamber when he came to it. He had dared to hope she would be, at least to quarrel with him. A quarrel would have lightened his spirit.

There were guards on the door: his own, he had been pleased to see when he came in, with eyes that would meet his, and minds that did not quail in fear of his presence. "Find Vanyi," he said to redheaded Alidan, "and tell her I'd welcome her company."

Alidan shifted his feet and looked uncomfortable. "My lord—"

"And when," Estarion wanted to know, "have I ever been 'my lord' to you, except when you were up to something?"

"My lord," Alidan said again. And when Estarion glared: "Starion, Vanyi said to tell you. She won't come to you at night any longer. If you want a woman, she said, you know where to find a sufficiency of them."

The world narrowed to a single, bitter point. Alidan, red Gileni and no coward, flattened against the wall. His face was grey under the bronze.

Estarion spoke softly. "That's not Vanyi speaking. That's my lady mother."

"It is Vanyi," Alidan said. "Believe it, Starion. She told me herself."

"With my mother at her back, forcing her."

"No," said Alidan. "She was alone, and she wasn't under binding. Whoever put her up to it, she wanted it. She said so."

"Bring her to me."

"She won't come," said Alidan. "She said that, too. You'll sleep alone, or you'll sleep with a yellow woman."

Estarion took a step forward. Alidan flattened further. But Estarion had no mind to strike him, and none, upon reflection, to confront Vanyi. She would be guarded with iron and with magic, and if she said she would not see him, then nothing short of a mage-blast would win him through to her.

"Coward," he said to the wall she had raised about herself. It returned no answer.

TWELVE

THIS COLDNESS, THIS THING THAT WAS GROWING IN HERSELF, WAS NOTHING that Vanyi could stop. There had been warmth once, gladness, mind that met mind and knew no walls between them. Loss of the child had altered everything: broken, darkened, marred it perhaps beyond mending.

She loved Estarion still, down at the bottom of things. But it was very far down, and the heart that beat there was a tiny thing, globed as if in glass. When mind or tongue shaped his name, the light about it was warm. But when her eyes looked on him, the wall came up between them. He was other, stranger, emperor. His touch, she knew, would burn.

So he had seemed when she first came to Endros: alien, exotic, not quite human. The quick light wit that masked the knots of old scars, the sudden temper, the smaller things—the way he stretched all over when he woke, like a cat; or the turn of his head when he was startled; or his inexplicable and quite insatiable fondness for sour apples—were walled in with her love for him. She could not touch them.

It was best, she told herself. He had to marry in Asanion. He was too loyal in himself; he would never look at another woman while she was there to distract him. If she turned him away from her, even taught him to hate her, then he would look for comfort where it best served him, and surely find it.

She would happily strangle any woman whom he called beloved. But she could not—physically could not—make herself go to him. Even to face him; to lay her hand over his heart, just so, and know the power that slept in him, and know, know surely, that the child of this night would not die unshaped and scarce begun.

No one tried to talk to her. Estarion's lords and servants were too shy of the priestess-mage or too scornful of the commoner. The guards had no time. The priests had troubles of their own.

That, if she would let it, was cure and physic for her hurt. She had the land-sense—it was the first thing any mage-born child woke to knowledge of, and she had sea-sense on top of it, or water-sense at least. She knew how the earth welcomed Estarion: which was both pleasure and pain, because he had been so sure that it would recoil from him, and because that surety had become a part of her. But something had gone, or was going, awry.

"He's only partblood Asanian," she said to the priests and priestesses who had come from Endros, half a cycle's journey into the Golden Empire, when there was no one else to listen or to intrude. "And we all know what happened to him here. Is he twisting the worldlines, do you think? Or finding them twisted, and tangling them further?"

"If that were all it was," said Shaiyel, in whom the land-sense was so strong that he could wade in the earth as if in water, "then I could mend it with a word." He flushed under their stares. He was young, younger than Vanyi, and almost as pale as she. He kept well out of Estarion's way. He was half Asanian, and he favored his mother, though his eyes were narrower and his cheekbones higher and his hair straighter than any proper Asanian's. He never could understand why people thought him arrogant. He was like Estarion in that. He knew what he could do. Why should he pretend that he did not?

"It's not Estarion," Iburan said. He lounged on a bench against the wall, great black mountain of a man, dressed with uncommon plainness in the white robe that priests of the Sun wore in this part of the world. His beard was braided but ungauded, and his hair was in a single plait. In a little while they would all attend the sunset-rite in the temple of this city—town, rather, as Asanion reckoned it, smaller within its walls than Endros but thronged with double and treble the people.

"It's not the emperor," said Iburan again. "Except that, by living and breathing and walking in this country, he brings it about. I felt something like it when his father came here. Asanion never felt itself joined to Keruvarion in a marriage of equals. It would rule or it would have nothing, no matter the will of its emperors or their blood-right to its throne."

"But it accepts," said Shaiyel. "My mother accepted my father, though he was a slant-eyed plainsman. We are all one, she told me. We must be, or the sun will fall."

Iburan's smile concealed itself in his beard, but Vanyi felt it. "Not quite the sun that rides in the sky. But the Sun that rules out of Endros—yes, that could fall too easily if the half of the prop beneath it breaks asunder."

"One would think," said dour Oromin, "that nigh a hundred years of inescapable fact would impress itself on an empire's mind."

Vanyi faded into the shadows. They were saying nothing that she had not heard innumerable times already, and never to any purpose. On a field of battle half begun, the heir of the Sun and the heir of the Lion, brought together out of all hope, had wedded their two empires. And spent the rest of their lives and the lives of their children struggling to keep that marriage intact. For a long while, maybe, they had been more successful than not. Then Ganiman died in Kundri'j Asan, and his son all but died taking vengeance.

Emperors in Asanion seldom died unaided. It was the way of their succession. But it was not the Sunlords' way.

Sunlords were too direct, she thought. They saw the world as a simple place, a pattern of light and dark under the sway of god and goddess. They did not understand Asanian complexities. Even that first heir of the two lands had had his mother's bright clarity of mind, and too little of his father's subtlety.

Estarion had no subtlety at all.

No matter what she thought of, she circled back to him. She slipped out of that room full of priests and useless chatter, and sought the way to the gate.

This was a proper palace, as convoluted as an Asanian's mind. She lost herself more times than she cared to count, before she found a servant to direct her toward escape. The man was subtly, exquisitely contemptuous. *Barbarian*, he thought at her, not caring if she heard.

And so she was. She did not thank him: that would have set her below him. But she bestowed on him a coldly brilliant smile.

She was learning the shape and the taste of an Asanian city. Villages in the Isles huddled together above the sea, their faces turned inward toward the well and outward toward the boats and the nets. Towns in the Hundred Realms warded themselves in walls, but under the peace of the Sun they had allowed themselves to go to green, in gardens within, in fields and farms without.

In Asanion the walls were manifold. This town of Shirai had three, and gates so placed that one had to walk far round the circle from one to the next. The streets within the circles were an inextricable tangle of blank walls, twisting turns, sudden squares, and crossroads often choked with market booths, or veiled women chattering at a cistern or worshippers thronging into a temple. Keruvarion had conceded mightily in suffering the worship of the goddess beside the god. Here the thousand gods had yet to diminish their number, for all the truth that was embodied in the emperor.

So many people crowded so close together could never be truly clean. The stench of them flooded Vanyi, all but drowning her. Their roar and seethe swept over her like a storm on the sea. She was seafolk, skyfolk. She was not made to live in such a place.

A thin thread of discipline kept her on her feet. She was tall here, and slight, borne along like a twig in a millrace. She did not try to fight the current. It fetched her up against a wall that had been the recipient of too many attentions; it reeked like a midden, or like a tavern in the morning after a long carouse.

But there was cleanliness within the wall, and quiet. She worked her way round to the gate. It was shut but not locked. It opened to the touch of her hand.

Which god was worshipped here, she did not know, nor did it matter. This was a holy place. Avaryan's temple would be full tonight, with the god's heir in the town, and the high priest from Endros come to sing the rite. Few people lingered here. A woman with a gift of fruit and flowers for the altar in the outer court. A circle of boys reciting lessons in front of their teacher. No priest that she could see, and no priestess.

The inner court would have been closed once to one of her sex. Maybe it was still. She did not care. The torque about her neck was passport to any temple in this world, even to the sanctuary, where the god's secrets were kept.

She did not need to go so far. This was a local god, perhaps, or goddess: it was hard to tell. The image above the altar was carved of wood black with age, clothed in robe upon robe of improbable, royal richness, and crowned and necklaced and garlanded with flowers. Its face was a mask of beaten gold, neither male nor female, blank, serene, unreachably beautiful. It had no eyes, only darkness. Its mouth smiled just perceptibly.

Here, she thought, was Asanion: a golden mask, an androgyne smile.

Strange how little it repelled her, or even frightened her. Maybe she had lost fear with the capacity to love, or in truth to feel anything at all.

She sat cross-legged on the floor. It was swept clean, she noticed, and sprinkled with scented water. Somewhere in the temple's depths, then, were priests with a care for their duty. She was aware of them now that she stretched her senses.

What she was looking for, she did not know. She had been led here as she had been led to Endros from the breast of the sea. The god's hand was light on her but firm. It did not ease the bleakness in her belly. Nothing could do that.

She let her body settle, her power open like a sail to catch the magewinds. They were treacherous here amid the crowding of so many minds, on land so long subdued that it hardly knew itself apart from the men who lived on it. And yet the winds were there, gusting and circling.

Voices. Mageborne, she thought; then shadows fell across the light. She was not visible, maybe: dark trousers, dark coat, dark cap, sitting motionless in shadow.

They spoke Asanian softly, barely above a whisper. "It is so?"

"It is so."

Men's voices both. The first was hesitant, the second eager—she would have said exultant. The eager one went on almost too fast to follow. "Oh, it is so! Out of the darkness he is come, the golden one, the Lion's child."

Estarion? Even in her half-trance, annoyance stabbed her. Could she never escape him?

"I don't believe you," the first voice said. "The yoke is heavier than it ever was. And now that one is come—the dark one. They say he has the eyes, but his face is a barbarian's face, like a black eagle. An army rides with him; the high ones bow down to him. How can any power free us from him?"

"Easily," said the second. "As easily as a knife in the dark."

"Not this time. They were innocents before. Now they know. They feel the hate we bear them."

"They are mages, too. And little good it does them. *He* is coming. He will strike them down."

"With what? Sorcery?"

Scorn, that, and a flash of fear. The second voice laughed. It was higher than the first, perhaps younger, and something in it spoke to Vanyi of more than simple courage: wine or dreamsmoke, or darker things. "He needs none of their sorcery. He *is*. He will throw down the false king and rule as the old emperors ruled, true blood and true spirit. No bearded barbarian mocking the throne of the Lion."

"You're dreaming. What did you get into this time?"

"Truth!" sang the younger man. "I saw him. Very well, if you insist—in my dream. But the prophecy is true. The time is come. The burning god will fall, and the Golden Empire win back its own again. Can't you feel it? Can't you hear it? It's coming—it's almost upon us."

"I hear the same old wishful wheezes I've always heard," the first voice said. "It's been, what? Fourscore years? Five? We're as strong under the yoke as we ever were. And now the black king is here. All the high ones fall in front of him. If there is a prophet—and I admit it, I've heard people talking, too—what is he but a madman? We've had those before. They never came to anything but a head on a spike."

"This one is different," the young one said. "You'll see."

"I'll see him strung up for the crows," the older man said. He sounded ineffably tired, but behind the voice was a spark of hope: that Estarion would fall; that this prophet, whatever he was—dream, delusion, living lunatic—would set Asanion free.

Vanyi drew a careful breath. They still had not seen her. The young one went away singing to himself. The elder—and he was old, she saw as he moved into the light, an ancient yellowed creature in a priest's threadbare robe, with a broom in his hands—the old man kept silent but for the singing in his mind. The same song in both, wordless, wandering, but full of hatred for the invaders out of Keruvarion. It was worn so smooth, cherished so long, that it gleamed like a bloodstone in water.

She drew shadows about herself. Even so, she thought that the old man sensed her presence as the very old can, or the blind, by other senses than sight. He tensed, peering. She made herself nothing, no one, wind and shifting air.

It took all the courage she had to walk to that guarded door, to say to the men there, "I would speak with his majesty."

Men? They were boys, youths whom she knew, who smiled at her and asked after her. Was she well again? "We worried," said the slim brown boy from the Nine Cities. "He's going to be glad to see you. All those simpering yellow women are giving him the jaundice."

She burst out laughing, though she had thought there could be no lightness in her. "And of course no one can tell, he being what he is."

The other guard, a hulking lad from somewhere north of Ianon, grinned blindingly. "We won't tell him you said that. Go on, he's waiting for you."

Vanyi halted in the doorway of the inner chamber, stiff as a hound at gaze. At first she could not see him for the cloud of veils and perfumes and golden eyes. There must have been a dozen of them, and a fat personage beaming at them all and proclaiming in a voice much too sweet to be natural, "Oh, what joy! What delight!"

"Out." That voice at least was unmistakable. It had a growl in it. "Out, I said!"

"But," said the personage. "Majesty. They came all this way—all the way from Kundri'j, purely for your majesty's pleasure."

"Then let them go back to Kundri'j and give pleasure to men who want it." Estarion rose up out of the veils, his eyes hot gold with fury, and the raw edge of it in his voice. "And tell his gracious lordship—tell him to pay your full fee. Doubled."

"Trebled," fluted the personage, "with additions for our hardship. To come so far for so little—the roads, the inns, the brigands—"

"*Out!*"

"Well roared," said Vanyi dryly in the ringing silence.

Estarion stopped sucking in breath, stopped moving at all. He stared at her as if he had never seen her before. "Vanyi?"

"So I was the last time I looked."

"Vanyi!"

He was on her before she could stop him, arms about her, stronger than she remembered, whirling her in a dizzying dance. "Oh, love! Oh, lady! You don't know—"

Her mind set itself to go rigid, to fight free. But her body had other intentions. Her arms knew precisely where to go. Her lips knew what they wanted, which was to silence him. The taste of him was piercing sweet.

She pulled back so abruptly that he staggered. He looked as drunken as the youth in the temple. Her hands smoothed his hair back from his face, combed through the curls of his beard, clenched at her sides. "This isn't what I meant," she said.

He blinked. He was always the slower to come to himself. "Damn those boys to everlasting hells. Bless them for sainted idiots. Among the three of you, you saved me from a fate worse than death."

"What was so terrible about it? All those ladies need is a bath and a few days in the saddle, to make them halfway human."

"Not my saddle," he said with honest desperation. "Vanyi, beloved, whatever I said, whatever I did—"

"I didn't come here to forgive you," she said, so sharp that she brought him up short.

"But—"

"You can't be anything other than you are. I won't ask you to be. And you shouldn't ask me to do what I can't do. I can't be your empress, Starion. I've known that from the beginning."

"You have not." The giddiness was gone. Estarion was Estarion again, and ready for battle.

She forestalled him. "No, Starion. No fights. Not now. I came—" Her voice died. "I came as your priestess. As your servant. Will you listen?"

He did not want to: it was transparent in his face. But he had his training. "I will listen," he said, so tight that she could barely hear him.

She told him. The temple; the voices. The prophet they spoke of.

"Nonsense," he said as the old man had, in very nearly the same tone. "People are always talking. And the boy was drugged, you say. Demented. It's nothing but Asanion, being Asanion."

"No," said Vanyi. The power moved in her. She opened it to him, willing him to see as she saw, fear as she feared.

He would not. "Even if there is substance in it, what difference can it make? I'm guarded day and night. I'm watched over like an infant. I can't even visit the privy without someone peering over my shoulder."

"You still don't believe," she said. "No one does. Your guards let me in with cries of delight. What if I'd been got at by someone with a gift for sorcery? I could have sunk a knife in you while you whirled me round the room, or poisoned you with my kiss."

"Not you," he said, so sure of her and of himself that she wanted to shake him. "You do love me still. In spite of everything."

"I'll never *stop* loving you!"

She clamped her mouth shut. He had enough sense, for once, not to reach for her. Maybe he was too stunned by the force of her outcry.

"Estarion," she said after a long moment, in the steadiest voice she could manage. "Do this one thing for me. Trust what I see. Trust nothing else, not even yourself."

"I can do that without your bidding. Asanion does it to me."

"Then let it. You aren't loved here, Estarion. Maybe you can witch them into it—you've the gift, I won't deny it. But the hate runs deep, and it runs strong. They'll have their prophet if they have to make him themselves. They'll do all they can to destroy you."

"I knew that when I was in my cradle. You're forgetting, dear love. I've seen what they can do to me and mine."

She shut her eyes and pressed her fists against them. Tears burned, too hot to shed. "Damn you, Starion. Why can't you be as easy to hate as they think you are?"

"They don't know me."

Her fists dropped. She glared. "You arrogant—"

He seemed not to have heard her. "What can any of them do to me that I haven't suffered already? Kill me? Then the god will take me."

"They can leave this empire without its emperor, destroy your kin and everything you love, roll over Keruvarion and crush it with bitter steel."

She heard the rasp of his breath, but his voice was light. "There is that," he granted her. "I'm guarded, Vanyi. I'm warned. What more can I do?"

"Show a little sense. Stop entertaining every whore in Asanion."

"Gladly!" His agreement was so heartfelt that she almost—perilously—smiled. "And?"

"And—" She stopped. He was seducing her. Keeping her there, tricking her with temper, leading to the inevitable, inescapable conclusion. Where was he safest? Under watchful guard. Who could guard him best?

"Not I." She hugged herself, trying not to shiver. "I'll speak to the guards," she said, "send one of them in to watch over you."

"I don't want to sleep with a guard."

"Then summon Ulyai, wherever she is. She's better for that than a dozen armed men."

"Ulyai hates cities in Asanion. She won't come inside the walls."

"She will if I tell her why."

"Vanyi—"

She would not hear him. She sent a messenger on the mageroads, a summons and a command. *The bright one has need. Come!* It touched the mind it sought, fierce cat-mind in the afterglow of a hunt, the rich taste of blood, the memory of the chase.

Some lord's park was less a deer. Vanyi felt her lips stretch in a grin as feral as Ulyai's own. This hunt was better, she told the cat. This was a mage-hunt, a man-hunt, ward and guard against the death that came out of the dark.

"She comes," Vanyi said. No matter that he knew. The words gave it substance.

Leaving him was as hard as anything she had ever done, and as purely necessary. He could not understand. She felt his anger swelling as she passed the door. She locked her mind against it.

THIRTEEN

KORUSAN DID NOT REMEMBER HOW LONG HE HAD BEEN LYING ON THIS HARD narrow bed that had been his since he rose to the second rank, in this cell with its tall thin window and its scrap of curtain for a door. But he remembered that he had been ill, memory that blurred into all the other illnesses. Most often it was fever, or a demon in lungs or heart or bones. This time it was lassitude that would not lift, and an ache without a source, that made his hands shake when he tried to curve them round a cup, and set him reeling when he would have sat up.

There were, as always, mages. They patched him together with threads of their magic, weaving over the other, older stitchings. He was as threadbare as an old cloak, and as like to fall apart.

He said so to the mage who tended him, when he gained strength enough to speak. It was the lightmage from the night by the gate, the last night he remembered clearly. She did not smile at his bit of wit. "You'll last as long as you need to."

"Am I your punishment?" he asked her.

She bent to the task of mixing a potion for him. It smelled less vile than usual.

"I am," he answered for her, since she would not. "Pity that you should suffer for telling me the truth."

"You knew it already," she said. Or he thought she said. The fall of her hair hid her face, and her voice was barely audible.

"Some things, one needs to be told."

"Some things were better left alone." She poured a measure of her physic and set the cup to his lips. He closed his hands over hers. She neither started nor pulled away. Her hands were cool. Her eyes met his. They did not pity him, which he was glad of, but neither did they warm for him.

So it would be with the women of the Olenyai, once they knew what this woman knew. "I would do very well among the wives of courtiers," he observed. "No fear of heirs who bear too faint a resemblance to their mothers' husbands."

"I suppose you are entitled to be bitter," said the mage. She wiped the cup with a cloth and laid it back among the jars of medicaments.

"You dislike me," said Korusan. Weakness made him blunt, and the potion made him bold. It was odd, to know both sides of that, and to know how little it mattered.

"No," said the mage.

"But I mean nothing to you, beyond the fact of my lineage."

"That's but a means to an end." She smoothed the coverlet over him. "Did you know that you are a legend to the people? They make a promise of you, and call you prophet."

He had not known. He was surprised that it could make him angry. "Whose idiocy is that? Your Master's?"

"You should be glad. The people are ripe for your coming. They have no love for the black kings."

"How can I be a prophet if no one sees my face or hears my voice?"

"Your face is a mystery, as every emperor's must be. Your voice is the voice of your servants."

"No servants of mine," said Korusan.

"We all serve you, my lord, from our hearts' center. You are the Son of the Lion."

He had taken joy in that name once, and swelled with pride when it was spoken. "I am the sum of my lineage," he said. "Which is nothing. How close did I come to death this time, when the old sickness took me?"

"Not close at all," she said, but she would not look at him while she said it. "You overtaxed yourself, no more. And it was a shock to discover . . . what you discovered."

Odd that she could not say it, when she could say so much else. "What greater shock will it be to mount the throne as emperor? Will I fall dead upon the dais?"

"Of course not," said the mage. "You are nowhere near as weak as you imagine."

"Oh, yes," said Korusan, "and I am so strong that I faint as easily as a girl, and rather more often."

"Maybe it suits some people to have you think so. Maybe they think it makes you more tractable."

He stared at her, speechless.

"You didn't ever think of that, did you? That maybe you aren't as feeble as that. An invalid could never be an Olenyas, or pass the tests of wood and steel, or live as a warrior lives, without ease or comfort. Keeping you slave to their mendings and magics—that keeps you slave to their will as well."

It could be true, he thought. And yet he knew his own blood, his own bones. He knew how brief his years must be.

Whether she read his thoughts, which mages said they could not do to a full Olenyas, or whether his eyes betrayed him, she said, "Oh, you won't live long. That's true enough. But you'll go all at once, not by these slow degrees."

"Why do you tell me this?"

She shrugged, a lift of a shoulder, a turn of a hand. "Maybe I don't dislike you. Maybe I feel sorry for you."

"Maybe you spy for the enemy."

She laughed. "Maybe I do! He loves our kind, does the emperor in Endros. He dotes so much on us of the Golden Empire that he won't suffer one of us in his presence."

"And yet he comes to Asanion. Or is that too a lie?"

"He comes," said the mage. "His mother drives him, they say, because she knows he'll lose us else. *He* loathes every step of the journey."

"Someone could kill him," Korusan murmured. "Then we would be rid of him."

The drug was taking effect. He wondered distantly if it was meant as the mage said, to weaken and not to strengthen him. But he was too tired to care. He heard her say, "Someone may kill him yet. Or we'll leave it for you."

For me, he thought. *Yes. That would be proper.*

When he woke again, the lightmage was gone. He had another nurse, a silent Olenyai woman who would not tell him what had become of her. He did not see her again.

In darker moments he wondered if she had been set there to say what no one should say, still less a mage of the Guild that would have wielded him as its puppet. If she had died for it, or if they had stripped her of her power and cast her out. Or if, after all, she had the reward of a gentler posting, away from the terrors of this conspiracy.

The weakness passed—quickly, his nurses said; too slowly for his patience. He was back almost to full duties when he was called from one of them into the Master's presence.

The Guildmaster was with the Master of the Olenyai as Korusan had expected, and no one else but a lone veiled guard. He knew the eyes above the veil, the fret of fingers on swordhilt, Marid's presence a greater comfort than he might have looked for. Was that friendship, then, this fancy that one man at least was not hungry for his blood?

Before the Master of the Olenyai, Korusan lowered his veil and stood in silence until he should be spoken to. The Master's own veil was down, his face a little gaunter than Korusan remembered, a little more weary; but it was the weariness of a hard task well begun. When he spoke, he spoke not to Korusan but to the Master of the mages. "He looks well. Will he continue so?"

"Now, I think, yes," said the Guildmaster.

"Good," said the Olenyas.

Korusan bit back words that would not have been wise. They could not dispose of him as they had a young lightmage, but they could master him with magic if they chose. Let them think him biddable, if reluctant; let them imagine that he was cowed.

"Prince," said the Olenyas, "we have somewhat that you should see. Will you come?"

Korusan bent his head, assenting.

He felt their eyes on him, and the cold brush of magic. He was still to them, empty of all but compliance. The eyes left him. The magic lingered, but after a time that too went away. Still, he kept up his guard and his veil, went where they led, said no word, and offered no resistance.

"This, prince," said the Master of mages, "is your empire."

Korusan regarded it as it lay on a table in a room somewhat less bare than others in this stronghold: it had hangings on the walls, new enough for the figures to be seen, and carpets on the floor, and a chair on a low round dais. That last had been brought in late and in haste, he thought; and likewise the table beside the chair, on which rested a single gleaming thing.

It was a mask of gold. It could not be the one that reposed in the palace treasury in Kundri'j Asan; that would be guarded incessantly.

By Olenyai. They were the trusted guards of emperors. They kept the treasuries, warded the inmost chambers, defended the Son of the Lion with their living bodies.

The mask was heavy as he lifted it. If it was not pure gold, then it was gold sheeted thick over lead. Its face he knew. It was his own. Its eyes were empty, blank.

"This is the mask of the emperor," the Guildmage said. "This you are born to wear."

They had had to remake it, he had heard, when the black kings came. Those were taller men than Asanians, leaner, longer-headed: too large by far to wear a thing made to Asanian measure. But this fit in his hands, seemed shaped for his face. "Then it is the mask of my ancestors," he said in wonder. "It is no makeshift nor forgery. But how—"

"It was given to us to be destroyed," said the Master of the Olenyai. "We chose not to obey the commands of kings who were not ours."

They would have called it treason, those bandit kings from the east of the world. "Yet the first of them was Lion's Cub himself."

"He broke faith," the Master said.

And that, Korusan reflected, was the greatest of all sins to the Olenyai.

He returned the mask to its place. The veil was a burden greater than gold; but that he had earned. That he would keep.

Nor did he sit in the chair that so clearly was meant for him. He took it from the dais and set it aside, and sat cross-legged where it had been. "I have as yet no throne," he said, "and no empire. Now what do you wish of me? To be persuaded to embrace your haste? Is there a purpose in it?"

He did not think that the Guildmaster was pleased. The Master of the Olenyai seemed to have expected this defiance. He raised his hand. A small company of veiled warriors came quietly from behind a tapestry, where must have been a door, and took station round the room. Guard-station, with Korusan in its center. It felt strange, awry, that he should be the guarded and not the guard; trapped in the center and not on the rim with Marid on his right and a second brother on his left and duty clear before him.

Korusan rested his hands on the hilts of his twin swords. They were solid, comforting. He was being tested, there could be no doubt of it. It was the Guildmaster's game, he suspected; Olenyai did not waste training-time in trifles. But perhaps the mage was not having all as he would have it. He was alone, no mages with him, surrounded by black-robed warriors.

The Master of the Olenyai took station at Korusan's right shoulder. "Prince and brother," he said, "be at ease. No harm will touch you. Only speak as your heart moves you to speak, and be silent as you will to be silent, and remember what we have taught you."

They had not taught him to sit as a prince in the hall of audience. But they had taught him to speak and to be silent, and to know what was sense and what was folly. He sat as straight as he might, composed his body as one should before battle, and waited.

There were but a handful of them, white-faced and staring, with the dazed look of men who had traveled far and long with their eyes blindfolded. Before that, maybe, they had traveled in curtained litters, taken here and there and round about until even the keenest-witted of them was hopelessly confused.

And here, where they had been brought at last, stood a circle of faceless men. Their eyes leaped to the one face bared among them all, that of the mage; but that was as blank as the mask upon the table. Then, as if reluctantly, they sought the center.

Korusan had leisure to study them. They were all Asanian, as indeed they must be. None bore the marks of rank. They looked like common tradesmen, priests of little temples, one or two in the garb of journeymen artisans, a smith from the look of one burly figure, the other perhaps a juggler or a player, with his long smooth hands and his mobile face.

When the Lion ruled in Kundri'j Asan, such creatures would never have been suffered in the presence of the emperor. But the High Court was all turned traitor, the Middle Court gone over to the enemy, the Low Courts fallen under the rule of the Sun-god's servants. Only the little people remembered what had been, who had ruled them before the black kings came.

Korusan's lip curled slightly behind his veil. The Sun-brood made much of its affinity for the common man. But in Asanion the common man despised his out-land conquerors and yearned for the rule of his own kind.

Korusan looked at the pallid faces, the fear-rounded eyes, and knew only a weary contempt. He was bred to walk among princes. Not to beg charity from sweaty commoners.

Having ascertained at last that he, seated in the center, must be the one they came for, they flung themselves before him. None of them was clean. But none dared so vastly as to touch him, still less to stare at his hidden face.

Save one, who bowed down patently for prudence's sake, but kept his eyes on Korusan. "And how do we know," he demanded, "that this is the one we've looked for for so long?"

Korusan did not pause to think. If he had, he would have stopped himself before he went too far. In one hand he took the mask of the emperor. With the other he unfastened his veil. He held the mask beside his face. "Do you know me now?" he asked.

The bold one dropped down flat. But he was bold still, and wild with it. "You're younger than the one I dream of. And the mask, golden one: it too is older than you."

"Surely," said Korusan. "It is a death-mask."

"Ah! Poor god. He died young."

"Emperors often do." Korusan's arm was growing weary. He set down the mask again and said, "You have seen my face, and I am both Olenyas and Lion's heir. For that, then, you must die."

They started. Not one had failed to look up when their fellow spoke, to give way to curiosity that defied even fear.

"But I choose when you die, and how," said Korusan. "Now I let you live, so that you may serve me."

Their gratitude was as rank as their fear. When he was emperor—if he came so far—he would command that petitioners be bathed before they approached him.

"You are the Lion's son," said the one who dared to speak, the bold one, the player with his half-trained voice and his half-mad courage. "You are the chosen of the gods. You will rule when the black kings fall."

But, thought Korusan, there were no gods. "I will rule when my line is restored." And how briefly that would endure, with no heir to follow him.

They waited, trembling, on their faces. No one else moved, not the Olenyai, not the Guildmaster. He must speak, or the silence would stretch, and turn awkward, and then humiliating, and then dangerous.

There were words in him. Whether they were useful words he did not know, but they were all he had. "Swear to me now, men of the Lion. Swear that you will serve me. If you betray me, you die. If you lose this battle that is before us, you die. If you fail me in anything, for any cause . . ."

He paused for breath that came suddenly short. Their voices rose, finishing what he had begun. "If we fail you, majesty, we die."

This was power, to sit so, and to look down, and to know that these lives were his: his to keep, his to cast away.

"I am the emperor who should have been. I am the emperor who is to be. I am the heart of the Golden Empire. They who dream that they conquered me, they dreamed only, and they lied.

"And now he comes, my people: the barbarian, the savage, the bandit king. He jangles in outland gold. He speaks with the tongues of apes and birds. He goes naked, shameless as the animal he is; he wears the fell of a beast. And he dares to boast that he rules us. Will you deny him, my people? Will you refuse him? Will you turn your backs on him?"

"Aye!" they cried.

"We are but the least of the least," the bold one said. "Our allies are hundreds, thousands strong. Asanion is full of us. Wherever he goes, there he must find us, the false king. Whatever he does, he must run afoul of us. Shall we slay him for you, majesty? Shall we lay his flayed hide at your feet?"

Korusan stiffened. "The usurper is mine. But all that you may do to aid us, you will do. Go; remember me. Fight for me. Take back this empire in my name."

"He does have a talent for this," the Guildmage said.

Korusan caught himself before he spoke untimely. He rose from the dais, taking no open notice of the mage, and stepped down to the carpeted floor. He was dizzy; he had to struggle not to shake. He drew long breaths, calming himself, bringing his temper to hand.

"He is bred for it," said the Master of the Olenyai after a perceptible pause.

Korusan turned, still refusing to acknowledge the Guildmaster, and faced the Olenyas. "I trust that this mummery has been of use."

"Of much use," the Olenyas said. "Those were unprepossessing enough, but they have a great following. And now they know what they follow. They will serve you the more assiduously hereafter."

"There are no lords among them," said Korusan.

"Lords we have," the Guildmage said, "and many. They have no need for this spectacle."

"No? I should think that they would need it more." Korusan straightened his robes and raised his veil once more to conceal his face. "Am I done? May I go?"

"The emperor may go as he wills," the Guildmage said.

Ah, thought Korusan, but who was the emperor?

FOURTEEN

Dark. Darkness and blood. Voices gibbering. Eyes—

Estarion flung himself headlong out of sleep.

The lamp flickered, burning low. Ulyai blinked at him. Her mind saw a cub under her gentling paw, and her tongue licking him until he settled, comforted.

He half fell on her, wrapping arms about her neck, burying his face in warm musky fur. His breathing quieted. The sweat dried cold on his body. The shivering came and went. "I can't remember," he said to her. "I—can't—"

But he could. That was the terrible thing. He could remember too well. Deep down, where the darkness was, and the long fall into death and the soul's destruction.

Not his death, not his soul torn asunder and scattered to the winds of the mage-world. Oh, no. He had caused it. His power had done it, had killed the mage who killed his father, and in killing, slain itself. His power was maimed and perhaps would never be mended. The soul it had destroyed was lost beyond retrieving.

They thought they knew, those people who loved and guarded him. They gave him wisdom, gave him compassion, lashed him with impatience when they judged he needed it. But they did not know the truth of what he had done. To sunder a soul from a body: that was terrible. To shatter that soul—that was beyond any hope of forgiveness.

In the beginning, when the horror was new, he had let himself fall into the blessed dark. They had found him, dragged him back, shown him the way to the restoration of his power. He was weak. He had let them. He thought he could atone, if only by living and remembering, and suffering that remembrance.

Instead he had forgotten, or chosen not to remember. It was simpler. It won him Vanyi, who was water in a dry place, coolness in the terrible heat of his desert. And it had lost her. There was no escaping what he was. Even his body betrayed him.

He struggled to his feet. Ulyai growled and batted at him. She kept her claws sheathed. He evaded them, staggering away from the bed. His knees were as weak as a foal's.

Standing steadied him. He pulled on a robe and let his feet take him where they would.

Ulyai followed him, but she did not try to stop him. He was glad of her presence. She held him up when he stumbled.

It was a peculiarity of Sun-blood that it sought the heights. Mountains if there were any. Roofs else, and the stars that seemed dim and strange, and the night air.

The roof of this house was made for standing on: it had a wall about the rim, and a garden of flowers sending their sweetness into the night. Estarion plucked one great moonpale bloom and bore it with him to the parapet and leaned on the rail. It was not far down. Five man-heights, maybe. Six. Hardly enough to break one's neck. For that one needed a tower, or a crag.

"It doesn't work in any case," Sidani said from the shadows of the roof. "Mage-blood saves itself. You'd find yourself flying, or landing as light as a bird on a treetop."

She came to stand beside him, leaning as he leaned. Brightmoon was down. Great-moon's light limned her face in blood, dyed her hair as red as any Gileni prince's.

"You've tried it?" he asked her.

She held up her clenched fists and her lean corded arms. Old scars seamed them, tracing the lines of the great veins. "I thought that this would be surer. It only made work for a healer."

"But you're not a mage. No more," he said bitterly, "than I."

Her brow went up. The irony was pure Sidani. "And why," she asked, "does death seem so much more alluring than the life of an emperor?"

And why not tell her? He did not know her at all, no more than he could know a hawk in the sky or a fish in the sea. She could be his blood enemy. She could be the prophet Vanyi spoke of, though he doubted that Asanion would follow a woman, still less a woman who was a barbarian.

"Do you know," he asked her, "that it's possible, if one is a mage, to do more than kill the body of one's enemy? That one can kill his soul?"

"Nothing can kill a soul."

"I did."

She neither laughed nor recoiled. "What makes you think that?"

"The man who killed my father hated us with a perfect hate," he said: "so perfect that I could only kill it by matching it. And in matching it, I destroyed it."

She pondered that. Either she chose to believe him, or she was better at feigning it than anyone he had ever seen. "Maybe it only fled too swiftly for you to follow."

"No," he said, though hope yammered at the corners of his mind. "I felt it shatter. It was indescribable. And where it had been, there was nothing. Not even the memory of a scream."

"They say you can't remember."

"I don't want to. Oh, there's darkness in plenty. I can't see my father fall. I don't know what I did when he died, or after his assassin . . . ended. But the ending: that I'll never forget. Not if I live a thousand lives."

"So. You're not as callow as you look."

He rounded on her. She smiled her sword-edged smile. "We were all young once," she said, "but it's fools who say it's either easy or simple. You looked the Dark in the face when you were twelve years old. You've been running from it ever since."

"Wouldn't you?"

"I've been running since before your grandfather was born."

Stories. But in this light, almost, he could believe them.

A rumbling drew his eyes downward. Ulyai leaned against Sidani, purring thunderously, while the strong old fingers rubbed the sensitive places behind her ears.

"You're not afraid of her," he said.

"Should I be?"

He bit his tongue. A beast as large as a small senel, fangs as long as daggers, claws that could bring down a bull at the charge: a fair lapcat, that. "She's not overfond of strangers," he said.

"I'm hardly that," said Sidani. "She's been my blanket, most nights, since we left Kurion."

"But—"

"Jealous, child?"

"No!"

Her teeth flashed white in the shadow that was her face. "Good. Then you won't mind that she found herself a he-cat in the forest of Kurion."

"There are no ul-cats in Kurion."

"Tell that to the forest king who, at Greatmoon's full, took a queen." Sidani regarded him in high amusement. "Surely you wondered what was keeping her so long."

"She goes her own way," he said stiffly. He looked down into the green gleam of eyes. They closed, opened again, in lazy contentment. "You are smug," he said to the cat.

"Well she might be. She'll bear her cubs in Kundri'j. They'll be purely delighted in the palace, to play host to a nest of ul-cats."

"Gods," said Estarion.

"So they will be. Asanians will worship anything, if it frightens them enough."

He shook her babblings out of his head. The last of the darkness went with it. She had meant that, maybe. She was more like Ulyai than anything human should be.

"Keep her with you," said Sidani, "until you come to Kundri'j."

A great weariness came over Estarion. "You too? Is everyone convinced that I'll fall over dead if I'm not guarded every living moment?"

"You won't fall. You'll jump. Or someone will push you."

"I'm not going to jump," he said.

"Not tonight." She turned her face to the great bloodied orb of the moon. For a moment he saw what she must have been when she was young. Haughty as a queen. Free-spoken as a man, or an empress. And beautiful: a beauty that smote the heart.

None of it surprised him. She was a northern woman. They were often so, in the kingdoms and among the tribes.

They were formidable when they were young. When they were old, they were terrible. This one drove him back to his bed with the edge of her tongue, and sat by him until he slept, and stood guard on his dreams. She and the ul-cat, one on each side of the gate, and nothing dark allowed to pass.

FIFTEEN

I NDUVERRAN WAS THE GATE TO ASANION'S HEART, A CITY OF GOLD AND LEAD, flowers and dung, fierce summer heat and sudden stony chill. The cities that Estarion had seen and heard of in the Golden Empire were all old beyond reckoning. All but Induverran. There had been a city of that name in this place for years out of count, but the walls that framed it, the towers that rose within it, were none of them more than fourscore years old. Even Endros was older than that; but Endros was a white city, with a purity that time and men's habitation could not sully. Induverran struck Estarion with an air both grandiose and shabby, as if the land's weight had overwhelmed the new-raised stones, or memory bowed and stained them.

That memory was clear always beyond the walls. Induverran that was now stood apart from Induverran that had been, nearer a little river that had shifted since the first city was built. The old city stood in ruins like the charred bones of a demon's feast, grown over but thinly though the land was rich round about. No one walked there. Birds did not shun it, but neither did they linger, or build their nests amid the fallen pillars.

Induverran's lord sat his senel on the edge of the ruined city. He was a prince of five robes, of blood as pure as any in the empire, and Estarion should have detested him. But he had a hard clear eye in that yellow-curled head, and when Estarion readied to ride out of the new city and into the old, he was there waiting, mounted on one of the golden stallions for which his domain was famous.

The senel switched his silver-tasseled tail and stamped. Lord Dushai quelled him with a hand on his neck. "There they fought," he said in creditable Gileni. "There the mages hurled their blasts of power, and the beast of their mingled magics stalked and slew. And there," he said, tilting his chin toward the open plain, "the armies met."

"But not in battle," Estarion said. "My forebears stopped them: the Asanian and the Varyani, riding down upon them out of the living air, and raising walls of magic and of light."

"It was too late for the city," said Lord Dushai.

"They did what they could," Estarion said, struggling not to snap. That battle was nigh a century past. He was its consequence, with his lion-eyes and his northern face. They had faced one another across the broken city, the emperor of Asanion and the emperor of Keruvarion, son of the Lion and son of the Sun, and looked to end their rivalry in blood and fire. But their children had forged a peace. It had cost the high prince of Asanion his sole empire. It had cost the heir of Keruvarion far more.

Sarevadin. Estarion said the name to himself, like an incantation. Neither man's name nor woman's, given by a great mage and queen to the child of her body: man-child as he had been then, tall, redheaded, northern-skinned prince with a great gift of magery. Woman as she had ridden out of the Gate between the worlds, heavy with the heir of two empires, magewrought and magebound, but the mages had had no power to sway her soul to their will. Only to rend her body asunder and make it anew, as they wished to do to the empire she was born to rule.

Estarion slid from Umizan's back. The stallion did not lower his head to crop the thin pallid grass, but followed as Estarion walked into the broken city. Others came slowly behind: Lord Dushai on his fretting, skittering mount, a line of guards, a thin scatter of hangers-on. No one else had been willing to leave the comforts of the new city for this bleak battlefield, not even Sidani who, Estarion had thought, would go anywhere.

The stench of blood and burning was long since washed away. The taint of magery was faded almost to vanishing. And yet a power lingered in this place.

Here it began. Here the two empires met, fought, were joined into one. Here, where the grass began to grow green, the emperors faced their rebel children, and knew what they had done. Treason. Betrayal of all that their fathers had wrought, in the name of unlooked-for peace.

"They loved one another, the stories say," Estarion said. He did not care overmuch who heard, nor expect an answer.

Nonetheless he received one. It came, it seemed, out of a stone, but in Sidani's voice. "Only love would explain it," she said.

She was sitting on the ground, wrapped in a mantle that had lost its color to years and weather. For once she looked honestly old, a thin and ancient creature who shivered in the heavy heat of Asanian summer. Or maybe she was living in another time, in another season, when the wind blew chill over the plain, and death walked, and powers moved in the earth.

"Were you there?" Estarion asked her, half expecting a lie, half expecting it to be the truth.

She gave him neither. "Cold here," she said. "So cold."

When he touched her, her skin was chill. And the air already nigh to furnace-heat, even so early, with the sun barely lifted over the horizon.

"You're ill," he said.

She did not hear him. She was in delirium, or in a trance. He gathered her in his arms. She was as light as a bundle of sticks, and nearly as fragile, who had seemed as strong as a swordblade.

"Lord," someone said. Godri. Alidan stood behind him, and others of the guard, and a handful of Lord Dushai's men. Lord Dushai kept a little apart, saying nothing. What the emperor chose to do, his stance said, was the emperor's concern. Estarion almost loved him then, though he would never like so perfect an Asanian.

"Lord," said Godri, "we can carry her. Let us—"

Estarion ignored him. Umizan waited, unwontedly patient. He would carry the fire's child, for so he thought of her. Estarion saw briefly, dizzily, through the senel's eye: a shape of flame, red-gold at the heart, but burning dim now, sinking into darkness and cold.

"She won't die," Estarion said fiercely. "Stop thinking it!"

Umizan's ears were flat, but he did not shift or fret as Estarion set the shivering, burning body in the saddle. She was conscious enough to rouse as she felt the senel under her, to grip the beast's sides with her knees, to wind fingers in the long plaited mane. He walked softly, as smoothly as ever senel could, bearing her as if she were made of glass.

Once she was stripped of her worn clothes and wrapped in a soft robe and laid in the bed that had been meant for Estarion, Sidani slept peacefully enough. Her brow when he laid his hand on it toward evening was as warm as it should be, no sign of fever or of unnatural cold. She breathed well and easily. Her sleep was deep and quiet, without dreams.

He exchanged glances with Ulyai, who had come to fill a solid half of the bed. "Watch over her," he said.

The cat laid her head beside the woman's and sighed. She had been negligent. She had let both the bright one and the fire's child go out alone while she indulged herself in a fine fresh haunch of plowbeast. An ul-queen did not stoop to apology, but she could regret an indiscretion.

She would watch over Sidani. Estarion could wish himself as happily occupied.

Lord Dushai, perhaps mindful that a man could grow weary unto tears of banquets, had not laid on the usual feast or the usual parade of beauties. Both were to be had, but he had woven them into a new thing, as new as the hall into which he led his guest.

That was not the long narrow chamber Estarion was used to. It was as round as one of the moons, ringed in pillars, and topped with a dome that seemed made of light. Nor was Estarion to sit at a high table, there to be stared at and remarked upon while he endured the fiery delights of the Asanian taste. There was a couch placed for him in the innermost of many rings of couches, a low table set between it and the couch beside, on which Dushai established himself, and in front of them the open center of the circle. Others reclined in the widening circles, some alone on their couches, some accompanied. His mother faced him across the open space, with Iburan seated upright at her feet. She raised a brow at him. He twitched a smile in return.

Servants brought food, drink. Estarion found that he was hungry. He was acquiring a taste for some of the Asanian sauces, though others were a sore test of his fortitude. The thin yellow Asanian wine went not ill with the more palatable of the dishes, and it was chilled with snow brought from mountains in the north and kept in deep cellars.

He had chosen to be cool, though it meant shocking his many-robed subjects. His kilt was of fine cream-pale silk broad-belted with gold and great plates of amber as yellow as his eyes. He was bare above it but for a pectoral of gold and amber and topaz, his hair plaited into the helmet-braids of the Ianyn kings. He had almost sacrificed his beard in the name of coolness, but contrariness forestalled him. Asanians never grew their beards, if in fact they had any. They reckoned it a barbarism. Therefore he kept his.

Barefoot, bareheaded, lightly kilted, he was as cool as human body could be, and almost content. The servant who had brought him wine set the flagon on the table and took up a fan, waking wind where there was none. He stretched out on the couch, propped up with cushions, nibbling a bit of spiced sweetness. People were staring in Asanian fashion, under lowered lids or out of the corners of their eyes. Poor creatures, wrapped in all those robes, compelled by custom to wear their hair unbound or knotted at their napes. The crop-headed, tunicked servants were happier by far than they.

His own people had had a little sense. Those who dared kilts, or who were entitled to them by blood and breeding, wore them with relief. His mother might have worn one herself, but she had greater care for Asanian sensibilities than he had. Her gown covered her from throat to ankle but left her arms bare. Its heavy raw silk revealed little of the body beneath, which was a pity. She had beautiful breasts, firm still and round though she had borne and suckled a son.

She bowed her head to the compliment, with a slight, wry brush of vision: himself as she saw him, a slender dark beauty with a noble breadth of shoulder.

Dark, yes, beyond a doubt. Slender—lean, for a fact, and not much hope of gaining flesh as he aged, if his mother's kin were any guide. They were all as ribby as spring wolves. Beauty . . . He laughed. Lord Dushai thought him amused by something someone had said. He let it pass.

His mother was pleased with him. And why not? As far as she knew, he had given up his corpse-faced commoner and accepted his lot, though not, yet, so far as to take to bed an Asanian woman. He did not even know where Vanyi was. Among the priests, most likely, or in the temple. She did not speak to him now; she did not touch his mind, nor respond when he sought hers.

No use to try. It only caused him pain. He drained his cup of snow-cold wine and held it out for the servant to fill. Lord Dushai addressed him, soft and clear under the muted murmur that was Asanian conviviality. "I have prepared an entertainment for you, majesty," he said, "which perhaps you have not seen before. We call it, if you will, a concourse of attractive lies."

Estarion's brows went up. This was new, and possibly interesting. He watched as black-clad servants brought lamps into the empty circle till it blazed as bright as noon. While they did that, others dimmed the lamps without, casting the hall into twilight.

He was aware of heightened alertness: his guards marking the deepening of shadows. The beginning of an ache marked those who were mages, and the wall they raised about him. He made himself ease, endure, await what would come.

Once the servants had arranged the lamps to their satisfaction, they departed. There was a silence. It was a peculiarly Asanian thing: no stirring of restless bodies, no sighs of impatience, no muttered commentary. Even his Varyani were quenched into stillness.

Thunder rolled. Estarion jumped like a deer. Dushai's amusement brushed him, startling not for that it existed, but for that there was no scorn in it. He settled slowly, willed himself to smile as if at a jest.

Drums and flutes and horns, and instruments he had no names for. A consort of musicians marched into the light, arrayed themselves round the edges, settled to the floor, and never a pause or a soured note. The music they played was Asanian, rather like the yowl of mating cats, but, like their wine and their sauces, it grew on one.

He was ready, more or less, when the players came in. Their like haunted the roads of Keruvarion, wandering bands full of, as Lord Dushai had said, attractive lies. But these were no mountebanks. And they did not speak their parts. They sang.

Their tale was in his honor, of course, and apt in view of the morning. They played out the tale of Sarevadin and of Hirel Uverias, the dark prince and the golden. The one who was Hirel was Asanian, a beautiful boy with the fierce unhuman eyes of a lion. The one who was Sarevadin was a wonder: while he was a prince, one was certain beyond a doubt that he was male, but when she rose up out of the mages' circle she was a woman, and no hint about her of the man that she had been. No magery, either, that Estarion could sense. It was all art.

He looked for a twist, for a stab of hostility in word or gesture. He found none. They were honest players, and their play an honest play. They did not touch on the tragedy of the Sunborn: the world he had sought to make, with the goddess bound in chains and the god triumphant over her, laid low by his heir's betrayal. He would have ruled alone, and set Asanion beneath his heel. His heir had set Asanion's emperor on the throne beside her, sacrificing all that she had been, because she saw no other hope.

This was all sweetness. Two princes loved one another across an abyss of enmity; two empires could never be reconciled but through the love of those who ruled them. An easy conclusion, for all the enormity of Sarevadin's sacrifice. A simple resolution. The old emperors were disposed of—Ziad-Ilarios of Asanion dead defending the life of Mirain's empress, that empress dead in spite of him, Mirain himself ensorceled in his Tower—and the Mageguild thwarted in its desire to rule the rulers they had made, and the lovers wedded on the field of battle. Soldier of the Sun embraced soldier of the Lion. Emperor clove to empress upon a golden throne. Joy ruled where had been only sorrow.

Estarion suppressed a snort. It was very pretty. Very convenient, too, for the tale-spinners. They never mentioned aftermaths. Emperor and empress growing old, emperor dying early as royal Asanians did, empress declining headlong to her own death, perhaps by her own hand, and Asanion chafing endlessly in the bonds of amity that they had forced upon it. Rebellions out of count, even a war or two, and their son dead in one such, and that one's grandson poisoned in the Golden Palace, and the last of their line presented with the consequences.

He would have liked it better if someone had come raging and foaming out of the shadows after the last aria and prophesied death, doom, destruction. Like Vanyi's prophet. That would have been nearer the truth.

The players finished their playing. The musicians concluded with a flourish. Asanians did not applaud; they rose and bowed. Estarion was pleased to follow their example. The players bowed in their turn, and it went back and forth, like a dance of odd birds.

Somewhat after he had had enough of it, he put an end to it by stepping into the light. The players were startled, but they masked it well.

The Sarevadin, seen close, was less ambiguous as to gender than before. The northern skin at least was genuine; the red Gileni mane was not. Estarion bit his tongue before he asked what could compel a northerner to make himself a eunuch. The player had pride in himself. He met Estarion's eyes willingly, if warily.

The Hirel was older than he had seemed. His lion-eyes were clever shapes of glass with plain brown behind them, and a dun-drab lock escaped from the yellow wig. He was no more reluctant than his fellow to look an emperor in the face: a remnant maybe of the part he had played.

"You did well," Estarion said to them.

He never understood why a word from him could mean so much. It was the fact of his rank, he supposed, and the fiery thing in his hand. These players wanted to kiss it, as people did in Keruvarion but never in Asanion. Or maybe the common-ers did; but he was not allowed to approach them, or to be approached by them. Emperors did not do such things here. They did not even speak to lords of the Lower Courts.

He had caused a scandal by addressing these players. He did not care. They were Asanian, mostly, but some of them had come from Keruvarion. This manner of singing the parts was a thing of the far west, where they had gone a season or two before, having an enterprising leader: the young eunuch, whose name was Toruan.

Relieved of his wig and his woman's dress, seated on the couch beside Estarion and partaking hungrily of meat and bread and fierce sauces, he was a pleasant, witty companion. He could deepen his voice almost to match Estarion's or lighten it to a woman's sweetness, but in itself it was soft and rather husky, not like a child's, but not like a man's or a woman's, either. It was, Estarion thought, remarkable. He said so.

"Training," said Toruan. "That's why they do it: for the voice, to keep it from spoiling. Catch it soon enough, train it well enough, and it grows into this." He indicated himself with a hand as elongated as the rest of him; but his chest was vast, now that Estarion had his attention called to it. The gown had shaped it into a convincing semblance of a woman's breasts.

"You chose this?" Estarion asked.

The eunuch paused. For a moment his face went still. Then he smiled. The pain in it was almost imperceptible. "Of course not, sire. My clan was poor. A sickness ravaged it, took all the hunters and laid low our herds and left us starving. I was the best of what was left. They sold me for a wagonload of corn. The one who took me was kin to a master of singers in Induverran. He heard me singing at my work. He had his kinsman come to listen; his kinsman bought me, and made me a singer."

"The selling of slaves is banned in Keruvarion," said Estarion, soft and cold.

"They went over the border to do it," Toruan said. "They were hungry, sire. Their children were dying. My father and mother were dead, and I wanted to see more than our hunting runs, and be more than a wild clansman. It profited all of us."

"It fed them for a season at the most. It robbed you of all your sons."

"I didn't know it would come to that," said Toruan. "When they asked me if I wanted to be a singer, I was so glad, I sang. Then they gave me wine. When I woke from the drug that was in it, I found my price all paid, and no way to unpay it. I should have killed myself, I suppose. But I never quite worked myself up to it."

Estarion's tongue had a will of its own, and that could be cruel. "I . . . know about prices," he said.

Toruan stared at Estarion's hands—at the one that gleamed with gold and burned with unmerciful fire. "Maybe," he said, "you do." And maybe, thought Estarion, he did not. Not such prices as these.

Toruan consented to bring his players and his repertory of sung-plays to Kundri'j Asan, if not at once and not in the emperor's train. "That wouldn't be proper," he said. He was northerner enough to break bread and share speech with the imperial majesty, but when it came to traveling with it, he went all Asanian.

Lord Dushai was regretting, maybe, his novel entertainment. Estarion could read none of it in his face. There were still the women to endure, kept long past their time by the emperor's whim, and while they waited they had eaten and drunk perhaps to excess. Some of them were openly importunate. When clever soft hands slid beneath his kilt, he fled.

The chambers he had been given were quiet. No one stared or whispered. No one called him to account. He had offended a high lord, scandalized that lord's court, and insulted its women. And he was, it seemed, to be left to rest in peace. Maybe that was his punishment.

Ulyai was asleep on the bed, although she opened an eye at Estarion's approach.

Sidani was awake. She had been lying so, it seemed, for a while. She looked much as she always had, neither young nor truly old, and the glance she turned on him was brightly ironic. "So, youngling. I take a fit and wake in your bed. Do I make the natural assumption?"

"It was the safest place I could think of," he said, "and the most comfortable."

She wriggled in it. "So it is. They've learned something since last I came here. This is a proper bed. They were always trying to drown me in billows of cushions."

"I had the servants get rid of those. Asanian beds aren't bad, once you get down to them."

"I never thought of that." She lay silent for a while. He hovered, wavered. The golden collar irked him suddenly; he extricated himself from it. Once it was gone, he found that he could breathe. He sat on the bed's edge. "Are you well?" he asked her.

"Was I ill?"

He shrugged a little.

"I was," she said. She sounded surprised. "I was cold, I remember that. I'd been thinking too much. Remembering."

"It put you in a fever," he said. "Iburan looked at you. He said it was nothing he could cure."

"No one can mend old age. Not even gods."

"You're not old."

"Infant," she said, "stop that. Of course I'm old. I'm ancient."

"You're not going to die quite yet."

"Alas for that." It was only half mockery. "Watching one's husband die is not pleasant. When one's son dies . . . that's harder. And when one's grandson is laid in his tomb, then, youngling, one begins to wonder if one isn't cursed. And such a curse! 'May you outlive all your descendants.'"

Estarion flung up his burning hand, casting the curse aside. The light of it made her blink. "Don't say such things," he said.

"What? Someone might be listening? Gods don't care. Men can't harm me."

"You are appalling," he said.

She grinned: a shadow of her wonted insouciance, but it was white and wicked enough. "Are you going to sleep, youngling, or do you have other sins in mind?"

His cheeks were burning. Still, he met her grin with one of his own. "You'll live," he said.

Godri had spread him a bed in one of the lesser rooms, with eloquent if wordless disapproval. Estarion went to it in something like gladness, once he had seen Sidani asleep again. Maybe he witched her into it. Maybe he did not need to.

SIXTEEN

THE NEW MORNING WAS IF ANYTHING MORE HEAT-SODDEN THAN THE ONE before. Estarion woke in a sweat, to sounds like muted battle. One of the voices was Godri's. The others he did not know, but he knew the cadence of Asanian speech. They had looked for the emperor in his bed, it seemed, and failed to find him.

He rolled to his feet, yawning hugely, stretching till his bones creaked. The battle was no longer quite so muted. He went out to face it.

Asanians were ridiculous about naked bodies. Bed-play to them was the high art, and they performed it, as far as he had ever been able to tell, in as many clothes as possible. They never bared more than faces and hands and feet, except in the bath; and then they pretended that they were robed to the eyes. They even wore clothes to sleep.

Absurd; lunatic in such heat as this. He entered the battlefield as he was born, with no covering but his skin. The silence was thunderous. Godri faced an army of Asanians, every one of them in a servant's tunic, and every one determined, it seemed, to pass or die.

On sight of Estarion, they dropped flat on their faces.

"Godri," he said. "Who are these people?"

Godri's eyes were battle-bright; his breath came hard. He steadied it enough to reply, "They say they belong to the Regent of Asanion. Who is, they say, on the road to Induverran this very moment. And who expects to see the emperor properly—as they say—bathed, clothed, and arrayed to receive him."

"And you object?" Estarion asked.

"They have," he said, "razors. And robes. And bottles of scent."

Estarion raised his brows.

"They informed me, my lord, that my services would no longer be needed. You are in Asanion now. Asanion will look after you."

When Godri was as precise as that, Godri was most dangerous. Estarion smiled slowly. "Will it, then? And I suppose I'm to wear the ten robes and the wig, and the mask, too? And sit on a throne in the hall? And speak only through a Voice?"

"Yes," said Godri.

"Pity," said Estarion, "that I won't be doing any of that." He shifted from Gileni to Asanian. "Up, sirs. Listen to your emperor. The bath I'll take. But no razors, and no scent. My squire will see to my robing. If his grace the Regent is displeased, then I take it upon my head."

There was one use for Asanian servility. It kept them from arguing with royalty. The Regent's servants were not pleased in the least, but they could not protest. The emperor had spoken. They must do as he commanded.

They bathed him in blessedly cool water. They did not threaten him with razors or drench him with scent. They did object to the kilt which Godri proffered. "That will not do," the chief of them said—safe, maybe, because it was the squire he spoke to.

"It will do," Estarion said.

It was a royal kilt, scarlet edged with gold. The belt that went with it was rich, gold leaved over thickly carved leather, and he suffered the full weight of northern ornament: rings, armlets, necklaces, earrings of pure and heavy gold lightened with a gem or two; strings of gold and ruby woven in his hair, and threads of gold in the curls of his beard. He was blinding; dazzling; glorious. "Since," he said, "after all, I am receiving the Regent of Asanion."

"He's not going to approve," Godri observed.

"Alas for his grace," said Estarion.

The hall was as cool as anything could be in this climate. Its lofty dome held off the worst of the heat, and its many-colored stone kept to itself the coolness of the night. A pair of servants wielded gilded fans, cooling Estarion with their breezes.

The chair on which he sat was not too uncomfortable as thrones went. Asanians knew the virtue of cushions, too much so when it came to their beds, but thoroughly satisfactory under his rump. He rested his foot on the living stool that presented itself: Ulyai, who judged herself more truly needed where he was than with Sidani. She was not forthcoming as to the woman's whereabouts. *Safe,* she informed him in the image of an ul-queen laired with her cubs. He decided to trust her. In the circumstances he had little choice.

His own escort was present only in part. Most of the courtiers were still asleep or amusing themselves as courtiers could in a foreign city. His Guard was halved to those on day-duty. His mother was there, of course, and Iburan, and one or two priest-mages. Not Vanyi. Everyone else in that hall was Asanian.

A small shiver ran down Estarion's spine. So many yellow faces. So many minds turned on him, and not one level pair of eyes.

This too was his empire. These too were his people. They did not ask that he love them, only that he rule them.

He sat a little straighter. The walls about his mind were high and strong, but his head ached in spite of them. He knew the pounding of his mother's siege-engines. Disapproval was too mild a word for her response to the sight of him in the finery of her people. Even Iburan had taken his beard out of its braids and abandoned his kilt for the stifling confinement of a robe. He looked like a cave-bear in a coat, vast and ruffled and surly. But he was proper as Asanians thought of it. He was covered in accordance with his rank.

Maybe Asanians did not feel the heat as other people did. They did not sweat that he could see, or grow faint. They seemed content to stand for hours out of count, not moving, not speaking, not meeting his restless eyes.

His grace the Regent was in no haste to appear before his emperor. First he must come to the city; then he must be borne through it in his litter; at last he must enter the lord's palace and be received by the lord, and offered refreshment, and bathed and robed with honor and conducted to the hall. While Estarion sat fasting, sweltering, barely breathing lest he say something unfortunate. In Keruvarion at least he would have had a hallful of petitioners to keep him occupied. Here he was given nothing to do but sit.

It was designed to drive an emperor mad. But he was mage and priest before he was emperor. There were disciplines in which he had too little practice, and exercises of the mind that prospered well enough behind full shields. One of them was to draw all of his self inward save a sentinel behind the eyes, and focus it, and quicken time until movement without was a blur. In that shifted time he ran through the Prayers of Passing, first the invocation, then the doxology, then the petition, and at the last the praises. And as the last great singing line sank into the silence of his self, the blur before him slowed, and the world ran level again with his awareness. A wind ruffled the hall. An army marched in upon it.

The other face of time's quickening was time's slowing. Estarion took his leisure to examine the invasion. It was not as numerous as at first it seemed, or so headlong. It was simply determined.

He knew the livery of the Regent's guard, armor ornate to uselessness, lacquered and gilded till it rivaled his own finery, and all of it crimson and silver, the colors of his lordship's house. He knew their master, memory as sharp as a knife in the flesh, prince of seven robes, crimson on crimson on crimson, and the man within them aged cruelly in the years of Estarion's absence. But the ones who came behind, he did not remember, unless they were the shadows of his dream. Cold reason named their kind. Bred warriors. Olenyai.

Black robes, black hoods, black veils shrouding faces to the eyes. Twin swords, baldricked one on either side. Hands ivory-pale, eyes gold or amber, and none of them taller than any other, and that was small in any country but this; but even that smallness was deadly.

Asanion had bred its princes for a thousand years and more, for beauty, for subtle wit, for impeccably civilized viciousness. These were its warriors, bred as carefully as princes, reared and trained in secret, forbidden ever to reveal their faces. They were the dogs and slaves of the emperors, the soldiery of its warlords, bought and sold in captains and companies, bound to their lords by oaths and gold and, it was said, deep-woven sorcery.

Estarion had seen none of them since he came to Asanion. The armed men whom he had seen were men like any other, guards as he knew them in Keruvarion, free men taken into lordly service. There were no wars where he had gone, no emperor but the one, and that was himself. There had been no need of Olenyai.

He had all he could do to force his eyes away from them, to hold his face still while the Regent performed the nine prostrations of the Asanian homage. His following performed them with him, concerted as a dance. But not the Olenyai. The shadow warriors did not sacrifice vigilance even for the emperor's majesty.

The pain behind Estarion's eyes was near to blinding. He saw as in a broken glass, a thin glittering shard that held a remembered face. "My lord Firaz inShalion Echaryas," he said. "Well met again, and welcome."

"My lord Meruvan Estarion Kormerian Ganimanion iVaryan," said the Regent, stumbling not even once, "well met at last, and welcome."

Tidily put, thought Estarion. He did not remember that he had been fond of this man. One was not fond of Asanian high princes. One hated them, or one admired them, or both. This prince was as high as any but the highest, and he paid the price of his blood and breeding. He had been beautiful once as his kind could be. Now he was all gone grey, worn and ravaged with the years. And yet he was younger than the empress, whose hair had not begun to whiten, whose beauty was just coming into its prime.

They blossom young, said a voice in the deeps of his mind, *and they wither soon. They're all the more deadly for that.*

Memory; but when or where, or who spoke, he could not tell. Nor had he time to hunt it to its source. Lord Firaz was speaking: long elegant phrases of greeting, gladness, judicious flattery. But there was a barb in the tail.

"My emperor will know that he is now in my domain, under, of course, the imperial majesty. Those of the east who accompany him are freed to return to their places. Henceforth he will prosper in the hands of his western servants."

Estarion drew himself up slowly. He cut across a further spate of nonsense, but carefully, in High Asanian as perfect as he could make it. "Is my lord Regent implying that I should send back my escort?"

"Its task is done," said the Regent, "majesty. Your majesty's servants have been sent to your majesty's chambers. Your majesty's guard stands before your majesty. Your majesty's regent—"

"My servants? My guard?"

"As your majesty sees." The Regent's hand gestured slightly, gracefully. The Olenyai bent their shrouded heads. It was not humility. Not in the least.

"And if I wish to keep my own people?"

"These are your majesty's people."

Estarion closed his eyes, opened them again. His mother listened in unmarred serenity. He shot a bolt through the walls of his mind. *You knew!*

She inclined her head a fraction. *Wait,* the gesture said. *Be patient.*

He was in no mood for patience. "Suppose," he said, "that we compromise. I keep my own Guard, and suffer your servants."

"These are your guard," said the Regent.

"We shall consider this," Estarion said, "later." He rose. "You are most welcome in our presence. But the sun approaches its zenith; the heat likewise comes to its height. Be free now till evening. Rest; seek what coolness there may be."

"That was peremptory," said the empress. There was no censure in her tone; simply observation.

"It was scandalous." Estarion prowled her antechamber. Her servant—as much a northerner as she, and blessedly silent—had rid him of his gauds and cooled him with a cloth dipped in water and herbs. The sharp green scent followed him as he paced. At the far wall he spun. "Mother, I'm not going to let him rule me."

"Are you clever enough to stop him?"

"You are."

She sighed. "Estarion," she said, "have you considered that it might be wise to yield? In body only. In spirit you remain yourself."

"I won't wear all those robes in this heat."

She frowned, but then, as if she could not help herself, she smiled. Here where only he and Zherin could see, she had yielded to simple sense and discarded her robes. Her beauty was garment enough in his reckoning, that and the pride that never forsook her, even when she slept. "I am not about to abandon you," she said, "if that's what you fear."

He would not admit that he had. "I don't want to lose my Guard. Or my squire."

"And your court?"

"They might be happier away from here." He began to pace again. "Mother, I can send them back. Most of them will be glad to go. But not Godri. And not my warriors."

"You do know," she said, "that under the compact of the empires' union, the heart of Asanion is Asanion's own. Firaz is doing no more than his duty—and granting you ample grace in demanding it no sooner than this. He could have met you at the border and not at the gate."

"He could have waited till I came to Kundri'j."

"He was wise to wait so long, but wiser to come so soon. Easier then for you to accept it, and come to the city in proper estate."

"If that's what he wants, then I'll ride in like a wild tribesman, and damn him and all his works."

Her gaze on him was level. He flushed under it. "Will you, Estarion?" she inquired.

"No, damn it." Her doubt stung him; her glance at his kilt and his braids. "Mother, I'm not a complete fool. I'll behave myself tonight: I'll even wear a robe. But he has to know that I'm not his puppet. I'll be as proper as I can be. I'll promise him no more than that."

"And me? Will you promise me to be more circumspect? Here they find it in themselves to endure your outland fancies. Kundri'j Asan endures nothing that is not Asanian."

"I'm not Asanian."

"You must learn to be."

His jaw set against her. "Maybe it's time they learned to see the world as it is and not as they would have it. The Golden Empire is gone. The Blood of the Lion is here, in me, black-faced bearded barbarian that I am. I am not ten robes and a wig and a mask. I am living, breathing, human power. And I rule them."

"Do you?"

Testing, always testing. He would hate her if he loved her less. He swooped down, set a kiss on her brow. "Can I do less than try?" he asked her.

She caught him before he could straighten, and held him with her hands on either side of his face. Her eyes were ages deep. The goddess dwelt in the depths of them. He was light and fire, Sun's child, bright noon to her deep night, man to her woman, son and emperor as she was mother and queen.

"My beautiful bright child," she said. The words were tender, but their edge was fierce. "I'll never call you wise. But neither will I stop you."

"Will you help me?"

"Only if there's wisdom in it."

"Then I'll try to be sensible."

"Sensible is even rarer than wise."

He grinned between her hands. "If I fall short of sense, then maybe I'll reach wisdom."

She cuffed him hard enough to bruise. "Puppy! Go, torment your servants, give me a moment's peace."

SEVENTEEN

THE BATTLE ROYAL BETWEEN GODRI AND THE REGENT'S SERVANTS WAS A ladies' walking-party to the war that Estarion found at the door of his chambers. The scarlet livery of his Guard held the way against the black regiment of the Olenyai. When Estarion came upon them, they were close to drawn swords.

His temper had, he thought, been holding up remarkably well. But this, after all the rest that he had had to endure, snapped the fragile cord of his patience. Just as a scarlet-liveried hothead went for a little snapping beast in black, Estarion let his temper go. *"Hold!"*

His battlefield bellow brought even wild Alidan up short, sword half drawn.

Estarion drew a very careful breath. "Put away your swords," he said.

Alidan obeyed him. The Olenyas glanced at another of his like, his captain maybe. That one lowered lids over yellow eyes. The blade snicked into its sheath.

Estarion noticed, but he forbore to remark on it. "Now," he said. "What is this?"

The Olenyai went still. The Guard burst out in a babble of furious voices.

Estarion's hand slashed them into silence, and singled out the decurion of his Guard. "Kiyan. And you—Olenyas. Are you their captain?"

"I am captain of this watch," said the voice out of the veil. A quite ordinary Asanian voice, no power or terror in it. And no title for the emperor, either.

"Explain this," Estarion said.

The Olenyas did not answer at once. Kiyan the decurion said, "Sire, they invaded your chambers, ordered your guards' dismissal, and informed me, when I came to settle it, that none but they will guard you. Is that so, my lord?"

"They have orders to that effect," Estarion said. And as Kiyan opened his mouth to speak: "But not from me. I have a matter or two to settle with the Regent. While you wait for that, let your two commanders come to an agreement. Both companies will guard me. Both, sirs; together and alike."

That was not at all to their liking. The Guard scowled; someone snarled. The Olenyai looked as supercilious as eyes could look in faceless masks.

A long look quelled the scowls. The Olenyai, who being Asanian would not meet his eyes, needed more. Estarion said, "My guards, my Olenyai. You are mine, no?"

"We are the emperor's," their captain said.

"Just so," said Estarion.

He stepped forward. They parted, Olenyai and Guardsmen alike. He escaped to the sanctuary of his chambers. Such as that was, with imperial servants infesting it and Godri brooding balefully in their midst.

Asanian custom permitted an emperor to receive a high lord in private, with no more than a servant or two in attendance. Estarion was careful. He put on the robes the servants chose for him, simple as such things went, inner and outer only, and thin enough almost to be endurable in the heat. He let them comb his hair out of its braids. He arranged himself as they—discreetly, politely, firmly—suggested, in a chair in one of the smaller rooms. It would have been a ghastly cupboard of a place, save that it opened on the garden. A fountain played just beyond, cooling the air and the ear.

Set up like an idol in a temple, watched over by a glowering pair of guards, bronze-dark narrow-eyed plainsman and black-robed Olenyas, Estarion received

the Regent of Asanion. Lord Firaz came in unattended, which marked either very
great insult or very great trust; his robes were no more elaborate than Estarion's,
and his manner was much less stiff than it had been in the hall. He insisted on a
single prostration, but then he let Estarion raise him and set him in a chair a little
lower than his own. He sipped the wine that the servant poured, great trust again,
not to ask that it be tasted before he ventured it. He even abbreviated the dance of
courtesies, restraining himself to a few dozen phrases in praise of the wine, the
weather, and the appointments. The wine was drinkable, the weather wretched, the
appointments no more and no less than they should be; but Estarion did not say so.
It was his part to listen, smile inscrutably, murmur inanities.

After hardly more than a turn of the glass, Firaz approached the meat of the
matter. "Your majesty—"

"Come now," said Estarion. "We're kin, or so I'm told. Let me be 'my lord' if you
insist; or if you can bear it, let me be myself: Estarion."

"My lord," said Firaz. "I rejoice to see you so well reconciled to our ways."

"But," said Estarion, "I am not. I do turn and turn about as my fathers did before
me: now of the north, now of the east, now of Asanion. None of them owns me. I
belong to them all."

"You are in Asanion now," said its Regent.

"I had noticed," Estarion said mildly.

Firaz took the warning: his nostrils thinned. But he was not one to be daunted
by imperial temper. "May I speak freely, my lord?"

"I would prefer it," said Estarion.

The Regent's eyes widened a fraction. Estarion tasted doubt, and a flicker of
respect. "Very well, my lord. If I may say so without risk of grievous injury to your
pride or to mine, your exhibition in the hall would not have been well received in
Kundri'j Asan."

"No?"

Firaz went on doggedly. "I believe that you knew it, and that you did it for precisely that reason. Are you determined, my lord, to turn this half of your empire
against you?"

"What if I were?"

"I would understand it," said Firaz. "I would not condone it."

"You don't think Asanion would be better served if it were rid of its pack of
mongrels and upstarts, and an emperor of the pure blood set upon its throne?"

Firaz astonished Estarion. He laughed. "Should I say yes, and die for speaking
treason? Or should I say no, and be hanged for imbecility? My lord, you are the
Heir of the Lion. It is written in your face. If your servants are blind, or if they do
not know you, then it were best you teach them to see. But not," he added, "quite so
much as we saw in hall this morning."

"Why?" asked Estarion.

"Modesty is not to be explained. It is."

"I wasn't naked."

"You were." Firaz stopped himself. "My lord, I see clearly that you are no fool, nor do you do aught but as you choose. I would venture to ask that when you choose in Kundri'j, you choose the wise man's portion."

"And that is to do as you dictate?"

"I do not dictate," said Firaz.

"Your servants do. They ordered my squire, the chosen attendant of my journey, out of my presence. Your Olenyai had dismissed my Guard, at your command and in defiance of my will."

"It was your squire, my lord, who led me here. I see a Guardsman out of Endros and an Olenyas of Kundri'j at your right hand and your left."

"I discovered," said Estarion, "that my titles have a certain worth, even in Asanion."

"They are your servants, my lord, and your warriors. They but come to fulfill their duty."

"So they do. There will be, I hope, no further objections to my escort or to its disposition."

"Will your majesty see fit to indulge Asanian eccentricities in the matter of clothing and of conduct?"

"That depends upon the eccentricity."

"Will your majesty consent at least to observe the fundamental proprieties?"

"I will not ride in a litter. I will not wear the mask or the wig. I will, if I choose, walk outside of the palace."

Firaz paused, perhaps to gather patience. "My lord, will you learn to be an emperor in Asanion?"

Cruelly hard, that, to ask so direct a question. Estarion was almost minded to be merciful. "If you will teach me, I will learn as I may."

"It was for that, my lord, that I came."

"Then," said Estarion, "begin."

The art of wearing ten robes was like that of wearing armor. The seventeen inflections of the imperial salutation made a pretty, if wearing, game for a clever mind. The myriad minutiae of the courtier's dance needed a lifetime to study properly; Estarion had no patience for them.

Some of his courtiers went back to Keruvarion, bored with the long sweltering days in a city without useful diversions. Asanian court games wearied them rapidly: most required a command of high court Asanian, and few outside of the bedchamber demanded more of the body than a languid shift from one side of a chamber to another. Hunting did not amuse the exquisites of Asanian courts. That was a sport for winter, they sighed. Water games shocked them: one had to be naked for those. Mounted exercise and sword-practice were difficult where every open space was a garden or a concourse of people, and the plain was a furnace from dawn till sundown. Estarion's soldiers braved it, and those of his escort who were determined enough to cling to him. The rest took their seneldi and their guards and their servants and began the long journey back to, as they called it, civilization.

He would happily have gone with them. But he was the cause and the source of this exile in Induverran. If he left it, it must be to come to Kundri'j. And that would not be until Lord Firaz, his tutor and his jailer, pronounced him fit for the High Court of his own empire.

Some things he would not do, here or anywhere, even in Kundri'j. One of them was to sit mewed in his chambers, speaking to no one save through guards and servants, walking nowhere save in walled gardens. That was the way of old Asanion, to keep its emperors as strongly prisoned as any miscreant, to cut them off from any stain of common earth.

That he would not endure. "Either I am emperor or I am not," he said to his Regent. "And if I am, then I go where I will, within the bounds of safety or of reason. I may go guarded—I suffer that. I may go in robes, if you insist. But I will go."

There was nothing that Lord Firaz could say to that, except to request that his majesty permit an Olenyas to accompany him. A request from Lord Firaz was a thinly veiled command. Estarion saw no profit in disputing this one.

He did not like the Olenyai. They were protected by some magic that made his head ache with a constant dull throbbing; it kept him from reading them, or from learning anything about them at all, except what their eyes betrayed.

"And yet," he said to Godri, "I think they're loyal. Not to me, not that, but to the rank I hold."

Godri, these days, wore a permanent scowl. "And if they ever take it into their heads to suspect that you don't hold it any longer, they'll cut you down without a thought."

"The day I let go my kingship, you can be sure I'll be too dead to care what yonder blackrobes do to my carcass."

Godri's grin was feral. It vanished quickly. "Just have a care they don't speed the day. I see them sometimes, my lord. Staring at you. Measuring you for your shroud."

"Maybe they're only wondering how I'd look in a black robe."

But Godri had no stomach for levity. He muttered something dark.

"Godri," said Estarion. "Do you want me to send you home?"

For a moment Godri's face lit like a lamp. When it darkened, it was even blacker than before. "I swore oath, my lord. I'll stay with you till death or your hand set me free."

"I'll free you," Estarion said.

"No!" Godri seemed to shock himself with his own vehemence. He stopped, collected his wits and his expression. "My lord," he said at length, as calmly as Estarion had ever heard him, "you may send me away. You are the emperor. But what is to stop me from coming back?"

"You hate this place," Estarion said.

"But," said Godri, "my lord, I love you."

Estarion had no words to answer that. Godri spoke it as plain fact, with no great passion. It simply was. Like, Estarion thought, the sun's rising out of the eastern sea; or the dance of the moons; or the silences that shaped the notes of a song.

Thus Godri stayed. His scowl was a constant of Estarion's wakings, his caustic observations an antidote to the gagging sweetness of courtiers' speech. The servants learned to walk softly round him. The Olenyai accorded him a remarkable degree of respect.

"He has killed, and killed well," one of them explained. It was all he would say, and more by far than Estarion could get out of the others.

Of course a tribe of warriors would value a warrior's virtue. Estarion wondered if that was why they thought so little of him apart from the fact of his kingship. He had never killed anyone. Not with his hands.

Sidani was gone. Estarion had not seen her since he left her asleep in his bed, the second morning in Induverran. He heard of her here and there for a day or two: she was telling her wonted stories, walking her accustomed paths, recovered it seemed from the sickness that had beset her. Then he heard nothing. She was not dead—he would have known, he was sure of it. She had risen one morning, gathered her few belongings, and taken to the road.

He had not truly known her: she was too prickly for that, her shifts too odd. And yet he missed her presence, her biting wit, her gift for saying the unsayable.

Wanderers wandered. It was their nature. Talespinners had somehow to gather their tales. And maybe she loved Asanion no more than he did, who had shown the raw wounds of her soul on the battlefield of Induverran. Of course she had not fought there. She could not be so old. But she was odd when it came to her stories. She called them memories, and reckoned them her own. These, he thought, had grown too much to bear.

That she had left was no more than sense. But she had gone without farewell. That hurt. He had thought she valued him a little: enough at least to take her leave when she must go.

Her absence, Vanyi's continued and relentless coldness, his own gilded imprisonment, came together into a knot of misery. It was another burning morning, another searing day in this cycle of Brightmoon called Anvil of the Sun. He woke from a bleak and lightless dream, as he had been waking every morning since he learned to sleep alone. He went to the bath, which was ready as it always was, and the servants waiting, eyes that would not look into his, faces that would not warm for anything he said.

The water of the bath was cool on his fevered skin. The servants' hands were deft and light. One of those behind him, finding the knots across his back and shoulders, worked clever fingers into them: pain melting into pleasure. He was barely awake, or he would have resisted. He wanted those knots. He had earned them.

He did not know the servants' names; they would not tell him. This one, a dun-haired eunuch, stroked the tension out of him, saying nothing, offering neither love nor hate. There was a strange comfort in it. Perfect service, nameless, faceless, unobtrusive.

As his back eased, he felt the rest of him growing calmer. All but one part of it. That, sensing his body's pleasure, rose to claim its share.

If he had been on his guard he would have quelled it before it began. But he was not entirely in his body. He drifted now in, now out of it, half asleep, half awake, haunted by the dimness of his dream. He watched the banner go up, distantly interested. Proper behavior would bid him do something discreet: sink down into the water in which he stood, exert the discipline he practiced too seldom, master the upstart.

He did none of those things. He stood slack, back arched into the hands that smoothed it with long slow strokes, and let his eyelids fall. There was a drugged serenity in it, a mingling of exhaustion and heat and hands that knew his most sensitive places.

How they came from his back to his front, he never knew. But what they did there woke him abruptly and completely.

He could not bolt. The Asanian held him too firmly. In that appalled instant he saw the whole of the plot against him. Why take his life if they could take his hope of heirs instead?"

"No," he said. Tried to say.

The Asanian took no notice. The rest of them went about their business; he was aware of them, a prickling in his skin. He tasted no hostility, nor anything but calm preoccupation. This terror, this shame, was no more to them than duty. His majesty had need; this one of their number fulfilled it.

He was going to start laughing, and once he started, he would not be able to stop. It was pure high comedy to be trapped so, in such a predicament, and no escape that he could see. The nether half of him was delighted. It had been far too long since he took notice of it.

Very, very carefully he closed his fingers over those clever hands. They froze. "No," he said much more clearly this time, if no more steadily.

The Asanian actually raised his eyes. They darted everywhere before they fell, but for a moment they met Estarion's. "This is not what I wish," Estarion said.

"My lord needs," the Asanian whispered. He was young, little more than a child; he had the nervous look of too much breeding, like a fine stallion or a lordling of the High Court. They bred their slaves here as they bred their princes, and for much the same qualities.

"My lord needs discipline," Estarion said.

"I do not satisfy?" the boy asked. His face was white. He began to tremble.

"There now," said Estarion. "There. You satisfy me perfectly. Just not . . . in that. We don't reckon that a need, where I was raised."

The Asanian's eyes flashed up again in pure incredulity.

"Not *that* kind of need," Estarion said. He still had the child by the hands. He drew him to his feet.

The Asanian was pallid with shock, but he seemed to have mastered the worst of it. "Ah," he said. "My lord prefers the higher arts. Will it be a woman, then?"

Estarion opened his mouth, shut it again. "I don't need anything. Anyone."

He saw the crossing of glances, the silent speech that was not magery, but was as clear as any words. They had decided that he was a witling or worse.

"Not now," Estarion said. "Later. Maybe. If it suits me."

That mollified them a little. It did not convince them that he was a rational being.

Maybe they had the right of it. He stood in the shallows of the bathing-pool and knew that if he did not do something, he would run raving through the city.

"Kundri'j," he said. "Kundri'j Asan." They stared at him in Asanian fashion, sidelong and in glances. "I have had enough of this," he said to them, but in good part to the air and the memory of his Regent. "It is time I left here. I must go. I must come to Kundri'j."

EIGHTEEN

KORUSAN HAD DWELT ALL HIS LIFE IN THE CASTLE OF THE OLENYAI, IN Kunzeran to the north of Kundri'j Asan. He had gone out in his training, ridden on the hunt, gone with the rest of the young Olenyai to the market in the town that was nearest. But he had never been farther than half a day's journey from the castle, and he had never walked in the city of the emperors.

To one place he went often, a place that he had made his own: the remnant of old forest that bordered the Olenyai's lands to north and east. He rode there of a morning in high summer, on the senel that he favored among those in the stable, and he rode alone as it best pleased him to do.

As he came under the trees he found one waiting for him. To the eye it was simply one of the brothers, an Olenyas like any other in robes and veils and twinned swords. But the carriage of the head and the glint of the eyes could belong to none but the Master.

Korusan knew the prick of temper, but he quelled it. He did not bare his face, nor did he speak.

The Master turned his mount beside Korusan's. They rode under the trees in silence. It was strangely companionable, for all of Korusan's displeasure at the loss of his solitude.

There was a place not far within, but off the wonted track, that Korusan had taken as a refuge. It was a clearing, not large, where a house or a small temple had been once. Part of a wall remained, and a bit of the floor, overgrown with creepers that flowered in the spring and fruited sweet in the autumn. Now, in summer, the flowers were gone, the fruit hard and green, but the shade was pleasant. There was water in a stream that ran beside the broken wall, grass for a senel to graze on, quiet to rest in away from the clamorings of duty.

Korusan had come here more than once with Marid, but he had not made it known to any other. The Master's presence surprised him in that it did not break the quiet.

Once he had loosened his senel's girth and unhooked the bit from the bridle and turned the beast loose to graze, the Master pulled off veil and headcloth. His hair was flax-fair, as tightly curled as a fleece; he dug fingers into it, smiling into the sun. "Ah," he said. "Here's a rare pleasure."

Korusan, moving more warily, freed his senel as the Master had, and bared his head. If he had been alone as he had hoped to be, he would have uncovered more than that; but modesty restrained him, even when the Master stripped to shirt and loose-cut trousers and waded barefoot in the stream.

The Master paused in dipping a handful of water, and slanted a glance at Korusan. "Do I shock you, young prince?"

"That depends on what you wish of me," said Korusan stiffly.

"You were always impeccable in your manners," the Master said: "more Olenyas than the Olenyai."

"Am I to consider myself rebuked?"

"Not at all," the Master said. "The young ones are always punctilious. It does them credit."

"I think," said Korusan after a moment, "that I am being made sport of."

"Is my prince offended?"

"No," said Korusan. He unbent sufficiently to put aside his outer robe, if not the inner, and to take off his boots. The water was shockingly cold. He did not stand in it longer than he must, to lave his face and drink a little. Safe on dry land again, he sat with knees drawn up, watching the Master out of the corners of his eyes.

The Master came out of the water and sat a little distance from Korusan, lay back on the grass, and sighed. "There will be no such pleasures for me again, I fear. Tomorrow I ride to Kundri'j."

Korusan went still, body and mind.

"Before I am Master of Olenyai," the Master said, "I am captain of the guard of the Golden Palace. That duty has never beset me: I had but attained the fourth rank when Ganiman died. But now I must take it up."

"I had heard," Korusan said carefully, "that a company of our brothers had ridden from Kundri'j under the Regent's command."

"Yes," said the Master. "They rode to Induverran, where the emperor is, to await his departure for Kundri'j Asan."

Korusan's heart began to beat hard. "Then," he said, "it is time. He comes."

"He comes," the Master said. "And I must command his guard."

"You should have gone to Induverran," Korusan said.

"No," said the Master, but without rebuke. "I rank too high. It was only the Regent who commanded, you see."

Korusan did see. But he said, "The Regent summoned you to Kundri'j."

"I summon myself to Kundri'j, to prepare for the emperor's coming."

Korusan was shivering, but his body burned with fever. He did not trouble to curse it. It was only shock. "So soon," he said, "and yet it has been so long. . . ."

"Did I say that you would accompany me?"

Korusan met the Master's gaze. "I say that I will."

The Master's eyes narrowed. "Would you risk yourself so, in the very face of the enemy?"

"Where else can I be, if I am to destroy him?"

"Here," the Master answered. "In safety, under guard, while your servants serve you."

"No," said Korusan. "This, no one can do for me."

The Master frowned.

"I must see him," Korusan said. "I must know what he is." He raised his hand, although the Master had made no move to speak. "Yes, I have seen the portraits, heard the tales, had his every act and thought laid out before me with tedious precision. I know that he favors sour apples, that he rides a blue-eyed stallion, that he has a training-scar on his right thigh above the knee. I know all that a spy can know. But I do not know him."

"Would you have him know you, and destroy you?"

"What can he know? I am an Olenyas, a blackrobe, a faceless warrior. And he is no mage, whatever he was in his childhood. He can work magics, if they are small enough, and he can read a soul if it is close and he is undistracted. More than that, he cannot do. So the mages say."

"Do you trust the mages, prince?" the Master asked.

Korusan paused for a breath's span. "I trust them well enough to believe that they have examined him and found him feeble. That they might have underestimated him, I grant you; but even they cannot read me."

"And that, prince, may be a fatal arrogance."

"Then I wager that it is not. I must see him, my lord. I must know my enemy."

The Master was silent for a long moment, eyes fixed on Korusan's face as if to limn it in his memory. "You were bred to hate him. Can you bear to stand guard over him, to dwell close to him, to be called his servant? Can you do that, prince? For if you cannot, then you have destroyed us all."

"I can do whatever I must," Korusan said, soft and level. "For if I cannot, then all your training has been in vain, and your hopes have failed."

"He is alien, prince. He is taller than any man you have seen. His skin is like black glass. He speaks Asanian with a barbarous accent, in a voice like mountains shifting. And for all of that, my prince, he has your eyes. Eyes of the Lion in the face of an outland beast."

"I have seen the portraits," Korusan said, still steadily, whatever his heart might be doing. "He has no beauty. He is merely strange. Strangeness I can endure, if I know that there is an end to it."

"I do not think," mused the Master, "that the mages would approve. They would call it folly to risk you so openly."

"And you, my lord?"

"I," said the Master, "do not approve. But I can understand. I too wish to see what kind of man he has become. He was an engaging child, for a foreigner."

"You knew him?" Korusan asked, startled.

"I guarded him. He coaxed my name out of me, but he never saw my face."

"And I have your face but not your name," said Korusan with careful mildness.

The Master raised his brows. "What, you do not know? My name is Asadi." He sighed. "Such nonsense, to conceal one's name. We never did so before the mages came among us."

"Before I came," said Korusan, "newborn of a mother who died before they took me from the womb, in a flock of mages. Would I know my own true name, my lord, if I had not insisted on it?"

The Master's lips twitched. "Perhaps not, my lord Ushayan inMuriaz. But your usename serves you well."

"It will serve me in the Golden Palace."

"And what of the truth that it embodies? All that any stranger may see of you is your eyes, and those alone suffice to betray your lineage."

"I will chance that," said Korusan. "Some of the Olenyai lines come close enough, and all of us walk faceless. Who will see aught but the veil and the swords, unless I wish him to see?"

The Master was wavering again toward resistance. Korusan steadied him with a last, strong thrust. "You are the captain of the emperor's guard. You have named me your emperor. I will enter Kundri'j; I will serve in the palace. Do you refuse me?"

He looked for anger, or for outraged pride. He received wry amusement: lifted hands, crooked smile. "You know that I cannot refuse my emperor."

Korusan looked hard at him, suspicious. "Is this a game you play?"

"Certainly," the Master said. "The greatest game of all: the game of kings." He rose and stretched, supple as a cat. "And it does please me to set a caltrop in the mages' path. They presume too much, my prince: of you, of all of us."

Korusan's heart eased its hammering. His fever was high still, dizzying him, but his mind was clear on top of it. He smiled slowly. "So they do, my lord. So indeed they do."

NINETEEN

Kundri'j Asan.

Estarion said the name to himself in silence, like the silence that rode with him. Even the clatter of hoofs on paving stones was muted, the clink of armor among the guards, the snort of a senel as it shied at a dangling pennon. The sky was the color of hammered brass, the heat a living thing, breathing heavy on his neck, and he robed ninefold; not ten, not on his last march, for he was not yet come to the throne, and he would not wear the mask that made the emperor. He was mere high prince, then, with his bared face and his nine robes. He cared little for the count of the damnable things, only that he wore them. It was that or wear armor, and he would not come as a conqueror.

Estarion could not have felt less like an emperor. His body was dripping wet, shoulders and breast and thighs rubbed raw between the weight of robes and the unfamiliarity of the high Asanian saddle. He had not inflicted that torment on Umizan. The beast he rode was one of Lord Dushai's own, placid to torpidity but blessed with a coat the color of pure minted gold. Umizan's contempt for the creature was the only distinct thing in this blurred and sun-battered world. The stallion would have broken his halter when this ride began, and taught his rival a lesson, if Estarion had not forbidden and Godri mounted him. He could not shed that born rider short of flinging himself down and rolling; and that, even in his fit of temper, he was too sensible to do. He contented himself with flattened ears and horns lowered not quite enough for threat, keeping to the place reckoned proper for the squire who rode him, and stabbing Estarion with darts of acute displeasure.

I too, brother, Estarion said to him behind words.

Ulyai would not even pass the first gate. She tried. She clung as close as Estarion's idiot mount would allow, from Induverran across the plain to Kundri'j. But as the walls drew closer, her ears went flatter, her tail lashed more fiercely. Before the bridge that spanned the river of Asanion, broad brown Shahriz'uan, she halted. Her muzzle wrinkled, baring fangs. She could not bear the scent or the sound or the sense of this city of all the cities in the Golden Empire.

Her eyes were as close to pleading as an ul-queen's could ever be: pleading afire with rage. She could not cross the bridge. Not unless he laid his will on her.

And that, he would not do. *Go,* he willed her. *Be free.*

A yowl escaped her, a cry of protest. She wheeled. Seneldi shied. She broke through them, running swift as a shadow on the grass. The last horned idiot veered and skittered. Then she was free. The plain was open before her, her freedom calling. She sped to meet it.

Estarion's heart yearned after her. But he was bound by his word and his damnable duty.

He shifted in the saddle. His mount plodded on. The sun beat down. The city swallowed him.

Nine circles in the circle of the river, Shahriz'uan in its chains of locks and bridges. Nine levels as in the courts of this empire, from lowest to highest, from plain white marble to burning gold. It turned its splendor toward him, its high houses, its thousand temples, its broad plazas and straight ways, even its gardens and its cool places. The walls were hung with banners, the fountains flowing with wine and sweet perfumes, the way paved with flowers or carpeted with richness, priceless rarities to be trampled under hoof and foot.

He would happier have seen that wealth fed to the people who were not permitted to line the ways, the poor and the sick, the maimed, any who fell short of perfection. They were there: he felt them. There was hunger here, and sickness in this unrelenting heat. Squalor behind the splendor. A reek of dung beneath the heavy scent of flowers.

The imperial majesty was not to see such things, not to know of them, lest they sully him. His Asanian teachers had not said so in as many words. They knew it, as he knew that majesty must see everything, the dark and the bright, and know the face of death as he knew life. How else could he rule? How else speak for his people in the courts of the god?

He passed through the nine gates, white marble, black marble, lapis, carnelian, jasper, malachite, ice-blue agate, silver, and last of them all, the innermost, bright gold. It drank the sun's heat and poured it forth again, a blinding brightness, a fire as terrible as that which burned in his hand.

His mount halted unbidden. He raised burning hand to burning gate. It did not rock and fall.

It was only stone sheathed in gold. The sun was only sun, fierce with the breath of summer on Asanion's plain. His hand was flesh, his arm, his shoulder itching where he could not scratch.

Laughter welled in him. The Olenyai who rode ahead, the point of the spear, understood at last that he was not behind them. The court in back of him, the Guard, the servants in their multitudes, had begun to knot and tangle.

He was a great discomfiture to the heart of the Golden Empire. He kicked the senel back into its amble, and passed through the gate.

From Golden Gate to the Gate of the Lion was an avenue of lions, great stone beasts crouched on guard. The gate itself was a frieze of lions on the hunt and in the pride, rearing rampant to form the lintel and the posts. There was a joy in them that struck Estarion strangely in this joyless place, a delight in their play, even a welcome for this lost mongrel child riding under them, into the prison that was the Golden Palace.

Lord Firaz was waiting beyond the gate, on foot, attended by courtiers in the robes of princes. He greeted Estarion with the nine prostrations and the nine great salutations, less the tenth that was for the emperor enthroned. Then he took Estarion's bridle and led him inward, pacing slowly, as princes did in the Golden Empire.

The chain of courts opened and closed before them. In one they left the seneldi. In another, Estarion's courtiers found themselves politely but firmly directed toward another way than the one on which he was led. In the next, all but the core of his Guard fell back; but the bulk of the Olenyai were kept back as well, and that was a comfort. Lightly guarded, with the Regent ahead of him still, not quite touching him to guide him, he came to the heart of the palace.

The Sunborn had built the hall of the throne in Endros in the image of this: the Hall of the Thousand Years with its thousand pillars and its roof of gold, wide enough for armies to march in, and a floor of panels inlaid with jewels and gold, that could be lifted up from golden sand and dust of jewels, ruby, sapphire, topaz, emerald. The throne was moated so, behind a black wall of Olenyai.

In older days the throne had been a great bowl of gold lifted on the backs of golden lions. That did not please its last trueblood emperor. He had had it remade, suffering its lions to stand as they had stood for a thousand years, but setting on their backs a broad chair. Two could sit there on an abundance of cushions, taking their ease, and behind them a marvel of jewelwork: a lion rampant upon the face of a golden Sun.

Estarion faltered. He had come well-nigh to the wall of Olenyai, hardly marking the glittering ranks of the High Court, aware chiefly of the man who led him and the guards who paced behind, and the throne to which he came. It was not the great work of magery that was the throne in Endros, and yet it had its own power. Hirel Uverias had made it to share with his Varyani empress. Their son had sat in it, and their son's son. Their names rang in his memory. Hirel and Sarevadin, Ganiman, Varuyan, Ganiman. And now, if he did not falter, Meruvan Estarion.

He was dazzled, or ill with heat. He saw a shadow on the throne, a dark man, dark-eyed, with a sudden, brilliant smile. Not a young man, for he had married late, but still in the prime of his manhood, and gifted with the light bold spirit of his Gileni mother. He bore the weight of robes with easy grace, wore the mask when he must and smiled at it after, and was all the emperor that the Asanians could have wished for. And they killed him.

The throne was empty. Lord Firaz had just begun to perceive Estarion's hesitation. Before he could pause or turn, Estarion finished the stride he had begun. Briefly he wondered if the Olenyai would hold the way against him. But they parted smoothly, with no sign of reluctance.

Lord Firaz halted at the foot of the dais. Estarion must mount alone. One waited beside the throne, prince of seven robes with a face as like to the Regent's as a brother's or close cousin's, and in his hands, upheld with the barest hint of waver, the tenth robe, the emperor's mantle, woven of silk and gold.

It was as heavy as worlds. How the Asanian had borne it, Estarion could not imagine. He was a small man even for one of his kind, and yet he laid the mantle about Estarion's shoulders, hardly trembling with the effort, and secured it, and sank down in obeisance. It was not Estarion's part to raise him, still less to thank him. He backed down the steps and past the Olenyai, into the first rank of princes.

Estarion stood erect in front of the throne, though the mantle's weight strove to bow him down. The court lay flat to a man, all but the Olenyai, black motionless stones among the pillars of the hall.

Then at last Lord Firaz came up. He held the mask, the dreadful golden thing that Estarion had refused. It glittered in his hands. Blind eyeless face, Asanian to the last graven curl of its nostril, and beautiful in the way of these people: broad low brow, full cheeks, straight nose, lips that seemed as soft as a girl's. It was all smooth curves, no planes, no angles. It grew no beard. It never aged or scarred, or suffered the shame of a flaw.

Estarion reached, startling the Regent, capturing the mask. It was gold, and heavy, and despite the heat of the air it was cool. He lifted it. Its eyes were narrow windows on a world gone strange. Olenyai backs. The clean line of a pillar. A lord still prostrate, hair thinning on his skull, sadly exposed within the circle of his coronet.

Estarion lowered the mask before it touched his face. He kept it in his hands as he sat, giving in at last to the weight of his robes. Lord Firaz had recovered himself. Estarion could not tell whether he approved, or whether he chose to take the bargain he was given. He spoke in a clear, strong, trained voice, words as numerous as the grains of sand under the paneled floor; but all of them came simply to this: "Behold, lords of the Golden Courts. Behold your emperor!"

It was no more terrible than receiving homage from the throne of Endros. Estarion had not expected that. His back grew tired; his rump protested the long hours of sitting. Worse was hunger, but thirst was worst of all. This was a test of imperial

hardihood, to bring him straight from the road into the hall, and set him down
without food or drink or pause to rest, and compel him to accept the full homage
of the High Court.

But he had done almost as much in Keruvarion, coming to audience from the
hunt or the practice-field, forgetting to send for wine or water, and laboring till
dark over matters of state. His mother was not here to call him away, nor did a servant creep up behind with a filled cup. That was not done in Kundri'j Asan. The
emperor must not appear to be a human man, with a man's needs of the body. He
did not even join in banquets, although his son and heir might do so.

Peculiar logic, Estarion thought, considering how many feasts he had suffered
on his journey here. Then he had been the Varyani emperor, but not yet full lord of
Asanion. Now that he would have welcomed a cup of water as a gift from heaven,
he was forbidden anything but homage.

A weaker man would faint, or call a halt to the ordeal. Estarion refused. He
received the respects of every lord in that hall, singly and in companies, father or
eldest brother with all his sons and brothers and cousins and hangers-on, each of
whom must be named to the imperial majesty, and his place affirmed, his authority
made certain by the emperor's decree.

There was none who came as that lord had come to the throne of Endros, defiant out of turn. Nor did his lordship appear among the princes of five robes. Estarion
was cravenly glad. These Asanians were making the best of the emperor they had.
They did not afflict him with hostility, nor did they try visibly to shame him.

The emperor did not speak at the giving of homage, which was a mercy. His
Regent spoke for him, or his Voice if he had one. Firaz did duty for both. He said
all that an emperor should say, in phrases as elegant as they were politic. No insults
there, that Estarion could discern; no errors in the myriad shades of inflection.

He could grow accustomed to this. The knowledge chilled him. So many years, so
many battles, so much hatred of Asanion and Asanians, and he sat here, surrounded
with them, and he accepted it. Worse than that: he knew that he was born for it.

Maybe it was a poison. Or a mage's trick; though the ache in his head was for his
empty stomach, and not for the touch of sorcery.

The last princeling came, made his obeisances, withdrew. Estarion sat unmoving, but no one else came forth. He was to rise, then. Stiff, struggling not to sway.
The hall stretched endless in front of him. He must walk the length of it, mantled
if not masked.

He could not do it. It was nearly sunset; he had not eaten or drunk since before
dawn. He was drained dry.

He essayed a step. He did not fall. Another. It bred another. Like Asanians in
their harems, spawning sons. That made him want to laugh, dizzily, weak with fasting. And was that a fast, then, this mere day's stretch? He had gone thirsty three
days running in the cause of his priesthood, and fasted longer, until his body was a
light and singing thing, and his soul stood all naked to the sun.

Pride, then. Stubbornness. He would not show himself weak to the court of his western empire. He hated them for testing him. He loved them as he loved anything that dared him to outmatch it.

He walked unaided from the hall down the passage that presented itself, into the room on which it opened. Servants waited there. The one who relieved him of the mantle won the most loving of all his smiles. The one who brought him water in a golden cup gained a prayer of thanks unto the hundredth generation. It was not a eunuch, either, which was Estarion's good fortune. Ungelded servants were rarer, he had noticed, the closer one came to the throne. Were they afraid that the emperor would be seduced as women were, and bear a child out of turn?

He was too wise to ask them that. He drank the cool sweet water, and never mind that the boy who brought it had sipped it first lest it be poisoned. There were cakes, too, and something with spices in it, and fruit, whole and sour-sweet. He was wise with a priest's wisdom. He did not gorge himself on either food or drink, but partook slowly, sparingly, letting each sip or bite settle well before he essayed another. The servants freed him from his robes while he ate, combed the tangles from his hair, indicated with Asanian subtlety that he could bathe when he was ready.

He wanted most to fall upon the couch that stood against the wall, and not wake till morning; but a bath was a potent enticement. He let himself be led into a chamber like a hall under the sea, all green and blue and sun-shot gold, with a play of tiled fishes, and a pool as wide as a lake, full of warm and ever-flowing water. He opened his mind without thinking, reached for the one who was not there, who had not been there in a bitter count of Brightmoon-cycles. *Vanyi, look. Here's a bit of your sea, all in the dry land.*

But she was gone, her mind closed away as if she had never been, or been part of him. He was alone.

Truly. None of his Guard had come so far, none of his court, his priests, not even his mother. She was in the queen's palace as was proper. If he would speak with her, he must summon her.

He opened his mouth to do it. Then he shut it, and likewise his mind. She had forced him to this. Let her know what she had done, and suffer its consequences.

TWENTY

VANYI WAS PROUD OF HERSELF. HAVING LEFT ESTARION TO HIS OWN DEVICES, she devoted the whole of her self to her duties and her priesthood. She was not even dreaming of him every night now, nor missing him for more than two heartbeats out of three. Sometimes, when they were still in Induverran, she had seen him from a distance. He looked well, if harried, and strikingly cool in the heat.

In Kundri'j Asan she did not see him. He was shut up in the palace behind the gates and walls of gold, where no woman walked and no commoner might go. She had her place in the temple of the Two Powers within the wall of lapis, in the third circle of the city. Its Worldgate was as potent as that in Endros, with holiness on it beyond its simple power, for it had been made by the Mageguild itself. This had been the guildhall, this house like any other in this circle of the city, neither the richest nor the poorest of those about it. Priests of god and goddess had kept it so after the Guild died out, altering it little save to set an altar in its central court. Common people did not know, maybe, what power dwelt here. Some came to worship, and the priests did turn and turn about in the rites, but most chose other temples.

It was a quiet place, for all its weight of memory. Vanyi could have been happy there, searching out its secrets, prowling its library that had been left when the mages went away. Her old fascination with the Guild was whetted here, tantalized with glimpses into their lore and their magics.

Iburan refused the place of chief priest although he far outranked the mistress of the temple; he was content to serve where he was needed, to stand guard on the Gate in his turn, and to go rarely to the upper city and the high temple of Avaryan and Uveryen. He never said, nor indicated by glance or strayed thought, but Vanyi suspected that he was not fond of the high priestess. She was a proud cold creature of princely Asanian blood, such as raised steadier hackles than Estarion's; nor did she make a secret of her dislike for Iburan. Great northern bear, she called him, and other things less flattering.

Thus he did service like penance in the least of the temples in Kundri'j, and bowed his head and was humble, and made no move to put himself forward.

"She has no power," he said to Vanyi not long after they came to Kundri'j. She remembered it afterward as the day the lightning fell. In that hour it was simply another breathless, airless, hideously hot day, its only distinction that its sky was the color not of brass but of lead. She could feel the heat building, hammer on the anvil of the earth.

This temple had a garden of strange flowers—fruit of Magegates, Iburan said, and as secret as the rest of it. Vanyi plucked a blood-red bloom with a scent that both dizzied and steadied her, like her lover's kiss. She almost cast it away, thinking of him, but tucked it in her hair instead and sat on the rim of a fountain. The spray of water was cool on her hand.

Iburan plucked a fruit the color of a maiden's cheek in Asanion, and bit into it. "She's no mage, my lady Himazia," he said when he had chewed and swallowed. "She knows this temple only as a nuisance, a tendril of my jurisdiction in the heart of her domain."

"They don't have priest-mages here," Vanyi observed. "Not as they do in the east."

"They don't like to believe in magery." He spat out the fruit-pit, knelt, buried it carefully in a bit of open earth, watering it with handfuls from the fountain. "There now," he said to it. "Sleep well; grow strong, and bear fruit."

"It's not that there are no mages," Vanyi said after a pause, due respect to his invocation. "They have too many, maybe. Every lord has his sorcerer in grey. Do you wonder, sometimes, if the Guild didn't die out after all, or subsume itself into our priesthood? What if it survived in secret, in Asanion? A mage killed Ganiman the emperor. Maybe he wasn't alone when he did it."

"We never found an accomplice," Iburan said. He sat on the fountain's rim a little distance from her, and washed the fruit's sweetness from his beard. "The Guild died a natural death. Anyone will tell you so. After it failed to raise a puppet emperor on the throne of the two lands, and was subjugated to the will of Sarevadin and her consort, it withered into nothing. Mages had no desire to join a guild of traitors. Those who were willing or able to bear discipline accepted the torque. The rest took teaching from the priests and went their ways, sworn and bound to work no harm."

"All of which I know," said Vanyi sharply. "I heard it the first day I went to our priestess in Seiun and told her I wanted to learn. What if she was wrong? Consider what Hirel did to the army of his brothers, any one of whom could have supplanted him or his half-bred son. He shut them in the palace, gave them all that they could ask for—but no women. No children. If the palace galled them, they could leave freely, on one small condition. They must leave their manhood behind and go out as eunuchs. His sisters were free to do as they pleased, but they could never marry, never bear children to challenge his heir. It was a brilliant solution. Merciful, even. What if he did the same to the Guild?"

"He did, in his way," Iburan said.

"And if the Guild saw it, and saw through it? What then? Mightn't they have pretended to dwindle and vanish, but only gone into hiding?"

"It would be difficult," said Iburan, "to conceal such powers as they would need to raise, simply to train their young mages. We would know. We'd have sensed them long ago, and disposed of them."

"Not if they used Gates," Vanyi said.

Iburan sighed, but not with temper. "So. You've thought of that, too? We've found nothing. You know that. You're a Guardian."

"I don't think," said Vanyi, "that we should grow lazy simply because we haven't found anything. They'd be expecting it, you know. The last Guildmage who would admit to it died when Varuyan was emperor. It's been a solid generation since. Time enough to dig in deep and build the walls high."

"Have you had a Seeing?" he asked her.

"No," she said. She was irritable: that surprised her. "You know that's not one of my talents. I'm just thinking. Maybe it's this place. It remembers. It doesn't like us much."

"That it doesn't." He was smiling. His beard hid the curve of his lips, but his eyes were warm, even wicked. "You are marvelously gifted with power; more, one might think, than you have any right to be."

That did not help Vanyi's temper at all. "I'm not too badly trained, and I have Gate-sense. I'm nothing more than that."

"But you are," said Avaryan's high priest in Endros. "It's time you admitted it."

"Why now?" she demanded. "Why here?"

"Because it pleases me," he said, "and because you've made a study of the Guild and its Gates, and your bones tell you to be uneasy. None of the rest of us is so troubled."

"Not even you?"

She had not meant her voice to sound as hard and mocking as it did. Iburan did not take umbrage at it. "Not even I. I'm jealous, I confess. If I were a shade less wise, I'd even be angry. Who are you, after all, but a priestess on Journey, and a commoner at that?"

Her own frequent words, spoken with exquisite irony. She blushed and glowered, and bit her tongue before she said something even more unfortunate than she had already said.

"Priestess," he said, wholly grave for once, "never let your lack of rank or lineage shield you from the truth. If your power tells you that you should be wary, listen to it. Heed it. Act as it bids you. And if you have need of me, wherever you or I may be, call on me, and I will come."

Vanyi shifted on the fountain's rim. Her body was as reluctant as her mind to accept what he was telling her. That she was not a priestess-mage like any other. That she was—could be—more than that. Maybe much more. More even than an empress.

Her body knew how to stop that thought before it ran wild. It had been long cycles since she had had a man, and would be longer yet, unless she let the priests restore the bindings. Her womb was open still, unspelled. It made a useful refuge from a harder truth.

Useful; and safe, which her body well knew. Even if she had not risked breaking her vows again, she would do no more than fidget under Iburan's splendid black eye. Everyone knew whose bed he went to when the temple did not keep him for itself. Everyone, that is, but Estarion. One way and another he had failed to notice, and people had failed to enlighten him. Wise of them. He would not be pleased to know how his mother found comfort in her widowhood. Sons could be odd that way. Every man's mother a saint, and every man's sister a maiden.

She stood up abruptly. "I have duties," she said; or something like it. She did not look to see if Iburan's smile turned mocking; or if he knew all of the reasons why she fled.

The Gate was at rest as Gates went, wandering with dream-slowness through its manifold worlds. This one could, if one but asked, come to the center and focus of the Gates' power, the Heart of the World. That stronghold stood amid bare and barren mountains under a moonless sky, on a world that had no name. Its center was a blaze like a hearthfire, but it was pure power. It had made the Gates in the beginning, and it had made an empress of a Varyani high prince, and in the end it had betrayed the mages who made it. Sarevadin was part of it, wrought in it. She mastered it and the Guild, and drew its claws; but not before it had killed her mother and her consort's father, and driven her own father mad. She never forgave the mages, never trusted them or granted them power in her empire. Therefore they dwindled and the priest-mages of Endros rose to take their place, but in sub-servience to the Sun's blood, and not in power over them.

The strength of the Gate here was such that three priests watched by night, two by day when the sun's power balanced that of the Gate. The other who watched now was a stranger, an Asanian girlchild, mute with shyness. Vanyi let her be. She would warm in time, as young animals did. Her magery was a bright and singing thing, as splendid as her outer seeming was dull.

They sang the rites together, the child's voice light, almost without substance, Vanyi's darker, smokier. The meeting of voice and power bred a silent amity.

They settled to prayer, content in one another's presence. Vanyi was aware in her body of the Gate at rest, the land under her, the air heavy with heat. The sky beyond the temple was like a roof, looming low, breeding thunder.

Well indeed, thought Vanyi. Please the god, the heat would break. She would be able to breathe again. People would stop snarling at one another; the city would retreat from its raw edge of violence. Nothing had erupted yet, perhaps for fear of the emperor's presence, but it was there, smoldering like fire under ash.

Almost without her willing it, her power divided itself. Part went on warding the Gate. Part ranged over the city, testing its mood.

She glanced at the Asanian priestess. That one seemed unperturbed. It was always so, her manner said. Kundri'j was an angry city. It smoldered; sometimes it burst into flame. Then people rioted, and the soldiers came, or if affairs were desperate, the Olenyai—this with a shiver of fear and sharp dislike. Now the emperor was here. People did not love his outland self, but his rank comforted them, and his presence in the palace.

Vanyi had no reason to be uneasy. She was not a seer. Old tales were rankling in her, half-rotted fears, treason overheard in the temple in Induverran, strangeness in the Gate of Endros. This Gate was at peace. Its stars, when they shimmered past, were simple stars. Its worlds were worlds without fear.

And suppose, she thought, the Guild survived. It had made the Gates. Suppose that it could wield them, shape them to show only what the Guardians wished to see, while it drew in secret from their power.

There was an insect in the Isles. The male possessed a maddening incessant buzz, but did not bite. The female was silent; she drank blood, and left great itching welts where she had been. Silence was the warning, people said. When there was no sound, no evidence of the creature's passing, then one did well to be wary.

Fine way to drive oneself mad, thought Vanyi sourly. *I hear nothing, therefore I fear everything.* The Gate and the temple were at peace. The sky was readying to burst, but that was nothing to fear under this roof, in walls of stone and magecraft.

Guildcraft.

She got up abruptly, paced from end to end of the sanctuary. Her companion watched her wide-eyed. She tried to smile. It only drove the child back into her shyness.

This house was built by mages of the Guild. This Gate was their Gate. These stones were imbued with their power, however thickly overlaid with the power of the priests. If they truly had not vanished, if they chose to come through, they would be idiots to emerge here, into the Guardians' arms.

Such Guardians. One a year from full priesthood, the other little more than a novice.

"I'm losing my mind," Vanyi said aloud. The little priestess did not understand her broad Seiun dialect. She said in Asanian, "I wish this heat would break."

"Soon," the priestess managed to say, great boldness in one so shy.

"Now," said Vanyi. The word had no power in it, nothing but hope approaching desperation, but she could make it happen. She could shatter this heat, these clouds, this terrible, breathless waiting.

Magery was not for compelling the sky to do one woman's will. Such threatened the balance that sustained the world. If she broke the storm too soon, one domain's crops could wash away, another's wither in drought. She was no god, to make such choices.

She felt the power building above her. The Gate's shifting was quicker now, its edges sharper. Vanyi's power firmed itself, weaving more tightly with the Asanian's.

"This is a mother of storms," the child said. "Watch for the winds. They're treacherous. They like to spin and roar, and then they eat anything they find. But don't be afraid. If one comes near us, we can coax it away."

And if one would not be coaxed? If it were driven by living will, by the malice of an enemy?

It was only a storm. When it had passed, the heat would have broken, the air would be clean and cool and blessedly sweet. Vanyi would get her temper back again, and she would stop vexing herself with shadows.

Break, she willed it. *Damn you, break.*

The Gate was pulsing like a heart. Vanyi sent out a summons. Three would serve better here than two.

She did not wait to see who answered, but began to match her breaths to the pattern of the Gate. When they pulsed together, she shaped the notes of the breaking-chant. Beat, pause. Beat, beat, pause. Beat, pause, beat. Breaking that perilous rhythm which, sustained, could shatter the Gate.

It fought her. The storm was in it, lending it strength. The little priestess chimed a descant. The Gate wavered. Had it been a living thing, Vanyi would have reckoned it confused.

That too was dangerous. Confusion could shatter more easily even than that relentless beat-beat-beat.

A third voice entered the weaving, a third power like a pillar of light. It shored them up; it mastered the Gate. *Iburan.* The name was pure power.

All at once, with a roar like armies charging, the storm broke.

It was glorious. Freed of fear for the Gate, secure in the threefold weaving, Vanyi rode the lightnings. Winds raged; she laughed at them. Rain lashed the roofs of the city, scoured the dust from its streets, churned its lanes to mud. The river roared in its bed.

The heat was gone, shattered. The land heaved a mighty sigh. The lightnings ran away eastward, drawing the winds in their wake. The rain came down more gently.

Vanyi slipped back into her body. She was kneeling before the Gate, the little priestess on one side of her, Iburan on the other, all three clinging together. The Gate was restless still, but growing quiet as she watched.

All of itself, her voice soared up, chanting the god's praises. Iburan's wove into it, drum-deep; and the little priestess' like the call of a bird. They sang the storm away and brought back the sun, bright in the blue heaven.

But the Gate remained the Gate. And Vanyi's heart was not at ease, however much she willed it to be so.

TWENTY-ONE

T HAT ONE IS STRONG," A DARKMAGE SAID.

The Guildmaster raised his eyes from the scrying-glass. They were red-rimmed; the lines of his face were slack with weariness. "Which? The black priest? We knew that long ago."

"No," said the darkmage. "The young one, the Island woman. I should fear her, I think."

"She is nothing," said the Guildmaster.

The darkmage looked as if he would have argued, but they had by then taken notice of the stranger at the door. Korusan suppressed an unbecoming stab of malice that even the great Master of mages had failed to mark his coming. They had been preoccupied—pressingly so, from the look of them.

He did not let his eyes wander to the scrying-glass, sorely though it might tempt them. He had yielded to one like it before, and been ill for days after. There was too much magic in him, he had been given to understand, and yet too little. Too much to be impervious to the lure of the visions in the glass, too little to defend him when they sucked at his soul.

"My prince," the Guildmaster said. "You are welcome in Kundri'j Asan."

No word of disapproval that Korusan should have come to this city. No suggestion of anger that he had dared it. "Is it not my city?" Korusan said. "Am I not to be lord of it?"

"In time," the Guildmaster said, "you shall."

Korusan circled the room and the gathering of mages, keeping his distance from the glass on its frame. "How marvelous," he said, "that you lair here, deep in the enemy's palace. And none of them suspects that you exist."

"One does," said the darkmage who had spoken before: stubbornly, Korusan thought, and not at all prudently. "She pries into the library we so unwisely left intact. She questions what none of her kind should question."

"She is no danger to us," the Guildmaster said. "What can she know but that we were once strong?"

"She knows Gates," the darkmage persisted. "She could almost be one of us."

"Had she been one of us," said the lightmage who stood beside him, gently enough but with an edge of impatience, "she would have been known, found, brought among us before ever the Sun-cult had her."

132

"There are few of our order in the Isles, and those hard pressed by Sun-magic and sea-magic. She could easily have escaped them. As," the darkmage said, "she has escaped you even yet."

"Hush," the lightmage said, with a glance at Korusan. The darkmage looked stubborn but held his tongue. He would take up the battle again later, his expression promised.

Korusan wondered if this one would go the way of the lightmage who had been too honest in the face of his questioning. "Who is this woman you speak of? Is it anyone whom I should fear?"

"No, no one," the Guildmaster said, even as the darkmage said, "A priestess, a mage—she was the emperor's lover, they say she is that no longer, she—"

Mages closed in on him, silencing him, easing him out of the circle and the room. It was smoothly done. Korusan observed it with interest and a glimmer of pity. Outspokenness was never a virtue in an Asanian, whether he be mage or prince.

"My prince," said the Guildmaster when the importunate one was gone, "you are welcome here as always, but perhaps you would choose to rest from your journey in greater quiet than we can offer."

"I have rested," Korusan said. "My Master bids you attend him."

The Master of the mages did not look pleased to be so summoned, even by the Lion's cub. Korusan was prepared for his resistance, and mildly disappointed when he acquiesced. "I will come," he said, "when I am done here."

Korusan inclined his head, all courtesy. "I wait upon your pleasure."

"You may go," the mage said, "my prince."

"I am bidden to accompany you," Korusan said.

"You accept a master's bidding?"

Korusan smiled in his veil. "I choose to accept it." He took the stance of the guard at rest, hands resting lightly on swordhilts, and set himself to wait. He was precisely in the path of any mage who wished to leave the room—fools, they, for trapping themselves where was but a single door. They must brush past him or walk round him if they would go about their duties.

They made no more workings while he watched, nor spoke unless it were from mind to mind. One of them covered the terrible beauty of the glass. Others cleared away the tools of their trade, odd small things that made Korusan's skin quiver. Their Master watched and said nothing. When the last of it was done and its doer had departed past Korusan, the Guildmaster still did not move.

Korusan was in comfort, now that the glass was hidden. He could fight patience with patience.

The mage spoke abruptly. "Have you looked upon your enemy?"

"No," said Korusan. His voice was sharper than he liked.

"He is here. You know that, surely. They enthroned him these three days past."

Korusan had known. He was being tested again as always, his temper tried to see if it would break. "It is not the throne that makes the king," he said.

"There are many who would dispute you," said the mage. "The throne, the power, the backing of the courts and the armies—all those, he has."

"But I," said Korusan, "have you."

"Do you, prince? You like us little, you trust us less. If you could dispose of us, you would do so and be glad of it."

"But I cannot, and I will not, while your purposes serve mine. You have wagered all on this last cast of the bones—my bones, frail as they are. Only remember: you have called me your prince. As your prince I may command you. And I will look ill upon your disobedience."

"We will obey you," the Guildmaster said, "while you show yourself our ally."

That would do, thought Korusan. It must. He stepped aside, and bowed slightly. "Come. The Master of the Olenyai waits."

The two masters of their orders conspired at nothing that Korusan had not heard before. It had chiefly to do with Olenyai deployed here, mages deployed there, and rebellions fomented through the satrapies of Asanion. Of the emperor in this palace they said nothing.

And yet it was the emperor who mattered. Korusan left them, gaining a glance from the Olenyas and no apparent notice from the mage. Perhaps they thought that he went to the cell that had been given him. He thought of it, would have been glad of it, but his mind would not let him rest. It leaped and spun, driving him through this stronghold within a stronghold, this chief of the postings of the Olenyai.

Inevitably it drove him out into the palace. His robe and his veils granted him passage wherever he wished to go, except perhaps the harem; but that he did not approach. It was empty, he had been told, for the Sunlord had no woman but the priestess who knew Magegates, and she had left his bed. The queen's palace, which was occupied, tempted Korusan slightly, but the guards there were women, and some had magic. He veered away from them.

He was circling, he knew that. Round and round about, narrowing slowly to a certain center.

The emperor of Asanion had lived for time out of mind like a prisoner in his own palace. He had his chambers, and they were many; his courts, and they were broad; his wonted ways and his expected duties. But he did not pass the walls. He did not walk free in the world. That was the price and the sacrifice with which he bought his power.

The outland savage was shut up as tightly as any son of the Lion. Korusan half expected to hear him roaring somewhere deep within, but the halls were quiet, the chambers cool in the heat of the day. There were foreigners about, black men and brown men, even a few women; priests with their torques, guards in alien livery, a lordling or two eyeing the splendors of the palace as if he had a mind to buy. None of them ventured to question the lone Olenyas. They were afraid of him, he thought, catching their glances and watching them shrink aside. Wise fools. It was not his robe that they needed to fear, or even his swords. All his body was a weapon.

Of the Olenyai here, some were strangers. Many were not. One greeted him with Olenyai effusion: eyes that smiled, voice that called softly in battle-language for there was no one near to hear. "Brother! How did you come here?"

Korusan moved smoothly into position on the other side of the door that Marid guarded, and permitted a smile to creep into his voice. "I rode," he said. "And you?"

Marid slapped his right-hand swordhilt, half in mirth, half in exasperation. "You know what I meant. I thought the mudrobes would never let you loose."

"I let myself loose," said Korusan. "Whose door is this?"

"I think you know," said Marid.

"He is within?"

Korusan must have sounded more eager than he meant to: Marid raised a hand. "Down, lad! You can't have his blood yet. We're all under orders. We're to guard him as if he really were the emperor, and show ourselves loyal, and not a thought out of line."

"Have you seen him?" Korusan asked.

Marid's answer was cut off before it began. Footsteps approached them. They froze in the stillness of sentries, eyes schooled to blankness. The one who passed wore scarlet and gold, and his face—Korusan labored not to stare.

"What in the worlds—" he began when the creature had gone within.

"That is the emperor's bodyservant," Marid said. "Lovely, isn't he? He's a savage from the desert. He's killed a dozen men, they say, and he maimed a thirteenth to win his place by the emperor's side."

Korusan widened his eyes at that. "Truly? And was he born with such a face?"

"Oh, no. Those are his manhood-marks and his killing-marks, and some of them are for a prince. He'll talk to us sometimes. He's almost human under the devil-mask."

How strange, thought Korusan. *How utterly foreign.* His stomach was tight, but for once it did not want to empty itself. Perhaps it understood that he was here, at last, where he needed most to be.

He set hand to the door's latch. Marid frowned at him. "You aren't going to. Are you?"

Korusan answered by opening the door. Marid did not stop him. Duty bound the other to keep his post, but Korusan had no orders yet, and no ban upon him.

He knew these chambers within as if he had dwelt there all his life. They were the heart of his teaching, the place to which he had been born, in which he hoped to die. He walked in them like a shadow, faceless, unregarded: simply another of the Olenyai.

They were trusting in Keruvarion. That too Korusan had been taught, with
some degree of incredulity; but his teachers averred that it was true. Now he saw
the reality of it. All these open chambers, unquestioning guards, servants walking
in and out; no locks, no bars in any place but one.

That one room had been the emperor's bedchamber. The bar was new, the lock
still bright from the forging. It did not yield to Korusan's touch.

"You! What do you there?"

He turned carefully, and not too quickly. The voice was sweet for all the bar-
barousness of its accent, speaking a rough but comprehensible Asanian patois. The
speaker was half expected, the tattooed savage in Varyani livery. He looked alarming, but his challenge held little hostility.

Korusan answered him in the same patois that he had spoken. "Do you hold his
majesty prisoner?"

The emperor's servant looked narrowly at him, then shrugged. "What, are you
new here? Of course we don't. That's where his father died. He won't go in, or let
anyone else go in, either."

Such innocence. Korusan almost admired him for it. "The last emperor died
these ten years past. Surely he does not bear the grief still."

"He can't forget. It almost killed him, too. He still has the black dreams."

"He is as weak as that?"

The savage's eyes glittered. "Only look at him, and you'll know that for the lie it
is." He calmed himself visibly. "There now. You people don't know him; and mages
are different, and Sunlords most different of all."

"It is clear to see," said Korusan, "that his servant loves him."

"So do all who know him." Someone called from down a passage. The savage
snapped alert. "There! He's looking for me. Do your duty, blackrobe, but don't try
to do it in there. He'll have your hide for a kilt."

Korusan followed the emperor's servant quietly, with steps that slowed, the
deeper he went into the maze of chambers. Still he was not challenged. There were
more of his own kind here, but they would reckon that he came under orders. And
so he did if he was truly their prince, with authority to command himself.

The black king was in a chamber that had been meant for guests, but that he
seemed to have claimed for his own. He must have come from High Court: his servant was divesting him of the robes.

Korusan had seen northerners since he came to Kundri'j. There had been
enough of those in the palace, and others in the city and on the road. He had
grown inured to black faces, arched noses, blue-black hair; he was prepared for
towering height.

This was not a giant as his kind went. He was only a head taller than Korusan, and
narrow, almost slight. He was long-legged like a colt, with some of a colt's awkwardness, as if he had not quite come to his growth; and maybe he would grow into
the shoulders that seemed so wide against the rest of him.

No beauty, no. Ugly indeed, with that sooty skin, that blade of a nose, that long mobile mouth half hidden in curling beard. His eyes were as keen a shock as Korusan had been warned to expect. They were all of the Lion, clear deep gold, no rim of white to lessen them, until he widened them at something that his servant said.

Korusan was braced for them, and for the coal of anger that burned his belly at the sight of them. He was prepared for strangeness, even for revulsion. But he had not expected to be captivated.

There was grace in that long body, something like beauty in the way the head turned, looking over his shoulder at the servant, who was struggling with the heavy masses of his hair. He smiled, white in that dark face, and said something in a tongue that Korusan did not know, that made the servant laugh. And Korusan was angry; no, Korusan was jealous, because neither of them had seen him, or cared that he watched.

He should have taken himself away, but he could not will his feet to move. This was the enemy of all that he was. This, taking its ease in these chambers that should have been Korusan's, casting off with patent contempt the robes to which Korusan was born. Holding Korusan rooted with the purity of a line, long straight back, long plait down the center of it, long hand outstretched to touch the servant's shoulder, to rest lightly on it. "There, don't fret, I'll be well," the Sunlord said in Gileni. Korusan understood: he had been taught that tongue, the better to know his enemy.

Likewise in Gileni the servant said, "How can I not fret, my lord? You keep to yourself too much these days; and you left court so suddenly, as if you were ill, or worse. Won't you come out to the training ground? Won't you do a round with the swords?"

"Later," the Sunlord said, as if he humored a child. His voice was deep, like a lion's purr, but it had an odd clarity. The servant seemed troubled, opening his mouth as if to speak, seeming to think better of it. He withdrew slowly, giving his master ample time to call him back.

His master did not take it. Korusan, unmarked and undismissed, watched the outlander decide that he was alone. He stretched first, languidly, as a cat stretches, and yawned. His teeth were whiter than an Asanian's, sharper, the eyeteeth long and narrow and perceptibly curved.

He dropped the robe that still covered him. He was lean, skin stretched over smooth muscle, long bone. There was no softness to him. He was all planes and angles.

So strange. Hardly like a human creature at all. Korusan saw the glare of gold as the right hand came up, the impossible thing, the brand the priest-mages made when one of Sun-blood was born, swearing solemnly that it was bred there. But no living thing grew gold in its flesh.

The Varyani emperor wandered toward a curtained wall, caught at an edge, hurled back the hangings with vehemence that made Korusan start. Sun flooded the room. Through the dazzle of it Korusan realized that this was a bank of windows, and they looked down on the gardens. One by one the outlander flung them open, letting in heat as well as light. He leaned on a windowframe, seeming to care not at all if anyone below should see his nakedness, and said to the hot golden air, "Sometimes I think that my dreams are real, and the Golden Palace all the world, and Keruvarion the delusion of a fevered brain. Sometimes I imagine that I've never breathed any air but this, never walked on ground not smoothed before me, never worn less than the nine robes of a high prince. Was I bred for this after all, do you think, and not for that other world?"

He was speaking Asanian, not perfectly but well enough. "Hound," he said, still to the air. "Patient, silent guard-hound. What do you think of me?"

Korusan went very still. It was foolish: his presence was known. But instinct had its own logic.

The Sunlord was dripping light. It ran down him in streams like water, pooling on the floor. Impossible. Sorcerous. Magic wrought to overawe the credulous, to frighten the yellow-faced spy.

But there was no denying the sight of it. Korusan slid toward it, essayed it with a fingertip. It burned and stung. He drew back carefully, keeping the corner of his eye on the barbarian. Emperor he would not call him, not naked and shameless, head fallen back, eyes closed, wallowing in his puddle of sun.

When the creature turned, Korusan was taken by surprise. He was cat-quick, and not above malice. "There, my hound. Run at my heel. See what I do, faithful slave that I am, and obedient emperor."

Pure insolence. Korusan would teach him manners. He smiled behind his veils, and followed the black king, not for obedience, but to see what he would do.

TWENTY-TWO

ESTARION HAD WON A FEW SMALL SKIRMISHES. LORD FIRAZ WAS WINNING the war.

He had had a bellyful of High Court this morning, walked out of it before he did something more unfortunate; and now he went back, dragging robes. He could not even say why he did it. Sun's heat, maybe, addling his brain while it made his body stronger. Or a pair of yellow eyes in a swathing of veils, and a subtle shimmer of contempt as they looked at him. It had not gone away when he commanded the Olenyas to play bodyservant, which the bred warrior did, and did well, with mute obedience. It was still there as Estarion made his second entrance of the morning, breaking in upon a court that was doing very well without him, throwing it into an exquisitely restrained flurry. He lost sight of the guardsman thereafter among all the rest, but he fancied that he could feel those eyes upon him still, judging him and finding him wanting.

High Court was excruciating as always. The emperor did not speak; his Regent spoke for him—as coolly now as ever, no shadow of rebuke, and chiefly in platitudes, greeting this lord who had come from the far western provinces, well-wishing that princeling for his taking of a new wife. His seventh, Lord Firaz murmured under cover of the man's prostrations, and a great heiress; which was well, for his properties were insufficient to support the tribe of his sons.

Estarion bit his tongue. Lord Firaz was revealing a surprising store of wit, much of it wry. His aplomb, Estarion knew too well, was unshakable, even for an emperor who fled and then came back, breaking every dictate of propriety.

The next petitioner to be presented wore five robes to the princeling's three. It was, Estarion realized, a child. He had thought it was a very small man: the infant carried himself so haughtily, refusing to bow beneath the weight of his robes, wearing an expression so rigid that surely it would shatter.

His name was almost longer than himself, with three princely houses in it, and one royal connection. "He is come," said Lord Firaz, "to beg your majesty's indulgence, and your forgetfulness of his father's sins."

Estarion raised a brow.

The child spoke for himself, which was just within the bounds of protocol. "My father," he said in a clear steady voice, "is dead. He regretted deeply his dishonor. He took his life as the canons prescribe. He died bravely, and courteously."

"How can death be courteous?"

Estarion had never spoken aloud in that place before. He fancied that his voice echoed, deeper than Asanian voices were wont to be, and barbarously accented. The child was too young or too scared to be shocked. He answered, "He wished your majesty to know that he atoned for his disgrace."

"What was that?"

"Majesty," said Lord Firaz, soft and smooth. "His father was that one who, so we are told, dared defy you in your court in Endros Avaryan."

For a moment Estarion's mind was blank. Then memory filled it. An Asanian lord paying homage out of turn. Estarion's great error, and the Asanian's greater one as his kind would reckon it, looking direct on the face of his emperor.

This son had his father's face, now that Estarion had eyes to see it, though soft yet and unformed. But he had not, it seemed, inherited his father's recklessness. Estarion regarded him in disbelief, and in swelling horror. "He killed himself? Simply because he tested me?"

"One does not test the emperor." The child sounded like no child then.

No, thought Estarion. *Let him have his name.* He was Nizad of the house of Ushavaar. Nizad said, "We will pay penalty as your majesty decrees. He is dead, his ashes scattered on the midden, and the honor is taken from his name. What more your majesty will have, we will pay."

"No," said Estarion. His heart was swelling, struggling in the walls of his chest. "No. I'll have them trying to kill me if that's their pleasure. I won't have them die for me."

"He defied you," said Nizad. "He deserved his death."

"He did not." Estarion pushed himself to his feet. "There is no dishonor. Do you understand? He only did as he thought best. The shame is mine. I spoke ill to him. I never thought that he would take his life for it."

Nizad raised wide astonished eyes. But never, quite, into Estarion's face. Estarion came down, dragging the world-weight of robes, and took the small cold hand. The Court was appalled. Again. He did not care. "I give you back your father's honor," he said. "All else that was his, I return to you. He was a brave man. I grieve that he took his life for so little a cause."

"You are everything," Nizad said. "You are the emperor."

Estarion sucked in a breath. There was no reasoning with them, any of them. "Go," he said: the first thing that came into his head. "Prosper. Prove that I'm no fool for shocking the Court speechless."

A normal child would have laughed, or smiled at least. Nizad dropped down on his face. Even his babble was flawless, not an inflection out of place. Estarion could pause to wonder at it, amid all the rest.

"They are not like us," Estarion said to Godri. "They are not like me. How can I rule them? I can't begin to understand them."

His squire looked a little strange himself, drawn and silent. "I don't think they understand themselves, my lord."

Estarion wanted to pull off the damnable robes and kick them as far as they would go. But he had done that already, too often. He had done everything that a rebel could do, or a captive, or a spoiled child.

"And for what?" he said aloud. "They still surround me. They still torment me. They still overcome me, no matter what I do."

Godri had nothing to say. Poor Godri. Estarion defeated him as Asanion defeated Estarion. But Godri loved his master, and Estarion hated his.

Hating it accomplished nothing. Estarion stopped, struck with the thought. It had occurred to him before; it had been beaten into his head. And yet. Suppose . . .

He began to smile. Godri's eye rolled like a startled senel's, which made Estarion smile wider. "Suppose," he said, "I gave them what they wanted. What then, do you think? Would they let me be, and take the chains from me?"

"I don't know, my lord," Godri said in a tone that indicated that he knew, and that Estarion would not like to hear the truth.

"You don't think they will," Estarion said. "But I have to try it, do you see? I'm trapped whatever I do. If there's one small chance that I can be free, will you fault me if I take it?"

"You'll do what you'll do, my lord, whatever I say to you."

Estarion drew him into a quick, hard embrace. "Oh, my poor friend! Such a trial I am, and you never say more than a word. I do love you for it."

"Maybe you should hate me," Godri muttered. But he smiled as if he could not help it, and when Estarion told him what he meant to do, the smile burst into laughter. Most of it was incredulity, but some at least was mirth. "It may only be another skirmish, my lord. But such a skirmish!"

Fortified by Godri's approval, Estarion prepared his battlefield with care. The servants surprised him by clothing him in the robes he asked for, and astonished him by bearing his message to the one for whom it was meant.

Lord Firaz came in good time, unruffled as always. Estarion wasted no time in nonsense. Having seen the Regent served with wine and cakes—both approved by the dun mouse of a taster—he said, "I've sent out a summons to the High Court. I'm to marry in Asanion, they say. Well and good. Let each lord and prince present his marriageable daughters. I shall choose as I best may, and get it over."

The Regent did not so much as widen his eyes. "Shall we say, then, that the ladies of the Court are to gather in, perhaps, a hand of days?"

"No," said Estarion. "Today. At the next turning of the glass."

"Sire," said his lordship with extreme delicacy. "These are ladies of the High Court, not—"

"Surely," Estarion said, "they've been prepared for this since I crossed the border into Asanion. They'll come to me in the sixth hour. Or will you tell me that every marriageable woman in the High Court is not now in the city, waiting on just this summons?"

"Your majesty is perceptive," said Lord Firaz. His tone was dry. It did not quite imply that his majesty was also precipitous. "Perhaps rather the seventh hour, when the day's warmth is diminished somewhat, and the hour of rest is past?"

"I have rested," said Estarion. He smiled. "Will you stand with me, so that I may choose wisely?"

The Regent bowed to the floor, not without irony. "As my lord wills," he said.

The hall of queens lay in the inner palace, behind gates guarded by women of the Queen's Guard and eunuchs of the Golden Palace, in walls as much of silence as of stone. Here the pillars were carved in intricate fashion with twinings of vines and flowers, and the walls behind them were thick with figured tapestries. The sun that came in, came in through narrow lattices; light here was lamplight, great banks and clusters of them, burning oil scented with flowers.

Estarion paused in the passage behind the throne. He had not been permitted to come so far before. A company of guards had gone ahead, eunuchs of the Golden Palace, and more of them surrounded him, and still more warded his back. What they feared, he could not understand. His father had been murdered in the emperor's chambers, in that room which Estarion had commanded to be locked and barred, and to which he did not go. If an assassin came, it would be a bold one indeed who ventured the protections of the women's palace. One who penetrated the outer palace had to fear only death: One who came as far as this would die long and slow, and he would die a eunuch.

From where Estarion stood, the hall was clear to see behind a shimmer of curtain, and filling with veiled women. They came with little evidence of haste and no more flutter than one might expect. Their fathers and their brothers were not permitted here, but must wait in mounting anxiety in the outer palace. Eunuchs guarded them, and mothers and aunts and cousins, some old enough, or bold enough, to drop their veils.

A tall figure moved among them, robed as an Asanian lady, but those slender dark hands were not Asanian, nor that unveiled face. Estarion had not known till he saw her how sorely he had missed his mother's presence.

He could not tell if she disapproved of his haste. It was too like him, she had been known to observe. He was like a cat, asleep or idling daylong, then leaping to the hunt, and never a pause between. Estarion admitted it. But he was not about to change his mind, even for his mother's sake.

The hall was almost full. Estarion's nursemaids, having ascertained that there were no rats behind the arras, consented to allow him past the door. He could see clearly through the veil, but no one would be able to see him. It was remarkably like being a child and spying on one's elders through the curtains.

He was to mount the throne, there to sit while each lady was brought to him and presented with due ceremony. But his mood was purely contrary. He dropped all but the innermost and outermost of his robes, which should be enough to satisfy even Asanian modesty, and left the bulk of his guards staring at the heap of them, and walked calmly round the veil.

They were, most of them, watching the throne and not the curtain behind it. He was well past the dais before anyone moved. A ripple ran through the hall, a whisper that in Asanion was appalling rudeness. And better than that, to his mind, mutters of doubt, objections, even resistance. How could that be the emperor? It was a lanky barbarian in a mere two robes, like a commoner with pretensions.

His mother turned at his approach. The light in her eyes made him want to weep. He had meant to kiss her hand with cool courtesy, but he found himself embracing her instead, clinging hard if not long. "Mother," he said in the language of her tribe. "Oh, Mother. They wouldn't let me go."

"You've grown thin," she said in the same tongue. "You're naught but a rack of bones. What have they done to you?"

"I've done it to myself." He mustered a smile. "It's not as bad as it looks. I've been out of the sun too long, that's all."

"I should never have forced you to this," she said.

A small prick of malice moved him to agree with her, but he mastered it. "Hush now," he said. He bent to set a kiss in each of her palms. "We're being rude, you know. Shall we bring out our best Asanian, and set about finding me a wife?"

"Maybe," she said, still in the speech of her youth, "maybe, after all—"

He could not let hope grow, that she would relent, that he could go home, win Vanyi back, be as he was before: innocent, and happy. "Come now," he said. "Here is Lord Firaz, and he promised he'd tell me who is rich and who is beautifully bred. Will you show me who is sensible, too, and maybe not excessively horrified to contemplate a barbarian in her bed?"

"Most of them are fascinated," Merian said, this time in Asanian. She took his hand: the left, that was like any man's. "Lord Firaz, what pleasure to see you here. Your ladies: are they well?"

They circled the hall slowly. Lord Firaz, having exchanged courtesies with the empress, proceeded to present each lady, her lineage and her connections and her prospects as a mother of sons, as if she were a mare in his stable and Estarion a stallion at stud. Merian was charming, setting the nervous at ease, coaxing smiles out of the shy or the sullen. Estarion did not say anything. He was noticing who darted glances at his face, and who managed to evade him in his course. He had never felt quite so much like a necessary evil before.

He met a pair of coin-gold eyes in a blue veil. They did not drop at once, or shrink from the sight of him. They belonged to someone whose path never quite crossed his. There was someone else next to her, one of the shy ones, no more than a bowed pink-veiled head and a strayed yellow curl. A very small, bent person in black had them in charge, herding them with skill, determination, and a talent for keeping them out of his majesty's way.

His majesty said something to the woman whom Firaz presented, words he never afterward remembered. The blue veil was losing itself in the crowd, and the pink beside it.

There was one great use and pleasure in the office of emperor. People did not get in his way. Estarion left his mother being pleasant to a woman whose name he had already forgotten, and went in pursuit of the lady who would look him in the face.

Her duenna was almost too clever for him. The fierce old thing led him a merry chase, making good use of a gaggle of plump startled maidens and a knot of guards, and a convenient pillar. Estarion stretched his stride round that, and almost laughed.

Trapped, and thoroughly: cornered for a fact. He knew how to fill an exit simply by standing straight and gangling less, and letting his shoulders be a wall. He tried not to grin. Asanians, like cats, did not show their teeth except to display their armament.

He bowed as an emperor might, for courtesy: an inclination of the head, a slight tilt of the body. "Ladies," he said. "Am I so fearsome a monster, that you should run from me?"

The shy one hid her veiled face in her sister's shoulder. The bold one looked straight at him, and she was laughing, surely, the more her duenna glowered. "You are not handsome," she said, "as the canons would have it. But you are very interesting."

She had a clear light voice, a little sharp maybe, but pleasantly so. Estarion raised a brow, which made her eyes dance the more, and said, "I would rather be ugly and interesting than handsome and insipid."

"You are not ugly," she said. "At all. Just . . . different. Does it come off?"

He looked down at his bare sufficiency of robes. "I should hope so," he said.

She did laugh then, clear and free. "Not those, my lord! That." She managed somehow, without moving or touching him, to make it clear that she was pointing at his hands, and not at their shape, or even at the Sun's gold.

He turned them. They were perfectly ordinary hands, burning brand aside: long and narrow like the rest of him, callused from rein and shieldstrap and sword. She set her small round hand beside them, all ivory as it was, with long gilded nails. "You aren't born that way, my nurse told me. They rub you with soot when you are born, and every day after, till the color takes, and you're all black, which is what they call beautiful. What color are you really? Nurse said white, like a bone. I think brown. If you were white, the soot would only turn you grey."

Estarion had never heard such nonsense in his life. "I'm all as nature made me," he managed to say. "Here. Touch."

He thought that she would not. But she stretched out a hand that shook only a little, and brushed the arm he bared for her. Timidly at first, as if she feared the stain; then more boldly, stroking light but firm, as one should stroke a cat.

"You have fur," she said, "like an animal."

"Like a man," he said. He should have been offended. He was merely amused. There was an innocence in her, coupled with a brazen boldness, that one seldom saw even in children, and never in maidens of breeding in the High Court of Asanion.

And yet slaves and servants did not dress in sky-blue silk sewn with silver, or betray glints of gold at ears and throat and wrists and ankles. The one who must have been her sister was all that she was not, modest and shy and ladylike in every particular, and her duenna was a smolder of resentment.

"Do you have fur," she asked, "all over?"

He had a rush of heat all over, in places he would rather not have thought of. "Not quite," he said. "Don't Asanians have any?"

"Not that they'll admit to." She looked him up and down. "I suppose I'll have my eyes put out, or my tongue, for being so impudent. If I have a choice, may I keep my eyes? I talk too much, everyone says so; my tongue would be no loss. But I do like to look at you. The others are so dull. All the same color, and soft, like bread before it bakes."

He laughed. The shy maid surprised him: she did not cringe, but lifted her head and looked at him. Her eyes were softer than her sister's, more amber than gold, and full of astonishing mirth. "What are your names?" he asked them both.

"I am Haliya," said the bold one. "And this is Ziana, and our dragon is Gazi, who thinks that I should marry someone proper, and not an outland conqueror. Ziana and I were born on the same day, to the same father, and our mothers were sisters, which makes us sisters, too, twice over. We're not rich, or not very, though we're noble enough. Our house is Vinicharyas. It used to be very great in Markad, but now it settles for being middling ordinary in Kundri'j."

"You are not ordinary at all," said Estarion. He liked to talk; too much, some people thought. But she was like a river in flood.

"We know who you are," said Haliya. "Are you going to have me punished? Nurse said that people are shockingly free with their emperors in Keruvarion, but she did like to tell stories, and not all of them were as true as one might wish."

"Emperors in Keruvarion are people like anyone else," he said. And at the widening of her eyes: "Well. Maybe not like anyone. But anyone can come up to me and talk to me. Look at me, even. Touch me. Make me feel like something other than a poppet on a stick."

"You do hate that, don't you?" Her sympathy tasted real, if not over-warm. "So do I. I tried to run away to Keruvarion once. My father whipped me himself, with his own hands. He was stiff for days after."

"And you weren't?"

"He didn't beat me very hard," she said. "It runs in the blood, you see: running away. Especially the womenchildren. I could hardly help it. I'm older now, of course. I know what's proper."

"I ran away once," said Estarion. "I wanted to be a tribesman by the Lakes of the Moon, and hunt the spotted deer."

"Did your father whip you when they brought you back?"

The chill that touched him was less than he had expected. He could answer her calmly, even lightly. "My father was dead. My mother decided that I had too little to do. She gave me a princedom to rule for myself, and no one to help or hinder, unless I acted abominably."

"And did you?"

"I sulked for days. But the princedom couldn't run itself. Its steward was old and growing feeble, and its lords and barons were trying the bonds of their fealty, and the merchants were padding their profits, and the people, the poor people, didn't deserve any of it. So I had to behave myself, you see, and do what I could. Without insulting the steward, starting a war among the barons, or driving the merchants out, because we needed them to buy the wool and meat and cloth that were our wealth, and to sell the things we needed: wood for the looms, iron for the needles, herbs and earths for the dyes."

She was listening with every evidence of interest, but he stopped himself. "There now," he said. "I was prince in Umbros till I'd learned my lesson, and then we found a princess for it, and I went back to the life I'd run away from. It wasn't so ill, once I'd thought about it."

"A princess?" Ziana asked, so unexpectedly that he looked at her sister. But the voice was not the same, not at all. This was soft and low, trembling with the effort of being so bold. "A princess to rule a princedom?"

Estarion found himself speaking more gently, trying not to frighten her. "She was heir to it, as close as made no matter. She would have taken her place long before, but she'd gone traveling to the Nine Cities to learn new ways of weaving and dyeing, and she had affairs that wouldn't settle all at once."

"She ruled," Ziana said as if to herself. "Do you hear that, Haliya? I told you that wasn't one of Nurse's stories."

"Of course she had a husband," Haliya said, "or a brother who could tell her what to do."

"She'd married in the Nine Cities," said Estarion, "that's true enough, but her husband wasn't minded to live in a shepherd's cot on the edge of the world, as he put it. She wasn't bitter about it, much. She had a daughter from him, to be her heir, and let him have the son, which they all reckoned fair, as such things go."

"I wish I lived in Umbros," Ziana said.

"It's not very elegant," said Estarion. "It's mostly moors and woolbeasts and shepherds. The palace is a manor house that grew. It's raw and cold in the winter, and what summer there is, is more rain than sun. We had fires in the hearths at High Summer, and winter rains by Autumn Firstday. No one had much use for silk, or for pretty things. They weren't sensible."

"Silk makes a great deal of sense," said Ziana. "It weaves strong and it weaves light, and it's warm when you want it, and cool when you want it. And it takes color like nothing else."

She was, in her way, quite as surprising as her sister. Estarion was enchanted.

"Ah," said Lord Firaz, sliding in beside him. "Sire, we had lost you. I see you have found Prince Alishandas' daughters. They are the jewels of Markad, born of mothers who were kin to the royal house. There have been mages in their line, and priestesses of the Sun—Orozia of Magrin, mage and priestess and friend to Sarevadin, was their father's grandfather's father's sister; and she was but the first of several."

"That is a noble lineage," said Estarion. Stupidly, maybe, but he was caught in amber eyes, and again in golden. Such wit and such willfulness; and here, where he had never looked for any such thing. He slanted an eye at his Regent. "I'm in a quandary, my lord. Here are two. How do I choose?"

"Why, sire, you take both," said Lord Firaz in some surprise. "You have no harem; that is hardly a disgrace, as new come as you are, but strict honor would dictate that you choose many ladies from the cream of the realm, to honor their families and to bear you strong sons."

"Many?" Estarion felt the slow flush rising. Bless his ancestry, it did not show. "How many?"

"Had you been high prince in Asanion," said Firaz, "you would have been expected to take a lady for each day of the year. Then on your accession to the throne you would double that number; and when your first son was born, treble it."

Estarion must have looked a perfect fool. He picked up his fallen jaw. "How on earth can any man please that many?"

Lord Firaz was amused: there was a glint in his eye. "He does his best, my lord."

"And Hirel had fifty brothers." Estarion shuddered. "I'm not Asanian. I'm Varyani. We take our women one at a time."

"In Keruvarion that is honorable, my lord. Here, it gives insult to all those fathers whose daughters might rise in the emperor's favor and enrich their families, and give them kin in the royal house—perhaps even on the throne itself."

Estarion had heard it before. Of course he had. But hearing and listening—those were not the same at all. "God and goddess," he said.

"Here we have a thousand gods," said Firaz.

"I won't—" Estarion stopped, drew a long breath. "Would honor be satisfied," he asked, "if I eased myself in gently? If I remembered the ways of the Ianyn kings, and chose nine ladies of beauty and lineage? Would that content the Court?"

"For a beginning," said Firaz, "it would, sire."

"Very well," Estarion said. "Choose me seven who you think will suit me, and who will find me, if not suitable, then at least endurable."

"Will my lord not choose his own?"

"I have," said Estarion.

The Regent's brows went up. "My lord honors me with his trust."

"I do," said Estarion. He stepped back, opening the way to the hall. The ladies did not seize it, he noticed. Their dragon, as they called her, seemed to have accepted the inevitable. Her scowl was no less fierce, but she had stopped flexing her claws.

TWENTY-THREE

THEY STOOD IN FRONT OF HIM. NINE OF THEM. NINE VEILS, NINE PAIRS of eyes, from warm amber to bright gold. Nine bodies so wrapped and swathed and swaddled that he could only guess at their shapes, though he had no doubt of their gender.

They had been parted from their protectors. Those would be deep in colloquy, one by one, with Lord Firaz and the empress, settling matters as honor required. The guards here were eunuchs of the palace, aged and discreet.

The room was small, smothered in curtains. Estarion followed his nose to one and swept it back. Light trickled in through a lattice. There was no catch, no opening. He snorted disgust and wheeled. They were all staring, women and eunuchs alike.

A chair stood against the wall. He sat in it, not to be at ease, but to keep from prowling.

This was not beginning well. He tried a smile, not too wide. None of them warmed, except Haliya, who was laughing at him. She raised a hand to her veil.

Women bared their bodies in Keruvarion with less ceremony, and less trepidation, than women in Asanion showed their faces. Estarion had no sympathy with it; or had had none, until he met those bright eyes. This was great bravery, and a great gift. She was giving him herself.

He did not know if she was beautiful. She was less plump than some, which Asanians would reckon a defect. There was a scattering like gold dust across her nose: remarkable. The color came and went beneath it. She was not quite brave enough to smile at him without her veil to hide behind.

The others, so exampled, unveiled themselves likewise. He was careful to notice each face, to say something to each maiden, whether she blushed or paled, stared hard at her feet or raised her eyes daringly to the vicinity of his chin. Ziana was the beauty that her sister was not: an amber loveliness that paled the rest to milk and water. When she blushed, she blushed rose-gold. He could not help what he did, which was to rise and take her hand, and kiss it as if she had been the empress and he but a prince of her court.

He let her go not entirely of his own will, to face her sister again. Of them all, he had failed to speak only to her. She felt it: he saw it in the angle of her chin, in the hard brightness of her eye. He brushed her gold-dusted cheek with his finger. "Does it come off?" he asked her.

She did not laugh as he had hoped, or delight him with her wit. She drew herself up, straight and stiff and cold. "If I do not please your eyes, my lord, I shall leave you. But do keep Ziana. *She* has no blemish."

"Nor do you," he said.

"I am not beautiful. I am too thin. My face is blotched with the sun. One of my teeth is imperfect: it broke when I fell climbing the wall in our garden. I have a scar on my chin from riding my brother's pony over a fence too high for him, and—"

He felt his brow climbing. It stopped her. Asanians could not do that, maybe: he had never seen it in them. "I should want you to be perfect?"

"You are the emperor," she said.

"I do hate it when people say that," he said.

"Then I won't say it," she said. "Your majesty."

She was small as Asanians were, barely shoulder-high. And yet he did not frighten her. She kept her chin up as if she wanted it there, and glared down her nose at him. "Are you going to send me back?" she demanded of him.

"Do you want me to?"

"My wanting has nothing to do with it."

"I will if you ask," he said, and now he was as stiff as she.

She widened her eyes, which truly were beautiful, and curled her lip. "But why should you? You own this empire and everything in it."

"I don't own you."

"You do." She looked straight into his eyes. "You can send me away. I don't mind. Maybe they'll let me go this time, and see how a woman can be a princess in Keruvarion."

"You do want that," he said. He did not know what he felt. Regret, maybe. Admiration for her outspokenness, so precious rare among her people.

"I wanted it once," said Haliya. "Then I thought I wanted to be a proper woman, and be a man's wife, and bear his sons. I'll not do that now."

"Why not, if I set you free?"

Her laughter was gentle, which startled him. "You really don't know, do you? You've seen our faces now. No one else will want us."

Estarion stood still. His heart had gone cold. "Then—all those ladies in all those cities—"

"Oh," she said, "they're safe enough, unless a man is remarkably silly about his honor. You didn't single anyone out, you see. You didn't say anything to them beyond the politest necessity. Whereas we've been your property since we walked through yonder door."

"That is ridiculous," Estarion said.

"It's custom. If you hadn't been the emperor, if you'd been a lord or even a prince, someone higher might be willing to take your leavings as concubines, or as servants to one of his concubines. We have no honor left, you see, that belongs to our kin. We only have what you will give. If that is nothing, then nothing is our portion. I don't mind," she said, "much. I know the way to Keruvarion."

She did mind. Even his little magecraft felt it. It was her honor she cherished, he knew that, and not his presence.

"I should set you free," he said.

"You can't do that."

"The emperor can do anything."

"Anything the emperor can do, he can do. He can't make a woman a man."

"Why in the hells should I want to—"

"She means," said a gentle voice, "that women live like this. Men go out, and ride, and run away to Keruvarion." Ziana blushed under his eyes. "Here, my lord, it's different."

Estarion threw up his hands. "You're going to drive me clean out of my wits. Then what will you do?"

"Madmen are like dead men," said Haliya calmly, but with a glint in it. "We'll be your widows. We can do whatever we like."

"Even go out, and ride, and run away?"

She lowered those bold eyes, but not before he saw how they danced. "I forget myself. Again. My lord."

"Oh, stop it," he said. "Could you bear to go to Keruvarion if you went with me?"

"In a carriage? With curtains? And guards?"

"On a senel. In trousers. With," he admitted, "guards. There's no escaping them."

"Will you promise that?"

He hesitated. She would not droop. She was too proud. But the light went out of her. He had her hands in his before he knew it, not tempted to kiss them, but not tempted to let them go, either. "I promise," he said.

Once Estarion had escaped as far as the queen's palace, he discovered that his jailers had lengthened his chain. He could go to his mother now if he wished, or speak to the women who were, in law if not in fact, his concubines. He was careful not to slight any of them. But he had begun with the sisters, and to the sisters he always returned.

It was perfectly decorous. There was a eunuch there always, and they sat demurely, hands folded in their laps, and watched Estarion pace. He amused them, he thought. The Asanian word for panther was the word for northerner, too, and Ziana called him by it, blushing at first as if she had let it slip out, then when he smiled, making it her name for him. Haliya did not call him anything but "my lord."

He came to her in the morning, not long after that first meeting, so early that she was just out of bed and not yet dressed. He could hardly burst in on a lady in her bower, even a lady who belonged to him. He fretted and paced, while the eunuchs watched and eyed his companion with mighty mistrust.

Godri would never have come so far if Estarion had not invoked the full force of imperial ire. But there was no one else whom Estarion wished to trust with this.

Just as he was ready to give it up, Haliya emerged, wrapped in veils. Her glance at Godri was astonished. She would have been warned that there was a second man in her antechamber. But she could never have seen a desert tribesman before, nor such a richness of warrior-patterns on his face.

He had too much delicacy to stare at her. He relinquished what he carried, and stepped back.

"Go," said Estarion, filling her arms with Godri's burden. "Put these on."

She clutched the bundle to her breast, but stood her ground. "What—"

"Just go," he said. "Or we'll dress you ourselves."

She wheeled at that and ran.

"She has a fair turn of speed, for a lapcat," Godri observed.

Estarion almost hit him. "That is a lady of Asanion."

"Didn't I say that?"

Estarion prayed for patience. He needed it. She was so long in coming that he began to suspect she would not come at all.

At last she appeared. The trousers fit her: he had hoped for that. The coat was loose to spare her modesty, but it showed a great deal more of her than her wrappings ever had. The veil was an expedient of his mother's for the road into the Golden Empire, much like the headdress of Godri's people, or of the Olenyai.

He took her hand before she could stop him. "Now," he said, "come with us."

She had to trot to keep pace, but she went willingly, eyes bright with curiosity. Her hand was hot in his, clinging tighter the longer he held it. Eunuchs trailed after, expostulating.

The wall of guards stopped them all. Haliya regarded them in astonishment. "These are women!"

"So they are," Estarion said, amused.

"But they're guards."

"Guards can be women," he said.

"Then—you—"

"Oh," he said before she fainted with shock, "these are my mother's. I borrow them when I come here. My own Guard is safely male; but I can hardly bring them to this place, can I?"

"But," said Haliya. "They have swords. And that's armor. Is this a play? Am I to be the fool in it?"

"This is a gift," he said, and held his breath. She could refuse. She could slap him for his presumption, and run back to her gowns and her veils.

Or she could let him lead her through the gate that had opened in the armored wall. It closed behind them, shutting out the eunuchs. Estarion let his smile break through at last, and stretched his stride.

There was a courtyard that, Estarion had discovered, abutted one of the stables and yet was safely within the confines of the queen's palace. It took a little doing, but a senel could be brought in, with a eunuch groom to be properly honorable.

Estarion regarded the mare with some surprise. Godri had chosen her, there was no mistaking it. She was one of his own: desert-bred, sand-colored as they all were, less ugly-headed than most, with the beginnings of horns on her brow, rare in a mare and much prized.

"Godri," said Estarion. "This is—"

Haliya pulled her hand free of his and ran to the mare, and flung her arms about the beast's neck. "No! Don't send her away. She's perfect. I don't *want* anything prettier."

Estarion blinked, taken aback. She had mistaken his intent too completely for words.

Godri laughed. "My lord, I think your lady has sense after all."

"She is an idiot," said Estarion. "To think that I would afflict her with a mount that was"—gods, the word tasted vile—"pretty. Pretty! That plowbeast I rode into Kundri'j is pretty. I'd have him for breakfast if I thought my stomach could stand it."

Haliya turned, still clinging to the mare. The beast preserved her aplomb admirably, even condescended to lip a strand of hair that had escaped the veil. Haliya glared. "Then why did you start to say—"

"I started to say," said Estarion, "that this is the best of Godri's herd, which is the cream of Varag Suvien. This is his queen, his beloved. He has given you a gift worthy of kings."

Her gaze dropped; her cheeks went scarlet. But she had spirit to spare. "Everyone else has tried to mount me on—on plowbeasts. With gilded feet. And ribbons."

Her disgust was profound. The mare snorted and caught her veil in long teeth, and plucked it off.

Godri had the wits to turn away. Estarion did not see the need to do the same. Haliya, bareheaded and vivid with defiance, mounted in creditable order. She did not ride badly, either, for a lapcat.

"How did you learn?" Estarion asked her afterward. She was damp from the bath, demurely gowned and veiled again, with her sister in attendance. "Did you steal your brother's pony and teach yourself to stay on?"

"I watched," she said. "From windows. Walls, sometimes. Even the roof, until Nurse caught me. I knew how to do it before I tried it."

"Did the pony think so, too?"

She bristled at him. "I'm dreadful. Aren't I? You didn't say anything, but I saw you laughing with that painted savage."

"That painted savage is a lord and warrior of Varag. He is also," said Estarion, "the only one in Kundri'j whom I can honestly call friend."

That quenched her a little, but she was not one to let go a fight. "You were laughing at me."

"We were marveling. Godri says you'll make a rider."

"I'm not one now?"

"Do you think you are?"

She lowered her eyes. Her fingers knotted and unknotted in her lap. "My lord," she said after a while. "Did you mean that? About the gift?"

"I don't say things I don't mean."

Not that an Asanian could believe it; but Haliya was kind enough not to say so. "I may ride every day?"

"All day if you want to. I've given orders. They will," said Estarion, "be obeyed."

The eunuch on guard did not speak, but Estarion knew he heard.

Haliya took her time in responding. That was Asanian, that restraint. He had stopped thinking that it was coldness.

She stood all at once, with an air of resolution, and stepped forward. She folded her arms very carefully about Estarion's neck. He sat still, not daring to breathe. She was warm; she smelled of spices. Her lips were cool on his.

He drew back as gently as he could. "Do I take it that that is payment?"

She did not slap him. That would have been predictable. She caught his face in her hands. They were not cool at all now; not in the least.

He was gasping when she let him go. So, to his surprise, was she. He wondered if he looked as wild as she did.

Her hands were trembling. She let them fall to his shoulders. "You burn," she said. "Like fire."

"They say I'm the Sun's child."

Her fingers tightened. She looked ready to fall over; he steadied her about the middle. She was a pleasant handful, small but not as a child is, and sweetly curved. He did not even care that she was a yellow woman. Gold, rather, and ivory, and that sheen of dust from the sun: brighter since she came to the riding court, and touched with rose.

"We burn," she said, "when the sun touches us. Some of us change, and learn to bear it. Some of us are flayed alive."

"You go golden," he said.

"Oh, I burn, if I stay in it long enough."

"Do I frighten you?"

"Yes," she said.

She did not sound afraid, nor did he sense it in her. And yet it was the truth.

He had forgotten everything but the light in her eyes. She swayed toward him. Her hair was the color of wheat in the sun. The scent of her was dizzying.

They were alone in the room. He did not know at first how he knew that. Here in the circle of her arms, the world was clearer than it had been since he was a child. And yet when he looked past her, he saw no more than a blur.

If he asked now, she would give him anything he asked for. Anything he wanted. And cycles since he held a woman in his arms, since he knew that sweetness above all others.

She did not love him. He was a mage here; even shielded, he sensed what was to be sensed. He interested her greatly. She liked him; that was clear to see. It warmed him. She would give him her body as she had given him her face, willingly, even proudly, without regret that it was he and not another who must be her master.

Very gently he freed himself from her embrace. It was cold without, and grey, and the clarity of his seeing was gone. He set a kiss on her brow, chaste as if she had been his sister, and said, "Child, you are honey-sweet. But I'm no woman's master, nor are you my slave."

Her eyes narrowed. "It's that woman, isn't it? The commoner. You want her to bear your firstborn."

Estarion's heart clenched. "How did you know—"

She laughed, bright and hard. "We may live in chains, but we have ears. Everyone knows about the Island woman. She didn't want to share you, did she? She's selfish."

"Everyone doesn't learn to be as generous as an Asanian woman," Estarion said, trying to be light.

"She's not beautiful," said Haliya. "You don't like beautiful women. Except your mother. You like them to be interesting instead."

"I don't see faces," Estarion said. "Or I didn't, before I came here, where faces are so hard to see. What is in this place that trammels mages?"

"I don't know," she said. "I'm not a mage."

"Aren't you?" He shook himself. "No. You have it in your blood, clear enough. You wouldn't know what you have, without another power to strike sparks from you."

"Oh, I know that," she said. "That's not magery. It's only being Vinicharyas." One of the gifts of which line was to strengthen a mage's power with the touch of her body on his. Even if he had but a trickle of power left.

The quality of his silence alarmed her. "Is it something I should be afraid of? Have I hurt you?"

"No," he said quickly. "Oh, no. I never meant to scare you. I was only marveling at you. Will you forgive me?"

She took her time about it, but in the end she did. "You're so interesting, you see," she explained. "And really, once one grows used to you, rather beautiful."

TWENTY-FOUR

RATHER BEAUTIFUL,'" ESTARION SAID. "SHE CALLED ME THAT. IT CAN'T BE for my face."

"The warrior-patterns wouldn't show on you," said Godri.

Estarion laughed. It was rusty: he was forgetting how. "Your father thinks they would. White paint, he told me, and gold. He thought gold would suit me very well."

"They'd cost you the beard," Godri said—with, Estarion noted, no little pleasure. Godri, good desert tribesman that he was, could not approve of the northern fashion.

"They might be worth it," Estarion said. "They'd shock Asanion to its foundations." He sighed and stretched. He had found a room with a window that faced westward, and disposed of the lattice with three very satisfying blows of a throw-ing axe. The axe was ancient and long resigned to exile upon a wall, but it had been pleased to do its duty again, albeit without due sacrifice of the enemy's blood. Nothing but dust and dead wood in that damnable lattice.

He folded his arms on the window-ledge and leaned out. The sun slanted long over the roofs and spires of the palace, and beyond them the descending circles of the city, and beyond those the river and the plain. The wind was almost clean up here, and almost cool. Summer, that had seemed so endless, was ending at last. Three days, and the sun would cycle round to Autumn Firstday.

His father had died on the night of that feast. Ten years ago, less three days. He flexed his burning hand. "Who'd have thought I'd stand here again," he said.

"You remember?" Godri asked. "From before?"

Estarion shrugged, almost a shiver. "Sometimes I don't know what I remember. What's dream, what's real, what's delusion. None of us is entirely sane, you know. We can't be. Not and be what we are."

"Mages?"

"Kings." He met the sun's glare. It was life, but it was death too, as all fire was. The Sunborn did not understand that. He tried to cast down the dark, naming it death and enemy. And so it was; but it was sleep also, and rest, and ease for the weary.

Nothing was absolute. Asanion was his prison, and yet he ruled it. He hated it; but he was learning in spite of himself to admire it. Even, in some part, to love it.

He turned abruptly. The room was dark after the brilliance of the sun. Godri was a shadow in it. "There's something," Estarion said, "I have to do."

Godri followed in silence. Estarion had made these rooms his own, but one suite of them was locked, its door barred. He laid his branded hand flat on the carved panel. Wood and gilding, carved caravans bearing tribute, memory that darted close and then away.

He did not have the key. That was in the keeping of the chamberlain. But he did not need it. He bore in his hand the key to every door. It was a power that tales did not tell of, and songs only hinted at.

The pain of the Sun's fire mounted almost beyond endurance, then suddenly subsided. The lock fell in shards. Estarion drew a shaking breath. "That was hardly necessary," he said to the air, or perhaps to the god.

The door opened to his touch. The hinges were oiled, the air within clean, touched but faintly with the taint of disuse. Death's stains were long since disposed of, Ganiman's body embalmed with spices and borne away into the east, to lie in the tomb of kings under Avaryan's Tower. The floor where he had fallen was clean, the bed mounded in cushions, no mark of his dying throes.

He had not died easily or quickly. Estarion had been there. Others remembered: they had told him. How he stood, how he would not speak, nor move, nor suffer any to touch him, but fixed his eyes on Ganiman's face. He had no memory of that. His mind had been far away, hunting a mage who was a murderer. He had not seen what the poison and the sorcery did to his strong beautiful father, withered and shriveled him, robbed him of voice and strength and wits, made of him a mindless mewling thing.

There was mercy, maybe, in that bar to his memory. When he saw his father, he saw him as he had been: tall robust handsome man, stern enough before his people, but lighthearted as a boy, and apt for mischief.

"The night before he died," Estarion said, "he led a whole regiment of his Guard on a raid against the queen's palace, abducted my mother and carried her away to this room, and held it against all comers. The uproar went on till dawn. People thought the palace was invaded; the eunuchs shrieked and wailed, and all the guards came out in arms. It was splendid."

Godri inspected an image that stood in a niche. "That's himself?"

Estarion did not need to look at it. "That's the Sunborn. Father was handsomer than that. Pretty, he said. He cultivated a beard and a severe expression. They only made him the more beautiful."

"You look like this one," said Godri. "Interesting face. He wasn't a tamed thing, was he?"

"And I am?" Estarion asked coldly.

Godri glanced over his shoulder. "Did I say that? You'll see reason now and then, when you've had your nose rubbed in it. Look at the eyes on him. Nothing reasonable about him at all."

"That was the god in him, I was always told." Estarion stood by the bed. He did not feel anything. It was not numbness, not exactly. More as if he had felt all that there was to feel, and there was nothing left.

Godri wandered on past the carving of Varuyan on senelback, thrusting a spear into a direwolf's vitals. When he paused again, it was in front of a painted portrait. "Hirel and Sarevadin," he said. It was not a question. "Was his majesty really that young?"

"He'd not turned sixteen when his son was born," Estarion said.

"Well," said Godri after a pause. "The yellowheads don't live long. I suppose they have to get in their breeding while they can."

Estarion stood very still.

Godri did not seem to notice. "The lady was beautiful, wasn't she? That Ianyn face, and that hair, like new copper. They say your father looked like her as she was before she was a she."

Estarion had no difficulty in untangling that. He eased by degrees. "That's the Gileni blood. Not like the royal Ianyn. All beak and bones, those."

"You'd be less of both if you fed yourself better." Godri came round to Estarion's side and looked up him, black eyes bright in the swirling patterns of his face. "Is it bad?" he asked.

"No," Estarion said, too quickly maybe. But when he thought about it: "No. He was on the throne when I came to it. He's round about the palace, sometimes. But not here. This is only where he left his body behind."

Godri shivered but held his ground. "You're healing."

"If you want to call it that," Estarion said.

"It was well you came here, even if it makes you ill. Some fevers are necessary. They burn away old scars."

"Maybe," said Estarion.

The fever that was in him would not let him rest. He went to his mother for a while. She tried to comfort him, but she had her own burden of memories, and her own troubles.

The harem was waiting on his pleasure. One was very fine upon the lute; another had a wonderful voice. None was importunate, or tried to lure him to the inner chamber.

Haliya was not there. She was tired, her sister said, and had gone to bed. "But if my lord wishes . . ."

"No," he said. He listened to the singer and the lute-player. He said polite things to the others. When enough time had passed, he sent them away.

Ziana was last and slowest to go. He almost called her back. It did not matter that she had no love for him. Her beauty pleased him, and her calmness soothed his temper.

And if she conceived his son, what then? Did he want her for his empress?

He returned to his chambers in a mood as black as the sky. No stars tonight, no moons. Clouds had come up while he tarried; there was rain in the wind.

Guards hovered. Varyani, no Olenyai. Those were hidden in shadows. "Go," he said to the ones he could see, those who had been his friends, while he could have friends, before he was emperor in Asanion. "Go, rest, carouse in a tavern, do something that isn't fretting over me."

"But," said Alidan, "it's our duty to fret over you."

"I command you," Estarion said. And when they would not move: "I'm strangling with all the hovering and the watching, and knowing how you hate it. Some of you at least, be free for me."

"And if anything happens?" Alidan persisted.

"What can happen?"

Alidan refused to answer that, and rightly. But Estarion was in no mood to be reasonable. He drove them out, even Alidan, who needed main force.

His chambers were full of shadows. Some of them had eyes. He rid himself of them by dropping his robes and baring his teeth. Whether for fear of his armament or horror of his shamelessness, they vanished with gratifying speed.

There was always wine on the table by the bed. Godri insisted on tasting it. "Dreadful," he said, "but nothing deadly in it, that I can tell."

Estarion knew that already. That was another magery he kept, to know what was in the wine he drank. Or maybe it was only a keen nose. He downed a cup, and then another. Godri combed his hair out of its tangles.

"Do you notice," Estarion asked him, "what the Asanians do? They don't comb it, except on top. They let it set into a mat."

"So could you," said Godri, "if you didn't want to wear the king-braids again."

"Sometimes I wonder if I ever will." Estarion poured a third cup. The wine was strong, but it barely blunted the edge of his mood. Godri was no lady's maid: sometimes he tugged too hard. The pain was welcome. Less so the brush of his fingers as he plaited Estarion's mane into a single braid, bound and tamed it for the night. Estarion's skin was as twitchy as his temper. He almost wheeled, almost seized those tormenting hands. But they went away. Godri smoothed back the coverlet of the great bed and bent to trim the lamp.

Estarion let his body fall into the bed. Godri drew up the coverlet gravely, but with the flicker of a smile. "Good night, my lord," he said.

Estarion's growl made the smile brighten before it vanished. Godri went lightly enough to his own bed in the outer room. Fortunate creature. His moods passed as quickly as they came. He was even reconciled to Kundri'j; or close enough to make no difference.

Estarion lay on his face. The wine soured in his stomach. The coverlets were heavy, galling. He kicked them off. Cool air stroked his back. He rolled onto it, then onto his side. Canopy and curtains closed in on him. He covered his eyes with his hands. The dark was no more blessed than the nightlamp's glow. He ran his hands down his face, neck, breast. His fingers clawed. He clenched them into fists, pressed them together in his middle, knotted himself about them. He was not weeping. That much fortitude at least he had.

The dreams would be bad tonight. He had no power to turn them aside. The wine worked in him, dragging him down into the whispering dark.

Fear. Terror. Panic.

Estarion clawed toward the light. His breath shuddered and rasped. His nose twitched with the sharpness of sweat. His body could not move. He willed his eyes to open. Slowly the lids yielded. They were like stone. A thin line of light pierced the darkness.

He was not alone. His head would not turn, his hands were dead things. But he knew. There was someone else in the room. Breathing. Watching.

Magery?

A drug? And how, if not in the wine?

His power was as numbed as the rest of him. It could not lift itself, could not batter down the walls that it had raised. He was locked within. Trapped.

Laughter shivered through him. Oh, he was a fine image of an emperor, trapped and spelled and stinking of fear. Rats faced death with more grace.

That it was death, he had no doubt. It stalked him through the dimness of the chamber, breathing faster as it drew closer, though it tried to be silent. It could not know what senses he had, when he troubled to use them.

He gathered all of himself that there was. He did not try to open his eyes further, or to flex his fingers. When the blow came, he must be ready. He must move. Must. Move.

Under the world-weight of lids, through the veil of lashes, he saw the shadow that crept across him. Veils, draperies. A woman?

No. That scent was male: strong with fear-musk, and something else, cloyingly sweet. Dreamsmoke and honey. Something gleamed. Steel. Wealthy assassin, that one, and a fool, to carry bright metal and not black iron or greened bronze.

Move, Estarion willed his body. Must move. *Must.*

Nothing.

The knife poised over him. No face behind it, nor eyes, hidden in veils.

Fear was gone. There was only the will. To move. To *move.*

Steel flashed down.

Estarion lurched, floundered, dragged lifeless limbs, but he moved. Away from that glittering death, and up, into the shadow that bore it.

Two shadows. He crumpled bonelessly to the floor. The shadow with the knife locked in battle with a second shadow. That one had eyes and a face, and warrior-patterns thick on it.

Estarion's body struggled against the spell that bound it. Life crawled back, marking its way in pain. He could move hands, feet.

The shadow-battle swayed toward him. The knife was gone, lost, but its wielder had the strength of desperation. And wanted, still wanted, the life that flopped and gasped on the floor. The assassin lunged. Hands clawed for Estarion's eyes.

Godri struck them back. They yielded; one dropped. Estarion saw the glint of metal, black now, assassin's iron, curved like a cat's claw. Something—something he must know—

Godri caught the wrist that bore no weapon. The black knife arced, slashed past the patterns of his cheek, but drew no blood there. It darted at his hand. He seized it. By the blade, the idiot, the brave, mad, damnable fool. Gods, what it did to his fingers—blood welling, his face blank, unwounded hand twisting, clasping the assassin's wrist. Bone snapped. A shriek tore out of the veils, but the assassin would not yield, would not let go of that deadly blade.

Shadow reared up behind the shadow of the assassin. The veiled one stiffened. If he had had eyes, they would, perhaps, have gone wide. He dropped like a felled tree.

Godri swayed. He had the knife still, fist clenched upon its blade. Blood dripped. He did not seem to notice. He dropped gracelessly to his knees, who had always been as graceful as a dancer. "My lord," he said. Were those tears upon his cheeks? "Oh, my lord!"

With all the strength that he had, Estarion shaped words. "Godri. Godri, let go. The knife. Let go!"

Godri stared blankly at his bleeding hand, at the thing that he clutched in it. "It's nothing," he said. "I'll get a bandage—wrap it—"

"It is poisoned," said a clear cold voice. An Olenyas kicked the assassin's body out of the way and stood over them both. His eyes were all gold. "You are a dead man, tribesman. Whatever possessed you to take an assassin's knife by the blade?"

Godri drew himself up on his knees. "You're talking nonsense, yelloweyes." His breath caught. He swayed again, steadied, spoke through gritted teeth. "Don't listen to him, my lord. Did that vermin strike you? Are you hurt?"

"He never touched me," Estarion said. It was easier now, or would be, if he had not seen how grey Godri was, how his body shivered, his unwounded hand clenched and unclenched.

"Gods be thanked," Godri said. His voice was thin; he needed three breaths for the three words. "Oh, my lord, I thought you were killed."

"Spelled," said Estarion. He struggled to sit up. The numbness was fading. He was clumsy yet, as if half of him was turned to stone, but he could wrap arms about Godri, and know how he shivered and spasmed.

Just as Estarion's father had. But there was no mage to hunt, no assassin to kill. The Olenyas had done that.

"Fetch a physician," Estarion said. "Quickly."

"What use?" asked the Olenyas. "He is dead. Nothing can mend him."

"A mage can," said Estarion. He was growing—not angry. No. There was no word for it. It was too perfect, too blackly brilliant. "You are not going to die," he said to Godri.

Godri did not answer. The poison was strong in him. Estarion could smell it, could taste it in the air. It was vile, cloying-sweet.

He called his power to him. It was slow, it dragged, it trickled where it should have been a thin but steady stream. It was not enough even to fill the cup of his skull. With sunlight, maybe, it might have been more. There was no moonlight tonight, and no stars. Rain fell like tears.

Estarion gathered up the limp body. It was still breathing. He was sure that it was. It could not have stopped so soon.

"Well for him," the Olenyas said, "that it was quick poison and not a slow. He had no pain."

No doubt, for an Olenyas, that was compassion. Estarion found himself on his feet, hands fisted in Olenyai robes, shaking the man within as if he had been a child's doll. The Olenyas made no move to resist. "Don't," Estarion said. "Don't—ever—"

"I am not to tell the truth?"

"My friend is dead!"

It was a howl. The Olenyas heard it calmly, dangling in Estarion's grasp. "That is truth," he said.

Estarion dropped him. He landed lightly, hardly ruffled, no malice in the steady golden stare.

"My friend is dead," Estarion said more softly, "and I could not make him live. My friend . . . died . . . for me."

"He died for idiocy. And," said the Olenyas, "for you."

"I could kill you," said Estarion. He was quite calm. "You could have come before. You came too late."

"I came with the speed I had."

"You were supposed to guard me."

"You sent us all away."

Estarion gasped for breath. He should weep. He could not remember how. "You shouldn't—have— I'll kill you. You'll let me. You'll all die for me."

"I will not."

That stopped Estarion. "You exist to serve me."

"I exist to serve the throne. That one," said the Olenyas, tilting his shrouded head toward Godri's body, "lived and died for you."

Estarion had him by the robe again. He was not as small as some, Estarion noticed. Maybe he was young. His voice was so dispassionate that it seemed age-less, but it was light, as if it had not long been broken from child's into man's. The skin round the eyes was smooth, unlined, and white as ivory. The brows under the veil were dark gold. Maybe Estarion could see something of the face: straight long line of nose, smooth curve of cheek and chin.

Asanian. Estarion's belly knotted with disgust. He thrust the creature away, stumbled past Godri, half fell where the assassin lay. The man's bowels had let go in death; he stank. Estarion swallowed bile, and stripped the veils from the face. Round unremarkable Asanian face, nothing to distinguish it from a hundred others.

"He was not of us," said the Olenyas.

It seemed to matter to him. Estarion stripped the body grimly, quelling the hot surge of hate. Calm, he must be calm. Later he could break. Later he could weep.

The dead man was plump and hairless—so that was true, they grew none save under the arms and between the legs, and shaved or plucked that. Full male; half unexpected, to find him no eunuch. No brands or marks or sigils but the knife that was in Godri's hand still. Nothing to name him or place him or bind him to anyone but himself.

"How do you know he's not Olenyai?" Estarion demanded of the one behind.

"No scars," the Olenyas said.

Estarion did not see how that could matter. He had scars himself. Anyone did, who trained at all for war. "Then what is he?"

"A fool," said the Olenyas.

"He was clever enough to come into my bedchamber, ensorcel me, and kill—" Estarion's voice caught. He must be calm. He must. Or he would be no use at all. "And kill my squire. That's not a fool. That's a mage, or a man who knows mages."

"Still," said the Olenyas, "a fool. He feigned to be of us. He is not. Those who sent him will be dealt with. You can be sure of that."

"You know—"

"We will."

Estarion rose. He was shaking again. "You will please," he said, "dispose of that carrion. And send for—send for Iburan. The priest, from Endros. You know him?"

"We know him," said the Olenyas.

"I'd rather my mother didn't know. And the ladies. Until tomorrow. Unless . . ." Horror smote him. "If there are more—if they've struck at her—"

"I shall see to it," said the Olenyas.

He was comforting in a strange fashion: so cold and so evidently unmoved, whatever Estarion said or did to him. When he had gone upon his errands, the room was suddenly very dark, full of the stench of death.

Estarion went back to Godri. He was growing cold, his body shrunken, all the quick grace gone out of him. He did not look as if he slept. He looked dead. Cold; empty. Lifeless.

Estarion smoothed the many plaits of his hair and straightened his limbs, as if he could care how he lay. The assassin's knife was locked in his hand. Estarion left it. Godri would have won the battle, if there had not been poison. He would have taken the small wound, bound it up, gone on unheeding as a warrior should.

"Asanion," Estarion said. "Asanion killed you. Asanion with its sleights and its poisons. Oh, how I hate this place!"

There were only the dead to hear. No guards. No servants. He had sent the guards away. The servants—and were they dead as well? Or spelled?

He sat on his heels beside Godri. "They should not have been able to do this to me," he said. "I should have known. My walls should have defended me."

Maybe they had. Maybe the dreams had been his walls breaking, his power resisting.

And what mage could do it? What mage would dare?

It was a drug, it must have been. A subtle thing, and slow, mixed in his wine or wafted in the air. Then it was a matter for the guards to discover, intrigue of the court perhaps, or a lord with a grudge. Asanion was full of grudges, and not the least of them that Estarion was lord of it and not an emperor of the pure blood.

Estarion's mind whirled and spun. It was better than weeping. Better than facing himself, and knowing that a man had died for him. A man who was his friend; whom he had loved.

The Olenyas came back alone. Estarion half rose, braced for battle, and barely eased to recognize the eyes in the veil. "Where is Iburan?" he demanded.

"Coming," said the Olenyas. "As are the rest. I bade them hold back until I had given you warning."

"Send them in," said Estarion. But as the Olenyas turned: "No. Wait. Do you have a name?"

The Olenyas paused. "Does it matter?"

"Yes."

The Olenyas turned back to face him. The golden eyes were level. Lion-eyes. So, Estarion thought: the Olenyai bred them, too. Was he a prince of them, maybe? Or simply an accident of nature?

"They call me Koru-Asan," the Olenyas said. "Korusan."

Estarion laughed, sharp and short. "Yelloweyes?"

"Golden," said Korusan. "If you please."

"They call me that, too, you know," Estarion said. "I've heard them talking."

"Your ears are keen," Korusan said.

"And my eyes," said Estarion with bleak lightness, "are as yellow as butter."

"As gold," said Korusan. He bent his head, which was Olenyai obeisance, or subtle mockery, and opened the door to the deluge.

TWENTY-FIVE

IBURAN'S PRESENCE, MASSIVE AND QUIET, WROUGHT ORDER OUT OF CHAOS. Estarion could happily have fallen into his arms and howled. But that was not given to a man and an emperor. He sat wrapped in a robe while guards and servants and a scattering of lordlings fussed and fretted. He watched them bear the assassin away to be hung from the wall with spikes, and Godri to be laid out with honor in the Hall of Glories.

It all went on without him. That was a wisdom he had come to long since. The emperor was necessary. He was the empire in his own person, his strength its strength, his progeny its hope of continuance. But for the workings of its days he was not needed at all, except to set his name to the greater ones, and to suffer the rest to go on as it would.

Iburan loomed over him. "Starion?" the deep voice said.

Estarion stiffened. He had wanted just this; now that he had it, he wanted to wound it, tear it, cast it away. "Godri is dead," he said.

"I grieve for that," said Iburan.

"Do you?"

Iburan sat at Estarion's feet. Easily, lightly, he laid his arm across Estarion's knees. Estarion could not escape him without oversetting him. There were shocked expressions among the servants; the lords whispered to one another. An emperor in

Asanion was touched by no one but his bodyservants and his women, and by them only as he gave them leave.

Iburan, who knew that very well, looked long into Estarion's face. "No," he said at last. "You're not well at all."

"Should I be?" Estarion inquired. "Consider where I am."

"Where we forced you to go." Iburan sighed. "It would have been worse if you had never come here."

"Not for Godri."

"Is one young man, however beloved, worth the breaking of an empire?"

"Tonight," said Estarion very quietly, very carefully, "I can't answer that as you wish me to. I can only see that he is dead."

"You are not," said Iburan.

"That too I can't answer as you would like. I'm changing here, Iburan. I don't like what I'm changing into."

"What you were in Keruvarion, that was half of you. This is the rest of it."

"Then the half of me is a cold, hard, cruel thing, and it would gladly see whole ranks of men rent with hooks, if but one of them knew what was to pass this night."

Iburan did not flinch. "The half of you weeps for the one you loved, and longs to avenge his death. That's no shame, Starion."

"You have been a father to me," Estarion said. "Can you give me no more now than empty words?"

"I give what you will take. What have you done to your magery, child?"

"Asanion has done it," Estarion said.

"No," said Iburan. "You do it to yourself. You've shut it all away. If you had had your defenses laid properly, this murderer would not have come. And if he had come, and eluded you, you would have known who he was, and who sent him. Now he is dead. His soul is fled. There is nothing for a mage to discover, except that he hated, not you yourself, but what he thought you were."

"His emperor," said Estarion, tight and bitter.

"His conqueror. Still they call the Sun-blood that, after a lifetime of years."

"So I am," said Estarion with a curl of the lip, "if conquest it must be, to inflict myself upon an empire that does not love me."

"They don't hate you," said Iburan, "who know you. And that's most of the High Court, these days, and much of the Middle Court."

"But not the people, who dream of prophets and of conquests undone, and conspire to be rid of me."

"Self-pity ill becomes you, Starion."

Estarion could not strike him. Not this man. Not that he was Avaryan's high priest in Endros, or that he had been a regent in Keruvarion, or even that he had been, in all but name, foster-father. It was simpler than that. "I know full well," Estarion said, "that you can break me across your knee. But I will not hear that you find me wanting. I have enough of that in myself."

"Then what will you hear? Your mind is locked shut."

"It always has been." Estarion leaned forward, nose to strong arched nose. "You left me here, Iburan. Why? You could have stayed; you could have been my bulwark. Instead, you left me alone."

"And how would it look," asked Iburan, "for the High Court to see me ever at your back, great black bear of a northerner, whispering in your ear? What then would they call you?"

"Conqueror," said Estarion. "Emperor."

"I came when you called me," Iburan said.

"Of course you did. There's no heir in the offing yet."

Iburan rose. The beard hid his expression, but his eyes were hard. "I shall always come when you ask, sire. Now will you ask me to go?"

"Gladly," said Estarion, all but spitting it.

Oh, well done, Estarion lauded himself. He had slain his friend with his folly, and lost his lover, and now he had driven away his foster-father. The faces about him now were all Asanian faces. All strangers.

And one that was no face, but a veil and a pair of golden eyes. They watched him steadily, a little fixedly, as if fascinated. When he drove the others out, that one stayed. "One must guard you," said the Olenyas.

"They won't try again tonight," said Estarion. But he did not order the Olenyas to leave him.

Dawn was coming. He felt it in his bones, both ache and pleasure. He wandered the rooms with his golden-eyed shadow. No danger hid there, no threat but memory. Here was Godri's armor on its stand, there his box of belongings, pitifully little to matter so much.

Estarion had no tears for him. He turned away from the memory and the grief and walked swiftly, he cared not where. To the garden in the end, because it had no roof, no barrier to the sky. Rain fell soft, hardly more than mist.

Korusan was still behind him, cat-quiet. "You'll get wet," Estarion said.

"I'll not melt," said Korusan.

Estarion turned, startled. Wit, in an Olenyas? There was no way to tell. It was black dark, the Olenyas a shadow on shadow. "Why do you hide your face?" Estarion demanded of him.

"Custom," he answered with no reluctance that Estarion could discern. "Modesty, once. And if one cannot see one's enemy's face . . ."

"One can't tell what he'll do next," Estarion finished for him. "That's not so. It's the eyes that give it away. And yours," he added, "more than most. Are you a prince of Olenyai?"

"Olenyai are warriors," the cool voice said, "not princes." Then: "When we hunt an enemy to the death, we veil our eyes."

"*Shiu'oth Olenyai*," said Estarion. "Yes, I've heard of those. They're vowed, yes? And sworn to die unless their enemy dies first."

"Sworn to die with him," said Korusan, "when they take the great vow. Life is not worth living, you see, once the enemy is dead."

"I could understand that," Estarion said.

Korusan laughed. It was an uncanny sound in the dark and the rain: young, hardly more than a child's, but old as mountains. "You understand nothing, my lord and emperor. What have you ever lost but what you could easily lose?"

"My father," said Estarion, sharp with the pain of it.

"Fathers die," Korusan said. "That is the way of the world."

"I gather you never had one," Estarion said.

"What, you think us born of the earth, or of a mage's conjuring? We are human enough, Sunlord, under the veils and the swords."

"How old are you, child?"

The Olenyas was not to be startled into anger. "I have fifteen years," he said calmly. "And you?"

"I thought everyone knew my age to the hour," said Estarion.

"Twenty-two years, twice six cycles of Brightmoon less two days and," said Korusan, "five turns of the glass, and one half-turn." He paused. Estarion held his tongue. "They say you will live a hundred years, if no one kills you first."

"You're here to avert that," said Estarion.

"Oh, yes," said Korusan. "No one will kill you while I stand beside you. I keep that privilege for myself."

Estarion laughed. It was the first true laughter he had known in Kundri'j. It swept the dark away; it brought back, however dimly, the light that once had been all he was. "None but you shall take my life," he said. "Here's my hand on it."

Korusan clasped it. His grip was warm and strong, strong enough to grind the bones together, had not Estarion braced against him. Estarion grinned into the night. This was terrible; it was wonderful. It suited his mood to perfection.

Korusan had been appalled when he followed the path of a suspicion and found a figure in Olenyai black, wielding a blade against the Sun's get. That was none of his plotting.

He was angry, first, while his body moved to do what was necessary. If this was one of the mages' puppets, he would take the price in their blood. Then he grieved, for he had conceived a liking for the Sunlord's servant. Neither anger nor grief got in the way of his lesser belt-knife. Swords were too great an honor for an assassin who dared robe and veil himself like an Olenyas.

After grief came stillness, and certainty. This life belonged to him. This prey was his; he would relinquish it to no other, no, not to death itself.

And, having claimed it, he was not about to let it escape him. He made himself the black king's shadow. He found himself admiring a creature who could stand in the rain until dawn, talking of everything and nothing. Of course he did not understand what Korusan meant by the oath he had sworn. He was too arrogant for that, and too much a child.

Korusan would be dead before he came to this man's years. His bones ached in the damp; old scars throbbed. But if a man could live as long as this one hoped to, then twenty-two was infant's years, and lifetimes in front of him still, and worlds to learn the ways of.

Most bitter of enemies he might be, but he was an engaging creature. Attractive, even, if one were fond of panthers. The grey morning showed him wet to the skin, hair a draggled tail, rain dripping from his beard, and eyes bright gold.

Korusan sneezed.

The lion-eyes went wide. "There now. See what I've done. I've caught you your death."

"I know where my death is," said Korusan, "and that is not in this place."

The Sunlord would not listen. He herded Korusan into warmth and dryness, got him out of dripping robes but not the veil, played servant as if he had been born to it. And if he knew what he served, what then would he have done?

He knew Asanian modesty. He observed it well enough, not even a glance aside, no touch that was not required. The robe in which he wrapped Korusan was black, and went round Korusan exactly twice, and trailed elegantly behind. The wine he poured was a vintage reserved for emperors. Korusan was startled that it stayed in his stomach.

"You're a delicate little thing, aren't you?" observed his lord and master.

Well for Korusan that his enemy recalled him to due and proper hate. He had been deadly close to conceiving a liking for the creature. "I could snap your neck before you moved to stop me," he said.

Estarion smiled down from that northern height. "I'll wager you could, if a sneeze didn't catch you. Your toes are blue. Why didn't you say something?"

And then, damn his arrogance, he went down on his knees and rubbed life and warmth into Korusan's feet. With his own hands he did it. Grinning, with all his white teeth gleaming. Thinking it a great lark, no doubt, to play the servant to his servant.

He was not even shivering, naked as he was but for a scrap of kilt. He was like a hearthfire, hot as fever, but Korusan knew that he was always so. Beast-warm. Beast-strong. His beard dried in ringlets. He was covered with curly fleece, breast and belly, legs and arms. But his back was smooth, and his sides, and his shoulders.

He was beautiful, as a panther is. Korusan shivered. Estarion leaped to his feet, all long-limbed grace, and fetched a blanket. Korusan flung it in his face. "Enough! This is unseemly."

"It will be more unseemly if you drop dead of a fever. I won't lose another guardsman, Yelloweyes."

"Golden," said Korusan.

A grin was all the answer he gained. Arrogant. Insolent. Thoroughly unrepentant.

Fool, thought Korusan, *to make himself so easy to hate.* So easy, and so unexpectedly difficult. One could despise his dreadful manners, and shudder at his alien face. But there was still that innocence of his, that transparent conviction that everyone must love him, simply because he was himself.

It would be a pleasure to kill him. But not now. Not too soon. Not until he could know why he died, and who had slain him.

PART THREE

Koru–Asan

TWENTY-SIX

GODRI WENT TO HIS LAST REST AS BEST HE MIGHT IN THIS CITY OF STRANGERS. There was no sand to inter him for the season of the death-vigil, but fire they could give him, and a pyre in the Court of Glories outside the hall in which he had lain in state. Estarion sang the words of the rite, first those of Avaryan's temple in Endros, then those of the desert and the tribes. He sacrificed a fine mare upon the pyre, to bear the soul to its rest, and when it was time to kindle the flame, he called down the sun.

Estarion watched him burn. How long it was, or who lingered, he did not care. He had no tears. That troubled him. He should be able to weep.

He was walled in guards, surrounded by them, watched and warded till his nape crawled. And there were mage-walls on him. Iburan's, no doubt, to defend him against a second assassin. He traced them in the ache behind his eyes.

His chambers were no refuge. No more was the harem. His mother was doubly and trebly guarded—they might, after all, strike at her, since they had failed with her son. In the hall of the throne, no one could approach him. Even the Regent stood outside the inner wall of watchers, speaking as Estarion no doubt would speak if he had the wits. Estarion wondered if Firaz counted this a victory in their long and almost amiable war, or a defeat. He could not come close enough to ask, even if the Regent would have answered.

Estarion's loss was not spoken of. Asanian courtesy. Grief was a private matter. One's servants spoke to the servants of the bereaved. Condolences came attached to gifts of minor value, a perfect blossom, a jewel, an image of the departed. Estarion was amazed to see how many small figures appeared in his chambers, the face of each painted with a reasonable likeness of Godri's warrior-patterns.

"They wish to be recorded," Korusan said of the givers, "as sharing your grief. So that you may suspect them less of wishing to slay him."

"No one wanted to kill Godri," Estarion said.

"That is understood," said the Olenyas.

"There are rites of thanksgiving in all the temples," said Estarion, "that I survived the attack. How many people will truly thank their gods, do you think? And how many will pray that the next attempt succeeds?"

"Do you honestly expect that everyone will love you?"

"I'd be content not to be hated."

Korusan shrugged. "Perhaps you should have asked to be born a commoner, or the lord of a little domain, where you could be adored and petted and never troubled with disagreement."

"Then I should better have been born a woolbeast. A blooded ram with nothing to do but grow fine wool and tup the ewes."

"You say it, not I."

Was he laughing? Estarion could not see his eyes, to tell. He was inspecting a tableful of death-gifts. His finger brushed a topaz on a chain. It was the exact clear gold of his eyes.

"Do you want that?" Estarion asked.

His hand jerked back. It was the first unguarded gesture Estarion had seen in him, the first that betrayed him as the boy he was.

"You may have it," Estarion said. "Everyone always gives me topazes. I have chestsful of them."

"Do you dislike them?"

"I like emeralds better. And opals of the Isles. Have you seen them? They're black or deep blue, and shot with fire."

"Like your hair with gold in it?"

"And red and green and blue." Estarion regarded him in some surprise. "You're a poet."

"I am a guard. What is there to do but study my charge?"

"I never thought of that," said Estarion. "Don't Olenyai do anything but guard? They sleep, surely, and eat. And practice weaponry."

"And unarmed combat, and the arts of the hunt."

"And the high arts?"

Korusan took up the jewel on its chain. His voice was as cool as ever. "I can read. I write, a little. I sang before my voice broke. Now I am like a raven with catarrh."

Estarion laughed. "That won't last. You'll sing deep, I think."

"Not as deep as you."

"That's northern blood. The priest, Iburan—he can sound like the earth shifting."

The topaz was gone, secreted somewhere in the swathing of robes. Estarion smiled inside himself. Strange how the world, like grief, could shift and change; how the hated shadow-watcher could become, if not a friend, then a human creature with mind and wits of its own.

"You didn't sleep last night," Estarion said, "and you've been my shadow all day. Don't you need to rest?"

"I slept while you were in Court," said Korusan.

"You've shadowed me since I came here, haven't you?" said Estarion. "It's hard to tell, if one isn't noticing. No faces."

"You see more than you admit to," Korusan said.

"Don't we all?"

The Olenyas moved away from the table. "It is a custom," he said, "for the imperial Olenyai to choose those who will stand in closest attendance upon his majesty. I asked to be chosen."

"Why?"

"I wished to see what you were."

"And what am I?"

"Interesting."

"Haliya says the same thing."

Korusan's eyes widened a fraction.

"A friend," said Estarion. "As Asanian as you, and as chary of showing her face."

"Your concubine," said Korusan. His tone dismissed her with the word. "And I am your servant."

"She talks like that, too. Or is that too insulting to contemplate?"

"You are not Asanian," Korusan said.

"Enough of me is," said Estarion, "to claim blood-right to this place. I hated that, did you know? I wanted to forget that I was ever anything but Varyani. I avoided mirrors, and cultivated hats and hoods, and let no one address me as Son of the Lion."

"You could have revoked your claim," said the Olenyas.

"Of course I couldn't," Estarion said. "It's mine."

"You are," said Korusan, "emperor."

"You hate me for it?"

"Should I love you?"

Estarion grinned and stretched, as if he could widen these walls with his hands and break through to open sky. "You are interesting," he said. "Fascinating. If you study me, may I study you?"

"The emperor may do as he wills."

"The emperor wills . . ." Estarion turned full about, dragging his damnable robes. His mood was as changeable as the sky, now sun, now clouds, now black night.

"Godri is dead," he said. "I should have died in his place. And the sun still shines. The clouds run over the vale of the river. The world cares nothing that I am lord of it, or that my people would cast me down."

"Or raise you up," said Korusan.

"I see," Estarion said in something very like delight. "The people would be death to me. You would be death to my self-pity."

"Does it give you pleasure to feel so sorry for yourself?"

"It gives me considerable gratification," said Estarion, "to think of throttling you in your sleep."

"Then we are alike," said Korusan.

Estarion flashed a grin at him. "Go away," he said. "Sleep. I promise I won't throttle you. This time."

The Olenyas went away. Estarion had not honestly expected him to. But he was tired: Estarion saw it in the droop of the shoulders in the black robe, in the slight drag of the step. A child, yes. A child who knew the use of the swords he wore, and who had slain an assassin with ease and dispatch and no slightest glimmer of remorse.

Other shadows came on guard. Estarion shut them out of mind and sight, and flung himself on the bed in the inner room.

The sun sank slowly into the west of the world. He felt it in his skin. That much was still his, the sun-sense, the land-sense. Asanion, and his father's death, had taken the rest of it away, locked him in himself. But the sun never left him.

He sat up, clasping his knees, resting his chin on them. He was smothering. Stifling. And tonight, if anyone came to kill him . . .

It was easier than he had thought. More fool he, for not thinking of it sooner. Dressed in his wonted armor of robes, he walked calmly and openly into the harem. His shadows halted perforce at the doors. He slipped into an empty chamber and bundled the robes into a chest there, and stood up in well-worn coat and trousers, with a hat in his hand. Still calmly, still openly, he walked through the maze of rooms and passages, empty of the thousand concubines that were the emperor's portion, bare and unguarded.

Haliya's riding court was deserted. She had been there earlier: the marks of hoofs were clear in the sand, a fall of droppings that the servants, careless or in haste, had missed. He circled it, keeping to the shadow of the colonnade. The door was barred but unlocked. The passage was empty. The gate opened to his touch.

He walked past the stalls and the drowsing seneldi, to pause in the shadow of the stable door. Grooms and servants walked past, some briskly, some idling in the long light of evening. He pulled the hat down over his eyes. What men did not expect to see, they failed to see. He squared his shoulders and put on the swagger of an emperor's guardsman at liberty, making his insouciant way to the stews and taverns of the city.

A shadow attached itself to him beyond the Golden Gate, well down the Way of Kings. He neither paused nor turned. But as the road narrowed and divided, he slid hunter-swift into an alleyway, doubled back, shot out a long arm to snare the shadow as it passed.

Olenyas. He had known that: the ringing in his skull was unmistakable. Nor did the eyes surprise him. All gold, and slightly more amused than angry.

"Yes," said Estarion. "You let me catch you. How did you know it was I?"

"Any fool would know," said Korusan. "No one else in this city walks like a hunting cat."

"Only half the northerners in my Guard," Estarion said.

"None of them needs a hat to conceal his eyes." Korusan shifted slightly. "If it does not trouble you overmuch, I would prefer to be throttled in my sleep, and not in a byway of the Upper City."

Estarion let him go. "You're not going to drag me back to prison."

"I would not dream of it," said Korusan.

"No?" said Estarion. "Back with you, then. I've no need of you."

"You have every need of me," said Korusan.

"Your emperor commands you."

"My emperor has sore need of guarding, if he will walk in his city, and his assassin's head barely cold upon its spike."

"They'll think I'm one of my own guardsmen."

"You reckon that an advantage? There is a fine art, my lord, to the disposal of a foreigner in Kundri'j Asan."

"In Endros we call it slugging and rolling. I've run the taverns all over Keruvarion. I can look after myself."

"I shall watch," said Korusan.

Estarion ground his teeth. "I order you to go back to the palace."

Korusan did not move. His eyes were level. Yellow eyes. Were Estarion's own so disconcerting?

He struck the boy's shoulder with his fist, rocking but not felling him. "Follow me, then. And keep your mouth shut."

Korusan's silence was eloquent. Estarion turned on his heel and stalked down the narrow street.

Kundri'j Asan after nightfall was a stranger place even than under the sun. The Upper City retreated into darkness and silence, broken only rarely by the passage of a lord in his litter, with his servants and his guards and his torchbearers. As Estarion descended, the streets grew narrower, the buildings meaner, the people more frequent with their noise and their smells and their crowding bodies. They jostled Estarion, pressed against him, groped toward the purse at his belt. He kept a grip on it and on the dagger beside it.

He should have been intolerably crowded. But it was freedom. No one knew him. No one fled from his path. Merchants importuned him, beggars plucked at him. Wanton women, all but naked save for the inevitable veils, leaned out of windows or beckoned from doorways.

He was not spat on, nor did a knife stab out of the dark. He smelled no conspiracy, heard no voices preaching riot. Of the prophet Vanyi had spoken of, he saw nothing, heard no word. But neither did he hear anyone speak of the emperor. His height and the color of his face brought silence where people stood together.

He had been where riot smoldered. Kundri'j was quieter than that. Happy, no, it was not that, no more than any city in Asanion. It seemed prosperous enough. The hungry were not starving. The beggars had the look of honest guildsmen. Priests and prostitutes shared street-space with no apparent hostility.

He should have been more easy as he walked, rather than less. He had been imprisoned too long. He had forgotten what it was like to walk where he would; and he had never been unknown as he was here. He could even, he suspected, have taken off his hat and met no recognition. The emperor was in his palace. He did not come down among his people, or sully his pure self with their presence.

There was something underneath. Thought, awareness, memory. Longing. Wanting something. Something that was gold, no shadow in it. Prophecy—prophet—

He halted, half stumbling into a doorway. Something squalled and fled. He started, clutched at the doorpost. He was dizzy. His power felt raw, aching, like a limb too long unused.

A shoulder slid under his arm; an arm circled his middle. Korusan was a fierce warm presence, a familiarity so sharp it burned, as if it had always been, time out of mind. He let himself lean on the Olenyas, lightly, while his body mastered itself.

"You are ill," said Korusan.

"I'm well," Estarion said, "for the first time in far too long. It takes me like this. You shouldn't mind it."

"Mad," said Korusan as if to himself.

"Sane," said Estarion. "Here, stop fretting. I was tasting the city; it was stronger than I thought. It's been cycles since I could even begin to do it. There's something in the palace, I think, that throttles magery."

The boy's eyes were a little wild. "There is something in me—that—" He silenced himself so abruptly that Estarion heard the click of teeth. "My lord, you will come back to the palace. You have had enough of—tasting the city."

"I have not," said Estarion. "I'm not even halfway to where I'm going." He stood straight and pried the boy's arm loose. "I won't take a fit again. My honor on it."

Clearly the Olenyas did not believe in the honor of emperors, but he did not try to stop Estarion from going on. He clung as close as Estarion's own shadow, all but pressed against his side. Estarion sighed and suffered him. He was comfort of a sort, in his robes and veils, armed to the teeth.

The city cast them up at a gate in the third circle, on a quiet street lit at intervals by lamps. That was wealth, to pay men to set up the lamps and keep them filled, and light them at dusk and quench them at dawn. No taverns here, spilling their light and their custom into the street; no tawny-breasted women at the windows. Here all the walls were blank, the gates iron-barred.

The one Estarion sought was unlocked. It opened to his touch, admitting him to a soft-lit precinct, outer court of a temple as it seemed to be, unwatched and unguarded.

But there were watchers. His nape prickled; his head throbbed. He walked boldly into the light, trailing his shadow. "Greeting to the temple," he said, "and goodwill to its priests."

His words fell in silence. He passed from the outer court to the first sanctuary, deserted likewise, lamplit, redolent of incense and the evening rite. The altar was heaped with fruits and flowers. He bowed before it, aware of his shadow's stiff stillness, and laid a coin in the offering-bowl. Prayer he had none, except his presence.

The door behind the altar was open like all the rest. It led to a vestry, and beyond that to the inner house. The priests were all asleep, it seemed, or out upon errands. Estarion might have wondered that they kept so poor a guard, except that it was this temple, and this house, and these priests. They knew him. They admitted him without question: almost pain, to comprehend that.

Only the temple's heart was closed to him. He felt its throb in his bones, the pulse of the Gate under the care of its guardians. He could have forced the door. That power was in him. He did not choose to summon it.

Korusan was clinging to his side again, eyes darting, knuckles white on the hilts of his swords. Estarion touched him; he started. "Down, lad," Estarion said, making no effort to be quiet. "You're safe here. Nothing will eat you."

"And what will devour you?" the boy demanded.

"Nothing," said Estarion. "These are my people here. This is my magic that sets your hackles rising."

"I see no people. I smell no magic."

"It doesn't need your belief," said Estarion, "to be." He moved away from the warded door, following the tug of instinct.

She had a room to herself in an upper corner of the house. The way there was dim, deserted. Once a figure trotted past him. He made no effort to be invisible. The priestess took no notice of him at all. Anyone who came this far, it seemed, was judged to be harmless. He would have called it arrogance, had he known less of palaces.

Her door was latched but not warded. He opened it slowly.

She was asleep. His breath caught at the sight of her in lamplight, clothed only in her hair, with her coverlets fallen on the floor. The room was narrow, bare, no more than a cell. The only light in it was the single lamp, the only ornament the torque about her throat. There was not even a rug for the floor. And yet it was beautiful, because she was in it.

After so much ivory and gold she was blue-white, her hair ruddy-dark, her face sharply angled, her body thin but full enough in the breast, narrow-hipped, long-legged, free in her movements as a boy. She was not tall, but she seemed so, even asleep: she had that gift, to seem larger than she was.

He bent over her. She did not stir. Her scent was dizzying. And nothing in it but herself; no perfume, no sweet oils. He kissed her softly. She sighed. He pressed a little harder. Her lips parted; her arms came up, circled his neck as they always had, always would.

Her body went taut. Her eyes snapped open. She thrust him away. "What in the hells are you doing here?"

He sucked in a breath. "Good evening, Vanyi," he said.

She scrambled herself up, as far away from him as the wall allowed. "What do you think you're doing? Get out of here!"

He sat on the bed's edge. He was perilously tempted to laugh, or else to weep.

Neither would have been wise. "I'm glad to see you, too," he said. "Have you been keeping well?"

"You've lost your wits," she said. "How ever did you escape? And what is that?"

He followed the line of her glare. Korusan stood rigid by the door, looking everywhere but at her. "That," Estarion said, "is my shadow. No one will kill me, he's promised. He reserves that pleasure for himself."

Her eyes narrowed. "You look dreadful," she said. "Don't they feed you?"

"You sound exactly like my mother."

"Damn it," she said. She rose, pushing past him. He did not try to catch her. She pulled a robe out of the clothing-chest and put it on, combed her hair with her fingers, knotted it at her nape. Estarion watched. Korusan endeavored bravely not to. She raked him with her glance. "You," she said. "Out."

He ignored her. Estarion bit back a grin. "Out, guardsman," he said.

The Olenyas took station just beyond the door. He could hear everything, surely, but there was no helping that. Estarion doubted that the boy spoke Island patois. He stretched out on the bed. "God and goddess," he said, "I've missed you."

"You should never have come here," she said.

"I'm safer here than I'll ever be in that gilded dungeon. Nobody recognized me in the city, Vanyi. Not one."

"Of course not. You're not in ten robes and a mask." She came to stand over him. "They must be combing the palace for you."

"Not at all. They think I'm in the harem."

He meant her to laugh at it, not to go bitterly cold. "So? And why aren't you?"

"None of them is you."

"I'm sure you've tested it," she said. "Repeatedly. To be sure. Is any of them pregnant yet?"

He sat up sharply. "No!"

"Pity," she said. "It must be tedious, keeping all those women happy. How many are there? A dozen? A hundred? Or do you lose count after a while?"

"Don't be ridiculous," he said. This was not going at all as he meant it to. She loved him, he knew it. He had felt it when he touched her, before she was awake to flay him with her tongue.

"And why shouldn't I be ridiculous? I'm your castoff, your commoner, the one who couldn't carry your baby. Now it's my turn, I suppose, and you're too polite to leave me out of your round."

He tried to be calm. She would think that. Of course. Everyone else did. "I haven't touched even one of them," he said.

"You don't have to lie to me," she said. "I'm jealous, yes, I admit it. I always did hate to let anything go, no matter how long it had been since I tired of it."

"Are you tired of me?" He rose. "Are you really, Vanyi? Or are you only bitter? Maybe you have a right to be. I should have escaped long ago, or brought you into the palace."

"In the harem," she asked, "with all the others? Well for you you didn't try."

"I wouldn't do that to you." He laid his hands on her shoulders. She did not try to elude him. That gave him hope, although her face was stony. "Vanyi, I swear by my father's tomb, I haven't touched any woman but you."

"Then you are a perfect fool." She wrenched out of his grasp. "I don't want you, Estarion. What will it take to convince you of that?"

"More than this," he said. "Your mouth tells me terrible things. Your body loves me still. Why won't you listen to it? I won't be in this place forever. We can go back to Keruvarion, be as we were. And when your Journey is over, you'll be my empress. Even Mother is almost reconciled to it."

"Listen to you," she said. "Your body tells me things, too. It tells me you don't believe yourself, not honestly. You want to believe it. You want me to fall into your arms, give you your night's pleasure, promise you what you can't take. You can't, Estarion. There's no going back, for any of us."

"There is," he said stubbornly. "Damn you, Vanyi. I love you."

"So you do," she said. "So much that you won't leave me alone when I ask, you creep up on me in my sleep, you all but rape me before I'm awake to know it."

"Rape?" The word caught in his throat. "That was rape? By the thousand false Asanian gods, I hope you never know anything worse."

She was white and set, hateful, hating him. He wanted to hit her. He wanted to weep in her arms for all that they had had, and that she would not let them win back. "Why?" he cried. "Why do you do this?"

"Because I must." Damn her calm. Damn her cruelty. "Take your shadow, my lord. Go back where you belong."

"No," he said. His hands clenched, unclenched. "Not without you."

"Then you will have to force me," she said, "because I will not go of my own will."

"Stubborn, obstinate, muleheaded—" He stopped for breath. "Vanyi! For the love of god and goddess—"

"For the love of your empire," she said, merciless, "no."

"When have you ever cared for my empire?"

"When have you cared for anything but what suited your whim?"

"God," he said, "and goddess. Godri is dead, Vanyi. I came to you—"

"You came crying to me, hoping I'd make it better. It's all I've ever been. A shoulder to cry on. A body to sate yourself with. You have a whole harem full of them now. Why do you trouble with me?"

"Because I love you!"

"If you loved me," she said, "you would go now. And not come back."

"*Why?*"

She turned her back on him.

He battered down the walls of his mind. He stretched a power gone soft and slack with disuse, and touched.

Walls. They were higher than his own, and stronger. When he pressed, they caught fire. They drove him stumbling back. They held him behind his own gates, warned him with lightnings when he ventured resistance.

A great anger swelled in him. Pain fed it, and grief, and the sheer bleak incomprehensibility of her hatred. For it was that. It could not be anything else.

"Very well," he said, soft and calm. "I shall not trouble you again. Madam." He inclined his head, though she could not have seen the courtesy. He left her standing there, cold hating obstinate woman, with her magic and her priesthood and her sacred solitude.

TWENTY-SEVEN

KORUSAN DID NOT SAY ANYTHING, WHICH WAS A VIRTUE ESTARION COULD admire. Nor did he follow Estarion back into the harem. Estarion was somewhat surprised at that. He vanished into the shadows of the passage.

Estarion walked through the riding court in starlight, and into the harem proper. Its halls were as empty as ever, echoing faintly with his footsteps. He paused where he should turn to take the outer way.

Had Vanyi not given him full leave, all but commanded him?

He passed the first door, and the second, on which a eunuch stood guard. The servant bowed before him. He had half expected to be forbidden, late as it was. But this was his harem. His whim ruled it. Everyone said so.

Word traveled swiftly here. It was the lifeblood of the harem to know when its lord walked in it. They were awake, all nine of them, and waiting for him. They had been waiting, it was evident, for long and long. The youngest, the pretty child with the ivory curls, had fallen asleep in Ziana's lap.

They did not ask him where he had been, or why he looked so strange. He did not doubt that he did. His face felt stiff; his jaw ached.

Any, he thought, or all. Not little Shaia; she was barely come to her courses. Haughty Eluya, sweet-voiced Kania, Igalla and Maiana and Uzia and Ushannin, beautiful Ziana and her unwontedly silent sister. Any of them or all of them. They knew that this was a choosing. Their tension was palpable, although they strove to conceal it.

He circled the room as he had that first day, setting a kiss on each brow. Eluya was like marble, enduring him. Igalla's eyelids fluttered as if she would faint. Ziana offered him her lips, full, rose-gold, enchanting. Her perfume was honey and *ailith*-blossoms.

As before, he came last to Haliya. She seemed to expect it, to be resigned to it. Courtesy commanded that each lady be greeted properly; then the lord chose his favored one. She half slid away from him, easing his return to her sister. The others were all looking at Ziana as Asanians did, sidelong, measuring her.

He caught Haliya in his arms. She was too startled to do more than stare. When he lifted her, she was astonished. So much so that she did not open her mouth until they were in the inner room, and the door was shut and the bed was waiting and he had set her on her feet beside it. "You don't want me!"

"Would you rather I didn't?" he asked, sharply maybe. Maybe only aggrieved.

Her answer was as forthright as the rest of her. She reached as high as she could, clasped her hands behind his neck, pulled him down.

"Beautiful, beautiful, beautiful."

Her wonderment made him smile in spite of himself. Asanians did not, after all, practice the high arts in their robes. They made an art of getting rid of them. She made short work of his coat and trousers, shirt and trews. Marveling at him; reveling in him. Stroking him as if he had been a great purring cat, running fingers through his loosened hair, playing with his beard. She was nothing like Vanyi. She was both more innocent and more skilled. She knew what gave a man most pleasure, but it was all new to her, all wonderful.

The hard core of anger neither softened nor went away. But he had come to do grim duty. She was making it a pleasure.

He could more than once have put an end to it. Her boldness was half fear, her art half instinct. She was a maiden. "We're very careful of that," she said, "when we have our training."

"You train? As if for war?"

She sat astride him. She was small, but her breasts were deep and full, her hips ample. He filled his hands with her. She filled herself with him, riding lightly, grinning down at him. "Am I not a brave warrior?"

"The bravest," he said, while he still could say anything.

Women in the east made more of their virginity than this western woman did. "For me," she said as they lay together, she in his arms, toying with the curly hair of his chest, "the hardest thing was to show my face. The rest of it was simple. I was so afraid you'd find me wanting. I'm not pretty, I know. I never was. I've been a great disappointment to my family."

"Even now?" he asked.

"Oh," she said. "Now they're all astonished. You were supposed to choose Ziana first. Is it that she's too beautiful? Are you trying the waters with me, to work yourself up to her?"

"She's interesting," he admitted, "to look at. But I like a woman who can talk to me."

"She's very witty. She saves it, that's all, for the inner room."

"Can she ride a senel? And shoot a bow?"

She struggled up. "How did you know about that?"

"Spies," he said. "Did you think the bow and the arrows just appeared on your mare's saddle?"

"I thought the grooms made a mistake and saddled her for one of the guards."

"A mistake they've made every day since," he said.

She hovered above him. Her hair streamed down, bright gold. It, like her eyes, like her breasts and her hips and her sweet rounded thighs, was beautiful. "I can be an idiot sometimes," she said. "Did you know that your eyes tilt up at the corners when you smile? And your tongue isn't pink, not really. It's a little bit blue."

"Isn't yours?"

She presented it for his inspection.

"Pink," he said, "all through. How odd."

"*You* are odd. You aren't all black, like a shadow. You're like glass. I can see underneath. What happens when you faint? Do you go blue?"

"My lips go grey," he said.

"We go green. And try to fall gracefully. It's an art."

He tangled his hands in her hair. "Is everything an art with you?"

"Everything." She swooped down to set a kiss on his cheek. "Oh, I do like you. Do you like me?"

"Very much," he said.

She did not say the next thing, the thing he dreaded. Maybe Asanians did not know about it. She wriggled down the length of him, doing things that he had not known a woman could do, with such delight in discovery that he could not help but laugh.

He had begun the night in grief and rage. He ended it in laughter. That was a gift. He had the wits to cherish it, and the one who gave it.

Estarion started awake. The bed under him felt strange, oversoft, scented with perfumes. He was alone in it.

He lay for a while, piecing together memory. Godri—Vanyi—Haliya—

He had dreamed that last. Surely he had. But this was not his bed, this billowing mound of cushions, and this was not his chamber, with its sweeps and swathes of curtains. He was naked in it, his body loosed, eased as only a woman could ease it.

The anger was still in him, the tight, hurting thing that thrust out guilt. Regret, he had none. They wanted him to choose. He had chosen. Haliya would do. She might even do well. As for the nonsense of love, that was forbidden him. Vanyi had made that very clear, clearest of all who undertook to teach him his duty.

He had been slow to learn it, but now he had it. He would be the emperor they wished him to be. And since this was Asanion, he would be emperor as emperors were in the Golden Empire. Cold. Devious. Ruling as spiders ruled, from the heart of the web.

Servants appeared, knowing by some art of theirs that the emperor was awake. They bathed him, dressed him, brought him food and drink. He had little appetite, but the wine was welcome. When he had drunk the flagon dry, Haliya was brought in to him.

The laughing wanton lover of the night was gone. In her place stood an Asanian lady in a furlong of silk, painted and scented and jeweled and refusing adamantly to meet his glance. Even when he rose and went to her and tilted up her chin.

"Haliya," he said. "Whatever has come over you?"

Her face was tight, her voice stretched thin. "I am not a maiden now. I must be a woman."

"Who told you that?"

"It is custom," she said.

"Custom be damned." Her eyelids were gilded. His finger, brushing them, came away tipped with gold. "I liked you as you were before. Surely you won't be living your whole life now in all that silk? And paint—you can't ride a senel with your face covered with gilt."

"A woman never rides a senel."

"Even if her lord commands her to?"

Her eyes flashed up then, as bright as they ever were. "Does my lord command?"

"Your lord commands," he said.

She grinned, brief but brilliant. She smoothed a fold of her outer gown. "I do look ridiculous, don't I?"

"You look very splendid," he said, "and very uncomfortable. I much prefer you in trousers on your mare."

She blushed scarlet under the gilt, startled him by pulling his head down and kissing him soundly, and left him with a lightness in her step that looked fair to turn into a dance.

Her gladness warmed him. Too much, maybe. He sent for another flagon of wine. It settled him, cooled his heart again, steeled him to be emperor.

Korusan stood guard on his proper chambers. Estarion did not know how to read the glance the Olenyas shot him, nor did he care. Much. It was not admiration, he did not think. Envy? Amusement? He was not about to ask. An emperor did not take notice of his servants, except to command them.

That resolution lasted exactly as long as it took him to endure his hour in the hall, and to hold audience with a company of princes, and—great wonder and rarity—to ride for a few brief moments in his garden. Umizan was more fractious even than usual. Estarion had to rebuke him, which was unheard of. "Brother," he said to the flattened ears. "Do you want me to set you free?"

The ears flattened to invisibility, and the stallion bucked, sharp and short.

"Yes," Estarion said, "and I don't want to lose you, either. But you're going mad here."

A blue eye rolled back.

"I can't escape it," said Estarion. "You can. Ulyai is long gone. I lay no blame on her: she only did what was wise. You can do the same."

Umizan half reared, curvetted, lashed his tail as if he had been a cat. But when he had done that, he went still. His skin shuddered. He snorted.

Tears pricked in Estarion's eyes, the first in long seasons. "Yes, brother. It's wise. In the morning I'll send you away."

Umizan's head drooped. Estarion stroked his neck, trying to comfort him. "It won't be forever, brother. Only as long as I'm pent up in Kundri'j."

"He understands your speech?"

Estarion regarded Korusan in surprise. The Olenyas had been watching here as he did everywhere else. Estarion slid from the saddle, keeping his arm about Umizan's neck, smoothing the long mane. "He is my hoofed brother," he said, "and he comes of the Mad One's line."

Korusan walked round the senel. Umizan's ear followed him, but did not go flat. That interested Estarion. Umizan did not like strangers, and he detested Asanians. This one he suffered even to touch him, to run a hand down his neck and flank, to exchange senel-courtesies, nose to shrouded nose.

"He is very beautiful," said the Olenyas.

"You may ride him if you like," said Estarion, out of nowhere that he could think of.

"He will suffer me?"

"Ask him," Estarion said.

Korusan stroked the stallion's muzzle, taking his time about it. He did not speak. Umizan blew gently into his palm. He took reins, wound fingers in mane, vaulted lightly astride.

He rode well. Asanians often did. His hands were light, which was not common. He put Umizan through the dance of his paces. There was no telling behind the veils, but Estarion thought he might be smiling.

He brought the stallion to a halt in front of Estarion. His eyes were bright but his voice was cool. "Yes, you should send him away. He does not thrive in this confinement."

"So. He talks to you, too," Estarion said. He did not know that he was jealous. Interested, rather. Wary.

"He is not difficult to understand." Korusan swung down, stepped away, leaving the senel to his master. He did not do it easily: there was a drag in the movement, quick though it was.

Estarion had won in hard battle the right to tend his own senel. Korusan lent a hand, capable in that as in everything else he did. They were almost companionable, walking up from the stable, man and shadow, emperor and Olenyas.

TWENTY-EIGHT

VANYI STOOD UNMOVING FOR A LONG WHILE AFTER ESTARION WENT AWAY. The trembling began in her center and spread swiftly outward, till it buckled her knees and toppled her to the floor, gasping, fighting the tears that she would not, must not shed.

But she had fought them too long. She had no defenses left. She wept hard and she wept long, till her throat was raw and her ribs ached. And when she had no tears left, she lay where her fit had cast her, and she began to laugh. Weak laughter, laughter that, in its way, both sobered and steadied her.

She went down to the Gate. It was not yet her time to stand guard, but one of the priests there was pleased to gain an early escape, and the others did not vex her with questions. There had been nothing, no sign, no suspicion, either before or after the attempt on the emperor's life. It must be as rumor said: an assassin hired by rebels, with a warding on him, a common enough magic, within the powers even of a streetcorner mage. It had nothing to do with Gates or with the great magics.

There were no mages strong enough to oppose the priests of the temple. Those who served lords and princes in Asanion were trained often enough in Endros or in the Nine Cities, or trained one another under the eye of the temples. The wild ones, the herb-healers and wisewomen and purveyors of village curses, could do no harm beyond their narrow reach. What harm they did was punished swiftly by priests passing through on Journey, or by hunters sent out from the temples, or by lords' mages who did not suffer rivals.

That much good the Sunborn had done. Magic was a known thing now. Dark magic and death-magic were forbidden or carefully circumscribed. The mageborn need not suffer the sins of ignorance; the sorcerers, those who came to power through the word and the work and not through the gift of birth, had leave to learn their arts in peace.

Vanyi, mageborn and temple-trained, let her power bathe in the shimmer of the

Gate. Its fire was cold and clean, its strength unwearied. She had been in the Heart of the World, that place like a fortress, where all guardians of Gates must go before they took up their charge. She had seen the flame in the hearth, walked in it and through it as part of her testing. She wondered now as she did then, that human creatures should have wrought such a thing, and made it everlasting. Not all or even most that was of the Guild was evil. It had striven to take power in the world, which was its downfall. In its day it had been a great and glorious thing, each mage a master of one of the faces of power, dark or light, and each paired with his opposite. That, the temples had lost. Some priest-mages served the god, some the goddess; they did not work together save in great need.

She was distracting herself from her folly, and from the lover she had driven away. And why not? This was hers, this duty and this calling.

As she stood her watch, a shadow paced through the door. It had been barred and warded; but the shadow took no notice of it. It wore a cat's shape, a cat's lambent eyes, its belly heavy with young.

Vanyi had been kneeling by the Gate. She rose slowly. The other Guardians were mute and motionless, as if enspelled. "Ulyai," she said, or willed to say.

Estarion's sister-in-fur heard: her ear cocked. She took no other notice. She approached the Gate as calmly as if it had been a door. It shifted, shimmered. She sat on her haunches to watch.

"Ulyai," said Vanyi. "How did you get in here?"

Ulyai set to work washing her paws. Where she had been, how she had hunted, there was no telling. She was no more magical than she ever had been, and no less.

The ul-cats of Endros' palace were a law unto themselves. They had their own courtyard and their own garden, lived and bred and hunted as they chose, came and went at will, and answered to none but the emperor or their chosen kin-without-fur. Ulyai had been Estarion's companion since he came back from his first sojourn in the west.

She had not followed him into Kundri'j. Wise cat. Yet now she was here, magical unmagical beast, watching the dance of the worlds.

Vanyi made no move to touch her. It was only prudence. She was as large as a child's pony, with fangs as long as knives.

She washed herself all over, meticulous as a lady's lapcat. Then she rose, stretched each separate muscle—was that where Estarion had learned it, or had she learned it from him?—and yawned enormously. The world-dance had slowed as it sometimes did. Ulyai's ears pricked. These were green worlds now, fields and plains and forests.

She crouched. Vanyi goggled like an idiot as the cat leaped long and high and light, into the Gate.

She caught herself the instant before she sprang in pursuit. The Gate pulsed and began to sing, a deep musical humming. Vanyi's magery uncoiled of its own accord, to slow the pulse, to damp the power.

Something.

Something watching.

Something flitting, shadow-quick, shadow-subtle.

Something in the Gate.

Not Ulyai. The cat was gone. Vanyi stalked the shadow through the flicker and shimmer of the Gate. Unwise, unwise, her training yattered at her, to do this alone, unwarded, unwatched—the priests with her worse than useless, rapt in a dream of Gatesong.

Nothing.

There had been something. Vanyi was sure of it. Something—someone—some power in the Gate, using it, passing through it.

All those worlds—might not they too have mages, guardians, wielders of Gates?

So they might. But this had a feel of this world, and not a beast, not a cat or a senel or a lesser creature stumbling into an ill-warded Gate. This shadow had moved with will and purpose, with intelligence, as a man would. A mage.

Priest-mages used Gates—rarely, with great caution, and never alone, for Gates were dangerous. But there had been none such since the emperor left Endros, no need and no occasion. If there had, she would have known; and likewise every other Guardian in the twofold empire.

She could not go to Iburan, even if he had been in the temple and not in the empress' bed. Not until she knew certainly what she had sensed. They had alarms enough, with the attempt on the emperor's life. They did not need this, which came to no more than a passage of shadows.

And maybe, she thought, she had dreamed it all. Her companions, who had seemed bewitched, were awake now and on watch; they remembered nothing, no ul-cat coming out of the night, no disturbance in the Gate. Both were her elders, and more skilled in magecraft than she; and she had had night-terrors of Gates before, eyes in the dark, presences on the edge of her senses. Nothing had ever come of them. She had too much magery, she always had. It made her see shadows where no shadows were.

Tonight in particular she was not the best of judges. She would wait and watch and see. If another shadow passed, another power betrayed itself, she would be ready. She would discover what it was that wielded Gates, and took no heed of wards or guards. And if it was not dream or delusion, was the Guild as she had feared for so long, feared and yes, hoped . . .

Then she would go to Iburan and the others. Then they would do what they must do.

TWENTY-NINE

KORUSAN SAT IN THE SHADOW OF A PILLAR, GLOWERING AT THE DOOR TO THE emperor's harem. He could pass it easily, if he were minded. Neither eunuch nor armored woman could stop him.

At the moment it did not suit his fancy to walk where, of men entire, only the emperor should walk. His majesty was within, doing what a man did in his own harem. He had taken an unconscionable while to work himself up to it, but since the night he went to the priestess in the Mages' temple, he had visited his concubines every evening and often nightlong.

Concubine. It was only the one, the Vinicharyas, and not the beauty of the pair, either. A fair number of wagers had been won and lost over that. Korusan had a fine new sword and a string of firestones, for opining that a barbarian would more likely choose a woman who could ride and shoot than one whose only skill was to please her lord in the inner room.

They said that the barbarian was not unskilled in pleasing his lady and servant. For a barbarian. The lady was looking well satisfied.

Korusan had seen her. She rode her hammer-headed mare without a veil, thinking herself safe from scrutiny. Her hair was the true gold and her eyes were like the beaten metal, but her face was a little better than plain, and her mouth was too wide, and where the sun touched her, she freckled. He did not think, from what he saw of her in tunic and trousers, that she was very much more remarkable beneath them. A good depth of breast, yes, and ample hips, but no more than any woman should have if she was to breed strong sons.

His scowl deepened. If he had been a mage, he could have burned down the door with his glare. His majesty was going about it with a good will, to be sure. And it was no secret where Korusan walked and listened, that the emperor had succeeded already in breaking the mage-bonds laid on his priestess. They had been strong enough to lose her the child, but she should never have conceived at all.

There were no bonds on the lady in the harem. She was young, hale, of good fertile stock—her father had a dozen sons and daughters innumerable, and four of the sons were born of her mother. Wagers now turned not on whether, but on when.

Korusan would get no sons. The pain of that was old now, the wound scarred over. It still ached when the soul's wind blew cold.

And that one, that upstart, that mongrel, could not fail even when he wished to. Such irony, thought Korusan. The Sun's whelp was getting sons behind that door, not even knowing that his shadow waited alone, nor troubling himself to care.

It would be a nuisance to dispose of the woman and the infant, if any of them lived so long. And suppose that there was no child. It was possible. Even Sun-bolts were not unerring to every target.

Suppose that the Varyani emperor went back to his priestess. She had driven him away ruthlessly—strong-willed as an Olenyas, and prickly proud. But suppose that she softened. She would not allow herself to bear a child until she was initiate; she wanted that, for a surety, and now that she had warning, she could guard herself against it.

She was besotted with the emperor. That was obvious even when she drove him out with curses. He was besotted with her. He talked about her endlessly, pacing and prowling, till Korusan knew every word she had ever spoken, every move she had ever made. He did not speak of his concubine at all, except to mutter that *she* was a sensible woman, *she* did not scream and strike at him for daring to breathe in her presence.

Korusan rose, working knots out of knees and back. The ache in his bones was fierce tonight. It was always there, gnawing on the edges, biding its time until it killed him. But he was its master still. He drove it out with a swift turn of the warrior's dance, leap and curvet, stamp and whirl and swift slashing stroke, down the length of the passage; and at the end a tumbler's leap and plummet and somersault. He came up breathing hard, laughing silent Olenyai laughter, striding out past astonished, staring eunuchs.

He had not expected to enter the temple as easily as the emperor had. Nor did he. There was a guard at the gate this night, a large and deceptively idle young clean-shaven northerner in a priest's robe and braid and torque. But there was no one watching the wall in the back, nor any magic to prevent a shadow from going over it.

The priestess was not in her chamber. Korusan tracked her by scent and sense and instinct to a room redolent with the scents of ink and parchment, bursting-full with books in their rolls and cases. A table stood in the middle of it, with a light like a star hanging in the air, magelight, clear and pure and blindingly bright. In that uncanny splendor her hair was the color of sweetwood, red and brown and gold intermingled, and her eyes the clear grey of flint. She had a pen in her hand and a roll of parchment before her, with words written on it, copied from the ancient and crumbling book at her elbow; but her head was up, her gaze fixed on the dark beyond the light. She did not look angry or sullen, or even sad.

As he watched, she lifted the hand that did not hold the pen, and traced an intricate pattern in the air. It shaped itself in red-gold fire, hovering after her hand retreated. She inspected it without astonishment, frowning a little, retracing one of its many woven curves. It flexed like a living thing, smoothed, flattened, sank down to the written page, and spread itself there, as if it had been a bird and that its nest. Korusan fancied that it tucked its lacework beak beneath a latticed wing and went placidly to sleep.

A shiver ran down his spine. He had seen mages at their workings. They had worked on him more often than it comforted him to recall. But this was magic so calm, so matter-of-fact, performed with such ease and apparent pleasure, that it took him aback.

The priestess smiled at her handiwork and applied pen to parchment, writing smoothly and swiftly, as one who did it often. He recognized the characters of the Gileni script, but not the words.

He came to stand at her shoulder, moving as soft as a cat or an Olenyas. He watched her become aware of him. She was not alarmed. What Keruvarion must be like, that everyone he saw who came from it would let anyone walk up behind, and know no fear: he could not imagine it. Maybe it was that so many of them were mages. They thought themselves invulnerable.

Out of curiosity, and because she needed the lesson, he leaned forward, peering at the image she had made with magic. She started most satisfactorily. "Who—" He met her eyes. Her mouth snapped shut. What came then was tight and hard, as through gritted teeth. "Tell him no. I will not go to him, summoned or unsummoned."

Korusan should not have been surprised. "He has not summoned you," he said. "He is with his ladies."

That might have been a misjudgment: she had a temper, and it thrust her to her feet. She was smaller than he. Interesting. He had thought of her as tall. She was so, if she had been Asanian, but for an easterner she was a small woman. "Then why are you here?" she demanded.

Presence of mind, too. Korusan was beginning to like this odd fierce creature. He shrugged at her question. "I had thought," he said, "that you might wish to know to what you drove him."

"Why? What profit is in it for you?"

He gave her a part of the truth. "I would wish that a lady of good family not bear mongrel offspring."

She very nearly struck him. He could have eluded her, if he chose to. She knew that: she showed him her teeth, and her flattened hand. "Sometimes," she said, "you people are repellent."

"And you, madam, are without flaw?"

She returned to her seat. She was not wary of him, which was either courage or great folly. She took up the pen and turned it in her fingers, but her eyes lingered on him. "You're his shadow," she said. "They all call you that. Do you dog his steps because you love him, or because it pleases you to hold his life in your hand?"

"I am his guard and his servant," said Korusan. "But for me, when the assassin struck, he would have died. Do your people understand life-debt?"

"We understand that Asanians are anciently inscrutable, and Olenyai worst of all. Does life-debt mean that you are bound to him until you set him free?"

"And he to me." Korusan inclined his head. "You understand much."

"He wouldn't agree with you." The pen snapped between her fingers. She laid down the shards of it carefully, as if she feared to break them further. "What do you want with me?"

"To understand you," he said.

"Why?"

"Because," he said, "my master loves you."

Her fists struck the table. "Stop it! Will you stop it? Bad enough that he hounds me and haunts me and drives me to distraction. Must I have his every slave and servant doing the same?"

"Why?" asked Korusan. "Has anyone else come to you?"

"No!" She lowered her head into her hands. It was not defeat, nor was it weariness. It was violence grimly throttled. "Go away," she said.

He went. She had not expected him to. But he was not Estarion, to resist will as well as word. She raised her head from her hands. The shadow of him lingered in the room: a shape of veils and silent movement, soft voice and wide bright eyes. Feverish, she thought. As if he were ill, or touched with something of his master's fire.

She swept up the first thing that came to hand: an empty scroll-case, solid and heavy. With all her force, she hurled it at the wall.

The silence afterward was blessed. She stared at the dent the case had made in the plastered wall, and called to mind each line of that faceless shape. He had eyes like Estarion's, lion-eyes as they called them here. She had thought them plain Asanian until she came to this place and found that eyes in the Golden Empire were much as elsewhere, more often yellow than brown, but never whiteless like an animal's.

Shaiyel was not unduly disturbed to be roused in the middle of the night, although the priestess with him blushed and hid her face from the light. It was a sin in Asanion, Vanyi recalled out of nowhere in particular, for a grown man to lie in bed alone. Shaiyel smiled at her, welcoming her, offering what hospitality a priest could in his cell: a seat on the stool, a cup of water from the jar.

She declined them. "Shaiyel," she said. "Tell me about eyes of the Lion."

His own widened. They were amber-gold, large, round, and quite human. "They are the mark of the blood imperial," he said.

"Always?" Vanyi demanded.

He clutched a robe about him and rose, pouring a cup of water, sipping it before he spoke. "There have been lines of slaves," he said, "but they never prospered. Too many defectives. Too many incorrigibles. It's something in the blood. It goes with the eyes, maybe; I don't know. I'm neither physician nor healer."

"What of the Olenyai? Do they have a strain of it, too?"

"Very little is known of them," Shaiyel said. "I suppose it's possible. I've never seen one who, as far as I could tell, was anything but plain Asanian. Purer blood than most, maybe, and better breeding; but there are lordly houses that can claim as much."

"Have you noticed the emperor's shadow?" She spoke of Estarion without her voice breaking. She was proud of that.

"Ah," said Shaiyel. "That one. He has life-debt. I wonder if Starion knows what that means."

"I doubt it," said Vanyi. So: that much was true. "Do you think that any of the old royal line survived?"

"Certainly," said Shaiyel, drawing her into a knot until he said, "Starion is the last of it. He even has the eyes. His son will, too, if he goes on as he's begun."

"No," said Vanyi, thrusting pain aside. "I don't mean Estarion. Could there have been others who were full Asanian? Didn't Hirel let one of his sisters marry?"

"Jania," said Shaiyel. "Yes. But that was far away in the west, almost to the sea. And her line died out, I heard, as the slave-lines did, and for much the same cause."

"And," said Vanyi to herself, "there's no way they could have gone among the Olenyai. The blackrobes don't take in strangers. Do they?"

"So we're told," Shaiyel said. "Their lines are more sacred to them than our altars are to us. We can break an altar if we must. They won't break their bloodlines."

Vanyi shook herself. "This place . . . I'm starting at shadows. He came this evening, you see. The Olenyas. He seemed curious, as if he were inspecting me. I think he wants to breed me to his emperor."

It did not come out as lightly as she wanted it to. Shaiyel touched her hand in sympathy. "There's no understanding Olenyai. Maybe he wanted to see what you were, and he'll come back again when he judges it time, and ask you the question that's in his mind."

"Probably not," she said. "I told him to go away. If he wants his fortune told, there are mountebanks in the market who can do it better than I."

"But is any of them the emperor's beloved?"

"I don't *want* to be—" She broke off. "Shaiyel, I don't like it, that he came to me. He's not what he seems to be. I know, Olenyai can't be read, they have a magery on them. But there's something under it. And it frightens me."

Shaiyel had no comfort to offer. She left him as soon as she could, sooner maybe than was polite.

Dawn surprised her. She had been walking nightlong, back and forth through the temple, round about its gardens, up the street and back again. When she realized that she could see her hand in front of her without the aid of the lamps, she was standing at the crossing, poised to turn back toward the temple.

She drew a breath. The city was waking about her. Some of it had never gone to sleep.

A woman without a veil, walking the open street, was a scandal, but a priestess in robe and torque, hair plaited behind her, was not reckoned as other women were. Once or twice people spat just past her. More often they bowed or gave her room.

The palace admitted her without question. Some of the guards were Estarion's own from Endros. It half warmed, half pained her that they were still there. They greeted her with pleasure, even with fondness. They were all full of the emperor's nights in the harem: not meaning to be cruel, but it was clear, was it not, that she had set him free. And it would be a wonderful thing, or a dreadful one, if he sired a son in Asanion, of an Asanian woman.

She was almost glad to enter the perfumed confines of the queen's palace. The empress had done what she could to make it bearable: torn down hangings, discarded cushions and carpets, flung windows wide. It was still a stifling prison.

Vanyi had to wait to be admitted. She did not mind overmuch. Servants brought breakfast, which she nibbled at, and offered diversion. She accepted the book. She refused the lute-player.

She was beginning to think that she had acted too quickly. What could the empress do? Vanyi had nothing more than vague suspicions, an intrusion in a Gate, an Olenyas with the eyes of an emperor. Plain sense would bid her consider that she was a woman still unbalanced from the loss of a child, further shaken by the loss of a lover, and prey to wild fancies.

Just as she gathered to rise and escape, a eunuch entered and bowed. "The empress will see you now," he said.

The empress had been celebrating the rite of the goddess: she was still in her robes with her hair loose down her back, and a look on her as of one who has not quite returned from the gods' realm to mortal reality. Vanyi, who had forgotten the sunrise-rite in her distraction, knew a stab of guilt. It did nothing to sweeten her mood. She managed a punctilious obeisance, even a proper greeting.

Merian forestalled it before it went on too long. "Enough. This may be Asanion, but I prefer the usages of Keruvarion. Will you sit? Have you eaten?"

"Your servants saw to it, lady," Vanyi said.

"Then you will pardon me if I break my fast in front of you."

Vanyi inclined her head. Merian's servants brought a much lighter repast than they had offered Vanyi, bread only, and fruit, and water scented with the sour-sweetness of starfruit.

The empress seemed to take an endless time about her frugal meal, chewing each minute bite, swallowing, pausing as if in prayer before she took another. Vanyi was ready to scream by the time Merian put down the last bit of fruit half-tasted and waved the rest away, and said, "Tell me."

"I know about Estarion," Vanyi said, which was not how she had meant to begin at all.

"Everyone knows about Estarion," said his mother. "Do you want him back?"

"No," Vanyi said, "damn it. Everyone asks me that, too."

"Including Estarion?"

"I'm the one who drove him to it."

"So you both may like to think." Merian sat back in her tall chair, as much at ease as she ever allowed herself to be. "My son is quite excessively dutiful, and quite clever at casting blame on others for the pain it costs him."

"I had a great deal to do with it," Vanyi said. "Don't try to tell me I didn't. It's what you wanted, isn't it? I hear she's even a hoyden, as Asanians go. He gave her a senel, and she rides it every day."

"She is quite charming," said Merian, "and very forthright in her opinions."

"I'm sure that delights him."

"It is what he is accustomed to."

Vanyi wanted to laugh, but if she did, she would burst into tears. "He does like a woman who will give as good as she gets."

"Even now," said Merian. She sighed. "He is changing. Asanion has altered him."

"For the better?"

"For the worse." The empress rose and began to pace. Vanyi had never seen her restless before. She walked to the wall and spun. "No. Not for the worse. I cannot reckon it, or him. He comes to me, he speaks, he is courteous, he is everything a son should be. And yet he seems to me to be walking in a dream."

"A nightmare," said Vanyi.

"Yes." Merian closed her eyes for a moment. "And since his squire died, there is no touching him at all, mind or body. He has closed himself off altogether."

"He . . . came to me," Vanyi said through a narrowing throat. "He wanted . . ."

"Of course you refused," said Merian. Vanyi could not judge her tone, whether she meant to lend comfort or to prick with scorn. "If you had accepted, you would have broken your vows."

Comfort or scorn, it did not matter. "So he went to the Asanian woman," Vanyi said. "And now he belongs to her."

"You should not envision her as a snare or a temptress," Merian said. "She is a child who was born to breed princes."

"And so she will," said Vanyi. "But I didn't come to speak of her. Or even, directly, of him."

Merian waited, one brow lifted.

"You know his Olenyas," Vanyi said. "The one who never leaves him."

"The one who bears the life-debt." Merian sighed. "I know him."

"Have you noticed his eyes?"

"Should I?"

"Have you?"

Merian half smiled. "You think that he is a lost heir to the Golden Throne?"

"Couldn't he be?"

"It is possible," Merian said. "And if it were, would he have slain the assassin who was striking at my son?"

"He might, if he had in mind more than simple assassination."

"Such as?"

"Revenge," said Vanyi. "Payment for all the years of Varyani rule in Asanion. That's why your husband died, isn't it? Because he dared to be emperor, and to be a foreigner. Estarion has an advantage his father lacked: the one thing, the sign that marks Asanion royalty."

"There is somewhat more to him, and it, than that."

"Of course there is," said Vanyi. "And there's more to this blackrobe than life-debt or loyalty or any other Asanian claim to virtue. He's shielded from magery—"

"They all are," said Merian, cutting her off. "They wear a talisman; they have done so for as long as anyone remembers."

"Yes, and who makes the talismans? Who raises the wards?"

"Mages," said Merian.

"Mages of the Guild?"

"The Guild is dead."

"What if it's not?"

Merian stood in front of her, eyes level upon her face. It was not a challenge. She was not, Vanyi thought, the enemy. "Do you have proof?"

"No," said Vanyi. "Not yet."

"Why do you think it, then? Might there not be mages in Asanion as elsewhere, who may be willing, for a price, to set a simple spell? Or they may be Olenyai themselves, those mages. Why not? It is a useful thing for a warrior and a guardsman to be protected against magic. We do the same for our own, when we think of it."

"I can't explain," Vanyi said, though she hated to show that weakness. "It has to do, a little, with Gates, and feelings in my bones. If I can gather proof—if I can prove that the Guild survives, and that it is using the Gates—will you stand by me?"

"What will you do if you find proof?"

"Confront them," said Vanyi. "Discover their purposes. If they mean the empire no harm, then well for them. If they're up to their old tricks . . ."

"You may of course be obsessed," the empress observed.

"I know that." Vanyi quelled her temper. "My lady, much of magery is in the bones and the instincts. We forget that, with our training and our tests, our rules and laws and vows."

"You would instruct me, priestess?"

The empress was not angry. Vanyi allowed herself the flicker of a smile. "I'm instructing myself. I have nothing more than a feeling and a fear. I tell myself that even if there is a threat, there's nothing at all that would suggest the Guild."

"Except that your uneasiness began in connection with Gates."

"Yes." Vanyi rubbed her aching eyes. "And the Guild made the Gates. I'm even hoping it's they, and not something else—something incalculable. There are a million worlds out there. Who knows what moves in them?"

"And the Olenyai?"

"Maybe there I am jumping at shadows. They're uncanny enough, and they know it. And that boy has lion-eyes."

"Everything in Asanion is shadow," said the empress. "And I am priestess of the dark between the stars, and I—even I—would give heart's blood to be in my own land again."

Vanyi would give her sympathy, but she had little enough to spare for herself. "So would we all," she said. "Lady, if you judge it wise, would you go to your son? Warn him. Tell him not to trust his Olenyai, and least of all the one who clings closest."

Merian took her time in responding. When she did, it came slow. "I will speak to him."

THIRTY

THE MESSENGER CAUGHT ESTARION AS HE DRESSED FOR THE HAREM. "Majesty, if you please, your lady mother would speak with you."

He paused. It was late, and Haliya was waiting. He had a new tale to tell her, that he had heard in court, and a song that would make her laugh. He was eager for her already; he had had to call off the servant who would have eased him when he thought of her.

"Tell my mother," he said to the messenger, "that I'll see her in the morning. I'll break my fast with her, if she will."

The messenger bowed to the floor. "Majesty, she said that it was urgent."

"And I have urgent business," said Estarion with a flash of temper. "In the morning. Tell her."

The messenger was Asanian. He could not argue with his emperor.

When the eunuch was gone, Estarion drew a breath. He should go, he knew that. But he was feeling contrary tonight. He wanted, needed, what Haliya could give. He would only embarrass his mother, or lose his temper, or say something they would both regret.

He approached the harem with a clear enough conscience. Haliya was not ready for him: the room in which they met was empty. He settled there with the wine and sweets that waited, drinking the wine, toying with the sweets. He had arrayed a whole army of sugared nuts, with banners of dried starfruit and a honeycake general, before the door opened.

It was not Haliya. He half rose. "Ziana. Is she—"

Ziana made obeisance with grace and composure. "My lord," she said.

"Is Haliya ill? Has something happened?"

"Oh, no," said Ziana. "She's quite well."

Annoyance made his voice sharp. "And she sent you to keep me busy while she sees to more important matters?"

Ziana raised her eyes to him. He would not call it hurt, what was in them, but he had not pleased her. "Nothing is more important than you, my lord."

"Then why—" He stopped. At long last his mind had caught up with the rest of him. She was wearing what a woman wore when she came to her lord in the evening. It covered her voluminously, but it was made to come off of a piece.

"My lord," said Ziana, "we talked about it, Haliya and I. We thought that you might not know. There are courtesies, you see. And prudences. Since the harem is as it is, and women are as they are, their lord cannot afford the luxury of a favorite. Oh," she said as if he had spoken, "he may have one, of course. But he can't see her and only her. It isn't fair to the others."

Estarion was speechless.

She went on bravely. "So, my lord, we decided that since you likely might not know, and since you have never had a harem before, we would help you. It's not strictly proper, mind. You should have had us all in together, and chosen one of us again, but not the same one as before. A truly dutiful lord would do that every night; we don't expect that, or even want it. Once in every hand of days is more than ample."

And he had spent every night with Haliya for a Brightmoon-cycle and more. "You must think me a perfect boor," he said.

"Oh, no, my lord," said Ziana. "You don't know, you see. And you do mean well. Haliya is very, very pleased with you. She's told me everything that you like, and I've thought of more that may delight you." She moved closer, which was great boldness, and dared to touch his cheek.

Her hand was soft and cool. He shivered. "I don't—" he said thickly. "I don't think—I'm made for this."

"Of course you are, my lord." Her gaze was kind. "Haliya said you could be shy. Who'd have thought it? So tall as you are, and so proud."

"I'm not tall inside," he said.

"But you are." She laid her hand over his heart. "We've decided, all of us, that you are beautiful. The canons deny it, of course. They call for ivory, not ebony; gold, not raven; smooth sleekness, not nerves and bone and angles. The lion in a cage, not the panther in his lair."

"You are beautiful," he said dizzily, "by any canon."

"I was bred to be," she said. "Haliya's colors are better than mine, but I have the bones. And amber is permitted, even preferred in some of the poets."

"I don't know that I want to choose," Estarion said.

"You don't need to. You have us both. And all the rest, too. Eluya looks like a tigress, but she has the softest touch in the world. And Ushannin learned the high arts from a great master in Ishraan, who named her her best pupil. And—"

He silenced the rest of her recital with a finger on her lips. "I'm not ready to think of more than one woman at a time," he said. "Even two are more than I know what to do with."

"You'll learn," said Ziana. "It's not so hard. And you're certainly man enough to master it."

She was not speaking in figures. Asanians were half appalled, half fascinated by northerners' size as by everything else about them. And while Estarion was not a large man as his mother's kin would reckon it, that was still rather more than an Asanian could lay claim to.

The swift heat rose to his cheeks, but never as swift as what rose below. He stood abruptly and turned his back on her. "I can't do this," he said.

"Of course you can, my lord," said Ziana. From the sound of it she was trying not to laugh. "You do want me. And I want you. Very much," she said.

The honesty of that, and the plea clothed in pride as in fine silk, made him turn to face her again. "Do you really? And why?"

"Because you are ours," she said. "You belong to us as we belong to you. And because you are beautiful. And because . . . I like the way you talk to me. Even when you are being rude."

"I'm rude?"

"Sometimes," she said. "It's refreshing. You always say what you think, you see. And we almost never do."

"Haliya does," said Estarion. "I think you do, too."

"It's our besetting flaw," Ziana said.

"Don't mend it," he said. "I forbid you."

"As my lord wills," she said demurely, but her eyes were laughing.

She was, in her way, as enchanting as her sister. He had known that before. He had not properly comprehended the wit that inhabited the amber beauty.

His body decided for him. It stepped forward; it found the fastening of her robes. He paused. She was trembling, but not with fear. She did want him. Goddess knew why, goddess knew how, but there could be no mistaking it.

He had taken Haliya, and she had been glad of it, and had accepted it. Ziana took him. She was honey and fire and swift intelligence. Such splendor as that was, to be lost in the body's pleasure, and to look into eyes that knew and cherished every moment of it, and every inch of him.

"I don't understand," Estarion said somewhere in the night, when his body rang like the bell after the peal, but his mind was wide awake. "I don't see how a man can love three women at once, and equally, and treasure them all."

"How does a father love his children?" Ziana asked. "He may have a dozen or a hundred. But there is enough of him for all of them."

"That's different," said Estarion.

"In its way," she said, "yes." His hand cupped her breast. She laid her own over it, lacing her slender ivory fingers with his long thin ebony ones. "I'm glad you say 'equally,' my lord. It's a great honor."

"It's you who honor me." He kissed the top of her head. Her hair smelled of honey and of *ailith*-blossoms. "I don't think I know myself anymore. I wasn't raised for this, or prepared for it."

"I think you were," she said. "Only you didn't know it."

"There's a spell on me. I know that." He felt it, wrapped about him, swathing his will and his power, smothering them. "It's in the stones, or in the air. I don't know which. But it's not meant to harm me. Simply . . . to bind me here."

"Isn't that what honor is, and duty? A binding?"

"Are they always sealed with magery?"

"I don't know, my lord," she said. "I know nothing of magic."

Nor did she. He clasped her to him and made himself laugh. "You have a magic all your own. See, I'm enchanted, enraptured, enspelled."

"Silly," she said, but she indulged him. And yet, in a pause: "You won't always stay here. You'll go back where you came from."

"I'm lord in Keruvarion, too," he said. "I have to travel through my empire." But not now. Not soon. Not while he could foresee.

"When you go back," she said, "take me with you."

"Your sister made me promise the same thing," he said. "Did you conspire in it?"

She frowned, shaking off his levity. "I know you'll take Haliya. She rides, and she can shoot a bow. I can't do either. Will you still take me?"

"Would you be willing to learn?"

"No," she said, "my lord. I'm afraid of seneldi. I know that makes me a great coward. But I would like to see a place where a woman can rule."

"Then you shall," he said.

"Promise."

"On my right hand," he said, dizzy again, drunken with her. She kissed his burning palm, a cool touch, soothing the fire. But not the fire that was in the rest of him.

THIRTY-ONE

THE EMPEROR DID NOT SEE THE EMPRESS MOTHER IN THE MORNING. FIRST HE was late in coming from the harem; then there was a matter of state too urgent to put off; and after that he was expected to sing one of the Sun-cult's rites in the great temple.

Korusan made certain that no more of her messengers reached him. It was simple enough. The slow wearing of time, the Regent's persuasions, Godri's death, Vanyi's rejection, seemed to have broken Estarion's resistance. He closed in upon himself. After his blue-eyed stallion was sent to run the fields and mount the mares in Induverran, he did not go to his riding court. With autumn the rains had come; there was little pleasure in walking in his gardens. He went to the harem still, but, Korusan noticed, somewhat less often than before. As the days ran on, he took to sitting in his inner chamber with a book unrolled on his knees, but the pointer never stirred by more than a line. One day he did not even open the book; the next, he left it on the table and sat quiet, staring at nothing, saying nothing.

He was alert enough in court and when he went to the harem. He did not seem to be dying of a broken spirit. He was quiet, that was all. Still. Unmoved and unmoving, neither content nor discontented, neither happy nor sad, simply being.

Korusan hated it. The bright, restless, eternally unpredictable barbarian was gone. In his place sat a poor shadow of an Asanian emperor. He still would not wear the mask, and he still kept his barbarian beard, but that had the air of habit too long ingrained.

On a grey raw morning between the harem and the High Court, Korusan found him in his bath, eyeing the razors in their case. He was testing one of them on his arm.

Korusan had no memory of movement, but the razor was in his own hand, the case clapped shut and his free hand clamped on it. Estarion was quietly amazed— that too so unlike him that Korusan wanted to shake him. "I'm not about to kill myself," he said.

"No," said Korusan. "Merely to lose yourself."

Estarion's brow went up. He tugged at his beard. "There's more to me than this."

"Will you become all Asanian?"

"Is that so unbearable?"

Korusan returned the razor to its case and secreted it in his robes. "I prefer you as you are."

"Barbarian."

"Barbarian," Korusan agreed, "and honest in it."

That gave Estarion pause. And Korusan: Korusan understood, at last, too much.

The summons came as he changed guard at midday, while the emperor held court and the grey rain came down. Marid brought it, walking lightly, with a brightness in his eye that was more than simple love for his swordbrother. "The Masters," he said. "They bid me tell you. It's time."

Korusan stood still. Marid stared back at him, amber eyes, black veil, restless fingers on the hilts of his swords. "At last," said Marid, "you shall have what is yours."

Korusan drew a careful breath. "I shall speak with the Masters," he said. "Guard well, guardsman."

Marid's eyes laughed with the irony of it. "I keep his life for you, prince."

"Hush, brother," said Korusan. "I am but a guardsman here."

"Indeed," said Marid, unrepentant, "guardsman."

Korusan prepared himself carefully. He put on his best robes. He armed himself with all the weapons that a warrior might carry: the swords and the dagger that anyone might see, the others that were known only to the Olenyai and to the dead, who had known the bite of them. When he was the perfection of an Olenyas, he went to his Masters.

Korusan passed the guards and the watchers and the hidden ones who made his hackles rise. That he was protected from them was little comfort. They were shadows on the edge of vision, voices on the edge of hearing, movements not quite sensed. His instinct, inevitably, was to hunt them down.

It was quiet in this stronghold within a stronghold. No women or veilless children dwelt in this place. They were all men and warriors here, doing their turn in the emperor's service; and they were trained to silence.

He found the Masters together in the room behind the hall. There were attendants of the Guild among the Olenyai, robed in violet and grey amid the somber black. Korusan chose not to notice. He was awaited: he was not challenged at the door, or forbidden entry. He entered with beating heart, chiding himself for a fool. Was he not the son of the Lion? Did they not call him lord and rightful emperor?

He was still but an initiate of two ranks' standing, and please the nonexistent gods, no mage at all.

A warrior did not trouble with preliminaries unless they served his purpose. Korusan bowed to his own Master for true respect, and to the Master of the Guild for careful courtesy, and said what he had come to say. "It is not time."

Neither of them betrayed astonishment. The mage seemed about to smile as one smiles at a child who thinks itself a man. Master Asadi lowered his veil, which was a mark of great trust in this company, and said, "We believe that it is time."

"No," said Korusan. He did not bare his own face. That was noted, he knew, although no one spoke of it.

"Why?" asked Asadi.

"Because," said Korusan, "it is not."

"Are you a seer," the mage inquired, "or a thaumaturge, to know the art of times and places?"

"I am the emperor's shadow," said Korusan, "and I hold his life in debt. How fare the rebellions, my masters?"

"Well," said Asadi, "and prospering. But they need their prince and prophet. They need your conscious presence."

"Soon," said Korusan.

"It were best you do it now," the mage said. "The people are fickle, and the emperor's mages are not all fools. The more we do, the greater our workings, the closer we come to setting you on your throne, the greater the danger of discovery."

"I see," said Korusan, "that you are afraid for your secrecy. Wise, that. Prudent. But the time is not yet come. Your magics are succeeding—they are your magics, I trust?" He received no answer, but he had expected none, nor needed it. "The emperor is mewed in the palace. He stirs forth less with each day that passes. He is learning to be content with his harem and his court and his confinement. He has no knowledge of aught but what he sees and hears, and that is nothing. When he is perfectly closed in, venturing forth no longer even to preside in court, then we may move."

"Then will be too late," the mage said.

Korusan studied the man. His face was sleek, complacent, deceptively harmless. His eyes were as cold as ever, as quietly merciless. They did not fall before Korusan's stare.

Korusan smiled. "You are a worthy opponent," he said, "but I am the Lion's cub, and I hold the Sunlord's life in my hand. I judge that we must wait. Now is too soon."

"When will it be time?" the mage demanded. "Can you judge that? The Sunlord may have little magery that he can wield at his will, but he casts spells with his simple presence. The light of his eyes can bind worlds."

"And you dare oppose him?"

The mage did not bridle at Korusan's mockery. "I have not his native power, but neither have I maimed and squandered what is mine. You, my young lord, have no magery, no power but what guards your mind from intrusion. You are easy prey for the spell that he casts."

That could indeed be true. There was a remarkable fascination in the black king, more than his oddities might account for. But Korusan was no fool or child, to be snared by outland magics. "When I am ready, I will kill him. I am sworn to it. His life is mine, mage. Remember that."

"I do not forget," the mage said. "Do you?"

Korusan laughed, cold and clear. "Never for a moment. Do you think that I sit idle? I have him in my power. He calls me friend, he tells me his secrets, he speaks to me as much as he speaks to anyone. I shall teach him to love me. And when he has learned it well, then, mage, I shall strike."

"Be swift, then," the mage said, "or we shall fail."

"We will not," said Korusan. "I shall slay him with my own hand."

"Soon," the mage said, like a chorus in a song.

It occurred to Korusan afterward to wonder that he had won so easy a victory. Perhaps after all the Guildmaster granted him the right of his lineage.

Or perhaps, he thought, the mages did not need his complaisance to do what they willed to do. Their spells were sapping Estarion's will with his strength. In time he might care too little to live. Then he would rob Korusan of the life that was Korusan's, take it with his own hand, and spare the mages the effort of disposing of him.

Not, Korusan swore to himself, while he had power to prevent it. Estarion must care that he died; must know who slew him. Else there was no purpose in aught that Korusan did, and he was but a puppet after all, to dance at the mages' whim.

THIRTY-TWO

TORUAN THE SINGER HAD COME BACK.

Estarion learned of it by accident. As he was returning from court by another way than the usual, in part to avoid a gaggle of lords who sought to waylay him, in part to vary the monotony, he heard the singer's name just as he turned a corner, and paused. Two of his Varyani Guard idled in the passage, new come it seemed from the city, warm with wine. "He's doing a play for the High Court tonight," one of them said. "One of Lord Perizon's men owes me a fortune at dice. I'm going to make him pay me off by getting me into court. How do you think I'll look in yelloweyes livery?"

"Beautiful," said his companion.

The other cuffed him. "Go on, laugh. I was a pretty thing before that bastard broke my nose for me."

"Lovely," his companion agreed sweetly. "The whole fathom and a half of you."

They would have brawled happily in the corridor, if one, the plainsman with his sharp narrow eyes, had not caught sight of Estarion. He pulled the northerner about, wide-eyed both, bowing arm in arm like players on a stage.

Estarion looked them up and down. "I don't suppose the two of you could be troubled to escort me to court tonight."

"No, my lord!" the northerner said. "Yes, my lord. My lord—"

Estarion left him still babbling. He was weary suddenly, as he was too often of late, weary to exhaustion. But he would be glad to see Toruan again. He mustered the will to send a messenger and the wits to inform the servants before he rested, that he would attend court that evening; and there was Ziana to think of. Or Eluya. It was time to change the guard again in the harem.

All the more reason to avoid it tonight. He stood while his servants freed his body from its robes and his hair from its inevitable knots, and when they went away, lay on the couch that was closest. Korusan was nowhere to be seen. The Olenyas on guard was the nervous one, taller and narrower than the run of them, with fingers that could never be still. After a while his twitching grew unbearable. Estarion ordered him out. He went without protest, leaving Estarion in peace.

Estarion drowsed, neither truly asleep nor truly awake. Some part of him resisted; protested; begged him to wake, move, do something. But he was too tired.

It was not Estarion's custom to attend court in the evening. His servants informed him so, at length. He took no notice. They dressed him in robes so heavy that he could barely move, and crowned him with gold, and touched his eyelids with gilt. He had not allowed that before. Tonight he did not care. He would have let them shave him, even, if Korusan had not taken the razors. Odd child; presumptuous. He still had not appeared. Estarion hoped that he was resting well, or whetting his swords on slaves, or whatever Olenyai did when they were not on guard.

The court at night was a restless glittering thing, lit with lamps, flashing with jewels and gold, murmurous with voices and music and even laughter, soft as the canons prescribed, and deep. No women's voices. No ladies, and no women of lesser repute, though those, Estarion had heard, might come forth later, after the wine had gone round.

His presence gave them pause, but only briefly. Custom, which was always their salvation, bade them bow as one, grant him the accolade of silence, then return to their dance of precedence. He was neither expected nor permitted to join in it. His place was to sit before and above them, and watch, and be silent.

His two guards and he were the only men in the hall who were not Asanian. And, when they appeared, Toruan and certain of his troupe.

The court quieted at their coming, settling to chairs and stools that servants placed for them, making a circle before the throne. As they had in Induverran, the musicians came forward first, took their places, began to play. The singers followed.

This was not the masque of Sarevadin and her prince, nor was it any tale Estarion knew. It was Asanian, maybe, yet Toruan sang in it. He was the lord in his palace, or perhaps the god in his temple, to whom the people came for guidance or for healing or for surcease from their troubles. He wore a white robe, which was royal or divine, and he carried a mask, an Asanian face, which sometimes he held before him and sometimes he bore at his side.

He did not speak to the people who came to him. Another did that. And what that one heard, he rendered differently to his lord. A man would ask for aid against his enemy, and the speaker between would sing to the lord of praises sung and tribute promised. A woman—a eunuch in a veil, surely—would beg him to heal her child of a sickness, but he would hear that she asked for his blessing on her womb. A youth would bid him attend to a great injustice, and he would hear that he must work stern justice in the youth's demesne. The people cried their grief. He heard only praises.

The people, given false coin or none to heal their ills, grew angry with their lord. Or with their god; it still was not clear which he was. They came together. They resolved to beg him, all of them at once, to listen, to hear them, to give them what they needed. Bread for their bellies, for they starved. Wine for their throats, for they thirsted. Healing for their children, for they were dying.

And he heard only praise. He smiled, he blessed them, he sang sweetly of their joy and their prosperity. The louder they sang of grief, the sweeter he sang of contentment, until their patience shattered. They rose up. They tore him from his throne, rent his mask asunder, slew him in a roaring of drums and a rattle of sistra and the thin, high, sweet descant of his unshakable complacency.

"That," said Estarion, "was quite the rashest thing I have ever seen. Preaching sedition in the High Court of Asanion—it's a wonder they didn't rend you limb from limb."

Toruan was somewhat grey about the lips, but he laughed. "Oh, they wanted to. But not in front of you."

"You're not safe after this," Estarion said.

"I am if you say I am," said Toruan. He drank off the wine that Estarion's servant had poured for him, and held out the cup to be filled again. His hand was shaking.

"Why?" Estarion asked him.

Toruan closed both hands about the newly filled cup. His eyes searched Estarion's face. "You didn't understand, did you?"

"I understood," Estarion said, amiably enough, he thought, but Toruan's fingers tightened till the knuckles greyed. "Granted that they keep me like a prisoner of state, can you honestly say that matters are as bad as you showed them to be? Or that I am that perfect a fool?"

"I never thought you a fool, my lord," Toruan said. "But you are cut off here from anything that hints of reality."

"Who put you up to this? My mother? The temple? My court in Keruvarion?"

The proud eyes lowered; the eunuch hid his face behind his cup. "I did receive a messenger from the empress mother. But that was after we decided to do it, my lord. We've been in the towns; we've traveled the roads. We know what people are saying to one another, and what they're threatening to do."

"Rebellion against the barbarian on the throne?"

"That, my lord, and more."

"Surely not," said Estarion. "I'm here; I came as I was ordered to come; I've taken what's mine, and done what's expected. Those are old grievances and empty threats."

"They are not," said Toruan, "my lord."

"So," said Estarion. "You were put up to it. Who was it who wrote the songs for you? Iburan? He's a fine fast hand with a verse, and he doesn't get on well with the high priestess here. He'd want to wake me up to that, I'm sure. As if there were anything I could do. I've no authority inside the temple."

"My lord," said Toruan, "I spoke to the priest, I confess it. He was your mother's messenger. He said that you'd protect us even if you were angry; you're too honorable, he said, and too honest to do otherwise. But we had our play all written. We were going to take it to Keruvarion."

"What, and foment rebellion there?" Estarion was not angry, not yet, but his temper was slipping its chains. "Isn't it enough that you've incited the High Court almost to riot? Not that they'd ever show it, but they were running over lists of poisons, and hiring assassins."

"You needed to know," said Toruan, as stubborn as ever a northerner could be, and as perfect an idiot. "The priest thought so, and the empress mother. You won't listen to them. They thought you might at least give me a hearing."

"So I did," Estarion said. "So did the court; and I'll be hard pressed to get you out of here unpoisoned. What do you want me to do? Go back to Keruvarion?"

"Open your eyes to what's outside of this palace." Toruan flinched a little at Estarion's expression, but went on stubbornly. "It's bad, my lord, and getting worse. They use your presence here as a weapon. They call you conqueror. They swell your Guard into an army, and have it raping and pillaging Kundri'j."

"When I was in Keruvarion," said Estarion, "they called me conqueror. They had me scorning to set foot in their country, and despising all that they were. At least now they have me here to carp at."

"They killed a tax collector in Ansavaar."

"They have a deplorable propensity for killing tax collectors. That was seen to, surely?"

"They overran the troops sent to punish them, and fortified the town, and there they sit. They've declared themselves free of your sway."

"Have they?" Estarion half rose, then sat again and sighed. "It will be settled. I'll attend to it."

"Then you'll attend to the rest, too? It's a plague, my lord. You know what sickness is, how it comes to a man, and he passes it to his wife, and she to her baby, and the baby to the cat, and round it goes. And maybe they all live, and maybe one or more of them dies. And that is the way of the world. But if it goes beyond the one house, if it runs through the town—then it's not so little any longer. It's pestilence. It wipes out whole cities, strips the land of its people, lays low the demesne. That's what this is, my lord. It's not a little thing, a rebellion that refuses to die of age and exhaustion. It's young in strength but old in rancor. It won't give way at a word, even if it's you who speak it."

"How odd," mused Estarion. "They spend all their strength to see me here, and now that they have me where they wanted me, they do their best to lure me out again. Aren't they ever satisfied?"

Toruan did not understand, or did not care to. He said, "My lord, I won't say you're badly advised, but you aren't hearing what goes on outside of the palace. It's worse than it was when you came here. Much worse. In some towns I'm afraid for my skin. They see it, you see, and start to growl."

"My guards have had no trouble in Kundri'j," Estarion said. "Nor did I, when I went out. I was barely noticed."

"This is Kundri'j," said Toruan. He looked about at the chamber in which they sat. "How do you stand it, my lord? You must be suffocating."

"One learns to endure it," Estarion said honestly enough, and somewhat to his own surprise. "Tell my mother that it was a valiant effort. She and her priest will see that you are protected. You may choose to take yourself and your people to Keruvarion, where your art is a new and wonderful thing. But," he said, "you may not be wise to give them your tragedy of folly. They don't hire assassins. They see to it themselves, and promptly."

"Our play was for you," said Toruan. He set his cup aside untouched, and dropped to his knees in front of Estarion. "My lord, we are yours, all of us, but we're a vanishing few in the mobs of Asanion. They've been stirred up. Their old hates are new again, and their fears are stronger than ever. Maybe you can't go out among them as you could in Keruvarion, but if you knew, if you kept yourself aware of them, all of them—"

"I am as aware as emperor can be," Estarion said. He was weary again, aching with it. He had hoped for an evening's pleasure, for an hour's brief escape from his troubles, and this well-meaning idiot had only made them worse.

He was not to blame. The empress had got at him, and Iburan, who thought himself subtle. They would know how little Estarion was deceived by their cleverness.

He dismissed the eunuch as politely as he could, sending him under guard to the empress' palace and charging the guards to defend him with their lives. It would, he hoped, suffice.

He almost smiled, thinking of the court, how appalled the lords had been, how hard they had fought to conceal it, because the emperor professed himself pleased. No doubt they thought him a simpleton.

He wandered his rooms, more restless than he had been since he could remember. Servants kept creeping out of shadows, begging to serve him. He herded them out. The guards were more tenacious, but they could at least be banished to windows and corridors.

He tried to sleep, but sleep would not come. He read a few lines in his book. He drank more wine than he should, enough to make him light-headed, and walked for a while on the roof of his summer-room, under a sky as restless as he was, until the rain drove him in.

As he came down from the roof, a shadow met him. He smiled with the first honest pleasure he had known since morning. "Yelloweyes," he said. "I've missed you."

Korusan did not say anything. That was like him. Estarion passed him, drawing him in his wake, chattering of he knew not what. It was a restlessness of the tongue, close kin to that of his feet.

Somewhere in the maze of rooms, between the room of silks and the armory with its golden panoplies, Korusan stopped. Estarion's shadow was cold without the Olenyas in it. He turned. Korusan stood as straight and stiff as the pillar beside him, with eyes that burned. *Fever*, thought Estarion. The boy was perfect Asanian: he hated to be touched. But Estarion was not to be thrust aside for this. "You're burning up," he said.

"It is nothing," said Korusan. But he shivered.

He was ill, there could be no doubt of it. Estarion considered the wisdom of knocking the child down and sitting on him and shouting for the physician. It would be a fair battle. Korusan was arming for it already, tensing under his hand. He lowered it from the brow to the shoulder, which was rigid. "You should have this seen to," he said.

Korusan's hand flew up. Estarion braced to be struck aside; froze as the boy's fingers closed about his wrist. "I am often ill," Korusan said. His voice was coolly bitter. "It is nothing to fret your majesty. It will pass as always, and leave me no worse than before."

"And while it's passing? How well will you guard me, when you can barely stand up?"

"I can stand!" he snapped, wavering as he said it, but not loosing his grip on Estarion's wrist.

Estarion tripped him, caught him as he fell, braced for a fight. Korusan offered none beyond a sulfurous glare. Estarion laughed at it and carried him inward.

The bathing-room was warm and quiet, its pool of ever-flowing water murmuring gently to itself. Estarion set Korusan on the rim and held him there. "Bathe," he said. "It will cool you down."

Korusan stared at the water as if he had never seen its like before.

"You do bathe, I suppose," Estarion said with tight-strained patience. "Or do you lick yourselves over like cats?"

Korusan hissed at him, so like a cat that he laughed. "We bathe. But not," the boy said, "in public."

"I'll turn my back," Estarion said.

Korusan lifted his shrouded head, as haughty as any emperor, and as short in his temper. Estarion met his glare, gold to gold. Something shifted. In Estarion, in Korusan; he did not know. Maybe the earth had shrugged in its sleep.

Gold, he thought. They were not the color of coins; that was Haliya, as close as made no matter. They were clearer, a color between amber and citrine, now as flat and hard as stones, now as soft as sleep. Thick long lashes, dark gold, and fine arched brows a shade lighter, and skin as clear and fair as ivory.

Korusan lowered the lids over those remarkable eyes, and raised them again, almost as if he were succumbing to sleep. Estarion caught him before he could tumble into the water. But he was steady on his feet. He was taut still, but not as rigid as before, easing slowly. He reached up past Estarion's arm, and with sudden force, sharp enough to make Estarion start, stripped off headcloth and veil.

Estarion's breath caught. Even after those eyes, he had not expected beauty such as this: an image carved in ivory. No line drawn awry, no mole or blemish, no flaw save two thin crimson scars that ran straight and deliberate from cheekbone to jaw. They only made him the more beautiful.

"If you had been a woman," Estarion said, "singers would be making songs of you."

"Not in Asanion," said Korusan. He ran fingers through cropped yellow curls, pulling out tangles with ruthlessness that made Estarion wince. "It is wanton to sing of a lady or an Olenyas."

"Or a prince of the court?"

"That," said the boy, "I am not." He said it strangely, but that was his fever: he was shaking again, cursing himself. With the same ferocity that had startled Estarion when he bared his face, he wrenched free and shed his robes and his weapons, all of them.

Beautiful, yes, and clad in scars and a single ornament, a topaz on a chain about his neck; and so young, caught between boy and man, slender but with breadth coming in his shoulders, taut-muscled as a swordsman must be, light on his feet as a dancer, even dizzy with fever. This time as he swayed, he caught at Estarion. His hands fisted in robe and tore.

Estarion had stopped trying to guess what the boy would do next. He was not afraid. Probably he should have been. A bred-warrior's body was as much a weapon as one of his swords, and if anything more deadly. But there was no death here, unless it were in Korusan's sickness.

The air was cool on his bared skin. He shivered lightly. Korusan touched him. A spark leaped, jolting them both. He laughed. Korusan recoiled; then sprang, lion-swift, lion-strong, bearing him down in a tangle of limbs and robes.

Estarion struck tiles hard enough to jar the breath from him, guarding his throat by instinct, seizing what presented itself: a shoulder, a wrist. Korusan twisted with boneless suppleness. His body was burning hot, fever-dry. Estarion let him hurl himself sidewise, guiding him, toppling them both into the water.

It closed over them. Korusan's legs locked about Estarion's middle. Estarion thrashed. Drown—he would drown—

He burst into blessed air, gulped, scrambled feet beneath him. Korusan clung with blind ferocity. Gasping. Weeping? Face buried in Estarion's shoulder, arms inextricable about his neck, chest heaving with sobs or with battling for breath. His weight was as light as it was strong.

Estarion's hand found itself stroking the boy's back. Its sleekness was all muscle, its bones just perceptible—thin as Asanians went, and smooth as they all were, like ivory. And cooler, maybe, than it had been.

He sank down carefully, braced against the pool's side, alert for mischief. But Korusan offered none. His breathing quieted. His clasp loosened, though it did not let go. It was trust, Estarion knew with sudden clarity. Estarion could thrust him under and hold him, and he would not fight.

His head moved on Estarion's shoulder, from side to side as an infant's will, seeking the breast. But no infant this. One hand crooked still about Estarion's neck. The other explored the long curve of neck and shoulder and arm, and up again, over belly and breast and throat. Pausing there, as if tempted; but tangling itself at last in beard. Estarion looked down past clenching fist into eyes gone wide, all pupil, in a face as white as bone, and the blood-red slash of scars.

Estarion traced the line of them with a fingertip. "Sword?" he asked.

"Knife," said Korusan. His voice was as cool as ever. It seemed to come from elsewhere than that stark face. "One for initiate. Two for honor. Because I showed myself worthy in the battle that made me Olenyas."

They fought to win the veils and the swords. Of course. Estarion should have known without asking.

"Are you all so beautiful?"

Korusan looked startled. That was rare. It made Estarion laugh, at which the boy scowled. "What does beauty matter?"

"Little," said Estarion, "if one wears veils to hide it. Is that why? To keep people from thinking you pretty idiots?"

"You who deny your own beauty: you think to be a judge of mine?"

"I'm not—"

Korusan tugged. Estarion swallowed a yelp. The boy's teeth bared. They were white and even, no flash of barbarian fang, but sharp enough as they sank into his shoulder. Estarion howled. "Hells *take* you!"

Korusan pulled his head the rest of the way down.

It began, Estarion observed with dreadful calm, somewhere in the vicinity of his tailbone. It felt most nearly like the spark of magery swelling into fire, searing up his spine, bursting through his skull. He would not have been surprised at all if this young lunatic had bitten off his tongue and spat it into the water; but he seemed content to settle for devouring Estarion alive. Lips first, cheeks, chin, throat—nip of teeth there, but not quite to draw blood—breast and still-throbbing shoulder, arms, hands, barely shying from the flame of gold. And breast again, and belly, and—

Estarion heaved them both up bodily, dripping by the pool. Korusan made no effort to steady himself on his feet, but sank down, arms about Estarion's knees. Estarion's banner was up and flying. He could not tell if Korusan was awed. He looked stunned, but that might only be fever.

Estarion pried him loose. He had to kneel to do it. It set Korusan eye to chin, which was better than what else he had been staring at. Estarion kept a grip on his wrists, though he made no move to break free. He was, Estarion noticed, a fair figure of a man himself, for one still half a boy.

There was nothing girlish about him, for all his beauty. If there had been, Estarion could not have done what he did. Taken vengeance. Kissed him hard and long. And when they were both reeling, drawn back. He held Korusan's wrists even yet. He let them go.

"You are velvet," said Korusan, "and steel."

"Steel," said Estarion, "and ivory."

"Your life belongs to me," Korusan said.

"And yours to me," said Estarion. It came from he knew not where, but when it was spoken, he knew it for truth.

Korusan rose. He neither swayed nor staggered. He drew Estarion up.

Estarion could stop it now. He knew that. He need only resist: pull free of that hand, speak the words that waited on his tongue. This was nothing that he had ever looked for, or wanted. He had seen how some men were with beautiful boys. He had not understood them. He was a man for women, always, since he was old enough to know what a woman was for.

This went beyond man and woman or man and boy or—if he were honest—man and man. It was certainly unwise for an emperor to discover a passion for his guardsman. It could very likely kill them both. And it did not matter in the least.

Korusan's fever had changed. It was a whiter heat now, a fiercer burning, and it knew precisely how to cure itself. Estarion, Sunborn, panther's cub, had never thought to be a cool spring or a healing draught. He found it wonderfully strange.

It was not like loving a woman. Vanyi was as fierce, Ziana as serpent-supple, Haliya as quick to know where was his greatest pleasure. None of them was so close to his own strength.

They grappled like warriors. They made a glorious shambles of the bed, tumbling from it to the floor, ending in a knot of cushions and carpets, gasping. Estarion was dizzy. Korusan was breathing quickly, stretched the length of Estarion's body.

Suddenly the boy laughed. It was edged with hysteria, but it was true mirth. He ran sharp-clawed hands down Estarion's sides. Estarion spilled him over, set knee on his chest, grinned down at him. He grinned back. "Am I a match for you?"

"Almost," said Estarion. He bent to seize another kiss. It lingered, softened. No war this time. No contest for mastery. Long, slow, impossibly sweet. Bodies so different, and so much the same.

Not all the dampness on Korusan's cheeks was sweat. Estarion tasted the sharper salt of tears. Korusan would have raged, had he known that Estarion knew. Estarion kept silence, and held him long after he had fallen asleep. Even in dreams he kept a shadow of tension, a memory of the warrior that he was. But not in his face. That was a youth's, a boy's, more beautiful than any girl's.

Estarion eased himself out of Korusan's arms. Korusan stirred, murmured, but did not wake. His brow was cool, his fever gone.

It had lodged itself in Estarion. He bathed quickly. His robe was rent, but there was another in the clothing-chest. He put it on. He bound his hair back in a thong, out of his face. He had not, yet, begun to shake.

His shoulder ached; his ribs stung. Vicious, that one, before he let himself be tamed.

What he did then . . .

Estarion was striding swiftly. His robe swirled in the wind of his speed. He nearly cast it off. A guard's eyes restrained him, and the gleam of lamplight on bronze.

The spear drew back before him. The guard—broad brown plainsman's face, name forgotten somewhere in Korusan's shadow—flashed a smile. Estarion had none to return.

There was no peace on the roof, no stars, and a thin cold wind blowing, cutting to the bone. The winter of Asanion was begun. Estarion barely felt it. His vitals were all fire.

The sun was coming. He should sing it into the sky. But he was empty of either prayer or song.

"Do I love him?" he asked the dark. "Do I even like him? Does it matter at all?"

The dark kept its counsel.

"I never meant this," Estarion said, "or anything like it. I'm bewitched, ensorceled. And I don't care. Why can't I care? Is he doing it to me? Will he kill me when he has me in his power?"

Korusan had had Estarion in his power many times this night, and had done nothing but love him. It was love, love as cats knew it, with claws. Estarion was a pitiful excuse for a mage, but some things could not elude him. The boy's heart was his.

Fierce, prickly, deathly dangerous, marvelous thing. Clasping him was like clasping a naked blade. Estarion had never known anything like it, or conceived of it.

Now he had it. Now he could imagine it. And he would not give it up.

The empress' palace was quiet, its guards alert, but silent when he bade them be. If she was not awake, she would be soon: the goddess' servants made a rite of the last darkness as did the god's priests of the first light. He advanced softly through the rooms, from latticed light to latticed shadow, through curtains that strove to snare him in silk, past guards who bowed if they were Asanian, or bent their heads if they were Varyani. Women and eunuchs all. No men here. None but Estarion.

His body was bent on proving it. Again. And he had called Korusan insatiable. He was like a man waked from too long a sleep: waked to find himself wrapped in chains, but those chains were falling one by one.

He must rule in Asanion. There was no arguing it. But he could not rule in Kundri'j Asan. It was stifling him, throttling him, robbing him of wits and will and magery.

His mother knew. He had been shutting her out as he had done to them all, all who could teach him to be wise.

The last door was shut and, he would notice later, barred. It barely gave him pause. Locks had never mattered much between them, not when there was such need as this.

The lamps burned low. He had night-eyes; dimness mattered little. He saw the tumble of her hair on the pillows, black untouched with silver; the curve of her cheek like the arc of a moon, the swell of her breast, the hand that moved upon it, broad strong-fingered hand that was no woman's that Estarion had ever seen.

Estarion froze. Shadow distilled itself into shape. It would tower over Estarion's slenderness. What Korusan was to Estarion, Estarion was to this: slight smooth-skinned stripling. But Korusan was stronger than he looked. Estarion was weaker. Weak to spinelessness.

Iburan opened eyes unclouded by sleep, or by guilt, or surprise. It was Estarion whose privates shriveled, whose cheeks burned.

"Fair morning to you," said the man who had been his foster-father. And, for what clearly was no single night, father in more than name. Even, maybe—

Estarion's hand flared to sudden pain. He gasped.

To have been such a fool. Such a perfect, utter, unconscionable fool. To have seen it full before his face, how they were always together, always in accord, never separated for long or at great distance. To have seen, and to have failed so utterly to see.

He wheeled.

"Starion!"

His mother's voice. He shut his ears to it, to everything but the truth.

He had been asleep. Now he was awake. He had been blind. Now he could see. He raised hands to his eyes, his lion-eyes. One hand that was dark. One that was burning gold. The agony of it was exquisite. It made him laugh. It was that, or shriek aloud.

"Starion!"

His name pursued him, but it could not hold him. This truth had shown him what he must do. He was free, and freed.

THIRTY-THREE

KORUSAN WOKE ALONE. HE KNEW AT ONCE WHERE HE WAS, AND WHAT defenses there could be if anyone struck to maim or to kill. There were more of those than anyone could imagine who was not Olenyas, to see a slender youth naked and forsaken in the emperor's bed.

Not even a servant hovered. He regretted that somewhat. The creature would have had to die for having looked on Korusan's face.

Estarion would die. But not yet. Korusan had been delirious with fever, but not so much as to have lost awareness of his purpose. To have gone so far, so soon . . . no, he had not intended that. Nor expected so easy a victory.

If victory it had been. His fingers flexed in the silk of the coverlets, remembering a very different silk, with panther-strength beneath, and the red heat of blood. No shrinking there, no priestly scruples, and if no art, then instinct enough to make in time a master.

Korusan had meant to take the outlander by surprise. And so he had. But the outlander had surprised him in turn. Not by being Asanian—gods forbid, if there were gods—but by being himself.

Love was nothing that Korusan had time to know. Obsession he had already, and no room in it for another. This, he had no name for.

"I have you now," he said to the air with its memory of Estarion's face. "You belong to me. No one else shall take you."

He smiled. No. No one else. Least of all a woman who could bear Estarion a son.

The Masters would be most displeased. He was to slay this upstart and any off-spring he might sire, and claim the throne to which his blood entitled him. To slay with love, to prevent the siring of offspring at all . . . they would not understand. They were not the Lion's brood.

Only Estarion, whose eyes were lion-eyes—only Estarion could comprehend it.

"I the darkness," said Korusan, half in a dream, "you the light. I the image of ivory, you of ebony. Uveryen-face, Avaryan-face, now the one, now the other, matched, opposed, lovers and warriors . . ." He laughed, although he wept. "You were to wake alone, I to escape before you could snare me in your magics. How dared you claim the part that was mine?"

"Did I?"

Korusan started, surging to his knees. Estarion leaned against the pillar of the bed, more like a panther than ever in his tautness that masked itself as ease. His expression was calm to coldness; and that, in fiery Estarion, was perilous.

"I thought you would be gone," Estarion said.

"So should I have been." Korusan composed himself with care, sitting on his heels, hands on thighs. "You should never have let me come to this."

"What?" Estarion's voice was sharp. "Guilt? Humiliation?"

"You."

"I'm sorry."

He was. Korusan bared teeth at him. "Do you regret me?"

Estarion looked down as if searching for a lie. Korusan watched his fist clench and unclench beside his cheek on the carved whorl of the pillar. It was the right, the branded fist. He had pain there: Korusan had seen it before, how he flexed it or, when he thought no one was watching, rubbed it along his side or his thigh, or simply held it beside him, knotted, trying not to tremble. It was a magic, the tales said, to keep Sun-blood from waxing too proud.

When Estarion spoke, he spoke slowly, eyes fixed on his feet. "I can't regret you or anything that I've done with you. I suppose I should. You're so young, and I—"

"Oh, you are ancient." The scorn in Korusan's voice brought the lion-eyes up, wide and improbably golden in that outland face. "You are ages old, ages wise, an elder, a sage, a patriarch." Korusan rose to face him. "You have seen but a fifth part of the life that your god has granted you. I have lived three parts of the four that have been given to me. I am *old*, Sunlord. I am a brief breath's span from the grave."

"That's not true."

"That is most true." And it was nothing that this of all men should know; but Korusan could not stop himself. "My blood, the blood that gives me this beauty you make so much of—it bears a price. We die young. Very young, Sunlord."

"Not that young," said Estarion. "You'll see forty. Fifty even, if you're fortunate."

"I shall not see twenty," Korusan said.

"Nonsense," said Estarion, flat and hurting-hard. "It's hard enough to tell with only eyes to go by, but the rest of your Olenyai aren't children. All the others are men grown."

"Not I," said Korusan. "Not my line. I am the last of it. After me there are no others."

"Then why—" Estarion stopped himself before he came too close to the truth. "Never mind. You're still sick, aren't you? You're seeing death in every shadow. You won't die. I'm not going to let you."

"No one has such power," Korusan said.

"I do."

Korusan laughed, because he always laughed at death and folly. He who had no magic still had eyes within, half of training, half of his own nature. He saw the death that slept in him, blood and bone. It was waking. Years and training, medicine and magic, had lulled it, but even the Sun's power could not drive it out. It was sunk too deep.

Estarion's hands on him were burning cold, both pain and exquisite pleasure. "You'll live," said Estarion. "My word on it."

"Great lord," said Korusan. "Bright emperor." His mockery was bitter. "Will you swear not to outlive me?"

"That's in the god's hands," Estarion said a shade too quickly.

"Spoken like a priest," said Korusan, "and like a king." He smiled. He felt Estarion shiver. "If I am not clad and veiled very soon," he said, "every servant in the palace will know my face."

Estarion let him go. Korusan paused, considering wisdom and unwisdom, and prices, and velvet over steel. Abruptly he spun, seeking the refuge of his veils.

It had all come upon Estarion at once: Toruan's message, Korusan's fever, his mother and Iburan proving him a fool beyond fools, then Korusan again, with death lodged in his bones. He did not pause to think. He had paused too long, thought far too much, until there was no reflection left in him at all. It had taken what magic was left him. He found none, though he delved deep. He was empty, ringing hollow. There was not even pain to mark where it had been.

What stirred in him, he told himself, was relief. An emperor did not need to be a mage, still less the poor maimed thing that he had been for so long. He had wealth to hire the greatest of masters, power to compel obedience even from the likes of the Lord Iburan of Endros, who danced the dance of dark and light with the empress mother of Keruvarion.

His servants were there to bathe and robe him, as they were every morning. He allowed the bath. He forbade the robes. When he received the Regent of Asanion, it was in royal richness, but such as it was reckoned in the princedoms of the east: embroidered coat, silken trousers, boots heeled with bronze and inlaid with gold. His hair was tidily plaited, his beard cut short.

Firaz seemed undismayed to see his emperor gone back to outland habits. "I shall see to the Court this morning," he said, "and assure them that your majesty is well."

"No need," said Estarion. "I'll tell them myself. Some of them will be needing to muster forces, armed and otherwise. It's time we dealt with this little matter of rebellion."

"Majesty," said Firaz, "there is no need to vex yourself. All that need be done, your servants shall do."

"I vex myself," said Estarion, "sitting in this silk-lined cage, hearing nothing but what my servants judge fit for me to hear."

"Ah," said Firaz. "That one shall be dealt with also, and swiftly."

Estarion's smile widened. "He already has, my lord. I saw to it last night. I trust there will be no additions to my undertaking."

The Regent inclined his head a fraction. Estarion watched him narrowly, but he did not look like a man startled in guilt.

Firaz had waged long war to make an Asanian emperor of an outland savage, but he was an honest man. God and goddess knew, if he was either traitor or enemy, it was much too late to escape.

Even in Asanion an emperor had to place his trust in something. Well indeed: Estarion would trust his loyal adversary. "When I came to Kundri'j," he said, "I rode at speed, and I kept the company of princes. In that, I think, I was mistaken. Tomorrow when I ride out, I ride as I was used to ride in Keruvarion, among my people, teaching them to know my face."

Firaz drew a sharp breath: a great betrayal, for an Asanian. "Majesty! That is deadly dangerous."

"So," said Estarion, "it is." He sat back, stroking his new-clipped beard. That was tension, but maybe the Regent would not know it. "I will go, Firaz. You will go with me or remain, as you will. But Kundri'j has held me long enough. It's time I saw the rest of Asanion again, and reminded it that it needs no dreams or prophets."

"In the teeth of winter, my lord? Will you not wait until the spring comes round again?"

"Will the siege in Ansavaar wait for a prettier season? I'm going to break it, my lord. I'd like to find a living city when I go in, and not a hill of starveling corpses."

"My lord, you cannot do that."

Estarion almost laughed. "Am I the emperor, my lord Firaz?"

Firaz bowed to that, but his back was stiff. "You are the emperor, my lord Estarion. And the emperor does not ride to battle."

"Then that tale is a lie which tells of Ziad-Ilarios at the battle of Induverran, and he not only emperor but Son of the Lion, of the pure and ancient blood."

"His heir was gone," said Firaz. "His empire was overrun. He had no choice."

"He had other sons—half a hundred of them, or so they say. And he put on armor and rode to war."

"You have no son," Firaz said, "nor any hope of one, if you are killed in pursuit of this folly."

"If I die," said Estarion, "I'll die free and sane, and not mewling like a beast. Which I shall be, good my lord, if I am pent much longer in this palace."

Firaz opened his mouth as if to reply, but shut it again. He bowed low. Perhaps it was contempt that held his face so woodenly still; but Estarion thought that it was not. He was afraid for his emperor. His emperor was touched, but he was not going to yield for that. "Now," he said. "The Court."

The Court astonished him. It was barely shocked to be addressed direct, and it received his commands with aplomb. It seemed like Firaz to have been expecting something of the sort, though maybe not so soon. Estarion could not tell among the bland faces, who was pleased to see him abandon the safety of walls and guards. Some, maybe, wondered if he were being subtle, to lure out his assassins. Others would be certain that he courted his death.

So he did. If Asanion killed him, he wanted to die under the sky, not smothered in silks. And maybe he would live. Maybe the rumors were all lies, and the rebellion a falsehood, a distillation of discontent that had not come yet to open battle.

If Asanion had a war-council to match that in Keruvarion, no one would admit to it. The emperor spoke, he issued commands, they were obeyed. It was convenient, in its way. No one but Firaz dared to tell the emperor what he could not do.

"It will of course be done," Estarion said, smiling sweetly. "Yes, my lords?"

None of them protested. None even met his eyes.

"Will they do it, do you think?" Estarion wondered when he had gone back to his lair again. "Or will they conveniently forget?"

"They will not forget," said Korusan.

Estarion slanted an eye at the Olenyas. He was robed and veiled and armed as always, no difference in him that Estarion could detect, but his nearness was warm on Estarion's skin. And only yesterday he had been a stranger, a voice without a face, cool and remote.

"What," Estarion mocked him, but gently, "will you hunt the laggards down yourself, and make them obey or die?"

"Yes," said Korusan.

"Do you ever laugh?" Estarion asked him. "Or dance for the simple joy of being alive?"

There was a difference after all: Korusan would meet his eyes and not slide away. "I dance," he said, "with swords."

"Everything you do is about killing," Estarion said.

"I am Olenyas," said Korusan.

Estarion sighed. He knew every inch of that body, and every scar on it; and he had enough of his own to know what weapons had caused most of them. He did not know Korusan at all. Except that he was doomed to die young. And that he danced with swords.

He would ride with Estarion, he and a company of his fellows. The Olenyai had not questioned their emperor's command, or even rolled an eye at it. They did flaunt it a little in the faces of his Varyani Guard, which marked them human after all, and which made the Guardsmen snarl. If Estarion could persuade those warring warriors to mingle freely and in friendship, he would have no difficulty with the rest of his twofold empire.

The servants had left Estarion with his shadow and a tableful of delicacies, none of which Estarion was minded to taste. He would not rest before the sun went down, or sleep tonight. There was too much to do. But for an hour, because the emperor did not eat in company, he was granted a respite.

He held out his hand. "Come here," he said.

He knew a moment of exquisite uncertainty, mounting to terror. Korusan was Asanian, and Olenyas, and incalculable. He might have meant not love at all, in the night, but something like war, and conquest: Asanion conquering Keruvarion in the bed and body of its emperor. If that was so, then he would refuse to be commanded; he would spurn Estarion, laugh, call him a lovestruck fool. So he was; so he could not help but be. He was besotted with a pair of golden eyes, an ivory face, a heart as gentle as it was prickly-fierce.

Then the Olenyas came. He did not laugh; he did not cast Estarion's weakness in his face. He was less savage than he had been in the night, and yet more hungry, as if he had been starving and here was his feast. It was wonderful and terrible, like riding a stormwind, or dancing with swords.

He could dance. Naked first in Estarion's arms, clad in nothing but the stone that had been Estarion's gift; robed again after with swords in hand, whirling from shaft of sunlight to shaft of shadow. Estarion found swords of his own and the slight protection of trousers, and waited in the light. Korusan spun out of the dark, swirl of robes, flash of steel. Estarion laughed. Korusan was silent, but his eyes were burning gold. They danced the dance of steel and blood, swift, swifter, swiftest, and never a pause or a shrinking, though the blades were deadly keen and the dance in bright earnest.

They both knew it. One false move, one misstep, and blood would flow. Now Estarion pressed harder; now Korusan. Korusan was a fraction the quicker. Estarion was a shade the stronger. He had the advantage in reach. Korusan could slide in beneath it if he let slip his guard, and slide away again.

Estarion was tiring. He had moldered in the palace too long; he had lost his edge. Sweat dripped into his eyes, blinding him. Korusan seemed as cool as ever, but Estarion heard his breath coming fast.

Without warning Estarion dropped both swords and sprang under and round the wall of steel, sweeping up the startled boy, whirling him about. He could have cloven Estarion asunder. Maybe he considered it, but then he let fall his own swords. Estarion set him down. The boy was furious—spitting with it. "Idiot! Lunatic! You could have been killed."

Estarion grinned, gulping air. "Oh, come. Don't sulk. It's no sin to be caught by surprise."

"I was not," said Korusan. From the sound of it, his teeth were clenched. "Had I been, you would have died."

"Not likely," said Estarion. He was gasping, running with sweat, beautifully content. "Gods! I've gone soft. We'll dance again, Yelloweyes. Every morning and every night, until I've got my wind back. Then we'll dance at noon, too, and whenever else there's time for it. And when we come to fight—"

Korusan was blushing. It could be nothing else. Head down, eyes down, and heat coming off him in waves. Estarion took pity on him. "Here, eat, while I wash the stink off. You're too thin by half."

"*You* are a rack of bones," said Korusan. But he did not try to hold Estarion back. When Estarion looked again, the feast was somewhat diminished, and Korusan had a cup in his hand, sipping something that smelled of thornfruit and spices.

THIRTY-FOUR

VANYI WAS AT GREAT PAINS NOT TO BETRAY HER HONEST OPINION, WHICH WAS that the two in front of her looked like children caught in mischief. That one was Avaryan's high priest in Endros and the other the empress mother only made it worse.

She made herself speak calmly. "You should have told him."

"Certainly we should have," said Iburan. He seemed torn between rage and laughter.

"One could argue that he should have been less blind," said the empress. She was pacing while the others watched, a restless panther-stride so like her son's that Vanyi's throat closed. "Whatever our failing, its result is interesting to say the least. I wondered if he would ever stir, once the palace had him in its net."

"More blindness?" Vanyi asked.

The empress spun on her heel. Her glance was sharp. "No, I did not know that it would do this to him. I hoped that it would heal his scars; that I had raised him man enough to rule as he was born to rule."

"Maybe," said Iburan, "it only needed time. He rides in the morning to settle the rebellion in the south."

That had the smoothness of long repetition; and the empress' reply, the harshness of long resistance. "He is not riding. He is running, as he always runs. Will he never learn that he cannot escape himself?"

"You do him an injustice, I think," Iburan said mildly.

"Then let him prove it to me!" cried Merian.

Both of the others let the echoes die. When Iburan seemed disinclined to break the newborn silence, Vanyi said, "There is something else, my lady. Isn't there?"

At first Merian did not answer. She looked young this evening, young and angry. Vanyi did not like her better for it, but it was easier to think of her as a woman and not as a figure of awe on a golden throne: a woman with a son whom she loved to distraction and sometimes despaired of, and a lover whom she could not marry. When she was empress regent she could not set any lesser man in her royal husband's place, not without forsaking her regency. Now that she had laid aside that office she was free to take a husband, but she needed the emperor's consent. And that, thought Vanyi, she was not likely to get.

That dilemma at least, Vanyi would never need to face. Everyone knew where Estarion spent his nights. If one of his women had not conceived a son, one would do it soon enough.

But not, she realized with a small shock, while he rode to the rebellion. Asanian ladies did not leave their guarded walls. They did not ride to war, even to wait in tents for their lords to return. And they were ladies, his concubines; not slaves or courtesans. They would remain behind.

Merian's voice startled her out of her reflection. She had to struggle to remember what she had asked, to understand the answer. "There is something else. He has done somewhat to his power. I would say that he had slain the last of it, but if he had, he would be dead."

Vanyi's heart clenched. Iburan spoke quietly, calmly. "He buries it deep, but it lives. Or, as you say, he would have died."

"When he came this morning," Merian said, "when he stood above us, I never even sensed him. It was as if he was not there. My body's senses knew him, but to my power he was invisible."

"Shields," said Vanyi.

"Shields leave a trace," said Merian.

"He's never been like anyone else," Vanyi said. "Why shouldn't he have found a new way to hide himself?"

"Completely?" Merian demanded of her. "So completely that he is not there at all?"

"Consider," said Vanyi. "When he was here before, he nearly died, and his power was all but destroyed. He needed years to heal even as much as he did. Then all at once, before he was properly seated on his throne, he came back to this place where he lost his power. You know how he is inside of walls. These walls are higher and thicker than any he's ever known, and his faithful servants have taught him that he'll never leave them again. That's false, even he should know that, but how sensible can he be when he's locked in a cage? I doubt he even knew he had the key, until this morning."

"Did we give it to him, do you think?" asked Iburan wryly.

"You opened his eyes to something," Vanyi said. She sighed. "You'll pardon me for asking, but why did you call me here? I'm not his bedmate any longer. I can't bring him back to hand."

"Can't you?"

She rounded on Iburan. "What are you asking?"

"I think you know," he said.

"I won't," she said. "I will—not—take another woman's leavings."

"Jealousy," he said, "is a simple woman's luxury."

"I'm a fisherman's daughter from Seiun. As," Vanyi said with bitter precision, "you and your lady have never failed to remind me. I am not and never will be empress."

"What you are," said Merian, "is his beloved. He loves you still. Never doubt it. If he does as his duty commands, and does it with something resembling pleasure, who are you to fault him?"

"Maybe," said Vanyi, "I love him too much to let you use me, and him, as you are suggesting. You want me to lead him by the privates, straight out of this rebellion and back to his harem and his properly pedigreed ladies."

"No," said Merian without perceptible anger. "I wish you to keep him safe: to guard him with your power, since he seems to have lost the capacity to guard himself."

"And lead him back to his ladies." Vanyi pressed palms to her aching brow. "My father warned me, you know. Never get too close to the gentry, he said. Gentry aren't like us. They're cold as fish and treacherous as the sea, and when all's done and said, they'll look first to their damned honor and then to themselves, and never mind the blood they've shed or the hearts they've broken." She looked up into their faces. Iburan's was gentle, as if he could understand. Merian's was eagle-fierce. "Sometimes I wish I'd married that fat lout down by the harbor."

"You would be miserable," said the empress.

"My misery would be simple," Vanyi said. "It wouldn't be this hopeless tangle."

"You would have flung yourself into the sea."

Merian's lack of sympathy was bracing, in its way. Vanyi hated her with hate so perfect that it lacked even heat. "I'll force myself on him. I'll ride with him. Will that be enough for you?"

"Certainly," said Merian. "His heir must be of Asanian blood. I bid you remember that."

"I never forget it," Vanyi said. "Not for one moment."

Iburan followed her out of the empress' receiving room. She ignored him, difficult as that could be.

In the outer chamber a eunuch trotted past them. He wore white and gold: emperor's livery, with the shoulder-knot of a messenger. Vanyi paused. Everything in her wanted to be out of this place, back to her temple and her duties and her peace, but instinct held her where she was. She could stretch her ears, if she wished. She noticed that Iburan was doing the same.

There were no endless circling greetings and formalities. From anyone else in

Kundri'j it would have been an insult, and the eunuch seemed to believe that it was. He did not know Estarion, or Estarion's mother.

Vanyi barely needed more than ears to hear him. His voice was high, and it carried. "The emperor bids you prepare to ride. He departs this city at sunrise."

The empress' response was calm. "Inform my son that I have been ready since the sun touched its zenith. I shall await him at first dawn."

The eunuch seemed disconcerted: when he spoke again, his voice was less strident. "The emperor also bids you know that the priest of Avaryan in Endros will accompany him. He bade me tell you, 'I cannot forgive. But I can comprehend.'"

Vanyi's eyes darted to Iburan's face. It was perfectly blank.

In the room within, the empress said, still calmly, "Tell my son that I understand."

Iburan began to walk as if he had never paused. Vanyi found herself swept in his wake. She could not find words to say.

Outside of the palace, in the empty street, Iburan said them. "Clever, clever child. And oh, so cruel. Who taught him that, I wonder? Asanion? Or his mother?"

"What's cruel about it?" Vanyi asked. "He said he understood."

"He said it through a messenger," said Iburan, "and he said it within an imperial summons." And when she still did not understand: "He treated her like a vassal. And more than that. He let her know that he won't prevent us. He won't even keep us apart. Can you see what that will do to us every time we come together? We'll know that he knows. We'll shrivel with guilt."

"I doubt that," said Vanyi, with an eye not quite on the bulk of him beside her.

He laughed, sudden and deep, but it was brief. "No, it won't stop us. But it will slow us a little. Parents who disapprove, those are spice to a pair of lovers. Children in the same condition . . . they dampen the proceedings remarkably. They have such expectations; and they never, never forgive."

"If he knew how you laugh at him, he'd be furious."

"I'm not laughing," said Iburan. "He's dangerous, you know. I don't think he realizes that; and the rest of us tend to forget. When he was young, before his father died, he promised to be a great mage and king. He may never be the mage now, after all that's happened, but the king is there still. If he learns to stop running—if he accepts all that he is—"

"And if he doesn't do either, he'll be deadly, because he won't settle to anything, but will drag the empires after him wherever he goes."

"He'll break them," Iburan said. He tugged his beard. It looked naked without its plaits and its gauds. He seemed to miss them, raking fingers through it, scowling at the darkening sky.

Suddenly he straightened. "Come now. We've packing to do."

Vanyi hung back. "Shouldn't I tell him I'm going?"

"And have him say no? Don't be a fool. He's ordered me to go; I have to have attendants, it wouldn't be proper if I didn't. Unless you'd rather wait on the empress."

"Thank you, my lord," said Vanyi, "but no."

"She's hardly a monster, child."

"Of course she isn't." Vanyi did not mean to sound so angry. "It's only . . . we never seem to agree on anything. Except that we love that damnable, arrogant, impossibly infuriating son of hers."

"You are," he said, "quite dreadfully alike."

"I am *not*—" Vanyi bit her tongue. He was grinning at her. "Sometimes I wonder who's really his father."

"You should have known Ganiman," said Iburan. There was sadness in it, but above and about that, a wry amusement. "Starion comes by it honestly. If anything, his father was worse."

"That's not possible," said Vanyi. She strode forward down the broad street. After a handful of heartbeats she felt him behind her, broad as a wall and nigh as strong.

THIRTY-FIVE

THERE WAS ONE DUTY THAT ESTARION COULD NOT AVOID, NOR OVERMUCH WISH to. He performed it toward evening of that endless day, late enough to be polite, too early to linger. He would have left Korusan behind, but the Olenyas refused to leave him until he came to the inner door of the harem. Estarion half expected him to pass it. He halted and crouched in a shadow as he often had before, with no more evidence of disgruntlement than he had ever shown, if certainly no less.

Once past the door in the scented quiet, Estarion drew a shaking breath. There was a word in Keruvarion for what he was. Soldiers gave it to women who sold themselves in the street. In Asanion it was prettier. Here he was lord and emperor, and duty-bound to sire sons; and when duty did not bind him, he was permitted his body's pleasure.

His ladies were waiting. Tonight, he thought, he would choose Haliya, and damn the proprieties. When he came back—if he came back—he would return to the round of his duty.

They were all together in their usual silence, but the undercurrent was odd. Not rancor, he did not think, or jealousy. But tension certainly, and the salt bitterness of tears.

He kissed each one of them, taking his time about it. It was not, surprisingly, little Shaia who had been weeping, but Igalla with her elegant bearing and her queenly manners, and Eluya. Almost he chose one of them, but there was Haliya, dry-eyed and stiff-backed, and Ziana looking rarely unplacid.

He did not delude himself that he was loved. But they were fond of him, maybe, and they fancied that he owned them. He never had been able to talk them out of that. If he should be killed or if he should fail to come back, they could look for little mercy from an empire that had defeated him.

He had been steady, or so he thought, until he found himself leading both Haliya and Ziana to the inner room. He had not meant that at all. A choosing, yes, for courtesy, and a farewell as brief as he could decently make it, but nothing more than that. He ached even yet from Korusan's fierce embraces.

Or maybe he had been clever. He could hardly be expected to take them both at once, or to take one while the other watched. They seemed to think otherwise, it was true, and not to be discommoded by it. Maybe he should have chosen all nine at once, and escaped while they untangled themselves.

Neither of the sisters reminded him that he was being improper, or that he should have chosen Eluya or Igalla. Ziana fetched him wine spiced and warmed as he liked it. Haliya eased him out of coat and trousers, found his knots and aches, and set to work. Some were patently not practice-bruises. She did not remark on them.

He had not known how tired he was until those clever fingers stroked away his tautness. He had not slept since—when? He could not remember. His eyelids drooped in spite of themselves. Ziana had his head in her lap. He heard her voice as from far away. "You cut your beard. I like it so, like a fleece, curly and thick." She combed fingers through it, lightly, making him shiver.

Haliya stroked the lighter fleece of his body, breast and belly and loins. The rest of him was all but asleep, but his banner rose valiantly to greet her.

This was whoredom, harlotry, weakness of body and soul. A priest should master his passions. A Sunlord should rule them.

A Sunlord should sire sons. That was all he was meant for, when it came to it. If he died tomorrow, or if he never touched a woman again, there would be no heir to rule after him.

Necessity. That was the name of it. Very pleasant, lying here, with beauty beneath his head and brilliance at his middle.

Korusan would not be amused. He was jealous, that one. Asanians did not train their men as they did their women, to accept what must be accepted. Men owned. Women were owned.

Korusan would ride with his lord. These ladies would not. The voice of guilt was growing faint. Shame he had never had. He was blessed in his lovers.

He said so, later, when Ziana lay on one side and Haliya on the other, and he was renewed as if he had slept the night through. Ziana smiled from the hollow of his shoulder. Haliya said, "Will you say that when you've had a thousand lovers?"

"I'll never have so many," he said.

"You said you'd never have more than one. It's a longer step from one to three than from three to a thousand."

"Not likely," said Estarion. "I can be as Asanian as this, with you to show me the way. Even nine of you—that's within the realm of possibility. But no more."

"I would like it, of course," said Ziana, "if there were never more than nine. I'd see more of you then."

He kissed the smooth parting of her hair. "I should hate to see less of you than I do." She mercifully did not point out that he had not visited her in a hand of days. First there had been obligations. Then evening Court. Then Korusan.

He sat up abruptly, startling them both. "I have to go," he said.

Neither protested. That piqued him a little. Surely if they loved him they would beg him to stay.

Ziana brought him his coat, Haliya his trousers. They did not play with him, not much. Not enough to tempt him to linger.

But as Ziana fastened the last jeweled button, as Haliya set his foot in her lap for the boot, they both paused. Golden eyes and amber met, parted, fixed on him.

"Take us with you," said Haliya.

He did not think that he looked angry. He even laughed. Ziana flinched. Haliya went stiff, and her hands on his foot tightened to the edge of pain.

"You know I can't," he said. He took care to be gentle.

"You gave your word," said Haliya.

"I promised that I would take you to Keruvarion. I'm not going there. I'm going south, and then maybe west, wherever need takes me."

"You will go to Keruvarion," Ziana said. "Once you're away from Kundri'j, nothing will stop you."

"Nothing but duty and necessity," said Estarion, "and a matter of rebellion in the provinces."

"I can ride," said Haliya, "and shoot. I won't encumber you. Your mother is going. She has women with her. Would one more be so great a burden?"

Ziana, who could neither ride nor shoot, was silent. Estarion spoke to her. "I promise you. When at last I go to Keruvarion, I'll take you, or send for you."

Her head bent. She did not weep. Tears were not a weapon she would use, if others served as well. He caught her hands that smoothed his coat, smoothed and stroked it. "You can't ride to war, my love. We'll all be on seneldi; the wagons will be only for baggage, and those we'll leave behind if we must."

"I ride," Haliya said at his feet. "I can fight. Take me with you."

Oh, he had trapped himself neatly, with Ziana to melt his heart and Haliya to bend his will. Ziana at least had sense to see the truth. "If you promise," she said, too low almost to hear. "If you send for me when you come to Keruvarion."

"On the Sun in my hand," he said, raising it to her cheek. She bore the touch of it, though her eyes went wide with terror. Maybe she feared that it would brand her.

He kissed the cheek where it had rested, flushed over pallor, unmarked and unscarred.

Haliya was not so easily put off. "Take me," she said.

"Why?" he demanded with deliberate brutality. "What can you do that a dozen others can't? I don't need you for my bed. I don't need you in my army."

He had struck, and struck deep, but she had her fair share of steel. Most of it was in her spine, and some in her voice. "Maybe you need me to remind you of what you're fighting for. Of what you have to come back to."

"I can't be trusted to remember it?"

"No."

His teeth clicked together. He could flatten her with a blow. Or he could laugh and pull her up, and keep his hands on her shoulders, and say to her, "You are impossible. And so is your whim. What will it do to your honor if I take you with me to war?"

"My honor is your honor," she said steadily. "I want to go, my lord. I won't make trouble for you."

"Your coming with me isn't trouble?" He lowered his brows. "If you come with me, it won't be as my bedmate. You'll ride in my mother's company, and you'll answer to her, and wait on her if she asks. If she bids you ride without a veil, you obey her. Do you understand?"

"Perfectly." She met his capitulation with admirable restraint. Her breath came quickly, but that might only have been discomfort. He unclamped his fingers from her shoulders. She kept her eyes level with his: one of her more interesting arts. "Is that the price, my lord? Not to see you at all?"

"You'll see me," he said. "I'm leading the march. But you ride with my mother."

She bent her head, but not her eyes. "And if you ask for me and she refuses, I am to obey her?"

"I could still leave you behind," he pointed out.

That quelled her, for the moment. She would whoop, maybe, when he was gone, and dance round the room. Or maybe not. There was Ziana still, watching and listening and saying nothing.

Haliya was the bolder, no question of it. Ziana, he suspected, was the braver. She accepted what she could not change. She had his promise, which he would keep. Her hand rose to her cheek, where he had sealed the vow.

That, when he left Kundri'j Asan, was what he would choose to remember: Ziana straight and still in the harem's heart, holding his heart in her hand.

PART FOUR

Meruvan Estarion

THIRTY-SIX

IT SHOULD HAVE FELT LESS LIKE FLIGHT; AND ESTARION SHOULD HAVE FELT LESS like an earthbear dragged out of its burrow. He was persuaded to sleep, if briefly. As he woke to a raw cold dawn, a palace in tumult, and for all he knew, armies gathering to cut him down, he reflected that maybe he had moved too soon. It was winter, the feast of the Long Night well past and the sky closed in with clouds and cold. Armies would go if he sent them, to put down the rebellion. He had no need to go with them. On a bare day's notice, none but his own outland Guard and his Olenyai were ready: tenscore of each, and the hundred of his mother's guard, pitifully small for an army, barely enough to defend him if he was beset. If he waited a hand of days, he could have ten times that number; a full cycle of Brightmoon, and ten times that would follow him, out of the imperial levies.

There were armies where he went, under lords who were his vassals. And he was not going to fight if he could help it. They said that Sarevadin alone, without her consort, could ride from end to end of the empire with a company of guardsmen, and no one would touch her or offer her harm; and everywhere she went, her people learned to love her.

He was arrogant and more than arrogant, to dream that he could do the same. He was not Sarevadin but the last and least of her descendants. And when she rode, she had left a son under guard in Kundri'j, and a consort of impeccably Asanian lineage.

The consorts he had, eight of them, and the ninth ready, no doubt, and waiting for him to ride. The son he would get, god and goddess willing, when he came back. He was not going to his death. He was going to preserve his empire. And, he admitted, here alone in the dark, to save himself.

Asanion had lost its horror. Its people were people to him now, lovers, even— maybe—friends. He could not rule in this palace as the old emperors had ruled, as prisoners of their own power. But he could rule this half of his empire.

He had gained something, then, from his sojourn in the Golden Palace. Even his magery seemed a little less blunted by the walls about him, his mind a fraction less blind.

He lay in something resembling content, counting his aches and bruises. Korusan had not been there when he came out of the harem. He had been disappointed, enough almost to snap at the Olenyas who waited to fill his shadow, simply because

231

it was not Korusan. But he had held his tongue. It was as well, he told himself as he calmed. He had much to do still, and then he should rest.

But if the boy had grown angry at the time Estarion spent with the women, if he had gone and would not come back . . .

Nonsense. Korusan had gone like a sensible man to prepare for the march and then to sleep. Estarion would find him in the ranks of the Olenyai, one pair of lion-eyes amid the simple human brown and amber and gold.

If his captain allowed it. If he was not commanded to remain in the palace.

He would come. He did as he pleased, that one. And he would please to ride with his emperor to war.

Korusan was not asleep, nor was he resting. He was facing the Master of the Olenyai yet again, for once without the mages or their Master. Master Asadi had done an unwonted thing when Korusan entered his chamber, offered him food and drink to break his night's fast. He took them, aware of what they signified. From master to brother of the second rank it was high honor. From Olenyai commander to emperor in exile, it was the seal of an alliance.

Korusan was hungry, but he ate carefully, and drank sparingly of the well-watered wine. He was aware of Asadi's eyes on him. The Master was eating as lightly as he, and with as much sense of ceremony.

Custom forbade that they speak of anything but trifles until the bowls and cups were taken away, the wine replaced with a tisane of spices and sweet herbs, hot and pungent, to warm the blood for the cold journey ahead of them. Korusan sipped gingerly but with pleasure.

At length he set down the cup. He kept his hands wrapped round it, for warmth, and looked into Asadi's bared face.

"Do you approve of what the Sunlord does?" Asadi asked him.

He nearly laughed. "I disapprove of his existence. As for this, I think that he may be wise."

"To leave his guarded palace? To walk into the net?"

"Better to walk into a trap than wither in a cage."

"You love him."

Korusan kept his face expressionless. "You can judge that?"

"I can judge my Olenyas." Asadi sighed, gazing into his emptied cup. Korusan wondered if he had magery after all; if he could scry in the dregs of his tisane. Absurd. Insulting, to look on the Master of the Olenyai as a village soothsayer. "It will come to a crux, my prince. Then you will be forced to choose."

"What choice is there?" Korusan demanded with a flash of heat. "I am not a traitor. I do not forget what I am."

"But how will you prove it, my prince?" asked Asadi. His voice was gentle. "Our allies will force you to a conclusion. I hold them off as best I may, but my strength is hardly infinite. They wish this Sunlord dead. They will kill him, or break his mind, unless you move before them."

Korusan's stomach knotted and cramped. He should have known it would do that. But he was master of it, just. "All of you have plans and purposes, plottings that you labor to bring to fruition. So too do I. Are you as great a fool as the mages are, to think me a brainless child, incapable of choosing my own times and places?"

"Hardly," said Asadi, "or we would never have yielded to you in this. And now the quarry leaves the lair. It will be more difficult for the spells to bind him while he rides under the sky."

"But also easier for death to take him," Korusan said, "where his defenses are dissipated, and any man may come at him. And he goes straight into the rebellion that the mages have fomented."

"So I argued," said Asadi, "and so I was permitted to conclude. But our allies are not well pleased."

"Let them be displeased," said Korusan, not without pleasure in the thought, "if only they grant me my will. Bid them loose their spells. We have no need of them."

"They will call it arrogance," said Asadi.

"And you?"

Asadi shrugged, one-sided. "I think that you may have more power over him than they believe, but less than you might hope. He goes where his whim moves him. Can you guide him?"

"I have no need," said Korusan. "He goes where I wish him to go."

"Into the fire, aye. And then, my prince?"

"And then," said Korusan, "we take him."

Asadi inclined his head. He did not quite believe it, Korusan could see. And if he was doubtful, the mages must be reckoning Korusan a traitor to all their cause.

Korusan lifted his chin and hardened his heart. So be it. Hate was older than love, blood stronger than the bond of flesh to flesh. He would do as he had always meant to do. Whatever it cost him.

The escort was waiting at sunrise. The emperor must be the last of them, for when he came, they would ride. Estarion did not find it difficult to drag his feet. Maybe he should wear the mail. Or the corselet. Or the full parade armor. Maybe his hair should be plaited, or knotted for the helmet, or—and at that his servants howled—cropped to the skull. Maybe he should go back to his bed and rise for morning Court, and forget that he had ever dreamed of escape.

In the end he wore mail, a glimmering gold-washed coat over supple leather, and he wore his hair in a priest's plait, with his torque for a gorget. He had a cloak for the people to wonder at if they ever looked up so high, white plainsbuck leather lined with golden fur—not lion, it was too clear a gold. Sandcat, the servant said: a lithe sharp-nosed creature the length and breadth of an Asanian's forearm, that lived in cities like a man. Estarion doubted that it went to war. Only men did that.

He pretended to break his fast. He drank the honeyed wine, picked at something that maybe had been roast plowbeast before they spiced and stewed it and wrapped it in thin unleavened bread. When it was well dismembered, he reached for the winejar to fill his cup again.

There was a hand on it before him, and eyes above that. Golden eyes.

The breath left him in a long sigh, even as Korusan said, "You grow too fond of the wine. If you will not eat, then drink this." He poured out warm thornfruit nectar, thinning it with water and a fistful of berries from a bowl.

Estarion eyed it with great mistrust, but he essayed a sip. "This is good!"

Korusan did not dignify that with an answer. He spread a napkin and began to fill it with the less fragile of the delicacies.

"What are you doing?"

"You must eat," said Korusan, "but you must ride, and the sun is rising. Will you keep your escort waiting?"

"My escort will wait as long as it must."

Korusan knotted the napkin and slipped it into his robes. Estarion wondered, brief and absurd, if the razors from the bath were still there somewhere, in a hidden fold.

The Olenyas tugged his robes into place, settled his swords in their sheaths, and said, "Your majesty is ready to ride."

His majesty was ready to upbraid him for an insolent child. He found himself, one way and another, striding through the maze of rooms. He gained followers as he went, guards, servants, people who not quite stared and not quite muttered and were, for Asanians, open in their curiosity. He hoped that he obliged them. He walked as tall as he knew how, and put on a swagger that was half despair.

Dank air struck his face. There was no sun. The sky was grey, with rain in its belly, or possibly sleet. He halted under it. If it rained—if there would be sun tomorrow—

The escort was drawn up in ranks, waiting for him. The black mass of the Olenyai, separate and haughty. The scarlet blaze of his Guard. His mother's strong women in their green livery, and she in front of them, warded in mail, armed with bow and knife and sword. Iburan was at her right hand in the plain robe he affected in Asanion, and his priests behind him. Some of them were women. One was Vanyi.

Estarion's jaw tightened. There was someone else in the empress' following, a small figure on a sand-colored mare. She had no escort that he could see. She had a mail-coat: where in the hells had she found that? The bow in its case he knew, and the arrows. He had given them to her. She had found a knife somewhere. No sword. He would have to find her one.

A groom held a mount for him. It was not Umizan: there had been no time to bring him from Induverran. Estarion paused to make this new beast's acquaintance. It was not one he knew, and not, he was pleased to observe, the golden plowbeast he had been forced to ride into Kundri'j. This was a tall striped dun with ell-long horns. Estarion smoothed the mane on the stallion's neck. It was striped like the rest of him, golden dun and glossy black. His eyes were amber, bright yet quiet. He breathed sweet breath into Estarion's palm.

Estarion mounted in a smooth long leap. The senel was steady under him. "Has he a name?" Estarion asked the groom.

The man dipped his head. "Chirai, majesty," he said.

"Chirai," said Estarion. The black-rimmed ears tilted back. Estarion gathered the reins. He could turn still, ride out of this court and into the stableyard, dismount, pull his walls about him.

Or he could urge the dun stallion toward the gate. His breath was coming in gasps. His hands were cold, even the one that burned and throbbed.

Idiocy. He was Estarion of Endros. He hated walls; he craved the open sky.

His senel settled it for him. As if he had given the command and not sat like a stone, Chirai moved softly forward. The rest fell in behind them.

The Regent of Asanion waited under the Golden Gate. There were men with him, lords of the High Court, and guards armed and armored. Estarion knew, looking at them, that they would stop him. They would offer battle; they would hold him captive until he died.

Chirai kept his steady pace. Firaz waited in silence. A spearlength from his mount's lowered horns, Estarion halted. "The emperor will pass," he said.

Firaz bowed his head. "Will the emperor reconsider?"

"The emperor must do as he will do."

Estarion barely breathed. Firaz looked full in his face, which was boldness beyond belief, had Estarion been Asanian. But he was not. He smiled a sword-edged smile.

"You are," said Firaz at last, "the emperor." It was a capitulation, and a challenge. Estarion acknowledged them both. "Guard my palace," he said.

"Fight well," said Firaz, "and return well to that place which is yours."

"So I do intend," Estarion said. He touched heel to Chirai's side.

Firaz bent his own senel aside. As Estarion passed man and mount, he said, "Take comfort, lord Regent. If I'm killed, the next emperor can only be more proper than I am. And if I live—why then, maybe I'll have learned decent manners."

"One does not learn propriety in battle," said Firaz, "my lord." He bowed lower than he ever had, down to his stallion's neck. "May your riding prosper, my lord emperor. Believe that I speak truly; that I wish you well."

"I never doubted it," said Estarion. "Believe that, too, my lord Regent."

Estarion emerged from Kundri'j Asan like a snake from its skin. Slow at first once he passed the Golden Gate and the lord who held it, with a tearing that was like pain. Then swifter, winding down the Way of Princes, rising from walk to trot to smooth rocking canter. Hoofs rang on paving stones. The silence of Asanian homage was profound and for once undaunting. The great fear was before him: the last gate; the bridge over the river, and the broad wall-less plain.

As he passed the gate and mounted the arch of the bridge, a thin rain began to fall. His cloak kept it out, but he was bareheaded, with nothing between him and the sky but a circlet of gold. He tipped his head back. He could fall, fall forever into the endless sea of cloud.

Rain kissed his face. His mount carried him with unruffled calm, down from the bridge and the river, stride by stride away from the ninefold walls. He fell out of the sky to the vastness of the plain, grey as clouds itself, and no walls, no walls as far as he could see.

His whole body shuddered. His mind shrank. It gathered all its force in its center; held, clenched in upon itself; and bloomed like a flower of fire.

He had power. He had magic—he, the maimed one, the blinded fool. He had never known truly how much he had, nor known how much of it was blunted within the walls of Kundri'j Asan. He laughed with the shock of it, half in incredulous joy, half in terror.

His escort spread behind him, Asanian, Varyani, divided as enemies must always be. But there was a yellow woman in the empress' following and an Olenyas in his own shadow, black robe amid the scarlet of his Guard.

His senel bucked lightly, startling him. He gave the stallion his head. The stallion swung from canter into gallop, and from gallop into flight.

THIRTY-SEVEN

VANYI HAD NO NEED TO ASK WHO WAS THE STRANGER IN THE EMPRESS' following. She was the only Asanian, and the only one mounted on a hornbrowed mare out of Varag Suvien. The headdress was Suvieni, too, the headcloth drawn up over the face and secured in a circlet. Vanyi knew who must have taught her that expedient.

So much, Vanyi thought, for Iburan's hope of wielding her in Estarion's defense. This chit of a child would see to that.

The first night out of Kundri'j, they stopped in Induverran. Estarion was reunited with his blue-eyed stallion: touching and unexpectedly amusing when Umizan met the senel whom Estarion had ridden from the city. The black charged upon the dun, ears flat, horns lowered, hoofs pounding. The dun stood with head up, alert but unalarmed. As Umizan surged for the kill, Chirai pirouetted neatly out of his path. When Umizan came back, raging, Chirai snorted as if in exasperation and eluded him again, and yet again. They danced the full circle of the field, until Umizan thundered to a halt, blowing and foaming, and stamped. Chirai flicked an ear, lowered his head, began coolly to graze.

Vanyi's sides ached with laughter. Even the Olenyai were amused. Estarion walked over to his sweating, seething, baffled blue-eyed brother, wrapped arms about his neck, and leaned against him till he quieted.

The rain had ended a little while since. Darts of sun broke free from the clouds, striking blue-black fire in Umizan's coat and Estarion's hair, turning Chirai's striped hide to bars of black and gold. Vanyi sneezed.

"Are you well?"

Vanyi glanced at the one who had spoken. Not so small, standing next to her: a palm's width the less, maybe, holding herself very straight in her desert tribesman's veil. She did not seem to know who Vanyi was. "Do you have a name?" Vanyi demanded of her.

She blinked at the sharpness, but she answered without hesitation. "Haliya. You?"

"Vanyi." It was not intended to be polite.

The Asanian's eyes widened. They were an improbable shade of gold, like coins. "Then you are—"

"Yes, I was his bedmate. I'd have thought you'd know."

Haliya blinked. Vanyi sensed no enmity in her, nothing but interest, and puzzlement that might be for Vanyi's rudeness. "Of course I knew," she said. "But he didn't say that you were beautiful. Your skin is like milk. Mine," she said with evident regret, "is more like well-aged cheese."

Fine ivory, Vanyi would have said, from what she could see of it. "He likes a pale-skinned woman."

"I don't think he cares," said Haliya, "as long as he finds her interesting."

There were people about, but none of them was listening. They were all watching Estarion. He mounted Umizan, bareback and bridleless, and rode him bucking and curvetting across the field.

Haliya sighed. "I broke my arm the last time I tried that."

"You didn't."

Haliya was difficult to offend. She laughed in her veil. "That's what he said, too, when I told him. But I did. I was a terrible child. Of course," she said, "when I went for that particular ride, it was my father's herd stallion, and no one ever rode him at all. I should have known what he'd do."

"I begin to see," Vanyi said slowly, and not without humor, "why he finds you interesting."

Haliya did a thing that left Vanyi speechless. She slipped her arm through Vanyi's and said, "I'm glad he brought you. I was afraid I'd be the only one."

Vanyi could not break free as easily as she might have expected. Haliya was strong, and although her eyes smiled, her grip was steely hard. "He didn't bring me," Vanyi snapped. "I came with the priests."

"I made him take me," said Haliya. "He didn't want to. He thought I should stay with the others."

"Why didn't you?"

"I wanted to ride," Haliya said. She sounded very young and very determined. "So he did mean it. He wasn't going to bring anyone for the nights. Is that a sickness, do you think? Or is it something they do in Keruvarion, to teach themselves about pain?"

Sometimes Vanyi wondered if Asanians were human at all. They did not think like anyone else she knew of, even syndics in the Nine Cities, who were surpassingly strange.

Haliya answered herself, since Vanyi was not going to. "He'll be choosing ladies in the cities, then. He didn't before, and he offended people. Now he understands what's proper."

"Don't you ever get jealous?" Vanyi demanded of her. "Can't you conceive of wanting him for yourself?"

"That's selfish," said Haliya.

"And you're a perfect saint?"

Haliya drew herself up, still holding Vanyi's arm, and said with dignity, "I do try to show a little honor."

"It's not honor where I come from," said Vanyi, "to let one's man go without a fight."

"Are you going to fight me? I'm no good with a sword, but I can shoot."

Alien. Vanyi pulled free and stood rubbing her arm. "The usual method," she said acidly, "is to exert oneself to gain the man's complete and total favor."

"So that's why he said he could only manage one at a time. He feared for his life."

Vanyi gaped at her.

Haliya patted her hand. "I suppose you can't help it. You're foreigners. You don't understand the right ways of doing things."

"I see you've met the lady of the Vinicharyas."

Vanyi paused in folding the vestments from the sunset-rite. She would have liked to pretend that she did not know whom Iburan spoke of, but there could be no such simplicities among mages. "She's very . . . original."

"I would call her interesting."

"So would his majesty." Vanyi smoothed the last white robe and laid it in the traveling-chest, and turned to face him. "Were you expecting bloodshed?"

"Asanian women don't fight over men."

"So she told me."

Iburan closed and locked the box in which they kept the vessels of the rite. His fingers traced the inlay of its lid. "She brought no maid and no attendants. That's shockingly improper for one of her station."

"Surely the empress is chaperone enough."

"The empress can't be expected to wait on her."

Vanyi did not like where this was leading. "I may be a commoner, but I am not a servant."

"You serve the god," said Iburan.

"I do that." Vanyi kept her eyes level on his face. He was not allowing her to read it, or the mind behind it.

"I have been thinking," he said, "that she's very much alone. And Estarion isn't keeping her with him."

Vanyi should not have felt that stab of vindictive pleasure. "She told me that. She seemed to think that he'd be warming his bed with a selection of provincial ladies."

"Not likely," said Iburan. "Not on this riding, when he's a clear target for any assassin who happens by. As, I'm thinking, is she. She's Asanian; she rides like a man; she's clearly been corrupted. She would be a potent object lesson, and a valuable hostage."

"He hasn't thought to set guards on her?"

"He's set his mother on guard, and the whole company of her escort."

"But?" said Vanyi. "There is a 'but,' isn't there?"

"I think," Iburan said, and he said it very calmly, "that she needs more than that. She needs someone who can ride with her, keep her company, ward her with magecraft."

"There's Shaiyel," Vanyi said. And before he could object: "Yes, he's male, but he's Asanian. Isn't he kin to the Vinicharyas?"

"Distant kin," said Iburan, "and a man."

"His wards are as strong as mine. His land-sense is better."

"He's not a woman."

"I'm not the only priestess in this army!"

Iburan let the echoes die.

"Why are you asking me?" Vanyi demanded. "Am I being set a penance?"

"Maybe," he said. "Maybe you need lessoning in humility and forgiveness, and in the virtues of priestesses. And maybe," he said, "I think that you can protect her as no one else can."

"Because I want to kill her slowly for having what I can't have?"

"She doesn't have it now, either." He sighed. For the first time she saw that he was not a young man: saw the glint of silver in his beard, the lines of weariness about his eyes. "You could leave us all. You have your Journey still. The Gates won't break or fall for want of you."

"Wherever I am," she said, "the Gates are in me. It's like the land-sense, my lord. I have the Gate-sense. I always have."

She had not told him anything that he did not know. "Will you go?"

"Of course not." Vanyi was too tired all at once to be angry. "This is my Journey. I have no other."

"Will you guard the Lady Haliya?"

Vanyi laughed without mirth. "I haven't taken her hide yet. I don't suppose I will. Hide-taking is for men. They can afford the simple pleasures."

"Young men," said Iburan. "Old ones are as vexed as women."

"Would you know?" Vanyi took his hand, startling him a little, and kissed it. "I don't know why I don't hate you, my lord."

"Hate is a simple pleasure," said Iburan.

She stared at him. Then suddenly, and this time truly, she laughed.

THIRTY-EIGHT

VANYI WAITED TILL MORNING. IT WAS NOT A FAILURE OF COURAGE. IT WAS sense. She would have one untroubled night's rest before she subjected herself to her penance.

And she did sleep. She prayed first, for humility and forgiveness, and the virtues of a priestess. The god gave her no answer, but she had not asked for one.

She was no humbler in the dawn's dimness, no more forgiving, but she had virtue enough to do as she had promised. As the escort arranged itself, Vanyi claimed her Senel and led him to stand beside the Suvieni mare. Haliya was mounted already, shivering in the chill. Her eyes were bright with excitement. She greeted Vanyi as if she were glad to see her, but to Vanyi's surprise she did not vex the air with chatter. Maybe she had a sense of Vanyi's temper, or maybe she was too full of words to decide which she wanted to burst out with first.

Estarion came out last as always. The golden mail was put away; he was in his old familiar riding clothes, with mail showing under them, and a sword at his side. He looked as if he had slept well. He was smiling, saying something that made Lord Dushai laugh, pausing to greet people: lords, servants, hangers-on. His shadow was occupied as it always was now, by an Olenyas. The same one, Vanyi saw, the one with the lion-eyes. Her nape prickled. There was something different about him—about the two of them.

Of course there was a difference. Estarion was himself again, or close enough. The trapped look was all but gone from his eyes. He moved with his old grace, laughed with his old lightness. He even smiled at his mother, although he barely inclined his head to Iburan.

Vanyi he did not see at all. She made sure of that. There was no need for him to know what duty she had taken. He greeted Haliya with more than civility, standing full in front of Vanyi, so potent a presence that she almost forgot every vow she had sworn. Haliya was dignified. She did not fling herself on him or demand that he keep her with him. She said, "This is barely proper, my lord."

He smiled. "I won't shame you, then. Am I permitted to kiss your hand?"

She sucked in a breath, outraged. "My lord!"

"Ah then." His regret seemed genuine. "Fair riding to you, my lady. Send me word if there's anything you lack."

"I have everything I need," she said.

He went away to lead the march. Haliya did not watch him go, or sigh over him. She gathered the reins and said, "You must tell me how you do that."

"What?" asked Vanyi. And after a moment: "My lady."

"I'm not your lady," Haliya said. "Was it magic?"

"You aren't supposed to know about that."

"I'm Vinicharyas. We know too much about it." Haliya nudged her mare into the line of riders.

Vanyi kicked her gelding in behind. She had thinking to do. It was not supposed to concern Estarion, or the way he had spoken to Haliya. Light. Easy. Tender—yes, he was that. But not passionate. He was not in love with her. If there was a word for a man who was happily in friendship with a woman, then he was that.

It would have been better, Vanyi thought, if he had been madly in love with her. Passion died. Friendship had a way of persisting.

It rained more often than not as they rode southward out of Induverran. Estarion took no visible notice of it. The rest of them endured, most in silence. They were riding swiftly, but not at racing speed, and not precisely as an army to war.

There were armies mustering. Estarion made himself known to them. They cheered him, albeit with bafflement, as if they could not quite understand that this was the emperor. The emperor was ten robes and a mask in the palace in Kundri'j. How could he be riding in the rain, bareheaded as often as not, and stopping to talk to commoners?

For he did that. It was something he had always done in Keruvarion, but in this half of his empire it was unheard of. His Varyani kept constant watch, but they did not try to prevent him. His Asanians looked sorely tried by it: hands twitching near weapons, eyes darting at every shadow. Vanyi heard the captain of Estarion's Guard say to the captain of the Olenyai, "Chin up, man. Do you think any of these mud-grubbers understands that that's the emperor in his own self?"

"They," said the Olenyas, "no. But others will know. And they can kill."

"Not while we're here to stop them," said the captain of the Guard.

Vanyi could admire his confidence. The land was quiet about them. Too quiet. As if it waited, or readied an ambush. Rumors told of violence, riots in the towns, people killed, a lord stripped of his escort and flogged like a slave and cast out naked upon the road. But that was west of their march, too far to ride in a day or even two. Estarion was dissuaded from turning aside. Matters were worse in the south, people said. He was needed more urgently there.

He did what he could, she granted him that. For those who rode with him, it meant sudden swift riding and then long pauses as he worked his way through a city or a town. He would have gone alone if his guards had let him. He even, more than once, climbed up on a fountain's rim or a market-table and spoke to as many as would listen. "You hear prophets giving speeches," he would say, "and prophets' disciples. Now hear what they're ranting against."

People thought him mad. Vanyi knew better than to think that he would care.

Vanyi, traveling unregarded in his train, found that she could not hate Haliya, or even despise her. Haliya was a child, an innocent, an infant in the ways of the world. And yet she knew more of men and their follies than Vanyi had learned in half again her years. It was training, she said. That was what women did. They studied their men.

She was in awe of Vanyi. She said so the first day, when Vanyi informed her that she now had an attendant. "Of course I should have one," she said, "but I can't have you."

"Why not?" Vanyi asked. "Because I'm a foreigner? A commoner? A rival?"

"You are a mage," said Haliya, with a tremor in the word. "You are the gods' voice. How can they waste you on me?"

"They think I need a lesson," said Vanyi.

Haliya would not believe her. "I should be waiting on you. Is that what you're telling me? You don't have to be delicate. It's more than proper. Since you are mage and priestess and—"

"Maybe," Vanyi said, "we can wait on each other."

Haliya stopped short. She looked shocked, then she laughed. "That's outrageous."

"So is his majesty."

"There is that," said Haliya, as if it settled things.

She was not one to show awe in stumbling and in awkwardness. She did it gracefully. She let herself be looked after, but she did her share in turn. She kept quiet when she thought that Vanyi wanted it. Vanyi did want it, to pray or simply to think, but Haliya seemed to think that she was working magic. She never asked to see any. That would be improper, her manner said.

They had to share a bed most nights, when they were crowded into a lord's small house. If the house was large enough they shared a room: more of that endless Asanian propriety. Vanyi half expected to be offered more than a warm presence when the nights were cold. That was a way of the harems, or so she had heard. But either the tales were false or Haliya did not presume so far. She was a tidy sleeper, and quiet. At first she woke when Vanyi rose to sing the sunrise-rite, but after a day or two she merely stirred and muttered and went back to sleep, or feigned it.

She was always up and dressed when Vanyi came back from her hour among the priests. If she broke her fast she did it then, while Vanyi was away. Vanyi did not ask. She nursemaided the child the rest of the day, and the night too. Surely Haliya could be trusted to fend for herself in the morning. She was in exuberant health by all accounts, ate voraciously at the nooning and at evening, and slept as healthy children sleep, deeply and long.

What first made Vanyi suspicious, she did not know. A hint of greenness about Haliya's cheeks, one rain-sodden morning. A servant coming late to clear away the remains of her breakfast, of which she had touched nothing, not even the sweet-berry pastries of which she was so fond. When Vanyi came in unexpectedly early— and maybe she did it by design, and maybe she did not—she was not at all surprised to find Haliya retching into a basin.

Haliya looked as guilty as a woman could look, and as defiant. She said, "I had too much wine last night. I should have known better."

Vanyi would dearly have loved to believe her. But there was no hiding the cause of her illness. Not from a mage.

Iburan must have known or guessed. Vanyi spared a moment to damn him, silently, to the deepest of the twenty-seven hells. Of all the guards he could have chosen for this duty, for all the reasons he could have chosen her, she was the least fit, and this the most unforgivable.

"You're pregnant," she said. "How long?"

Haliya raised her head. She looked dreadful; she was actually green. Vanyi had no pity to spare for her. She swallowed painfully, and grimaced. "I think six cycles," she said. "Maybe seven."

"You knew when you left Kundri'j."

Vanyi's voice was absolutely flat. Haliya shied at it, but nothing could stop her tongue from running on. "I wasn't sure. I've missed courses before. They came on early, you see, but they never have been regular about it."

"You knew," said Vanyi. She was being unreasonable, she knew it. She did not care. "Does he?"

Haliya went even greener. "Oh, no! Don't tell him. Please. He'll send me back."

"And so he should." Vanyi throttled an urge to seize her and shake her. It was not mercy. She knew that if she did it, it would empty the rest of the little idiot's stomach. "I lost a baby on the ride to Kundri'j. Do you think he'll take even a moment's chance of losing this one?"

"They say that wasn't the riding. It was the magic on you. The priestess-thing. The bond."

True; and bitter beyond bearing. "What did you think you could do? Lie? Hide it till the baby was born?"

Haliya was recovering in spite of everything. She straightened; the color crept back into her cheeks. "I wasn't going to lie. I was going to tell him when we got back to Kundri'j, or when we came to Ansavaar."

"And I wouldn't have guessed?"

"You won't tell him, will you? It would be a dreadful nuisance to send me back now. You'd have to go, to keep me safe, and we'd have to be so careful. If anyone found out that I was his lady, and that I was bearing his son—"

"What makes you think it's a son?"

"It has to be," said Haliya. "You see why I have to stay, and why we can't tell him. He'd want me to go back, you see. And I'd be dead or taken before I got there."

And good riddance, Vanyi thought. But there was more of her awake now than shock and petty malice. It was not Haliya's fault that she had done what Vanyi failed to do. She had conceived, probably, the first night Estarion lay with her. The night Vanyi drove him away.

Vanyi had brought this on herself. She was learning, a little. She could see what her folly had won her.

Haliya could not even be smug, so that Vanyi could hate her. "I know I should have stayed in the palace. But I couldn't bear to stay, and to know that he was gone, and maybe that he'd die. He could. They hate him out here. He travels like the sun, in a mantle of light, but that only makes it darker where his light doesn't fall."

Vanyi was not in a mood to listen to poetry, however prettily conceived. "You had better pray," she said, "that he doesn't take it into his head to keep you warm of nights. Men are only blind when we most want them to see. He'll know in an instant."

"That won't happen," said Haliya.

"You hope it won't. Hoping isn't happening."

"It won't," Haliya said. She peered into Vanyi's face. She was a little short-sighted, Vanyi suspected. It gave her an all too charming air of preoccupation. "You really don't know," she said. She sounded incredulous and yet resigned, as if to the foibles of foreigners.

"What should I know?" Vanyi demanded.

But Haliya was choosing to be maddeningly Asanian. "He was well taken care of, that night before we left. Too well, I thought. That's art to the high art, but there shouldn't be blood in it. He had hardly anything left for us."

"Who is she?" Vanyi asked. She was proud that she was calm, that she was thinking clearly, not screaming at the walls. "Someone else in the harem?"

"It's not a she."

Vanyi blinked. "Of course it's a she. He doesn't incline toward men. Even that lordling from Umbros, back in Keruvarion—beautiful as a girl, everyone was sighing over him, and he had nothing in his pretty head but wailing love-songs under Estarion's window—he got a smile and a word and a summons home, and that was that. Why would it be a man? How could he be . . ." She stopped. "Blood, you said? He drew *blood?*"

"Not much," said Haliya with that damnable Asanian aplomb. "More like a brawl in a pride of lions. It sounded like that, people said. Lots of scratches. Bruises in interesting places. They thought it was murder, but it was only the two of them."

Vanyi had thought herself beyond shock. This she had never expected, never foreseen, never prepared for. "How could I not know?"

She was not aware that she spoke aloud until she had done it. Haliya was kind. "It was a surprise, wasn't it? I'd have sworn he wouldn't, either. But you can tell, the way they stand together."

"*Who?*"

"The blackrobe," said Haliya. "The Olenyas. Or didn't you notice him? I think he's young under the veils. And beautiful. Those eyes go with beauty more often than not. I expect he's fascinating, too."

Vanyi's knees gave away; she sat down. She had seen. She had refused to see. The shadow in the emperor's shadow. The bond that no mage could mistake, unless she willed it. They were lovers. Not two who kept one another warm of nights; not friends who happened to be lord and concubine. Lovers.

"There," Haliya said. "Don't faint. He won't take harm. Olenyai are sworn to defend their lord to the death. It was that one who saved his life, the night the assassin came, though it was too late for the squire from Keruvarion; so there's life-debt in it, too. That's strong bonding, and strong protection."

"Pray," said Vanyi. "Pray to any gods you worship, that you speak the truth."

Haliya did not understand. She thought it jealousy, which was nothing an Asanian woman would admit to. And yes, Vanyi conceded, it was that; but only the shell of it. The core was cold fear.

She watched, now that she knew. She saw how it was. It was not the bright shining thing she had shared with Estarion and slain by her own fault, because she was both wise and a fool. This was a meeting like matched blades. They had been open with it, she and her emperor. The Olenyas had nothing open in him. He was all shadows and secrecy. But he was there, unfailing, fixed on Estarion as a cat fixes on its prey.

When she lost the child she had not known she was bearing, she had thought she knew what it was to be emptied. But Estarion still loved her; she was sure of it, and secure in it, even in casting it away. When he went to his harem, she had been jealous, bitterly so, but even then she knew that he would have preferred to go to her. Haliya bore his child, did the one thing that Vanyi wanted most to do, and now never would; but Haliya was not Vanyi, not his first woman and his first love.

The Olenyas was a new thing, a terrible thing. Vanyi was not afraid of any woman in Estarion's harem. She feared the Olenyas. She told herself that she was starting at shadows, dreading a harmless man because she could not see his face or touch his mind. What danger could he be? He was oathbound to protect Estarion. He could not bear a child or share the throne, or claim any part of the woman's portion. And while he preoccupied Estarion, no new woman could come to claim the emperor's heart. Vanyi should be glad of him.

Estarion did not look like a man enslaved by a devil. He was bone-thin, who had never had flesh to spare, but he was thriving. This riding suited him, this edge of uncertainty, even the wet and the deepening cold, till of a morning they woke to a world of glass, rain that had frozen into ice, and no riding anywhere until the sun had warmed the road. He passed the time in walking about the place in which they had passed the night, a town called Kitaz, ignoring his wall of guards, wandering into a wineshop and a leatherworker's and a jeweler's.

Vanyi wondered if he could sense the powerful discomfort of those he spoke to, unless they could convince themselves that he was not the emperor. Asanians did not want their royalty among them. It belonged in palaces, out of sight and, except for wars and taxes, the common mind. Royalty in their own muddy streets, haggling over a trinket, drinking their thin sour wine and thinner, sourer beer, was so far out of the way of the world as to be incomprehensible.

He had his shadow, always. They did not touch one another or exchange glances. They had no need.

She caught herself peering for marks of the lion-brawling Haliya had spoken of. Of course there would be none to see when he was in leather and mail, but he did not walk as if he were in pain. Servants, who knew everything, said nothing of uproars in the royal rooms. That his majesty did not sleep alone, they accepted as natural and proper. Like Haliya they approved of his choice of bedmate, although they wondered if the Olenyas kept his veils even then. None was quite bold enough to settle the wager. The tales were terrible of what befell a man who looked on a blackrobe's face.

She felt like a spy, or like a jealous wife. There was no one she could talk to. No man, certainly, even Iburan. This was not a man's trouble. Haliya did not understand. The empress . . .

Maybe. But not until Vanyi had more to tell of than vague fears and shameful jealousies.

On the morning of the ice, she walked in Kitaz herself. She had no intention of dogging Estarion's steps, but she found herself in his wake as often as not. It was a small town for Asanion, one broad street with a fountain in the middle, a tangle of lanes and alleys, a pair of temples and a market and the lord's house on the hill. His lordship was absent. Doing his duty in the Middle Court, his steward said. Hiding, Vanyi suspected, and hoping that the disturbance would go away.

When the royal progress came to the market, she worked her way ahead of it. The jeweler's shop attracted her with its glitter; she braved the jeweler's scowl to admire his work, which was very fine for the provinces. He could hardly order her out, priestess that she was, and she conceded a little to his modesty by wrapping her scarf about her face.

As she lingered and yearned over his treasures, contemplating her thin purse and her thinner excuse for needing anything so frivolous, the shop filled with light.

It was Estarion, that was all, bringing the sun in with him, and trapping her as neatly as if she had planned it. Which she most emphatically had not. He was not aware of her, not at first. He had turned to grin at someone outside, as at a victory. "See," he said. "No assassins."

His guards must have tried to enter in front of him. He always loved to thwart them. It was a game of his, that he had forgotten in Kundri'j but now remembered.

She did something to make him turn. Breathed. Twitched. Let fall the trinket in her hand. He came round like a cat, uncannily quick. The light that came to his face made her gasp. Not now, she thought in desperation. Not still.

Then his face went cold. And that, which she had wished for, was worse. Much worse. "Lady," he said.

"Majesty." She eyed the path to the door. He stood full in it. She never thought him uncommonly tall, not beside Iburan and his northern guardsmen, but he towered in this place, his head brushing the roofbeam. The door was barely wider than his shoulders. They had broadened since he rode out of Endros.

He was not as much the boy now as he had been. His face was leaner, its lines more distinct. He would never be pretty, nor would anyone call him handsome, but his beauty was coming clearer, the fierce beauty of the hawk or the panther.

She looked at him in something close to despair. She would never stop loving him. There was no use in trying.

At least she had not thrown herself into his arms. She wanted to, desperately. But it was the body's wanting. The mind knew that that was over.

Was it?

She spoke to silence the voice in her head, said the first thing that came to her. "Are you going to buy something for Haliya?"

"For her sister," he said. There was a slight but perceptible pause before he said it.

"I think," said Vanyi, "that this might do." She lifted what she had dropped. It was not the most elaborate trinket in the lot, but it was the most interesting. It was a pendant for the neck or the brow, plain bright silver like wings of flame, set with a jewel like silk turned to stone: bands of gold and amber and bronze that shimmered as the jewel turned.

Estarion moved closer. She almost fled, but there was nowhere to go. He did not touch her as he took the jewel from her fingers. "It's exactly the color of her hair," he said.

"I thought it might be."

He slanted his eyes at her. They were as bright as the jewel, but less changeable. "They tell me you're keeping Haliya company."

"Iburan ordered it," Vanyi said. If she sounded ungracious, then so be it.

He went a shade colder at the name, or maybe at Vanyi's words. "I'm glad she's well protected."

"You're not afraid I'll murder her in her sleep?"

"You wouldn't do that," he said, and he sounded like himself again. "I'll free you from her if you like. My lord high priest should have known better than to burden you so."

"It was to be a penance," said Vanyi. "It is still, most ways. But I don't want to be free of it."

"Even if I say you may?"

"You're not my high priest," she said.

He did not like that: his lips tightened as they always did when he reined in his temper. "But she is my . . . concubine." He choked on it. She was rather nastily glad. She would atone for that, but first she would enjoy it.

"Do you think I'll corrupt her?" Vanyi inquired.

"I think it must be agony for you to look at her."

"She's quite pleasant to look at. And you," Vanyi said, "have a high opinion of yourself."

She almost wished that he would hit her. He wanted to: she could see it. But he laughed. "I do, I confess it. I don't expect you to pardon me: I'm hopelessly unpardonable. But can you think of me, a little, with priestly charity?"

"How do you think of me?"

"You know," he said.

"No," said Vanyi. "I don't know anything. I thought I knew you once, when we were young together. But that was long ago. Maybe I never knew you at all."

"We're not fighting," he said as if to himself. "It's a beginning, I suppose."

"Or an ending."

"No," said Estarion, as if his royal will could make it true.

Vanyi looked up at him. He was so close that she had to tilt her head. She could have touched him, laid her hand over the beating heart, traced the line of his cheek. She could say the word and he would come to her hand. She had the power. It was as strong as magic, as certain as the laws that bound the worlds.

A shadow shifted behind him. Eyes fixed on her, lion-gold in faceless mask. They were not angry, nor did they hate. They laughed at her. They knew her as Estarion never would, nor ever could. All her sins and petty failings, her pride, her vanity, her penchant for stepping beyond her proper bounds.

Estarion shifted. He was not with her any longer, although he stood as close as ever. He was in the shadow's shadow.

The power was gone. The Olenyas held it, swallowed it.

Vanyi let him. Cowardice, wisdom, she did not care what anyone called it. A child who had never been born, a child who must be born, both bound her and held her helpless.

The Olenyas did not know that. She would have wagered gold on it. Nor was she about to tell him. He had his emperor. She had more. She had the emperor's heir, and the mother of the heir, safe in her charge. She had the empire that would be.

THIRTY-NINE

WHEN THE ICE HAD MELTED FROM THE ROAD AND THE SUN SHONE DOWN almost warm, Estarion led his escort southward again. He was numb still, mind and power, but the land-sense had little to do with the arts of mages. He felt the earth as if it were his body. Great aches and bruises, knots and tangles of dissension, a pain like sickness that spread outward from no common center. What he rode to was not the worst of it, but it made a beginning.

He was waking as if from sleep or from a long illness. The sun and the sudden warmth, in what should have been black winter, speeded a healing that had begun when he left the Golden Palace. He caught himself singing as he rode up a long slope. The scouts who ranged ahead were out of sight. His escort spread behind.

He glanced over his shoulder. Those whose faces he could see, flashed smiles. He smiled back. His Varyani were as glad as he to be out of Kundri'j.

"I'll have to do something about that," he said to Korusan, who rode at Umizan's flank. The Olenyas was mounted on Chirai. Umizan would not permit his lord another mount, and it had seemed a waste of good senelflesh to leave the dun behind. So Korusan had charge of him, and not unwillingly, either, as far as Estarion could see.

Estarion hooked a knee over the pommel of his saddle, riding at his ease. "I can't live in horror of my own palace. What's to be done, do you think? Pull down the Golden Palace? Build a new capital?"

"First you need a solid empire for it to be capital of," said Korusan.

"Granted," said Estarion, "and a solid self to rule it. Sometimes I despair of that."

"A rather cheerful despair," Korusan observed.

Estarion unhooked his knee and swung down his leg and touched Umizan into a gallop, all in one swift reckless movement. Umizan reached the crest of the hill in three long strides, and plunged into a deep bowl of a valley.

No scouts, no token of alarm. Safe, then. Estarion let the stallion run as he would. The road was steep but smooth. A town huddled at the valley's end where it opened into sky, but the land between was cropland, fallow with winter. No one passed there. People kept to their walls and traveled as little as they might, between winter and the rumor of war.

He was well ahead of his escort. A glance back showed them on the crest, spreading out as if to scan the valley. Then they poured down into it.

Umizan slowed to a hand gallop, tossing his horns. Estarion laughed into the wind. It had a bite to it. Rain again by morning, his bones judged, or even snow.

What at first he had taken for a cairn or a shrine set up by the road, stirred as he approached it. Umizan shied and skittered sidewise. Estarion clutched mane, clamped knees to the stallion's sides. Umizan wheeled, snorting, horns lowered.

Estarion glared down the lance-length of them. Bright black eyes glared back. "That took you long enough," said a voice he had thought never to hear again.

"Sidani?" Estarion slid from the saddle. The stallion stamped, still in a temper: and well he should be, fool that he had made of himself. "Sidani," Estarion said. He felt the grin break out. "Where in the hells have you been?"

"Ansavaar," she said. She nudged the stone at her feet. It shifted, yawned, opened eyes that gleamed green.

"Ulyai!" Her snarl and slash drove him back. He gasped, shocked. It was Ulyai—he could not mistake her. "Ulyai. Have you forgotten me?"

"Hardly," Sidani said. She pointed with her chin. Ulyai's back rippled. Three pairs of eyes appeared above it, two green-blue, one blue-gold. Three pairs of ears pricked. One by one the cubs tumbled over their mother's flank and rolled to the ground. Her foreleg caught and pinned two. The third, the one whose eyes would be gold when they were done changing, eluded its mother's grasp and leaped upon Estarion's foot, attacking it without mercy.

He swept the little beast up, wary of claws and infant fangs, and met snarl with snarl. The cub's jaws snapped shut. It stared wide-eyed.

It was darker than the others, almost black. "Yes, I look like you," Estarion said to it. Him. It was a he-cub. He let Estarion ease him into the crook of his arm. In return Estarion let him gnaw gently on his thumb. The cub began to purr.

"I expect you can explain this," Estarion said after a while.

"I expect I can." Sidani shouldered one of the two she-cubs and lifted the other onto her mother's back. She looked much the same as ever. Thinner, maybe, but then so was Estarion. He saw no sign of the sickness that had beset her in Induverran.

Estarion looked over his shoulder. His escort had come up at last. He called out to them. "Look! See who's been waiting for us."

His Varyani were far from displeased, but his Asanians did not know what to make of it. He laughed at them. "Here's a friend I've been missing. Guard her well, guardsmen. She's as kin to me."

Fine kin, Korusan thought, eyeing the wanderer woman as she chose one of the remounts—a cross-grained, slab-sided gelding that seemed to know her, for he lunged with teeth bared, and then stopped, skidding, and all but fell over on his rump. She grasped him by the horns and shook him; he let his brow rest briefly against her breast. She swung abruptly into the saddle, taking no notice of the reins, and wheeled the beast about.

She had Estarion's reckless temper, that was certain, and his fondness for monstrous cats. All through her juggler's tricks, the ul-cub kept her place about Sidani's shoulders. Estarion had another as dark and gold as he was, and the dam played mount to a third, pressing up against the black stallion's shoulder. The Varyani mounts snorted and sweated but endured; likewise the Lady Haliya's mare and Korusan's dun. The rest of the Olenyai were not so fortunate. Those who were not forcibly dismounted were run away with, or fought a pitched battle of man against maddened senel.

The woman surveyed the carnage with an ironic eye. It paused on Korusan, went briefly strange; then passed on. She sent her gelding forward with a touch of the heel, caught Estarion's glance, drew him after her. They divided in a long circle, seeming slow but in truth very swift, herding together the scattered seneldi.

Korusan followed slowly. Chirai was uneasy but willing, snorting and brandishing horns as he passed the ul-queen. She sat to watch the spectacle, and ignored him with queenly disdain. Korusan endeavored to return the courtesy. He had heard of the palace cats of Keruvarion; who had not? But their living presence was unnerving.

All his brothers' mounts were caught, and all of his brothers who had been borne away. It was bitter to be so humiliated before their rivals from Keruvarion. They bore it well, sitting straight and stiff on their shuddering seneldi. The emperor faced them. He seemed to be searching for words to salve their pride.

The wanderer rode her borrowed gelding down the line of them, with the cub draped purring over her shoulders. "There now," she said, her own voice like a purr, both rough and sweet. "It's only ul-cats. They won't eat you. Not while you serve your emperor."

Cleverly put. It gave the Olenyai time and grace to set themselves in order, but it warned them also, and showed them on which side they might find this stranger. They took the road again with the wanderer riding beside Estarion, talking a great deal of nothing, to the emperor's evident pleasure. The two of them had met, it seemed, over an escapade of his, and parted over one of hers. Where she had been since, or how she had come upon Estarion's own ul-cat and delivered the beast of cubs, she was not telling. She was very skilled at that. Almost, Korusan thought, as if she were Asanian.

The town at the valley's mouth would not let them in. It was no indication of disrespect, its lordling said. There had been sickness; it might be plague. He invited the emperor's escort to pitch camp in his fields and offered a penful of skinny woolbeasts for their dinner, but more than that he would not do.

He was lying. Estarion could not be such a fool that he failed to know it, but he refused to storm the walls. "They're not in open rebellion," he said, "and I'd rather camp under the sky than sleep under another roof."

It could have been worse thought of, Korusan admitted. Their camping place was broad, level, and easily defended. They had tents, there was wood and dung for their fires, and the woolbeasts were not too stringy once the cooks had done with them.

Estarion did not fulfill Korusan's greatest apprehension, that he would take his ul-cats to bed with him. The cub was too young to leave his mother for long, and she was content to idle by the fire with the wanderer for a companion. The emperor's tent was blessedly empty of animals.

The emperor's desire tonight was hot but brief; he fell almost at once into sleep. Korusan propped himself on an elbow, warm in the other's warmth, and considered the sleeping face. It had become a part of him. He knew no other way to think of it.

He laid his palm against Estarion's cheek. Estarion did not stir. He curved his fingers into claws, raked them softly through the curling silk of the beard, down the smooth line of neck and shoulder, round to the breast. Over the heart they closed into a fist.

"If the world were empty of you," Korusan said, "I should not wish to be in it." His mouth twisted. "I meant to snare you. I snared myself."

Oh, most certainly he had. He did not know when it had struck him. Perhaps that first morning, when he woke alone, and knew himself empty without Estarion's presence. Perhaps even before that—perhaps from the moment he saw this outland emperor, this upstart, this rival, this enemy he was sworn to destroy.

Estarion did not love him as he loved Estarion. Estarion's heart burned like the sun. Worlds basked in it, and it had warmth to spare for them all. Korusan's was a fiercer, frailer, narrower thing, a spark in the night. It had room for one love, and one great hate. Both of them the same. Both fixed here, in this heart under his hand, in this beloved enemy who slept oblivious, like a child or a blessed saint.

Korusan rose slowly. Estarion did not move. His branded hand lay half across him, glinting gold in the light of the lamp. Korusan turned his face away from it.

Robed, veiled, hidden in shadow, Korusan slipped from the tent. The fire had died down. The camp slept but for the sentries and, rising from beside the embers, the woman Sidani. Brightmoon was high amid swift-running clouds; Greatmoon hung low in the east, the color of blood. The twofold light struck frost and fire in her hair, now white as the bright moon, now red as copper. Her eyes gleamed on him. Her voice came soft, blurred as if with sleep. "Hirel?"

Korusan stopped. He had misheard. She had not given him that name.

She drew closer. They were nearly of a height. "Hirel? Hirel Uverias?"

"He is dead."

The words came flat and hard. She laughed. Moon-touched, he thought. "You promised me. If there was a way, you would come back. I never knew you'd come in the same body."

And how in the hells had she known whose face he bore? He felt stripped naked, he in his robes and his swords and his veils.

"Madam," he said with control that he had learned through hard lessoning, "you are mistaken. I am Olenyas; no more, if no less. The last of the Golden Emperors is dead."

"No Olenyas ever born could claim those eyes." She was close enough now that he felt the heat of her body, breathed the startling sweetness of her breath. She must have been beautiful in youth, a beauty to break the heart. It was in her still, here under the moons. She raised a hand. He shied, but she was too quick. The air was cold on his bared cheeks.

His hands leaped to his swords, but he did not draw them. Her eyes held him fast. Great eyes, dark eyes, eyes to drown in.

"I always forget," she said, "how beautiful you are."

"You must die," he said, gasping it. "You see my face."

She laughed. "I am dead, child. Years dead. Here," she said. "Look." She held up her hand.

Gold, gold turned to ash and grey scars; but there was no mistaking the shape of it. He had kissed its image just this evening, held its burning brightness to his cheek till he could bear it no longer: and Estarion smiling, not knowing that Korusan's trembling was pain—willing, joyful, fire-bright pain. They branded their emperors in Keruvarion, branded and ensorceled them; or the god did it, if one believed in gods.

"I tried to cut it out," said the madwoman, soft and deceptively calm. "I took the sharpest knife I had. I heated it in fire and began to cut. It was no worse than the burning I was born with. But the god was having none of it. The gold goes all the way to the bone, did you know? and wraps about it. And when I thought to cut off the hand, it was the knife that went instead, flared up and went molten and poured away. Thus the scars. The cuts healed clean, but molten steel is a match for any god. It took away the fire, and that I was glad of; but now it burns like ice."

"Gods," said Korusan. "You—are—"

"Sarevadin." She smiled. Yes: he saw it now. Estarion favored her, and in more than face. "You always were slow to know me."

"I am not Hirel!" Korusan snapped. "I am Koru-Asan of the Olenyai, and you are stark mad."

"Of course I am. All the dead are."

He gripped her shoulders. They were bone-thin, fire-warm, and very much alive. "You are no more dead than I."

"Exactly." She closed long fingers about his wrists, not to resist, simply as if it were her whim to know the swift pulse of blood beneath the skin. "Whose get are you? Jania's?"

His teeth clicked together.

"I never did approve of that expedient," she said. "Fifty brothers were a great inconvenience, but it was hardly kind to keep them locked in prison their lives long, and no sons to carry on after they were dead. Did any outlive me, do you know?"

"The last took his life before the fourth Sunlord died," said Korusan. He was falling into her madness, hearing her as if it were nothing to him but a tale.

"Ah," she said. "He lived long, for an Asanian. But Jania—I won the field there. We married her to a man in the far west of the empire. He was a good man, I made sure of that; he cherished her."

"She hated you," said Korusan.

"She did not," said Sarevadin. But then, slowly: "Maybe she did. She had hopes of me before I changed, and after, when I was as you see me, I let her brother send her away. She had the spirit that covets empires. Pity she wasn't born a man, and that she had so many brothers."

"Had she been a man, Asanion would never have fallen."

"Oh," said the old one, the empress who had been, who should have been dead, "it would have fallen, cubling, in blood and fire."

"So may it yet."

"In the end, yes. All things end. But not in this generation. He's a charming child, isn't he? He looks like my father."

"He looks like you."

"So he does, though I was prettier, even when I walked in man's shape. The god meant me for a woman, I think, but changed his mind. For a while." She brushed Korusan's cheek with her unbranded hand. The touch was like bone sheathed in raw silk. "Do you love him, youngling?"

Korusan wrenched away. The terror of it was not that she was dead and yet she lived. It was not even that she was the enemy, the one whom he had been born to hate—more even than Estarion. It was that he felt the power of her, the same power that was in her grandson's grandson. To dwell in his blood. To make herself a part of him.

Korusan was not her consort, not that great lord and traitor. Hirel Uverias was dead. Korusan might wear his face, and bitter penance that was, but he was no one but himself.

"You can't deny the blood," said Sarevadin.

He whirled away from her, back into the tent and the dimness and the blessed quiet. He shuddered with cold that pierced to the bone. So it was, fools and children said, when one spoke with the dead.

He lay again beside Estarion, pressed body to fire-warm body. Estarion half woke, smiled, gathered him in. He struggled not to cling. Estarion was asleep again already, his arms a wall against the dark.

FORTY

IT SNOWED BY MORNING, BUT LIGHTLY, DRIFTING FROM A LEADEN SKY. ESTARION had them all up and riding by full light. A great restlessness was on him. It made Vanyi's skin twitch.

The heat of him made nothing of cold or snow. He was everywhere, it seemed, with and without his yellow-eyed shadow: now in the lead with Sidani, now riding back to speak with one or another of his escort, now bringing up the rear.

Haliya had been avoiding him with remarkable subtlety, managing always to be where he was not. Not that it was difficult. She needed but to stay close by Iburan, and make herself small when Estarion rode past.

But on this raw grey morning, Iburan's mare came up lame. He fell back to the rear and the remounts, calling to the others to go on, he would follow. Vanyi would have stayed to guard him—and in great relief to be freed from her other and more onerous duty. But he sent her away. He had Shaiyel and Oromin and a pair of the empress' warrior women, and he would tend his mare before he sought out another that would carry his bulk. He did not need Vanyi. Haliya, the leveling of his brows reminded her, did.

Haliya took what refuge she could among the empress' women. She was the only Asanian among them, and the smallest but for Vanyi. As Estarion roved rearward for the dozenth time, he checked Umizan's stride and swung in beside her.

Vanyi roused with a start to find her mare sidling toward Umizan with clear and present intent: ears flat, neck arched in the way mares had when they came into heat. Umizan would have been more than senel if he had been oblivious.

Estarion did not even see the mare or the woman who rode her. His eyes were on Haliya. Haliya looked as serene as an Asanian woman could in her veils and her modesty, but Vanyi caught the trapped-beast dart of her glance.

Vanyi let slip a finger's width of rein. It was enough for the mare. She slashed at Umizan's shoulder. He veered, snorting and tossing his horns. Estarion cursed; and met Vanyi's eyes.

She would have wagered gold that, had he been as fair as she, he would have blushed scarlet. "Good morning, sire," she said.

Haliya's gratitude was an intense annoyance. He was blind to it. They were on either side of him now, hemming him in.

Vanyi was not going to make it easy for him, or for his lady, either. She called her mare to order. It took time, and sufficient attention to keep her eyes from fixing on his face as they were sorely tempted to do.

She was aware even so that he looked from one of them to the other, and did battle with training against transparent cowardice. "My ladies," he said at length, stiffly. "Are you well?"

"Very well," said Haliya with perfect steadiness. "And you?"

It went on so, an exquisite dance of Asanian courtesies. Vanyi would not have believed Estarion capable of it.

Unless, she thought, he suspected something. He would not get it out of Vanyi, and Haliya was bred to keep secrets. In the end, and none too soon, he went back to the lead and the woman whose mysteries were nothing to do with him.

Haliya breathed a long sigh and let herself slump briefly against her senel's neck. "Oh, gods," she said, "I was so afraid he'd want me tonight."

"Not likely," said Vanyi. "Not with me here, watching him think about it."

Haliya did not understand, but she knew enough of Vanyi now to believe what she said of Estarion. Haliya's hand crept to her middle. It often did that of late. Vanyi was not finding it easier, the longer it went on. This should have been her child, her secret, her fear of being sent back to chains and safety.

Grimly she reined herself in. She had brought this pain on herself. She would bear it as she must, with a priestess' fortitude.

Simple to say. Unbearably difficult to do.

Korusan was wretchedly ill. It was the cold and the snow, and the fever that would not go down for any will he laid on it. He had managed to conceal his weakness from Estarion: rising before the emperor, pulling on his garments and his weapons, mastering himself enough to mount and ride. Estarion might have questioned him, but he took refuge in silence. When Estarion rode back to speak with his ladies, Korusan did not follow. Chirai's gaits were soft, his responses light. Folly to expect that a beast would understand a man's troubles, but the stallion seemed to be moving more carefully, smoothing his paces to spare Korusan's pain.

For there was pain. It was deep, in the bones, and it gripped with blood-red claws. He did not allow himself to be afraid. When the pain set deep, the mages had told him, there would be nothing that they could do. They had kept him alive his life long, nursed him through all his sicknesses, warded him with their magics and mounted guard on his bones. Now their protections were failing. He could feel them unraveling, fraying like silk in a cord.

He should have been dead in infancy like his brothers, or feeble of mind and body as his sisters had been. He was the last of his blood, the last child of the Lion. And he was dying.

But not now. Not, fate willing, too soon to do what he must do.

He was aware always of the madwoman's eyes on him. Sarevadin. He would have dismissed it as a folly of night and madness and newborn fever, but in the cold snow-light he knew that it was true. She even moved like Estarion, sat her mount as he did, with light long-limbed grace, held her head at that unmistakable, arrogant angle. How anyone could fail to see, he did not know. It was as clear as lightning in the dark.

She was dead, and he was close enough. It was said that the dead knew one another, even when they walked among the living. She tilted a smile at him, sweet and wild.

It widened for Estarion as he rode back from the excruciation of two ladies in one orbit. He returned it with ease that knew only innocence. Blind, blessed fool, not to know his own dead kin.

Estarion could not keep still. People noticed it, he saw how their eyes rolled on him, and how they looked at one another and sighed. He tried to keep down the pace, for the seneldi's sake if not for the riders', but Umizan was willing, and he was possessed of a bone-deep urgency.

The land pulled him southward, and stronger the farther he rode. The canker that was in Ansavaar was distinct and persistent, but there was another, closer, and it rankled deeper as the day went on.

When they halted to rest in a wood protected from wind and blowing snow, Estarion called in the chief of the scouts. The man was Olenyas, shadow-silent and shadow-quick. It vexed his Asanian propriety sorely to see his emperor go down on one knee in unmarked snow, but Estarion was in no mood to care for outland decencies. He smoothed the snow with his hand and took up a stick, and drew the shape of the land as his land-sense knew it. He marked the ache that was in Ansavaar, and the closer, stronger one that was on the road he followed, and looked up into the amber eyes. "What is this?" he asked, thrusting his stick into the latter marking.

The Olenyas would never show surprise, but he paused before he spoke. "You do not know, sire?"

Estarion bared his teeth. "If I did, would I ask?"

"That is a map, majesty," the Olenyas said. "Or so it seems."

"Indeed," said Estarion. "And this?"

"A city, sire. A day's ride from here, perhaps more in the snow. Pri'nai."

Estarion regarded the stick propped upright in the snow. "Yes," he said slowly.

"Yes, that is what they call it. Pri'nai." He rose. "Can we get there by evening?"

The Olenyas seemed to have decided that all foreigners were mad, and Sunlords maddest of all. "We would be hard pressed to do it. And we would leave some behind. Your priest—his mount—"

Iburan could fend for himself. But Estarion was not entirely lost to sense. "No, we'd best not try to get there in the dark. And it will be dark early tonight. We'll camp as late as we can, and ride before sunup. We'll be in the city by midmorning."

"Unless the snow worsens," the Olenyas said. "Sire."

"It won't." Estarion swept his foot across the map, obliterating it. "It will clear by morning. We'll have the sun with us when we reach the gates. Then," he said, "we shall see what waits for us in Pri'nai."

FORTY-ONE

THE SNOW ENDED IN THE MIDDLE NIGHT, THE CLOUDS SCATTERED BEFORE A sudden wind. By dawn when Estarion was up and pacing, waiting for the rest to rouse, it was bitter cold, the stars like frost in the paling sky.

The sunrise was brilliant but empty of warmth. It found them on the road, hoofbeats muffled by the carpet of snow. Estarion was barely aware of them. He knew that Korusan was near him, that Sidani was beside him. He sensed the coming of another like a shiver on the skin: Iburan on a tall Ianyn stallion, towering over Umizan. Estarion would not glance at him. Even when he said, "There's trouble ahead."

"The whole west is trouble," said Sidani.

"Granted," Iburan said equably, "but there's worse here."

"We're riding under arms," Estarion said, "and in battle order."

"So I noticed." Iburan paused. "What drives you, Starion?"

"You need to ask, my lord of mages?"

"I need to ask," Iburan said.

That was meant to shame Estarion into sense. It pricked his temper, but it cleared his head a little. "Do you feel the land, Iburan?"

"I feel the trouble in it. Blood has flowed on it. Hate rankles in it."

"Yes," Estarion said.

"And you think that you can stop it?"

"If not I, then who?"

Iburan was silent.

"You don't think I'm arrogant?" Estarion asked.

"I think that you may be both more than anyone thought you, and less."

Estarion stiffened.

"Oh, he is that," said Sidani. "Who trained him? You? You didn't do badly, as far as you went. But you didn't make a Sunlord of him."

They rounded on her, both alike and both astonished. The irony of that did not escape Estarion.

She grinned at them. "Oh, he's emperor enough, priest—and more since he came to Asanion. He's still not all that he could be."

"He's young," Iburan said with a touch of sharpness. "He'll grow into it."

"Will you still be saying that when he's a greybeard? Because he'll be then as he is now."

"And how is that?"

Estarion wondered if she enjoyed the spectacle as much as he did. Iburan in a temper was a rare thing; Iburan struggling to keep from roaring was a wonderful one. She sat her evil-tempered gelding with grand insouciance and laughed. "Oh, such outrage! Look at him, priest. Isn't he a pretty thing? Fine wits, fine mind, and a light foot in the dance. He knows how to make people love him; and that without magery, because he assures himself that he has none. Why is that, Iburan of Endros? What makes this prince of mages so eager to deny the whole of himself?"

Estarion's laughter died soon after she began. She could not be saying what she said. She knew nothing of power, or of Sunlords, or of anything but wild stories. It was too much like hope; too much like all his prayers, before he had forgotten how to pray. "Woman, you are a fool. I have no power worth the name, nor ever shall again."

She waved him to silence. He had obeyed before he thought, for pure startlement.

Iburan answered her slowly, as if Estarion had never spoken: that too a goad to his temper. "He slew with power. He was slow to recover."

"So simple," she said. "So easy an escape. If you failed, or if you left his training half done—why then, it was never your fault, but his."

"We taught him all that we knew," Iburan said. Growling it. "And who are you, old woman, to cast reproach on me?"

"I am no one," said Sidani. "No one reproaches you. But one might wonder if you knew what you were doing. He was—he is—no common mageborn child. And yet you raised him as one."

"How else was I to raise him?"

"As his father's son."

"So," grated Iburan, "we did."

"Has he entered the Tower in Endros?"

Iburan looked ready to spit at her. "No one enters that Tower."

"Sun-blood do."

"I am not Sun-blood."

"So," Sidani said. She sighed. "One never allows for these things. If Ganiman had not died—if he had had time to tell the child what he must know—"

"And how do you know?" Estarion broke in.

She laughed. "Dear child, sweet child, I was old when your grandfather was born. I know what all the dead know."

"Mad," said Iburan.

Estarion's temper set in pure contrariness. If she knew—if, O impossible, it could be true—"*Is* she mad, priest? Or does she know something that none of us has known?"

"The Tower is halfway to the other side of the world," she said. "And that's a pity. You're half a Sunlord now, and half a Sunlord you remain, until you pass that door."

"It has no door," Iburan rumbled, but they took no notice of him.

"And what will I gain," Estarion asked, "when I come there?"

"Maybe nothing," she said. "Maybe all the power you think you've lost."

Estarion drew a knife-edged breath. All his power. All his magic. All his strength—to kill again. To slaughter souls. "I don't know if I want it," he said.

"Then you are an idiot," she said. She kicked her gelding into a gallop.

He watched her go. She was safe enough, he thought distantly: the scouts were well ahead, and the road was straight and clear.

"Sometimes," mused Iburan, "I wonder . . ."

"What?" Estarion snapped. Shock made him vicious; shock, and hope turned to gall. The woman knew nothing. No one, no power, even the Sunborn's own, could make him a mage again.

The priest shook off Estarion's temper. "She's no danger to you, whatever nonsense she babbles."

Estarion turned his back on all thought of Iburan or Sidani, hope or magic or the Tower that his firstfather had made. This was Asanion. Such things were nothing here.

The sun was dazzling on the snow. He narrowed his eyes against it. The others rode with heads down, trusting their mounts' sure feet, or wrapped veils about their eyes. They looked stiff with cold.

He felt it, but dimly. Half a Sunlord, was he? Then the whole of a Sunlord must burn like a torch.

"Quick now!" he called to the rest of them. "The faster we ride, the sooner we're in the warm."

"Warmer than any of us needs, maybe," Iburan muttered.

Estarion laughed at him. Somewhat to Estarion's surprise, he laughed in return. For a moment they were easy, as if there were no walls between them.

But even before this quarrel, there was the matter of the secret that Iburan had kept, worse betrayal than any trespass in an emperor's bed.

"If you had told me," Estarion said, "I could have forgiven you."

"Could you?"

"All of you," said Estarion with sudden heat, "every one of you—priests, princes, madwomen, all—never a one of you sees me as anything but a child or a ruined mage. When will I be a man? When my beard is grey? When I'm dead?"

"When you learn to forgive the unforgivable," said Iburan.

"Then there are no men," said Estarion. "Only saints and children."

"Even saints can err," said Iburan, "and I'm no saint. What I did, I did for love of you."

"No, priest. You did it for love of my mother."

"That too," Iburan said willingly. "But you were first. When your father brought you to me, and you hardly higher than his knee and hardly old enough to leave your mother's breast—all eyes and questions, and power shining out of you like light from a lamp—I knew that I would love you. Him I served gladly, for he was my emperor, but you I served with my heart."

Estarion drew a breath that caught on pain. "When I saw you I was terrified. You were the largest man I had ever seen. Mother's father was taller, and some of my uncles; but you were like a mountain looming over me. Then you smiled. And I loved you. Father was my father, soul and body both. You were my teacher, and my heart's friend."

"So am I still," said Iburan. "So shall I always be."

"Why, then? Why didn't you tell me?"

"Cowardice," Iburan said. "You never ask why I did it at all."

"What's to ask? She was beautiful and young, and widowed untimely; and you were thrown together in my incapacity. You'd be more than man if you hadn't warmed to her."

"I did try to resist," Iburan said. "For your father's honor. For your sake."

"And she?"

Iburan glanced back. Maybe he met the empress' glance; maybe he had no need.

"She wore you down," Estarion answered for him. "She's wise, and cold when she has to be. Her goddess isn't the bright burning god we worship, you and I. *She* would keep the secret, for her own purposes. But you should have told me."

"I feel," said Iburan after a pause, "quite properly rebuked." His expression was rueful, but there was something new in his eyes. Something, Estarion thought, like respect.

"I misread you," Iburan said. "And I misjudged you."

He had not. But Estarion was not about to confess to it. He bent his head stiffly. He did not say anything. Iburan bowed and wheeled his mount, returning to his place. It was not, Estarion took note, at the empress' side, but farther back, rearmost of the circle of mages.

Estarion's mind shifted itself away from little troubles; and it was little, this fret of his over his mother's choice of lovers in her widowhood. He was aware of Pri'nai like an ache in his own body, a wound that festered deep and would not heal. Whether it was that he was coming closer to it, or that his land-sense was growing keener, he did not know.

He was well in the lead now, with no memory of parting from his escort. Sidani waited ahead of him with Ulyai at her gelding's heels and the young ones tumbling over one another in the snow. When he came level, the two she-cubs sprang into their panniers on the gelding's saddle. The he-cub leaped, aiming for Umizan's rump. Estarion swept him out of the air. He settled purring on Estarion's saddlebow.

Sidani did not speak as they rode on side by side. Only a lingering shred of prudence kept Estarion from kicking Umizan into a flat gallop.

Pri'nai stood at a meeting of roads, where the great southward way met the traders' route into Keruvarion. Yet there was no one on the road. No travelers, no traders, no farmfolk walking to market. The houses they passed were silent, but not empty: they were full of eyes.

"They know we're coming," Sidani said. Her voice was startling after so long a silence. There was no other human sound, only the cold clash of metal in mail-ring or harness, the thudding of hoofs, the snort of a senel. No one was singing or talking. Hands were tensed on weapons; vanguard and rearguard had drawn in, wary.

One of the scouts came back from beyond the hill. "Gates are open," he said. "Guarded, and heavily, and they're stopping people who come in or out. But there's no fighting."

"It's inside the city, then," Estarion said.

"I think, sire," the scout said, "maybe. There's a feel to it I don't like. Nobody out, and nothing moving outside the walls. It's brooding on something."

"I'll go in," said Estarion.

"Sire—"

"I'm going in."

He went in. Not slowly, not quickly after all his haste to come so far. He led his escort down from the hill toward the city of the crossroads. It stood in a ring of gardens, orchards and vineyards bleak in the snow, and the white mounds of tombs amid the bare branches.

The northward gate was open. Guards filled it. Troopers' bronze and officers' steel gleamed above it. If all the gates were so guarded, then Pri'nai was ringed with an army, and all of them in the black and bronze of the lord of Ansavaar.

And if Ansavaar itself was in revolt, then Estarion was well and truly destroyed; for this was the army which he had come to command.

He might have sent men ahead to prepare his coming, as he had done in every city he had entered since Induverran. But in this he had chosen to come unheralded. He knew better than to think that he was unexpected.

The wind caught his standard and unfurled it. Golden sun flamed on scarlet, the war-banner that had not flown in the twofold empire since Varuyan was emperor. One of the Olenyai bore it. Not Korusan. The boy would not leave Estarion's shadow, or speak, or lift hands from swordhilts. He was ill, Estarion thought, or beset with some trouble. Estarion would put him to the question. Later.

Estarion wore mail and the scarlet war-cloak taken hastily out of the baggage, but his helmet rested on his knee. He did not intend to need it. He kept Umizan to a sedate canter, advancing lightly toward the gate and the guards. No one rode in front of him. He was a plain target, and so he meant to be.

A spear's length in front of the line of guards, he brought Umizan to a halt. They knew him: none would lift eyes to his face. "The emperor," he said, making no effort to shout, but knowing that they could hear him all along the wall, "would enter Pri'nai. Will the lord of the city admit him?"

There was a silence. Estarion sat calm in it. He heard behind him the soft snick of swords loosened in scabbards, and a seneldi snort. The cause of that came to stand at Umizan's shoulder, tail twitching, inspecting the guards as if to choose the tenderest for her prey.

"Every city," said a voice at last above the gate, "is the emperor's, and every lord is his servant."

Estarion looked up at the captain of the guards. The man did not look down. "Is it a quandary," Estarion inquired, "to stand above your emperor?"

He won no answer. Ulyai moved forward, growling at the nearness of the city, but unflinching. Umizan followed her. The guards melted before them.

After the quiet without, the clamor of the city was deafening. The walls contained it and sent it ringing back, a dance of echoes that made Ulyai snarl and the seneldi squeal and skitter. People fled the restless hoofs. Those who could dropped down in homage; the rest vanished into doorways or darted down passages. No one lingered to watch the emperor ride by.

The clamor had a source, and Estarion sought it. Pri'nai's center was a broad open space, a court of temples and of the lord's palace, with a fountain in it, silent now in winter. Here were the people of the city, a milling, shouting, restless crowd, all turned to face the wide stair that mounted to the palace. Guards rimmed it. Further throngs filled the top of it and vanished through the open gates.

Estarion halted on the edge of the square and beckoned. His trumpeter edged forward, wary of Ulyai, who pressed close against Umizan's side. He passed Estarion with a glance half of boldness, half of panic. But boldness was stronger. He raised his trumpet to his lips and blew.

The crowd parted. Slowly, with much jostling, it opened a path to the dais. Silence spread as people went down in homage.

Estarion rode the length of that road of living bodies. His back tensed against an arrow that did not fly, a stone that was not flung. The desire was there, and the hostility, but it did not burst the bonds of fear, the power of a thousand years of emperors.

Estarion dismounted at the foot of the stair. The guards parted as they had in Pri'nai's gate. The press of people thrust and jostled and cursed itself aside.

The hall of the palace was dim after the brilliance of sun on snow, lamplit and windowlit, seething with lordly presences as the square had been with commoners. At the end of it stood a dais, and on the dais a tall chair, and in the chair, the lord of Ansavaar. There were others about him, a man before him with a scroll of the laws, and at his feet a huddle of men in chains.

They all stood frozen at the emperor's coming. He considered lingering in the doorway, but that was cruel. He did not pause or slow until he stood upon the dais and the lord of Ansavaar bowed down at his feet. "Up," he said, "my lord Shurichan."

Shurichan of Ansavaar rose with practiced grace, shying from the ul-cat's shadow. Ulyai ignored him, taking station at the dais' foot.

He was a young man, taller than some and broader, and a rarity in an Asanian lord: a man who not only knew how to fight but evinced a fondness for it. He wore armor over his fivefold robes, and his princely coronet circled a helmet. "My lord emperor," he said. "Well come to Pri'nai."

"So one might think," Estarion said. He leaned against the chair in which Shurichan had been sitting, and folded his arms. "Now, my lord. Go on with your justice."

"Majesty," said Shurichan. "I can hardly—in your presence—"

Estarion tilted his head. He eyed the chair, and the man who had sat in it. Shurichan betrayed no expression.

Estarion looked about. There was a stool nearby, on which a scribe might have been sitting: he was on his face now, rusty black robe, rusty black hat. Estarion hooked the stool with a foot and drew it to him, and perched on it. "Now," he said. "Go on."

Shurichan was nicely shocked. He fell rather than sat in his high cushioned chair, and composed himself with visible effort.

Estarion watched him narrowly. Resentment, yes; his court of justice had been disrupted, his office lessened by the insouciant presence on the stool. But anger, no. And no move to protest.

Interesting. Estarion surveyed the men on the dais, the cat at its foot, the guards returned to their vigilance, the crowd of lords rising slowly from the edges inward but slow yet to resume their clamor. His escort had spread among the guards, ringing the dais, and his mages among them in a broad and broken circle. They were fully on guard; the wards had been raised about him since he left the hill above Pri'nai.

Within the wards, in the court of justice, men waited in chains. They were ragged, beaten and bruised, cowering in terror or glaring with defiance. Common malefactors, Asanians all, and nothing to mark them from any hundred of their like; and yet Estarion's heart went still. Here, he thought. Here: not south of here, not in the siege of that lesser city, nor west where he had forborne to go. Here it came to the crux. He felt the force of it in his bones.

The men about him, lords, scribes, judges, rose one by one in order of precedence and returned to their places. The scribe whose stool Estarion had taken settled without apparent discomfort on the dais, set his tablets on his knees and raised his stylus, and waited.

The herald of the court glanced at his lord, and then swiftly, almost shyly, at Estarion. Estarion smiled. "Read the charges," he said, "if you will."

The man looked flustered, but he obeyed.

They were couched in the excess of Asanian ceremony, dense as weeds in a garden. Estarion was learning to find the flowers in the undergrowth, to pluck the essence of the charges from the knots of the law.

These were rebels. They had conspired against the imperial majesty; they had raised insurrection in Pri'nai and the towns about it; they had named themselves followers of one they called prophet and prince, lord of the Golden Empire, son of the Lion. And the one they followed, their prophet, their prince—he huddled among them in the wall of their bodies.

Estarion rose. The herald faltered, but Estarion's gesture bade him continue. His voice rang clear in the stillness as Estarion stepped down among the prisoners. They shrank from him. None sprang, though one looked as if he thought of it: a young one with a split cheekbone and an arm that dangled useless, and the eyes of a slave to dreamsmoke.

The one they sought even now to protect was a poor thing, a huddle of torn silk and tarnished cloth of gold, crouched with his arms over his head. Estarion lifted him by the wrists. He came as limply as a poppet made of rags, but once on his feet he stayed there, trembling. His hair was a brass-bright tangle, his face bruised ivory. His eyes were gold, and enormous. They were not lion-eyes, although to one who did not know, they might seem so, large-irised as they were. He was as beautiful as a girl, as delicate as girls in Asanion were supposed to be.

He looked remarkably, uncannily like Korusan. But Korusan was steel. This was silvered glass, so brittle that a breath would shatter it.

"Who are you?" Estarion asked him. His voice was gentle, and not through any will of his own; he should have been merciless. But it was difficult to be cruel to such a child.

The boy trembled until he nearly fell. Estarion held him, shook him. "I know what they say you are. You know as well as I, that that is a lie."

"I am," the boy whispered. "I am. Lion—prince—I prophesy—"

"But I am the Lion's heir," Estarion said. "There is no other."

"I am," the boy said. He was weeping, shuddering, sick with terror. "They said I was. They said!"

"What were you before they told you the lie?"

"I—" The boy swallowed. It must have hurt: his face twisted. "I was—he owned me. Kemuziran. He sold spices. And slaves. And—and—"

"And you," Estarion said. "You're a purebred, aren't you? The line they breed still, for the beauty and for the likeness to the Lion's brood. No Lion, you. You were bred to be a lady's lapcat."

A man, or even the beginning of a Lion's cub, would have stiffened at that and remembered his pride. This son of slaves flung himself weeping into Estarion's arms. "They made me! They said I'd die if I didn't do it!"

Estarion had hardly expected this armful of wriggling, howling child. He pushed the boy away, not roughly, not particularly gently. The boy stopped sobbing, raised great tear-stained eyes.

"'They'?" Estarion pressed him.

"The others," the boy said, hiccoughing. "They bought me and they taught me. They told me what to say. They said—they said—I could be—I could—"

Estarion held his burning hand under the boy's nose. "Would you want that?"

The boy shuddered and shrank away. It was not artifice, not the sleight of the courtesan. Estarion was sure of it.

"That is what they thought to give you," Estarion said. "Can you clasp the sun in your hand? Can you bear empires on your shoulders? Can you, little slave, sway the hearts of kings?"

"They told me," the boy said. "I would die if I refused them."

"You will die because you obeyed them."

"No," the boy said, weeping again. "Please, no."

The recitation of the charges had died away some time since. The boy locked arms about Estarion's waist and clung, burying his face in Estarion's cloak.

Estarion sighed and let him be. The rest of the prisoners watched, slack-jawed or frozen-faced. Guilt was as sharp as a stench, and hate with it, and fear.

"You," he said. The dreamer spat, aiming for Estarion's face, but the spittle flew wide. Estarion smiled, sweet and terrible. "I might forgive you your sedition, but this I do not forgive. A man will do anything at all, who stoops to the corruption of children."

"Such an innocent," the dreamer drawled. His patois was broad, his inflection an insult. "They say a king can be an idiot where you come from. Who set the coins in your eyes? The were-bear who follows you about?"

"No," said Estarion. "My father. And his father before him. And before them all, the Lion's cub, the Golden Emperor. I'm of his blood."

"Traitor's blood," the dreamer said. "No Lion's get, you, but liar's. Barbarian, outlander, stealer of thrones: you should have stayed in your own country."

"This is my own country," Estarion said. He gripped the chain that locked the dreamer's collar, and hauled him up. "You are a fool and a teller of lies. Your dreams are the smoke's children. You know nothing of your own."

"And what are you?" the dreamer mocked him. "Not even a mage, and barely a king."

Estarion dropped him. He fell in a clatter of chains. Estarion faced the lord of Ansavaar and swept his arm round the huddle of prisoners. "Take these," he said. "Lock them in prison. In the morning, flog them. Then set them free."

"Majesty?" Shurichan frowned. "Majesty . . . free them?"

"They do not deserve death," Estarion said. "Death is for the great; for renegades, for traitors, for destroyers of thrones."

"And these are not traitors?" Shurichan demanded.

"These are fools and children. I will not ennoble them with death, or make them martyrs."

Shurichan blinked. He did not understand. His way was more direct: and there was irony in Asanion. Treason won death. Life in disgrace—that, Estarion thought, he had never heard of.

"That is . . . very cruel," Shurichan said at last, dubiously, as if he thought that he should approve, but could not bring himself to it.

"I call it justice," said Estarion.

"And that?" Shurichan asked.

Estarion looked down at the child who clung still, convulsively. "Him we keep. He's too great a temptation, with those big eyes of his. Ready a room for him. We'll keep him in comfort."

"But—"

That was great daring, to protest even so much. Estarion smiled at it. "Look at him, Shurichan. What can he do but seduce his guards? He won't want to be free. He'll welcome the safety of prison. No one forces him there; no one threatens him with thrones."

Shurichan bowed, veiling his eyes. Estarion pried the boy loose and gave him over to the Olenyai. He shrieked at sight of them, and struggled, till Estarion laid a hand on his head. "Hush, child. They won't hurt you, or let you be hurt. Go with them, let them protect you."

"I want to stay with you!" the boy wailed.

It was great pleasure to see the faces of the men who would have made this child their puppet: to know how perfectly they were nonplussed. "The next time you make an emperor," Estarion advised them, "choose a woolbeast in fleece. It will serve you better, and cover your backsides, too."

The prisoners were guarded as the emperor himself was, by both Varyani and Olenyai. Korusan did not find it difficult to take a turn of the watch, the one which happened to coincide with the nightmeal, nor did his companion object when he took charge of the feeding. That gained him the key to the cells, which he omitted to return.

Sentry-go with a Varyani could be interesting if the foreigner was hostile, or if he was inclined to chatter. Often he was both. This one, as luck would have it, was silent for one of his kind. He did not seem to object to the existence of Asanians, nor did he shy from Olenyai veils. He accepted the place of outer ward, granting Korusan the inner duty, which was to pace slowly along the passage, glancing at intervals into the cells.

The prisoners were kept apart lest they conspire to escape, and there were mage-bonds on them: Korusan's own wards itched in response. After several revolutions he glanced toward the corridor's end. The Varyani, a plainsman with a suggestion of Gileni red in his dark hair, stood facing outward, still as a stone. He glanced back when he heard the scrape of the key in a lock, but Korusan ignored him. Boldness, he had been taught, could be better concealment than stealth.

The plainsman did not protest as Korusan opened the door and slipped within. Nor did he leave his post.

Korusan stood in the dimness of the cell, waiting for his heart to cease hammering. The only light came from the cresset without, slanting through the bars onto the recumbent figure of the prisoner.

The man was asleep, twitching in the fashion of one too long forbidden dreamsmoke. He snapped awake as Korusan knelt by him. His eyes were blood-shot, blinking rapidly until he gained control of himself.

"You know me," said Korusan, soft and cold.

For once the dreamer was not smiling. He looked greener even than his condition might account for, as he stumbled up and then flung himself flat.

"Why did you lie?" Korusan asked him.

He raised his head, but kept his eyes fixed on the floor. He seemed to swell as he crouched there, gaining color and force. "For you, my lord. For you I did it."

"What? Found a slave's brat and called him emperor? Set him up to supplant me?"

"No!" the dreamer cried, but softly, as if he had sense enough not to rouse the Varyani's suspicions. "No, my lord, it wasn't like that at all! We needed a diversion, you see. A feint. A target for them to strike at, and be complacent, and think that that was all we had."

"None of them guessed," said Korusan, more to himself than to the fool on the floor.

The fool heard him nonetheless, and answered him. "They didn't, did they? I'm a good liar. I should be: I was a player before I became your servant."

Korusan curled his lip at the thought of this man as his servant. "You could have been the worst liar living, and still the mages would have shielded you. They would not wish their plots known to their enemies."

"But I lie well," the dreamer insisted. "I do. They said so. They hardly needed to put a magic on me. Just to keep me safe, they said. To free me to be your sacrifice."

Korusan recoiled. "I do not want a sacrifice."

"Why, bless you, my prince, of course you don't. But you shall have one. It's needed. The people will follow you all the more gladly once they've seen how we were willing to die for you."

This creature was unbearable. He actually shone, he was so full of his own glory.

"You are all idiots," Korusan said fiercely. "If you die, and I come to my throne, I will repudiate you. You lied in my name. You turned my honor to dust."

There was no quelling the dreamer. "Oh, yes, you have to deny me. I can't besmirch your brightness. But I die happy, knowing that my death helped to make you emperor."

"You are not going to die," snapped Korusan. "He will flog you and let you go. Fool, I thought him. Now I know him wise."

"I'll die," the dreamer said. "I'll make sure of it. Wait, my lord, and see."

Korusan restrained an urge to thrust him down and set foot on his neck. He would have welcomed the humiliation, and worshipped the one who did it to him. Korusan left him instead, shut and locked the door with taut-strung care, returned to his post and his silent companion.

To whom he said, "I thought I might get sense from him, once the drug had worn off. He utters nothing but lies and lunacy."

"His brain's well rotted," the Varyani agreed, "and the rest are witlings. It's a piss-poor excuse for a conspiracy, this one."

"But it suffices," said Korusan.

"It does, at that," the Varyani said. "And tomorrow we put an end to it."

Tomorrow, thought Korusan, it would hardly have begun.

FORTY-TWO

FULL OF YOURSELF, AREN'T YOU?"

Estarion paused. He was clean, warm, and about to be fed; he had rid himself of servants and won a few moments' solitude. The rebels' puppet was asleep, with one of Iburan's mages seeing to it that he stayed so. The rebels were in much less comfort, and under strong guard.

Sidani nudged a squalling ul-cub toward its mother. Ulyai, having laid claim to his lordship's bed, was amply content to nurse her young ones in it. She blinked lazily at Sidani, yawned, set to washing the he-cub's ears.

Sidani leaned against the doorframe, eyebrows cocked. "You think you did well in milord's court."

"I think I had no choice but to do what I did." Estarion scowled at the robes laid out for him, and looked longingly toward his baggage. The coat, maybe, embroidered with gold. Or—

"You should have killed them, and done it then. Not dragged it out till tomorrow."

"What, and made martyrs, but taught no lasting lesson?"

"Lessons are best taught quickly."

"Maybe." He pulled the coat from its wrappings and shook it out, and sighed. No. Not for this. He must be as Asanian as he could manage, however it galled him.

"Where's your shadow?" Sidani asked.

"Resting." Estarion dropped the robe he had been wrapped in and reached for the first of the ten.

"Are you sure of that?"

He whipped about, plait lashing his flanks. "What are you saying?"

She shrugged. "I wonder if you ever noticed whose face he wears."

"What, the Lion's mask? Yes, he has it. I'd be astonished if he weren't a cub of that litter."

"And it doesn't concern you that he might have ambitions?"

"Korusan?" Estarion laughed. "Korusan's ambition is to reach his twentieth year. If he manages that, he'll go for Master of Olenyai."

"Not emperor?"

Estarion went still. "He loves me."

"Do you love him?"

"Is that any affair of yours?"

"Do you?"

He thought of driving her out. But Sidani was not a tamed creature, nor one to yield to mere proprieties. He set his teeth and answered her. "If anyone holds my heart, it is one who does not want it. My Goldeneyes . . . have you ever been the half of a thing, and known that there was another, and it was nothing that you ever expected?"

Sidani's eyes closed. Her face was stark. "Yes," she whispered. "Yes."

Estarion stopped, drew a breath. He had not looked for that of all answers. "You don't call that anything as simple as love. It has no name. It is."

Her eyes snapped open. "You have no right to understand so much."

"Why? Because I'm young and a fool?"

"Because he isn't dead yet. You haven't had to live without him."

"I hope I never may."

"Then you'll be dead within the year."

Estarion shivered. He was naked and the room, though heated with braziers, was chill. "Are you prophesying?"

"I hope not." She moved toward one of the braziers and stood over it, warming her hands. "Go carefully, young emperor. Watch every shadow. There's death here, surer than ever it was in Kundri'j."

"Yes," he said. He put on the first of the robes. It was silk, and cold, till it warmed to his body. When he reached for the second, he found her hands on it, and her eyes behind that, daring him to refuse.

She helped him to dress, unplaited his hair and combed it and netted it in gold. Somewhere she had been a body-servant, maybe, to have learned such lightness of hand. When the tenth robe was laid atop the rest, she turned him to face her. Her grim mood was gone. She smiled her old, wild smile. "Oh, you're a beauty, you are. If I weren't five times your age, I'd have you on the cushions in a heartbeat."

He was as reckless as she, when it came to it. He swept her backward and kissed her thoroughly, and set her on her feet again. She looked wonderfully startled. He left her so, walking lightly to the ordeal of the banquet, trailing robes and gold.

There were robes for Estarion again in the morning, and gold, but of Sidani there was no sign. Estarion wondered if he had frightened her into flight. That would hardly be like her; but who ever knew what she would do?

The night had been quiet. Korusan came in as Estarion readied for sleep, looking bruised about the eyes but protesting that he had slept. Estarion forbore to press him. It was not true, what Sidani had suggested. This was Olenyas only, whatever his face, and he lived to serve his lord. And if that was love, to see him so, and love was blind, then so be it. Estarion could not be other than he was; he could not learn to start at every shadow.

Korusan was in one of his muted moods, when he wanted rather to fold himself in Estarion's warmth than to dance the battle-dance that always ended in another dance altogether. Estarion was content to hold and to be held. He fell asleep so, though he thought that Korusan lay awake. The golden eyes were open, the last he remembered; and when he woke they had not changed, nor did the boy seem to have moved nightlong.

They went out together, man and shadow, in a swelling crowd of attendants. The cold was less this morning but still keen enough to cut, the square of the palaces as crowded as it had been before, but its center, by the fountain, stood open. Lord Shurichan's men had raised a platform there and set the whipping-posts upon it, and ringed it with guards.

For Estarion there was a throne on the steps of the palace. The high ones waited there, muffled against the cold. He knew his mother's slender height in a cloak of ice-white fur, Iburan's massive solidity, the thickset golden-armored bulk of Lord Shurichan, the liveries of guards: Ansavaar's black and bronze, Keruvarion's scarlet and gold, plain Olenyai black.

When he came into the sun with Ulyai and her cubs at heel, all that throng bowed down like grain before a gale. All but his Varyani. He grinned at them. None of them smiled. The strain of dwelling in Asanion was taking its toll.

He sat in the tall chair. Ulyai stretched at his feet; her she-cubs, unwontedly subdued, crouched in the hollow of her side. The he-cub snarled at the press of people and sprang into Estarion's lap, where he settled, tensed as if on guard. Estarion rubbed his ears until he eased a little, but he would not relax his vigilance.

Merian came to stand beside and a little behind him. He slanted a glance at her. "Trouble?" he said.

"Possibly." She rested her hand on his shoulder. It would be a pretty picture: mother and son, empress and emperor, her white cloak and his scarlet against the gold of the throne. "Are you speaking to me again?" she inquired.

"Did I ever stop?"

"Often." She sounded more amused than not. "You could have forbidden me my pleasures."

"And made them sweeter? Pity I didn't think of that."

She laughed softly. She looked young this morning and beautiful in white and green, with gold in her hair. It was impossible to hold a grudge against her, however great her transgression. And what had she done but love a man worth loving?

She should have told me, whined the small mean thing that laired in Estarion's heart. But her laughter was too sweet, and she too much beloved, for all the sparks they struck from one another. He reached impulsively, caught her hand, set a kiss in the palm.

She smiled. "I think that you quarrel simply for the pleasure of forgiving me after."

His heart was too full, almost, for speech. But he found his famous insouciance and put it on. "What's life without a good fight?"

She leaned lightly against him, arm about his shoulders. He knew better than to think that any of it was uncalculated. She guarded him so, and claimed him for her own. But there was love in it, and pleasure in his nearness; a pleasure that warmed him even in the bitter wind.

A stirring on the crowd's edges marked the coming of the prisoners. The banners over them were Estarion's, and Shurichan's flying lower, as was fitting. Guards with spears opened the way before and behind. Of the captives there was little to see: a bobbing of bared heads, a pause and a flurry as one of them stumbled. The people were deathly silent. In Keruvarion they would have been roaring, surging like the sea. Here they were still. Watching. Almost, Estarion thought, like an ulcat poised to spring.

Shurichan's troops were scattered through them, and his own who were not needed to guard his person, and on the roofs waited a line of archers with bows strung. If any in that throng either rose in revolt or sought to free the prisoners, he would meet with the point of a spear, or fall to an arrow from above.

The executioner mounted the block and readied his whips. One by one the prisoners ascended to face him. He was big for an Asanian, almost as tall as Estarion, and broad, and startlingly young, with the long gentle face of a woolbeast. He went about his work with peaceful deliberation, taking no notice of the struggling, cursing captives, or the cries of the cowards among them. They would believe, maybe, that Estarion mocked them with clemency, and meant to see them flogged until they died.

The last of them stumbled to his place with the aid of a guard's spearbutt. The executioner shook out the thongs of a many-headed whip, smoothed them, laid the whip carefully on the table beside the rest. He turned toward Estarion, bowing low.

"He is ready," Lord Shurichan said, "majesty."

Estarion hardly needed to be told. He raised his branded hand. The sun caught it, shot sparks from it. People flinched. His lips stretched back from his teeth, but not in pleasure. None of this was pleasure. But he would do it. He could do no less, and still be emperor.

Justice, he thought as the whip rose and fell. Some of the prisoners screamed. Some cried and pleaded to be let go. His stomach was a hard cold knot. His jaw ached with clenching. The ul-cub in his lap had dug claws into his thigh. He welcomed the pain.

They said that when the Sunborn wrought summary justice, he opened his mind to the one who suffered it. Lest, he said, he grow too fond of exacting punishment, and too free of his power to do so. No one had ever pretended that he grew the softer for it, or the less implacable.

Estarion had no such greatness in him, and no such steel. But he would not put a stop to this. These were fools; and fools they must be seen to be.

The last was the dreamer, blue with cold and bleak with want of dreamsmoke. He kept his air of insolence for all that, shook off the guards who would have dragged him to his punishment, walked there on his own feet and in his own time, and held up his hands to be bound to the post. He managed as he walked to catch Estarion's eye and hold it. Estarion met the hard yellow stare with one as hard and, he hoped, as flat. The dreamer shrugged, turned his back, barely flinched as they stripped the robe from it. His shoulders were narrow and yellow-pale and thin, sharp-boned like a bird's. He did not seem to mind as the others had, that he was naked. He grinned over his shoulder and wriggled his bony backside.

He did not scream until the tenth stroke, and then in a strangled squawk, as if it had been startled out of him. It took the edge off his mockery. Still he walked away when it was over, though his back was laid open with weals that would turn to scars, branding his shame until he died.

Estarion rose with the ul-cub on his shoulders. The crowd was quiet. The guards were watchful but at ease. They did not like what he did; they had argued loud and long against it. But his mind was fixed. He would go to the scaffold and speak to the prisoners, and let it be known in Pri'nai that the emperor's justice was more than a cold word out of Kundri'j. It was here, present before them, and with his face behind it.

He began to descend the stair. His guards were ready for him, likewise his Olenyai, and his mother and his mages. They did not have his consent, but they defied him. If he would indulge this folly, their eyes said, he would go full guarded, or he would not go at all.

He could not quarrel with them now. And too well they knew it, as surely they knew what comfort they were, warding his back with power as with weapons.

Half of the way down, he paused. The prisoners stood on their scaffold, held upright if need be. Some were waking to awareness that this was all they would suffer; that they were alive, and would indeed walk free.

There was a stir behind Estarion. Ulyai growled. Estarion glanced back. One of the guards had stumbled. His fellows caught him. He steadied, muttering curses at his own clumsiness.

Estarion smiled thinly. He was all nerves and twitches. His captives stood waiting for him, their rebellion broken. He had not won in the south, nor yet in all Asanion, but he was lord in Pri'nai; that he had proven.

The way was open as it always was, the people on their faces in homage. He would teach them to stand like men. But first he must show them a Sunlord's clemency.

He sprang lightly onto the scaffold, disdaining the steps that led up to it. He had caught his guards for once off guard. That made him laugh. Ulyai lofted herself up beside him and crouched, tail twitching, muzzle wrinkled in a snarl. Poor queen of cats; she hated Asanian cities with a deathless passion. Her son, riding on Estarion's shoulders, howled ul-cat glee.

No, Estarion realized too late. Rage. The cub dug in claws, reversed himself, and sprang. Estarion spun. The dreamer went down in a flurry of claws and teeth and steel.

Steel?

The air was full of wings, wind, knives. Ulyai roared.

"Starion!" Iburan's voice, great bull-bellow. "Starion! 'Ware mages! *'Ware mages!"*

Not mages, Estarion thought as the world slowed its turning and the wind died to a shriek. Not only mages. A Gate. And in the Gate, death.

They boiled out of the air, men in white, armed with knives. They sang as they came. They sang death, they sang oblivion, they sang numbing terror. All their eyes fixed on Estarion's face.

Claws hooked in Estarion's knee. He snatched up the he-cub, who was still snarling, bloody-mouthed but richly content. He did not spare a glance for the dreamer. Ul-cats, even as young as this, did not leave living prey. With the cub again on his shoulders, he leaped down into the roil that had been his escort. His throat was raw. He was shouting. Howling. "Here! I am here! Take me, fools. Take me if you can!"

He stumbled. Body. White. Assassin—but—

The world reeled. That was fur that hampered his feet, a great sweep of cloak spattered bright with blood. There was a body in it.

"No," he said. He said it very clearly. Battle raged about him. None of it touched him.

He knelt beside his mother. She breathing still. The knife in her breast pulsed with the beating of her heart. No blood flowed there; the blade stanched it. It was not the only wound, not by far. The rest were less clean, if less deadly.

Her head rested on Iburan's knee. The priest looked immeasurably weary; his head had fallen forward, his beard fanning on his breast. Her eyes wandered from his to Estarion's. "Take," she said, a bare breath of sound. "Take the knife."

"You'll die," Estarion protested.

"Yes," she said. "Take it."

Estarion tossed his head in furious refusal. "No! We'll get you out of this—call healers—mages—"

"I am mage," Iburan said, "and healer. I can do nothing."

"Of course you can." Estarion looked about. A wall of black and scarlet circled them. White pierced it briefly, but fell to the flash of a sword. Arrows were flying; one arced over him singing. And the people—the poor people—would be dying, trapped like cattle in a pen.

"Hold her," Estarion said to Iburan. "Keep her alive." He thrust himself to his feet. The scaffold was at his back. He gathered, leaped, half fell to the splintered wood of the floor. He cast a glance about. The dreamer was dead. The rest were gone—alive, he hoped, and under guard.

The battle was not as fierce as he had feared. The knot of his guards was the worst of it. People fled the fighting, trampling one another, sounding at last like human beasts, yelling their terror.

He was calm. Perfectly, icily, immovably calm. His mother was dying. Mages had killed her. They thought maybe to deceive him, to feign their coming through the crowd of his people, his Asanians. But he had felt the Gate; he had known the wound it rent in the earth of his empire.

Something stirred in him; something shifted. It was not anger. No. Nor fear. Nor even irony. These rebels whom he had punished had been no more than a mask, their punishment a pretext. Now the enemy had shown his hand.

Mages.

Mages of the Gates.

He looked down. Iburan looked up, and deliberately, coolly, drew the knife from the wound in the empress' breast. She sighed. And her heart, her great wise heart, burst asunder.

Estarion's skull was beating like a heart, beating fit to burst. He clutched at it, rocking, dislodging the ul-cub. The cat fell yowling.

The empress was dead. Godri was dead. His father was dead. All dead, all slain. Because of him. Because of Estarion.

He howled. There were no words in it, only rage. And power. Raw, pulsing, blood-red power. He had driven it down deep and bound it with chains of guilt and terror, and sworn a vow beyond the limits of memory. Never to wield it again, never to take a life, never to destroy a soul.

He had done it, and done it surpassingly well: he had shut the door of memory, and made truth of the lie. Even mages had not seen the deception. They called him cripple, feeble, maimed, and all but powerless. But his power lived, far down below his remembrance, waiting. Yearning to break free.

He was dizzy, reeling, stunned with the shock of magic reborn, but he was master of it still. He remembered the ways of it. He drew it like a sword, great gleaming deadly thing, and raised it, and poised.

Mages, yes. Gate: so. Land weeping with pain, people a knot of shadowy fear. He soothed them with blade turned to gentleness, calmed them, brought them under his shield. And turned then. Outward.

So it had been when his father was dead, before the dark came upon him. This clarity. This bright strength with its edge of blood. It was never as they had taught him, those who called themselves masters of mages. They feigned that it was difficult; that a mage must struggle to see what was as clear as sun in a glass, and as simple to encompass. Here were mages, little lights like candles in a wind, and the threads of their lives stretched spider-thin behind them. To cut, so, one had but to raise the sword. To snuff them out, one needed but a breath.

No. That too was memory, though dim. One should not wield the sword so; and never the breath that was the soul. There was a price—prices.

And what was the price of his mother's life, his father's, his friend and brother's?

Not so high. Not, again, so bitter. They had suffered death of the body. He would slay souls. And in that, be doomed and damned.

So simple. So very simple.

Starion.

Iburan. Again. And another.

"Mother?" Gladness; soaring, singing joy. "Mother! You live?"

No. Faint, that, but clear. *Starion, no. Never be tempted. Never for me.*

"Mother!" No answer. *"Mother!"*

She was gone. He raged and wept, but she would not come back for him, nor for any mortal pleading.

Mages bobbed and glimmered like corpselights. He caught the stink of them: self-delight and surety, and contempt for his frailty. They could not even see the light that was in him. They were too weak. He struck them blind, and they never knew.

He writhed in the darkness, twisting and coiling like a dragon of fire. A magelight darted at him, wielding what no doubt it reckoned deadly power. Estarion batted it aside. It reeled. He caught it. He considered the thread that spun from it, the light that flickered in it, and gently, most gently, plucked thread and minute guttering spark from the bubble of light, and pricked the bubble with a sharpened claw.

So simple. So precise. Body, soul, he left entire. Magery he took away. And when the last corpse-pale glimmer was gone, he drifted alone in the dark.

That too he had forgotten. What peace was here; what quiet, where no storms came. He coiled, uncoiled. So supple, this shape, freed from the stiffness that was humanity. He had thought it madness to linger here. It had been madness to depart.

Now at last he would stay. The dark was sweet and deep, the silence blessed, and absolute. *Peace,* his soul sang. *Peace.*

FORTY-THREE

V ANYI HAD A FEW BREATHS' WARNING. SHE SHOULD HAVE HAD MORE THAN that. Her Gate-sense had been uneasy for long days now, a broad sourceless uneasiness, but nothing on which she could set hand or mind. Estarion's insistence on making a spectacle of himself was purely Estarion, and no more foolish than anything else he might have taken it into his head to do. He was guarded with all the vigilance that any of them might muster; she was part of the wards, set among a faceless rank of Olenyai, weaving her strand of autumn-colored silk into the greater web.

The warding that the blackrobes wore was a hindrance, until realization came to her in a blaze of sudden light. Olenyai wards were made for shield and guard against attack. In the face of power that would weave with them and not oppose them, they yielded with astonishing ease. She was just finding the way of it, just beginning to know the pride of her accomplishment, when the web of the world began to fray.

She had never seen the opening of a Gate, never thought to see it. Yet there was no denying it; no hoping that it was something else, something less, something that did not pierce straight to the heart of the wards and shatter them. The breaking was not even deliberate. Estarion's mages had armed themselves against attack of steel or magery, but not against the forging of a Gate. It drained the power out of their working and wielded it for itself, drank deep of the resistance that some of them—fools, idiots, blind brave hopeless innocents—mustered against it.

But not Vanyi. The Olenyai shields protected her, woven with them as she was. She dropped out of the web half stunned but conscious, and able to see with eyes of the body. She saw the battle begin, white-robed assassins against Guardsmen in scarlet, Queen's Guards in green. No Olenyai. The assassins veered aside from them. She saw the empress fall, and Iburan go down with her. She saw Estarion leap shouting to his mother's side. He wore a sword; he seemed to have forgotten it, or he was trusting his guards beyond life and hope. Or he had merely taken leave of his wits. When he struggled back to the scaffold, bright target for any assassin with a bow or a throwing knife, Vanyi remembered how to move.

She struggled within a suddenly solid wall of bodies. Yellow eyes fixed on her, hard and flat as stones. No lion-eyes; all of these were plain Asanian.

Even yet she had the key of their wards. She set it in its lock and turned it carefully, not too swift, not too slow. Beyond the circle the world was breaking—the empress dead, the mages fallen, blood feeding the Gate, and above them all, miraculously unharmed, the emperor.

She slid hands between two stone-still Olenyai and opened them like the leaves of a door. Beyond their circle was havoc. More magery; more Gate-work, taking its strength from the cattle-panic of the people as they fled the blood and the battle.

Estarion stood erect on the scaffold. His face was perfectly blank. His eyes were pure and burning gold.

"God," Vanyi said, her voice lost in the tumult. "Oh, goddess."

No one else seemed even to see him. His guards held off the assassins, taking bitter toll in blood and lives. He was no man to them then, no living, breathing, fallible human creature, but prize and victim of the battle. Those who fought to guard him, those who fought to kill him, were oblivious to him else. And mages, both his own and those others, knew that he had no power for the wielding.

She had heard his outcry in his riding: how he was nothing to anyone but a child or a ruined mage; a weak thing, a thing to be guarded and protected, with no strength of his own.

They were all going to regret that, she thought, remote and very clear. He was like a mountain asleep under the moons, motionless, lifeless, deep sunk in snow. But his heart was sun-bright fire. And soon, between one breath and the next, it was going to shatter.

Vanyi wrenched eyes and mind away from him. The ring of guards had widened. The assassins were falling back. The Varyani captain and the captain of Olenyai had matters well in hand; they had even, gods knew how, brought Lord Shurichan's men under their command. Within the ring, Estarion's mages were beginning to recover. But there were others among them, and that mountain of fire above them, and no knowledge in any of them that there was danger apart from steel or simple magery.

Down! she cried with her power. *My mages, my people—for your lives' sake, down! Shield!*

Oromin touched her with incomprehension, but shielded as if by instinct. Shaiyel and his little priestess were now clear in her awareness, now locked in walls. The others fled before the lash of Vanyi's urgency. But one resisted.

Iburan, Vanyi pleaded. *Shield yourself. He's going to—*

And where are your shields? Iburan lashed back. And when she wavered, struck so fiercely that she must shield or fall.

And the fire came down.

In the world of the living was nothing to see. A scattering of priests fallen on their faces. A battle that went on unheeding. A lone motionless figure on a scaffold, with the wind tugging at his scarlet cloak, and the sun in his eyes.

But in the world of power, even behind the strongest of shields, that figure was a tower of light. Corpse-candles danced and flickered about it. Mages, and none of Vanyi's kind, either. If they had heard her call to shield, they had chosen not to heed it. And they paid.

So would she have done if she had laid herself open to him. He stripped the mages of their magery as easily as a child strips a sea-snail of its shell, but left them alive to know what he had done to them. He shut down the Gate without even thinking of it, healed the rent in the land and the air, and as an afterthought, in passing, herded the last of the assassins into the swords of his guard.

And then was silence.

Vanyi dragged herself to her feet. The fighting was ended. The people were fled, all but the dead. No one stood in all that wide and windy place but Estarion's Guard and Lord Shurichan's best, and a handful of stumbling, staggering priest-mages, and she.

Scarlet pooled on the scaffold. Not blood, thank god and goddess, but the emperor's cloak, blood-red for war. Estarion lay as if asleep. He did not wake when she touched him. His ul-cub crouched beside him, bristling, but did not snarl or threaten.

A shadow fell across her. She looked up into Olenyai veils, and eyes all amber-gold.

A great anger swelled in her. It was not reasonable, she knew it was not, but she was past reason. "You," she said. "Where were you when he needed you?"

"Fighting," the Olenyas said. His voice was as cool as always, but there was a tremor in it. "I could not come to him."

Yes, he was shaking, and trying not to. She had no pity to spare. "Look after him now, then. And by all gods there are, if you lay hand on him except to guard him, I'll flay your hide with a blunt knife."

"He is not," said the Olenyas, as if he struggled with the words. "He is not—he is not dead."

"We all may wish he were," Vanyi said, "before the day is out. See to him, damn you, and stop fluttering."

That stiffened his back for him. He called up others of his kind, and did as he was bidden.

She looked up. She was being stared at. Dark eyes, yellow eyes, eyes of every shade between. No sea-grey or sea-green or sea-blue. That mattered suddenly, very much. They were all alien here. And they were all begging her to do their thinking for them.

The empress was dead. Estarion was worse than that, maybe. Iburan was alive, half kneeling, half sitting with the empress' body in his arms. But as Vanyi came down off the scaffold, he sighed and slid sidewise. She braced herself against the weight of him, and gasped. "You're hurt!"

"Assassins' knives," he said calmly, "as we know too well, are poisoned. Not that that need have stopped me, you understand, but it slowed me when I should have shielded. Do you know what I was to him? A stinging fly. He plucked the wings from me and let me fall."

"No," said Vanyi.

But that was her tongue, being a fool. She hardly needed power to know that his magery was gone. He was all dulled for lack of it, his great body shrunken. The eyes he raised to her were wry. "I always did misjudge him," he said. "Here I thought I could stop him, or at least slow him down, and he never even knew I tried. You're going to have your hands full with him, Vanyi."

"I?" She thrust the thought away. "I'm not anyone to deal with a Sunlord gone mad."

"Who else is there?"

"Oromin," she answered promptly. "Shaiyel."

"No," said Iburan. He sighed. It bubbled; he coughed. "They don't know—they can't master him. You have the power. No one—else—" He coughed again, a froth of bright blood, struggling to say more, all that there had been no time to say. That she had more magery than she would ever admit. That he had meant her to follow him—but not now. Not so soon. Not until he was ancient and august and tired, and she was fit to take his place.

"No," she said. But he only smiled, damn him; and the life pouring out of him as she watched. She must not weep, nor could she linger. She set the burliest of Estarion's northerners to work fashioning a litter, and the rest to taking up the dead and clearing away the flotsam of the battle. Iburan might have called that taking his place. She called it plain common sense. Someone had to make order of this chaos. It had nothing at all to do with magic, or with mastering emperors.

Somewhere in the midst of it Lord Shurichan appeared. There was not a mark on his armor, not a drop of blood on his prettily drawn sword. He had ambitions, Vanyi saw, to take matters in hand. He was the only great one left standing, and the only man of rank in that place.

Just as he drew breath to issue orders, she set herself in front of him. She was markedly smaller than he was, and markedly female, but he could hardly ignore the hand that plucked his sword from him and returned it to its sheath, or the voice that said with acid clarity, "My lord Shurichan. How convenient that you should appear. I was just about to send a messenger to inform you that the battle is over; it's safe to come out."

His mouth was open. He shut it.

"I commend your prudence," Vanyi said, "and I forbear to remark that a lord of a province who fails to stand at his emperor's back when that emperor is threatened might find his loyalty called into question. You were taking the road of greater sense, I presume, and trusting to your men—who are as brave as a lord can wish for, and as faithful in defense—to guard his majesty. Since of course if he emerged alive, you would be present to aid him in your fullest capacity; and if he should, alas, fail to survive the consequences of his rashness, why then there would still be a lord in Ansavaar, and the empire's unity would be preserved." His face had gone crimson as she spoke; now it was vaguely green. She smiled sweetly. "Set your mind at rest, my lord. Everything has been seen to, and at no cost to your comfort. Surely now you are weary from so much excitement; you should rest. These gentlemen will assist you to your rooms."

A company of Estarion's Varyani took station about him. The smallest topped him by a head. He looked, she thought, like a gaffed fish. By the time he reached his chambers he would be bellowing; but that was no concern of hers. If Estarion came out of this alive, he would soothe the man's ruffled feathers. If he did not, then Vanyi would fret about it when she came to it. Estarion dead and his heir nine cycles in the womb, and no surety that the child would live to be born—

She would not think of that. Shock and the suddenness of attack kept order now, but once it had faded, there would be war.

Not if she could help it. She straightened her back and set her jaw and did what she had to do.

There was an ungodly lot of it, and no sleep till it was done. Somewhere amid the endless hours—it was dark beyond the window of the room in which she had taken station, but how long it had been so, she did not remember—some of Estarion's Guard came to her. Shaiyel was there. He had come ostensibly to tell her that Iburan lived still, but she could have ascertained that with a flick of magery. He thought to guard her; when the guardsmen entered, he was working his subtle western way round to coaxing her to sleep.

They were the young hellions she had always liked best, with redheaded Alidan in front. He looked tired and unwontedly grim, his fire banked for once, but no less fierce for that. He had a captive, a figure in soiled and blood-stained white, chained, gagged, and stumbling. The man behind him dragged another such. They flung both at Vanyi's feet.

The assassins lay unmoving, save that one of them twitched as he struck the tiled floor. Alidan kicked him. He jerked and went still.

"Do you need to be quite so emphatic?" Vanyi asked.

"With these," Alidan said, all but spitting, "yes." He hauled the man onto his back. Man, no. The hair was cropped, the breasts were small, but the face was too fine even for a boy's. The robe was torn. There was another under it, or a shift, neither blue nor purple but somewhere between. And the other, who was male, wore grey beneath the white.

Vanyi drew a long slow breath. She did not need the touch of power on minds that had been stripped naked and left to find their way unwarded; she did not need to sense here two of those who had threatened Estarion with magecraft. The robes were proof enough.

"Guildmages," she said. "They were to rise up in triumph, I suppose, and cast off their disguises, and proclaim the Guild's return."

The man was nigh dead; his life ebbed low. The woman opened bruised and swelling eyes. She did not speak. Her mind offered nothing but contempt.

"Half a mage I may be," Vanyi said, "but I'm more now than you. Is there another invasion coming? Should we look to be besieged?"

The answer flickered in the shallows of the ruined power, tangled in a weed-growth of nonsense. Vanyi swooped to pluck it out.

It fled darting-swift. She made a hedge of her power's fingers, and snapped it shut. On nothing.

The woman's eyes stared up. Life faded from them; but even in death they gleamed with mockery.

The other was dead and growing cold. Vanyi straightened, swallowing bile. "See if you can find more of these. And quickly, before they're dead, too."

"There are no more," Alidan said. He sounded more angry than regretful. "These were the only two who lived. They waited, I think. To mock you."

"They were fools," she said. "Shaiyel, go with these men. Find what there is to find."

He was willing, but he hesitated. "And these?"

Her shoulders ached with keeping them level, her neck with holding up her head. "Search them. Then dispose of them."

There was nothing to find, of course. Their minds were wiped clean. That was a mage's trick, to leave no trace of themselves behind, even in the helplessness of death.

But she had learned enough. She had proof that the Guild yet lived, and ways, maybe, to track them down. They had built a Gate. It was fallen now—Estarion had seen to that. But she had memory of how it had come, and how it had stood, and how it had broken. She needed time, which she did not have, and leisure, which was forbidden her, but she would search out the truth. She swore a vow on it, alone in the dark before dawn, with the weight of empires on her shoulders, and the emperor clinging to life in a guarded chamber.

Haliya was with him. Vanyi had been aware of that from the first: how the little idiot crept through all the tumult, melted the guards with tears, and established herself at his bedside. She had not done anything foolhardy, and she did not make herself a nuisance. Now and then she bathed his brow, as if that little could bring down the fever that raged in him, or tried to coax water down his throat.

She was harmless enough where she was. If anyone ventured the chamber, he would be dead before he touched either, emperor or empress who would be. And if Estarion woke, he would not threaten her, Vanyi did not think. Even if he woke raging.

Vanyi need not approach him while Haliya was there. It was cowardice, she knew that, but she clung to it.

Of Korusan there was no sign. He had been with Estarion in the beginning. Now the Olenyai who stood guard were all strangers.

Vanyi might have pursued that, but her solitude was broken. There were disputes for her to settle, lordlings to placate, merchants of the city to soothe. All of them repeated the rumor that the emperor was dead, that he must be seen to be alive or they could not answer for the consequences. She put them off as best she could, but there were more behind them, always more, and no rest to be had.

And Estarion lived so his life long. Vanyi thanked the god that she was not born to it; that she could walk away from it. Soon. When there was someone to take the burden from her.

FORTY-FOUR

PEACE WAS BLESSED FOR HALF OF AN ETERNITY, BUT THEN, IN THE WAY OF things, it began to pall. Estarion knew first a glimmer of restlessness, an ache that might have been boredom. The dark that had been so sweet now seemed an unrelieved monotony. A single star, even the flicker of a candle, would vex less than this endless night.

He stretched, flexed. The darkness yielded, but still it conceived no light.

And should he wait for it? *Light*, he said, thought, willed. And there was light. One star, then another, then another. Once begun, they gave birth to one another, a blooming of stars like nightlilies in the fields beneath Mount Avaryan. All creation was stars, and all dark was turned to light.

And it was not enough. He floated in a sea of stars upon the breast of Mother Night, and it was only light, and he was only he, naked fish-sleek self whose heart was fire.

Beyond light, beyond dark—what was there, what could there be? All that was not light was dark; all that was not dark was light. And where they met, they wrought a wonder: a miracle of living flesh.

He was flesh. He lived. He breathed: great bellows-roaring, drumbeat of the blood along the white tracks of the bones. He counted each one; all those that were whole, the arm that had been broken long ago and set just perceptibly out of true, the ribs cracked and cracked again but healed the stronger for it. He traced their curve with fingers of the soul. And there, see, the chalice of the skull, a goblet full of fire, light within light, flame within flame, lightnings leaping from promontory to promontory. The Sun itself was in it, in what had been mere mortal brain.

Even that was insufficient. There was world beyond this world of the self. He opened his eyes to it.

And screamed.

"Hush, dear lord, hush. Hush."

The hands on him were agony, the voice a dagger in his skull. Everything—everything—

"Too much! *Too much!*"

"Hush," said the other. The Other. The half that was himself, but was outside himself. He struck it away; he clung with the strength of terror, till the creaking of bones, soft awful sound, brought him somewhat to his senses.

Korusan's face of flesh was a blur. Within was both darkness and flame, and pain, such pain—

"Peace," said the soft cool voice. Soft like velvet on the skin; cool like water, but with still the edge of agony.

Estarion lay gasping in his arms. The world was itself again, or near enough. It was Korusan who made it so, Korusan in his black robes with his veils laid aside.

Gently—Estarion would not have said cautiously—he laid his hand on Estarion's cheek. "My lord," he said.

Estarion closed his eyes and let that touch hold him to his body. "Oh, unmerciful gods."

"You wished to die?"

Estarion's eyes snapped open. "Better if I had!"

"My lord—"

Estarion spoke much more quietly, much more carefully. "I have the great-grandmother of headaches."

"That would indeed," Korusan said dryly, "make a man wish himself dead."

"How much wine did I—" Estarion broke off. "No. Oh, gods. I didn't dream it, did I? She's dead. My mother is dead."

"She is dead," said Korusan.

The storm of weeping swept over him, battered him, left him abandoned.

Korusan held him through all of it, saying nothing. When even the dregs of it were gone, and Estarion lay exhausted, Korusan lowered his head and kissed him softly.

It was not meant for seduction. It was comfort; warmth of living flesh before the cold of the dead.

Korusan straightened. His cheeks were flushed, but his eyes were somber.

"Tell me," Estarion said. "Tell me everything."

Korusan frowned. Estarion saw himself in the boy's eyes: waked screaming from a sleep like death, shaken still, sweat-sodden, grey about the lips; but grim, and clear-headed enough, for the moment.

Korusan told him. Merian dead. Iburan alive but like to die—the mages sustained him with their magic, but he was failing. Assassins dead and burned; two mages caught, but dead before they could be questioned.

"Guildmages?"

Korusan frowned more darkly. "Yes." He went on with the rest, which was simple enough. "Your empire is secure, or no less so than before. Your priestess has it in hand. She does all that must be done."

"My—" Estarion struggled against a sudden thickening of wit. "Vanyi?"

"The Islander. The fisherman's daughter."

Estarion did not think that he would ever smile again. But warmth welled and spilled over, and maybe a little touched his face. "Ah, Vanyi. She'll be my empress yet."

Korusan did not say anything to that, but his grip tightened nigh to pain.

"But you," Estarion said, "are the half of myself."

The golden eyes closed. The face, the beautiful face, was as white as Estarion had ever seen it, but for the flush that stained the cheekbones. Fever again. Estarion uncoiled a tendril of the fire that was in him, took the fire of fever to himself. He was not even aware that he had done it until it was done. It was a shock, like cold water on the skin, or joy at the bottom of grief.

Korusan shivered.

"You are ill," Estarion said.

The boy laughed, breathless, bitter as always. "Am I ever not?"

"No longer," said Estarion.

"No," said Korusan. But what he meant by that, Estarion could not tell. He would have had to break the wards that were on the boy's thoughts, and that, he feared, would break the boy's mind. Later, when both of them were stronger, would be time enough to take down the wards, to heal the sickness, to put all fever to flight.

Now . . .

He sat up slowly. Korusan, at first resisting, suddenly let him go. He swayed. The ache in his head was blinding. Wind roared through his soul, wind of wrath, wind of grief.

He pulled himself to his feet. He did not remember this room, although it must be the one in which he had slept before this all began, the lord's bedchamber in Pri'nai. Memory of trifles was lost to him. But the great things, the grim things, the ranks of the dead—those he would never forget.

His hands were full of fire. It dripped from them, splashing on the floor. Each droplet congealed into gold, rayed like a sun.

He clenched his fists. The fire welled in them. He willed it to subside. It did not wish to. Its anger burned.

Korusan's eyes were wide and blank.

"Warrior child," Estarion said to him. "Lion's cub."

Korusan blinked, started, came to himself. The quick flash of temper was deeply comforting.

"Yelloweyes," Estarion said, "don't tell anyone."

"What?"

Estarion flexed his throbbing hands. They bled fire still, but more slowly. "This. It's not . . . it's nothing to be afraid of. But I'd rather you didn't tell anyone about it."

"Liar."

Estarion went stiff.

"Your magic," said Korusan. "It has mastered you. Has it not?"

Estarion set his teeth. "Not yet. Not, gods willing, ever."

"I heard the priests talking. They were afraid that it would be so. That the magic would be too strong and you too weak, and it would consume you."

"No," said Estarion. "I won't let it."

"Is it a matter for letting and not-letting?"

"*Yes!*" Estarion winced with the pain of his own outcry. And maybe it was a lie, maybe it was the feeble wishing of a fool, but he would not yield. Not while he had wits left to resist. "I will . . . not . . . give in. I will master it. It will be my servant. On my hand I swear it."

"Gods willing," said Korusan.

Korusan held the throngs at bay while Estarion drowned himself in drugged wine. Laughing, making light of it, but with a sharp edge of desperation. He had shown himself in the doorway of his chamber, smiling, upright, very much alive; he protested when his nursemaid coaxed him in again. But when the door was shut and barred, he downed the wine with rather too evident relief, and toppled headlong into sleep.

Once he was safely unconscious, his Vinicharyas crept out of hiding. She had fled there when he showed signs of waking, leaving the field to Korusan. As she had then, she said nothing, seemed not to know that the Olenyas was there. She sat where she had sat before, at the bed's side. What she thought she could do, Korusan did not know. He doubted that she did, either.

He left her to it. Tight-coiled terror had held him until he saw Estarion awake and speaking sense. Now it was gone.

He slipped out by the servants' way. In a corridor lit by a single guttering lamp, he leaned against the wall and shivered. Estarion had taken the fever, and with it the little warmth that was in Korusan's thin blood. He wrapped arms about ribs that stabbed with pain. Broken. Maybe. Who was to tell now, with sickness set deep in his bones?

His stomach spasmed. There was nothing for it to cast up: and that was well for his veils.

He pulled himself up, back flattened against the wall. The pain grew no less, but his will remembered its strength. He was the Lion's heir. He yielded to no master.

Plain obstinacy set him to walking. Training kept him erect, even lent him a semblance of grace. Between the two, he walked out of the palace as the Olenyas he was; and even, somewhat, convinced himself that he was strong.

He had the watchwords and the secret ways; they had been given him in Kundri'j Asan, for all the cities where the rebellion was strong. He did not think that he was expected here. The watchers admitted him unquestioned, as much on the strength of his eyes as on that of the words and the signs. They looked less wary than they ought.

The Master of Olenyai stood in a room like a guardroom, empty of any furnishings but a tier of lamps, but full of strangers. The Master of Mages faced him, looking unwontedly ruffled. The air had the thunder-reek of battle.

Korusan neither wavered nor hesitated. He was too angry to be afraid, too fevered to be cautious. He strode to the center of the circle, dropped his veils, and faced them all.

He had shocked them properly. He raked them with his eyes: Master and Master, black veils of Olenyai, blank faces of mages, faces of strangers who were lords of the empire. He lashed them with his voice. "Who gave you leave to loose the attack?"

The lords stared openly at his face. Mages and Olenyai neither moved nor spoke.

Save the Master of the mages. "It was time," he said. He granted Korusan no title, no mark of respect.

The Master of the Olenyai lowered his veil slowly. The lordlings flinched. "Your lives are mine," he said to them. "Remember it."

Korusan looked into that face which he had come to know so well, with its nine thin parallel scars, the last of them still faintly livid. His own two ached as scars will in the cold, although it was warm here with the heat of bodies and braziers. "Did you countenance this?" Korusan asked.

"I did," said Asadi, "my prince."

"I did not," said Korusan, soft and still.

"It was time," the Master of mages said again. "You were not within our reach, to consult. And," he said, "it was our thinking that you were best left untold, lest he or his mages discover our intent."

"You are saying," Korusan said very gently, "that you did not trust me."

There: that was a cause of the battle that had broken off with his coming. He saw the tightening of Olenyai hands on swordhilts, the tensing of mages' bodies.

"It is true," said the Master of mages with calm that was either great arrogance or great folly, "that you appear to be entirely his putative majesty's creature. Could we endanger your semblance for the sake of a warning that, in the end, you did not need? You were not by his side when he fell."

"I was kept from him," said Korusan, "by my brothers." He glared at them, and at Marid most of all. "You knew!"

"We wanted to tell you," said Marid. "But when we were told, it was already too late; you were with him, and it wasn't safe."

Korusan turned back to the mage. "So. It was you who decided it. And it will be you who rule when I am emperor, yes?"

"If you are emperor," the mage said. "Is he dead, prince? You had him in your power—held him as he lay helpless. Did you finish what we began?"

Korusan's lungs were full of knives. He could not speak. There were blades in his throat, and his tongue was numb.

"He lives," the mage said. His voice was calm, expressionless, with an edge that might have been contempt. "You held his life in your hand, and you let it go."

"He has seduced you, prince," said another of the mages. It was a woman, a lightmage. He had not seen her before. "You are snared in his spell. For they do weave magery, those of his blood, all unknowing, and as they breathe, to make themselves beloved."

"When would you have given us leave to begin?" her master asked. "You forbade us in Kundri'j, before he had bound you. Now that you belong to him—"

"Koru-Asan is no one's slave," said the Master of the Olenyai, soft and deadly.

Master of Olenyai and Master of mages stood poised on the edge of a new quarrel. Korusan found his voice somewhere and beat it into submission. "No, I did not kill him. If I am enslaved to him, then so is he to me. I will take him when and as I please, and ask no one's leave."

"So you said in Kundri'j," said the Master of the Guild. "And we gave him to you, laid him at your feet, and you pleased to let him live. There are good men dead because of him, strong mages destroyed, an empire in worse disarray than it has ever been."

"Blame him not for that," Korusan said, clipping the words off short. "You would not wait for me to take him from behind. You must open your Gate, proclaim your presence to every mage in every temple from westernmost Veyadzan to the Eastern Isles, declare open war upon the body of the empress mother, rouse the emperor's wrath and with it his magic—and you cry foul against him for your own immeasurable folly?"

"And how long would we wait?" the mage shot back. "Years, prince? Decades? While you wallow in his bed, come crawling at his bidding, weep tears of bliss when he permits you to kiss his fundament?"

Korusan could not kill him. That would be too simple. Marid would happily have done it for him. He restrained his swordbrother with a glance, and looked the mage up and down. "I had wondered," he said, "whether you were arrogant or a fool. Now I am certain. You are a perfect idiot." He drew his lesser sword, the left-handed blade, and stepped forward. The mage went grey-green. He held it before the man's eyes. "Your life is mine. Tempt me and I take it, magebound or no."

The blade flashed down, up. The mage gasped and clapped hand to brow. Blood dripped into his astonished eyes.

Korusan granted him a modicum of respect for keeping silence, though a blade as sharp as this wounded to the bone first and woke the pain long after.

The mage vanished in a flurry of light robes and dark. Korusan turned his back on them. The lordlings and the Olenyai waited in varying degrees of stillness. "You will wait," he said, "until the empress has had her death-rite. Then I promise you, we bring all of this to its end."

The Olenyai inclined their heads. The lordlings went down on their faces.

He swept his blade clean along the edge of his outer robe and sheathed it, and looped up the veils again. Some of the mages had left their master and faced him. He could not read them, whether they pondered threat or submission.

"You thought that you had simple enemies," he said to them: "a Sunlord who had slain his own magic and left himself open to your power, a son of the Lion so enfeebled by the failing of his blood that he would be your puppet, your creature, and your slave. Long years you labored to create us both: he the weakling, easily destroyed; I the weakling, easily mastered. I will take what is mine, mages. Have you no least doubt of that. But I will take it as I will, and when I will, and where. You will serve me then. You will do as I bid."

He had no care for resentment or anger or thwarted pride. They gave him all of that. But they gave him also silence, and slowly, one by one, the lowering of proud eyes, the bending of stiff necks.

He turned on his heel. There had been bodies between himself and the door. They barred his way no longer.

Sheer white-hot will kept him on his feet through the maze that was that house, past the watchers and the guards, into the twilit street. People passed, scurrying from the shadow of him. His stride slowed. He stumbled, caught himself.

He would come to the palace again. He had willed it, therefore it must be. But it would be no easy journey. The knives in his lungs had sharpened. The ache in his bones was fiercer now, almost too much to ignore.

He was not dying. He would not allow it. He would walk, so, one foot before the other. Walls helped him; where they were not, he willed the air to hold him up.

It was no more difficult than the run through the mages' wood that had begun his initiation into the Olenyai, nor any more impossible than running from that ensorceled place into the test of wits and will against the mages' snares. Certainly it was no less simple than standing robed, veiled, two-sworded, Olenyas, and yet naked before a pair of golden eyes in a black eagle's face. All that, he had done. This too he would do.

He was aware of the shadow as it moved. Oh, he was feeble: he should have known it before ever he saw it, sensed it waiting, slipped round to catch it by surprise. He tried to leap aside, but his feet were leaden heavy. He stumbled and fell.

No blade swept his head from its neck. "Sweet Avaryan!" said the shadow in a voice he knew. He had not known how cordially he hated it, or even yet how weak he was, till he felt her hands on him, pulling him up, and no will in him to resist.

The Islander draped his arm about her neck. She was smaller than he but sturdy enough, no doubt from hauling nets since she was big enough to stand. One hand gripped his wrist. The other circled his middle and closed on his belt. So joined, like drunken lovers, they swayed and staggered homeward.

Such as home was, a palace sunk in the stillness of exhaustion, guards alert to every shadow, and its heart a dead empress, a dying priest, an emperor drugged into a stupor. Korusan was recovering somewhat, but Vanyi was too strong for him. She half carried, half dragged him into a chamber that must be her own, and lowered him to the narrow bed. She was gentler than she looked.

He struggled to sit up. "I cannot—I must—"

She held him down with one hand. He struck it aside and surged to his feet. Pain ripped through him. He gasped. The gasp caught on hooks and tore.

It was true, what they said. One could cough up one's lungs. One did it in racking agony, in bloody pieces.

His veils were gone. A basin hovered in front of him. Hands held it, and eyes behind that, eyes as grey as flints.

"Yes," she said. "Now you have to kill me. You can wait till you're done dying."

"I am not—" he said. Tried to say. His throat was raw, his voice scraped bare.

"Stop it," she said. Damnable arrogant peasant. "The blood's given out, hasn't it? It's a miracle you've lived as long as you have."

"Kill me, then," he whispered, since he could not say it louder. "Get it over."

"Oh, no," she said. "You belong to Estarion. He's the one to say whether you live or die."

"What? Is he your god?"

She smiled a blade-thin smile. "No. But I think he's yours." That outrage laid him flat. The knives at least were not sunk so deep, the pain faded to a dull roar. He was weak beyond bearing, but he would live, he thought, for yet a while.

She laid the basin aside without apparent revulsion at its contents, and bent over him. Her hands ran down the length of him, not touching. His flesh quivered. Magery. Hers was less repellent than the others he had known, the pain of it sharper, but it was a clean pain.

"Goddess," she muttered. "You're a patchwork of ill-matched magics. What were they trying to do to you? Kill you quicker, or kill you more slowly? Or couldn't they make up their minds?"

He refused to answer. She took no notice. "That's half the trouble. Look, there, that mending goes to war with this, and this—" She spat a word that must have been a curse. "Hedge-wizards! Why in the hells couldn't they have let you crumble away in peace?"

"Perhaps I wished to live," he said.

She paused. She seemed surprised that he could speak, even in a croak. But she did not know Olenyai hardihood.

"You are a pretty thing," she said. "That must be why he fancies you."

He bit his tongue. He was feeling stronger. More magery; but again it was different. He could, in a fashion, see through it into the mage herself: a tang that was jealousy, a white heat that must be her magic, a great bright singing thing that seemed to be part of Estarion, and yet was not.

It was for that that she healed him. Because she fancied that she saw it in him also, and because she thought that he had power, somehow, to guard the emperor. She, like the Guildmages, believed that there had been a test; that Korusan had passed it, and proved himself bound to Estarion. And no one so bound could turn traitor. It was not possible.

Nor was this that she did. She could not make him whole. That was beyond any mage's power. But she could give him a few days' life—cycles, she was thinking, even years. But his bones knew better.

He rose carefully, drew a breath. It did not catch. He flexed his shoulders. They ached, but no more than they should.

She sat on her heels, watching him. He could kill her now. He had his swiftness back, and his strength. She was unarmed, unwary, bone-weary as mages were after a working. She would die before she mustered wits to move.

Estarion loved her. There was no accounting for it—she had neither beauty nor lineage nor sweetness of temper to endear her to any man, let alone an emperor— but Korusan could hardly escape the truth of it.

"I let you live," he said to her, "because I am not ungrateful. And because you belong to him."

"I do *not*—"

Her anger startled him; it made him laugh, which startled her. They stared at one another in sudden silence.

"I begin to understand," she said, "what else he sees in you."

Not until he was long away from her did it strike Korusan what she had done.

He was Olenyas. He was—or he thought he had been—warded against magic. And she had worked magic on him. Easily, potently, as if there had been no defenses on him at all.

He should be alarmed, but he was grimly delighted. Guildmages scorned her for her common lineage, her lack of training in their arts of magic. And she made nothing of their magics on him; spat contempt at the weaving of them. She was more than they could imagine, greater danger than they might have anticipated.

It would be a pleasure to see their faces when they learned what this priestess-witch was. Even if he died thereafter, he would die in some measure of content.

FORTY-FIVE

WHEN ESTARION WOKE FROM HIS DRUGGED SLEEP, HE WAS ALONE. BUT THERE was a memory of presence—piercing to senses that, dulled for so long, were grown painfully keen. Haliya. As easily as he breathed, his magery followed the trail of her out of the room and through a maze of passages to the women's chambers. He did not track her within. She was safe there among his mother's guards.

Wild joy smote him. Mage—he was a mage again. But then with memory came the stab of grief, felling him even as he rose.

Merian was dead. He had quarreled with her endlessly, fretted the bonds of love, duty, honor, flown in the face of them all until surely she would learn to hate him. But she never had, no more than he had hated her for what she was: empress, priestess, mother of his body.

Robed as a priest but cloaked as a king, he went in to the hall where she lay. They had given her a bier worthy of her royalty, coverlets of silk, great pall of cloth of gold. She lay in the stillness of the dead, her beautiful hair woven into the many plaits of a northern queen. Gold was on her breast above the pall, and gold in her ears, and gold set with jewels on her arms, her wrists, her fingers.

Her panoply, she had always called that, like the armor that a king wore into battle. When she would be in comfort she wore an old threadbare robe, her hair loose or braided down her back, and no jewel but the armlet that her royal lover had given her before he made her his empress.

That she wore still, a plain thing amid the rest, copper that was much prized among her people, inlaid with golden wires shaping a skein of dancing women. She was the tall one, the one whose beauty shone even through the rough unskillful work. For her Sunlord had made it himself, given it to her in shyness that by all accounts was alien to him, and in accepting it, she had accepted all of him—not the man alone but the empire he ruled.

Now they danced together on the other side of the night. Their son knelt by her bier, hands fisted in the pall, and wept.

He wept hard, but he did not weep long. He raised his head. Her guards, tall women in bright armor, had averted their eyes. Tears glistened on their cheeks.

He scrubbed them from his own. His eyes had burned dry. He would not weep again.

Rage swelled where grief had been, rage as white and cold and pitiless as the sun that pierced the high windows of the hall.

It thrust him to his feet. It drove him through the palace in a train of startled people, animals, even a lone brainless bird that had escaped its cage.

The rebels who had begun it all were gone. He began to order out the hunt; then paused. They were but puppets. Whether they thought they acted of themselves, or knew that they were a feint, it did not matter. He knew. He had memory of the Gate, and of the powers that sustained it.

First he must look to the care of his mother's body. She would not be burned as priests of the Sun were; she was priestess of the goddess, and would be given to the dark and the silence. He did not know that he wished her entombed here, unless he made the whole city her tomb; and that was madder even than he was minded to be. A place waited for her in Endros Avaryan beside the body of her lord, in the tomb of the emperors beneath the Tower of the Sun. Yet that was far to go, and revolt between, that might swell to war. And there was the matter of revenge for her death.

Sunlords are above revenge. Her voice, his memory tricking him in a dart of sunlight.

Sunlords had never needed revenge; never, until Estarion, been the playthings of hidden enemies. Sarevadin who had been taken by mages and stripped of all but the raw self, had known by whom she was taken, and why. Hers had been open war, mage against mage and no quarter given.

He was prey to poison, treason, assassins. They had taken his father, his mother, his servant. They had robbed him of youth and strove now to rob him of manhood.

No more.

"My lord."

A priest, a mage in torque and braid, tawny head bent. Estarion stared at him, empty for the moment of speech.

"My lord, will you come?"

"To what?" Estarion asked him. "Treachery?"

The priest's head flew up. He was not pure Asanian: that pride was a plainsman's, and those eyes, yellow though they were, narrow above the high cheekbones. Power shimmered on him, bright with anger. "Yes, my lord, there has been treachery. The high priest of Avaryan in Endros is dying because of it. Will you deign to visit him on his deathbed?"

No, Estarion thought. There was no reason in it, no mortal sense.

The priest had no pity for him. "I would not have troubled you, sire. But he insisted."

How odd to be despised. How rare. He was loved or he was hated. Sometimes he was feared. But scorn—that was a new thing.

"Take me," he said.

They had laid Iburan in a room that must have been a servant's, with a bed as narrow as a northerner's, and no softening of silks or velvets. Braziers there were none. He did not need them. He had his priests and his priestesses, and the heat of their power.

He lay in the midst of them, burning with fever. His body could bear no touch of coverlet; his weight upon the bed was pain. The torque about his neck burned as if it had been molten, but none of them had dared to take it off.

He should have been dead long ago, but he clung to life with fierce persistence.

Estarion thrust through a wall of pain, and dropped to one knee beside the bed. The face that had been so beautiful was ravaged with poison. The body was grossly swollen, suppurating with sores. It stank.

Just so, he thought, remote and burning cold. Just so had his father been.

"They lack imagination, our enemies," he said.

Dark eyes opened in the ruined face. They warmed at sight of Estarion. The voice was a husk of itself, but there should have been no voice at all. "Starion. Still angry with me, then?"

"No," Estarion said. "Never again, foster-father."

Iburan's eyes filled with tears. They scalded as they overflowed. With infinite gentleness Estarion wiped them away. Even that cost Iburan pain.

"I took your power," Estarion said. He had not known till he said it. The horror came after; the bleak hatred of himself. "I have killed you."

"My own fault," said Iburan, "for getting in the way."

"Mine," cried Estarion. "My fault. Oh, Avaryan! It's I who should be dead, and not you."

"Stop that," said Iburan. "Time enough when we're all dead, to squabble over the bones. Now listen to me. While you were dealing with mages—and dealing surpassingly well, too; you were a marvel to watch—I happened to notice a thing or two. It slowed me down when I should have been getting out of your way, which was foolish of me, but I learned somewhat. Watch your Olenyai, Starion. If they aren't part of this, they know enough to damn them in any court of justice."

Estarion did not care. Iburan was dying, Merian was dead. What did anything matter but that?

But Iburan's intensity held him, and his hand, clasping Estarion's wrist with a shadow of its old strength. "Listen to me, Estarion. Watch them. The one they set to spy on you—the young one with the lion-eyes—"

"He's no spy," Estarion snapped, forgetting to be gentle.

Iburan paid no attention. "He'll kill you if he can. He's been ordered to do it."

"He loves me," Estarion said.

Iburan sighed. His breath rattled; he coughed. "No doubt he does. He hates you, too. Watch him, Estarion. Promise me."

The light in Iburan's eyes was fading, his grip weakening. It was only the mages' light, Estarion tried to tell himself, flickering as it was wont to do.

"Starion," said Iburan, "when you sing the death-rite for her—remember—how she loved best the hymn of the morning star. Sing that for her, for me."

"You'll sing it yourself," Estarion said with sudden fierceness. "You won't die. I won't let you."

He called his power. It was white fire, hot gold, sun's splendor. The priest-mages fell back, struck to fear. They remembered too well what that torrent of magery had done. Its consequence lay before them, dying powerless.

"No."

It was simple, barely to be heard, and it had no magic in it. But it checked the calling of Estarion's power. It held him motionless.

"Starion, don't. I'm too far gone. And, son of my heart, much as I love you, I think it's time I left you. I've guarded you, bound you, held you back till I nigh destroyed you. Better for you that I go. I've no fear of the dark land. She's waiting for me there, and her lord, my lord, whom I loved."

"You said you loved me more."

That was unworthy, but Iburan did not say so. He smiled, a stretching of cracked and bleeding lips. "Ah, child, that's why I leave you. The god never granted me a son of my body; and yet I never felt the lack."

Estarion's throat locked shut. He forced the words through it. "The god granted me a father twice over. Now he takes you from me as he took the other. Exactly—as—"

"That's merely justice," Iburan said. His fingers slipped from Estarion's wrist.

Estarion caught them, cradled them. "Foster-father—"

Iburan was still smiling.

So easily, after all, he went. Between one breath and the next: he lived, and then he did not. He slipped the flesh and all its torments as lightly as a lady sheds her garment, dropped it and rose winged, leaping into the light.

So could he have done at any time since he knew that he was dying. He had waited for Estarion. And Estarion had indulged himself in trifles. In sleep. In ramping about. In being a great roaring idiot.

So let him be for yet a while. He looked down at the empty, stinking thing that had been the greatest mage and priest in this age of the world. He kissed its brow, which already had begun to cool. He smoothed the beard, still beautiful on the ravaged breast, and folded the hands over it.

He straightened. The priests—his priests—returned his stare. Some were weeping. Some were angry. Some were both.

"I give him the Sun," he said. "By your leave."

"You have no need of that, Sunlord," said the proud one. Shaiyel, that was his name. He had not put himself forward before. In the clarity of grief, Estarion knew why. Anyone of Asanian blood in Keruvarion learned to walk softly round the emperor.

The taste in his mouth was bitter. He smiled through it. "And yet I ask your leave."

"Then you have it," said Shaiyel.

Estarion inclined his head. Shaiyel was not forsaking contempt for anything as simple as this, but he could grant justice where justice was due.

Estarion drew a breath. His power beat like a heart. He spread his hands above Iburan's body. The fire tried to bleed out of them; he held it back, though it burned and blistered.

The priests began to chant. It was not the death-chant but the sunrise-hymn, the song of praise to the god at his coming.

A shiver ran down Estarion's spine. The god was in him. Never so close before this, never so strong. It would master him; it would burn him to ash.

Then so be it.

He laid himself before the god. *As you will,* he thought, sang, was. *All, and only, as you will.*

He was the fountain and the source. He was the burning brand. He was the fire in the corn; he was the light on the spear. He was bright day in the dark land.

They were with him, all of them, not only the few who wrought the circle here. Priests and mages, servants in the temples, initiates on the world's roads, guardians at the Gates, attendants upon lords and princes—all gathered in the bright blaze that was his power. All knew what he wrought here; all wove themselves within it. He, their heart and their crown, took the body of the god's servant. He lifted it up, and it weighed no more than a breath. He filled it with light.

It burned like a lamp made of straw. Like a lamp it was beautiful, and like straw it was consumed. The shape of it lingered yet awhile, a body of light. Then it too crumbled and sank into ash.

The light died. The circle withered and fell away. There was a great stillness.

Estarion looked down upon an empty bed. The impress of the body was in it still. "Great bear of the north," he said. "Great mage and priest. Dear god in heaven, dread goddess below, how I loved you."

The god's departing left him cold and ill and bleakly, grimly content. He did not remember what he said to the priests. He supposed that he had said something; they seemed a little comforted. One, the priestess who looked rather like Ziana, wept in his arms. He left her folded in Shaiyel's. They would all grieve together, once he had freed them from the vexation of his presence.

When he noticed again where he was, he was far from them, surrounded by strangers. He blinked, clearing his sight to a frightened face, a voice babbling of something: "My lord, if you will eat, you have not touched a bite since yesterday, you should—"

Lord Shurichan, solicitous to silliness, transparently terrified lest he be found guilty of the empress' murder. He was guilty of much—Estarion could hardly approve of an agreement or three that he had made in the event of the emperor's death—but in that he had taken no part.

How simple to see the truth; how blinding the pain that came after it, the power swelling and pulsing, struggling to break free of encumbering flesh.

He was growing stronger, or more skilled. He swayed, but caught himself before anyone could wake to alarm. There was no mage near to recognize the hesitation for what it was. Only simple men, Asanians, who determined that he was weak with fasting, and herded him to a chamber and saw him plied with dainties until he ate simply to be rid of them. He drank considerably more than he ate. Korusan would have had something to say of that, but Korusan was nowhere about.

Dizzy with wine and wrath but steady on his feet, Estarion went in search of his guardsman.

He found the boy where he belonged, standing guard over Estarion's chambers. The sight of him woke something. It might have been rage. It might have been joy—black joy, that cried to Iburan's bright spirit: *See, he is mine. He loves me!*

Estarion pulled him within, shut the door on goggling faces, got rid of veils and robes and encumbrances, and flung him down on the floor, as if he were the whole empire of Asanion and Estarion an army arrayed against it.

Korusan was not acquiescent. That weakness was not in his nature. But he allowed it. He did not struggle, though he could have fought free and felled Estarion if he had been so minded. He yielded because it was wise to yield, but, great dancer that he was, he yielded as it best pleased him, guiding where he seemed to be guided, leading where he might have been led.

And when they lay breathless, tangled in robes and rugs and one another, Estarion raised his head from Korusan's sweat-slicked breast. "Only you," he said, "could give me this."

"A fight?" asked Korusan.

"I'd have raped a woman," Estarion said.

"You would not." Korusan pulled him up and kissed him. "You are royally drunk. Who fed you so much wine? I will have his ballocks for it."

"You can't have them," Estarion said. "I need them. If not—for raping women—"

"You are incapable of any such thing. Now will you stop it before you grow maudlin? Tears are shameful enough. Tears soaked in wine are a disgrace."

"That too you give me," said Estarion, "brisk as a slap in the face. What would I be without you?"

"Dead," said Korusan. He wriggled free, sprang to his feet. But he did not move once he was up, standing half turned away, as if he did not know what to do next.

He had grown since first Estarion saw his face. He was a little taller, his shoulders visibly wider. He was less a boy, more the man that he was meant to be. But beautiful still. That would not change, however old he grew.

Estarion rose behind him, folded arms about him. "There now. I'm not going to die just yet."

Korusan was rigid. "And if I am? What will you do, my lord?"

"You aren't, either," Estarion said through the cold clenching in his middle. Not this one. Not this one, too. "See, you don't even have a fever. You're as well as I've ever seen you."

"Ask your priestess how that is. Ask her how much it cost her magic, to make me so."

Estarion started. "You went to Vanyi?"

He had not seen her with those about Iburan. She should have been there. She would tear herself with grief, that she had not.

"She came to me." Korusan's breath caught. It might have been laughter. "Or I fell at her feet. I shall have to kill her, my lord. She saw my face."

"Kill her," said Estarion with deadly lightness, "and I kill you."

"And then, no doubt, yourself." Korusan sighed. His stiffness eased a little; he leaned back against Estarion. "She would almost be worthy of you, if she had any lineage to speak of."

"How perfectly Asanian," Estarion said.

"I am perfect Asanian," said Korusan.

FORTY-SIX

THE SUN SET IN A SKY AS LUCENT AND AS BRITTLE AS ICE. THE CITY WAS QUIET, but it was the quiet of exhaustion. Where the rebellion would flare again, or when, no one knew. Not even Estarion.

He had begun that bleak day beside his mother's bier. He chose to end it there. In the morning he must sing her death-rite. Then she would go to the embalmers, who would prepare her for the long journey to her tomb.

Tonight she lay in peace. He dismissed the guards, who granted him that right, to keep the last vigil alone. His tears were all shed. He was as still as she was, and nigh as cold. His flesh felt little enough of it; the Sun's fire warmed it. But his heart was as hard as her cheek beneath his hand, and as icily chill.

Someone breathed close by. He whipped about.

Ulyai padded out of the shadows beyond the candles' light. Her cubs followed in a wary line, and behind them the woman whose name, after all, he did not know, nor anything of what she was. To his newborn mage-sight she was a dark glass, clear to the bottom and yet revealing nothing but a shadow of his own face.

The ul-queen stretched herself at the bier's foot. Her she-cubs pressed close. The he-cub sought the colder comfort of Estarion's knee. So high already. He would be tall, that one.

Sidani walked past Estarion as if he had not been there, round the bier, to bend over the figure that lay on it. Estarion had ceased to be astonished at anything she did, but this verged on impertinence. He opened his mouth to say so.

"She had Asanian blood, you know," the wanderer said, "and royal at that. Hirel never knew that he had a daughter among the tribes. It mattered little to them; it was carelessness in a chieftain's daughter, or willfulness, to bear the child of the one they called the little stallion. That's how you come by your eyes, youngling. She carried the Lion's blood, too—as much as your father did."

"When did Hirel ever—"

"On a time," she said, "when Sarevadin, proud idiot that he was, had slain a mage with power, and lost his own in return. It should have killed him. He found the Zhil'ari instead, and his companion found a diversion to sweeten the evenings. In the end they came to Endros and the Sunborn, and Sarevadin had healing, of a sort, though he hardly knew it then. He'd lost his magery beyond retrieving. He'd gained something that, once known, was more by far."

Estarion looked at her and knew that she was mad. But it was a seductive madness, of a most persuasive sort. It tempted a man to give himself up to it as if it were true. "Is that a secret, lady? That those who kill with magery become greater than mages?"

"Goddess forbid," said Sidani. "We'd have a world full of warring mages else, blasting one another to ash in the hope of becoming gods."

"You make no sense," Estarion said.

"I make perfect sense," she said. "You're a great killer of mages. Has it made you hungry for more?"

He could have killed her for that. He held himself rigid; smiled, even, wide and feral. "You can't imagine what it's made me."

"Oh, but I can." Her own smile was sweetly terrible. "You are a menace, child. You think that you have yourself in hand; you imagine that you can go on as you are now, a little colder maybe, a little harder, but shouldn't an emperor be cold and hard? That's pride, too, and folly."

"You know nothing," he said, low in his throat. "You are a nameless gangrel woman with more addlement than wits."

"I had a name once," she said. She laid her hand on the empress' cheek. "So beautiful," she said, "and so cold. How Mirain would have raged to see a priestess of the goddess upon the double throne, mother to its heir, regent of its empire. He was madder than any of us, and blinder. He could never see the dark for the blaze of the light."

"You speak treason," Estarion said.

She laughed long and free. "Oh, that word! So easy on the tongue; so deadly on the neck. I've spoken worse than that in my day, and to haughtier kings than you."

"How can anyone—"

He caught himself. She grinned, reading him as easily as she ever had. "You're nothing to some I've seen. You're a gentle one for all your fierceness; you wear another's skin too easily to be honestly cruel. Cruelty takes a certain lack of imagination, you see."

"I'd have thought it took the opposite."

"No," she said. "That's mere cleverness. True wit needs more."

"I have little enough of any of that," he said, neither wry nor precisely angry. He was tired suddenly, tired of everything. Even of what he knew she would say, that he was a master of self-pity.

But, being Sidani, she did not say it. "You were broken young, and you mended crooked. Surgeons know what to do when they see the like. They break again, then set anew, and this time set it straight."

"You'll break me?" Estarion asked. Humoring her, he told himself. Passing the long night in this strange painful amusement.

"You're broken already," she said. "Are your hands bleeding gold?"

He clenched them, pressing them to his thighs. "No!"

"You're a dreadful liar, child." She came round the bier again and took his hands. He mustered every scrap of will to resist her. None of it mattered in the least. Her fingers were cold, but there was heat within, a thread of fire. They pressed just so, and his hands unfolded.

The left hand was trembling; blisters had risen on it, grey against the dark skin. The right was all gold, roiling and flowing in the bed of the *Kasar*.

"Sages," she said as if to herself, "would set the seat of power in the loins, or in the heart, or behind the eyes. And so it is, in all of them and none. But in Sun-blood, wherever it begins, it ends in the hands. There's the god's wit for you. Where else is pain so intense, or so delicately modulated?"

Estarion had an answer for that. He bit his tongue, but she read it, perhaps in his branded palm.

She laughed. "Yes, there, too. But the god set fire there long ago, and in every man—and in a woman it's not so easily got at, though it's hotter once it starts, and lasts longer. The hands it had to be. Do you think you're being brave, bearing pain that would lay strong warriors low?"

"It's no worse than it ever is," Estarion said.

"Liar," she said tenderly. "Ah, child, what a muddle they've made of you."

"Isn't that what we all are? Muddle and folly?"

"Everyone doesn't threaten empires with his muddlement." She touched the *Kasar* with a finger. He gasped: not that it cost pain, but that it cost none. A ripple of coolness spread outward from her touch.

"How—"

She was not listening. "And you are a threat, youngling. Never doubt it. You'll carry on for a while, and think yourself safe; but when you break again, you'll break past mending. A Sunlord broken is a terrible thing. Pure power, and pure mind-lessness."

Yes, a deep part of him whispered, looking down into the sea of fire. "No," he said aloud. "What do you know of this? What do you know of anything?"

"What do you know, my lord emperor? Have you looked on the face of the Sun-born in his sleep? Have you stood in the Tower that he made?"

"It has no door," Estarion said. "And if it did, what good would it do me?"

"Why," she said, "none, for all the use you'd have made of it. A door is a simple thing to make. It's what it opens on that matters. Mirain made that Tower of magery, and sealed it with the Sun's fire. His own fire, child. The same that burns in you and leaves trails of golden droplets wherever you go. It's not simple power such as mages know, that they draw from earth and air and wield through their bodies. It's a different thing, both stronger and stranger. Training alone doesn't master it. It needs more. It needs what is in the Tower."

"And what is that?"

"Strength," she said. "Knowledge. It's woven in the stones. It holds the Sunborn in his sleep, and guards the bones of his descendants. A night on the crag of Endros would drive a man mad; and so it still might, if anyone dared the Tower. But a man who is a Sunlord—he needs that madness, that snatching out of himself. It's the source of his power."

Estarion laughed, startling himself. "Oh, you are a master of talespinners! You almost had me believing you."

"I hope so," she said. "It's almost too late for you. And that 'almost' is more hope than surety."

"Oh, come," he said. "Now you're trying to scare me, as if I were a child with the night-terrors. I need lessoning in reining in my power, I admit it. But once this rebellion is put down and the empire is quiet, I'll withdraw to a temple; I'll submit myself to its mages; I'll learn to master myself."

"You have no time," said Sidani. "Even tomorrow's sunset might be too long. Look, you're bleeding again. That's blood, child: blood of power."

"Then I'll bleed dry, and be no worse than before."

For the first time she seemed impatient. "*Tcha!* You are the most exasperating infant. Power doesn't bleed like blood, not in Sunlords. It kills you, yes. But first it kills whatever else it lights on, and it grows stronger instead of weaker, the longer it bleeds, until there's no will left, only the power. What you were when it killed a mage's soul, what it was when it plucked mages free of their power as if they had been sea-spiders in their shells—that's the barest beginning. Your high priest is dead because you had no mind to notice that it was he and not a Guildmage standing in your path. What, when you begin to feed on your priests here, and after them, priests and mages wherever your power finds them? And when they are gone and your hunger still unsated, what's to do but seek the souls of simple men, and consume them?"

"No!" cried Estarion, struggling against her grip, trying to block his ears, his mind, his awareness that whispered, *Yes. Yes.* "It's all lies. You're raving. How can you know this? *Who are you?*"

"Sarevadin."

That was not her voice. It was colder by far, and somewhat deeper. It came out of the darkness, a shadow, golden-eyed. Another came behind it.

He almost wept at the sight of them—and no matter the riddle of their coming in together, priestess and Olenyas, and standing there as if they had been so for a long while, watching, listening, waiting for their moment. "Korusan! Vanyi. Thank the god and goddess. I've fallen prey to a madwoman."

Then the name that Korusan had spoken pierced through the veils of befuddlement. Korusan spoke it again. "I know what she is. I followed her here, and your priestess after me. She is Sarevadin. Look, take her hand."

She had let Estarion go. Instinct cried out to him to thrust himself as far away as he might, but something made him do as Korusan bade. She did not resist him, did not seem dismayed, stood smiling faintly as he seized her hand and turned it palm up.

Gold and ash. Gold—and—

He was not even awed. What struck him first was pity, and horror of the quenched and twisted thing. "What did you do to yourself?"

"I tried to cut it out," she said.

He raised his eyes from the ruin of the *Kasar* to the ruin of her face.

No; not ruin. He had always thought her beautiful, with her proud bones under the age-thinned skin. "You look like your portraits," he said.

"Not much, any longer," she said.

"No," said Estarion. Obstinacy was a refuge. It kept him from having to think. "We all know you're dead, you see. And we look at the portraits and see the hair, like copper and fire, and take little enough notice of what's under it, except that it's a woman, and beautiful."

"You'd never hide as I did," she said.

"Why?"

She knew that he did not mean himself, or his eyes that could never be mistaken, not in such a face as his, but the fact of her abandoning it all, throne and empire and the power that she was born to hold. They had always understood one another. They were of the same blood.

"If you were given a chance at freedom," she asked him, "would you take it?"

"That would depend on the price," he said.

"I paid in my lord's life. I thought that I should die with him, and leave our son free to take the throne for which we bred him. I failed in courage once I'd taken the sword and set myself to fall on it; so I killed myself who was Sarevadin, but left the body alive. I became no one and nothing."

He looked at her. Something monstrous swelled in him, something that was not joy, nor terror, but a welter of both. "Then I have no right to any of this. It is yours. You are the empress who should be. You are the elder heir of the Sunborn."

"I think," she said after a long pause, "that this is your revenge on me for keeping my secret so long."

Estarion was too numb with shock to be appalled. "You don't want it?"

"Youngling," she said, "do you?"

He sucked in a breath. Her hand was still in his, forgotten. He laid his own over it, *Kasar* to *Kasar*. It was a perilous thing to do, but he was past caring. The lightnings jolted through him. He was fiercer than they. She stood like a rock in a tiderace, head tilted back, half glaring, half laughing in his face.

He had not stood face to face with living blood of his Sunborn blood since his father was slain. He had forgotten, if he had ever known, what it was to know that whatever he was or willed to be, there was one who was his equal. Or—and that was stranger yet—his better.

"Now will you believe me?" she asked him.

He had almost forgotten what brought them to the quarrel. It was like her to remember.

"It is true, Starion." Vanyi, hard and clear. She stood behind Korusan still, her white robe like a shadow of his black one. "You will lose yourself in your power, unless you master it."

"And that needs the Tower in Endros?" Estarion spoke to them both, all, it hardly mattered. "If I ride out now, will I be alive when I come to it?"

"There is another way," said Sarevadin.

Estarion's glance leaped to Vanyi, caught on Korusan's veiled face. That the women had conspired to trap him—he could credit that. But he did not think that the Olenyas had had any part in it. The boy's eyes were wide, blank, astonished.

"Gates," Estarion said. "But the Mageguild wields them."

"Did I say it would be easy?" Vanyi was trembling as if with exhaustion, or with fury held rigidly in check. "You don't know what you look like to eyes that can see. The whole of the mage-realm pulses as you breathe. She"—she would not name the name, Estarion took note of that; had she perhaps not known until he himself did?—"says that there is a way to tame your power, to teach you what you have to know without the years that you don't have. You don't even have days."

"I may be stronger than any of you can guess," he said.

"You are a worse idiot than we could have imagined." Sarevadin slapped him lightly, just enough to sting. In the swift flare of his temper, she grinned her wild white grin. "There is a way, young one. Yon priestess says that she can raise a Gate. That's dangerous; I don't pretend it isn't. But if we move quickly, and if we move as I know how to move, we'll be there before the Guild knows what we've done."

"There," said Estarion, "but not back again."

"You'll take us back," she said. "Or we'll all die together."

"All?" Estarion asked.

"I'm going," Vanyi said. "I know Gates, and I can stand guard while you do—whatever you do."

"But you're not—"

"She's not Sun-blood," Sarevadin said. "She's not male, either. She'll not lose her wits in my father's Tower."

Her father. One forgot, or could not encompass it. This was Sidani the wanderer woman with her wild wit and her scurrilous tales, putting guardsmen to the blush with the songs she could sing. And it was Sarevadin the empress, great beauty of her age, great mage, great queen, great lover and priestess. This, standing by the bier of another empress, bidding Estarion do the maddest thing that he had ever done.

Walk through a Gate in defiance of the Guild that had risen against him. Enter the doorless Tower. Look on the sleeper who must not be waked, and mend his power that was broken, or die in the trying. With a priestess on Journey for defender, and a madwoman for a guide.

He spread his arms. "Well? Shall we go?"

"No," said Sarevadin.

His jaw had dropped. He picked it up again.

"It needs time," she said, "and your mother wants singing to her rest. And you should sleep. Tomorrow when the rite is sung and the feast is done, we go. Go light on the wine, youngling. You'll want your head clear for the working."

The hot flush crawled up his cheeks. He fought it with temper. "All this desperate urgency, and you'll dally at the end of it?"

"You will dally," she said. "We will labor long and hard to make ready. Gates aren't raised in a heartbeat; Gates warded with secrecy are slower yet."

"But I can—"

"You cannot," she said, flat and implacable. "You will sleep, if I have to lay a wishing on you, and you will play the emperor as your people require, and when it's over, you will find us waiting." She softened somewhat. "Don't worry, child. You'll have enough and more to do, once you're in the Tower."

FORTY-SEVEN

KORUSAN ESCAPED IN ESTARION'S SHADOW. THEY ALL SEEMED TO HAVE forgotten him, the women caught up in the working that they must begin, Estarion in a temper at being sent to bed like a child. He went obediently enough, Korusan noticed, for all his snarling; he took with him the he-cub, which his dam did not appear to take amiss.

Korusan did not follow Estarion to his chambers. At first not caring where he went, then only seeking solitude, he found himself in what seemed to be an ancient portion of the palace, dank and dim and long untenanted. A torch was thrust into a wall at one of the turnings. Korusan lit it with a flint that he carried, with much else, secreted in his robes, and the steel blade of one of his lesser daggers. It caught sullenly, but burned bright enough for the purpose.

The cold was deep here, set in the stones. The walls were faded and peeling, the tiles of the floor broken or gone. The air was heavy with age and dust.

A stair presented itself. Korusan climbed it. His lips twitched in spite of themselves. Estarion, when vexed with the need to think, always climbed as high as he could, and perched there above the babble of the world; and then, as often as not, did no thinking at all, but simply basked in the sun.

No sun tonight, but stars like flecks of frost, and Brightmoon riding high. Her light was cold and pure and, Korusan thought, rather prim. She had no rival in the sky: Greatmoon would not rise until just before the dawn.

Korusan stood on a roof that ended in a crumbling parapet. It gave way behind him to a landscape of peaks and sudden valleys that was the newer palace, but before him was nothing but a stretch of winter-bare garden, a high wall, and the roofs of the city. Every so often a guard walked the wall. The man did not see the shadow on the roof, or else did not reckon it worth remarking on.

Korusan sank down, wrapped in his robes. He was shivering, the ache in his bones returning after its few hours' grace. He drew up his knees and clasped them, and rocked.

Now, he thought, was the time. Sarevadin had shown herself to her grandson's grandson. He had offered her his throne, and she had laughed him down. And given Korusan, at last, the key to what he must do.

He should go to the Master of the Olenyai. Once Estarion was gone on his wild hunt, the field would be free; the empire would be theirs, to win and to hold. And if Estarion came back, he would come back to a battle long since lost; and if he did not, then he was dead, and nothing that his people did could matter.

They would think so, Olenyai and mages both. The mages would find a way, no doubt, to trap Estarion in his Tower, or at the least to confine him to Keruvarion. Estarion in Endros would set Asanion free.

And yet. Korusan rocked, frowning at nothing.

Suppose, he thought. *Suppose that there was a way . . .*

The Sunborn was alive. The mages said so. Mages could lie, but in this they swore to truth. The great mage and traitor, the Red Prince of Han-Gilen, had laid a sleep on him within his own Tower, because he would not yield to the constraints of peace. That sleep preserved him, unaging and undying, until the end of days. Or, some said, until he was called anew to war. He was always a warrior king, was Mirain An-Sh'Endor.

And if he woke, what then?

He had been mad when he fell into his sleep. Mad as Sarevadin feared that Estarion would be: conquered by his magic. It seemed to be a hazard of Sun-blood, that the Sun overwhelmed the man.

Suppose . . .

Korusan counted the aches in his bones. The priestess had given him days, who might have had but hours before he died. He dreamed no longer that he would live to wear the mask of the emperor. If his own frailty did not kill him, the mages would see to it that he died before he took thought for rebellion.

Then they would rule. Or not. He cared little. He did not have Estarion's soft heart for the people who lived outside of palaces. Veilless, swordless, halfwit multitudes; they were no kin of his. If he freed them from the barbarian yoke, then that was no more than his duty. He could not be expected to love them on top of it.

Mages of the Guild would be no worse for the empire than mages of the Temple. And Asanion would be Asanion again. Let Keruvarion have its conquerors. The Golden Empire would suffer no rule but its own.

Estarion could live, if that were so. Emperor of half an empire, to be sure; but so had he been before his mother pricked him into entering Asanion.

Korusan's arms tightened about his knees. Estarion alive, not dead. Estarion alive without Korusan. For Korusan would be dead, and soon. That was as certain as the cycles of the moons.

Korusan alive without Estarion was inconceivable. Estarion without Korusan . . .

"No," said Korusan, loud in the stillness. "He is mine. No one else shall have him. No woman, no man, no throne or empire. No one."

Estarion stalked snarling into his chambers, with the he-cub stalking at his heels. His vigil was broken, his mood ungodly. And it was barely midnight; long hours yet till dawn.

He had stripped, flinging garments and ornaments at anything that would stop them, before he knew that he was not alone. The ul-cub crouched in front of a small huddled person with eyes even yellower than the cub's. They watched one another with equal, wary intentness.

"Did he grow overnight?" Haliya asked, looking up into Estarion's face.

Estarion bit off sharp words. She looked cold sitting there, even wrapped in furs, white and amber and spotted gold. He, naked, was like a fire burning. He knelt and wrapped arms about her.

Haliya was tense in the circle of his embrace. "He has a name now, I think," she said. "Has he told you what it is?"

"No," Estarion said, startled. "You said you weren't a mage."

"I'm not," she said. "I'm a Vinicharyas, which is something different. He'll tell you when he's ready, I suppose. Do you have a fever? You're hot as iron in the forge."

"That's Sun-blood," he said. "The colder it is, the hotter I burn."

"And you're angry," said Haliya. "She got at you, didn't she? That horrible old woman. She says she's dead. Her body just hasn't admitted it yet."

"Her body has been failing to admit it for fifty years." Estarion shuddered in his skin. "I used to worship the memory of her. The reality . . . it's so much more. And so much less."

"That's usually the way of it." She eased a little, enough to stroke his face. "The dead should stay decently dead."

Her hand was small and cold and yet surprisingly strong. He turned his head, kissed her palm. There was no desire in him, not for her, not tonight, but he was not sorry, after all, that she was here. Friends had been simple for him once, and many, and since he came to this cursed half of his empire he had lost them all. But he had gained Haliya.

She was warming as he held her. Her shivering had stopped.

"You were with me," he said, "while I slept, and worse than slept. You kept running away before I could wake. Did I frighten you so much?"

"No," she said. It was not precisely a lie, but she could not meet his eyes while she said it. "I didn't want to trouble you."

"You could never do that," he said.

The he-cub thrust in between them. Haliya went rigid. The cub sprang into her lap. He filled the space between them. Her face was white beyond the cat's shadow-dark head. Estarion let her go, moved to thrust the beast away.

"No," she said, catching his hand. "No, don't."

"You're terrified of him."

Temper brought her eyes flashing up. "I will learn not to be. He's young, he's small. By the time he's grown I'll be as brave as you."

"By the time he's grown he'll be big enough to ride."

She put out a hand. It trembled, but it stroked the cub capably enough. He filled her lap and flowed over, lolling in her furs, butting against the curve of her belly.

Estarion was not terribly surprised. Not then. Not after all the rest. Ulyai's son traced the shape of her with remarkable clarity.

She must have conceived the first time Estarion went in to her, or the second. Unless—

No. She had been a maiden. She had known no man since. And he knew already how determined the Sun's arrows could be.

He laid his hand where the life in her was strongest, where it swam and rolled and dreamed.

It, no. He. Bright web of Sun-blood, its center a spark of fire. He would be mageborn; was mage already, waking to the touch of the *Kasar*. Her hand leaped to cover Estarion's. "He moved! He kicked me."

"He hasn't before?"

"Oh, yes," she said, "but never so hard. He knows you, my lord."

"Estarion."

"My lord Estarion."

She was laughing at him, crazy with relief. He narrowed his eyes. "That's why you were afraid. Why you hid. You didn't want me to know."

"I was afraid you'd send me back."

"So I would have," he said.

"You can't now," said Haliya. "It's safer here than anywhere out there."

"Gods," he said. "If my enemies knew . . ."

"They don't," said Haliya. Her face was hard, her voice was iron. "Nor shall they. I won't give them another target."

"You won't be able to hide it much longer," he said, "even wrapped in furs and hiding among the women."

"They guard me well," she said. "Especially your mother's armored women. And your priestess."

"Am I the only one who didn't know?"

She barely flinched. "Your priestess has known for a long time. The others either guessed, or I told them when your mother died. They had to know, to guard the heir."

"The heir." His tongue stumbled on the word. "You . . . really . . ."

"I won't lose him," said Haliya. "Vanyi has promised me that. He will be born alive, and he will be born strong."

"Vanyi knows." Estarion did not know what he felt. Pity, maybe. Fury, that she had tricked and trapped him, and never told him that it did not matter; that if he died, it was not ended. There was an heir. The line would go on. "She let me think that I was all there was."

"Maybe she thought it would be easier for you if you didn't know."

"Or easier for you," he said, "or for herself. She's a bitter, cruel creature sometimes, like the sea she comes from."

"And you love her," said Haliya.

She said it without pain, and without jealousy that he could perceive. "I love you," he said. He meant it. And not only for the child pressing against his hand, seeking the light of his presence.

"A man can love many women," said Haliya. "A woman finds it easier to love one man. I love you, I think. I like you more. Love's uncomfortable; it burns out. Liking is made to last."

"You'll teach him well, this son of ours," Estarion said.

"And you." She let fall her armor of furs and flung arms about his neck. The ul-cub spilled squalling to the floor. She did not notice.

His altered senses would have known her for a Vinicharyas even without the proof of her name. She made the world a clearer place while she held him in her arms. He was quiet there, at rest if not content.

Even his power was gentled, tamed and harnessed to his will. But this new clarity forbade him to dream that he might not after all be bound to seek his healing, or his death, in the Tower. There was no hope of escaping that.

He did not know that he wanted any. It was comforting in its bleak way, this knowledge that in two days, three at the utmost, he would most probably be dead.

She said nothing of it. She knew—he felt it in her. Vanyi had told her. Vanyi was not one to spare any creature pain, if she reckoned that pain necessary.

Haliya yawned, sighed, like the child she still in great part was. He carried her to bed. She would never be the singing fire that Vanyi was, or even Ziana; she did not need to be. Tonight she was content to hold and to be held, warm in his warmth, quiet in his quiet that she had made.

He closed his eyes, briefly as he thought. When he opened them, the air had changed to the chill that promises the dawn, and Haliya had left him. Servants were waiting with lamps and candles and the robes of the rite.

He was calm, greeting them. He submitted himself without protest; but it was not the empty passivity of his time in Kundri'j. He allowed this. He willed it. Tonight, by the god's mercy, he would end it.

PART FIVE

The Tower of the Sun

FORTY-EIGHT

DARKNESS WAS THE GODDESS' PORTION, AND SILENCE. BUT AN EMPRESS MUST have the light and the singing for her honor's sake, now that she was dead.

Merian had never been one to shun the sunlight. She had mated with it, keeping the rites of the moon's dark, but when they were past, she stood in the sun when it was strongest, and loved it for its bright fire. Her child was the sun's child, but night's child too, with his dark face and his sun-gold eyes.

He gave her honor, and the music she had loved, singing the death-rite over her in the bitter-bright morning. The shell of her was cold under his hands, with ice in its still heart. He could have warmed her; burned her as he had her lover. But she would have the darker comfort of the tomb, and her emperor's bones beside her under the black Tower of Endros. Her cortege was chosen, her bier in the making. When the embalmers had done with her, she would go, across the long leagues of empire to the City of the Sun.

He would go before her. Tonight, at sunset and Greatmoonrise, god and goddess passing in the door of the night, the Gate would open. He would do what he must do. She might find him there when she came, laid on the stone beside his father.

He was calm now, empty even of grief. Some thought him numbed with wine, but he had touched none since before the death-vigil. He had not eaten, either, or drunk aught but a little water when he woke. There would be a feast after this rite. He would pretend to eat, although he did not need it. The sun was enough, and the cold clean air.

The hall was full of people, a glitter and shift of myriad minds in his magesight. He was seeing almost wholly with it, had been since he left his chambers. It was a potent effort to see with eyes of the body, to look on dull flesh, mere stone, plain light of lamps and candles. So much simpler, so much more beautiful, to ignore the flesh and look on spirit bare.

And he had reckoned himself content without magery. It had come close to killing him, in soul if not in body. No spell of the Golden Palace, that, but a twisting in his own will.

And yet, he thought as the rite left him standing still and silent, and the choir of priests and priestesses sang the last of the great hymns: and yet it was an ill thing, what he had suffered this empire to become. He had not begun it, no, nor done more than continue what his fathers had done before him. But he had fostered it.

There should have been one empire, one people, and there were two, eagle of the Sun and lion of Asanion yoked to the single chariot. They hated one another. They spoke of conquest and of conquerors. Keruvarion looked in scorn on fallen Asanion. Asanion turned on its Varyani emperor—not its own, never its own, always the barbarian, the alien, the foreigner—in murderous resentment.

They must be one. He might have said it aloud. No one heard him: the priestesses' descant soared high and piercing clear over the deep voices of the priests, drowning any lesser voice. He shaped the words again in the silence of his mind. *They must be one. Whatever comes of this that I do, whether I come back alive or lie dead in the Tower, the empires must be one empire. Or they break and fall, and shatter into warring shards.*

And if that would be so, then there could be no Golden Palace set apart, and no Palace of the Sun in the heart of the Hundred Realms. Kundri'j and Endros must not be separated. There must be a new city, a city that was of both and neither, set between the empires. And a new court, not Court of the Sun and Courts of the Lion but both together, Varyani, Asanian, and no distinction made between them.

And was he the Sunborn, to conceive such a purpose? He would be dead when the sun rose again, or worse than dead. Nothing that he thought or willed or dreamed could be. He was a broken thing, a marred beginning. He would never come to more than that.

But his son might. He would give the child that, write it down when the rite was done, entrust it to the child's mother. Who would, god and goddess help her, be empress when he was gone.

The hymn soared to its crescendo and faded. He must sing the last words, the words that sealed the rite. For a terrible moment he had no words at all, no memory, only darkness and silence.

Then again he was full of light, and in the light, the music, and in the music, the words. "Dark lady, lady of the silence, Lady Night: come now, take your child, grant her rest. May the sun be gentle upon her. May the wind caress her. May the years tread light upon her bones."

Vanyi heard the singing from the heart of her own working. She was never there; there was always a duty to keep her away, always something to be done in Estarion's name. She should resent him profoundly. But she was not a reasonable creature when it came to Estarion. He knew what prices she paid—she had felt it when Iburan died, a tendril of thought that uncurled to touch her, then shrank away. He had expected her to be enraged.

That, not the necessity of her absence, roused her temper. So little he knew her. So ill he judged her.

And had she done anything to prove him false? What he had done in Asanion was as much her fault as anyone's. If she had not driven him away, he would not have gone to his yellow women. Haliya would not be huddled in her phalanx of guards, watching her emperor sing the empress mother to rest and reflecting in spite of herself upon the child she carried—how he too would sing these words, if the gods willed. She knew no sadness in the thought, and no fear that Vanyi could discern. She was not expecting to be empress as Merian had been. Women in Asanion did not rule like men, with their faces naked to the world.

This would be empress-by-right if the night's working failed. This would rule, whether she willed it or no. This child, this innocent, this creature who was neither mage nor simple woman, but something between.

"She won't do badly," said Sarevadin, startling Vanyi back into herself. The walls of the palace chapel closed in once more, the wards set but not sealed, the substance of the Gate gathered but unformed. There was nothing to see with eyes of the body, and little with eyes of the mind but a mist of raw power under a shield and a ward. It was lumpen to the touch of her senses, inert.

Sarevadin crouched in front of it as if beside a wanderer's fire, arms resting on knees, eyes fixed on Vanyi. The angle of the light caught the scars on her neck, brands of the torque that she had worn as priest and priestess, until she cast it away. "She's a child," she went on, "but she's wiser than she knows, and stronger than she thinks. He chose her with his temper, true enough; but a Sunlord always judges best when he's not trying to think."

"Are you saying," Vanyi asked, "that Sun-blood is better brainless?"

"Often," said the Sunborn's child, "yes. If the god exists—if he's not the dream of a mage afraid of his own power—then I think we may be one of his more splendid failures. Or maybe we're the joke he plays on the world's fools. My father honestly believed that he was sent to bind the goddess in chains and raise up an imperishable empire. I learned what folly that was; I lost my magery to it, and my very self. But I had my own idiocy. I thought that I was to make one empire of two, I and my lord. I thought that I had done it; or close enough, once my lord was dead and I had killed my name. When I left, I meant to leave forever—to become nothing, a nameless thing, a leaf on the wind.

"And I did, priestess. For a lifetime of simple men, I did. Then I wandered back through the empire I had forsaken and by then nearly forgotten. I paused by a river, and saw a young man fishing. He looked like any other princely idiot with a line and a hook and a bag of Islander tricks, which made me smug, because I had brought the Isles into the empire.

"Then he turned his eyes on me. I had no name yet. I refused to have one. But he forced me into his orbit. He made me remember. He spelled me as my father spelled the princes he would conquer, or as I would trap my lords of the warring empires. I was the biter bit, priestess. I was a Sunlord's slave."

"What are you trying to do?" Vanyi asked her mildly enough, all things considered. "You don't need to snare me in lies. You won't snare him. He's past that."

"Well," said Sarevadin, unruffled. "It's not untrue. He did startle me. He did remind me of what I'd been. And he's lethally charming when he wants to be."

"So are you," Vanyi said. "I don't suppose you'll tell me how you got in here. There are wards. Or didn't you notice?"

"Isn't it a little late to wonder?"

"You aren't a mage. I think that much is true. But you're something else." Vanyi's eyes narrowed. "You *are* magic. That's it, isn't it? That's what the mages did to you. They shattered you and made you anew; but when they did that, they made you a new thing: a human shape, a human soul, but sealed with power. I could sever myself from my magic, if I were driven to it; or Estarion could, as he did to the mages who fought him. You can't do that. Every part of you is woven with magery."

Sarevadin shrugged. Perhaps she truly did not care; perhaps she had known it for so long that it no longer seemed to her a wonder.

"And," said Vanyi as the truth unfolded in her, "that's why you didn't die when Hirel did. You can't, can you? Not while the power is in you. You made yourself age, for a disguise. Left to yourself, you'd still be as you were when you left Endros. And that wasn't as a woman of threescore years should be. In yourself, in truth, you haven't aged since the mages made you anew. Have you?"

Sarevadin smiled. "Are you going to remake yourself, priestess, and be immortal?"

Vanyi shuddered. "Gods, no. I've earned the scars the years have given me. I want to die when my time comes, and go where the dead go."

"If that is anywhere," said Sarevadin, "and not to oblivion."

"Oblivion would be pleasant enough," Vanyi said. "You're barred from it, yes? You tried to enter it, and it refused you. And Hirel went without you. Will you ever forgive him for that?"

"No," said Sarevadin. She was no longer smiling. "You should be less wise. You'll live longer."

"Are you going to kill me, and kill Estarion, and take back your throne?"

Sarevadin shuddered precisely as Vanyi had. "I'm going to keep you children alive. We made a royal mess of things, my father and I; we need you to patch it together. Estarion will, you know, if he doesn't shatter before morning. And you, if you don't do something ridiculous."

"And if we do," said Vanyi, "you'll live. You'll do what must be done. Promise me that."

"I promise nothing," said Sarevadin.

"Then I give you nothing," Vanyi said. She stretched out her hand, limbered her power. "No Gate. No help. No defense against the mages."

She would do it. She was angry enough, and tired enough of all of it. She was not royal, not even noble. She cared nothing for honor or duty or any such foolishness.

Sarevadin sighed. She was looking younger; or maybe it was the light. There was a faint coppery sheen in the frost of her hair. "Avaryan defend us from stiff-necked commoners. If we're trading threats, then shall I threaten to separate you from your magic?"

"Then I'll be no good to you," Vanyi said. "And Estarion might object. He's stronger than you."

"But younger," said Sarevadin, "and completely without guile. I learned trickery from the greatest of masters."

"So do it," Vanyi said. "What difference does it make whether he destroys himself now or later?"

"There now," said Sarevadin. "Where's your insouciance? We're going to win this game, priestess. Win it or lose it splendidly."

"I'm not a Sunlord's get," Vanyi said. "I don't know about bravura. All I know is stubbornness."

"That will do," said Sarevadin.

Korusan waited for Estarion. He seemed to do a great deal of that, some of it voluntary, some not. Korusan could not tell which this was. He could have been at the death-rite. Should have, perhaps. But he chose to stand guard on the empty chambers. They echoed without Estarion to fill them. He wandered through them, pausing to touch a vase that Estarion had liked, a cup that he had used, a cushion on which he had sat.

When he had walked the circle of rooms, an Olenyas stood waiting for him. Marid. He was almost still. In him that was ominous. His eyes held no malice, his stance no danger; but no friendship, either. None of the warmth that should be between brothers. He said, "The Masters summon you."

"Do they?" Korusan almost laughed. It was not mirth. "Tell them that I shall come to them."

"Now?"

"After sunset."

"They said now."

"I am in trouble, then?"

Marid's eyes widened in honest surprise. "Of course not. How can you be?"

Easily, thought Korusan. Aloud he said, "I shall come to them after the sun has set."

He thought that Marid would protest. But his swordbrother sighed, shrugged. "He's to die tonight. I heard them say it. With or without you, they said. Some are wondering if you really are the Lion's cub."

"That," said Korusan, "I am. Have no doubt of it."

"They say he has you bewitched. Is he such a master of the high art as that?"

"No." Korusan leaned against the wall. It was not that he had grown weaker; he was past that. He should sleep, maybe, if the pain would let him. "He has no art. He is all instinct."

"I had a northerner once, for curiosity. It was like coupling with a panther."

"So it is." Korusan considered Marid slantwise; thought of killing him. Thought of dying, and of taking Estarion with him. "Tell them. After sunset."

"You're ill again," said Marid.

"Go," said Korusan, "or I drink your blood."

Marid stiffened. If he had reminded Korusan of the bond that had been between them, Korusan would indeed have slain him. But Marid was wise, or too angry to speak. He bowed with precision that came close to insult, and did as he was bidden.

When he was gone, Korusan let himself slide down the wall until he crouched on the floor. His veils stifled him. He flung them off. The air was cold on his cheeks. The brands of his rank stung like fire. They had magic in them, maybe, to discern his treason.

He was no longer Olenyas. Son of the Lion he was born, Son of the Lion he would die. But the brotherhood of the sword that had bred and trained him, kept him alive when he should have died, shaped him for their ends—they had never been his, nor he theirs.

He should have known it long ago. It was written in his face, branded in his eyes. His kin was the one whom he was sworn to destroy. No one else bound him. No one else could command him.

He drew a breath. It stabbed, but it would do, for a while. He felt light; free. He had no masters. He had no brothers but the one, who was his lover, whose life belonged to him. But for that one he was alone.

He would keep the robes, because they were warm; and the swords, because he would have need of them. He moved to rend the veils to shreds, but paused. They too might serve a purpose. He thrust them into his belt and settled to wait.

The feast of the dead would go on till dawn, with wine and singing and merriment that increased as the feasters undertook to forget the death that had brought them here. Estarion left them long before the sun went down. If any noticed, he did not know of it. They would expect him to grieve in solitude. And so he had, and would again, if he came back a living man.

They were building the Gate: Vanyi, the priests and priestesses who had been Iburan's and were now, in default of another, hers, and a strangeness that he knew was Sarevadin. He felt their working in his bones, as he felt that his presence would be no help to them. His power burned too fiercely. It would seize them all and wield them, and in the end destroy them. Wiser to keep apart and bind his magery, and pray that it would not burst its bonds before he came to the Tower.

Korusan waited for him with the patience of a child or an animal. The boy had taken off his veils. There was meaning in that; but he gave Estarion no chance to ask what it was. "Dance with me," he said before Estarion was fairly past the door.

Yes, thought Estarion. In the dance was forgetfulness. He should worry, maybe, that they danced with swords, and Korusan an Olenyas, a spy, possibly a traitor, against whom he had been warned. But Korusan was his, heart and soul. He knew that as he knew his own name.

They danced as they always danced, without rest, without quarter. Estarion was stronger, and longer of arm. Korusan was swifter. Deadly swift now, with death in his eyes.

Estarion matched him stroke for stroke. He laughed as he did it, because if he died it did not matter, and if he lived, he would die soon enough.

They locked blades. Korusan's eyes held fast on Estarion's. His wrist wavered a fraction. Estarion's sword sprang free, flashed round, halted a hair's breadth from the boy's throat.

Korusan smiled. "Yes," he said, a mere breath of sound. "Slay me now."

Estarion let fall the sword and pulled him in. "Idiot child," he said. "I'll never kill you. I'll keep you alive till you grow old with me."

"That will never happen," said Korusan against his breast.

Estarion bent his head over the yellow curls. They were damp with exertion, scented with something faintly sweet: spices, or the ghosts of flowers. "You're growing tall," he said. "Look, your shoulders are nigh as wide as mine."

"Never," said Korusan, "as tall as you."

"That's the northerner in me. I'm small among my kin, as you are tall among yours. That makes us even."

Korusan tilted his head back. "Do you love me?"

"You know I do."

"Do I?" Korusan looked hard into his eyes. Estarion did not look away. He had no shame to hide, no lie to dissemble. "Do I know that, my lord? You are all the world to me. To you I am an afternoon's diversion. If I died, you would mourn, and raise your beautiful voice in the rite for me, and lay me in my tomb; and then you would forget me."

Estarion recoiled, wounded. "Do you think so little of me?"

"I think that you are greater than I. My heart has room only for you. Yours contains a world."

"You're calling me a whore," Estarion said, lightly he thought, but Korusan lashed out with temper.

"Always you laugh at me. Always you reckon me a child. If I were a man grown, would you cast me off as men do their boys who are boys no longer?"

"Are you trying to make me hate you?" Estarion asked. "You can't do that."

"No? Even if I told you that I have been sent to slay you?"

"I knew that already," Estarion said. "You haven't killed me yet. I don't think you will."

"I will," said Korusan. "I have sworn it. I hate you, beloved. I scorn you. I spurn your name beneath my feet."

Yet as he said it he clung with fever-passion, pulling Estarion's head down, kissing him until he gasped. Estarion laughed. "You're eating me alive."

"I hate you," said Korusan. "I hate you with all my heart. I will slay you, and mount my throne above your grave."

"I love you, too, dear lunatic," said Estarion.

Korusan thrust back, furious. "You do not believe me! I am your enemy. I am the Lion's son. I was bred to destroy you."

"And I am the Sun's child," Estarion said, "and the other half of you. The throne is mine, and shall be till I die. Not even you can take it from me."

"Mad," said Korusan in despair. "Mad, mad, mad."

"Hush," said Estarion. "Love me."

He had not been certain that Korusan would obey. But the boy was his, whatever the blood he claimed. He yielded as all men must, to the will of the Sun's son.

FORTY-NINE

SUN AND GREATMOON SAT FACE TO FACE ON EACH HORIZON, WINTER-GOLD and blood-red, the sun its wonted fiery disk, the moon a shield of blood. One could, if one blurred one's eyes just so, see how the sun reached across the arc of heaven to embrace the moon, god embracing goddess, light bending to its will the power of the dark.

There was none of that here where no windows were. Estarion's power had taken flight of itself to look on sun and moon and open sky; he dragged it back to the walls and the wards and the circle of watchful faces. Vanyi had brought in everyone whom she thought she could trust, who had power to sustain her Gate. It was a surprising number. Her priests and priestesses, of course, and some from Estarion's Guard, and a handful from the guard that had been his mother's and must now be Haliya's. But also the dark-robed priestesses who had walked soft in his mother's shadow, and a pair of nervous, darting-eyed Asanians in Lord Shurichan's livery. One wore the robe of a tame mage. He looked even less at ease than the other, who was a servant of rank, with a spark of magery that burned low but steady.

When Estarion came to the circle, Vanyi had already begun to draw them together, to make them one mingled skein of magic. His coming nearly shattered it, but she seemed to have expected that; she pulled him into the center with hand and power and held him there, willing him to be still. He did not resist her. He had never stood beside her in a great working, or even in a lesser one. He had never been mage enough to venture it.

Here, closed in the circle, he could see with both eyes and power, with no fear of losing the capacity for either. She had done as he had, dressed for comfort rather than for state; like him she had chosen well-worn riding garb and plaited her hair behind her, and worn no ornament but the torque of her priesthood. She seemed at ease in the midst of her magic, frowning slightly, oblivious to him except as a force to be constrained lest it shatter the circle. She was something more here than she was elsewhere, and something less, ageless, sexless, almost pure power.

Strange then to realize who, and what, stood a little apart from them though still within the circle. Sarevadin truly had no age, no sex; if Vanyi seemed made of power, this was the truth of it. She was calm, neither helping nor hindering, watching Vanyi with a flicker of amusement and a glimmer of approbation, as a mother watches a child, or a master her pupil.

Estarion had had training, however Sarevadin disparaged it. He knew that this should be one mage's working, that the rest were there simply to provide Vanyi with strength as she needed it. Therefore he did not do as he longed to do, seize the power that Vanyi had gathered and shape it more swiftly, and raise the Gate in his own time and not in hers, that seemed so crawling slow.

He could have done it more quickly, and more enduringly too. But this was not his working. He lacked Vanyi's affinity for Gates, her sense of the moment when at last all the power was gathered, the wards at their strongest, and no force beyond them could know, or knowing hinder.

That moment sang in his blood, when sun and moon poised in the last movement of their dance, before the sun sank beneath the rim of the world and the moon sprang into the sky. Greatmoon was a cry like trumpets, the sun a ringing of bronze upon bronze. Vanyi smote her hands together, and the earth shook. What had been raw shapeless power rose up taller than a man and broader, looming over the lone small woman who presumed to master it. She raised her hands joined palm to palm. Estarion moved on instinct, laid his branded hand upon her shoulder. In the same instant Sarevadin did the same. Vanyi buckled under the weight of twin suns, but she was stronger than they. Slowly, as if she parted the leaves of a great door, she spread her hands apart.

Wind howled. It rocked her, but the others held her, and her hands never wavered. Lightnings cracked. None of them touched her. The force of the Gate plucked at her. She braced against it, even when it strove to coil about her, grip her, suck her into itself. Estarion's hand was white pain, her shoulder under it rigid. The Gate, half opened, was a cauldron of twisting, seething, boiling fires. It blinded him; it roiled in the pit of his stomach. His throat burned with bile.

Her hands were at their farthest extent, flattened as if against the posts of a door. Her will snapped out. *Help me!* Estarion raised his free hand, fighting against sudden, leaden weight, and gripped what felt, as it looked, much like a doorpost.

He set his teeth and pushed. It pushed back. It tempted him to let go her shoulder; but that, he must not do. Holding to her with his right hand, with his left he thrust the gate wider, past the stretch of her shorter arm. When his arm was straight, trembling with strain, he glanced at her. The Gatefires had died down a little. Her face was a shifting pattern of lights and colors, but it was discernibly a face, tight-lipped, intent. "Now," she said.

He hesitated a fraction of a breath. Then he let go.

The Gate pulsed. His arm snapped up again, but stopped half extended.

Vanyi sagged briefly under his hand, leaning against him, before she remembered to be prickly-proud. "It's done," she said. Her voice was crisp. "Best we move quickly. This is a warded Gate, and therefore secret, but even that may not be proof against the mages who first mastered Gates."

The circle shifted. One of them, the priest Shaiyel, came out of it to face Vanyi. "I'll keep the watch. The others should rest. If you need them later . . ."

"You'll know." She smiled. "You did well, all of you. Places are prepared for you, with wards to keep you safe until we come back."

Not if, Estarion noticed. Until. She had her own degree of arrogance, and no little penchant for acting the empress.

She waited until the last of the circle, but for Shaiyel, had retreated slowly, with many glances back at the wards, at the Gate, at the three who stood before it. Shaiyel withdrew to the edge of the wards, shaping the words and the gesture that would seal them anew.

A shadow slipped past him. Two shadows. One, feline, flung himself on Estarion, purring raucously. The other, robed but unveiled, turned a defiant face upon him.

"Yelloweyes," Estarion said, "you can't—"

"Wherever you go," said Korusan, "I go."

"Even to my death?"

"There above all else."

Estarion glanced at the women. Sarevadin had her blank blind look, as if she had forgotten where she was, or when, or why. Vanyi seemed merely interested; but that too was a mask.

"I don't trust him at all," she said, "but he belongs to you. You bear the burden of him."

Estarion wondered where she had learned to be so hard and cold. Not, he prayed, from him. He brushed the boy's cheek with a finger. It was fevered as it so often was, but the eyes were clear, unwavering. "Damn you," Estarion said. "If you kill me, you'll die a grimmer death than you ever dealt me."

"I would not wish to live if you were dead," Korusan said.

Estarion looked from him to the Gate. Death was in it. He saw the flicker and shift that was its shadow. Sudden joy filled him; a fierce, reckless, heedless delight. "Come then," he said. "Come with me and die."

"Not," said Vanyi, "if I can help it."

Estarion barely heard her. He seized Korusan's hand, caught another—Sarevadin's, fire-hot, fire-strong—and sprang.

"You blazing *idiot!*" Vanyi's voice, stripped to raw panic. Her hand, locking on his belt. They plunged into the maelstrom that was the new-made Gate.

He was drowning. Stones dragged him down—Korusan, Sarevadin, Vanyi, the ul-cub with claws sunk in his leg. He struck out with the one leg that was free, and with arms—wings—something—some untrammeled part of him that beat against the surging of the flood.

Wings, then, improbable as they were. And if he was winged, then this was not sea but storm-wild air, this turmoil the boiling of clouds, this tumult the thunder rolling in his blood. The winds that tore at him were worldwinds, sweeping him through the chaos of the Gates.

Small things rode him, clinging like grim death. He roared laughter, soared, swooped, soared again, riding the storm. It was mighty, but only in resistance. It was terrible, but only in battle. If he eased to it, yielded to its buffeting, it lost its power to destroy. It bore up his wings. It carried him from cloud to cloud, each cloud a world, each levin-bolt the fire of a Gate.

One of those who rode him crawled to his ear, shrieking into it. He would not have heeded anything so shrill, but the words forced themselves through the exultation of his flight. "Stop! Damn you, stop! You'll lose us in the worldwinds!"

He would not. But he had let himself forget why he flew here.

While he paused, struck with remembrance, Vanyi flung a bridle on him. He reared against it, but the bit was burning cold in his mouth, the reins implacable, drawing him about. Like a rebellious stallion he fought her; like a strong rider she turned his battle upon itself. And still the worldwinds bore them all.

A new hand took the reins. A new voice spoke in his ear. "Such a senel you make; and such wit, to gift yourself with wings. Tame yourself now and fly."

Sarevadin wore a new shape here, one that he had known in portraits since he was a child: northern face, copper-bright hair. But whether it was she or he, woman or man, he could not tell. Now it was the one, now the other. But the smile was the same in both, white and wild, and the bright dark eyes. "I know the way," said the Twiceborn, shifting, woman to man to woman. "Gates wrought me. Power is woven in me. I'll bring us to the Heart of the World."

Not the Tower of the Sun? Estarion wondered. But he did not speak. The bit forbade him, and the grip upon the reins, and the legs clamped to his sides, driving him on.

The storm was above him. Road rang beneath his feet—his sharp cloven hoofs, for he had willed this shape, and it was so. Worlds sped past him, but the road was outside of them. Magic quivered in it, on it. Magic rode him, nor could he turn aside.

He was pursued. How he knew it, at first he was not certain. Then his ears, straining back, caught the sound of feet; his nostrils, flaring, caught a scent like blood and burning.

"Mages," said Sarevadin, settling briefly to woman's shape.

And Vanyi behind her, holding to her, turning to peer past a pair of golden-eyed shadows: "We're warded against them."

"Not here," Sarevadin said. "Wards are no use on the mageroad." She—he—dug heels into Estarion's sides. "On, young one. On!"

He ran. Four legs were swifter far than two. Wings, he had lost or forgotten; no time now to win them back again. The burden he bore was light, though there were three of it; the fourth ran at his heels, darkness golden-eyed. He had been born amid the worldwinds, in the silence between Gates. He had come from Gates with the child of the Sunborn, to bind his soul to the Sunborn's heir. Here he was not so young as he seemed in the world beyond the Gates, nor so small, but he remained an ul-cat, with magic in his blood.

He stretched his stride. The ul-cub matched it; danced, even, laughing as a cat will, batting at his heels with half-sheathed claws. He started, bucked, learned at last what swiftness was.

Vanyi clung for dear life to an impossibility: a senel who was Estarion, and a shifting shape that was indubitably Sarevadin. The Olenyas clung to her with the rigidity of perfect terror. The worlds whirled past. Some were dark and some were light, some green and some bleakly brown, some full of water and some full of air, and all strange, all alien.

She had lost control of this venture before it was fairly begun. It was different to be in a Gate than to be outside of it, standing guard upon it. Here all laws were broken, all sureties undone.

Yet, once she had looked fear in the face and given it its name, she knew a strange delight. She was here, riding the mageroad. She was alive to know it, and strong in her power, and the Gate that had brought them here was hers.

Pursuit was gaining, though Estarion outran the worldwind. The watchers wore any shape they chose, but now, as if to honor Estarion's own choice of shape, they ran as direwolves. Magelore had it that they were empty of intelligence; they existed simply to catch trespassers upon the worldroad and dispose of them. But the eyes in the lean grey heads were bright with malice, and the teeth were bared in wide wolf-grins. They were hungry for manflesh, senelflesh, even—maybe—catflesh.

The first of the watchers drew level with the ul-cub. He slashed sidewise with dagger-fangs, and raked with claws. The watcher howled and tumbled from the road, bleeding fire. The others neither wavered nor slowed.

One of the arms deathlocked about Vanyi's waist let go. Steel hissed from sheath. Korusan held the longer of his swords poised along his thigh. She undertook not to shrink from that keen-honed blade hovering a handspan from her leg. If he was truly a traitor, he would plunge it into Estarion's straining flank and kill them all. And she would not be able to stop him.

A watcher sprang. The sword swept down.

Sarevadin bent forward over Estarion's neck, pulling Vanyi with her—him—both, neither. Hair the color of new copper lashed Vanyi's face. She gasped, blinded, and felt teeth close on her foot. There was no pain at first, simply the knowledge that pain would come, and the thought, dim and almost wry, that if Estarion bucked at the slash of teeth in his heels, Korusan's sword might cut off her foot. Would she bleed power then, or plain blood?

She kicked as hard as she could. The teeth tore free. She would not feel the pain. She must focus on holding to her rocking, heaving seat and keeping out of the way of the Olenyas' sword. He was an artist with it. He wasted no movement, indulged in no flourishes. Every cut found flesh, or what passed for flesh.

If these had been true wolves, they would have given up the chase long ago, even if they were starving. These would not pause until they downed their prey. Were there more of them? Or did each that fell give space to another, so that their number never varied?

Sarevadin muttered a curse. There was a long rent in the trousers, blood bright against dark skin. The face that half turned was as male as Estarion's when Estarion was not wearing a stallion's horns, and as keenly carved, red-bearded, black-eyed, furious. "This will get us killed," he said. She. Shifting again, impervious to her own strangeness. She flung herself from Estarion's back, so sudden that Vanyi toppled bruisingly forward, locking arms about the straining neck. She struggled to look back. The watchers had paused, but not to devour Sarevadin. She—he—ran in the midst of them, slapping them with a bare and burning hand, kicking those that lunged to snap at his unprotected throat.

Vanyi hauled back on the reins. Estarion jibbed. "I'll be polite later," she snapped at him. "Slow *down,* damn you!"

He plunged to a halt that nearly flung her over his head. Before she was properly settled, he wheeled. And changed.

The road was hard. She got up stiffly, nursing a bruised tailbone. Estarion took no notice of her. He was running in his own shape toward the pack of direwolves, dagger in hand, shouting something indistinct.

Sarevadin shouted back. In man-form he was a little smaller than Estarion, a little narrower, and no less hot-tempered.

"Gods," said the Olenyas. "How like they are."

So they were, even when, again, Sarevadin was a woman, shoulder-high to Estarion, glaring down her nose at him. The watchers crouched whining at her feet. She laid her hand on the head of the one that had led the pack, and said distinctly, echoing in that eerie place, "What did you stop for? We're almost there."

"What in the hells did *you* stop for?" Estarion shot back.

Her direwolf leered at Estarion's ul-cat. The cub crouched low and snarled.

Sarevadin quelled them both with a glance. "This was getting out of hand. It's one thing to teach you how to run. It's entirely another to kill more watchers than can restore themselves."

"But these—things—the mages—"

"These are watchers," she said with taut-strung patience. "They won't harm you; they're only here to guard the road."

"But—"

"Watchers watch and guard, and keep young idiots moving. Guildmages close in ahead and behind, from the thresholds of their Gates. You have to be in control of yourself when you meet them, or they'll devour you whole."

"You've led us into a trap," Estarion said, flat and cold.

"It's easy to think so, isn't it? You can't stay here. You can't go back—the watchers will stop you. Now will you run?"

Estarion looked as if he would have argued, but the ul-cub had his wrist in its jaws and was pulling him about. One of the watchers nipped at his heels. He kicked like the senel he had briefly been, spat a curse, and bolted.

He swept Vanyi in his wake, and Korusan with not-blood dripping still from his sword. The pack ran behind, and Sarevadin among them.

They were warding, Vanyi realized almost too late. Protecting their erstwhile prey from enemies behind and, as some of them edged ahead, from danger before.

The worlds spun faster. Too fast. She struggled to stop, but the road had her. She could not slow or turn, or alter any moment of it.

Estarion veered. She cried out. And fell.

Quiet.

She half sat, half lay on stone. Stone arched over her. Fire burned, blessed warmth after cold she had not even known she suffered.

"The Heart of the World." Sarevadin's voice, no longer shifting, and her face as Vanyi had known it in Asanion, pared clean with age. She stood by the fire that seemed so simple and was so great a mystery, for it was no mortal flame but the light of power that ruled the worlds. She warmed her hands above it.

Estarion circled the wide bare hall with its walls that seemed painted or hung with tapestries, until they shifted and changed and showed themselves for Worldgates. They, like the fire, were simplicity to the eye, mystery to the mind. He made as if to touch one that showed a place of water and green things; it changed to a hell of fire. He drew back carefully and turned. "Why are we here? Is this a betrayal?"

"All who would master the Gates must begin here," said Sarevadin. "All roads of the Gates lead to this place."

"That may be true," said a cool bitter voice, "but I smell death here." The Olenyas had found himself a shadow to be part of, and the ul-cub to share it. He had sheathed his sword but kept his hand upon it. He moved from his chosen shadow into Estarion's. "If you have led us ill, you will answer to my sword."

"Gladly," said Sarevadin. She beckoned with her scarred hand. "Come, children. We're dead if we linger. They know we're here; they'll be moving to close the Gates."

Vanyi, stretching her bruised power, gasped. The quiet here was illusion, the stillness a mask. Below that frail semblance was naked chaos.

The Heart of the World, that core of magic in all the myriad worlds, hung on the thin edge of ruin. Was it their coming that had done it?

Even as she shaped the thought, the Heartfire roared to the ceiling, then sank almost to embers; blinding bright, then blind dark. "Swiftly!" cried Sarevadin. "Take my hands!"

Estarion had her right hand, the Olenyas her left. Vanyi, slowest to move, hesitated between Estarion and his guardsman, yearning toward the one, shrinking from the other. Hating herself for both.

That moment cost her dearly. The fire roared up again. The worldwalls throbbed, flickering dizzily from world to world. She lunged toward Estarion, just as he sprang into the fire. Her hand caught his; tore loose.

She stumbled and fell to her knees. The floor heaved and rocked. Worldwind howled over her. Mages were in it. Watching. Waiting. Listening. They wanted— something. The Tower. The magic that was in it. The advantage that they reckoned to gain, somehow, from Estarion's healing. Or, and more likely, his death.

She clung to stones that surged like the flesh of a living thing. Shadows danced in the fire. One of them had a voice. "Can't move us through. Can't—move—"

Sarevadin. And Estarion, breathless, tight with what might have been pain. "Can't move back, either. You may be made of fire, but I'm half flesh. And my guardsman is all human. Get us out of here. It's killing him!"

Vanyi crawled across a floor turned treacherous, clinging where she could cling, slipping where it fluxed and slid. Her power was as bruised as she, and as helpless. She set her teeth and struggled on.

The fire was a sheet of blinding heat from floor to heaving, quivering vault of roof. Vanyi, well outside of it still, felt the heat of it on her face, searing her hair, crisping the flesh on her bones.

She had walked into this fire when first she mastered Gates. It held no power to harm a mage. Yet now it was worse than deadly, and they were in it, trapped in it. She could just discern their shapes: Sarevadin still unscathed but seeming helpless, Estarion clutching a writhing body to his breast, crying, *"Get us out of here!"*

Vanyi thrust a dart of power at the fire's heart. It sprang back, piercing her with agony.

"No one can get us out," said Sarevadin to Estarion. "Except you."

"I can't," he gasped. "I don't know how."

"What does knowing have to do with it? Open the Gate!"

"What Gate?"

"This!" The shadow that was Sarevadin wrenched his shadow-hand from the shadow-Olenyas and held it up. Vanyi shielded her eyes against a blaze that made the fire seem a dim and lifeless thing. "This, that opens all doors. That is itself a door."

"Open your own!"

"Mine is broken." She hauled him about within the fire. *"Open it!"*

"I don't—I can't—"

Vanyi touched the fire. Her fingers blistered and charred. She bit her lip until it bled, and pushed against the pain.

She could see them through the veil of it. Estarion held Korusan as if he had been a child; the boy's head was buried in the hollow of his shoulder. He raised his branded hand. His power flared more wildly even than the fire in which he stood. He must control it. Master it. And when he had done that, walk through the Gate that he had made.

She could do nothing. The fire was too strong. He was bred of it, and he could scarcely endure it. She could not imagine what torments racked the Olenyas.

She raged until she wept, beat on the fire with fists of power, gained nothing but blistered hands.

He raised the *Kasar* above his head. His hand trembled; he steadied it. He drew it down the fiery air.

The fire parted, folded away before that fire which was hotter than it could ever be, shrank and cooled and dimmed until it was simple Heartfire once more. A Gate opened in the midst of it, and Sarevadin set foot on the threshold. Estarion paused. "Vanyi!"

"Go!" she screamed at him in anger that came from everywhere and nowhere. "You don't need me now. Go!"

"Vanyi—"

She would have plunged into the fire, whatever it did to her, and pushed him through the Gate. But Sarevadin, poised in the Gate, caught hold of him and flung him through.

FIFTY

VANYI WAS LOST. KORUSAN WAS UNCONSCIOUS OR WORSE, A SLACK WEIGHT UPON Estarion's shoulder. And where they stood was nothing like the worldroad. It seemed a perfect void, save that something held him up beneath his feet, and something else tugged him onward.

Sight grew slowly. There was little to see but the shape that led him. Its hair was copper-bright again, its gender indistinct. That maybe was the truth of the Twice-born; what she—he—was in the world of the flesh was but a shadow.

Warmth pressed against his leg. The ul-cub had followed him yet again, moving easily through these Gates that racked human flesh and drove human minds mad. So led, so guided, he passed out of the darkness and into light.

He stood inside of a vast jewel: flat beneath his feet, faceted about and above him, everywhere netted and veined with splendor. No lamp had ever burned here, nor ever would. The stone burned with its own white light.

Carefully he lowered Korusan to the floor. The boy struggled suddenly, all but oversetting him. He found himself crouching and Korusan standing over him, gripping his shoulders with terrible strength. White rimmed the golden eyes. The face was the color of bone.

Korusan let go. Estarion straightened slowly. The boy seemed to have forgotten him, sliding through the shadowless light, veering wide round the ul-cub and the motionless, voiceless Sarevadin, toward what lay in the jewel's heart.

Black stone like an altar, or like the slab of a tomb. A sweep of white and gold: cloak of leather and fur undimmed by the years. And laid upon it, clad as a northern king, the sleeper.

He was asleep, truly, not dead. The fire of his life was banked low, the pulse of his heart slowed to the beat of the ages, the wind of his breath stilled to the faintest of whispers. And yet he lived, and living, dreamed.

Estarion knew that face. It met him in every mirror. Though all the portraits showed Mirain clean-shaven, his beard had grown with the slowness of his sleep. It was a little longer than Estarion's, curling in the same fashion. His hair was plaited along his side, his hands folded on his breast. He would not be a tall man, standing; somewhat taller than Korusan, maybe, compact and smooth-muscled, with a warrior's strength, perceptible even as he slept.

He seemed harmless as any sleeper was. And yet this Tower was his, this light that beat in it, this mighty stillness. Estarion's power touched the edge of his dreams and leaped back startled, stung as if with fire.

"Yes," said Sarevadin. "He's angry still. It's been a long night's sleep for him, and memory as keen as if it were yesterday. I'd wager little on the life of anyone who woke him now."

"Can he be waked?"

Estarion did not mean to ask it, but his tongue was as befuddled as the rest of him. She answered as calmly as ever. "Of course. He'd wake raging, and he'd sear you to ash in doing it, but wake he would. It's easy enough to do. Just command the spell to break."

Estarion bit his tongue. "Is he . . . supposed to . . . calm down while he sleeps?"

"After an age or two," she said, "maybe. Mages drove him to the edge before he was brought here. I doubt there's much left of him by now but anger. The Red Prince hoped that he'd dream his way back to sanity in this place that was built of his own best magics, and then, if there was a world left to wake to, go out to do the god's will."

"So he thought he did," said Korusan. He had drawn back from the sleeper, swaying on his feet. "Who is to teach him that the god is a lie and a dream?"

"You can say that here?" Estarion asked him.

"Here above all." Korusan stopped swaying and drew himself erect. "Is this not a place for learning the truth?"

"Such as," said Sarevadin, "that you are sworn to destroy all that the Sun has made?"

"My lord knows," said Korusan. "I told him."

"Does he truly, cubling? Truly and surely, in his bones?"

"I know," Estarion said.

They paid no heed to him, standing face to face beside the bier of the Sunborn. Estarion saw a memory, or perhaps a dream: this same two, this same battle of wills, but Sarevadin was young, as young as he, and heavy with the child who would be his grandfather's father.

"You are not my lord," she said, "and yet, young lion, you are. You love as he loved. But your Sunchild can never be yours entirely. We ended that, you and I, when you lived in that other body. We made a new thing. We wrought—"

"Failure," said Korusan, too cold for contempt. "And now he has brought me here. Is he a fool, do you think? Or merely eager to die?"

Estarion would not hear the flatness in those words, the hate that burned beneath them. He would remember the love that had been no lie, the despair that would lighten once he had his power again, his strength, his throne.

He felt the rising of the power that was in this place. It was part of the sleeper, and yet apart from him. It was all that he was not: coolness in fire, stillness in rage, darkness in light. It flowed softly over Estarion's rent and ruined magic. It soothed like a healer's touch. It guided him through the intricacies of his self. It began to make him whole, as he was meant to be.

He would have lain down beside the Sunborn and let the Tower work its healing. But Korusan stood between, and Sarevadin now old, now young, laughing in the boy's face. "Ask yourself, cubling. Are you the fool? Are you looking to die at your lover's hand?"

"Together," said Korusan. "We die together."

"Korusan," said Estarion through the mist of power. "Koru-Asan. What is this talk of death? You'll live while I live."

"And die when you die." Korusan drew his swords. They glittered in the strange light, but never as bright as his eyes. "I am dead, my lord. The fire in the cold place—it lodged in me. It consumes me."

"You're raving," Estarion said. Moving here was like swimming through light. He reached, paused as blades flashed into guard. "Here, stop that. What you're feeling is that you're whole. You've never known what that is."

"No," said Korusan. "I die." He slapped the left-hand blade into sheath, shook back the sleeve. His arm was a patchwork of bruises, wrist and elbow blackened, swollen.

Estarion caught his breath. He reached again. This time no sword prevented him. He laid hand on Korusan's arm.

Pain rocked him. So much broken, so much mended, and broken, and mended again.

Korusan smiled, bright and bitter. Bruises had begun to shadow his face. His blood was breaking its bonds. His bones were crumbling.

"No," Estarion said.

"Yes," said Korusan. He sheathed his right-hand sword and spread his arms. "Come, my love. No need to weep."

Estarion's eyes burned and stung, but not with tears. He stepped into his lover's embrace.

Iron hands flung him back. Sarevadin sprang on Korusan, impossible, shifting, young-old creature shouting words in no tongue Estarion knew.

She had hurled him into a corner of the Sunborn's bier, knocking the wind from him. He gasped and wheezed, struggling to breathe, to straighten, to stagger to his guardsman's defense. Steel flashed. A knife. The hand that wielded it was black with bruises, but ivory-white about them.

"No," said Estarion very softly. He knew the trick. Who did not? A sweet word, a proffered embrace, a dagger in the back. It was perfect Asanian.

Not Korusan. Not his gold-and-ivory princeling, his dancer with swords. He had slept in those arms for nights out of count, stood naked within reach of Olenyai steel, offered his life to it again and yet again. And Korusan had never harmed him.

They battled like brawlers in a tavern, black robes, dun leathers, long-limbed alike, wily-vicious alike, wielding teeth and nails when steel had failed. Estarion, though still gasping, found that he could move. He waded in.

They turned on him. But he had fought such battles before Asanion made an emperor of him; memory was swift and clear, here in his own Tower, in his own city, in this half of the empire that was truly his. The one who was armed was more immediately dangerous. The one who was not seemed confused that he eluded and would not strike her. He kept the corner of his eye on her, closing in on Korusan.

Korusan's eyes did not know Estarion at all. Maybe they were blind. His face was patched blue-black and ivory. His breath rattled as he drew it in. He coughed. Estarion tasted blood on his own tongue.

His power was slipping its bonds again—even here, where no Sunlord's power should be aught but mastered.

Korusan slashed. His hand was clawed with steel. Estarion darted in past it. Too slow, too slow. Burning pain seared his arm.

The second thrust aimed for the heart. Estarion reeled back. "Korusan. *Korusan!*" No use. There was death in those eyes.

Sarevadin sprang again between them. She was as mad as the Asanian, and as murderous.

She at least was unarmed. He clamped arms about her and held grimly. She was strong, but not strong enough. She was a shield against the Olenyas: he hesitated, lowering his blade a fraction, seeming to come a little to himself.

"Put me down," said Sarevadin. She was breathing hard, but she sounded like herself again.

Estarion did not loosen his grip. "Give me your word you won't kill him."

"Only if he swears he won't kill you."

"That's between the two of us," Estarion said.

"Not with you it isn't. You've an empire waiting for you. Or have you forgotten?"

"Would to the gods I could."

She twisted in his arms. For a woman so ancient she was wonderfully supple. She slid down a handspan. He shifted his grip. She drove an elbow backward into his belly and tumbled free.

She did nothing at first but stand just out of his reach. While they struggled, Korusan had drawn back to the Sunborn's bier. He stood over it, knife in hand still, held loose at his side. He seemed rapt in contemplation of the sleeper's face.

As they watched, Estarion working pain out of his middle, Sarevadin immobile and seemingly empty of will, Korusan touched the still brow. Estarion gasped. But the spell did not break. The sleeper did not wake. His dreams quivered with anger, but so had they done since his haven was invaded.

This Estarion would become, if he did not master his power. He traced in pain the line of the wound in his arm. The Tower had driven Korusan out of his wits. It was no more than that, but no less. And Estarion had brought him here. Estarion bore the guilt of it.

Korusan bent. His whisper was clear in the stillness. "How like my beloved you are, and how unlike. He is a soft thing, for all his strength. You . . . " He laughed, low and surprisingly deep. "You are steel in the forge. Would you rule again, great king and liar? Would you conquer all that is?"

"He'll kill you," Sarevadin said.

Korusan set a kiss on the Sunborn's lips, mocking yet also, in its strange way, reverent. "May every man be given such a death. And maybe," he said, "I would draw blood before I died."

"Maybe not," she said. "Try it and see."

Estarion was beginning to understand.

She was farther away, and seemed for the moment disinclined to move. Korusan had laid his hand on the Sunborn's heart. Was it beating stronger? The air had a strange taste, like the moment before thunder. The light had dimmed by a fraction.

"Yes," said Korusan. "A son of the Lion stands in your own stronghold. He would set you free, that all may fall. All of it, O bandit king. Sun, dark, Keruvarion, Asanion, lion and black eagle—all that is. And look!" he said. "There is a stranger on your throne. He bears the Lion's eyes. He was born of the night's priestess. All that he is, you fought to avert. They have betrayed you, your son and your son's sons."

There was a singing in the air, faint and eerily clear, like shaken crystal.

Estarion's bones were glass. One stroke and they would shatter.

Was this what it was to be Korusan? This exquisite pain, this perfect despair? To know that he would never be more than he was now; that before he could be fully a man, he would die.

"I am the last," said Korusan. "No son can be born of my seed. When I am dead, the Lion is gone, and you are victorious.

"And yet," he said, "I too shall have my triumph. I take with me the son of your sons. When the Lion falls, so shall the Sun."

But, thought Estarion, it would not. Haliya in Pri'nai, walled in guards, made sure of that. He almost said it, almost betrayed the one secret that Korusan must not know. Not now. Not until he was sane again. For if he knew—if he found a Gate—

One could love what one most feared. One could even love what one hated. He had learned that in Asanion.

He moved softly. He knew better than to hope that he could take an Olenyas by surprise. But that he might come close while that Olenyas was absorbed in rousing what must not be roused—that, he could pray for.

His power strove to rage out of its bounds. Only the Tower constrained it now. He was as vast as the crag, his body a tiny brittle thing, creeping over the shimmering floor toward the man on the bier and the shadow above him. He willed himself down into the feeble flesh, his sight to narrow to the compass of his eyes, his awareness to focus upon this one, deadly moment.

Steel came to his hand. Olenyai dagger. He nearly cast it off in revulsion, but his fingers clenched, holding fast. He thrust it into his belt beside his own sheathed blade. The sound did not bring Korusan about. He had spread his hands over the sleeper, tracing the shape of the body.

"He knows," Sarevadin said, the shadow of a whisper. "They taught him well."

She had not moved, nor would she. She would let it happen. She would watch, and when the time came she would die; and she would have the rest that had eluded her so long.

Estarion did not want rest. He wanted—he did not know what. But not this.

He gathered himself and sprang.

Korusan wheeled. Estarion fell on him. He twisted. In the last possible instant, Estarion saw what he did. No need of spells or chanting if they fell full on the body of the Sunborn, and Estarion bleeding power in a spray of molten gold.

Estarion wrenched, heaved. They crashed to a floor that seemed harder than stone, smoother than glass. Light pulsed in it. Korusan lay still. Stunned? Dead?

Estarion shifted atop him. He surged, hands clawed, springing for the throat.

Estarion caught them. Pause, again. Blood rimmed the golden eyes. A bruise spread across the curve of the cheekbone, swollen, nigh as dark as Estarion's own hand. "Korusan," Estarion said. His voice caught, for all that he could do. "Yelloweyes. It's I. Wake; see. I've healing for you."

"You do not." Korusan arched his back. The pain tore at Estarion's bones. "Let me die," Korusan said.

Estarion's eyes blurred. He was not seeing with them, not truly, nor feeling with the heart that beat in his body. No.

"If you do not kill me," Korusan said, "I will wake him."

Estarion tossed his head from side to side. It ached, ah, it ached. He was breaking, mind, heart, power, all at once. "Wake yourself. You're dreaming, youngling. Wake and let me heal you."

"Will you let me kill you?"

"Would it comfort you?"

"No," Korusan said. He twisted, thrust sidewise, broke free. He had drawn his swords. One flew gleaming from his hand. Estarion caught it unthinking. It was the longer, the right-hand sword.

He dropped it at his feet. "Come here, Yelloweyes."

Korusan lunged.

Estarion did not believe it, even seeing it, even knowing the track of that blade. Even with the sting of the older wound, even in the face of all that he had seen, heard, suffered, he could not believe that this of all men intended his death.

Straight to the heart. No pause. No wavering. And worst and most terrible, no regret.

Unarmed, unable to move, Estarion looked into the face of his death.

And knew himself a coward. He dropped. The sword flashed over his head. He surged up. His hands locked about Korusan's throat. "Yield," he pleaded. "My dear love, give it up."

The sword shortened, stabbing. It slid on the toughened leather of Estarion's coat. He pressed his thumbs against Korusan's windpipe.

"Don't," he said. "Don't make me do this."

The golden eyes neither wavered nor fell. Korusan was smiling. He let go the sword. It clattered to the floor. His hands fell to his sides. Estarion began to ease his grip.

A claw raked his side. He gasped.

Korusan's smile was wide and sweet and quite empty of reason. He struck again with the dagger that had been hidden in his sleeve. His lips shaped words. *Hate you*, he said. *Love*—

Blood trickled down Estarion's ribs. If there was poison on that blade . . .

He was sobbing. For breath. Of course. His cheeks were wet. With sweat: naught else. "Stop it," he whispered. "Oh, my love, stop it."

Korusan slashed, caught Estarion's cheek so swift there was no pain at all, stabbed downward. *Die with me. Beloved, die—with—*

Estarion's fingers flexed on the boy's throat. He could not, oh, merciless goddess, he could not. Korusan thrashed. One hand dropped. Estarion felt—could not see, had no need to see—the narrow deadly blade like a needle, angled to pierce his heart.

And it would. So much Korusan loved, so much he hated, that he would die, and take his lover with him.

"No," Estarion wept.

They were body to body as they had been so often, locked like the lovers they had been, would always be. Korusan tensed against Estarion. His smile widened. His blade thrust again for the heart.

Estarion's body chose for him. It twisted, arched, took the needle in the meat of the breast—pain no greater than any that had come before, and no less. His thumbs thrust inward with terrible ease. And snapped the boy's neck.

FIFTY-ONE

VANYI STOOD ALONE IN THE HEART OF THE WORLD. SHE WAS THIRSTY. THAT was so small a thing, and so absurd, that she laughed, a bark in her dry throat.

The Gate that Estarion had made had closed when he passed it. The Heartfire burned like simple fire, with even the illusion of wood beneath it. The worldwalls had returned to their slow cycling, shifting now one, now another, in a stately dance.

She could walk through any or all of them and find herself anywhere. She was tempted. To forget duty, honor, pain, priesthood, to become nothing and no one in a world empty of humanity . . . there was a dream for a black night.

She should have been prostrate with exhaustion from the raising of the Gate and the running of the worldroad. In any other place perhaps she might have been. Here, where all power had its center, she felt as she might in the midst of a long day's working, with much completed, but much still to do.

The way to the Tower was shut but not barred. It should have been locked against any but Sun-blood. Had the Olenyas done that? Or had Estarion left it so, to let her through?

Idiot. She called in her power to secure the Gate. It flooded her, nearly drowned her. She gasped and struggled.

It slowed. She shut herself off from it, willing her heart to stop pounding, her hands to stop trembling. Everything was stronger here, with the Heartfire to feed it. Even a mage sure to arrogance of her own mastery could be taken by surprise.

She opened a sliver of gate to let the power trickle in. With it came awareness, and widening of senses that had focused on herself and her troubles.

Watchers. Not the wolves of the worldroad that had proved themselves loyal to the Sunchild. These were wolves of another sort, two-legged, skilled in magery. They were eager, like wolves on the hunt; hungry, yearning toward sweetness. What that sweetness was . . .

They were swift to shield, but not swift enough. Sealed behind her own strong walls, she studied what she had brought in with her, snatched swift and secret from the mages who watched: a web of greed woven with malice and old ranklings, and in it surety. The emperor had taken the Olenyas with him into the Tower. Through that one they would enter, slay the Sunlord, gain mastery over the one who slept. Even enspelled, Mirain was a mighty power. The mage who mastered him was master of aught that he desired. And if that desire was the Mageguild's power, its strength reborn, its puppet on the throne—then so might it be.

"You do lack imagination," Vanyi said. She did not trouble to keep it to herself. "You tried that once, and failed resoundingly. What makes you think you'll win it now?"

The Heartfire flared. Power beat on her shields. She rocked before it but did not fall.

"You are cowards," she said, "and always were: working through slaves and servants, hiding behind walls, lurking in Gates. Now you leave everything to a dying child, while you shiver in shadows."

They beat harder. She would crack, but not, she prayed, too soon.

"You're afraid of the Tower and the sleeper. You think that you can rule both—but no one can do that, unless he bears the *Kasar*. You haven't found a way to counterfeit that, have you? And you never will. You are small men, cravens and fools. True bravura would have attacked the Tower long ago. Maybe no mortal man can master it, but who's to say it can't be broken, and the sleeper taken in its fall? He may be a mage and he may be mad beyond recovery, but he's no more than a man."

"And would you do better?"

He came out of a Gate, one that had shown a mountain against stars and a constellation of moons, blood-red, sea-green, foam-white. He looked like a merchant grown discontented with prosperity. He fostered that impression: well fed, well clad, sleek, yet petulant about the eyes. There was a new and livid scar upon his brow.

To a mage who could see, he was both more and less than his body's seeming. He walked in power as in a cloak, as one who is master of it, and certain of that mastery. Yet he was not content with it. He was one who wanted. It almost did not matter what, or why, only that what he did not have, he wished to possess.

That too might be a mask, a temptation to contempt. Vanyi armored herself as she might. She would not be anything to incite the admiration of an Asanian with pretensions to rank: undersized Islander woman in clothes that, though serviceable, were near enough to rags. Of her power, little showed itself that might not be reflected glory of the Sun's blood.

Behind the mage who must have been the Guildmaster came others robed in violet or in grey. They were all Asanian. She did not find that surprising. The Guild had been born in the Nine Cities, but those had given themselves to the temple. Asanion never had.

They spread in a circle about her, but not, she noticed, between her and the fire. Maybe they feared it. Maybe they thought that she did.

She did indeed. But she feared more what they might do if they seized the Tower and the king who slept in it.

She was a very poor guardian of this Gate. Her strength was not for battle. Her knowledge was in making, not in breaking.

She remembered the tale as it had been sung in Shon'ai by a eunuch singer. His clear voice rang in her memory. Mages in the Heart of the World, battle of power that turned to battle of steel and fist, and ended in the Tower of the Sun.

This was the same battle. They had won a truce only, Sarevadin and her lion's cub. Now it was broken. Now it would end.

Vanyi shook herself free of despair that was a working of mages, even through her shields. The mages' Master shrugged slightly. "Our slave will do what must be done in the Tower," he said. "Do you think that you can stop him?"

"He's not your slave," she said.

"He serves us," said the Master.

"I think not." Her feet ached with standing. She sat cross-legged in as much comfort as she could feign. "You shouldn't trust the emperor's Olenyai. They serve the throne, and nothing less."

"The throne belongs by right to the one who serves us."

"The water-blooded offspring of a female line? A man whose seed has failed, who will sire no get? What, after him? The bastard of a slave?"

She had pricked his temper. Good: it weakened his magery, eased its grip upon her. "He is the emperor."

"Then he cannot serve you," she said reasonably. "Quite the opposite."

They were closing in behind. No doubt they had knives. They could not even live their own tale; they must thieve from another.

She had a dagger, but it was small, good for little but cutting meat. She had her power, which was no greater than it should be. Her best weapon, her tongue, would not be useful much longer. They would see that she was delaying them, and ride over her.

Unless . . .

She rose slowly, with as much grace as she could muster. She opened her mind by degrees, touching the Gates one by one. Her Gate-sense was overwhelmed here, where all Gates began and ended. She thrust blindly with her power.

The worldwalls stilled. The Heartfire burned steady.

The mages glanced at one another. She felt the leaping of thoughts, the forging of the web that bound mage to mage.

Now, she thought, while the web was still half woven. A dart—there, where the web was not weakest but strongest. And in the instant of confusion, mind and body gathered, leaped.

Pain.

She shut it out.

Agony.

She willed it away.

Torment.

She flung herself through it.

Estarion fell to his knees. Korusan writhed in his arms. Death-throes; no life, no sense left, only the broken, witless shell. He clutched it to him and wept.

A body tumbled out of air, spun, righted itself. It had come through a Gate. The Gate slammed shut, bolted with power.

He stared blankly. The body had a name. Vanyi. And a voice, grating in his ears. "What in the hells—"

She was not looking at him, or at the death that he had made. He followed the line of her gaze, because it was less pain than that dead face.

Sarevadin stood where Korusan had been standing, bent over the body of her father. She seemed intent, almost curious, tracing the lines of his face, murmuring something that had the cadence of a chant.

Vanyi's breath hissed between her teeth. "He's waking."

And Sarevadin was singing him out of his sleep.

If a woman wanted to die so much that she did not care what died with her own death—if she were years gone in madness—might she not turn on all that she had been? Might she not undo the magics that she had wrought at such great cost, and rouse the power that she had sung to sleep? Would she even know what she did, save that she saw her death, and moved to embrace it?

The Tower healed the wounds of Sunchildren. If life was a wound, and healing was death, and death came only through the sleeper's waking, then the Tower itself would feed Sarevadin's will. It would do as it was wrought to do—even if it destroyed itself in the doing.

Vanyi was moving, trailing tatters of light. She gathered it in her hands, knotting swiftly. Sarevadin's hands lowered over the sleeper. If she touched, if she spoke his name, he would wake. Wake angry. Wake in a torrent of fire.

Vanyi flung her net of magic.

It fell short and shattered on the floor. Its strands of broken light blurred into the shifting, pulsing patterns of the stone.

Estarion laid Korusan aside gently, without haste but with speed enough. He was moving as he moved in the dance, slow to his own senses, swift to those of the world without. The flames were rising. The sleeper breathed in time with them. His fingers flexed on his breast. The faint line of a frown creased his brow.

Estarion glided forward. Vanyi had fallen. She had put all of herself into the net; she had no strength left to stand. She stirred, but feebly.

Sarevadin swayed. Her face was rapt.

Estarion closed arms about her and gasped. She was wise, and wily in her madness. She was shielded against his power.

He set his teeth. His body convulsed, but he held. His power fluxed. His blood was boiling. His brain was like to burst from his skull.

And he held. She could not finish her working while he killed himself on her shield. She poured power into it. He poured it away. It roared through blood and bone. It battered the barrier of his skin. It found exit in the *Kasar*.

He barred it. He did not know how. He did not care. He shut the Gate that would have saved him.

"Stop it!" she shrieked at him. "You'll burn alive!"

And he would not when the Sunborn woke?

She raked nails across his face.

So low she had sunk, she who had been both prince and princess, Sunlord and Sunborn empress. He counted the sting of those small wounds with all the rest, and laughed. It was pain, not mirth. His throat was full of fire. He could hold no more of it.

And more came. He would break, he would die.

Or he would grow to hold it.

As a flower grows, or a child, because it must; because its nature is to become greater than it is. Swiftly, of necessity; slowly, in the order of things, little by little, each small part of it full and complete before the next began. One could lose oneself in the wonder of it.

His body was healing. His soul would not. Grief was nothing that even mages could mend, except with forgetfulness.

And still the power came. She was draining it out of herself, and out of the working she had made, and—dear god—into the spell that bound the Sunborn.

She had not been waking the sleeper at all. She had been fighting him. Estarion, mistaking her, had come deathly close to breaking the spell himself.

The flow of power had stopped. Sarevadin was not empty; she could not be while she lived. But she was weakened, and sorely.

Vanyi was weaving her web again. She took its strands from her own substance, plaiting it with threads of stonelight. She murmured to herself as she wove. It sounded less like a spell than like a string of curses.

"Help her."

He glanced down startled.

Sarevadin's eyes were open, no anger in them, no scorn of his idiocy. "She's not strong enough to do it alone. Help her."

Estarion tossed his aching head. "What can I do? What if I go wrong again? What if I finish what I began, and wake the Sunborn?"

Her brows drew together as if with temper, but she sighed. "I don't suppose I should expect you to trust your power, after all you've done to it. But you have to learn, and quickly. She thinks she's enough. She's not. With you she may be."

"What can I—"

"Shut up and do it."

He could not. He did not know how.

Sarevadin climbed the ladder of his body. He tensed to thrust her away. She caught at his arms. Her hands were burning cold. "Do it," she gritted. "Do it, damn you."

He loosed a thread of power. It met Vanyi's shields and snapped back.

Sarevadin shook him, nearly oversetting them both. *"Do it!"*

He could not. His touch was too strong. Even the brush of it frayed the web.

"Fool of a boy," muttered Sarevadin. She closed her eyes. He clutched her before she fell. But she was firm enough on her feet, with him for a prop. Power hissed and crackled about her. It stung. He was caught; he could not let go.

Her power seized his with ruthless strength and wielded it. Full in the heart of the weaving. Darting through the knots and plaiting, needle-thin, needle-sharp. Drawing them in. Making them strong. Plucking the net from the hands that had made it, and casting it over the man on the bier.

He tossed beneath it, raising hands that clawed to rend it to rags. He was not awake, not yet, but his anger was roused, and it ruled him.

Sarevadin crooned: to herself, it might have been, or to the web that strained and tore. Estarion's power was in her hands still. She poured her own through it, taking from it what she needed: youth, strength, raw unshaped will. She gave it shape. She wove the web anew, and herself into it, as Vanyi had.

Vanyi had kept her soul apart from the making. Sarevadin's soul was the making. Her life was her power. Her body was wrought of it. She shifted as she had on the worldroad, woman to man to maiden to youth to shape of both and neither. And still she wove, singing her wordless song.

The sleeper fought her with mindless rage. His dream had turned to fire.

She sang it down. She cooled it with water of the soul, sweet spring of light, soft rain on parched earth. She sang calm; she sang sleep. She sang a soft green stillness into which his wrath subsided. She bound it there. She gave it dreams; dreams of peace.

The Sunborn lay still under the pall of power. He was not all resigned to it: one hand had fallen to his side, clenched into a fist. But he was bound. He would learn perforce the ways of peace, who had ever been a man of war.

Sarevadin sighed in Estarion's arms. She was herself again, fragile with great age, and her eyes were calm, almost happy. More truly so, maybe, than they had been since Hirel died.

She smiled. Her voice was a thread, almost too thin to bear the weight of words. "That will keep him for a while. Do you trust me now, a little?"

"I always trusted you," Estarion said.

"Don't lie. It makes you twitch." She shifted; he settled her more comfortably. She weighed no more than a child. "You'd better lay me here. It's a long way down to the tombs, and I'll be dust before you come there."

"You're not dying," said Estarion, but his heart clenched. She was withering as he watched.

"They said I couldn't die. They didn't think I'd strip myself of power. They didn't know I could. No more," she admitted, "did I, until I did it." She smiled. "I'm not sorry I tried. It gave you yourself. And it gave me . . . it gave me . . . "

"Death," Vanyi said. She was white and shaking, but she was alive. She stretched out a hand, not quite daring to touch the cheek that was thin skin stretched over bone. "Wouldn't a simple cliff have done as well, with rocks at the foot of it, and the sea to sweep you away?"

Sarevadin was beyond answering, but her eyes laughed.

The Sunborn's bier was broad enough for two. Estarion laid her on it, gently, and straightened her limbs. He had nothing to cover her with, but she was too frail to bear the weight of cloak or pall, even if it were made of light. Her life was ebbing softly, slowly, like water from a broken cup.

Her body sank with it. Flesh melted from bone. Bone crumbled to dust. No pain went with her dying, no fear, no thought but joy. And that was a splendid, soaring, bright-winged thing, casting off the memory of flesh, leaping into the light.

FIFTY-TWO

THE SUNBORN DREAMED AGAIN HIS LONG DREAM. BESIDE HIM ON HIS BIER LAY a shape of ash that fell in upon itself and scattered in the wind from the Gate.

Estarion whirled. There had been no Gate, once Vanyi was in the Tower. Yet the wall behind him was open, and beyond it the Heart of the World. Mages stood there, one in robes that mingled dark and light, and those behind him like guards, some in violet, some in grey; and in a half-circle about them the black shadows of Olenyai. One Olenyas stood beside and a little behind the master of the mages, hands on swordhilts, so like Korusan that Estarion almost cried his name. But Korusan lay beyond the bier, crumpled, twisted, dead.

Vanyi's voice shocked Estarion into his senses. It was clear, hard, and perfectly fearless. "I forbid you to trespass here."

"Are you Sun-blood," demanded the Master of the mages, "to permit or forbid?"

"Are you Sun-blood," she countered, "to set foot in this place? Men go mad here, mage. Men die."

"Old jests," said the mage. "Old nonsense."

"Then come," she said. "We killed your spy. Our own madwoman is dead. The Sunborn is not likely to wake in this age of the world; and no thanks to your plotting for that."

The mage's eyes widened slightly. He seemed for the first time to see the bier, the Sunlord beside it, the body of the Lion's cub with the ul-cub crouching over it as if on guard.

The Olenyas had seen it long since. His eyes were on Estarion, level, betraying no emotion.

"Yes, I killed him," Estarion said. "It was my right. His life was mine, as mine was his."

The Olenyas inclined his head. "Majesty," he said.

Estarion stiffened. He was being given—something. He did not dare to hope, yet, that it was acceptance. "Do you serve me, Olenyas?"

"I serve the emperor," said the Olenyas.

"You," said Estarion as knowledge came clear, voice and eyes and set of the body in the robes, "are the captain of Olenyai in the Golden Palace."

"I am the Master of the Olenyai," said the Olenyas, "majesty."

Estarion drew a breath. "Am I the emperor?"

The Olenyas paused. Estarion did not breathe, did not move. Nor, he noticed with distant clarity, did the mages. Their Master looked as if he would have spoken, but did not dare.

"Yes," said the Olenyas. "You are the emperor."

They won their veils in battle and their rank in combat, man to man. In slaying their prince and champion, Estarion had won their service. He even bore their brand: the sting and throb of the long cut in his cheek, that Korusan had made before he died.

It gave him no joy. "If you are mine," he said, "then serve me now. Take these traitors to my throne. Kill any who resists."

The mages seemed unable to believe what they had heard. Even after their allies closed in upon them, taking them captive; even, some of them, when they broke and ran, and swift steel cut them down.

The Master of mages was quicker than his fellows, and closer to the Gate. As the Olenyai closed in, he bolted for what he thought was safety.

Estarion sprang to seize Vanyi and fling her out of the mage's path. She ducked, slid, broke free. The mage hung in the Gate. Her power pulsed, holding him there. He raised lightnings against her.

She hurled them back at him, reckless, in a blind fury, as if all of it were seething out of her—grief, rage, guilt, fear, hate, love that had bent awry and turned to pain.

The mage seized on that pain and twisted. She lunged into the Gate, went for his throat. He laughed in his bonds. He had trapped her.

He caught her in midleap. She kicked and flailed. He held her just out of reach of eyes and throat, and while she raged, forgetful of power, he smote her with his magery.

She sagged. He drew her in. He would kill her with his hands, bind her with his power, seal her to his will—any or all of them. Estarion, helpless on the far side of the Gate, barred from it by magewalls, could only watch and rage.

The mage clasped her tightly. His power uncoiled.

She erupted, body and power. He toppled astonished. She bound him as he lay, her movements swift, furious, and heaved him up.

He hung again in the void of power that was the Gate, wound in cords like a spider's prey. And like a spider's prey, he looked living on the face of his death. Shadows gathered about him. Watchers: dim shapes like wolves, grinning wide wolf-grins.

The ul-cub yowled and sprang. The watchers scattered. The cub in the Gate was larger than they, black beast sun-eyed. He bared his fangs at the mage. The mage began to struggle.

Vanyi stood back, watching, saying nothing.

The mage spoke with remarkable steadiness under the circumstances, but there was no mistaking the desperation in his voice. "Let me go," he said. "Lady, priestess, whatever you wish, whatever I can give—"

"What have you given us," she asked him coldly, "but death and betrayal?"

"I erred, I confess it. I'll serve you faithfully. Only let me go."

"No," said Vanyi.

He offered her gold. He offered her slaves. He offered her empires—and what right, Estarion wondered, had he to do that? She ignored him. He offered her magic. She clapped hands over her ears. He offered her the Gates and all that was in them, if she would set him free.

"Take him," she said to the ul-cub.

The cat flowed toward him. He began to scream.

"Goddess," she said in disgust. "Nothing's even touched him."

Nothing, Estarion thought, *but terror.*

The ul-cub circled the mage, tailtip twitching. He fought harder against his bonds. They snapped. He dropped, still screaming. The ul-cub sprang.

It was a clean kill. One spring, one snap of jaws in the neck. The ul-cub stood atop the body, treading it with half-flexed claws, as if to ask it why it jerked and twitched.

Slowly it stilled. He sniffed it. His nose wrinkled. He stepped away fastidiously, shaking a paw that had drawn blood, pausing to lick it clean. The watchers had stood back in respect, but once he had retreated they closed in, surrounding the body. Their chieftain sniffed the blood on it, tasted it. He barked once. The pack fell yelping on the feast.

The ul-cub ignored them. He sprang out of the Gate and flung himself at Estarion's feet, and set to washing himself thoroughly, with much snarling and sneezing at the stink of mageblood.

Vanyi followed the cat, walking steadily. Only Estarion, maybe, saw how pale she was, how pinched her face. He yearned to clasp her to him, to stroke her pain away. But he had grown wise: he did not touch her.

When she turned again to the Gate, she was calm. She said to the Olenyai, "By your emperor's leave, take the prisoners back to Pri'nai. He will follow when he is finished here."

The Olenyai glanced at Estarion. He hesitated. The Gate sang faintly to itself. The watchers were still feeding.

Below the Tower was the crag of Endros and the river, and his own city. He had but to find the door to that doorless place, and walk out of it, into his palace.

Or he could pass the Gate, enter the Heart of the World, walk from it to Pri'nai and Asanion and rebellion that was not ended for that its prophet was dead.

His heart shrank from facing Asanion again. Even Haliya, even his ladies in Kundri'j—he was duty to them, no more. Asanion would never be his, would never learn to love an outland conqueror.

He knelt beside Korusan's body. He had straightened it when he laid it down, so that the head did not hang awry on its broken neck. The face was quieter than it had ever been in life. Not at peace, no. Peace was alien to emperors, or to princes of the Lion's brood.

Estarion was the last of that blood, but for the child in Haliya's womb: he with his dark hands, his alien face. He was the Son of the Lion.

He kissed the cold lips. "I loved you," he said. "Not enough. Not as you loved me. No one can love like that and live. But as a Sunlord can love—so I loved you." He lifted the body, cradling it. Already it had begun to stiffen.

He could not lay it on the bier. It was not fitting. Yet he did not wish to take it from the Tower.

His power was in him, filling him like wine in a cup. It flexed a tendril of itself. The Tower responded. Where had been blank luminous wall, a niche stood open, like the tombs of the kings in the crag below. Estarion laid Korusan in it. It fit him precisely.

As Estarion drew back, the wall closed again. Through it as in a glass he could see the shadow that had been his lover, his enemy, his kinsman. He kissed his burning palm and laid it against the stone. He did not speak. All that he could say was said. There was nothing left but silence. They were waiting still, Olenyai and mages beyond the Gate, Vanyi and the cat on this side of it.

He spoke to the Olenyai. "Let your prisoners go."

The Olenyai did not wish to obey, but he was their emperor. The mages responded variously to freedom. Some stood still, as if they did not dare to move. Some shook themselves like ruffled birds. A few stepped apart from their erstwhile jailers and faced Estarion through the Gate. Those would be the strongest of them, or the most determined in rebellion.

"The battle is mine," he said to them.

"But the war may not be," said a woman in grey. Her shadow-brother stood behind her, hands on her shoulders, and fixed Estarion with a cold stare.

He gave them fire-heat. "You have a custom, yes? Whoever defeats your master in battle of magecraft becomes master in his stead."

The lightmage was not pleased to answer, but answer she did. "That is so."

"Then by your law," said Estarion, sweeping his hand toward Vanyi, "this woman is your master."

Vanyi opened her mouth. The lightmage spoke before she could begin. "That is none of ours. She belongs to the temple."

"She is a mage," said Estarion, "and a master of Gates."

"Estarion—" said Vanyi. She sounded as if she could not decide whether to kill him quickly or let him die slowly, in the most exquisite agony she could devise.

"She defeated your master in combat," Estarion said to the mages. "Fair, I would hardly call it, but there is no question as to the victor."

Some of the mages looked as if they would have argued, but the lightmage, who seemed to hold rank among them, silenced them with a slash of the hand. "What are you proposing, Sunlord?"

Another merchant, this one, and settling in to haggle. He was in no mood to indulge her. "This is your trial, mage. I judge you guilty. You have earned death, but I am weary of killing. I give you all to this priestess-mage. Your Guild is hers, to break or to keep. But if she breaks it, then you die."

"And if I won't kill them?" Vanyi demanded.

"Then I will." There was iron in his voice, the taste of it in his throat like blood. "Let them live, and be master of them. Refuse to master them, and they die."

She looked long at him, studying him as if he were a stranger. Maybe he was. He was not the fragile young thing that had come to this place. He was not whole, either, not surely, not yet. But he was beginning to be what he was born to be: mage, priest, emperor.

"If I do this," she said, "you'll lose all hope of making me your empress."

His belly knotted. He had been going to command her in that, too; to name her empress in despite of the woman in Pri'nai. No one else was more fit to rule.

"Haliya might surprise you," she said, reading his thoughts as she always could, even when he was shielded; as he had been able to read hers even when he had no power to speak of. It was not magery. It was love.

"Yes, I love you," she said. "I always have. I always will."

"And your price is the Guild—the deaths of its mages?"

She flinched. He had not meant to say that. It had come out of him, out of the high cold thing that he was becoming, here in the Tower of his fathers. She seized his hands. "You won't let them live? Even for me?"

He looked down at her. He never remembered how small she was. Not much taller than Haliya, but tall in the soul, and great in power. Very great. She made so little of it that even mages failed to see the truth.

"You don't want me," he said, reading it in the eyes that lifted to meet his. "Not except for yourself; not for what I am or the titles I bear. You were never made for empire. But power and the Gates—there you are mistress and queen."

"Not queen," she said.

"No," he said. "But Master of the Guild, yes. It won't be easy. There are more mages, maybe, than any of us imagines. I wager you'll find them on all the worlds of the Gates, or near enough. And they're mostly Asanians. They hate foreigners, and they despise the lowborn."

She was shaking as if with cold. She was no fool, to be fearless of what he wished on her.

Wished, no. He wanted her at his side, sharing his throne, his bed, his heart.

Wisdom was a bitter thing.

"If you don't lead them," he said, "and keep them rigidly in hand, they have to die. I can't trust them. They contrived the death of my father; they nearly killed me. I won't leave them free to destroy my son."

He had startled the mages and brought the Olenyai quivering to attention. He would have laughed, if he had remembered how.

Vanyi took no notice. Her eyes were full of tears, but they were as hard as his own, and as clear. "You've changed," she said.

"For the worse, I'm sure." She caught his irony; her lips twitched. She still held his hands. He turned them to clasp hers. "I envy you. I have my empire, and my power is mine again. You have the high magic. The Gates are yours, and all the worlds they command."

"If I can master them."

"You doubt it?"

Her lip curled. "I'm not a prince's get. I don't know what I can do until I do it."

"Nor do I," he said, "and I'm a Sunlord's get."

"You don't leave me much choice, do you? Empress or Guildmaster. What if I want to be a simple priestess on Journey?"

"The mages die," he said.

She drew her breath in sharply. "And you? What are you going to do? Hide in Endros? Hope your troubles go away?"

She thought she had him. It was fair, he supposed. "I . . . thought I might rest. For a while."

"While your empire falls about your ears? That's wise, yes."

"Of course," he said, "before I can rest, there's a little matter of civil war. And a pair of empires that must be one. And two cities that will submit to the mastery of another that is neither Asanian nor Varyani, but both. Once that's built, then I'll sleep for a cycle, and go hunting for a season, and forget that I was ever born to rule this monstrosity of an empire."

She gaped. She would never forgive him, he thought, for mocking her. Then she laughed. There was pain in it, but it was real enough for that. "Confess, Estarion. You didn't know you'd say that until you said it."

"I didn't," he said.

"We know each other well," she said. She let go his hands, ran hers up his arms, stroking them, as if she could not help herself. "If I take the Guild, you've lost me. I won't come to your bed. I won't be your lover. What I will be . . . I'll be your friend, Meruvan Estarion, but not your servant. I'll serve you as I can, as the needs of the Guild allow. But if I see that your commands will serve the Guild ill, I'll oppose you."

"Even to death?" he asked her.

"If I must."

Her hands rose to his shoulders, crossed his breast, came to rest over his heart. It was beating hard. "I can't promise you," he said, "that I'll always do what's best for the Guild. If breaking the Guild will serve my empire, I'll do it. Even if it kills you."

She bowed her head, raised it again. This was no easier for her than it was for him. But she had courage at least to match his, and will as strong. She took his face in her hands, pulled it down, and kissed him. "For remembrance," she said.

If he had had tears left, he would have wept. She let him go, turned, walked toward the Gate. She stepped through it. The watchers watched but did not move. She stood before the mages. "You heard," she said. "Now heed. You saw what came of your Master. Remember it."

They would remember. Estarion would never forget.

The ul-cub rose from his crouch by Estarion's feet, stretched from nose to tail, and eyed the Gate. He was thinking of his mother and his sisters, of milk and meat and sleep.

Yes, Estarion thought. *Sleep.* The long night was past; the dawn had come. He looked about, to remember: black bier, bright walls, shadow in the stone.

Beyond the walls the sun was rising. It brought light into this place of all places, great tides and torrents of it, flowing over him, singing in his blood. He filled his hands with it, and bore it with him through the Gate, and in that cold hall of all suns and none poured it out upon the stone.

The mages did not understand. The Olenyai, maybe, did. Vanyi looked ready to strike him. "This is not your place," she said.

"All places are mine," he said, "and none, as they are for any man. I'm lord of a world. May I not bear tribute from it to the Heart of all worlds that are?"

She did not trust him. That was pain, but it was just. She was his equal now; and that both pricked and pleased his pride.

He met her glare with the flicker of a smile. "Welcome me to the heart of your realm, mistress of mages."

Her glare did not abate. He would not have been surprised if she had flung him back where he came from, cat and guards and all. "You have nerve," she said as if to herself, and not kindly, either.

His smile widened. He did not mean it to. With all the grief on him, the guilt, the blood on his hands, he should never smile again. But there was a pool of sunlight between them, here where sunlight never came, and she was wonderful to watch, mantled in her magic, wrestling with her temper.

She mastered it. Sparks still flew from it, but when she spoke she was civil, if not precisely gracious. "Welcome," she said, "to the Heart of the World." And after a pause, in which no one seemed to breathe: "My lord emperor."

That would do. For a beginning.

SPEAR OF HEAVEN

Rudyard Kipling would have known where this came from.
So would the lamas of Shangri-La.

ONE

THE CHILD SLEPT, AND DREAMED OF WORLDGATES. IN HER DREAM SHE SAT IN front of one, right on the threshold, and watched the worlds shift and change. She liked the green ones, and the ones that were all sea-wash and blown spume, and the ones where it was always morning, with the sun just coming up, and birds—or things like birds—singing in the unchanging light. But the fire-worlds were splendid, and the worlds of ice, though they made her shiver, and the worlds that were always night, with torrents of stars.

They were always changing, never twice the same. A million worlds. Mother said it, and Great-Grandfather, and Vanyi who ought to know, since they were Vanyi's worlds, or Vanyi's Gates at least. Kimeri did not know what a million was, except that it was very many.

She dreamed of a million worlds, and of sitting as she would have liked to sit if there had not always been Guardians to chase her away: not quite touching the Gate, and feeling all the other Gates inside herself, and the worlds inside of them, millions and millions and millions. She made a song of it, because songs were what she liked to make, this cycle.

And as she sat and watched and sang, one of the Gates was gone. Like that. One moment there, like a bead on an endless string. The next moment, nothing. Except . . .

She would cry, she thought, when she woke up. But not until then. In her dream there was no one to notice, no one to hold her and pet her and tell her there was no need to cry.

She hugged her dream-knees to her dream-chest. The dead Gate was hurting worse now. It had not hurt at first; it had been too different, and too surprising. She had not known what it was until she felt how it crumbled and fell in on itself like the dry husk of an insect that she had found on a windowsill, that Great-Grandfather had said was dead. Dead was gone, except for a smear of dust and a bit of a wing.

Not gone, said a voice that was not a voice, not really. It came from inside, from the place where Gates were. *Not gone. Not dead. I am. I am . . . I still . . . help me!*

Kimeri tried to answer, but the voice, whoever owned it, could not hear her. *Help me,* it begged. *The Gate—I can't—help me!*

"I can't," said Kimeri aloud, because maybe that would make the voice hear. "I'm too little. I can't do anything."

Help me, the voice said. *Help me.*

No matter if it was a dream. Kimeri hurt. The Gates hurt, because one of them was dead. And inside the dead Gate was—someone. A voice. A person who could only cry for help, and could not hear when Kimeri answered. She was too little, and she was only dreaming. She could do nothing at all.

She began to cry.

It was universal law, Vanyi thought. In time of crisis, everyone capable of contending with the disaster was either asleep, abroad, or overburdened. A Gate was broken, a Guardian lost, and the one Guardian who could be spared to watch over the inmost of the nine Gates in the Mage-hall of Starios was a silly chit of a boy with a horror of young children. Particularly young children who, he insisted, had appeared out of nowhere, sound asleep and weeping in it, on the threshold of his Gate.

The Master of mages in the Empire of Sun and Lion, Guardian of all the Gates, priestess of Avaryan, right hand of the emperor who sat the throne in Starios, went in her own person to the hall of the ninth Gate, and found the child as the boy had said, drawn into a knot almost within the Gate. In spite of herself, Vanyi caught her breath. Even a handbreadth more, and the Gate would have taken the child.

The young Guardian had fled. "Coward," Vanyi said to the space where he had been. The emperor's youngest heir—for it was she, the tangle of honey-amber hair was unmistakable—was deep asleep, and crying as if her heart would break.

Vanyi lowered herself stiffly to the floor, gathered the dreaming, sobbing child in her lap, and rocked her, crooning, "There, little terror. There."

The little terror woke slowly, hiccoughing, choking on tears. Vanyi shook her to steady her breathing, and slapped her once, not too hard, to get her attention. Her eyes opened wide, amber-gold and quite beautiful, even bleared with weeping; and angry, too, and bright with stung pride. "I'm *not* a baby," she said fiercely.

"Did I ever say you were?" Vanyi asked in her driest tone.

That, as Vanyi had hoped, subdued the child's temper, if not her pride. But she could hardly help that, with the breeding she had.

"Now," said Vanyi, "suppose you tell me what you're doing here."

Kimeri looked about. She did not seem surprised, but then Vanyi had not expected her to. She would have crept in, of course, when the Guardian's back was turned, and fallen asleep watching the Gate. She had done it before. She would do it again, no doubt, as long as her keepers persisted in falling asleep at their posts.

"I was asleep," Kimeri said. "I didn't mean to be here. A Gate died, Vanyi. It hurts."

Vanyi told herself that that did not surprise her, either. Seeing that the child was who she was, and what she was. "A Gate died," Vanyi agreed somberly, "and you should have stayed home, where you would be safe."

"I'm safe here," Kimeri said. "Gates won't hurt me. Even Gates that die."

"O innocence," said Vanyi. Innocence stared at her with eyes the color of amber, in a face the color of old ivory. It was too young to understand. She smoothed the amber curls and sighed. "I had better return you to your keepers before they add their own panic to the rest."

"They don't know I'm gone," Kimeri said. "You won't tell them, will you? They'll carry on till nobody can think."

"You should have thought of that before you escaped," said Vanyi.

The golden eyes lowered. Vanyi knew better than to expect that the child was chastened. Quelled, yes. For the moment. It would have to do.

The Guildhall was rousing to uproar as awareness of the Gate's fall spread outward. Vanyi was needed in a dozen places at once, for a dozen different tasks, all of which only she could perform. No Gate had ever fallen except as the Guild willed it—not ever, not in a thousand years. The shock resonated from Gate to Gate, from Guildhall to Guildhall across this one of all the worlds.

It had not gone outward yet, she thought, affirming it as she knew how to do, from within. The worlds beyond this were quiet still, untroubled by the fall of a single Gate among the many. But that quiet would not hold. Her bones knew it, stiff with cold that was only in part born of the night's chill and her own advancing years.

All of that beset her; and she rose with the child in her arms, and said, "Come then. I'll take you home."

Home for Kimeri—ki-Merian, Merian of Asan-Gilen as she would be when she was older—was the palace that rose in the heart of the city as the Guildhall rose on its sunset edge. Vanyi brought her to it on the back of a mettlesome seneldi mare, riding without bridle or saddle, since fetching either would have meant waking the groom who slept in the back of the stable. Kimeri would have preferred a mount of her own, but Vanyi was in no mood for such nonsense.

The guards at the palace gate were awake and too well trained to ask questions. They barely widened eyes at the sight of the Master of mages mounted bareback and bridleless with a small amber-gold child riding behind. They bowed low to the mage, a fraction lower to the child, and let them in without a word.

TWO

I AM GOING."

"You are not."

There was a pause. It was not the first, nor was it likely to be the last in an argument that had gone on since the night was young. It had begun with the two of them sitting reasonably civilly face to face across a game of kings-and-cities. The game now was long forgotten, and they were on their feet, he by the window where his pacing had taken him, she by the table, stiffly still, with her fists clenched at her sides.

"I will go," she said. "You gave me leave."

"That was before the Gate fell. The Gate which, I should remind you—"

"Yet again," she muttered.

He ignored her. "—has just this night fallen, and none of us knows why, or how. I won't risk my heir in an expedition that has gone from mildly dangerous to outright deadly."

"Oh, and am I your only heir?" she demanded with bitterness that was as much a part of her as her golden lion-eyes. "I've done my dynastic duty, Grandfather. I've given you another royal object to protect until it stifles."

He turned his back on her and stared out of the window into the dark. He all but vanished against it, dark as he was, and dressed in plain dark clothes as he had come from a walk in the city. The only light in him was the frosting of silver in his hair, and little enough of that.

She was all light as he was all dark: all gold, golden skin, golden eyes, golden hair cut at the shoulders and held back from riot by a fillet of woven gold. But, as he turned to face her again, he had the same eyes, lion-colored, and much the same face, black-dark to her honey-gold: strong arched brows, strong arched nose, stubborn chin. His beard was greyer than his hair, but not overmuch.

"Daruya," he said a little wearily, "no one ever forgets that you have given the empire an heir. It's still a remarkable scandal."

"What, that I wouldn't name her father, let alone marry him? Believe me, Grandfather, you wouldn't want him playing consort to my imperial majesty, when I come to it, which pray god and goddess won't be for long years yet. He's a beautiful, brilliant political idiot."

"And married," said the emperor, "to a woman older than he, much wealthier, and possessed of considerable power in the western courts." Her eyes had widened.

He smiled. It was not a gentle smile, though there was affection in it, and a degree of amusement. "Yes, I know his name. You thought I wouldn't learn it? I've had four years to hunt him down."

She sucked in a breath. "You haven't killed him."

"Of course not," the emperor said. "What do you take me for?"

"Ruthless," she answered.

He laughed with a tinge of pain. "Well, and so I am, when I have to be. The man's an idiot, as you say. And you knew it when you bedded him?"

"I knew that he was fertile, though even if he hadn't been, I was sure the god would find a way to alter it. I wanted his looks and his intelligence for my child."

"And you didn't want a man who could bind you with the name of wife." He came back to the table, studied the pieces laid out on the board, shifted the black king to face the golden warrior. "I could have forced you to marry a man whom I chose, to cover the shame of a child born without a father."

"There's no such shame," she said, "in the tribes of the north."

"Then it's a pity you aren't a tribesman, isn't it?" He looked into her furious face and sighed. "We're all rebellious in our youth. My rebellion was to refuse to rule the western half of my empire, then to insist on ruling only there, and nearly breaking the whole with my stubbornness. My son's was to hunt aurochs at a gallop in country too rough for speed, and to break his neck doing it. Yours is mild to either of those. You gave us a scandal, no more, and an heir of your body. No breaking of necks or empires; merely of strict propriety."

She snatched the warrior from the board and flung it at him. He caught it in a hand that flashed gold—like her own, like her daughter's. Like that of every heir to the throne of the Sun. They carried gold in their right hands like a burning brand, born there—set there by the god, the priests said. She did not know. It burned, that she knew, and worse, the more she fought it.

"I'm going with the mages," she said. "They'll go still, you'll see. They have to find out what broke their Gate. I can help them. I have a gift for Gates, and for that kind of magery."

"So do they," he said, "and they aren't heir to the empire."

"You promised me," said Daruya. "When you refused me the right of Journey, when I became a priestess—you promised that I would have one later."

"As I recall," he said, "what I refused you was permission to run away to sea when you were pregnant with ki-Merian. I very nearly had to chain you in the temple then."

"But you didn't," she said. "I stayed home. I did my duties like a proper humble heir to the throne. I delivered my daughter, I nursed her myself, I raised her and weaned her and taught her what I could. Now she's old enough to be separated from me. I'll leave her here, I'll surrender her to you. But I'm going with the mages."

"No," said the emperor, impervious to her sacrifice. "Not since the Worldgate broke."

Daruya heard a sound behind her. She whipped about.

Vanyi smiled thinly at her. Daruya flung up her hands, the one that was simple human flesh, the one that flashed gold. "You too, Guildmaster? And what did he pay you to keep me in my cage?"

She gave Vanyi no chance to answer. Some time after she was gone, while the storm of her passing was still rumbling on the edge of awareness, Vanyi said, "Well. I presume you've told her she can't go."

"You always were unusually perceptive," said the emperor. He was not angry, nor particularly bitter. Wry, that was all, and a little sad. "I can't let her, of course. Whether or not she's been so generous as to leave an heir to come after me."

"Which, from the look of you, won't happen for another forty years at least." Vanyi spoke without envy. She had not grown old with excessive grace. Her hair, once the color of sea-moors in autumn, red and brown and gold intermingled, was winter-grey. Her pale skin was gone paler with age, the lines of laughter and of care drawn deep. She looked her threescore years and more.

He, who was but a little younger, seemed a man still in his prime. He made a gesture as if to deny her, but she stopped him. "No, don't say it. We're what our breeding makes us. I like to see how little you've changed, except to grow into yourself. It comforts me."

She left the door and came into the room, and sat in the chair that Daruya had long since vacated. He stood with his hands on the back of his own chair, staring down at her from his not inconsiderable height. "You think she should go?"

"No," said Vanyi. "Not in the least. While the way was open, while it was a simple expedition to the other side of the world, what better ambassador than the heir to the empire? But now . . . we don't know what we're going into. We don't even know what broke the Gate."

"And yet you'll go?"

"You can't forbid me," she said calmly.

"I wouldn't try," he said. "That was our pact from long ago. The empire for me. The Mageguild for you, and the mastery of Gates. Alliance wherever we could. But where we could not . . . well. We've never been enemies, have we?"

"Once or twice," she said, "we did disagree on policy."

His lips twitched. "Rather more often than that, I recall. But enmity—we never came to that."

"No," said Vanyi. She sat back in the tall chair and sighed. "I shouldn't even be here. The Guild is in an utter taking. You'd think it had never seen a crisis before."

"It's got used to having you in command," he said.

"Don't flatter me," she said with an edge of annoyance. "I'm running out on responsibility, much as your granddaughter would love to. Did you know that your great-granddaughter spent the night in the Guildhall, on the threshold of the ninth Gate?"

She had taken him completely by surprise. He looked so startled that she laughed; and that roused his temper, which only made her laugh the harder.

He shook her into some semblance of quiet. She looked up into his face, suddenly so close. He would kiss her, she thought. It was a fugitive thought, from nowhere that she could discern. It fled as swift as it had come, as he let her go and stepped back. She could not see that it cost him any effort.

Forty years, she thought. Forty years since she last shared his bed, and lovers enough in between, and she could still go all to bits when he laid hands on her.

He seemed long since cured of her. There had never been any hope in it to begin with, a fisherman's daughter from Seiun Isle dreaming that she could wed as well as bed the Lord of Sun and Lion. They had parted long ago, and properly enough. He had taken nine concubines in Asanion, half in obedience to the custom of that ancient empire, half in defiance of it.

The obedience was in the taking. The defiance was in the setting free, in giving them to choose whether to marry or to go where they would. In their own western country they would have had no choice but to remain in his harem; but in his eastern realm they could take the freedom he gave and do as they pleased with it.

Most had chosen to marry among the lords and princelings of the east. Vanyi had reason to suspect that not all of them had gone maiden to the marriage bed; but none of the husbands had objected that Vanyi ever knew of.

One of the royal concubines had desired no husband. She had gone away to rule a princedom in the east of the world, had prospered and grown old and adopted a daughter to rule after her.

Only one had remained with the emperor, and that was exactly as he wished it. She had borne his son and heir, and held in great honor the name and the title of empress. She was aging sadly now in the way of her people, but she was still alive and still hale, and he was devoted to her. Of that, Vanyi had no doubt at all. She had only to read it in his eyes.

He took no notice of her abstraction. "Where is the child now?"

She had to stop and remember Kimeri and the Gate, and the nurses' snoring as the child crept through the door into her own chambers. "I brought her back," said Vanyi, "and put her to bed, none the worse for her night's wandering. There's a binding on her now, and I called one of the palace ul-cats to enforce it. She won't go anywhere again until morning."

"God and goddess," said the emperor. "She's as bad as her mother."

"I wouldn't say that," Vanyi said. "She was sleepwalking, it seems. She doesn't remember coming to the Guildhall. The Gate's fall brought her, I think—she's got Gate-sense."

"All the Sun's brood do," he said. He sounded faintly angry, though not at Vanyi.

"Poor Estarion," she said with rough sympathy. "It always ends in your lap, no matter where it begins. It's your doom, I think: to be the one who holds it all together."

He shrugged. Self-pity, Vanyi knew, was an indulgence he had given up long ago. He had been emperor since he was twelve years old, when he saw his father dead of poison in the palace of what had been the western empire, when western Asanion and eastern Keruvarion were united only by force and by ancient enmity. He had spent his youth and all his manhood uniting those two hostile realms into one empire, building his city on the border between them, bringing their courts together, making their disparate peoples one people. Now he had his reward. For five whole years he had had no call to war; for three seasons, no assassin had tried to take his life.

Strange how little he showed of all that. He had scars in plenty, but his coat and trousers hid them. His face was still more young than old. He kept from his youth a kind of innocence, a resilience that never seemed to fail or to harden, no matter how sorely he was tested.

If he was aware of her thoughts, he gave no sign of it. He sighed and said, "She's punishing me, you know. For letting her father die and her mother go away as soon as she was born. So she had an heir without a father, and meant to leave the heir as she was left, but I was cruel: I wouldn't let her."

"That was brutal, yes," said Vanyi, dry as winter grass. "You left Varuyan to find his own way as all sons must, even princes. If that was into marriage with a pretty fool, and into an aurochs' horns while that fool was pregnant with his daughter, that was his fault. Not yours."

"I know that," he said a little sharply. "Not that Salida was—or is—as much a fool as you insist. She's Asanian; she's practical. She didn't have the will or the strength to raise a Sunborn daughter. She knew it. She also knew that if she stayed in the palace, she'd be immured there, condemned to be nothing more than a dowager princess. If she gave up the child, surrendered her rank and her dowry, went back to her kin, she could marry again; she could have children that honestly were her own, and not the get of a god."

"Granted," said Vanyi. "But she could have spared something of herself for her firstborn: a word, a letter, some intimation that she remembers the girl's existence."

"We decided, she and I," said Estarion, "that it were best if she did no such thing. Less pain for her. Less difficulty for the child whom she so wisely gave up."

"That wasn't wise," Vanyi said.

He said nothing. She could not tell if he agreed, or if he was being stubborn, or if he had simply tired of the subject. He wandered back to the window. There was something of the caged beast in the way he stood, but a beast resigned to its captivity, its yearning shrunk to a dull ache.

"You were all the father she ever needed," Vanyi said, not to comfort him, but because it was the truth. "Haliya has always been a mother to her. But that's never enough for the young. They're the strictest traditionalists of all."

She could not see his face, only the broad line of his shoulders, and the heavy braid that fell between them. His mood to the touch of her magery was surprisingly calm. He said, "If Haliya loses the child of her heart, I don't know that she'll recover."

It was calm, then, over grief. No use to say that he had known it when he married. His line lived long, if sudden death did not take them, and he had taken an Asanian wife, of a people who blossomed early and died young. It had been necessary, one of the many necessities that bound two empires into one.

Vanyi gentled her voice as much as she might. "Is she so frail?"

"You should know as well as I. You saw her yesterday."

She ignored the snap in his voice. "She's grown old, to be sure, and I'm sorry for it. But I think she's stronger than you imagine."

"Strong enough to withstand the cruelty of a child?"

"That's what mothers are for. Grandmothers, too."

He carefully did not observe that Vanyi had never been either. She would have borne his son, if she had not miscarried. There had been no children after, of any of her lovers. Her choice. Her grief, when she had leisure for it. Which mostly she did not. The Gates were her children, the mages her kin.

"And I should go back to them," she said. He was a mage, if not of the Guild. She did not need to speak aloud the thoughts that were clear for him to read.

He turned in the window. "You will go?"

She almost smiled. "O persistent. Of course I'll go. I've watched my mages girdle the world with Gates, walking or riding or sailing from each to the one that must be built after. Now I want to see for myself what's on the other side of the world."

"And what broke the Gate there." He spread his hands, the dark and the golden. "I have no power to stop you."

"Of course you do," she said. "But you won't use it."

"Because I promised," he said, a little wearily, a little wryly. "I'm cursed with honesty: I keep my word."

"There are worse things to be cursed with," she said. She rose from the chair, creaking a little.

"Thank you," he said.

She blinked.

"For bringing ki-Merian home," he explained—not even a hint of rebuke that she, the mages' Master, should fail to read a simple thought. "She'll have better nurses after this. More wakeful."

"Less susceptible to her sleep-spelling." Vanyi caught the flash of his glance; she smiled. "Yes, I know they're all mageborn, and those that aren't, are ul-cats, with magic in their blood. Maybe she needs a simpler guardian: one too mindblind to notice when she's working her magics."

"I'll think on that," he said.

He would, too. That was the great virtue of the emperor Estarion. He listened to advice. He might not take it—but he did listen.

THREE

Once Daruya's temper had carried her out of her grandfather's sight, she calmed as she always did, into a kind of sullen embarrassment. She went to lair in her safe place, the stable that housed her own seneldi, the herd that she had bred. There in the dark and the hay-scented quiet, she slipped into the dun mare's stall and sat on the manger, elbows propped on knees, chin on fists. The mare, accustomed to Daruya's presence at odd hours, chewed peacefully on the remains of her supper.

Daruya let the mare's peace seep into her mind, blunting the sharp edges of anger. "I don't know what it is," she said. The mare flicked an ear, listening. "Whenever I stand in front of my grandfather, I shrink till I'm no bigger than Kimeri, and no wiser, either. And then we fight. Or I fight. He just smiles in that way he has, and lets me howl, till he decides it's time to shut me up."

The mare nosed in the corner of her manger. Daruya stroked the black-barred neck, ruffling the mane with its stripes of black and gold. This was a queen mare: unlike the bulk of her kind she had horns, though not the ell-long spears of a stallion; hers were a delicate handspan, straight and sharply pointed. Daruya brushed one with a finger, pricking herself lightly on the tip. "I wish," she said, "that he could see anything of me but my worst. He thinks I'm an utter child, spoiled and irresponsible."

"And aren't you?"

Daruya flicked a glance at the stall door. A shadow leaned on it, regarding her with golden eyes. He was faceless else—veiled, hooded, black-robed from head to foot. He inspired no fear in her at all, and no surprise. "Chakan," she said. "What are you doing up at this hour?"

"Much the same as you are, I suspect," he said. His voice behind the veils was light, even laughing. "Let me guess. He won't let you go to the other side of the world."

"Worse than that," said Daruya. "The Gate we were to pass through is broken, and the mages don't know how, or why. Vanyi and the others are still going, but to the Gate before the one that broke. I'm to stay home. Just as I always do."

"I wouldn't say that," said Chakan, folding his arms on the half-door and resting his shrouded chin on them. "You're not kept a prisoner. Not even close."

She glowered at him. Chakan the Olenyas was a cheerful soul, for all his black veils and his face that none but another Olenyas or a heart's friend might see, his robes and his twin swords and his long bitter training. She knew that he grinned at her behind those veils—his eyes were dancing.

"But there," he said. "I cry your pardon. I'm supposed to indulge your temper, and here I persist in being reasonable."

"I hate you," she said.

"Of course you do." He straightened, stretched, yawned audibly. "Are you contemplating a suitable punishment for his majesty? An aurochs hunt, maybe? I'd rather a boar, myself, it being spring and all, and the aurochs not in rut until the fall. They're dreadfully peaceable at this time of year. A boar, now—a boar will rip you to pieces no matter what the season."

She never could help it with Chakan—he always made her laugh, even when she wanted to kill him.

He knew it, too. "There now," he said. "It's almost dawn. If you won't hunt boar, and I think you shouldn't seeing as to how we'd have to rouse out the whole hunt, and they're all sleeping off their night's carouse—shall we ride instead? I've a fancy to see the sun come up from the Golden Wall."

"If you wanted that," said Daruya, "you should have left at a gallop an hour ago."

"Bet on it?" he asked.

Hells take him. He knew exactly how to twist her to his will. "Six suns, gold, that we don't reach the top before the sun is up."

"Done," said Chakan.

Daruya took the striped mare. Chakan had his own gelding saddled already, waiting in the stableyard and sneering at the stallion in his run. The stallion, who knew the cranky little beast, ignored him as a king should.

It was very dark, but the stars were brilliant, and Brightmoon rode the zenith. They rode down from the palace hill through a city already awake, the markets rousing and setting up, the bakers baking the day's bread, the smiths working the bellows in their forges. Asan-Gilen, city of the two empires, which everyone called Starios—Estarion's city—was properly said never to sleep. Rather, it changed guards. Even as the merchants set about opening their stalls, the nightfolk drifted yawning to bed.

Some of them knew Daruya and greeted her, either with silence in the western fashion or with a word and a dip of the head in the way of the east. By the courtesy of Starios, none detained her, nor was she ever beset with crowds. Unless of course she wanted them.

Spoiled, Chakan would say to that, and arrogant, too. Odd, she thought, that he could say such things and barely ruffle her temper, but if her grandfather even hinted at them, she flew into a rage.

She shut down the thought. The processional way, wide and all but empty in the not-quite-dawn, ended in the Sunrise Gate, the gate that looked on Keruvarion.

That was shut still, but the lesser gate beside the great one opened to let them through, with a grin and a salute from the guard. She found herself grinning back. The wind blew straight out of the east, full in her face. It smelled of morning, and of green things, and of open places.

Chakan's gelding was already out, already stretching into a gallop on the grass that verged the emperor's road. Daruya's mare tossed her unbitted head and snorted, and launched herself in pursuit.

East out of Starios they ran, across the fields new sown with spring, through the arm of forest that stretched out toward the city, and then up, veering off the great way to a narrower path. It wound upward through the trees, till the trees gave up the pursuit. The land here was stony, the way steep, tussocked with grass. Once, and then again, the seneldi leaped streams that crossed the track.

The sky, that had been all dark and stars and bright arc of moon, greyed as they rode, till it was silver, and the stars were gone, and the moon a pallid glimmer. Chakan's gelding stumbled in landing, after the second stream; but he steadied the senel, and who went on undismayed, racing the sun.

Daruya let the other take the lead, narrow as the way was, and difficult. Her mare was reasonably content to settle to the smaller senel's pace, flattening her ears and threatening his rump with her teeth only when he seemed to slacken. Daruya, after all, was not trying to win the race.

This steep rock that they climbed was the Golden Wall, not for its color, which was green in spring and brown in summer and white with snow in the winter, but for that it marked the border between Keruvarion in the east and the old Golden Empire in the west. Estarion had set his city just beyond the shadow of it, where it sank into a rolling land of field and forest, athwart the traders' road from east to west. There was a little river running through it, tributary in time to Suvien the mighty that was the lifeblood of Keruvarion, opening westward of the city to a lake on which the people fished and the high ones kept their summer villas.

All that, Daruya could see as she reached the summit of the ridge. Her mare snorted and danced. Chakan laughed aloud. The sun, just rising, shot a shaft of light straight into his eyes.

Daruya slid from the saddle and let the mare go in search of grass. She was breathing hard, and all her black mood was gone. She spread her arms to the sun. The morning hymn poured out of her, pure white song.

When the last note had rung sweet and high up to heaven, she stood still with her arms out, head flung back, drinking light. It had a taste like wine.

Awareness came back slowly. Chakan was sitting cross-legged on a stone, watching her in Asanian fashion, sidelong. His eyes were the same color as the sunlight. "Sometimes," he said as if to himself, "one . . . forgets . . . exactly what you are."

The exultation of light gave way to a more familiar irritation. "Oh, not you, too. I get enough of that from my grandfather."

"You do not," he said, and he sounded like Chakan again, immune to the awe of her rank. "He is utterly matter-of-fact about anything to do with being a mage or being a Sunchild. It drives some people wild. He should be a figure of awe and terror—not a quiet-spoken man in a plain coat, who can drink light like water, and make the stars sing."

"That's just magery," she said.

"No," he said. "Mages can work great wonders, I'll never deny it. Sunlords are different. The god speaks to them directly."

"Not in words," said Daruya.

"Does he need them?"

That silenced her. She paced the rough level of the summit, turning slowly as she went. Away eastward stretched forest and plain, the wide reaches of the Hundred Realms. West was a broader level, forest that gave way quickly to tilled fields and clustered towns. Below on its own hill and on the level about was Starios beside its lake.

The sun had reached all she could see, turned it to gold, melted mist that clung to hollows. She could if she wished gather the light in her hands. She knotted them behind her. The right hand with its golden brand was burning fiercely; she shut her mind to it. Chakan, if he knew, would say that the god was talking.

And did she not want to be what she was?

With a sudden movement she pulled off the fillet that bound her brows, worked fingers into tangled curls. Priests and royalty did not cut their hair. She had cropped hers short not long after Kimeri was weaned—chiefly, Chakan had opined, out of petulance that the child's birth had not been more of a scandal. People expected Daruya to do outrageous things. Often they forgave her, because she was their princess, and beautiful: the Beauty of Starios.

It was quite maddening. "Sometimes I think," she said to the wind, "that all royal heirs should be brought up far from court, in ignorance of their rank, until they're old enough to bear the weight of it."

"It's too late to try that with Kimeri," said Chakan.

"Yes, and I was going to leave her with the burdens while I ran away. Is that what you were thinking?"

"No," he said.

He did not point out that she could read his thoughts if she tried. In fact she could not. Olenyai were protected against magery; and Chakan, like some few of his kind, was born shielded, unreadable even if he had wished to be read. It could be disconcerting, if one heard his steps, saw him approaching, but sensed nothing in the mind at all, not even the shadow of presence that marked the rest of the Olenyai.

Daruya found it restful. He asked nothing of her as mage or woman—he had never wished to bed her, that she knew of, nor been anything but friend and, as much as anyone could be, brother. She had brothers in blood, or so she was told, sons of her mother and her mother's husband, but none of them had ever come forward to claim the kinship. Chakan was more truly kin, Olenyas though he was, bred and shaped to serve his emperor.

She, bred and shaped to be empress in her turn, said less bitterly than wearily, "All priests, even royal priests, are given a little freedom, a bit of Journey to teach them the ways of the world. I've not been allowed it. Yes, I know it wasn't safe before—there were still wars, rebellions, assassins coming right into the palace and dying on Olenyai swords. But that's over. After forty years of war, we have peace. We've had festivals from end to end of the empire, to celebrate the wars' ending. It's time now, if it will ever be—time for me to have the rest of my training."

"It's not," mused Chakan, "as if you'd never had training elsewhere. You've ridden to war with your grandfather. You've accompanied him on all his progresses since you were old enough to sit a senel, and sat in his councils and attended his courts. You've done your year in the temple in Endros Avaryan, and gone up to the Tower at the end of it, and come into your power before the bier where the Sunborn sleeps."

"But that's not everything," she said. "It's not complete. You know how a smith makes a sword—how he forges the blade over and over, and shapes it, and makes it into an image of what it will be. But it's only a bar of steel until it's tempered. Then, and only then, is it a sword."

"You don't call all that tempering?" He went on before she could answer. "No, maybe it wasn't. You know enough for a whole college of mages, and a court of lords, too. But you haven't turned that knowledge to use. You need to grow yourself up, I think."

"That's what *he* says," said Daruya. "He doesn't understand that I can't do it here. He's here, do you see? He'll pick me up if I stumble. He'll smile if I make a mistake, and be oh so forbearing, but I'll always know that he could do it better and faster and stronger. I need to be somewhere where he can't meddle."

"Does it have to be the other side of the world? You could ask for a princedom anywhere in the empire. He'd give it."

"He gave me this embassy," she said. "Now he's taken it away."

"He's only being sensible," said Chakan. "Whoever's broken a Gate isn't likely to balk at killing an emperor's heir."

"Does it need to be the act of an enemy? It could have been the Gate itself that was flawed."

"All the more reason to be cautious, then, if as I'm told the expedition goes to the Gate nearest the one that fell, and goes overland from there. That Gate could fall, too, and with the heir to the empire in it."

Daruya shivered in her bones, but fear was a little thing to this yearning of hers to be out, off, away. "And if that happened, would it be any worse than my getting killed in battle, or being stabbed in my bed by an assassin, or breaking my mind in entering the Tower of Endros? My grandfather *led* me to battle and the Tower. What's the difference in this, except that he won't be there to pick me up if I fall?"

"The difference could be exactly that," said Chakan. "Or that you want it so badly. That much wanting is dangerous. It closes off sense."

"Maybe it's something I have to do," said Daruya. "Have you thought of that? Maybe I'm called to it."

"If so, then you just realized it."

Daruya walked to the edge where the Wall fell sheer, down and down to the plain of Keruvarion. She poised there, rocked lightly by the wind. Chakan said nothing, made no move to pull her back.

He knew her too well. She would never leap unless she knew she could fly. Death was not what she yearned for. Not at all. Life—she wanted life, great gleaming handfuls of it. More than she could ever have under the emperor's loving tyranny, his light hand that weighed more than the world.

"I need to do this," she said. "I *need* it, Chakan. I don't feel death in it. Only necessity. And I think the expedition needs me, now more than ever. The place it goes to is all strange to us, and its people are afraid of magic. Or, no, maybe not afraid, but wary of it; inclined to hate it, because they don't trust it. If something happened to the Guardian because of that, and broke the Gate, then it may be that I can use what I am for once, use it to teach these strangers that magic is nothing to fear or hate."

Once she had said it, it sounded hollow, bombastic, a child's arrogance. Chakan said nothing of that. He said, "What can you do that the Master of mages can't?"

"Be my grandfather's heir," she answered without even thinking. "Speak for him with the authority of his own blood."

"So you won't escape him even on the other side of the world."

Daruya hissed at him. "I'm not trying to run away from my inheritance! I just want to stand on my own feet."

"And make your own mistakes." He lay back on his flat stone. After a moment he slipped the fastenings of his veils and let them fall free, baring his face to the wind and the sun. It was a handsome face, beautiful in fact, as Asanians of pure blood and long, close breeding could be: smoothly oval, white as new ivory, nose straight and finely carved, lips full, chin as sweetly rounded as a girl's. And yet it was not a girlish face, not at all. The right cheek bore healed scars, four thin parallel lines running from cheekbone to jaw; and a fifth, matched to the rest, so new that it still bled a little.

Daruya caught her breath at that. "You didn't tell me you were being raised to the fifth rank."

He slanted a glance at her. "I didn't know. My Master called me in in the middle of the night, ordered me to unveil, and marked me as soon as he saw my face."

"He didn't by any chance say why?" she said.

"Eventually," said Chakan. "I'm to take ten Olenyai to the other side of the world, to guard the mages."

Daruya's fury was so perfect that it did not even blur her senses. "Mages don't need guarding."

"For this they might," he said. He laced his fingers beneath his head, raised a knee, looked utterly off guard. That, she knew, was a complete deception. She was fast, and Olenyai-trained—but if she leaped, he would meet her in the air, and give her a ferocious fight.

She might have welcomed it. But she was stalking other prey. "Tell me why they chose you."

"Because I'm very good at what I do," he said honestly. "And because I'm used to mages."

"And," she said, "because they can't get at you with magic. That's it, isn't it? That shield of yours—they want it. Maybe need it, if it's mages they fight."

"They also want my skill with the swords, and the ten bred-warriors I can lead. I'm going to ask for Rahai. He's so good with his hands, he never has to use his swords."

He was happy, hells take him—full to bursting with his good fortune.

She sprang. To her startlement, he did not meet her in midair. When she struck the rock with bruising force, he was gone.

She lay winded, gasping for air. His voice sounded above her head. "I was thinking. You can't wear the robes and the veils—you're too tall. But there's another way."

She rolled onto her back, still wheezing. "What—in hells—"

"It is a pity you overtop the tallest of us by a head," he said, maddeningly roundabout as Asanians were when one most wanted them to be direct. "Your eyes would do. Your skin is darker than most, but in veils that's less noticeable. Do you think your daughter will be another long tall creature? She's shaping for it already, poor thing."

"You babble like a flutterbird," said Daruya. She could breathe again, if shallowly. Her ribs hurt. "I can't play the Olenyas. It would cost you your honor at least."

"It would cost me my life," he said with no perceptible apprehension. "It might be worth it, mind, for the splendor of the trick. But not unless you're mage enough to make yourself smaller."

She cut through his nonsense with a voice like a blade. "You said there was another way."

"There might be," he said. "It would cost, too, seeing as to how I'm sworn in service to the emperor, and the emperor has forbidden you to go."

"Swear yourself in service to me," she said.

"I can't do that," said Chakan. He said it lightly, but there was no yielding in it.

She sat up carefully, glaring at him. "You'd sacrifice your honor to dress me in Olenyai robes, but you won't honorably swear yourself to the heir of the blood royal?"

"Robes are the outer garments of honor. Oaths are its heart. I'm sworn to the throne, and through it to the emperor. When you are empress," he said reasonably, "I'll serve you till death, with all my heart."

"But you'll break your oath if you help me escape the emperor."

"I will not," he said. "You'll serve the emperor on this embassy, though he may think, at the moment, that you won't."

Daruya's head was spinning. It might, to be sure, be the shock of her fall. But one did not have to plunge middle first onto a rock to reel before Asanian logic.

He held her and patted her while she emptied her stomach on the stones. "There," he said. "Next time you attack me, do it somewhere where you can land soft."

She snarled at him. He smiled sweetly, sadly, and buried the evidence of her foolishness, producing from the depths of his robes what looked for all the world like a gardener's trowel. Probably it was. Olenyai robes could conceal anything, and often did.

When he was done, he crouched in front of her, arms resting on knees. "You do want to go, and he did give you leave, though he rescinded it. I'm thinking he might be overcautious as you say—emperor or not, he's a grandfather, too, and he dotes on you. I'm also thinking you may have the right of it; they'll need you out there, your Sun-blood and your training, and your power to speak for the emperor in the emperor's absence."

"You think too much," muttered Daruya.

He grinned at that. "Yes, don't I? I never learned to shut myself off and be simple muscle. It's a flaw in a warrior. It's rather useful in a commander."

"If he lives long enough to become one." She leaned forward, no matter what it did to her ribs and her uncertain stomach. "Are you going to roll me up in a blanket and hide me in the baggage?"

"Very near," he answered. "I'm not visible to mages, yes? One told me once—unwisely, I'm sure—that I cast a kind of shadow; when someone stands in it, he vanishes, too. Suppose you dressed in black, not Olenyai, not exactly, but cloaked and hooded, and rode one of my remounts. You can become a shadow, yes? If you blur the eyes and I blur the mind, what will anyone see but a troop of Olenyai and their seneldi, and nothing more?"

Daruya wanted it to be so easy—wanted it with all that was in her. But she had learned to be wary. Yes, even she, with her name for recklessness. "If I'm caught, there's hells to pay."

"Don't be caught," he said with grand assurance.

"It's not sensible," she said.

"Of course it is," said Chakan. "Not that I don't think your grandfather is perfectly right, as far as he goes. You should stay safe where he can protect you. But that's no way to fly a hawk. You have to let it off the fist, or it never learns to hunt."

"Asanian logic," she said. "And I've nothing left in my stomach, to cast at your feet."

"I'll survive the lack," said Chakan. He sat on his heels, comfortable, quite clearly pleased with himself. "The Guildmaster means to leave as soon as may be— before sunset today, I'm told. You'll have to be quick if you're to do it; and clever, too, to make your farewells without being caught."

"I can mask my face and my thoughts," she said. "I was trained to rule an empire."

He was impervious to irony as to the weapons of mages: it sank into the shadow of his self and vanished. "Well and good. We meet in the Guildhall in the hour of the sixth prayer. You'll be a shadow, remember. A whisper in the air."

She stood. It was amazing how elation could kill pain, even of ribs that, she suspected, were cracked. She met his grin with one at least as wide. Hers had edges in it, the sharpness of teeth. "You could have told me this before you let me play the ranting fool."

"But you needed to rant," he said. "And who knew? You might see sense. This isn't sense that we're up to."

"No. It's necessity." She reached out a hand for him to grasp, pulled him up. In the moment of unbalance he shifted, treacherous, seeking to pull her down. But she was ready for him. She set her feet, made herself a rock in the earth.

He laughed up at her, for, standing, she was much taller than he. "No, it won't be as splendid as if you were one of my Olenyai, but riding as my shadow—yes, that will do. We'll sing it when we're done, like the song of the prince and the beggar's daughter. She was dead, you see, but he loved her withal."

"I don't intend to die on this journey," said Daruya, "or for a long time after. I'll live to take your oath from the Throne of the Sun, Olenyas. You have my word on it."

"And the word of a Sunchild," he said, half laughing, half deadly earnest, "is unalterable law."

FOUR

THE HALL OF THE NINTH GATE WAS QUIET. WITH ITS GATE HIDDEN BEHIND a veil, a curtain of white silk no paler than the walls, it seemed but an empty chamber, the hall of a temple, perhaps. Its floor of inlaid tiles made a map of the world as mages knew it. Half was wrought in intricate detail, with cities marked in colored stones. One that was gold, heart of the west, was Kundri'j Asan. One that was a firestone, heart of the east, was Endros Avaryan that the first of the Sunlords had built. Between them lay a great jewel like a star: Asan-Gilen, Estarion's city, that had brought together the realms of Sun and Lion, and given them a place where neither claimed the sovereignty.

The other half of the map was vaguer, its shape less clearly defined. Its cities were few. Crystals marked the Gates, a thin line across the broad mass of the land. Mages had traveled to each place, the first sailing in ships across the wide and terrible sea, coming to land and building the first Gate. New mages had come through the Gate, traveling on foot across a vast plain, and at each Brightmoon-cycle's journey, building a new Gate through which yet newer mages could come.

The eighth Gate was set on the knees of mountains that to its builders had seemed mighty. But those who followed discovered that the mountains were but foothills, and low at that. They climbed to the summit of the world, and nearly died in doing it; but when they would have turned back, too feeble to build their Gate, strangers found them and led them to safety.

There in the mountains that touched the sky, they found a valley, and in the valley a kingdom: the Kingdom of Heaven, its people called it. There was the ninth Gate, the Gate that had fallen. On the map it was unharmed, a crystal of amethyst— the color, said the mages who came back, of the sky above the mountains' peaks.

Vanyi stood pondering the color of the sky and the integrity of a crystal and other such inconsequentialities, while the others came together near the veil of the Gate. They were not many as expeditions went; dangerously few, if they were to be an army. Six mages, three of the light and their twinned mages of the dark. Ten black-robed Olenyai with their commander. Mounts and remounts for them all, since there were no seneldi on that side of the world, laden with such baggage as they could not live without; the Guardian of the eighth Gate would provide what more was needed for the ascent into the mountains.

All together they crowded that end of the hall, with much clattering and snorting. One senel in particular, a handsome dun mare, was being difficult. The Olenyai commander took her in hand, gentling her with soft words.

Vanyi recognized his voice and, as she came out of her reverie, his hands, strong for their smallness and beautifully shaped. Her brows rose. She had hoped that the Master of Olenyai would send his best, but she had not expected him to send Chakan.

Chakan the prince, some called him, because he was so free of the emperor's courts and counsels. He had been raised with the princess-heir, and was as close to her as a brother. He managed somehow to avoid the malice and the envy of courts, to be both foster-brother and perfect servant. His only flaw, in Vanyi's estimation, was that no mage could read him.

He made Vanyi think of another who had worn the veils and the swords, who also had been born with shields against magic. But that had been no Olenyas, for all the purity of his blood and the strictness of his training. He as much as duty and empire and her own obstinacy had taken Estarion from her.

That one was long dead. Estarion had killed him, killed the last descendant—save only himself—of the Golden Emperors. This was no long-lost Son of the Lion. The eyes in the veil were yellow gold, to be sure, but they were not lion-eyes, not so great-irised that they seemed to have no whites at all unless they opened wide; nor did they bear such a weight of bitterness as Koru-Asan had borne. Chakan of the Olenyai, for all his gifts and his skill, was an innocent, and devoted to his emperor.

Which, no doubt, was precisely why the Master had sent him. Vanyi liked him. She even trusted him—as long as he was not called on to do anything that would run counter to his emperor's purposes.

Vanyi met eyes that were true eyes of the Lion, set in the face of a black king from the north. Estarion regarded her unsmiling. She had not seen him come in. He could walk like a shadow when it suited him, even before the Master of the mages.

"Did you lock your granddaughter in her rooms?" Vanyi asked him. "I thought I'd see her by now, trying to beg or cajole or threaten me into taking her in spite of you."

"I left her in an imperial sulk," he said, "but I didn't think it necessary to lock the door. She understands her duty, however much she may resist it."

"I hope so," said Vanyi. She held out her hands. He took them without constraint, and set a kiss in each palm. Her breath caught. She turned it into a flicker of laughter. "I'm going to miss you. Who'd have thought it?"

"Maybe you'll find someone there who'll give you grand arguments, and slap you down when you get above yourself."

"*I* get above myself!" She mimed mighty indignation. "You, sir, were arrogant in the womb."

"Well," he said, "it's an honest arrogance." He went somber all at once, as he could do; looking suddenly much older, though never as old as he was. "Guard yourself, Vanyi. Whatever breaks Gates can break mages, too. Even Masters of mages."

"Oh, I'm too mean to die," she said; but she too sobered, gripping his hands tightly and then letting them go. "We have to know what broke the Gate, before it breaks another. If it's a weakness, you see—if we're doing something amiss in the building—we have to know, before there's too much passing back and forth of mages, and we lose more than a single Gate, or a single Guardian."

"And well before those who aren't mages begin to cross," he said, agreeing with her. "I've a pack of merchants already clamoring to explore this whole new country. They don't care that it takes a mage to direct a Gate, and a mage to guide the crossing. They're drunk on dreams of profit."

"They'll dream for yet a while," she said dryly. "You too, my lord emperor. I'll come back, I give you my word."

"Alive?"

"What, afraid of windy ghosts?" He looked so stark that she patted his cheek, a touch that stopped just sort of a caress. "Yes, I'll come back alive, or close enough to make no difference. Don't wait about for me. I'll be taking my time at it."

"Not too much," he said. "And send me word when you can."

"That I can do," said Vanyi. She stepped away from him. It was an odd sensation, not quite like pain. Well, she thought; they had been apart often enough, and once for a whole hand of years, while he fought his wars in the far west of Asanion, and she ruled mages in the raw new city that would be Asan-Gilen. But that had come after a quarrel, and they had parted with bitter words. Parting in amity, when god and goddess knew when they might meet again—that was harder.

Best get it over. Mages were drawing back the veil that hid the Gate. It was sleeping, showing no passage of worlds, only a grey nothingness.

As she approached, it began to wake. She felt it in her bones.

Likewise she felt a wrench, a little like envy, a little like grief, that after a moment she recognized as not her own. It came from Estarion, standing on the map, with his foot beside the broken Gate. There was a shadow just behind him, a cat as large as a small senel, as dark and golden-eyed as he was himself: one of his ul-cats, the king of them from his size and his air of lazy power. He blinked at Vanyi and yawned, baring fangs as long as her hand.

Estarion took no notice, seemed to be aware of little apart from Vanyi and the Gate and his own solitude. He did not look like a king or a conqueror. He looked like a man who must remain behind while his friend journeys to the other side of the world.

Looks were deceptive, she thought, drawing nearer to the Gate. Meruvan Estarion was emperor to the marrow of his bones. As she was mage and Master of the Gates. She raised her hands. The Gate woke to the touch of her power, woke and began to sing.

Daruya thought silence, thought shadows, thought nothingness. It was a delicate balance, a sensation not a little like the moment before one was disastrously sick—a dissonance between the fact of her existence and the illusion that she was not there at all. She was cloaked for further safety, wrapped in black, with her face shrouded, though not in an Olenyai veil. Her one indulgence and indiscretion, the mare she rode, seemed to have attracted no attention even when she indulged herself in a flurry of temper. Striped duns were not uncommon, and Olenyai were fond of them. One of the bred-warriors even had a rarity, a silver dun, grey bars on white.

For all her care and caution, she nearly forgot herself when she realized that the emperor was there. He must have come in under the same sort of protection that concealed her. She strained her ears to hear what he said; relaxed in every muscle when he spoke of her being safely shut up in her rooms. She thrust aside the niggling of guilt. He trusted her—he had not locked her in.

No. He trusted his own vanity, his conviction that she would yield to him simply because he asked. By the time he found out that she was gone, it would be too late to call her back. Then she could prove how groundless his fears had been, and how much he needed her where she was going.

The Guildmaster had left the emperor standing alone and come to wake the Gate. Daruya, divided between watching Vanyi and sustaining her deception, still kept her eyes on the emperor. He was watching Vanyi. He always did. A blind man could see that they had been lovers, could still be if either one of them were even a fraction less stiff-necked.

Her grandmother the empress was excuse, not obstacle. Haliya, great lady and queen, knew perfectly well how it was between her husband and her husband's friend and frequent rival. It had never troubled her. Little to do with men and women did. She had not even blinked when Daruya came to her first, pregnant and defiant and scared, because her plan had worked and now she was not so sure she wanted to face the consequences. Without Haliya's quiet good sense, those consequences might have been even less pleasant than they were.

Daruya had visited the empress before she came to the Guildhall. She did so every day and at much the same time: after the daymeal was done, when the emperor was occupied with matters of state, but before the empress held her own court. Today Daruya had thought of turning coward and staying away, but she found her courage and her cunning. If she did not go to see her grandmother, people would wonder, and perhaps be suspicious.

Haliya was lying on a couch in her day-room as she too often was of late, fully and properly dressed in the Asanian manner, except for the threefold outer robe that she would assume when she held her audience. She seemed tiny in the swathing of robes, shrunken, bleached to the color of old ivory. All but her eyes, which were the true Asanian gold, bright and vivid still in the withered face.

She had grown so old so suddenly. Her hair had been white for as long as Daruya remembered, but as late as Autumn Firstday she had been riding with the emperor's hunt, keeping pace with him through the wild coverts, and shooting a fine big buck for the evening's feast. Somehow, in the winter, the life had drained out of her.

They did not say anything of consequence. Daruya did not confess what she was about to do, nor did she hint at it. Sitting her senel on the threshold of the Gate, feeling the Gate-music that throbbed in her center, she remembered the softness of her grandmother's cheek as she kissed it, the sweet husky sound of the voice that like the eyes was still perversely young, the scent of *ailith*-blossoms that the empress had always loved.

Daruya would not be there in full spring, to fill the empress' rooms with flowering branches. But in the autumn, when the fruit was heavy and sweet—then, she promised herself and the memory of her grandmother, she would come back. She was not going away forever. Only for a while, because she must.

The Gate sang its deep pure song. Vanyi matched the measure of her power to it. She felt the resonance that rang sixfold from the mages who would cross with her, the quiver of discord that was the company of Olenyai with their beasts and baggage.

A strong sweet note rose through the dissonance, smoothed it, shaped it into harmony. She started a little in the working, but caught herself. Estarion had made himself a part of the Gate-magic. He was no mage of the Guild, nor could ever be; that was forbidden him as emperor. But he was mage and master.

She was wise enough not to resent the help he gave, though it stung her pride. Six mages and a Master should have been enough to open this Gate. Still, his strength was welcome. It made her task simpler, spared her power for when she would need it most, past the Gate's threshold on the worldroad.

The grey blankness of the Gate had shifted, transmuted, come alive. As with all Gates, it strove ever to change through the turning of the worlds. But she had set her will on it. It fixed on the eighth Gate of that other half of this world, holding pace like twin seneldi in a race, each desirous of outrunning the other, but held level by their riders' compulsion.

The Guardians on the other side were holding likewise, their task the less because their Gate was lesser, bound in servitude to this one. Any who passed that Gate could only come here, although from here he could pass anywhere in the worlds, even to the Heart of the World itself, which was master of all Gates.

In the moment when the two Gates matched, Vanyi brought them all together with a word. Two mages passed first, and then the Olenyai and the animals, and after them the rest of the mages. She was last of all, and Estarion who would not pass the Gate.

They did not speak, even when, briefly, they were alone. He was holding the whole force of the Gate in the hands of his power, even that part which she could well have held. It was by no means the limit of his capacity, but he showed the strain a little: a tightness about the nostrils, a rim of white about the eyes. It did not prevent him from smiling his old, white smile. She took the memory with her into the Gate.

FIVE

THE STORM STRUCK AS VANYI CROSSED THE THRESHOLD. SHE KNEW A moment of calm, a vision of the worldroad as it should be: grey road, grey land, grey sky, and before them the glimmer of the Gate to which they traveled. Then the sky shattered.

All Gates were present in her awareness, no more or less to it than the parts of her own body. But as a body convulses with pain of a blow, now the Gates reeled. The whole great chain of them, from world to world, shivered and cracked and began to break.

The road heaved under her feet. She staggered. Shadows milled ahead of her, men, beasts, the glimmering shapes of mages with their power laid bare. She started toward them, wavered, turned back.

The Gate through which she had come was there still, though its lintel sagged. Estarion stood in it, arms braced, holding it up. His power surged toward her like a tide of light. "The chain!" he cried, faint amid the howl of the storm. "The Gates— let me—"

Her own power reared up like a wall. The tide crashed against it and recoiled. As it rolled back upon Estarion, she thrust the wall behind it. It struck the Gate with the clap of stone on stone, locked and barred and sealed it until she should open it again.

Estarion would suffer for that. But he would not die—and die he would have done, if he had done what he was setting out to do, and tried to restore the chain of Gates with his sole and unaided power. No man, even the Lord of Sun and Lion, was strong enough to do such a thing alone.

All such thoughts encompassed but a moment of the worlds' time. Even as she thought them, Vanyi was wheeling away from the sealed Gate, back to the tumult upon the worldroad. One at least of the seneldi was down—dead, and its rider beneath it, unnaturally still. Shadows beset the rest, driving them together. Mages fought with bolts of power. Olenyai fought with swords, useless against shadows— far better for them were the amulets they wore, that protected them against magic.

The watchers of the road were nowhere to be perceived. She called them, received no answer. If they had come, they could have driven off the shadows, the dark things without substance and yet with deadly strength. Even as she fought through a road turned to clinging mire, catching her feet and causing her to stumble, a shadow enfolded a lightmage, Jian who was youngest of all.

In desperation Vanyi formed and aimed a dart of power. But she was too far, too weak, and the shadow too swift. She felt, they all felt, the mage's fear, her resolve to be strong, to resist pain; pain mounting to agony, till nothing was in the world but that, and agony beyond agony, and abruptly, without warning or transition, nothing.

Jian was gone. Her darkmage cried out, a raw, anguished sound, and flung himself at the shadows. They slipped away from him, eluded his grasp, his power, the maddened stabbing of his dagger. They seemed to mock him. With a spring like a cat's, one of them fell on the darkmage who was farthest from him, who had stopped to stare aghast, and was too slow to escape. His lightmage, leaping to his defense, fell into the shadow's maw.

A blaze like the sun blinded them all, even Vanyi in the raising of her power. Shadows withered and died. The road's heaving steadied. The chain of Gates, at the point of rending asunder, subsided into a kind of quiet.

In the center of it, soft and calm but rather strained, a voice said, "I can't hold this for long. Do you think you could all stop goggling and get a move on?"

"God and goddess," said Vanyi, astonished that she had any voice at all, let alone one that could be heard in this place. The road was solid underfoot. She forced her creaking knees to drive her forward. "You heard her. *Move!*"

They were deadly slow, but once they had begun, they gained speed. Those who were mounted pulled those on foot up behind, even the one who struggled and fought and tried to fling himself back to the place where his lightmage had died.

A tiger-patterned gelding—no, it was a mare, a horned queen mare, and a black shadow on her back—wheeled in front of Vanyi. The mare's rider thrust out a hand. Vanyi caught it, let it and the mare's movement swing her up. Even as she settled on the crupper, strong muscles bunched beneath her and surged toward the glimmer of the Gate.

The light was dying behind them, the road breaking apart. The mare's hind feet found purchase in the last of it before it melted into nothingness, and thrust them through the wavering Gate.

Light. Solidity. A waft of scent, pungent and strange.

They had come through. The Gate was fallen: its posts were broken, its lintel shattered. But they were on the other side, in a place so strange that Vanyi could find no thing to rest her eyes upon, except a pair of Guardians, mute and still: one on her feet and looking whitely shocked, one sitting up as if he had fallen and just now come to his senses.

Her arms, she discovered, were locked in a deathgrip about the rider's waist. Grimly she pried them free. She slid from the back of the motionless senel. No one else was moving, not even the animals.

She counted. All seneldi present and safe except for the one that had died early in the battle. One Olenyas lying too still across a saddle. Three mages—she bit back a cry. Of six that had left the Guildhall, only three had come through the Gate: darkmage and lightmage, slender elegant Miyaz and quiet-eyed Aledi, and one lone stark-faced darkmage, young Kadin who had lost his lightmage to the shadow.

Her eyes returned to the rider who had brought her out of the Gate, the rider whose light had kept them alive to come this far. Now that there was no way back, all concealment was gone, hood and veil thrust aside, golden lion-eyes holding hers with remarkably little defiance. "You did need me," said Daruya.

"I'll tan your hide," said Vanyi.

She turned slowly. The place was beginning to make sense. It was a temple, she knew that already: safest, her mages had said, for the raising of a Gate, and least likely to attract attention with its comings and goings. Ah, but such a temple. Every level surface was carved and painted and glittering with gilt. She could, if she struggled, recognize the shapes of leaves and flowers, birds, beasts, men, things that were all of them and none and everything between.

At the end of the hall opposite the broken Gate stood the greatest monstrosity of all. It was supposed to be a god, she supposed. Its shape was manlike, but it had—she counted—a full score of arms, each hand clasping a different object: a sword, a flower, a bow, a basket of fruit. Its face was fully human and yet profoundly alien, a smooth mask of beaten bronze, high-cheeked, proud-nosed, thin-mouthed. Its eyes were black and quiet. Its lips were smiling.

It indeed. The full breasts were a woman's, but the organ below, vastly and proudly erect, was indubitably a man's.

She stared at it. She had never, she thought in a dim corner of her mind, been so purely aware that she had come to a foreign place. No, not even when, fresh from the boats and the fish and the peasant simplicity of the Isles, she came to Endros Avaryan that the Sunborn had built, and came face to face on the public street with a young man who happened to be the emperor. And she had thought him strange, with his face like a northern tribesman's and his startling eyes.

Estarion had been as common as seawrack compared to this. And yet it was all part of her own world. The same sun shone through louvers in the roof, catching fire in the gilding. The same moons would rise in the same sky. No sun like an orb of blood, or twin suns, or triple, or more. She could have traveled here, given a year or five and a ship and a herd of strong seneldi.

She was in shock. Gates were broken, mages dead. Her power had strained itself to the utmost in doing what little she had done. Estarion had done more, before she trapped him on the other side of the Gate; and Daruya, rebellious, reckless fool, but for whom they would all have died.

It dawned on her, slowly, that Daruya was receiving a shock of her own. One of the packs in the baggage stirred, shook itself, sat up on its senel's back. "Mama," said ki-Merian fretfully, "my head hurts."

SIX

CHAKAN SWORE BY ALL THE ASANIAN GODS THAT HE HAD HAD NOTHING TO do with this second shadow among his baggage. Vanyi was inclined to believe him. He confessed without shame to the concealment of the princess-heir, but the princess-heir's daughter had come entirely of her own volition.

Kimeri said as much when Vanyi pressed her. "I had to come," she said. "The Gate's crying. Can't you hear it?"

And that was all she would say, except to burst into tears herself, wailing, *"Mama!* My head *hurts!"*

It was nothing, Vanyi assured herself, but a headache—the child had taken no harm, by the god's mercy. Once Kimeri was put to bed in the elder Guardian's own chamber, with a warm posset in her and a cool cloth on her brow, they held their council there, speaking soft so as not to wake the sleeping child.

There were four of them: Daruya, Vanyi, Chakan, and the elder Guardian looking worn and haggard. The younger had insisted on standing watch though the Gate was broken. The rest, mages and Olenyai both, slept as they could in rooms that had been prepared for them, or tended the seneldi in the stable, or mourned their dead in quiet corners of the temple.

None of those here suggested that they move elsewhere, even to the outer chamber. Daruya, who had never struck Vanyi as the most attentive of mothers, stayed fiercely close to her daughter, with a look about her that defied any force of hells or heaven to harm a hair of that head. "Not," she said, "that I fear anything here. All threats to us are in the empire or on the worldroad."

"I'm not so sure of that," Vanyi said. "Something here is breaking Gates. Did you feel it? It was coming from outside—but not from the Gates in Starios."

"Then," said Daruya, "it's only this chain of Gates—only the ones bound to the Gate we departed from."

Vanyi opened her mouth to correct her again, but paused. She had felt all Gates from the worldroad, she was sure of it, and all had felt the blow. And yet . . .

"It was strongest on this road," she said. "So strong that maybe it deceived us into thinking it was greater than it was. If it's only the Gates on this continent, the ones that we built and bound to the ninth Gate in Starios, then—"

"Then we're safer than we thought," said Daruya. "And so are the rest of the Gates, and the Heart of the World."

"Certainly," said Chakan, "no one will be assailing us from within the Gate. Nor will we be running back to Starios through it."

How like him, thought Vanyi, to say what none of the others would say. They were trapped here. Oh, they could go back, take the year and more, journey overland, find a ship, journey overland again. But the few moments' walk from Gate to Gate—that was ended, for who knew how long.

"Estarion will be beside himself," she said. "Both of his heirs fled to the far end of the world, and no quick way back."

Daruya shot her a lambent glance. "You don't think he'll just walk through the gate of his *Kasar* and drag us all back home?"

"You know I don't," Vanyi said levelly, "or you'd be doing it yourself."

"I can't," said Daruya, too shocked with the discovery even to be angry about it. "It's all bound together somehow. When I came through, I felt it close behind me—everything. Every Gate and every road. There's no way back. Except the simple human way." She glared, though Vanyi had not said anything, nor changed expression. "I didn't plan this!"

"Certainly not," said Vanyi. "You're only an idiot when it comes to yourself. We were all fools for not expecting that the child would try to follow us. She's always had a fascination with Gates."

"She was under guard," said Daruya. "I saw to it myself—set priest-mages over her and commanded them not to let her out of their sight. I hope Grandfather rends them all limb from limb."

Chakan sat softly on the end of the bed and tucked up his feet. "It is interesting," he mused, "that she eluded priest-mages. You can do that. Your grandfather certainly can. Would you be willing to wager that your daughter is as strong as either of you?"

"She's so young," said Daruya. It was not a denial, not of what he said. She smoothed her daughter's curls, gently. Kimeri smiled in her sleep. Daruya's face set. "Wherever the fault lies, both of us are here. I may choose to think that the god wanted it so. Why else would he have allowed it?"

Maybe he did not care. Vanyi was too circumspect to say it. "Well then," she said. "Here we all are, and here we stay until we know it's safe to raise a new Gate. I'm going to go on as I intended, into the Kingdom of Heaven. The source of the trouble is there, by all the evidence I've seen, and we're expected there."

"Maybe not now," said Daruya. "Maybe that's why the Gates were broken."

Vanyi grinned ferally. "Then we'll surprise them. They don't know us if they think a little matter of fallen Gates will keep us away from the expedition we've been planning since the first Gate went up."

"We are a tenacious people," observed Chakan. His glance took in them all: the white-skinned Island woman with her sea-colored eyes, the wizened brown Guardian from the Nine Cities, the tall princess-heir of both Keruvarion and Asanion, and even himself, the Asanian bred-warrior. "And we are that, do you notice? All these years of fighting, and now we're entirely *we,* and those out there are *they.*"

"Even the worst of warring clans will unite against a common enemy." Vanyi sat back in the chair that she had chosen, and rubbed her weary eyes. "Faliad, have you have word from the other Guardians?"

"Not since before you came," the Guardian said. He looked as tired as she felt, but his voice was strong enough. "They were well enough then, except for the Guardian in Shurakan—what we call the Kingdom of Heaven."

"Only the one Guardian?" Vanyi asked sharply. "There were to be more."

Faliad lowered his eyes. "Yes, Guildmaster. There were. But we had lost one to a fever, and another was recalled to Starios. Before any others could be sent for, the Gate fell. There was only Uruan to guard it, and he died in the breaking."

Kimeri stirred in her sleep. Faliad fell silent, but she was only dreaming. She pressed close against her mother, sighed, and was still.

"It seems," said Vanyi after a while, "that we made mistakes. Maybe building these Gates was a mistake. No mage ever built them in chains as we did, with intent to open them to those who weren't mages. Nor were lesser chains bound to greater Gates. It may be that in making so many, and interweaving them in such complexity, we weakened the fabric of the whole."

"No," said Daruya with such certainty that Vanyi shot her a look. But she was oblivious. "Somebody did this. I felt the thrust of will on the Gates, just before they started to fall. Somebody wanted them down."

"Can you prove that?" Vanyi demanded.

"Not if you didn't sense it for yourself."

Vanyi stiffened. She was Master of the Gates. How dared this haughty child tell her that she knew nothing of them?

She caught herself before she spoke in anger, knocked down the anger, and sat on it. When she was sure that she could speak reasonably, she said, "Maybe you saw what I was too preoccupied to see."

Daruya accepted the concession with surprising grace. "I was slower than you were to understand what was happening, and much slower to act. Too slow, or people wouldn't have died." That was grief; she caught it and hid it as soon as it escaped. "I had time to look, and to see what came at us. There was human will behind it. I know the taste and the smell of it. It was human, have no doubt. And it hates us."

"Us?" asked Chakan. "Foreigners? Gates? Mages?"

"All of them," Daruya answered.

"Yes," said Faliad slowly. "Yes, there is hate for us here. It's not so strong in this place, where all the traders' caravans come through, and strangers are a common thing. Out on the plains, in Merukarion—Su-Akar is their name for that country—strangers are mistrusted, and keep to their own places, apart from good native folk. They call us demons, in particular our Asanians, since demons here have yellow eyes. Our northerners they call gods, because the dark gods look so, taller than mortal men, and black as night without stars. Me they endure: I look like some of them. The rest recall the people of the Hundred Realms, with their bronze faces and their narrow eyes. Some are redheaded, did you know? like red Gileni."

Daruya, who was kin to the Red Princes of Han-Gilen, inspected her hand. It was long and narrow, with tapering fingers, the color of pale honey. She turned it palm up. The gold in it caught the lamplight and blazed. "The Guild would have done better," she said, "to appoint only Guardians who were plainsmen."

"We considered that," said Vanyi, "long ago. We decided not to hide ourselves. They'd find out in the end, whether we wanted it or no; best that we be honest from the beginning, and be as foreign as in fact we are."

"So they think that we're all in league with demons and dark gods. Wait till they see our emperor. They'll want to sweep us from the earth."

"They already do," said Chakan. "Or if not us, then our Gates at least. You will go on, lady? In spite of that?"

He was addressing Vanyi, his eyes on her—demon-eyes, she thought. They seemed very human to her, for all that they were as yellow as a cat's. "Yes," she answered him. "We go on, and the sooner the better. For now I think it best if we sleep. We'll want to be awake and thinking clearly when Estarion comes roaring down the mindways. He's going to be in a right rage."

"With the grandmother of headaches," said Chakan. His voice was light, but his eyes were wide with alarm. "Ai! I won't want to live, by the time he gets done with me."

"He won't have time for you," Daruya said. "He'll be too busy tearing into me."

"You both should have thought of that before you colluded in this escapade," said Vanyi coldly. Neither had the grace to look abashed.

She pushed herself to her feet. "Well. Enough. Faliad, come with me. Olenyas, you got her into this, you guard her till she gets out of it. Me, I'm going to bed. I might even manage to sleep."

"Sleep well," they said together. She looked sharply at them, but neither showed any sign of mockery.

She sighed, considered another spate of advice, left them instead, without another word. When she glanced back, Daruya was sitting as she had been for much of their council, cradling her daughter. The Olenyas lay across the door with his swords clasped to his breast.

"They'll do," she said. She was reasonably content, all things considered.

Faliad, poor man, looked ready to drop. She sent him to bed and made sure that he obeyed her. He took the younger Guardian's cell as the Sunchildren had taken his own; Vanyi plied him with wine that she found there, until he fell asleep.

She was weary to exhaustion, but there was no sleep in her. She wandered through the temple, peering at its strangenesses until they palled on her. By the time she found the door and opened it on a narrow street, it was dawn.

No, she thought. Dusk, with the lamps just lit in sconces along the walls that lined the street. This was the other side of the world, where day was night, and night, day. There was still light in the sky, but it faded fast.

The people walking by were not so strange. They were, as Faliad had said and she knew from her mages' accounts of their travels in this land of Merukarion, as much like plainsmen of the Hundred Realms as made no matter. There were differences, but those were small: shorter stature, broader build, lighter skin—and yes, one or two even of the few she saw here had hair the color of copper. The rest were dark, of course, or grey with age.

They were like Asanians in that they did not stare, except sidelong, under lowered eyelids. She was not dressed as they were, and her skin was white—white as a bone, they said in the empire. Her hair had been red once, but not the red of copper; a darker color by far, like moors in autumn, with brown lights and gold. Now it was all gone to ash.

She leaned against the doorpost and watched the people pass. No hatred touched her, and no fear. Wariness, that was all, and a veiled curiosity, a whisper of thought: *There's another strange one in Shakryan's temple. I wonder how they conjured it up? Is it a ghost? A ghoul?* A shiver at that, but of the more pleasant sort. But then, as the thinker came level, disappointment. *Only an old woman. Poor thing, she has a disease. It took all the color out of her.*

Vanyi laughed at that, but silently, drawing back into the shadow of the doorway lest she alarm the passersby. Northerners used to think that of her, too, even when she was young. Even Estarion had, at first: Estarion with his black-velvet skin and his black-velvet voice and his astonishing eyes.

"Damn," she said aloud, as she always did when she could not get him out of her head.

And there he was in it, as if she had invoked him: spitting mad, she noted, and yes, as the Olenyas had predicted, he had a glorious headache. Not one bit of him was muted by coming from half around the world.

She let him rage himself to a standstill. She could, if she put her mind to it, see him where he was, still in the Guildhall, with the sun shining through the high windows of her own morning-room. They must have taken him there after the Gate collapsed: he was sitting on the couch she liked to nap on, stripped to breeches, his hair worked out of its plait, and a gaggle of mages and priests hovering, looking frantic.

He took no notice of them at all. His eyes glared straight into hers. She heard his voice as if he stood in front of her. "Damn you," he said. His tone by now was almost reasonable. "*Damn* you, Vanyi. You've got both my heirs on your side of the world. And I can't get there. My way is no more open than yours is." He flung up his hand, a flash of gold. "It's locked tight shut."

"I know," said Vanyi. "Your elder heir said as much. Eloquently."

His eyes glittered. "And the younger? What did she say?"

"No," he said quickly, before Vanyi could answer, "don't bother. I don't want to know."

"Believe me," Vanyi said after a pause, "if I could send them back, I would. Were you the one who taught them the shadow-trick? Even the baby's mastered it."

"No!" That much vehemence was too much for him: he winced and clutched his head. "God," he said much more softly. "Goddess. What a ghastly mess this is."

"It would be worse," she said, "if Daruya hadn't been there to keep the road steady till we could all get past it. She's worthy of her training, Starion."

"If her training had been adequate, she wouldn't have gone at all."

"Granted," said Vanyi, silencing him before he could go off in another rage. "I'll undertake to complete it as I can."

"Has she left anyone a choice in the matter?"

He was wry, which was reassuring: it meant that he was getting his temper back in hand. He ran shaking fingers through his hair, pulling out the last of the plait.

Vanyi regarded him in something resembling sympathy. "We can still talk," she said. "That's not so ill."

"But I can't *be* there." He leaped to his feet, scattering priests and mages, and paced out his frustration. "If we muster all our power, ward it with all our strength, then raise another Gate—this time let me go through it. If the Gate alone isn't enough, the *Kasar* may be—"

She stopped him before he could go any further. "You will not! I don't even dare raise one here. It's deadly, Starion. And don't tell me how strong you are," she said, as he opened his mouth. "I know it to the last drop of power. It might be enough. But it might not. We can't have the emperor dead, no matter where his heirs are, or how long it will take them to get back unless we raise the Gates again."

He was looking fully as rebellious as Daruya, and about as young. But he had more sense, or more cynicism. The rebellion faded from his face. He raised his hands, sighed. "Hells take you for being right. I'll go mad here, waiting."

"Of course you won't," she said briskly. "You'll be too busy. Isn't today your judgment-day? You must be late already."

"I put it off," he snapped. Good, she thought: he was thinking, even with his temper as chancy as it was. "See here, Vanyi. We've got to do something."

"And so I shall," she said. "I'm going over the mountains, just as I planned to. Do think, next time you want to talk to me. The people here are sure I'm a lunatic, or a god's plaything."

"Wise people," said Estarion. "Vanyi, you're not—"

"I have to go," she said.

Even as he began his protests, she cut him off, raised the shields about her mind, withdrew into the temple, in the dimness and the strangeness and the scent of incense. Someone was chanting. The younger Guardian? Or did they keep a priest or two here, to preserve their pretense of holiness?

She was too tired to hunt down the voice and ask. She could, in fact, have slept where she stood. Speaking across the world was harder than it looked while one did it.

She found a bed, it little mattered where, and fell into it, clothes and all. Not even fear could keep her awake, nor her creaking bones, nor grief for the mages whom she had lost. She laid them all on the breast of Lady Night, and herself with them. If she had dreams, she remembered none of them, till it was morning again, and fear and pain and grief were locked once more about her neck.

SEVEN

VANYI THRUST ASIDE THE REMNANTS OF BREAKFAST, UNROLLING THE MAP that Faliad had brought for her, anchoring it with cups and bowls and a jug half-full of the local ale. The others—all of them, mages and Olenyai and Sunchildren—craned as best they could, to see what was drawn on the fine parchment.

She ignored them. "So," she said. "Here we are, out on the western edge of Merukarion—Su-Akar, we should be calling it, I suppose. This is the town called Kianat, and here are the mountains that are only foothills. What's this?" She peered. " 'Here be demons'?"

The younger Guardian of the fallen Gate, whose name was Talian, spoke quickly. "There are, truly. The mountains are full of them. They haunt the peaks, and lure travelers astray."

Vanyi shot her a glance. She was flushing under the sallow bronze of her skin and wishing transparently that Faliad were here to spare her the ordeal. But the elder Guardian, having slept little if at all, was standing watch in the outer temple.

Vanyi decided to have mercy on this younger fool. "Ah well, we're mages. We'll raise the wards and chant the spells and keep the demons at bay."

"Lady," said Talian with shaky determination, "you may smile, but this isn't our own country. It shares a world and a sun with us, yes—but it's as alien as any world on the far side of Gates."

"That's well enough put," said Vanyi, unperturbed by the girl's presumption. She turned back to the map. "So. Demons in the mountains. There's a pass, this says, that seneldi can cross. Yes?"

"In this season," Talian said with a little less trepidation, "lady, yes. You won't want to delay too long, or go too slow. The snows close in early at those heights."

"There really are no seneldi here?" asked one of the Olenyai.

"Really," said Talian. "They have a kind of ox that draws their wagons, but no swift riding animal."

"Then how do they wage their wars?"

"On foot," Chakan answered for the Guardian, "and well enough for that, I'm sure. Our traders, once it's safe for them to come here, should make a great profit from the sale of seneldi. A whole new realm, empty of them. Remarkable."

"It is strange," Talian agreed, "like everything else here. They don't have mages, either."

"Everyone has mages," said Vanyi. "How can they help it? Even where there's no Guild to teach the spells, mages are born, and grow up to wield the lightnings."

"There are none here," said Talian.

"None that anyone will admit to, you're saying." Vanyi frowned at the map. "Suppression, then. Witch-hunts, I'd wager. Children disposed of when they begin to show the gifts."

"It could be, lady," Talian said. "They are afraid of magic; they won't talk about it, or let it be mentioned."

"It took mages to break the Gates," said Vanyi.

"But need they have been native mages?" Chakan met her glare with limpid eyes. "Consider, lady. Between the Mageguild and the priesthood of god and goddess, our part of the world has made magery a known and regimented thing. We take it for granted. Here in Merukarion, how do we know what's common and what's not? The gift might not appear here, for whatever reason. If there are mages, who's to say they're not renegades of our own country, who hate the Guild and mean to break it as they can?"

"Possible," said Vanyi. "But my bones don't think so. They tell me it's something else, something that comes out of here." Her finger tapped the map where it marked the kingdom of Shurakan. "Tell me about the Kingdom of Heaven."

The Guardian looked briefly rebellious, as if she wanted to remind the Guildmaster that she had been told everything that anyone knew. But she controlled herself. Maybe she reflected that everyone here might not have shared the counsels of the Guild, and that they should know what they confronted before they went out to face it.

"The Kingdom of Heaven," she said after a pause, in the tone of one teaching a lesson to a circle of intelligent children, "is called Su-Shaklan in their language. Our tongues are more comfortable calling it Shurakan. It keeps to itself, people say here, to the point that while it permits foreigners to pass its guarded gates, it does so only on sufferance, and never allows them to stay past a certain fixed term. That varies according to the purpose for which the strangers come. Ambassadors may linger a season; two, if they come too near the winter, when the passes are shut and the mountains impenetrable till spring."

"Why are they so wary?" asked Chakan. "Have they had enemies so bitter that they fear all strangers?"

"I think not," Vanyi said. "Consider where they are. Here are the mountains, so high they touch the sky—there's no air to breathe, it's said, and anyone who climbs so high, unless he's a mage and spell-guarded, will die. And they have no mages, we're told. And here's their kingdom, a valley no larger than a barony in our empire, and a small one at that. It's green, warm, rich, everything that's blessed, and more so after the barrenness of the mountains. They've made themselves a haven, difficult to reach, small enough to crowd quickly. Strangers would be rare there, but when they came, they'd threaten to strain the little space, and drive its people out by simple force of numbers."

"And," said Talian, "their minds are walled as high as their country. They're afraid of new things, strange things. Their kingdom is old—ancient, they say—and set in its ways. And they fear and hate magic. Their first rulers were a god's children, king and queen, brother and sister, who fled some calamity that had to do with magic, and led their people to the valley, and set up a kingdom that would be forever free of the taint. The word for magic in their language is the word for evil, and for the excrement of their oxen."

The mages were appalled. Chakan laughed.

He caught Vanyi's eye and sobered, if only a little. "Well, Guildmaster. There's your reason for the breaking of Gates, however they went about it. How in the million worlds did they let one be set up there at all?"

"There is a faction in their court," Vanyi said, "that wants to be sensible, not to mention practical, about the existence and practice of magic. It's a heresy, I suppose, but it's strong, and it's been ruling Shurakan. Its leaders welcomed our mages and allowed them to raise the Gate."

"Ah," said Chakan slowly. "So. This, you didn't tell the emperor."

"Or me," said Daruya, startling them all. They had forgotten her, as quiet as she had been, sitting in a corner with her daughter playing at her feet. "If you had, my grandfather would never have let me come here even before the Gate fell. He wouldn't have given you a company of his Olenyai, either."

"No," said Vanyi. "He would have wanted to come himself with an army at his back, and whole temples full of priest-mages to bring the Shurakani round to the error of their religion."

"He is not as bad as that," Daruya said stiffly. "A company of cavalry, yes, he would have wanted that, and more Olenyai. And a priest-mage or two, such as he is himself, in case you forget."

"And himself," said Vanyi. "There's the trouble, child. He'd have insisted that he was the only right and proper ambassador to such a benighted people, and run right over me, too, because he is strong enough to do that. He'd want to conquer these people as he conquered the whole of our half of the world, because it's in his blood to do exactly that. How not? He's the god's child. He was born to rule the world."

"And I wasn't?"

Vanyi faced her full on. "You, I think, for all your crotchets and your persistent conviction that you have to be a scandal in order to be noticed, are at heart a more reasonable creature than he is. And if you aren't, you'll refuse to conquer Shurakan simply because your grandfather *would* conquer it—purely for its own good, of course, and because he's the god's however-many great-grandson, supposing that you accept the dogma that Mirain An-Sh'Endor was the god's son in truth and not the bastard-born offspring of a northern priestess and the Red Prince of Han-Gilen."

"They still repeat that slander?" Daruya was surprisingly calm about it. "Ah well. You explain this"—she flashed her golden hand, dazzling Vanyi briefly—"and then we consider who sowed the seed of the Sunborn. Meanwhile, what if I decide that I can't resist the urge to be a conqueror, either?"

"I doubt that," said Vanyi. "Men conquer by force of arms. Women have other methods. Some of which I hope you'll see fit to use."

Daruya eyed her narrowly. She gave nothing back to that stare but a bland expression and a faint smile.

"He can't come now," said Daruya, "even to drag me back home in disgrace. By the time we have the Gates back up, we'll have had time, I should think, to fend him off. Unless you're going to give him a new war to fight, somewhere in his own empire?"

"I should hope not," Vanyi said tartly. "He can find his own war. His own places to meddle in, too."

"And a new heir?"

The girl was trying to goad her into an indiscretion. Vanyi gave her smile a little more rein. "I suppose, if he had to, he could see to that for himself. With as many females as he has, flinging themselves at his feet—"

"He does not!"

Vanyi laughed aloud. "Oh, there's nothing like a sinner for outraged virtue! Of course he does, silly child. I suppose he looks horribly old and decrepit to you, but to any woman who's not his granddaughter, he's a big beautiful panther of a man—and he brings with him a promise of empire. Many's the woman who'd leap at the chance to bear a Sunlord's heir. She'd have to wait to share the throne, but share it she certainly would, with the empress growing so frail."

For a moment Vanyi wondered if Daruya would spring. But she had more control than that, if not much more—not enough to find words that would suffice. Vanyi hoped that she had made the child think. It would do her good.

In the barbed silence, Chakan said, "So. We're to have guides through these mountains?"

Talian answered him with evident relief. "Certainly. Pack animals, too—some of their hairy oxen."

Chakan raised a brow. "You found men here who would endure the company of demons and dark gods?"

"Some men," said Talian stiffly, "are less superstitious than others. Even here. And greed is as potent an encouragement here as anywhere."

"Greed for gold?"

"Gold isn't what they crave," said Talian.

If Chakan found the Guardian's coyness annoying, he showed no sign. His face of course was never to be seen by anybody but his brothers and, Vanyi was reasonably certain, Daruya, but his eyes were limpidly clear, betraying nothing but calm curiosity. "Oh? What do they value above gold?"

"Silk," said Talian. "Silk of Asanion, in the most gaudy colors imaginable. One bolt of it can buy a princedom here. Or a troop of guides through the mountains, with oxen and provisions."

"Remarkable," said Chakan. "Silk, so precious? I wish I'd known that. I'd have brought a bolt or three to do my own trading with."

"Warriors will stoop to trade?" Talian asked, shocked out of discretion.

Chakan's eyes laughed. "Warriors do whatever they must do to win their wars. If the weapon of choice is silk—why, so be it."

Talian clearly did not know what to say to that. Vanyi found the silence blessed, but doubted that it could endure for long. She broke it herself before anyone else could be minded to try. "We leave as soon as we can be ready. The guards are waiting, I hope?"

"They have been sent for," said Talian.

Poor child. She had not found any of them comfortable guests. Vanyi had a brief, wicked thought of commanding the girl to accompany her. But although she could be ruthless, she was not needlessly cruel. Talian was only a child, just past her making as a mage, when she gained no twinned power, became neither darkmage nor light, but showed herself for a Guardian of Gates. It was a false belief among the young mages that Guardians were weaker than twinned mages, lesser powers, mere servants of the Gates; but from the look of this one, she believed it. The Olenyai alarmed her. The Guildmaster rendered her near witless with terror.

Vanyi took pity on her, after a fashion. "Fetch the guides here. If they're to lead us where we want to go, it's best they know now what we are—all of us at once."

"Demons, dark gods, and all," said Chakan, impervious to her withering stare.

He, with his Olenyai, had eaten before they came in, when they could do it without the hindrance of veils. They had no breakfast to abandon. None of them was obvious about it, but now that Vanyi took the time to notice, they were standing idly, comfortably, casually, in a circle that encompassed both herself and the emperor's heirs. There was a placid deadliness in the way they stood, hands well away from swordhilts, faces hidden behind the black veils, yellow eyes calm, fixed on nothing in particular.

All but Chakan, who took an easy stance beside and just behind Daruya's chair. Kimeri looked up from playing with what looked like a ball of string, and smiled. He did not do anything that Vanyi perceived, but the child got to her feet, dusted herself off conscientiously, and held up her hands. The Olenyas swung her whooping to his shoulders, where she sat like an empress on a throne.

Vanyi wondered very briefly if there was more to that than anyone would admit—if the child had been fathered by the Olenyas. But her bones said not. If Olenyas and princess-heir had been lovers, it was utterly discreet and long over.

They were guard and princess, friend and dear friend, or Vanyi was no judge. But nothing more than that.

Pity, rather. An Olenyas in Daruya's bed might be better protection than an army of mages.

No one spoke while they waited for the Guardian to come back. The mages were still stunned by the Gate's fall. Miyaz and Aledi seemed to cling together. Kadin, who had lost his lightmage, sat with them and yet irrevocably alone. He had eaten nothing, drunk little. His fine dark face was grey about the lips. His long fingers trembled as he picked up his cup, paused, set it back down again.

Vanyi watched him but did not speak to him. It was too early yet. A mage who lost the half of himself died as often as not, either from grief or by his own hand. She did not think that this one would do that. He was a northerner, from Ianon itself that had been the Sunborn's first kingdom. He had pride, and strength of spirit.

The mark of his clan was painted fresh on his forehead—a good sign, even if it were no more than habit. His beard, that had been chest-long and plaited with gold, was cut short, his hair cropped to the skull in mourning. Again, good enough. He could have turned the blade against himself.

They would all suffer if he did. Six mages and a master had been ample for the embassy that Vanyi had in mind. Three of them dead left the rest overburdened, even if Kadin came through this grief intact. If he did not . . .

She would think of that when she had to. She let her eyes return to the map, tracing and retracing the ways they must take. Guides they might and must have, but she never trusted to one expedient if several would do.

"Daruya," she said abruptly. "Come here."

Daruya came, for a wonder; what was more, she seemed inclined to pay attention as Vanyi set about teaching her the map and the journey. But, thought Vanyi, this mattered to the girl. It touched her pride.

Pride was useful in swaying kings, and kings' heirs.

EIGHT

THE GUIDES WERE A WOMAN AND HER THREE HUSBANDS. DARUYA AT FIRST would not believe what her magery told her she was hearing; surely her gift of tongues was failing or turning antic. But the woman's mind quite clearly perceived the three men with her as husbands—men who shared her bed and stood father to her children. They were brothers, sturdy-built middling-tall men like heavyset plainsmen, with bronze skin seared dark by sun and wind, and narrow black eyes, and black hair worn in cloth-wrapped plaits. Their wife was much like them, near as tall as they and quite as solid.

She did the speaking for them all. Her name was Aku, which meant Flower; she named her husbands, but Daruya paid little attention. Names were not what they were. They were stolid, at least to look at, but there were festoons of amulets about their necks, and they eyed the Olenyai in what they fancied was well-concealed terror. The Olenyai, without the mages' gift of tongues, had leisure to observe, and to be amused. Daruya hoped that one of them would not take it into his head to do or say something appropriately demonic, and lose them their guides before they even started.

The woman seemed fearless enough. She was brusque, striking a hard bargain with Vanyi, whom she had singled out without prompting as the leader of the expedition. That spoke well for her perception, since Vanyi had not been trying to look conspicuous. The other mages in their robes—lightmage silver, darkmage violet—were far more impressive than she was in her plain coat and trousers and boots; and the Olenyai were alarming, faceless black shadow-men with golden demon-eyes. Vanyi could have been a servant, an old woman of no particular height or distinction apart from a certain air of whipcord toughness.

But Aku knew, and for that, Vanyi let herself be haggled with. Daruya might have done it herself, for the matter of that, if she had had occasion. At the moment she seemed to have been included with the Olenyai in the class of demons, in the minds of the men, and as young and therefore insignificant in the mind of the woman.

Old age held great power here. Daruya made note of that.

At length the bargaining was concluded, the guides given half a bolt of scarlet silk in payment, the rest to follow at the end of the journey. Daruya rose in relief and gathered up Kimeri, who had fallen asleep in Chakan's lap. Kimeri murmured, burrowed into Daruya's shoulder, and went back to sleep again.

"Poor baby," said Chakan. "She hardly knows where or when she is."

"She knows it very well," Daruya said. "She wore herself out, that's all, creeping through the storm in the Gate."

He looked as if he would have said more, but he did not. She was glad. It frightened her that ki-Merian of all people was so docile and sleeping so much. She could find no wound in the child, of mind or body, nothing but tiredness and a desire to be near her mother. But that was disturbing enough. Kimeri was the least clinging of children, and the least inclined to sleep when she could be up and doing.

Daruya did not want to say anything of that, even to Chakan whom she trusted. She busied herself with the flurry of departure—a last meal eaten in haste, farewells said to the Guardians, gathering and mounting and forming their caravan in the temple's inner court. The seneldi were snorting and rolling their eyes at strangers, hairy oxen as Talian had called them: great shaggy beasts, taller than a tall senel, with broad curving sweeps of horns, and feet as broad as banquet-platters.

There were four of them in the court, wearing harnesses that translated into saddles and bridles of a sort, as each guide approached his beast and mounted by climbing its harness like a ladder. He had only one rein, and a stick that he used to turn his massive mount and to drive it forward.

Daruya, fascinated, almost forgot to mount her own fretting, head-tossing mare. Chakan passed Kimeri up to ride on her saddlebow, still asleep and dreaming peacefully of riding her pony in the empress' perfume-garden. Once the mare felt the twofold weight she settled, though she still snorted at the oxen.

Vanyi was speaking, not loudly but clear enough to be heard over the stamping and snorting of the animals. "We're shadow-passing through the town for convenience's sake—this many seneldi appearing from nowhere would raise a frightful riot. Daruya, will you anchor the casting?"

That meant riding in the rear and securing the edge of the working. It also meant great trust, and a degree of concession that she had not expected so soon. She sat her mare nonplussed, until she found her tongue somewhere and put it to use. "I'll ride anchor. Chakan, you too. I can use you."

Vanyi's approval was quick, sharp, and surprisingly warm. Daruya began to wonder exactly how surprised the Guildmaster had been to find her with them in the Gate—and exactly how unwelcome she had been. Not at all, maybe. Vanyi did not share the emperor's concern for his heirs; or at least not his concern that they be kept close, and therefore safe. Vanyi in fact cared little for royalty at all, that Daruya could discern. She was a commoner, and an Islander into the bargain. Kings to her were a blasted nuisance, no good at all for mending nets or catching fish or sailing a boat in the teeth of a gale.

Daruya, who had learned from Vanyi herself to do all three, caught the thread of power as it spun toward her, and drew it taut. On it she strung a web of shadow. It was the same working she had used to conceal herself on the way through the Gate, and she used Chakan's shield as she had then, but this was wider, stronger. Anyone not a mage who looked at the passing of their company would see four oxen with their riders, the train of pack-oxen that waited outside the temple, and a confused image of guards, riders, caravanners, but no clear faces and no certainty as to their numbers.

With five of them working the concealment, it was a simple enough thing, and no great effort. Daruya was able to see the town as they rode through it, to be startled at its earthen plainness. After the wild extravagance of the temple, she had expected the rest to be as gaudy.

The temples were eye-searing spectacles, to be sure, and there were a great number of them, but in among them the houses of the people, large and small, were simple blocky shapes of mud brick, unadorned even by a scrap of gilding over a lintel. The people were of like mold: dressed in grey or brown or at most a deep blue, hung with amulets but boasting no other adornment—until she saw a procession of what must be priests. They marched in a long undulating line, matching pace to the deep clang of a bell, chanting in a slow drone. Their heads were shaven and painted like the carvings in the temple. Their bodies were bare in what to her was a wintry chill, but for the simplest of robes, a length of cloth, saffron or scarlet or a searing green, falling to the ground before and behind, open else, and hung about with a clashing array of gold, silver, copper, great lumps of amber, river pearls, firestones cut and uncut, strung together without art or distinction. They made an astonishing spectacle, the more astonishing for that passersby seemed to take no notice of them except to move out of their way.

The caravan bade fair to run afoul of the procession, but just before the two collided, the priests swayed aside down another road. The caravan paused, waited for the rest of the procession to pass.

Daruya, forced to leisure, took in as much of the town as she could see. It was built on level ground, but beyond it reared the wall of a mountain, so sheer and so high that it seemed to crown the sky. Snow gleamed on its summit and far down its slopes—small wonder the air was so cold here. There seemed no way over or past it.

She was warmly dressed in gleanings from the temple's stores, her coat lined with fur and a cloak over that, and a hat on her head, but still she shivered. Kimeri, cradled in her arms, nuzzled toward her breast. It ached as if in answer, though the child had been weaned since her second year. Daruya brushed the warm smooth forehead with a kiss, and swayed as the mare started forward again.

They left Kianat unseen and took the caravans' road to the north and west. It was steep, and in places it was very narrow, but it found the pass that went over the mountain and climbed it, higher than Daruya had ever been in her life.

And when they came to the top, the second day out of Kianat, all unshielded now and riding openly as they were, demons and dark gods and all, Daruya caught her breath. What she had fancied to be a lofty mountain was, indeed, but a slave and a servant to the peaks that marched away before her, wave on jagged snow-white wave of them, mounting up and up into the pitiless sky.

It was beyond imagining. She was ant-small, mote-small, crushed under the immensity of mountains and sky. But the sun that rode over them, casting fire on the snow, was her own, the face of her forefather. Its fire burned in her hand. Her blood was full of it.

That raised her head before it bowed too low, and straightened her back. She bore the weight of the sky. She faced the mountains' vastness and gave it tribute, but no fear; no submission.

"Here," said Chakan, "be demons."

They had made camp just below the top of the pass, where the land dropped away to a brief level. That this was a frequent resort of caravans, Daruya could well see. There was grazing for beasts, with a well-cropped look, and stone hearths to build fires in, with walls about them that kept out the wind. The guides unloaded a heap of tanned hides that, sewn together swiftly with strips of leather and secured to the walls, made roofs for a cluster of huts about the yard in which the beasts would be penned. They were not to graze all night, it seemed, for the reason Chakan had hinted at.

"Just until sundown," he said, "and then they come in, no matter how hungry they still are. Demons eat oxen, we're told, and would discover a taste for senelflesh if given the opportunity."

"You were told all that?" Daruya asked, prodding at the fire she had built of dried ox-dung and dried grass and a flash of magery. "You don't speak their language at all."

"No, and I'm not turning mage, either, to know what their babble means." He squatted on his heels, warming his hands at the blaze. "Still and all, signs are clear enough, and the three husbands seem to think that when a demon wants to know something about his cousins of the peaks, the demon should get an answer however he may. Besides," he added, "I asked a mage to translate for me. We're judged not to be the man-eating kind of demon, did you know that? The Old Woman— that's what they call the Guildmaster—has us enslaved, and we're condemned to live and eat like mortals until she lets us go."

"Including me?" Daruya asked with lifted brows.

His eyes danced. He was grinning behind the veil. "Why, of course. You're the chief of us. We're your husbands, so hideous that our faces must never be seen lest they drive men mad; but you're merely mortally ugly, so you don't hide yourself or your little demon, who they think was conceived of the night wind and suckled on milk of the snow-cat. They're not far off, are they?"

She bit her tongue. He would laugh if she said what she wanted to say, which was that if she was ugly, then what in the world did they reckon beautiful?

Vanity. It stung her nonetheless. She had been the Beauty of Starios for as long as she could remember. It could be a nuisance when men young and not so young, and not a few women, flung themselves at her feet; but she took no displeasure in what her mirror showed her, all honey and amber, and queenly proud.

Chakan read her much too easily for a man with no magery at all. "Beauty's an odd thing. Changeable. Madam Aku's a great beauty here."

"She's built like a brick," said Daruya, with a snap in it.

"Maybe a brick is beautiful," said Chakan serenely, "where they don't value gold. Silly of them, but there you are. It could be worse. They could have decided that it would be an act of virtue to murder us in our beds."

"They may yet," said Vanyi, lowering herself to sit beside the fire. She had a flask in her hand, which she passed to Daruya.

Daruya sniffed, then tasted. Wine, and good wine, too. She drank a swallow, then two, and handed the flask to Chakan. He did not hesitate, but slipped it under his veils and drank with practiced ease.

"Dinner's coming when it's had time to cook," Vanyi said. She looked about, drawing Daruya to do the same. This was the largest of the huts, with room enough for a good half-dozen people. Through the open side, the one that faced the yard, she saw the beasts being herded in, in dusk that had fallen with startling suddenness. The seneldi did not like to be crowded together with the oxen, but they were getting better about it. There was only a little squealing and kicking, and only one bellow as Daruya's mare gored a dilatory ox.

It was a shallow gore, and little blood shed through that shaggy pelt and thick hide. The mare looked very pleased with herself. With the contrariness of her sex and her kind, she settled to share a heap of fodder with the offending ox, as peaceful as if the beast had been a herdmate, and one she honored, at that.

Daruya sensed nothing beyond the circle of huts but empty spaces, height and cold and raw wind. Her head ached vaguely with the thinness of the air, and her breath came shorter than it should, but that was nothing to take particular notice of. If there were demons, they avoided this place.

Even so, she ate with little appetite and slept ill. Height-sickness again. One or two of the Olenyai and both the elder mages were in worse state than she. She fretted for Kimeri, but the child was no more and no less well than she had been since the journey began.

Kimeri kept wanting to fall asleep. She did not like it, and at first she thought it was something her mother or Vanyi was doing to keep her quiet. But they were worried. They tried to hide it, but she knew. She could not think of anything to say that would make them feel better. Certainly not that she kept seeing Gates and feeling them inside of her, broken and hurting, and a Guardian who thought he was dead.

Something happened when they went over the pass. She stopped being so terribly sleepy. She still saw Gates, but the mountains were stronger, a little. She could look at them, at their sharp white teeth against the purple sky, and even, almost, forget about the Guardian. But only almost. The Guardian was inside of her, too, now, like the Gates.

The mountains outside of her were stubborn. They tried to make her think that they were the only thing that mattered, but she knew better. "There are people like you at home," she said to them while everybody was making camp for another cold restless night, but nobody was paying much attention to her.

She was too wise to wander out of sight, too restless to stay where she was put. She climbed on top of one of the big patient oxen, the way she had seen its rider do, up its side with the harness like a ladder, and sat on its back that was as broad as a table. The mountains stood all around the place where they were, a high valley full of new green grass, with bits of snow in the hollows, and a spring that bubbled out of a tree-root and filled a bowl of rock; stood and stared.

The seneldi had decided after a great deal of fuss that the oxen were sort of distant cousins. The oxen thought the seneldi very silly. They got on well enough, and Daruya's mare had made friends with the ox that Kimeri was sitting on, the big queen ox who told the others what to do.

Now as they grazed side by side the mare threw up her head and snorted. The ox kept on grazing peacefully, but she was awake inside her armor of horns and shaggy hair. Kimeri looked where they were looking.

Something sat in the branches of the tree that overhung the spring. It looked a little like a bird and a little like a man and a great deal like neither. It had feathers, white and grey and silver and faint grassy green, and a wide round face with wide round yellow eyes, and very sharp, very pointed teeth. It showed them to her, and flexed curved claws like a cat's, and hissed.

The senel was ready to bolt, but the ox sighed and yawned and chewed her cud. Kimeri decided that if the ox was not afraid, then neither would she be. It took some deciding. This was a demon. She had heard the guides talking about them, especially their yellow eyes and their long fangs. The guides thought the Olenyai wore veils to hide fangs just like these, though of course Olenyai were only men, with plain Asanian faces and ordinary Asanian eyes, yellow and gold and amber and ocher-brown.

This was not a man at all. It did not have a babble of thoughts like a man, but neither was it the wordless nowness of an animal. It felt most of all like a mage when he worked his magic—a singing presence, a flicker like a fire on the skin. But it was not as strong as a mage, not as solid on the earth. She thought of ice, that was like stone but very different.

She must be careful, she thought. She was Sun-blood—she burned too fierce sometimes for magical things to bear. Things like spirits of air, or fetches on their masters' errands, or demons of the mountains come to see what trespassed in their country.

The demon was surprised that she did not shriek and run away. She was supposed to do that, all the earthborn did. Even earthborn who were demon-eyed. She stayed where she was. The demon tried jumping up and down on its branch. It had no weight: the branch never moved. That was interesting. The demon started to chitter and gnash its teeth.

"Why do you do all that?" she asked it. "You can't hurt me."

The demon stopped. Its big yellow eyes blinked. It filled her mouth with the taste of blood, like iron but strangely sweet. That was the blood of an earthborn man, fresh from his throat that the demon had torn.

"That was because he was afraid," Kimeri said. "He let you eat him. I'm not afraid of you."

Her great-grandfather would know what to say to that. It was a long word. Arrogance, that was it.

"But it's true," she said. "You don't need to drink blood. You have the air up here, and the wind off the snow."

Blood was sweet, the demon told her. It was warm.

"Mine would burn you," she said. She clambered down off the ox's back, holding on to harness and pelt, and went to stand under the tree. The demon stared down at her. She stared up. "You won't be drinking any blood here. If you do I'll tell my mother. She's much stronger than I am. Her blood is like the sun."

The demon shut its big round eyes. When it opened them, they were all of the demon that was left; then they were gone, and so was the demon. But it was near— she felt it, it and its brothers and sisters and cousins.

"Remember," she said to them. "No bad tricks. I'll know it was you, and I'll do something about it."

NINE

THERE WERE PEOPLE IN THIS COUNTRY. WHAT SEEMED INHOSPITABLE BEYOND believing and beautiful in the coldest way imaginable, a jagged landscape of peaks and lofty valleys, snowfields and icefields and sudden plunges into green oases, had its own thin tough populace. Villages clung to the sides of crags or huddled round the warmth of a valley. There were fortresses on peaks that should have been too steep for any creature to climb, inhabited often by wind and dust and sky, but often again by a dirty scrabble of people whose only pride seemed to be in the sharpness of their weapons.

The people were like the land they lived in, harsh, stark, often cruel, but showing flashes of sudden beauty. In a town so steep it had no streets, only ladders from
house to stone-built house, and no open space but the level in its center, where its
market was set up and doing a brisk trade, Daruya heard a singer whose voice could
have called the stars out of the sky. The singer was blind, and therefore oblivious to
Daruya's strangeness; he sang on even when the rest of the listeners drew back, giving her demon-eyes a wide space.

She heard a hiss and a scuffle behind her, where Chakan was insisting on guarding her back. She glanced over her shoulder. The Olenyas had a wizened townsman
by the throat. He shook the man as a hound shakes a rat. Something fell tinkling:
a fistful of coins that wore familiar faces.

"Right out of my purse," said Chakan, almost too amused to be angry. "It's no
defense to be a demon, it seems. Not against thieves."

The thief struggled in his grip. He laid the point of a dagger against the man's
throat, just under the chin, and hissed. The man went grey. Chakan laughed and let
him go. He bolted.

"That should warn off the rest," said Chakan.

Daruya had her doubts. She had observed that demons in this country were as
fair game as any other travelers. She had also noticed that they seemed to have no
fear of theft among themselves. It was only dishonor, she supposed, to steal from
one's own kind.

Her own valuables were wrapped in silk and hung between her breasts. A thief
would have to pass a heavy coat and a leather tunic and a pair of shirts to reach the
treasure. She wished him well of it if he came that far; he would have earned it.

The singer's song ended on a wailing note. It wound up and up, spiraled down,
and faded. She plucked a coin or two from Chakan's hand and tossed them into the
bowl at the singer's feet. They would be safe there, since the singer was not a
foreigner.

Daruya was still pondering thieves and honor and the relation of foreigners to
both, as their caravan scrambled up yet another steep and stony pass. The town on
the crag was far behind. Shurakan, the guides said, was far ahead: at least half a
Brightmoon-month of journeying, as much time as lay behind them since they left
Kianat. It went slow; it always went slow in this country of endless up and down
and very little level.

This pass was like a knife-cut in the earth, a thin slash in the mountain's side.
Steep as it was, its walls nearly sheer, closing in on them as they went on, it seemed
likely to narrow to nothing and so trap them, and leave them at the mountain's
mercy.

She let out her breath at long last as the narrow wall—barely wide enough for
the oxen to scrape by—began to widen again, and the slope to soften slightly. The

caravan, with her in the middle, kept on at its plodding pace; no wall in front of it yet, and light still in the gap. Echoes ran up and down the walls: snort of senel, grunt of ox, thud of hoofs, low mutter of voices as Vanyi, up ahead, conferred with Aku the guide.

There was no getting closer. The way was too narrow. Daruya tried stretching her ears to more than simple human keenness, but Vanyi was too canny a mage for that; she and her companion rode as if globed in glass. Daruya had to content herself with straining to catch the odd word, and praying for the walls to open before she went out of her wits—the more so for that the one word she caught was *ambush*.

Her eyes ran up the walls of the cleft. Too steep surely for any man to come down, and too high to leap. If she were a bandit or mountain lord, she would close off the ends of the cleft and trap her prey within. But no one had done that. Her magery, seeking, found nothing. The way was open behind as in front.

She did not ease for that. Eyes were on them, unseen, not truly hostile but not friendly, either. The beasts were quiet, which was well. She combed her mare's mane with her fingers, shifted in the saddle, stretched a kink out of her shoulder. A glance found Kimeri riding on Chakan's crupper. The child had wanted a mount of her own this morning—sure sign that she had come back to herself. Maybe tomorrow, Daruya thought, she would have one of the remounts saddled and let Kimeri ride it for at least a part of the day.

The walls of the cleft opened slowly and sank by degrees into the land beyond, until they rode through a stony valley, steep-sided, with grass growing amid the remnants of winter's snow. They paused to drink from a stream, found it clean and bitter cold: snow-water. The sun was high enough to reach beyond the walls of the valley, and warm enough that the guides took off their coats and their furred hats and rode in their shirts.

Daruya, less hardy, still pulled off her hat and let the wind run fingers through her hair. A gust blew it in her face, a heavy curtain of amber-gold curls. She laughed for no reason that she could name, and shook it back.

Her laughter ran its course. There were smiles about her, in Olenyai eyes or mages' faces. But she was watching the summit of the ridge, where sunlight dazzled and shadows seemed to dance. Shadows born of living bodies, and within them a glitter of metal, and awareness keen and sharply pointed and very clear.

She said to Chakan, very calmly, "Look up. No, not there. Up. East wall."

The soft hiss of sword from sheath was his answer, and his voice, as calm as hers, and no louder. "Eyes up, Olenyai. We have company."

It was not a good place to be at the bottom of. The east slope was too steep for a senel, but not for a man with the surefootedness of the mountain born. There were men and weapons ahead, too, and behind. They were nicely trapped.

Daruya caught Vanyi's eye. The Guildmaster raised a brow. Daruya tilted her hand till gold caught the sun and flashed. Vanyi smiled a cold white smile.

Briefly Daruya considered the guides, and the lack of magic and mages in

Su-Akar. *Let them learn*, she thought. She had not called in her power in long and long, not since the Gate. It came gladly, swift as a hawk to the fist. The sun fed it.

She was aware of Vanyi calling her own magic, a weaving of dark and light, shadow and sun; and the mages summoning each his own, even Kadin who never spoke, never sang, rode always mute and wrapped in grief.

His gladness was a dark thing, tinged with blood. He wanted to take life, to kill as his lightmage had been killed. She brushed him with a finger of power, bright Sungold to his black dark. He recoiled in startlement. She gentled him with patience, pressing no harder than she must with raiders closing in on every side. *Softly*, she willed him. *Be calm. You'll have revenge—but not now. These fools are unworthy of you.*

He begged to differ, but she was stronger. He subsided, sullen but obedient, letting her direct him as she judged best. She was not his lightmage, yet the familiar force of matched yet opposing power comforted him, filled a fraction of his emptiness, muted his grief.

Instinct had taken her to him, as if even she, priestess-mage and Sunchild, had need of the dark one, the power that lay in shadows. Yet she could not bond with it; could not be his lightmage. That was forbidden her.

She would ponder that later, when there was leisure. For now she took it as it offered itself, and used it as it asked to be used. Hilt to her blade of light, haft to her spear of the sun, bow to the arrow of power that flew flame-bright from her hand.

It was beautiful and terrible. Mere earthly arrows shot down from above flared to ash and vanished. Swords melted in a fire hotter than any forge. Men shrieked—pain, in those who found themselves clutching white-hot hilts, and fear in archers whose bows crumbled in their hands, whose arrows were ash in the quivers. What they saw, Daruya saw through them: a small odd caravan trapped in the valley that was so perfectly suited for ambush, mounted on strange beasts, and guards in black ringed about a towering shape of light.

Back of the light was shadow. It waited to take what the light left, to drown souls that held no more substance than a moth's flutter. Seductive thought, alluring prospect, to be rid of these bandits with no fear of reprisal.

But Daruya's training was too strong. One did not slay with power. Above all, one did not destroy the soul, even of an enemy. The price for that was the power that had destroyed so much, but not—cruelly—the life of the mage.

The shadow struggled, resisting. She reined and bound it and loosed a last, blinding blaze of light. There was no harm in it, only terror. The bandits broke and fled.

"Well done," said Vanyi dryly.

Daruya quelled a hot retort. She had done it again: swept in and done what needed doing without regard for the Guildmaster's precedence. In the Gates it would have been death to wait. Here, she should have yielded; should have waited upon the rest.

Vanyi did not say any of that. She did not think it, either, that Daruya could discern. She simply nudged her senel forward past the still and staring guides. The others, mages first, then Olenyai, followed slowly.

Only Daruya did not move; and the guides. The men had a look she had seen in battle, in warriors who had seen too much, whose minds had stopped, leaving them blankly still. The woman was stronger, or more resilient. She flinched at the brush of Daruya's glance, but she steadied herself, lifted her eyes, met Daruya's.

Daruya was prey to both arrogance and impatience, as her elders never wearied of telling her. But she was not a fool. She spoke very carefully, choosing her words as meticulously as if she had been addressing the emperor of a nation with which she could be, if she failed of diplomacy, at war. "I swear to you by all that I hold holy, that I have harmed not a hair of their heads, nor done aught but win us free of ambush."

Aku's eyes narrowed. "You did it? Only you?"

Daruya felt the flush climb her cheeks. "If there is blame, yes, it is mine alone."

"But the other could," said Aku. "Could have done the same."

She meant Vanyi. Daruya hesitated. To lie, to prevaricate, to tell the truth . . . "She did nothing."

"She would have," Aku said. Perceptive, for a woman who had no magic. She was no longer quite so afraid. "I see that you're very foreign."

"Very," said Daruya, a little at a loss. She thought she understood what the woman was getting at. But she could not be certain—even knowing what thoughts ran through that brain, both the spoken and the unspoken. "We're still mortal," she said. "Still human. We're not gods, nor demons, either."

"So you say," said Aku. She struck her ox with the goad, urging it forward onto the track the caravan had taken. Her husbands, stirring at last, fell in behind her.

Daruya, left alone, baffled, a little angry, had the presence of mind to sweep the land round about. Nothing threatened. The bandits were still running. Already the tale had grown, the caravan swelled into an army of devils armed with thunderbolts. By the time it passed into rumor, it would be a battle of gods, into which the bandits had fallen by accident and barely escaped alive.

None of which mattered now, with guides who could turn traitor and lead them all into a crevasse. What dishonor would there be in that? Not only were they foreigners; they were mages.

Fear would be enough, Daruya hoped. And common sense. Aku had that. She would want her payment, her scarlet silk. And maybe she would see the profit in seeing this journey to its end, the tales she could tell, the travelers who would pay high to pass through the mountains with a woman who had guided a caravan of demons safely into Shurakan.

And they were safe. Whether word spread swifter than they could travel, or whether they were simply blessed with good fortune, they met no further ambush. No one tried to rob them in the villages, nor were they fallen on in camp and forced to give up their valuables. The snows that were not uncommon even at this time of year veiled the upper peaks from day's end to day's end, but never came down upon their track. All their passes were open, the ways unblocked by snow or rockfall or avalanche.

The luck was with them. Kimeri heard the Olenyai saying that to one another, in whispers so as not to frighten it away.

They could not see the demons who followed, spying on them, or clustered round their camp at night, round-eyed as owls, staring and wondering. The mages, who should have been able to see, were not looking. The guides had made themselves blind, because seeing made them so afraid.

Demons kept bandits away, though her mother's magic helped. The one whom she had come to think of as her demon, the white-feathered one that she had met at the spring, actually chased off a ragged man who was too desperately hungry to care about the rumor of fire and terror. Kimeri was angry at the demon for that. She made sure there was food for the man to steal, left some of her supper and some of her breakfast behind, and hoped he found them and was not too frightened to eat.

The demon understood anger, but its memory was very short. It was like the wind: changeable. But its fascination for her went on and on, and made it as solid as it could be, almost solid enough to touch.

Other demons came and went. There were different kinds. The ones with feathers were actually not common. Most had a great quantity of horns and teeth and claws, and scales and tails and leathery wings, and always the yellow eyes. The ones that drank blood looked at the men and the seneldi and thought hunger, but Kimeri's demon warned them off with growls and teeth-gnashings. It was not the largest demon and certainly not the most terrible to look at, but the others seemed to listen to it. Maybe, she thought, it was like her: royal born.

When her mother actually let her have a senel to ride all by herself, the demon came to sit on her crupper. The bay gelding did not like that at all. Kimeri calmed him down, shaking for fear her mother would think he was too much for her and make her ride like a baby again, the way the demon wanted to ride. But he was a good senel, sweet-tempered and quiet, just not prepared to carry a thing that had substance but no weight, and looked so odd besides. Once she had explained, he pinned his ears and fretted but gave in, and put up with the demon. The demon helped by being quiet and not moving around too much, except when it forgot and stood up on the senel's rump and made faces at demons that peered down from the sides of mountains.

It was a very happy demon, riding behind Kimeri, being invisible to everybody else. Sometimes she thought Vanyi might know it was there, but Vanyi said nothing. Kimeri was careful not to talk to it aloud, and when she talked to it in her head to make sure nobody else could listen. It took a little thinking to manage that, but it was not hard once she began.

At first the demon never thought in words, but the longer they went on, the clearer the demon's thoughts became, until they were having conversations, long hours of them, as the senel climbed up and climbed down and scrambled from mountaintop to mountaintop along the roof of the world. Demons had been there always, like the rocks and the snow and the sky—"From forever," the demon said. It liked the thought of forever, played often with it, turned it around in its head like a bright and shining toy. "Forever and ever and ever. We fly in the air, we swim through the earth, we dance on the waters that come out of the dark. We are here always. Always."

"Do you go anywhere else?" Kimeri asked it once in her head, after they had ridden through a valley with a waterfall. The demon had shown her how it danced on water. She had set out to try it, too, but her mother had caught her just as she began, and scolded her for getting wet, and made her change all her clothes, even the ones that were dry. "Do you only live in the mountains?"

"Where else is there to live?" the demon asked.

"Why," said Kimeri, "everywhere. There's a whole world beyond the mountains."

"The mountains are the world," the demon said.

"No," said Kimeri patiently. "The mountains are the roof of the world. The world is much larger than they are. There's the plain out past them, and the ocean, and more mountains, though not so high, and more plains, and rivers, and forests, and home, where I come from."

"You come from the mountains," the demon said. "You come from the thick places—the low mountains, the ones on the edge of the world, where air is heavy and easy to ride on."

"That's not the edge of the world," Kimeri said. "That's only the edge of the mountains."

"The edge of the world," the demon said.

It was a stubborn demon. She tried to show it home, the palace, the plain and the forest, even the Gate. But it insisted that home was the mountains, and the palace was like the palace in the place she was going to, which the demon thought of with a shudder. "The walled place," it said. "The place that burns." It meant wards, she thought, because it said the mages' wards burned, too, but only a little, and once she let it ride with her, it could ignore them completely.

But the wards that made it so afraid were Great Wards, or something like them—wards stronger than any few mages could raise. It scared itself right off the senel and into nothingness, scaring her so much that she thought she had killed it. But it came back a long time later, after they stopped to camp, and it acted as if it could not remember what had scared it away. It would not talk about the walled place again; she did not ask, for fear that it really would go away and not come back.

TEN

"THE BURNING PLACE IS NEAR," THE DEMON SAID. IT WAS ALMOST AS HARD TO
see as it had been the first time Kimeri saw it. Quivers ran through it, ripples
of fear, but it clung stubbornly to the back of her saddle.

She would be afraid of the place herself if she had not heard her mother and
Vanyi talking about it. To them it was a human place, that was all, and maybe it was
dangerous, but it was nothing to frighten a mage. Demons, who were mostly air,
had more to fear, and more to be wary of.

Her demon stood up on the senel's rump. "Stay here," it said.

It was not talking to the senel. It caught at her hair with claws like a brush of
wind. "Stay in the mountains," it said. "Don't go down to the burning place."

"But," she said, in her head as always, "what would I do here?"

"Be," the demon answered. "Be with me."

"I'm not going to get hurt in the burning place," she said, trying to comfort it. "I
have my own burning inside of me, that keeps me safe."

"Stay in the mountains," said the demon. "We can fly. We can play with the
wind. You can sing, and I can dance. Stay."

She was usually careful not to act as if there was anyone with her, but now she
turned and looked at the demon. It looked like a shadow on glass, with eyes that
glowed like yellow moons. Its whole self was a wanting.

She remembered that some of its kind drank blood, and some had claws that
could rip an ox to pieces. But not her demon. It wanted her to stay, that was all, and
keep it company.

"I learned words from you," the demon said. "Who will talk with me, if you go
away?"

Kimeri's throat started to hurt. Her eyes were blurry. "I have to go."

"You can stay," said the demon.

"No," said Kimeri. An idea struck her. "You can teach the others words. Then
they can talk to you."

"I want you," the demon said.

"I have to go," Kimeri said. "I have something to do. I can't not do it. Even to
talk with you, and play on the wind."

The demon's claws tightened in her hair. They were more solid now, but still no
stronger than the wind. Gently, because she did not want to hurt it, she let out a

flicker of magery. The demon tried to cling, but the burning, even as little of it as there was, was too much for it. It wailed and let go.

"I'm sorry," said Kimeri, "but I can't stay. I'll try to come back."

"That is not now," the demon said.

There was nothing that Kimeri could say to that. She had more than a demon to think of, a Gate and a Guardian and a place where they both were, as terrible in its way as the burning place. She could not stop her throat from hurting and her eyes from filling up, but she could not do what the demon wanted, either.

It was too much for a very young person, even a princess with a Sun in her hand. The wind whipped the tears from her eyes, and kept the others from asking questions and being awkward. But her senel's saddle was too cold a comfort, his mane too rough to bury her face in. She made her way to where her mother was riding, talking to Chakan; pulled herself over behind her mother's saddle and wrapped her arms about that narrow middle and clung.

Kimeri was acting strangely again, clinging and refusing to let go. Daruya worried, but magery found nothing wrong except a sourceless grief. Homesick, she decided, and afraid of this bleak steep country that seemed to go on and on without end. It was disturbing enough for a grown mage; for a child it must be terrifying.

She gave what comfort she could, and it seemed to be enough. Kimeri grew calmer, though she still did not ask to go back to her own saddle. Daruya let her stay where she was, glad of her warmth and her presence.

It seemed that they had been traveling for whole lives of men, ascending each mountain only to find another beyond, crossing each pass into a new and higher country. The air blew thin and bitter cold. Spring lagged behind, then vanished in endless fields of snow.

This was the summit of the world, as high as any simple man could go and live. Mages could have gone higher, but even Vanyi was not moved to that degree of curiosity, not with what she faced, ahead in Shurakan. There were peaks above her, white jagged teeth, and sky the color of evening although it was midday. Both moons were up, Brightmoon a white shadow of the sun, Greatmoon like a shield of ruddy copper, hanging above the crenellations of the Worldwall.

Those who needed mages' help to breathe had that help and welcome. That was most of them now, all but the guides, who were born to this country. They kept formation as they had from the beginning, Aku leading, the men bringing up the rear. Their expressions were unreadable. Since Daruya disposed of the bandits to such spectacular effect, the ease that had been growing between Vanyi and Aku had vanished.

Aku was still civil, would still converse with Vanyi, answer her questions, perform her duty well and fully. But there was no warmth in it. A mage, like demons, like foreigners, was nothing that Aku wished to call friend.

It was not even hostile, that withdrawal. It was, that was all, like the language Aku spoke, the clothes she wore, the way she harnessed and rode her ox. Vanyi, speaking Aku's tongue through a trick of magery, wearing the winter garments of the Hundred Realms, riding a senel, was no more kin to her than one of the animals.

Vanyi was stubborn. She did not take refuge in aloofness, did not sequester herself with her mages and let the guides do as they pleased. She kept on riding beside Aku, kept on asking her questions, kept on pushing against the barrier that Aku had raised. It never moved, but neither would she desist.

She was as bad as Estarion, she supposed. She did not want to conquer, only to know and to understand. But she wanted that understanding. She fought for it, even against such determined resistance. There were hatreds enough in the realms of Sun and Lion, tribe fearing tribe, nation despising nation. But never minds closed and locked as these were. Never such perfect refusal to accept a stranger, still less a stranger who was a mage.

If Shurakan was as bad as this, she thought more than once, it might kill them out of hand, lest their alien presence pollute the land's purity.

And now as they crept across the roof of the world, Shurakan was close at last. Vanyi sensed nothing but rock and snow and cold, but Aku pointed to a peak like a spearhead, leaf-shaped, clean and hard and white against the sky. "That is Shakabundur," she said, "the Spear of Heaven, that stands guard on Su-Shaklan."

Aku's face was unreadable. Her mind offered nothing to the reading but a deep relief. The journey had been no joy to her, even with the prospect of riches in return for it.

Vanyi suppressed a sigh. It was tempting to pay the guides off now and go on alone, with their destination in sight. But she was not that great a fool. There were leagues yet to go, she judged; two days at least, and likely more, before they came to the valley—and who knew what between. One bridgeless chasm could set them back days, as they tried to find a way round.

She urged her senel forward. The gelding's ribs were beginning to show, what with long marching and short commons, but he was healthy enough. They had not lost any of their seneldi, even on the steepest tracks. That was good fortune. God and goddess approved of the journey, the priests would say—though not Estarion, who was lord of them all. Estarion did not approve in the least.

There was no warning at all. One moment they were scrambling along a precipice. The next, they found themselves on the very edge of it, and the mountain dropping down and down and down into a vision of misty green. After white snow, black rock, sky so blue it was near black, the mist and the greenness seemed utterly alien.

"Su-Shaklan," said Aku beside Vanyi. Vanyi raised her eyes from the vision of green to the white spearhead of the mountain that stood guard over its northern flank, then let them fall again into the country called the Kingdom of Heaven.

And no wonder, if it struck all travelers so. It was beautiful beyond comprehension.

"You must go there," said Aku, pointing. Vanyi followed the line of her hand to the cliff. For a moment she saw nothing but sheer drop; but slowly she perceived the line of the track, twisting back and forth down the precipice, shored with ledges. The bottom was out of sight, obscured by mist and distance.

Vanyi brought herself sternly to order, and faced the guide and what she had said. "You're not coming down with us."

"You have no need of us," Aku said, "and we are not of that country, nor welcome in it. We agreed to bring you here. We've done that. We'll take our payment and go."

And if Vanyi refused to pay, she made it clear, it would be simple enough to arrange a fall over the precipice. The three husbands were sitting their oxen with perfect casualness, just near enough to separate Vanyi from the rest, just far enough away to maintain their unthreatening air. She considered that they were sixteen to the guides' four, but the guides had the advantage, at the moment, of position. She shrugged. She had never intended to play the guides false, whatever they might think.

"Chakan," she said. "Pay them as they ask. Half the bolt of scarlet, on the whitefoot ox."

"We're taking the oxen," said Aku calmly. "We'll leave you what's yours."

"Oh, no," said Vanyi, just as calm, with a hint of a smile. "We bought and paid for those oxen. And those packs. And those provisions. We'll keep them, if you don't mind. We may have need of them."

Daruya, bless her intelligence, had spoken a word to the Olenyai. They were as casual as the husbands, hands not too blatantly near to swordhilts, sitting their seneldi in a loose, easy, and quite impenetrable formation around the huddle of oxen.

Aku inclined her head slightly. "We need to eat," she observed, as if to the air.

"You have your own ox," Vanyi said, "and I notice that his pack is remarkably large and heavy." She smiled again, a fraction wider. "My thanks for a journey well guided. May your gods prosper you."

Aku understood the dismissal. She shrugged slightly, spreading her hands in a gesture half of resignation, half of respect. "Prosper well," she said, "if the gods allow."

ELEVEN

THE DESCENT INTO THE KINGDOM OF HEAVEN WAS HEART-STOPPINGLY STEEP. They dismounted to begin it, dropping one by one over the side of the mountain and picking their way along a narrow thread of a track, with a wall of stone on one side and empty air on the other. Daruya at least was aware that the guides were left behind and in no friendly mood. But no great stones rolled down from the summit to sweep them aside, and no arrows flew. They were as safe as they could be on so steep a slope, with seneldi that, though surefooted, were not mountain oxen.

Kimeri had been notably reluctant to begin the descent. She kept lagging behind, looking back at the summit. There was nothing there; the guides were gone, heart-glad to be rid of their charges.

Chakan, in the rear, met Daruya's glance. His own was watchful, his pace just quick enough to keep the child from stopping. He would guard Kimeri and see that she was not lost or fallen. Daruya sighed and fixed her mind on the track.

Climbing could be exhausting, but going down was worse. One had to brace constantly, even where the track pretended to be more or less level, running sidewise along the cliff-face. And one could see where one was going—downward a league and more, and god and goddess knew whether they could reach the bottom before night caught them all and pinned them to the precipice.

It had been morning when they began, not long after sunrise. At noon they halted. There had been halts before, too many of them in Daruya's mind, but necessary. Even the Olenyai could not go on without pausing, not on such a road as this.

This pause was longer, with time to eat leathery dried oxmeat and still more leathery dried fruit, and drink water that still tasted faintly of snow though it had been carried in leather waterskins since last night's camp. The beasts had a handful of corn each, which finished out the store of fodder. If there was no grass below, only green illusion, they would starve.

It occurred to Daruya as she sat on the stony ground and tried to chew a strip of meat somewhat tougher than the sole of her boot that they should long since have seen what they descended to. Morning's mists should have lifted. The valley should have opened below them. Yet it was still hidden; still featureless, an expanse of misty green with the Spear rising out of it.

"Wards," said Vanyi beside her, rubbing legs that must have ached as fiercely as Daruya's, grimacing as her fingers found a knot. "And Great Wards, at that. Do you feel how strong they are, and how old? They're anchored in mountains, with the Spear for a capstone."

"So they do have mages," Daruya said.

"Not necessarily. Mages could have been here long ago, set the wards, and died or gone away. The people who live here now might not even be aware of what protects them."

"How do we get in, then?" Daruya demanded.

"We knock on the door," said Vanyi, unperturbed.

"Are you sure there is one?"

"I'm assuming it. Our mages got in, after all. It can't be closed to people who come peacefully—just to invaders with weapons."

Daruya's eyes slid to the Olenyai, each with his two swords, his bow and quiver, and his other, carefully concealed armament.

"We'll get in," said Vanyi. "Swords or no swords."

The air grew warmer as they descended, until they had all packed their hats away, and their coats. The Olenyai kept their robes and veils, but the others were down to tunics and trousers or mages' robes when at last they came to the bottom of the cliff. It was a broad shelf of rock, bare of grass, and beyond that only air. A bridge stretched across it. Of what lay on the other side they could see nothing but mist.

The bridge was no solid work of stone such as they built in the empire. This was a wavering makeshift of wood and rope, swaying in the wind that swept down off the mountain. It was wide enough for an ox, more than wide enough for a senel. Whether it was sturdy enough . . .

Daruya's stomach ached with clenching. Her eyes burned. She should be able to see across the chasm. She could see perfectly well to the bottom of it: a long, long fall, and a tumble of rocks, and a river, its roar muted with distance. The drop was much deeper than the bridge was long; it had to be. And yet the bridge seemed to vanish into infinity.

She turned her face to the sky. It seemed very far away and very pale. The sun hovered on the rim of the precipice, as if it hesitated to abandon her in the trackless dark.

No one else was moving, either. Chakan had Kimeri on his shoulders and was calming his fretful senel with strokings and soft words. Vanyi stood on the first plank of the bridge. She stamped. The bridge echoed. "Solid enough," she said through the echoes. "We'll have to make sure none of the seneldi puts a foot through."

Or shied and leaped over the utterly inadequate rail of stretched rope and fell to its death. Daruya swallowed. Her throat was dry. She stroked the dun mare's neck. The mare was quiet enough, slick with sweat from the descent, and mildly annoyed that there was nothing to forage.

"Come then," Daruya said to her. "Let's get it over."

She rode past Vanyi, deliberately closing ears and mind to objections. The mare hesitated as her hoof touched the bridge, but she had always been valiant. Daruya urged her gently forward. She snorted, lowered her head to examine this oddity to which she must trust her weight, and advanced gingerly upon it. The echo made her stiffen, but she did not halt.

Daruya kept her eyes on the road directly ahead of her and tried not to think of the fact that the rails, chest-high on a short man, were knee-high on a rider mounted on a tall senel. If she fell, she would keep them both alive and bring them safely to earth. Her magery was strong enough for that. But it would be less trouble if she forbore to fall.

Nobody had followed her yet. They were all waiting to see if the bridge would hold her. She could not hear them breathing.

The mist ahead seemed impenetrable, but it came to her slowly that there was something in it. A shape—shapes. One on either side of the bridge. Massive, looming figures, narrow and tall. Men? Giants? Demons?

The mare was unafraid of what lay ahead. All her tension was for the unsteadiness of the bridge and the hollow booming of her hoofs and the sough of wind in the ropes. Daruya supposed she should have walked, but riding seemed more queenly somehow—more like the act of a Sunchild entering a new country.

The tall shapes grew slowly clearer. The faint maddening humming in her skull was the warding, she realized. She had never felt one so strong before, or so removed from human source. It might have been a power in the earth, for all the sense she had of the mages who had raised it.

She was glad suddenly that she had not yielded to temptation and flown on wings of magery, avoiding the bridge altogether. The wards would have armed themselves against her. But because she came quietly, riding as any woman could ride, they did no more than rattle her teeth in her skull. Even that muted with the raising of her shields.

It was not a warding against mages, then. Only against magery.

The mist was thin now, revealing glimpses: green of grass and tree, white of— was it roof? Tower? And directly before her, vast shapes of men, stone-stiff and stone-still, tall pillars that seemed to hold up the sky. Their faces were weathered and worn. Their hands were rigid at their sides. They stared blankly, eternally, across the bridge and the chasm.

They had been painted once—brilliantly, from the look of them. Under the paint was grey stone, bones of the mountains. All their power was in their stillness, and in their height even above one who rode on senelback. The Great Wards were not in them; they signified them, no more.

At first she did not see the men who stood beyond the pillars, dwarfed by them. But she heard them: the song of metal on metal in the armor that they wore, and the ring of armed feet on stone as they advanced. She halted her mare between the pillars and waited for them.

Fear was a dim and feeble thing. Curiosity was stronger by far. The armor that these men wore was as fantastical as the temples in Su-Akar. Every edge of it was flared and fluted. Its surfaces were carved, gilded, colored in eye-searing patterns. It covered them from head to foot. On their heads were helmets like temple towers, some visored with scowling demon-faces, a few open. Those she stared at. Plainsmen again, she thought, high-cheeked, narrow-eyed, bronze-skinned; taller than the men in Su-Akar, as tall as in the Hundred Realms, and while not slender, not nearly so broad and thick. They grew beards here, the first that she had seen in this part of the world: a thin straggle by northern standards, confining itself to chin and upper lip. They looked only vaguely ridiculous, and very stern.

Behind her the bridge boomed. The others had decided at last to cross it, more slowly than she had, but determined once they began. She stayed where she was. The guards would have to shoot past her to strike any of the rest.

"Greetings," she said in the language that her magery had taught her, "and well met, men of Su-Shaklan."

"Greetings," said the guard in the center, whose thin beard and mustaches brushed his breastplate. His armor was even more ornate than the others', his helmet higher, with a winged golden thing on the crest: dragonel, perhaps, or dragon proper. He did not say that she was well met. "You will give me your weapons if you wish to pass this gate."

Haughty man. She gave him in return the hauteur of an empress born. "I am unarmed, as you should see." All but the magery that she could not use, not here, and the small dagger in her boot, which she used for cutting meat. She lifted her chin a fraction higher. "Now may I pass?"

"Not alone," said the captain of the guard. His eyes slid past her to what she was already aware of, the knotting of people and animals at her back and on the bridge.

She nudged the mare aside. Vanyi's mean-eyed gelding pranced past her, snorting and tossing his horns. The mages followed, and the Olenyai, and Kimeri riding beside Chakan. Daruya remained where she was.

"If you would enter Su-Shaklan," said the captain of the guards, "you will give to us your weapons. None but a man of the kingdom may go about armed."

Daruya held her breath. Olenyai swords were more than edged blades; they held the honor of their master. They were not to be parted from, even in sleep.

And yet, one by one and following their commander's lead, the Olenyai surrendered their swords, their bows, their knives, and such other weapons as they could be seen to carry. That there were more, and many, hidden in the black robes, Daruya knew for a certainty. Either the guards did not know, or they did not care what weapons a stranger concealed.

She suspected the former. No one judged an Olenyas rightly at first. The robes and the veils were alarming enough, but the men in them were small, more often slender than not, and little given to posturing. They never saw the need.

They had given up their swords for the emperor's sake, for this embassy that he had sent. They would not forget the sacrifice. Nor would they hesitate to exact a price, if they could.

For the moment they were quiet, keeping their demon-eyes lowered, playing the humble strangers. It was not ill played. The guards ignored them, speaking to Daruya. "These animals of yours. They are clean?"

As clean as they could be after such a journey, she almost answered; but they were speaking of ritual. While she wondered how to reply, Vanyi said, "They are clean in the eyes of our gods. I speak for them as for the men who follow me."

The guards accepted that. Like the guides, they saw her grey age and reckoned her wise. The captain even inclined his head to her, mighty concession to a foreigner in this of all places in Shurakan. "And the woman, too? And the child?"

"All who are with me," said Vanyi, no sign of a smile in her voice, but Daruya sensed her amusement even through her shields and the hum of the wards.

The captain turned abruptly on his heel. "You will come," he said.

TWELVE

FROM THE OTHER SIDE OF THE GREAT WARDS, SHURAKAN SHOWED ITSELF clear, unveiled and unconcealed. The pillars of its gate stood on the rim of a valley like a goblet, slopes and terraces descending half a league and more to a lake like a blue jewel with a broad rim of green. Beside the lake was a city of dark roofs and white towers. Other, smaller cities and towns and villages scattered through the valley and up the slopes of its sides. On the terrace just below and northward of the pillars, under the Spear of Heaven, rose a second city. Its towers were airier than those of the city in the valley, its walls higher, broader, running along the edge of the terrace. Between terrace and walls, the city stood nigh half a league high; only a bird would wish to fall from that wall.

Vanyi's mages of the Gates had named both cities to her, and she to Daruya a few evenings since beside a fire in the mountains. That in the valley was the Winter City, that on the height its companion of the Summer. The high ones, the lords and princes, court and king and queen and all their followers and dependents, traveled from one to the other in the long round of the year. Winter saw them below in the green warmth of the valley, drinking sweet water from the lake and hunting on the forested slopes to south and west. Summer brought sullen heat and pestilence and stinging flies, and sent the court fleeing up the mountain to cool airs and clean stone amid which they set their gardens. Only the poor remained below, and the holy men and women in their temples, and the folk who tilled the rich land beside the lake, preparing for the harvest and the winter and the lords' return. Then the Summer City was silent in its mantle of snow, and only the hardy remained, and the holy ones in the temples, and those commanded for their sins to hold the city until summer came round again.

It was summer now—the very day of High Summer, Daruya realized with a start, the greatest of festivals in the empire, and she had forgotten it. The Summer City was full of princes. On this longest day of the year, with the sun sinking fast below the mountains but light lingering in the pellucid sky, the streets were thronged with people, in the music of bells and drums. They all wore the faces of plainsmen as she knew them in the Hundred Realms, familiar and yet subtly strange: features both stronger and finer, hair dark but often with a ruddy sheen, men as tall as she and broad with it, women walking proud in long coats and wide-legged trousers. Many wore the open-sided robes of temples, men and women shaven-headed alike, bare alike beneath the robes, and no more shame in them than she might have seen in kilted tribesmen of Keruvarion's own mountains.

They had no fear. It was an odd thing to think as she rode among them walled in guards, but it was true. They stared at the strangers, commented openly on demon-eyes and shadow-gods and foreign horrors, seemed not to care if they were understood, or if the strangers might take revenge for what was said of them. They looked on what to them was superstition and terror, and they shrugged at it. They were the people of the Kingdom of Heaven. Their gods defended them. Nothing could touch them or do them harm.

And yet a Gate had fallen here. They knew fear of that, surely, and hate. She did not find it in the faces that she passed. Even the poor seemed decently fed and reasonably content.

They had entered the city through its eastern gate, the gate of the dawn that looked upon the pillars and the mountain wall. Once past the gate they turned northward and made their way up a road not much wider than a cart-track in Asanion. Here it was a broad thoroughfare. Blank walls lined it, set with elaborate gates. Those that were open looked in on the jeweled extravagance of temples, or on gardens full of flowers, lit with lamps in the dusk.

Ahead of them rose a greater wall than any, strung with lights like a necklace of firestones. Its gate was of bronze, the pillars like those of the kingdom's gate, mighty man-shapes in postures of guard. These were freshly painted, their armor gilded, their helmets ornamented with lamps.

As with all gates once the sun had set, this one did not open for them, but one lesser, to the side of the great gate, where new guards waited to relieve the old. The guardians of the pillars turned without speaking and went back to their duty, unmindful of the dark or the hour. The guardians of the palace—for it could be nothing else—took them in hand with as little ceremony.

First they wished to separate the strangers from their animals. Daruya would have protested that people who had never seen a senel could not know how to care for a herd of them, but Vanyi was before her. "Kadin, go with them. Show them what to do."

Daruya could hardly quarrel with that. Kadin surveyed the persons waiting to take charge of the beasts, and was surveyed in turn. He was by head and shoulders the tallest there, and dark to invisibility outside the light of torches, but for the gleam of his eyes. After a long moment a man in a coat that swept the ground, which seemed to indicate rank here, held up his hand and said, "Show us."

The others eased at that, as if at a master's command. Kadin went away with them, with seneldi and oxen following. Vanyi and Daruya and Kimeri, the two remaining mages and the Olenyai, went onward on foot into the lamplit palace.

Daruya would remember little of that first sight of the Ushala, the palace of the brother-king and sister-queen in the Summer City of Shurakan. Lamps, she remembered those, burning perfumed fat and faintly rancid oil. Corridors that went on and on. Courtyards walled in darkness. Expectation that, tired and filthy and road-weary as she was, she must face the king and the queen and be as royal as they.

But she was not asked to suffer that. She was taken through the heart of the palace and out into its gardens and thence to the walls, where stood a row of houses. Guesthouses, the guards said, with an intonation that made her think *pest-houses,* houses set apart for the victims of a plague. All but one were dark. That one was waiting, ready for them, and it was surprisingly pleasant. Its rooms were not large but airy and clean, clustered round a courtyard in which was a fountain, and flowers sending sweet scents into the night. There were servants, soft-footed quiet people who offered baths, food, drink, rest.

Daruya took them all, one after the other. Vanyi stayed with her, and Kimeri. The others went away with most of the servants to baths and food and rest of their own. Chakan would have stayed, but the servants were persuasive, and Daruya commanded him. "You're dropping on your feet. Go and sleep, and come back to nursemaid me in the morning."

Vanyi she could not compel so, nor did she overmuch wish to. There were great basins full of steaming water for both the women, and a smaller one for Kimeri, who for once was too tired to object. The servants were quiet and skilled. Daruya fell asleep under their hands; woke with a start to find herself lying on soft cloths, having the aches stroked out of her.

Vanyi lay almost within reach, much wider awake than she, and palpably on guard. Daruya knew a moment of shame—she should have been as wary, she who had her daughter to think of. But there was no danger here. All her senses assured her of it.

They were still assuring her of it when she woke to a dazzling-bright morning and Kimeri bouncing on her stomach, caroling, "Mama, see! See where we are!"

Daruya barely had time to scrub the sleep out of her eyes before Kimeri was dragging her to the window through which all the light was coming. It dazzled her; and yet it was not sunlight. That was away out of sight to the eastward. She was receiving the full force of it reflected from the Spear of Heaven, blinding white and seeming to hang directly before her, with a brief dip of valley between.

The house, she realized with the sluggishness of the barely awake, was built into the palace wall. There was nothing below her window but eventually—very eventually—the valley's floor.

Kimeri scrambled up onto the window's broad sill, laughing with delight. "Mama, isn't it wonderful? We're as high up as birds!"

"We were higher in the mountains," Daruya said. "And on the bridge."

"But we couldn't *fly* there." Kimeri leaned out as if she intended to do just that.

Daruya barred her with a stiffened arm. She had not been this animated since Starios, nor this openly inclined toward mischief. It was a relief in its way, but Daruya found herself wishing that the child could have clung to her unwonted docility for a day or two longer. "You won't be flying here," Daruya said sternly. "You'll scare people. They don't have any magic, and they don't know about people who do."

"I can teach them," said Kimeri.

"Not today," Daruya said. That quelled her, for a wonder. She let herself be swung back into the room and inspected. Rather to Daruya's surprise, she was clean, combed, and dressed, and yes, fed. The servants were marvels indeed, if they could accomplish that much with this young imp.

Kimeri wriggled, impatient with motherly fussing. "May I go now, mama? Chakan says I can play in the garden with Hunin if you say yes."

"I say yes," said Daruya. "But only the garden, and only as long as Hunin says you may."

"Yes, mama," said Kimeri meekly.

Her tone warned of disobedience, but not for the moment. Daruya decided to let it suffice. Hunin was the eldest of Chakan's Olenyai, sober and sensible. He would keep Kimeri in hand, nor hesitate to call on a mage if there was need.

With Kimeri there probably would be.

Daruya sighed and let her go. Time enough to worry when the child lost patience with her limits and went about testing them. For now Daruya would see what could be had in the way of bath and breakfast—another bath, yes indeed; after so long with nothing to bathe in but icy streams and water in waterskins, she meant to be clean from morning till morning, and every moment between.

Vanyi's waking was easier and somewhat earlier, her bath simple and brief, her breakfast likewise. Once she had disposed of both, she said to the servant who attended her, "I would speak with the queen. Whom shall I send with the message, and when may I be granted audience?"

The servant did not change expression, nor ask why Vanyi wished only to speak with the queen. He had been expecting the question, then, and he had an answer ready. "Madam should speak with the Minister of Protocol, since it is he who determines who shall and shall not address the children of heaven. This unworthy person may send one yet more unworthy with a message, if madam wishes."

"Madam does wish," said Vanyi. "Madam is called Guildmaster, or lady, or if one is suitably familiar, Vanyi."

"Lady," said the servant, bowing in the manner of this country: hands folded on breast, head bent low. She doubted that it was proper to bow in return.

The message went out as promised, but the answer was slow to come back. While Vanyi waited, she discovered that none of them was being held prisoner. They could come and go as they wished, not only in the palace but in the city. The guards who had brought them to this house had left them in the care of the servants, none of whom showed inclination to be a warrior or a jailer. They made no objection to Vanyi's ordering the house as she pleased, with Olenyai on guard, mages established in an inner room to set up wards and begin their search for the destroyers of Gates, and seneldi stabled, after some negotiation, in the house next door. Pastures they could not have, but they were given ample grain and fodder, and the courtyard was large enough for them to run in, two and three at a time.

It would do, Kadin conceded; he kept his position as groom and guard. He was avoiding the other mages. Naturally enough, Vanyi thought, though it grieved her. It would throb like a raw wound to see Miyaz and Aledi together, weaving their powers of dark and light. He made no effort to enter their sanctum, slept in a room in the house that he had made a stable, devoted himself to the care of the seneldi. He had even, since he came to the city, put off his violet robe and put on the kilt of his people. He wore it with an air that defied his Guildmaster to challenge it.

She did no such thing. When it was time for him to be a mage again, she would see that he did so. Now he would mourn as he must, without her to meddle. Jian had been lover and wife as well as lightmage. He was entitled to a certain extravagance of grief.

"A visitor, lady," said the servant whom, by the time the sun reached zenith and sank slowly westward, Vanyi thought of as her own. She was sitting in the room she had been given, watching the play of light over the valley and testing the strength of the Great Ward. It had no weaknesses that she could find.

When the servant spoke, she started out of a half-dream. "A messenger?" she asked.

"A visitor, lady," the servant repeated. "A guest who bids you welcome to

Su-Shaklan. We have given him the cakes of welcome, and the tea. Will the lady receive him in the room that is proper for such things?"

The lady would, and with alacrity, no matter what the servant thought of that. Vanyi was not noble born, to care for such silliness—unless of course it suited her.

The visitor was waiting for her in a room that faced the garden, nibbling the last of a plateful of cakes and sipping a tiny cup filled with the hot herb-brew of Shurakan. He was not, as she had still dared to hope, an emissary of the queen, not openly or obviously. He was a priest in a saffron robe, with a pattern of flowers painted on his shaven skull.

It took a moment to see the face between the robe and the paint. It was not a young face, wizened and weathered, but its eyes were bright, its smile sweet, showing an expanse of toothless gums as he rose and bowed. He did not bow as low as the servant did, Vanyi noted—there were degrees of reverence, then. This seemed to indicate respect but not servility, and a measure of equality.

His voice was sweet and rather high. It was not a eunuch's voice. There were eunuchs here, her Guardians had said, and all of them were priests, unmanned in the service of one of their bloodier goddesses. But he was not of that sect. His voice had a trained purity, as if he were a singer.

"Lady," he said, "it is well you are come, and well that I see you, come at last to Su-Shaklan. I greet you in the name of the gods and the gods' children, and all who are in this kingdom they make blessed."

It took Vanyi a moment to understand him. Magery could teach a language, but not its odder nuances. Some of these were very odd. She did not try to rival them, but said, "Greetings to you also, priest of the gods. My name is Vanyi, Master of the Guild of Mages in the empire of Sun and Lion."

The priest's eyes narrowed a fraction. He was wincing, she realized, and in the most delicate manner possible. "Lady. Ah, lady. We do not use such words here, if we are most properly polite. I am named Esakai, priest of Ushala temple, where the children of heaven pay their devotions."

He was telling her something, subtly. That she must not speak of mages here, yes, she had expected that. He had responded as a courtier might in requesting an outland barbarian not to relieve himself on the palace floor. The same delicate revulsion; the same careful consideration for the stranger's ignorance.

But that was not all he was getting at. "Are you a messenger of the queen?" Vanyi asked him.

The tilt of his head and the lift of his brow reminded her that they were both standing, and he was old, and his feet were no longer as sturdy as they had once been. She chose not to ignore him. Rudeness was not what the occasion called for; and if he meant to divert her, then he had misjudged his target. She sat in the chair opposite the one he had occupied, thus allowing him to sink back into it with a barely audible sigh of relief.

Which too was subtlety. She countered it again with blunt directness. "The queen sent you, then?"

"Oh," he said. "Oh, no, lady. Of course not. The daughter of heaven needs no unworthy mortal to speak for her."

"Then how does a mere mortal gain audience with her?"

"Why, lady," said the priest in limpid innocence, "he does not. Mortals are unworthy to gain the attention of the gods' own children."

"In my country," said Vanyi, "our ruler also is descended from a god, but he never shuns the company of his people. He walks among them as one of their own, and they love him for it."

"So do our people love the children of heaven," said the priest, unruffled, "but the children of heaven would never lessen themselves by walking on common earth."

"That was so once," Vanyi said, "in part of our empire. Its emperors, as they were then, became so rarefied that they had to take the earth to themselves or perish. The last of them mated with the sun-god's child and begot a new world in which the gods walk with men, and men give the gods their power to rule."

"How strange," said the priest. "How . . . unusual."

"That may be," Vanyi said. "But surely people do speak to the queen? She condescends, I'm told, when need demands."

"Ah," said the priest as if she had explained a matter that puzzled him sorely. "Ah, lady. The queen speaks, yes, for herself and in the times that she chooses. She never sends messengers or begs mortals to attend her. They come when the Minister of Protocol bids them come, and she comes as she wishes, or not."

Slowly Vanyi worked her way through the tangle of alien logic. "The queen chooses when and to whom she speaks. The Minister of Protocol decides who will speak to her, if she chooses to speak, which is her right and her decision. Therefore the queen sends no messengers. The Minister of Protocol, however . . . "

"The Minister of Protocol abides by the will of heaven. The queen and the king her brother may speak or not speak. That too is the will of heaven."

"I think," said Vanyi dryly, "that the Minister of Protocol has a great deal of power. Has he sent you to instruct me?"

"I came by the will of heaven," said the priest, "and of my own curiosity, to see what manner of people you are. The lowly mortals name you demons. I'm thinking that you are no such thing. But you are very strange—and your shadows most of all."

"What, my blackrobes?" Vanyi allowed herself to smile. "They're warriors of that empire which had to wed itself with the Sun or die. No demons; no creatures of terror. Merely men, bred and trained to defend their emperor."

"Very strange men," the priest said. "Were their mothers bred to demons, to make them strong?"

"We have no demons in Asanion," Vanyi said, "which is the name of their country. Nor in Keruvarion, which is the name of mine."

"There are demons everywhere," said the priest, "except in Su-Shaklan. Our prayers keep them out."

Their Great Wards kept them out, Vanyi thought. She did not say it. "Still, in Asanion, men look as these men do, as the lady does who rode with us, though she's taller than any of them. Their faces are like hers. They veil them for honor and for custom."

The priest shuddered delicately. "Ah, poor things, to be so ugly. Maybe they do descend from demons, though they deny it. Demons are very strong."

"Daruya is reckoned beautiful in our country," Vanyi said with a hint of sharpness, catching herself a moment too late, suppressing rueful laughter. She was as vain as that girlchild, and on her behalf, too.

"Ah," said the priest, mildly nonplussed. "You are strange."

"But human," said Vanyi, "and desirous of addressing the queen. Might the Minister of Protocol be persuaded to grant me a few moments of his time?"

"This mere mortal could hardly say, lady," said the priest.

"Venture a guess," Vanyi said with a flash of teeth.

The priest blinked. "Oh, that is beyond me, lady. It has been a great pleasure to speak with you. May I return, if your charity permits? I should like very much to hear more of this empire of yours, where demons call themselves men, and kings walk in the dust without fear of soiling their feet."

Vanyi inclined her head. She could keep him there if she tried, but she was not minded to do that. He would go back to his Minister of Protocol, she was sure, and report every word that they had said. Then, with any luck at all, the Minister himself would be curious enough to summon her—or to send a messenger with a better head for the heights.

She could wait. For a while. Then, with or without the mighty Minister, she would do as she had meant to do since she conceived this expedition.

THIRTEEN

DARUYA WAS BORED.

Everyone else had things to do. Vanyi was pressing for an audience with the queen. The mages had raised their wards and begun a working to discover what had broken the Gates. The Olenyai took turns on guard. Even Kimeri had occupation in plenty, what with the garden, the stable, and the discovery that Kadin the mage had no objection to the presence of a small girlchild as he went about his business with the animals.

Daruya was the odd one, the one who had no duty and no occupation. Vanyi did not need her to assist in the campaign for an audience with the queen—if anything she was a hindrance, what with the need to explain who she was and what she was and why she had come, and the delicacy of balancing her rank as princess-heir with the queen's rank as ruler of Shurakan. Kimeri needed her only to be there and to offer praise of the flowers she brought in great untidy armfuls, or the spotted cat-kit she retrieved from the straw of the dun mare's stall, or the bit of harness she had mended all by herself. The mages certainly did not need her; she had proved already, too often, that she overwhelmed their subtle workings with her great blaze of power. And when she went into the city, to the house where the Gate had been, to see what was there, she found Kadin in the empty echoing place with no need or want of her, and a shrinking from the light of her power that made her blind angry and inexplicably inclined to weep. She had nothing to do and no purpose here but to wait, and to hope that when Vanyi won through at last to the queen, Daruya would be permitted to speak in the emperor's name.

There was only so much she could do to occupy herself in the house they had been given. The servants needed no assistance, and looked askance at any offer of it. Kadin was not displeased to let her help with the seneldi, but she could not spend every moment of every day in their company. The Olenyai neither needed nor wanted her to take a turn on guard.

For a full hand of days she kept her patience reined in. She wandered about the palace, finding no obstacle to passage, merely polite stares and respectful bows. People spoke when spoken to. Some even addressed her before she addressed them, greeting her, inquiring as to her health and the health of her companions. They all seemed to know a great deal about the embassy, even to understand that it was an embassy and not an invasion of demons from beyond the Worldwall. It was not a matter of importance, they indicated with glance and gesture and inclination of the head, but it was pleasant to see strangers here where strangers came so seldom.

"You'll take back the tale of us, I'm sure," said one exquisite courtier in a coat that trailed behind him, from beneath what had at first seemed a towering helmet but revealed itself to be an edifice built of his long lacquered hair. "Your empire would wish to know how we order the world in Su-Shaklan."

"It is curious, yes," Daruya replied with careful courtesy. "It's always eager to learn the ways of strangers."

"It will learn much from ours," said the courtier. "Why, it might even become civilized, and your emperor be judged worthy to address our children of heaven."

Daruya stared at him. It dawned on her with the slowness of incredulity that he was calling her a barbarian and her emperor an inferior monarch, unfit to stand in the presence of Shurakan's divine rulers. Her first impulse was to laugh; her second, to box this idiot's ears. She suppressed both. "My emperor is the son of a god," she said stiffly.

"Ah," said the courtier, polite. "How pleasant. Is it a god we know?"

"We call him the Sun," she said more stiffly still.

"Ah," the courtier said again with an expression of mounting ennui. "A great god, yes. Very great. But not one of ours."

They were not interested. That was the maddening thing, the thing that Daruya would never have credited if she had not seen and heard it. This little sipping-bowl of a kingdom fancied itself great; looked on the mighty realm of Sun and Lion, and smiled as at the fancy of a child; called its lords mere barbarians, and disparaged its god with a shrug of sheerest indifference.

How tiny this realm was, how minute the concerns of its people, how very narrow their minds. She would have been happy to open their smug little skulls with an axe.

The palace was too small for her grand fit of temper. She walked right out of it, with an Olenyas to keep her shadow safe: Yrias, who was young and diffident and too shy to stop her. He would be her protection against Chakan's wrath when the captain of Olenyai discovered that she had ventured the streets of the Summer City without him.

They were as steep as ever and as narrow, and as straitly walled. It was like walking between cliffs in the mountains, except for the gates that opened here and there, and the people who went back and forth in a jostling crowd. No one rode here, even on an ox; they were all afoot, many laden down with mountainous packs or trotting between the shafts of a wheeled cart in which sat a toplofty noble or a painted-faced lady or a mound of roots and greens for the market.

Common people, Daruya had come to realize, dressed as she did, in trousers and hip-long coat. People of rank wore coats of increasing length, until the princes swept about in elaborate garments that trailed behind them, worn over the same simple shirt and wide-legged trousers as that affected by the lowest urchin—though of cut and color befitting their station. Her good plain clothes, which in

Starios would have marked her for what she was, here made her seem a commoner, and not a wealthy one at that.

The distinction was not as sharp as it might have been. She saw a princeling give place to a man in a coat that hung only to his knees, because the latter was larger and older and walking with ponderous dignity. The prince acted as if he were doing the man a favor; the man acted as if he had expected that favor and would have been shocked not to receive it.

Age mattered, she had already observed. Size did, too, it seemed. And dignity. But a prince was still a prince. The queen and the king still were thought of as equal to the gods. Everyone bowed to divinity and yielded place to it, but when priests walked past, unless they marched in procession, they had no more precedence than anyone else. It all seemed very complicated and very hard to make sense of.

There were temples everywhere. Asanion's thousand gods seemed to be mirrored here in Shurakan, if not doubled and trebled. Every god had his priesthood, too, and every family gave at least one child to a temple. She saw a gaggle of such children in the care of an erect, stern woman, being herded toward a sweetseller's stall. They were reciting as they ran, in eerie unison: "The gods are all. The gods are one. We are all one in the eyes of the gods."

Priests all wore the same robe, although its color might change with the god and the temple. Children of princes stood equal there to children of beggars. Daruya stopped to ask the woman who herded the children, waiting till each had been given its fistful of sweetness and squatted in a line to eat it, perched like birds on the low wall that ran from the sweetseller's stall to that of a maker of shoes. "You *are* all one?" Daruya asked. "Truly?"

The priestess stared at her, curious but not hostile, and unafraid of her yellow eyes. "All of us," she said, "yes. Hush now, Kai-Kai, you know you like the redspice buns better than the honeytits."

The child sulked but ate her bun, reminding Daruya forcibly of Kimeri in a similar fit of indecision. Daruya smiled at her. She would not smile back, though she stared as hard as the priestess had. "So everyone is the same in the gods' eyes. And yet you have divisions; you have princes and you have beggars."

"Of course," said the priestess. "That's how the gods ordered the world. But we're all the same in the end. We all die."

"Even your children of heaven?"

The priestess' lips thinned. "You are a foreigner. You don't understand."

"But I would like to."

"No," said the priestess. "You only think so." She gathered her charges together abruptly and swept them onward, most still eating, and all sticky-fingered.

Daruya stayed where she was. She had meant to discomfit the priestess, there was no denying it, but she had not intended to feel guilty about it. It was time these smug self-satisfied fools had a comeuppance.

On the other side of the street, between a goldsmith and the extravagantly gilded gate of a temple, was a place that looked interesting. Its gate opened on a courtyard, which was a garden as they often were here. Low tables were set in and about the garden, so low that they had no need of chairs, and people sat at them on silken rugs, sipping from little cups or nibbling what looked like rarefied examples of the sweetseller's wares. Nearly all of the people were men, and few of them were priests. The coats that Daruya could see trailed in long sweeps on the clipped grass or the patterned stones of pavement.

This, she saw as she drew closer, was a teahouse—tea being what people drank here when they did not drink gaggingly sweet wine or, even worse, the milk of oxen. It was a poor excuse for a quencher of thirst, being but hot water poured over a handful of mildly bitter herbs, but they made a great fuss over it, with ceremonies devoted to it, and whole houses that served nothing but tea and sweet cakes.

In Starios this would have been a tavern frequented by the lordly sort. Daruya had spent many an evening in such a place, drinking and gaming and seeing what trouble she could get into without incurring her grandfather's wrath. It was to the upper room of one that she had taken a certain gold-and-ivory beauty of a lordling, and conceived an heir without the complication of a husband.

Shurakani teahouses were quieter places, from the look of this one. Her arrival caused a mild flutter—very mild. She was not asked to leave. When she sat at a table, a soft-footed servant glided up, deposited on the table a delicate night-blue pot and an even more delicate gilt-rimmed cup, and glided away.

The pot was almost too hot to touch. The cup was cool, no larger or more substantial than an eggshell. The scent that wound with steam from the spigot of the pot was as delicate as the rest, with a suggestion of flowers.

She thought of calling for ale, and raising a tumult until she got it. But she was too well trained to do that. Pity. She was bored, and growing more bored by the heartbeat. She poured tea into the cup, found it an exquisite shade of golden amber. Its flavor was subtly bitter and subtly sweet. It was like the tea of ceremony, somewhat, but darker, stronger: more fit for use.

Conversations that had paused with her presence had resumed. They were not all as quiet as she might have expected, considering the elegance of the teahouse and its servitors. One table crowded with young elegants was discussing in detail the wares of a certain house of pleasure on a street called the Path of the White Blossoms. At another, three or four grey-mustached men discoursed lengthily on the nature, number, and kind of the gods.

"Incalculable, innumerable, and ineffable," said a man who sat alone near Daruya. He had been watching her for a while; she had been undertaking to ignore him. That was rather difficult, as it happened. He was not as young as the young elegants, not nearly as old as the grey philosophers. His hair was black with ruddy lights, worn in a club at his nape. His mustaches hung just below the line of his shaven jaw. His shoulders were broad beneath his coat, which was long enough to gather in folds on either side of him as he sat cross-legged on the grass. She thought he might be tall: he sat eye to eye with her, and she sat higher than most of the men round about.

He met her stare with one as frank, and grinned at her frown. "What, stranger, do I offend you? Don't people take one another's measure in your country?"

"How do you know what country I come from?" she demanded.

He laughed and gestured in a graceful sweep: her hair that escaped all bonds she set on it, her eyes, her face, her height that was rather extraordinary here. He had long hands, she noticed, and tapering fingers; but they were not either weak or effeminate. They looked, in fact, quite strong. "You would be one of the people from beyond the Wall," he said. "The demon's daughter, I'd suppose—and is that one of your husbands behind you?"

Yrias' indignation was so sharp that Daruya started. It was on her behalf, of course—it always was. She wanted to slap him. Instead she said to the man who spoke so boldly, "None of them is my husband. They're my guards. And I am not a demon's get!"

"Oh, surely," said the man with no evidence of contrition. "You are human, yes, the priests say that you say so. Pardon me for needing to confirm it."

"I suppose," she said with acid precision, "that it's only to be expected. You know no race but your own."

"What, there are others?"

He was laughing at her. People who laughed at Daruya never escaped unscathed. Yet, because he was an innocent in such matters, she said sweetly enough, "Ah, but you people have never seen any faces but your own. I have kin who look like you. And kin who look like my warriors, or like me. And kin who are taller than I, and black from head to foot. All bow to the Lord of Sun and Lion, who rules from the city in which I was born."

"Truly?" The man swept up his pot of tea and his cup and a basket fragrant of sweetness and spices, and established himself boldly and shamelessly at her table, facing her across it, favoring her with what no doubt he reckoned an enchanting smile. "Tell me more of all these people who sound like men and demons and dark gods all mixed in together."

"They're all men," Daruya said, snappish. "And you are presumptuous. Did I invite you to share my table?"

"You answer when I ask questions," the man said as if that countered her objection. He dipped cooled tea from her cup into the roots of a blossoming tree and filled it again, and held it out to her till she had perforce to take it. He smiled as she sipped, transparently approving. "My name is Bundur of House Janabundur."

She raised her brows. Was she supposed to be awed? "My name," she said, "is Daruya of House Avaryan."

His brows rose in echo of hers. "That is a proud house?"

"That is the royal house," she said. "Is yours?"

He shrugged, nonchalant. "I'm not the king, and not likely to be, for which I praise the gods. Are you likely to be queen?"

"If I outlive my grandfather," she said, "yes."

"And he let you come here. That was generous of him."

She felt the slow flush climb her cheeks. He saw it—she traced it in the gleam of his eyes. Narrow black eyes above proud cheekbones. He did look remarkably like a plainsman. A very handsome, very presumptuous plainsman. Sharply, angrily, she said, "I am my grandfather's envoy."

"You, and not the woman who is said to lead your embassy?"

Oh, he was a clever man, and he knew it, too. "Vanyi leads. I speak for the emperor when the time comes."

"Emperor," he said, musing, downing a cup of his own tea and a cake from the basket as he did it. "That is a king, yes? But more than a king?"

"A king of kings."

"How can there be more than one king?"

"In the same way that there can be more than one god. Kings are common in the world. Emperors are rarer. There were two, for a while. Now there is one."

"One killed the other?"

"One died. His son married the daughter of the other. Their son was emperor. And so it continued."

"Ah," said Bundur. "An emperor is only a king after all."

"He is not," Daruya said. "Kings bow to him. He rules kings. Your whole kingdom would fit into a minor barony, with room left to graze whole herds of oxen."

"Our kingdom is the heart of the world," said Bundur, "its model and its pattern. Your emperor should have let his sister rule also, as the gods decreed."

"Our emperors have no sisters. Or brothers. The god gives each royal descendant one child, and one child only. That child rules."

Bundur tossed his head. "No! You don't say it? What did your first king do to offend the gods?"

"Rather a great deal," said Daruya with sudden wryness. "But that was supposed to be a gift."

"I think he cursed you." Bundur had to drink another cup of tea and devour another cake to calm himself. "What if your child dies?"

"Your child's child inherits."

"And if there is none?"

"The god provides," said Daruya. She found herself running her hand along her thigh. Her right hand, with its burning brand. She was not tempted to turn it palm upward to show him what she carried, the god's seal and his promise that her line would not perish from the earth. It was no secret in the empire, but neither was it for every eye to goggle at.

All the more so here. Her tea had cooled, but she drank it. It was wet; it quenched thirst after a fashion.

"Do you have sisters?" she asked Bundur abruptly.

"Seven of them," he answered with some complacence. "Three gave themselves to temples. Two married into families of distinction. One is still unbound by either husband or god. One was our sacrifice."

Daruya frowned.

He saw fit, at that, to explain. "You don't have that? When sickness comes, or the gods' displeasure, one child takes it all on herself. If she lives, the plague or the curse is ended. If she dies, likewise. The rest of her family is safe."

"That is barbaric," said Daruya.

"It's great honor," he said, unoffended, "and great courage. It increases the distinction of the house. I would have been the sacrifice myself, but I had no brothers. I wasn't allowed."

"If she had had no sisters, would it have been allowed?"

"Of course not," said Bundur. "There must always be one sister and one brother. The gods decreed it."

"Even if only one child is born?"

"Then," he said, "the master of the house takes another wife. Or the mistress another husband. Or they adopt a child, if those expedients fail."

"How utterly strange."

He regarded her in mild surprise. "You don't do that? Ah—but of course. Your gods allow one child. What do you do when none is born at all?"

"In our line that never happens. In other lines, the lord takes another wife. Or adopts an heir."

"See, then? We're more alike than you think."

"Our women don't marry more than once at a time."

"Yet your men take many wives?"

"Only in Asanion," she said, "where the people look like your demons."

"Ah," said Bundur. "Demons. They do as they please."

He seemed to think that that explained everything. She drew breath to set him right, sighed instead, let it go.

"You have no husband," he said, "and yet you have a daughter."

She stiffened. Her hand, reaching for the pot to fill her cup again, stopped short of pouring tea over the table and into his lap. "I have a daughter," she said, tight-lipped. "Is that a sin in your country?"

"Only if you bear no son to keep her company."

"There will be no son," said Daruya, "whether I marry or no."

"Do you know that?"

"I know that." She filled the cup. Her hand was steady. She was proud of it. "Women of my country are not in the habit of discussing intimate matters with strangers in teahouses."

"Ah, so you are different. I thought so."

Her glare should have shattered him where he sat. He only smiled. "If this were my own city," she said deliberately, "and you had said such things as you have said to me, you would be whipped and cast out."

"But this is my city," he said, still smiling, "and I speak as I reckon it proper to speak. You're sadly ugly, lady of the yellow eyes, but supremely interesting. May I speak with you again?"

She could not speak at all, for outrage.

He rose and bowed as low as she had ever seen a man bow in this country. He must wash his teeth in his own piss, she thought viciously, to keep them so white and to display them so freely. "I'll visit you," he said.

She lunged. But he was gone, deceptively swift. She found herself on her knees, trembling with rage, in a circle of silence. All the eyes that had been fixed on her were now fixed scrupulously elsewhere. The voices began again after the faintest of pauses.

She set hands to the table to hurl it in the nearest politely averted face. A brawl would be splendid, would be glorious.

Would be most inadvisable in this country where her rank mattered nothing and her lineage met with massive indifference. If, that is, she could have started one at all. Teahouses did not seem given to the wilder extremes of conduct. One needed wine for that, or bad ale—the worse, the better.

Carefully, meticulously, she gathered herself together and rose to her feet. It did nothing for her temper to discover that Bundur, damn him to the lowest of the hells, had paid her reckoning, or that, if he had not, the teahouse would not have accepted her good imperial gold.

"You will want to change that," said the polite personage in charge of the proceedings, from her seat under the tallest of the flowering trees. "The Street of the Moneyers takes gold sometimes, to melt down for the goldsmiths. One of them can give you proper coinage of our kingdom."

Daruya could have overturned that table, too, and the woman with it. But she was still in command of herself, still mindful of her position, although she would have given all her despised gold to have been able to forget. She said something not too rude—the personage did not bridle, and did not call for the watch, or whatever did duty for that here—and got herself out before she said or did something truly inadvisable.

FOURTEEN

WHILE DARUYA WAS DISCOVERING THE EXTENT OF HER SELF-CONTROL, VANYI was testing her own against a master of obstruction.

It had taken her five days to reach the Minister of Protocol. Five days of incessant campaigning, intriguing, and outright threats, against a phalanx of functionaries who made the Golden Palace in Asanion seem a haven of simplicity. But she had ruled the Mageguild for forty years, and she had learned to cut through obstruction with a sword of purest obstinacy. If a functionary would not pass her to the next highest of his kind, she did it herself, got up and walked to the office that she saw in the functionary's mind. If the one above him, growing wise, sought to prevent her by slipping out the back door, he found her waiting there. If he set guards on her, she called her shadows forward. Olenyai, even swordless, were dangerous fighters. No one in Shurakan could match them. Shurakan, after all, had never known war, nor had occasion to make an art of it.

And so, step by step, she won her way to the gate, as it were: to the Minister of Protocol, who alone barred her way to the queen. There she found herself halted.

The Minister of Protocol did not affect the trappings of power. He wore a coat that fell discreetly to his ankles, the color of clouds, with the merest suggestion of embroidery about the hem. His shirt was simple, his trousers undistinguished by excessive width or richness of fabric. He wore his hair in a severe knot at his nape, and his thin beard and greying mustaches at an unassuming length, barely past the collar of his coat.

She, who had mastered the art of discretion for herself long since, regarded him in jaundiced approval. He offered her tea. She accepted it and the cakes that came with it, ritual welcome everywhere in Shurakan. One could judge the degree of one's welcome, she had been told, by the quality of the tea and the kind and quantity of the cakes.

If so, then she was barely welcome here. The tea was simple, without adornment of flowers or sweetness. The cakes were plain redspice buns just touched with honey, and there were only two for each of them. But, considering the Minister of Protocol and his studied simplicity, she suspected that the frugal refreshment was a statement not of her insignificance but of his desire to be thought a harmless fool.

That was a game she too could play. She drank her tea and ate both of her buns and sat waiting for him to begin, wearing an expression of mindless amiability.

He might be the most powerful man in Shurakan, but he lacked one thing that

Vanyi had a world's worth of: time. Her whole duty at the moment was to speak to the queen. His was manifold, and not all of it could wait for him to conquer her with superior patience.

It was he, then, who spoke first, after the pot had been emptied and the basket of buns stripped bare. He chose the weapon of directness, as she had expected. The subtle never understood how predictable they could be when they tried to take Vanyi off guard. "Tell me why it is so urgent that you speak with the queen."

"Surely," said Vanyi, still wearing her amiably vague expression, "her majesty is accustomed to greeting embassies from outland royalty. It's a frequent duty of our imperial house."

"Surely," he responded with a thin smile, "their celestial majesties are both accustomed to receive strangers in audience, when the press of their duties permits. You can be received . . . " He consulted a book that lay on his worktable, not the rolled and cord-bound books of Vanyi's part of the world but a strange thing, plaques of horn as long as a man's arm and as wide as his hand, hinged and jointed together. His finger ran down the long closely written columns. "Their majesties will admit you to their presence on the fourth day of the eighth round of the bright moon."

Even with magery Vanyi needed a moment to render that into the reckoning she knew. When she did, she heaved a mighty sigh. "Oh, come, don't be ridiculous. That's five rounds of the moon from now. I'll confer with her majesty within this round, and sooner if possible."

"Their majesties," said the Minister of Protocol, "have many matters of import to occupy them. You are fortunate that they can see you before the new year."

Or, his tone implied, that they would see her at all.

He was a subtle man, enclosed within himself, but he let her see what passed behind his bland face. He loathed magic, despised mages. He believed that foreigners should summarily be cast from the kingdom. But for deep-grained courtesy and a not entirely illogical suspicion that Vanyi might prove useful to him or to the rulers he served, he would have refused to contend with her at all.

She sat back in her chair, rather thoroughly at ease. "Very well then. Tell me why I shouldn't just walk past you and hunt out the queen for myself."

"Tell me why you refuse to speak to the king."

Vanyi raised a brow. "Rhetoric for rhetoric, is it? Would the king allow me to pollute his presence?"

"The son of heaven is no friend to what you are," said the Minister of Protocol, "but he knows the value of circumspection. He would admit you. As he will, on the fourth day of the eighth round of the moon."

"By which time," said Vanyi, "with any luck at all, our embassy will be finished and we'll be gone. Don't you want to hurry us through and be rid of us?"

Clearly the Minister of Protocol would not have minded that. Equally clearly, his duty required that he impede her in any way he could. "You may not address the daughter of heaven alone in the absence of her brother. That is never done."

"No?" Vanyi inquired. "That's odd. I distinctly heard one of your underlings granting a party of priests an audience with her majesty at the same time that same underling arranged for his majesty to participate in a rite of purification for a temple."

"Those were minor matters," said the Minister of Protocol, unruffled. "Embassies are of greater import, and involve both children of heaven inseparably."

"But ours is a minor embassy, you've all been careful to make that clear to us. Our empire is as nothing to your celestial kingdom. Our emperor can never be equal to your queen and her king. Our gods bow at the feet of your myriad divinities. All of which," said Vanyi, smiling sweetly, "is so self-evident that surely even you can't deny we're insignificant enough to speak to the queen alone."

"That is not done," said the Minister of Protocol.

"Why? Are you afraid she'll let us corrupt her?"

"The children of heaven are incorruptible."

"Therefore you have nothing to fear."

"What is there to fear?" asked the Minister of Protocol. "What haste compels you to press for an audience before the time their majesties have allotted?"

Vanyi kept her smile, though it hurt. "I don't suppose," she said, "you know what became of the man we lost here, or the Gate he guarded."

"One of your people has died? Please accept my condolences."

Vanyi met his blandness with blandness. "Let's suppose you do know, since I've been assured that all knowledge in Shurakan comes to you before it reaches their majesties' ears. You don't think that would have ended it, did you, to break our Gate and kill our Guardian?"

"No rumor of such has come to me," said the Minister of Protocol. His mind was as blank as his face, and as smoothly innocent. "You speak of . . . that, yes? That art of yours." His nostrils thinned. "It was suffered here by the grace of the daughter of heaven and by the silence of her brother. If it failed, or if its servant proved too weak for his task, that is no concern of ours. So it was agreed when her majesty permitted the building of the temple that housed your Gate."

"Oh, I'm not blaming you," Vanyi said. "But if you do know anything of it, or if the queen does, we'd welcome the knowledge. The man we lost was dear to us."

"And his Gate," said the Minister of Protocol, "dearer still."

That was false, but Vanyi saw no profit in saying so. "You do understand why I should speak to the queen. What would destroy a Gate and a Guardian might not hesitate to destroy a kingdom."

"If that kingdom were such as the Gate was, perhaps. Ours is clean of such taint."

"Is it?" Vanyi asked. "Su-Shaklan is warded by magic. How else do you think it's kept itself so safe for so long?" She stood, bowed slightly: an inclination of the head. "I'll speak with you again. And then, I'm sure, with the queen."

———

"And you left him? Just like that?" Aledi the lightmage was not surprised, not as well as she knew Vanyi, but she was amply bemused.

Vanyi rubbed her aching eyes and thought of asking for a cool cloth to cover them. It was brutal work, waging war with ministers of protocol. "I launched my bolt and got out, yes. I thought I was being clever—showing him who was master. Probably I was a coward, not to mention a fool. If he believes me, I've talked myself out of a rather valuable weapon on our behalf."

"I doubt he will," Miyaz said. He looked tired himself. The room in which they were sitting, the inner one in which the two mages had drawn their circle and set up their magics, had already acquired a faint reek, somewhat of sulfur, somewhat of flowers, that spoke of power wielded often and strongly.

"They don't believe in magic here," he said. "They curse it and they fear it, and yet in their hearts they know there's no such thing. It's profoundly disconcerting."

Aledi rose from her cushion and knelt behind him, working the knots out of his shoulders. He rolled his head back onto her breast and sighed. She kissed the yellow-curled crown, just where the hair was thinning. "It's worse than disconcerting, at least to me," she said. "It's frightening. Kadin goes out, you know, and prowls—poor boy, he's all broken inside since Jian was lost. We found him in the house of the Gate. He was sitting in the middle of it, in dust and cobwebs that looked as if they'd been there for years and not for Brightmoon-cycles. He said what we were all feeling. 'People say it's haunted. But there's nothing here. There might never have been a Gate at all.'"

"Is he still there?" Vanyi asked a little sharply.

"Oh, no," said Aledi. "We made him come back with us. It wasn't the first time he'd been in that house. He went there the first morning after we came to the city. It's always the same, he says. Always empty."

"I sent him," said Vanyi, "that first day."

The two mages stared at her. Aledi looked mildly hurt. Miyaz was only weary. "I rather thought so," he said. "Why did you send us today?"

"To see if you felt what he's been feeling," Vanyi said.

Aledi bent her head, hiding her face in Miyaz's hair. Her voice came muffled, ashamed. "I was afraid to go before you commanded me. It was so much easier to stay here and make the circle, and not think about what we made it for."

"Today you were ready to think about that," said Vanyi. "Would you be willing or able to raise a circle in the house of the Gate itself, to see what you could find?"

Aledi shivered. Miyaz looked pale. "We'll do whatever you bid us do, Guildmaster," he said.

Vanyi considered them through the pounding in her skull. She had to make herself remember why she had brought these of all possible mages. The three who had died, Kadin who lived broken and grieving, had been stronger, wiser, bolder in the wielding of their power. These two were to have given her the graces of courtiers, well-bred as they were and raised to the Asanian High Court; they were to have been ambassadors more than mages, fellow warriors against the Minister of Protocol rather than against the less-than-shadow that had broken the Gate in Shurakan.

But she needed mages now, when she must be ambassador and win through to the queen by proper channels. Forcing her way with magery would only prove to the Shurakani that mages were to be feared and hated.

While she wasted her strength on the Minister of Protocol, these two had to be strong enough to raise and sustain wards about this house and to bolster Kadin in his watch on the house of the Gate. They were mages of great skill—she would hardly have chosen them otherwise—but she wondered, looking at them, if that skill would be enough. She said to them, "For now, rest easy. I won't ask you to do anything but what I've had you doing here. But be ready to help Kadin if he needs you—whether he asks you or no."

Asanians had one virtue, preserved even in the melding of their empire into Keruvarion. They took orders, and if they asked questions they did not press for answers. Miyaz closed his eyes and to all appearances went to sleep. Aledi clung to him and kept silent.

Vanyi levered herself up. The circle of power was quiet, the lamps that marked its wards burning steady. She could sleep, she thought, if no one interfered. Sleep would be a pleasure.

Her mind reached to the limits of its wards and found no danger. It touched Daruya—in a snit as usual, but not in trouble that Vanyi could discern—and Kimeri playing contentedly with a companion or two. Nothing to fear there, either. The other children meant her no harm beyond a small, shivery, delightful conviction that they had made friends with a demon-child. Only Kadin was cause for anxiety: he had gone back to the house of the Gate, to sit in the dimness and the empty silence that matched the condition of his heart.

He was not thinking of death, not at the moment. He was not thinking of anything at all.

Better nothing than death. Vanyi could not help him; he was not ready for that yet, if he would ever be. She left him alone, drew in the boundaries of her power, became simply herself again, and a bone-tired self at that.

Vanyi.

She started out of a drowse. A moment longer and she would have been asleep.

The voice spoke again, soft round the edges of her shields. *Vanyi, let me in.*

Temper would have refused, but habit opened a Gate in the wall of her mind. He entered as he had so often before, fresh and morning-bright—it was that on the other side of the world, and for an instant her yearning to be there was as sharp as pain.

"Estarion," she said without voice. "You woke me up."

He did not look remarkably contrite. "Oh, it's night there again, isn't it? Everything's backward. Do people have their faces in their bellies or on the backs of their heads?"

"Don't be silly," she snapped, but he had lightened her mood. Eased her headache, too, without her even being aware of it: a touch like a cool hand, a fading of pain. He never asked permission, never thought he needed to.

He looked about this room that was her mind's conception of itself, noted what had changed and what had not, and said, "I dislike this Minister of Protocol. What a fish-faced fool!"

"So he would like us to think," said Vanyi.

"He reckons himself clever and subtle and wise, and I suppose he is, by his lights. He's still a fool." Estarion leaned against a wall, insouciant as any young bravo in a tavern. His mind-self was much as his bodily self was; he did not affect the image of youth, nor feign more beauty than he had. That was rare, but it was also Estarion.

Vanyi resigned herself to his presence. She was not entirely displeased by it, though she would have welcomed the sleep that he had put to flight. He was a fairly restful guest. With her headache he had taken some of the dragging tiredness, smoothing it away as easily as he breathed.

"Do you know," he said, "you've done a great deal for so short a time in this place. I doubt a stranger would get so close to me in a hand of days."

"A stranger from the other side of the world would find you in her sitting room before she was well settled in it, pouring out wine and besetting her with questions."

"Well," he said, shrugging. "I suppose so. I've never been particularly careful of my station. Perhaps I should get myself a Minister of Protocol?"

"You already have one," said Vanyi. "He's sweet, elderly, and erudite, and you drive him to distraction."

"What? Who? Rezad? Is that what a Minister of Protocol is—a chancellor of the palace? Well then. Rezad definitely won't keep the filthy commons from my presence, and I'd have his liver for breakfast if he tried. He knows it, too. He's very wise, is Rezad."

"And very long-suffering."

"Rezad is Asanian. He expects to suffer for his emperor. If he didn't, he'd think there was something wrong."

Vanyi sighed. "This Minister of Protocol is no Rezad. He's going to give me what I ask—but I'll have to fight for it."

"Which is precisely why I call him a fool. It may be his duty to protect his queen and her king from importunate strangers, but an ambassador deserves greater consideration."

"An ambassador from you in particular?"

He flashed his white smile. "Oh, but I'm nothing on this side of the world! It's courtesy, that's all. Not to mention common sense. If I'm as terrible a monster of a mage as he must think, I could be mounting armies of dragons and preparing to descend on his kingdom."

"Are you telling me you aren't?" He grinned at her. She resisted the urge to slap him—too common an urge, and too easy to gratify. "Estarion, I need to sleep. Are you going to get to the point or will you go away and let me rest?"

He looked briefly guilty. Too briefly. "I wanted to see that you were well."

"And your heirs? Both of them?"

It was difficult to catch him off guard. He regarded her calmly, arms folded. "I see that they're well. Have you tanned their hides yet?"

"No," said Vanyi. "And I won't, unless they try something like that again. Daruya got us through the Gate. We'd have died without her. Did you know she was that strong?"

"She's Sun-bred and priestess-trained. All appearances to the contrary, she has remarkable discipline—when it suits her to remember it."

There, thought Vanyi. He was colder than he needed to be. Irked, and afraid, too. His heirs had abandoned him; that pricked his pride, at the very least, and roused him to the fact that if he lost them both, he was an emperor without an heir.

She did not soften her voice for that, or treat him more gently. "I know what Daruya is. I helped to train her. I'll tell you what worries me more. Ki-Merian. She hid herself from us all, and survived a Gatestorm that should have killed a child so young and so untrained."

"The god protected her," Estarion said. "And her own power, too." He drew a long shaking breath. "God and goddess. What I wouldn't give for an ordinary, common, simple, mischievous child without a drop of magery in its blood . . . "

"You'd be bored silly before the hour was out," said Vanyi. "Live with it, Estarion. You're a mage and the father of mages. They do what it suits them to do, and they make fools of us all when they're minded, and if they outlive us, why, it's a miracle, and the god's own mercy. We have nothing to do with it."

"That's a lesson I've never been able to learn." He straightened, unfolding his arms. "I'll let you sleep. I only wanted to know—"

"I know," said Vanyi. She said it more softly than she might have, after all. "Go on. I'll do what I can to keep your descendants alive and sane. If it will console you, I think they do that very well for themselves, all things considered."

He was consoled, perhaps. His farewell was like a brush of a hand, a flicker of a smile. She took them both down with her into sleep.

FIFTEEN

KIMERI IN SHURAKAN MISSED THE DEMON OF THE MOUNTAINS VERY MUCH AT first. But it was out there beyond the wards that were so little really to a mage with any power at all; and she was here, where it could never come. Someday she would find it again. She did not think that would be very soon.

She dreamed about it now and then. She saw it teaching words to the other demons of the mountains. None of them was as quick of wit as it was, and most of them still ate travelers for dinner, but it seemed content after its fashion.

It never did try to pass the wards into Shurakan. That, it was sure and Kimeri supposed, would shake its poor airy self to pieces.

She, who was fire and earth and water, too, was happy in Shurakan. That was a little surprising. She still had her other dreams, the ones about Gates, and the Guardian was still caught in the broken Gate. She tried more than once to go where the Gate was, but an Olenyas always caught her.

Once it was even Vanyi who was standing on the other side of the door Kimeri was going out of. Vanyi was coming in: she had her clothes on that she wore when she went to the palace and tried to talk to the queen. Kimeri should have been more careful, but she was looking for Olenyai and not finding any; she forgot to look for a mage.

Vanyi herded her straight back in, saying something about mothers who let children run wild in enemy territory. Kimeri had heard that before. When she could stop, which was all the way in and most of the way to Vanyi's rooms, she said in complete exasperation, "You have *got* to let me go out."

Vanyi's brows went up. "Have I, your highness?" she asked. "And why is that?"

She was being nasty and sweet at the same time. Kimeri was aggravated enough to tell her the truth. "Because the Gate isn't dead, and neither is the Guardian. He's trapped inside it. I've got to get him out."

"You've been having dreams, haven't you?" said Vanyi. But before Kimeri could say yes, she had them every night, and they were horrible, Vanyi went on, "There now. When people die, especially if they've been killed, we always want them to be alive again. We dream about it, we wish for it. But it doesn't bring them back."

"He *is* alive," Kimeri insisted. "I know he is. I hear him. He's trapped in the Gate. He doesn't know how to get out. If I went there, I could—"

"Maybe you could," said Vanyi, "someday, when you're older. If there's anyone to rescue from a Gate that's broken. But not now. It's not safe."

"He's trapped," said Kimeri. "He hates it. He wants to get out."

She was almost in tears. That was never a wise thing with grownfolk. It just convinced them that she was a baby, and too young to know anything.

Vanyi said things that she meant to be soothing, and handed Kimeri over to the servants and told them to feed her a posset and put her to bed. And never mind that the sun was only halfway down from noon. Nothing Kimeri said made any difference to her at all. She simply was not listening.

Kimeri thought about a shrieking fit, but that was the sort of thing babies did. She set her teeth and did what she was told. "Grownfolk never listen," she said to the walls when she was finally alone.

But it was not all like that. Vanyi was out most of the time, and so was Kimeri's mother. Kimeri could not go out in the city, and all she could do to help the Guardian was tell him in her dream that she was trying, and she would keep on trying. And yet, in everything else, she had more freedom here than she had ever had at home.

It started with being able to spend as much time as she liked in the stable with Kadin, which no one had ever allowed before. It got better when she found out that there were children round about, and what was better yet, none of them had nurses to make their lives miserable.

They did have nurses, that was true, but those were indulgent when they were not outright lazy. Children here could do much as they pleased, provided they were sensible about it and kept out of grownfolk's way. When they grew very big—seven whole summers' worth—they had to go to the temples to school, and many never came out of the temples again. But before then they were as free as birds.

Kimeri, who had always had armies of nurses hovering and fretting, found it wildly exciting to slip away from the stable, where Kadin never took much notice of her anyway, and find the places where the children liked to gather. Those were usually places where grownfolk never came, odd corners or dusty passages or rooms full of things that no one knew the names of, the makings of games that could range from one end of the palace to the other.

The first time Kimeri went to a gathering place, she had a friend to speak for her. His name was Hani; he was older, almost old enough for a temple, but he was not as tall as she was. She found him straddling the wall of the stable the day after she came to the city, staring at the seneldi. He was much too curious to be afraid, and he was not shy at all. As soon as Kimeri saw him he grinned, showing a mouthful of more gaps than teeth, and said, "You were our protect-us-against at prayers this morning. What are you really?"

"Kimeri," she answered, not knowing what else to say. Then because he was thinking that she did not know his language: "That's my name. I'm a person. What are you?"

"But what *kind* of person are you?" he asked her.

"A Kimeri person," she said. "Me. Myself. I'm not a demon. That's stupid."

"All right," said Hani, sliding down from the wall and landing neatly on his feet. He had straight black hair cut staight across his forehead and straight around his head just below his ears, and he was wearing a coat and a pair of trousers much like the ones she was wearing, and altogether he looked like a perfectly ordinary person from the Hundred Realms. But so did everybody here. There was nobody who looked like an Asanian, as Kimeri did, or like a northerner, which was what Kadin was.

Hani stood in front of her, and he looked and sounded older but he was definitely smaller. He looked her up and down. After a moment's thought, he stretched out a hand and tugged at one of her curls. She let him. He was curious. He had never seen curly hair before, or hair the color of yellow amber. "You're very funny-looking," he said. "What did they do to you to make you look like this?"

"I was born this way," she said. "You don't look funny to me. Lots of people where I come from look like you."

"Of course they do," said Hani. "People look like that."

Out in the courtyard, where Daruya's mare was loose with two of the Olenyai geldings, the mare decided that the geldings had been taking too many liberties, and went after them with teeth and horns. Hani watched them with his narrow eyes gone wide. "They're going to kill each other!"

"Of course they're not," said Kimeri, feeling superior. "The striped one is a mare. She's telling the other two to stop thinking they're as good as she is. Mares," she explained, "are the center of the world."

"Why?"

"Because they are," said Kimeri. "There, see? They're all quiet again, and the geldings are behaving themselves. They know how they're supposed to be."

"They look like mountain deer," Hani said, "except that they're so much bigger, and they have manes, and long tails with tassels on the end. And their horns are straight instead of branched, and much shorter than the stags'."

"That's because they're geldings, and mares don't usually have horns at all. You should see the stallions. They have horns two ells long, and sharp as spears."

"Do they kill people with the horns?" Hani wanted to know.

He was not particularly bloody-minded, she noticed. Just curious. "Sometimes," she said. "When people get in their way, or are cruel to them. You don't whip a senel, my mother says. Seneldi are our hoofed brothers. We treat them like people, and they carry us because they love us."

"Would one carry me?"

"Why, of course," said Kimeri.

And one of the geldings did, because Kimeri asked; and Kadin came to see what they were doing, but said nothing, which was much better than Kimeri would have got from a nurse. Kadin was a mage, and a northerner besides. He saw nothing alarming in riding seneldi around a perfectly safe and completely closed-in yard, even if they did leave off the bridles and saddles.

Hani found Kadin terrifying, but he put on a brave face for Kimeri. She let him think he convinced her. Northerners were so very tall and so very dark. Even Asanians were a little afraid of them, and Asanians were used to them.

After that, Hani was her friend. He took her to the palace, and got in trouble for it, too, what with the other children being sure he had taken up with a demon. But he was one of the oldest, and while he was far from the biggest, he could knock down and hammer on anyone who argued with him. He did that to a boy or two, and she did it to another boy and one of the girls, and when the two of them were finished, they all decided to forget what Kimeri looked like and treat her like a person.

The others never quite came close enough to be friends. Hani was different. He found her much more interesting than anyone else he knew, and even if he did not believe most of her stories of what the world was like outside of Shurakan, he liked to listen to them. He had his own stories to tell, too, and he knew all the fascinating places to play.

One of his favorites was one of the hardest to get to. First of all it was in the part of the palace where the most people were, though they only gathered in that particular place once in a Brightmoon-cycle. The rest of the time there were people muddling about, cleaning the floors, feeding the incense burners, braiding flowers into garlands to hang from everything a garland could hang from.

But once one got past those and slipped through a heavy curtain like chainmail, one was in the best place. A lamp was always lit in it, to honor the god whose house it was. The god himself stood on a plinth, all carved of wood and set with glittery stones and painted and gilded and dazzling in his gaudiness. His robe came off at every cycle, and priests put a new one on.

The day Hani took Kimeri to see the god, he was wearing cloth of gold. "That's a good omen," Hani whispered, being very careful not to wake any echoes. "His robe is the same color as your hair, see?"

Kimeri stood in a shadow in that shadowy place and smelled the incense, and felt rather strange. She felt that way in temples in Starios, too. "There are gods here," she murmured.

Hani blanched, but he kept his chin up. "Why, of course there are. This is their place. Are you going to come and see the best part, or are you afraid?"

Kimeri, who was not afraid at all, gave him a disgusted look and walked across the patterned floor. She walked the way she had been taught to hunt, very, very quietly, putting each foot down from the toes backward. Hani, tiptoeing behind her, made a great racket. He was scared, but he was excited, too, and a little irked with her for being so much braver than anybody else. She could have told him that gods' children would hardly be frightened of gods, but he had already refused to believe that she was the sun-god's child.

It was very quiet in the room, which was actually a tall, wide alcove in a much larger space. The lamp flickered in a draft, making the shadows leap and dance.

Hani's heart was thudding—Kimeri could hear it. Her own beat as it always did, maybe a little faster because she was excited, that was all.

They reached the wooden god and stared up. He was a terrifying thing to look at, with his four sets of arms and his scowling face, but Kimeri rather suspected the scowl was a mask. He felt stern to her, but not unwelcoming. The flowers he was festooned with were almost too sweet-scented. She stopped a sneeze before it burst out and betrayed them.

Hani, heart still thudding but perfectly in control of his courage, led her by the hand around the plinth on which the god stood. The shadows were very black there, but when she sharpened her eyes and used a little magery, she saw how the god stood in a niche, and the niche was a hollow half-circle. Hani set hand to wall and felt his way around behind the god. It was dusty in there, and it smelled of old wood and new paint and something sharply pungent that came from the god's robe, and of course flowers everywhere. But there was plenty of space, plenty of air to breathe. Kimeri noticed the shape of a door in the very back, and just across from it, in the god's leg, another door.

Hani, blind in the dark, groped for the catch that Kimeri could see perfectly clearly. He was thinking that he could be quiet and keep from letting her guess what he did. He did not know mages, she thought a little smugly. The catch made a distinct click, and then the door was open, with a ladder leading up into the god's body.

He tugged her in. The scent of old wood here was overpowering. "Climb," he whispered, hardly to be heard if she had not been a mage's child. He thought he was helping her by setting her hands on the rungs of the ladder and nudging her feet toward the wall that was the inside of the god.

She climbed. Hani was behind her, panting so loud she wondered how anyone could keep from hearing him.

It was not a long climb. The god was not terribly tall, merely tall enough to be imposing. The top of him was almost big enough to be a room—his head, and there were windows, long and narrow like Shurakani eyes. Someone long ago had spread cushions underneath them to lie on, dusty but comfortable.

Kimeri looked out of one eye, Hani out of the other. The floor was surprisingly far below. The light of the lamp was hurtfully bright after the dark inside the god. Kimeri shut down her magesight and let herself see with ordinary eyes.

Hani nudged her with his elbow. "See this?" he whispered.

She looked at what he was holding. It looked like a trumpet, except that it was soft, made of cloth. Its bell was bronze.

"That's a speaking trumpet," Hani said. "A person sitting here can talk into it, and his voice comes out of the god's mouth and sounds like the voice of heaven. That's how they make prophecies here when the priests think it's time."

She was supposed to be shocked and amazed, but she did not see why she had to be. "We don't need to pretend at home," she said. "Our prophets are real. They make prophecies in their own voices, and priests write them down."

"So do the priests do here," said Hani, a little annoyed. "The prophecies are real. The god inspires them. But the people believe them better if they come from his mouth, instead of from somebody who might look like you or me and be somebody's brother, or his cousin."

"How silly," said Kimeri. "Prophets *are* one's brother or sister or cousin. What else would they be?"

Hani opened his mouth to reply, but froze. The curtain of the god's shrine was sliding back with a great rasping of metal and grunting of men who heaved away at it. When it was drawn about half aside, it stopped, and people came through. What they were up to was clear enough to see: they were carrying enormous sheaves of flowers, baskets and baskets of them.

"Oh, dear," breathed Hani.

Kimeri would have agreed with him, except that she remembered the door behind the god. She tried to tell him about it, but he clapped a hand over her mouth. "Don't move," he whispered. "Don't breathe. If they find out we're up here . . ."

His visions of dire fates were clear enough to shut her up. The least of them showed him being whipped while she got a royal spanking.

The people with the flowers were in no hurry at all. They brought lamps with them till the space beyond the curtain was blazing with light. They settled down to weave garlands and gossip and pass round skins of something that made them warm and giggly. The lamps gleamed on their heads, which were all shaved bare, and in their eyes, and on the flowers they were weaving and the flowers that others were taking down from the rafters and the plinth and everywhere between, including the god's hands.

Once or twice Kimeri was sure that one of the garland-takers had looked straight up into her eyes, but the man turned away without saying anything. She crouched down a little lower and tried not to breathe.

All the dead and dying flowers being moved meant a great deal of dust and a scent so strong it made her sick. She did her best to keep her stomach where it belonged. She needed to go to the privy, too. But worst of all she needed to sneeze. She needed it so badly that her eyes itched and watered and her nose hurt, and her throat felt as if she had swallowed a bone sideways. She held her nose, but that meant breathing through her mouth, and that was noisy. And the sneeze kept on fighting to come out.

The inside of the god exploded.

She was still holding her nose, but the sneeze had shocked itself to death without ever coming out. Hani crouched with streaming eyes, yellow-grey with shock. The people outside were gaping and goggling. Some of them had fallen over. Hani's sneeze had gone through the speaking trumpet and come out like the god's own.

He grabbed her before she could say anything, and nearly threw her down the ladder, scrambling so fast to follow that he trod on her fingers. Outside she heard people yelling, arguing—"The god spoke!" "No, he didn't. Someone got inside." "What? If it's a demon—" "We *have* demons in the palace. Haven't you seen them?"

Sooner or later one of them would remember how to get inside the god, and come running to look. Kimeri shut her eyes and woke up her magery and dropped.

She landed light, with Hani almost on top of her, too scared to notice what she had done. He was still holding on to her hand. He half pulled her arm out of its socket, yanking her through the door—and then stopping cold as he remembered that he had nowhere to go.

The door in front of them had a perfectly visible catch, if one had magesight. Kimeri opened it and dragged him through and shut it tight.

They were in a passage like a dozen others, narrow and dim-lit and dusty. Hani was blind in it, but there was light farther on. Kimeri pulled him toward it.

"Do you know where we are?"

Kimeri looked around her. They had gone through a great many passages, because Hani was sure there were people running after them, and would not hear Kimeri when she tried to tell him that the priests had never even found the door behind the god. People never listened to her. She looked at him sullenly and set her chin. "You're the one who knows everything. Where do you think we are?"

"I don't know."

It cost a great deal of pride for him to say so. She was glad. "I thought you knew every crack and cranny of the palace."

Since he had said so in the same exact words, he could hardly call her a liar. He glared at her instead. "I don't know *every* one. Just the ones that are important."

"This one is very important. We're in it."

"Then why don't you get us out of it?"

Kimeri was ready to burst into tears, but she was not going to let any nit of a boy see her cry. "I can't find my way, either. I haven't learned to do that yet. I get all twisty when I try."

He thought she was talking about being a girl and being too silly to tell where she was. He did not know anything about being a mage and being too young. If she told him, he would not believe her. Nobody believed in mages here.

That made her angry, and anger made her walk, she did not care where. Forward was good enough. He could follow or not. She did not care.

He did follow, of course. Being lost made him scared. Being scared made him angry, but not as angry as Kimeri was at him for getting them into this in the first place. She stalked ahead and he stalked behind, and neither of them said a word.

They walked for a long time. Sometimes they took turns because Kimeri got tired of going straight. They were going in circles, she thought. Not the way they would in the woods, the way people got lost when they went hunting, back to the same place over and over, but the way walls could turn and twist and bend in on themselves and keep people from ever finding the way out.

Once she thought they had found it, but when they looked out at the blessed light it was coming in through a high window in the wall, and the room they were in was as empty as the rest, and there was no door but the one they had used to get in.

Hani stamped his foot and flung himself down on the floor. "We've got a curse on us! The god's punishing us for climbing inside his statue."

"He never punished you before, did he?" Kimeri asked reasonably.

The last thing he wanted was for her to be reasonable. "I never climbed inside him with anybody else before."

"You mean I'm the curse," said Kimeri. "Because I'm a foreigner and I look funny. I'm *not!* We're lost because you don't know as much about the palace as you thought you did."

"We're cursed," he repeated. His face looked pinched and nasty. His eyes were slits. "Cursed, cursed, cursed."

"We are not!"

"Are."

"Are not." Kimeri started to hit him. He spat at her. She whirled and ran away.

She did not care where she ran or how fast she did it. She careened around corners and through doorways. She heard him behind her—running and calling and trying to apologize—but she would not listen. He was only scared to be left alone.

There was furniture, suddenly, to dodge around, and instead of stone underfoot there were carpets. There were still no people. People were all somewhere else.

Except for the one she fetched up gasping against, who had come out of nowhere and stepped right in front of her. It was a tall narrow person with strong arms that caught her and held her even when she struggled. She was not thinking about that; once she did, she stopped.

The arms stayed strong, and kept holding her. She looked up. A woman looked down. She was not old like Vanyi but she was not quite as young as Daruya, either, and she had a way of looking older than she was. Her face was narrow and her lips were thin and she looked very severe, particularly when she frowned.

Kimeri burst into tears. It was not anything she thought about doing. It just happened.

The woman did not push her away, but held her and let her cry. When she was almost cried out, the woman said in a voice that was both rough and sweet, "There. That's enough, I think."

Kimeri sniffled hugely and swallowed the rest of her tears. The woman gave her a cloth to wipe her face. She used it. Her face had been very dirty: the white cloth was quite black when she tried to hand it back.

"No," the woman said. "Keep it. Give it back to me later."

And clean, she meant. Kimeri sniffled again, but that was the last of it. "Lady," she said huskily, "can you tell me where I am?"

"Do you have a particular need to know?" the woman asked.

"I got lost," said Kimeri. "I can't find my way out."

The woman's face was no less stern, but her eyes were a little warmer. "I know how that feels. I've been lost here often myself. Have you been about it long?"

"Forever," said Kimeri, fighting back the tears again. This was not a person to cry much in front of. She was like Vanyi that way, and about as sharp in the tongue, too.

"It's always forever," the woman said. No: she was not quite as sharp as Vanyi. But almost. "Here, I'll show you the way. Does your friend need help, too?"

But Hani was gone. Coward—he had recognized the room and known how to get out of it and run while Kimeri was getting the front of the woman's coat wet. "I hate him," she said. "I just hate him."

"That's often how we women feel about men," the woman said. "We never can stop living with them, for all of that. He'll come creeping back, you'll see, and worm his way into your heart again."

"He won't," said Kimeri. "He hates me."

"I think he likes you and is afraid of me." The woman looked bemused at that. "People often are. It's a puzzlement."

"I suppose it's because you're so tall," Kimeri said, "and so narrow. And you look so severe. But you aren't really, are you? If he's so afraid of you and he's still my friend, he should be trying to rescue me from you."

"He's a rarity in a male: he's wise. Do forgive him for it. It's a virtue we see too little of."

"I hate him," said Kimeri.

"Of course," the woman said. She was laughing inside, which made Kimeri hate her, too. A little. Before she took Kimeri's hand and led her out of the room and down a passage and across the corner of a garden and up a stair and to a door. "And past that," she said, "is the court of the strangers where your house is."

Kimeri knew that it was. She could feel her mother near, and Vanyi, and the others all together. None of them even knew that she was missing.

The woman started to draw her hand out of Kimeri's, but Kimeri stopped her. "What's your name?" she asked. She could see it in the woman's mind, as clear as everything else that she might ask, such as what the woman was and what she was doing here, but it was not polite to say so. Polite mages asked, and let people tell them.

The woman's brows quirked. "My name is Borti. What is yours?"

"Merian," Kimeri answered, "but they call me Kimeri—ki-Merian, because I'm little. But I'll grow."

"That," said the woman, looking her up and down, "you will."

"May I see you again?" Kimeri asked.

Borti smiled. She did not look severe at all then, or even very old. "Yes, you may. Come to this door and take the way I showed you, and if I'm free I'll be in the room where you met me first. I'm often there at this time of day, and usually alone."

Kimeri knew about alone-times. She needed them herself. She gave Borti her best smile and let her hand slip free. By the time she opened the door she was running. But she paused to look over her shoulder at Borti, who stood where Kimeri had left her, watching. She lifted a hand, the one that burned sun-hot, and ran through the door.

SIXTEEN

NOT LONG AFTER HER FORAY INTO THE TEAHOUSES OF THE SUMMER CITY, Daruya began to make a habit of going to the stable in the mornings and riding whichever of the seneldi seemed to need it most. It was dull enough work when she thought about it, riding in circles within the same four walls, but there was an art to it, like a dance of rider and mount. Her mare in particular had a talent for it.

It took the edge off boredom, certainly, and filled the mornings. She was close to happy, one bright cool morning, trying something new with the mare: a flying trot, legs flashing straight out, reined in by degrees until all the mare's swiftness and fire contained itself into a powerfully cadenced trot in place. The mare was amenable to a degree, but found it much more enjoyable, once contained, to lighten her forehand until she sat on her haunches. If Daruya urged her forward then, she reared up and sprang on her hindlegs. If Daruya sat through it, she came back lightly to a standstill, enormously pleased with herself.

At last, after considerable negotiation, Daruya coaxed the mare to permit half a dozen strides of trot-in-place. The mare bestowed them with the air of a lady granting an enormous favor. Daruya praised her lavishly, which she felt was no more than her due, and sprang from her back, and nearly jumped out of her skin.

A stranger, a Shurakani, stood watching, grinning at her. After the first shock she recognized him: the man from the teahouse, whose name right at the moment was emptied out of her skull. But not the eyes. Not the clear strong presence of him. He was larger than she remembered, broader in the shoulders, and he was quite as tall as she.

"That's a splendid display," he said without even taking the time to greet her. "You should offer it as an entertainment for princes. They'd give silk to see such a rarity."

"I am not a hired entertainer," Daruya said stiffly. The mare snorted and rubbed an itching ear on Daruya's shoulder. She turned her back on the intruder and tended the senel, taking her time about it.

He was not at all dismayed by her rudeness. He watched with perfect goodwill, and had the sense not to offer to help. She took off the mare's saddle and bridle; he stood by, curious. She walked the mare to cool her; he followed. She sponged the mare with water from the fountain; he watched. She led the mare into the house that had been made into a barn; he strolled after, with a moment's hesitation as he realized that all the walls had been taken down and partitions set up, and the house filled with strange horned beasts.

Daruya was used to it. She led the mare to her stall, fed her a bit of fruit, and stood smoothing the damp neck, ignoring the watcher with strenuous concentration.

She was still aware of him. It was impossible not to be. He regarded the seneldi warily but without fear, walking down the lines of stalls. The first nose that thrust inquisitively toward him, he shied at, but he came back bravely enough and stroked it. He was prepared for the next, and for the one after that.

The seneldi approved of him. He found the itchy places behind ears and at the bases of horns, and he was respectful of flattened ears and snapping teeth. He had brought nothing sweet for them to eat, which was a count against him, but they made allowances for ignorance.

He made a circuit of the stalls, coming to a halt at last outside of the one in which Daruya was standing. "These are marvelous animals," he said. "And the way you ride them—astonishing! Would you teach me?"

"Everyone asks that," said Daruya, addressing the mare's mane, which she was combing and smoothing with unnecessary precision. "It's easiest if you learn as a child."

"But not impossible to learn as a man grown?"

He sounded plaintive. She refused to be swayed by it. "It would take years to learn to ride as I ride. Just to stay on—that's possible, I suppose."

"It would make a beginning," he said.

She shot him a glance. "Right now?"

He was startled—his eyes went wide. But he laughed and spread his hands. "Why not?"

He had not the faintest conception of what he was getting into. She thought briefly, nastily, of setting him on Vanyi's gelding and letting him loose, but it would hardly do to kill or maim a man of high house in Shurakan, simply because he was presumptuous. She fetched the starbrowed bay instead, a plain, sweet-tempered, imperturbable animal who made no objection to being saddled and bridled and subjected to the weight of a large and substantial man who had never sat a senel before.

He had, however, sat an ox—and not badly, either, Daruya had to admit. There was no finesse in the way he scrambled into the saddle, but he balanced well, he took quickly to the commands to start and stop and turn, and he could ride the gelding on a circle and keep him there. He might, with time, come to have a decent seat on a senel.

He knew it, too. His expression reminded Daruya forcibly of the mare after her most impressive leap on her haunches: pure self-satisfaction. Daruya felt much less charitable toward the man than she had toward the mare. "You have talent," she said, because she could not lie about that, "but you have no art."

"No? Then will you teach me?"

She did not want to. It would take time to do it properly, far more than she had or meant to have in Shurakan, and she could not for pride do it otherwise than properly. But he annoyed her. "I'll teach you," she said, "if you can be taught. Beginning here." She slapped his back. He stiffened in outrage. She showed him the count of her teeth. "You're slouching. Sit up straight. No, not as if you had a rod for a spine. Softly, flowing with the movement of your mount. Now let your legs fall as they want to, softly, always softly. Ankles, too. Let them follow as he moves. Yes, like that."

She worked him to a rag. It was only a brief span by the sun's ascent, and it was a bare few moments' exercise for the bay, but the man slid from his back and nearly fell as his knees buckled. "By the gods! I'm destroyed."

"You've barely begun," said Daruya. "And you still have to cool him and unsaddle him and take him to his stall."

"You are merciless," said Bundur.

"You asked for it," she said.

But she lent him a hand, not out of pity for him, of course not, but out of concern for the senel. He gained back much of his strength as he worked, which was the object of the exercise—and a curse on his cleverness, he saw that, too. When he was done, he had most of his arrogance back. Enough to say, "Tomorrow, again?"

"You won't want to," she said.

"Yes, I will. Tomorrow?"

She wondered if the Shurakani had a god who protected fools and innocents. "Tomorrow, then. If you can walk this far."

As it turned out, he could. Just. And once he had pulled and hauled and heaved himself onto the senel's back, and gasped as he perceived the full and painful extent of his folly, he rode creditably enough. "My muscles are so insulted, they've expired in protest," he said from the saddle.

"Sit up," said Daruya. "You're slouching again."

"O cruel," he sighed, but he obeyed.

He came back the next morning. And the next. Sometimes early enough to watch her ride—and to mourn his own ineptitude. Sometimes so late that she feared—hoped, she corrected herself in considerable irritation—that he was not coming at all, until she saw him striding through the door. Then she was snappish, because her heart had leaped so suddenly, startling her. He never seemed to notice.

What he thought of her, he did not tell, and she did not try to read as a mage could. Because it mattered too little, she told herself; because, her heart muttered to itself, it could all too easily matter too much.

He never stayed longer than it took to saddle, ride, and put his mount away. He talked freely enough and most engagingly, but he never said a word that was not perfectly proper. However bold his eyes might be, his tongue was as circumspect as any woman could wish. He never offered to accompany her wherever she might be going afterward—to the house, usually, or to wander in the city. He did not, ever, bring a friend and ask her to increase the number of her pupils. That rather surprised her. Most ambitious princelings would have been flaunting their new accomplishment all over the court.

For all she knew, he was doing that—but keeping the rest from besetting her. She was not invited to court, nor was she courted by various of the palace functionaries as Vanyi was. She was quite the isolate, quite perfectly the nobody, and she was determined to be happy in it.

Chakan did not approve at all. She took her time in telling him all that she was doing in the stable from sunrise till nearly noon, which was an error. He came to her, half a dozen days after Bundur first appeared in the stable, and set himself in front of her as she debated between a jar of honeyed wine and one of Shurakani ale to go with her daymeal of flat bread and softened cheese. She chose the ale, filled a cup, held it out.

He refused it with a snap of the hand. "What is this I hear," he demanded, "of your entertaining a Shurakani noble in the stable every morning?"

Daruya found that her mouth was open. She closed it. "What in the worlds—" Her temper caught up with her tongue. "You of all people are concerned for my virtue?"

He dropped his veil. His face was white and set. "Do you know who that man is? We've been following him when he leaves here. He goes directly to the king's apartments, as often as not. And when he doesn't go to the king, he goes to other notables of the king's faction."

"Why shouldn't he visit the king?" Daruya demanded. "He's a prince here, even I can see that. Princes keep company with kings."

"Did you know that his mother is the king's half-sister?"

Daruya stiffened. No, he had not told her. But she had not asked. "Well then. Why shouldn't he visit his uncle, if he's so minded?"

"His beloved uncle," said Chakan, "has shown himself to be a powerful opponent of foreigners in Shurakan, and a devoted hater of mages. If he had his way and were not restrained by the queen's moderation, we would all be flayed and our skins spiked to the walls."

"Oh, come," said Daruya. "Now you're talking nonsense."

"I am not. You may think that this city is a haven of innocent goodwill, but there are powerful factions in the court that would kill us as soon as hear our names spoken."

"And how do you know that?"

"We listen," he said. "We watch. We stand guard. You're watched from sunrise to sunrise, and not only by us. Everywhere you go, you have at least two shadows: your Olenyas and a king's spy. You'd be dead now if it hadn't been for Yrias. He's driven off more than one attack on you while you meander happily through the city."

"Those were footpads," said Daruya, "or simply the curious, trying to see how easy it would be to steal from me."

"They were not," said Chakan. "They were in the pay of the king's faction. As you can be sure this princeling of yours is. What better way to keep you in hand than to occupy you all morning, every morning?"

"God and goddess! I'm not tumbling him in the hay. I'm teaching him to ride a senel." Daruya came desperately close to flinging her ale in his face. But she was stronger than that; and he looked as if he was expecting it, which made it worse. "If he really were under orders to keep me busy, don't you think he'd outright seduce me, and stay with me all day into the bargain? He doesn't even try to coax secrets out of me, except the ones that have to do with riding."

"He hasn't had time to do more," Chakan said. "He will, you can be sure of it."

"I say he won't. He wants to learn an art that no one else here knows. What's reprehensible about that?"

"Nothing," said Chakan, "if he were not the king's sister's son."

"He is also," Daruya pointed out, "the queen's sister's son."

"No," said Chakan. "They're children of the old king, both. But the queen's mother, who was also queen, died bearing her. The king married again to beget the canonical second child, who was the king. His wife had been married before, and had a daughter. The daughter was this man's mother."

"How complicated," said Daruya. "But he's the queen's kin, one way and another."

"Half-kin," said Chakan. "Children of different wives seldom love one another. And this man is the king's sister-son."

"He means me no harm," Daruya said stubbornly. "I'd know if he did."

"Would you? They have arts here. They don't call them magery, but what's a name? Who's to say he isn't concealing his mind from you?"

"I can read a great deal more of him than I can of you."

He hissed in disgust. "Yes, and his face is open for anyone to see, too. There's a Great Ward on this kingdom that reckons itself free of mages' taint. Gods alone know what else it's lying about to our faces—even to yours, my lady of Sun and Lion."

"He's not lying to me," she said through gritted teeth.

"No? And you had no idea he was the king's nephew."

"I didn't ask."

"You shouldn't have had to."

"I didn't need to. He's not my enemy."

"You know that?" Chakan asked, viciously sweet. "You know that for an incontrovertible fact?"

Daruya could be as vicious as he was, and as nastily reasonable. "So come and watch his lessons. Look as deadly as you please. See if it makes any difference."

"Oh, I will," he said. "I promise you I will."

Daruya hated to quarrel with Chakan. He never fought fair, and he always turned and swept out before she could flatten him with a final blow. He was properly rattled this time: he forgot to veil his face again with the flourish that temper put in it. It was a victory, but a small one.

Maybe he was right. She was sure that he was not—but doubt had a way of creeping in and gnawing at the roots of one's surety. Mages' courtesy kept her from reading the mind of every man she met, but she did not go about blind, either, least of all with strangers who might be enemies. Bundur was not an enemy. Truly, she would know. Other motives he might have had for visiting her that first time, but he had come back because he wanted to learn to ride a senel.

Maybe too because he wanted to observe her. Why not? She was a foreigner. She had no easily visible function in the embassy. He would have wanted to assure himself that she was no danger to his kingdom.

And maybe he wanted to see what kind of creature she was. There was nothing like her in his world. Maybe he kept coming back because he found her interesting. A man might do that, even with a woman of respectable virtue.

A little more of this and she would be getting aggravated because he had not ventured anything improper. She had thought about it more than once. He was a very handsome man. But he thought her ugly; he had made that very clear. Interesting, but ugly.

Goddess, she thought. Men were such maddening creatures. How did any sensible woman stand them?

Chakan was there the next morning, standing like a stone beside the wall of the riding-yard. Daruya ignored him as she put the mare through her paces. She kept on ignoring him as she took first the brown gelding, then the whitefoot black, and rode them.

Bundur was late. Very late. It was nearly noon, and no sign of him.

Chakan had an air of grim satisfaction. She almost screamed at him: "How could he know you were going to be here?"

But she knew the answer before he spoke. "They see everything we do."

She had been going to visit the city. There was a festival, she had been told, with music and dancing and a procession. She went back to the house instead, had a bath so long she was shriveled and sodden when she came out, and thought about cutting her hair again. In the end she let it be but had the servant twist it into a myriad small plaits, each tipped with a bead of lapis or malachite or carnelian. They swung to her shoulders, brushing them when she turned her head to consider her reflection.

Odd, by the lights of Shurakan, but becoming. It was a fashion of the north of Keruvarion; in its honor she put on what went with it, the kilt and the gauds. The servant was scandalized. Women did not bare their breasts here.

How backward, she thought. It was a warm day for Shurakan, almost hot. She was not going anywhere, or at least no farther than the garden, where she intended to lie in the sun and brood on the faces of treachery. Vanyi was gone, waging her war among the functionaries. Kimeri was out playing somewhere in the palace— safe, and annoyed when her mother brushed her with a finger of magery; Daruya would have something to say to Chakan, when she could bring herself to speak to him again, of how he let the daughter run wild while he overprotected the mother. The Olenyai were either guarding Daruya or occupying themselves. The mages were inside their circle, discovering the usual nothing at all about the breaking of the Gates.

The sun was hot and blissful on her skin. She had been starved for it these past days, what with skulking in the house and riding within walls, or wandering about a city that left little space for the sun to get in. She lay on the cropped grass, basking in light. She slept a little, lightly, dreaming of gold and of lions.

She woke suddenly. Two shadows stretched over her. One was Olenyas, barring the second, much taller and broader. That one was taking little notice of the obstacle.

Still half-asleep, she slid behind those bright black eyes and saw what he saw: golden body all but bare, glittering with gold, in a pool of light as solid as water.

Malice sparked, fed by the light in his eyes. She stretched luxuriously, as a cat will, muscle by muscle.

Ugly, did he think her? But interesting, he had said at that first meeting. Most interesting, lying with arms stretched above her head, grinning ferally at him.

"Go away, Yrias," she said. "This man is safe enough."

The Olenyas' eyes were narrow, mistrustful. But he was an obedient guardsman. He withdrew to the edge of the grass—near enough to leap if he was needed, far enough not to intrude.

Daruya rolled onto her side, propped on her elbow. "You didn't come for your instruction this morning."

Bundur's breath was coming just a fraction fast. She watched him take himself in hand. He did it very well, she thought. "It's festival day," he said. "I had duties I couldn't escape."

"Marching in procession? Waiting on the king?"

He did not start at that or look guilty. "Standing in court, too, while the children of heaven bestowed gifts of the season on an endless parade of worthy recipients.

Your chief ambassador was there. She caused a stir—foreigners have never appeared at such a function before."

"And how did she manage it?" Daruya inquired. She hoped she sounded casual. She was seething. Vanyi had plotted such a coup, and not brought the rest of them into it?

"She did it on the spur of the moment, I gather," he said, pricking her bubble of temper rather thoroughly: "heard about the event, decided to observe it, and walked in as calm as you please. The Minister of Protocol was beside himself."

"I can imagine," Daruya said. "Was she thrown out on her ear?"

"Of course not," said Bundur. "We're not barbarians. Somebody found a gift for her, and she had it from the queen's hand—but the Minister of Protocol got her out before she could make any speeches."

"Maybe she wasn't going to deliver any," Daruya said. "She'd made her point, hadn't she? That would be enough for her. The queen's seen her, knows she's here— the queen can do with the knowledge as she best pleases."

"Which could be nothing," said Bundur.

"That's the queen's right," Daruya said with the certainty of one who had been raised to be an empress. She sat up and clasped her knees. Bundur looked faintly disappointed. He had been enjoying the sight of her with rather too much pleasure, once he had got over the first shock. She let a bit of edge into her voice, to call him back to himself. "I suppose you came to beg for a late lesson?"

"Well," he said, "no. I'll be there tomorrow, never fear. Today I wondered—" He looked unwontedly diffident, even embarrassed. "I should have come much earlier, but I was being an idiot about it, I suppose. I wondered—on festival night we have a dinner, which we prepare according to very old custom. It's eaten with one's family, and a friend or two, no more." He stopped. She did not help him with word or glance. He let it all out in a rush. "Would you share dinner with us in House Janabundur?"

"Just me?" she asked. She caught Yrias' eye. "I can't do that."

"No, no," he said hastily. "You and your kin who are here, and your captain of guards—he's your friend, yes?"

"How do you know that?"

He was blushing: his skin was darker than usual, more ruddy than bronze. "It's known. One is like a brother to you. He, your daughter, your lady ambassador— they're welcome, and should come."

"It's short notice," she said.

"My fault for that. But festival shouldn't be spent alone."

"I was going to go to the city," she said, "and watch the processions."

"That's done, too, after the dinner is over. Everybody takes lanterns and puts on a mask and goes out, and dances till dawn."

That was tempting. More than tempting.

And to dine in the house of the king's sister-son on the night when people dined only with friends and close kin—what magnitude of coup might that be?

Maybe it was a trick. Chakan would say so. But if Vanyi was with her, and Chakan himself, and Kimeri who was a weapon of remarkable potency, surely they could protect themselves against any danger Shurakan might offer.

She looked up into Bundur's face. It was empty of guile. Which could of course be a sleight in itself, and probably was. But she saw no enmity there. What she did see . . .

Ah, she thought: the power of northern fashion in a country that reckoned women's breasts a secret to be kept for the inner room. She was too wise to flaunt them any more than she already had. She tilted her head, beads on braid-ends sliding on bare shoulders, and feigned deep reflection.

Just as a shadow began to cross his face, she said, "Very well. One dines at sunset, yes?"

"At sunset, on festival night," said Bundur.

"Does one do anything in particular? Bring a gift? Offer flowers? A prayer?"

"A gift isn't necessary." Which meant that it was. "Flowers are welcome, and prayers, always."

"I see," she said. "At sunset, then."

"At sunset." His voice was a little strange—thick. He was excited. Not, she hoped in the depths of her stomach, because she had fallen into a trap and would be dead by midnight.

Chakan was sure that it was a trap. Vanyi, most strangely, was not. She had made her point indeed, let the queen see her and left the woman to make the next move in the long game. When she came home to a near-war in the dining-room between Daruya and Chakan, she ascertained its cause at once and stopped it with a pair of words. "We'll go."

Chakan rounded on her in such fury that Daruya flinched. Vanyi did no such thing. "Down, young lion," she said. "Draw in your claws. You don't have the faintest understanding of what this means."

"I know that it lures us all to the house of strangers, shuts us therein, and leaves us easy prey to the king's assassins."

"So it might," said Vanyi, "if it were any other night and any other festival. This is the festival of the summer moon. It's for kin; for heart's friends; for lovers. Enemies are never hunted on festival day. No wars are fought, no feuds pursued. If a man meets his brother's murderer in the street on festival night, he smiles and wishes him joy and goes on. In the morning they go back to killing one another—but while the festival's peace is in force, no man ever breaks it."

"What better chance," demanded Chakan, "to destroy the unsuspecting with the semblance of perfect peace?"

"Not during the festival," said Vanyi.

"In the mountains," he said, "no one steals from anyone else. But foreigners are fair prey. Theft from them is no dishonor. How can it fail to be the same here? We're outlanders. We don't keep festival. We can be killed, and no one will look askance."

"This isn't the mountains," Vanyi said. "Honor is truly honor here. We've been bidden to keep festival in the highest house in Shurakan short of the royal house itself. If it's the house most closely connected with the king, then so much the better. The queen is at least not disposed to murder us out of hand. The king would happily see us dead and burned. Let his sister see us, know us, learn that we're not monsters, and maybe she'll talk to him, and maybe, for a miracle, he'll listen."

"Minds like that never open," said Chakan. "They're locked shut."

"Maybe," Vanyi said. "Maybe it doesn't matter, if we can get a foothold in the king's faction. It's not just a matter of finding out who broke the Gate here, Olenyas. When we do that, when we've got the Gate up and working again, then we'll want to use it. And we'll need friends here, to keep us from being attacked all over again. Those friends may be in House Janabundur."

"Or they may not," said Chakan.

"We can't know that till we go there, can we?" Vanyi dismissed him with a wave of the hand. "Go. Get ready to guard us tonight. I need to talk to Daruya."

He snarled, but he went.

Daruya rather wished he had not. Once he was gone, the door shut and an Olenyas on the other side of it, Vanyi fixed her with a profoundly disconcerting stare. "Well?" Daruya snapped after it had gone on for quite long enough. "Are you thinking what everybody else seems to be thinking? No, I haven't been tumbling the master of House Janabundur in a senel's stall."

"I don't doubt it," said Vanyi imperturbably. "He's a handsome buck, isn't he?"

"I can't say I ever noticed," Daruya said. But she felt the heat in her cheeks. She had never been a good liar.

Vanyi saw it, raised a brow at it. "Maybe you didn't know you were noticing. He'd be old to you, I suppose. He must be thirty winters old, give or take a few."

"He has twenty-seven summers," Daruya said stiffly, "and that is hardly old at all. He rides a senel very well for someone who was never on one before this past Brightmoon-cycle. But then he's ridden oxen since he was Kimeri's age. The skills do translate."

"As do a few other things," Vanyi observed. She inspected the daymeal that had been laid on the table some untold number of hours ago, picked out a fruit that was still fresh and a loaf that was not too dry, and ate each in alternating bites. In between she said, "Consider this. When our mages first came to Shurakan, a faction in the court welcomed them, admitted them to the kingdom, gave them a house for the Gate, and gave them leave to come and go as they pleased. Through the Guardian of the Gate they invited an embassy from the guild in Starios, and promised to receive that embassy with honor and respect.

"Then the Gate fell. The faction fell, too, it seems, either just before the Gate or just after. Certainly I've seen no evidence of it. We've been admitted, yes, and given a place to dwell in, and freedom of the city. But no one comes to us with any direct purpose except curiosity. I got at the queen today, but only because I'm a brash foreigner and I seized a chance. They won't let me loose to do that again. To all appearances we came here on our own, uninvited by any person or persons in Shurakan, and we're being treated as humble petitioners to their celestial majesties, not as invited ambassadors." She finished the loaf, deposited the fruit-pit in a fine bronze bowl, poured a cup of the inevitable tea. "I haven't said any of that to the Minister of Protocol, you know. It isn't something I'll say to someone whom I'm not sure I trust.

"And in any case," she said, "if this faction is indeed discredited, its members, if they live, are lying low. They aren't letting themselves be seen to speak with us or approach us. Unless one of them, their leader even, is the man who will be our host."

"I don't think he's that subtle," said Daruya.

"Does he need to be?" Vanyi asked. She paused, as if she needed to ponder what she said next. "I think you ought to know what it means when a man comes in his own person, without a messenger, and bids a woman and her kin to dine with his kin on festival night."

Daruya could well guess. The catch in her throat was temper. Of course. "It's a dreadfully public way to ask her to bed with him, isn't it?"

"Not if it's marriage he has in mind."

"That's preposterous," said Daruya. "I'm a foreigner. I'm nobody that his benighted people will acknowledge: no family, no kin, no power in the kingdom. And if that isn't enough, I'm hideously ugly."

"None of that would matter," said Vanyi, "if he thought he had something to gain. Or if he could persuade his enemies to think exactly that. Is there a better way to blind them to what he's really doing, if he's leading his faction back to power and using us as his weapons?"

"That's supposing there's a faction at all, and he's part of it. He's the king's sister-son. Could he turn traitor to his own kin?"

"He might not think of it that way. His faction—if it is his—believes that Shurakan can't be forever shut within its walls, and has to learn to contend with foreigners on their own ground. Even foreigners who are mages."

Daruya could not see it. She tried; she battered her brain with it. But she could only see Bundur riding the starbrowed bay, trying to sit gracefully in a jouncing trot.

Vanyi broke in on the vision. "I'm thinking that we've been kept here in careful isolation, handled at arm's length, and ignored as much as possible. Someone is keeping us from being cast out altogether. That someone may have sent us a message through your Bundur—or may be that gentleman, as innocuous as he seems. No nobleman of his age in Shurakan is a complete innocent. I'd say none could be completely honorable, either, but I haven't seen all of them yet, to be sure. He's up to something, if it's only a campaign to get you in his bed."

"That's all it probably is," said Daruya. "I'll tell him he doesn't need to make a grand performance of that—I'll bed him happily enough, and never mind the priests and the words."

"What if he wants those? For honor's sake?"

Daruya laughed a little shrilly. "Then he's a fool. I didn't marry the man who sired Kimeri. I haven't married any man I've bedded since—and many's the one who's hoped for it. It's not greatly likely I'll marry this one, either. Who is he at all but a petty princeling of a kingdom on the other side of the world?"

"And you will be empress of all the realms of Sun and Lion," said Vanyi. Her tone was perfectly flat. "Which, if your grandfather has his way, will include Shurakan and the lands between. With armies to hold them. And Gates to march the armies through."

"Then maybe," said Daruya with sudden bitterness, "it's as well the Gates fell when they did, and they should never be raised again."

"What, you don't want to conquer the world?"

"I don't want to make a fool of myself," snapped Daruya. "My grandfather never troubled his head with such nonsense. I'm vainer than he is, and weaker, too."

"Which," said Vanyi, "may be your great strength." And while Daruya stared at her, for once emptied of words: "Go get dressed. It's getting late."

She sounded exactly like a mother. Daruya bristled, but as Chakan had done long since, she obeyed. There was, she told herself, no great profit in refusing; and yes, the sun was low, slanting through the windows and pouring gold upon the floor. She took a handful of it, part for defiance of Shurakani propriety, part for warmth in a world that could grow too quickly cold.

SEVENTEEN

HOUSE JANABUNDUR STOOD ON A PROMONTORY OF THE CITY WESTWARD OF the palace, sharing its eminence with an assortment of temples, one or two other lordly houses, and untold warrens of common folk. It was very like the kingdom it was built in, Daruya thought, waiting at the gate in the last rays of sunlight for her company to be recognized and let in.

They had done their best to look like the ambassadors of a mighty empire. Chakan had brought half his Olenyai and left the others to guard the house by the palace walls; they could show no weapons, but their robes were impeccable, their veils raised and fastened just so, their baldrics oiled and polished and crossed exactly. Vanyi had put on the robes of the Mageguild's Master, as she almost never did. They were cut in the Asanian fashion of robes within robes within robes, seven in all, grey and violet interleaved, and the outermost was of silk and woven in both violet and grey, a subtle play of color and no-color that shimmered in the long light. Her hair was plaited and knotted at her nape, bound with a circlet of silver; she wore no other jewel but the torque of the priestess that she had been from her youth, plain twisted gold about her throat. Kimeri, clinging to her mother's hand, wore a gold-embroidered coat and silken trousers, with a jeweled cap on her head and rings of gold and amber in her ears.

Daruya had caused the servants an hour's panic, but the result, she rather thought, was worth the trouble. She had traveled light perforce, and brought nothing suitable for a state occasion. By dint of ransacking the embassy's stores and taking the market by storm, the servants had made do handsomely. The shirt and trousers were her own, of fine white linen woven in Starios; and the boots were made in Shurakan, white leather golden-heeled. The coat over them, like Kimeri's, was new-made of silk from Vanyi's stores, a shimmer of fallow gold brocaded with suns and lions, gold on gold on gold. Along its hem and sleeves ran a wandering line of firestones. Her hair was in its braids still, but its beads were amber and gold. There were rings in her ears and about her wrists, plates of amber set in gold. Her belt was gold, its clasp of amber. But lest the eye weary of so much white and amber and gold, she wore a necklace of amber beads interwoven with firestones, shimmering red and blue and green.

She smoothed the long coat with the hand that did not hold Kimeri's, a nervous gesture, quickly suppressed. Chakan had struck the gong that hung in front of the gate; its reverberations sang through her bones. Kimeri fidgeted. "Mama, can I take my boots off, please? My feet hurt."

Daruya swallowed a sigh. The boots were new, of necessity, and made for the child, with room to grow in—and they were stiff, and she had walked half across the city in them. "When you get inside," said Daruya, "we'll ask if it's not too unpardonably rude for you to go barefoot to a festival dinner."

"Why would it be rude?" Kimeri wanted to know. "My feet *hurt.*"

Daruya was spared the effort of a reply by the scraping of bolts within and the opening of the gate. An aged but still burly porter scowled at them all impartially, but said nothing, merely stepped back and bowed, hands clasped to breast.

Vanyi interpreted the gesture as an invitation. She entered in a sweep of robes. The others followed a little raggedly, Olenyai last and darting wary glances at the walls that closed in beyond the gate.

That was only the entryway. The wonted court opened beyond, lamplit, with the inevitable fountain. A servant waited there, elderly and august, to lead them up a stair to a wide airy hall full of sunset light.

Daruya saw nothing of it at first but the light, which poured through a long bank of windows framed in a tracery of carved wood and molded iron. Slowly she accustomed her eyes to the splendor. The room was long and high but not particularly wide, stone-vaulted, with slender pillars holding up the roof. The floor was of the patterned tiles that were so common here, the walls hung with embroideries, too bright and many-figured to make sense of in a swift glance. At one end of the hall, near a broad stone hearth, a table was set.

No one sat there, although the plates and cups and bowls were all laid in their places. There was no one in the room but themselves and the servant who had brought them, and that one was retreating, bowing, saying nothing.

Chakan hissed and flashed a glance at Daruya. She refused to indulge him. None of them knew the custom here. In Starios the host would have been standing at the table, the family seated, awaiting the guests. Shurakan might well do otherwise: leave guests alone in an empty room while the family mustered outside and entered in a body.

They emerged from a door at the far end of the hall, as the guests had entered in the middle. Bundur led the procession. Daruya told her heart to stop beating so hard. It would never have been such an idiot if Vanyi had not vexed it with her tale of festival dinners and offers of marriage.

He was not at all ill to look at. As if to counter her white and gold, he wore shirt and trousers of the shimmering black near-silk that they wove here from the floss of a seedpod, and a coat of scarlet embroidered with black and bronze. His head was crowned with scarlet flowers. They should have been incongruous; they were merely splendid.

A group of women walked behind him. The eldest, with her silvered hair, must be his mother. She looked like him, with the same proud cheekbones and robust figure; her garments too were black, her coat the color of bronze. Two younger women accompanied her, one with the free hair of a maiden, the other wearing the shortened coat and severe plaits of a new widow and leading a child by the hand. It was a boychild as far as Daruya could tell, not as tall as Kimeri but seeming older, with a thin, clever face.

Bundur spoke words of greeting, which Vanyi answered. She gave him the gift she carried, a length of gold-green silk; he received it with open admiration and an honest gleam of greed, and passed it to the eldest of the women. She was his mother, yes, the Lady Nandi, and the younger women were his sisters: Kati who had not yet chosen a husband, and Maru whose husband had died in the spring of a fever. The child's name was Hani; he was not Maru's son but Bundur's. Daiuya stiffened at that.

"His mother chose not to keep him," Bundur was saying to Vanyi, ostentatiously ignoring Daruya, "and left him to me."

"The mother lives? You're married to her?" Vanyi asked.

"The mother is a priest of the Blood Goddess, who forbids her devotees to marry. I wouldn't have married her in any case," said Bundur: "we weren't mated except in the flesh. And since no priest may keep a child in the temple, I took this one to raise as was only proper. He'll go to a temple himself, come winter solstice."

"I don't suppose you've asked him if he wants to go," Daruya heard herself say.

It was the child who answered. "Of course I'll go, lady. I want to learn everything a priest can learn."

"Will you be a priest?" asked Daruya.

He shrugged. "I don't know. I don't think so."

"My mother is a priestess," Kimeri said in a clear voice, rather cold. "Ours can marry and keep their children if they want to. I'm going to be a priestess when I grow up, and have a daughter, and keep her, no matter what her father says."

"Her father might say no," said Hani.

It dawned on Daruya that these two knew each other, and not happily, either. They were as stiff as children could be who had had a quarrel, and Kimeri was itching for a fight. "*You* won't be the father," she said nastily, "so what would you know?"

"Children," said Lady Nandi, "this is festival, when all enmities are laid aside."

Neither looked particularly contrite, but they subsided, shooting occasional, baleful glances at one another. Kimeri was thinking openly at Hani. *Coward, coward, coward.* Daruya had a vision of some outrageous prank in the palace, and Kimeri left alone to face the consequences while Hani bolted for safety.

Hani saw it differently. He had run for help but found none, and when he came back Kimeri was gone. He was too stiffly proud to say so. Kimeri was too angry to read him properly.

Daruya bit her tongue and kept out of it. She had not even known that Kimeri was playing in the palace. Of course the child had to have been; she was never home, and Daruya had yet to see her in the stable in the mornings.

That would stop, Daruya resolved to herself. An Olenyas would accompany the imp hereafter, and keep her out of trouble if he could. An Olenyas should have been doing so from the beginning.

Another weapon in her war against Chakan. She stored it away and focused on the festival, which after all was a feast of amity.

Bundur held out his hand. She found herself taking it and being led to the table and seated in the center, with Vanyi on her right hand and Chakan—too startled to resist—beyond her, and Bundur on her left, and his mother and his sisters beyond. The children had their own place at the table's foot, with a feast suited to their taste, and bright boxes set in front of them that proved to be full of games and toys and manifold amusements. They seemed to arrive at a truce, however temporary: when Daruya looked toward them they were playing together, arguing softly but without perceptible rancor over the untangling of a puzzle.

"Children are good fortune," Lady Nandi said in her strong sweet voice. "Don't you think?"

She was addressing Daruya, showing no particular revulsion at either her ugliness or her foreignness. Daruya blessed her long and often bitter training for vouchsafing her a harmless answer. "A child is the hope of its house."

Lady Nandi greeted that ancient banality as if it were priceless wisdom. "Truly! And yet my son tells me that you intend to have but the one?"

She wasted no time in getting to the point. Daruya rather liked her for it. "It's not a matter of intention," she said. "The god so far has given one child to each of his descendants, one heir and one only. I don't expect that I'll be any different."

"Our gods are kinder," said Lady Nandi.

"I don't doubt it," said Daruya.

There was a pause while servants brought the first course: platter after platter, bowl after bowl of fragrant and often cloying delicacies. Daruya watched in dismay as her bowl was heaped with the pick of them. Bundur selected with his own hands the roasted wing of a bird, and a slender pinkish object that was, he said with relish, a bird's tongue, and something shapeless that he promised would give her a taste of heaven. It gave her a taste of salt and mud and peculiar spices. It was, Bundur told her while she struggled to keep a courteous face, the nest of a bird that dwelt in cliffs above the city.

There were words to speak as they began, a chant from one of their sacred books, which Bundur led and the women responded to in chorus. It had something to do with war in heaven, and with an army of birds, and a goddess' two children fleeing the field of battle.

For all the quantity of food that filled her bowl, she discovered, watching the Shurakani, that no one ate more than a bite of each offering. The bowls were taken away almost full. "For the poor," Bundur said, as if she had asked.

Odd custom, but not unappealing. The second course was the same, and the third. The first had been devoted to creatures of the air. The second was comprised of creatures of water: fish broiled and spiced, fishes' eggs, the legs of a fen-leaper. The blessing-chant took up the tale of the goddess' children, who fled from the realm of air through river and fen to the protection of the waterfolk, and there were kept alive while all their people perished. In the third round of the feast, over the fruits of the hunt, mountain deer and boar and the strong flesh of the cavebear, Bundur sang of the deer that led the children of heaven to the secret place in the mountains, and the sow who gave her piglets to feed them, and the bear that sheltered them in its cave until they gathered a new people and founded the kingdom of Su-Shaklan.

Last of all came a mountain of sweet cakes and a palace of spices, and the delicate flowery tea of ceremony, neither given nor shared lightly. Over it the Lady Nandi spoke the blessing, the words that formed the center of the festival: " 'Rule in joy,' the goddess said to her children, 'and rule in memory of sorrow. Do not fight, nor give yourselves up to hatred, nor take the life of any living thing but to feed your bodies or to defend your souls. Remember; and keep this festival in the name of peace.' "

"In peace," the others echoed, Bundur's deep voice, the women's lighter, the children's lightest of all. Vanyi's too, Daruya noticed, and Kimeri's. But not Chakan's. And not her own. By the time she thought of the courtesy, it was too late. The prayer was ended. The cakes were going round, and the tea, and Bundur was smiling at her.

"So," he said, "what do you think of our festival?"

"We have nothing quite like it," she answered. "There's High Summer, when we celebrate the birth of the Sunborn, and Autumn Firstday, when children come of age and heirs come into their inheritance, and Dark of the Year, when we all do penance for our wrongdoings. But no festival like this, when every year people try to remember to love one another."

"You're a warlike nation, then?"

"No," she said. She was aware that the others were listening; that she was being judged by what she said. But then she always had, who had been born the emperor's heir. "We've had wars, and many—there's no help for it in a realm as vast as ours. But we've had peace, too; long years of it. I remember the Feast of the Peace, when my grandfather ended the last of the wars, and all enemies were brought together in one place and made into one people. They weren't all happy about it, but they came, and they swore not to fight again. Nor have they."

"How long has that been?" Bundur asked.

"Five years," said Daruya. "It looks like lasting, too, though there've been small skirmishes here and there. Some people never do understand when a war is over."

"We haven't had a war in a dozen generations," Bundur said.

Daruya smiled thinly. "Yes, and whom would you fight with? Your mountains protect you. We don't have such mountains where I come from. It's mostly open plain. Armies have fought across it for a thousand years."

"You must feel naked," said Bundur, "and defenseless."

"Not any longer," she said. "We're all one empire. You could begin walking by the western sea, and by the time you came to the shores of the east, you'd have been traveling for half a year. And safely, too. Bandits don't hunt the emperor's roads."

"Do they infest the lesser ones?"

"Not if he can help it."

"He must be a very busy man, to look after so vast a realm."

Bundur did not believe any empire could be that large—he was indulging her, and transparently, too. "The emperor has lords and servants in plenty. And someday," she said, "I'm going to take you there and show you how wide it is, you who can't imagine anything larger than your tiny goblet of a kingdom."

His face lit from within. "You would do that? You would show me the world beyond the Wall?"

She was a little surprised. She had been threatening him, she thought; but he acted as if she offered him a great gift. "You actually *want* to see the world?"

"You thought I didn't?"

She lowered her eyes. Her cheeks were warm. Damn him, he did that to her much too often. "You all seem so smug. Self-satisfied. Content to think that Su-Shaklan is all the world you need to know."

"Oh, no," he said. "Su-Shaklan is the heart and soul of the world, yes, but some of us do want to know what else there is."

"You might not like it," she said. "It's very wide. And in places very flat. And no one there has ever heard of Su-Shaklan."

"No one here has heard of your empire, and you do rather well despite it," he pointed out.

"You think so?" she asked.

"I think," he said, "that you are like the sun in a dark place. You gleam, do you know that? All gold, even in the shadows."

"That's the god in me," she said. "No god of yours, as everyone is so careful to remind me."

"Maybe we can be taught," he said.

She laughed, short and cold. "Do you want to be? You might be corrupted."

She was aware of his mother, listening, and his sisters. They offered no objection, betrayed no disapproval. She might have been a player on a stage, performing for their pleasure.

He spoke as if they had been alone. "If I can be corrupted by a single foreign woman, however fascinating, then I deserve whatever fate I suffer for it."

"What do they do to heretics here? Burn them? Flay them? Spike them to the walls?"

"That depends on the heresy."

"They flay mages, don't they? And bathe them in salt, and keep them alive and in agony, till the gods have mercy and take them."

"Not in this age of the world," he said. "We have none of that kind." *Ah*, she thought: even he could not say the word. "But some of us lack the ancient animus against them. Not all of them are evil, we believe, and not all of what they do is foul."

"I'm glad to find you so enlightened," she said levelly, "considering that I am a mage of a line of mages, and all my blood is afire with magery."

"We call that the gods' fire here," he said.

"It's the same," said Daruya, "no matter what name you set on it."

He lifted a shoulder, flicked a hand: shrug, dismissal of the uncomfortable truth. "You're a priest, yes? You're consecrated to your god."

"All the Sun-blood are," she said.

"So," said Bundur. "Your god lives in you. That's a heresy in some sects here, but not in all. Not in ours."

"Are you saying," she said slowly, "that you can sweeten what we are to your people by calling us priests and our power the gods' power?"

"Isn't it the truth?"

"Well," she said, "yes. But—"

Vanyi intervened, and none too soon, either. "We used that expedient in Su-Akar. We were told it wasn't necessary here."

Bundur turned his attention to the Guildmaster, apparently unruffled by her meddling. "Once, it wasn't. Things have changed."

"So I see," she said.

He smiled. His teeth were white, and just uneven enough to be interesting. "We'll speak of that. But this is festival night, when we should forget our troubles. Will you come into the city with us?"

Vanyi looked as if she might have pressed him for more, now that he had begun. But she was no less wise than Daruya. She let be, for a while. "We were intending to see the dancing."

"With us," he said laughing, "you can do better. You can join in it."

"Well now," she said, "I don't think—"

"Come," he said, sweeping her up, and Daruya, too, and whirling them out of the hall. "Masks, cloaks, festival purses—come! We'll revel the night away."

It was a mad, glad night, night of masks and laughter, sudden lights, sudden shadows, dancing and singing and long laughing skeins of people winding through the city. Daruya was swept right out of herself, whether she would or no. With her alien face hidden behind a mask, her alien mane concealed by the black hood of a reveller, she was no stranger at all. No one stared at her; no one whispered, or called others to come and see the demon walking free in the streets of the Summer City.

For all the wildness of the festival, her companions clung close together. Bundur's hand was strong in hers, fingers wound together, inextricable. When she danced, she danced with him. When she ran, he ran with her, and the others behind.

She had no wish to be free of him. He seemed like a part of her, the moon to her sun, whirling ever opposite, ever joined, but never touching save at arms' length. More than once some stranger tried to pull her loose; Bundur laughed and spun her away and shouted something that she could not make sense of, something about festival right. It always sent the other spinning off to a new quarry.

The music was all bells and drums, with once in a while the moaning of a great horn. It sounded odd, but after a time it seemed fitting—particularly after she had drunk a beaker or two of another wine than she had had in Shurakan before. This was strong, heady, and not sweet at all. If anything it was sour, like the yellow wine of Asanion. What color it was, she could not clearly see. Pale, she thought, not red, not blood-colored. Gold like sunlight. It burned going down, and warmed her to her fingers' ends, and made her feet light in the dance.

Bundur drank off a whole jar of it, dancing round a fire that leaped and capered in a square. There were masks all around it, laughing, clapping their hands, beating on drums. It came to Daruya with a shock of cold that she was standing alone and he was far away, across the fire. He whirled on the other side, arms wide, singing in his deep voice.

She ran, lifted, sprang through the fire. It reached for her as she flew. She laughed at it. "Cousin," she said to it. "Soul's kin." It warmed her but could not burn. It was never as hot as the fire in her blood.

She landed lightly, reaching for Bundur. Their hands clasped. The fire leaped out of her and wrapped him about.

He gasped. He was burning—but he was not. The fire filled him and did not consume him.

"Mageborn," she said, but in her own tongue, the language of princes in Starios. "Fireborn, Sun's blood. You—too—"

He understood, but in his bones, where he refused to listen. In himself he knew only that there had been fire coming out of her, and it was gone. They stood on cold paving, with the dance going on around them, and the fire—simple mortal flames again—casting ruddy light upon them all.

No fear, she thought. Even in the refusal of knowledge, no fear.

He pulled her away from the flames, but not back into the dance. She tried to twist away. The others were gone. She could not find them. The fire—

But he was too strong, and he was running, dragging her whether she would or no. This was the trap, her mind gibbered. Now he had her alone. He would take her away, hold her hostage, demand an empire's worth of ransom. Chakan would be gratified.

Stupidity. He was running away from the fire and the knowledge it held. He dragged her because he lacked the sense to let her go. He was lordly drunk, pure mazed with wine, and still too much the gentleman to throw her down and rape her as many a self-respecting princeling might have done.

Although, at that, he might not be so drunk that he thought she would allow such a thing. She would have gelded him if he had tried.

He ran, and she ran with him, weaving through the crowds. There was a giddy pleasure in it, once she gave herself up to it. Running, darting, dancing when they fell into a skein of dancers, running loose again, from end to end of the city and back, from fire to fire, dance to dance, sunset-side to sunrise-side, till movement was all there was and all there need be. So was the sun in its dance with the moons. So were the stars, wheeling in their courses. Such was the festival, this feast of the peace in the Summer City of Shurakan.

EIGHTEEN

I T HAD NOT BEEN A PLEASANT MORNING. FESTIVAL WINE WAS STRONGER THAN it looked, and hit harder; and Vanyi, having fallen into bed just as dawn paled the eastward sky, was roused much too soon after sunup to greet a guest. Esakai of Ushala temple, fresh and bright-eyed as if he had slept the night through, wanted to wish her a bright morning and was disposed to linger. He was curious as always, questioning yet again the preposterous belief the mages shared with Asanion, that there was no war in heaven between the light and dark, between good and evil; that the worlds hung in a balance, and that both light and dark were faces of the same power.

She was never completely averse to debating theology, but in the morning after a night of revelry it was more difficult than usual. She trapped herself, one way and another, into inviting her guest to breakfast. He might have stayed till noon if Daruya had not come to her rescue.

Daruya, trained in a harder school than Vanyi had been, got rid of the man in the most amiable way possible, but with admirable dispatch. He seemed hardly aware of the speed of his dismissal; he was still smiling when Daruya thrust him out the door, and still trying to persuade Vanyi that perhaps balance was not the way of the worlds.

Once he was gone, Vanyi found herself wishing for a less taxing escape. Daruya shut the door and barred it with an air of ominous purpose, dropped into the chair that Esakai had vacated and filled an empty bowl, tasting as she went, with a young thing's ravenous hunger. She had come to bed later than Vanyi, if in fact she had slept at all. Her hair was out of its myriad plaits, new-washed and curling more exuberantly than ever; she was back to the plain trousers and the worn coat that she wore among the seneldi, her only ornament the torque of Avaryan's priesthood. She looked stunningly beautiful, and completely unaware of it.

She filled a cup with tea, grimaced but drank it. "This has to be the most vile excuse for a tipple that man ever thought of," she said. "I even find myself missing Nine Cities ale."

"You aren't either," Vanyi said. "That stuff is undrinkable by human creature. This is rather pleasant once you get used to it. It's subtle."

"I'm not." Daruya spread a round of bread with herbed cheese, folded it over, devoured it in three bites. "You were wrong after all."

"What?" Vanyi asked. "About tea?"

Daruya's glance was disgusted. "Of course not. About that man."

Vanyi opened her mouth to play the idiot again, and to ask if the child meant Esakai; but that would press her temper too far. "What did he do, try to bed you?"

"No!" Daruya snatched up a fruit, hacked it open, scooped a handful of blood-red seeds. She ate them one by one, frowning. "No, he didn't. We danced, that was all. And I had to carry him home and help his servants put him to bed. He was drunk to insensibility."

"Mean drunk?"

"Charming," said Daruya. "Full of delightful nonsense. And never, even once, trying to lay his hands on anything he shouldn't."

"Ah," said Vanyi. "You're insulted."

That won her a molten glare, but Daruya's tone was mild. "From all you said, I thought he'd at least offer a proposal of marriage."

"Oh, no," Vanyi said. "That's not how it's done. The young man and the young woman keep company, and dance round the festival fires. The families discuss the colder aspects of the arrangement."

Even through her wine-caused headache, Vanyi was tempted to laugh. Daruya looked suddenly horrified. "You didn't—they didn't—"

"As a matter of fact they did," said Vanyi. "His mother took me back to the house—over my objections, I should add, and in spite of the fact that she was right, the children did need to get to bed. She brought out much too much of that damnable wine, and showed herself for a master negotiator. If their majesties ever send an embassy to your grandfather, I'll wager they send the Lady Nandi. She's as deadly as any courtier in the empire."

"I hope," said Daruya, thin and tight, "that you told her to take her wine and her fever-dreams and vanish."

"I thought of it," Vanyi admitted. "But she's persuasive. It's not, as she says, that her son can't find a wife in Shurakan. Many's the noble family that would give silk to buy him for their daughter."

"Then I wish her well of him, whoever she is," said Daruya. She sounded defiant. Vanyi, studying her, began inwardly to smile.

She kept the smile from her face. "He wants you," she said. "It's peculiar and considerably awkward, her ladyship and I agree, but they have a belief here, a doctrine that rather reminds me of some of our own. You know how their rulers are paired, king and queen, brother and sister; and they shudder at the thought of a single child. In their philosophy, souls are twinned, too, and for each man there is another matched to him. Sometimes it's a man—did you know they allow that here, and don't frown on man wedded to man or woman to woman?"

"That is strange," said Daruya, but not as if she paid much attention.

"It would explain your grandfather," Vanyi mused, "and his Olenyas with the lion-eyes, all those years ago. And Sarevadin the empress and her Asanian prince. And—" She shook herself fiercely. "In any case, my lord Bundur is convinced that you are the other half of his soul. He insists that he felt it the moment he saw you, and he's been adamant that he won't consider any other woman for his wife."

"He's out of his mind," said Daruya. "And if that's his doctrine, why in the world do women take handfuls of husbands here, and men marry only once but take women to their beds as often as they need to, to get themselves their pair of children?"

"I asked that," Vanyi said. "Nandi replied that the soul-bond is precious rare, and good sense does dictate that people marry for practicality's sake."

"Then let him be sensible," Daruya said, "and marry one of those nice respectable ladies. Even if I wanted to be his wife, it would be impossible. I'm a foreigner, I'm a mage, I look like a demon's get—and I'm the heir to an empire he's barely even heard of. I can't stay here and be the next matriarch of House Janabundur."

"He knows all of that," Vanyi said. "So does his mother. It doesn't matter."

"It might matter when my grandfather hears about it. He'll be livid."

"I should think that would be an incitement to do it," Vanyi said dryly.

Daruya bared her teeth. "Shouldn't it? But this time I think I'll actually be the obedient granddaughter." She raised her voice slightly, and the voice of her mind very much indeed. "Grandfather!"

Vanyi should have expected the young chit to do that. The ringing note of the mind-call nearly shattered her skull, but then, paradoxically, mended it. It was like being tempered in a forge.

There was no mercy in Sun-blood. But she had always known that. She felt the call reach the one it sought, felt the shifting of that powerful mind, wheeling like a dance of worlds, fixing itself on this place, this room, the two of them in it.

With an effort of will she brought him into his wonted focus. Not the great mage and emperor on his god-wrought throne; not the terrible warrior at the head of his armies. Simply Estarion, that dark man with his golden eyes, saying to his grand-daughter as if they stood in the room together, "Good evening, grandchild. Is this important? If not, you have some explaining to do."

Daruya did not even blush. "Oh, and is she angry, Grandfather?"

"Rather," he said. In this meeting of minds he put on a garment, a robe like woven sunlight, and divided himself briefly to soothe the woman in his bed. Quite a lovely woman, and amenable enough once she had had the circumstance explained to her—she was a priestess-mage, and not so young as to be jealous of a man's grandchild.

"She sends her regards," he said to Daruya, "and asks if you're still willing to put your stallion to her Suvieni mare."

"By all means," said Daruya with remarkable grace. "My regards to her, too, and, Grandfather, do you know that people here are trying to marry me off?"

He barely reeled with the shift; his eyes widened, and then, to Daruya's visible outrage, he laughed. "Are they, now? And is he worth it?"

"Is any man worth it?" she shot back.

"Most people would think so," he said mildly. He sat in a chair as if he were a solid presence in that room, and investigated the remains of breakfast. He pointed to one of the fruits in the basket, the blue-green one with the thorny rind. "What in the hells is that?"

"Fen-apple," Vanyi answered. "It looks poisonous, doesn't it? It doesn't taste bad. A bit tart, is all. They slice it and dip it in honey."

"They're going to marry me to a man in this kingdom-in-miniature," Daruya said sharply, "and you waste your time making faces at fen-apples?"

"I don't call it time wasted," he said, "if it gives me time to think. Who is this man, and why is he aspiring to your hand?"

"His name is Bundur," said Daruya, still with a snap in her voice, "and his mother is the king's half-sister. He thinks that our souls are mated, or some such nonsense, and he insists that he'll have no wife but me. He also thinks that I'm ugly, but because I'm interesting, it doesn't matter."

"How unusual," said Estarion. He might, for the matter of that, be speaking of the fen-apple, which he was examining from all sides. He had tried to pick it up, but his ghost-presence was not solid enough for that. "Is he ugly by our reckoning?"

"He looks like a Gileni nobleman," Daruya said. "In a word, no."

"Ah," said Estarion. "You have too much nose, then. And are too tall and too narrow. And much too oddly colored."

"And I have a demon's eyes." She shut them, drew a breath. "Grandfather, if you forbid it, he'll leave me alone."

"I never noticed that that made any difference to a determined lover," he said. "Particularly if, as I've been told, nobody here has the least regard for our lineage or our power."

"They do have regard for age," she said, "and for authority in a family. Even if I pretend that I have to send to you for permission—that would take years—"

"You should have thought of it before you summoned me," he said. "Now you'll have to lie about it."

She gaped at him.

"If Vanyi approves of this man," he said, "and if he comes of a decent family, and means you well, I can't see that I have any objection to his marrying you. It would give Kimeri a father, for one thing. For another, it would be useful for the embassy to have one of its members married to the king's kinsman."

"But you've never even seen him," she said with growing desperation.

"Vanyi has," he said. "I trust her judgment." He slanted a glance at Vanyi. "Do you like him?"

"He'll do," Vanyi answered. "He's good-looking, he's clever, and he can play politics—but he's honest about it. And he dotes on your granddaughter. Can't take his eyes off her."

"He can't believe any woman can be so hideous," Daruya said. She looked as if she would have liked to seize her grandfather and shake him. "Grandfather! You can't allow this."

"Granddaughter," he said, "you won't take anyone in my empire. If this man will do, then take him with my blessing. It will be a very pretty scandal that you had to marry a barbarian from the other side of the world, and wouldn't take any man, lord or commoner, in your own realm."

"Oh, no," she said. "I won't let you sway me with that. I don't want to marry anybody."

"You should," said Estarion. He stretched, yawned. "Ah me. I'm tired. They're trying to start a rebellion in Markad again, would you believe it? People are laughing in the rebels' faces, and the rebels are getting progressively more rebellious. All six of them. Maybe I should marry them off to ladies in Ianon, who will keep them nicely occupied and beat them soundly when they get out of hand."

"I think you should, at that," said Vanyi. "Unfortunately I don't think this man will beat our princess when she needs it. He's too much in love with her."

"I'd kill him, of course, if he laid a hand on her," said Estarion, as amiable as ever. "I wish you joy of the wedding."

He was gone before Daruya could say a word. Vanyi laughed at her expression. "Well, child. I'd say you were fairly effectively outflanked."

"You did this," Daruya said with sudden venom. "You colluded with him. You *told* him."

"No, I didn't," Vanyi said. "By my honor as a mage. I never said a word to him, or asked him to help. Though I admit I was less confident than you that he'd see your side of it. He wants you well matched, and with a man who will love you as well as keep you sensible."

"He doesn't know the first thing about Bundur."

"But I do," said Vanyi. "I like him. I think you do, too."

"What does that have to do with it?"

"When it comes to wedding and bedding," Vanyi said, "rather a great deal." She levered herself to her feet. "I'll leave you to think about it. But do bear in mind that this is a prince, and a power in the kingdom—and he favors our embassy. If you refuse him, you've insulted him terribly."

NINETEEN

ARUYA THOUGHT BEST WHEN SHE WAS IN MOTION. MOTION THAT, THIS TIME, took her to House Janabundur and halted her in front of its gate. She had not intended to come here, still less to let the porter admit her, but once it was done, it was done. Lady Nandi was not at home, the servant told her with careful courtesy, but the master of the house could be summoned if she wished.

She did not wish. She heard herself say, "I'll see him."

"Lady," the servant said, bowing her into a room she had not seen before, and leaving her there.

It was a receiving-room. She knew the look. Cushions to sit on, a low table, tea in a pot, the inevitable cakes that every house kept on hand for welcoming guests. The walls were hung with figured rugs, some of which looked very old, and all of which were as intricate as everything seemed to be in this country. Each told a story, sometimes simple, sometimes fantastic. She liked the small purse-mouthed man with the long mustaches, engaging in combat with an extravagantly streamered and barbeled dragon-creature. It was a most peculiar combat: it ended with the man and the dragon in a cavern, drinking tea and eating cakes in delightful amity.

She was smiling when Bundur made his entrance. It took him aback, which made her laugh.

"Lady!" he cried. "You devastate me. No howl of rage at the very least? No rampant display of temper?"

"I'm saving that for a larger audience," she said.

"Intelligent." He poured tea, handed her a cup. She sighed and sipped from it. It was the flowery tea of ceremony, of course. He said, watching her face, "You don't like tea."

"I'm getting used to it." She tilted her head toward the dragon tapestry. "What does this mean?"

"Why, whatever you want it to mean." But before she could frown: "It's an allegory, or so I'm told, about the folly of war. Personally I prefer the literal interpretation, that a warrior went to destroy a dragon of the heights, and they fought a mighty battle, but in the end, when neither could overcome the other, they declared a truce. Then after they had had a long and satisfying conversation, they decided that enmity was foolish, and became friends."

" 'Know your enemy, find a friend.' " Daruya shrugged. "We have that story, too, though we don't put a dragon in it."

"Wisdom is the same wherever you go." He emptied his cup and set it down. He looked well, she thought, considering the condition in which he had been put to bed. "So, then. Are you going to say yes?"

"Aren't you being a little bit precipitous?" she asked him. "You're supposed to circle all around it, yes? And wait for our elders to conclude the agreement."

"No," he said. "Not once everyone's been told."

"I'm not going to say yes," she said.

He betrayed no surprise, and no sign of hurt, either. "But of course you are. You just don't know it yet."

"No," she said.

"Yes," said Bundur. "What concerns you? That I'm a prince in this kingdom, and you're a nobody? That you're a queen in yours, and I'm a nobody? That's a perfect balance, I should think. Or is it that I'm older than you? Eight years is nothing—or is it nine?"

"Eight," she said. "Closer to seven. I'm not a child."

"Of course not. If you were, I wouldn't be asking for you. So that's not what troubles you. Your daughter? I balance her with my son. Each has need of a sibling. Marry me and they can be brother and sister forever after."

"I don't want to marry anybody," said Daruya.

"Of course you don't want to marry just anybody. You want to marry me."

"You," she said in mounting incredulity, "are the most arrogant, cocksure, headstrong, stubborn, obstinate—"

He was grinning, and wider, the longer the catalogue grew. "Surely," he said when she ran out of names to call him. "And you love me for it. I'm exactly the man for you. Else why did you refuse all those men in your own country, which you say is so vast and has so many people? You were waiting for me."

"Oh!" said Daruya in frustrated rage, flinging the cup at him. He caught it deftly, avoided the spray of tea that came with it, set it down with the care due its fragility.

"You see?" he said. "We match. You fling my mother's best cup, which is a hundred years old, last work of a master. I catch it. A perfect pairing."

"Why?" she shouted at him. "Why do you insist on this travesty?"

"No travesty," he said, as calm as ever. "Destiny. I argued with it, too, you know. I had a long discussion with several of the gods. They all told me what I knew already, which was that you were meant for me. I saw that the first time I looked on your face, there in the teahouse, and reflected that ugliness can be its own kind of beauty."

"I am *not* ugly," she gritted.

"No," he admitted freely. "You aren't. It was only that first time, before I learned to see you as you are, and not as something out of nature. Now I think you quite beautiful. In your strange way."

"I'm not flattered," she said. "I'm not going to marry you."

"Of course you are."

He smiled. His eyes were limpid, amiable. He was no more yielding than the mountain he was named for, Shakabundur that was rooted in the deeps of the earth and clove the sky. He did not care what she said or how she said it. He was going to have her.

Why then, she wondered with a shock, did she not feel more truly trapped? She was angry, yes. Furious. She wanted to knock him down and slap the smile from his face. But she felt as she had in the festival, without even the excuse of wine and the dance. As if they were supposed to be here, face to face, bound and in opposition. She had not even the luxury of rebellion. As easily rebel against the color of her eyes, or the shape of her hand.

Her hand. She raised it. There was pain in it, but not as it had been before. The burning was muted, the throbbing dulled almost to painlessness.

The brand was still there, the *Kasar* with its glitter of gold in the pale honey of her skin. Its power was not gone; she felt it like the weight of the sun in her palm. But the pain that had been with her since her earliest memory, that she had been taught would never leave her, was sunk so low that it might not have been there at all.

Bundur was staring at it. Had he seen it before? She could not recall. She did not flaunt it. A man, seeing flashes of it, might think he imagined them, or she was carrying a coin in her hand, or wearing an odd fashion of ornament.

She answered him before he could ask. "Yes, you see what you think you see. I was born with it. All of my line are. It's the god's brand."

"It's splendid," he said.

"Do your kings carry such a thing?" she asked. She meant to mock, but not entirely.

If he caught the mockery, he disregarded it. "No. Our kings and queens are known for what they are, but the god doesn't mark them, except in the soul."

"I carry two brands, for my two empires," she said. "Sun in the hand, for Keruvarion, and eyes of the Lion, for Asanion, which was the Golden Empire. Our gods are given to displays, I suppose. It makes it easy to tell who's meant to rule and who is not."

"But it makes it difficult to get away from it when you need to."

She stared at him, surprised. No one had ever understood that before.

He smiled and laid his palm against hers, unafraid, unaware that the brand could burn. His hand was broader, stronger, the color of bronze. It was warm. His fingers wound with hers. His face behind its smile was austere, proud, with its sharp planes.

"Your people," she said, "must be kin to our plainsmen. Did they come across the sea long ago and settle here, or did they begin here? How old is this world of yours?"

"Old," he said. "Ancient beyond telling. And yours?"

"Maybe older than that. Maybe younger." She clenched her fist. It wound their fingers tighter. "I'll bed you if you want it. Happily."

"I don't want that," he said. "Not for a night or a season. I want it with honor, in the marriage bed."

"Why?"

"Because it should be so. Because you are worthy of it."

"I the outlander. I the ugly one. I the mage."

"All of that. And worthy. Do you not want me because I'm ugly to you, too?"

"No. I don't want to marry."

"Why?"

Her own question, returned with that ceaseless smile. "I don't. That's all. Some-day I'll have to, to get myself a consort—then it had better be someone suitable, who can share the throne and the duties, and rule in my name when I can't be everywhere at once. How would you do that? You know nothing but Shurakan."

"I could learn," he said.

"And leave Shurakan?"

"Even that," he said steadily, "I could do if I must."

She wrenched free in sudden disgust. "You don't have the faintest conception of what you mean when you say that. You're not getting a wife if you get me, you lovestruck fool. You're getting the heir to an empire, and the whole empire with her. If you were ambitious I'd understand it. But you don't even know what my empire is. Nor do you care."

"I said," he said, "I can learn. And if we're talking of politics, be politic now and think. I may not understand your empire, but I understand Su-Shaklan—and Su-Shaklan is about to become rather more than dangerous for you and your embassy. Do you know that there are many who hate and fear foreigners, and you above all? They're growing in numbers, and they're growing powerful. The king has been resisting their persuasions, but he's weakening fast. The least he'll do, once he gives in, is lock you in prison. His counselors are begging him to kill you outright."

"I know that," she said impatiently. "I've known it since we came here."

"You don't know how close the king is to the edge." Bundur took both her hands, though she resisted, and held them. "Listen to me. I visit the king often—he's my mother's brother, it's expected. We're fond of one another. But he's immovably con-vinced that foreigners mean nothing but harm to Su-Shaklan, and foreigners of your ilk more than any other. This morning he told me that if I want to keep you safe, I had best marry you soon, and bring you all under the protection of Janabundur. Otherwise he can't promise that any of you will escape this place alive."

Daruya's lip curled. "Oh, do tell me another. Why in the hells would the king tell you that, if he hates us so much? He'd be locking you up for a madman, for wanting to marry me at all."

"He understands the soul-bond," Bundur said. "He doesn't like it, he doesn't approve of it, but he can't deny it. 'Marry her,' he said, 'and seal it for all to see. Or see her hunted down and killed with all the rest of her kind.'" His hands tightened, bruising-hard. "Lady, Daruya, he's not an evil man, but he's a righteous one. And he's beat upon day and night by those who hunger for your blood and the blood of all mages. It's an old, old hate, from the beginning of the kingdom. He fights it, but he can't fight it much longer."

"Then how come you can?"

"Maybe," he said, "because I'm not the king. My mind is my own. I can use it to think, and my eyes to see. You're no more evil than any other child of men."

"If no less." *Damn*, thought Daruya. Her fingers were locked with his again. They seemed to think that that was the way of nature.

This must be what Vanyi felt when she was with Estarion—and forty years had done nothing to ease it, either. What Estarion felt with Vanyi, Daruya could not presume to know. He loved his empress, of that she was certain. He had refused an Asanian harem for her, but as she grew old but he did not, he had taken other lovers, with the empress' knowledge and consent.

The first one or two, Daruya had reason to suspect, had been of the empress' choosing. The empress was Asanian. She would have been perturbed, even offended, if he had forsaken all the pleasures of the bedchamber, simply because she was not herself able to share them.

But none of those lovers had been Vanyi. With Vanyi it would have mattered too much.

Getting with child had been simple compared to this. Daruya chose the man, she found him willing, she took what she needed and bade him farewell, and that was that. He went back to his doting wife. She went back to her grandfather, and to the splendor of a scandal.

This would be a scandal only insofar as the man was a foreigner. Her grandfather approved it, the more fool he. The Master of the Guild wanted it—pressed her to do it. They all saw the advantage in it, the embassy saved, and their lives, too, if Bundur spoke the truth. None of them seemed to comprehend that when a woman married, she married, one could hope, until she died.

Or she might not. She might leave her husband. Daruya might leave Shurakan when their embassy had done what it set out to do; leave him, go back to Starios, be princess-heir again without the pressure of urging that she marry and be respectable. Her child would have a father-in-name. The man who held that name . . .

"This is impossible," she said. "We can't do it."

"We can," he said, as she had known he would.

"Then why," she inquired acidly, "don't you marry Vanyi instead? She'd do anything to further this embassy. She's not bound to any one place, she's not heir to any empire, she's not young, either, but she's strong; she'll live another thirty years, and keep you well satisfied, too."

"The Lady Vanyi is not soulbound to me," said Bundur, "or I might consider it."

"If I said the words with you," said Daruya through clenched teeth, "I could not promise to stay with you, or even to stay married to you for longer than necessity requires."

"I could take that risk," he said.

"You don't know what you're saying."

"On the contrary," said Bundur, and for the first time she saw a hint of temper, "I do. Give me credit for a little wit, my lady. I understand all the arguments against this—I've had them from my kin, too. None of them matters. Nothing matters but that my soul bids me take you."

"And that we're in danger if I don't."

"Well," he said. "If you weren't, I wouldn't push so hard or so fast. Too fast for you, I know. But the king never cries the alarm without excellent reason."

"I'll think about it," said Daruya, pulling free as she always seemed to be doing, and leaving him before he could call her back.

TWENTY

KIMERI DECIDED THAT SHE DID NOT HATE HANI AFTER ALL, EVEN IF HE WAS a coward. He kept saying that he had been going to get help, but she went away before he could come back—very well, she would say she believed him. It was true that he was afraid of the tall woman, though why he should be, she could not imagine. The woman was of high rank, but then so was Kimeri; and Kimeri's mother was as tall as most men, and quite terrifying, too, when she was in a temper. Kimeri would be that tall someday, everybody said she would. She was looking forward to it. Then Hani would be afraid of her, and she would show him what an idiot he was.

They had called truce for the festival, and had a splendid time, even if Hani's grandmother had dragged them back home much too early and put them to bed in the same room. They were going to be sister and brother, Hani's grandmother was thinking, because Kimeri's mother was going to marry Hani's father. Kimeri had her doubts about that. Hani's father was big and handsome, and he made the room brighter when he came into it, but Kimeri's mother was very clever about escaping from people who wanted to marry her.

Kimeri had the same dream as always, the same dark place, the same presence that she knew was the Guardian in the Gate. As always, she was glad to wake up, but sorry, too; the Guardian's sorrow, because while she dreamed he had company, but while she was awake he was all alone. It was hurting more, the longer he stayed in the Gate, but at the same time it was hurting less, as if he had stopped caring about being alive again.

She was surprised to wake up and find the walls all wrong, and the bed not the bed she had got used to. She was in Hani's house, and Hani was sound asleep in the bed next to hers. Kimeri thought about waking him up, but if he stayed asleep she could have all of the tea with honey in it that a servant brought as soon as she got out of bed, and most of the redspice buns. She ended up leaving him some of each, because she was not as selfish as she might be.

There was an Olenyas sitting in a shadow the way they liked to do, waiting for her. It was a different one than had been there when she went to sleep. "Rahai," she said, touching his shoulder. His eyes were dark for an Olenyas', almost brown. They smiled at her. He got to his feet in the way she tried to copy but never could, as if he had no bones at all, and followed her when she walked out of the room and the house.

He knew where to go once they were outside, which saved her trouble, because she wanted to dawdle and not pay attention to where she was going. The city was all quiet and rather tired, with bits of festival garland scattered everywhere, and sleepy-eyed people sweeping it up. Nearly everybody was still asleep, or just awake with a pounding headache. Grownfolk woke up like that when they had had too much wine the night before.

She wandered a bit, because she needed to think. She thought about going to the house where the Gate was, since she was outside the palace anyway, and Rahai might not stop her. But something said, *Not yet. Soon, but not yet.*

She thought of arguing, but the *soon* was very soon; she felt it. She kept on walking, then, without Rahai saying anything. He had no headache. He had been asleep while everybody danced and played. She felt a little sorry for him, but not too much. Olenyai had their own games and their own festivals, and those kept them as happy as men could be; and meanwhile he was wide awake and pleased to be guarding her on this fine summer's morning. Bits of thought trickled through the protection all Olenyai had: right-here-nowness, high clear sky with a cloud here and there, mountain walls, air like wine chilled in snow. Shadows that were people, people-harmless, people-who-might-harm. Those latter he watched, ready to defend if there was need, but there never was.

They came to the palace eventually and went inside. The guards on the gates looked blurry-eyed and headachy. Kimeri gave them a festival gift, a touch that took the ache away. None of them knew where it came from, but that was the way it should be.

Rahai tried to lead her straight through to where the house was, but she was not ready to go there yet. Vanyi was there, just about to wake up. Her mother was just coming in, thinking about Bundur and not knowing she was doing it, nor wanting to if she had known. She was all in a tangle about him, wanting and not wanting, being part of him and not wanting to be a part of him at all.

Maybe she *would* marry him, Kimeri thought. She had never been like this about a man before, especially one who wanted to marry her. If she liked a man, she bedded him; if not, she told him to lose himself, and shut the door in his face. Kimeri had never seen her in a such a confusion of wanting-not-wanting.

She did not want Kimeri to see her that way, either. Kimeri got out of her mind before she noticed the intruder, and went looking for somewhere to go that would not get in Daruya's way.

The palace children were still asleep, like Hani, or being fussed over by their parents or their aunts or their cousins. Servants were up and working, but none of them would speak to Kimeri unless she spoke first, and they certainly would not play with her.

But there was someone who might be glad to see her. Whom she felt she might talk to, and maybe, finally, be listened to. That someone was awake and had no headache, and was mildly bored herself. She was in the room she had told Kimeri to come to, reading a book she had read too many times before, and thinking about too many things at once. How Hani could be afraid of her, Kimeri could not imagine. Even if she was the queen.

She thought Kimeri did not know. She still thought it when Kimeri slipped through the back door, the one that was not supposed to open on anything at all, and Kimeri did not like to tell her she was wrong. She might be insulted.

She smiled, not knowing what Kimeri was thinking, and Kimeri was glad of that. "Good morning, child," she said. "Good morning, shadow-man."

Rahai bowed. He did not understand Borti's language, since he had no magery to teach it to him, but he could tell when he was being spoken to. He was wary, his eyes watching everything at once. Kimeri tried to tell him silently that he had nothing to be afraid of, but his protections kept him from hearing magewords. He stayed close, on guard.

Kimeri ignored him. Borti, studying her, did the same. "Good morning," said Kimeri. "Did you have a good festival?"

Borti's smile stayed the same, but the thoughts in the front of her mind were full of sad things: a fight with a man who must be the king, a great number of people smiling but looking as if they had fangs, fear she could not put a name to. Kimeri tried not to listen, but when a person thought so loudly, it was very hard to shut one's ears inside.

Borti's thoughts were deeply troubling, but aloud she said, "I had a pleasant festival, I suppose. And you?"

"Very pleasant," Kimeri said more honestly than Borti had. "My friend is my friend again—you know, the boy who ran away. He's a coward, but I can forgive him that. He's only a boy."

"Wisely said," said Borti. She reached for the box on the table next to her and opened it. A great odor of sweetness and spices wafted out. "These were a festival gift. Would you like to share them with me?"

Rahai slipped in before Kimeri could, and tasted one. Kimeri frowned at his rudeness, but Borti seemed to understand, and even to approve. After an endless while he got out of the way and let Kimeri sit down and try the sweets. They were odd but wonderful, like Shurakan.

"You didn't have a shadow-man before," Borti said. "Did your mother give him to you for the festival?"

"Oh, he's not a slave," said Kimeri quickly. Rahai could hardly be insulted, since he did not speak Borti's language, but she did not want Borti to think the wrong thing, either. "He's a bred-warrior. He serves the emperor, and my mother since she'll be empress someday, and me since I'll be empress after her. He thinks we all need guarding."

"And you didn't before?"

"I slipped away then," Kimeri confessed. "This time I didn't. Everyone's getting more afraid instead of less, the longer we stay here."

"Do you know why that is?" Borti asked.

She did want to know, not the why, but whether Kimeri knew it. Kimeri supposed she should be clever and pretend not to know, but she hated to tell lies. "Because we have enemies, and they hate us. They're going to do something soon, aren't they?"

"They might," Borti said, meaning they would.

"Something like breaking the Gate," Kimeri said. "That's what they did before."

"Gate?" asked Borti. "Which Gate is that?"

She was testing again. Kimeri hated it when people played the testing game, but she decided not to get angry yet. "The Worldgate, the Gate the mages made. But mage is a dirty word here, isn't it?"

"Some people think so," Borti said. Thinking louder than ever: that it was foolish, but who knew what mages really were, or what they could do? Except raise their Gates. She had seen the one in Shurakan. It was strange, but it had not felt evil. It looked like a door, but on the other side of it was a place that could not be as close as it was—a place on the other side of the world.

She came back to what Kimeri said. "The Gate is broken, you say?"

"You didn't know it?" Kimeri asked her. "I thought everybody knew. That's why we came here the way we did. We didn't have a Gate to come through. Vanyi has been trying to get to y—to the queen and tell her, and ask her to help find out who did it. Her mages can't find anything at all."

Borti's eyes narrowed. She looked frightening then, if Kimeri had been the kind of person to be scared by a face. "Is it so? Has the Gate broken and no one has told me? How did it break? Do you know that?"

"Something broke it," said Kimeri. "I don't know what. Nobody does. But nobody knows what happened inside it, either. Except me. The mage who was Guardian— they think he's dead. Even he does. But he's not. He's trapped inside the Gate."

"How do you know that?"

Kimeri swallowed the bit of sweet she had been chewing. It was too sweet suddenly, and too sticky. It gagged her going down. But once it was down, it stayed there.

Nobody ever listened to her, or paid attention when she talked about Gates. But Borti did—Borti was fixed on her without the least doubt in the world that she knew what she was talking about. That was so strange that for a moment Kimeri had no words in her, and no way to speak them if she had.

Her voice came back all at once, and her wits with it. "I know because I'm a mage, too. I felt the Gate break. I saw it trap Uruan. He's still in it. I dream about him all the time, about how he's in there, and he thinks he's dead. He's scared, when he remembers to be."

"Why haven't you tried to get him out?"

"I don't know how," said Kimeri. "Vanyi won't even let me talk about it. The other mages pat me on the head and say 'Yes, yes' and don't hear a word. Even Kadin—he says maybe so, but what difference does it make? Dead is dead."

"And yet you leave him there. Surely there must be something you can do."

"They won't let me go outside the palace," Kimeri said. "Except for the festival, and then they watched me every minute. I did try. I did." She was almost in tears. "He doesn't feel anything, not really. He just dreams, and makes me dream, too. I try to help him then. I try to make him feel better."

Borti was not the kind of person to melt when a young person cried, or even to pay much attention to it unless it flung itself into her arms. Which Kimeri was deliberately not doing. "Can you show me?" Borti asked.

Kimeri blinked at her, shaking away tears. "Now?"

"No," said Borti a little too quickly. "I mean, can you show me where the Gate was?"

"I don't know if I can get out," Kimeri said.

"Can you come here?"

"I think so," said Kimeri slowly. "I did before. If it's night—if you don't mind that people say the house is haunted—"

"Ah, and so it would be," said Borti. She was amused, but scared, too. "Tonight? Before the Brightmoon rises?"

"I can try," said Kimeri.

The voice inside of her was singing. *Soon. Yes, soon.* She told it to be quiet, before somebody heard, and unmade it all.

TWENTY-ONE

TONIGHT WAS A NIGHT OF THE GREAT MARRIAGE: WHEN BOTH BRIGHT-moon and Greatmoon were full, dancing in the sky together, the blinding-bright white moon and the great blood-red one, so splendid together that they blocked out the stars. Here where the world was so much closer to the sky, the moons seemed near enough to touch. Near enough to knock out of the sky and shatter on the earth, and pour out their blood, white and red, in shining rivers.

Kimeri was dizzy with excitement. She had got out of the house as she had come through the Gate, by making herself a shadow. None of the Olenyai had followed her. Her mother and Vanyi were singing the rite of the moons' rising; the mages were with them, even Kadin. She should have been there, but she made sure to vanish before anyone could start looking for her.

By the time the Olenyai understood that she had escaped, she was deep in the palace, almost to the room at the end of the hidden passage, and Borti was running toward her, wrapped in a cloak and a hood. "Quickly," Borti said, catching Kimeri's hand as she ran past. "People will be following."

Kimeri lightened her feet to run faster, and kept up easily with the woman's long stride. They went by ways that Kimeri did not know, with many twists and turns and doublings-back. Borti knew the palace as well as Hani had ever pretended to: she never hesitated, and never paused when there was a turn to make. In almost no time at all, they had passed through a gate and found themselves in a dark and deserted street.

Greatmoon was up, casting a glow like fire into the sky. Brightmoon would follow in a little while: Kimeri could feel her below the mountain walls, climbing slowly, taking her time. The sun was still close to the horizon on the other side of the sky, staining it a different red than Greatmoon did, more rose-red, fading to palest green and then to purple as it sank. The stars were trying to come out, but tonight they would not last long, not with both moons to drown their light.

Borti paid no attention to the splendor in the sky. She was even more nervous than she had been in the morning, and her thoughts darted almost too quick to follow. More about the king, about the fight they had had, about people who smiled with their faces but who thought terrible things. She was thinking that she should have stayed in the palace, but that she had to come out, she had to get away, it was only for a little while, then she would go back before she was missed. Which did not make sense to Kimeri, since Borti had already been missed: or why had she wanted to run so fast?

She slowed down in the street, just a little, enough to seem purposeful instead of panicked. "You have to lead me now," she said. "I've never been to the house where the Gate is—was."

"Is," said Kimeri. She let her feet go heavy again, and turned where her dream told her to go. It was hard, because the dream, like a bird, flew the straight way, but the streets were not straight at all. They twisted and turned, went up and down, round and about, and stopped in blind walls or closed gates. She had to thread her way through them, less quickly or surely than Borti had come through the palace. But she did not get lost, and she only ran into one wall, and that turned out to have a door in it, which opened into another street. At the end of that was a stair, then yet another street, and then at last, when they were both winded and ready to rest, a house that looked from the outside like any other house. But no people lived in it. No lights hung in strings along its roof, and no lantern hung by its gate to welcome people as they went past.

This street had people in it, but only a few, and they were not paying attention to a cloaked and hooded woman leading a cloaked and hooded child by the hand. Kimeri decided to venture a light, since the moons' light shone too dim yet, with Brightmoon just up and Greatmoon keeping more light than it shed. Her left hand was clutched tight in Borti's. She freed the right from her cloak and unfolded her fingers from her palm.

The sun in it shone dazzling. She damped it quickly, till it was just bright enough to see by, like a shaded lantern. She felt Borti's start of surprise, the stab of fear that disappeared as quickly as it came. Borti was brave, to be so calm about magery, and without warning, too.

By the light of the *Kasar* they went up to the gate. It was latched but not locked. There was a warding on it, with a taste of Kadin and a hint of Vanyi. Kimeri slipped a bit of shadow-thought into it, until it was sure they were no one and nothing but a night wind and a glimmer of moonlight. Then she slipped through, pulling Borti after her.

The house was dark and cold, as if summer had never come inside. It smelled of dust and of old stone. Kimeri knew people had lived here, and not long ago, either: mages, Guardians, coming and going through the Gate and into the city. The house had forgotten them.

A spell was on it, a spell of dark and of forgetfulness. It tried to weave itself around Kimeri, but she was ready for it. She sent it running with a flash of the *Kasar*. In that clean bright light they walked through empty, dusty rooms. Furniture was as the Guardian had left it, a bed that had been slept in, a chair drawn back from a table, a scroll on it with weights on the corners, the page half written on. Kimeri could not read yet. She was saving that for when she had time to learn it properly.

There was a loaf of bread on the table beside the scroll, green with mold, and a knife beside it, and a withered wheel of cheese. The black wrinkled things in the blue bowl must be fruit.

Borti's hand was cold in Kimeri's. She was not afraid of a mageling with a handful of light, but ghosts made her bones shiver. She thought she saw them in every shadow, every flicker of light as they moved.

Kimeri could not think of a way to comfort her. There was a ghost in the house, after all, if only one. She felt him in the innermost room. It was like the room the mages had taken in the house in the palace, deep inside, walled all around and windowless, but larger—a good deal larger, to hold the Gate. It had been a shrine, Kimeri guessed: the walls were splendidly painted and the floor had tiles like the speaking god's shrine in the palace. There was no god here. Only a blank grey wall with the faintest suggestion of an outline drawn on it: posts and lintel, the shape of a gate.

There was a lamp-cluster here, with oil in the lamps, and flint and a striker hanging from the hook on the base. Kadin kept the lamps filled, Kimeri thought. She wondered if he ever used them. He could make magelight, even darkmages could do that; or he might like sitting in the dark.

He was not there now. He was singing the moons into the sky. Kimeri lit the lamps by thinking about it, because it seemed the right thing to do. Their light was warmer than the light of the *Kasar,* and gentler. The lines of the Gate were fainter in it, but the grey of the wall seemed more silvery, as if there were a Gate there still.

Borti's voice came soft, no more than a whisper. "Are there words one says? An invocation, a calling up of the dead?"

"He's not dead," Kimeri said. She hoped her voice was not too sharp. "Can you see where the Gate was?"

"I see a wall," Borti said.

"That was it," said Kimeri. "Does it look a little odd to you?"

"It's painted grey," said Borti. "Like rain."

"Like rain," said Kimeri. "Yes. See, it shimmers. The Gate is broken, but somehow it's still here. Like a ghost of a Gate. He's keeping it here by being in it."

Borti shivered, but she was strong. She did not run, or think about running. "I don't see anything."

There was nothing to see. But he was there, in the greyness that looked like a wall but was not. Kimeri wondered what would happen if she touched it with her hand. She was not sure she needed to know.

"Uruan," she said, which was the Guardian's name. Names had power, all the mages said so, and the priests, too. "Uruan, can you hear me calling?"

He was trapped in the Gate, drifting, dreaming. All he could see was grey, nothingness, no sight, no sound, no taste, no scent, no touch. Kimeri tried to push through the grey, to give him the touch of her mind's hand, the sound of her voice. "Uruan!"

Borti gasped. Kimeri, half in her body and half out of it, saw how the wall changed, how its grey turned silver. There was a shape in it. A body. A face. Uruan was a red Gileni: he was easy to see, dark bronze against the grey, with his bright mane.

"*Begone*, foul fiend from the hells below!"

The voice was a brass bellow. It rang in the empty space. It knocked Kimeri down and set Borti spinning, crying out. Uruan struggled in his prison, waking out of his dream into a madness of panic.

Kimeri scrambled to her feet. She was too furious to be afraid. A man stood in the doorway, a preposterous figure, shaved head and shaved face painted half black, half white, and the rest of him ordinary Shurakani brown, which was easy to see because he was naked. Maybe he thought he was dressed: he was hung everywhere with jangling ornaments, amulets, images, fetishes, things that smelled of black dark and things that smelled of bright light, all jumbled together and jangling against one another. He was dancing from foot to foot, a rattle in one hand, a long and dangerous-looking knife in the other.

"Oh, goddess," said Borti. She was laughing, though she sounded as if she wanted to cry.

Kimeri was not laughing at all. The man's jumble of amulets matched the jumble of his power, and it was power, magery all twisted and odd, half real, half pretended. He was aiming it at the Gate. At Uruan, who was a half-thing himself, half alive and half not, and like to become nothing if the man kept on.

"Stop it!" Kimeri yelled at him. "Stop it! You're killing him!"

The man turned the force of his power on her. It swayed her, and she could not see for a bit, but she was stronger than it was. He was dancing and hopping from foot to foot, waving his knife about as if he had the faintest idea how to use it. "Demon! Creature of darkness! Back to thy hells, and thy foul spirit with thee!"

"Oh, come," said Kimeri, too angry to be polite. "That's silly. I'm not a demon, and that's not a foul spirit, that's a man trapped in a Gate. What in the world are you?"

"He's an exorcist," Borti answered for him, since he seemed unable to speak. Demons, it was clear, were not supposed to talk back, still less tell him exactly what was what. Borti went on, "He sends demons back where they came from, and lays ghosts to rest."

"He's not much of an exorcist," Kimeri said tartly, "if he can't tell a demon from a Sunchild, or a trapped Guardian from a creature of the hells."

The exorcist blinked. His magic was in rags. Under it he was not a bad man, simply ignorant. Kimeri was not inclined to be kind to him for that. Even when he said in a completely different voice than the one he had been using, soft and rather diffident, "Have I made a mistake? This isn't the haunting I came to be rid of?"

"Who sent you?" Kimeri demanded. "This is our house if it's anybody's. *We* certainly didn't want an exorcist."

"We send ourselves," the exorcist said. "Every night of great moment, when the moons are full or the moons are new, or one or both is in a position of power, somebody comes to dance the haunting away."

"It never works, does it?" Kimeri said. "It's not going to work now." She advanced on him and plucked the knife out of his hand. It made her fingers tingle. It had a black blade; at home it would have been a darkmage's instrument, and not a pleasant one, either. Usually its blade was poisoned.

This one was not. She broke it across her golden palm and flung the pieces away. "You shouldn't walk around waving darkblades as if they were kitchen knives. Don't you know they can drink souls?"

The exorcist opened and shut his mouth. "I don't—I didn't—"

"Obviously," said Kimeri. "So you people think there's a ghost here, and he walks when the moons are up. He doesn't, really. He's trapped in the Gate. It's just his fetch that walks, trying to find its way out. If you hadn't interrupted, we might have been able to help him."

The exorcist looked completely crestfallen. He was not very old, Kimeri saw, for grownfolk. He was maybe as old as her mother. He was full of himself, all fresh and newly initiate, and this was supposed to be his first great charge.

It served him right, she thought nastily, for being such an idiot.

He tried to scramble together his dignity, and his crooked magery with it. "You are a demon," he said in as steady a voice as he could manage. "You were set here to test me."

"I am not," said Kimeri. "I told you that already. People look like this where I come from. Now will you go away? We're busy."

That was the wrong thing to say. He had his power all together, and his temper to make it stronger. He rolled it into a ball and threw the lot of it at her, so fast and so hard she could barely get out of the way, and even more barely see where it was going. Her own power lashed out desperately, all anyhow, and struck it sidewise.

There was a blinding flash, a clap of thunder. Kimeri was knocked down again. But her body did not matter. Her power was flying into the broken Gate, locked with the exorcist's, and Uruan was right in its path. Holding himself there. Seeing his death, wanting it, wanting to be gone, away, out of this agony of half-existence.

"No," said Kimeri. She said it in her ordinary voice. In the howling of Gatewinds, no one should have been able to hear it at all, but it was clear, its sound distinct.

The Gate was awake. It should not be—it was dead. But neither should Uruan be alive, and he was. Somehow he and the Gate together had kept it all from falling apart.

The bolt of power struck them both. Something ripped. Something else tore. It might be the inside of Kimeri's head. It might be the fabric of the Gate, or the thing that had bound the Gate, knocked it down and fallen on it. Through the gap, something fell—something large and breathing and bruised, that looked around, laughed once as a madman might, and crumpled to the floor.

So that was what Uruan really looked like. He was more like the people here than anybody else in the embassy, copper-bright hair and all. He looked like the prince in Han-Gilen, which was not surprising, since the prince was his elder brother. His face at the moment was grey, as if he had brought some of the nothingness with him, but that was only shock and unconsciousness. He was very much alive, and very much there, lying on the threshold of the new-waked Gate.

Kimeri scrambled to her bruised knees. Borti was struggling up, too, and the exorcist was starting to come to himself. They were both staring at the Gate. It was awake but not focused. On the other side of it was night, with stars; but no stars that shone on the world Kimeri knew.

They were quiet, and that was what mattered. Kimeri asked them to guard the Gate for her. They did not exactly agree, but she felt as if they had. They were inside of her somehow, as they were in the Gate. It was strange, but it felt right; they belonged there, they and the Gate both. Nothing would touch that Gate, or pass it, or hurt it, as long as they were there and she was there. She was content with that; she hoped that everyone else would be, too.

TWENTY-TWO

KIMERI SHOULD HAVE KNOWN BETTER THAN TO EXPECT THAT ANYBODY would be reasonable about the new-waked Gate. Especially with Uruan back, as they all thought, from the dead. Borti had to make the exorcist help her carry him, since Kimeri was too small and too tired from everything she had done; then they had to go by back ways, because a naked exorcist and a hooded woman and a yellow-eyed child carrying an unconscious man through the streets at night was suspicious to say the least. Kimeri had enough power left to cover them all with shadows, which helped.

Vanyi and Daruya both met them halfway to the house in the palace, with Olenyai and mages behind. Kimeri could have hidden from them, but she was too glad to see them, even if she would get a right tanning when they had time to think about it. At least she did not need to explain anything to start with; Uruan was enough to engross them all, and Borti and the exorcist rather faded into insignificance. They were swept along whether they wanted it or not, but no one asked questions, nor said or did anything but keep them under guard.

The house was warm and welcoming, Olenyai in it to let them in and bar the gate behind them, lamps lit in the dining-room, which was the biggest room and the one where everyone could gather, but no servants anywhere. They had all disappeared.

The Olenyai brought in a pallet and spread it for Uruan, and he was laid on it.

People tried not to crowd. Vanyi bent over him, and Daruya, running their hands down his body, tracing it in power.

"Alive," said Vanyi, saying what they all knew. "And well, except for shock. He'll sleep it off and wake sane."

Daruya sank to her heels, hands on thighs. Her eyes found Kimeri, who was trying to find a shadow to slip away inside of. "Merian," she said.

Her tone was mild, but she never called Kimeri by her grownfolk name unless Kimeri was in trouble. Kimeri came forward slowly, holding her courage in both hands. Just outside of her mother's reach, she stopped.

"Ki-Merian," said Daruya. "Can you explain this?"

Kimeri swallowed. They were all staring, mages, Olenyai, Borti and the exorcist, too. "I told you he was in the Gate," she said. "You wouldn't listen."

Daruya's brows drew together. "You told me you were having nightmares. You didn't say what those nightmares were."

"I told Vanyi," Kimeri said.

Vanyi flushed, which was startling. "God and goddess. So she did. I thought she was babbling, or telling stories."

"Because I'm too young," Kimeri said. "I know. Nobody would listen."

Except Borti, but Kimeri did not think she wanted to say that. Not yet. Kimeri was in enough trouble by herself.

"Well then," Daruya said, "since we didn't listen, and that's our fault, suppose you tell us how you woke the Gate and got the Guardian out of it."

"I didn't mean to," said Kimeri, trying not to whine. "The exorcist was trying to lay the ghost and exorcise me, and I tried to stop him. The Gate woke up. Uruan fell out of it. The Gate's still there. But it's not opening on anything but stars."

"A blind Gate," Vanyi said. She sounded afraid. That, like her blush, was not like her at all. "We're warned in all the books of Gates, not to let that happen."

"Do they ever say why?" Daruya asked. Odd to see her the calm one, and Vanyi flustered.

"No," Vanyi said. "Only that they're dangerous; that they open on the living heart—whatever that means. They don't say."

Kimeri could feel the Gate in her. In her heart? Maybe. She was not going to tell Vanyi that. Vanyi might try to do something about it, and that would be dangerous. Kimeri knew that because the stars knew it: the stars in the Gate.

"Can we use the Gate?" Daruya asked. "Can we get back to Starios through it? If we can do that—"

"No," Vanyi said again. "That much I do know. A blind Gate leads nowhere. If you try to use it, you'll end up as Uruan did: trapped till something sets you free."

Daruya might not have left it at that, but someone started pounding on the gate, so loud that they heard it even this far back in the house. There was shouting, Olenyai voices, and another voice over it, deep and clear at once. "Damn you, you sons of the Pit! Let me in!"

"Let him in!" Daruya called in Asanian, rising so fast Kimeri hardly saw her move, and running toward the door; then stopping as if confused, blushing and going white, then blushing again.

Bundur ran in trailing hot-eyed Olenyai, ignoring them completely. He looked wild, his hair down out of its knot, his coat as short as a commoner's and torn besides, and a cut on his cheek that he seemed unaware of. He was talking before he had come all the way into the room. "You have to come, you mustn't stop, you've got to get out of here."

Now it was Daruya who was in a flutter and Vanyi who was calm: the order of the world was back in place again. "Stop babbling, take a deep breath, and start from the beginning," Vanyi said.

Bundur took the breath, and shut his mouth, too, but he still did not seem to see anything much but Daruya's face. When he spoke again he sounded much calmer. "The king is dead." Maybe only Kimeri heard Borti's gasp. Maybe not. "Do you remember the people I told you of, the ones who want to expel all foreigners and kill the mages? It seems my uncle was more difficult to bring round to their way of thinking than they thought he might be. They've killed him and set up their own king."

"The queen?" Vanyi asked.

"Dead," said Bundur. "As far as anyone knows. She hasn't been seen since the murderers broke into the palace. They'd have got rid of her first, even before they issued their ultimatum to the king. They're still dealing with resistance from the queen's people—but once they've broken that, they'll come here."

Vanyi's eyes went vague: she was using her magery to see. "Not for a while yet, but yes. We'll be a fine symbol of the new reign, with our bodies spiked to the walls and our heads over the gate."

Bundur shuddered. Somebody was retching—Aledi, with Miyaz holding her head. He looked as if he would have liked to join her. "Listen to me. There's one way I know of to keep you safe. Come back, all of you and all the belongings you can gather, to House Janabundur. I'll keep you there."

"And die when they come for us," Daruya said.

Her eyes seemed to steady him, though they were burning gold. "No," he said. "Not my wife, and my wife's kin and servants."

She shuddered as he had, but with less of a greensick look. "It can't be that easy."

"Custom is strong," he said, "and it will confuse them—at least long enough for us to think of other ways to defend ourselves."

Daruya raised her hands as if to push him away, then knotted them together and twisted them. "What if it doesn't work?"

"It will," he said. He was sure. He was also out of patience. "But you have to come now. They've closed the great gates—I just got in before the bars went down. They'll be securing the lesser ones soon."

"And we have seneldi to move." That, for some reason, seemed to calm Daruya down, get her thinking. "We'll go through the stable. Vanyi, Kadin, we'll move everything the fastest way, and keep a shadow over it."

Bundur had not expected that. Kimeri watched him think that he had not been planning to take in all their livestock, too, but nobody heard him when he tried to say it. Then it struck him what it meant. Daruya was going to marry him. Kimeri would have gone over and held him up if he would have let her.

As it was, his knees buckled, but he stiffened them somehow and ran with the rest of them, scrambling together everything they could. Not much from the house—clothes to change into, one or two of the packs of trade goods that Vanyi had brought in, weapons for the Olenyai; and Kimeri wondered what the guards of Shurakan would give to know how the bred-warriors had got their swords back again. From the stable they had to take more: grain for the seneldi, bales of cut fodder slung across unwilling backs, saddles and bridles and the rest.

By that time the tumult inside the palace was loud enough to hear with human ears. Kimeri kept a grip on Borti. Nobody had been taking particular notice of the woman—Kimeri helped them with that, and helped to think she was some kind of servant, or maybe the exorcist's assistant, until the exorcist saw the seneldi and bleated something incoherent and bolted. He would be safe. His magery was all tangled up, but it was good enough to hide him while he needed to be hidden, and when he found an open gate he would run back to his temple.

Borti had no such escape. Her brother-king was dead. The people in the palace were hunting her. She was safest where she was, with a hood hiding her face and a shadow hiding all of them, creeping along the wall toward a gate that might, with the gods' help, still be open and unguarded when they got to it. The seneldi came quietly, with a magery on them, but even that could not keep them from rolling their eyes and snorting at the sudden reek of death from inside the palace. Someone had opened a door and died in it. Several other people ran out, looking for enemies to kill, but they saw nothing but moonlight and darkness and an empty yard.

Borti stumbled. Kimeri kept her on her feet, using magery when bodily strength was not enough. She kept trying to run inside, as if it would do any good at all to die as her brother had. She was not thinking; something in her had gone blank and blind. Mages would have to mend that when they got to House Janabundur.

The gate had a guard, but Chakan killed him. It was almost too quick to see: one moment he was alive, the next he was not. His soul hung about, bewildered, till a gust of wind caught it and blew it away.

Once past the gate they mounted quickly. Rahai tossed Kimeri into the saddle of the starbrowed bay; she pulled Borti up behind her, with Rahai pushing, not asking questions. He was a wise man, was Rahai. Borti had no kind of seat on a senel, but she could balance herself, even tranced, and she clung to Kimeri.

Bundur was riding, too. He rode well—he wanted to gallop down the twisty street, but Daruya stopped him. There were people in the way. The shadow would not hold if they went too fast or ran into anyone. They had to walk, mostly, and trot in the few stretches where it was level enough and empty enough. They were still faster than if they had tried to go on foot, though Bundur did not like to admit it.

The city was quiet. It was only the palace that was in uproar. The people would wait till it was over, then decide what to do. Kings had died this way before, though not for a long while. Shurakan had got used to peace, but it had never forgotten the scent of blood in the air.

House Janabundur waited for them. It was remarkably like Kimeri's earlier homecoming: the same warm welcome, the same barred gates, the same gathering in the largest room. But there were differences. The seneldi had to be put somewhere and taken care of. The back garden did for that; Lady Nandi sighed for her flowers, even after Kadin assured her that these seneldi were civilized and would eat only what he gave them permission to eat. They liked having a space to roam in, even one as small as that, and settled happily enough to their fodder and the handful of grain that Kadin fed each one in turn.

He stayed with the seneldi. The rest of them went up to the hall where they had dined on festival night. It was only yesterday, Kimeri thought. It felt years gone.

They had to have tea and cakes—they could not be welcomed without them. Everybody choked down a sip and a bite, even Hani creeping out of bed to see what the commotion was. It seemed natural for him to set himself beside Kimeri and keep quiet while Bundur told his mother that her brother was dead.

Lady Nandi had expected it. "I knew," she said, "when the whispers grew so loud, and everyone so sure that he would yield. I knew he never would." Her eyes were dry, her voice steady. She kept all her tears inside until she should have time to be alone. Then she would weep. "He believed that the haters of foreigners were right, mind you, and that foreign presence could only destroy what we have built here. But he was also the king. The king is above the fears of simple men."

But not the queen, Kimeri thought, with Borti gripping her hand till it hurt, sitting on the other side of her from Hani. No one really saw her yet, though the shadow was wearing thin. Kimeri was tired, even with the Gate inside her to make her stronger. The queen had been afraid, and was becoming afraid again as she woke from the horror that had held her speechless. But she was brave, as always. She fought her way through the fear. Kimeri helped. She held the light where Borti could see it, and guided her out of the dark place.

All the while she did that, the others talked. Kimeri's mother was being stubborn again. "Did I say I'd agreed to marry you?" she was saying to Bundur. "Marry Vanyi. She'll take you."

"With all due respect to her ladyship," said Bundur, "I don't want her. I want you."

"Stop that," said Vanyi, so sharp and so sudden that they started and fell silent. "That will be enough out of you, Daruyani. You will do as your heart is bidding you do, so loud even I can hear it, and that will be that."

"Not tonight," Daruya said, obstinate still. "At least give me time to think about it."

"Time for the palace to discover and stop you? I think not." Vanyi was on her feet. She was not a tall woman and not usually imposing, but when she wanted to she could stand as tall as the mountain that guarded Shurakan.

Daruya stayed where she was, sitting at the table, but somehow she was as tall as Vanyi.

They all waited for Vanyi to say something devastating, something that would break Daruya down and trample on the shards. But Vanyi said nothing at all. Simply stared at her, long and long. Then turned her back on her in profound contempt.

The silence was deafening. Lady Nandi thought for a moment, then stood as Vanyi had, and turned her back, too. So did Chakan.

That cut Daruya to the bone: Kimeri heard her gasp of shock. After Chakan, the rest followed. They did not understand Shurakani, but they understood what had been happening, and this was what they thought of it. Even they, who should never have cared to wed their lady to a foreigner.

That left Kimeri and Hani, and Borti by now visible but ignored, and Bundur. Kimeri got up slowly, turned even more slowly. It hurt; it wrenched at the place where the Gate was. But she had to do it.

Behind her she heard her mother's breath catch. "Not you, too?"

Bundur did not say anything. He was too much in love to be contemptuous, but he was hurt, hurt enough to want to wound. And he let her see it.

Daruya's anger was like a breath of fire, sudden and whitely hot. "Damn you! Damn you all! I'll do it!"

TWENTY-THREE

THE WORST BETRAYAL, ABSOLUTELY THE WORST OF ALL, WAS CHAKAN'S. He tried to slip out of Daruya's sight, but she caught him and dragged him with her into the room she was given to dress for her wedding, and shut the door in the face of everyone who tried to follow. She did not notice what kind of room it was, except that it was small, lamplit, and seemed to lead to another, which would be a bath from the scent of warmed water and herbs that came from it.

She backed Chakan against the wall, well aware that he could have escaped if he had put his mind to it. He eyes were not contrite at all; they were laughing as they had not since he came to Shurakan.

"Why?" she demanded of him. "Why you? You were the one who warned me against him!"

"The emperor wants you to marry him," Chakan said.

His laughter, she realized, was as much at himself as at her. "You're not his slave," she snapped.

"I serve him," he said. "And he approves this match."

"Do you?"

"It doesn't matter."

"It matters profoundly."

He looked away, which was not easy as close as they were, eye to blazing golden eye. "You need this marriage to keep you safe. Your grandfather and the Guild-master approve it. Whatever I may think, you have to marry this man or endanger the embassy."

"I don't matter to you, do I? Except as the heir to the throne you serve."

He would not look at her even then, even at such a blow. His voice was soft, without expression. "I was bred to serve. I can do no other."

"Chakan!"

The pain in her voice rocked him. She saw it. She also saw that his eyes were fixed on the floor beside her foot, and that his face, what she could see of it, was rigid.

She spun away. Her throat was tight, but she had no tears to shed. She never did for the things that truly hurt. "Go," she said.

He did not pause; did not speak. He simply went.

For a little while then she was alone. He did that—damn his hide, he told the others to let her be. She turned slowly. It was a small room indeed, very small, little more than a closet. There was a clothing-stand, and garments spread over it. Her eyes avoided them. Beyond, in a room no larger, was a basin full of water, steaming gently, and all the appurtenances of the bath.

Her anger was gone. It had left with Chakan. She took off what she was wearing, dropped it where it fell, lowered herself into the water. It was hot—almost too hot. She welcomed its nearness to pain.

She was wallowing. She knew that perfectly well. Her grandfather would have taxed her with it if he had been there. Her grandmother, too. Haliya had great compassion, but not for young things who, in her mind, were taking their fits of temper altogether too far.

Of course they were all perfectly right. This marriage would save the embassy, if only for a little while—long enough to find other expedients. It would confuse the faction that had killed the king, and confront it not with a defenseless party of foreigners but with a powerful, indeed royal, house and all its allies and dependents. It was supremely practical and quite devastating.

If she were the proper obedient creature that Chakan was, she would swallow her objections and submit. What difference did it make, after all? She would leave when she wished to leave. She did not have to take her husband with her, or even remember that he existed, except as a convenience, a name of respectability. Lovers would find it an added spice to bed another man's wife.

She sank down till the water lapped her chin. The trouble with all of that cold practicality was quite simple and quite inescapable and quite substantial. Bundur himself. He was not the kind of man one could forget. He had somehow, without her knowing precisely how, crept in under her skin and set up residence there.

No man had ever done this to her before. Those who adored her, worshipped her, fell breathless at her feet, she had always dealt with as gently as she could, and sent toward women who would indulge their follies. Those who had the sense to regard bed-play as the game it was, she took to her bed when she wished, eluded gracefully when she did not. She had never been thrown into such confusion, never so lost her temper with anyone except—god and goddess help her—her grandfather.

"Does that mean I love him?" she asked the ceiling. The ceiling, plain plastered surface, returned no answer. She slid completely beneath the water and stayed there, counting the heartbeats, till she had to breathe or burst.

People were staring at her. Some looked ready to bolt for help. Others—Vanyi foremost—knew her too well to think that she would ever take her life in such ignominious fashion. She stood up in the basin, water sheeting from her, and reached for a drying-cloth. Some of the people staring were servants; they scrambled to serve her.

They were all women, she noticed. Two of them were Bundur's sisters. They tried to pretend that they were not staring at her, how strange she was, the color of pale honey all over, and curly golden patches under her arms and between her thighs as well as on her head. She was thinner than they liked to see, lithe like a boy, with training scars that she had never tried to hide, and a real scar taken in battle: the deep gouge of an arrow in her hip.

"It wouldn't have scarred," she said with careful amiability, "if I'd let the healers at it; but I had to keep riding, you see, and fighting, and being too brave for belief."

The sisters regarded her without comprehension. She tried a smile. They did not smile back. They disliked her, and no wonder. This, soulbound to their beautiful brother. This, accepting him with the strident opposite of grace, needing to be dragged kicking and struggling into the arms of a prince who could have had, willing, any Shurakani bride he chose.

Daruya could have asked why he had not taken one of those willing brides, except that she already had, and had been answered. He wanted her. He had a strong streak of the contrary in him, too.

"In that," said Vanyi, "the two of you are beautifully matched."

Daruya's smile was very, very sweet. "Aren't we?"

"Ah, child," Vanyi said sighing. "Times are when I'm glad your grandfather is as long-lived as he looks to be. You'll need all those years to grow out of your crotchets."

That stung. Daruya kept her smile, but with an effort. "Maybe I wasn't meant to inherit."

"You're not that fortunate," Vanyi said. She took the ivory comb from the hand of the servant who wielded it, struggling with hair that curled in most unnatural and lively fashion. She did not make undue effort to be gentle, but neither was she baffled by all the sudden knots and tangles. She made order out of them as competently as she did all else, and with dispatch, too.

There was no time for braids. A cap had to do, of deep blue silk embroidered with golden beads in a pattern much like the Sun in her hand. The garments that went with it were of like color and kind, fashion of her own country for once, but close to what the women wore here. Soft plain shirt of raw silk tucked into loose trousers the color of the sky at evening, but brocaded all over with golden suns. Shoes for her feet, silken slippers such as a lady would wear in her palace, deep blue, golden suns. And over them the coat, blue silk, brocaded suns round the edges, but sleeves and coat proper sewn of panels of silk the color of bronze and copper and gold, and each, again, sun-brocaded. She had not even known that Vanyi carried such a thing in her baggage, or that it would have been cut to Daruya's height and slimness.

She stood up in it while a servant clasped the amber necklace about her neck, and met Vanyi's calm ironic stare. "I had it made today," the Guildmaster said. "It's the same pattern as your riding clothes, more or less. Easy enough for a handful of good needlewomen to manage."

"It's very handsome," Daruya said.

"It suits you," said Vanyi. From her, that was high praise.

It was deep night by the time they all gathered again in the hall with its ancient hangings, in front of the dragon tapestry. There were a great number of them to Daruya's eyes, what with all the embassy that had survived the Gate, and the servants and the women of House Janabundur, but not—to Daruya's faint shock—Bundur.

She knew a moment's wild hope that he had turned coward and fled. But he would hardly do that now, after all he had done to win her. As she took the place she was pushed and prodded to, in front of the rest, Bundur appeared at the inner door. He was wearing the black-and-bronze splendor of the festival. The cut on his cheek had been stitched up neatly and washed clean. His chin was shaven, his mustaches brought to order, oiled and persuaded to hang politely on either side of his mouth. He had not, she noticed, succumbed to any urge to make his hair fashionable. It was sleeked smooth and clubbed at his nape as always, bound with cords of green and glimmering bronze.

He was really quite beautiful in his way, like a big sleek cat. He was not prostrate with nerves that she could see, though he was trembling around the edges of her magery—a trembling to match her own. He smiled as he came toward her and held out his hand. Her own hand had reached to clasp his before her mind came into it at all.

Lady Nandi stood in front of them with an air of solemn ceremony. She spoke words that Daruya did not afterward remember. Nor, she thought, did Bundur. Something about the gods; something about souls and bonds and women and men. Nothing about love, Daruya did notice that. Was it nothing they thought of here? Or did they so take it for granted that they saw no need to name it?

He had both her hands now, or she had his. *Damn,* she thought. *Damn, damn, damn.* But beneath that: *Yes, yes, yes.*

Bundur repeated the words his mother spoke. His mind was not thinking of them. Only of her face, of the golden shining thing that she was, for all her tempers and crotchets and follies.

But you don't know me, she tried to say. *You don't know me at all.*

I know what matters, he said deep inside of her. *I know what you fear.*

Her heart clenched. "What? What—"

"Say after me," Lady Nandi said with considerable patience: "'Thy soul mine, my soul thine, from life unto life, to the worlds' ending.'"

Life unto life? But—

Bundur's eyes were dark, resting on her, driving sense, logic, even rebellion straight out of her head. She heard her voice speaking, faint and breathless but clear. "'Thy soul mine, my soul thine, from life unto life, to the worlds' ending.'"

Nothing happened. It was not a spell, not a magery. It described, that was all; told the others what was true, or what they believed to be true. What Daruya believed . . .

No one cared. She had said all that she needed to say. The lady said the rest. Then not the lady. Someone else, a woman whose face Daruya had seen somewhere before, but she did not know where. A narrow face, stern, with eyes that cherished some deep anger and some deeper grief. But the voice was clear, level, deep for a woman's, and firm. "I bless you both in the name of all the gods; I grant you the grace of heaven, and such protection as heaven may give. May you prosper and live long, and be reborn as children of the gods."

Daruya came out of her fog abruptly—as abruptly as Bundur had. No one was staring at them any longer, but at the woman in the dark plain cloak with its hood on her shoulders, and garments under it that might have been a servant's. She returned their stares with massive calm. Her hands rose—narrow hands, beautiful as her face was not, with slender elegant fingers—and came to rest on Daruya's head and on Bundur's. She was tall; she did not have to reach far, nor did she struggle to follow as he knelt, drawing Daruya with him whether she would or no. "May the gods protect you," she said, "and honor your marriage."

Bundur's head bowed under her hand, then came up. "I should think they would, now," he said. "Borti. Lady. How in the world—"

"She helped me wake the Gate," Kimeri said from beside the stranger. "*She* listened to me."

"Imp," said Vanyi, with mirth in it. "Oh, imp! Have you been hiding her all this time?"

"Yes," Kimeri said, keeping her chin up and her eyes level, not on Vanyi but on her mother. "She insisted she had to say the blessing. To make it stick."

"It will now," Bundur said. Laughter burst out of him, rich and infectious. "Borti! Thank all the gods. We were sure you were dead."

"I might have been," the woman said. The queen. Daruya read that in the minds around her, the queen's strongest of all. How like Kimeri, she thought, to find and befriend the person in Shurakan whom they needed most, and to produce her in the very nick of time, too, and never a word before then.

The queen said, "I fled, I thought, to distract myself from fear of what would happen—what did happen while I was gone. The gods were guiding me. Or this child of theirs was."

"Does that mean we're kin?" Kimeri asked. "I like that. Mother, can we be Borti's cousins? Avaryan must be her goddess' brother at least. Or maybe he *is* her goddess."

"In the end all gods are one," Daruya said. She rose from her knees, where she should not have been; no queen was equal to the princess-heir of the Sunborn's line. Borti was not indeed much shorter than she. "Lady," said Daruya, inclining her head. "I thank you for your blessing. It was generously given."

"It was my thank-offering for my escape," Borti said. "As little thankful as I feel now—I live, and that, I'm sure, no one expected. Nephew, half-sister, you have full freedom to cast me out. The king they've raised in the palace will be bringing in his sister to claim my place and my office; she'll want my life if she can get it, and the life of anyone who shelters me."

"I don't think so," Bundur said. "They were going to crown Shagyan, which would have brought in Mandi, but he developed a backbone when they murdered the king. They hacked it, and him, in two. Paltai took the crown from the king's hand and set it on his head before anyone else could move."

"And Paltai," said Borti, "has no sister." Her eyes closed; she drew a breath. "Goddess! And we thought his family cursed by heaven, because it begot only sons."

"Heaven curses the king who rules alone," said the Lady Nandi. "That was ill done, to let him take the crown and keep it."

"Not for us," said Bundur. "Not for many who may accept a deed done before they could prevent it, but who may be inclined to support us if we challenge it."

"Dare we challenge?" Lady Nandi demanded.

"Dare we not?" he shot back.

"I think," said Vanyi, "that this needs a council of war, and sustenance to help it along. Here's the wedding feast spread, and it looks splendid considering how hastily it was cobbled together. Shall we eat it while we talk?"

Everyone looked startled, but no one quarreled with her eminent good sense—Daruya least of all. The queen's presence here changed everything. It was no longer only a wedding in haste, an expedient adopted to save the lives of a mere foreign embassy. Now they were honestly at war with the faction in the palace.

And in war, even weddings could lose themselves to necessity.

They sat to a feast that, with Brightmoon setting and Greatmoon hanging low and dawn paling the eastern sky, could well do duty for an early breakfast. Hasty it might have been, but there was plenty of it, too much for most until they discovered a quite unexpected hunger. Even the Olenyai partook of it, as awkward as that could be for people whose honor forbade them to unveil before strangers.

For a while no one spoke except to call for another basket of bread, or to ask a neighbor to pass the wine. Borti ate, too, as they all did, reluctantly at first and then as if she were starving. No one stared, or waited on her with slavish adoration, or treated her otherwise than as a kinswoman of rank. Daruya might have expected more servility, as rigorously as these people had kept their rulers from the taint of foreign eyes, but the ruler in her own person stood no more on ceremony than Daruya herself did.

It was well, Daruya thought, filling a fold of bread with spiced meats and cheese and handing it to Borti while she prepared another for herself. She could almost ignore the man on her other side in considering this stranger who was a queen. A ruler who kept to the strictures of old Asanian royalty, or who believed too much in her own divinity, might be difficult to deal with. This plain sensible woman with her solid appetite and clear affection for Kimeri was much to Daruya's liking—and would be to Estarion's, too, Daruya suspected.

Gods. She was thinking of what Estarion would like, and not sulking over it. Had she grown up so much? Or had she merely replaced Estarion-as-adversary with Bundur? Her husband, they were all thinking when their eyes fell on the two of them. Her protector from the king's murderers.

It made her ill to read such thoughts. She flung up her shields and rested in the quiet behind them, listening to voices that were only voices, watching faces that showed little of the minds behind.

"So then," said Vanyi, taking the lead as she always seemed to do, "we're best advised to wait, you think."

"Yes," said Lady Nandi. "Now that you have the protection of our name and kinship, no one from the palace will move directly against you, since that is also against us."

"And in any case," Bundur said, "the fighting isn't likely to get this far. Palace coups here always restrict themselves politely to the palace."

"Then I didn't need to marry you at all," Daruya burst out. "We could simply have come here and been safe."

"No," he said. "You would have been pursued—maybe not at once, but soon enough. Now that you are part of House Janabundur, that changes things. That gives you power in the kingdom; it equips you with allies and defenses, to all of which you're entitled, since as my wife you rule this house and everyone in it."

"I do not," Daruya said. "Nor would I displace the lady whose house it is."

"But that is the way of the world," Lady Nandi said. "If you wish me to continue, but in your name, then that's well, and sensible of you, too. But you rule. You are House Janabundur, as is your husband."

"You do see," Bundur said. "Don't you? Before, you were an outlander, nothing and no one, no matter what power you might hold in your own country. Now you hold the power of the second house in Su-Shaklan."

"You'll pardon me if I don't let it go to my head," Daruya said.

"I'd never forgive you if you did," he said. He was grinning at her again. His white teeth and his bright dark eyes could make her knees buckle. Damn them. Damn him.

"I see," said Borti beside her, "that these two are indeed soulbound. It's an old binding, and strong. I've never seen a stronger."

"Nor I," said Lady Nandi with the same air of resignation with which she had confirmed Daruya's sudden new rank. "And she fights it, which only adds to its strength."

"No." It escaped before Daruya could stop it. She bit her tongue before it betrayed her further.

"Unfortunately, yes," Vanyi said. "As far as I can tell, and mind you I've never thought of matings in quite this way, your kind of resistance simply encourages it."

"Then if I give in, it will go away?"

"It doesn't work like that," Vanyi said.

Daruya had thought not. She finished rolling meat and cheese in bread, and bit into it. Her hunger did not care if she was angry or happy or a mad mingling of both.

"So we wait," said Vanyi, taking up where they had left off. "And see what the palace does."

"And watch, and keep Borti hidden," Bundur said. "That, we have to do, I think. They'll be hunting her for a goodly while, and wanting her dead."

"Luckily," said Borti, "very few people have any idea what I really look like. They only ever see me in court, when I'm robed to immobility and weighted with wig and crown, and painted to look like a mask of the goddess. Who would know a tall plain woman in a servant's coat, doing servant's duties in Janabundur?"

"You can't do that," Bundur said, shocked.

She laughed at him. For a moment they looked very much alike. "Of course I can! I do it more often than anyone would want to know. It's a convenient way to learn what people are saying, and it gives me something to do. It's massively dull on the throne and behind the screens that are supposed to protect me from common eyes, with ministers speaking for me, and making all my decisions, too."

"Not all of them," Vanyi said, "I don't think. If you speak, you're listened to. When it suits you to speak."

"When I'm given knowledge enough to speak." Borti sighed. "When I stop to think—now I have leisure for it—I realize that we used to see much more of our common subjects. We've been closed in, walled about, cut off. Cleverly too, and imperceptibly, till it was too late for my brother and almost for me."

"It was a common expedient once in our Golden Empire," Daruya said, "when a man wished to be emperor, to do just as your traitors did, and cut off the emperor who was, and destroy him."

"But not any longer?" asked Borti.

"The Golden Empire is gone," Daruya said. "I'm all that's left of it, I and my daughter. Now we have assassins, though not of late, and the occasional rebellion. Our rulers walk out where anyone can see, and everyone knows their faces."

"That was true here, once," said Borti. She looked suddenly exhausted, hollow-eyed and pale under the bronze sheen of her skin. "I shall sleep, I think. Then think again, and consider what to do."

"So should we all," Lady Nandi said, rising. Her glance at Bundur was bright, suddenly, and full of mirth that echoed his own. "With possible exceptions."

No, thought Daruya. But her mouth was full of spiced meat and festival wine, and Bundur was pulling her to her feet, and the Shurakani were singing, out of nowhere and none too tunefully, what must be a wedding song. The sun was coming up—it was morning. How could there be a wedding night?

Bundur swung her up in his arms, swept her clean off her feet. He was laughing. They all were. Except Daruya, who was rigid with shock and resistance; too rigid to fight. Even when he carried her away, and no one followed, not one. Not even an Olenyas.

TWENTY-FOUR

BUNDUR SET DARUYA ON HER FEET. SHE WAS STILL STIFF, STILL FURIOUS, BUT all too wide awake to the absurdity of resistance. Awake too to where she was. A room with tapestried walls, a broad hearth swept clean, a low table, cushions, and a curtained alcove. Behind the alcove was the bed.

He did not drag her to it. Once she was steady on her feet, he went to the hanging that bled light, and slid it aside from a window. Sun, topping the Worldwall, washed him in brightness. He stretched, yawned, pulled the cords out of his hair, and shook it down. He turned, smiling.

God and goddess, Daruya thought. She was terrified—panicked. Her eyes darted without her willing it, looking for escape. The door was barred. Another door—a bath? Another portion of the suite?

She could not move at all. He wandered to the table where things were set for tea, including a little brazier and a copper pot full of water, singing as it came to the boil. He folded his legs under him and made tea, his big hands deft with the delicate pots, the bronze spoon, the dried leaves of the herbs, and the pinch of flowers.

"The trouble," she said, out of nowhere in particular, "is that I can't—let—myself love a man. Not without fighting with him endlessly, trying to make him hate me and leave me, or at least let me be. It's so much easier to choose lovers as one chooses one's dress for the day, for its color or its style or its suitability to the weather. And come nightfall, one can take it off and forget it, and put on another."

He was listening, but not discomfiting her with his stare. He lidded the teapot and set hands on knees and waited while the herbs and flowers steeped. Their fragrance wafted toward Daruya in a breeze from the window: sweet and pungent, with a faint green undertone.

"I've never felt this way before." She could not stop talking, filling the awful silence with a babble of words. "I've never wanted to be near anyone all the time—thought of him when he's not there—remembered his hands when I should be thinking about something else altogether. I'm losing myself. I don't want that. I hate it."

"Time makes it easier," he said.

"You know that?"

He raised his head and looked at her. His eyes were too bright to bear. "Not . . . from personal experience. I'm still rather lost myself. But I've been assured on excellent authority, one does grow accustomed; one learns to keep the self and the other, both, without losing either."

"You can't feel that for me. I'm all edges. I make a great deal of noise. I wound your pride with every word I speak."

"But not with every word you think," he said, "or every glance you turn on me. Fear makes you say all those words that wound."

"I wish," she said tightly, "that you would lose your temper. Just once. And stop being so bloody understanding. It makes me sick."

"Am I too much like your grandfather?"

She leaped. He caught her. He was stronger than she, and he had skills she had not expected. She could not fling him down and pummel him. "Who told you?" she gasped. "Who told you that?"

"The Lady Vanyi," he answered. "She says I well ought to drive you wild: I'm too damnably like him. But steadier, she says. I don't think she means it as a compliment."

"She's been desperately and hopelessly and unrequitedly in love with him for forty years," said Daruya.

"Not unrequited," he said. "Not the way she tells it. Though I suppose I'd have to ask him for his side of it. They do best as they are, that's all."

"Then can't we?"

He laughed. "Oh, you are clever! No, we can't. Do you want to? Really? In your heart?"

"In my heart," she said, "I want to be a child again, and never to have heard of what's between men and women at all. I'm afraid of you. Every time I look at you I feel as if I want to drown."

"Oh, that's only love," he said. It came out light, but she could sense the weight of fear beneath. He, too. He was afraid. Of her; of what she did to him, so close, with those hot-gold eyes of hers, and all that outrageous hair.

It was happening again. She was blurring into him. She wrenched away, body and soul, and backed against the wall. "I can't do it," she said. "There's no maiden-blood to show here, not with my daughter for proof that it's long since shed. Can't we just . . . not, and pretend we did? Aren't the words and the blessing enough, and the name of wife that the queen gave me?"

"Do you want it to be?"

"I want," she said. "I want—I don't—"

Oh, damn her traitor feet. They were taking her straight back to him, and her hands were seizing him, pulling him to her. They were exactly of a height. But he was much broader. She measured the span of his shoulders. He smelled of spices, of the herb they liked to sprinkle in the bath, of wine and tea-herbs and flowers. And under it, subtle but distinct, musk and maleness. It was different, a little, from other men she knew. Foreign. Sweeter, less sharply pungent. Or was that because he fit so well?

Horribly well. The skin of his face looked faintly weathered but felt smooth, molded tight to the proud bones. His eyes were shut—narrow eyes, but long, the lids folded as a plainsman's often were, so that they seemed to tilt upward. Open, they would be dark, almost black.

He was breathing shallowly. Breath that caught as she ran a finger down the line of his mustache, tugging it gently. His hands were fists at his sides. Every muscle in his body was bent on not seizing her as she had seized him; on not sending her back into panic flight.

"Too late for that," she said. "I did it already."

His eyes snapped open. "You can read my mind."

"I thought you knew." Fear, elation: she was a mage, he was sure of it now, he would thrust her away, shun her in horror of what she could do.

He did none of that. He shivered, yes, but he raised his hands, took her face between them, met her eyes. His thought-speech was clumsy but astonishingly clear in a man without training in magery. *I love you.*

It echoed down to the bottom of him, truth within truth within truth.

"You know nothing of me," she said. "How can you love what you don't know?"

"I know what the soul knows." Aloud, that, because she spoke aloud. "We believe that souls are eternal, but bodies come and go; souls are born and reborn, over and over, on the wheel of the gods."

"That is horrible."

"Beautiful," he said. "We were lovers before, but perhaps I treated you badly; perhaps you loved me too much, and cost us both that turn of the wheel. Now you flee and I pursue. But it's all one, do you see? We were bound before the wheel began, and will be again, until the wheel is gone."

"When I die," she said in a voice that tried not to shake, "I want to lie on the breast of Mother Night, in the god's peace, and never wake."

"But of course you want that—but only for a while. After night is dawn again. You'll be up and doing, loving and being loved, casting your bright soul on the wheel where it serves best. You're never one to be content with simply being."

"That's too easy," she said. "Too simple a wisdom. You prattle it like a child its lessons. I'd rather a round of honest bedplay, and a goodbye after, without the facile philosophy."

"It is not facile." Ah, at last: she had goaded his temper. But too briefly. He calmed himself again, and that was not easy with his banner flying as high as it was, urging him to seize her and rape her where she stood. "You don't understand. I can't expect you to. You're an outland woman who follows outland gods."

"Now you're talking down to me. Stop it."

He stiffened. "You *are*. Is the truth such an insult?"

"When you put it that way, it is."

"I don't know how to talk to you," he said. "All I know how to do is love you."

"I'd rather you talked more and loved less."

He saw the lie in her eyes. It brought his smile back, his wicked, innocent, brilliant smile. "You do love me," he said as if he had just discovered it. "You do. You did from the first. Didn't you?"

"Of course not!"

But he was exploring her face as she had explored his, with delicate fingers, tracing the arch of her brows, the shape of her eyes, so round and so shallow-set beside his, the curve of her cheekbone, the fullness of her lip. There was nothing in the world but that touch, so light it barely brushed her skin, so hot it burned.

"Honey," he murmured, "and gold. Why, you are beautiful."

He was surprised. She hated him for it, or tried. She was blurring into him again, feeling his wonder, his delight in her strangeness, in discovering beauty where he had never thought to find it.

"The Spear of Heaven in the morning, all fierce and burning gold," he said. "The she-tiger in the wood, snarling defiance at the hunter. But a tall lily, too, in a queen's garden, soft as silk, soft as sleep."

"Poets have made love to me before," she said—gasping it, with none of the edge of viciousness that she had intended.

"I'm no poet," he said. "I'm telling you what I see. I didn't marry beauty. I married my soul's self. But to find it—oh, that's wonderful." He paused. "I suppose I'm quite ugly to you."

"Why, you're as vain as I am," she said. "Of course you're not ugly. You're not pretty, but then I never cared much for pretty men, even when I chose one to father my daughter. I like a solid man with substance to him, good bone, a bright eye—"

"Like one of your seneldi?"

She had flattened his poetry into plain practicality, but he had turned it to laughter. "—a thick mane," she carried it on, "long and glossy, and a fine slope of shoulder, a strong back, good haunches, a straight leg and a sturdy foot . . ."

"But I have no horns," he said as if he lamented it, "and my tail is not even a nubbin. I'll never make a stallion."

God and goddess help her, he had her giggling. And finding fastenings, and discovering that there was not much to his clothes, but enough if one were in a hurry to get him out of them. The coat fell easily. The shirt had buttons, which needed wrestling with. The trousers were held up by a belt, and a cord under that. He did not wear trews.

He was a goodly stallion. But—

"They scarred you! Who cut—who—"

He gaped. Stared, as if she had found some mutilation that he had never known he had.

Understanding dawned. He went scarlet under the bronze of his skin, from the peak of black hair on his forehead all the way down to his breastbone. "It's . . . something we have done to us when we're newborn. They consecrate us to the gods. It's only the foreskin. The rest of me is quite as it was made, and quite able to—to—"

Quite willing, too. And not so odd, maybe. Barbaric, but not ugly, not really. To cut a man *there*, even if he were too young to know what was being done to him . . .

"I *am* ugly to you," he said, wilting as he spoke, all over.

"No," she said. "Damn it, no." She got out of her clothes, not being too careful of fastenings, to set them level and give him something else to think about.

It succeeded; that much she could say for it. He had modesty like an Asanian, a body-shyness that she had never had; her grandfather had seen to that, brought her up with and around northerners who went naked as often as they went clothed. It had not kept Bundur from letting her undress him, but it did strange things to his composure to be seeing her as naked as he was, and so different.

The women had seen how tall and narrow and boyish she was. He saw as he had seen in the garden not so very long ago that she was a woman; slender certainly but full-breasted enough, breasts that were still round and high and firm though she had suckled a child. Her skin was finer than he was used to, its texture softer, but the golden down on it was strange to him—he had little even between his thighs, was all smooth bronze. What he would have made of a true northerner, and a male at that, she could not imagine. Some of them were pelted like bears, with beards to their breasts.

"Am I ugly to you now?" she asked him.

"No," he said. "Oh, no."

"Nor are you to me." She took his shaft in her hand, warm heavy solid thing, coming alive to her touch. Beautiful, even so altered. As all of him was. As it had always been—yes, since first she saw him, sitting at a table in the teahouse, daring her to flay him with her tongue.

She could cut him to the bone now if she said but a word. Or two. Or three. She knew exactly which words they would be. And she said none of them.

He had skill. She had not expected otherwise. When she moved toward him he was there. There was a moment of hesitation; awkwardness, not-fitting. Then, as each found the rhythm of the dance, each fit to each, matched—

"Like riding a senel," he said. His voice was deep, full of laughter even in the midst of loving.

She locked legs about his haunches and drove him to a gallop: then back, slow and slow, grinning to match his grin.

Beautiful, his mind said. *So beautiful when you smile.*

"So ugly when I scowl?"

He laughed, outside and in. *Always beautiful. Always. And well you know it, too.*

"Then we are matched," she said. "Perfectly."

Haven't I always said so?

"Insufferable," she said. "Intolerable. Beloved."

TWENTY-FIVE

URUAN THE GUARDIAN SLEPT STRAIGHT THROUGH THE NIGHT AND THE DAY and the next night. When he woke with a raging thirst and a desperate lunge toward the privy, Kimeri was there. She helped him as she could, with him too caught up in his body's needs to be amazed that the golden power of his dream was a child, and a very young one at that, even if she was the Sunlady's heir.

Vanyi he knew better, and greeted with a recollection of his princely manners, though he nearly fell on his face trying to bow to her. She got him back into bed and saw him fed rich broth and strong tea, and answered the questions that babbled out of him. She was afraid that his mind had got scrambled in his long imprisonment, but Kimeri had no such fear. He was only weak, and having trouble understanding that he had been inside the Gate for more than a full cycle of Greatmoon—forty-nine days altogether, since he insisted on counting.

"It was no time at all," he kept insisting, "but it was an eon and then another. *She* was there," he said, tilting his chin at Kimeri. "She was the only light in that dark place."

Kimeri wanted to duck her head, embarrassed, but what he said was true, mostly. "That was the god who's in my blood. He kept making me dream about you."

"And so kept me alive and bound to the Gate." He could have been blaming her for it, but there was the beginning of a smile on his face, and in his eyes that had seen too much nothingness. He focused them on Vanyi, frowning. "What are you doing here? I was trying to get through before the Gate broke, to tell you not to come; it was getting too dangerous. The palace—"

"The palace was perfectly quiet when we arrived," she said, "but last night they killed the king and set up another."

He sat up, though his face went green and he reeled, trying to get to his feet. "Then where are we? We're not in the house of the Gate. I can feel it—it's somewhere else. Are we in prison? Has the faction that favors us won after all? They were all to be killed or silenced."

"We're in House Janabundur," said Vanyi, "and safe, for now. Stop trying to get up and gallop off."

"Janabundur? But that's—" Uruan went perfectly green but not unconscious, and folded up. The Olenyas on guard scooped him back into bed and laid a sheathed sword, very gently, across his chest.

He understood the message. His lips quirked wryly. "All right. I'll stay put. But, Vanyi, Janabundur is the king's—the old king's—clan-house. Not that its lord isn't disposed to be friendly; he is, and he's honest in it, but there would be better places to hide in plain sight."

"I don't think so," Vanyi said. "His lordship offered for the princess-heir and won her, with the emperor's consent, too. They married after we brought you here. Marriage in this place, it seems, can make a native out of a foreigner, and a power out of a nobody, and a proper noble lady out of a mage."

"The princess-heir? *Daruya?* Married to—" Uruan started to shake. It looked like convulsions. It was laughter.

Vanyi waited it out with more patience than she had ever shown Kimeri. Kimeri herself sat on the bed and tucked up her feet and watched him till he stopped giggling and wiped the tears away. "Really? Lord Shakabundur *married* her? She didn't throttle him for his presumption?"

"Really," said Kimeri. "She only tried to strangle somebody once. He was pushing her when she didn't want him to, and trying to get him to kiss her. Great-Grandfather said she should have gutted him instead." Since he could hardly argue with that, and did not seem inclined to, she went on, "She likes Bundur. She makes a great deal of noise pretending she doesn't, but that's because she's afraid. She's not used to liking men who want to marry her."

"Let alone marrying them." Uruan cradled his head in his hands, after assuring the Olenyas that that was all he wanted to do. The sword retreated but stayed within reach, poised to stop him if he tried to get up again. "God. Goddess. I gather the Gate's not passable?"

"It, and the whole chain of Gates from here to Starios," Vanyi said. "We had to walk in from Kianat, with a broken Gate behind us. Something here began it, but we've found nothing, except you."

"One redheaded fool trapped in a Gate." He closed his eyes, but he was not asleep. His mind was wide awake and very keen. Kimeri helped with that. The Gate inside her made it easy to run a thread of feeling-better through him, and keep it running till he had all he needed. He did not know what was happening, though if he had asked she would have answered. He thought it was something Vanyi was doing. "I'll do what I can," he said. "You can use another mage, yes? And I know people here. Some of those who were favorable to us might still be; and if Lord Shakabundur is with us, we're stronger than we've ever been."

"You're running no errands tonight," said Vanyi sternly. "Believe me, when I need you I'll use you. Until then, you'll rest and eat and make yourself strong."

He looked for a moment as rebellious as Daruya could ever be, but he was older, and better trained. He lowered his eyes and said, "Yes, Guildmaster."

Daruya woke toward sunset with every memory intact, Bundur beside her, and a scowl on her face. He smiled back. "Good evening, madam," he said. "Are you always so cross when you wake?"

She snarled and went to the garderobe that was past the bath, and stopped to plunge her head into cold water in the basin, and came back a little brighter of eye. He sat up in bed, raking fingers through his thick straight hair.

She hunted, found a comb. He sat still while she plied it, finding it much easier to make order of hair so thick when it was straight and not curling everywhere at once. It was waist-long, cut level—if it had never been cut, she thought, it might have been as long as he was. Combing it was like combing silk, or a senel's mane.

When it was smooth she plaited it in a single braid as if he had been a priest. He did not protest, though she had never seen a man with a braid here. He liked the feel of it, less clumsy than a knot at the nape, more easily managed than a long tail bound with a bit of leather or ribbon.

Then he wanted to comb her hair, for which she pitied him. Each knot untangled only bred a new one. But he insisted, and it gave him pleasure, like playing in gold. "Do women cut their hair short in your country?" he asked. "Your Guildmaster and the woman with her wear the long braid, I notice. Your men, too, those whose hair I can see."

"Royalty never cut their hair at all," Daruya said, "nor priests once they take up their office. I was sick of knots and tangles and hours with combs and brushes. I hacked it off when Kimeri was born."

His brows lifted. "All of it?"

"Right to the skull," she said with remembered satisfaction. "It was wonderful. Cool; light; simple to keep clean. Everyone howled."

He took a curl in thumb and forefinger and stretched it straight. Left to itself it fell just below her shoulders. Straightened, it was halfway to her waist. "Why did you let it grow again?"

"Laziness," she said. "Contrariness. I discovered I'd started a fashion; half the young idiots in the court were going about with heads cropped or even shaved bald, as if I'd ever intended to go that far. I think I'll be glad when it's long enough to make a decent braid. It gets in the way as it is."

"I can imagine," he said. "I remember when I came out of the temple to inherit Janabundur, how I regretted the simplicity of a bare skull. But I was glad, in the end, to leave that behind. It gets beastly cold in the winter."

Daruya tried to see him in a priest's robe, shaved clean. He would have been much younger; awkward, all angles, with big hands and feet, and a blade of a nose. Charming, rather. She leaned back against him, because he was warm and solid and it seemed like something she should do. His arms settled about her. He nuzzled her hair. They did not kiss here; she remembered how odd she had thought it, but how little she had been moved to teach him the art. There had not seemed to be any need of it.

She was comfortable. That alarmed her, but not enough to move. Comfort had never been anything she expected to have with a man. Arguments, yes. Resistance. His will striving to bend hers. Not this calm accommodation, or this conviction that she would do what he wanted, because she too wanted it.

He had much to learn of what she was. But not now. Not . . . quite . . . yet.

Tradition in the empire would have given a newly wedded pair three days of solitary lovemaking. In Shurakan they were given two full hands of days, and kept strictly apart, too, which as Bundur pointed out, favored the cause of protecting Daruya and her companions from enemies in the palace.

"Unless of course they find Borti," he said. Seclusion did not prevent the family from communicating with bride and bridegroom; they could speak, even eat together, as they were doing, the third morning after the wedding.

Borti looked up from slicing a scarlet fruit and feeding bits to Kimeri and Hani. Her face was blandly innocent, her accent slightly but distinctly countrified. "Why, and what would the great ones want with a children's nurse?"

"Not, I hope, what they'd want with a queen," Daruya said. If anyone had expected marriage to smooth her edges, he was disappointed. She was still Daruya; still all prickles and sharp words, and she did not spare Bundur any more than the rest. But something was different. Some tension eased, and not only that of a woman who needed a man for her bed; some resistance softened. As if, thought Vanyi, she had stopped fighting the inevitable and faced the fact that she was a woman, and royal born at that.

It was a young change yet, and might not hold. But Vanyi decided to let it hearten her. Estarion would be gratified; he had hoped for such a result.

They did match well. The awkwardness of new lovers was missing, the fumbling, the distraction, the obsession with one another. The bond between them ran deeper than that. Daruya had been fighting it since she came to Shurakan; had fought it maybe lifelong, as if her soul knew where the other half of it was, but the rest of her had refused to listen.

She was still fighting, but not against that. She would always fight; that was in her blood. Now maybe she would choose more useful causes.

As Vanyi reached for the pot to refill her cup of tea, one of the servants glided in and bent toward her. "Lady, one asks for you. Are you at home to him?"

"Who is he?" Daruya, stretching her ears and making no effort to pretend otherwise.

"Lady," said the servant with a deeper bow than he had accorded Vanyi, "it is one from the palace, a man who comes quietly but walks with the gait of rank."

"The Minister of Protocol," said Daruya. She half rose. "Should I—"

"I'll see him," Vanyi said. And at Daruya's frown: "You're in seclusion, remember. It suits us to keep you that way."

Daruya sat down again. It was not acquiescence. Bundur, Vanyi noticed, kept out of it. Wise man.

"Yes," Vanyi said as if Daruya had spoken. "As long as we can use the marriage-days as a shield against intruders, we gain time to think our way out."

"Little enough of that we've done so far," said Daruya.

"You think so?" Vanyi asked. "I'd say we were doing well. We're keeping Borti hidden, we've got Uruan back up to strength, and we have watchers in the house of the Gate in case someone comes there, thinking it deserted, and tries something. Now we have a visitor from the palace."

"Who, I hope, simply wants to exchange pleasantries with you, and not arrest you for high treason." Daruya gestured to the Olenyas who hovered nearest. "Chakan. Go with her."

Chakan bowed, scrupulously correct as he had been since his quarrel with his lady. That would take some smoothing over, thought Vanyi; but it was not her place to say so.

She could easily imagine what Daruya would say to that: When, pray tell, had Vanyi ever cared whether it was or was not her place to say whatever she had a mind to? But Vanyi could take refuge in proprieties when they served her purpose, or when it was simply practical.

The Minister of Protocol waited in an antechamber with tea and cakes and carefully schooled patience. He was not accustomed, clearly, to wait on the convenience of others.

Vanyi found his presence and his continued good health interesting. Palace coups in Shurakan, she had been assured, were civilized; no one died except by strict necessity, and those who could continue to serve did so. It reminded her in a way of the Olenyai and their honor, which was sworn to the throne and not to the one who sat in it.

She did not have to like it or him. She spoke abruptly, without greeting. "What do you want?"

He blinked at her discourtesy, but answered as he could. "You must understand, lady, that while I am utterly orthodox in my convictions, I am not in sympathy with those who would destroy all that even hints of magic."

"Is that what's happening in the palace?"

"It is what is going to happen soon. The new king has ordered the palace to his satisfaction. His followers are free to pursue the purposes for which they raised him to the throne."

"And those are?"

"To drive out all foreigners. To destroy all taint of magic in Su-Shaklan."

Vanyi considered that. It was nothing surprising, nothing unexpected. But to hear it spoken so baldly by this of all men—that brought it home, and forcefully. "How far are they thinking to go?"

"Far," he said. His hands, raising the cup to sip cooling tea, were not quite steady. "They seek even to suppress some of the odder cults and priesthoods among our own people: the exorcists, the spirit-speakers, the counters of the dead, even some of the oracles and prophets and the holy ones of the heights. All those, they say, are workers of magic."

"Some of them probably are," Vanyi observed.

"Only in the broadest sense," he said. "Too broad, in my mind. I mislike what it may lead to."

"Indeed," Vanyi said. "Broad interpretations can become very broad, until they include anyone whom one doesn't love, and any doctrine that one disapproves of."

The Minister of Protocol bobbed his head: Shurakani agreement. "Yes. Yes, that is what I see. Already they make lists, name names, reckon up their enemies and their unfriends."

"Are you telling me," Vanyi asked, "that I should get my people out before the whole palace falls on us with fire and sword?"

"No, lady," said the Minister of Protocol. "That would destroy you certainly. The guards of the borders have been instructed to slay you if they see you. In the city you are safe; in this house you are protected still by the name of Janabundur. No one yet is willing to challenge it or those who hold it."

"But for how long?"

"Lady, I do not know." A mighty admission, and a great abdication of pride. "I know only that you, through your kinswoman, are now of Janabundur, and Janabundur has great influence among those who might wish to avert what comes."

"The lord of the house is in seclusion," Vanyi said, "till the days of his wedding are over."

"His lady mother is not. And his sisters. Nor are you yourself."

Vanyi poured tea, to give her hands something to do while she pondered. His mind was as readable as ever—to the same point as ever, neither deep nor shallow, but beneath was a darkness she could not penetrate.

Did he know that the queen was here? His thoughts were innocent of such knowledge. They saw much amiss in the kingdom, a king whom he reckoned more puppet than ruler, weak and vain, and puppetmasters without let or scruple. They would trample the ancient orders and courtesies in the name of the gods and the ban against magic.

She held great weapons, she thought, sipping tea that she barely tasted. The queen. House Janabundur. Her own magery, and the power of all her mages. The Olenyai, warriors in a mode that was unknown here. Even Gates, if she could open them again.

But the palace ruled Shurakan. Its armed men might not be equal, man for man, to any Olenyas, but there were hundreds of them to her nine bred-warriors. Its power might—must—encompass a force that could break Gates.

Yes. It must. She had no proof, no certainty, but her bones knew. Whatever had broken Gates, its wielders had slain the old king and given the crown to one of its own.

The Minister of Protocol waited, silent, for her to finish pondering. She spoke abruptly; he started. "I'll speak to the Lady Nandi. More than that I can't promise."

"It will help," he said. "Not all of us in the palace are bound to the new lords. Those of us who can will assist you. Come or send to us discreetly, in my name. I will come at once, or my messenger if I am detained."

"What do you want?" Vanyi demanded of him. "The new king killed, his followers likewise? Yet another new order?"

"Lady," he said. "Lady, he who is king is king. But he should not permit his people to indulge in excess."

"Ah," said Vanyi. "You want us to sweep the rags and the gutter-leavings out of your palace. What do we gain in return?"

"You will not be hunted," he said, "nor expelled. And the haters of what you are will be constrained as before by the bounds of law and custom."

"That's not enough," she said. "Give us freedom of the kingdom—swear that we'll not be made prey to the hatred of the ignorant. Or," she added, catching his eye, "of those who fancy themselves wise. Allow us full status as ambassadors, with full respect and full privileges."

"If you succeed," he said, "that will be inevitable."

"Swear to it."

"By the gods and the goddess, and by the children of heaven," he said without hesitation. "Set us free of those who would run to mad extremes, and you will be accorded the rank and respect of friends. You are already possessed of privilege, as the kin of Janabundur."

Vanyi inclined her head. "We're allies, then. I'll send to you when I've spoken to Lady Nandi."

TWENTY-SIX

LADY NANDI WAS CARDING WOOL AS WOMEN DID HERE, WITH HER DAUGHTERS for company, and Borti with a spindle, spinning thread out of the wool. They made Vanyi think, with unexpected poignancy, of women in a fishermen's hut on Seiun Isle, waiting for the men to come back from the boats.

Odd to think that these were royal ladies, and one a queen. Queens in the empire did not spin or weave. They led councils and commanded armies, and held regencies when they did not rule in their own right. If they indulged in any stolen leisure, they rode seneldi and hawked or hunted; embroidered tapestries, or made music, or read from books. Weaving was a guild and a craft, and not the province of a princess.

Here the women of the house, even if they were of high rank, spun and wove and sewed, and dressed their kin and servants in their looms' weaving. They did not weave rugs or embroider tapestries. That was an art, and practiced in the temples, which seemed here to do duty for guilds.

Vanyi could remember how to spin, if she thought about it. She had not done it in years out of count. She had never threaded a loom; that had been her mother's task, while her mother lived. After she died, Vanyi had turned rebel and sought the sun-god's temple and become a priestess. Novices of Avaryan's priesthood did what they were bidden to do; Vanyi's tasks had been the planting and harvesting of vegetables for the pot, and the mending of nets, and long hours of study in the arts of magecraft, for that was and had always been her great gift.

She sat on the stool that was nearest, while the women carded and spun. Sun slanted through tall windows, warming the room, making stronger the heavy scent of wool. Someone had begun to thread the loom, but stopped halfway; the threads were a deep crimson, nearly black unless the sun shone on it. The wool that Borti spun was dyed a soft green. Vanyi wondered if the two colors were meant to be woven together. It did not seem likely, but with weavers one never knew.

It was peaceful here, even with her presence to make the servants uneasy. The high ones were placid, unruffled, their hands deft in their tasks. Borti spun a fine thread, Vanyi noticed, of even thickness; yet she seemed hardly to be aware of what her hands were doing. Her eyes were on the windows, her gaze full of sunlight, but under the brightness the shadow ran deep.

She grieved for her brother and lover, her king who was dead. They had not agreed on policy, they had quarreled often, but Vanyi knew how little that could matter between two who were friends and lovers both. She withdrew delicately from the other's thoughts, save for the flicker of emotions across the surface. "The Minister of Protocol wants an alliance," she said.

The servants lowered their heads and made themselves invisible. Lady Nandi said, "I thought he might."

"Have you spoken with him?" Vanyi asked, a little sharply perhaps.

"I know him," Lady Nandi said. "He would hardly approve of all that the new king's counselors are doing. Does he wish us to appear in the court and listen to what people are saying there?"

"Would you want to do that?"

"I had thought of it," Lady Nandi said. "It might not be excessively wise after what was done to my brother—and no one has come to me, who am, in their knowledge, his only living kin, to offer me the death-scroll and bid me fetch his body."

"You might," said Borti quietly, "go to the palace as one who has the right, and ask for those things. They won't harm you, I don't think. There's another thing these hotheads, most of whom are young, hold as truth revealed: that women are weak and must be indulged and protected."

"And I am old," said Lady Nandi, "and the old are weakest of all."

Surely, thought Vanyi. The lady was little smaller than her son, and he was a big man, rock-solid and built to last. But a young male, blinded by grey hair and a lined face, might be persuaded to see frailty where there was none. Vanyi would exploit it herself if she had the chance; though Nandi would do better in this, there was no denying.

Lady Nandi had no magery to read Vanyi's thoughts, but her wits were quick. She smiled at Vanyi. It was a wicked smile, much younger than the face it shone on; she had been a hoyden in her youth, or Vanyi was no judge of women. It might not be so surprising after all that the woman had let her beloved and only son take a wife as wild as Daruya.

"I think," Lady Nandi said, "that I may be driven to stumble to the palace on my ancient feet and beg weeping for my brother's remains. My daughters will follow, of course, with loosened hair and distraught faces. And servants with a bier."

"Pity is a powerful ally," Borti observed. "Our brother would laugh. He did love a scene well played."

Nandi bobbed her head. "Oh, he did indeed. Will you come? A servant's coat, a properly humble bearing . . . no one will know you."

"No," said Borti. Her voice was harsh; she softened it with a perceptible effort. "No, it's too chancy. If even one servant recognizes me, I've lost us everything."

"I would trust you not to be indiscreet," Nandi said.

Borti's hands faltered in their spinning. Her face was calm, even cold. "I thank you. Trust is no easy thing to earn. But I won't risk it. When you bring him back, with all such news as you can gather, and goodwill in the court, too, I'll perform the rites with you. If, of course, you permit."

"I permit it," said Nandi with formal precision. "I wish it."

"Make them pity you greatly," Borti said. "Win their hearts for us."

But before the Lady Nandi could risk herself on such an errand, before she could even finish preparing to go, a guest was brought to Vanyi as she tried to read in the library that was next to the hall. She never remembered afterward which book it had been, or even what kind of book it was. The man who stumbled and fell at her feet was a preposterous creature, naked but for festoons of charms and amulets; his face and body were painted, often garishly, but the bright scarlet and the livid blue were blood and bruises. He had been beaten, and badly; it was a wonder he was walking, let alone running ahead of the servant.

Vanyi abandoned her book with open relief and knelt to turn the fallen man onto his back. Her hands were as gentle as they could be. Even at that, he groaned and struggled, but stilled as he understood that she meant him no harm.

As she had expected, it was the odd creature who had helped to bring Uruan back from the house of the Gate: the exorcist, who appeared to have no name, or none that his sect would let him confess to. There was a scent of magery on him, weak but distinct.

His eyes opened in the bruised and swollen face. Much of the paint had rubbed away; the features under it were unremarkable except where they were swollen out of their wonted shape. His nose was broken, Vanyi noted, and he had lost a tooth or two.

"You were lucky," she said, "that they didn't break anything more vital."

He blinked at her, struggling to make sense of her. His magery, as ill-trained and twisted as it was, recognized hers, but he did not know what he was seeing; only that she seemed more real than the world about her. She made no effort to soften the effect. He would learn what it was that made him see her so; or he would not.

"Tell me why you came here," she said when he kept staring, blinking, poised on a thin edge of pain and panic. "Why here, and to me in particular?"

Her voice anchored him as she had hoped it would. "I ask you for sanctuary, lady of the mages," he said.

"Why?"

"Because," he said, "I'll be killed else. They've stripped my temple bare and burned it. They've beaten or killed the priests. They're doing it all through the city, wherever the whim strikes them. They say—" He had to stop and swallow bile. "They say that they're cleansing the city and the kingdom. Of—of—"

"Of evil magic?"

His head bobbed assent, unwisely: he gasped with pain and dizziness, and retched. But his stomach was empty. Those who beat him had seen to that.

"Why did you come here?" Vanyi asked. "You don't know us."

"But you are—that. What they said we were."

"What, mages? We're no more evil than any other mortals."

"Mages," he said. "M—mages. And strong. And they said—I heard them say—they can't touch you, not while Janabundur speaks for you."

"Not yet," Vanyi said.

"So I came to you," he said. "You can fight. You have light and dark in your hands like swords, and demons at your call. And gods; and the little goddess."

"What—" Vanyi laughed, but not with mirth. "I suppose you could call the imp that."

"I want to fight with you," he said. "I want to see them fall as my temple fell, in bloody ruin."

He was fierce as only the young can be, and muddled beyond belief. "I'm not going to kill anyone right at the moment," Vanyi said, "and never with magic, in any case. It's forbidden."

He did not understand. He said, "I want them to fall."

"From what I can gather," Vanyi said dryly, "your temple was sacked and burned by half the rabble in the city."

"They were led," he said. "Led from behind by those who called themselves pious and lovers of the gods. Lovers of their own greed, I call them. I saw how they took the best things for themselves, and stood back for the mob to scrape up the leavings." He scrambled himself erect, mustering a surprising degree of dignity. "I have no magic such as you have, but I can serve you and run errands for you and be your hands and feet."

Vanyi looked at him and sighed. She did not need servants; she had more than enough. But there was no graceful way to turn him out, not as battered as he was, and in such need of a bath and a physician.

"Ah well," she said. "What's one more mouth to feed? Go on, follow the servant, bathe yourself, and rest. I'll send someone to look after your hurts."

"I don't need to rest," he said, though he was wobbling on his feet. "I want to serve you."

"Later," she said. "Now, off with you."

Kimeri heard the exorcist come in. She listened as he spoke to Vanyi, and was ahead of him when he went to the servants' wing, where they had a bathhouse and an extra room or two. In the big wooden tub, with his amulets off and his paint washed away, he was a perfectly ordinary, rather skinny and gangly person with a spectacular crop of bruises and cuts, and that poor broken nose.

"I'm sorry I can't mend your nose," she said, clambering up on the rim of the tub. He had been left to get himself clean, which was not very kind of the servants. They thought exorcists were as bad as mages, and smelled worse. It did make it easier to talk to him, since there was no one about to stop her, except her Olenyas; but it was Rahai again, and Rahai never got in the way unless she tried to leave the house.

The exorcist almost drowned himself trying to bow in the water while scrambling away from Rahai's shadow.

"Stop that," Kimeri said. "You'll hurt yourself. And stop thinking that I'm a goddess. I'm a god's get, but I'm nothing to fall at the feet of. I'm not even a beauty yet."

He was so confused that he obeyed her. By the time he thought about what she had said, he was safe on the ledge in the tub, scrubbing gingerly at the last of his paint. He kept looking at Rahai as if the Olenyas were something to be afraid of, but since Rahai was doing nothing more threatening than standing by the door, he at least stopped trying to hide under the water.

"I'm sorry about your temple," said Kimeri. "And about your nose. Vanyi's going to send Aledi to look at it. Aledi's got a little healing magic. You'll be afraid of her: she's Asanian, and her eyes are yellow. But she's very gentle."

"Your eyes are yellow," the exorcist said.

"That's because my father is Asanian, and my mother is mostly Asanian, and so were her mother and father. But I'll be taller, because my great-grandfather's mother was from the north, where everybody is as tall as a tree."

"North is the Spear of Heaven," said the exorcist. "There are no man-trees there."

"Not in your north," Kimeri said. "You should get out of the water now, before your bruises get stiff. Do you mind wearing clothes? Everybody seems to, here."

He did not mind wearing clothes. All the amulets and the paint were really only for formal occasions; his temple had been having one of its great exorcisms, when they tried to drive all the evil out of the kingdom for another turning of the moons. Evil had found them instead, and broken the temple. Kimeri watched him think about that as he climbed into the shirt and trousers and coat. He left his amulets in the box the servants had set out for them. He was not afraid that anyone would steal them. They all had curses on them, and everybody knew it.

All but one, which he put on. It was a leather cord with a stone on it, smooth and round and grey, with a hole worn in the middle. "To keep my soul safe," he said.

If he thought it would, then it might. Kimeri thought the stone was rather pretty.

Aledi came in then and chased Kimeri out, not meaning to be impolite, but she was thinking much too clearly that small children had no place in the middle of magic. Aledi did not understand Sunchildren at all. Kimeri could not expect her to. She was Asanian, and High Court Asanian at that. But it stung.

Hani could not play with her. He had lessons in a temple near the house, just for the morning but enough to keep him away when she needed him. She was too young for lessons, even if she had been Shurakani. She was supposed to do what young children did, which, as far as she could see, was nothing at all but be chased out of people's way.

If she could have gone outside of the house, she would have been able to find something to do. But the Olenyai would not let her. It was too dangerous, they said. People were hunting mages. They were burning temples and chasing people out of houses and beating up anybody who looked or sounded or acted different. The air, even in the house, had a foul smell, like blood mixed with the thing that men and women did, that her mother was doing with Bundur and not bothering to hide.

Except that what her mother and Bundur did was a joyful thing, like singing. What the people were doing in the city was ugly. It made Kimeri want to scrub herself over and over, to take the stink away.

Kimeri went to where her mother was. She stayed outside while they finished what they were doing, then waited a little longer, in case they started again. They got up instead and put on their clothes, and talked about eating.

She went in. Bundur was sitting on the windowledge. Kimeri's mother was braiding his hair. Kimeri climbed up on his lap, not even asking him if he minded, and buried her face in his shirt. He smelled of clean man and clean wool and the thing that, in this place, was joy. He did not push her away but gathered her in, though he looked a question at Daruya.

"She's . . . what I am," Daruya said after a little while. "She knows what's happening in the city."

He was shocked. "All of it?"

"All that matters." Daruya's hand brushed Kimeri's head, bringing calm. "You should be flattered. She never goes to people she doesn't trust."

That was not exactly true, but Kimeri did not say it. He was warm and solid, and yes, she trusted him. He made her feel safe.

He kept on being solid and warm, and being glad that she was there. That must be what it was like to have a father. Great-Grandfather felt the same way about her, mostly, and he understood her, too, and Bundur did not, yet; but this was different somehow. This was nearer to her, with her mother in it, being part of it and part of him. While she was with them, the ugliness could not touch her, or make her afraid.

TWENTY-SEVEN

THAT NIGHT WAS FULL OF FIRES AND SHOUTING, BROKEN TEMPLES AND shattered gods and mobs that raged from end to end of the city. House Janabundur was as safe as a house could be: it was high up on a hill, with no roofs overlooking it, and its walls were strong and its gates were barred. Olenyai guarded them, side by side with Janabundur's strongest servants. Daruya was not surprised to see how many of those there were, or how loyal. Janabundur had an army of its own if it chose to raise one. Many of its best men had been finding their way to the house over past days, coming from houses in the city, farmsteads in the valley, holdings along the mountain walls. They brought with them bundles that, when opened, revealed well-kept weapons and armor of leather plates strengthened with bronze.

It was not war, Bundur insisted. Fools in the palace had raised the mob, and would pay dearly for it, come the cold light of morning and the colder eye of the law. He had no comprehension of the discrepancy between a rule of law and a palace coup leading to rampage and riot. "The law has always banned magic," he said. "They've spread the net so broad that they're sweeping in innocents. Then, when every sane person recoils from what's been done in the name of law, another law will save us all: the law that protects the innocent, and the law of the human heart, which is always contrary. They'll be favoring mages, you'll see, out of pity and guilt. Out of that we'll make a new decree, one that softens the strictures against magic."

"It should remove them altogether," Daruya said.

"Someday," he said, "it may."

They could not sleep in one another's arms: Kimeri was between them, and Hani, who had crept in to have his own fears soothed away. It was peculiarly comfortable to lie all of them in a bed, demurely clothed, the children asleep in the circle of their parents' protection, lulled by their voices.

Morning came with crawling slowness and a sense as of a long debauch barely begun. Daruya had been in a siege once, in her grandfather's wars. She remembered this sense of being trapped in walls and yet sheltered by them, the determined cheerfulness, the refusal to consider what would happen if the enemy broke through their defenses.

Hani would not go to his lessons this morning. Bundur took both children to the kitchen, where a hound bitch had whelped in the night. Daruya was glad to be away from him, to be herself again for a little while, and yet she missed him keenly, the touch of his hand, the smell and the taste of him. She had not been out of his sight since she married him, nor he out of hers.

Truly, then, it was past time. She put on her riding clothes and went to see which of the seneldi would be amenable to a canter round the garden.

Daruya brought her dun mare to a neat halt precisely in the center of the circle that had marked the limits of her exercises. As she dismounted, Kadin came through the gap in the hedge. He too was in riding clothes, but no senel followed him.

It was not noble of her, but whenever she saw him she shivered. His grief seemed to shape all that he was; that, and the darkness that was his magery. She, bred of the Sun, could with utter ease have matched him, light to his shadow.

It was not the matching of souls that bound her to Bundur. It was another kind of twinning, one that by the laws of her inheritance she could not accept. She had never known exactly why, unless it had to do with her firstfather's conviction that light and only light must rule, or with Vanyi's refusal to submit the Mageguild to the emperor's will. The Guild served him when it could, which was often, but it remained distinct. All worlds were its concern; it would not bind itself to the lord of this one, however great a mage he might be.

And yet, faced with this darkmage whose power so craved the light that would complete it, Daruya suffered sore temptation. She was all edges and angles, shocked by the marriage that had been thrust on her, the murder of a king, the fall of Gates. One more shock surely could not matter, one more transgression, one more count against her in the minds of her people.

She was tired of being wild. It struck her as she stood there, loosening the saddle-girth and rubbing an itch out of the mare's neck. She was weary of resisting; of breaking law and discipline simply because they discommoded her.

The trouble, she thought, was that Bundur would not fight back. He yielded; he smiled; he slid smoothly round her and showed her her own face in the mirror of his mind. She was usually scowling. She was always rebelling. It was her art and her gift.

But here in the face of a rebellion that would put all the rest to shame, she sickened of it. Kadin did not know what he did, how his darkness lured her, how even his grief made it easy to succumb. He would not want her for a lover; twinned mages need not be bedmates, or even friends. They raised power together, that was all. They made each other complete.

No, she thought. Resistance again; she almost laughed at that—bitterly, again. She was a pattern of repetitions. Could she not vary it?

Kadin was oblivious to her maundering. He caught the mare's bridle as Daruya began to lead her out of the hedged circle that had become the riding-ground. "Lady," he said, "wait."

Daruya paused. She had grown accustomed to men who were her own height or smaller; it was odd to have to look up. He was keeping his hair cropped short, she noticed, but letting his beard grow. That was like a northerner, as was the gold ring in his ear. Northerners felt naked without their beards and their gauds.

"Lady," Kadin said again. "Daruya. If I named a quarry, would you hunt with me?"

For all her noble intentions and her real weariness, her heart leaped. "A hunt? Where?"

"In this city," he answered. "For breakers of Gates."

"Yes," breathed Daruya. "Oh, yes." But—"Did the Guildmaster send you to me?"

"No," said Kadin. "I came to you first."

He was speaking the truth: he opened himself to let her see it. He also let her see why. Vanyi would wish him to be cautious, to be circumspect. Daruya, he thought, would be eager for a wild hunt, for the revenge that twisted like hunger in his belly.

He approved her wildness; admired it. She was not as flattered as she might once have been—and not long ago, either.

Still. A hunt, and a quarry. "Who is it?" she asked. "Where did you find him?"

"I'm not sure yet," said Kadin. "I know that my magic has found a place, a lair of . . . something, and a remembrance of fallen Gates."

"You really should have gone to Vanyi," Daruya said, but not as a rebuke. "If it's this uncertain still—you could be catching the death of the one who did it, killed in the confusion. Maybe he was the target of it all."

"I think not," Kadin said. "It's strong. The uproar stripped its shields, I'll wager, and I was hunting just when the shields went down. It doesn't know they're down; it's made no effort to raise them again."

"A trap," said Daruya.

"Possibly," he said. His eyes were bright. His teeth flashed in his beard. "Will you hunt with me, Sunlady?"

She should not. She should go to Vanyi, speak to Bundur and his mother, talk it to death.

Then sit in this cage while the others pursued the hunt.

Ah well, she thought. He had asked; and he was strong, both mage and man. What danger in simply finding the quarry, so that he could bring sure word back to his Guildmaster?

Even the voice of temptation knew what folly that was. Kadin would not play scout in this. He hunted to kill.

All the more need of her to keep him from doing something rash. She unsaddled and rubbed down the mare and stabled her with the rest, took the hooded cloak Kadin offered her and hid her alien face in it, and drew shadows about her besides. He was a shadow beside her, following the scent that he had found.

TWENTY-EIGHT

THE CITY WAS QUIET IN THE WARM NOON, AS IF IT RESTED FROM ITS EXERTIONS of the night. A pall of smoke hung over it; some of the markets were shut, and some had suffered at the hands of rioters. There had been efforts to keep order: streets with guards strolling or standing, wearing the colors of one noble house or another, or else the shaved head and saffron tabard of a temple. Not one of the temples that had been attacked; those, Daruya suspected, were mostly the poorer or smaller, too weak to fight back.

Where guards were was greatest quiet, shops unlooted, houses or temples unburned. Even so, too much of the city had suffered, she saw as she ghosted through it with Kadin. Once or twice she saw desultory parties of looters behind broken gates, gutting temple or house and setting fire to what they left behind. They did not think that they were serving the gods or upholding the law. They were smashing and seizing, that was all, and taking pleasure in it.

She had been sheltered from it in House Janabundur. How much, she had not known till she passed through the middle of it. It was no consolation that everyone who could had retreated behind walls and barred the door. Too many had not been able to, or had seen their walls breached and their door battered down.

The cold part of her, the part that was bred to rule, took note of who had been the targets. Smaller temples, temples of the odder or more exacting gods, particularly those without the numbers or the weapons to mount a defense. Houses of simple citizens, physicians, herb-healers, astrologers, diviners. Foreigners of any and every description. None was as foreign as she: all were of Merukarion or of the mountains. They had been driven out of houses or hostelries, beaten, robbed, even killed.

And she had been safe. She had lain abed with her Shurakani prince, while people died.

Guilt was no alien thing to her. But guilt for being powerless and accepting it—that was new.

She was doing something now. It was dangerous, it was badly advised, but it was something. She was not idling in House Janabundur and letting the city rack itself to pieces.

Kadin led her with a hunter's speed, a hunter's quiet. Her magery touched his, found what he followed. It was more memory than present reality: a scent, a taste, a quiver in the air. As he drew closer to the source of it, he needed her to keep him hidden, to steer him round obstacles. He was blind, focused on the one thing alone, the thing that had an air, however faint, of magery.

He stopped abruptly. She nearly collided with him. His face turned from side to side. His eyes were shut, his nostrils flared. He turned till he faced straight away from the sun, and stopped, standing stiff, like a hound at gaze; but his eyes were closed still.

Daruya looked where his power was focused. It was a temple; she had learned to recognize the shape of the gate in the blank wall, and the fact that it was open, inviting strangers in. It could dare that: the street was guarded, the guards alert, armed with pikes. People passed, going to and from the market at the street's end, where the guards were thickest and trade was almost brisk. Daruya caught a scent of roasting meat, baking bread, spices, flowers. Ordinary scents of the Summer City, eerie now with the stink of smoke and blood beneath.

Her stomach growled. She quelled it, and a completely unexpected urge to laugh. The body always had its say, no matter what the mind might think.

Kadin moved away from her so suddenly that she was left flatfooted. He had forgotten his cloak of shadows; he slipped along the wall, hunter-wise, but there was no mistaking his size or his foreignness. She darted after him, shadow-shrouded, before anyone could see and raise the alarm.

At the temple gate he paused. Daruya felt it with him: the faint hum of power, the skin-prickle of wards. Magic, in a place devoted to the destruction of mages?

It was not strong, not a Great Ward. It was set against a hostile mind, but not against a mage wrapped in shadow and shields. Both of them slipped through carefully, for such wards were delicate. Daruya did what she could to seem no more than a gust of air, a trick of the light.

Inside was a temple like many another: outer court, inner court, shrine and sanctuary, garden and cloister and dwellings for the priests behind. It was not a large temple, nor particularly small. Its god was more human-faced than most, but its body, though standing upright, was that of a mountain ox, and on its head were great sweeping horns. A white she-ox lay in a golden pen inside the shrine, chewing her cud. Devotees might purchase a twist of green fodder and offer it to her with bowings and prayers, and seek her consort's favor for their petitions.

If the ox saw the intruders, she did not betray them. Kadin ran soft-footed past her, round a knot of worshippers, through the god's shadow, and into the deeper sanctuary. Daruya heard sounds from within, the ringing of bells, the echoing hum of a bronze gong, the sound of voices chanting. She could not make out the words, if words there were.

So were the gods worshipped here, ceaselessly, in a long drone of chants. She had felt before this the power that rode the chanting, the strength of focused will that came close to magery. But never so clear. Never so distinct.

The sense of it on her skin was strikingly familiar. She had known just that brush as of wind, just that shiver beneath, as she approached a circle of mages in a lesser working. Guard-magic, she thought; a touch of wind-magic. Her own power woke to what it looked on: the swirl of winds in the upper air, a gathering of clouds above the mountains. Left unattended, they would swoop down into Shurakan in a storm of wind and hail, in a roll of summer thunder.

The inner chamber was open, unguarded save by the shimmer of wards. Daruya looked past Kadin to a circle of men—yes, all men, no women—in crimson tabards, each sitting on his heels, hands on thighs, head bent, eyes closed, chanting. The light of magic on them was as bright as a beacon to her inner eye.

And they did not know it. True mages—Guildmages, priest-mages—would have done their working behind a layering of wards, one for protection of their bodies, one for shielding of their minds from intrusion, and one for the working itself, to turn aside the unwary or the hostile. The warding here was weak, little more than a prayer for safety. The mind-shields were all but nonexistent. Thoughts babbled without direction and without focus, like a river beneath the ice that was the working.

They had no faintest conception of what they were doing. They were praying away a storm, they thought, and asking their god to guard the city, to defend their temple against the wrath of the mob. Here and there, like a spark on flint, was a thought of greater intensity: fear of mages, relief that they were nigh gone from the city, a wish that their kind had never been.

Suppose, thought Daruya, *that the sparks found tinder:* Gates open and vulnerable, mages passing through. Suppose that this and nothing else was the source of the Gates' fall.

No. It was too simple, the circle too weak. There was real magery in it, but feeble, undisciplined. What she had felt in the Gate had been greater—had been a real and present malice, directed at the Gate and at the mages within it. She did not sense it here.

Kadin, it seemed, did; or did not care that there was a difference. The drawing in of his power sucked at her, reaching for the light that was in her, seeking it to complete itself. Her power trembled in response.

She clamped it down, got a grip on Kadin, set her teeth, and hauled him back out of the doorway. He was too surprised to fight, too intent on the circle and on the calling of his power. She struck him with her own magery, a swift, fierce blow that rocked him on his feet.

"What in the name of—" he began, making no effort to be quiet.

She clapped a hand over his mouth. "Shut *up*," she gritted, barely above a whisper.

He struggled. She held on. Her power was stronger, even holding together shields and shadows. If it did not give way to the seduction of his darkmagic—if the priests or their guards did not rouse to the presence of strangers in their temple—if she could get him out before he unleashed a blast of power upon the men who, he was certain, had killed his lightmage—

The chanting went on, endless, unvarying. Its magic spun and wove into a circle of dim light, stretching and elongating, curving up past the temple's roof. Weather-magic, and no awareness at all of the world's balance. Rain that did not fall here must fall elsewhere; that much a child knew. But these pious priests did not. Ignorant, blind, utter fools.

And Kadin wanted to blast them from the earth. "They're not worth it," she hissed in his ear.

They killed Jian.

Deprived of his mouth to speak, he resorted to mind-speech. That too was perilous—more so than a whisper. Guards might not hear soft voices, but wards woke to the inner speech of mages.

"We don't know that," Daruya whispered as fiercely as she could. "Come out of here. We know there's magic working in Shurakan—that much you won for us. Now let's take it to the Guildmaster. She'll know what to do about it."

Kadin's resistance was beyond words, his body coiled to fling her aside, his power poised to leap, to destroy, to kill. That such use of magery would destroy him, he knew. He was glad.

"No," said Daruya, almost aloud. She caught a trailing edge of his magery and did a thing no Guildmage would ever stoop to: looped and bound him with it. He raged, he fought, but the harder he fought, the tighter the bond grew. Enough of that and he would strangle his power, turn it inward on itself. Then he would have the destruction he yearned for, but all within.

She had gambled rightly. He wanted to die, but not without purpose. Not unless he took his enemies with him.

They got out of the temple, though it cost Daruya high, sustaining shadows, shields, and mindbond, and dragging a large, reluctant, half-stunned darkmage bodily past the blind eyes of guards and the oblivious faces of worshippers. The white ox watched her, mildly curious. If she ever came back, she would bring the beast a gift of sweet fodder, in thanks for keeping her secret. She swore that as an oath in the silence of her mind, where only a god—or a god's white ox—could hear.

Kadin was nearly unconscious by the time he stumbled into House Janabundur. Daruya was in little better case. But she found Vanyi first, before her knees gave way: dropped the darkmage like a rolled carpet at the Guildmaster's feet and crumpled beside him, still awake, still aware, but no more strength in her than in a newborn baby.

There was someone else there. She could not see him at first; her power was too sorely strained. It came back slowly, feeding itself on her stillness. She was kneeling at Vanyi's feet, yes. Vanyi was standing face to face with one who was not here in body at all, and yet was visible: the more so, the longer she stared.

How dark he was, she thought, how bright a gold his eyes. And how young he seemed. He had always been ancient to her: her grandfather, her emperor, source and cause of her rebellions. He was not a young man, no; his hair was flecked with grey, his beard silvered. And yet he looked not much older in truth than Bundur.

If he had been any less meticulously and brutally trained, he would have been dancing with frustration. "You see?" he said. "*You see?* There is magery in this wretched little kingdom."

"They don't know that's what it is," Daruya said. Her voice was faint, breathless.

"They have little discipline," said Vanyi to Estarion, "except in the raising of wards. That's what deceived us for so long. But with the uproar in the city, they got careless. Or their wards weren't strong enough to hold against the force of hate and fear that was beating on them. Then they betrayed themselves."

"And lured yonder darkmage into a trap," said Estarion.

"They didn't mean that," Daruya said. "Can't you hear me? *They don't know.*"

"I hear you," he said, as maddening as ever, as if she were no older than Kimeri. "I commend you, too, for saving him from himself."

"How do you know what I did?"

"There now," said Vanyi, coming between them as she so often had before. "He's got eyes, and he knows Kadin. It's not hard to guess what you two were up to, considering the storms that have been shivering the Great Ward from end to end and shaking loose whole scores of lesser wards. This whole kingdom is infested with them. Every temple and shrine and holy man's hut must have at least a warding or two, if not more."

"It's prayer to them," said Daruya. "When they work magic, they think it a miracle, and the gift of a god."

"And isn't it exactly that?" Estarion sat on a cushion, for all the world as if he were there in the flesh. He looked comfortable but tired—as he would be, for it must be late night in Starios, and he did not look as if he had slept.

Daruya had no sympathy to spare for him. "But they don't know," she said, stubborn. "They don't see what they are or what they do. They just do it."

"And hate us, and pray their gods to destroy us—and so, in their minds, the gods do." Vanyi sighed. "They won't thank us for telling them what they're really doing."

"They won't believe it," said Estarion. "That kind never does."

"Unless we can prove it to them," Daruya said. "Somehow. Show them that they're as much mages as we."

"That's for later," said Vanyi. "Much later. Now we have a greater urgency to face: to be rid of the mages who broke the Gate."

"We don't know it's those mages," Daruya said. "It could be any circle of priests in Shurakan—any holy man, if it comes to that, who has reason to hate mages and Gates."

"It could," said Vanyi, "but I think not. Do you know what temple that is?"

"Should I? It has a god like an ox with a man's face, and a white she-ox for his consort."

"Yes," said Vanyi. "That is Matakan, whose father is the greater moon, and whose mother is the white moon-goddess, the mother goddess of Shurakan. The king and the queen are his kin. His chief power is the blessing of crops and the fields, and the guidance of princes. His legend calls him friend of the earth, brother of the children of heaven, and destroyer of unclean magics."

"Magic," said Daruya in dawning comprehension. "Ox-droppings. Excrement of Matakan—the evil that he casts out when he consumes the fruits of the earth."

"Exactly," Vanyi said. "What would you like to wager that Matakan's temple is the place where the new king's faction gathered before it seized the palace, where behind wards they conceived their plots and broke the Gates?"

"I saw none of that," said Daruya. "I saw a circle of priests turning aside a storm. They hate mages, yes, that's underneath everything they do, but there's no clear intention in it. No malice."

"Not in the priests you saw," Estarion said. "But wouldn't those be the lesser ones, the ones who aren't needed to hold the palace? They perform the offices, keep the storms at bay, while their masters go about the greater business of their order."

That made too much sense. And it had to come from Estarion, at whose every *Yes* she shouted, by instinct, a vehement *No!*

Not now. She was too tired, there was that. And he could not do anything here but talk, no matter how solid he seemed.

"So," said Vanyi, "we find the masters. That should be simple enough. They'll be in the palace, ruling it and its king."

"And warded, guarded, and praying you'll fall into their hands." Estarion reached but did not try to touch her. "Prayer here is magery. Remember that."

"I'm hardly likely to forget it," Vanyi said. Her voice was tart.

Kadin stirred suddenly at her feet, thrashed, flailed at air. Daruya flung herself on him and wrestled him into stillness.

The silence was much larger than it should have been. Much deeper. Much more . . . numerous.

Kadin was awake, but he was quiet, breathing hard, staring toward the door. Daruya followed the line of his gaze.

What Bundur must be seeing, she could well imagine. His wife on the floor with the black mage, in a posture she had more than once assumed in the marriage bed. The Guildmaster standing over them. And the stranger who sat by the wall, the dark man with the lion-eyes, whose like he could never have seen before, nor ever imagined.

Estarion looked both real and unreal. Solid, yet not quite there—as if he were more distant than he should be. His edges shimmered.

A demon, Bundur was thinking. A dark god. Both and neither.

"Grandfather," said Daruya steadily in Bundur's language, "this is my husband."

Estarion inclined his head. He had grace; he carried himself as one who had been emperor from his childhood.

Bundur saw it. Understood it. "Sir," he said, a little abrupt perhaps, but courte-ous. And to Daruya: "This is your emperor?"

"This is the Lord of Sun and Lion," she said. She rose carefully. Kadin sat up but offered no violence. She could forget him, she thought, until she had dealt with the rest of it.

They were measuring one another, her grandfather and her husband. Finding one another immensely strange, and very foreign. There was no leap of liking, no meeting of minds that she could discern. And yet somehow they agreed.

Maybe it was simply that they knew her and acknowledged her failings. Estarion had that look about him. So did Bundur—a quirk of the lip, a glint of the eye.

"And how," Estarion asked, "do you contend with the hottest temper in my empire?"

"As I do with all forces of nature, sir," Bundur answered: "swiftly, thoroughly, and with great respect."

"Is it worth the trouble?"

"I married it," Bundur said. "Sir."

"Ah," said Estarion, "but did you think you were going to tame it?"

"Of course not," said Bundur.

Estarion smiled his sudden brilliant smile. "You're a wise man, I see. And remarkably courageous."

"She's no danger to me," said Bundur.

"No? Then she must love you for a fact." Estarion settled more comfortably, stretched out on the cushions, propped on his elbow. "But I was thinking of your courage in standing here, talking to the most foreign of foreigners, and knowing that I'm not, strictly speaking, here at all."

"You're not here?" Bundur sounded puzzled. "I can see you, hear you."

"But I have no bodily substance. I'm a working of magic, a figment of your mind's eye."

"Grandfather—" Daruya began, half angry, half afraid.

He ignored her. So did Bundur. Bundur's vitals were knotted to the point of pain, but he was strong. He held his ground. She dared not touch him, still less ease the pain, for fear he would revolt.

"Tell me," he said, "O shape of air and darkness, if what I hear is true. Is it magic that they practice in the temples? Are the greatest haters of magic its most devoted practitioners?"

"I'm no oracle," said Estarion, "but from all I've heard and seen, it's true."

Bundur's knees gave way. There was a cushion close enough to fall to; he dropped onto it with something resembling grace, and sat for a moment, simply breathing. At length he said, "I thought I was stronger. I thought I knew what it was to live among mages."

"Even mages are never quite prepared for everything that can happen," said Estarion. "And you were taught from childhood to hate mages and to reverence priests. To discover that they're the same thing . . . that would break most men's minds."

Bundur laughed shakily. "I've married a demon's child, I've consorted with mages, I've seen a dark god in my own sitting room. What's another terrible truth, to that?"

"Not all priests are mages," Vanyi said, sharp and clear. They listened to her as they would not have done to Daruya: stopped their stallion-dance and stared. She glared back. "No, young Shakabundur, not even in our country, which isn't half as preposterous a place as you're coming to think it is. It's just a few priests and a particular form of prayer, and a fairly universal talent for raising wards. We would be a threat to that, we and our Gates, not least because we can name it for what it is."

"You think the leaders know," said Daruya.

"Know or suspect," Vanyi said, "and believe themselves righteous because their gods answer their prayers. Maybe they didn't know before they saw us. Who's to tell, till we can ask them?"

"You're not going to do that," Estarion said quickly.

Vanyi's brows went up. "And why not? Do you think we should cower here till they fall on us and destroy us?"

"I think you could let them come to you."

"I could," she conceded. "It's a decent stronghold, this. Well armed, well guarded; good walls, no easy way in. They'll come here, of course, before too long. Once their other quarry is hunted out and disposed of."

"Promise me you won't do something rash," said Estarion.

Vanyi looked at him. Simply looked. He withstood her stare far better than Daruya could have, but even he could not find a grin to set against it. She said, "I won't do anything that isn't necessary."

"That's not what I asked," he said.

"That's what you'll get."

"Gods," muttered Bundur. "And he's her king?"

"More than king," Daruya said. "But she's the Master of mages."

"My sorrow," said Estarion, flashing a glance at them, "that I ever let it be so. Damn you, Vanyi—"

"Damn you, Estarion," said Vanyi. "Go away and let me work."

"Not till you promise to be sensible."

"I'll be exactly as sensible as I need to be."

"If you get yourself killed," he said, low and fierce, "I'll haunt you till I die myself."

"The way you're haunting me now?" Vanyi wanted to know. "Avaryan help us. I'm like to die of it."

"Don't," he said.

"What, you care that much?"

It was mocking, but it was not. Estarion met it with sober certainty. "Always, Vanyi." He paused. "You didn't know?"

"I didn't dare." She rubbed her eyes. She looked as if she was suddenly, cripplingly exhausted. "Go home, Estarion."

This time he obeyed her—if anyone could call it obedience. It looked like the yielding of royal will to royal whim. Daruya herself could not have done it better.

TWENTY-NINE

VANYI ENTERED THE PALACE WITHOUT CONCEALMENT, AND WITH NO PARTICular care to be either nameless or faceless. She had had some difficulty escaping House Janabundur—everyone was determined to keep everyone else safe, and never mind how many of them had already rebelled against it—but after all she was the Guildmaster, and the oldest woman in the house besides, which mattered more to the Shurakani. She had her way. She also had a pair of Olenyai at her back, but that was more help than hindrance. They kept her from having to fret about attacks from behind.

The palace, like the city, was quiet, almost too much so. It was waiting for something, she thought. Her arrival? She would have laughed at herself, but there was cold in her bones.

The Minister of Protocol's workroom was empty, its table tidy, dusted, and clean. He had not been there that day, or the night before, either. She followed the memory of him, brazening her way past guards and chamberlains, going invisible when she must. She was taking no great care to hoard her magery. This was her gamble, her last cast of the dice. That she knew who had cast down the Gates through the circle of priests. That that one was waiting for her as a spider waits for its prey, crouching in the center of its web.

Fear had no part in it. She had been considering this for a long while now, perhaps since she decided to come to Shurakan in spite of the Gate's fall. Someone would have to lure the enemy out. Her mere presence in the kingdom had not been enough. She must force the meeting, and the confrontation.

If she had guessed rightly. If the enemy was the one she thought, and not someone else, someone unexpected.

The palace was a warren. Not as much of one as the Golden Palace in Kundri'j Asan; nor was it as large as Estarion's palace in Starios. But there was a great deal of it, a great many doors and passages, staircases, rooms that were full of people and rooms that were echoingly empty.

Vanyi followed the thread of presence that was the Minister of Protocol. Either he had been wandering lost for long hours, or he liked to ramble. Or it was yet another aspect of the trap. If she gave in to tedium and retreated, the enemy had won a respite. If she persevered, she was caught. In either event, the enemy won.

Which was exactly what Vanyi hoped for. She pressed on past weary feet and aching head, staring strangers, guards who barred her way and found themselves confronted with the threat of Olenyai swords. Neither bluster nor insults swayed the veiled warriors. They spoke no Shurakani; only the common language of hand on swordhilt and a few fingerbreadths of bared steel.

The trail led her into darker, narrower ways, perhaps older, certainly the province of servants and lesser ministers. Rooms were crowded together here, with larger ones at intervals, full of the scents of cooking and the clatter of plates and bowls. It was the hour for the daymeal. Vanyi had eaten, but not in a while. She regretted not thinking to bring at least a pouchful of fruit or a round of bread to nibble on. She had thought—hoped—to be seized at once and taken to the one she must see.

Foolish of her. An enemy clever enough to hide from mages who were actively hunting a destroyer of Gates, had more than enough sense to lead her on a merry chase before going to ground.

Indeed, and it was growing less merry by the heartbeat. She stopped abruptly. The Olenyai drifted past her, halted. One circled round to guard her back. The other poised just ahead of her, alert, though the corridor was empty.

Think, she told herself. What was this for? Why a trail this long and this convoluted, if they both knew how it had to end?

Subtleties within subtleties. The enemy might be afraid of her. She was a Master of mages, after all—and that one knew what the title meant.

Or she might be hunting the wrong quarry. Why then would he run? He should not even know she hunted him.

Unless he ran from someone else.

But who—

She began to run.

Back the way she came. Back through the twisting, turning passages. She forgot that she was a woman of venerable years, with stiff knees and shortening wind. She ran like the girl she had been.

The Minister of Protocol's workroom was no longer empty. The Minister of Protocol sat in it, upright at his worktable, smiling. And very dead.

The smile was rictus. Certain poisons induced just that expression, and just that blue cast to the lips. Vanyi was glad, at least, that he had had no pain. She had feared much worse.

She said so, taking a great deal too many breaths to do it, to the seemingly empty room.

"But, lady," said a gentle voice, "death is death."

"Some deaths are worse," she said. "And some, if your sages are to be believed, cast a man lower on the wheel of lives. Is it easier to die if you believe you'll be reborn?"

"One would think so," said Esakai the priest of Ushala temple. He had been using no magery to conceal himself, only a fold of curtain over an alcove. He came forward slowly, leaning on a staff.

He looked no different. Elderly, gentle, amiable. No hatred in him, no terror of what she was.

He regarded the Minister of Protocol with honest regret. "I do wish he could have lived," he said. "But he was obstinate. He would not see reason, even with the authority of the gods behind it."

"What reason was that, if it was too unreasonable for this of all men?"

"Why," said the priest, "that truly he was not well advised to ally himself with you. Your magery is difficulty enough. Your Gate is deadly. What is it after all but an instrument of conquest, conceived to destroy our kingdom?"

Vanyi gaped. Of all reasons she had expected, this was the last. Hastily she mustered wits and voice. "*That* was why you broke the Gate? Because you were afraid of armies invading through it?"

Esakai's thin white brows rose. "You expected any other reason?"

"It's too logical," Vanyi said.

"Lady," said Esakai sadly. "Oh, lady, how little you must think of us, if you believe that we can only fear you because you possess powers we were all bred to despise. That is no trivial thing, mind, but it's not all we can think of. We remember what you've told us of the empire you come from, how vast it is, how small we are, and how insignificant. It could consume us in an instant. And so it will, unless we resist it."

"No," said Vanyi. "That's not what I meant. You've let your mobs destroy half of Shurakan in the name of the gods' will against mages. If invasion were all you were afraid of, you'd have done none of that. You'd have marched on Janabundur—regardless of the power of the name or the house—and dragged us out and made examples of us."

"Yes," said Esakai, "and given your king-above-kings all the cause he would ever need, to fall on us and destroy us."

"He can't come through the Gate," Vanyi pointed out. "It's broken."

"And so shall it stay, while we have the power of the gods to help us. But, lady, if he has armies of dragons as the tales say, he needs no Gate, and no long march overland, either. We won't chance that. We'll see to it that no mage can ever live safe in Su-Shaklan, and we'll wield you as we may, to gain your emperor's promise that he won't conquer us."

Vanyi had been aware of the armed men closing in behind her, the drawn swords, the pikes, the hum of chanting that bore magery in it. The Olenyai would have sprung to her defense. She held them back. "No," she said. "Hold; be quiet. Get away if you can. This is strategy, and planned for."

From the roll of their eyes, they knew it already. One might approve. The other might be thinking her a raving idiot. There was no telling; they were shielded against magery.

But they were quiet, which was what mattered. To Esakai she said, "It's very odd, you know. One of the first things I did when I began building Gates to span this world was to inform the emperor that whatever he did, he was never to think that he could use my Gates to further his conquests. He'd do it the old way or none, foot-slog and senelback. My Gates are not his to use, nor are my mages his servants."

"He honored that agreement," she said, "though I gave him precious little to sweeten it: promise that he could use Gates himself, to see what was on the other side, and promise to share what we learned. He'd never bring his armies to over-whelm Shurakan."

"Unless," said the priest, "he were given what he considered reason. However slight. And his heir is here—the one who will rule after him, if the gods ordain. Might she not be the beginning of his invasion?"

"Believe me," said Vanyi, "Daruya would sooner die than be her grandfather's puppet."

The priest shrugged slightly, contemplating the dead man as before, with an expression of honest grief. "So would this man, and we gave him his wish. We can-not endanger our kingdom. Surely, lady, you understand that."

"I understand that you barely comprehend what you did in breaking the Gate. And your servants don't comprehend at all that the prayers they chant, the circles they dance in, are workings of magery. What will happen when they learn the truth?"

"The gods defend them," said Esakai, "and through them this kingdom."

"All priests are blind," said Vanyi, who was herself a priestess of the Sun.

He did not know that. He sighed, pitying her. "You thought to be a sacrifice. I name you hostage. Let your people pay the price to gain you back—let them depart from Su-Shaklan and never return."

"It's not going to be that easy," said Vanyi. She was feeling odd. Her breath had come back, but shallower than before. Her chest was tight. Her arm ached. Had she struck it against a wall somewhere, or strained it careening round a corner?

But she was where she needed to be. "Let me send these warriors as messen-gers," she said. "They're safer so; I don't know how many of yours it will take to subdue them if you let them stay, when your own guards try to carry me off."

Esakai believed in the Olenyai no more than any other Shurakani; he could only see their small size and their quiet bearing. But it served him to be rid of her guards, however weak they might seem. He agreed to it.

They did not, but she commanded them. "Tell Daruya," she said. "She's not to come galloping after me. There are subtler ways to win this war."

One of them, who was slightly the taller and rather the elder, inclined his head. "I'll tell her," he said. "She won't like it."

"Of course she won't," said Vanyi. "I expect her to control her temper and think, and do what's sensible. She can do it if she tries."

"Yes, lady," said the Olenyas. His voice was perfectly bland.

She was sorry to see them go. They had been like a wall at her back, visible and tangible protection against the dark. Without them she was utterly alone.

She was bait, and this was the trap: trap within trap. She could only pray that Daruya would understand the message and see what she must do. It was more trust than most would have given that wildest—and many would say least—of the Sun's brood. But Vanyi had never quite believed that Daruya was as feckless as she seemed.

It was a frail thing to rest her hopes on, but it was what she had. She smiled at Esakai. "So then. Am I to be shut up in a dungeon, or may I have dinner and a bed?"

"You are our guest," said Esakai, "until we are given reason to think otherwise."

She bowed, ironic. "My thanks, sir."

THIRTY

DAMN THAT WOMAN, THOUGHT DARUYA, *TO ALL TWENTY-SEVEN HELLS.*
They were all in the hall, even the children—happenstance, chiefly, since it was evening and the daymeal was past. The women were sewing by lamplight, the children playing on the floor, Bundur reading from a book of old stories. Daruya listened, wondering how any of them could be so calm with Vanyi gone to the palace and not yet come back, and no word from her, no message, nothing. The mages, who should have been either fretting over their Guildmaster or arming for the fight, were sitting on the edge of the lamplight, Aledi and Miyaz close together, Kadin well apart and utterly silent, and the Gileni Guardian, Uruan, seemingly asleep. Even the exorcist was there, looking surprisingly ordinary, playing with the children.

Hunin and Rahai burst in with signal lack of ceremony, and the rest of the Olenyai after them. The hall seemed suddenly full, and not only with bodies; the air had the scent and the taste of a storm that was ready to break. Daruya stood up with the swiftness of relief, and half stepped toward the Olenyai. "Where is she?"

"In the palace," Hunin answered. "She sent a message. You are not, lady, to gallop to her rescue. You are to remember that there are subtler ways; to think, to be sensible. And then to do what you must."

"And you *let* her send you away?" demanded Daruya.

"She commanded us," said Rahai, and not happily, either. "She was captured and is being held hostage."

"In return for what?"

"She didn't say," said Rahai.

"You didn't ask?"

He met her ferocity without blinking. "She didn't tell us. They were speaking Shurakani. I caught the word for hostage, but the rest was babble."

"I think," said Uruan from the edge of the light, "that they were meant not to know, so that they couldn't tell us. She doesn't want us to surrender whatever it is they want." He faced the Olenyai. "Did you know the men who captured her?"

"It was one man," Hunin said. "He came here more than once: a priest of the palace temple. Esakai, his name was."

"What is this?" Bundur demanded suddenly, his Shurakani voice running swift on the heels of Hunin's Asanian. "What are you saying? What is this about Esakai the priest?"

"He is saying," said Daruya, reining her patience tight, "that Vanyi has been captured and held hostage, and that she doesn't want a rescue. He doesn't know what she's hostage for. He thinks she doesn't want him, or us, to know."

"I can guess," Uruan said in Shurakani. "All foreigners out of the kingdom, and all mages dead or exiled."

"It might be more than that," Daruya said. She clenched her fists. "*Damn* her! I knew she'd do something like this. What is she trying for? To get herself killed and make a martyr, and bring down the wrath of the whole Mageguild, and the empire, too?"

The Olenyai did not understand her. The Shurakani, who did, did not know what to say. She started to stamp in frustration; caught herself. "Damn," she said, but much more mildly. "Uruan, come here. We're wasting time, talking in two languages and getting nothing said. Translate for us."

He was willing, even glad to oblige. He was still haggard and a little wild about the eyes, but he was in better case than Kadin. His ordeal inside the Gate seemed to be fading like a black dream; and he was strong as all his kin were, with a fierce resilience.

He would do. He rendered her outburst into Asanian, word for word. She could have done without quite so faithful a translation, but she had asked; she could hardly call back the asking.

Chakan responded at once and firmly. "The Guildmaster would do no such thing. She asked you to be sensible. To think."

"I am thinking," said Daruya. "I'm going to fetch her."

"You are not."

It came from both sides, in two voices, in two languages: Chakan, Bundur. They stared at each other in astonishment and swift anger—gods, even in that they were alike.

Suddenly they laughed. Chakan recovered first, and spoke in Daruya's furious silence. "She was not, whatever you may think, telling you not to do it so that you actually would. She has a better opinion of you than that."

"Not that I've ever noticed," Daruya muttered.

"I have." Bundur glanced at Chakan. "The warrior is right. She thinks she can accomplish something in the palace, and safely enough to send her guards away."

"Or unsafely," said Daruya. "These aren't her warriors. They're my grandfather's and mine. It's not her place to get them killed."

"Daruya," said Chakan, "as logical as that might be, it's not like Vanyi. She's in the palace, yes. She knows who's been breaking Gates—he's holding her hostage." He turned toward Bundur. "My lord, do you know this priest?"

Even in a temper Daruya could note the enormity of the concession: Chakan the Olenyas had granted a foreigner his title.

Bundur could not be aware of the exact degree of the honor, but he seemed to notice that he had been admitted to favor. "I know this priest," he said through Uruan. "He's one of the oldest of the old guard, well known to everyone, with no enemies that I've ever heard of. I'm amazed if what your warriors think is true, that he's been the mind behind the attacks on mages. It seems unlike him."

"Yet he is of the old way of thinking, yes?" Chakan inquired. "And he has the art of seeming less than he is—that's not uncommon. Who notices a harmless old creature doddering about, mumbling a word here, casting a smile there? What if the word were that mages were to be destroyed and the foreigners cast out, and the smile were directed at those who did so with utmost dispatch?"

"He needn't have done anything himself," said Daruya. "He could just suggest. And hint. And deplore. Oh, so many foreigners, so many mages, and that ghastly Gate of theirs . . ."

She stopped. They thought her finished: Bundur said something, but she was not listening.

Gate, she thought. That was how it had begun—not with mages killed or hunted out, or foreigners expelled. With a Gate, through which an embassy was known to be coming, an embassy from a great and distant empire.

Suppose . . .

"Suppose," she said, "that mages aren't what he fears most. He's afraid of them, there's no one in Shurakan who isn't, but they aren't his great fear. No; he dreads what their magic has made. Their Gate. Their door to other worlds, that opens on a particular city in a particular realm. Now suppose he's given word that an embassy has asked and been granted leave to use that Gate to enter Shurakan. The embassy is to be made up of mages—whom all Shurakani hate and fear—and of the heir to that foreign empire, which is ruled by mages who are also priests." She paused. They were all silent, staring at her.

"Don't you see?" she said. "We were thinking to honor Shurakan by sending our best and highest: the Master of the Mageguild, the princess-heir of Sun and Lion. What if Shurakan didn't see the honor? What if it saw something else?"

"Conquest," said Chakan. "Yes."

"Not all of us saw that," Bundur said. "Not even most. We were honored, as far as we knew how to be."

"But a few saw the Gate, and saw armies riding through it," said Chakan. "So did the emperor, for the matter of that. Vanyi prevented him from doing more than think, but would Shurakan know or trust that she would do it?"

"I would wager," said Daruya slowly, "that she thinks she can convince her captor of that, and talk him round—or at least confuse him enough to let us escape."

"Not escape," Bundur said. "Or exile, either, I don't think. She wouldn't give up that easily. She thinks she can gain time somehow, maybe for us to bring back the queen."

"There is that," said Daruya. "Borti—majesty—what do you—?"

There was no answer. Borti's chair was empty. And Hani was alone on the floor in a wrack of scattered toys, looking dazed and somewhat sleepy. Daruya throttled an urge to seize him and shake the truth out of him.

His father spoke before she had mastered her voice. "Hani, where did Kimeri go?"

Hani blinked. "I don't know," he said. "She went away."

Bundur would have pressed, but Daruya forestalled him. "No, don't. The imp put a wishing on him. If he ever knew where she went, or even when, he's forgotten."

Bundur's eyes rolled like a startled senel's. She caught him, shook him till he looked her in the face. "There. There, stop it. You're supposed to be reining me in, not the other way about."

He gripped her arms hard enough to bruise, and sucked in a breath. But he was calmer; he was seeing sense again. His hands loosened but did not let go. "I'll tan her hide," he said.

"You'll have to wait till I'm done first." Daruya glanced about. No one else was gone. If they were quick—if they raised a hunt—

"They might only have gone to the privy," said Chakan, "or the imp might be getting into perfectly reasonable mischief with the hounds or the seneldi."

Daruya did not believe it, much as she wanted to. But she let him send his hunters through the house, to discover what she had known already: that her daughter and the queen of Shurakan were gone. Together, she was sure. To the palace, most possibly. Where Daruya could not in good sense go—not while Vanyi was there and doing whatever she was doing to protect the embassy.

It was nothing different from what she had done since she arrived in Shurakan: waited, fretted, found nothing useful to do with herself.

And the queen, whom she barely knew, whom she did not truly trust, had taken her daughter and vanished. Another hostage; another prisoner. Another and most compelling reason to do as Vanyi forbade, and descend on the palace with fire and sword.

There was a hand on her. There were two. One was broad and bronze-dark, one smaller, narrower, ivory-pale. She met two pairs of eyes: narrow and black, wide and yellow-golden. Such unlikely allies. They did not know or like each other, or even speak the same language. And yet, when it came to Daruya, they agreed altogether too often.

"Wait," said Chakan.

"Be patient," said Bundur. "You'll have your gallop, I'm sure, and your cup of blood, too, that you seem so thirsty for. But wait a bit. Give Vanyi time to work."

"If she's not dead," said Daruya, "or too badly hurt to do anything at all."

"You'd know," Chakan said.

She would. Damn him for knowing it. And damn Vanyi for forcing her to think about sense. And damn Borti, and damn Kimeri, and damn her own self, because she could do nothing at all but wait and seethe and, when she had wits enough, pray.

THIRTY-ONE

BORTI IN HER PLAINEST SELF SEEMED NO MORE IN THE MIND'S EYE THAN A servant. Kimeri being nobody in particular struck anyone who looked at her as simple child-shaped object moving in shadow of adult object, and therefore safe and not to be noticed. It was easier than wearing shadows, and harder for mages to track, though they would after a while.

They walked into the palace as if they belonged there, which in fact Borti did. Vanyi's traces were in front of them, clear to a mage's sight, like the track a star leaves when it falls. She was safe, Kimeri had made sure of that. She was eating a very good dinner and talking to the priest who thought he was her captor, and thinking about going to sleep. Her thoughts were very clear inside the palace; outside of it they had been blurred, shadowy, not quite there.

The palace was warded, of course. For people who insisted that they were not mages, Shurakani were very good at raising wards. Kimeri could only do mindshields and shadows and nothing-in-particular, yet. She did not know how to protect a whole palace or a whole city.

She was shaking inside. Not because Vanyi was caught, or because she was in the palace and it was full of people who hated what she was. No; she was used to that. But she could see inside the priest's mind, and it was all gentle and pious and very determined, and he was going to make a magic in the night that would break every Gate in every world.

He did not really know that that was what he would do. He thought he was going to pray to his gods to keep the Gate in Shurakan closed forever, and invaders on the other side of it.

As soon as she could do it without making anybody notice, she let Borti know that she was there. They were in a passage that was empty, with empty rooms opening out of it, and an empty stair at the end. There was no light in it, but Kimeri could take care of that.

Borti stopped when the clear yellow light welled out of Kimeri's burning hand, and stared, shocked to her bones. "Child! Where in the world did you come from?"

"I've been right beside you," Kimeri said. "You couldn't go away all by yourself. You could get caught. They'd kill you."

Borti paid no attention. "You must go back," she said.

"You're going the wrong way," Kimeri said. "You need to go where Vanyi is."

"I am going where the king is," Borti said.

"You can do that after. We have to find Vanyi first. And the priest. He doesn't know what he's going to do."

"Then I'm sure she'll keep him suitably confused," said Borti. She sighed. "Child, you should have stayed with your mother. I can't trust a guard to take you back. Unless one of your shadow-men came with you?"

"They're all with Mother," Kimeri said. "You don't understand. Esakai is going to sing a prayer, and he thinks he's going to keep anybody from ever opening the Gate again. He's really going to break Gates everywhere. All of them."

Borti blinked. "Gates? All? How many are there?"

"Millions," said Kimeri. "Mages only use a tiny bit of them, but they're everywhere, on all the worlds. And they'll all fall down if Esakai says his prayer."

"Is that so terrible?" asked Borti. "It would be inconvenient, I suppose, not to be able to go from end to end of the world in a step, but people weren't meant to do that in any case. Gates are unnatural. How can it hurt any world to be rid of them?"

Kimeri was glad she was used to grownfolk who were willfully stupid. If she had not been, she would have stamped her foot and screamed. Instead she said, "Gates aren't unnatural. They're part of the worlds. Mages find them where they are, that's all, and open them. If they all break, anything can happen. Worlds might—might fall in on themselves, and Things come off the worldroads." She was shuddering. She tried to stop. "Terrible Things, Borti. Things that nobody should ever want to see."

She was scaring Borti. She had to make that better, or Borti would not want to move at all. "It might not be that bad," she said. "It might only be, if enough Gates are broken, the rest won't be able to shut. And new Gates might open by themselves. Most of them probably will open here, because this is where the first Gate broke, and it's the weakest of them all."

Finally she had said something that Borti could understand, mostly. "If Esakai tries to shut the Gate, he'll not only fail, he'll open Gates all over Su-Shaklan?"

Kimeri bobbed her head the way people did here, to say yes.

"Oh, goddess," Borti sighed. "It's like an old story. The more they try to make things better, the worse things get."

"Well," said Kimeri, "maybe the prayer will fold this world in on itself, and we'll all fall off the wheel together and have nowhere to be born again. That's not so bad, is it? Being unborn is like not knowing you exist at all. Hani told me that."

Borti shivered. "It's . . . a little more complicated than that. You don't want that to happen, you really don't."

"But if it has to," Kimeri said, "it will. Can we go find Esakai now?"

Borti thought about it for much longer than Kimeri thought she needed to. But she was not a mage, though she had a bright and shining soul inside her; she did not know how to think about magery, except with fear wrapped around it. She had to cut through the fear first, then see what she had.

After a while she asked, "How long do we have before Esakai says his prayer?"

"A while," Kimeri admitted, not wanting to, but she hated to tell lies. "He'll wait till middle night, to make it stronger, with dreams in it."

"We have time, then," said Borti. "We'll go to the king first. He may be interested to know what his allies are doing, since they don't know it themselves."

"I don't think—" said Kimeri.

"Child," Borti said, and she sounded exactly like Kimeri's great-grandfather when he had made up his mind and that was that, "I would have time to take you back to Janabundur, too, if I pressed it close."

She did not. But Kimeri shut her mouth and kept it shut.

Borti bobbed her head, satisfied. "Come with me, then. How good can your manners be? Paltai was never a monster, but he is frightfully stiff about protocol. He'll be worse, now he calls himself king."

"I can be very polite," said Kimeri, "even when I have to go to the privy and I'm in High Court and I can't."

Borti gaped at her, then laughed, hardly more than a snort. "Yes, we'll stop at a garderobe, too, before we visit Paltai. Come, child."

Paltai the pretender king was a handsome man, like Bundur but not so big, and with a much more fashionable air. He grew his mustaches to his breastbone and wore his hair in a lacquered tower, even in bed. He looked rather ridiculous, except for his eyes. Those were cold and clever, and they did not look as if they had ever worried about hurting anyone.

Kimeri wondered how he got the crown on the edifice of his hair. At the moment the glittering thing was sitting on a cushion next to his bed, where he had been playing with a servant when Borti walked in through a door that maybe he had not known was there. The servant squawked and ran away. The king scrambled all the bedclothes together around his middle and glowered at Borti, who was all he could see; Kimeri was wearing shadows again. "Woman! Did I summon you? Out, and come back in the morning."

He thought Borti was a servant, and not a very bright one, either. Borti knew it. She smiled, not a pleasant smile at all, and said, "Paltai. I'm devastated. You don't recognize your last mistress but six?"

The black eyes blinked, reckoning names and connecting faces. None of them was a plain-faced servant of early middle years. But one had been a strong-faced queen whose maids had a particular talent with paint and perfumes.

Borti showed her teeth, which were not bad for a woman her age in Shurakan. "Not much to look at, am I, without a little help from my ladies. Still, I'd thought better of you. You claimed never to forget a face or a lover."

"I never forgot you—as I knew you then," he said. "You were magnificent. You look sadly fallen now."

"I always looked like this when I wasn't being beautiful for a bedmate." Borti sounded calmer than she was. "Do you think you can rule Su-Shaklan without a queen?"

He did. But he was not going to tell Borti that. "When I've had time to settle the kingdom, I'll take a bride."

"I'm sure," said Borti. She did not believe him. "Tell me, Paltai. Did you know that your mage-killers are working magery themselves?"

"Are they?" He was not shocked at all. He was amused. "Who told you that? Your pet mages?"

It sounded like "your pet ox-droppings." Kimeri wanted to giggle, but that would have given her away.

Borti was not even thinking about giggling. "I've seen what mages do. I've seen what the priests do. It's the same thing, Paltai."

"Except," he said, "that mages do it of their own will, in overweening pride, and priests do it of the gods' will, in fitting humility."

"Such humility as this?" Borti picked up a shimmer of folded silk. It slithered down into a coat twice as long as Borti was tall, and it was real silk, worth more in Borti's mind than Kimeri could easily imagine.

Kimeri realized something that she had been too busy to notice. Paltai was a priest. His hair was a wig and his mustaches were false. He was pretending to be beautiful as he thought of it, and enjoying looking the way he meant to look when he had been king for years and years. It made him feel more like a stallion.

It was a twisty feeling. She did not like it. She was much happier when he got up, taking his blankets with him, and took off his wig and his mustaches and looked like a priest again—peculiar with his bald head and shaven face, both of them starting to grow out in a furze of black down, but not as peculiar as he had in the wig.

And she could see that the crown went on his head, and fit, too, though he only rested his hand on it and stroked its tall jeweled peaks.

He was telling Borti who was king now, and enjoying thinking about it. He was a little sorry to have had to kill Borti's brother in order to be king, but not very much. He had never liked the man—had found him stiff-necked and stubborn.

He liked Borti better. He liked her rather a great deal, in fact, which was good of him. But she was in his way, and he could see that she was going to be difficult. He edged his hand toward a cord that hung by the crown.

Kimeri tugged very lightly at Borti's coat and whispered, not even aloud, though Borti heard it that way. *Let's go now, quickly. He's ringing for the guards.*

Borti's face did not change, though she heard Kimeri. She did not move, either. "This magic that the priests work is dangerous. They're trying to close the foreigners' Gate beyond all opening; they'll open it instead, and open Gates all over Su-Shaklan, with the gods know what waiting to come through."

"So your mages tell you," said Paltai, his mind tight shut. "You owe them gratitude for sheltering you, certainly, but credulity was never a flaw in your character. Have they bewitched you?"

"I believe that they know their own art and its failings," Borti said. "And that they have honor, as difficult as that is to believe." She steadied herself, and throttled the temper that had always got her in trouble. "Paltai. People who could kill one king can very easily kill another—and if they remove any thought of the queen, why not remove the king, too, and establish a rule of abbots and priests? Wouldn't that be logical? Do you want to be their proof that the line of kings has failed, and the children of heaven have been forsaken by their mother and by all the gods?"

She had not even ruffled the king's composure. It was too enormous for that. "The gods have chosen me. No priest will question that."

Borti drew breath to argue, but Kimeri could hear the guards coming. She caught at Borti's hand and pulled her, no matter how strange it might look to Paltai to see Borti being tugged away from him by a blur and a shadow.

Borti came, which was more than Kimeri had quite dared to hope for. She was sad and upset and furious, but she could see what was in front of her. And that was a fool who believed more in himself than in the gods.

The guards were at the door, hammering on it. The king ran to open it. They would know where the passage was that had brought Borti here. Kimeri kicked herself for not thinking about that till it was too late. And if the guards caught Borti, Borti was dead, just as dead as her brother who had been the king before Paltai.

There was nowhere to go, nothing to do. Except one thing. Kimeri had not known she had it till she reached inside and it was there. It was in the Gate, and part of it. It showed her how to begin. She took a deep breath and did it.

Guards poured into the room, bristling with pikes and spears and swords. There was nobody there but the king. Nobody in the hidden passageway or hiding behind the curtains. Nobody anywhere near that room, not even wrapped in shadows.

THIRTY-TWO

VANYI HAD GOT RID OF ESAKAI AT LAST, BUT NOT THROUGH ANY DOING OF HER own: he was going to the temple of Matakan, where the priests raised the circle that would bind the Gate. He left her under guard, in reasonable comfort, with food and drink and a bed. And he left her warded. It was an effective ward, not strong but strong enough, that tangled her gently and inextricably in strands like spidersilk when she tried to lay a wishing on the guards and walk out of the room.

Clever, clever working. It used her own strength against her. The harder she fought, the tighter she was bound.

She had outsmarted herself. Her brilliant plan to lull Esakai into thinking he held her hostage, then to trust Daruya to move against the priests in the temple while Vanyi escaped and sped to Daruya's aid, was no use at all if she could not get out of her prison.

And time ran on. The priests were gathering. She had no way of knowing what Daruya was doing—the tangle of wards robbed her of any useful magery. Her body at least was behaving itself. It was more tired than it should be, but the tightening in her chest was gone, lost somewhere in the wards.

Something plucked at them. They quivered and tightened. The touch came again, subtler this time, slipping through them like a thin sharp-bladed knife, pausing, then slashing, sudden and swift. In the instant of the wards' breaking, the power—for power it had to be—caught Vanyi in a vast but gentle hand, and lifted her as a woman might lift a fledgling from the nest.

The hand vanished with breathtaking suddenness. Vanyi, robbed of its strength, staggered and almost fell.

The floor under her had changed. She had been standing on rugs. Now she stood on patterned tiles. The walls had grown both higher and wider. Much higher. Rather wider. Where the bed had been stood a monstrosity of wood and paint and gilding, several times taller than a man.

She had companions. The Queen of Shurakan, drab as a servant and grey with shock, and ki-Merian regarding them both with a worried expression. It took a moment to realize that the child was glowing like a lamp at dusk, a pure golden light that neither blinded the eye nor overwhelmed the mind: sunlight as it shone in the palace courts of Starios on a fine day in spring, just after the snows had gone but before the *ailith*-boughs burst into blossom.

Kimeri did not seem aware of the power that filled her full and overflowed. Nor did she wonder at what it had done: taken a Master of mages out of a warded trap and set her down far from there, and the queen too from the look of her, reaching as if to touch walls that were no longer there.

Avaryan and Uveryen, thought Vanyi, too astonished for awe. *God and goddess. What that child can do, not even knowing it's impossible . . . she's a living Gate.*

Vanyi should have seen it long since. But she had been blind as they all were, looking at a child of three summers, almost four as the child herself insisted, and deluding themselves that she was anything like an ordinary young thing. Vanyi should have known better. She had heard the tales of what Estarion had been when he was a child, and she had seen his son and his granddaughter—mages born, with the Sun's fire in them even in the womb. None of them had been as purely mageborn as this one, she did not think. Unless they were better at hiding it, or had more determined guardianship.

None had been so surely bound to Gates. And none had been caught in a Gate as it fell, not so young. Vanyi had seen what Daruya could do on the worldroad, the glorious blaze of her power that she raised in that place as easily as she breathed. Suppose that that power had roused her daughter's power as well. Then suppose that Kimeri's magery had begun to grow, fed by the Great Wards and by the troubles in Shurakan, and by the Gate she had awakened and left blind after the Guardian was rescued from it.

Suppose that the Gate was not blind. Suppose that it was part of the child. Suppose . . .

Vanyi was dizzy. She found herself sitting on the floor, with Borti slapping her face lightly and Kimeri clinging to her hand, pouring magery into her. "Your heart tried to stop," Kimeri said. "Don't let it do that again."

Vanyi felt very strange. She could not shape words at all, and yet her mind was dazzlingly clear. The pains in her body, in her arm—idiot. Of course. Any herb-healer knew what that meant.

Her heart was beating oddly. It was scarred, distended, as if it had tried to shake itself to pieces but been forestalled. But when—?

When she argued with Esakai. It had been happening for a long while, but quietly, as these things did. She had refused to notice. She was getting older, she tired more easily, how not? There was nothing wrong with her.

Kimeri was beginning to be frightened. "I can't make it better," she said, half in tears. "I don't know how."

"This is close enough," Vanyi said. Ah: words again. And breath that did not seem to tighten her chest every time she drew it in. She tried standing up. Dizziness hovered, but she drove it away. She could walk: she circled the place, which was a curtained sanctuary, she saw, in a larger temple.

"Vanyi," said Kimeri. Her voice trembled a little. "We have to go now, if you can. They've started the magic."

So they had. Vanyi found that the palace wards were not as strong as they had been, or else and more likely the child's power pierced right through them. She heard the opening notes of the chant, felt in her bones the shifting of powers about the circle.

The outer sanctuary was empty. She strode toward it.

"By the time we could run there," Kimeri said behind her, "it would be all over. We have to go the other way."

"No," said Vanyi. "You're staying here, and I'm going there."

"You'll die," Kimeri said. "Your heart will burst if you run."

So it would. Damn the child's clear sight. But if she used the Gate—

She was, abruptly, elsewhere. It did not grow easier with use. The dizziness this time at least did not fell her, and her battered heart stumbled but steadied. She saw it with her mage's eyes as a great bruised fist.

She forced herself to understand where she was. Another temple, a god with an ox's body and human face and stance, a white ox drowsing in a pen heaped high with offerings. People staring—painted images, she would have thought, but they breathed. Their eyes were blank, bedazzled, lost in dreams of woven darkness and light.

The weavers of the magery stood together where the Gate-magic had set them, staring about as blankly as Vanyi must have the first time she was swept away by the Gate. One or both had had the presence of mind to catch and hold the priests in the sanctuary as soon as they all appeared out of air, but that might have been instinct, or magery wiser than its bearers.

Daruya came to herself before Kadin. Her face woke to an expression of pure, fierce glee—swiftly conquered as she guessed who must have brought her here. "Vanyi! So you needed me after all."

"Not I," said Vanyi. She tilted her chin. "That one."

Kimeri looked little enough like a child caught in mischief. She was urgent but polite, as she had been trained to be. "Mama, could you tan my hide later? They're breaking Gates in there."

"And if they break Gates," Vanyi said, "they'll very likely break her. Though I can't be sure. I've heard of a living Gate—it's supposed to have been possible, long ago, if a mage were powerful enough. But I've never seen one, or heard more than the mention."

She was babbling. Daruya did not not tax her with it, or silence her, either, but went straight to the point. "Kimeri. Shield yourself, and stay shielded. And stay close to me. It's you they'll break if they can—you've got the Gate inside you."

And how, Vanyi wondered, did she know that?

She was Sun-blood. They were all outside of ordinary human reckoning, no matter how human they seemed—no matter how young or wild or foolish.

Kimeri went to her mother as she had been commanded. She took the hand her mother held out: the burning hand, that flamed so bright as they touched that it put every shadow to flight. The temple afterward seemed black dark despite the many lamps that were lit in it, and the light of the Sun's youngest child, as coolly golden as ever, and as steady. Daruya shed no light but what had been in her hand; she was shielded. "Kimeri," she said, warning, reminding.

Kimeri's light went out abruptly. She seemed shadowy without it, insubstantial, small gold-and-ivory child with wide yellow eyes, more like an owl's than a lion's.

A shadow shifted, startling them. Kadin glided toward the inner sanctuary, toward the sound of chanting that came clear now that Vanyi listened. There was nothing human in the way he moved. He was pure hunter, pure panther.

Grief stabbed Vanyi, sudden and unexpected, twisting in her struggling heart. He had been a beautiful boy, quiet but brilliant, with a great gift for weaving shadows. Jian had cast light in his dark places, heart as well as power. Without her he was a shell of himself.

Vanyi had hoped that he could be healed; that he could find another lightmage and be, if not what he was before, then strong enough, and whole. It had happened before with twinned mages left alone by death of body or power. But not often. Not when they were bound in heart as in magery, as Kadin had been with Jian.

There was little left of him now but air and darkness and a great hate. She watched Daruya run after him—saw the brightness that yearned to fill the dark, and the dark that would have welcomed it. She thought briefly, wildly, that it was possible. That this darkmage could join power with the heir of the Sun—law, custom, compacts be damned. What did Daruya care for any of them?

But the dark was empty of aught but vengeance. The light was too searing bright, its bearer too much the child of Avaryan. Even as the two powers met, they recoiled. Kadin stumbled. Daruya nearly fell.

They recovered almost as one. Kadin flung himself toward the door of the inner sanctuary. Daruya caught at him, too late.

When Vanyi was in great extremity she was at her calmest, and at her coldest and most clearheaded. There was a way, she reflected, to break any ward ever raised, even a Great Ward. One had to be mad to try it, or so set on a goal that one took no notice of the wards at all. One leaped, body, power, and all, full into the center of the warding.

And, if one was fortunate, one died. If one was not, one suffered as Uruan had in the broken Gate: one was trapped and unable to escape.

Kadin was not fortunate. Nor was he trapped. As he touched the wards, as they flared to light and life, his power snatched at Daruya's and seized it. Kimeri's was woven in it, and in Kimeri's was the Gate.

All together they struck the wards. No such defense had been made to withstand the full power of Sun and dark, wielded by one who cared not at all whether it killed them. The light of the Sun seared the wards from end to end of their expanse. The darkness in Kadin opened wide to swallow them.

And they were through, into the sanctuary.

The circle in its actual presence looked like a gathering of priests about an elder. In magesight it was like one of the peaked round towers that were so common in Shurakan, its many pillars holding up a tall conical roof adorned with a glitter of ornaments, a spikiness of cupolas, a bristle of rods that called away the lightnings from the rest of the tower. The king's crown of Shurakan was very like it in shape and semblance.

This was a tower of prayer—of magic, many-pillared but rising to a common center. That was Esakai, anchoring the chant with his voice, thinned with age as it was, but true.

He faltered not at all as his wards were broken, his shrine invaded. His priests were rapt in the chant. Their minds were pure prayer, pure magic.

Mages never let themselves be so lost in their workings, not even when they raised the circle. It was dangerous: it could cost them power and sanity. But it was a mighty sacrifice. It left them all open to the wielding of the one who led them, the one who preserved will and awareness, and directed their power as he chose.

"As *you* choose," said a voice, clear and cold and seeming inhuman. But it was Daruya's, familiar enough yet unreachably strange. This was the Sunchild pure, stripped of passion and of petulance, speaking with the clarity of a god. "You choose this, Esakai of Ushala temple. You work your will upon this edifice of magic. No god speaks through you or wields you. Only your own desire."

"You are blind and deaf to my gods," Esakai said—chanted, weaving through the drone of the priests. "You know nothing. You are nothing. You shall be nothing."

Nothing, nothing, nothing. The echoes throbbed in the heart of power, sapped it of strength, drained light away, and made darkness dim and frail.

Vanyi's own power lashed out in pure denial. She would *not*. She refused.

She almost laughed. Daruya, great artist of refusal, wove power with Vanyi's and strengthened it immeasurably. She saw the humor in it, too: laughter, painful but true, and levity that turned the priests' chant to a shimmer of wry mirth.

Truly, Vanyi realized. The chant had faltered. Priests were giggling or grinning or simply looking surprised.

"Yes, laugh," said Daruya with sudden fierceness. "Laugh at this liar who bids you work magic in the name of his gods. No god speaks to him. He is a mage, no more, no less. A worker of his own will on the gods' creation."

"You are a demon," sang Esakai, "sent to tempt us. See, my holy ones! See how this child of the realms below has twisted and mocked all that you are."

"I am the Sun's child," said Daruya. "You are a mage, and a ruler of mages. Your kind drove the goddess' children to Su-Shaklan and taught them to hate the very name of magic. You defended yourselves with lies and deceptions. You named yourselves priests, hid in your temples, worked your magics in secret, under the name of prayer. But they are still magics. You are still mages. You cannot deny the truth of what you are."

There was more than conviction in her voice. There was power. She spoke truth as only a mage could speak it.

It swayed those priests who had fallen already out of the chant, but the rest were bound still, held by the power of the one who led them. The circle was diminished, but it held.

Beyond the world of the senses, where magery came into its own, Vanyi felt the trembling of ground beneath her feet. Gates were woven with the substance of every world. This prayer, this working, sought to unweave it, thread by thread on the loom of the worlds, Gate by Gate. One by one, from Shurakan outward, through the place where its Gate had been, the Gate that was now a living thing.

Vanyi heard a child's voice, soft, frightened. "Mama. Mama, I'm all strange inside."

Daruya had Kimeri in her arms and such an expression on her face as no enemy should ever live to see. Kimeri was bleeding light. The swifter the chant, the swifter she bled. Her center was darkness, shot with stars: the Gate, and the focus of the working.

Shadow swept across the circle. Silence rode it. Kadin the darkmage wielded it, smiting it as he had smitten the wards on the door, with the same perfect heedlessness of the cost.

He had won through the wards. The circle was stronger. It took its strength from the toppling of Gates. The chant wavered, the Gates ceased to fall, but only for a moment. It rose again, mightier than before. Kadin fell reeling back.

He caught himself, sprang forward once more. He would do it again and yet again, till he destroyed himself.

Vanyi called in all the power she had. She felt the gathering of Daruya's magery, bright blazing thing, feeding Kadin's darkness, giving him all her temper, all her pettiness, all her rebellions both lesser and greater—all her weaknesses melded into one great strength.

She made of it not a weapon but a vision. Clarity. Truth unalloyed, driven straight and clean and true, direct to the heart of the circle. Full into the mind and soul of the one who led it, the priest who believed that he served his gods.

He could refuse it, but Daruya was a master of refusal. She knew precisely how to force it past his resistance. He could blind himself to it, but she of all people knew the art of opening eyes and mind that were shut, locked in stubborn certainty. He could even try to run away from it—but she caught him and held him and made him see exactly what he had done, the good and the ill, the piety and the folly. Gates opened rather than broken, powers roused that had never known the name of Shurakan, worlds shivered on their foundations, that must break under the weight of his beloved kingdom.

He had fallen silent in shock and resistance. The chant went on without him. It had its own power now, its own will to completion. The magic wove itself, unweaving worlds.

Vanyi cut across it with her own strong force of truth, her dart of power into each separate mind, rapt, entranced, lost in the working, it did not matter. She spared nothing of her strength.

She met a force of darkness, darkmage striking with the same truth and the same vision. He too spared nothing, not even mercy. Minds shrank in horror from what they had done, from what they were trying to do. He showed them their folly bare. He turned them on themselves, and their working with them.

One by one and then together, they fell from the working.

But the working was too far advanced. It sustained itself. It fixed on the focus that was the youngest of all the Gates, the one that dwelt in living flesh. It poised to strike, and in striking to fell them all, Gates, worlds, whatever was woven in its substance and so must be unwoven.

One last time the darkmage sprang. He made himself a shield. He took the force of the working full in his center.

It pierced him through. It unmade him. It shattered him from center to farthest extent, body, mind, and power.

And it veered aside not a hair's breadth.

Kimeri could do nothing. She was in pain beyond anything Vanyi could imagine, rent from within and without, and that only by the beginning of the working. Her mother held her in silence more terrible than if she had raged or wept.

Estarion would have Vanyi's hide if she let both his heirs be destroyed by a mageworking gone mad. She thrust her sluggish body toward them, with its stumbling heart, its blurring sight, its cold feet. She was dying, that was perfectly obvious. She would do her best to take the working with her.

Kimeri gasped. It was loud in the silence. She struggled in her mother's arms. Daruya, taken off guard, dropped her.

She stumbled as her feet struck the floor, but she did not fall. Her whole body shook. Her face was stark white, her eyes white-rimmed. She raised her hand, the one that flashed gold. "No," she said remarkably clearly, remarkably steadily. "I don't want to. I won't."

The working had no awareness to know what she said, or how she resisted. It struck her hand.

And stopped. She did not pause to be amazed. She pushed against it—only the one hand, only the *Kasar,* with wisdom that must be instinct—and it gave way. It yielded. It flinched, even, before that palmful of burning gold.

She braced her body and leaned into the working as if it had been a vast unwieldy creature, an ox that stood in her way and sought to trample her. She pushed it back and back.

Just as she began to waver, as the working began to resist, Daruya set her hand above Kimeri's. Gold as bright, but larger, woman-large, with strong power behind it, and the force of the god. Between the two of them they drove the working inward toward the place where it was born, the circle's center, the man standing alone there, with his priests fallen or stunned or fled. It shrank as it retreated. Sun's power withered it, Sunchildren's will overwhelmed it.

They might have tried to bend it aside from the man in the circle. Or they might not. Vanyi had loved the Sun's brood for forty years and more, served them, protected them, been as kin to them. But she had never understood them; never been part of them.

Whatever they willed, whatever they intended, the working, shrunk now to the breadth of a javelin and as sharply deadly, pierced straight through the priest's heart.

He made no effort to escape it. Vanyi hoped she would never see such despair again, such perfect awareness of what, all unwitting, he had done. Even before the spear struck, he willed himself out of life, casting his soul upon the wheel, seeking life on life of expiation.

Not in truth because he had tried to unmake the worlds. Because he had failed, and in failing brought both magic and ruin to Shurakan.

THIRTY-THREE

THE POWER WAS FALLEN THAT HAD RULED SO SHORT A TIME IN SHURAKAN. THE people of the Summer City, both city and palace, woke as from a dream to find their city half in ruins. In the palace, lords and servants wandered as if lost.

All of them had seen the vision that Daruya forced upon the priests in Matakan's temple. All had known exactly what it was that they followed, and exactly what it was that they feared.

She had never meant it to spread so far. The priests' working had woven it into the fabric of the realm. They had the truth now, whether they wanted it or no.

Most of them forgot it soon enough, either because their minds could not absorb it or because they refused to accept it. Some few died of it—her fault, and her grief forever after. The rest had learned something, if only that magery was indeed something to fear.

The queen, who had seen and known it all, was strongest, too. It was she who saw to the tending of the fallen priests, both the dead and the living, and the cleansing of the temple. Inevitably, people discovered who she was. They began to trickle in as the night reeled into dawn, to look on her face that had gained nothing of beauty in the long hours since she slept. None offered to speak to her, still less to denounce her or to sink a dagger in her heart.

Word spread, soft on the morning wind. *The queen lives. She sits in the temple of the ox-god who defended White Moon-Goddess and led her into Su-Shaklan. Now he defends her child. He blesses her; he protects her as his own.*

The king came in the evening. He did not come willingly, not he whose pride deafened his ears to the gods' voices. His allies were humbler or more sincerely afraid. They understood that their leader was dead, his body laid before the god, and his priests dead or vanquished. Their alliance was broken. They looked about them and saw lords who had come out of their houses with armed men at their backs, and the lord of Janabundur foremost. They saw a court diminished to nothing, its ministers suddenly and numerously indisposed, and its Minister of Protocol dead, who would have had the power to impose order on confusion.

They came to the queen one by one, mute, as suppliants to a goddess, or transgressors to a ruler from whom they could not expect forgiveness. She forgave them—how could she not? Without them she had no court and no kingdom. And she was fond of them, as one is of one's erring children, one's foolish servants.

Last and most lonely and most stiffly proud came the king. He had been left all alone in his splendid new palace, without even a bodyservant to wait on him. They were all gone. All fled, or huddled in and about the temple in which the queen sat.

When he came, she was sitting at a table in the abbot's workroom, trying to eat a roast fowl. Kimeri, none the worse for her night's terrors, was up from sleeping the day away, and nibbling a wing. The others were still asleep or pretending to be, in priests' cells that had been emptied for them, with Olenyai come from House Janabundur to guard them—except Rahai, who insisted that he was going to guard Kimeri and nobody else.

People kept looking at her strangely and muttering about her being a Gate. She was not, not exactly. She was a mage and a Sunchild who happened to have a Gate inside of her, along with the Sun's fire and her magery. Vanyi wanted to pummel her with questions, but Vanyi was not going to be pummeling anybody for a while. Aledi had got there just before she fell over, and kept her heart beating when it tried again and determinedly to stop.

Vanyi was still alive, but it had been a near thing. She should have told Aledi long ago that she was having trouble with her heart; it was nothing a healer-mage could not mend, not if she knew about it soon enough. As it was, Vanyi was going to be well, but it would take her a long time, and she would have to be very careful. No mage-battles. No arguments, even, most of all with Aledi, who stopped being gentle when she had to contend with difficult invalids.

So Vanyi was in bed trying to get better, and Daruya was asleep, and Kimeri was with Borti, who did not seem to mind that Kimeri was a living Gate. Borti was tired almost to tears, and fighting it, which made her look stiffer and more queenly than ever. She could persuade the priests to keep people out while she got a little rest, but they would not stop lingering and staring and offering her reverence.

"You'd think I'd be used to it," she said crossly round a bite of roast fowl, "but it's downright embarrassing to have them groveling as if I were Moon Goddess herself, and not just the least of her children. If I'm not careful she'll take offense, and I'll be worse off than I was before."

"She won't mind, I don't think," said Kimeri. "They're scared. They don't know what you'll do to them. They helped the others kill your brother, after all, and they would have helped kill you, if they could have caught you."

"They thought they were doing the gods' will," Borti said. "Don't they think I understand that? They were preeminently wrongheaded, but they meant well. And I need them. They prove that I've a right to my title."

The king came just then. Hunin brought him, because Miyaz the darkmage had insisted. Miyaz had been a prince of five robes in the High Courts of Asanion: he knew how to tell when a queen would want to be left alone, and when she would want to have a visitor.

The king looked ruffled and surly. His extraordinarily long coat was dirty all along its trailing hem, and somebody had thrown a basket of ancient vegetables at him. He had wiped the worst of it off his face, but his coat was sadly stained.

He had not worn the crown, at least, to come over to the temple. That would have got him killed. He was not much loved in the Summer City. He was a false king, and no son of heaven.

The daughter of heaven, plain tired blunt-spoken Borti with her dinner in front of her half eaten, looked at him and sighed. Particularly when he said nastily, "So now you accept the service of demons."

He meant Hunin, who was laughing behind his eyes. Hunin did not think much of this poor shift for a king.

Borti could see that. She said to Kimeri, "Tell your warrior that I apologize for this my kinsman. He's not so ill a man, not when he's getting his own way."

Hunin approved when Kimeri told him that in Asanian. He said, and Kimeri said for him to Borti, "That is the way of princes, lady." He bowed as low as he would for a princess of seven robes in Asanion—not quite as he would for a nine-robe princess, which was what Kimeri was, and certainly not as for an empress, but from an Olenyas to a foreign queen it was a great honor. Kimeri said so.

Borti smiled at him. "Thank you," she said. He bowed again and made it clear that he was part of the wall, since she had to be polite to the king.

She bit her lip. She was trying not to laugh. "Such a prince of servants!"

She was learning to understand Olenyai in spite of their yellow eyes and their black veils and never being able to see their faces. She barely even thought of them as demons any longer. Kimeri was proud of her for that.

The king was getting impatient, but he was too scared to show much of it. Borti looked him up and down. "Paltai," she said, "you idiot. You should have come here in a priest's robe. No one would have noticed you then."

He stood stiffly, reeking of ancient bloodroot and defunct ox-garlic. "I came in what was on my back. The servants are gone, and have taken the keys to the wardrobe with them."

"But there's another key in the—" Borti stopped, then started again. "The king would know where to find his own key. And how to convince a priest of Ushala temple that it would be to his best advantage to lend a robe for a good cause."

"There are no priests in Ushala temple," said Paltai. "They're all gone, and the doors are locked. Every door in the palace is locked, except those that lead from the king's chambers to the gate."

Borti's face stayed calm, but inside she was exultant. She had not dared to hope for that, not even in her heart, where no one else—except Kimeri, but she did not know that—could know. A lord's servants could tell him that they were no longer serving him. They did it by locking everything but the way out, and leaving him to find it before he froze or starved, since he could not get at his clothes or his dinner. It was a very rare thing, but it had happened before, if not to a king.

Paltai had to tell Borti that it had happened to him. That cost him a great deal of pride. But he was not too proud to do it. Real pride would have stayed in the palace till someone came to drag him out, or else slunk away to hide and brood and work mischief later. Paltai was more honest than that.

He also thought Borti was soft in the heart. He was gambling on it, that she would not have him killed or sent to exile in the mountains. He had earned that, and would have had it if Kimeri had been the one to decide, but it was Borti's place to say what she would do with him.

She thought about it for a long while, while he stood stiffer and stiffer, till he started to tremble. He had been too angry and arrogant to be afraid. Now, in front of Borti, as ordinary as she looked and as indecisive as she seemed, he was suddenly terrified. Something about her reminded him at long last that she was the daughter of heaven, and his allies had killed her brother, who was also her husband and her king.

After a long while she said, "There are many who would say that this upheaval in the kingdom is my fault and my brother's, not only for letting foreigners in but for failing in our duty to the gods. Since we had no heirs—since the goddess never granted us children of our bodies." She paused. That was an old pain, and one that went deep. "I am not so old yet that I cannot bear a child. I may be barren—"

"You aren't," said Kimeri. It was neither wise nor polite, but she hated to see Borti hurting. "It wasn't you. It was the king. His seed was weak."

They both stared at her. She stopped herself before she started to fidget. "I can see," she said. "I can't help it."

"Child," said Borti. "Oh, child." Kimeri could not tell if she wanted to laugh or cry. She did not know which, herself. She made herself look back at Paltai, who was looking at Kimeri with wild speculation, seeing in her a power he could use. Borti said, "No, Paltai, don't think of it. This child is my kin, if somewhat distant. She too is a daughter of heaven."

"And an heir?" Paltai asked with a twist of the lip.

"Not to this kingdom," said Borti. "And since I may not after all be barren, and my brother-king is dead, I'll be needing a consort, to do my duty to the goddess. It would have to be someone of known ability to beget children, of high family, of the blood of heaven."

"It is a pity," said Paltai, "that Lord Shakabundur is so recently unavailable."

"Yes, it is, isn't it?" said Borti. "I blessed his wedding, too. They're soulbound beyond any doubt, and beyond any hope of changing it."

"What's to prevent him from doing stud-service in the palace for the kingdom's sake?"

"Why, little, I suppose." Borti sighed again. "Paltai, you do have a terrible tongue on you. Hasn't anybody ever taught you to be sparing with it?"

He started as if she had slapped him. In a way she had. He was not used to that: it made him angry. But he bit his tongue and did not say any of the things he was thinking.

Borti saw. She smiled. "I could ask Bundur to favor me, of course. It's been done before. His lady might even allow it—one never knows. But there is another way. You've been king already. Would you return to the palace if I sanctioned you before the people?"

She had astonished him. He had been thinking that she was playing with him, taunting him with his failure, asking him to help choose his supplanter. He was really quite foolish, Kimeri thought, and he did not know Borti very well at all.

"There is a certain logic in it," Borti said. "Granted, you saw my brother killed by your allies, and seized the crown before anyone else could move. You made no effort to prevent the sack of the city, nor were you able to hold your place once it was known that I was alive. You were a very poor king, taking all in all.

"But," she said, "within your limits, you're not a bad choice. Your family is royal kin. You have children but no wife, which proves your ability to beget heirs to the crown, and offers no impediment to your taking the place of consort."

"Not king?" Paltai asked. He had come back to himself, sharp, wary, and beginning to believe she meant it.

"The king is dead," said Borti. "The queen has need of a consort. You were a wretched king, Paltai, but you would make a reasonable husband, all things considered."

He looked away. His tongue wanted to cut her till she bled, but the rest of him was telling it to be sensible. "I . . . don't know if that's wise," he said finally, which was not what he had started to say at all.

"Probably not," Borti said. "I don't think I care. I've always been inexplicably fond of you, and you're a pleasant bedmate. You would have to be oathbound, of course, and purified before the kingdom."

He shivered. Purification in Shurakan was not an easy thing, not for sins as great as his. He would have to shed blood and endure a great deal of pain if he wanted to be soul-clean by his people's reckoning. Even so he said, "It would be worth the trouble, to father the next children of heaven."

"I thought you might think so," said Borti.

They understood one another. Liked one another, too, better than they would ever admit. Borti would not forgive her brother's death. This was her revenge, and very clever, making Paltai give up the crown but live always in sight of it—but there was more to it than that. Someday maybe Kimeri would understand.

Paltai was ready to say yes, but he was not quite willing to let Borti know it. "What about them?" he demanded, with a stab of his chin at Kimeri. "We'll never be rid of them now, since they've won your crown back for you."

"We would never have been rid of them in any case," Borti said, not looking at Kimeri but very much aware of her. "Once they had come, they were going to keep coming, no matter what we did. I'm going to treat them like people of honor, and if necessary shame them into doing the same for us."

"Will you let them build their Gate again?"

"I don't think I can stop them," said Borti. "I may be able to control them, to a degree. After all, we know now that our priests can break Gates. If we allow the one, and set limits on who and how many may pass it, we'll give them what they want but keep them aware that we can take it away."

"We never did want to invade you," Kimeri said. "Really we didn't. We just wanted to see what was here."

"So would a child say," said Paltai.

Kimeri looked at him hard, till he flushed even darker than he was already, and ducked his head. "We aren't all perfectly honorable," she said, "but we are honest. When we say we'll do something, we do it. We keep our word. We're very simple people, I suppose."

"Or else," mused Borti, "with mages to keep everybody honest, honesty is easier." She shook herself. "No, Paltai, I won't be filling my court with mages and turning this into a realm of magic. But we do have to discover our own honesty, and our own magics. Since we've lied to ourselves for so long."

"You didn't know," Kimeri said.

"Now we do." Borti stood, wiping her fingers where they were greasy from her dinner. "Go and bathe, Paltai. When you've done that, and have rested, we'll let the kingdom know that it has a queen again in truth, and that the queen has a consort."

Paltai did not like being told what to do, but he had wits enough to know that he was outmatched. Borti's smile was warm, but it was absolutely implacable. He would do as she said, or he would be disposed of.

They would get on well together, all in all. He knew that; it made him smile after a while, wry and rather pained, but real enough. "Yes, divine lady," he said, and only about half of it was mocking.

THIRTY-FOUR

VANYI WAS THOROUGHLY ANNOYED WITH HERSELF. SHE HAD HAD TO BE carried from the sanctuary like a blasted invalid, and she had not been allowed to do so much as raise her head. If she wanted anything she asked for it, and Aledi gave it to her, or Miyaz while Aledi rested, or, the past hour or two, the youngest of the Olenyai. It was not pleasant to have to ask him to carry her to the privy. She was years past anything resembling prudery, but damn it, she was a grown woman; why in the hells did she have to be packed about like a baby?

"Because," said a warm deep voice, "you had no more sense than one, carrying on while your body was trying to kill itself. This is fair punishment; you can't dispute it."

Vanyi would have snapped erect if a pair of all too familiar hands had not held her down. An all too familiar brush of magery soothed her hammering heart and brought, if not calm, then a kind of resignation. Another came in behind it, less familiar but in its way immeasurably stronger.

She looked from Estarion to the priest-mage who had come in behind him. The latter could have been a Shurakani in a Sun-priest's torque; he was a plainsman from Iban in the Hundred Realms, and he was chief of the healer-priests in Starios. He was neither ghost nor sending; he was very solidly there.

So was Estarion. "You're not supposed to be here," Vanyi said. She was half in a fog already, what with the healer's working, and not even a by-your-leave, either. But she kept enough of her mind alert to focus on Estarion.

"I'm not here," he said. "I'm in Starios, being emperor. You're being visited by a simple citizen of the empire who offered to try the Gate now it's open again."

"The Gate's open?" She stretched out a finger of magery, but the healer slapped it back. She snarled and subsided. "We haven't done anything to rebuild it. It's a blind Gate—and Estarion, about that—"

"It's open," he said. "All Gates are open as they always were, though there are cracks in the walls in the Heart of the World. Mages are mending those. The Gate in Starios is up and strong, and when I told it to open on Shurakan, it did. Your Guardian met me on this side. I brought two pairs of mages to give what aid they could—the twins from the Lakes of the Moon, and your Guardian's cousin Iyeris and her lightmage. They're in the house of the Gate, making it habitable again with help from the people of Janabundur. Did you know that exorcist of yours has Gate-sense? He might be worth training as a Guardian. Imagine," he said, entranced with his own vision. "A Shurakani born, being Guardian of its Gate."

Somewhere far down below the fog of healing, Vanyi was furious. She was the Master of the Guild. She was the ruler of the Gates. How dared he order her mages about? How *dared* he meddle with her Gates?

He sat on the edge of the bed, perfectly pleased with himself, having broken every pact they had ever made. He only made it worse by saying, "All of this, of course, is by your leave. The Guild was struck hard when the Gates started to fall— it was all they could do to hold themselves together. They cried out for any help they could get. I happened to be nearest. I tried to do everything as you would wish."

"You came here," Vanyi said. "Do you have the least idea in any of the worlds what will happen if people here discover what you are? They're already certain that we mean to conquer them out of hand. Your presence will only confirm it."

"Then we had better not let them know who I am," said Estarion placidly. "Later, of course, we should propose an exchange of state visits, here and in Starios, and an alliance of goodwill between our nations. At the moment I'm a messenger from your Guild, guard and escort to the healer whom you so badly need. You can receive messengers, surely? That's not forbidden?"

Vanyi closed her eyes. "Hells," she said, but without force. "Esakai was right. None of us will ever be rid of you."

"Not even if you die," he said. "Remember that." He took her hand. He was warm, sun-warm, and strong. "Haliya sends her love and her sympathies."

"And her I-told-you-sos?"

"She saves those for people who can argue with them."

She looked at him. Her mind was empty. She was healing, being healed. Slowly; Aledi had been right, it could not be quick, not as foolish as she had been.

He smoothed her hair back from her brow, easily, tenderly, as if she had been one of his children. Now that he was quiet, she could see how worn he looked. It had not been easy in Starios, either, when the Gates began to fall.

"And when you began to die," he said.

"Stop reading my mind," said Vanyi.

"I can't help it." Nor could he, since he did not want to.

She sighed. It was good to have him here, and never mind the difficulties, the politics, all the rest of the nonsense that hovered on the other side of the healer's magery. He bent over her. His face was all the world; and she could not touch it. She could not reach so high.

"You will be well," he said. It was a prayer, and an emperor's will.

Daruya had not meant to sleep till evening. There was so much to do—the Gate to look after, the mages, Vanyi—and she had dreamed straight through the day and into the night. Troubled dreams, most of them, full of shouting and confusion. Gates falling, walls tumbling in the Heart of the World, mages dying or being caught in Gates as Uruan had been. She kept trying to hold it all together with her two hands. Both of them in the dream were branded and burning with the *Kasar*, a living fire that ate at flesh but never consumed it.

She woke with relief to lamplight and quiet and the blessing of memory. The Gates were safe. She and Kimeri between them had seen to that.

Kimeri was with the queen, and content. Vanyi was asleep and very much alive. They had brought in a new healer—Daruya knew the mark of a healer-priest's power, as distinct in the mind as the *Kasar* itself. The Gate was up, then, and open, and letting people pass.

Bundur was not thinking about her at all. He was in the palace. It had been locked tight, which seemed to be the Shurakani way of telling its king that he was not welcome. The king was gone. Bundur was finding everyone who had keys, and seeing that those keys were set to the locks and the palace opened up again. The queen was coming back to it; she would find it waiting, all cleansed and opened and giving her welcome.

Daruya should not mind that he was occupied in doing his duty—she had done the same in following Kadin through Kimeri's Gate. But he was not thinking of her, either, or missing her presence. That stung.

She rose, washed the sleep from her eyes and her face, and put on her clothes. They were clean, a little damp about the edges. Her hair was a hopeless tangle. She did not even try the comb that was laid on the table beside the bed; she raked fingers through instead, tugging out the least of the knots, and gave up the rest for lost.

Someone had left her a basket with bread in it, a bit of cheese wrapped in a cloth, and a bowl of spiced fruit. She ate, and drank from the bottle beside the basket—water, nothing more.

Up, awake, dressed, and fed, she ventured forth into the temple. It was dark, save where once in a great while a lamp was lit, and seemed echoingly empty. The white ox was not in her pen; she had a stable to rest in at night, out past the priests' cloister. The god did not appear to notice her absence.

"How like a man," said Daruya. Her voice woke echoes in the shrine and sent something fluttering and squeaking through the rafters.

She paused by the white ox's enclosure. Someone had cleaned it and washed it, as must be done every night, and taken away the heaps of offerings—food to the kitchens, fodder to the stable, valuables to the treasury. A faint scent of ox remained, a suggestion of ox-droppings—like magic, it could never quite be denied. The gilded bars were cool, and just high enough to fold her arms on and to prop her chin. The god's image glimmered above her.

She felt light and oddly empty, as she always did after a battle. She was not startled to hear a step behind her, soft but making no attempt at stealth. It was not Chakan: him she would not have heard at all.

She turned, prepared to greet a priest, or maybe someone from Janabundur.

Priest indeed, but not of any god in Shurakan. He was here in the flesh: she could feel the warmth of him and catch his scent, which was different from that of the men here, sharper, with a suggestion of seneldi, a hint of ul-cats. He leaned on the bars of the ox's pen, chin on folded arms as hers had been, and studied the god who loomed above them. "Fascinating," he said.

"Does the queen know you're here?" Daruya asked.

Estarion slid a glance at her. "Vanyi asked me much the same thing. The answer is no, and will continue to be no. I brought Lurian to look after Vanyi, and mages to tend the Gate. I'm going back, and quickly, too."

Why, she thought, he was defending himself—as if he thought he had any need to do any such thing. Estarion the emperor never stood in need of defense. He did as he willed, and that was that.

Estarion in the temple of Matakan seemed no older than Bundur. He was not the emperor here. He was simply Estarion.

"Grandfather," said Daruya in sudden comprehension. "You've run away."

He raised a brow. "What, you didn't think I could?"

"What if the Gate falls again? We'll all three of us be trapped on this side."

"That would be interesting, wouldn't it?" He yawned and stretched like one of his enormous cats, from nose to nonexistent tail, and stood grinning at her.

"You look," she said, stumbling over the word she wanted. Damn it, then. She would say it. "You look bloody irresponsible."

"That's exactly how I feel." He was still grinning. "I've shocked you. Imagine that. Maybe it's time I did the running away and you did the ruling in Starios. You're old enough, more or less, and steady enough, no matter what you want people to think."

"That," said Daruya through gritted teeth, "is exactly what drives me wild. You never see me as anything but good, loyal, solid, dependable, dull—"

"—despite all evidence to the contrary," he finished for her. "Not dull, no. Not you. You're a golden splendor of a child. But underneath all the sparks and the temper is a right worthy queen. You show it when you have to, you know. In Gates as they break. In temples when priests are praying the worlds to pieces."

"I had to do it," she said. "Nobody else would."

"Nobody else could."

"Except Kimeri."

"Kimeri is not quite four years old. You are what she will be when she's grown to a woman—crotchets and all, though if she's as like you as I think, she'll be utterly dutiful and obedient and quiet, because you've always made so much noise about being a rebel."

Daruya flushed. "And she'll despise me for it. That's what you're telling me, isn't it?"

He regarded her in honest surprise. "Of course not. Children will do the opposite of what their parents either want or expect. It's the way the world is."

"I don't want her to be like me."

"Nor do you want to be like you. Do you?"

Temper flared as she unraveled that. She bit back the angry words. He was waiting for them, ready to smile at them, and say something that would make her look a perfect idiot.

No. Not this time. Not either of them—not she with her outbursts, or he with his maddening calm.

God and goddess. He was exactly like Bundur. So complacent. So perfect in his superior wisdom.

With Bundur it was a pretense, a prince's mask. With Estarion—

The very same. It was easier to see here, without the dazzle of his rank to blind her. And, she admitted with creeping shame, the flare of her temper whenever she saw him or thought of him.

It had not always been this way. When she was as young as Kimeri, she had adored him. She had followed him everywhere, got underfoot in everything. And he had allowed it. Only when he fought in battles did he forbid her to follow— and she obeyed, because he showed her exactly how terrible battles were.

Somehow as she grew older it had changed. She had begun to resist him, at first to prove that she was herself, apart from him, and could do as she chose and not as he expected. Until rebellion became the expected, and she was trapped in it. And he was always the one whom she resisted most strenuously, and the one who seemed least perturbed by it.

She could never crack the polished surface of his composure. No, not even when she drove him to a rage. It was always a calm, reasonable, rational rage. He always forgave her. He never seemed to hate or scorn her, no matter what she did or said.

She did not want to tell him so. He would only tell her that his own youthful sins were far worse than her own. For all she knew, they had been. Even in that she was never his equal. She could only follow, and be the lesser.

That was foolish, too. It was wallowing, and a ripe rotten sea of self-pity it was, too.

She tried something. She said as calmly as she could, "I suppose you expect me to go home with you when you go."

"Actually," he said, "I don't. You're a lady of this kingdom now. You have duties here."

She was gaping. She shut her mouth. "Responsibilities. But I have them in the empire, too."

"None that can't wait," he said, "or be done through Gates, by messengers."

She did her best to comprehend what he was saying. "You . . . want . . . me to stay here? On the other side of the world? With people who know how to break Gates?"

"You may not want to stay," he said. "There is that."

Her eyes narrowed. "You're going to take Kimeri back, then. Aren't you?"

"Only if you ask. And if she consents."

"I won't—" She broke off. "You can't mean you're letting me decide for myself."

"Why not? You've been doing just that for rather a while now."

"But I don't want—" She stopped again.

This time he spoke before she could go on. "Do you want to go back?"

"Bundur wouldn't come. Kimeri might not. She likes it here."

"Child," he said with all the gentleness in the world. "I'm not asking you what they want, or what I want. I'm asking you, Do you want to go back to Starios?"

"Yes," she said at once. Then: "No. No, I can't. Vanyi can't travel, there's the embassy, there's Kimeri—she likes having a brother, and I—"

"And you like having a husband." He smiled. "It's pleasant, isn't it? Even if you went into it screaming denials."

She nearly screamed denial of that, but that would have been too easy. "You didn't want to marry Haliya, did you?"

"Not at all," he answered. "Not at first. I wanted Vanyi or no one. Least of all a yellow woman. Who was sure that I was going to marry all eight of her fellow concubines, that being the absolute smallest number of women an emperor in Asanion could possibly have in his harem. Even when I convinced her that I wanted only her, she was still certain that I'd take other wives later."

"Ziana," said Daruya.

"The beautiful sister, yes. But she didn't want to marry, not really. She preferred the princedom I gave her, and the daughter she adopted, and the freedom that she'd hardly dared to dream of inside an Asanian harem."

Daruya knew that very well. She had spent summers with Ziana before that lady died. But it sounded different coming from Estarion, who had taken the lady as his second wife in Asanian law, then sent her to be ruling princess in Halion. People whispered that he had put her aside in all but name, but Ziana had never thought so. Nor, it seemed, had Estarion. He had given her what she wanted most.

"You give too much," said Daruya. "You don't take enough."

"Why, what should I do?" he asked with all apparent honesty. "Run away? Leave you the regency?"

"If you have to," she said steadily.

"Maybe," he said. "In a while. Once matters are settled in Shurakan. Would your lord like to see the world beyond his mountains?"

"He intends to," said Daruya. Her heart had quickened a little. "Would you—really—?"

He held out his hand. The *Kasar* glittered. "Shall we swear a pact? When Shurakan is settled—in a year and a day, perhaps?—you'll come to Starios with your lord, and take the regency."

She kept her own hands on the bars of the ox's pen. "And you? What will you do?"

He shrugged, smiled. "I don't know. Wander. Be nobody in particular. Explore the worlds beyond the Gates."

Yearning struck her so hard that her knees buckled. To do that—of all things one could dream of, that, she wanted most.

He saw. His smile widened. "And when I come back, as I give you my solemn word I shall, then you have your freedom to go where you will. A full priestess-Journey, seven years long, if that's your wish."

"I've wished for that . . . " Her voice died. She flogged it to life again. "I could even run away to sea?"

"Even that," he said.

And his hand was still up, still waiting. She clasped it, *Kasar* to *Kasar*. No bond was stronger than that, no pact more potent. "A year and a day," she said, "until I come to Starios. And while you journey—a hand of years?"

"Not so long, I think. Another year and a day. Or two."

"You never had your priest-Journey, either," she said. "A hand of years. And then I go on my own way." And what Bundur would say to that—if he thought he had any say in it—

He would lead the way through every Gate. He had it, too, that eagerness rigidly curbed, that longing to fly free.

"God and goddess," said Daruya. "I married my grandfather's image."

"And your own," Estarion said. He pulled her into his embrace. She startled him, nigh hugged the breath from him. He laughed with what little he had left, and kissed her forehead, and left her there, blinking, astonished at them both.

THIRTY-FIVE

WHEN THE QUEEN HAD RETURNED TO THE PALACE AND TAKEN HER consort, and the mages had rendered the house of the Gate fit to live in, and Vanyi was up and walking and doing her best to outwit the healer-priest who stood watch on her, Daruya climbed with Bundur and the children and two of the Olenyai, up the Spear of Heaven. It was a full day's journey to the mountain, even on senelback; the seneldi waited in camp on the mountain's knees, with Yrias to guard them and keep them from straying.

Daruya had seen little of Bundur in the days of the queen's return. For all her magery and for all her resolve to be a woman and not a petulant child, she could not help feeling as if a distance had grown between them.

He seemed oblivious to it. And yet it was he who said to her as they woke of a morning and he prepared to go yet again to the palace and the court, "If I asked you to run away with me, would you go?"

Her heart leaped, but she was wary. "Where would you run?"

"Not to your empire," he said, reading it in her eyes. "Not yet. But there's yonder mountain my namesake, and it's calling me. I've a mind to climb it."

"Even to the snows?" she asked.

"Even so far, if you like," he said.

"I would like," said Daruya.

Which was why they were here, scrambling up the steep stony track, still well below the line of the snow. It would have been only the two of them, but Kimeri was not to be denied, and Hani refused to be left out. They would go as far as a place Bundur knew, and share the daymeal; then they would go back down with their Olenyai, and Bundur and Daruya would go on till they met the snow. The summit they could not reach, or so Bundur thought. The air was too thin.

But he had never climbed a mountain with a mage. Daruya meant to stand on the Spear's very tip and greet her forefather the sun, and see all the world spread out below her.

This was a more earthly pleasure, much like the journey into Shurakan, climbing the side of a mountain with a pack on her back, for they would not come to the snow till nearly sunset, and would have to camp there, up against the sky. It was still almost warm here below. Her boots felt hot and unwieldy; her coat was rolled and fastened to her pack, and she climbed in her shirt, and would have shed even that if it had been a little warmer. The Olenyai, wrapped in robes and veils, must have been sweltering.

From the mountain's side she could see little of what was ahead, but if she looked back she saw the whole of Shurakan, deep green goblet of a kingdom, rimmed with snow. Clouds ran swift below, and broke like breakers against the mountain walls. The Summer City on its terrace seemed far away and yet very clear, a circle of walls enclosing roofs and turrets.

One tower flew a streamer of scarlet, a minute flash of gold: House Janabundur with its banner that Chakan had raised, golden sun on scarlet silk. It was the custom, he insisted, when a Sunchild was in residence and making no secret of it; therefore he would have it here in this foreign country. Some of the court already had admired the fashion and considered flying banners of their own, oblivious as all Shurakani were to the distinction between an imperial heir and a mere and minor lordling of the court.

Daruya smiled at the banner and at the one who had insisted on it. He was carrying Kimeri on his back, making nothing of the child's light weight; his eyes returned her smile. The grim guardsman of the first days in Shurakan was gone. He was the Chakan she remembered, on guard always but willing to ease into laughter. And he seemed to have decided, if not to trust Bundur, then at least to regard him with less suspicion.

They scrambled up a last and nigh impossible slope, slippery with stones and scree, and teetered on a sudden narrow rim, and descended into a ring of startling green. It was like an island in a sea of clouds, a tiny valley, even a forest in miniature, a grove of gnarled and knotted trees that bore sweet fruit. A little stream ran through it from the living rock, a cavern overhung by the arch of a tree.

Daruya stood on the valley's edge, struggling for breath yet trying to laugh. When at last she could speak, she said, "Bundur! This is just like the dragon's cave in the tapestry."

"This is the dragon's cave," he said, and very pleased he was with it, too. "This is where the Warrior Sage fought with the dragon, and won by losing, and the dragon taught him to brew tea from the leaves of the cloudfruit bush." He gestured toward a tangle of low thicket. "There, see. Cloudfruit."

"And water, and mountain apples, and grass to sit on," said Kimeri, standing on her own feet again and running toward the stream. Daruya reached by instinct to catch her, but Bundur had no fear; nor did her power. There was no dragon in the cave, and no cave-bear, either, though she heard the squeaking of cavewings deep within.

The Olenyai paused in following the children toward the water. They exchanged glances. Chakan dropped veils, headcloth, outer robe. He folded them, tucked them under his arm, and grinned at Bundur, who was struggling not to stare and failing miserably. "No fangs," he said in atrociously accented Shurakani. And trotted after the children, lithe in shirt and trousers, with his swords slung behind him. Rahai strode in his wake.

"Gods," said Bundur. "They're no more than children."

"Rahai is older than you," Daruya said. "And he won't live as long." She paused. "An Olenyas' face is his honor. Who sees it, unless he be friend and kin, must die."

Bundur went very still. "And what am I? Friend or prey?"

"Both," said Daruya. "It's an honor—and a warning."

"Ah," he said. "I serve you well, or I return to the wheel of souls on the blade of an Olenyas' sword." His eyes followed the bred-warriors where they dipped water from the stream, forbidding the children to drink until they had proved it safe. They did look like children themselves, as small as they were and seeming slight, with their cropped yellow curls and their smooth ivory faces. But the scars of rank on their cheeks—Chakan's five, Rahai's four—betrayed the truth; and the twin swords, and the way they moved, light and supple, like hunting cats.

"I suppose," mused Bundur, "they took the veils at first because no one reckoned them dangerous. Are they beautiful in your country?"

"Very," said Daruya.

"They're pretty," Bundur said. "You are beautiful."

She widened her eyes at him. "What? I thought I was ugly but interesting. Now that I'm beautiful, am I dull, too?"

She was only half laughing. He caught at her, pack and all, and turned her round to face him fully. "Is that what you think? That I've grown bored with you?"

"No," she said, but slowly. "I think you've been too busy to be bored."

"Too busy to notice you, or to see that you're fretting as if in a cage." She would have spoken to deny it, to say that she had enough to do among the mages, looking after her daughter, tending Vanyi, standing guard on the Gate. But he laid a finger on her lips, silencing her. "You were bred to rule over princes, and we keep you locked up like a novice in a temple. If it's in your heart to go back to your empire, go."

Her eyes blinked against sudden tears. Foolishness: her courses were coming on, that was all. "Do you want me to go? Have I become an inconvenience?"

"No!" He had spoken too strongly, or so he was thinking—idiot man. He softened his voice. "Lady, I would keep you here your whole life long, and love you every moment of it. But you were never born for a realm so small. It stifles you."

Guilt stabbed. She had not told Bundur of her pact with the emperor. There had been no time, and no suitable occasion.

If she did it now, he would think she mocked him. If she did not, she truly would be making a fool of him, who had never done her aught but honor.

She bit her lip. "Bundur—"

"You'll leave when your time comes," he said. "I know that. I expect it. But if you think you have to endure until then, out of loyalty or honor or even pity—"

"Bundur!" He stared at her. "Bundur," she said, less sharply. "I will leave, yes. I gave the emperor an oath that in a year and a day I'd go back to his city and take his place while he rested. He's been emperor for half a hundred years—it's horrible, when I think of it. I wonder that he didn't run away long since." She was babbling.

She made herself stop. "I also promised him . . . you'd come, too. I wasn't thinking at
the time, I wasn't remembering—you can be so proud, and I—"

"Daruyani," he said. He had loved the full form of her name ever since he
first heard it; but he kept it for great occasions. It was too beautiful, he said, to dull
with use.

Her eyes were blurring again. Loving a man was nothing like bedding him. It
was awkward; it was difficult. It kept reducing her to tears.

"Daruyani," said Bundur, "I told you long ago that when you went to your own
country I would go with you, if you asked. But if you only think to ask for fear of
offending me, then I refuse. I won't burden you with unwanted presence."

"I want you," she said. Her voice was rough. "You'll have to learn our language;
you'll be needing it, to be my consort. You'll have to learn our laws and our customs, and all our ways."

"Am I such a barbarian as that?" he asked, trying to be light, but his eyes were
glittering.

"You are exquisitely civilized," she said, "and very foreign. The courts will find
you exotic, and call you beautiful."

His cheeks flushed darkly. It was one thing to know himself a handsome man.
Beauty—that was difficult, if one were a man, and possessed of a certain kind of
pride.

She linked arms about his neck. They fit well, they two; they were eye to eye,
standing on the edge of the grassy level. She thought briefly, mischievously, of
plucking loose the cords that bound his hair and letting it fall straight and shining.
But that would embarrass him in front of the children and the Olenyai.

Later, she thought. Tonight, under the stars, on the edge of the snow. "They'll
call you beautiful," she said, "but none of them will lay a hand on you. Unless of
course," she added after a moment, "you want it."

"And will you kill them then?"

"I might."

"Am I allowed to ask what I can do to a man who lays a hand on you?"

"You can kill him," said Daruya.

He began to smile, long and slow. "I like your country, I think. Here, you could
take another husband, and I would have to suffer it."

"And in some parts of my empire," said Daruya, "you could take other wives,
and I would be expected to smile and be kind to them, and share your gracious
favors."

He knew her well. He heard the edge in her voice. It widened and deepened his
smile. "You like our country, too, then, where no man takes more than one wife."

"I suppose that means we're well matched."

"Very well," said Bundur. He sounded enormously complacent, much pleased
with himself and his world. She would slap him out of that. But later. When he
was not so charmingly entranced with her.

"Yes," he said, with his eyes full of her face, and his mind full of wonder that it should, after all, be beautiful. "We are matched." His brows drew together. "It doesn't make you angry still. Does it?"

She did slap him for that, but lightly, barely hard enough to sting. "Idiot," she said. "Of course it does. But only when you ask."

She caught at his hand and tugged him forward. The Olenyai were well ahead, with water-bottles full, carrying them up to the cave. Kimeri was carrying something taken from Chakan's pack; Hani had something else, balancing it gingerly as he picked his way through the grass.

As Daruya realized what they carried, she burst out laughing. Kimeri had the little brazier with its lidded jar of coals, Hani the pot and the cups for brewing tea; and that would be the packet of the herb that rested so precariously on top of the heap of cups. They were going to brew tea in the dragon's cave, for luck and for friendship, and because no one could ever do anything in Shurakan without a cup of tea.

She looked back at Bundur, who was following slowly. His somber expression had vanished. He grinned at her, and a fine set of white teeth he had, too.

"And what," she wondered aloud, "would a dragon look like, if he were flesh and not myth? Might he look like a prince of Shurakan?"

"He might," said Bundur. "Or she might look like a princess of Sun and Lion, from the other side of the world."

She stopped, briefly outraged. Dared he liken her to a ravening beast, however prettily subdued?

Indeed. And rightly, too. She shrugged, sighed, smiled, and went to drink tea in the dragon's hall.

TIDES OF DARKNESS

ONE

THE HEIR TO THE PRINCEDOM OF HAN-GILEN, HIGH LORD IN THE HUNDRED Realms, child and grandchild and great-grandchild of mages, noble and royal prince of a line of princes, was drunk. Royally, imperially, divinely drunk. But not, he was happy to observe, therefore incapable of pleasing the three delightful creatures who tumbled squealing with him into a vague blur of bedclothes and curtains. They were not his bedclothes or his curtains. He had better taste. But they were adequate, and the three ladies were considerably more than that.

The dark one could sing. The golden one could dance. The sweet brown one had hands of surpassing skill, and lips . . .

He drifted in a sea of wine. He sang with the dark woman; he watched the golden one dance. The brown woman stroked and teased him, holding him just short of release. He groaned aloud; she laughed. He seized her and tumbled with her in a cloud of scented silk.

Oh, this was a very fine brothel indeed.

The wine was wearing off. Pleasure, even at the hands of so skilled an artisan, could not last forever. He had the mage's curse: he could not fall into oblivion after. His mind was bitterly, brilliantly clear; and there was no wine in the jar beside the bed. Not even a drop to lift him out of himself again.

But he was no simple man, to be discommoded by a want of wine. He could send one of the women to fetch a new jar, or he could call for a servant. Or he could reach into the heart of him, where the magic was, and open the door that was there, and leap joyously into a world in which wine bubbled in fountains.

His three companions shrieked as the Worldgate cast them from lamplight into the full glare of the sun. It was a somewhat softer sun than they could have known before, but bright enough, and warm. The garden about them was full of strange sweet scents. Wine poured into the bowl of a stone fountain, rich red wine of a purer vintage than their own world could offer.

The brown woman and the gold were creatures of the moment; they drank till their lips were stained as if with blood. But the dark woman said, "I hear it's death to open Gates, unless you are a Gate-mage and consecrated in the temple."

He laughed. He had not drunk the wine, but he was dizzy with magic and with the sweetness of doing a thing so sternly and strictly forbidden. "No one will know," he said with sublime confidence. "Nobody knows what I can do. I'm the scapegrace, the fool, the pretty boy who knows nothing but the simplest magics. But I have Gates in me. Look, can you see? See them in my eyes."

She would not look. She was afraid. She gulped wine, choking on it. He was still laughing, because he would not have any of them think he cared for a whore's timidity. He whirled on the greensward that was not quite grass, among the flowers that had no kin in the world in which he was born. The Gates inside him spun into a blur of light.

The light winked out. He gasped. He was still on the greensward, but within him, in his magic's eye, he saw another vision altogether. There was a world—he had visited it, maybe, when he wandered alone through the halls of his magic. It had been beautiful, a world of sea and spume and sky. Now it was all ashen. Gaunt black birds flapped over a barren land; bones tossed in the dead sea. The stench emptied his stomach; he retched into the grass.

None of his companions came to comfort him. They were light women, toys to be used and cast away. They cared nothing for him, only for the gold he brought and the wine he gave them, and maybe a little for such pleasure as their kind could take.

There was a sour taste in his mouth and a bitterness in his heart. He gathered the women and flung them back through the Gate—back to the world from which they had come.

The fountains bubbled mindlessly into their basins. Somewhere, something trilled that was perhaps a bird, and perhaps not. Out of sheer contrariness, he turned the largest fountain to ice, and its wine to water.

He should not have done that. Opening Gates, that was direly forbidden. Changing the worlds beyond Gates, unless one were a Gate-mage or one consecrated by them, was so deeply banned that he did not even know the penalty for it. Death, he supposed. Or worse, if such a thing could be.

Gates never betrayed him. He was part of them. But guardians watching over Gates could find the tracks that he had so unwisely left and follow them to their end.

If the guards had been women, he might have charmed them into mercy. These were men, and not young, with a look about them of people who had never in their lives known a moment's levity. They seized him in a grip that he did not try to break, which was half of magic and half of human strength. They lifted him and carried him through Gates, not swiftly or easily as he could do, but by the long way, through the emptiness between worlds. He made no effort to tell them how they should do it. Mages never listened. They knew only what they knew, and that was all there was to know.

"Indaros."

The voice was much sweeter than its tone. It was a beautiful voice, and its owner more beautiful still, with an extravagance of hot-gold hair imperfectly contained in a fillet, and a face carved in ivory, and wide-set golden eyes. He raised himself in the windowless cell into which his captors had cast him, and stared frankly at her. "You don't look a day over seventeen," he said.

She had twice those years at least, and no more care for his frivolity than the guardians who had brought him here. "Indaros," she said again. "Get up."

He had intended to rise in any case. He unfolded himself, stretching till his bones creaked, and yawning vastly. "I feel vile," he said. "Is there a bath to be had? Or at least a change of clothes?"

She looked up at him; he was much taller than she. Nevertheless she managed to make it clear that he was far beneath her.

And so he was, being a mere prince-heir, albeit of a great princedom, and she heir to an empire—and, some said, to all the worlds beyond the Gates.

"No bath," he said regretfully. "Well then, you'll just have to stand the stink of me. Though I'd rather die clean, if you don't terribly mind."

"You won't die," she said. "You'll only wish you had."

He laughed. His mirth was honest, if a little wild. "Oh, do kill me. It's no trouble."

She frowned slightly, looked him up and down, and walked completely round him. He hoped that she was edified. He had, before sleep and pleasure and prison cell, been dressed in the perfect height of fashion. It was sadly wilted and stained now, but there still was no denying that his coat was distinctively cut and slashed, with dags and ribbons fluttering at carefully random intervals; or that it was a particularly striking shade of green. Or that the trousers had one leg green and one leg nearly as bright a coppery sheen as his hair; or that his shoes were thickly sewn with copper bells. They chimed gently as he shifted his feet.

"It would be a pleasure to kill you," she said as she came round to his front again, "but it will be an even greater pleasure to cure you of this . . . whatever afflicts you. Are you color-blind?"

He blinked at her. "You're sparing my life because you think I have bad taste? Oh, my wounded heart!"

"You have a heart to wound?" She dismissed him with the flick of a glance. "Enough. You've been judged. Be ready when your escort arrives."

"Escort?" he asked, arching a brow.

She was already gone. There was no lock on the door, he noticed. The seal she had laid on it was wrought of magic, and it was stronger than he could break.

That cracked his composure beyond retrieving. He was the most insouciant of princes; he had made it his life's work. But this quiet woman with her maiden's face and her Sun's fire of magery had got beneath his skin. "Judged?" he demanded of her absence. His voice rose. "*Judged?* Where is my trial? My defender? My noble judges? I'm a lord of rank. The law grants me a fair trial. I demand it. I insist on it!"

The echoes of his bellow died. There was no answer, only a lingering scent of her scorn.

He could not bear that, either. He flung himself against the door. He was not a small man, nor for all his infamous indolence was he weak, but the locks were made of magic. They never even shifted.

He was lying on his face when the escort came. He was not asleep. A mute and mind-shielded servant had brought clothing not long before, and a basin with it, and water enough for a bit of bath. He was fresher, cleaner, but notably less fashionable now; the paint was scrubbed from his face and hands, and his lovely soiled garments had left with the servant. The coat and trousers and boots he wore fit him well but were distressingly plain, without even a bit of embroidery to enliven their dullness. They were riding clothes, he could hardly have failed to notice. But he had not been given a weapon, even a knife for cutting meat. The belt was bare of anything but the grimly unornamented buckle.

He was cold inside, and empty. Transgressions had consequences, his father had taught him well enough. But one had to care for those consequences, which he never had. Still he had never broken two of the strictest laws of mages in swift succession—or worse, been caught at it.

He heard the door open and felt the mage-wards go down. If he had been inclined, he could have burst through the space where they had been, flung open a Gate, and vanished from the world. But he was not as far gone as that.

His fear was fading. The Lady Merian had let him live. She was the guardian of all the Gates, upholder of the laws, judge, and, he did not doubt, executioner. When he transgressed, he transgressed first against her.

He rose to face his jailers. They were not the mages he had expected, but his father's guardsmen in green and gold, regarding him with stony faces. He knew them all by name, had roistered in a tavern or three with most, but that mattered nothing now.

His cell, he discovered as he walked out of it in a wall of guards, was a priest's cell in the Temple of the Sun in Han-Gilen. He hoped he could be forgiven for not recognizing it; he had no call to that order, nor had he seen more of the temple than its outer reaches. With luck he would not see it again.

"It seems you have no call to anything," his father said.

This was both better and worse than facing the Lady of the Gates. She was a stranger, and accordingly distant from his faults and foibles. This was his father, and his mother coming into the smallest of the audience chambers with a thunder-reek of magic and a distracted look about her. She hardly seemed to see her son as she sat beside her husband, raking tangled black hair out of her face.

The prince paused for her coming, but spoke again all too soon. Daros watched the play of expression across the stern dark face, and the gleam of morning sunlight in the bright hair. He looked little enough like either of them. They said he threw back to some long-ago prince or—if they were ill enough inclined—to some princess of exceptional beauty and equally exceptional fecklessness.

"Feckless you certainly are," said his father, following his thought with the ease of a mage and the arrogance of a prince. "You have no useful skills; you serve no useful purpose. You refused the priesthood. You turned your back on the mages. If you have any calling at all, it appears to be that of tavern-crawler."

"And libertine, Father. Don't forget that."

The prince looked ready to erupt, but his princess spoke before he could burst out in rage. "Don't lecture him, Hal. He won't listen. He knows his sins as well as we, little though he pretends to care about them."

"I *don't* care about them," Daros said tightly.

She smiled. She was not beautiful; her face was too strong for that. But when she smiled, she warmed even his heedless heart. "Of course you care, child," she said. "You're afraid it will hurt. Can you tell us why you took three rather expensive whores through a Gate, and what you hoped to accomplish by changing what you found there?"

"It was only a game," he said—sulkily, and hating himself for it, but his mother always had been able to reduce him to a child.

"A game that you well knew was forbidden," his father said, though the princess tried to hush him.

"Yes, and why?" Daros demanded. "What harm did I do? Who was hurt or killed by what I did? It was just a Gate, and just a garden. Why are Gates banned? What are the mages afraid of? That anyone but they will discover secrets?"

"You know the answers to that," his mother said. "Your very failure to understand those answers is proof that the laws are necessary."

"How do you know I don't understand? What if I'm sure I did no harm?"

"Are you?" She rubbed her eyes and sighed. "Most of the mages wanted you put to death. It wasn't compassion for me that stopped them, or even the fact that you are the only living child of the Prince of Han-Gilen. You have cousins in plenty, after all; and I would mourn you, but never fault them for upholding the law. No; it was the Sunlady herself who revoked the sentence. Piddling useless thing you may be, she said, but you opened a Gate without spells, workings, or great raising of power. You did it, in fact, as casually as if the Gate had been an earthly door. She wanted to know why no one had ever enlisted you among the Gate-mages."

"No one ever asked," Daros said.

"Because you were never available to be asked." His mother looked him in the face for the first time since she had come into the room. He gasped in spite of himself. Her eyes were clear and hard and brimming with magic. But they could not pierce the barriers he had raised. "Why?" she asked him. "What do you fear? We've pampered you, indulged you, spoiled you shamelessly. What would cause you to keep such a secret?"

He shrugged uncomfortably. "It's not a secret. It's only . . . really, no one ever asked. They all weigh me light. Even you."

"Why—" But she stopped him before he could answer. "It doesn't matter. You've been tried and sentenced, and your sentence has been commuted from death to one less final."

"A fate worse than death?" he asked. "A state marriage?"

His father looked again as if he would erupt; again his lady forestalled him. "That was considered," she said. "Imprisonment, too, and excision of your magic."

He shuddered at that, for all that he could do; his stomach twisted until he gasped with the pain.

They saw, of course. He could not tell if they were gratified.

His mother said, "We considered many things, but she silenced us all, and spoke your sentence. You will be exiled, Indaros Kurelios. You will be given to a guardian who cannot be tricked or cozened or circumvented. Until he deems you ready to return, you will remain with him, under his rule, bound to serve him to the utmost of your capability. If you fail in your duty, or if you try to escape, you will be put to death."

Daros kept his face steady. He was growing afraid again. "Who—" His voice caught. "Who is my jailer? You, Father?"

Prince Halenan did not answer. The Lady Varani said, "We declined the honor, since we've done so badly for these past nineteen years. You'll be sent to another, who will, says the Lady of Gates, keep you in such order as you can ever be kept in."

"Who? One of my myriad uncles? One of the cousins? Suvayan is dour enough, and hungry enough, too. He'd keep me in chains. That would please you all, wouldn't it?"

She shook her head wearily. "Stop it, Daros."

If she had been cross, or even conspicuously patient, he would have defied her. But she was honestly and visibly exhausted. She had not slept, he realized, since his transgression was discovered. Maybe none of the Gate-mages had. More softly then, and somewhat less insouciantly, he asked, "Who, then? Where am I to go?"

"You will go to Han-Uveryen in the north of the world," his mother said. There was grief in it, but she did not yield for that. "You will be squire and servant to the lord of the holding. Your life will be in his hands. He will rule you absolutely and command your every breath, until your sentence shall be served."

Daros barely choked at the name of the holding, although he had heard of it, dimly. It was as remote as human habitation could be, far away in the land called Death's Fells. He focused his mind on another thing, a thing of rather greater importance. "How long a sentence will it be?"

"As long as your new lord sees fit to keep you," his father said.

"My new lord," said Daros, rolling the words on his tongue. "What great mage and lord of the world would make his home in that godsforsaken place?"

"Watch your tongue, boy," his father said through clenched teeth. "And above all watch it when you come to him. He was an easygoing man when I knew him, but that was years ago. He won't have kept that ease, I think, living in the Fells. He'd never have mercy on a transgressor of Gates. He made the laws for good and suffi-cient reason, and he set his granddaughter's daughter in command of them."

Daros' mouth was open. He shut it. "*He* made the—You're sending me to the emperor? I thought he was dead."

"He is very much alive," his father said.

"Gods," said Daros. "He must be ancient. When did he hand the empire over to his granddaughter? Was I even born yet?"

"Barely," his mother said. "He is still emperor, though he's surrendered his priesthood and given the regency to Daruya and her consort. He is also still the greatest of the mages, and a master of Gates. You'll walk soft in his presence, child, and accord him the respect he deserves, whether or not it suits your fancy. Am I understood?"

Daros bent his head. "I understand you," he said.

Her glance was distrustful, but she held her peace. So, perhaps by her will, did his father.

"You leave now," she said after a pause. "The guards will take you where you must go."

She had dismissed him. No embrace, no kiss, no farewell of mother to son; only the cold words and the cold stare. She was a mage of Gates; he had transgressed the laws by which she lived. What he had done was unforgivable. Only now did he begin to understand the meaning of the word.

His father's wrath he had expected; Prince Halenan was notoriously short of patience where his son was concerned. But the Lady Varani had never been so cold before, never kept so remote a distance. "But I did no harm!" he cried to her, hating the whine in his voice.

"You did more harm than you could possibly comprehend," she said. She turned her back on him: rejection so complete, and so mortally wounding, that he could only bare his teeth in a grin, salute them both, and bid his guards conduct him where they would.

TWO

DAROS' DEPARTURE HAD BEEN ARRANGED TO ATTRACT AS LITTLE NOTICE AS possible. The guards quick-marched him through the more obscure portions of his father's palace, down dusty corridors and through empty rooms, to a court in which he had played as a child, far from his nurse's quelling eye. He had thought to find a Gate there, or mages prepared to open one, but instead there were a company of men-at-arms and a string of packbeasts and a gathering of mounts and remounts.

They were profoundly ordinary animals, the lot of them. He did not see one of his own fine seneldi anywhere, nor any that might have been worthy of a prince. Not only, it seemed, was he to travel the whole of the long journey into the north as simple men did, on foot or on the cloven hooves of seneldi, but he was also to be forbidden any mark or privilege of rank.

At least he was not to go in chains—or not in chains that men could see. When he stretched out a tendril of magery to test the minds and mettle of his guards, he met a wall. It surrounded him completely, and confined his magic to the narrow borders of his unassisted self.

Ah well, he thought as he greeted the guards—none of whom returned the greeting—and mounted the nondescript senel that waited for him. It was a gelding, and one of his stunted horns was crooked; his brown coat was drab, his amber eyes profoundly disinterested in anything but his task of plodding along with his nose to the tasseled tail of the senel in front of him.

Indaros set himself to endure the ordeal. It was a long way to the Fells, and a senile old man at the end of it. If he could not escape before he came to Han-Uveryen, surely he would have no difficulty there. The Emperor Estarion was older than mountains, and had long since withdrawn from any semblance of imperial rule. Some even whispered that he was dead. Great mage and emperor he might have been, but that was long ago. He would be no match for the young and determined heir of a line of mageborn princes.

Daros had frequent cause to remember that as the journey stretched from days into Brightmoon-cycles. His guards were all mages, and all chosen for their strength of will; they sustained wards that prevented any rescue, or even recognition. He had nothing to do but ride and think and try to charm his guards—and charm them he did, at least into offering conversation. They would not loose the mage-bonds; even his best smile and his sweetest words failed to budge them. But it was not as grim an ordeal as it might have been; when they camped in the nights, they were rather convivial, and more so as they left civilized places behind.

The world grew bleaker the farther they rode; although it was still summer in the Hundred Realms, in the Fells it was well advanced in autumn, with chill wind and cold rain and an occasional grudging glimmer of sun. The land was no more delightful than the weather: an endless expanse of grey-green moor, surging into ridges and dropping suddenly into black tarns. Nothing stirred here but, once in a great while, a hawk wheeling in the grey sky. What quarry it pursued, they never saw; birds there were none, and creatures of earth were too small and quick to catch. They ate what they had brought on the packbeasts, and drank from rills and tarns. The land suffered them to cross it, but gave them no part of itself.

Of human creature they saw nothing. There were people in this country, Daros had been assured: dour tribesmen, kin to the lords of Ianon. But his escort kept well away from their forts and walled villages. If they had need of anything from the towns, a company rode to fetch it. He was never let out of sight, nor suffered to walk among people who might, gods forbid, have granted him relief from the relentless companionship of his guards.

On a day in which the rain was edged with sleet and touched with spits of snow, the captain of guards drew rein at the summit of a hill. "There," he said. "Han-Uveryen."

Daros peered through veils of rain. As if to oblige him, they lifted for a moment, uncovering the long rolling slope and the track of a little river. The river flowed into a lake; by the lake rose a crag. On the crag squatted a hill-fort.

Its walls were of stone as grey as the sky. A low square tower rose above them. No banner flew there; no light, either magewrought or earthly fire, burned to welcome the travelers.

Maybe, thought Daros, its lord was dead and his servants long gone. Then all this journey would be in vain; he would be forced to return through Gates to warmth and light and the arms of his friends and kin. Maybe even his mother. Maybe even she would speak to him again, since he had served as much of his sentence as he could.

It was a lovely dream as they rode in the bite of sleet, with wind working edged fingers through coat and mantle and chilling him to the bone. He could warm himself with a fire of magery if he chose, but he did not. He wanted the whole of the misery, to remember; so that he would never have to endure it again.

Han-Uveryen rose above them at last, perched on its crag. Ice dripped down from its battlements; the road that ascended to it was steep and slippery. They dismounted and led the seneldi, heads bowed against the wind that swooped down off the crag and did its best to fling them into the lake.

The gate, for a wonder, was open. There were people within, northern tribesmen, tall and dark, with grim faces. They had been warned of his coming and told of his crime and its punishment. They surrounded him, neatly easing out the guards who had brought him to this place. Those he was not to see again; they would rest and restore themselves, then return to the blessed warmth of the southlands.

He had no such fortune. These new guardsmen towered head and shoulders above him: true northerners of pure line, with hair to the waist and beard to the breast, and skin as dark as Mother Night. They were not to be charmed by a sweet smile or a ready tongue, nor had he any part in their canons of beauty. He looked into those cold black eyes and saw a manikin cast in bronze and dipped in copper, worthy of nothing but their contempt.

He grinned at the image. These were not mages. They were common mortal tribesmen, schooled in war but not in magic. The bonds upon him had all but fallen away. He could raise lightnings, walk in minds—but not open a Gate. He knew; he tried, and ran headlong into a wall. It was some little while before the headache passed from blinding to merely excruciating. Its message was abundantly clear. The one power he wanted and needed most, he was not to have.

He had expected grim stone, soiled straw on cold floors, stark barracks full of smoke and unwashed men. He was startled to find himself in a haven of warmth and light. The walls were stone, yes, but hung with tapestries of remarkable quality. There were rugs on the floors of the smaller rooms, and woven mats in the hall, and furnishings that would not have looked out of place in the hunting lodge of a prince in the Hundred Realms. The fire was contained in a broad hearth that funneled most of its smoke up out of the keep and away; what little remained served only to impart a pleasant pungency to the air of the hall.

The high seat was empty. The man who sat nearest it was younger by far than the emperor; he was pure northerner as the rest were, clashing with gold and copper in the antique style, with no garment but a kilt to warm him in the winter chill. Beneath the beard and the braids, Daros saw as he drew closer, the man was hardly older than himself.

He must be royal kin: he had the look, and the arrogance, too. The guards bowed to him. Daros did not deign to.

The northerner's expression was impossible to read, obscured as it was in curling black hair, but his eyes had narrowed slightly. "The emperor is waiting," he said without greeting or preliminary. "Raban here will direct you."

Raban was the tallest and grimmest of the guards. Was that satisfaction on his face behind the beard?

Daros' shoulders hunched. He straightened them with an effort. Something that he had done—perhaps as petty as his failure to offer proper obeisance to the nobleman in the hall—had hastened the time of reckoning. He rebuked himself for the stab of fear. The emperor was only an old man, however lofty his legend.

The old man, Raban informed him with rather too much pleasure, no longer lived in Han-Uveryen. "He's gone up the mountain," he said. "You'll find him there."

The mountain rose on the far side of the lake. Clouds and rain had veiled it, but as Raban brought Daros to the battlements to see where he must go, the wall of cloud lifted.

He caught his breath. This was a land of plains and sudden mountains, but this high peak he had never expected. It reared up and up, cleaving to heaven. The jagged summit was white with snow.

"He's up there," Raban said. "You'd better leave soon, if you want to be on the mountain before dark."

Daros considered all the possible things that he might have said, and rejected them all. He only said, "Show me the road."

He had not won the northerner's respect, but maybe he had lessened the man's contempt by a fraction. He was allowed a cup of spiced wine, almost too hot to drink, and a fresh loaf and a wedge of cheese, before he was cast out into the cold.

There was no escort. He was alone. They had saddled a senel for him—a considerably better beast than he had ridden from Han-Gilen—and filled its saddlebags, but given him no packbeast. If he did not find the emperor before his ration was gone, he would be thrown upon his own resources.

The sleet had stopped, at least. But the road was treacherous, and the cold was closing in, promising to be bitter once the sun's feeble warmth was gone.

The senel had been blanketed with a thick mantle of the northern wool that was the softest and strongest in the world. Its price in the markets of Han-Gilen would have taxed even his princely purse. He was simply glad of its warmth now, wrapped about him and trailing over the mare's rump. The striped dun trod lightly on the icy track, wise and surefooted and impervious to the cold. She picked her way round the lake, rising to a smooth trot where the track allowed it. He let her do as she chose; she knew this country better than he.

He had never been alone before. Even at his most solitary, he had been surrounded by the appurtenances of a prince: servants, guards, hangers-on. Now he was the only human thing within his eyes' reach.

He was forbidden Gates, but there was nothing at all to prevent him from escaping as any mortal could do, well mounted for a run into the Fells. But he was less tempted than he might have been. He was curious. He wanted to see what was on the mountain. A tomb, he would wager, and old bones in it, and mocking laughter at the boy who had gone so trustingly into the jaws of the jest.

Let them have their pleasure. He was not quite as soft as they thought, nor as ignorant of the world beyond the walls of a tavern.

He had ample opportunity to regret his foolishness as the dun mare carried him up the mountain. The way was steep and the sun sinking fast, and the road was long still before him.

He lit a fire with his magic to warm himself and his mount and to light the way once the dark had fallen. He was beyond weariness. He would find the tomb or the house in which the ancient was kept, pay his respects, then run, and be damned to the consequences.

He climbed from sunset into starlight, on a track that grew ever steeper. Greatmoon rose in a tide of blood; Brightmoon ascended like a white jewel in its wake. In that doubled light he saw as easily as by day.

He paused at intervals to rest the senel and to let her drink from rills that ran headlong down the mountain. She grazed a little then on bits of green hiding among the rocks; he fed her handfuls of grain, but for himself he took nothing but a little water. He had left hunger down below in Han-Uveryen.

Exhaustion hovered on the edge of awareness. He refused to give way to it. He would sleep when he found the emperor. The sooner he did that, the sooner he could escape.

He came on the shepherd's hut at dawn. The storm had cleared in the night; the cold was bitter enough to crack bronze. The hut stood against an outcropping of cliff, overlooking a surprising expanse of green, a deep bowl of meadow in the mountain's side. A chain of springs and pools surrounded it, steaming in the frosty air; the reek of sulfur was strong, but that of green things came close to overwhelming it. Even from the track, the heat of the springs was unmistakable, a waft of warmth and scented breeze.

The shepherd's flock grazed in the meadow, long-fleeced grey creatures too dim of wit to notice a stranger above them. As Daros paused on the track, the shepherd came out of his hut: a tall man, broad of shoulder, wrapped in a cloak of the same rich wool as the one Daros wore. He was a northerner: Daros glimpsed his profile, like that of a black eagle. His hair was thick and long, black threaded lightly with grey; his beard was a little greyer but still more black than white. He had a pair of buckets on a yoke, with which he drew water from the spring nearest the hut; if he was aware at all of the one who watched him, he showed no sign of it.

Daros slipped from the mare's back and left her rein dangling, and stood in the man's path. He trudged up it with his head down, lost in his own thoughts.

Just before he would have collided with Daros, he halted. The buckets were large and must have been heavy, but his shoulders barely bowed with the weight of them. He had the look of a man who had never known a moment's sickness, though he was small as northerners went: no taller than Daros. There were no marks of age in his face; he was in his prime, and strong with it.

He raised his eyes. Daros fell back a step. The man's lips twitched. He must be well aware of the shock of first meeting: that face so purely of the north, but those eyes of another tribe and nation altogether—eyes of the Lion, startling yet unmistakable. The Lady Merian had them, softened somewhat, like golden amber. These were the true pure gold, bright as coins in the night-dark face, large-irised as an animal's, and full of wry amusement.

Ancient, Daros thought as he fell on his face. *Senile.* Oh, indeed.

The Emperor Estarion lifted him with easy strength and set him on his feet, and said in a voice like a lion's purr, "Sun and stars, boy, I can't be that appalling a prospect!"

"You can't *be*," Daros said. The words tumbled out of him through no will of his own. "You can't be a day over thirty."

"Forty," said the emperor. "Don't be charitable."

"But you're at least—"

"Oh, I'm as old as this mountain." The emperor straightened as if to belie his own words, and stepped around Daros, toward the hut.

Daros followed him. The shock was wearing off. It would be a while before he recovered completely, but he could think again, after a fashion. Here was a jest indeed: a man not only strong enough to keep him in hand, but young enough, in body at least, to give him a fair fight. In magery . . .

He was strong. Daros staggered with the strength of him. Tales that called him the greatest of mages had not gone far off the mark, at all. He was so strong, and so sure in that strength, that he did not even trouble to conceal his thoughts.

For an instant Daros looked out of those eyes and saw himself as the emperor saw him: young and callow and altogether feckless, but with just enough spark of native wit in him to make him worth the uproar he had caused. The emperor was relieved at that. He had risked much, and gambled somewhat wildly, in suffering Daros to live.

"*You* decided my sentence?" Daros burst out.

"They all wanted you dead," said the emperor. "I reckoned it worth letting you live for a while longer, to discover what this gift of yours is, that eluded every mage who might have brought you into a temple."

"I have no calling to that life," Daros said. "My father says I have no calling to anything but trouble."

The emperor grinned. "I always did like your father's way with a word. Come in to breakfast. You must be famished."

Daros had felt no hunger at all until the emperor spoke of it; then his stomach clenched into a knot. The emperor grinned even more widely at his expression, and led him into the hut.

Breakfast was woolbeast stew, hot and savory with herbs and a tongue-searing hint of western spices. The emperor warmed it over a stone hearth while Daros tended his senel; they sat in the hut with the morning sun slanting through the open doorway, and ate in silence that was, to Daros' startlement, companionable. He was an easy man to keep company with, this lord of Sun and Lion.

Daros ate three bowls washed down with remarkably palatable ale, sat back and belched politely, and said, "I thought I'd find a tomb or a deathbed."

"Why, have they declared me dead in the southlands?"

"No one knows," Daros said. "You've not been seen for twenty years."

"Ah," said the emperor. "You're asking if I've been tending woolbeasts since before you were born. It's a good life. Peaceful. Useful, too. That cloak you're wearing came from these beasts."

"But you ruled the world," Daros said.

"So I did," said the emperor. "For years out of count I did it, from the time I was a child. When I left it, I was older than most men live to be; but it seems I have the family curse, to be unbearably long-lived. Either we die young, for foolish cause, or it seems we live forever."

"Truly? Forever?"

"Do I look like dying at any time soon?" the emperor asked.

"No," Daros said. "You look younger than my father."

"I looked like this fifty years ago," the emperor said. "I'm frozen in time, boy. Are you horrified yet? Are you about to open your Gate and run away?"

Daros' teeth clicked together. "You aren't supposed to—"

The golden eyes narrowed. For an instant Daros saw the man who had indeed ruled the world: a lord of power and terror. Then he was the shepherd of Han-Uveryen again, sitting back on his stool, sighing and shrugging and saying, "It seems we both do a number of things we aren't supposed to do. Don't try to run away, boy; the Lady of Gates has set guardians on all the worldroads, with orders to kill anything that passes there without her leave. They most certainly will kill you."

Daros needed no worldroads; his Gates were a different thing, and perhaps a thing that mages had not known before. But he had no intention of letting this man know that. As amiable as he was, he was still Daros' jailer.

Daros bent his head and lowered his eyes and pretended to be suitably cowed. The emperor did not trust him: he could feel that. But he was let be. That was enough, for a while.

THREE

MERIAN WAS INTOLERABLY WEARY OF GATES. SHE HAD LIVED AND BREATHED them for as long as she could remember; they were in her, part of her. But of late she had begun to understand how an emperor could give all his glory and power to his granddaughter and her consort, turn his back on them, and walk away.

This was no time to dream of flight, or even of escaping for an hour or a day, finding a quiet place and simply being whatever she pleased to be. At best she could steal a moment to dream—and when she did, she was startled and somewhat dismayed to see who waited for her there.

The Gileni boy was disposed of—well, she reckoned, though the rest of the Gate-mages begged to disagree. Her great-grandfather would keep him in hand. He would also, she hoped, learn what the boy could do; useless idle thing that he was, it seemed he had a gift for Gates that was little less than Merian's own.

And there he was in her dream, this eve of Autumn Firstday, idling about in a garden of singing birds. He was as lovely as ever, with that face cast in bronze and those narrow uptilted dark eyes and that hair like new copper—mark of his lineage, and pride of his beauty, too. She had not troubled to notice the rest of him while she judged him, but her eyes had been marking every line. Under the soiled and ridiculous finery, he was not at all an ill figure of a man.

She had understood long ago, when she was younger than this boy, that there was no room in her for both Gates and lovers. It was her duty to produce an heir; she was royal born, she had no choice in the matter. But unlike her mother, who had bred her as if she had been a senel, Merian could not bring herself to do the necessary.

Maybe, she thought, she should let the dream lead her. The boy was as royally bred as she, and a famous beauty. He had magic in more than the usual measure—how much more, it might serve her well to discover. And he had a name for prowess in the bedchamber. The women of Han-Gilen, both noble and irretrievably common, had never an ill word to say of him, except that he could not choose just one of them. He had to have them all.

She fled the dream and the thought. All Gate-mages who could come to the city of Endros Avaryan had gathered for the rite of Autumn Firstday: celebration in the temple and feasting after, and then, as night fell, a council.

There were a dozen of them in Merian's receiving room in the old palace, drinking wine or ale and nibbling festival cakes. Lamplight and magelight illuminated faces of nearly every race that this world knew, from ivory-and-gold Asanian to night-dark northerner. But they were all mages of Gates, bound together by the same duty.

"I still say," said Urziad of Asanion, "that all worlds but ours are empty of human life."

"Something builds gardens and palaces," said Kalyi of the Isles. "Something sets rings of stones on headlands and leaves the wrecks of ships by alien seas."

"We know that there were people once," Urziad said. "But we've been standing guard over the worlds for close on fourscore years, and none of us has seen a living soul. The worlds are empty, all but ours."

"The worlds around Gates are empty," Ushallin said. "That doesn't mean the worlds themselves are. Maybe the Gates are shunned as evil; maybe people are afraid of them. Maybe—"

"Maybe all the people are gone," said Urziad.

"But where? What would have happened to them?" Ushallin asked. She came from the Nine Cities; she was a skilled opener of Gates. She asked difficult questions, too, that none of the others could answer.

Kalyi at least was willing to venture a guess. "They may be greater mages than we can ever dream of being. Or they decided long ago to dispense with Gates, and left them behind as useless remembrances."

"Hardly useless if they can still be opened," Ushallin said. "It seems that we've been left alone amid all the worlds of Gates. What if there is a reason for that? What if something comes to Gates sooner or later, and devours all thinking beings in the worlds beyond them?"

A shudder ran round the circle. Urziad made a sign against evil—catching himself just too late. "Surely we have more to occupy us," he said, "than fretting over children's nightmares."

"But are they?" Merian had been silent for so long that she startled them all. "Are they simple nightmares?" she asked them. "There are notes in the histories, commentaries on the people of Gates; there were meetings, conversations, suggestions that there might be embassies and alliances. But since my great-grandfather's time, there's been no mention of any such thing. It's all empty worlds and silent shores. There has to be a reason. What if this is it? They've withdrawn or been driven back from the Gates. Something is stirring there, something enormous. Haven't you felt it? It comes in the hour before dawn, or in the drowsy center of the afternoon, when we're least on guard. It feels like a storm coming."

They were silent. She looked from face to face. They were all respectful, but there was no spark of recognition in them. They had not sensed what she had sensed.

They were good men and women, and strong mages. But she would have given much just then to speak with one who understood the deeper matters.

The mages of Gates knew only what they had seen in living memory: empty worlds, open Gates, freedom to pass where they would—within the laws and the bindings, which none of them thought to question.

But there was one who remembered the times before, when the Guild of Mages ruled the Gates, and Gate-mages were unknown in the world. Merian excused herself as soon as she respectably could, and took refuge in her garden, sitting by the pool that was always still even when the wind blew strong. It reflected starlight at midday and the moons' light at night, whether the moons were in the sky or no.

He was sitting between the moons, wearing the face he wore in dreams: much the same as the one he wore awake, black eagle with lion-eyes. They were lambent gold, those eyes; they smiled at her.

"Great-grandfather," she said.

"Youngling," said the emperor. "You're troubled tonight."

He was always direct. It had served him ill in dealing with the more subtle of his subjects, but Merian found it restful, in its way. "Is he still with you?" she asked. She had not meant to say it, but it escaped before she could catch it.

"He's your trouble?" Estarion asked, though not quite as if he believed it.

She shook off folly—both his and hers. "He troubles me, but not in this."

"He should," said Estarion. "He's a living Gate."

"So I gather," she said.

"Did you also gather that he's not the idiot he pretends to be?"

"I did hope that there was more to him than he was letting us see," she said.

"There is a great deal more," said Estarion, "though he might not thank us for perceiving it. I was a considerable shock to him, but he's recovered since; he's decided that I must be at least a fraction senile, since I prefer a shepherd's cot to the delights of my own cities."

"I thought so once," she said, "but not of late. Were mages as blind when you were young as they are now?"

"If anything, they were blinder." He raised himself up out of the pool, and stood dripping moonlight. "What are they not seeing now?"

"Gates," she answered him. "The worlds weren't always empty. Were they?"

"Ah," he said. "So you've noticed that, have you? I wondered if anyone would. No, when I was as young as this spoiled child you've saddled me with, we all knew that the worlds were populated, though there was considerable debate as to whether any of that populace were mages. None of them traveled as we traveled, that we ever knew. None came into this world. And none ever spoke to us or acknowledged us. But the oldest mages, who had the tales from long before, said that there was a time when the Gates saw a great deal of travel, and mages were aware of presences on the worldroads, going their incomprehensible ways."

"But none of them came into this world, or spoke to anyone from it."

"Not in those days," he said.

She frowned. "Tell me what you're not telling me."

"Not now, I think," he said. He smiled, but she knew how little hope she had of moving him. "This I can tell you. The boy knows something. He may not even be aware that he knows it."

"Would he divulge it to you?"

"I doubt it," he said.

She hissed at him. He only went on smiling. "You are always welcome in my house," he said.

He was gone before she could speak again. She considered flinging herself on the ground and indulging in a fit of pure useless fury. But she was too old for that, and maybe too much a coward.

Instead she walked through the Gate that was in her, and stood on a windy mountaintop, looking down into a starlit bowl of valley.

Estarion knew she had come. She felt the brush of his regard. What the other thought, she did not know him well enough to tell. If his reputation was to be trusted, he would not even be aware of her; but she placed little trust in rumor. Not about this one.

She waited out the night on the mountain, wrapped in a cloak of darkness and stars. The Gates lay quiet within her, save that, on the edge of awareness, she knew a glimmer of unease. Nothing troubled her, neither man nor beast nor bird of the air.

At sunrise she walked down to the shepherd's cot that was all the palace Estarion wanted in this age of the world. He had gone out before dawn, striding long-legged across the valley; he carried a staff and a bag, and had a bow slung behind him, as if he were going hunting. He had not taken the boy with him. The boy, she was well aware, had roused to see him going, then rolled onto his face and plunged back into sleep.

A creature of cities, that one, to sleep while the sun was in the sky. He had made a nest for himself in a corner of the hut, a heap of furs and blankets, but he had kicked them off as he slept. She had a fine view of his shoulders and back and buttocks, and his ruffled bright hair that was growing out of its dreadful close cut.

She sat on her heels and waited as she had on the mountain, with the patience of a mage. While she waited, she explored the Gates, searching out the strangeness. It kept eluding her, until she began to wonder if she had sensed it at all.

After quite some time, the sleeper began to twitch. His shoulders flexed; he wriggled, as if to burrow into his bed. He groped blindly for coverlets.

She was sitting on them. He opened a clouded eye and stared blankly at her. She stared coolly back. The eye went wide. He scrambled up, still half in a dream, and seemed torn between the prince's urge to bow and the fugitive's urge to escape.

She stood between him and the only door. He was still too aggravated with her to offer royal courtesy. He settled for standing in the tumble of his bed and glaring at her.

"I would think," she said, "that with your master gone out hunting, you would be expected to look after the flock."

He started as if struck. Shock of remembrance chased guilt across his face and hid behind outraged temper. "Are you my master, too?"

"I might be," she said, "if you prove to have a Gate-mage's gift."

"You don't want me," he said. He sounded just barely bitter.

"No? You imagine you're the only scapegrace who ever vexed his betters' peace?"

"I don't imagine I'm worth much at all."

She looked him up and down. It was a pleasant occupation, and one she was not inclined to finish overly soon; particularly when the slow flush crawled from his breastbone to his brow. "What is this play of worthlessness? Is it a fashion? A game? A way of tricking the dark gods into ignoring you?"

He shrugged, sullen. "Maybe it's the truth."

"You know it's not." She pulled a shirt from beneath her and tossed it at him. "Get dressed. I'll help you with the flock."

That startled him. "But you don't—"

"I did a year of my priestess-Journey here," she said. She tossed breeches in the wake of the shirt. He caught those, glowering, and pulled them on with rather more than necessary force. She caught herself regretting the breeches and the shirt, and the leather coat that went over them. They suited him better than his old finery, but his skin suited him best of all.

He was more adept at looking after woolbeasts than she might have expected. He was less sulky, too, once he had set to work. There were pens to mend and feet to trim and the ram to feed where he lived in his solitary splendor; young ones to count and older ones to look over for signs of trouble. There was a peaceful rhythm in it, that she remembered well.

The sun was high when they were done. They had not exchanged a word since they left the hut. When they went back to it, to dine ravenously on cheese and last night's bread and flagons of bitter ale, the silence had set into crystal, too beautiful to shatter.

Yet shatter it she must. As pleasant as this idyll had been, she had duties waiting, and mages calling down the worldroads, needing her for this urgency or that. She drained the last of her flagon, sat back on the bench in front of the hut, and turned her face and hands to the sun. Her left hand was ordinary enough, but the right burned and flamed, bearing a sun of gold in its palm: the *Kasar*, brand and painful price of her lineage. "Tell me what you sense in Gates," she said.

His silence changed abruptly, to the temper of heated bronze. Yet when he spoke, he sounded as light and useless as he ever could pretend to be. "What should I be sensing?"

"Tell me," she said.

"Nothing," he said. "Nothing at all."

She moved so swiftly that he could have had no warning. Her hand clamped over his throat. She gave him the full flare of her royal temper, fierce enough that even he had the wits to blanch. "Stop," she gritted. "*Stop* lying to me. There is something out there. You have seen it. Tell me what it is."

"You're not my master," he said.

She flung him down and set a knee on his chest. He made no effort to resist. His eyes on her held no fear. She kissed him hard, until he must have bruised, and flung herself away.

He lay where she had left him. His expression was blank, stunned. Slowly, as if in a dream, he said, "Something sweeps across the worlds. It feels like a storm coming, or like the sea rising. Moons shatter in its wake. What rides ahead of it . . . it rapes and pillages, burns and slashes and kills. People are dying, and worse than dying. You feel them, don't you? I hear their cries when I sleep. I see the flames even awake."

Whatever she had hoped for, it was nothing as distinct as this. She groped for the rags of her voice. "How long?"

"Since I came to this place," he said. He sat up. His mask was gone. There was still not a man beneath, but the boy was less feckless; he had seen things that harrowed the heart. "When you caught me, I felt something—saw a broken world. I didn't want to think anything of it. But after I came here, where there is little to do but tend woolbeasts and sleep, I saw more and more." He peered at her. "You don't see it. None of you does. Even he doesn't know."

"I think," she said, "he does." She would give way to that fit of anger later. "I'm beginning to feel it. The rest sense nothing."

"That's the guard on the Gates," he said. "It protects you mages."

"And not you?"

"I'm not bound by rites or vows," he said.

"No?"

"I'm not going to swear to anything," he said, "or be bound to anything."

"Indeed?"

She was aggravating him in spite of his best efforts: his nostrils had thinned and his lips were tight. "Indeed, your royal highness."

Her lips twitched, which piqued him even further. She forbore to laugh aloud. These matters were not for mirth, however amusing it might be to test his temper. "I do think it best that you remain as you are: renegade, apart from orders and guilds. But I would ask a thing of you, for this world's sake if not for my own: that you will tell me of your dreams, and take me into them if you can."

"Not likely," he said, biting off the words.

"Tell your master, then," she said, "and let him choose whether to tell me."

"What if he won't?"

"That is between the two of us," she said levelly.

He glowered at the sky, which was growing a thin fleece of cloud. Even without wishing to walk in his thoughts, she could feel the roil of confusion, the anger and defiance and childish resentment, mingled hopelessly with that same fear for the world which had brought her to this place and this aggravating person. He did care for what might come; his masks were a defense. Beneath them he was remarkably, almost shockingly passionate in his convictions.

She escaped before he caught her in the inner halls of his self. She was just in time: he focused abruptly, sat straight on the bench, and said, "I'll do what I can. I won't be your servant. Bad enough that I'm his—I don't need two of you ordering me about."

"No?" she asked silkily. "Is he not your emperor? Am I not the heir of his heir?"

"When you are empress on the throne of Sun and Lion," he said, "I will give you reverence as your rank deserves. But while you are mistress of Gate-mages, I am none of yours. You can kill me after all, if you like. You won't change my mind."

"Nor do I intend to," she said. "I am thinking . . . if I give you freedom of Gates, will you promise, for the world's safety, to do nothing that will endanger you or any of us?"

He sucked in a breath, shocked out of all sensible speech. She resisted the urge to shake him until he stopped gaping at her. In time he mastered himself; he found words to say. "You're—letting me—"

"With conditions," she said. "You go nowhere alone. Either my great-grandfather goes with you, or I, or another mage of suitable power and good sense. Observe that stricture, and the worlds are yours. Search among them; find what you can find. Bring back such knowledge as you gain. And guard yourself. It would be a pity to lose you."

"It would? What if I won't suffer a nursemaid? If I go out alone, what will you do? Kill me after all?"

"I doubt we'll need to," she said.

He eyed her suspiciously. "You can't be changing the laws this easily. Are you that afraid?"

"I am that uneasy," she said.

"You're afraid." That seemed to comfort him in some odd way. "Very well. I'll do it. Not for you, princess; don't delude yourself. I don't want to see this world burned to ash, and all its people taken away into darkness."

"Yourself among them?"

His eyes flashed at her under the lowered brows. "*I* could escape."

She had to incline her head at that; it was a just stroke.

He thrust out his hand. "Allies?"

"Certainly not enemies," she said as she completed the handclasp.

FOUR

Estarion knew when Merian left his house, and knew quite well what Daros did afterward. He was rather surprised that the boy did not leap at once into a Gate and vanish among the worlds. That had been his plan, and Estarion had watched while he refined it and elaborated on it. He was quite a subtle creature when he wanted to be, and astonishing in his gift for Gates. Did he know how strikingly unusual it was? Estarion would have said unique, but he shared not inconsiderable portions of it with Estarion himself, and with Merian—and with no one else that Estarion knew of, in their world at least.

Daros should have taken his freedom and run with it. But he was devotedly contrary, and he had no intention of gratifying anyone's expectations. Therefore he stayed about the hut, tending it and its garden as a good servant should, and waiting conspicuously for its master to return.

Its master would do that, but in his own good time. He had been hunting as the children believed, but his hunt was for nothing as simple as the mountain deer. He hunted among Gates, following the track of a shadow.

It was a subtle track, well hidden, and protected behind strong walls. The strength of the magic that sustained it made him catch his breath. He was strong; there was none stronger in his world. To this, he was but a feeble child.

He had not felt either young or weak in longer than he cared to remember. It was rather refreshing. He shielded himself as best he might, and hunted with all the stealth of which he was capable. That was considerable: even Merian could not find him unless he wished to be found.

The darkness ran in tides like a sea. It seemed to come from farther out, beyond the reach of his world's Gates, but with each ebb and surge it drew closer. It had buried worlds that he had walked on not so very long ago, distant worlds, far down the worldroads. It lapped the shores of several that he had passed by, or that he had not marked before. He prowled soft-footed round the edges, glimpsing bits of worlds: a flash of green, a spray of foam, a stretch of stark red sand.

It struck him without warning, falling on him from behind. Such substance as it had was like a great cat made of darkness visible, fanged and lethally clawed. He twisted, lashing out with a crack of power. The thing drank it as if it had been water, waxing with the force of it, rising up over him. He flung himself out and away.

The thing smote him so hard that his senses reeled. He was dimly aware of a Gate, and of falling. Then darkness was about him, black and deep.

The gods' curse had fallen on this land between the river and the desert. Their demon-servants stalked the night, rending any who ventured the darkness. The king was dead because of them, foraying out one long blue evening to avenge the slaughter of his people, and returning at dawn on the shoulders of his guards, so torn and broken that the priests despaired of mending his body for its journey into everlasting.

The king's wife had taken the scepter in her lap, close against her womb that had borne him six sons, but none of them had lived to see the men's house. She was all there was to rule the city, now that he was dead; his brothers had died of sickness and war, and his nobles were not of the true line. Kings and lords of other realms up and down the river were as sore beset by the unknown enemy as she, and as incapable of either war or invasion. And above all, in the end, the priests favored her. They fancied her a weak and pliant woman, a wife but not a queen.

She had played that part well while she lived as the king's wife. Now for this past year of her widowhood, she had smiled and listened and pretended to be awed, and ruled as her husband had done, with care to do nothing too untoward—not yet. In secret she brought out the weapons that had come with her from her mother's house, and began anew the exercises that she had practiced in her youth. She was not so young now, and not so supple, but she set her teeth and persevered; her servants, who were loyal, helped her as they could.

Even a queen might leave her city by daylight, if she professed a fondness for hunting on the river. However dread the night, the day was still safe; and a hunt was welcome—to bring in fresh meat for the pot and to restore spirits too long confined within walls of mudbrick and fear.

It was also opportunity to practice her archery, which was difficult within the palace. She could manage to be separated from the rest of the hunt, to wander among the reeds until there seemed no other boat in the world, and no other people but the boatmen and servants who accompanied her. They were all part of her secret, and glad of it, she reckoned as she ran her eyes over their faces. It was a warm day: they were gleaming with sweat, though even the rowers were resting, letting the current carry them along the reed-grown bank.

When they were well out of sight of the city and the hunt, she bade the boatmen steer the boat to the bank and moor it there. This was rich country for waterfowl, thick with flocks so numerous and so bold that they barely troubled to shift themselves out of range.

She would hunt them later. At the moment she had a desire in her heart to walk for a while between the green land and the red, between the nurturing earth and the stark hostility of the desert. It was a thing her husband had done, to remind himself of what his country was: rich yet precarious, and sharply divided from the world of gods and jackals.

The division was sharper than ever now, the desert more inimical. It was searingly bright in this hot and sunstruck morning: red sand and sharp stone and a clutter of scrub, and cliffs rising sheer beyond, a wall between the river and the deep desert. After the flocks that teemed on and above the river, and the fish and the crocodiles that fought their perpetual war in the water, this place seemed empty of life, save for a falcon that hovered against the sun.

She bowed to him, in homage to the god that he was. The air here was harsher, drier than it had been beside the river. Dust caught at her throat. Her maid offered her a skin of water, but she declined. She was thirsty, but not enough, yet, to act upon it.

She began to feel, deep in her heart, that she was called to this place. The gods were speaking, if she had ears to hear. Something waited for her, something wonderful. She went forward eagerly, with great lightness of spirit.

Only her maid and the captain of her guard went with her into the red land. She left the rest on the edge of the green, with orders to wait for her return. They were not unhappy to be left behind; the desert was a dread place, and more so since the night had become full of death.

There was a track out upon the sand, narrow and barely visible. She did not think that humans had made it. It led, she knew from long ago, up over the high hill and through a narrow cleft, to a valley with a spring and a shy hint of green. Gazelle came there to drink from the spring, and lions, too, and jackals questing for carrion.

Vultures were circling as she struggled up the steep slope. Lions' kill, she thought, but the lions must be gone: she caught no sound or scent of them. The call was strong in her. She could not have turned back even if she would.

She went on cautiously, with her bow strung and an arrow fitted to the string. Her guard would have gone ahead of her if he could, but the track was too narrow.

She reached the top with heart beating as much from excitement as from the exertion of the climb. She dropped there and crept forward like a snake over the stones, until she could see through the cleft into the valley.

It was almost devoid of green in this season, but the spring bubbled from its rock, ran into a pool hardly larger than a woman's hand, and sank back into the sand. A human figure lay by that bit of dampness, sprawled on its face. It was dressed in the kilt and broad belt of the people of the river, but the length and breadth of its body, and the night-darkness of the skin, spoke of a man from the south, where the sun had burned the earth's children black.

At first, with crushing certainty, she knew that he was dead. But as she watched, his hand stirred, long fingers closing into a fist, then opening again. Completely without thought, drawn irresistibly, she rose to go down into the valley.

The captain of guards caught her arm. "Lady! He could be one of the night's demons."

"In the full light of day?" She stared at his hand until it removed itself from her person. "Bring your spear, and be on guard. But don't harm him unless he threatens me."

He was not happy, but he was a good servant. He lowered his eyes, firmed his grip on his spear, and followed her down into the valley.

It was a large man indeed, and very dark. His hair was thick and plaited to the waist. Its blue-black waves were threaded lightly with grey, but his body was a young man's, taut and strong. With care, and very much against her captain's wishes, she turned him onto his back.

She had not seen a face like that before, not on the blunt-featured men of the south; this had the profile of the hawk that had come to circle overhead, driving off the vulture with its divine presence. The shadow of its wings seemed for a moment to enfold him.

She closed her eyes briefly. That face—that hawk's shadow. She knew it. How or where or when, she did not know. But to her heart he was no stranger, no more than one of her souls.

Her mind was very clear, not clouded at all. "Help me," she said to her captain, and to the maid who had trailed behind them both. Among the three of them, however unwilling two might be, they lifted him and carried him the long hot way to the river. When they came in sight of the rest of her guard, those strong young men came to relieve them of their burden; they carried him to the boat, and laid him in the shade of the canopy.

He had stirred now and then on the journey, but he had not roused. Once he was laid in the boat, he sighed and was still, except for the rise and fall of his breast as he breathed.

That was the gods' mercy. They could be kind to one of their own.

That this was a god or a son of gods she had no doubt whatever. She would offer him honor, and not lock him in the granary as half her advisors bade her do; the rest would prefer that she have him killed before he could wake and doom them all.

None of them, not even the priests, could see what she saw. When she looked at him, she saw the sun's fire encased in the dark wood of the south. A night-demon, she was certain, would be dark to the heart of it.

She tended him herself. Tomorrow she would have duties that could not be escaped, but for this day she would do as she pleased, and as the gods willed. She saw him bathed in cool water and scented with oils, his hair combed and plaited and his beard smoothed into order. Only his right hand would not yield to their ministrations. It was clenched tight about a gleam of gold: some treasure, perhaps, that he guarded even in his dream.

When he was clean, the queen's servants laid him in the bed that had been the king's, in the colonnade that opened on the garden. Coolness washed him there, the breeze of fans wetted in water, and sweet scents, and relief from the glare of the sun.

The priests would not speak their spells over him to heal him, nor would they pray to the gods on his behalf. She said such prayers as a queen might say, sitting beside him, watching as the light shifted slowly from the blaze of noon to the softer glow of evening.

In that long light, at last, he stirred and gasped. He opened his eyes.

They were full of the sun. She fell before them, on her face as even a queen should do before a god. She heard the catch of his breath, the rustle of coverlets as he rose, and felt the warmth of his hands on her, raising her. She would let him lift her to her feet, but she would not look at him. One did not stare a god in the face.

She could stare at his hands clasping hers, and as he let her go, at the thing that he had guarded with such care. The sun again, but set in his hand, burning in it as fiercely as it ever did in the sky. It cast sparks of golden light across her face, and glinted on the walls and the floor.

He clenched his fist about it once more and said in a voice as warm as it was deep, "Don't be afraid." The words had a strange sound to them, as if they had begun in a language she had never heard, but had shifted and transmuted into words that she could understand.

"One should fear the gods," she said, still with her eyes turned resolutely down.

"God? I? You worship the sun here?"

"Is not the sun most greatly to be worshipped?"

"We do believe so," he said.

She was silent.

When the silence had grown almost awkward, he said, "Tell me if you will— where is this?"

"You are in my city," she said, "by the river that feeds the black land. We found you in the red land, where gods and demons walk. We cry your pardon if we acted in error."

"No," he said. "No, you did well. That's no friendly country, this red land of yours."

"It is not ours," she said, politely, but firm nonetheless. "This is ours: the green and the water, and the black earth. It was blessed once. Now . . . one thing we do fear, even more than gods. We fear the night."

He stiffened just visibly. "What do you fear in the night?"

He must know, as gods did. But it seemed he needed to hear it spoken. "We fear the things that walk in the dark; that rend flesh and devour souls. My people believe that you must be one such. But I see the sun blazing in the darkness."

"Ah," he said. "No wonder you won't look me in the face. I won't blind you, lady, or suck out your soul. I am a man, though one or two of my forebears were gods."

She did not believe him, but she nerved herself to look up.

If he was a man, he was like no man that she had ever seen. He was smiling at her. His golden eyes were warm. He did not frighten her, but neither did he put her at ease. "You came from the gods' country," she said, "from the land beyond the horizon. Don't deny it; I see it in you. You are not of mortal kin."

"Not of this world," he admitted. "The things you fear—I came hunting them. Your world is in great danger."

"You hunt them?" she said. She was not daring to hope, not yet. "You have weapons that will kill them? Powers? Magics?"

"I don't know," he said. Her face fell; he brushed it with a fingertip, a touch as light as a whisper of wind. "Lady, we've only now become aware of them; we don't know what they are, where they come from, or anything but that they are destroying worlds. If I can discover the truth, I will. But you shouldn't hope for too much. I'm only one man."

"But surely," she said, "there are others where you come from. They can come here, too, yes? They can join us in our war."

"There are others," he said, but his face for once was somber. "Whether they can come here . . . I barely managed it, and the darkness had had no warning of my coming. I don't know whether I can go back, or whether my people can find me. There are so many worlds. And none of my people knows—none of them believes—that any of them is occupied."

She did not understand him, except that he was troubled, and that he might not be able to summon reinforcements. The rest was a matter for gods.

This she understood: that he was still weak from his passage from the gods' world to that of men; and that she was sorely remiss in her hospitality. She summoned the servants, bidding them bring food, drink, cooling fans, and a basin of water in which had been scattered a handful of sweet-scented petals.

He partook of it all with regal courtesy, and gracious manners that began to win over the less suspicious of the servants. He even knew how to dismiss them so that they were not offended; they told one another in her hearing that he was tired, he had had a long journey, he must rest.

She was of the same mind, but when she made as if to go, he stayed her with a word. "What may I call you?" he asked. "Lady? Queen? Majesty?"

"Tanit," she said before she could catch her tongue.

He bowed to her. "Tanit," he said. "And I am Estarion."

"Seramon," she said.

"Estarion," he said.

Her tongue could not shape those sounds in that order. "Seramon," she said, struggling.

He shrugged and smiled and spread his hands, the one that was dark and the one that cast shards of light over the wall. "Seramon," he said.

FIVE

ESTARION WAS GONE.

Daros had indulged in a fit of pure pique, devoting himself after Merian's departure to all the tasks he had been given, and all of Estarion's, too. By sunset of that day, he was too exhausted to do more than eat a bite of bread and fall into his bed.

Morning brought a soft mist of rain and no relief from solitude. He might have reveled in it, seized it, and escaped, but the thought persisted that this was a test. They wanted him to bolt. Therefore he would not.

By the sixth day he was deathly weary of his own company. Woolbeasts had no conversation. The senel had no interest in it. The stores of necessities—ale, salt, grain for grinding into flour—were running low. Every cycle of Brightmoon, either Estarion had gone down to Han-Uveryen to fetch provisions, or the fortress had sent a packtrain up the mountain. The moon had come to the full the day after Estarion went away, but no train of beasts had come winding up the trail. Obviously they expected the men on the mountain to come down.

On the seventh day, he ground the last of the grain, baked a day's worth of bread from it, and knew that either he went down the mountain to beg at the castle—and begging it would be, without Estarion to speak for him—or he went through Gates as they all seemed to wish him to do. Then of course, if he did that without a chaperon, he would be caught and killed, and they would be rid of him at last.

Unless . . .

She was in the midst of something that, from the taste that came to him through a tendril of magic, was both tedious and obligatory. It felt in fact like a court function.

He made so bold as to borrow her eyes. Yes—there was the great hall of audience in Starios of the kings, that Estarion had built between two great and warring empires. He glimpsed the regents on their twinned thrones below the golden blaze of the throne of Sun and Lion: Daruya like an elder and somewhat darker image of her daughter, and her consort not greatly unlike Daros' mother: tall and strongly built, with broad cheekbones and narrow black eyes. The court stood in ranks before them, glittering in regal finery.

Merian was enormously and unbecomingly bored. Courts of the law, imperial audiences, embassies, those she could bear; they were interesting. But High Court was dull beyond belief.

He was tempted to linger in this hidden corner of her awareness, where even she had no inkling of his presence. It was a surprisingly pleasant place to be. Her mind was not at all as he had expected; there was nothing either dour or repressive about it. It reminded him of the water garden in his father's summer palace: bright, melodious, full of sudden delights and fluid order. The wall she had built about it was thick and high, overgrown with thorns; but the heart of her was wonderful.

He hated to leave it. But she would be furious if she knew, and just then he did not want her anger. He slipped free, curved round, presented himself for her notice.

His wards were almost not enough to shield him against the full glare of her attention. She was Sun-blood, and that was pure blazing fire. She did not even give him time to speak. "Have you found him? Where is he?"

Daros could not make his mind shape words. She caught hold of him, opened one of the Gates in him, and stepped through it.

She did it to punish him; she could perfectly well have opened her own Gate. But that would not have proved that she was his master.

He allowed it because he was still so enthralled by what he had seen inside her. They stood in the shepherd's hut, with the rain dripping sadly from the eaves, and stared at one another.

She was as splendid as a firebird in her court dress, all gold from head to foot. He in plain worn leather, with no ornament but the copper of his hair, bowed as a prince should to an imperial heir.

Her lips narrowed at that. He had not meant it for mockery, but he was set too long in the habit of insolence; he could not perform an honest obeisance.

She seized him and shook him. He did not stiffen or resist, but let his head rock on his neck. *"Where is he?"*

It dawned on her eventually that if she wanted an answer, she had to stop rattling his teeth in his skull. She let him go. He dropped to his knees. "I don't know," he said through the ringing in his ears. "I came to ask you. This isn't a test? You aren't tempting me into running through Gates?"

"Why would I—" She bit off the rest. "You would think that, wouldn't you? You haven't seen him at all?"

"Not since the morning you came," he said.

"And you let this happen? You haven't gone looking?"

"You forbade me to go alone," he said.

He thought she would strike him, but she struck her hands together instead. "You could have summoned me!"

"Isn't that what I just did?"

She did not like it that he was being reasonable and she was not. He watched her gather herself together. After a while she said, not too unsteadily, "No one knows where he is. That's not terribly unusual—he vanished for the whole of a year once, before we found him on a ship on the eastern sea. But my dreams have been strange. This morning when I woke, I wanted to ask him something, and he was nowhere. He is not in this world."

Daros could not claim to be surprised. "He must have done it while we were engaged with one another," he said. "Otherwise one or both of us would have known. And if he did that . . ."

"There are worlds beyond worlds," she said. "And he can hide himself wherever, and whenever, he pleases."

"Why would he do that?" Daros asked. "Is he testing us both?"

She shook him off. "No. No, that's absurd. He wouldn't play that game now. Which means—"

Daros finished the thought for her. "He's trapped somewhere."

"Or dead," she said starkly.

"No," said Daros. "You would have known if he had died. So would I, if he'd died in a Gate. Power like that doesn't just vanish when the body dies."

"Unless the power itself had been consumed," she said.

But he was stubborn. "He's still alive, somewhere among the worlds. I'm going to find him."

"He might not thank you for that," she said. "If this is a hunt, and you come crashing through his coverts, you'll only make it worse for all of us."

"Lady," Daros said, and he thought he said it quite patiently, too, "either you want me to find him or you don't. Either he's safe or he's not. You can't have both."

"I don't think he's safe," she said. "I'm going hunting. Will you come?"

"You think I can be of any use?"

"You can sense the thing that I suspect he was after."

"Ah," he said. "I'm to be your hunting hound."

"Call yourself what you will," she said. "We leave as soon as I can gather a few necessities."

"Gather a few for me," he said. "Unless you'd rather wait a day or two while I fetch them from the castle?"

"I'll fetch them," she said. "Be ready."

She melted into sunlight. He stood for a moment, simply breathing. The Gate inside him begged him to open it now, and vanish before she came back to plague him.

He was growing wise at last, or else he was turning into a coward. He gathered a change of clothes, a waterskin, one of the woolen cloaks; he rolled them together round an oddment or two, and the half-loaf that was left from his morning's baking. That bundle, with Estarion's second-best bow and a quiver of arrows, and a long knife, was all he could think to take.

She took her time in coming back. He began to wonder if she would; if she had thought better of it and gone alone. But the Gates were quiet. She had not passed through them.

He was napping when she came, propped against the house-wall in the sun. Her shadow, falling across his face, woke him abruptly and fully. He was on his feet, shouldering weapons and bundle, before his eyes were well open.

Her golden robes were gone. She was dressed much as he was, in coat and trousers, with a small bag slung over her shoulder. She had brought no weapon but a knife at her belt. Her hair was plaited tightly and wound about her head. She looked even younger than she had before, but strong, too, and a little wild.

She said no word. He had the briefest of warnings: a flicker in the Gates. She gathered him with her magic and swept him with her through the walls of the world.

They stepped from sunlight into firelight in a hall of stone. Now it seemed as vast as a cavern, now hardly larger than the shepherd's hut on the mountain. "This is the Heart of the World," he said. "I've heard of it. I've never been here."

"Never?"

He ignored the bite of Merian's disbelief. "You would have known about me if I had."

"So we would," she said grimly. "Now sit. This place belongs to us, to Gate-mages. It's as safe, and as shielded, as any place can be. You will remember it, where it is, how to come to it. This is where we will meet if either of us is separated."

He had always known where it was, but he held his tongue. He sat where she bade him, on a bench that he could have sworn had not been there a moment before. She stayed on her feet, frowning at the fire. It was hot; it danced as flames should. But it was no mortal fire. Power of Gates was contained in it, and worlds spun like sparks.

"We will find the trail here," she said. "You will be obedient; you will set aside whatever arts and fashions you may be enamored of, and be my servant until the emperor is found."

"And then?" he inquired. "Do I finally die?"

"Do you want to?"

He did not answer.

"If by fecklessness or folly you endanger the emperor, or prevent us from finding him at all, I will kill you with my own hand. Find him, help me bring him home safe, and I may see fit to free you from your bonds and your sentence. Then you may go back to your taverns and your women."

"For how long? Until our world flares into ash like all the rest?"

"That won't concern you, will it? Your service will be done. When the fire comes, if it comes, you can die with a flagon in your hand and a doxy on your knee, and never know a moment's grief."

Daros could hardly give way to anger. He had cultivated his reputation with great care; he had made certain that no one ever overestimated him. It made life simpler and much more pleasant.

But here, with this daughter of gods, he wearied of the game. He rose, quick enough to startle her, and stepped past her toward the hearth and the fire that was not fire. She spoke; he took no notice. He was sifting the sparks, searching among the worlds for a thread of gold, a memory of passage.

The blight on the worlds had spread. He saw it as black ash and blinding smoke, a darkness in the heart of the fire. The size of it, the breadth and sweep, caught his breath in his throat. No mage had such power; even if all the mages of this world banded together, they would not come near to the strength of this thing.

It was not a living will, though living will must drive it. He thought of walls and of shields—of a shieldwall, and an army behind it.

As if the thought had unlocked a door, he glimpsed . . . something. He was just about to grasp it when her voice shattered his focus. "Daros! You fool. Get back!"

Her hands were on him. He was leaning over the fire; his cheeks stung with the heat. She dragged him back.

He was glad of the bench under his rump, but not of the woman who bent over him. "Don't you know enough not to startle a mage out of a working?" he snapped at her.

That rocked her back on her heels. She could not have been reprimanded for such a thing since she was a tiny child.

He pressed such advantage as he had. "Lady, I don't think we can do this alone. We can hunt for the emperor, yes. But the other thing, the thing he was hunting— it's coming toward us. If you would have a world to bring him back to, you would do well to call on your mages and set them to work building such shields as they can. They can do that, yes? Even if they don't see or believe in the reason for it?"

"It has been done," she said.

He flushed.

She was not inclined to be merciful. "You will leave the searching of the shadow to the mages. Your task is to find your master. Do you understand?"

"Yes," he said tightly.

"Good," she said. "See that you remember."

He lowered the lids over his eyes before she saw the extent of his defiance. The shadow was the key, he was sure of it. If Estarion was not inside it, then he was very close to it. "Do I have your leave to hunt?" he asked. And added, after a pause, "Lady."

"Hunt," she said. "But watch yourself. Don't fall into the fire."

For answer he sat more sturdily on the bench and knotted his hands between his knees. He was well away from the fire, if not from the lure of its myriad worlds.

She set hands on his shoulders. So mages guarded one another in workings. And so, he thought, could she keep him chained to her will.

She did not know all there was to know of Gates, or of his magic, either. He sent a part of himself down the safe road, threading the loom of worlds. The part beneath, after a careful while, he sent back toward the shadow.

He had done such a thing before, more than once, to elude his father or his mother, or to escape the testing that would have bound him to Gates or temple. But he had not done it in such close quarters, under such a watchful guard. The lesser hunt must seem to be all the world, and the greater must leave no trace at all. To divide himself so, he needed every scrap of power he had, and every bit of discipline that he had taught himself. That was more than anyone knew. Whether it would be enough, only time would tell.

The lesser hunt skimmed the sparks of worlds, finding no trace of what it sought. The greater one skirted the edge of shadow. It was a shield, he was certain now, but how it was sustained, what had wrought it, he could not tell.

He sought the source, the life behind the wall. It was elusive; it warded itself well, shields within shields. He looked for a face, a mind, anything that he could grasp, to draw him behind the shield.

He was not strong enough. Merian wore at him with the weight of her watchfulness. If he could have focused on the shadow alone, he could have found its makers, but the fruitless hunt through worlds not yet touched by shadow kept him from discovering the truth.

He must find Estarion. The emperor had gone hunting the shadow; Daros was sure now that he had found it. He was strong enough to face it; nor need he bow to any will but his own.

Daros let go the greater hunt and focused himself on the lesser. He pressed it as close to the darkness as he dared under Merian's eye. There was a hint, a glimmer—

It dropped away. He pulled back in frustration, into the hall again, beside the fire that never shrank or went out. But if all the worlds were laid waste, would it not, itself, vanish into ash?

Merian set a cup in his hand. It was full of honeyed wine. She gave him bread to sop in it, to fill his belly with care, quenching a hunger as strong as it was sudden.

He ate and drank because he must, but his mind was not on it. "I have to go back," he said.

"Not now," said Merian. "You'll rest first."

"But I almost found him. He's there. I couldn't—quite—"

"I saw." She pulled him to his feet. "Come and rest."

He fought her, but his knees would barely hold him up. "Stop that," she said, "or I'll carry you over my shoulder."

He did not doubt that she would do it. Sullenly but without further objection, he let her lead him out of the hall.

This was a castle after all, with stairs and passages, and rooms that seemed mortal enough, if ascetically bare. One of them had a bed in it, and a hearth on which she lit a mortal fire. He lay because she compelled him, and suffered her pulling off his boots and covering him with a blanket as mortal as the fire, worn and somewhat musty, as if it had been long unused.

The starkness of it comforted him. It was real; there was no magic in it. He was deathly weary of magic, just then.

He lay on the hard narrow bed in the stone cell. Merian was gone. He was aware of her in the hall of the fire, holding council and audience from afar with the army of her mages. She had kept a part of herself, a thin thread of awareness, on guard over him, but that could not constrain his vision.

He stood on the shores of a wide and heaving sea. It was a sea not of water but of shadow, of darkness given substance. Things stirred beneath, great beasts rising from the depths and then sinking again with a sound like a vast sigh.

Because he was dreaming and knew it, he set foot on the surface of the darkness. It felt firm and yet yielding, like a carpet of moss on a forest floor. It was darkly transparent, showing the play of shadow within shadow in the depths beneath.

Slowly as he trod those swelling hills and sudden hollows, he began to distinguish among the shapes below. They were worlds, each floating in a bubble of darkness. Those that were nearest the surface came clearest to his vision. Some of them he knew, others were strange. He stooped to peer through the dark glass.

It was a war. He had never seen one; there had been no more than bandit raids in his world since before he was born. Yet he had heard of battles, and seen them through the memories of those who had fought in them.

Armies faced one another on a wide and windy plain. The beasts they rode, the armor they wore, were strange, but there was no mistaking what they were or what they did. One side was smaller by far, and had a desperate look. The other came on like a black wave.

There, he thought. He bent lower, peering as closely as he could. The dark warriors were all armored, their faces hidden, their shapes not quite human.

The sea surged, flinging him off his feet. A vast shape rolled over the world and its warriors. An eye opened, as wide as one of the worlds. It turned and bent, as if searching.

He was tiny, a mite, a speck of dust in the vastness of the worlds. He was nothing; no more than a breath of wind. The dark thing need take no notice of him. It was far too great a beast for such a speck as he was.

It rolled on beneath and left him gasping, tossed on the restless sea. He was lost; the land was gone. In concealing himself from the great guardian, he had concealed himself also from the Heart of the World.

SIX

MERIAN LEFT THE BOY TO SLEEP FOR PERHAPS TOO LONG. THERE WAS A GREAT deal to do, and her mages, while willing to be obedient, lacked belief in the task. Even after she had let them see as much as she had seen, she still sensed the current of doubt and heard the murmur among them: "She's a great mage, we all know that, but we also know that she is a living Gate. What if the Gate in her has driven her mad?"

That murmur would grow if she loosed her grip on any of them. There were always doubters and naysayers; nor was every mage her friend, though she had ruled them since she was little more than a child. If she was wise, she would give up this foolishness and return to her palace, and let the emperor find his own way home. Had he not done so before, and more than once?

But this was not the same. There was an urgency in her, a sense almost of desperation, as if there were no time left—as if each moment that she let pass she wasted, without hope of replenishment. She must find the emperor; there was no hope otherwise.

This was nothing that she could say to any of her mages. They were blind to it, and worse than blind.

"It could be said," said Urziad from amid the Heartfire, "that you are deluded and we see the simple truth."

"My old friend and frequent adversary," she said, "so it could. Do you believe it?"

"I believe that what you see terrifies you," he said. "I dislike that you place your trust in a useless frippery of a boy."

"He believes in what I see," she said.

"Surely that should tell you how well to trust it, and him."

"The emperor also believes," she said. "And before you tell me that he's a senile old man who has been questionably sane from his youth, do recall that no mage now living can equal him."

"Except you," said Urziad.

She shook that off, however true it might be. "I think this boy may be stronger than any of us imagines. He's the hunting hound. I'm his huntsman. Will you see to it that there is a world for us to return to?"

"I would prefer that you never left at all," Urziad said.

"So would I," she said. "But needs must. Be watchful, my friend."

"For your sake," Urziad said, "and for no other reason."

"Gods grant it be enough."

He vanished from the Heartfire. She stretched and sighed. There was no measure of time here, but in the world of the sun her forefather, the day had come and gone. It was deep night, almost dawn.

The boy had had long enough to sleep. She went up to the room in which she had left him. He was sprawled on his face, perfectly still: the pose of one who had raised laziness to high art.

She laid a hand on his shoulder to wake him, and gasped. He was rigid. The skin of his neck was cold.

She heaved him onto his back. He was still breathing, shallowly. His face was grey-green, his eyes rolled up in his head.

She hissed at the folly of the child. He had fallen into a mage-dream; it had swallowed him whole. And she, worse fool yet, had left him alone. She should have known what he would do.

If there had been another mage to stand guard over her, she would have gone hunting him down the paths of his dream. But she was alone, and time was wasting. She flung him over her shoulder—grunting a little for he was not a light weight, but she was stronger than most men would have liked to know. She carried him out of the cell, down a passage, and a stair, to a cavernous room in which glimmered a pool of ever-flowing water.

The water was cold—icy. A flicker of magic could have warmed it, but she had no interest in his comfort. Quite the contrary. She stripped him of his clothes and dropped him unceremoniously into the pool.

For a long moment she knew that she had erred; that he was too far gone. He sank down through the water, limbs sprawling, slack and lifeless.

Just as she was about to dive to his rescue, he jerked, twitched, thrashed. Eyes and mouth opened; he surged up out of the pool, gasping, choking, striking at air.

She moved back prudently out of the way and waited for him to find his sanity again, such as it was. He scrambled to the pool's edge and lay there, breathing in gasps, skin pebbled with cold.

When it seemed clear that he would refrain from attack, she wrapped him in a cloth and rubbed him dry. His eyes were clouded still; he submitted without resistance. Only slowly did he seem to see her or to know who she was; even then he only stared at her dully.

Her heart constricted. Not, she told herself, that she cared overmuch whether he lived or died, but she needed him alert and sane, to hunt for the emperor. Indaros with his mind gone was of no use to her.

Little by little the light came back into his eyes. He straightened; he shuddered so hard that she heard the clacking of teeth. When he spoke, his voice was raw. "How long—"

"Part of a day and most of a night," she said.

"Not so bad, then," he said with a small sigh. "Lady, what I saw—" He was shaking uncontrollably. "Armies, lady. Wars. And something . . . I don't know what it is, how they raise it, what sustains it, but it rolls ahead of them. We aren't strong enough, lady. Not even all of us together."

"We are going to have to be," she said grimly. "Show me."

He opened his eyes wide. They were as dark as the night between stars, and shimmering with bubbles that were worlds. Before she could speak, move, think, she was deep within his memory.

He was strong, she thought distantly. Stronger even than she had imagined. As strong as she. Untrained, yes, but far from undisciplined. He had taught himself— really, rather well.

She gathered everything that he had told her, found Urziad where he drifted on the tides of dream, and sent it all to him, whole, as it had been sent to her. His shock knotted her belly.

There would be no doubt among mages now. Not after this. She struggled free, raising every shield she had.

In the silence, alone within herself, she stood staring at the boy from Han-Gilen.

No—let him be the man and mage that he so evidently was. Let her give him his name, Indaros Kurelios, prince-heir of a small and yet powerful realm. "Why?" she asked him. "Why hide yourself so completely?"

"I never wanted temples," he said, "or orders of mages. It seemed they never wanted me."

"I am thinking," she said slowly, "that it's great good luck for us all that that was so."

"What, that I'm a coward and a layabout?"

"Stop that," she said. "This needed someone outside the walls. Someone who could see unimpeded; who could go where none of us was able to go."

"Does that mean my sentence is commuted?" he asked sweetly.

"You still broke the law," she said.

He sighed, shrugged. The color had come back to his face, the insouciance to his manner. She was growing used to it; it grated on her less now than it had. "And the emperor is still missing. I know he's somewhere on the shores of the shadow—but where, I can't tell."

"We will find him," she said, "if we have to walk on foot from world to world."

"I don't think there's time for that," he said.

"What else can we do?"

He bit his lip. It was odd and rather gratifying to see him so far removed from his easy insolence. "I can track him. I think . . . if you ward me and protect me from the dark, I can find the trail he left. It's still there; I can almost see it. But it will fade soon."

She searched his face. He was speaking the truth, or as much of it as he could know. "Do it," she said. "Do it now."

He bent his head. She was prepared this time for the swiftness with which he acted. He had no deliberation; he knew no rituals. He simply gathered his magic and flung it forth. It was inelegant, but she had to admit that it was effective.

They flew on wings of bronze over a dark and tossing sea. What he followed was as subtle as a scent, as faint as a glimmer in the corner of an eye. She could find it only through him.

That piqued her. He was royal kin, but she was royal line.

He was her hunting hound. She let him draw her onward through the swirl of worlds. They clustered near the edge of the shadow, gleaming like foam on a dim and stony shore.

She who was a living Gate had never seen nor imagined such a thing as this. There was no worldroad, no simple skein of worlds. It was a much greater, much more complex thing, too great for mortal comprehension.

He rode these shifting airs as if born to them. She, earthbound, could only cling to him and be drawn wherever he went.

He circled a cluster of worlds far down that grey shore. The tide lapped but did not quite overwhelm them. They gleamed like pearls, or like sea-glass.

He had begun to descend. Broad wings beat and hovered. His eyes were intent, fixed on the worlds below.

Without warning the sea rose up and clawed the sky. It seized the tiny thing circling in it, struck it, smote it down.

They whirled through darkness. Winds buffeted them. His wings were gone. He clung as tightly to her as she to him, rolling and tumbling through infinite space.

She flung out a lifeline, a thread of pure desperation. It caught something, pulling them up short, dangling in the maelstrom of wind and shadow. Hand over hand she climbed up the line, with his dead weight dragging at her until he gripped the line below her. She hesitated, dreading that he would let go and fall, but he was climbing steadily, if slowly.

Light glimmered above them. Wind buffeted them, striving to pluck them free. Her fingers cramped; her arms ached unbearably. She set her teeth and kept on.

The thread began to rise as if drawn from above. The wind howled, raking flesh from bone and body from spirit.

The Heart of the World hung below her. She reached for it with the tatters of her magic, seeking the power that had sustained her and every Gate-mage since the dawn of the world.

Just as she touched it, the darkness struck. It had been waiting like a great raptor poised above its prey. It roared down with power incalculable.

There were wards, walls, structures of magic so strong and so ancient that they had been reckoned impregnable. They melted as if they had been no more than a wish and a dream. All the woven elegance of spells and workings, remembrances of mages eons dead, great edifices of art and power, crumbled and fell into nothingness.

The Heart of the World was gone. It had whirled away below her, drowned in darkness. The place where it had been, woven in the core of her magery, was echoing, empty.

This could not be. The Heart of the World was not a place, nor a world. It was a living incarnation of magic.

The dark had devoured it, swallowed it, consumed it. It was rendered into nothingness, just as the worlds had been beyond the lost Gates.

Shocked, shattered, stunned almost out of her wits, she fell into light. A grunt and a gasp marked Daros' fall beside her. She was far too comfortable on real and living ground to move or speak. That was cool stone under her, or—tiles?

Tiles indeed. She knew them well. Painfully she lifted her head. The two of them lay in a heap in the innermost shrine of the Temple of the Sun in Starios. The light about them was pure clean sunlight flooding through the dome of the roof. For a long blissful moment she basked in it, sighing as pain and fear melted away. Her whole being was a hymn of thanks to the god who had freed her soul from the black wind.

Daros groaned and rolled onto his back. His eyes narrowed against the light, but he did not flinch or cover them.

Movement caught Merian's eye. A pair of priests stood staring at them. Both were young, in the robes of novices; their eyes were wide, their mouths open in astonishment. One of them held a basket of flowers, the other clutched an armful of clean linens. They had come to tend the altar.

She rose stiffly. The novice with the flowers dropped onto his face, hissing at his companion to do likewise. "Lady!" he bleated. "Lady, forgive, we didn't recognize you, we—"

"Please," she said, cutting across his babble. "Go on with what you were doing."

He took it as an order, and no doubt as a sacred trust. The young and eager ones invariably did. Daros, to her relief, said nothing; he creaked even more than she, and when he followed her from the shrine, he walked lame. He did not complain, which rather surprised her. She would have expected, at the very least, an acid commentary on the ailments of mages.

Her aches eased as she walked, though the void in the heart of her felt as if it would never heal. He said nothing of what he might be suffering, if indeed he felt anything at all. He was not bound to Gates as she had been; the Heart of the World was no great matter to him as it was to her—and as it would be to every mage of Gates in this world.

She had taken the inner ways of the temple, away from the eyes of priests and the faithful; there was not even a servant to stop and stare. They descended by narrow steps into a maze of tunnels, lit by a wisp of magelight that bobbed ahead of them.

Daros stumbled. She was almost too late to catch him. His weight dragged at her; his breath rasped in her ear. He had overtaxed himself—fool; child. But she was worse than that, for allowing him to do it.

There was nothing for it but to press on with what speed she could. The urgency in her had come close to panic. It took all the discipline of both mage and priest to keep walking, and not to drop the stumbling, gasping boy and run back into the light.

An eon later, though not so long by the turning of the sun, they came out at last in a forgotten corner of the palace. There was still some distance to go before they were truly safe; she paused in the dim and dusty cellar, plotting her path from a memory decades old.

She heard no footstep, sensed no presence, and yet her hackles rose. She could not whip about: Daros impeded her. She had to turn slowly, every sense alert, braced to drop him and leap if she must.

She nearly collapsed in relief. Her stepbrother lifted Daros in strong arms, taking no notice of his feeble protests, and said, "The others are in the autumn garden. Can you walk that far?"

"Easily," she said.

Hani's glance raked her mistrustfully, but he shrugged, sighed, turned to lead her onward.

The autumn garden grew in a corner of the palace wall, where the sun was warmest in that season, and there was shelter from the first blasts of winter. Flowers grew there even into the dark of the year; the fountains flowed later than in any other of the gardens, and birds sang long after they had left that part of the world.

It was nearly summer-warm when Merian came there, the sun shining in cloudless heaven, the water singing into the tiers of stone basins. This world knew nothing of darkness or loss—not yet. It was almost painful in its beauty.

By the lowest of fountains, on the porch of the little house that ornamented the garden, her mother sat with Urziad and Kalyi and the high priestess of the temple with her golden torque and her eyes that, though blind, could pierce to the heart. Their faces mirrored the shock that seemed set indelibly in hers. That they were alive and conscious spoke of their strength and the strength of their power. Through their eyes she could see the losses: mages dead or broken, Gates fallen, spells and magics in ruins.

The princess regent stirred, drawing Merian's eye. She shared the gift or curse of her line: she seemed hardly older than Kalyi, who was but a year past the Journey that had made her priestess as well as mage. People said that Merian was like her mother, though paler; she was gold and ivory, but Daruya was honey and bronze. Merian bowed to her as the chief of Gate-mages should to the regent of Sun and Lion. Even as she straightened, her mother drew her into a bruisingly tight embrace. "We thought we'd lost you, too," she said. "Whatever possessed you—"

"I did." Daros had startled them: he was conscious, struggling free of Hani's grip, swaying on his own feet. "I found him. I found the emperor."

Daruya wasted no time in foolish questions. "Where?"

"On the edge of the shadow," he said, "almost inundated by the tide."

"And you left him there?"

He faced her with a perfect lack of fear. "Lady, he's trapped. I barely found him, and I knew where to look. Before I could come closer, the tide drove me away. I did try, lady. I'll try again, but first I have to rest." That was not a thing he admitted easily; he was young and male and proud. But he was brave enough to tell the truth.

"You will not try again," Daruya said. "No one can. Do you understand, boy? The great Gates are gone. The Heart of the World—the center of our magic—is lost."

"But that's not—" Daros shut his mouth just before Merian would have shut it for him. He bent his head, concealing the rebellion in his eyes.

It seemed the pretense deceived the rest of them, though Merian was in no way taken in by it. Daruya addressed him as if the rest of it had never been said. She was not belittling the great loss; she was making it bearable by focusing on what might possibly be salvaged out of the ruin. "The emperor is safe? Only trapped?"

"I couldn't tell," Daros said without too palpable a sense of relief. "I could only see that he was alive, tossed in the storm-wrack."

"That's the best we can hope for," Daruya said levelly, "and better than many of us can claim. We've lost too many mages—in body or in spirit—and all our greater Gates. Thank the gods and the foresight of those who built them, many of the lesser Gates are still standing—they were built and sustained through the power of this world, which is still intact. We'll keep them open, but closely guarded, for as long as we can. Every ward and shield that we can raise, we will raise. And we will pray that when the war is over, we can find our emperor again, and bring him back." She drew herself up and stiffened her back. "You will rest and restore yourselves, both of you. Tomorrow I will have need of you—as of every mage with strength or wits to fight. Until then, be as much at ease as you can."

Daros bowed as if in either weariness or submission, but Merian did not believe in either. She kept her own tongue between her teeth and undertook to seem more convincingly obedient than Daros. He was out on his feet; she was a little tired herself. Sleep would serve them both well, whatever came after.

SEVEN

OF ALL THE OUTCOMES DAROS HAD EXPECTED, TO FIND HIMSELF A GUEST IN the palace in Starios was one of the more unlikely. He was given every comfort, even a pretty maid if he should be inclined; somewhat to his surprise, he was not. He was worn to the bone, and above all he needed sleep. His lack of interest had nothing to do with a certain haughty royal lady.

He slept like the dead, a sleep blessedly free of dreams. In that sleep, the raw edges of his mind began to knit, and powers taxed to the utmost began slowly to heal. When he woke, he felt as if he had been beaten with cudgels, inside and out.

He fully expected to find Merian sitting beside his bed, but the person there was almost a stranger. He knew the face, of course; Hani the prince, son of the regent's consort, was known even to layabouts in taverns. "Am I under guard?" Daros asked him.

The prince raised a brow. He looked remarkably like Daros' father, though his hair was black rather than copper; his voice too was very like, deep and soft, but the accent was of another country altogether. "Do you feel the need to be guarded?"

"That depends," said Daros. "Am I safe here? I seem to remember a sentence of exile."

"You're not in Han-Gilen, are you?" Hani yawned and stretched. "I'm to tell you that after you've rested sufficiently and bathed, and one presumes eaten, though that wasn't mentioned, the Lady Merian will see you."

Daros' lips twitched. It was like Merian to remember a man's bath but not his breakfast. "I'd best get to it," he said. "By your leave, my lord."

"Ah," said Hani, shrugging. "I don't stand on ceremony." He snapped his fingers. Servants came at the run with bath and clothes and, yes, breakfast.

The bath was welcome. The clothes were good but plain—not court dress. Daros widened his eyes somewhat but offered no other commentary. Neither the servants nor the prince remarked on the myriad bruises that stained his skin, though their hands were gentle, to spare him such pain as they could.

Hot water and clean clothes restored him rather well. Breakfast set him truly among the living. He did his best not to fall on it like a starving wolf. Bread so fine, cakes so sweet, had not passed his lips since he left Han-Gilen.

He ate less than he wanted but somewhat more than he needed; then he was ready to be taken to the princess. Hani was his guide; the servants, dismissed, vanished wherever servants went when their lords did not need them.

He was sure, well before he came there, that he was a prisoner after all, and he was going into a cell deep in the bowels of the palace. But his guide brought him out of the tunnels and into a different place, which had the air and the proportions of a noble residence. He supposed that it was Merian's house, or perhaps her brother's.

It was a handsome house, well kept, and apparently deserted. But he sensed human presence elsewhere within the walls, and not only in the room to which Hani led him.

It was a library, and she was in the middle of it, half-buried in books, shuffling rapidly among a half-dozen scrolls and scribbling on a bit of parchment. She glanced up, preoccupied, and said, "Hani. Where did you put Vanyi's book?"

Hani slipped a scroll from the bottom of the heap, unbound it, and handed it to her without a word. She did not thank him, or acknowledge Daros at all.

He could sulk, or he could peer over her shoulder to see what she was reading. He recognized a history or two, a very old grimoire of which he had thought his father had the only copy, and what seemed to be a compendium of songs and gnomic verses.

"What are you looking for?" he asked her.

"Help," she said. "Wards alone won't be enough. But nowhere is there any word of such a threat as this."

"Don't you have priests and mages to do this hunting for you?" Daros asked.

"They are," she said: "all those that aren't flattened by the loss of their center."

He was not sure he understood. "The Heart of the World? But—"

"You really don't feel it, do you?" She sounded almost exasperated. "When it went down, weren't you rent to the core of you?"

"No," he said. "I can feel a gap in the fabric of magic—an emptiness where once was a nexus of Gates—but it doesn't touch me at all. The worlds are still full of Gates, and most of those are still open. Those that are shut, the shadow took, just as it took your nexus."

"To the mages of Gates," she said, "the Heart of the World is the very heart and center of what they are. The other mages, lightmages, darkmages—their power is born and nurtured here, in this earth, this sun. But the power of Gates was contained there, in the Heart of the World."

"Not for me," he said. "Nor for you, either, or you wouldn't be sitting here, being impatient with me. How badly are your mages hurt?"

She seemed surprised that he would care. "There are a dozen dead. Another hundred might as well be. The rest look as if they will recover. The lesser Gates are still alive; that sustains them. But how—"

"I'm not a Gate-mage," he said.

"That is obvious." She shook herself. "You're a great Gate—as I am; as, it seems, Estarion is. It's inside you. You can still leave the world."

"So can you."

"Yes," she said, but not as if it mattered. She turned back to the books in front of her. "I had been hoping to find something that would show us how to find the emperor."

"I know that," Daros said. "I remember where I found him. I could find it again."

"But should you? The danger is worse than ever. If the shadow can swallow the Heart of the World, it most certainly can swallow you."

"It can swallow him, too, and whatever world or place of magic in which he's found refuge," said Daros. "Lady, the sooner we get him out, the better. I don't know that anything can live, once the dark tide has rolled over it."

"We must know what it is," she said. "Else how can we fight it? But how can we do that, if even you can't go near it without being battered half to death?"

All his bruises twinged at once. He set his teeth against them and said, "I know where he is now. I don't need the worldroad, or the sea of night, either."

He thought she might seize him, maybe to strangle him, maybe to kiss him, but she did neither. "If you go, you may not be able to come back. You said he was trapped. What good would it do to join him in his prison?"

"Maybe none," he said. "Maybe a little, if we discover what the enemy is. Who knows? Maybe we can even destroy it."

"As well expect a gnat to destroy a mountain," she said. She rubbed her eyes as if they troubled her, and drew a long shuddering breath. "If we only knew what it was!"

"The Forbidden Secrets," Hani said abruptly.

They both rounded on him. He met their stares calmly. "There is on the far side of the world," he said, "an order of—priests is not the proper word. Devotees? Adepts? They call themselves the servants of the Great Oblivion; they worship the night without moons or stars. Their fastness stands on the summit of heaven. It's said that only those blessed of their gods can visit it, still less live there, because the air is too thin for simpler mortals to breathe."

"Would they know of Gates and dark tides?" Merian demanded. "Are they mages?"

"Some may be," he said. "I only heard of them as a story long ago, before we came to live in this empire. But I've heard since of the knowledge that they keep, that they say was passed down to them by their gods. What that knowledge is, only the initiate knows; it's not even known how it's conveyed, though most likely it's written in books. Still, there are rumors of what may be in it, whispers of strange things, dark things, things that feed on stars."

"Things that feed on stars." Merian stroked the scroll in front of her, absently, as if it had been an animal. "The books, scrolls, inscriptions, whatever they are, are forbidden, you say. I gather their guardians will be somewhat reluctant to present them for our inspection, even with an imperial decree. It's not their empire, after all, or their emperor who is lost."

"Even to save the world?" Daros asked.

"My own mages hardly believe that," she said. "Do you think devotees of a hidden order on the other side of the world will be any more willing to hear me?"

"You could ask," he said.

Innocent, her eyes said, and she did not mean it as a compliment. He shrugged. "You *could* ask," her brother said.

"Find them," she said, "and ask them, if you have such hopes of them."

"I may do that," Hani said.

He wandered off. Daros would have liked to follow, but he was curious as to why she had summoned him. Surely it could not have been to watch her scowl at books that told her nothing.

At length she seemed to recall his existence. He had been reading the grimoire with widened eyes and guiltily beating heart, for he had never been allowed to touch its mate in his father's library. When he had tried, he had scorched his fingers, and been thrashed soundly into the bargain.

This had no wards on it, or none that could trouble him. Nor was there a great deal in the book to appall him. The magic was dark and the rites nearly all of blood, but he had seen worse elsewhere. Nothing in it spoke of shadows across the worlds.

Just as he came across a spell for opening Gates, which required the blood of a virgin boy and the soul of a saint, Merian said, "I set you free."

Daros blinked. "You— What?"

"You're free," she said. "You can go. Your sentence is commuted."

"But you just said—you need me!"

She raised her eyes to his face. They were tired, but there was something more, something that he could just begin to read. "I have no time for you," she said. "You lack training; your discipline is rudimentary. There's no leisure to train you, and none to protect you against the trouble you will inevitably get into if left to yourself. One of my mages will take from you your knowledge of the emperor's whereabouts, then bind your power within the circles of this world. You should suffer little inconvenience."

"You need me," he said stubbornly. "You said so yourself: I'm not bound by the limits of mages. I can go where they don't think to go, do what they can't imagine doing. I can find the emperor while they're still groping in the dark."

"But," she said with sweet reason, "you don't want or need to be involved in this war. Don't you miss your taverns? Your wine? Your women?"

"No," he said, and it was mostly the truth. "I want to finish what I started."

"Do you? Do you really?"

He paused. This was not a light thing that he was doing. Her eyes on him were bright gold. The tiredness was still in them, but she was stronger than he had thought. "I want to finish it," he said.

"If you would do that," she said, "I can't have you bumbling about like a weanling child. You will swear yourself to me by the laws of mages. I will not bind you with priest's vows, or with the lesser vows of my order. But you will be my sworn man. You will answer to me; whatever you do, you will do by my leave. If you cannot do this, then you will leave, and be bound, and never trouble my peace again."

Daros opened his mouth, then shut it. He could see the trap about him, the jaws open wide. She had plotted this with skill that bade him remember precisely who and what she was. She was royal born, bred to rule. She would use every weapon that she found to hand, however flawed, however ill-balanced it might be.

"I think," he said after a while, "that my decision was made some time since. You made sure of it, didn't you? You need me—but you don't want me free to do as I please."

"You are a spoiled and insolent child," she said, "without sense or discipline. You are also a gifted mage, a master of Gates, and the key to the emperor's return. I will use you, and if necessary destroy you."

"So you said," he said, "when you first sat in judgment over me." He knelt at her feet and held up his hands. "I swear myself to you, Lady of Gates, to serve you as I may."

"You will serve me," she said, "with your heart and your hand, with your strength and your magic, to death or beyond, while the world endures. Do you swear this, on pain of dissolution?"

"I swear," he said steadily.

She took his hands. Her fingers were cool and firm, but in the palm of her right hand was a living sun. She laid that against his own palm, and then against his heart. He gasped; it was as if she had pierced him with a white-hot blade. "You are bound," she said, "and freed. No power but mine may compel you. No oath can bind you, unless I choose to allow. You are my servant. Serve me well; and may the gods defend you."

He knelt with the blade of the Sun in him and a weird high singing in his ears. He had done many things that were irrevocable; trespassing in Gates was not the least of them. Yet this was something more. For once he did a thing for a purpose other than his own pleasure.

He wanted suddenly to run far and fast, and hide where no one could ever find him. He had hidden for so long, pretended to be of so little worth, that it was as if he had been stripped naked in front of the High Court.

Well, he thought, as to that, he was not at all ill to look on. Might not his mind and his magic be the same?

He let her raise him. She did not at once let go. Her eyes seemed caught in his face, as if something there enthralled her.

Daros the libertine would have slain her with a smile. Daros the royal servant lowered his eyes before she could see the smile in them. He was sure now of several things, but he did not think that she wanted to know any of them.

This was her house, that she shared with her stepbrother; he kept it up, oversaw the servants, looked after her with quiet competence. He had a wife and children, but they lived on the other side of the world, in the country in which both he and his father had been born. Here he seemed to have neither wife nor mistress; ladies of the court pursued him, but he was adept at evading them.

Daros did not go to court. Merian went as seldom as she could; she much preferred the company of priests and mages. Of late, with the great loss among the Gates, the mages needed her more than ever. If she had no time to tame a reckless boy, she had even less to trouble with courtiers.

Of Daros she expected little, but he decided the first day that he would keep himself at her disposal. She rapidly grew accustomed to his presence in her shadow.

The shadow on the stars was growing stronger and coming closer. In his darker moments he was almost tempted to give way to it, but he was far still from despair. He wanted to live, for however long his world might have. He did not believe as too many of the mages did that now the Heart of the World was gone, this world was safe; the darkness was sated, and would not come closer. It would come—later rather than sooner, maybe, but there was no escaping it.

He was remarkably light of heart. "Better dead than bored," he said to Hani a Brightmoon-cycle after he swore himself into Merian's service.

Hani was a man of middle years and impeccable reputation, but behind the stern mask of his face he was still a wild boy. They were sharing a jar of wine that evening, while wind and rain lashed the walls. A fire burned on the hearth; there were cakes and fruit and roast fowl to go with the wine; and Merian had gone to bed, freeing them to be frivolous. Hani knew even more scurrilous songs than Daros did; he had taught Daros the most reprehensible of them.

In the silence after the song, Daros sensed as he often had of late that the tide was rising beyond the sphere of the moons. He said nothing of it, but Hani was a mage. "Will it be soon?" he asked.

Daros shrugged. "Who knows? Nothing's stopping it—but maybe there's a mage somewhere, or a Power, or a god, who can stand against it."

"You don't sound troubled," Hani said.

"Should I panic? We won't live any longer if I do."

Hani peered at him through the haze of the wine. "Ah. I keep forgetting. You're the living image of youth and ennui."

"I was," Daros said. "I set every fashion, and my whims were all the rage. I'm sadly fallen now. It seems I have a purpose apart from the cultivation of extreme taste. My old circle would be appalled."

"Are you?"

Daros laughed. "Terribly! But there's no help for it. I've become that most dreadful of creatures: a dutiful servant."

"May the gods avert," said Hani piously. He filled Daros' cup again, and then his own. They drank to duty—and to the horrors of courtiers. And with that, for a whim, to the tides of the dark, that came on inexorably, for all that anyone could do.

EIGHT

FATHER," SAID HANI, "WHAT DO YOU KNOW OF THE FORBIDDEN SECRETS?"
The regent's consort was an older, somewhat smaller image of his son. He had never had Hani's lightness of spirit, or else years of ruling at his lady's side had cured him of it, yet Daros did not find him either dull or excessively stern. He had been visibly glad to receive Hani, that bright morning a handful of days after the first storm of the winter; he greeted his son's companion with grave politeness, as if Daros' reputation did not precede him wherever he happened to go.

When the courtesies had been observed, Hani came direct to the point. His father's brows drew sharply together; the air chilled perceptibly. "Why do you wish to know of this?"

"My lord," Daros said, "we've all been looking for something, anything, that might tell us of what we face. These books or whatever they may be—do you know where they are?"

"Only in legend and rumor," the prince consort said. "The secrets and their keepers have an ill name in my country."

"Are they in Shurakan?" asked Daros.

"No," the prince consort said. "Such things would not be allowed there, even after the ban was lifted on mages and their workings. Rumor places them in the mountains that claw the face of heaven, far to the north of Shurakan."

Daros had been a poor scholar, but he had a tenacious memory. His mind saw the globe of the world, with the empire of Sun and Lion gleaming golden on half of it, and to the east of it the blue ocean, and the other side of that the land over sea, a broad plain rising up into mountains as lofty as stars. Deep in the midst of them, set like a jewel amid the snows, he saw the hidden kingdom of Shurakan beneath the mountain that was called the Spear of Heaven. North of Shurakan was a waste of ice and crag and stone. It was bleaker by far than Death's Fells, and even more remote.

He did not know precisely when he passed from memory to living vision. He was aware of the small audience chamber in the palace, and of the men in it; he knew when a servant brought food and wine, and when a messenger came from the regent with a matter that was of too little importance to call the prince consort away from his guests. All that, Daros was aware of, but in the same moment he was flying on wings of air above the jagged teeth of mountains.

The others had fallen silent, watching him. They did not, as Merian might have done, attempt to interfere. He felt Hani's presence like a warm handclasp, following him where he flew.

"Fascinating." That was the prince consort's voice, that deep burr with its accent of Shurakan. "She told us what he could do, but the reality is . . . fascinating."

"One can see why they bind mages with oaths and orders," Hani said.

"I don't think most of them are as strong as this."

"Not nearly," Hani conceded.

And all the while, Hani followed Daros over the mountains. Daros was hunting; he took little notice of the two who watched and judged. There was a nest of shadow among these peaks. It was not precisely the same as the dark thing that had swallowed so many worlds, and yet Daros would have reckoned that they were kin.

Hani's satisfaction warmed him. He did not give way to hope, not quite yet, but this was the closest to it that any of them had had.

His flight slowed. He hovered above a range of mountains. They were not as high as some about them, but still they rose halfway to heaven. On the side of a crag, built sheer into a cliff, he found what he had been seeking: a line of walls and the jut of a tower.

He might have descended to peer closer, but Hani held him back. "Not till we have reinforcements," he said.

He was only being wise. Daros sighed and withdrew, leaving the mountains behind, returning to the clear pale light of late autumn in Starios.

Father and son regarded him with expressions that struck him as altogether strange. Respect; a little awe. No one had ever been in awe of him before.

Mercifully, they did not speak of it. Hani said, "Merian has to know of this. Mother—"

"I'll see to that," his father said.

Hani clasped his father's hands and pressed them to his forehead. Daros bowed. The prince consort was already on his way out of the room.

Merian had been instructing young mages in the lesser arts. They, thank the gods, seemed barely shaken by the upheavals among their elders. As Daros paused by the door, he was nearly flattened by a swooping mageling, with a second in hot pursuit. He caught the first with his hands and the second with his magic, depositing the latter firmly on the nearest stool. He set the former beside her, smiled sunnily at both, and made his way through the swirl of airborne magelings.

Merian was in the midst of them, sitting at ease a man-height above the floor. She lifted a brow as Daros rose to join her, but did not pause in the flow of her instruction. He exercised himself to be patient, to listen; it was interesting, what she told them, and who knew? It might be useful.

It spoke well for the magelings that they barely blinked at the presence of a stranger. From the progression of whispers round the room, he would wager that any who had not known him when he came in would know him when the lesson ended.

Merian finished in leisurely fashion, admonished them to practice their lessons, and sent them out. Not all went willingly. Somewhat after the door had shut behind the last of them, Daros heard a squawk. One of the eavesdroppers had met the bite of Merian's wards.

"Tell me," she said.

"Surely you already know," said Daros.

"Only what Hani knows," she said. "He was with you, not in you. You think you've found some knowledge of the shadow?"

"Or something like it," Daros said. "I wasn't close enough to discover more."

"Can you go there?"

"Yes," he said with as much patience as he could muster.

She slanted a glance at him, but did not upbraid him for impudence. "Of course you can. Some of my masters of mages are tugging at the leash—they're clamoring to examine you, to discover everything that you can do. They'll wait till this is over, if there's a world left for any of us."

"I'm nothing remarkable," he said. "I'm an untrained, undisciplined mage; it's nothing more than that."

"We think it is," she said. "But there, we'll have that quarrel later. You'll lead an expedition of mages through your Gate. They will find what is to be found. You will guard the Gate."

He bit his tongue. He was sworn to her service; it was not his place to protest what orders she might give. But he had not surrendered his spirit. He spoke carefully, with, he hoped, a suitable degree of submission. "Will we leave soon?"

"Tonight," she said. "My mages are preparing themselves. If there is anything you would do—eat, rest—you should do it now. Your Gate will open at sunset."

"It will be dawn in those mountains," he said. "Do they want to invade the castle by day?"

"If the night's children are within," she said, "day is best."

He had to grant the wisdom of that. "May I have your leave to go?"

Her glance was suspicious, but she did not tax him with it. "Go," she said.

He ate; that was well thought of. He would rest when all was done. He found the mages in one of their halls, a room like the one in which Merian had instructed her pupils: wide, high, bright with light from its tall windows. There were six mages; they were all young, with the look of warriors rather than scholars. One, a woman of the Isles, was dancing in a shaft of sunlight, in a whirl of blades. No living hand wielded them; they hummed like a swarm of bees.

Daros walked carefully wide of those. The others prepared themselves in less dangerous ways, either sitting apart with eyes closed and mind focused inward, or conversing quietly by a window.

Those three looked up as he came toward them. No awe there, only a long, slow, measuring stare, and a slight curl of the lip from the yellow-haired Asanian with the well-worn weapons. He was not wearing either the robes or the veils, but his cheek bore the thin parallel scars of an Olenyas, a bred warrior. There were five scars: he ranked high, though not as high as the master of his order.

Daros had training in the arts of war; no one of royal or noble lineage could escape it. But he was not the prince of fighters that this man must be. He bowed slightly and smiled, a salute of sorts, and said, "Good day to you all."

They nodded or bowed in return, civil but no more. Even that was better than he had expected. "My name is Daros," he said. "If we're to fight and die together, should I know yours?"

They thought about it. At length the tall woman from the north named herself and each of her fellows. She was Irien; the Olenyas was Perel. The others were Kalyi of the Isles and Adin from the Hundred Realms and the twins Sharai and Lirai who had been born in Shurakan. They had the same face and accent as Hani and his father, or for that matter Daros' own mother.

"It is said," said Perel, "that you have no weight or substance whatsoever; that your spirit is a leaf blown on the wind."

Daros smiled. "It's also said that I've never left a woman unsatisfied or a tavern-keeper unpaid. Surely that counts for something?"

"We're trusting our lives to you," Kalyi said. "Tell us why we shouldn't be afraid."

"Of course you should," he said. "Fear will keep you honest. We know nothing of this place to which we go—only that dark powers built it and live in it still. I'll find what they keep, and learn what I may. May I trust you to protect me?"

"But you were not—" Irien began.

"Let him tell us," said Perel. "What is this plan of yours? Is it better than ours?"

"I have one use in the world," Daros said. "I'm a fine hunting hound. Whatever I seek, I find. Does any of you share that gift?"

They glanced at one another. All six were about him now, drawn together in a circle. It might be protection; it might be a threat. He chose not to be afraid.

"None of us is a hunter," Perel said. "We are all warrior-mages."

"Warriors to hunt a secret." Daros sighed, shrugged, smiled. "Ah well. I'll hunt, you'll guard. Who leads you?"

Their eyes slid toward Kalyi. He bowed to her. "Madam general. I will find the book or whatever it is that holds the knowledge we need. The rest is yours. Only be sure that when my hunt is over, all your troops are within reach. When we go, we'll go as fast as we can."

Again they exchanged glances. "Better," said Perel.

Irien lifted a shoulder in a shrug. "Certainly not worse. Though if he's our Gate, the last thing we want is to risk him in the fight."

"I'm not going to fight," Daros said. "I'm going to hunt. *You* will fight. Keep me safe, and bring us all out alive. That's all I ask of you."

"A simple thing," said Perel. "Indeed." Suddenly he grinned. "I like this plan."

"*She* won't," Kalyi said.

"She told us to trust the Gate," said Perel.

"So she did," Irien said. "Though I don't think she meant—"

"She meant that we should trust him," Perel said. "I'll risk it. After all, if he endangers us, it's a simple matter to kill him."

Daros laughed and applauded him. "A man after my own heart! Shall we two go, and leave the rest safe here?"

"You trust me as far as that?" Perel asked him with an arch of the brow.

Daros' flick of the hand took in the scars on Perel's cheek, and the number and quality of his weapons, both open and hidden. "I think I can trust you to keep me both safe and honest."

"We will all do that," Kalyi said grimly. "If you can rest, do it now. There's not much time left."

"Madam," said Daros with a bow and a flourish. Her glance was sour, but he thought there might be a hint, a merest glimmer, of softening about the mouth.

He would rest, for a while. They would not go without him: they could not. He was their Gate.

He went back to his room in Merian's house. It had been cleaned; the bed was fresh and scented with herbs. A bag waited by the door. He did not doubt that it was filled with whatever the servants had decided he would need.

He had been asleep on his feet, but once he lay down, he remained stubbornly awake. He was not afraid, not enough to trouble him. The Gate within had fixed on the place where he must go, but he was aware also, deep down, of the emperor's presence, nearly lost in shadow. Part of him wanted to go, to find Estarion, to bring him back. The rest knew that he could not do both at once.

He must have dozed: he opened his eyes, and Merian was sitting on the bed beside him. For a moment before she could have been aware that he had roused, he saw a face that she had not shown him before: soft, reflective, a little sad. He wanted to kiss her, to make the sadness go away.

She came to herself with all her armor intact, and the hard bright edge that forbade anything so familiar as a kiss. Because he was born contrary, he took her hand and kissed it, and held it to his heart. She let it rest there for the whole of a breath before she snatched it away. "Are you a general?" she demanded. "Or a lord of mages?"

He raised his brows. "Why, no. But I am a hunter."

"So I've been told." She knotted her fingers in her lap, glaring at them as if they had been as intractable as he. "You have no gift for obedience. I could bind you, and so compel it, but like an idiot, I prefer to trust your sworn word. Will you be obedient to Kalyi and do as she bids?"

"If her bidding isn't mad or suicidal, yes," he said.

She looked ready to slap him. She breathed deep, straightened her shoulders and face, and said, "She has convinced me to let you lead the expedition. But if she sees the need for a change, you will do exactly as she tells you. Do you understand?"

"Yes," he said. Then: "Is she in a great deal of trouble?"

"Not as much as you," she said. "Come back alive, with knowledge that we need, and I may—I may—forgive you both."

"Forgiveness is worth fighting for," he said. He kissed her hands again, quicker than she could elude him, and sprang to his feet. The shadows were growing long. He held out his hand. "Come with me," he said.

She was taken aback by his presumption, so much so that she had yielded before her wits recovered. He offered no insolence past that of taking her hand in his. Hand in hand they went to find the rest of the hunt.

NINE

THEY WERE ALL EXPECTING A RITE OR A GREAT WORKING. DAROS HATED TO disappoint them, but he needed his strength for what might come. The six of them gathered about him, linking arms in a circle, strong as a shieldwall. Merian reluctantly retreated. He was sorry to let go her hand, but this was a deadly thing they did. The imperial heir could not risk herself so recklessly.

He kept his eyes on her as he opened the Gate within. The last he saw of that place was her slender figure in the fading sunlight, the gold of hair and eyes washed over with the color of flame, or of blood.

He brought them to a sheltered place just below the crag, a hollow in the stone that was not quite deep enough to be a cave. Merian had warned them, but they were greatly disconcerted to travel so quickly, without resort to the worldroad.

There was a little time for them to recover while he ventured up the track that led from the hollow. It was not quite dawn; the air was thin and cold. He was glad of the cloak that he had brought from the Fells, and the small working that let him breathe here on the roof of the world.

He peered up the steep slope. The castle loomed above. No light shone from it; no banner flew from its turret. Yet there was life within, a flicker of living presence.

He looked for wards, but found nothing that spoke to him of any such thing. Did they trust in the remoteness of this place, and in the terror of its name?

"It could be a trap," Perel said, coming up beside him. He had recovered first of all the mages; he was still a little white about the lips, but his eyes were steady, staring upward. "They'll lure us in, then strip us of flesh and souls."

Daros shuddered in spite of himself. "You know something of them?"

"I've made a study of the dark arts," Perel said.

"Darkmagery?"

"Nothing so innocuous," said Perel. "Black sorcery, forbidden arts—we've banished them from the empire. But they're still alive in the world beyond our borders."

"So I see," Daros said.

The Olenyas looked him up and down. "You do, don't you? No wonder the mages are in such a taking. You're not supposed to exist. We want all our mages neatly bound up in packets and arranged on a shelf. Not racketing about the world, being much too strong for anyone's good."

"I hope to be worth something here," Daros said dryly. He cast his magic up like a line. Part of him was shuddering in instinctive horror; part was raising wards, forging armor of light. This was indeed kin to the thing beyond Gates. It drew its strength from the old dark powers, from blood and putrefying flesh, from sacrifice of the living soul, and from surrender of all light to the devouring dark.

One learned in the Hundred Realms to understand the dark as soul's twin to the light, bound together with it, inextricable and inevitable. Without dark there could be no light; without light the dark could not endure. This was nothing so beautiful or so balanced. It was to the Dark Goddess, and darkmagery, as diseased and rotting flesh to the clean-picked bones of the vulture's prey. It was a perversion, a sickness.

He had never understood the old zeal of the priests of the Sun against the powers of the dark. When he heard tales of the Sunborn, Merian's firstfather, that told of his relentless hatred of all that was of the dark, he had been suitably censorious; for after all, as great a king and conqueror as the man had been, his beliefs had been sorely misguided. Now at last Daros saw what the Sunborn must have seen.

He swallowed bile, gagging on it, and forced himself to look at what crouched above. It was a fortress of age-worn stone, built into the crag. He counted a score of living beings within—men, he thought, though he could not be sure. They were bound with cords of darkness.

He was not hunting men, even men whose souls had been walled forever against the light. He needed knowledge—truth of what had overwhelmed the worlds. If not a book, then an image, a song, an inscription, anything at all.

The mages had recovered: he sensed them behind him. He did not turn to look at them. Wordlessly he began to climb.

Long before he came to the top, he knew that this place needed no protection but itself. The track was narrow, and in places sheer. It needed the agility of a mountain cat, or of a mage, to ascend that path. The slightest slip or slackening would cast him down a thousand man-lengths, and shatter him among the crags.

The castle was aware of him. Its people, no; he would have sworn to that. But the stones themselves, and the darkness woven through them, knew that a stranger had come.

He made himself as small and as harmless as he could: innocuous, insignificant, no danger at all. He cloaked himself in that surety. He was a breath of wind gusting up the mountain, a glimmer of sunlight falling across the gate.

A firm hand of magic closed about him. "Let me," Kalyi said. He resisted; he had not learned to trust anyone else's power. But he was not altogether a fool. He relinquished the wards and the shield to her, however reluctantly, and turned again to his hunt.

The gate was wrought of iron, enormous and impossibly heavy. Yet it was balanced so lightly that if it happened to be unbarred, the thrust of a hand could shift it. Perel and Irien moved past the rest, laying hands on it, raising powers that made the small hairs prickle along Daros' arms and down his spine. The wall and tower above them seemed to stir in its sleep, half-rousing, opening a blurred eye and peering down.

They passed through the gate as if through a wall of mist. There was darkness within, thick and palpable, and a faint charnel stink. The mortar that bound these stones had been mixed with blood.

They paused in a shadowed court. At a glance from Kalyi, the twins slipped away along the colonnade. Adin and Irien went ahead. Kalyi, with Perel, stood still by the gate, enfolding Daros in the cloak of their magic.

Daros sighed faintly, trying not to breathe too deep of the tainted air. The walls, the tower above him, even the brightening sky, weighed heavy on his spirit.

He turned slowly. The heaviness was stronger—there. Ahead and to the left, toward a corner of the colonnade. His guardian hounds went with him, Perel ahead, Kalyi behind. His shoulderblades tightened. But her knives were not for him—not while he served her order's purposes.

It was a great effort to set one foot in front of the other, to go deeper into the maw of the castle, and not turn and run. He was aware in his skin of the twins in a dim hall, wrapped in shadows, watching as a skein of men with shaved heads and black robes wound, chanting, among the pillars. The shiver along his ribs was the presence of Irien and Adin, seeing to it that the way ahead was clear: dim passages, sudden turnings, ascents or descents that seemed set at random to catch the unwary.

They had begun to veer off the track, diverted without knowing it, shifted subtly aside by the power that waited in the castle's heart. He could warn them, or he could follow the straight way and let them be drawn to some semblance of safety.

His own guards slowed little by little, almost imperceptibly. He caught a hand of each, and set a spark in each mind: a binding to follow him wherever he led. Perel yielded to it with a twist of wry amusement. Kalyi resisted; but Daros was in no mood to be gentle. She, thank the gods, had wits enough to give way before she broke, though he would pay for his presumption.

Better to face her wrath later than to pay for her weakness now. His companions' rites and vows made them vulnerable. The power here knew mages and priests of the Sun, and turned on them as on an enemy. Daros it seemed not to perceive at all. He was small, he was harmless, he carried no taint of the Sun's priesthood. It took no more notice of him than of a rat in the wall.

Even ignored, he felt the power growing darker, deeper, eating away at his memory of light. He must come to the center of it, but whether he would be alive then, or sane, he did not know. He could only press forward.

These halls were deserted. The order must once have been numerous and strong: the castle was ample to house hundreds, even thousands. The score that were left huddled together in a tower near the outer wall.

There were guards ahead of him, but they were not human. They crouched like great beasts athwart the path that he must follow. Their eyes were shut, their bodies still; they might have been carved of stone. Yet they were alive, although they slept. Their dreams were all of the terrible light, how it burned, how it destroyed what they were bound to protect.

He was a shadow, a breath of wind, a skitter of leaf across the floor. The sun did not stain him. The light did not rule him. He was utterly a part of this place and this darkness.

The guardians of the secret crouched on either side of its door. To the eye they were a pair of stone lions, each sitting upright, one paw uplifted, one resting on the globe of the world. Their eyes were living darkness.

Daros paused between them. They focused outward, not on him at all, and yet the force of their watchfulness buckled his knees. It was all he could do to shield himself and his companions, and walk forward, and keep both his fear and his purpose buried deep.

The door had no earthly substance. It melted before him. The heart of the darkness was almost painfully ordinary. It was a room, bare, with no beauty of carving or gilding. There was no inscription, no carving or painting, no book, nothing that might contain knowledge as his people understood it. Only a wooden table such as one might see in any poor man's house, and on the table a bowl no more beautiful than the room. It was made of unfired clay, the color of drab earth, and not well shaped, either; its rim was crooked, and it sat awry.

Kalyi moved away from Daros. He reached too late to pull her back. The shield stretched and snapped. She staggered and fell to her hands and knees in front of the table.

The thing that came down had neither shape nor substance. It seemed to grow out of the bowl, pouring over the table, hovering above Kalyi's bent head. It reared like a snake. Daros cried out, scrambling together his power. The dark thing struck.

He leaped, not at Kalyi, but at the table. The bowl writhed in his hands like a living thing. He could see—he could feel—know—understand—

He thrust the bowl at Perel and spun. The dark thing coiled about Kalyi. He struck it with an arrow of pure light.

It burst asunder. The floor rocked underfoot.

"The book!" Perel cried. "Where—"

Daros gathered all six of them together, wherever in the fortress they were. Something was surging up from below, some child of old Night, waking from a long sleep to a terrible wrath.

"Take the bowl," Daros said to Perel, quite calmly. "Bring it to her. The secret is in it. Tell her."

"But—"

Daros silenced him with a lift of the hand. The truth was as clear as daylight, as sharp as a sword. It was in the bowl, which contained all the world. He knew where he must go. What he must do . . . that would come to him in time.

The Gate in him was open. It must be shut before the child of Night came up out of the earth. He thrust Merian's mages through, and the bowl with them. The floor bucked under him; he struggled to keep his feet. The Gate had begun to fray.

His heart was hammering. He sucked in a breath and leaped. Even as the Gate swallowed him, the tower crumbled in ruin. A vast maw opened below, jagged with teeth. The castle whirled down into the oblivion to which it had been consecrated.

Daros too fell into dark, but it was no earthly night. The devourer of Gates had found him. Only one spark of light offered refuge. He spun toward it. Darkness clawed at him. It burned like hot iron, shredding flesh and spirit. He twisted wildly. The spark was close—so close—if he overshot it—if he fell short—

Hope was all he had, and knowledge that had flooded into him when he touched the bowl, knowledge more complete than could ever have been written in a book. He clung to it as he whirled down through the darkness.

TEN

THE TOWN WAS CALLED WASET. IT WAS A GREAT CITY IN THIS COUNTRY, THIS narrow line of green between the river and the desert. To Estarion's eye it was little larger than a village, full of small brown people like none he had seen before. They were somewhat like the people of the Nine Cities, but browner, thinner, with long dark eyes in sharp-cut faces. They chattered like birds as he passed, staring, pointing, running after him. And yet the oddity of his breeding that had vexed him all his life, Asanian eyes in the northern face, did not frighten them at all.

They were calling him a god. Gods to them wore the bodies of men and the faces of beasts and birds; he, taller than any man they knew and darker by far, with his eagle's beak and his lion-eyes, was perfectly in keeping with their belief.

Tanit was the queen of these people. There was sorrow in her, for she had lost her husband to the things that ruled the night, but she was not consumed by grief. Estarion, searching in her eyes for the image of a memory, saw a man rather too much older than she for easy companionship, loved more like an uncle than a lover, but she had felt herself well served by the bargain.

Estarion understood royal marriages. He had had nine properly noble wives, and had loved a commoner whom he could not marry. Of all the things that made a man, love was the one he had thought of least since he left his empire behind. Now he could not help but think of it; he had thought of it since first he saw the queen bending over him, with her odd and striking beauty and the clear light of her spirit shining through.

This was a hot country. The women dressed sensibly for the heat: wrappings of thin white cloth about their bodies, baring the breasts more often than not, or if they were young or servants, they went naked but for a cord about the middle. They were easily, casually delighted to be women, and they loved to be admired. Those whose eyes he caught were more likely to smile than to turn away.

Tanit would not meet his glance, unless he startled her into looking up. Yet of them all, only she drew his eye, and she held it for much longer than was proper. She was not the most beautiful and she was far from the most alluring, but when she was there, he could see no other woman.

She saw him settled in her palace, which would have been a middling poor lord's house in his empire, but it was reckoned very great here. Her servants were as adept as he could ask for, and the house was clean—bright and airy, with painted pillars and a courtyard full of flowers. The food they served him was simple, harsh gritty bread and thin sour beer; they promised a feast later, but this was part of the rite of welcome.

He ate and drank for courtesy, and because he was hungry and thirsty. The servants kept changing. They were all making excuses to wait on him, to look on the god who had come from beyond the horizon.

It had been a long while since he was in a palace, but old habits died hard. The manner, the smile, the habit of charming servants, because servants could make a lord's life either effortlessly easy or unbearably difficult, wrapped about him like an old familiar mantle.

He was offered a bath and a clean kilt; the servants there were women, and young, and frank in their approval. They made him laugh, and be as glad as ever that his blushes never showed.

The queen found him so, clean and decorously kilted, with a pair of maids taking turns combing his new-washed hair. It was thick and it curled exuberantly, even wet; it gave them occasion for much merriment. On a whim he had let them shave his beard with their sharp flaked-stone razors; it had been long years since his cheeks were bare to the world, but in this heat he was glad of it, even as odd and naked as it felt.

He was rubbing his newly smooth chin when she came. Her stride checked; her eyes widened a fraction. That surprised him. He did not share the curse of excessive beauty that beset the boy from Han-Gilen, but it seemed that the canons were different here. She was frankly enthralled; and that made him blush.

She recovered more quickly than he. He was a god, after all, her shrug said. Her words were properly polite. "I trust my lord is well served?"

"Very well, my lady," he said.

She bowed slightly, regally. She had not the piquant prettiness so common here; her features were more distinctly carved, her face longer, more oval, her nose long and slightly arched. Her skin was like cream intermixed with honey. She was beautiful, and yet she did not know it at all. In her own mind she was gawky, gangling, too long of limb and plain of face to be anything but passable.

He would change that canon. It was fair recompense for her conviction that he was as beautiful as a god. He smiled and bowed slightly where he sat, and said, "Your pardon, lady, that I can't rise to do proper reverence. Your maids are lovely tyrants."

"I did command them to do their best for you," she said with her eyes lowered, but her voice had a smile in it.

"Sit, then, lady, and ease my captivity."

She sat on a stool near the bath, perched on its edge as if poised for flight. As she settled there, a small brown animal came stalking through the door.

It was a cat, or a creature like a cat; but unlike the palace cats of Starios, who had been large enough for a child to ride, this one was hardly longer than Estarion's forearm. Nonetheless it had the same keen intelligence and the same white-hot core of magic. It, unlike the humans here, would meet his eyes, gold to gold; it blinked slowly, deliberately, and said, *"Mao."*

"Mao," he replied gravely.

The cat blinked again and crossed the room in three long leaping strides. The third launched it into his lap. He hissed as it landed; its claws were needle-sharp. But he did not recoil, nor would he ever have flung the cat off.

It unhooked its claws from his stinging thigh and sat, and began to bathe itself with great concentration. It did not mind that he ran a finger down from its ears to its tail, finding its fur smooth and pleasingly soft. He found a spot that itched; it began to purr, as loud almost as one of his long-gone ul-cats.

As if that were a signal, a second cat, larger and somewhat darker, appeared from a corner that had been empty an instant before. It coiled about his feet, purring even more loudly than the first.

"The god and goddess welcome you," Tanit said. She sounded unsurprised and rather pleased.

The maids were less circumspect. "Now we know you're truly to be trusted," said the impudent one with the flower in her hair.

"I'm honored to be approved by such noble judges," Estarion said.

"So you should be," said Tanit. "These are the divine ones, the gods who walk in fur. They graciously accept our service, and bless us with their presence."

"Yes," Estarion said. "I see the fire of heaven in them. They're powers in your world."

"They are gods," she said.

He inclined his head and slanted a smile that caught her before she was aware. She smiled back. It was a wonderful smile, brightly wicked, though all too swiftly suppressed.

It was not time yet to touch her, but he could say, "Beautiful one, you should never hide your splendor. It well becomes a queen."

Her lips set in a thin line. "There is no need to flatter me, my lord."

"I tell you the truth," he said.

She rose abruptly. "Come, my lord. The feast is waiting."

His hair was combed but not plaited. He bound it out of his face with a bit of golden cord, and let the rest be. She was already at the door. He followed her with an escort of cats: both of the gods-in-fur of this place had elected to follow him.

It was good to be favored by cats again. He would like to be favored by the queen; but that, the gods willing, would come.

The court of Waset was waiting for him in a hall of painted pillars, seated at tables banked with flowers. The mingled scents of flowers and unguents and humanity were almost overpowering. He did his best to breathe shallowly as he walked down the length of the hall, beside and a little behind the queen.

The courtiers were not as open in their admiration as the children of the city, but they were wide-eyed enough. He saw the marks of grief on many of them, scars of loss and remnants of shadow. As fierce as the sun of this world was, it still had to give way to night; and in the night came the terror.

But it was daylight still, and they gathered in a guarded city. They dined on roast ox and fresh-baked bread and fruits of the earth, flavors both familiar and unfamiliar, and one great joy of sweetness. This world like his own had honey, and that was very well indeed.

They did not have wine; he regretted that. Their beer was a taste he had no great yearning to acquire. But he endured it. He had eaten and drunk worse in his day, and lived to tell of it.

He was not asked to entertain this court. That was for the musicians and the dancers, the singers with the voices like mating cats, and last of all, as the shadows lengthened, the small wizened man in the white kilt, whose voice was larger than all the rest of him put together.

He told the tale of the darkness. "It began to come upon us in the days of our late king, may he live for everlasting. There had always been walkers in the night, powers that had no love for the day, but this was a new thing, a terrible thing. It came out of the lands of the dead, from the horizons to the west, running with jackals in the night and vanishing with the coming of the day.

"For a long while no one knew it for what it was. The night was as dark as ever, and there were lions, crocodiles, nightwalkers and things that snatch children from their mothers' arms as they sleep. But this was stronger, darker, hungrier. It crept through villages and stole all the men and women who were young and strong, and slaughtered the weak and the children. Men would wake to find their gardens stripped bare or their herds gone, and the herdsmen gutted and cast before the doors of their houses.

"When our king had been on his throne for two hands of years, the night that had been perilous became truly terrible. Until then the dark things had never come close to the city; they skulked along the edges and raided the border villages, but round about our walls, men were safe. In that year, the dark things raided closer, and took more men and women, and in their wake left a hideous slaughter.

"Word came in from Gebtu, from Ta-senet, from Ombos—even from the chieftains of the south. They were all beset. It was everywhere, that horror. Traders were few on the river; they no longer came from far away. Every man was driven into his own town or city. Each kingdom had no choice but to protect its own. Trade, embassies, even wars and quarrels—all were ended. The world had closed in upon itself, and we were shut within our own boundaries like cattle within the fences of a field.

"Here in Waset, as everywhere, people had begun to take refuge in the city, and little by little the villages emptied of their weak and their fearful. The brave and the obstinate remained, and fools who swore that there was nothing walking the night. But none of them walked or sailed far, not any longer.

"In that tenth year of the king's reign, the river's flood that gives us the rich black earth for the tilling was the lowest that it had been in the memory of the oldest of the river-god's priests. It barely rose above its banks, barely dampened the edges of the fields. The gods' curse was on us, and for all that we did to propitiate them, they only sent us a plague on the cattle and an army of walkers in the night.

"The enemy had no face. It was shadow incarnate, darkness visible. It had no name to give it substance; it was living nothingness. But in that void were claws, and teeth to rend both flesh and souls.

"A priest went out one night. He was a very holy man, consecrated to our lord the sun, and the light of the god was upon him. He thought to speak with this thing if he might, to discover what it was, and perhaps to bless it and invoke the grace of the god upon it, and either overcome or destroy it.

"They found him in the morning with no drop of blood in his body, and his head sundered from it and laid in his lap as he sat against the wall of the city. His eyes had been taken away, made as if they had never been. To this day, men who saw it wake screaming from their sleep."

There was a silence. Tears ran down the queen's face, tracking through the paint which she wore like a warrior's armor. Estarion did not mean to trespass, but her pain was so strong, her memory so distinct, that he saw what she saw: not the priest who had died before she came to be the king's bride, but the king himself, drained of blood as the priest had been, but not only his head was severed and his eyes unmade. Each separate limb was torn from the rest. They had found every part of him except one, and that seemed a brutal mockery: his manly organ was lost, nor was it ever found.

All of those who went out with him were gone, save the men who had been nearest him. They had heard nothing, seen nothing in the suffocating darkness, until it was gone and the dawn had come. They were alone, with their king strewn at their feet.

"No one knows what this is," the queen said at length, "or what it wants of us or of the world. The dark gods—they want blood and souls. Their needs are simple, their rites known, though spoken of in whispers. This seems to want what the dark gods want, but all efforts to propitiate it have only made the night more terrible. Sometimes it lets a fool or a wanderer live, or satisfies itself with the stripping of a field or the running of a herd. It has no pattern to it, no weaving of earthly sense."

"And yet," said a portly personage who sat not far from the queen, "it is not random or capricious, like the wind across the red land. It has will; it has malice, living and potent. None of us has power to stand against it."

That was manifestly true. The only magic here resided in the cats who deigned to share Estarion's lap. There were priests in the hall, but they were not mages; nor was there a mage anywhere among these people. They were defenseless against any power that chose to advance against them.

No, he thought; not altogether. The sun's light protected them, and it seemed that the walls of the city had some power, too, or else the enemy did not choose, yet, to pass through them.

They were all staring at him. His expression must be alarming. He smoothed it and said, "I don't know what power I have against this; but whatever I do have, I place at your disposal."

They glanced at one another. These were courtiers, nobles and priests, and like all their kind, they were born suspicious. "Suppose," said one of those nearest the queen—not the priest who had spoken before, but an elegant man in a heavy golden collar—"that you tell us who and what you are, and why you have come. With all due respect, of course," he said, bowing in his seat.

Estarion bowed in return. "I come from beyond your horizon. My name is difficult for your tongue to encompass. Your lady has named me Seramon; that will do, if it pleases you. I am a priest of the Sun, and the Sun is my forefather. I was hunting shadow on the other side of your sky, and found it lapping the shores of this world. My own world is not yet threatened, but will be soon. If it can be stopped here—if it can be driven back—" He drew a breath. "What I am . . . have you workers of magic here?"

"Indeed," said the priest, "we work magic who serve the gods."

Estarion raised a brow. He could hardly call the man a liar, but there was not one grain of honest magic in that well-fed body. "May I ask what you reckon among the magical arts?"

"He's a spy!" someone cried, back among the pillars. "He wants to know our powers, so that he can destroy us."

"I have no fear," said the priest, although his breath had quickened a fraction. "Am I to understand, lord, that you also are a worker of magic?"

"I am," said Estarion. "And you?"

"I am a master of the hidden arts," said the priest. "In the morning, perhaps we may meet in a less public place, and speak as master to master?"

"I would be honored," Estarion said.

"Show us now!" cried the man who had spoken before. He had come out from the pillars and stood in the light: a young man no older than Daros, with the passion of youth and the suspicion of a much older and wiser man. "Show us what you are. But promise us one thing: that you'll harm none of us here. Swear to it!"

Estarion bowed to that wisdom, however headlong the expression of it. "I will not harm you," he said. "You have my word."

"By the Sun your father?"

"By the Sun my forefather," Estarion said.

He rose. Some of those closest drew away, but Tanit sat still, watching in silence. He stepped down from the dais into the space where the dancers had been. It was empty now, lit by a shaft of sunlight through the open door. It was still some time until evening, but the shadows were growing long. All too soon, the night's terror would come.

He gathered the light in his hands and wove it as if it had been a garland of flowers. Breaths caught round the hall; he smiled. It was a simple magic, such as a child could perform, but it awed these courtiers. He bowed and presented his crown of light to the queen, offering it with a smile.

She stared at it. It shimmered, taking life from the Sun in his hand, the burning golden brand of his line. Slowly she stretched out her finger to touch the crown. It did not burn; that startled her. She lifted it with sudden decision, in hands that trembled just visibly. "It is beautiful," she said.

"Beauty for beauty," said Estarion. He flicked a finger. The crown lifted out of her hands and settled on her brows. Brave woman: she did not flinch.

He smiled sweetly at them all. "As for the great workings and displays of higher powers, I beg your indulgence; among my people they are not reckoned among the entertainments proper to a royal banquet."

"And why not?" the young man demanded. "Is there truly nothing else you can do?"

"Hardly," Estarion said.

"Then show us!"

Estarion sighed. He had been a fool to do as much as he had; it forced him to play out the game. He paused to gather the threads of his power. People were stirring, beginning to mutter. The boy with the loud voice curled his lip.

He never said what he had been going to say. Estarion brought down the lightning.

He broke nothing, burned nothing. When all of them could see again, they stared at the floor in front of him. In it was set the image of the Sun in his hand, as broad as his outstretched arms, gleaming like molten gold.

He raked his glare across the lot of them. "What more would you have, my lords? Shall I cleave the tiles under your feet? Lift the roof and leave you naked to the sky?"

"No," the boy stammered. "No, no, my lord. Please pardon—I didn't know—"

"Of course you didn't," Estarion said with edged gentleness.

That ended the banquet: even without the shock he had given it, the sun was sinking low. Those who did not live in the palace were eager to be home before the fall of dark. It could not be said that they fled, but they left quickly, without lingering over their farewells.

In a very little while, there was only Estarion in the hall, and the servants waiting to clear away the tables, and Tanit sitting like an ivory image. Her crown of sunlight had not faded with the day; it shone more brightly than lamps or torches.

He took her hands and lifted her unresisting to her feet. She looked up into his face—rather a long way, for although she was tall for a woman of her people, that was not even as high as his shoulder. But he never thought of her as small. She had a queen's spirit, high and proud.

"You are a king of your people," she said as if it had only just occurred to her.

"I was," he admitted, "somewhat more than a king."

"I see it," she said, "like a shining mantle. You left it, yes? To become a god."

He laughed in spite of himself. "I left to become a rootless wanderer, and then a shepherd. I'm no great lord of any world now."

"A god is somewhat more than a lord," she said. "You were sent to save us. The others don't understand. They're afraid. But you would never do us harm."

"I would hope not," he said.

The cats came padding down the table, among the plates and cups and empty bowls. The she-cat leaped to his shoulder; the he-cat sprang into her arms.

No magic? Maybe not as his own world would reckon it. But this queen of the people had power in no little measure. He paid it due reverence.

ELEVEN

WITH THE COMING OF NIGHT, SERVANTS DREW SHUTTERS ACROSS THE windows of the palace and hung amulets and charms on the lintels of the doors. Priests walked the walls, chanting and sending up clouds of incense. Guards took station in strong-walled towers. The bright and airy city of the day became the fortress city of the night.

After so many years, there were few left who could not sleep even amid such fear. Estarion would sleep soon, but first he had to know what the night was in this world. He saw the queen to her rooms, but did not go at once to that which he had been given. He went up instead, to the roof.

The last light was fading from the sky. He saw the jagged line of cliffs across the river to the west, blacker than black, limned in deep blue and fading rose. Stars crowded the vault of heaven, not so bright as those he had known, but far more numerous, scattered like sand across a blue-black shore. This world had but one moon, smaller than Brightmoon, and wan; it rode high, but what light it cast was dim and pallid.

There was no other light in the world. The city was dark, walled against the night. Children here had grown to bear or beget children of their own, without ever seeing stars or moon.

Nothing yet stained the darkness. The night was clean, for a while. Not far away, a bird hooted softly, calling to its mate. Across the river he heard yipping and howling. Jackals, those would be: creatures like shrunken direwolves, scavengers and eaters of carrion.

Tonight he did not wait for the shadow. He was more weary than he had wanted anyone to know. He would rest, if he could, and in the morning call on the priest who laid claim to magic.

He slept after all, as deeply as if drugged. If he dreamed, he did not remember. When he woke, the shutters were open; sunlight poured into the room. Servants were waiting to tend him, and there was breakfast: the perpetual bread and beer.

He felt sleepy and slow, but he roused as he ate. He must be as keen of wit as he could be before he faced the priests. They, even more than courtiers, drove straight to the heart of any weakness.

The servants saw to it that he was dressed in kilt and belt and broad pectoral of gold and colored stones. They plaited his hair with ropes of gold and red and blue, and painted his eyes in the fashion of their people. They declared him beautiful then, and fit to be seen, but insisted that he not go alone.

"That would not be proper," said the eldest of them, a man much wizened by years but still bright of eye. He crooked a finger at one of his subordinates, young and strong and as tall as men grew here. "You belong to him. Serve him well, or pay the price which I exact."

The young man blanched slightly, but bowed and acquiesced. He carried a fan and a rod like a shepherd's staff, and walked ahead with an air of granting his charge great consequence.

Estarion was glad of the guide, and somewhat amused by the swagger the man put in his stride. He reminded Estarion a little of Daros, in his youth and bravado and his conviction that if he must be anything, it must be bold and bad.

The city had a temple for each of its nine greater gods, and a lesser temple or shrine for a myriad more. The temple of the sun was the largest and highest, a good three man-heights of hewn stone in this city of mudbrick and reed thatch. Its walls were thickly and brilliantly painted, inside and out; whole worlds of story were drawn there, tales of gods and kings.

Estarion, priest of another sun in another sky, found this place remarkably familiar. Its priests wore no torques like the one he had given to the altar of the god when he left his throne, and they shaved their heads and wore no beast's flesh or wool, only cream-pale linen and reed sandals. Yet their chants and the scent of their incense recalled the rites of his own god; their temple with its progression of courts was rather like the Temple of the Sun in his own city.

He was at ease but not complacent when they came to what must be the shrine. It was a long hall, its roof held up by heavy pillars; a stone image stood at the far end, and before it the table of an altar.

Priests stood in ranks in front of that altar. They were all dressed in simple linen, all shaven smooth: row on row of shining brown heads. The priest whom he had met at the banquet was seated behind and somewhat above them, surrounded by a circle of older and more august priests.

It seemed Estarion merited a full conclave. He decided to be flattered rather than alarmed. There was no more magic here than there had been in the queen's hall; what little there was, he could attribute to the cat which, having followed him from the palace, now walked haughtily ahead of him down that long march of pillars.

He halted at sufficient distance to keep all of them in sight. The cat sat tidily at his feet. It was the he-cat; he had, between last night and this morning, acquired a ring of gold in his ear. It gave him a princely and rather rakish look.

The priests regarded all of them, Estarion and the cat and the servant with the staff and the fan, as if they had been the children of Mother Night herself. They had heard the tale of the banquet from the one of their number who had seen it with his own eyes. They were afraid; and fear, in any mass of men, was dangerous.

Estarion smiled at them. "Good morning to you," he said.

The priest from the banquet bowed stiffly. The rest did not move or speak. They were a guard, Estarion began to understand; a shieldwall. Those whom they protected might have laid claim to a dim and barely perceptible glimmer of power. In Estarion's world it would not have sufficed to make its bearer even the least of mages, but here, maybe, it was remarkable.

Two of them boasted this ghost-flicker. One was an old man, toothless and milkily blind. The other was hardly more than a child. Estarion inclined his head to each. "My lords," he said.

The young one started visibly. The elder's clouded eyes turned toward Estarion and widened. Estarion saw himself reflected there: a pillar of light, towering in the darkness.

The old man came down from the dais. The younger one made as if to guide his steps, but he took no notice. He could see all that he needed to see. He stopped within reach, peering up, for he was very small and shriveled, and Estarion was very much taller than he. "You," he said in a thin old voice, "are nothing so simple as a god. I cry your pardon for the foolishness of my son; there are some with eyes to see, but he is not one of them. He does mean well, lord. Do believe that."

"I believe it," Estarion said. The plump priest, he noticed, was struggling to keep his temper at bay.

"We will not be mountebanks for you," the old man said, "nor strive to awe you with our poor powers. Some of us may be willing to learn what you can teach. Most will refuse, and I think rightly. Men cannot and should not pretend to the powers of gods."

Estarion bowed as low as to a brother king. "I see that there are wise men in this country," he said.

"Ah," said the old priest, shaking off the compliment. "I don't call wisdom what's only common sense. Any one of us can turn a staff into a snake, or water into blood—but you, lord, could overturn the river into the sky, and set the fish to dancing. We'd all be wasting ourselves on trifles. There's only one thing I would ask of you."

"Yes?" said Estarion.

"Promise," said the priest, "that whatever you do here, whatever you came for, you will do no harm to our people or our queen."

"I do promise," Estarion said.

"I believe," said the priest, "that you will try to keep that promise. Break it even once, however excellent your reasons, and even as weak as we are beside you, we will do our best to exact the price that such betrayal deserves."

"That is a fair judgment," said Estarion.

"Good," the priest said. "Good. This gathering was meant to cow you, of course, and overwhelm you with numbers and power; but I do hope that it helps you to understand: we serve the gods and the city, and the queen's majesty. As long as you do the same, we are allies."

The alternative was perfectly clear. "I see we understand one another," Estarion said. "That's well. I too am a priest of the Sun. It would be a great grief if we could find no common ground."

"You must tell us of your rites and your order," the priest said, "as far as you may, of course. But not this moment. My brothers have duties that they've been neglecting in order to put on this show of force, and I don't doubt that you have things that need doing. May we speak again under less nervous circumstances?"

"Certainly we may," said Estarion with honest warmth. "Good day, reverend sir, and may your god bless and keep you."

"And yours," said the old priest: "may he hold you in his hand."

Estarion had much to ponder after he left that place. Not least was the plump priest's expression as Estarion and the old man parted on the best of terms. There would be war in the temple after this, he had no doubt. He had been sorely tempted to stop it with a blast of cleansing fire, but it was neither the place nor the time for such excesses. He must trust that the old man could look after himself, and hope that the city and the queen were not forced to pay for the outcome.

He said as much to her that afternoon when she had taken a few moments' rest in the garden of her palace. She was dressed for the day in court, in fine linen and a great deal of gold; her face was a mask of artful paint. She still had the loose, free stride of a hunter or a warrior as she walked down the path from the pool to the little orchard that grew along the wall.

"Seti is neither as feeble nor as innocent as he seems," she said. "He was high priest for more years than I can count; when he handed the staff to his son—yes, that fat fool is the heir of his body—he surrendered no part of his actual power. If he approves you, the rest will follow. Some may snarl and snap, but none of them is strong enough to stand against Seti."

"Or so you can hope," Estarion said.

"So I know," she said, politely immovable.

Estarion bowed to her knowledge of the place and the people. "I'm a difficult guest, I know. I hope I've not created factions that will bring you grief."

"There are always factions," she said. "This may bring out one or two that we had been needing to know of."

"There is that," he granted her.

She passed under the shade of the trees, which was a little cooler than the fierce heat of the sun, and inspected the green fruit clustered on a branch. Her gown clung tightly to her body, so sheer and so delicately woven that it concealed nothing, only made it all the more beautiful. Her blue-black hair was plaited in a myriad small plaits, some strung with beads of gold or lapis or carnelian; they swung together as she moved, brushing her bare shoulders.

He would have loved to touch them, to run his fingers over the sweet curve of them, and know the softness of her skin. He was startled to discover just how keenly he wanted it.

She would not thank him for the liberty. He kept his hands to himself. She seemed to have forgotten him, but he sensed the spark of her awareness. She knew exactly where he was and what he did there.

He wandered back toward the pool, in part to test her, in part to cool his feet. The water was not particularly cool, but it was cooler than the air. He laved his face and arms, and stroked the bright fish that came crowding about him. They slid over his fingers with oiled smoothness, butting him with their heads but offering no insolence.

They seemed content in their captivity. He was not. This world was lovely, even with the heat; its people were well worth knowing. Yet he was not one of them. The shadow's strength had grown even in the scarce day's span since he fell out of it onto the harsh red earth. Whatever had held it back through a king's reign and into the reign of a queen was fading fast. His fault, maybe, for falling through the Gate. Maybe he had drawn the darkness' attention; maybe he had shown it a clearer way in.

There were no rents in the fabric of the world. The Gate through which he had come was gone, swallowed up in his deepest self. The tide of shadow darkened his sense of the stars, though it did not yet dim the sun.

He withdrew into himself and sighed. He was no nearer than before to knowing what the shadow was. What hope he had of defending this world, he did not know; he did hope that it was not too arrogant to think that he had been sent here, that the gods had given him this task. His own world, however great his fear for it, was as well defended as a world could be. It had hundreds, thousands of mages; it had its god-born rulers. It was a great fortress and deep well of magic. This world had, as far as he could tell, one lone Sunborn mage from beyond the sky, a tribe of small mageborn cats, and no more. Unless a warm heart and a strong spirit could be enough, the people here had no defense.

"If that scowl is for me," said the queen, "I'd best call my guards."

Estarion blinked and focused. Her face was stern, but her eyes were glinting. He found a smile for her and put away the scowl. "Do please forgive me," he said. "I was pondering imponderables."

"It looked as if they might be unthinkable."

"That, too," he said. He groaned, stretched, creaked. "Is there a place where a man may go to practice with weapons?"

"The court of the guards," she said. "I'll have you taken there. Is there a particular weapon that you prefer?"

"Something strenuous," he said. "I feel a need to wear myself out."

"You will certainly do that, at this time of day," she said. "Will you listen to a simple native, and hear another way? It's cool and pleasant on the river, and the cooks are always glad of fresh fowl for the pots. Will you come hunting with me?"

"Sitting at leisure in a boat? Lady, you're very kind, but—"

"You can take an oar if it suits your fancy."

It was a tempting prospect. Estarion loved boats and rivers and fishing; he was not averse to hunting waterfowl, either. But when he let loose the smile that tugged at his lips, it was for her, the beautiful one, that he said, "Very well. I yield to the royal command."

Estarion wielded an oar with skill that came back to him as he went on. At first he scandalized the boatmen, but when they saw that he knew what he was doing, they gave way grudgingly to his whim.

The boat was made of reeds, and floated high on the water. There was a high pointed prow and a high stern, and a canopy amidships, beneath which the queen and her escort could take their ease. Estarion chose not to indulge himself. He sweated in the sun with the rest of the oarsmen, pulling in unison to the beat of a drum.

It was good clean work, and it soothed him wonderfully. The tension poured out of him; the knot in his belly loosened. The thoughts and fears that had roiled in his head were quiet for once.

It was better than sleep, that day on the river. They brought back a boatload of waterfowl and the carcass of a young river-beast: a rich hunt and welcome. The river had been kind; they had lost no man or boat, nor even an oar, to crocodiles, and their quarry had been too numerous to count, all but flinging themselves on the hunters' arrows.

"He brings us luck," Estarion heard one of the boatmen say. They were all cordial now; he had proved himself to them, though he had done it with perfect selfishness. He had only wanted to lighten the burden that had fallen on him.

They all ate well that evening, but as before, with the coming of dark, everyone fled to the safety of his own walls. Estarion did not linger, either. His arms and shoulders ached; his hands stung with blisters. Yet he was wide awake, and he felt remarkably well refreshed, as if he had slept a whole night through.

He let himself be put to bed, to mollify the servants. Well after they had gone, he lay where they had left him. The sounds of the palace died one by one. Voices quieted, footsteps ceased. The strains of a flute, which had come and gone since he came in from the hall, slowly faded away.

He rose softly and put on a kilt, and took up the weapons he had brought from the other side of the sky: knife and short sword, bow and quiver, all made with metals that were not known here.

It was still light as he passed through deserted halls and empty streets. He walked without stealth, but with no desire to be seen. Only the cats could see. The two that were with him as often as not had elected to follow him; their cousins and kin flitted through the long shadows, calling softly to one another.

They were weaving wards about this city. It was subtle and rather marvelous, and quite elegant, like the creatures that wrought it. Their weaving tonight laid a path open for him to follow from palace to city gate, then out to the long stretch of fields along the river.

The gate melted before him. A large brindled cat perched atop it until it was gone; then the cat winked out, vanishing into the air with a sound like purring laughter.

The she-cat stopped just outside the gate, but her mate went on with Estarion. The cat had no fear. Estarion would not indulge in it until he had good and sufficient reason. He raised wards of his own about them both, a shield and a mantle wrought of magic.

He walked away from the walls, down the road to the river and then along the bank to a place that would do as well as any. It was far enough from the city to be out of reach of the wards upon it, but near enough that he did not have to walk far in the dusk. A line of boats was drawn up there, huddled together as if they too were afraid of the dark. He settled in one, sitting near the stern, gazing out over the river to the shadow on shadow that was the farther shore.

Every human creature might be shut away in safety, but night birds sang and jackals howled, and far away he heard the roar of a river-beast. The sunset faded to black; the stars came out in their myriads.

The cat curled purring in his lap. He stroked the sleek fur and leaned his head back, filling his eyes with stars.

The shadow came like a mist, a thin dank fog creeping across the river. The sounds of the night died one by one, save for the howling of jackals in the desert. Jackals, people believed here, were the guides and guardians of the dead. By morning, Estarion well might know whether that was so.

It made him almost happy. He would prefer to live, and this world might be the better for it, too, but he was not afraid to die. It was a passage through a gate, but only the soul could make the journey. The body was cast off, useless and forgotten.

The fog had a scent, a mingled effluvium of dust and damp and old stone. It was not itself deadly; plagues had not come with it in any tale that Estarion had heard. It flowed off the river, dimming the air about him, darkening the stars.

He had strong night-eyes; he needed no light to see. He sat still, save that he had, ever so softly, drawn the short sword from the sheath at his side. The cat sat up and yawned and began to wash his face.

The cat's calm deepened and strengthened Estravion's wards. He sat straighter, but did not rise to his feet. The cat finished his toilet and sat staring, still calmly, at the thing that came over the water.

The fog was nothing to be unduly afraid of. There was that about it which hinted of spells and powers embedded in it, enchantments that would feed madness and swell fear into blind panic. Because he had no fear, the spells did not touch him.

Could this alone be what had driven so many people mad, and rent their king limb from limb? Some of the darker spells had that power, but he could not believe that it was as simple as that.

He waited, as the stars wheeled slowly above the shadow. The fog lapped at the walls of Waset, curling tendrils round it but not venturing within. The river murmured to itself.

Something was coming. The cat sprang from Estarion's lap to the boat's prow. He rose then, sword in hand, power coiled within the circle of his wards.

They rode over the river as if it had been solid earth: half a hundred shadowy riders on strange beasts. Even to his eyes they were difficult to see, black on black as they were, but from a glint here and a gleam there he was able to give them shape. They were human, or near enough: two arms, two legs, a head, encased in armor of strange fashion, and armed with weapons, some of which he recognized, some not. Their beasts were like the crocodiles of this river, but much larger, much longer in the leg, and much more agile and quick.

What army they came from, or by what Gate they had entered this world, he could not tell; but they had no scent or sense of this earth. They overran the shore, riding swiftly and with the air of those who knew their way. They struck for a village that had been safe before, as close to Waset as it was; it was nearly in the shadow of the northern wall.

Estarion slipped out of the boat, set his shoulder to the stern, and sent it sliding toward the water. It slid smoothly in the rich black mud, but the splash of its launching stopped his heart in his throat.

The army did not pause or turn. He pulled himself into the boat before the current carried it away, found and softly shipped the steering oar, and let the river bear him down toward the embattled village, touching the oar only to keep the boat on its course.

They reached the village before him, riding like a storm in the night, yet eerily, supernaturally silent. They went for the storehouses and the fields. The former they stripped bare and loaded on beasts that they had brought with them, riderless, for that purpose. The latter they swept past, save one, which they raked with a strange dark fire. Then Estarion knew what those shadowy shapes were which the riders carried, which he had not recognized before: they belched forth flame, but flame transmuted into living, searing darkness.

There was nothing random about this raid. They left the villagers' houses alone, save, as with the fields, for one. That one they cracked open like an egg.

Estarion's fingers tightened on the steering oar until surely it would snap in two. For now, he must only watch and learn. Gods, he hated to be wise; but for this world and for his own, he must not betray himself to these marauders until he knew surely what they were.

The villagers cowered in the ruins of their house. Their little bit of fire barely flickered in the gloom. One of the raiders stamped it out. As Estarion's eyes struggled to adjust to the deeper darkness, something stirred among the raiders. He could swear it had not been there before, but it was incontestably present now: a loom of shadow, with no shape that he could discern. It flowed rather than walked; it poured itself over the huddle of villagers.

The cold that came out of it, the sense of sheer inimical otherness, made Estarion—even Estarion, who feared little in any world—gasp and cower in the flimsy safety of the boat. The cat pressed trembling against his side.

The dark thing sucked the warmth out of them, and the blood, and last of all the souls. It crunched them like bones, savoring every shrieking scrap. When they were gone, it shrank to a point of darkness, sprouted wings, and flittered into the night.

The raiders dismembered the shriveled and bloodless bodies with the skill and dispatch of butchers in a cattle-market, or priests in a sacrifice. Their movements had an air of ritual; they arranged the limbs in a pattern that Estarion could not quite see. When they were satisfied, they turned their beasts, both ridden and laden with spoils, and rode into the deepest darkness.

The earth breathed a sigh. The stars recovered their splendor. The moon shed its pale light again. The raiders were gone, departed from this world—until night came once more, and once more they would rule the darkness.

TWELVE

JUST AFTER SUNRISE, EARLY RISERS FOUND THE GOD FROM BEYOND THE SKY in a boat, asleep, with the lord of the palace cats draped purring over his middle. The boat was drawn up on the riverbank beneath the city's walls; it looked as if he had been there all night. And yet he was whole of limb, and as the boatmen stood over him, murmuring among themselves, he opened eyes that were as bright and sane as they ever were—although one sensitive soul avowed that they were sadder, and touched with a glimmer of godly wrath.

He greeted them with his white smile, and with words that were princely courteous. Those with amulets clutched them for protection, but his wits had not been devoured by the night. He was the same golden-eyed god that he had been the day before.

Tanit had learned that he was missing when a maid roused her at dawn. Her guest's servant was standing in her antechamber, trembling so hard that he could barely stand. It was a while before she could coax any sense out of him. Even then it came out in gasps. "I was asleep," he said, "across the door, as I should be. He had to walk over me. I woke up and he was gone. He's nowhere here, lady. I looked and looked. All night I looked. He's not in this house. Lady, I failed, I failed miserably. I deserve to die."

"We shall see about that," Tanit said—coldly, to be sure, but her heart was so constricted and her breath so shallow that it was the best she could do. She bade the maids look after him, and took her door-guards and braved the sunrise.

She came to the boat not long after the boatmen found him there. It was the only crowd along the riverbank this early in the day, with the sun barely risen and the dark barely put to flight; and he was standing in the middle of it, head and shoulders above the rest, like a pillar of black stone with eyes of hammered gold. She wanted, suddenly, to burst into tears.

She had been queen too long to be a slave to her own foolishness. The boatmen retreated before her; they recognized her even in a simple gown, with no more than eye-paint, and no crown. Their relief was palpable. This god was more than they were prepared to contend with, particularly at this hour of the morning.

She held out her hand to him. "Come," she said.

He took her hand and let her lead him away from the wide-eyed boatmen. She should have let him go once she was sure that he would stay with her, but her fingers had a mind of their own. They liked to rest within that big dark hand, with its warmth and its quiet strength.

They stayed there all the way to the palace, through the hall of audience and, with complete lack of conscious will, into her chambers. He sat where she bade him, which was more for her comfort than for his: she was not in the mood to crane her neck in order to see his expression. He was glad to be fed bread and cakes and bits of roast fowl that he shared with the cat, and to drink palm wine—the last a surprise, and a pleasant one, from his expression. She had learned from the servants that he was not fond of beer.

When he had eaten and drunk, she sat across the small breakfast-table from him and said, "Tell me why you're alive and sane. Are you one of the walkers in the night?"

"You know I'm not," he said, but without apparent offense. "I did see them—or one manifestation of them."

"And yet you live to tell of it," she said with careful lack of expression. "A village almost under the walls was struck in the night. Were you part of that?"

His eyes closed; his face tightened. "I saw it," he said.

"You did nothing to stop it?"

"I could do nothing," he said through clenched teeth; "that would not have made matters immeasurably worse. I watched; I don't know that I understood, but I will remember what I saw. Lady, may I summon certain of the priests, and such nobles as are familiar with your lore of magic?"

It was polite of him to ask. She considered refusing, because after all she was the queen. But he was a god. "Do as you will," she said. "I will give you the rod that permits a lord to wield power in my name."

"That is a great trust," he said.

"Yes," she said. Her maid Tisheri, ever wise, had found the rod that Tanit spoke of, a reed staff bound with bands of gold. Tanit gave it into his hand. "Guard it well," she said.

He bowed low. "My thanks, most gracious lady," he said. Then after a pause: "May I gather them here? Your authority will give my words more weight."

"Do I want them gathered here?"

He knelt in front of her. She did not know where that snap of temper had come from, and his lack of anger only made her the more cross-grained. When he took her hands—again, gods help her—she lacked the will to pull free. "Lady," he said, "I am a guest, and here on your sufferance. I ask your pardon if I've overstepped."

"You haven't," she said. "I'm being foolish. It's been too long since I yielded my will to a man's. I've forgotten how to do it gracefully."

"And I," he said with a glint in his eye, "was a king too long. I give orders without thinking."

"They are wise orders," she said. She looked down at their joined hands. He began to draw away, but she held him fast. "My lord, we should agree before we go on, as to how we shall manage this matter of authority. I know I am only a woman, but—"

"Lady," he said deep in his throat. "I'll hear no more of that. In my country, the regent and ruling heir is a woman; and her heir, in turn, is a daughter and not a son. You are not 'only' a woman. You are a lady and a queen."

She had never been so soundly and yet so pleasantly rebuked. "If I am a queen," she said, "then I may command you and be obeyed. Yes?"

"Yes," he said gravely, but with a glint in it.

"Then I command you to go, and do what you must, and come back when you are done."

He bowed over her hands without too terribly much mockery, and kissed the palm of each, and let them go. Long after he was gone, she sat staring at those palms, as if the mark of his lips should be branded there in streaks of fire.

They were only her ordinary, long and thin, cream-brown hands. Whatever memory they held, it was not visible to the eye. Which was well—because if anyone knew what she was thinking, the scandal would keep the court buzzing for days.

She could not stop thinking it. That the command she had wanted to give was not the one she had given, at all. And that if she had bidden him do that other thing . . . might he perhaps have consented? There had been a look in his eye, that she had thought she could not mistake.

There was no time or place for that, not in this world. She gathered herself together and rose. There was a council to prepare for and a day to begin. It was some little while before she understood what was causing her heart to flutter so oddly. It was not only that beautiful and godlike man. It was—before the gods, it was hope. For the first time since she was a child, she began to think that the night would not always be cursed; that the walkers in the dark might, at last, be banished from the world.

The Lord Seramon had called eight priests and nobles to his council: nine, with the queen. The old priest from the Temple of the Sun was there, and his son who could not in courtesy be left out, and the young one who was almost, in his dim way, a mage. There was a priest of their queen of goddesses, too, and the commander of the royal army, and two young lords who had been born at the same birth and were eerily, uncannily alike, and last and perhaps most baffled, the servant whom the chief of the queen's servants had given the Lord Seramon. He was no slave or menial; he was a free man of good family, who won honor for his house by serving in the palace.

Tanit had had them brought to her audience chamber with escort of honor and all due courtesy. They were barely courteous in return. Only Seti the old priest seemed at ease. The rest shifted uncomfortably, and either declined refreshment or hid behind it as if it had been a refuge.

The Lord Seramon was last to appear, accompanied as usual by cats. Their lord rode regally on his shoulder. He bowed to them all, and deepest to Tanit, and took the chair that had been left for him. "I thank you, my lords and lady," he said, "for coming at my call. I have a thing to ask of you. You may refuse; no shame will attach to it. But if you accept, the night may be a little less dark, and your people a little safer."

None of them brightened at his words. Seti spoke for them all, gently. "My lord, what can we do that you in your divine power cannot? Surely you can cause the sun to shine all night, and keep the darkness forever at bay."

"If I am a god," the Lord Seramon said, "then I am a minor one. The Sun is my forefather, not my servant. I could set a dome of light over this city, but I would have no strength left for any other working, or for defense against the attack that would come. The enemy that devours your children shuns the light. But the enemy's servants can endure it, even wield it if they must."

"You . . . saw the enemy's servants?" Seti-re made no effort to conceal his disbelief. "Yet you live; your body is whole. You seem sane. Are you certain that it was not a dream?"

"It was quite real," the Lord Seramon said. "I saw another thing, too, that interested me greatly. Because of it, I should like to ask that you yourselves, and such of your servants as are both brave and strong of will, may dispose yourselves like an army, and take turn and turn about in the villages."

"Indeed?" said the priest of the Mother. He seemed no more enamored of the Lord Seramon than Seti-re. "Are we to be a sacrifice? Or will we be given a weapon?"

"You will have a weapon," the Lord Seramon said, "and a comrade in arms." He bent his gaze toward the door. The others, as if caught by a spell, did the same.

A company of cats trotted purposefully into the hall. Being cats, they did not march in ranks, nor did they match pace to pace. Yet they were together, there was no mistaking it, and they had about them the air of an army. There were twice nine, and not all palace cats; some had the lean and rangy look of cats from the city.

They advanced two by two, and chose each a lord or a priest, and two gold-earringed beauties lofted lightly into Tanit's lap. She knew them; they were often to be seen about her chambers, and were much spoiled by the servants.

"These are the nobility of their kind," the Lord Seramon said. "Their cousins and kin will come to those whom you choose to fight in this army. Listen to them, my lords and lady. Let them guide you. They have power against this enemy that besets you."

The priest of the Mother laughed. "*This* is your great plan? These are your weapons? The gods do love them, lord, but what power can they raise against the walkers of the night?"

"Great power," the Lord Seramon said. "Did you never wonder why this city has not been attacked? It has walls, yes, but walls are nothing to this enemy. Your cats guard those walls. They take their strength from the sun, but the night is their mother. They rule on both sides of the sky."

Tanit shivered lightly. The cat in her lap seemed no more divine than ever, if no less; she was coiled, purring, blinking sleepily at her kin. Lightly Tanit laid a hand on her back. She arched it, bidding Tanit stroke it, yes, just so. Her purring rose to a soft roar. She reminded Tanit suddenly, vividly, of the Lord Seramon.

"I do believe you," Tanit said. "And yet, my lord, I ask you: If the cats have such power, why have they never defended the villages?"

"Because, lady," said the Lord Seramon, "they, like me, have limits to their power; and, being cats, they seldom think of gathering forces. It's their nature to hunt alone."

"Yet they guard our city together," she said.

"Each protects what is his," he said. "It happens that, in so doing, they protect all. They've agreed to ally themselves with your people; their power is yours to use. In return they ask for free rein among the mice and rats in the storehouses, and a tribute of milk and fish."

One of the twins snorted as if he could not help himself. "My lord! Pardon me, but that's absurd. You're a god; you may talk to a cat. What of us? We're only human."

"Listen," the Lord Seramon said. One of the cats at Kamut's feet rose on its hindlegs, stretching its long body, and flexed claws delicately, terribly close to his shrinking privates. The cat met his stare with one as golden and as steady, and quite as full of intelligence, as the Lord Seramon's own.

Kamut gasped and stiffened, but it seemed he could not look away. The cat yawned, splitting its face in two, curling its pink tongue, and raked its claws gently, ever so gently, down Kamut's thigh. Four thin lines of red stained the white linen of his kilt.

To his credit, he did not flinch or cry out. The cat sat once more, tail curled about feet.

"I . . . am only human," Kamut said after a long pause. "But *she* is a cat."

The Lord Seramon smiled that white smile of his. "Yes, young lord, you do understand. Will you be a captain in this army? I count a score of living villages within a day's walk of the city. All have been raided; but their houses still stand, and their people are holding on. Even one of you, with your allies, should be able to raise wards that keep the village safe, though the fields may be more than your strength can manage."

"It is a risk," Seti said. "If the dark ones fail to gain their sacrifice, they may strip the fields in revenge."

"The fields could be guarded," Tanit said.

"No man will leave the safety of walls at night," said the Mother's priest, with a slant of the eye at the Lord Seramon.

The Lord Seramon's mouth curved upward briefly. "No man will, but cats have no fear of the dark. The fields can be guarded. But you might wish to consider that wards of such size and extent may attract the very thing they're meant to repel. If I were to be asked, I would counsel that your people decide among them what they can spare—which fields, which houses—and withdraw from those."

"This is all very well," said the captain of the guard, "but defense only serves for so long. There comes a time when attack is the only wise course. Can this enemy be attacked? Can he be fought? Or will he wear us away until there is nothing left?"

"The raiders can be fought," the Lord Seramon said, "but how and with what numbers I don't yet know."

"A *minor* god," Kamut muttered to his brother.

The Lord Seramon laughed. "Very minor! But strong enough, I hope, to be of some use. So, then, my lords. Will you join with us? A wall is the first defense. An army within the wall—that comes after. Will you be the wall?"

"As weak a stone as I may be," Seti said, "I will hold up my part of the wall."

"And I," said Kamut, rather surprisingly; his brother Senmut echoed him.

They all agreed, even Seti-re, and the Mother's priest, whom Tanit would have expected to refuse. It was a spirit of rivalry: they were not to be outdone.

The Lord Seramon left them to plot their strategies. She could admire the skill with which he did it. They were not even aware of his silence or, after a while, his absence. He withdrew so quietly that even she hardly knew when he was gone. One moment he was there, watching and listening. The next, he was not.

It took this new and strange guard a rather long while to settle on how it would begin. Tanit was very weary when at last they scattered to the duties they had agreed upon. Her head ached; there was a dull pain in her belly, where so many children had grown and died.

Her maids would have put her to bed with a cool cloth on her brow and a potion to make her sleep, but she was in no mood to rest. She went hunting a minor god.

He was on the palace roof, where the maids spread the linens to dry on washing-day. It was bare now but for the pots of herbs that rimmed it. He stood on the edge as if he would spread wings and take flight, gazing out over the city and the fields and the river.

In the bright light of day he seemed both more mortal and less. The sun caught the threads of silver in his hair. There were scars on his back and side, down his arm, cleaving his face from cheekbone to chin. Scars of battle, worn almost to invisibility. She tried to imagine battles among the gods. Were their weapons like the ones she knew, or did they wield bolts of fire?

He glanced at her. "We have swords and spears," he said, "and bolts of mages' fire."

A shiver ran down her spine. "Do you know every thought I think?"

"Only the ones aimed like an arrow," he said.

Not only her cheeks were hot; her whole body flushed. If she could have sunk through the floor, she would have done it.

His hand was cool on her cheek, shocking her into a shiver. "Dear lady," he said so tenderly that she could have wept, "you have nothing to be ashamed of."

"No?" She looked him in the face. "Am I such a child to you?"

"Never," he said.

"I am no goddess, my lord."

"And I," he said, "in my own world, am no god."

"It has been so long a while," she said through a tightening throat, "since—and I cannot—a queen may not—"

"May she not?"

"Will you corrupt me?"

"I might seduce you," he said.

She gasped. His effrontery was astonishing. And damnably charming, because he did not care, at all, for the ways of men in this world.

"The ladies of your court are free of their eyes and their favors," he said. "Surely a queen may make what laws she pleases."

"What if she does not please?"

He tilted up her chin and kissed her softly on the lips.

She should have struck him. Not held him when he began to straighten, and deepened the kiss until she was dizzy with it.

He tasted of strange spices. There was a quality to him, like leashed lightning, or sparks that flew in the air when the hot winds blew out of the red land. Magic, she thought; divine power. And yet he was as warm as any mortal man, solid, real to the touch; he did not vanish like a vision or a dream.

"You swore that you would never harm me," she said to him.

"I shall keep that oath, lady," he said.

"Then why—"

"Lady," he said, "there are gods above us all. Maybe it amuses them to bring us together across the worlds; maybe they have a purpose for us, which our wits are too feeble to understand."

"Maybe this was never meant," she said, but she did not believe it even as she said it. She did not want to believe it. She wanted—she yearned—

"Why are you afraid?" he asked her. "Am I so terrible a monster?"

"You are beautiful," she said.

"And you," he said, "were married to a man whom you admired and cherished, but for whom your body felt nothing."

"I am not young," she said as steadily as she could. "I have borne ten children. None lived long enough to walk the black earth. Now I have a thousand children, and they need my loyalty undivided."

"Would a king divide his loyalty by taking a wife?"

"A king is a man," she said.

"A queen is a woman."

He was seducing her. That soft rich voice, those luminous eyes—they cast a spell. She had known him two days, but every one of her several souls reckoned that a lifetime.

"Gods are quick to love," she said, "and just as quick to leave. Mortals, who have so much less time to waste, are slower with both."

"Many things have been said of me," he said, "and not all have been to my credit, though they may have been true. But one charge has never been laid against me: that I was light in love. A king must marry well and often. So I did. But when I left the throne, I left that behind me. My bed has been solitary since long before you were born."

Then it may remain so, she meant to say, but the words would not shape themselves on her tongue. "I may take a consort," she heard herself say. "I will not take a lover. That would dishonor my husband's memory, my family's reputation, and my own good name."

Once she had traveled with her husband to the cataract of the river, where it roared headlong through a wilderness of stones. She had seen how flotsam, caught in the torrent, whirled and dived and for long moments vanished, but then suddenly reappeared an improbable distance downstream. So her heart felt now, hammering in her breast. It had spoken, not she. Half of it wanted him to recoil in horror and go away and let her be. The other half wanted him to say what in fact he said.

"Are you telling me that I should marry you?"

"I am telling you that I will not take a lover," she said with what little breath was left in her.

Two days, she thought. *Two lifetimes.*

"Will your people be appalled if I say yes? Will you?"

"Why would you—"

"Life is short," he said, "and the night is long. And from the moment I saw you, I have loved you."

"I—" She could feel the water closing over her head, hear the rush and roar of the cataract. "Life is short," she said faintly.

"Will your people be horrified?"

"If their queen takes a god for a consort? They'll reckon it a great good omen. The nobles and the priests will be less than amused."

"Nobles and priests can be managed," he said.

She met his eyes as firmly as she could. "If this is a jest, my lord, or a mockery, then may the greater gods repay you as you deserve."

There was no mirth in his gaze, no mockery or contempt. "I never jest in matters of the heart," he said.

She laid her hand over it. It was not beating as hard as hers, but neither was it as strong and slow as she knew it could be. Once more she found that she could see beneath the veil of him. The light was as clear as ever. He was a pure spirit. The beauty of him, within even more than without, made her catch her breath.

"You will be consort and not king," she said. "Can you endure that?"

"I would expect nothing else," he said. And with a flicker of lightness: "It's still a fair step up from shepherd."

"And a long step down from king of kings."

"Ah," he said, shrugging. "I gave that up."

"You are a very odd man," she said, "but for a god, not so strange at all."

He laughed at that. He took her hands and pressed them to his lips and said, "I'll see that this goes easily."

"No spells," she said. "Promise."

"May I smile? Wheedle? Be charming?"

"No magic," she said. Then added: "Except the magic that is yourself."

"That will be enough," he said.

THIRTEEN

Tanit went to Seti as soon as she could, which was near evening. The day had passed in a blur. She supposed that she had held audience, met in council, overseen the servants, and performed the myriad other duties of her office. She also supposed that the Lord Seramon disposed of himself in some useful fashion. He was seen round about in the city and in one or two of the nearer villages, and down by the river in the evening.

Her heart would have taken her there and begged him not to risk himself again by night, but her colder spirit bade her let him be. He could look after himself. This that she had determined to do was not at all as simple as she had led him to think.

Seti was preoccupied with the evening rite and sacrifice. She waited for him in a bare cell of a room outside the temple proper. A young priest waited on her; she wanted nothing, but he seemed content to amuse himself in conversation with her maid. She half-drowsed, sitting upright, spinning in her mind the things that she meant to say to Seti.

When he came, it was as if it had all been said, and she could pay her respects and go away. But she was not quite as foolish as that. He greeted her gladly, and opened his arms for an embrace and the kiss of kin. His cheek was dry yet oddly soft under her lips, like age-worn leather. "Granddaughter," he said. "It warms my heart to see you."

"Grandfather," she said to her mother's father. She insisted that he sit in the one chair the room afforded. She could be at ease on the floor, curled at his feet, as she had done when she was small.

"Tell me," he said.

She laughed a little. "Am I so obvious?"

"Maybe," he said. "And maybe it will be night soon, and time's flying. What's in your heart, child?"

"Too much," she murmured. She lifted her eyes to him, though he could not see; she suspected that he knew, somehow, or felt in the air what movements she made. "I am going to do a thing that will shock every priest and noble in this city. Except, I think, you."

"Oh, I'm not past shock," he said. "What is it? Are you going to take the god to your bed?"

She started and flushed. Even knowing how perceptive Seti could be, she had not expected him to see direct to the truth.

"I knew the moment you met," Seti said. "There are stars that dance twinned in heaven, and souls that are matched, each to each. Even the walls of worlds and time, mortality and divinity, simple human and great magic, matter nothing to them."

"That is very beautiful," she said, "but we live in daylight, and the court and the temples will be outraged."

"So they will," Seti said. "Does it matter?"

"No," she said slowly. "But—"

"What do you think I can do? Command them all to accept what none of them can change?"

It sounded absurd when he said it, but she said, "Yes. Yes, I had rather thought that."

"I can command respect," he said. "Once I might have commanded more. You would do better to win over your uncle."

"Seti-re will never listen to me," she said. She was not excessively bitter. It was fact, that was all. "But he will still listen to you. If he says the words that unite us, no one else will dare object."

"You are set on this? It's not simple enough to take a lover?"

"A lover would give them a weapon against me," she said, "and weaken us when we need most to be strong. A consort proves before the gods that this is no decision taken lightly."

"You are stubborn," said Seti, "and determined to make matters as difficult as possible."

"If I don't do it," she said, "the court will—or my uncle, who has never been my dearest friend."

"Indeed," he sighed. "Tell me, child. What do you truly hope to gain? Is this your revenge on us all for expecting so much but giving so little in return?"

"That would be the taking of a lover," she said. "This begs the gods to be merciful to our city."

"By binding one of their own to it?"

She bent her head.

"He consents? Freely?"

"It seems so," she said.

Seti sighed. "Child," he said, "I will see what I can do."

She kissed him, less formally this time, and smiled. "Thank you, Grandfather," she said.

Estarion had found that day astonishing and disconcerting and in parts delightful, like the lady who had issued so remarkable an ultimatum. Of marriage he had no fear—he had done it nine times over. But that was long ago, and he had not lain with a woman in years out of count. It was the only thing that had made him think that he might, after all, be old.

Now it seemed he was not old but perhaps merely rebellious. He had had one great love in his life, and she had denied herself to him, because she was a commoner and a priestess and a mage of Gates, and he must marry where his empire required. When that duty was done, when those ladies had grown old and died, he had wanted nothing more to do with any of it.

He was a man for one woman. He had always known that. She was long dead—she had lived an ample span, but she was mortal after all, and aged and died as mortals did. He still mourned her, though her death had had no grief in it. She had gone not into darkness but into light, soaring up like a bird into the luminous heaven.

There was a doctrine in the Isles from which she had come, and in the lands beyond the sea: that souls did not live only once; that they came back again and again, striving to perfect this life which they had been given. He wondered, even as he passed through palace and city and to the nearer villages, whether this was she, after all, with her bright spirit and her strong will, and her solid common sense. Or maybe it was only that he was made for such a woman, and when he met her like again, his spirit called to her and wanted her for its own.

For he did want her. He had turned his mind away from the harder truth: that he was not of this world. If he could escape from it, he would do so. She could not bind him, not against that.

That would come when it came. As the day waned toward evening, he knew that she went to Seti; he could imagine what she said to him. For his own part, he went to the one who could make matters most difficult. It was reckless, perhaps, and she would not be pleased to hear of it, but he was in no mood for prudence. That was a lost virtue in this world under the shadow.

Seti-re was at dinner. He dined alone tonight, but he dined well. He had a roast fowl and a platter of fish and the inevitable bread and beer. The priests who guarded him never saw the shadow that passed among them. Nor, while he savored his dinner, did Seti-re. It was only as he picked at the last of the bones and sipped his third cup of beer that Estarion let himself take shape out of shadows.

Seti-re started so violently that his cup flew out of his hand and shattered. Estarion made it new again, raising the shards and knitting them together, and set it gently on the table.

The priest stared at it. He seemed unable to take his eyes from it, or unwilling to look into Estarion's face. He was afraid; and fear filled him with rancor.

"My lord," Estarion said, "whatever our differences, may we not work together for the preservation of this city?"

"Is that truly what you are doing? You have the others well ensorcelled, but the gods protect me. I see you for what you are."

"Indeed?" said Estarion. "What am I?"

"Do I need to say it?"

Estarion raised a shoulder in a shrug. "Truly I mean you no harm. I was sent here to help; I will do everything I can, for the gods who sent me, but also for love of those to whom I was sent."

"Love?" said Seti-re. "How can you love what you barely know?"

"Some would say that love is easiest then—that only the best is apparent, until time dulls the sheen. As for me," said Estarion, "I have found much here to admire, and no little to love."

"Words are easy," Seti-re said. "Actions prove them."

"Indeed," said Estarion. "Will you say the words that join me to your queen as her consort?"

He had caught the priest utterly off guard. Seti-re stared, speechless. Just as Estarion began to wonder if he had any wits left, he said faintly, hardly more than a gasp, "If that is a jest, it is in extremely poor taste."

"No jest," Estarion said. "This too I was sent for; this I do in all joy."

"You want . . . me . . . to say the words." Seti-re looked as if he had bitten into bitter herbs. "You honestly imagine that I would consent?"

Estarion smiled. "Yes, sir priest. In fact I do. You are not a fool, and you have honest care for the city, whatever you may think of its queen. Or," he added, "of me. I frighten you. I am sorry for that. I would wish us, if not friends, at least to be allies; to make common cause against this enemy that threatens us all. My world, too, sir priest, and all worlds in its path."

"I believe that you are part of it," Seti-re said. "That you came not to save us but to destroy us."

"There is a thing that I can do," Estarion said, "which would place me utterly in your power if I break my word to the queen and the city. If I do that, will you lay aside your enmity?"

Seti-re eyed him narrowly. "What can you do? Offer your throat to my knife?"

"Better than that," Estarion said. "I will give you a part of myself to keep. If I betray my oath, that part will be snuffed out, and I will be gone."

"Dead?"

"And gone," said Estarion.

Seti-re drew a slow breath. Estarion resisted the temptation to discover what he was thinking. That was part of his good faith: to force no magic on this or any man.

At length the priest said, "I would have complete power over you. Or is this a trick? Will it be I who will suffer, and you who will laugh me into scorn?"

"By the god who begot my forefather," Estarion said, "and by the Sun he set in my hand, this is no trick. I offer it in good faith. Will you accept it?"

"You trust me as far as that?"

"One must give trust in order to receive it," Estarion said.

"What will you do?" Seti-re asked after a long pause.

Estarion realized that he had been forgetting to breathe. When there was air in his lungs again, he reached into the heart of his magic and drew forth a gem of fire. It was cool in his hand, hard and round like an earthly stone, but the center of it was living light. It pulsed with the beating of his heart.

Seti-re's eyes were wide. He trembled as he took the jewel that held the key to Estarion's life and soul. And yet he said mistrustfully, "*This* is your great weapon?"

"You know it is," Estarion said gently. "You can feel it thrumming to the center of you. That much power you have, turn your back on it though you will."

"But what am I to—"

Estarion wrought a chain of light, quickly, and strung the jewel from it, and presented it with a bow. It looked like a necklace of gold and fire-opal, luminous and beautiful but perfectly solid and earthly. "Guard it well," he said, "and beware. If you misuse it, it will repay you in kind."

Seti-re's lip curled, but he did not argue the point. He held the jewel gingerly, staring past it at Estarion. "Why does a god want a woman of her age, who is barren? Even though she is a queen?"

"Because she is herself," Estarion said. "Will you say the words?"

"Do you think you can compel me?"

Estarion smiled with awful sweetness. He held up his hand. In it lay a pebble. It was nothing like the fiery jewel he had given Seti-re, but within its grey dullness was a faint shimmer. "Trust for trust," he said, "and hostage for hostage. We bind one another, sir priest, and have each the power of life and death over the other."

Seti-re laughed suddenly. He was no more amiable than he had ever been, but in this laughter was genuine mirth. "Lord, you are devious! I almost begin to like you. What will you do with yonder stone? Swallow it? Fling it in the river?"

"Keep it," said Estarion, "against the time when our alliance is ended. Will you say the words?"

"I will say the words," Seti-re said. "On one condition."

Estarion raised a brow.

"That my enemies are your enemies. That if I call on you, you will answer, and aid me against them."

"If I may do so without harm to the queen or the city," said Estarion, "I will do it."

"Then I will say the words," said Seti-re.

FOURTEEN

T HE NEW GUARDIANS OF THE KINGDOM WENT OUT THAT EVENING WITH THEIR small furred allies, and disposed themselves among villagers who were more often baffled and suspicious than glad to be so protected. Tanit would have preferred to go with them, but the queen belonged in the city. She walked its streets at evening, unable quite to suppress the shiver of fear as the shadows lengthened, and saw how the cats built their walls of air. She could see those walls, how they rose and joined to shield the houses and people within.

"You have eyes to see," the Lord Seramon said. He came up on the city's walls, the walls of stone, not long after she had ascended there, and found her marveling at the intricacy of the wards.

"I'm not needed at all," she said. "This is entirely the cats' doing."

"Your people need to see you," said the Lord Seramon, "to know that you defend them."

"I think," she said, "that you gave me this title to keep me from demanding one less noble but more useful."

"You were queen of Waset long before I came here," he said with the flicker of a smile.

She hissed at him, but without rancor. Her hand had slid into his, entirely of its own accord. They stood together while the sun sank ever closer to the horizon.

Just when she was thinking that it would be wise to retreat to the palace, he said, "Seti-re will say the words that make me your consort."

"How in the gods' name—"

"We exchanged assurances," he said, "and agreed on an alliance. He has great love for this city, however poorly he may express it."

"He is my mother's brother," she said. "He arranged my marriage to the king. He was never altogether satisfied with the outcome."

"Because he couldn't control you?"

"And because there was no son and heir for him to raise and train in the temple."

The pain of that was old, and worn smooth. He did not shame her with pity, but he nearly broke her with the tenderness of a gesture: the soft stroke of a finger down her cheek. "You are what, and where, the gods will."

She spoke past the ache in her throat. "It will be dark soon. You may choose to spend the night under the sky, but I in my cowardice prefer the safety of a roof."

"Tonight we shall be cowards together," he said.

"Don't you want to see the wards go up across the kingdom?"

"I see them," he said in his deep purr of a voice.

She remembered then, as already she tended to forget, that he was not of her world. The awareness shivered in her skin, but somewhat oddly, it did not frighten her.

He followed her down from the walls, walking as a guard would, just behind her. They moved in a cloud of cats: his two, her two, a shifting circle of the city's defenders. At the palace gate, most of them faded into the twilight.

She had not been out so late since she was a reckless child. Even in the safety of the city, even knowing how well it was protected, she battled the urge to run through the gate and hide. She walked sedately as a queen should, pausing to greet the guards and to settle a matter brought to her by one of the servants, and to pray for a moment before the image of her husband's ancestor, the first king of Waset. His worn stone face grew dim as she prayed, veiling itself in dusk.

She looked up from that ancient face to the living one of the Lord Seramon. He was crowned with stars—the first that she had seen since, young and rebellious, she had gone up on the roof of her mother's house and looked full into the eyes of the night.

Darkness was terrible. Darkness was death. And yet in that face which was so dark, she found only comfort. He smiled at her. She wanted to melt into his arms, but she was not made for such softness. She turned from him, but without rejection, and led him into the royal house.

No human creature died that night, and no animal, either, nor was any villager stolen from his house. One field was stripped, but those near it were untouched. The wards had held.

There was festival in the villages. The people did not understand precisely what had saved them; only that priests and nobles had wielded magic, and that a god had shown them the way.

That their queen should take the god as a consort, they found perfectly right and fitting. The court reckoned it a scandal: three days he had been there, a shockingly brief time to come so far or to presume so much. But Tanit had expected that. She could see it, too: how sudden it was. Yet in her heart there was nothing sudden about it at all.

Seti-re brought them together in the temple before the gods and the people. He

was a good and proper ally; he put on a face, if not of joy, then at least of acceptance. He set her hand in the Lord Seramon's and blessed them in the names of
the gods, and performed the sacrifice of a white heifer and a black bull-calf, pouring out their blood over the altar-stone.

Tanit was in a world outside the world. She saw herself in royal state, robed and
crowned, with her face painted into the mask of a goddess, and her hair hidden
beneath an elaborate structure of plaits and beads and gold. She saw him beside
her, more simply dressed, but wearing royalty as easily, as naturally as his skin. How
strange that he the god should keep no more state than any noble bridegroom, but
she who was inescapably mortal should wear the semblance of divinity.

His fingers laced in hers, his eyes warm upon her, brought her back into her
body. "From before time I have known you," she said.

She had spoken in silence, in a pause in the rite. Seti-re looked affronted. But he
mattered not at all. The Lord Seramon bent his head. "From beyond the horizon
I came to you," he said, "and when the worlds have passed away, still I will belong
to you."

Those were the vows that bound them, far more than blessings spoken by any
priest. They were truth so simple, so pure and absolute, that there could be no
breaking them.

She did not, even then, feel constrained. For this she had been born. Whatever
came of it, she would never regret the choice that she had made.

The wedding feast had been prepared in haste, but the cooks had outdone themselves. There was a roast ox and a flock of wild geese roasted and stuffed with dates
and barley, heaping platters of cakes made with nuts and honey and sweet spices,
plates and bowls of greens and roots and fruit both fresh and dried, and an endless
procession of lesser delights. At evening the guests did not flee as they had so often
before. The bold would go home under protection of the wards, and the rest would
stay in the palace until the sun rose.

Estarion would not have been startled to discover that he was expected to play host
to all of them through what should have been the wedding night. He had known
stranger customs. He was seated apart from the queen, among the great men of the
kingdom; she sat with a flock of ladies, as blankly unreadable as a painted image.

He set himself to be charming to these men who eyed him in wariness or hostility or, here and there, open speculation. He was somewhat out of practice in the
art of seducing courtiers, but it was not a skill one could altogether forget. These
courtiers were far less jaded than those of Asanion, if not quite as easy in their
manners as those of his northern kingdoms. They were not warriors, but neither
were they purely creatures of courts. They made him think of small landowners
and gentlemen farmers of the Hundred Realms: bound to the earth, the river, the
hunt; shaped in small compass, but not petty of either mind or spirit.

He liked them. They were as flawed as men of any other world, but there was honesty in them, and care for their people, even under the long weight of the shadow. He had learned the names of each, and would learn their lands, their cares, their kin—later. Tonight he learned their minds, how they thought, what they hoped for; what, apart from the darkness, they feared.

Not long after sunset, a servant bent toward his ear and murmured, "Lord. It's time."

He had been listening to a tale told by a lord from a holding upriver, of hunting terrible long-toothed beasts in the cataracts of the south. "They can bite a man in half," the lord said, "and fling a calf out of his skin with a toss of the head. They have a taste for manflesh; they'll raid boats and steal the boatmen's children. Once I heard tell—"

The servant touched Estarion's shoulder, polite but urgent. "Lord!"

He excused himself as courteously as he could. No one took offense, even the teller of tales: a grin ran round the circle, and they vied in wishing him well. The warmth of their regard followed him out of the hall.

The servant led him not toward the queen's chambers as he had expected, nor to his own, but to a part of the palace which he had yet to explore. It was older than the rest, lower, darker, less airy and elegant. Its walls were plastered and painted, but the paint was fading. The air smelled of dust and age, overlaid with the scent of flowers.

They entered a chamber that might once have been a royal hall. Squat pillars held up the roof. The center was an island of light, banks of lamps arrayed in a broad circle, rising up toward the pillars and suspended from the ceiling. The extravagance of it, the soft clarity of the light, made all the richer the carpet of flowers that spread across the worn stone of the floor.

A bed was set there, strewn with fragrant petals, and beside it a table and a chest, the accoutrements of a royal bedchamber. She was not there. But for the servant, and the cat who coiled purring at the bed's foot, he was alone. In a moment, the servant effaced himself and was gone.

Estarion smiled. He had a fondness for the unexpected, if it was not too deadly. He took off his kilt and jewels and laid them in the chest, which was empty, and unbound the ropes of gold and strings of beads from his hair; then plaited it again in a single thick braid, bound off with a bit of cord. He sat cross-legged on the bed, and waited in the patience that priests and mages learned in youth.

Soft airs played across his skin. The scent of flowers was almost overpowering. Within himself he felt the wards upon city and kingdom. The darkness was late in coming; the night was quiet, the stars untainted. He knew a prickle of unease, of old and intractable suspicion: a deep mistrust of stillness in the heart of war.

Such quiet could be a gift, if a general had both wisdom and courage. Old habits were waking, fitting themselves to him like familiar garments. Yet he was calmer than he had been then, less impatient, less inclined to indulge his temper. He had learned to wait.

Almost he laughed. Patience indeed! Three days in this world, and he had bound himself to it with no honest thought for the consequences. And yet he could not find it in himself to regret it. What he had said to her in the temple was true. This had been ordained; this was where he was meant to be, and she, in this age of both their worlds.

He looked up in his island of light, into her face. She was standing on the edge of the darkness. Her mask of paint was gone, all but the jeweled elaboration of the eyes. Her hair was free, blue-black and shining, pouring down her back to the sweet curve of her buttocks. She was wrapped in a gown of sheer white linen, such as he had seen before. As before, it concealed nothing. The dark aureoles of her nipples, the triangle of her private hair, were but thinly veiled.

Her eyes were wide and dark, and blank, almost blind. Yet he knew that she saw every line of him. He frightened her a little with his size and darkness, the breadth of his shoulders and the strength of his arms and thighs. She was avoiding, with care, the thing that both frightened and fascinated her most.

He rose. He heard the faint catch of her breath, but she did not retreat. When he knelt, she eased a little. He was not so towering tall then, or so inclined to loom. He smiled at her. He might have thought that all those sharp white teeth would alarm her, but she warmed to his warmth, and smiled somewhat shakily in return.

She advanced into the light. Her feet bruised the blossoms strewn on the floor, sending up a gust of sweetness. She knelt in front of him, and lightly, almost trembling, brushed his lips with hers.

The leap of his body toward her took him aback with its strength. He mastered it before it flung him upon her. It seemed she sensed nothing. While he knelt rigidly still, she traced the lines of his face with her fingers. Her touch was like the brush of fire over his skin. She followed the track of a scar, the curve of his lip; she hesitated ever so slightly between smoothness of cheekbone and prick of close-shaved stubble. She coaxed his mouth open and stroked a salt-sweet fingertip across his tongue, and counted his teeth as if he had been a senel at a fair, catching her finger on the sharp curve of a canine. Her own were not so many; they were blunter, and her tongue, running over them, was pink.

Her scent was musk and spices. He breathed it in while she explored his body, downward from his face across neck and shoulders and breast, down his arms, along his sides. She turned his hands palm up, the dark and the gold, and assured herself that indeed it was gold, born in the flesh, rooted deep in bone and sinew. The fire in it, so much a part of him that it had long ago ceased to be pain, flared suddenly, then just as suddenly eased. He met her eyes and fell down and down, headlong into joy.

The love of man and woman was an awkward and often ridiculous thing. Tanit, in teaching herself the ways of his body, the things that were subtly or not so subtly different, knew that she was putting off the inevitable. With Kare the king, it had been a thing she did out of duty. She lay as still as she could, and did as he bade, and waited for it to be over. Then in a few months, either the blood and the pain came, or the child was born and drew a breath and died.

With this man who was not exactly a man, with his blue-black tongue and his predator's teeth, she caught herself thinking thoughts that she had never imagined she could think. Her maids did, and ladies of the court, too—their gossip was full of it, how this man's face or that man's eyes or another man's private parts made their bellies melt. She had never melted for anyone—until, so brief a time ago, this stranger from beyond the horizon lay unconscious at her feet.

He was fully conscious now, kneeling subject to her will, with a look about him that made it clear how great an effort it was to remain so still. He had mastered even *that* part of him. How she knew that it was force of will and not lack of desire, she could not tell; she only knew that it was so.

Her heart was beating hard. Her skin was now hot, now cold. Her belly—yes, her belly was melting as she looked at him, his beauty and strangeness. His eyes were as deep as the river. His lips tasted of honey, drowning her in sweetness.

His breast, his legs and arms, were lightly pelted with curling hair. She ran fingers through that on his breast. He quivered; then stilled. He was waking below. His will was weakening, or he had loosed its bonds.

She should cast off her gown and lie on the bed and let him get it over. But the fear in her would not let her do that—fear, and something else. Something that was inextricably a part of the melting in her middle. She wanted—she needed—

He rose in one long fluid movement, sweeping her up with such effortless strength that she laughed, borne as on a wave of the river. Her arms linked about his neck. She had gone from fear to a dizzy delight, a singing brightness in which nothing mattered, no darkness, no terror, only those eyes meeting hers and that body warm against her. For long moments she was not even certain which body was his, and which hers. They were all one, all woven together, flesh and manifold souls.

It was not as awkward as she had feared. Her body knew, after all, how to dance the dance. When it was ridiculous, he laughed as hard as she, rolling together in the banks of flowers.

He ended on his back, she sprawled along the length of him. He shifted; she stirred. She gasped. He was inside her, filling her, just on the edge of pain; until with a sigh she let the pain go. He had sobered. His eyes were softer than she had ever thought they could be. She kissed the lid of each, and found the long slow rhythm, the ebb and surge of the world.

When the release came, she cried out in astonishment. She had never—she could never—

It broke like the crest of the river in flood. She sank down and forever down, cradled in his arms, in a sweetness of crushed flowers. He was breathing lightly, as if he had been running. Skin slid on skin, slicked with sweat. She lifted a head that felt impossibly heavy. His eyes were shut, his head tilted back, but she could feel his awareness like a brush of fingers down her spine. Was this what it was to have magic?

"This is what it is to love a mage," he said. He kissed the crown of her head. "Beautiful lady."

"Splendid man."

He laughed softly. Her heart was singing—and so, her bones knew, was his. They would raise the light, and break the darkness. She knew that, just then, in that night in which the shadows never came.

FIFTEEN

TELL ME OF YOUR WORLD," SHE SAID.

They lay together in the long stretch of night before dawn. She had slept; he had rested in the quiet. Deep quiet, empty of enemies.

She had awakened in his arms, rumpled and beautiful. Her thoughts murmured inside of his. The words grew out of them. "What is it like? Is it like this?"

"A little," he said. "The sky, the sun—they're very like. We have deserts and rivers and green country. Mountains, too; and seas, which are rivers that fill the world, and taste powerfully of salt."

"We know of seas," she said. "The river flows into one. They say it's green. Someday I mean to see it and know for myself." And after a pause: "Tell me more."

"There are two moons," he said. "One is red, like blood, and so vast that in some seasons it seems to fill half the sky. The other is white and small and very bright. Long ago people believed that the red moon was the darkness' child, and the white moon was born of the light. Now we believe that darkness and light are twinned; that one cannot exist without the other."

She sighed on his breast. "And you? You believe that?"

"I know that in my world it is true."

"That is rather wonderful," she said. "Fitting for a world full of gods."

"There are men, too. And women."

"But not you."

"I was born," he said, "of a line of divine madmen. The first of them was a renegade without a father, a priestess' son when priestesses were put to death for violating their vows of fidelity to the god. But she had lain with the god, or with a man who had been possessed by the god—no one ever truly doubted that, not once they knew him. He was . . . not as other men were. He won himself an empire, but saw his own heir turn against him, make alliance with the son of his great enemy, and so cast him down. The two of them imprisoned him in a tower of magic and enchanted him into sleep, and so took him out of the world but not out of life. With that act they made a greater empire, and ruled it together. Their son inherited, and his son after him, and after him my father. Then I was born, and I was to be all that was most splendid in our world: mage, king, priest of Sun and Shadow.

"When I was twelve years old, a rebel killed my father. I destroyed the murderer, but nearly destroyed myself. It was long years before I was whole again. I was emperor for a mortal lifetime. I saw my son born, and I saw him die. I raised his daughter to be my heir, and she raised hers. When their time had come, I left the empire to them, and walked away."

"Such tales," she said. "Such brevity. I'll make you tell me the whole of every story."

"Only if you promise to tell me yours."

"Mine is nothing," she said. "I come from a lordly family near the border of Tasenet. My mother is the old priest's daughter and the high priest's sister. I was married in youth to the king. The king died; there was no one else to rule the city. Now I am queen, and the rest you know."

"Such brevity," he said. "This is why there are singers and poets: because we who live the tales have no gift for telling them."

She laughed her rich bubbling laugh. "My singers will make a legend for you and spare you the trouble. May you be the son of a god and a goddess? Were they gloriously beautiful?"

"My mother was," he said. "She was a chieftain's daughter of a wild tribe, a priestess of the dark goddess. My father saw her dancing by the fire one night as he tarried with the tribe during a hunt. He loved her then and ever after. It was a scandal in its day: he had resisted every marriage that anyone tried to make for him, and when at long last he did marry, he married for love."

"Ah," she sighed. "You can tell a tale after all. Will I be a scandal among the gods? Will they be horrified to discover that you gave yourself in marriage to a mortal woman?"

Estarion's lips twitched. One corner of his mouth turned irresistibly upward. "My heir will be absolutely appalled. She was as rebellious a child as a king should ever hope not to have. She chose her daughter's father for his beauty and lineage, used him like a fine bull, and sent him home to his wives when she had what she wanted of him. It was years before even I learned who had fathered her child. But then she found a noble consort, a man of perfect probity, and married him and adopted his son and became everything that she had formerly professed to despise. She's a better ruler than I ever was, and more truly suited to it, but a more humorless creature I've seldom known."

"Humor is not a virtue in a ruler," Tanit said.

"Isn't it? I do love that child, but if she learned to laugh, she might be happier."

"Maybe someday you will teach her."

"I'm afraid it's far too late," he said wryly. "Her daughter, too—poor things, they're children of grim duty from the cradle. They honor me as an ancestor, but it's been a relief to them that I've retreated from the field. I'm much too light-minded for the cares of empires."

"Now you mock yourself," she said. She folded her hands on his breast and propped her chin on them, and contemplated his face. It seemed to give her no little pleasure. "The gods have no humor—all the priests assure us of that. It seems to me your heirs are very proper goddesses, and you are a properly fallen god. The priests will not be reassured."

"Should they be?"

"About this? Maybe not. They'll do well not to take you for granted."

"Such a delicate balance," he said, "between scandal and contempt."

"You are not only light-minded," she said, "you are wicked. What shall I do with you?"

"Love me," he said.

Her smile bloomed, slow and wonderful, transforming her face from loveliness into breathtaking beauty. Dear gods, he loved her. He had not known such fullness of the heart since he had loved a priestess who was a commoner, long ago in the turning of the worlds. With her too it had been the matter of a moment: a glimpse, a glance, a word spoken.

They had not been lovers long, though they had remained friends until the day she died. This one was sworn to him by vows that he meant to keep.

As if she had followed his thoughts, she said, "You'll leave me in the end."

"No," he said. "No, I will not."

"Of course you will." She sounded undismayed. "Your blood and kin will call you, and you'll go. Only give me what you can, and help our kingdom as you may, and we'll all be content."

"Even you?"

Her gaze was level under the strongly painted brows. "I never looked for this, never hoped or dreamed for it. Every moment that I have it is a gift of the gods. When it ends, I'll weep. I'm not made of stone; but neither am I a crumbling reed. I'll carry on, my lord, and remember that I loved you."

"I might surprise you," he said, "and stay."

"Don't make promises you can't keep," she said. "You've given me yourself while you can. That's enough. Now love me, my lord, and be glad of these hours together. Long after they're gone, they'll hold us in memory."

He shook his head, but he was not inclined to argue with her, not just then. The sun was coming. The shadow had let this world be for one blessed night. She was ready to be loved again, and he, he discovered, was ready to do the loving. He

laughed for the simple joy of that, and took her in his arms again, and kissed her as
deep as either of them could bear.

She wrapped arms and legs about him and took him in her turn. She was no
meek submissive woman; not she. He loved her for it, as for everything that she
was or promised to be.

The shadow did not come back the next night, either, nor the next. People began to
say that it was gone; that the god's coming, the walls of magic he had taught them
to raise, the marriage he had made with their queen, had driven the enemy away.
They would hardly lay aside years of fear and hiding, not in three days or four, but
the young and reckless took it on themselves to go out at night, to see the stars; and
there was festival in daylight, feasting and rejoicing, until between weariness and
simple need to bake the bread and brew the beer the festival ended and the people
returned to their daily tasks.

When ten days had passed with no taint on the stars, even the most wary began
to wonder if it were true—if the darkness had been driven away. It had become a
game and a fashion to brave the night. At first it had been enough to ascend to the
roofs, and the boldest slept there in the cool and the breezes. But youth was not to
be outdone. Gatherings of young men walked beyond walls and wards, embold-
ened by an ample ration of beer and palm wine. Then some headlong soul took it
into his head to embark on the river with lamps and torches and a troupe of musicians as mad as he was, for a carousal that echoed over the water and sounded
faintly within the palace.

Tanit was ready to call out the guard, but the Lord Seramon stopped her.
"They're safe enough tonight," he said.

"And tomorrow night? Will they be safe?"

"I don't know," he said.

"You think it will come back."

"I know it will," he said.

She did not know why her heart should sink. She had had no illusions; she had
not imagined that this was more than a respite. But her heart had persisted in hoping against hope.

She rose from their bed and clapped her hands for her maid. He lay for a while,
watching her, but when Tisheri had come, he disentangled himself from the coverlets and vanished in the direction of his own chambers. He would be back. There
was less need for words between them, the longer they were bound together.

Tisheri did not approve of what she clearly was going to do, but it was not a
maid's place to gainsay her queen. She dressed Tanit and arranged her hair, and
adorned her in some of the lesser jewels. Then, with paling face but determined
expression, she accompanied her lady out into the night.

The royal boat was waiting, the boatmen yawning but steadfast, and the Lord

Seramon standing at the steering oar, a shadow on shadow with a gleam of golden eyes. At first she thought with a small shock that he had come out as naked as he had left his bed, but when he moved, the torchlight caught the folds of a dark kilt. She rebuked herself for the quiver of regret.

It was very dark, even with torches. The stars were small and far away. The moon hung low. The world was a strange place, so full of hidden things, and yet while he was there, her fear could not consume her. She could see beauty in this darkness, as she saw in him.

The revelers on the water were not too far gone in wine and beer to be astonished that the queen and her consort had joined them. The tone of their carousing muted sharply; they were suddenly, painfully constrained. Tanit had herself lifted into their boat; they hastened to find a seat for her, to offer drink and what little food there was, and to cover their naked drunken women as best they might.

She kept her amusement carefully veiled. As she had expected, once they were burdened with the task of entertaining her, they grew much less enamored of their exploit—particularly the ringleaders, whose fathers were lords of her council. One tried to hide; the other covered his embarrassment with bravado, and might have offered impertinence if her consort had not appeared at her side.

The Lord Seramon was even more terrifying in the dark than in the light. His presence dampened the last of their enthusiasm. But when they would have ordered their boatmen to turn toward the bank, the Lord Seramon said, "Oh, no. It's not so very far to dawn. We'll see the sun rise on the river. Isn't that what you had in mind?"

Tanit doubted that they had thought so far ahead, but they would hardly say so to him. They were all too neatly trapped, and had no choice but to give way to his whim.

He folded himself at her feet, smiling at the young idiots from the city. The musicians, less far gone in beer and perhaps wiser, too, began to play a softer tune than they had been playing heretofore. Their singer had a remarkably sweet voice. The sound of it in starlight, trilling out over the water, was like nothing Tanit had known.

In a strange way it made her angry. The night should be hers, just as the day was. The shadow had robbed her of that.

She would take it back for always, not just for what brief time this respite gave her. She would have the stars and the moon, and the river flowing black but aflicker with starlight. The night was glorious. She would claim it for her own, as she had claimed this child of gods who lay at her feet.

SIXTEEN

DAROS FELL FROM DARKNESS INTO DARKNESS. THE SPARK OF LIGHT THAT HAD drawn him winked out just before the Gate took hold of him. He fell, rolling and tumbling, with his magery in tatters and his wits all scattered. He fetched up with bruising force against something that might, perhaps, be a wall.

He lay winded, throbbing with aches. He did not think his neck was broken. He could move his fingers, his toes. He could roll groaning onto his back.

Almost he might have thought he had fallen back into the chamber of the rite in the dark fortress, but he knew deep in his bruised bones that that was gone. This was a different room in a different world. Tall slits of windows surrounded it. Strangeness flickered in them, like flame, if flame could be dark.

A pale blue light welled slowly. In this darkness it seemed as bright as moonlight. He sat up with care. His hands were glowing with that sickly light; it seemed to come from within him, though he had done nothing, raised no magic, nor willed it at all.

Something stirred in the circle of light. It unfolded, straightened.

It had a man's shape: it stood on two legs, lifted two arms. But it was not quite a man. The face was too long, the chin too sharp, the mouth lipless. The nose was a sharp hooked curve. Its eyes were round and huge, like an owl's. They blinked at him.

His power was drained almost to nothing, but he had enough, just, to raise a shield about his mind. And none too soon, either. The blow that struck it swayed him to his knees.

He crouched on the cold stone floor. He had no weapon, no magery to wield. The creature stood above him. In some remote way he supposed that he should be afraid.

It lifted him to his feet. Its hands were four-fingered, like a bird's, and the fingers were very long, thin pale skin stretched over bones that flexed in too many ways, in too many places. It brushed them over his face, ruffling his hair. It spoke in a voice like a flute played far away.

He had the gift of tongues; it was common enough among mages. He understood the words, though there was a strange stretching, as if they did not mean quite what his sore-taxed magic tried to make them mean. "Recover quickly, please, and go. You are not safe here."

"You brought me here," he said, realizing it even as he said it. "Now you send me away?"

"You are not what I expected," the creature said.

"I disappoint you?"

The owl-eyes blinked slowly. "You are young," it said. "Your spirit is light. What I called . . . it was strong; a sun burned in it."

A bark of laughter escaped him. The creature recoiled as if an animal had snapped in its face. "I know what you called. I was hunting him. Shall I find him for you?"

"I called you," the creature said. "You, too. You both. He would come, you would come. One more would come. But not only you."

"Why?"

"I need you both," it said. "You are young, your spirit is light. He is a little less young, and strong—so very strong. Almost as strong as you."

"I am not—"

"You will be." The creature straightened. What had seemed a cowl, veiling its head, unfurled and shook itself free and rose, fanning like the crest of some great bird. It glowed in the blue light, shimmering in bands of white and blue and icy green.

He was gaping like an idiot. The creature loomed over him, beautiful and unspeakably strange. And yet, looking into those round pale-golden eyes, he saw a spirit that was not, after all, so very different from his own. "You are a mage," he said.

"Mage," it said. "You may call me that. Mage."

"Mage," he said. "What do you need of us?"

"I need you," it said. "This place—this prison—this thing I am compelled to do—"

Daros' head ached with making sense of alien words. He had little power left, barely enough to be certain that the walls of this place were more than stone, they were wards as well. What they guarded, what they forced upon the prisoner . . .

That was the knowledge he had brought from the citadel. The darkness was made, and magic had made it. There were oaths, covenants—

"But you are not a dark god," he said. "You're a mage, no more if no less. How could you have brought *that* into being?"

"Simply," it said. "You could do it. Be afraid of what might come from beyond the stars; ward your world. Build the wards to renew themselves. Bind them with darkness because it is stronger for this than light. Let the darkness grow too strong. Then—then—" It stopped, as if it had lost the courage to go on.

"Then see the darkness gain a will of its own?"

"Not its own will," the Mage said. "What I was afraid of—it came. My wards brought it, my darkness. It found me and took me prisoner. It compelled me to do its bidding."

"It? What is it?"

"Will to conquer," it said.

He did not understand.

The Mage furled its crest and lifted him without effort: though its limbs were stick-thin, they were strong. It cradled him as if he had been an infant. He struggled, but it ignored him. It flung him through one of the many narrow windows.

It was, as he had thought, a Gate. The Mage's awareness was about him, its power on him, though its body could not leave its prison. Enfolded in that half-alien, half-familiar magic, he slipped through mists and shadow onto a wide and barren plain. Wind blew across it, sighing with endless regret. Clouds veiled the stars, if stars there were.

A city rose on the plain. It was a city of night, lit by no moon or star. There were people in it—human people. He could have no doubt of that. Weak with exhaustion though his magery was, the Mage's power sustained him, and lent him a little of what he lacked.

It bore him on silent wings, soaring above the walls and towers, the dark windows and blank doorways. People moved through the streets, passed through the doors. They were blind: they had no eyes. There were no mages among them.

They labored with grim and endless persistence. What they did, he could not always understand. They ground grain, they forged metal. There were no fields to till; the grain must come from lands where the sun shone: lands that were raided, stripped and emptied of their riches. Just so were the people made captive, bound and enslaved, their eyes taken and their minds darkened and their souls held prisoner.

It was conquest, and absolute. "But why?" he cried to the power that cradled him. "Who would do this?"

It carried him onward, up through the levels of the city to a nest of towers at its summit. There was darkness visible, lightlessness so profound that he felt it on his face like the weight of heavy wool, clinging close, trapping his breath.

It tore away. He saw again with mage-sight, clear in the darkness. He looked down into a hall that, though alien in its lines and the shape of its pillars, was surely royal. Figures stood in ranks there. They were cloaked, cowled. He looked for faces, but saw none.

They were not like the Mage. They were men, he could have sworn to it—yet men who could not abide the light. They lived in darkness. Darkness was their element. They wielded it as a weapon. They clung to it as a haven.

They would blind the stars, and darken the sun of every world. They sang of it, a slow rolling chant, very like the chant of the priests in the citadel on his own world. The god or power to which they sang was the darkness itself. The Mage had opened its way into the worlds, fed it and nurtured it, and made it strong.

They had no magic, these men who lived in night. They were empty of it; and yet that emptiness lured the dark, and gave it substance.

He began to see as he hovered above them why they had captured the Mage; what they needed of it, that they were so utterly lacking. The Mage was a weapon in their long and holy war. Light into darkness, darkness into silence, silence into oblivion.

He fled before it engulfed him. He twisted free of the Mage's grip, broke the wards, and with the last strength that was in him flung himself through the Gate.

Death's wings beat close, so close that they brushed him with the wind of their passing. His bones cracked with the cold of it. He was stripped bare of will and wit. One thing was left, one memory, one presence. It drew him irresistibly from darkness into darkness.

He opened his eyes on the Mage's face. Its crest was upraised like a strange crown. "You are strong," it said, "but not yet wise. Do you see, young mage? Do you understand?"

"No," he said. His voice was a strangled gasp.

"The fabric of what is," it said. "I tore it. My world is gone, my people . . ." It made a strange whistling sound, like wind in a wasteland, eerie and unbearably sad. "They who came, they worship the void; they bind their souls to nothingness. They conquer in order to destroy. They would unmake the worlds."

"It seems they're succeeding," he said.

"You are too light of spirit," it said. "You do not know that you are mortal—even now, even believing what I tell you. You expect to live forever."

"I do believe that my soul will," he said. "Or are they going to destroy that, too? Will they even slay the gods?"

"Everything," said the Mage. "All that is."

He shivered. "There is no hope, is there?"

"Most likely not," the Mage said, "but I am alive, and I cannot keep myself from hoping. I called you to me, you and the other, with the strongest spell that was left to me. I set it to find the one thing that could stop this tide of nothingness."

"I? And my emperor?"

"He is an emperor?" The Mage seemed . . . disappointed?

Daros thought he could understand. "He's been a shepherd since before I was born."

"Ah," said the Mage in evident relief. "Kings and kings of kings, they are no use to us. It will not be pride or power that wins this war, if it can be won."

"I am a prince," Daros said. "Is that an impediment?"

"You are a well-bred animal," said the Mage. "It seems hardly to trouble you. You must go now—I have held us out of time, but now it turns in spite of me. I give you this. Keep it safe; when the time comes, you will know its use."

Daros found that his hand was clenched about something narrow and strangely supple. When he looked down, he saw that it was a feather, glowing blue in mage-sight. He slipped it into the purse that hung from his belt. Even as his hand withdrew, the Mage and the room and the myriad windows whirled away. He spun like a leaf in a whirlwind.

He gave himself up to it. There was nothing else he could do. He let his body go slack, his limbs sprawl where they would. His mind held its center.

He burst through darkness into blinding light. It stabbed him with blessed agony. It was so wonderful, so glorious, and so excruciating that he dropped to the splendid stabbing of stones, and laughed until he wept.

Something jabbed his ribs. It was not a stone. Those were under him, blissfully uncomfortable. This was alive: it thrust again, bruising several of his myriad bruises. He caught it, still blind with light, and wrenched it aside. The gasp at the other end, the grunt of a curse, told him what he had known when he closed fingers about it: it was a spearhaft, and there was a man gripping it.

Men. He could see now, a little, through the streaming of tears: shadows against the light. They were human. They were small; Asanian-small, lightly built and wiry. Their hair and eyes were dark, their skin reddish-bronze, rather like his own.

They all were dressed in kilts, and they all had spears. The man who had brought him so rudely to his senses stood disarmed, staring at the point of his own spear, angled toward his heart.

Daros lowered it slowly, grounded the butt of it, and used it as a crutch to lever himself to his feet. The spearmen fell back before him. The tallest came just to his shoulder.

He had never towered before. It was an odd sensation; he was not sure that he liked it. Towering was for northerners. He was a plainsman; he was accustomed to being a tall man but not a giant.

He resisted the urge to stoop. They were staring, but not, he realized, at his height. He shook his hair out of his face.

The copper brightness of it made him pause, then smile wryly. Of course they would stare at that. Even plainsmen did, and they were born under the rule of red Gileni princes.

This was not his world, even a remote corner of it. He could feel the strangeness underfoot, the heartbeat of earth that was never his own. The sun was very hot, and he was dressed for the roof of the world. He stripped off his woolen mantle, his coat of leather and fur, his tunic, his shirt, his fur-lined boots, and—with the flick of a glance at the men who watched—his leather breeches. Even the light trews felt like a burden, but he kept those. He did not know how modest men were here, nor would it do to offend before he had even uttered a greeting.

He looked almost as battered as he felt. Bruises stained his skin along the ribs, down the shoulders and arms. One knee was a remarkable shade of purple, shading to livid as it ascended his thigh. He was not particularly lame on it, which was rather odd.

He gathered his garments into a bundle and bound it with his belt, fastened his purse with its precious burden about his middle, and said politely, "Good day, sirs. Would any of you have a sip of water to spare?"

The man he had disarmed had a half-full skin at his belt. He held it out, word-lessly. Daros bowed, smiled, sipped. He drank three swallows: far less than he wanted, but enough for courtesy, from the flicker of the man's eyes. He bowed again and returned the waterskin to its owner.

While Daros slaked his thirst, the man seemed to have reached a conclusion. "Tell me, lord, if you will," he said. "Do you come from beyond the horizon?"

Daros' gaze followed his. The horizon was a jagged black line beyond a wilder-ness of sand and stone. The sky above it was a vivid, almost unbearable blue. A winged thing hung there, in shape like a hawk. With no thought at all, Daros lifted his hand.

The hawk came down to it, plummeting out of the sky, braking with a snap of wings, settling lightly on his fist. Its claws pricked; he paid no heed to that small pain amid so many others. He looked into that wild golden eye, that pure feral mind. It had no fear of him. It was kin.

It leaped from his fist into the freedom of the air. He lowered his stinging hand. Beads of blood gleamed on it, scarlet on bronze.

The men about him sighed, all together. Their captain's suspicions had not eased, but it seemed he had had the answer he sought. "Come, lord," he said. "Come with us."

Daros sensed no danger in any of them, not unless he offered a threat. He tucked his bundle under his arm and offered his weaponless, nearly naked self for their inspection. "Lead, sir," he said. "I follow."

They led him away from the sand, over a sharp blade of hill, and down to startling, glorious green: the valley of a broad river, bordered in desert. There were villages along the river, and towns, and one town larger than the rest, which here might pass for a city.

He would have given much for a senel to carry him, but he saw nothing of that kin or kind. They had cattle, not unlike the cattle of his world, but he saw no one on the backs of those. People traveled afoot or in boats, or once in a chair on the shoulders of brawny men, as men went in this place. They were still small and slight beside him.

He walked because he must, though he was going blind again, this time with exhaustion. When they paused for water, he drank three measured sips, and rather to his surprise, was offered three more. They had bread with it; he ate a little, but it was coarse and gritty and its taste was strange. He was hungry, but not hungry enough for that.

The sun was much lower when at last they came to the city. He walked because he had no choice. People stared; a murmur followed him. "A god. Another god."

He was too tired to wonder what they meant by that. The shade of walls was welcome, even redolent of crowded humanity.

They took him inside a house, large as houses went here, with a guarded gate and high thick walls. It was cool inside, and the stench of the city was less; he caught the sweetness of flowers. His companions left him there, and quiet kilted people took him in hand. They brought him to a cool dim room, bathed him and dried him and laid him in a bed, and cooled him with fans until he slid into sleep.

He slept long and deep. If he dreamed, he did not remember. He woke with the awareness of where he was and how he had come there, complete in his mind, like the magic that had poured back into him like wine into a cup. It was horribly weak still, and his head ached abominably, but he had known worse after a long night's carouse.

The servants were ready for him to rise. They had bread and thin sour beer, fruit and cheese, and a pot of honey. The bread was not so ill, dipped in the honey. He was starving. He ate every scrap, to the servants' manifest approval.

He smiled at them. They smiled back. One offered to comb his hair—an honor the man had won against the rest, from the look of him. The color of it fascinated them. They had already satisfied themselves that it was real, running curious fingers over his brows and lashes and the light dusting of stubble on cheeks and chin. They presumed no further, which was well; he was not in a wanton mood this morning.

Fed and combed and shaven, and dressed in a kilt of lovely lightness and coolness, he was judged fit to be brought before the lord of the house. He was not moving so stiffly now; the raw edges of his magic were healing. He kept it close within himself, letting slip only enough to understand and be understood.

The servants led him through halls and courts, past people who stared, some openly, some behind the screen of fans. Many were women; some were lovely by any canon. They returned his glances with a clear sense of welcome. He was a great beauty, they agreed in murmurs that he was meant to hear. They wondered aloud if all of him was as beautiful as the parts that they could see.

Courts, it seemed, were the same in every world. He prepared his most proper and princely face for the lord of this one, as well as his patience, if he should be required to wait upon his highness' pleasure.

In that rather insouciant frame of mind, he entered a room of painted walls and heavy pillars, lit by shafts of sunlight. The lord was sitting just on the edge of one such blaze of brilliance, erect in a gilded chair. There was a creature in his lap, a very small but very magical cat. It eyes were the image of his, clear gold.

Daros laughed for pure delighted astonishment. "My lord!"

The emperor grinned at him, wide and white in a face that had lost half a score of years with the shaving of its thick greying beard. He shifted the cat to the floor at his feet and rose, sweeping Daros into a strong embrace.

Daros' eyes had spilled over. Foolishness; but he was tired still, and a little overwrought. The emperor held him at arm's length, looked him up and down, and said, "Avaryan and Uveryen, boy; something's been at you with cudgels."

"It was a long hunt," Daros said. He sighed. He was not particularly weak in the knees, but Estarion set him in the chair and stood over him, searching his face with eyes that saw everything Daros had to tell.

His hands came to rest on Daros' shoulders. Daros had no power to rise or to turn away. He had never been less inclined toward easy insolence.

"Show me," said Estarion.

Daros had brought the purse with its few oddments and its one great gift. He drew it out carefully. It weighed as light here as in that place between worlds, but in sunlight its appearance was transformed. It was pure and stainless white, and it shimmered like moonlight on water.

Estarion did not venture to touch it. A slow breath escaped him. He nodded slightly; Daros put the feather away, with a little regret and a little relief.

There was a silence. Daros broke it after some little while. "You really are the lord of this place?"

The emperor's brow arched. "That surprises you?"

"Knowing you, my lord," said Daros, "no. Are you working your way back up from shepherd?"

"I do hope not," Estarion said. "This is a little different from any occupation I've held before: royal consort."

"Royal—ah!" That did surprise Daros. "Does time move differently here? How many years is it since you came?"

"It's barely two Brightmoon-cycles," Estarion said, "and yes, that's mortal fast work. Come and meet her. Then you'll understand."

Daros set his lips together and settled for a nod. Nothing that he could say would be exactly wise. Estarion had a look that he could hardly mistake. Whatever this royal lady was, she must be beyond remarkable, to so enchant the lord of Sun and Lion.

She was in a small court near the wall that surrounded the house, kilted like a man and armed with a spear, doing battle against three men. Daros recognized one: the captain who had found him in the desert yesterday.

She was fast and strong. She was as tall as the captain, slender without slightness, but he could have no doubt that she was a woman. Her breasts, in Han-Gilen, would have been reckoned perfect: neither large nor small, round and firm, with broad dark nipples. Her face was a narrow oval, her features carved clean, beauty without softness, as pure as a steel blade.

Oh, he understood: he would have been astonished, seeing her, to discover that Estarion had not taken her for his own. She was no callow child; she was younger than Merian, perhaps, but not by overmuch. If he had come there first, he might have had thoughts of claiming her for himself.

It was too late for that now. She finished her fight, and well, but he saw how she was aware of Estarion, how her face and body changed subtly in his presence. This was a woman in love, and with all that was in her. Nor was it unrequited. The force of the bond between them rocked Daros on his feet.

He had heard of such a thing, but never seen it. His mother, his father—they were reckoned a love-match, but not with the absolute purity of this. They were two who had joined for love and for policy. These were the halves of one creature.

She flattened one of her opponents with a sweeping blow, knocked one of the others onto his back with the butt of the spear, and froze the captain in midstroke with the tempered copper point of the spear against the vein of his throat. He bowed and surrendered. She smiled a swift vivid smile.

Daros was in love. It had nothing in it of lust; he would never touch what these two had, even if he could. As she turned toward him, he bowed to her as to the queen she was.

She raised him with a queen's dignity. Her smile lingered, illumining her face. "Welcome to my city, my lord," she said.

"You are most kind, lady," he said.

"It's only your due," she said, "as my guest and my lord's kinsman."

He bowed again, over her hands, and could find no more words to say.

Estarion was laughing at him. Let him laugh. Even the infamous libertine of the Hundred Realms could stand speechless before such a woman.

SEVENTEEN

THE MAGES CAME BACK TO THE TEMPLE IN STARIOS, BATTERED AND half-stunned but safe. But Daros was gone from the world.

Merian had known from the moment he vanished. It was a tearing deep inside her, as if some hitherto unnoticed and yet essential part had been rent away. Even the Heart of the World had not wounded her so deeply—and it was far more to her and to her mages and this world than he could ever be.

She would kill him when she found him. With her own hands she would do it. He had broken every oath, every promise, every binding that anyone had laid on him. He was beyond incorrigible.

He was most likely dead, if not worse. The shadow had him. When she was not in a right rage, she might allow herself to mourn him. He had been a human creature, after all, and a lord of some worth in the empire.

"Lady?"

Perel's voice called her back to herself. Her mind was wandering; she could not remember when last she had slept. Her eyes fell on what he had brought back from the roof of the world.

It looked like a bowl, hollowed laboriously out of hard grey stone. The inside of it was stained, no doubt with blood. It was heavy and cold in the hands.

There was nothing in it. Nothing at all. It took magic and swallowed it; spells and workings cast upon it vanished as if they had never been.

It was a monstrously dangerous thing. "How like him to fling it in my face and disappear," she said.

Perel, for reasons best known to himself, had returned to the robes of his caste, black on black on black, and veiled to the eyes. Those eyes had a bruised look, but they kept their faintly sardonic expression. "It is a rather cryptic message to send before flinging oneself into the void. He did see something there, I think: something that he knew you would understand."

"I see nothing," she said.

His brows went up. "Might that not be the message?"

"You are as exasperating as he is."

"Not quite," he said. He bent toward the bowl. "We went in search of knowledge. We brought down a stronghold and brought back . . . this. I don't believe we failed, cousin. He said it was a key, although to what, he didn't say."

"To madness," she muttered. She propped her chin on her fists and glared at the thing. "Mages can make no sense of it. Priests bid me shun it. Servants of the Dark Mother swear that it's none of hers. Even my brother and his father know nothing of this. I need that maddening boy—and he, gods curse him, is nowhere among the living."

"I think," said Perel, "that he's not dead. Whether he's worse than that, I can't tell you—but if he were, you would know."

"How would I—"

His glance spoke all the volumes that he had failed to find on the roof of the world. She wanted to slap him. "I do not—"

"Don't lie to yourself," he said.

She flung herself away from the table and the bowl, round that shielded chamber in the temple of the Gates. The shields oppressed her, the riddle she could not solve, the one who was not there to tell her what it meant.

She needed to be elsewhere. A ride, a hunt, even an hour in a garden—

She was the general of this war. The defenses of this world were hers. She did not know what the enemy was or how to fight it. This should have aided her; should have told her what she needed to know.

She needed to be royal, to be a commander of the armies of mages. She wanted to be where he was. Even if that were the pits of the darkest hell.

She went in search of her mother. It had nothing to do with maternal comfort. She needed to remember why she could not abandon everything, as he had, and go hunting shadows.

The princess regent was closeted with her chancellor and his secretaries, engrossed in the minutiae of empire. Within moments of showing her face, Merian had a clean page in front of her, inks and pens to hand, and her mother pacing, dictating a letter to an imperial governor in Asanion.

Details of taxes and tribute raised a wall against her greater troubles. She was almost sorry to finish the letter and look up into her mother's eyes. They were piercingly keen. "Put that away," said Daruya, "and come with me."

The chancellor bowed. His secretaries paused in their work, rose, and did reverence. Daruya acknowledged them with a nod. She swept Merian with her out of the workroom and through the maze of passages to a sunlit gallery overlooking the garden.

Even as late in the year as it was, flowers grew in this sheltered place, and bright birds darted among them. Daruya sat her daughter on the bench there and stood over her. "Tell me," she said.

Her directness was bracing. Merian had wanted it; she could hardly complain that it lacked a certain tenderness. Daruya was not tender. Honed steel never was.

"Have I been dutiful?" Merian asked her. "Have I been a proper royal heir?"

"In most things," Daruya said, "yes. There is the matter of an heir of your own."

Merian laughed. It was not mirth, exactly; more startlement, and a stab of guilt. "I may be proper in that respect, too, if the gods are kind."

Daruya straightened and breathed deep. "How unsuitable is he? Is he a commoner?"

"Not at all," said Merian.

"Is he old? Lame? Feebleminded?"

"None of those, Mother," Merian said. "He's a remarkably good match, as breeding goes."

"Then what is the impediment? There must be one, or you'd not be moping and glooming at me instead of rousing your mages to war."

"There is a small matter," Merian said, "of his having vanished into the shadow."

Daruya sat on the bench beside her daughter. She was not slow of wit, nor was she blind. "Ah," she said. "His lineage is impeccable, and a reputation, even one as . . . remarkable as his, can be outlived."

"A man has to live to do it," Merian said.

"Do you believe he's dead?"

"I don't know," said Merian.

"No? You are a mage."

"He's gone into the darkness," Merian said.

"So has our emperor," said Daruya. "We have to expect that they'll find one another, and hope that they come back."

"Are you comforting me, Mother?"

"No," said Daruya. "I'm comforting myself. That doesn't make it any less true. Are you waiting for me to give you leave to go hunting them? You won't get it. We need you here. You will be the Gate for them, if they can come back through the shadow."

"I hate you," Merian said mildly.

"Of course you do. I'm your mother."

Merian sighed. "Duty is a horrible thing."

"Yes," said Daruya.

"And I should go back to it." Merian stood. "Have I whined excessively?"

"No more than you ought." Daruya smiled, which was rare enough to catch Merian by surprise. "You've chosen well. He's had an unusually feckless youth, but then so did I. He'll be a strong man."

"I thought you despised him," said Merian.

"Only a fool would do that," Daruya said. "Go. Muster your mages. The tide is coming. You have reason now to survive it."

"Selfish reason?"

"Hardly selfish," her mother said. "You're taking thought for the continuance of the line."

"Am I? He doesn't even know. He thinks I despise him."

"Does he despise you?"

"I think he dislikes me intensely."

"That need be no impediment," said Daruya, "in a state marriage—and still less in such an arrangement as I had with your father. He's notoriously free of his favors. You are beautiful, and royal. I doubt there will be a difficulty."

Merian set her lips together. There was no profit in protesting to this of all women that she did not want to be bred like a prized mare, still less by a man who disliked her. She would have a lover or nothing.

She well might have nothing, when all was done. She left her mother still sitting in the sun, and returned to the temple and the shielded chamber and the enigma of the bowl.

It mocked her with its plainness and its perfect emptiness. Yet there was knowledge in it. He had found it. Both Perel and Kalyi had sworn to that. Truth was in this thing, if only she knew how to read it.

She had a council to sit in and young mages to teach. At evening she dined with her brother Hani. He was in a taciturn mood; they ate in silence and parted early.

She had been sleeping in the temple in the Brightmoon-cycle since the mages came back, taxing her mind and wits with the riddle that Daros had sent her. Tonight, partly for temper but partly for exhaustion, she stayed in this house. She was aware of Hani's presence nearby and the servants below, and the city all about them. There were no wards on the house but what any mage would set on the place where she was minded to sleep. After so long in the heavily walled and shielded precincts of the temple, she felt oddly naked, as if she had laid herself bare to the stars.

It could be dangerous to be a mage on the verge of war, and to sleep within such light wards. She courted that danger tonight. Sleep was a Gate, and dreams could bear one to the worlds beyond. Walking, she had found no answers. Perhaps in sleep, something would come.

She composed herself in all ways, buried her fears and anxieties deep. Her power gathered in her center. She opened the Gate of sleep and passed within.

He was asleep on a low frame of a bed, in a room of shadows and dim lamplight. His skin was darker, his hair brighter than she remembered, shot with streaks of gold. His face was less girlish-pretty but no less beautiful. Something had stripped the silliness from him.

There was shadow on this world, but she sensed it dimly, beyond strong wards. The nature of them, how they sustained themselves, intrigued her, but before she could study them further, he sighed and opened his eyes.

They were dark, unclouded with sleep. The strength of power in them made her catch her breath. They came to rest on her as she stood over him. A slow smile bloomed.

If he disliked her, in this dream he showed no sign of it. "Lady," he said. "Oh, I am glad . . . lady, I thought never to see you again."

"In dreams we can see whatever we please," she said, as much to herself as to him.

"That depends on the dream," he said. He stretched, arching like a cat.

She had no power over herself at all. She lay beside him. She was as naked as he, gold to his copper, ivory to his bronze. His skin was warm under her hand, solid and strikingly real. When she raked nails lightly down his ribs, he shivered convulsively.

He tasted of salt, with an undertone of sweetness. He did not fling her off, nor did he shrink from the kiss. Not in the slightest. It was she who recoiled, poised above him, wide-eyed and wild. "That is not what I—"

"No?"

"Whose dream is this? Am I in your—"

His smile had come back. It made her dizzy, and drove the words out of her head. He closed his arms about her, but gently. She could have broken free if she had wished to. She did, truly she did, but when she tensed to pull away, she found herself stretched along the length of his body. Her breast on his breast. Her loins on—

He did not move to finish what she had begun. That was altogether unlike his reputation—but then he had never, in any tale that she had heard, been accused of taking a woman against her will. He was hot and hard between them, and his breath came somewhat quick, but he lay still.

She knew what one did. She was a mage, and no child. But she had never—

"Never?"

He was in her thoughts, soft as wind through grass. His surprise quivered between her shoulderblades.

"Never!" she snapped. But she did not wrench herself away.

"May I . . . ?"

No! her mind said. But her body, arching against him, cried, *Yes!*

He guided her softly, without haste. When she stiffened, he let be. After a while she eased a little; then he went on. The pain she had expected. The pleasure, so soon, she had not. She cried out in astonishment. He nearly let her go, but she held him fast. She knew this. She had been born knowing it.

It was so very, very real: the gusts of pleasure, the hot rush inside her, the gasp and muffled cry in her ear. Somehow they had shifted. It was his weight on hers, his body above her, his face gone suddenly, briefly slack.

He dropped beside her. She was thrumming like a plucked string. She barely had strength to lift her hand, and yet she had to do it, to stroke the sweat-dampened hair out of his face, to let her fingers drift across his lips.

He smiled with all the sweetness in any world. His eyes had been shut; he opened them, turning them toward her. The night was in them, and a glimmer of stars.

"I have to know," she said. "The message—what—"

"Nothing," he said. "Nothing at all."

She woke knotted in bedclothes. Her body was still throbbing. She fought to calm the beating of her heart. There was an ache in her secret places.

She stumbled to her feet. The water in the basin was chill—it made her gasp and shiver, but it cooled the heat in her. She washed herself with shaking hands, all over; and caught her breath.

There was blood on her thighs. The ache—the not-quite-pain—

Her courses. They were early. Had they bred this dream, then? She finished her bathing and did the necessary, then wrapped herself in a robe against the creeping cold. It was nearly dawn. She could try to sleep. Or she would take her aching self and seek out the library, and try to find something, anything, that might answer the riddle he had set.

Memory kept intruding. Lamplight on the high arch of his cheekbone, the proud curve of his nose. Salt taste of sweat. Fullness of him in her, fitting her perfectly, bringing her up and up to—

She shut that door and bolted it. The books told her nothing—just as he had. Nothing at all. She was left with memory that would not let her go, and a thoroughly improper desire to bring back the dream.

Of course she did not. She needed answers, not fruitless rutting born of impulses that should have been mastered long since. The books had none. The bowl offered nothing. The Gates were shut, the world walled off—yet she felt the shadow rolling toward it. There was no time for love, however real it had seemed, and however certain her body was that it wanted more.

EIGHTEEN

WIND HOWLED ACROSS THE PLAINS OF VOLSAVAAR, FAR IN THE WEST OF Asanion. Snow had fallen in the night; the wind had whipped it away by morning, bringing bone-cracking cold. Even in a mantle of magery, Merian shivered.

She sat astride a slab-sided mare, with Perel beside her and the lord of Kuvaar a little ahead, looking down into the cleft of a valley. There had been a city there ten days ago, set on a crag at a meeting of roads. The traders' route from inner Asanion ran westward here, crossing that from the north into the south, and fording the river that flowed from the mountains of gold and copper. It had been a rich city, rough-edged on this border of empire, but fat and prosperous.

Now it was gone. The land was scorched bare, the walls battered down. Towers lay in ruins, in a cawing of carrion birds.

"Every man of fighting age," the Lord Zelis said. "Every woman able to bear a child—gone. All the dead are the old and the sick, and the children. Not one was left alive."

"It's the same in Varag Suvien," said Perel, "and in the Isles, and in Ianon—whole cities destroyed in a night, all across the empire."

"Across the sea, too," said Merian. "All shattered in the same way, and all in the night. This was the first, but a mountain fastness near Shurakan was next—on the other side of the world. Then Ianon and Varag Suvien, half a thousand leagues apart, both on the same night. There's no pattern, nothing that tells us what will be next, or where."

"They left traces here," Zelis said. "Tracks that make no sense, and vanish within a bowshot of the walls."

"Your mages? Did they find anything?" asked Perel.

"Nothing," Zelis said. "The city was not warded. People here put little trust in mages; they reckon that strong walls and a trained army will be enough."

"And in Ianon they reckon that there have been no such wars since the time of the Sunborn," Perel said, "and in the Isles mages are still shunned as changelings and drowned in the sea."

"Whereas in the heart of the empire," said Merian, "we were so flattened by the loss of our great Gates, and so broken by the blow to our magic, that we never took steps to keep the enemy from coming in through Gates of its own. It slipped through the gaps in such wards as we had, and caught us unawares."

She sent the mare down from the top of the hill. The senel snorted and flattened ears and shied, but she was obedient enough. However reluctant she was, she did not spin and bolt.

Behind her, Perel said, "By your leave, my lord, your mages will meet in the morning in the holding. We'll see to it that there's no second attack here."

"Then . . . the Gates within the world are open for them? Not only for you?"

"We will bring them," Perel said in a silken purr, "from the places to which they've fled. You will be protected, whether they will or no."

"For that we thank you," said Zelis.

Merian sighed as she rode down to the ruined city. The empire had been at peace too long. Mages waged no wars, knew no adversity. They had become toothless scholars, working their magics for no greater stakes than curiosity. What threats had come upon them had barely taxed their powers. Those few that rebelled, or that seized too much, seeking their own gain, had been put down before they could grow strong enough to offer a threat.

Now this great enemy came, and none of them was ready. She rode the snorting, shying mare through the wilderness of devastation. There was a reek of smoke and burning, but not of decay. What the fire had not charred to ash, the carrion creatures had picked clean.

She felt no magic, no power. Nothing. No lost souls wandered the ruins. If this had been but one spate of destruction, she might have looked for an invasion, the beginning of a mortal war. But it had struck everywhere, all over the world. It came from the other side of the stars.

This city had fallen the night after she dreamed of Daros. She had been hunting him again through dream and shadow, but the shadow had been too deep. It had rolled like cloud across the stars, blinding her eyes and her magery. Lost in it, befuddled by it, she had wandered until dawn.

Word of the destruction had reached Starios on the third day, after Vadinyas fell in Ianon. The lord there was royal kin, and his daughter was an apprentice mage in Starios: one of the youngest, but very gifted, to her father's great pride. She woke screaming, and screamed until her voice was gone. Not even the chief of healers could bring her out of the darkness into which she had fallen.

In desperation they had called for Merian. She was not a healer, but she was Sun-blood; she could bring light where no other mage could. She went far down into the child's darkness, and brought her back, leading her by the hand. Merian washed her in light, gave her the sun to hold. Clutching it, speaking through tears, she told the tale of her kin and her people taken, the weak slaughtered, the land swept with lightless fire.

Then word came in from Volsavaar, from Varag Suvien, from the Isles. It was the same word, the same tale, without variation. The walls of the world were breached. The enemy had broken them down through Gates that owed nothing to any working of mortal mages.

Merian had come to Volsavaar first, because it was the first to be struck. She had come through the Gate within her, because it was swiftest and safest. No enemy had waited there, no darkness set to trap her. Yet she had felt the shadow, had known that if she tried to open a Gate from world to world, matters would have been otherwise.

She rode from end to end of that dead city, then back up the long road to the hill, where Perel and the lord of Kuvaar waited in silence. "You will do what needs to be done here," she said to Perel. "I think I know where they will strike next."

His eyes widened in the Olenyai veils. "Lady?"

He never called her by her title unless he was less than pleased with her. She chose to keep the title and ignore the displeasure. She turned to Zelis. "May I borrow this mare for yet a while?"

He bowed. He was baffled, but like all Asanians, he rested secure in one surety: she was the heir of the Lion, and was to be obeyed. She inclined her head to him, leveled a hard stare at Perel, and opened the Gate once more.

It was early afternoon in Volsavaar, but the sun hung much lower in the sky in Anshan-i-Ormal. Merian's Gate brought her to the marches of the sea, to a wild and stony coast dashed by winter waves. A storm had blown off to westward; the sun was descending in a tumble of cloud-wrack.

Merian rounded on Perel. He had slipped through the Gate behind her, as sly as a shadow. "Do you crave exile, too?" she flashed at him.

His golden eyes were bland. "I have no gift for calming children. Ushallin will come in the morning and hold yon mages' hands. She will explain to them, with far more tact and diplomacy than I would ever be capable of, that unless they perform the office for which they were trained, they will be stripped of their power and whatever wealth it may have gained them, and sent home in disgrace."

"A penalty for which you may set the example."

"I don't think so," he said. "I was born a mage, cousin, but I was bred and raised an Olenyas. I'm of more use here, guarding your back, than herding mages in Volsavaar."

She hissed. "I am cursed with disobedient men. Stay at my back, then, and don't get in my way."

He bowed with correctness so punctilious that it skirted the edge of insolence. She turned her back on him, the better for him to guard it, and rode along the headland to the place that was calling her.

She was not a prophet; she had little prescience. But she had seen a pattern in the cities that fell, a shape in the web of lesser Gates that crossed this world. The shadow had struck in the gaps, in outlands, where mages were weak. But there was more to it than that.

"And that is?"

She did not turn to face Perel. Her thought had shaped itself where he could catch it if he wished. "Strength," she answered him.

She could feel his puzzlement, his brows raised under the headcloth. "Mages are weak here," he said. "Wards are feeble or nonexistent. Where is the strength?"

"In mortal hands," she said. "Strong backs, Perel. Fertile wombs. If you were taking slaves, what would you look for? Where would you go?"

"Where magic is weak," he said slowly, "and men and women are strong. To the outlands of empire. But how—"

"They have to strike here tonight," she said. "The tide of the lesser Gates, the turning of moons and stars—it's centered in this place. They'll break through just . . . here."

She paused on the edge of the headland. A sea-city crowned the promontory. There was a harbor below, a sheltered circle, full now with ships moored or drawn up against the aftermath of the storm. The walls were high and strong, topped with towers; she saw the gleam of metal, helmet and spearpoint. A chain protected the mouth of the harbor, breaking the storm-surge and, in gentler weather, keeping out invaders and pirates.

There were no wards on walls or harbor. She sensed a spark of magery here and there: a healer, a soothsayer, a seller of love-charms and pretty potions. Its Temple of the Sun was tiny and deserted, its priest too ancient to perform the rites. The greater temples of the city were dedicated to the sea-gods, and those fostered no orders of mages.

This was a proud city; she might even have called it arrogant. As she rode through its gate, she took note of the strength of its guards, tall robust men with fair skin and sea-colored eyes. They raked those eyes over her, stripped her naked with them, and grinned approval, but they neither knew nor feared her. Perel in her shadow attracted more notice. They took count of his weapons, recalled a legend or two of black-veiled warriors from the distant east, noted that he was no taller than a boy of twelve summers, and dismissed him as they had her.

She would not waste either power or temper on hired brawn. She took the straightest way through the city, which was somewhat convoluted: there were three walls, with gates at different points along them, to slow the advance of invaders.

The citadel rose high in the center, a tower of iron and grey granite, with a banner flying from its summit: gold sea-drake on scarlet.

There were a good number of people in the streets, and most seemed well-fed and well-muscled. Women did not go armed, but all the men did. She saw children everywhere—many naked in the winter's cold, but seeming impervious to it.

The gate of the citadel was open like the gate below. Its guards were just as arrogant and no more inclined to offer courtesy to a pair of yellow-eyed foreigners. They were, however, more wary. They barred Merian's way with spears. "No riding-beasts in the citadel," they said. "No weapons, either."

Merian shattered their spears with a flick of the hand. "I will speak with your lord," she said. "Bring me to him."

They were not fools. She was glad to see that. They knew a mage when they saw one. "You will wait," said their captain, and with somewhat of an effort: "Lady." As he spoke, one of his men departed at the run.

She did not have to wait overlong. During that time, Perel amused himself by honing each of his swords, then the daggers he carried about his person. He was on the third when the guardsman came back. The man's face was pale. "He says for you to go down to the city and wait, lady. He'll summon you when he can."

"Indeed?" said Merian. "How lordly of him."

She rode forward with Perel behind her. The guards, loyal to their lord, tried to bar her with their bodies. She flung the Sun in their faces. While they reeled, blinded, she rode through the gate and into the courts of the citadel.

The lord was in his hall, entertaining a goodly gathering. She recognized at least one notorious pirate, and would have wagered on a dozen more. The lord himself, she knew slightly: he had appeared in court some years since, to be confirmed in his demesne and to swear fealty to her mother as regent. He was a large and handsome man, a fact of which he was well aware. His black hair was thick and curled in ringlets, mingling with his great black beard. There were rings of gold in his ears and clasping his heavy white arms; a massive collar of gold lay on his wide shoulders. A jewel flamed on each finger; he was belted with plates of gold crusted with sea-pearls.

The roar of carousal died as she rode into the hall. She had brought the Sun with her, and a fire of magic that sent guards and servants reeling back. She halted in front of the high seat and looked into the lord's startled face. "My lord Batan," she said. "Your city is prosperous. I applaud you."

"You are bold, lady," he said. He grinned. "I like that. Here, come up. Sit with me. Adorn us with your beauty."

She held up her hand for him to kiss. He froze at sight of the Sun in it. She watched the race of thoughts across his face, and arrested it with a cool word. "I am not here for dalliance. This city will be dust and ash by morning. Would you save it? Then listen to me."

"Ah, great lady," said Batan. "Your fears are flattering, but you needn't fret for us. We're well defended here. Who's coming for us? Raiders? Pirates? Rebels and renegades? We're armed against them all."

"Against this you are not." She urged the mare forward, up the steps of the dais, until she stood over the lord in his tall chair. "Where are your mages? Why are your walls not warded?"

"Lady," he said, barely cowed by the sight of her looming above him, "with all due respect, mages and fighting men have little in common."

"Indeed?" said Perel. Merian had not seen him move, but he was off the back of his senel, leaning lightly on the arm of Batan's chair, with the point of a dagger resting against the great vein of the lord's throat. With his free hand he conjured a flock of bright birds that scattered, singing, through the hall. "Warrior and mountebank, I, and occasional imperial errand-runner. Do believe her, sea-lord. I've seen what this city is about to be, and it is not a pleasant sight."

"We are defended," Batan said.

"Not against this." Perel lowered the knife but kept it ready, angled to pierce either eye or throat if the man moved untimely. "You should not have let your mages die off or settle elsewhere. Strength of arms is all very well, but this requires strength of magic."

"Indeed? Then why isn't—whatever it is—choosing mages for targets? Is it hungry to taste good clean steel?"

"It shatters cities," Merian said, "and takes slaves. It comes from beyond the stars. I can defend you, but I ask a thing in return."

"Of course you do," said Batan. "What do you need of me, beautiful lady?"

"A hundred of your best fighting men, with mounts for them all. And leave for my guardsman here to do whatever he deems necessary for the defense of this city."

"Men and mounts," said Batan, nodding slowly. "And provisions? How long a campaign?"

"One night," she said. "From dark until dawn."

"Then you won't be going far."

"Just out of sight of the city," she said. "If there's a level of land within that distance, with room enough to build a city, that will do best. If not, we'll make do with what we can find."

"I know of a place," he said. "It was a city once. They say mages broke it in a war, ages ago, when mages still fought wars."

Her eyes widened slightly. She knew nothing of such a city, or of such wars as he spoke of. They must be ancient beyond imagining, forgotten in the mists of time.

Now they would live again. "Yes," she said to him. "That will do very well. Choose your men now. We mount and ride within the hour. It were best we be in place before nightfall."

"I do like a strong woman," Batan said. Perel's dagger had withdrawn; he rose. His armlets and collar clashed as he flung them on the floor. His people were staring, mute, comprehending only that there was a battle ahead of them. He singled out ten of them, swiftly. "Fetch your men. First court, now."

They flung off the fumes of wine and idleness and leaped to do his bidding. Merian nodded approval. Perel was not pleased with the task she had given him, but for once he did not object. This was battle—he would defer to his general, however little he liked his orders.

When she came to the courtyard, she found her hundred men already gathered. One more joined them: Batan on a seneldi stallion as massive and beautifully arrogant as he was himself. He was armored as they all were, cloaked against the cold, but grinning delightedly at the prospect of a fight.

She found that she was grinning back. Gods knew she was no pirate, but after so long in fretting and in waiting, she was more than glad to be taking some action, even if it should prove completely useless.

The sun was sinking, but there was time, Batan assured her, to reach the ruins and set up camp. They could ride at speed, with no need to spare the seneldi. The evening was clear, if cold; the wind had died to a brisk breeze.

As they rode at the gallop through the city gate, the wards rose into a high and singing fortress, a flame of golden light in the long rays of the sun. Merian sighed and let herself slump briefly on the dun mare's neck, before she straightened and urged the senel onward. The mare was desert-bred: that pause in the lord's hall had been as good as sleep and grazing to her. She would need water and forage soon, but with the god's good favor, she would have it.

The ruined city lay somewhat over a league away, perched on a crag over a swirling maelstrom of waves. Its walls were broken, its towers tumbled in the winter grass. There was still a fragment of citadel, and enough wall to shelter this small an army. While they made camp, pitching tents and building fires and posting sentries, she walked the line of the old walls, gathering power as she went.

It had been some while since she made such a working, a great illusion and a subtle lure for the darkness. She could feel the stretching at the edges of her magic, the strain of arts and powers unused or little used, but she was not taxed unduly, not yet. If she had been less in haste, she would have brought with her a company of mages from Starios. It was only Perel's stubbornness that had given her such support as she had.

Too late now for regrets. If—when—she did this again, she would do it properly. Now she had to hope, first, that her workings would rise and hold, and then that she had guessed rightly; that the enemy would come here and not somewhere altogether unforeseen.

Batan followed her on her round of the walls. He did not vex her with chatter, but his eyes were a little too intent for comfort. She closed them out while she brought her magics together and raised the walls anew, stone by stone at first, then swifter, as the magic found its stride. The earth woke to the working, and drew up power of its own, startling her, but she had wits enough to make use of the gift as it was offered.

She built a city of air and darkness. Each of the men who camped in it she swelled to a dozen, then a hundred, populating the city with strong warriors. Herself she scattered through it, so that she was a myriad of women, young and strong, with babes at the breast and babes in the belly, and flocks of children.

When she was done, she encompassed multitudes; and this broken city seemed alive again, if any had looked on it from without. From within, without magic, there was little to see, save a flicker of shadows.

A few of the men were white-rimmed about the eyes. Those had enough power to sense a glimmer of what she had done. She mounted a heap of rubble that might once have been a stair, and waited for them all to take notice of her. The sun was nearly down; swift dusk was falling. She mantled herself in light, damping it lest she alarm the men, but letting it seem as if she had caught the last glow of the sun. "Men of Seahold," she said, "I thank you for this gift that you have given me. You are the shield and bulwark of your city, and its greatest defense. It may be that you will have to fight tonight. Don't be astonished if shadows seem to fight beside you. You may die; you may be taken captive. This will not be an easy battle, if battle there is. If any of you would withdraw, you should do so now. I can send you to safety while it is still possible."

"What will we be fighting, lady?" asked a whip-thin man with a terribly scarred face. "There's no threat from the land, and nothing will come at us by sea, not on this cliff."

"It will come from the far side of the night," Merian answered him, "and it will do its best to enslave you. You are bait, captain; if I've laid the snare properly, this invasion will pass by Seahold altogether and fall on us here."

"Ah!" said the captain. "Bait we understand. Deadly danger, risk of being boarded, captured, sold in the Isles—what! Are you shocked, lady? Do you think your laws can bind a pirate?"

"I think," said Merian, "that those laws might be enforced more strictly hereafter—but also that some sentences might be commuted for services rendered to the empire. If you survive. If this gamble succeeds."

"We are all gamblers here," another man said. Grins flashed white, spreading fast, for none was to be outdone by any other.

She had them. They were no cowards; they did not know enough to be afraid, nor maybe would they quail even if they had known. They took their ease as seasoned fighters could, alert but wasting no strength in fretting.

She settled on the broken stair, wrapped close in her mantle. Batan brought her a cup of wine, spiced and steaming hot, and a loaf of bread that must have been brought from the city. There was cheese baked in it, still warm, savory with herbs and bits of sausage. She ate every scrap, and sipped the wine slowly, until she was warm from her center outward.

Batan watched her, smiling slightly, as the twilight deepened and the stars bloomed overhead. In a little while both moons would rise together, but now there was only a gold-and-crimson glow along the eastern horizon.

His regard was deeply respectful, but offered more, if she would take it. If she had been another woman, she might have welcomed the warmth. But she was the cold daughter of the Sun, who carried the god's fire in her, but took none of it for herself.

She drew her cloak more tightly about her and shifted a little away from him. He shrugged, then smiled ruefully. He did not retreat to the greater conviviality of his comrades.

He was guarding her. She decided to allow it. When the fight came, if it came, she would need his strong arm and his skill in weaponry, until the trap was sprung.

They all settled to wait. The light in the east swelled so slowly that it was barely perceptible. Then the blood-red arc of Greatmoon's rim lifted above the horizon. Brightmoon blazed in its wake.

The silence was absolute. The phantom city grew stronger, more real, in that twinned light. No shadow came. Nothing stirred but the wind and the crashing of the waves.

Merian felt herself slipping into a doze. She shook herself awake. *He* was on the other side of dream, calling to her. But she could not answer. Not tonight. Not without betraying them all.

NINETEEN

A S THE MOONS CLIMBED THE SKY, SHADOW CREPT TO COVER THEM. IT SEEMED at first like mist or cloud, but it was too deep, its edges too distinct. It was like a curtain drawn across the moons.

The dimmer their light grew, the more campfires seemed to burn within the ruined walls. The city of shadows was stronger. It was feeding on old magic sunk deep in the earth, tapping roots that had grown there in times before time. It was stronger than Merian now, and had grown apart from her. It no longer drew from her strength.

There was danger in that, but no more, surely, than she had courted in baiting this trap. The fabric of the world was tearing. Things were pressing on it, seeking entry from without. Every instinct screamed at her to raise wards against it, but she must not. She did not want to keep it out. She wanted to draw it in, trap it, and if possible destroy it.

The tone of the waiting had sharpened. The darkness grew deeper, though the moons rose higher. The sea battered the cliff-wall. She could taste the salt of spray.

They came in the deepest night, when the only light was a struggling flicker of firelight. They rode through the tatters of the world's walls, an army of darkness mounted on beasts like nothing this world had seen.

The riders were human. Sworn and bound to darkness though they were, they were men. They were not mages. They were as mortal as men could be. The shadow was darkness absolute—but these riders had not wrought it. They wielded it, perhaps served it, but it was not theirs as the illusion of a city was hers.

They fell on it with a bombardment of weapons so strange that they caught Merian off guard. Siege-engines, even mage-bolts, she would have known how to face: feigned the proper response of mortal walls, and allowed them slowly to crumble and fall. This was like a blast of dark flame. It seared through the illusion. The western side of the camp caught the edge of it and puffed to ash.

There was no light, not even heat as she had known it. It simply destroyed whatever it touched.

Batan's men had no mage-sight. They could not know what had attacked them: their fires, dying too swiftly, revealed nothing but enveloping darkness. Those who had been in the western tents stumbled through the heaps of ash where they had been, naked and blind. The armor that they had worn, even to the garments beneath it, was gone, but the dark fire had harmed not a hair of their heads.

The raiders had stopped. One of them raised a weapon like a thick spearhaft and cast from it another bolt of lightless flame.

This time Merian was ready. The wall that met it had the strength of stone. It trembled before the assault, cracking and crumbling.

Batan barked orders to his men. Merian cast a magelight over them, shielded against the attackers, but clear enough that they could see as she saw. They spread across the field, weapons at the ready. As they moved, they doubled and trebled and doubled again. Her working had found its strength once more, rooted deep in this crag. Her armies of air were gathered. The living men took it for a dream, or understood and yet were not afraid.

Pirates, she thought with something very like admiration. They always landed on their feet, whatever deck they fell to.

The enemy broke down the walls, battering them relentlessly until not one stone lay atop another. If it astonished them to find an army arrayed against them, they betrayed nothing of it. The foremost rank raised their flame-spitting spears with a lack of haste that reeked of contempt. Swords and spears, even arrows, were no proof against them.

The earth quivered underfoot. Far below, beneath even the ancient magic, fire surged and swelled like the sea: fire of earth, born of the sun's fire.

Merian called it up. She grasped it with both hands, the hand that was mortal flesh and the hand that was immortal gold. She drew it into herself, filling her body with living flame.

Batan's men howled and sprang to the charge. The enemy lowered their spears. Merian loosed the fire.

They went up like torches. Their beasts, their armor, burned with a fierce white flame. The light ate them alive, devoured them whole. Nothing remained of them but a drift of ash, swirling in the wind.

Merian stood astonished. The wind blew the cloud of ash away. There was nothing left, not one thing. She had destroyed them utterly. Even the shadow was gone; the stars were clean, and the moons shining as bright almost as day.

"It can't be that easy."

Merian had called council as soon as the sun came up, gathering it in the fire in front of Batan's tent. She could see each one where he or she was: her kin in Starios, Ushallin in Kuvaar, Kalyi in the ruins of Yallin in the Isles, and Perel in Seahold, which had passed a peaceful night within the protection of his wards.

It was her brother Hani who had spoken, from the library that she missed with sudden intensity. "If a simple spell of fire could destroy them, they would never have come as far as this. Someone else would have lit them like torches long ago."

"I took them by surprise," Merian said. "They may come warded next."

"I'm sure they will," her mother said. "But do think. If they're so vulnerable to light—if they travel in a cloak of absolute darkness—we have a weapon against them. Light is our simplest magic, one that even the least of mages can raise. We can muster our mages with that knowledge."

"It is useful," Hani granted her, "but I can't help thinking, wouldn't it be better to track them to their lair and destroy them? If all we do is defend, they can keep coming and coming. We should attack."

"We need to know more," said Merian. "I saw men, not mages. Someone or something is behind them, and that has power enough to blind the stars, to break or ignore Gates, and to overrun worlds."

"Still an enigma," her mother said, "but a little less of one than before. If we can capture one of them, discover what he knows . . ."

"We'll try," Merian said. "They may come back here to find out what became of their raiding party. I'll be waiting for them."

"You'll have reinforcements," Daruya said, "but we can't spare many. We're spread dangerously thin as it is."

"We may be able to predict where they'll come," Merian said. "If we have mages ready to spring through lesser Gates at the first indication of the enemy's coming, we'll be able to do battle wherever he is."

Daruya nodded briskly. "Yes. That's well thought of. I'll see to it. Look for the newcomers before sunset."

"They'll find us here," Merian said. "I'll have men fortifying this place as much as they can—walls seem to be of some use, and better walls of stone than walls of air."

That ended the council. Merian lingered by the fire. She hardly needed its warmth: the magefire was still in her, burning with a steady flame.

Batan's shadow fell across her. Those of his men who had been touched by the dark fire were laid together in one of the larger tents; he had been with them until a moment ago. His face was grim. "They're blind," he said. "They flinch and scream when the sun touches them, but they can't see it. Their eyes are sealed shut."

Merian rose stiffly. She was weary; she had not slept since before she could remember. "Let me see," she said.

There were a dozen of them. The skin of those who were not already white-skinned seafolk was blanched to the color of bone. Their eyes were indeed sealed shut: the lids had melted into the faces. It might have seemed that they were eyeless, save that Merian could see the wild shifting of the eyes beneath the skin. When she came into the tent, bringing with her a shaft of sunlight, those nearest her writhed and moaned as if in pain.

Her lips tightened. Her anger was too deep for speech. She knelt beside the first man. He shrank from her; his skin shuddered convulsively. When she touched him, he shrieked.

She withdrew her hand, sat back on her heels, and drew a careful breath. The power she had was Sun's power, power of light. These men had been so poisoned that the touch of it was agony.

"Darkmages," she said. She spoke across the long leagues of the empire. "Mother. Send a darkmage. Quickly."

Daruya's mind touched hers, brushed it with assent, slipped away. She felt the press of power on the Gate within her. *Here,* she bade it. *Outside.*

She smiled in spite of herself at the one who came in, though she frowned immediately after. "Hani. You can't—"

"My father is taking his turn in the library," her brother said. He was dressed for travel in leather and fur, the common garb of Shurakan; his straight black hair was plaited behind him. He knelt beside her.

She had not even thought of him when she asked her mother for a darkmage. She never saw him so; he was her brother the scholar, the quiet and perpetual presence either in Starios or in Shurakan. He did not flaunt his power; even in councils of mages he spoke more often as a scholar than as a darkmage. Yet he was strong though he had come to it late; and he was skilled, as a scholar could be who had studied both the theory and the praxis of his art.

When he laid his hand on the wounded man's brow, the man twitched, then sighed. Hani echoed that sigh. "This is an ill working," he said, "well beyond my power to heal. Better all these men be taken where healers can look after them. There's too much broken, too much twisted. This horror of the light—it goes to the heart of them. Can you see?"

Through the mirror of Hani's power, she could. Without that, she was blinded by her own light. "We'll send them to the Temple of Uveryen in Kundri'j," she said. "You will stay here. If we manage to capture one of the enemy, he may be even more appalled by a lightmage than one of these men. We'll need you then."

"Very likely you will," he agreed. He fixed her with a hard stare. "And now, sister, you will rest while I see to what needs to be done."

"I can't rest," she said. "There's too much to—"

"I'll do it. You're out on your feet. Tonight we need you alive and conscious. Shall I throw you over my shoulder and carry you to bed?"

She glared. He was more than capable of doing just that, and rather too often had. "I can walk," she said tightly.

"Then walk."

There was a tent for her, pitched long since. Her belongings were in it—rather more than she remembered bringing with her. Someone had laid out bread, salt fish, strong cheese. She was not hungry, but she ate as much of the bread as she could choke down, and made herself swallow a bite or two of fish, and drank the sour wine that had come with it.

While she ate, she felt the rising of power, the opening of the Gate that took the wounded men away. She heard men talking: Hani and Batan, the latter at first brusque, then softening before her brother's unshakable good humor. The lord of Seahold was out of his depth, and not liking it; but she saw in him no taint of treachery. He would keep his oaths to the throne, however little it pleased him, and however poorly he understood the reasons.

The gods had been kind, to set this lord here, where such a man was most needed. She could rest. Hani would see that all was done that must be done.

She fell asleep to the sound of men arriving, masons and carpenters with the tools of their trade. They would build a wall to bolster her magic.

Her dream was drenched with sunlight. She caught a scent of flowers, and heard water lapping, waves of a lake or broad river on a green shore. The air was breathlessly hot, a great blessing after the damp and biting cold of winter by the sea.

He was standing on the bank, more deeply bronze than before, almost black against the dazzling white of his kilt. Sweat sheened his broad shoulders and ran in a runnel down his back. His hair had grown since last she dreamed him. It was cut in a way she had not seen before, straight across the brows and straight above the shoulders. A plaited band bound it above the brows. It was odd, but she rather liked it.

He had a bow in his hand and an arrow nocked to the string; he was watching a flock of birds that swam together on the water. They were large birds, grey and brown and white; their call was an odd and almost comical honking. In his mind was the thought that their flesh, when roasted, was very good to eat.

He was alone. She might have expected hunting companions, servants, a guard or two, but in this world of dream, there was only he.

He turned. The splendor of his joy weakened her knees. He caught her as she sank down, lifting her in a long delicious swoop. His laughter healed her of weariness and fear, cold and anger and the lingering touch of the shadow.

When he would have set her down, she drew him with her, body to his body, swept with a white heat of desire. He was ready for her after a moment's startlement: beautiful dream-lover, giving her her every wish.

They lay naked in a bed of reeds, breathing hard, grinning at one another. He stroked her hair out of her face, letting his hand linger, caught in curling golden strands. "It's been so long," he said. "I thought I'd lost you, driven you away with my wantonness. You are no light woman, and I—"

"I yearned for you," she said, "but our dreams never met."

"You don't hate me?"

He sounded so plaintive that she kissed him to console him. It might have led to other ends, but he was not as potent as that, even in dream. "I don't hate you," she said. "I'm rather sure I love you."

"You—"

"Yes, it is appalling, isn't it?" She meant to sound light; she hoped she did not seem too brittle. "Don't be afraid. I won't trouble you to love me in return. Give me what you have to give, and that will be enough."

"What I have to—" He broke off. "Lady, every day I remember that one night. Every night I sleep, hoping to see you again, but knowing—dreading—that my dreams will be empty. That you gave way to my importuning, but when it was over, you fled in horror, loathing everything that I was. I never meant to violate you so."

"Violate—" Now she was doing it: sputtering witlessly, too startled for sense. "I wanted every blessed moment of that. Every one. And every blessed inch of you."

She had struck him speechless.

She drove him back and down and sat on him, stooping over him, glaring. "Have you really been tormenting yourself ever since?"

He nodded.

She slapped him, not quite hard enough to bruise. "Idiot! Indaros of the thousand loves, they call you—didn't one of them teach you how to tell when a woman is desperately in love with you?"

"But," he said, "she usually is. But she's not you. She's not—*you.*"

It made no sense, and yet she understood it. "You never loved anyone before."

"Not with my heart and soul," he said. "Not with the worship of my body. Not with the surety that if she truly hates me, truly I shall die of it. It's not . . . very pleasant."

"What? Loving me?"

"Being afraid that you hate me. If you merely dislike me, or find me a hideous nuisance, I can bear that. If you find me useful in the manner of a stud bull, as your mother did your father, that's endurable. But hate—that I can't endure."

"I do not hate you," she said, though from the sound of it, he might think she lied. "Damn you, we're quarrelling. We're worlds apart, there's a sea of darkness between, I fought a battle last night and face another one tonight, and you can bicker with me as if we were a farmer and his wife."

"You fought—" He had seized on that; of course he had. "It's come there?"

"Ten days ago," she said. "No—eleven now."

"We haven't seen it in five cycles of this world's moon," he said. "The world is closed in; it's globed in shadow. The only Gate away from it is the gate of dreams. But the attacks have stopped."

"It hasn't been that long since—" She stopped. Time ran differently on the other side of Gates. She of all people should know that. "Tell me what you know of this!"

"The bowl I sent you—didn't it reach you?"

"Yes!" she snapped. "And there is no answer in it. None. At all."

"But that is the answer," he said. "Nothingness. That's what the shadow is. You can't fight it. There's nothing to fight. It's absolute oblivion."

"Last night," she said, "we were attacked by men. Lightmagic destroyed them utterly."

"Those are its servants—they are mortal. The shadow is not. As long as it exists, its servants will keep coming, and worlds will be destroyed."

"How many of them are there? How many servants?"

"Legions," he said. "They make more with every world they conquer. They serve darkness absolute. They are sworn to utter destruction. What you did to that raiding party—you should take care, lady; they'll come in ever greater numbers, craving the blessing of oblivion."

"What, they'll make me a saint of their cult?"

"A goddess," he said. "A queen of destruction."

She shuddered. He held her close to him, babbling apologies, but she silenced him with a hand over his mouth. "Stop that. I'm not fragile. I would rather not be what these madmen must think I am. But if it will serve this world or any other, I will exploit it to the utmost."

"Cold-hearted royal lady." But he said it tenderly, cradling her, covering her with kisses.

She caught his face in her hands and stopped him. It was not easy at all. She wanted to take him by storm. But this dream had given her all that she could have wished from the bowl of nothingness. She must take it back to the waking world. She could not tarry here, where her heart yearned to be.

"Beloved," she said, brushing his lips with hers. "You know I have to go again. As time runs between Gates, it could be an hour before I come back, or it could be a year. Do trust me—that I will come back. That I do love you."

"I do," he said, though he gasped as he spoke. "I do trust you. I love you with all my heart."

Such heart as he had, she might have thought once. But she knew him better now. With dragging reluctance she let go, relinquishing the dream, leaving behind the sun, the heat, the joy of his presence. She lay again in the winter cold, in the roaring of waves, in the midst of bitter war.

TWENTY

ATAN'S MEN HAD WROUGHT WONDERS WITH FALLEN STONE AND SHIPS' timbers. It was not a large fort, but the wall was stout, and the tents within had been shifted out of range of the enemy's strange weapons. It happened that Merian's tent had become the center, where the general's tent was wont to be; it stood over the deep well of the city's magic. She woke in the embrace of it, and came out to find herself in the beginnings of a sturdy hill-fort.

The sun was still high, but had begun to sink toward the low swell of hills to the westward. The air was a little warmer than it had been, the wind a little less knife-edged. She kept the warmth of her dream inside her, wrapped about the fire in the earth. For a long moment as she stood in front of the tent, she remembered his arms about her and his voice in her ear, at once deep and clear: the kind of voice that could sing the full range from flute to drumbeat. She wondered if he sang. Surely he did. Princes were trained to dance, to fight, to sing.

She was losing her sense of what was real and what was not: forgetting that this was but a dream. Her body felt as if it truly had been locked in embrace with a man. She ached a little, was a little raw, but more pleasurably than not. Places in her that had been shut and barred were open, filling with magic.

There was a cult of priests in Asanion who worshipped the gods of love, and made of it a rite and a sacrament. They professed that the act of love was a great working in itself, and that mages who joined so could double and redouble their power.

She did not feel as strong as that, but certainly she was stronger than she had been before she slept. She sought out Hani where he stood with Batan, overseeing the raising of the seaward wall. It was the last to go up, because it was the least likely to meet with attack, but they were not making it any less strong for that. There was an army of men at work, stripped in the cold, laboring feverishly to be done before the sun sank too much lower.

Batan bowed to her. Hani smiled. He was more at ease the closer to danger they

came. When death threatened, he would be perfectly calm. Had she noticed before
how much like the Gileni prince he looked? That line came from his part of the
world, long and long ago. In this proud bronze face, she could see it.

"It pleases me to see you well, lady," Batan said, breaking in on her reflections.
"It seems the rest did you good."

"It did that," Merian said, coolly as she thought, but Hani's glance sharpened.
She ignored it. Batan's expression at least did not change. She was keenly aware just
then of the weight of a man's eyes. This one wanted her, and would take her if he
could, but not until the battle was over.

She was flattered. She was also inclined to geld him with a blunt knife. She
regarded him without expression, until he flushed and looked away.

Be kind, Hani said in her mind. *He's a man—he dreams, as all men do.*

He could dream. She did not put it in words, not precisely, but Hani understood.
He shrugged, half-smiled, sighed.

By nightfall the walls were raised, and the laborers rested under guard in the camp's
heart. Most of them would rise to fight when the time came; weary they might be,
but they had their pride. They would defend what they had built.

They had all eaten while the sun was still in the sky, even Merian, who surprised
herself with hunger. She ate a solid ration and washed it down with well-watered
wine. It stayed with her, feeding her strength, as the sun set and the darkness
descended.

It was a long, cold night. Moons and stars shone undimmed; the sea quieted little by little. The men took turns to rest and share the fires. The guard on the walls
changed again and yet again.

She had miscalculated. Wherever the shadow had gone tonight, if it had gone
anywhere at all, it had not come here. She had driven it away.

Yet she did not put an end to the vigil. She was too stubborn; they had worked
too hard. This hook was baited, and strongly.

It came well after midnight, yet swifter than before. Stars and moons winked
out. A gust of icy air rocked the tents on their moorings. A hammer of darkness
smote the raw new fort. In the same instant, wave on wave of warriors stormed the
walls.

Merian lashed them with light. Her bolts struck shields. They cracked and
buckled. She struck them again, again, as the forces behind them smote the walls.
It was a battering of hammer on hammer, anvil on anvil.

Hani's magic poured like water beneath hers. It melted away the shields and
lapped at the feet of the darkness. Light stabbed through the rents that it had
made.

The enemy's slaves burned and died. But the darkness had swallowed the stars.

Hani raised wards about the walls. The remnant of the enemy retreated. The defenders stood alone in darkness impenetrable, lit by their feeble sparks of fire.

Merian was almost startled to see the sun rise. It burned away the dark, and showed a ring of blasted heath round the walls. Seahold was still safe—Perel's wards had held—and nowhere else, as she cast her mind afar, had seen attack. She had succeeded: she had drawn the enemy's attention to this one place.

She could not keep it there forever. If it were possible to divide the enemy, to lure them to a number of guarded places, that might be a wiser course—"Now that we know they can be lured," she said to her brother.

Hani was looking bruised about the eyes. He had worn himself thin in a long day of building and a long night of magical battle. Still, he kept his feet reasonably well, and he seemed to have his wits about him. "Another council?"

"In a while," she said. "I need to think. Will you ride out with me?"

He had strength enough for that. Batan, gods be thanked, had let go his iron resolve at last, and dropped into the first tent he happened upon. The camp was under the command of one of his seconds, a man in utter awe of the mages. He would never have presumed to object to their desertion.

They rode past the circle of the enemy's attack to the place where their track began, and then a little beyond it. There was a hill of sere grass and a ring of ancient stones: another place of power, such as seemed unwontedly common in this harsh country.

"Maybe we should have studied the mages of Anshan," Merian said. "Were they as old as the dark brothers of the mountains?"

"Older, I would think," Hani said. "Even the stories are dim and all but forgotten; all that's left are ruins like these, spread in a wide circle within the borders of the country, and a name for them all: the Ring of Fire. I can't remember anything of any enemy they may have fought, or whether they knew Gates. Mostly they fought one another and subjugated lesser mortals. They might have been gods."

"They drew their power from the earth," Merian said, "and from the fires far below. It's still here, waiting to be tapped. What if—"

Merian broke off. Hani's eyelids were drooping shut. He kept his seat on the senel's back as an old campaigner could, with no need of conscious awareness.

She let him sleep. She was fiercely, almost painfully awake. The longer she was in this place, the more its power filled her. She was drawing it as a tree draws water from the earth, through every root and vein.

It was not lightmagic, but Hani seemed to have no awareness of it. The enemy must not, either, or they would never have come here. She was conceiving a plan, but she needed time and solitude—which through Hani's exhaustion she had won for herself.

She left her mare, and Hani slumped in the gelding's saddle, and sought the center of the stone circle. The sun was warm inside the ring. Buried in the grass she found another stone, flat and smooth, somewhat hollowed in the middle. It was like a shallow basin filled with clear water, though no spring bubbled through the rock, nor had it rained since Merian came to this country.

The water was full of light. Merian dipped her hand in it, found it icy but not unbearable. She laved her face and sipped a little. Its taste was cold and pure, but as it sank to her stomach, it warmed miraculously. She drew a long wondering breath. She felt as if she had slept the night through.

The warmth settled deep within her, below her heart. She sat beside the stone, basking in the sun, and let her thoughts drift free.

Visions stirred in the water. She bent toward them, drawn through no will of her own. She saw a ring of cities, and foregatherings of mages, and great battles against powers that came by sea and land and air. Some were dark, though she could not tell if any was darkness absolute. They forged weapons of light and shadow, and wielded them against their enemies, and sometimes won and sometimes lost, but always kept their pride and the pride of their cities.

They were all gone long ago, sunk into the grass. Powers faded, cities died; wars destroyed what weariness and neglect did not. Mages were seldom born now in Anshan.

The water shivered, though no wind had touched it. The ancient visions dissolved. A face stared up at her, a very strange face, somewhat like an owl's and somewhat like a man's. The round yellow eyes blinked once, slowly. "Help," it said clearly. "Help . . ."

Merian bent closer to the water, but not so close that her breath disturbed it. The vision moved likewise, until its face filled the basin. "You are the rest of him," it said. "You must meet. The worlds that float in void—they must touch. You must bring them together."

"Who are you?" Merian asked of the creature. "What are you?"

"Mage," it said. "He knows. Listen! Speak to him. He knows."

It was not human, this vision. It did not think as humans thought. Merian struggled to understand it. "He? Who is he?"

"The rest of you," the Mage said. Was it ever so slightly impatient? "You can end this. But you must listen."

"I am listening," she said as respectfully and patiently as she could.

"Listen," the Mage said.

Its eyes flashed aside. It gasped. Before Merian could speak again, the vision vanished. Darkness filled the basin, darkness absolute.

She recoiled from it. Something caught her. She whipped about.

Hani blocked the blow before it knocked him flat. He seemed much rested and blessedly strong. She rested for a moment in that strength, before the power in the earth and the heat of the sun began again to restore her.

"Shall I call council?" he said.

"No," she said. "After all, no. But I need more builders, and more mages. The Ring of Fire will rise again."

"Have we time for that?"

"I think we do. We're not the heart of their war yet. These are raiding parties. I'll wager that the army itself is still worlds away."

"I hope you win your wager," Hani said.

So did she; but she was not about to confess it. When she mounted the mare, Hani was close behind her, swinging onto the gelding's back.

By day mages and makers rebuilt the Ring of Fire, the chain of hill-forts and sea-holdings round the rim of Anshan. By night they stood guard against the dark.

Merian remained in the first of the ruined cities, which had a name again: Ki-Oran, Heart of Fire. That had been its name in older days, the men of Seahold assured her. A fort had risen within the walls, a small citadel and quarters for a garrison.

The enemy had begun to raid abroad in Anshan, in the smaller towns and the fishing villages. Those, unlike the forts and cities, had no mages to ward them. They fell in black ash, their strong people taken, the weak slaughtered. What had become of those who were stolen, mages feared they knew: Batan's twelve wounded men were still in Asanion, healing slowly and incompletely when they healed at all.

Yet there was no lack of men to offer themselves for defense. Men in Anshan were all either pirates or bandits at heart, and they knew no fear. Given a fight, even a fight they could not win, and faced with a fate that truly was worse than death, they laughed long and hard, and brought their brothers and cousins to join them in the villages. They were bait, the lure that kept the sea-dragons away from the fish, and it was their pride to be so.

Merian had not forgotten the strange vision in the water, but its meaning eluded her. There was too much else to think of: finding mages to ward every village without weakening the guard and the wards outside of Anshan; building forts and strongholds; raising a wall of light-magic that would, she hoped, keep the raids within its circle.

The gaps in the web of lesser Gates were closed, except here. It was a monstrous task, and strained the mages to the utmost. They were warding a world. Everywhere that human creatures were, they must be, and be strong.

Winter deepened. In the deepest of it, the raids grew less frequent. Then for a while they stopped. But only fools celebrated a victory. The world was still under shadow. The greater Gates were gone, the Heart of the World destroyed. A few brave souls had tried to raise the nexus again, or find some sign that it could be restored, but those that survived the attempt would never heal completely. Where the nexus had been was a maw of darkness, growing inexorably wider, deeper, stronger. It swallowed magic; it devoured mages. It was beyond any mortal strength to conquer.

With the first breath of spring, the shadow-warriors came back. Already in sheltered valleys, fighting men had turned farmer and were plowing the steep rocky fields. When Greatmoon waxed again, they would plant.

"Man's got to eat," one of them said to Merian. She had ridden out of Ki-Oran to the village where the enemy had struck anew. The raiders had taken five men but injured none; the village's young mage had driven them off.

He was in his house under a healer's care, with his magic half burned away. The enemy had new shields, stronger and more deadly. Merian would speak with him when—if—he came to his senses. Meanwhile she had left her escort to walk through the fields, past the men and oxen engaged in the plowing.

It was one of these who had paused to greet her. He was not as young as some; he had a stocky, sturdy look to him, and a roll to his stride, as if he had just come off a ship. Yet he seemed at ease with the oxen and the plow, and his furrows were straight and clean.

He was not in awe of her, and he was frankly admiring of her beauty. It gave him clear pleasure to stand with her, looking out across the rolling field. "Fighting's good," he said, "but a man's got to eat before he can fight. We can't stop farming just because there's a war over us."

"We could feed you from the rest of the empire, if it were necessary," Merian said. "You are our shield and bulwark. There's no need to trouble yourselves with lesser things."

"We're proud to be your defense, lady," he said, "but we take care of our own."

He was not to be shaken. Merian accorded him respect and let him be.

She strode on round the edge of the fields, alone for the first time in quite some while. She was a little tired, a little light-headed; it was not an ill sensation, but it was rather odd. If she stopped to think, the lightness was not in her head but in her center. She almost felt as if, if she spread her arms, she could lift and fly.

There was no more magic here than in any other tract of earth. The closest fortress in the Ring of Fire was a day's ride distant. Yet she was brimming with light, drinking the sun. The *Kasar* in her hand was burning so fiercely that she kept glancing at it, expecting to find a charred ruin. But her hand was its wonted self: slender, narrow, with long fingers; ivory skin, golden sun.

She was quite startled when her knees declined to hold her up, and even more so when her head decided that, for amusement, it would expand until it had encompassed the sun.

It was dim suddenly, and cool. There was a roof over her, low and thatched, and a light hand laving her face with something cool and scented with herbs. She struggled to sit up. The hands became suddenly iron-strong.

They belonged to a burly man in a leather tunic, one of the warrior-villagers. A woman appeared behind him, so like that she must be kin; she carried a wooden bowl, from which wafted the scent of herbs. She set it down beside the pallet on which Merian was lying, and looked hard into her face. "Good. You're awake." She flashed a glance at the man. "Let her go."

The man ducked his head and backed away. She nodded briskly and dipped a cup in the bowl. "Drink," she said.

It was a tisane of herbs. The taste was faintly pungent and faintly sweet; it cleared Merian's head remarkably. She saw then that her escort crowded outside the house, which must be one of the larger houses in the village. Two of them stood on either side of the door, glaring at the pair who nursed her.

"Out," the woman barked at them. "*Out!* When she wants you she'll call you back."

They growled but retreated. The woman returned to Merian's side as if nothing had happened, and went on pouring the tisane into her.

Merian endured three more sips, but the fourth gagged her. She pushed the cup away. "Tell me what you don't want my men to hear."

"What, did you want them breathing down our necks? This house is small enough without those great louts in armor."

"I am not dying," Merian said. "I'm not even ill. I'm a little tired, that's all. The sun made me dizzy."

"You certainly aren't dying," the woman said. "Do you really think it isn't obvious?"

Merian did not understand her. "What isn't—"

The woman's eyes widened. "You honestly don't know, do you?"

"What don't I know?"

The woman paused, breathed deep, lashed her with a question: "Do you remember when you last had your courses?"

"Yes! They were—" Merian broke off. It had been—cycles? Since the morning that she woke and—

"Oh, no," she said. "That's impossible."

"So they all say," the woman said dryly. "I've been stitching cuts and birthing babies in these parts since before my own courses came, and believe me, royal lady, it is possible."

"But I have never—"

"I took the liberty of examining you," said the woman, "and lady, you have. If you don't kill yourself running hither and yon, you'll bear the child in the summer."

Merian sat dumbfounded. Those had been dreams. She had not gone to him in body. She had had no slightest inkling—

Had she not? That great well-being, that sense of doubled strength: was that his child in her, doubly mageborn and conceived in magery?

Impossible.

Her hands spread across her belly. Was it a fraction less flat than it had been before? Was there a spark of life within? Was it floating, dancing, dreaming, waiting for her to become aware that it existed?

She truly had not known. She had dreamed of him again thrice—gone to him, loved him, lain in his arms. They had spoken of little beyond one another. It was not for knowledge that she had sought him.

The last dream had been but a handful of days ago; he had been nursing wounds, remembrance of a lion-hunt. He had killed the lion, and been lauded for it, too; its skin had been their bed. She had kissed each mark and scar, and healed him as much as he would allow, which was not much at all.

"I want to remember," he had said, "to remind myself why prudence is a virtue. And why I should try harder to practice it."

"There are those who would faint if they heard you now," she said.

He laughed. "Wouldn't they? It would almost be worth it, just to see their faces."

She had laughed with him, and made love to him gently, to spare his hurts.

It had not been a dream. None of it had been.

But how—

She escaped the village and the sharp-tongued healer with the too-keen eyes. Her men had heard none of it, gods be thanked. She assured them that her brief indisposition was only lack of sleep and magic taxed to its limit. They pampered her, fussed over her, and tried to slow their pace back to Ki-Oran, but that she refused to submit to.

Her mind was a roil of confusion. This she had never expected or planned for. Later, yes, if he lived, if he came back to this world, if what she had dreamed was true. But not now. Not in the middle of a war.

Yet now she was aware of it, there was no denying it. She was carrying a most royal child: heir at one remove to the princedom of Han-Gilen, and at two removes to the empire of Sun and Lion. She had done her royal duty at last, done it well and most thoroughly—and her lover had met with her mother's approval, too, which was as great a marvel as any of the rest of it.

TWENTY-ONE

THE DARKNESS HAD BEEN GONE SO LONG FROM THE VALLEY OF THE RIVER THAT people began to believe that it was gone forever. The gods had done it, they said: the two who were in Waset, who had come from the far side of the horizon with the Sun in their hands, to drive back the powers of the night.

They tried to build temples, to worship their saviors. Estarion put a stop to that with firmness that struck even Daros to awe. But he could not stop the steady stream of people who came to leave offerings on the palace steps in the mornings, or the crowds that followed both of them wherever they went, bowing and praising their names. Nothing that they could do would lessen it, least of all any display of magery.

It was rather wearing. Dreams were no refuge: *she* was seldom in them. Daros needed further distraction, but there was little allure in taverns or in the arms of women who were not she.

He approached the queen one morning, half a year of this world after he had come to it. Estarion was elsewhere; she was preparing for the morning audience, being painted and adorned like the image of a goddess. She smiled at him, somewhat to the distress of the maid who was trying to paint her lips, and said, "I hear that your recruits are doing well."

"They are," he said. He had been training young men in the arts of war, finding them apt pupils, as farmers and herdsmen went. Weapons were not particularly easy to come by; they had no steel, not even bronze, and copper was rare. But what they could do with stone and bone and hardened wood, they did well enough.

He said as much. The queen nodded. "These things that you have, it's a pity we can't get them. But we make do. You do expect the enemy to come back?"

"The shadow is still there," he said, "on the other side of the sky. But I didn't come to speak of that. There's another thing that's struck me strangely. Traders are coming back, plying the river. People are even traveling again. But there have been no embassies. Why is that?"

"Perhaps we're out of the habit," she said. "It's been years since king could speak to king. The enemy kept us all within our borders. Common people could travel, but embassies were always prevented in some way: slowed, stopped, killed."

"They were dividing you," he said, "the more easily to conquer."

"Yes," she said.

"Do you have spies, lady?" he asked her. "Have you talked to travelers? Do you know what's happening in your neighbors' kingdoms?"

She regarded him with those great dark eyes, as if she needed to study him. "I do have spies," she said. "I do listen. My neighbors are holding their realms together as I am mine. None of them is strong enough yet to think of war, if that's what you fear—though they may do so before much longer, and knowing that I've allowed you to raise and equip an army."

His stomach tightened. "Lady, that's for the shadow, not for them."

"One may hope they understand that," she said.

"Lady," he said after a pause, "I came here to ask your leave to mount an embassy, to visit the kings and talk to them. The enemy divided you out of fear—because an alliance was in some way a threat. While the enemy is gone, if you can unite in common cause, he'll come back to find you much stronger and far more ready to stand against him."

"That is so," she said. "I have considered it. But there's been no one I can trust to send, who has the skill to speak as an envoy. My lords are as closed in upon themselves as my brother kings. We all are—we've forgotten how to speak to one another."

"I haven't," he said. "I was raised and trained for this." As was Estarion, but he did not say that. Estarion did what he chose, as he chose. Daros did not pretend to understand him.

She was still studying him. "You think you can do this?"

"I know I can." He hoped he did not sound excessively cocky.

"I will give you a boat," she said, "and boatmen, and a retinue suitable to your rank and station. Waset's good name will be in your hands."

"I'll not harm it," he said.

"I think you will not," said the queen.

Later that day, as Daros instructed the latest band of recruits in the rudiments of archery, Estarion happened by with casualness that was just a fraction too studied. He distracted the recruits rather excessively. Their awe of Daros had begun to wear off; he was familiar, if terrifying. The queen's consort was an eminence so lofty that he stole away their wits.

Daros called a halt to the proceedings before someone put an arrow through his neighbor, and dismissed the recruits. They withdrew with dignity, but well before they were out of sight they scattered like the boys they still were, whooping and dancing across the field to the city.

Daros would have liked to run with them, but he had an accounting to face. It was taking its time in coming. Estarion had wandered across the field to inspect the line of targets, taking note of the bolts that clustered in the center of one or two. "Good shots," he observed.

"They grew up hunting waterfowl," Daros said. He set about retrieving arrows, both those in the targets and those that had flown wide. Estarion lent him a hand.

When every bolt was found and put away in its quiver, they walked slowly back toward the city. Daros almost dared hope that there would be no reckoning after all; that Estarion had come simply for the pleasure of his company.

That was foolish, and he knew it even as he thought it. A moment later, Estarion said, "You're not a bad general of armies. Will you be trying your hand at diplomacy next?"

"You don't think I can do it?"

Estarion smiled thinly. "Why, lad. Don't you?"

"Isn't that what a prince does?"

"The general run of princes, yes. Is it a custom in your country to conduct the affairs of the realm in brothels and alehouses?"

Daros stiffened. "I haven't touched a woman of this world since I came to it, nor set foot in a tavern. I've been the very model of a prince."

"So you have," Estarion said blandly. "It's a remarkable transformation. I commend you."

"Yet you have doubts about this venture."

"No," said Estarion. "In fact I don't. I'm jealous. I can't go—I'm needed here."

"You want me to stay, so that you can go."

"No," Estarion said again. "It's only . . ."

Daros waited.

"We can ill afford to lose you. Promise me something. If one or more of the kings is hostile, promise that you won't try to force an alliance."

"I won't do anything dangerous," Daros said. "I'll swear to that."

Estarion's glance was less than trusting. "What you call merely dangerous, the rest of us would call lethal."

"I'll pretend I'm my father," Daros said. "Would that content you?"

"You're not capable of that much prudence."

"How do you know?"

Estarion cuffed him hard enough to make him reel. "Curb the insolence, puppy. If you can be wise and circumspect, and speak softly to these kings, then you'll do much good for this land. But if you grow bored or lose your temper, you may harm it irreparably. Do you understand?"

Daros set his teeth. He deserved this; he had earned it with his years of useless folly. And yet . . . "Surely I've at least begun to redeem myself since I came here. Have I been feckless? Have I been foolish? Have I been anything but dutiful?"

"You have not," said Estarion, "and that is a matter for great admiration. But one would wish to be certain."

"What? That I'll be resentful enough to prove you right?"

"Prove me wrong," Estarion said. "Because if you don't, I'll deal with you as painfully as I know how."

He was not jesting. Daros was torn between wanting to laugh and wanting to hit him. He settled for a baring of teeth. "I'll prove you wrong," he said. "My word on it."

"Good," said Estarion.

They were almost to the walls, but their pace had slowed. Daros had meant to be silent about another thing, but he was feeling spiteful. "I know you wish you could go. But your heart wouldn't be in it, would it? It's been a long while since you waited on the birth of an heir."

Estarion stopped short. He did not knock Daros flat, which rather surprised him. The emperor's voice was mild, almost alarmingly so. "I should have known you'd see that."

"Should it be a secret?"

"She's lost ten children, six of them sons, either miscarried or dead at birth. She's terrified of the omen if she dares celebrate this one."

"Yes," said Daros. "But she won't lose this child. Will she?"

"Not while I live," Estarion said.

"Nor I," Daros admitted. "I . . . laid a small wishing on her this morning, when I went to see her."

He braced himself, but Estarion only sighed. "Of course you did. So did I. She's wonderfully well protected."

"It's a son," Daros said. "Have you thought about what he will do to the line of succession in your empire?"

"He will do nothing," Estarion said. "Daruya will rule after me in Keruvarion and Asanion. This is the heir to Waset, son of the queen and her consort."

"Do you think Waset will ever understand what blood has come into its royal house?"

"Waset understands that its queen is mated to a god. And maybe," said Estarion, "this is proof that we will overcome the darkness. Sun-blood continues itself when it's most needed—always. Even here, it seems, on the other side of the horizon."

Daros bowed his head to that—not a thing he did often, at all, but he had a modicum of respect for the god who had begotten Estarion's line. "She is worthy of that blood," he said.

Estarion was not a jealous man. He smiled, by which Daros knew that he was in the royal good graces again. "Come in to dinner," he said. "Then don't you have an expedition to plan?"

"By your leave," Daros said.

"You'd do it regardless," said Estarion, "but I'll give it, for my vanity's sake." He flung an arm about Daros' shoulders and pulled him through the gate.

That was when the moon was halfway to the full. When it touched the full, the queen's own golden-prowed boat waited at the quay of Waset, with her picked men in it, and the best of Daros' recruits. There was also a deputation from the temples of the city, led by none other than the high priest Seti-re.

Daros would infinitely have preferred another companion, but it seemed that this was to be his first lesson in the art of being politic. Seti-re wore his accustomed slightly sour expression, although he lightened it considerably for Daros' benefit. For some unfathomable reason, though he did not like Estarion at all, he was in awe of Daros. Almost Daros would have said that he was infatuated, but it was not quite as fleshly a thing as that.

He was not the most comfortable companion for an embassy, but Daros had too much pride to object. He bade farewell to the queen and the queen's consort, not lingering over it; he hated endless good-byes. They had little to say to him that was not the empty form of royal show. All the things that mattered, they had said to one another in the days before this.

It was a strange sensation to ride the river away from Waset. It was all he knew in this world, and the one man of his own world was there, standing on the bank, unmoving for as long as he was in sight. The shadow of him remained in memory long after the river had curved, carrying the boat away from the city and the people in it.

The current was rapid in this season. The great flood of the river had passed, leaving its gift of rich black earth for the farmers to till, but the river was not yet settled fully into its banks again. Between the current and the oars, the boat seemed to leap down the river.

Daros should have sat under the canopy amidships with the rest of the embassy, but he had no great desire for Seti-re's company. He found a place near the high prow, leaning on it, watching as they skimmed through the black land. The fields were full of people and oxen, plowing, planting, tilling. Sometimes they paused to stare at the golden boat. Children and dogs ran along the banks, calling in high excited voices.

It was the same cry, as long as the boat sailed through this kingdom: "The god! The god is on the river!"

He thought of hiding, or at least effacing himself on the deck, but it was somewhat too late for that. He smiled instead, and called greetings to those who were close enough to hear. They answered, sometimes incredulous, sometimes delighted.

It was two days' swift passage to the border between Waset and Gebtu. The first night they stopped and moored near a town that offered them the best of its hospitality: a roasted ox, the inevitable bread and beer, and singing and dancing and a remarkable number of lovely women.

Time was when Daros would have taken his pick of the women. Certainly they were not shy in preferring him to other men. But he had no more desire for these than for the beauties of Waset.

He slept alone on the boat, with the boatmen and the stars, and the moon riding high overhead. He was becoming accustomed to a lone white moon, and no Greatmoon to turn the night to blood. Its cool light bathed him and flowed over the water. There seemed to be no shadow on the stars, but all Gates were still shut. This world was enclosed in a bubble of darkness.

There was still a gate, the gate of dreams. He sought it, and her; and found her waiting, asleep in a narrow bed in a small bare room. Those walls needed no ornament but the gold of her hair, spread across the coverlet, and the beauty of her face and body as she woke slowly.

Long before her eyes were open, she was aware of him. Her smile bloomed, rare and wonderful. He bent over her and brushed her lips with his. Her arms enfolded him and drew him down.

Part of him knew that he was mad or worse, besotted with a dream. Yet another part, the part that touched on his magery, insisted that she was real. Dream had brought him to her, but when they joined body to body, they did so in living truth. Certainly after these dreams, he was sated as if he had indeed spent the night with a woman, but there was never any stain of spent seed on bed or body. Yet sometimes there were marks of teeth or nails on his skin.

Tonight they spoke of nothing but one another: her pleasure, his delight in her. They chose to forget the troubles that beset them, the war they both fought, the enemy that threatened both these worlds. There was nothing then but the two of them, and a joy so deep that he woke close to tears.

He was lost, conquered, besotted. He was in love with a dream and a vision, and no woman in the waking world could equal her.

TWENTY-TWO

THE KINGDOM OF GEBTU WAS NOT AS PROSPEROUS AS WASET. THE SHADOW had been no more relentless there, but Gebtu had felt more keenly the loss of its young men and the stripping of its harvests. Beggars in Waset were few; the queen saw to it that the ill and the indigent were given a ration of barley from the royal stores, to bake their bread and brew their beer. Here it seemed the king did no such thing. Gaunt women and swollen-bellied children sat by the roadsides, begging from passersby, and swarmed on boats that ventured within reach of the bank.

And yet the city, when they came to it near the end of the third day out from Waset, was more splendid than that clean and well-fed but rather simple city. The walls were built of stone rather than brick; the gates were inlaid with gold, and the palace was notably more imposing than the palace of Waset.

A high and haughty prince of men received the embassy at the quay. His heavy collar of gold and his gold-sheathed staff proclaimed his rank; his belly was ample and his expression loftily noble. His retinue was large, rich with gold and colored stones, and arranged in meticulous ranks. Every one of them went down in prostration as Daros stepped from the boat to the shore. The nobleman bowed slightly more slowly than the rest, so that it was clear who was the lord and who were the commoners.

Daros kept his face carefully empty of expression. He would wait and watch and see what was to be seen; time enough later to act.

There was a chair waiting, and strong bearers to carry it. For an instant Daros had a fierce, almost painful longing for a senel. But there was no such beast in this world, that any of these people knew: nothing large enough to carry a man, only the tiny gazelle and the antelope of the desert, that were very like the senel in shape, but scarce a fraction the size.

With an inaudible sigh, he folded himself into the chair, which was not made for a man of his size, and suffered the bearers to carry him, rocking and swaying, from the river through the streets of the city.

The king of Gebtu might have kept a mere envoy waiting for days, but a god required more delicate handling. Daros was offered food, a bath, and rest, in that order; he accepted the first two but declined the third. The servants had been terribly cowed when they began, but he wheedled and smiled and coaxed until they could wait on him without collapsing in a fit of hysterics.

As they finished their ministrations, the door-guard announced a guest. Daros' smile of greeting was genuine. Seti-re was a familiar face, and welcome for that if for nothing else.

The priest was much more at ease here in this palace than he had been in the boat. He dismissed the servants with a flick of the hand, and put in a twist that made their eyes roll white.

"Clever," Daros said when they had gone. "Now only half of them will spy on us; the rest will hide to avoid the curse."

"Are you laughing at me?"

The man was quick to his own defense. Daros softened his smile and said, "Oh, no. Not at all. Is there news?"

"Nothing from Waset," said Seti-re, mollified. His eyes kept wandering to Daros' face and fixing there. It was beastly uncomfortable and rather distracting. "The king will summon us soon. I knew him long ago; he was a priest for a while in the temple in Waset, sent there by his father to learn the greater arts and the more famous magics. He proved to have some little talent for them."

"I had heard that," Daros said, "and that he was meant to be a priest, until his elder brothers were taken by the dark enemy. I've been trusting that you will help me with him, help me to talk to him in ways that he'll most willingly hear. I'm not a priest, you see, and I don't speak the language."

Seti-re stood a little taller for that. "My lord, a god can speak any language he chooses. A god such as you . . . he'll be captivated. Though he might ask to see some of your arts. Will that be a difficulty?"

"Only if he asks me to do something I can't or won't do."

"That would be true of any god," Seti-re said.

"Ah," said Daros. "I hoped I could trust a priest to understand such things."

Seti-re almost smiled. "My lord, if I may ask a great favor? You need not grant it, of course, in your power and divinity. But I would ask . . . may I speak as high priest of your cult?"

"You are high priest of the Sun in Waset," Daros said. "Can you be both?"

"If you will allow, my lord."

Daros looked him in the face. He held steady, though he had gone grey, shaking with fear. "You want power," Daros said, "but that's not everything, is it? You think you love me, because I carry the curse of a pretty face."

"No!" Seti-re had gone from grey to crimson. "May not a man choose the god he wishes to worship?"

"Because he has what men call beauty?"

"You have great beauty," Seti-re said with dignity, "but that is only fitting for a god. You are a young god; your power is great, but it startles you somewhat still. Yet you carry yourself with grace, and you seldom mock even the great fools of the world. May not a mere mortal find that admirable?"

"How odd," Daros said half to himself. "I've been found admirable twice since I decided on this expedition—and that is twice in my life. Sir priest, if you would worship me, you should know the truth. Where I come from, I'm reckoned a fool and a wastrel. I am—I was—a frequenter of taverns, a lover of loose women. I was caught transgressing great laws, and sentenced to exile and hard servitude. I broke that sentence to come to this world, and for that my exile is now, it seems, irrevocable."

"Of course you are exiled, my lord," Seti-re said. "How else would a god suffer himself to live among mortals?"

"A wastrel god," Daros said. "A useless prince."

"Not in this world," Seti-re said.

Since that was true, and since Daros had made much of it to Estarion, he shut his mouth with a click.

For a man who had no humor, Seti-re had a surprising store of wry wit. "You see, my lord?" he said. "There is no escaping the truth: that you are a god, and worthy to be worshipped."

The king of Gebtu was a man of middle years, as Daros had expected. He still kept his head shaved in priestly fashion, but covered it with a wig of numerous plaits, and cultivated an odd small beard on the tip of his chin. His court was extravagant, numerous, and visibly rich; Daros the setter of fashion easily recognized his like in these languid nobles.

They were not so languid now, for all their pretense. A god among them was a potent threat to their cult of ennui. They found Daros profoundly satisfying, a truly godlike god. He assisted them by drawing sunlight to him, wrapping it about him like a mantle. They blinked, dazzled, and the less bold dropped to their faces.

The king held his ground, only narrowing his eyes against the figure of living light that was his guest. When Daros halted, Seti-re advanced a few steps more and bowed before the king, and said, "My lord of Gebtu, I bring you the son of the Sun, the god Re-Horus."

Indaros, Daros thought, but he held his tongue. People did odd things here to plain Varyani names. Re-Horus he would be, then, as Estarion was Seramon.

He suffered the king's scrutiny as he did everyone else's, standing straight and offering no expression to be judged or found wanting. When he had had enough of it, he let fall his cloak of sunlight. He did not speak. That was for the king to do.

The king seemed inclined to sit still until Daros' image was graven on his brain—or, as they would have said in Waset, on his liver. Daros shifted slightly, easing his stance. At that, the king blinked and came to himself. "I welcome you to Gebtu, my lord Re-Horus," he said.

Daros inclined his head slightly. "Lord Kamos," he said. "I thank you for your hospitality."

"My lord," said the king, "if a temple would be more to your liking, or the service of priests—"

"No," said Daros. "No, my lord king. I'm well content."

That pleased the king: he lightened visibly. "That is well," he said. "And my sister queen in Waset—she is well?"

"Very well," Daros said.

"It is true, then? She has taken a consort?"

Kamos knew it was true, but he was not speaking for himself. For the ears of the court, Daros answered, "She has taken my lord to her heart, my master to whom I am sworn, a great lord and king beyond the horizon."

A long sigh ran down the hall. Fear sparked in it. The gods had come to Waset. Now one of them stood in their hall, looming over the tallest man in Gebtu, with face of bronze and hair as bright as fire.

Daros softened his voice almost to a croon, and set a little magery in it, too, to soothe their fears. "We came for all this world, not only for Waset—to lead your people against the darkness, and destroy it if we can. The enemy fears you, my lords; fears what you can do when joined in alliance. I have come to ask if you will turn that fear to living truth. Will you ally with us? Will you join against the enemy?"

"The enemy is gone," the king said.

"For a while," said Daros, "but he will come back."

"You are sure of this?"

"I am sure," Daros said. "This is a gift of greater gods than we, this breathing space. I don't doubt you've heard that I've gathered an army in Waset—or that you've wondered whether that army is meant to invade Waset's neighbors. I swear to you, it is not. I've gathered it against the common enemy of us all; and I come now to ask if you will join your army to it, and be willing to make alliance with others of your neighbor kings."

"There are no alliances," Kamos said. "There have not been since my father's day. Alliances break; kings fall apart from one another. Only one's own kin and kind may be trusted."

"So the enemy has taught you," Daros said. "He separated you, kingdom by kingdom, the more easily to conquer you. If you gather together, if you unite yourselves, you may have strength to oppose him."

"How can one oppose the dark itself?"

"With light," said Daros.

"Firelight? Torchlight?"

"Sunlight," Daros said, "and strength of will."

"The sun cannot shine at night," said Kamos.

"No," said Daros, "but the light of the gods can—the light of magic."

"We do not have that power," Kamos said.

"If I give it to you," said Daros, "will you swear alliance with Waset, and help me unite your neighbors to the north?"

"With Waset," Kamos said slowly, "we were friends and kin once, when that was possible. We might be so again. But to unite the rest . . . my lord, your power is great, but can you truly hope to bring together all the kingdoms of the river?"

"I can try," said Daros. "With your help, I might succeed."

"Will you make me a god?"

Daros found that his mouth was open. He shut it.

"Gods stand beside the throne of Waset," Kamos said. "How much stronger would Gebtu be if its king was a very god. Can you do that, my lord?"

"That is not within my power," said Daros. "I can give you the light. You have the capacity for that." And that was true. This man was as much a mage as any in this world. It was the feeblest of powers, but enough, just, for the simplest of all arts, the summoning of light.

A thought was waking in Daros' heart. He could not speak of it, not yet; it was not clear enough for words. But soon. He chose silence now, waiting on the king's response.

Kamos answered him after a long and reflective pause. "I will consider what you have said, my lord. Will you rest a while with us?"

"I will remain for three days," Daros said, "before my duty bids me go."

"That will have to be enough," said Kamos, not willingly; he was a king, and kings were not accustomed to observing any strictures but their own. But a god stood higher in rank than a king.

The king withdrew to ponder his choices. Daros, after three days on a boat, was restless; he refused to be kept mewed in his rooms, however richly ornamented they might be.

The guards at the gate tried to keep him in. They were terrified of their captain and in great fear of the king, but Daros' presumed divinity won him passage. He hardly even needed to fling the gate open with a gust of mage-wind.

He was not alone on his ramble through the city. A man had followed him from the palace: not a tall man but sturdy and strong for one of these light-boned people. He was young, younger than Daros; boys grew to manhood early here.

Daros did not confront him, not yet. He was a comfortable enough presence, silent and observant, as a guard should be. He left Daros free to think his own thoughts as he walked those streets, broad and clean close by the palace, but narrow and reeking as he moved outward toward the walls. It was as if whatever the king could see he kept in excellent order, but once it was out of sight, it vanished from his awareness.

Kamos was not a weak king. As kings went in this world, he ruled well. But Daros had hoped for better. His fault and his folly: he was his father's son in spite of everything, and had seen the rule of Sun and Lion in the great cities of another empire, on the other side of the sky.

Daros had not come here to teach a king how to rule. Nor was there time if he had intended such a thing. But the temptation to do something, say something, was overwhelming.

There was a thing he could do. He did not know that it had been done before, but the part of him that knew his magic was sure that it was possible. He would have preferred another place, and another king—or better yet a queen—but maybe, once the gift was given, this king would wake to the failings of his rule.

Or maybe he would close his eyes to them altogether and become a tyrant.

Daros must hope, and trust in his magic, which had led him here. He walked the circle of the walls, then back through squalor to wide avenues and noble houses. He was aware on the edge of his mind that people followed him, stared at him, tried to touch him—but his companion held them off with a hard eye and a raised spear.

He halted by a cistern, one of many in the city. Its lid was off, and jars abandoned by it: the women who had come to draw water had fled at the sight of him. He was sorry for that, but he did not think it would be wise to call them back.

He sat on the rim. The water was not far below; it shimmered darkly, reflecting the sky. It made him think of darkmages, how soft and deep their power could be.

He was not a darkmage. He was not sure that he was a lightmage, either. He seemed to partake of both. Or maybe he was something different.

The sun, even so close to the horizon, fed him its strength. The water, born of the river that was the lifeblood of this land, made him stronger. Even the stones and the beaten earth had become part of him, though this was never the world to which he was born.

He looked up from the water. The young man from the palace was watching him steadily, wary but not afraid. There was a brightness in him, a spark even stronger than that in the king. "You're the king's son," Daros said, for it was clear to see. "What is your name?"

"Menkare," the prince said, "my lord."

"Did your father bid you watch me?" Daros asked, though he could have had the answer for the looking.

"No, my lord," said Menkare. "You're full of light. Even after your spell ended in the hall, it stayed, under your skin. Is that because you are a god?"

"It's because I am a mage," Daros said. "Come here."

The boy came, light on his feet, alert, but obedient to the god's will. When Daros took his hand, he barely stiffened. He had a bright clean spirit, and a mind that thought in lines like shafts of sunlight in a dark hall. He was little like his father, except in the magnitude of his gift.

Daros was not devout, but he knew the gods existed—and not only mages who were thought to be gods. Looking at this son of the king, he knew why he had come here, and what he had been brought to do. He opened the gate of his magic and let it flow through their joined hands, into the brightness at the heart of this prince. It was headlong, eager; it took the full force of his will to keep it flowing slowly, lest it burn away the boy's mind.

Menkare's eyes were wide. "What—my lord—"

"The gods' gift," Daros said. "I give it to you."

"But—"

"There are greater gods than I," said Daros, "and this is their will. They ask that you not speak of it until they give you leave. Can you do that?"

"Yes, my lord," Menkare said. "But—"

"Come," said Daros.

Menkare followed slowly, stumbling a little. He was full of light, brimming with it. It streamed through his veins and flooded his brain, his heart, his lungs and liver.

He could not wield it yet. Daros had not given him that. He must grow into it, become accustomed to it. But when the shadow came back, if the gods were kind, there would be a new mage in this world.

Daros had been walking perfectly steadily and thinking perfectly clearly. He was astonished to find himself on his back and Menkare standing over him, and the gate-guards lifting him. He could not move at all.

His magery was intact. He had done it no harm. But every scrap of bodily strength that he had had was gone.

They carried him in and put him to bed. Menkare's glance swore the guards to silence. He stayed with Daros, as quietly watchful as ever.

Daros had a voice if he would use it, and words enough, too, but he elected to be silent. Sleep came swiftly, sweeping over him like a tide of night.

TWENTY-THREE

S LEEP RESTORED DAROS' STRENGTH AND BROUGHT HIM BACK TO HIMSELF. He woke to find Menkare asleep beside his bed, curled on the floor like a hound pup. The magic in him had settled more deeply: he looked to Daros' eye like a mage indeed, albeit young and unschooled.

Was this how Daros looked to the mages of Gates and temples?

Daros lay for a long while, feeling out the channels of his body, assuring himself that they were all as they should be. His power was fully itself. He had surrendered none of it. The price, then, was the body's strength—which could be inconvenient if he was to bring magery to this world without magic.

At length he rose carefully, relieved to discover that his knees would hold him up. His hair had not gone white; he had not poured away his youth. He was still his young and potent self.

Such vanity: his knees nearly gave way, but only with relief. He did love to be young and strong and beautiful.

He stooped over Menkare. The prince woke slowly, blinking, frowning up at Daros' face. "You changed me," he said. "My dreams—"

"You were a seed. I made you grow."

"What . . . am I a god?"

"If by that you mean a mage," Daros said, "yes. You are."

"That's not what I wanted," Menkare said. "You should have given it to my father."

"This gift was not for him," said Daros.

"*He* wants it."

"I'll give him what he can bear," Daros said, "and ask him for a thing in return. Will you come with me? Will you help me make these kingdoms one?"

Menkare sparked at that, very much in spite of himself. Yet he said, "I'm not sure I trust you."

"Or your brothers, once you're away and the field is clear for them to claim your place?"

Menkare laughed without mirth. "No, I don't trust them at all—but I'm not afraid of them, either. You, I think I fear."

"I am strong," said Daros, "and I am not of this world. It's wise to be wary of me. But I mean you no harm."

"You'll have to prove that."

"Then you will have to come with me, so that I can do it."

This time Menkare's laughter was genuine, if somewhat painful. "I'll go with you. How can I not?"

"How indeed?" said Daros.

Kamos took most of the three days to make the choice he could not help but make. In that time, Daros made himself familiar with the court, learned the names of the lords both greater and lesser, and became acquainted with each of Menkare's dozen brothers. Some were older, some younger. Two others were sons of the king's foremost wife.

She summoned him late on the second day, with her eldest son as her messenger. The summons was no great secret, but neither was it trumpeted aloud in court.

Women here did not live apart from men, nor were they kept in seclusion as they still were among the higher nobility of Asanion. But they kept to their own places, ruled their own realm of the house, the nursery, the ladies' court. He had met none of the queens, who had their own palace and their own court; he was sure that that was deliberate on the king's part. Kings, unless they were Estarion, had a certain predilection for keeping their women away from excessively attractive men.

That did not prevent the queen from sending her son to fetch the god from beyond the sky. She received him in a cool and airy room, seated on a throne much like her husband's, attended by a guard of women whom, for an instant, Daros took for northerners of his own world.

He had seen people from the south of this world: large, strong, very dark, though not the true blue-black as Estarion was. Their faces were broad and blunt, their lips full, their hair as tightly curled as a woolbeast's fleece.

These women were of like blood, but they were leaner, even taller, and their features were carved clean; and once his eyes had found their range, he saw that they were not so dark. They were deep brown with an almost reddish cast. He could not tell if their hair was straight or curled: it was shaved to the elegant skull. They wore kilts like guardsmen, and carried spears.

They were glorious. He smiled for the pure joy of seeing them, even as he bowed before the queen.

She was a woman of this country, as he would have expected. She looked a great deal like her son. He would not have called her beautiful, but she was pleasing to look at; her eyes were clear, with a keen intelligence. "You like my guards?" she asked. Her voice was warm and rich, much lovelier than her face.

"Your guards are splendid, lady," Daros said. "Where do they come from?"

"From a tribe far to the south," she answered him.

"There are tribes far to the north of my world," he said, "who are quite like these. Their women are warriors, too."

"Would those be my guards' gods, perhaps?"

"Anything is possible," said Daros.

The queen smiled. "And you? Do you belong to a tribe?"

"My people live in cities," he said. "My father is a ruling prince—I suppose you would reckon him a king, but my family takes a certain ancient pride in eschewing that name and rank."

"A prince among gods," said the queen. "We are honored."

Daros bowed to the compliment.

"You come bearing gifts," she said. "My husband is in great confusion of mind over that which you offer him. He hopes to be a god, but fears to be denied it."

"I can only give him what he is able to accept," Daros said.

"Is he as mortal as that?"

"All men are mortal," Daros said. "Some are . . . less so than others. He has a considerable gift, for a man of this world, but I can give him only a little more."

"Will that be of use against what comes?"

"I hope so," said Daros.

"You hope? You don't know?"

"Prophecy is not my gift," he said.

She sighed and rested her chin on her hand, narrowing her eyes, searching his face. "My eldest son says that when you go, you've asked him to go with you. As what? As a hostage?"

"As an ally," said Daros.

"Will you do that in every kingdom? Take the heir to serve your cause?"

"I will do what the greater gods bid me, lady," Daros said.

"It would be a wise thing," she said, "to take such royal hostages, both as threat and promise. But if you take my son, I would ask something in return."

"Yes, lady?"

"Give me what you would give my husband."

Daros had expected that. It was not easy for him to say, "Lady, to kindle a fire, I need a spark. Your lord has it. You, alas, do not. You are mortal. But," he said before she could speak, "this I can give you: I will keep your son safe. While I live, while I endure in this world, he will come to no harm because of me."

She read the truth in his face. It did not please her, but she was no fool. She bowed to it. "I will accept that," she said.

The king of Gebtu received his gift on the last day of Daros' sojourn in his city. It was given him in the court of the highest temple. Seti-re served as priest of a rite that Daros would have preferred to avoid; but Seti-re insisted.

"Gods live in ritual," he said. "A god without a rite is no god at all."

There was a great deal of chanting and incense, passes of hands and turns of a sacred dance. When Daros was close to eruption, Seti-re's glance gave him leave to do the small thing, the simple thing, that all this mummery was meant to conceal.

The king knelt in the center of the court. He had taken off his crown and his wig, and bowed his bare and gleaming head in submission before the god. Daros laid his hands on it. The spark within the king was no greater than ever, if no less.

Daros gave the king what he had to give. It was not the shining flood that had filled Menkare, but a glimmer of light, a gleam in darkness. It fed the spark, swelling it into a coal.

He withdrew then, before the coal burst into flame. Kamos was trembling violently. Daros soothed him with a cool brush of magery.

The rite rattled and droned and spun to a lengthy conclusion. The king remained kneeling through all of it. Only when it had ended, when silence had fallen, did he rise, staggering, but he shook off hands that would have supported him. He walked out of the temple, eyes blank, face exalted.

That exaltation carried him through the feast of parting. Daros managed to avoid speaking with him. Seti-re did what talking was to be done, chattering of anything and everything, and seeming oblivious to the silence on either side.

Only at the end did Kamos cut through the babble, reach across the priest's ample body, and grip Daros' wrist. "Tell me what I can do," he said.

"You can bring light in the darkness," Daros said, "and fill hearts with hope."

"Yes," the king said, rapt. "Yes." He raised his free hand. Light flickered in it, feeble enough but unmistakably there. He laughed with a child's pure delight.

"Remember also to bring hope," Daros said, "and to look after your people. That is the price I ask, lord king. Will you pay it?"

"Yes," said the king. "Oh, yes."

Daros did not believe him, but chose to let be. He had what he needed: an ally, and the king's son beside him when he set sail again on the river.

He left that day, though the sun was nearer the horizon than the zenith. The king did not try to keep him, nor seemed inclined to keep his heir. The lesser princes were more than glad to see their brother go.

Menkare did not look back once he had set foot on the boat. "My father is a happy man," he said as they sailed in the long light of evening. He, like Daros, had a fondness for the solitude of the prow rather than the close quarters of the deck.

"One may hope he will remain happy," said Daros.

Menkare smiled thinly. "His new toy will keep him occupied for a while. By the time he discovers that you gave him a single dart and me the whole quiver, we can hope that he's inclined to be forgiving."

"The alliance has been sworn in the temple, witnessed by all the lords and priests," Daros said. "I sealed it in other ways, which will become apparent if anyone tries to break it. It will hold at least until the enemy comes back again."

"I won't ask how you sealed it," Menkare said after a pause, "only be glad that you did—and hope it holds as long as you say."

"It will hold," said Daros, as much prayer as assurance.

"And meanwhile? Will you give godhood to every king's heir from here to the river's delta? Can you do that?"

"Only if there is a seed of magery to nurture and grow."

"I have a thought," said Menkare. "Men of this kind—they're drawn toward temples, yes? My father was. I was; I never went, because my mother didn't wish it, but the call was there. If you search in temples, you may find what you need."

"I have thought of that," Daros said. "I can't give this gift too often—its cost is too high. But if I can give it even a dozen times, that's a dozen more mages than this world had before. I can teach them as we go—then bring them back to Waset, where is a greater master than I. Then, if the gods give us time, each of you can return to your kingdom and raise walls against the enemy. Then—"

"I think," Menkare said dryly, "that it's enough for now to think of learning to use what I've been given. Let the rest come later—and other godlings with it."

Daros bowed to that. He had run ahead of himself; not wise, but sometimes he could not help it. There was a grandeur in it, a plan that was, without doubt, divine. But whether he could accomplish it before the shadow came back—who knew? Certainly not he. He was not prescient. He merely clung to hope, and left the rest to the gods.

TWENTY-FOUR

THE SEA OF THIS WORLD WAS GREEN, AS TANIT HAD SAID—WAS IT INDEED A year since last Daros had seen her? He stood on the edge of the vast delta, in a land of marshes and reeds and breathless heat, and there before him the waves surged and sighed. They were salt; he had tasted them to be certain. Yet they tasted also of the river, the black mud and the myriad reeds, and the cities that ran in a skein from the cataracts to this wide green ocean.

He had a small fleet of boats now, and a retinue to rival a king's, of every nation from Waset to the shores of the sea. Twelve of them were mages, a dozen out of hundreds that he had seen in temples and palaces, cities and villages. Only Menkare was a prince. To Menkare's surprise, only Kaptah and Ramse were priests. The rest were lords of courts, royal or noble guardsmen, men of cities or villages. They had come in a dozen ways, but this they had in common: they had been drawn to him, called by the flame of magic in them.

Two of them were women, and both of those were villagers. Merit's husband had been taken in the last raid before the enemy withdrew. Nefret was to be married, but she left her young bridegroom and her kin and her village in the delta, and came to Daros with as much a gift of magic as he had ever seen in this world. She was almost a mage in his reckoning, a healer—even as young as she was, she had been the herb-healer and midwife for her village—and, as the gods would have it, a seer.

She stood beside him on the shores of that grey-green sea, and said in her light child's voice, "We should go back tomorrow."

"I had intended to," he said.

She shook her head slightly. Her eyes looked far out over the water, but she was not seeing waves or spume or sky. "All the way back. Back where you came from in this world. Back to Waset."

Daros' heart constricted. "What do you see? What—"

"It's coming," she said. "Not tomorrow. Not in a few days. But soon. It's coming back."

He did not need or want to ask what she meant. He knew. Even without pre-science, he could feel it.

The others had drawn in close. The rest of the following, the guards, the priests, the crews of the boats, were scattered across the sand. All those nearest Daros were mages, and all sensed what he sensed. How not? Their gift had come through him; he had taught them what they knew. They were raw, young, no better than callow recruits in a sorcerous army, but this was difficult to mistake.

The enemy gathered on the other side of the sky. Gates were stirring. All too soon they would open. Then this world must be ready; must be armed and prepared for them.

Seti-re was sitting on a stool that one of his acolytes had brought, with the waves lapping his bare feet. He started slightly as Daros came to squat on the sand beside him. To the eye he had changed little in this year. He was still smooth, plump, slightly sour about the eyes. But the sourness within had turned perceptibly bitter. High priest of Daros' putative cult he might be, and much feted and feasted by kings because of it, but he had had to see the gift of magic given to others—to villagers, even women—but never to him. There was nothing in him from which it could grow.

He was still besotted with Daros' beauty, which he maintained had only grown greater with the passage of time. But for that, Daros might have found this new bitterness disturbing. Bitter men knew no loyalty, in the end, but to themselves.

"My lord priest," Daros said after a while.

"My lord," said Seti-re. For once he was not staring at Daros, but at the restless face of the sea.

"We're going back to Waset, my mages and I," Daros said, "to build walls of light before the enemy comes back."

Seti-re bowed where he sat. "As you wish, my lord."

"I have a thing to ask of you," said Daros, "if you will do it."

"Whatever my lord wishes," said Seti-re.

"No," said Daros, sharply enough that the priest's eyes flicked toward him. He held them with his own stare, willing the man to see what he needed to see. "This must be your free choice. We are not going back to Waset in boats. We are going as I came to this world—by magery. I can take you and any other who will go, but if you choose, there is another thing, a greater thing, that you can do."

Seti-re had brightened in spite of himself. Maybe Daros' smile had something to do with it—he had armed it and aimed it for conquest. "What can I do, my lord?"

"We will be building walls of light in Waset," Daros said, "but if the alliance is to hold and the kingdoms are to sustain their defenses, we need an anchor—a second place of strength. Will you go to Sakhra, and speak for me there?"

Seti-re frowned, in thought rather than in bitterness. Sakhra was the northernmost of the skein of cities, the stem of the lotus before it fanned and flowered into the delta. "Why are you asking me to do this? Shouldn't it be one of your godlings? Perhaps the prince from Gebtu?"

"We need strength," Daros said, "and loyalty, and a talent for speaking to kings. Sakhra's king may come to think that since his city is so far from Waset, he may not be so firmly pressed to observe the terms of alliance—and once the enemy comes, it will be all the more tempting to withdraw within his borders again."

"The same may be said of every king from Sakhra to Esna."

"Yes," said Daros, "but if my high priest is in Sakhra, and I am in Waset, and there are visible proofs of the power that runs from end to end of the river—might he not think twice before he breaks his oath?"

"Visible . . . proof?"

The eagerness in him was almost as strong as magery. "I cannot make you a mage," Daros said, "but I can give you a working that will serve you, when you have need."

"Such as you gave the king of Gebtu?"

"Not quite the same," Daros said.

He stooped and sifted the sand. A pebble came into his hand, smooth and round and silver-grey. A hole had worn itself in the middle. He made a cord of sunlight and shadow and the coolness of spray, plaited it tightly and made it solid and lasting, and set it in the priest's hand.

Seti-re stared at it. Daros saw how he did not quite dare laugh. He was thinking of a moment with Estarion, a promise—a gift given and received, and power bestowed where there was no power to match it.

"When you set your will on this," Daros said, "it will let you summon light. But have a care. If you use it overmuch, or use it against me or mine, it will feed on your spirit as fire feeds on dry tinder."

Seti-re closed his fingers over the stone. A shudder ran through him. It had begun to thrum in harmony with that other one which he kept always about his person, which held within itself the essence of Estarion's spirit.

Daros had given him nothing so powerful, but he need not know that. His bitterness was sweetened somewhat. He was reminded yet again that he had power, real and solid: power over the lives of the gods themselves.

Of all the kings and lords and priests whom Daros had met and wooed and cozened in this long journey, this one remained the most difficult. The power of a name and the promise of divinity had carried him down the river. He had raised the princes of the dead in Abot and called down the sun in Henen. Kings had begun to come to him almost as soon as he began, either in their own person or through noble emissaries. His task had been done for him as often as not by the power of rumor and the terror of the few magics that he had been pressed to perform.

This strange country, many days' journey long and yet hardly wider than its wonder of a river, lay ready and waiting to be brought together. But Seti-re was never as wholly won as even the most doubtful of the kings.

He was a key, of sorts. In Waset he stood highest save only the queen. On the embassy he was second to one whom men called a god. Even without magic, he held power.

Daros had no prescience. That was almost an article of faith. But in giving this man such power, he had done a thing that could not be undone. Whether it was good or ill, he did not know. He only knew that he had had no choice but to do it.

When dawn touched the sky, rising over lush and level green, the fleet gathered to sail upriver. But Daros and his mages did not embark on the boats, nor did Seti-re and the company of his priests. While the boatmen and the guards from a dozen kingdoms watched, Daros opened a Gate.

He had not known until he did it whether it was wise or even possible. But although the shadow pressed hard upon the borders of the world, the light still ruled within.

He sent the priests first, wrapped in living light. As far as they knew, they simply stepped from shore of reeds to court of the temple in Sakhra, before the astonished eyes of priests performing the morning rites. Seti-re would be pleased: he had appeared as gods were rumored to do. No doubt they would be calling him a god, too, after this.

Daros brought his mages to Waset with much less fanfare, drawing in the circle of them, binding them with power, and setting them in a dim and quiet hall within the palace of Waset.

Estarion was waiting for them. Daros had sent no word ahead, but he had not expected to need it. Any mage in this world would have known what Daros had done, the moment he opened the Gate.

He stood in the midst of his huddle of startled and speechless magelings, and looked into the eyes of the Lion. Estarion had not changed in the slightest. After so long among the people of the black land, Daros was somewhat taken aback by the emperor's size and strangeness; but then, he thought wryly, if he could have seen himself, he would have been no less disconcerted.

"My lord," he said lightly. "Well met again at last."

"Indeed," said Estarion. Several of the magelings had flung themselves flat. He raised them gently, soothed them as if they had been children, and handed them off to the servants who had come in behind him.

They all went willingly except for Menkare, who would not shift from his place at Daros' back. Estarion smiled at him, which could not have reassured him at all, and said, "Your lord is as safe with me as he can be in this world. If I promise not to eat him, will you go to the place that has been prepared for you?"

Menkare opened his mouth to refuse, but Daros said, "Go, my friend. This I must face alone. I'll come to you after."

"Will there be anything left of you to do it?" Menkare muttered. But he went as he was bidden.

After he was gone, there was a silence that Daros had no intention of being the first to break. He took advantage of it to shut and secure the Gate, and set his magery in order, and brace himself against whatever blast Estarion might level upon him.

There was little he could do against the force of those eyes on him, raking him to the center and taking from him everything he had done since he left Waset. He let it go freely, with neither shame nor guilt. Most if not all of it Estarion already knew; Daros had spoken with him often. But he had never quite got round to telling Estarion the full extent of the magelings' power.

At length, Estarion let him go. He stiffened his knees before they buckled.

Estarion's voice when he spoke was remarkably mild. "You've grown," he said.

He did not mean in body, though Daros was not quite the child that he had been when he came to this world. "I know of no laws against the making of mages," he said.

"There are none," said Estarion, "because no one knew it was possible."

"No one needed to know," Daros said. "When any village child may be born with magic, and most of the royal and noble houses are thick with mageborn lines, what need for anyone to make mages where there were none?"

"There is a rumor that you've been making gods in order to challenge the powers that exiled you."

"That's true, isn't it?" said Daros. "The enemy exiled us both."

"You think a dozen untrained magelings will be of any use against what we face?"

"I've taught them the art of raising wards," Daros said. "That's useful enough."

Estarion had to grant him that. But he said, "You've taken a great deal on yourself."

"I did what I had to do," said Daros. "As did you, when you gave your soul's key into the hands of a man who could turn traitor in an instant." Estarion stiffened. Daros bit back a small tight smile. "Now I've given him the key to the alliance. He's in Sakhra, no doubt being worshipped as a god, but also, we can hope, holding its king to the oaths he swore."

Estarion raised his hands. Daros steadied himself for the blow, but Estarion seized him and pulled him into a bone-cracking embrace. "Damn you," said the emperor. "*Damn* you. If my son grows up to be half the man and mage that you are, he'll be the despair of everyone who loves him—and the salvation of a world."

Daros for once had no words to say. Estarion held him at arm's length and shook him until his teeth rattled. "You have done better than I ever dreamed you would—and taken greater risks, at far higher cost to you, than you should ever have done."

"I had to," said Daros. "There wasn't anything else I could do."

"That may be," Estarion said. "The gods know, no one else could have done it. Now come with me. My queen is waiting, and another whom you might like to meet."

Tanit did not waste time in words. She had been sitting with her scribes, going over the accounts, but at their coming, she rose and held out her arms. Daros never paused to think; he swept her up and spun her about and set her down as gently as if she had been made of glass.

She was grinning as widely as he must be. "You look splendid," she said.

"And you," he said. He looked her up and down. She was as slender as she had been when he first met her, lithe and strong. There was a light in her that had not been there before, a deep and singing joy whose cause watched him bright-eyed from the arms of his nurse.

He looked like his mother. He was darker, that was to be expected; in fact he was much the same color as Daros. His hair was black and curling; his eyes were round and dark. He would be tall, Daros thought, and maybe he would have a keener profile than people were wont to have here.

There was no gold in his hand. The *Kasar* had passed down in another line. But that mattered little to a mage's eyes. He was mageborn—splendidly, gloriously so. Daros, meeting his eyes, felt as if he stared direct into the sun.

The child crowed and held out his arms, as imperious as ever Sun-blood could be. Daros was an obedient servant: he took the child from his nurse and cradled him, not too inexpertly.

"Menes," Estarion said, "greet your cousin Indaros."

"'aros!" that half-year's child declared. He grinned at Daros, baring a pair of teeth.

Daros was literally held hostage: this latest heir of the Sun gripped a lock of his hair, as fascinated by its brightness as any other person in this world. Once Menes had examined it from all sides, he gnawed happily on it, and screamed when his nurse ventured to pry him loose.

"Let him be," said Daros. He did not raise his voice, but the lash of magic in it both drove back the nurse and silenced Menes' howls. "And you, sir, may touch but not eat. I am for pretty, not for dinner."

Menes scowled, but Daros was a score of years ahead of him in both power and rebellion; and he had been shepherding magelings for a year of this world. Even a child of the Sun was no match for that.

"Here's another use for mages," Daros said to the child's father. "Surely you didn't think mortals would be strong enough to raise this one."

"I had rather thought to do it myself," Estarion said.

"I hope you may," Daros said.

Estarion looked as if he would have said more, but wisdom forestalled him. Surely he of all people would know how uncertain the worlds could be.

TWENTY-FIVE

DAROS HAD BEEN IN THIS WORLD FOR NIGH ON TWO OF ITS YEARS. HOW LONG it had been under his own sun, he did not know, unless he could believe his dreams. That world had barely completed half a year, passing from autumn into winter and from winter into spring.

The first dream of her had been so real, so vivid, that he had been sure for a long while after that it had been no dream at all. Then, just as he began to believe that he had deceived himself in everything—her presence, the love she had given him—he had dreamed of her again. For her it had been a much shorter time, and much less fraught with doubts and desperation. She was Sun-blood. She never doubted herself.

It was comforting, in its way—as the sun's heat could be, even when it flayed flesh from bones. After that he accepted that she would come when the dreams allowed, and tried not to drive himself wild with waiting for her.

On the night after he came back from his embassy into the north, Daros dreamed of Merian again. She had only come to him twice in all of that year, and now a third time she passed through the gate of dreams.

She was unusually distracted; she was as glad as ever to see him, but she had little to say. Her voice kept trailing off.

He tried to charm her. He told her tales that he had heard on his journey, then when those failed to draw her attention, he began to tell her of the journey itself, of the kings, the alliances, the making of mages. But she was not listening. After a while he let himself fall into silence, and simply held her.

She sighed and cradled her head on his shoulder. He stroked the golden extravagance of her hair, and kissed the lids over those beautiful eyes. Her profile was as pure as ivory against the sun-darkened bronze of his skin.

She stayed so all through the night, so close and so vividly real that when he woke in the morning, he could have sworn that her scent still lingered. Of course she was not there, nor had been except in his dream.

The night after that, at last, the shadow came back. It raided a village upriver, where the barley crop had been unusually rich that year, and its harvest had filled the storehouses. The shadow's servants took those stores, all of them, and blasted the storehouses to ash; then they raided the village through wards that had grown lax with time and disbelief, and took all the men and every woman of bearing age, and left the children to drown in their own blood.

Daros had never had a weak stomach. But when he saw that heap of bodies, each rent limb from limb, hacked and mutilated out of all recognition, he choked on bile. Most of his magelings had gone green; one or two were already retching.

Estarion, old warrior that he was, walked expressionless among the carnage. "I've seen worse," he said after Daros nerved himself to follow, "but not by much."

"It's a message," Daros said a little thickly. "Those years of attacks—they were only raids. This is war."

"Maybe so," said Estarion, "but if it really is war, they'll be wanting to end it quickly—sweep over us and destroy us and be gone. They'll be conquering worlds, not simply villages."

"Maybe they are," Daros said. "Maybe they need this world more for its grain and slaves than for its service to oblivion. They left it alone for a while to grow and ripen. Now comes the harvest."

Estarion's glance was almost respectful. "That's an appalling thought, but it's frightfully logical. There's no other reason for this world to have been subjected only to raids for so long. It's been feeding the armies."

"And in letting it be, they told us that there are other such worlds, slave-worlds." Daros stopped. "What if we could raid the raiders?"

"You think we can track them to their stronghold? We can't get past the wall of darkness that surrounds this world."

"We might," said Daros, "if we attached ourselves to the next party of raiders."

"Are you saying we should let ourselves be taken?"

"Why not?"

Estarion cuffed him, and not lightly, either. "Because, puppy, without us this world has no human mages of any skill at all, and the cats, being cats, may not choose to go on protecting every town and village."

"Not if you stay and I go. I'll leave half of my magelings here to bolster you, and take those who are strong enough to stand with me." And, Daros thought, there was another thing he could try, but he was not ready to tell Estarion of that. It would involve too many explanations, and confessions that Merian's kinsman might not be pleased to hear.

"And what then?" Estarion demanded. "You'll go into darkness, you and those children, and very likely die there, blinded and in chains."

"I might," said Daros, "but I've been there. I know what to expect; what to guard against. If the Mage will help—and it well might—I'll be safe enough, considering."

"Yes, considering that that's the most insanely ill-advised plan I've heard in gods know how long."

"I can see that it's mad," Daros said, "but I don't think it's as unwise as that. How long can we hold on here? Shouldn't we try to end it sooner rather than later?"

"Certainly it will end for you," Estarion said.

"Then tell me what else we can do!" Daros said with a flash of heat. "These people are being kept like cattle. Worlds are falling all around them. Theirs will go in the end, when there's nothing else left to conquer. No wards or simple magics can stop it."

"And you can?"

"'Know your enemy.'" Daros recited the words in the singsong of the schoolroom. "That lesson I learned—even I, the despair of my tutors. What do we know of this enemy? Where does he come from? Who leads him? Even what face he wears—has any of these people ever seen it?"

"None who survived," Estarion said.

"None of them was a mage until I came to meddle with them. I went to the dark world once; I came back. I'll come back again."

Estarion stood silent in the sweet stench of death. In those few moments, his face had aged years. "There are worse things than death," he said.

"This world will know them," said Daros, "if I don't do this."

"I'll think on it," Estarion said.

Daros sucked in a breath, but held his tongue. This was as much as he would gain, for now. He clung to what patience he had, and followed Estarion back through the heaps of the dead toward the huddle of guards and mages that had accompanied them from Waset. All of them, save only Menkare the prince, had retreated as far as they could from the horror in front of them.

Estarion's glance was eloquent. Even if Daros could endure the enemy's world, these children could not. They were born to sunlight; the dark was their greatest fear.

Daros turned his back—as great an insolence as he had ever offered this man—and closed his mind. He would do this thing, whether the emperor willed or no.

It was late in the day before Daros was able to speak to the queen. She was closeted with her council, and then with Estarion; and Daros had preoccupations of his own. His mages were in sore need of comfort.

"It's different," Nefret said. She had not wept on the field, nor did she in the palace, in the room in which they had gathered. She looked as if the tears had been burned out of her by the same fire that had consumed the village. "When we were mortal, it was terrible. Now that we have this gift—this curse—it goes beyond that. We can feel—we can see—"

"Shields," Daros said. "Remember what I taught you. You must wall your mind and protect the fire within you."

"And then?" she demanded. "Then it eats us from the inside out?"

"Then it makes you stronger," he said. "I made you for this; I trained you to fight this war. You are strong enough. If you had not been, you could never have endured the gift that I gave you."

"Maybe we don't want it," she said.

Some of the others murmured agreement. He lashed them with a bolt of magic. They gasped. None flinched—that much he was pleased to see. "What I have given," he said to them, "I can take away. But have a care! If I take it, I may take everything that makes you yourself. Seven souls, you believe you have. This power is woven with them all."

"The gods are not kind," said Kaptah the priest from Henen. He was not one of those who had agreed with Nefret. "Lord, did they strike elsewhere? Has that knowledge been given you?"

"They struck villages near Ombos and Hiwa, and Imu in the delta," Daros said. "But they struck no cities, and no villages within sight of cities."

"But they will," Menkare said. "If this is war, these skirmishes will come more often and more strongly, the longer they go on."

"Yes," said Daros. "Tell me, prince of Gebtu. Would you come with me to the enemy's stronghold, and take the war to him there?"

"The enemy is on the other side of the sky," said Menkare.

"So he is," Daros said.

Menkare thought about that. A slow smile bloomed. "Yes," he said. "Yes, that's absolutely mad. I would do it, my lord."

The others glanced at one another. "And I," said Kaptah.

Ramse, the elder of the two priests, shook his head, though not in refusal. "We can't all go. Someone has to stay and defend our cities."

"Half of you will remain," Daros said, "and look for obedience to the Lord Seramon. The rest go with me—but only if you understand, fully and freely, what we will do. We will let ourselves be captured, bound, and carried away. It's no failing of courage if you refuse. The defense of this land is a great charge in itself—and if I fail in what I do, it may be the greatest of all."

"We understand," Nefret said. Her eyes were burning. Her husband, her brothers—the enemy had taken them. She had no real hope of seeing them again, no wise woman would, but even the prospect, however remote, struck fire in her spirit.

The queen received Daros between a much lengthened council and a newly fearful sunset. She had her son with her, drowsing in his cradle, and his nurse and the chief of her maids in quiet attendance.

She knew why he had come: it was in her glance. Yet she smiled, because the sight of him made her glad. "I missed you," she said after he had paid her reverence and sat at her feet. "Waset is a much brighter place when you are in it."

"There is no queen like you in all the kingdoms of the river," Daros said.

She laughed a little. "Oh, hush! My husband will never believe it, but any spy would think that we were lovers."

"That we will never be," Daros said, "and that's well—for lovers are common enough, but a friend is a great rarity."

"I should hate to lose you," she said, suddenly somber.

"I don't intend to die," he said. "My lord and I, and my new-made mages—we are going to save your world. We were brought here for that. We will do it."

"My dear friend," she said tenderly. "Don't say that just to comfort me. I know what happened out there. The dark is back, and worse than ever. You'll catch blame for that, you and my lord."

"Not if we can help it," said Daros.

"It was bad. Wasn't it? He wouldn't let me go. I'm still somewhat out of temper with him because of it."

There was no eluding her clear eye. "It was bad," he said. "It won't be as bad again. We've strengthened the wards that had grown lax, and secured the granaries and the cattle-pens. Some of the fields not yet harvested will be lost, but there's no helping that."

"No, there is not." She sighed, but she was neither discouraged nor particularly weary. It was the sigh of one taking up a burden again after a lengthy respite. "So we're at war again."

"I know a way to end it."

She raised a brow. She knew what he would say, but he had to say it.

"If you will give me leave, I'll take six of my magelings and follow the enemy to his own world, and do my best to stop him there."

"You, and six new-hatched magelings." She did not sound too terribly incredulous. "Against—hundreds? In the dark?"

"Light is their most bitter enemy. My magic is born of the light. Let us find their center, the one who leads them, and we'll destroy him. Then if we can set their Mage free, they lose all their magic; they become no more than mortal. We'll have them—bound to their own world, unable to leave it, to raid or bring war to any beyond them."

"And the dark that they serve? Will it leave us then?"

That, Daros could not answer. Not exactly. "Without their strength to sustain it and the Mage to drive it onward, it will at least stop advancing. Then simple wards should hold it off—maybe forever. Certainly for a very long time."

"Still a death sentence," she said, "after all."

"Maybe not for you or your son, or your son's sons. Maybe not for thousands of years."

"Do you reckon that a risk worth taking?"

"Seven lives, to save a world? There's nothing lost if we fail, but everything to gain if we succeed."

"Seven lives," she said. "Six godlings and a god. He forbade it. And you come to me?"

"He said that he would think on it."

"Ah," she said. She closed her eyes. "Then so will I."

Daros began to rise, but she held him down. Her grip was strong.

"He loves you like a son," she said. "He still grieves for the child of his body who was lost for a foolish and empty cause, long ago. To send you to almost certain death—that will tear at his heart. But if he judges that there is no other hope, he will do it. He will let you go."

Daros said nothing. She did not need to hear his doubts.

No matter; she read them in his face. "Promise me, dear friend. Do nothing until he's done thinking on it."

"There may not be that much time," Daros said.

"Can't you trust him? Can you trust anyone but yourself to do what is necessary?"

Daros flushed. "I am not—"

"You are as arrogant a young pup as was ever whelped in a princely house." Her voice was mild, her tone without censure. "Give him three days. He will have done all his thinking by then—and so will I."

Daros did not like that at all, but she had shamed him into acquiescence. He kissed her hand with rueful respect. "You are as implacable as he is," he said.

"Of course I am," she said. "I'd never be able to stand up to him if I weren't."

He laughed a little painfully, bowed low with no mockery whatever, and left her with her maid and her nurse and the son for whom she had prayed through all the years of her youth.

TWENTY-SIX

You MAY GO," ESTARION SAID. HE SPOKE WITH NO PLEASURE AT ALL, WITH such a face as he must have worn in grim judgement over the courts of empire.

Daros had never expected to be given leave, or so soon, either. They had passed a brutal night, with raids on half a dozen villages, barely beaten off, and a new and alarming thing: attacks on the wards.

Daros had been standing guard on Waset's walls, holding it with magery while Estarion sustained the web of wards in the greater kingdom. His magelings had known the first test of their new existence, weaving their fledgling powers with either Estarion's or Daros'. Daros had divided them quite deliberately into the half who would go and the half who would stay. He kept Menkare and Kaptah and Nefret, Ay and Huy who were brothers from Sekhem, and Khafre the captain of the king's guard of Ipu. They were all trained in war, all but Nefret, and she, the healer and seer, was perhaps more valuable than the rest.

They had done not too badly that night, but by dawn they were out on their feet. Daros saw them to bed before he turned toward his own too long forsaken chamber.

Estarion was waiting there, seated cross-legged on the bed. He had made the decision that he had no choice but to make.

"We can't take many nights of this," Estarion said. "Gods know, I think you're mad, and I think you'll die, if you're lucky—but without this gamble, there's no hope."

"If it can be done," Daros said, "I'll do it."

"I don't doubt it," Estarion said dryly. "You may have your six magelings. Do your best with them, as fast as you can. You're leaving tomorrow night."

"We can leave sooner. We can—"

"Don't be a fool," Estarion said. "You're out on your feet. Today you'll sleep. To-night and tomorrow, you'll prepare those children of yours. We'll hold on mean-while. There is one other thing. A price, if you will."

Daros held his breath. Of course there was a price.

"My cats and my cats' allies," said Estarion. "They're not mages, not as yours are. But give them what you can. Help as you may, for the defense of Waset."

Daros bowed his head. He was willing, even glad to do that. But first he must rest. He was falling asleep where he stood. He needed to sleep long and deep.

And he needed to dream. Dreams might hold the answer. He let himself be put to bed, barely even startled that the servant who tended him had been an emperor in another world, another time. Estarion could be whatever it suited his fancy to be.

Daros had tried before to force the dreams of Merian, and failed. They came when they came. But this was urgency beyond simple desire. He shaped himself into a prayer to whatever god would hear, and offered whatever that divinity would take, even his life, if he could only walk in dream where he needed to walk.

It seemed that one of the gods heard him. He passed through deep water, through darkness that though absolute was not the nothingness that the Mage had wrought. It was a living thing, the breast of Mother Night.

Merian was on the other side of it. She stood atop the tower of a hill-fort, look-ing down into the crash and roar of a sea. Wind whipped back the golden masses of her hair, and plucked at the folds of the mantle that she had wrapped about her.

He in kilt and bare feet, long accustomed to the heat of a hotter sun than had ever shone in this sea-smitten country, felt the cold like the cut of a knife. The chattering of his teeth brought her about, even in the roar of the gale. Her eyes were wide, her expression flat astonished, but she kept her wits about her. She opened her cloak of wool and fur, drawing him into blessed warmth. Her arms clasped him close; he gasped as she crushed the breath out of him, but he uttered no protest.

She loosed her grip a little and tilted her head back. He had to kiss her; he could not help himself at all. "I'm not dreaming you," she said. "You're real. You *are* here."

"I can't stay long," he said, "or linger for loving, not now. Will you forgive me?"

"Maybe," she said. "What is it? Why are you so somber?"

"The world we've been living in," he said, "is about to fall. I have a plan—the emperor says it's madness, but he's given me leave, because there's no other hope. I think there is a little, if you will help me. Are you terribly beset here?"

"Not quite yet," she said. "We've lured them all to Anshan. This is Ki-Oran—"

"Ki-Oran!" For a moment it seemed to Daros that the tower rocked underfoot. "Gods! You're madder than I am."

She frowned. "You've heard of this place?"

"My father's library," Daros said. "I used to make a game of reading the books he'd forbidden. He has books that tell of the mages in Anshan. They're nonsense mostly, written long years after the fall, but there's a little honest meat on the bones of the stories."

"Your father's library," she said slowly. "We never even thought—"

"He keeps it quiet, mostly," Daros said, "even—sometimes especially—from mages. As useful as the temples are, and as much as he approves of the orders of mages, there are still things, he says, that most of them were better not to know."

"*I* should know."

"And they call me arrogant." He smiled to take the sting out of it and brushed her lips with a kiss.

She was too preoccupied to return the kiss. "I'll send word to him—ask him, command him if I must—"

"Lady," he said firmly, so that she looked up startled. "Whatever the books can tell you, I doubt there's anything you haven't learned already, if you're here, alive, and sane. Are you using the Ring of Fire?"

"Yes," she said. "How did you—"

"It's logical. Lure the enemy in, keep him contained. We've done something like it, though with nothing like the power you can bring to bear. That lack of power is killing us. Therefore, while we're still alive, we've decided to take the war to the enemy."

"With what? Have you armies? Weapons? Magic?"

"A realm half a thousand times as long as it's wide, encompassing the banks of a long river. Reed spears and a copper blade or two. My lord and I, and a dozen fledgling mages, and perhaps twice that many who can make fire if they're pressed to it."

"You're mad."

"So your kinsman said. But he can't think of anything better."

"Tell me," she said, "that you're not planning to let yourself be taken in a raid."

"Is there any other way?"

"You don't know," she said. "You really don't know. When they take slaves—they blind them and take their souls. We saved a handful of men, kept them alive, but they were beyond any power to heal. Some of them are dead now. The rest are eyeless, mindless, stripped of will or understanding. Nothing that we've done has made the slightest difference."

He stiffened; his breath came suddenly short. But he was not about to turn coward. "We're warned now—I thank you with all my heart. We'll take measures to protect ourselves."

"Even if those are enough," she said, "what do you think you can do in the dark world? Go up like a torch? Take as many of the enemy with you as you can, before the rest overwhelm you?"

"Something like that," he said. "I was thinking—lady, if mages from this world could find us there, we could join together, find and destroy the leader or leaders, and free the Mage from its prison. Then maybe we could bind the darkness, once the powers driving it were taken away."

"My kinsman is right," she said. "You are mad."

"Do you see any other way?"

"No," she said as unwillingly as Estarion had. "Damn you, no."

"Can you help?"

"I would have to ask. This isn't something I'll lay on anyone who isn't as mad as you are."

"Yes, we need good madmen," he said. "But don't take too long, please, lady. Our world hasn't much time left."

"Your—" She broke off. "Come with me."

"I don't think I can," he said. "I'm dreamwalking. I'll wake soon. Can you do it? Will you?"

"You'll trust me?"

"With my soul."

"Don't make light of it," she said sharply.

"That, I would not do," he said. "Lady, will you come to me as soon as you may?"

"I will try," she said.

He kissed her, lingering over it, nor did she try to break free. There was more than desire in it. There was a gift, a pearl of magic that he set in her heart. Hardly had he done that when the dream took him away, reft him out of her arms.

Merian stood alone in the bite of the wind. Her cloak was gone, and he in it. She drew the magic of the place about her, warmer than any wool or fur, and paused to gather courage. Then she said calmly to the air, "Perel. Come. I need you."

He came as soon as he could. It was a long hour, but Merian put it to good use. She had sent word to certain others, lightmages and darkmages both, and bidden them wait upon word from Ki-Oran.

By the time he arrived, she had prepared everything that could be prepared. He came through the Gate that she had opened, full-armed and on guard, though she had sent him no word that she was in danger.

She wasted no time in preliminaries. "Perel," she said, "if I asked you to be taken by the enemy, would you do it?"

He stood where the Gate had brought him, just inside the door of her workroom, wrapped in Olenyai black, with only his eyes to be seen. They had widened slightly, but he betrayed no other sign of startlement. "You have a plan?"

"The heir of Han-Gilen does."

That did astonish him. "He's here? He's come back?"

"No," she said, "but he dreamwalked here, to ask me this. He's trapped in a world within the shadow, he and the emperor. They're about to fall. He thinks—he hopes—that if he can be taken to the enemy's own world, he can fight from there, and close their Gates, and bind or destroy them at their source."

"That boy has a finely honed deathwish," Perel observed. "Which is all very well for him, but what makes you think that I share it?"

"Don't all the Olenyai?"

"Most of us prefer to stay alive. All of us would rather be unmaimed."

Perel advanced a step or two into the room. Merian rose from the worktable.

Once again she had surprised him profoundly. She was not greatly swollen with the child yet, but in shirt and breeches, she was obviously not her old slender self. She met his stare and said flatly, "I'll thank you not to make a public outcry of this. Nobody else knows, except my loyal people here."

He bent his head to her will. "Only tell me one thing. Please, by all the gods, swear to me that it's not Batan's."

"It is not Batan's," Merian said, "or any other pirate's. Don't fret, cousin. Even Mother won't object to the breeding of this child."

"She might take issue with the timing of it," Perel said.

"Yes—that I didn't do it fifteen years ago." Fifteen years ago, she thought, Daros was a youngling child.

Perel did not press her to name the father; nor had she expected him to. Olenyai were bred like fine animals. Once she had assured him that this child was properly bred, he had ceased to fret over it, except on her behalf.

"I am thinking," Merian said after a pause, "that if lightmages and darkmages went in together under shields, then the slavetakers could be persuaded that they had been duly bound and blinded. Once you were there, you would find Daros and his people, join forces, and do the rest according to his plan."

"That supposes," said Perel, "that they can be found at all, and once found, that all of them are sane and whole. We know nothing of this world, where it is, what it is. We'll be going in, quite literally, blind."

"He knows," she said. "He's been there. He'll set a beacon in the Gate, for only us to find. That will guide you to the enemy's world, and once you've passed the Gate, guide you to him."

"Even so," said Perel, "without knowing what to expect—"

"He gave me this," Merian said, "through the dreamwalking." She held out her hand.

Perel took it warily, braced against the lash of sudden pain or power. She gave him what Daros had given her, the flash of knowledge wrapped in memory: the dark world, the stronghold, the men in it.

Perel let go her hand. He drew a long breath, and let it out slowly. "No name, no words in their language. No knowledge of what or who leads them, or how, nor very much of why. Their weapons, we know, are stronger than ours. What does he think he can accomplish by invading their stronghold?"

"He believes," she said, "that some force is driving them, and some power ruling them. If that can be removed, the rest won't matter."

"You're asking us to gamble a great deal on a guess and a dream."

"Yes: I'm asking you to gamble your lives on the defense of this world."

He flushed. She had stung him; he was as close to anger as she had ever seen him. "I would die for you, lady of the Sun, and for the empire you'll someday rule. But I want that death to be worth something. If I throw my life away, what good does it do you?"

"Very well," she said, and her voice was as cold as her heart. "Go. I'll find someone else to lead the expedition. For it will go, Perel. It's a vain hope, but it's action beyond simple defense. It might even succeed."

"Did I say I would not go?"

"Weren't you hinting at it?"

"I do not hint," he said stiffly. "I'll go. I'll pick my mages—will you give me a free hand?"

"I've spoken with a number of mages who confess themselves willing. You may choose others, if that's your wish."

"Lightmages as weapons, darkmages to shield them. Masks of illusion for us all." Perel straightened his shoulders. "How many?"

"Enough to be a threat. Not so many that the enemy senses that threat until the knife is at his throat."

"Twice nine," Perel said, "and I. If we're taken like slaves, we'll not be able to bring worldly weapons. That could be a difficulty."

"The enemy has weapons, and probably to spare," she said. "But none of them, in himself, has magic."

"That does give us an advantage," Perel conceded. "Very well. When do we go?"

"Tomorrow night," she said. "You'll be cast like a lure. With luck and the god's favor, the enemy will seize you."

He bowed. He was not happy with her at all, but he would do what she needed him to do. That was the way of the Olenyai—just as it was the way of imperial blood to use him with ruthless disregard for his life or sanity.

She was not happy with herself, either, but so be it. She gave Perel a gift, because she trusted him, and because in her mind he deserved it. "This child is his—the Gileni's. For her sake, will you serve him as if he had been of the blood royal?"

"How in the worlds—"

"I'm not entirely sure," she said, "but it appears that one can do more than walk in dreams."

Her cheeks were warm. He saw the flush: his lips twitched. "I am glad," he said, "that I don't have your gift for dreaming true."

"I think the gift is his," she said. "He's a mage unlike any other. Will you help him?"

"I will help him," Perel said with a sigh.

"You have your mages," Merian said.

She had tracked him through thickets of dream, past lies and delusions, wishes and fears. He was perched on the prow of a boat, sailing down a broad deep river. Small brown men filled the boat, and one large and very dark one at the steering-oar, golden eyes full of the sun.

But she had not come to Estarion, however it gladdened her heart to see him. He looked splendid, strong and young, laughing and trading banter with the men in the boat.

Daros was drowsing, smiling a little, full of sun and empty of fear. She slipped inside the stream of his thought and warmed herself in his sunlight. His smile bloomed all around her.

She hated to darken that brightness, but time was short. "Twice nine mages," she said, "and Perel. Will that be enough?"

"It will be ample," he said with swift joy and a strong surge of relief.

"They'll set themselves in the enemy's path tonight. That will be somewhat after you go, if all goes well. Once they're past the Gate, they'll find your beacon. You'll command them after that. Perel knows; the others understand."

"Are they dismayed to be taking orders from the rakehell of Han-Gilen?"

"Not all of them," she said. "Some allow as how you've earned a little respect through serving the emperor so demonstrably well."

"How very kind of them," he said.

"Most charitable." She could not kiss him, here inside him, but she could envelop him in the sensation. He was warm to the tips of his toes. "Beloved," she said. "Stay alive, and unmaimed if you can. Come back to me."

"I will," he said.

"I'll hold you to that," said Merian.

TWENTY-SEVEN

DAROS WARMED HIS HEART WITH HER MEMORY, AND WITH THE HOPE THAT she had given him. Nearly a score of mages, the best and the strongest, and an Olenyas to lead them—he was richer than he had dared to dream.

And yet, like the madman he was, he could not help but think that his magelings had been chosen for this; that they would prove themselves before men and gods. He roused from the last of his dream and turned his eyes toward them where they sat together. They did not cling to one another; none of them wept or trembled. They looked as soldiers should before a battle: a little pale, a little shaken, but strong.

It was a peculiarity of this very peculiar country that if one wished to travel downstream, one rowed; but to travel upstream, one raised a sail, because the river flowed northward and the wind blew from the north. On this hot bright morning, the wind was like a blast from a furnace, carrying them swiftly upstream toward a village near the border of Esna. The queen had chosen it; she had had kin there before the enemy took them. This would be revenge, after a fashion.

Daros was very calm. He had never fought in a battle, but he had trained long and hard enough, for a layabout. He had lived two years in this country, training fighting men, making and training mages. He was as fit and as ready as he would ever be.

The village was a trap, handsomely baited. Its storehouses were brimming with barley; its cattle-pens were full. The men who appeared to dwell in the houses had the look of soldiers, and their women were sturdy and strong. They greeted the newcomers with respect, and Daros and Estarion with somewhat more than that.

The boat could not linger if it was to return to Waset before sunset. But Estarion did not give the order for it to depart.

Tanit had said that he loved Daros as a son. Daros did not doubt it. He loved this man—as a father? Perhaps. As dear kin certainly, and as his lord, and yes, his emperor. He offered the obeisance of a prince of the Hundred Realms to the lord of Sun and Lion, and rose into a long and tight embrace.

"Stay alive," Estarion said in his ear, soft as a lion's growl. "Stay as sane as it's possible for you to be. Come back with all your limbs intact."

"Keep this world safe, my lord," Daros said in turn, "for your son if not for me."

"For both of you," said Estarion.

Then he would go. He took his place not on the deck but among the oarsmen as they prepared to row downriver against the wind. As the river bent, bearing them out of sight, he flung up his hand in a last farewell. The flame of gold dazzled Daros even from that distance, as if the sun had come down to rest upon the water.

The boat of the Sun sailed away. Daros' tiny army remained like bait in the trap. They settled as best they could. There was no time to teach them more than they already knew; that would never be enough, but it would have to serve.

They had their shields, and their small workings of illusion, so that when the enemy looked at them, he would see what he wished to see. They could not hope to carry weapons with them, but Daros had a gift from Estarion, a steel knife such as this world knew nothing of, and with it the Mage's feather that he had brought from the place between worlds. He had hung them both on a cord about his neck, and concealed them with a small working.

Apart from those few things, the only weapon any of them carried was his magery. They rested if they might, slept if they could. The seeming villagers went about the daily tasks of tending the cattle and the fields, baking bread, brewing beer. At the time of the daymeal, there was bread, beer, roast goose, a bit of green stuff, and dates from the palms that grew tall around the village.

Daros ate for strength, as did they all. None of them knew when they might eat again. All too soon the sun set; they set wards enough to escape suspicion, but weak and ragged as they had been in other villages when the enemy struck.

Kaptah sang the sun to its rest. He had a pleasant voice; it was comforting, in its way, but there was great sadness in it. Only the gods knew when any of them would see sunlight again.

The magelings drew in a little closer. They were all in the same house near the western edge of the village, as the enemy was wont to come from the west. It was small and the air inside was close, but no one wanted to open the door. That would be done for them soon enough, if their trap was laid as well as they hoped.

Khafre ventured a little magelight as the night closed in, but Nefret damped it with a flick of magery that won murmurs of respect from the rest. "Have you forgotten?" she said sharply in the darkness. "They hate the light. Use the eyes you were given!"

Khafre ducked his head, abashed. She had reminded him, and the rest of them, too, that they had mage-sight.

They did not see Daros swallow a smile—he made sure of that. "Sleep if you can," he said, "but remember to keep your power on guard."

They all nodded. Each was a soldier in his own fashion; they knew the wisdom of hoarding their strength.

The enemy came in the deep night. Daros felt the opening of Gates like the opening of wounds in his own body. They were out in force: they struck up and down the river, not only here. Elsewhere they met stronger wards, though not yet as strong as they would be once the enemy had taken the bait.

All the magelings were awake. Menkare and Khafre had risen, setting themselves shoulder to shoulder nearest the door. Daros was farthest back, cut off from escape save past the others.

When the dark fire struck, their shields were up. The door puffed into ash; the roof of woven reeds vanished, leaving them open to the stars. Daros caught his breath at the force of it, even through shields. Ay, just out of his reach, gasped and crumpled.

Daros reached for him—too late. His shields were broken. Ay convulsed, and began to scream.

Daros seized Ay's brother and dragged him off, caught the next mageling who was near—Nefret, who would have tried to heal a man who was past healing—and swept the rest of them out into the roiling darkness.

Shapes of shadow swarmed upon them. First Nefret, then Huy was ripped from his hands. Bands that felt like iron closed about him and clamped tight.

He sensed the spell in them, strong as a drug, invoking sleep. His shields held, but he went limp as they expected. He could not see through the dark shapes that surrounded him, to discover what had become of the others. Except for Ay—Ay was dead. He had felt the spirit's flight even before he left the broken walls.

He was remarkably calm. It was a terrible thing to be helpless, bound and blinded even to mage-sight. Yet he had wished for this, and planned it, though he had hoped not to be separated quite so swiftly from his magelings.

Slowly he made sense of the darkness. Two robed figures were carrying him, gripping the bands about him as if he had been a bundle of reeds for a boat. They were moving: from the scent of mud and water and reeds, away from the village and toward the river. There were others nearby, moving likewise. Their gait was human, and steady, undismayed by the blind dark. None of them spoke. His captors were on foot, but some of those beyond them were mounted on the strange scaled beasts that he had seen before.

Their Gate lay across the river, and the road to it was not quite in this world. If he strained, he could hear the river running below. His captors' booted feet trod air above the glide of the current.

They passed into the dark world, into perpetual night, and cold that bit deep before his shields closed it out. They did not carry him far. He felt the loom of walls, heard the deep creak of hinges in a gate.

He dared open his eyes to mage-sight. His captors appeared to sense nothing: they paced onward as they had before, through a vaulted corridor and a roofless court, then up a long stair. There were others behind and before them. Not only his magelings had been taken. From the sound of many feet, the captives were numerous. Nor could they all have come from the village outside of Esna.

The stair ended at last in a high wide gate and a cavernous hall. It was not the one in which he had been before. There was nothing royal about this. It had the look and smell of a barracks.

It was vast. Its edges were lost in gloom, even to mage-sight. Broad galleries rose toward the roof, and a webwork of ladders connecting one to another.

The train of slave-takers coiled in a skein round the hall and stopped. Daros' two captors lowered him to a floor of grey stone. The bonds about him snapped free. Hard hands heaved him to his feet. All about him, others did the same. Khafre, Menkare, Nefret—all there, and alive. Huy, then Kaptah: they were somewhat farther away, among others of their country.

Only they had eyes. All the rest were blind, every one—within as without. They were bound by a slave-spell, their souls lost, all will taken away: row on row of blank and eyeless faces.

There were hundreds of them in this one room, of many in this city, on this world. Thousands all told; thousands of thousands. The sheer magnitude of it went beyond horror. There was no word for what had been done here, to the folk of world after world.

The takers of slaves withdrew. Something in the way they moved made Daros certain: they too were slaves, bound like all the rest. Slaves taking slaves—there was a hideous economy in it.

The soul-lost formed in ranks and stood still. Daros' magelings managed in that surge of movement to set themselves about him. They were pale and shaking, but they were masters of themselves still. Their shields had held, even Huy's, though he was rigid with grief for his brother.

They stood so long, so motionless, that Daros began to fear that they would not move at all for hours, perhaps days. If that was the case, he would have to make his move long before he had intended to, slip away and pray that he could find a hiding place in a world he did not know.

But there was, at last, movement. Figures emerged onto the first gallery.

These were not slaves. Even the guards, great looming figures, walked with volition. Those whom they guarded wore robes that Daros remembered, like darkness cut and sewn into garments.

The robed ones were men. He who led them had let fall his hood. He was white-skinned like a man of Anshan in Daros' own world, but as pale as such a man would be who had never seen the sun. His hair and beard were black; heavy black brows lowered over dark eyes.

He had eyes, though they were all dark, whiteless and strangely blank. It seemed that he could see, though he was not a mage. He looked out over the hall and the ranks of slaves. His face wore no expression.

He was not a mage, but great power was on him. He wore it like a cloak. Perhaps, Daros thought, that was precisely what it was. And if that was so . . .

The man spoke. His words meant nothing. Daros could not shield himself, protect his magelings, sustain the illusion that he was as eyeless and witless as all the slaves about him, and wield his gift of tongues, all at once. Even his power had limits.

The words must have been a spell of command. Daros felt the tug of it. Others near him began to walk, trudging out of the ranks of slaves, toward the far end of the hall. Menkare too was moving, and Khafre, and Nefret, but not Huy or Kaptah.

There was nothing he could do but hope that whatever he went to, he could come back to this place, to the rest of his mages. Those chosen seemed the strongest. They had the look of warriors, or of warriors' women.

He walked where the spell bade him. In so doing, he had to pass beneath the gallery. The man on it was a cold presence, a power that was not magery but was not entirely human, either. It was almost like metal—like a machine.

Daros had that to ponder while he walked slowly out of the hall and down a corridor, then a stair. They went far down, much farther than they had come up. Still he did not sense the weight of earth overhead. They must be descending the steep face of a crag.

They came out into the lightless air, in a reek of smoke and heated metal. There were forges nearby, vast perhaps beyond imagining, but this court showed only the loom of a wall and the waiting presence of the guards. As each of the enslaved approached, he was stripped of whatever garment or ornaments he might possess, swept with cold fire as if to cleanse him, and dressed in a long dark garment rather like that of the men in the gallery. Then he was led, not into another hall, but through a gate and out onto the plain that Daros remembered.

Daros had kept his hidden weapons through stripping and cleansing. The knife was cold against his breast, the feather too light to be called weight, but the presence in it was as strong as the darkness itself.

The place that they had come from was a city behind a high wall. The place that they went to, he remembered all too well: the citadel on the crag, high above the dark plain. The way to it was long and steep, but there was no pause for food or water. Slaves and soul-lost must have no need for such. Daros and his remaining mages were still mortal; they could only grit their teeth and endure.

The citadel swallowed them. As the gates of iron clanged shut, Daros knew a moment of pure and craven terror. To be free, to be away from there, to be in the light, any light—he would have unleashed the lightnings, if a vanishingly small part of him had not kept him sane. This was precisely what he had wished: to be in the heart of this realm, within reach of those who ruled it. The gods were looking after him; this was proof.

It seemed they were to be soldiers in the guard of the dark realm. They were taken to barracks less vast than those in the city; these were like enough to guard-halls in castles of Daros' own world. A hearth in the center radiated heat without light; bed-niches lined the walls. A second hall past that boasted long rows of tables, and benches on which the ranks of slaves all blindly sat.

Here at last was food and drink: harsh dry bread, salt meat, flagons of clear liquid with a distinct, astringent taste. Except for that strangeness, he would have said that it was water.

It restored his strength considerably. Menkare next to him, and Khafre and Nefret beyond, sat somewhat straighter and seemed less grey about the face.

They dared not speak, even mind to mind. Blinded slaves crowded close. Most of those nearby were men and women of Menkare's world, but round about them Daros saw casts of face that he had not seen before. There were perhaps people of half a dozen worlds, all human in some fashion, but none was of his own kind. Nor was any a mage, even to the minute degree that he had found in the country of the river. Magic was a rarity in the worlds, it seemed.

That, even apart from the shadow that had cut off world after world, would explain why Gate-mages did not meet their own kind wandering the worldroads. If there were others, they were vanishingly few. People of the worlds shunned Gates, out of lack of understanding or, if they knew of the dark armies, out of fear.

He fought down the surge of despair. This army of slaves was a single night's harvest. There would be myriads more in this citadel alone, and more to come as each band of raiders returned through Gates. Merian's mages would come. She had promised; he could trust that she would fulfill it.

There was no reckoning night or day in this place. It was always dark, unlit by moon or star. They were fed at what must be regular intervals. They were taken to the barracks and expected to sleep after every second meal. In between, they served as menials in the citadel.

Others like them, who Daros suspected had been there longer, stood guard at doors and gates, or accompanied various of the lords both within and outside of the citadel. Yet others were taught to ride the scaled beasts with their vicious jaws, and to fight with weapons both familiar and alien.

The lords had eyes, all of them. The slave-soldiers did not, but they were not truly blind. Daros, finding occasion to sweep a corridor that led to one of the practice-courts, marked how lethally swift they were, and how faultlessly the best of them struck targets with throwing-spears and darts and, most fascinating of all, the weapons that hurled the dark fire.

Both teachers and overseers were blinded slaves, but they seemed to have more will than the ranks they commanded. The ranks were mute, but the overseers could speak; they gave instruction and issued orders, speaking a language that must be that of the lords; but it addressed itself to each slave in his own tongue. Daros heard it in the tongue of Shurakan, which was rather strange; his mother had spoken it to him when he was small, but once he was grown, he had spoken chiefly the common speech of Keruvarion.

Daros had not yet managed to approach the lords. They kept to themselves in the upper reaches of the citadel; if they had servants, none was of Daros' company. Newcomers were not permitted in the lords' halls; the doors between were heavily guarded.

He wondered what they feared. Their slaves? All of those seemed utterly subjugated, except his tiny band of mages. The Mage was not on this world; it dwelt apart in its prison. If he turned his thought toward the feather on its cord, he could sense that potent presence, and see, if briefly, that strange face with its eyes bent upon him.

The Mage was aware of him. He took a little comfort from that in this darkest of places. What good it would do, what help it could be, he did not know, but any hope was better than none.

TWENTY-EIGHT

DAROS COUNTED DAYS BY THE NUMBER OF TIMES THAT HE LAY DOWN TO sleep in that lightless place. His sleep was dark, his dreams unformed. After the second—night, he supposed he could call it, though the night here was perpetual—his magelings had begun to lose their courage. They had managed to stay together through the times of labor, and had claimed bed-niches side by side. They gave each other strength. But night unbroken, even with mage-sight, was a terrible burden on the spirit.

On the third night, Daros woke from a restless half-doze to the sound of weeping. It was silent; it sounded within his mind, with a flavor of the guardsman Khafre. He had seemed the strongest of all, but the soul that opened itself to Daros was deeply horrified by the dark and the eyeless slaves and the strangeness of this bleak world. He, like all his people, was a creature of sunlight. Even in death they sought the light.

"That is your strength," Daros said to him. Daros had brought sunlight into his dream, setting them both in Khafre's own world, standing in a field beside the river, under the pure clean blue of the sky. Menkare was there, and Nefret, and Kaptah looking somewhat shocked. Huy—

"Gone," Kaptah said heavily. "He broke. They killed him."

Daros had not known. He had been shielded too closely. His fault; his folly.

He must not let it crush him. "And you?" he asked Kaptah. "Can you hold on?"

The priest spread his hands. "Have I a choice?"

"Keep this place in your heart," Daros said. "It will strengthen you when nothing else will."

Kaptah bowed.

"Light is strength," Daros said to them all. "The enemy has a horror of it, is even destroyed by it. In light you can take refuge."

"Sometimes I think I'll forget what light even is," Nefret said. "We can't last very long, my lord. This place is too alien to anything we know, except the darkest of dark dreams. If we had a plan—anything to do except wait for the rest of your gods—it would help immensely."

"I had thought of that," Daros said. "You keep the bond with Kaptah—don't lose it. You others, explore as you can; if you can discover the secrets of this place, we may be able to use them."

"And you?" she asked.

"I will penetrate the lords' towers, and learn what I can. There may be a way— did you notice the other slaves? Some are warriors. And some, who are closest to the lords, have will, or something like it. If I can find my way among them, gain their trust, learn their secrets—"

"Alone?"

"Until my brother mages come," Daros said, "yes. It won't be long now."

"And then?"

She was asking all the hard questions. "Then we bring light to the dark land," he answered her.

She did not ask him how. Maybe she had had enough of questions.

Anger made her stronger. Anything that did that, Daros reckoned was worth the price.

The sixth night promised to be no better than the rest. His magelings gathered in the place of brightness as they had done every night. They fed on sunlight and spoke of small things, things that had nothing to do with the dark world.

Daros left them to it. He had tried, the past few nights, to dreamwalk into Merian's presence, but the shadow on this world was too strong. This was the heart of it. It was born in this place, and rolled forth in waves to drown the worlds.

Khafre and Menkare had explored the citadel as best they could. They had found a warren of guardrooms and slaves' quarters, and a maze of deep storerooms under armed guard, and stables for the scaled beasts. They had come across nothing of great use. The armories were heavily guarded. The troops in training either fought with blunted or feigned weapons, or performed their exercises under heavy guard and surrendered those weapons when they were done, to be locked away in the armories.

Daros had yet to penetrate the defenses of the lords' towers. There were wards as well as guards. Both were vigilant. Once he came close to slipping in behind a lord who was coming out, but the lord's guards closed in too quickly. Daros barely escaped into a side passage before he was caught.

That night, the sixth night, he left his magelings to rest in their illusion of light, and went dreamwalking, however futile it might be. The beacon he had set in the Gate was still there; no one had found it, nor had the mages passed it. Time that passed so differently from world to world was not serving him now. Even with the expedients that he had given them, his magelings could not hold for much longer.

The ways of dream were dark and strange. He wandered through dim and twisting corridors, across landscapes of torment, through a chamber of echoes and weird howling. He dared not venture too far: he could lose his waking self in the darkness, and never return to his body.

Just before he would have turned back, the faintest of grey glimmers caught the corner of his eye. He drifted toward it. It grew no brighter, but it grew larger. In a little while he saw the Mage's prison. It was the same as he remembered, round like one of the towers of the dark citadel, and each of its many windows a Gate, but the Mage could pass through none of them.

Daros stepped through one of the windows onto the dark stone floor. The feather on his breast stirred. It drew him toward the shadowed center.

The Mage lay there. Its eyes were open, but perhaps they could not close. Its long strange body seemed to have fallen in on itself. Bonds of shadow confined it; it breathed shallowly, its lipless mouth open.

It was conscious, but that consciousness had retreated far within. Its power raged and surged, bound as it was, compelled by a will outside of its own.

That will led back in direct line from the prison to the citadel in which Daros' body lay. It stretched like a cord across the roads of dream, to one of the towers of the citadel, the highest and grimmest and most heavily guarded of them all.

Because Daros was in dream and not in flesh, he could swim along that cord as if the dark had been water and not lightless air. It undulated a little in the currents of worlds; magic pulsed through it, seeping into him, making him subtly stronger.

It slid through a high slitted window of the tower. Windows, thought Daros, in that place without light: everywhere else in the citadel were shafts to let in air, but no windows. Only here.

He made himself as invisible as he could, mingling his awareness with that of the Mage and letting the cord draw him through the window into . . .

Light?

It was dim. In any world lit by a sun, it would have been the deepest of twilight. But here it was dazzlingly bright. It bathed the body of a man who sat upright in a tall chair. The room about him was full of a myriad things: a great thick-legged table, smaller chairs, stools, boxes and shelves and bins of books in numerous shapes and forms—startling in the dark; proof indeed that these lords could see. Directly in front of the man, on the table, whirred and spun a thing of metal.

The light came from this, and so did the darkness. It spun them both out of the cord that came from the Mage. The light dissipated here. The darkness spread. Some of it streamed back down the cord to bind the Mage ever more tightly. The rest spread like black water through all the worlds.

The man looked like the other lords that Daros had seen. He was older, perhaps; his beard was shot with white. He had an air about him that Daros had seen in men of great power: the surety that when he commanded, men obeyed.

As Daros drifted, insubstantial, in the air, another man entered the room. He shielded his eyes with a dark cloth, which concealed most of his face, but he also was of the kin and kind of the lords of this citadel.

The man in the chair rose. The spinning thing faltered. The other man slid into the chair, and the whirring resumed, spinning darkness, dissipating light.

Daros followed the first man as he made his way slowly, stumbling with weariness, out of that enigmatic place. He recovered a little strength as he went. His steps steadied; his shoulders straightened. He descended a long stair with no nobler purpose, maybe, than to find a bed and fall into it.

But when he reached the landing, a man met him. "Trouble?" said the lord from the tower.

"Yes," said the other.

The first man sighed gustily. "Lead me," he said.

Daros knew that hall. He had seen it before, where the dark lords gathered. There were only three there now, waiting for the lord from the tower. A small figure knelt before them.

Daros nearly shocked himself out of the dream. It was Kaptah. He had been stripped of the dark robe that all slaves wore. There were bruises on his body, and his eyes were blackened and swollen—he still had them, for what good they would do in the dark.

The lord from the tower circled him slowly. He was tightly bound, his arms drawn cruelly behind his back, and his spine arched just short of breaking. He could not move, but he managed to radiate defiance.

"He was found among the least of the slaves," one of the lords said, "caught wandering apart from his company, spying near the storehouses in the city of the newest slaves."

The lord from the tower brushed a hand over Kaptah's eyes. "He has not been rendered fit to serve us. How is that? Who allowed it?"

"He was found," the other replied. "He came in from one of the worlds that we harvest. The rest who came with him are as fit as any other. It's only this one."

"Make him fit," said the lord from the tower, "and then feed him to the nightwalkers. Unless there is a reason why you trouble me with this?"

"There is a reason," said one of the two who had been silent. He aimed a blow at Kaptah's head.

Kaptah did not mean to respond as he did: Daros could see that. But his shields had been wrought too well. The blow did not strike flesh. There was a flash of sudden light and a sharp scent of lightning. The lords recoiled. Kaptah's captors were less dismayed than the lord from the tower, and swifter to cover their eyes.

The lord from the tower hissed. His eyes had squeezed shut; tears of pain ran down his cheeks. "Another one of *those*? But that world is free of them. We were assured of that."

"It seems the assurances were false," said the man who had struck Kaptah. His face was tight with pain; his hand trembled in spasms.

"Pity," said the lord from the tower. "That world was useful. Now we have no choice but to offer it in sacrifice to the dark, and find another both rich and untainted."

"That . . . is another matter," said the man who had struck Kaptah. "Our advance has halted."

The lord from the tower rounded on him. "It has done what?"

"We are halted," the other said with a goodly degree of courage.

"And how may that be?"

"There is a world," the first of Kaptah's captors said. "All Gates lead there— even those we would divert elsewhere, when we pass through them, we find ourselves there. It's foul with lightmagic; reeks of it. Our warriors need cleansing after every raid."

"Then," said the lord from the tower with a snap of impatience, "why have you not destroyed it?"

"We can't," said the lord who had struck Kaptah. "We have tried. It's walled and guarded. We can pierce it; strip storehouses, take slaves. But no Gate will open beyond it."

"Maybe it's the end," said the first lord: "the last world, the world that the gods will take, and so swallow all that is."

"It is not," the lord from the tower said. "That end is still far away. I have a suspicion . . . " But he did not go on. He bent over Kaptah. Quite without warning, and quite without mercy, he snapped the priest's neck.

Kaptah's shields had risen, but not fast enough. They crackled about the lord's hands. He hissed but held his ground. Kaptah dropped, limp. He was dead before he struck the floor.

"Watch for others like this one," the lord said. "Destroy them when you find them. As for this other trouble, let me rest a little. Then call the conclave."

The other three bowed. Two of them took up Kaptah's body to dispose of it. The third ran the errand that the greater lord had commanded of him.

Daros hung in the air of that hall, with no more substance to him than if he had been air itself. He had had no strength, no capacity to act, when the third of his magelings died through his fault—because he had brought them here, and they were not strong enough, and so they broke and were betrayed. Only three were left, and no sign of the mages from his own world.

He saw the darkness beneath him, the depths of despair. The light he had given his magelings was not enough. He was a greater mage than any of them, and because of that, his weakness as well as his strength was greater.

He could not be weak now. He could not falter even in the slightest. These men without magic somehow had mastered a greater working than any mages of any world had ever ventured.

It was something to do with the thing of metal and glass that spun light and dark, and the lord who called this conclave. The Mage was a key, but there was more. He must know more. He must—

"My lord. My lord Re-Horus!"

Daros plummeted into his body. Shapes were stirring about him, slaves rising, shuffling toward the dining-hall. The guards were watching—more closely than before? He could not tell.

Menkare caught his eye. There were questions there, a myriad of them, but none of them could escape, not now. Daros looked away—guiltily, he supposed.

Far above them in the tower, the conclave was coming together. Daros had to be there. Somehow, if he could find a corner to hide in, he must dreamwalk again. Or—

He was to labor in the kitchens this lightless day, in the drudgery of grinding grain and baking bread. As soon as he could, he found occasion to be sent to the storerooms for another basket of grain. But when he left the kitchens, he went not down but up.

He risked much—too much, maybe. But he could not stop himself. He must know what was said in conclave.

The Mage's feather stirred under his robe. It was whispering, speaking words he could almost understand. He closed his hand about it. It tugged, drawing him onward.

He was mad enough, and desperate enough, to do as it bade him. He was less than a shadow, no more than a shifting of air in those silent halls. He passed as he had in dream, but his body was solid about his consciousness. The well of his magery was deep, and brimming full.

It was the Mage leading him, taking him by ways he had not gone before, deep into the citadel. First he went down, into deserted passages and dusty stairs; then he began to ascend. The way was long, the darkness suffocating. Mage-sight showed nothing but blank walls and empty corridors.

There were wards, but the Mage had wrought them. They let him pass unharmed. His thighs were aching, his lungs burning, when he came to the end of that endless stair. The door yielded to his touch, sliding almost soundlessly into the wall.

He was in the highest tower, as he had known he would be. This door opened on a small gallery, hardly more than a niche. The hall of the conclave lay beyond it.

They had gathered but not begun. He counted a score of them in that great empty space, dwarfed by the vaulting. They reminded him somewhat poignantly of the priests of the dark on his own world, in the castle of the secret, which he had destroyed. But those had been the last feeble remnants of a forgotten order. These were commanders of an army that had driven the dark across the worlds.

They were all of the same race and kin, and no doubt the same world—this one, he could suppose. While they waited for the greater lord, they spoke softly among themselves. Daros stretched his ears to hear.

Most of what they spoke of was remarkably ordinary. They spoke of wars, of course; of the management of estates; of rebellious offspring and difficult servants. They did not speak of wives, or of women at all, which was odd. Did they have no women? How then did they get children?

That thought begged him to pursue it, but two men near him were conversing of something that caught his attention. "The captive," one said. "I hear it's weakening. It's not feeding Mother Night as strongly as before."

"And I hear," said the other, "that it's stronger; that it's working its way free. The high ones are working harder to keep it bound."

"It's dying, I heard—freeing itself the only way anything can. The high ones are working harder because there's less power to work with. And there's a rumor—a whisper—that we may have found the End."

"I don't believe that," the first man said. "Something's blocking us. We're going to break that block soon."

"Now that is true," said the second with a gusting sigh. "We should never have given so many worlds to Mother Night—arrogant of us, to think that there would only be more, and the more we destroyed, the more we would find."

"But isn't that the point?"

A third man had come up beside them. He was younger than they; his beard was soft and rather sparse. But perhaps because of that youth, he had a harder, wilder look to him. "Isn't that what we're for? Haven't we sworn ourselves from the first origin of our people to the service of the Night? Isn't it our dearest ambition to render all that is into darkness and silence?"

The others greeted him with a mingling of wariness and faint contempt. He was young, their tone said, and reckless, and none too wise. "Indeed," the second man said, "that is our purpose before the Mother. But while the flesh constrains us, we must have means to live: air to breathe, food to eat, slaves to serve us. Do you, like a child, believe that this world exists by itself? That it sustains us in blessed darkness without need of intervention?"

"Of course not!" the boy said irritably. "I know that this foul flesh needs the fruits of light to live—that the air of this world would bleed away without certain expedients. But if the End has come, shouldn't we be rejoicing? Why are you conducting yourselves as if this were a disaster?"

"Because," the first man said with conspicuous patience, "the wall we've met is not the End. Something is barring the way. Our source of power is willing itself to death. And our slave-worlds are now too few to feed us all."

"Are they?" said the boy. "Well then, cull the slaves. The fewer we have to feed, the more there is for us."

"We need them," said the second man. "Without them we have no food, no weapons, no armor, and no war. The last culling—of both worlds and bodies—was meant to leave room for new and fresher ones. Instead, we ran headlong into a wall."

"So break the wall," the boy said.

His elders growled to themselves and walked pointedly away from him.

He stood forsaken. For an instant Daros thought he caught a flicker of hesitation. Then the boy bared his teeth. "Aren't we strong enough to break down a simple wall? Are we not the destroyers of worlds?"

They did not pause or respond. He aimed a slap of laughter at their backs. "Cowards! Mother Night has opened her arms, and you're too craven to embrace her."

"Better craven than dead in the light," one of his elders said as he departed.

TWENTY-NINE

THE LORD OF THE TOWER CAME LATE TO HIS OWN CONCLAVE. HE DID NOT look as if he had rested; his face was haggard, his shoulders bowed with the weight of worlds.

Others followed him into the hall. If the lords who waited had the look of warriors, these made Daros think of priests. They carried themselves differently; there was a subtle tension between them and the rest.

The one who led them—for Daros had begun to be certain that he was, if not a king, then something very like one—had somewhat in him of both warrior and priest. He carried a tall staff, which served to support his body as well as his authority. The thunder of it on the stone floor called the conclave to order.

The murmur of voices broke off. The silence was complete. In it, the king ascended what Daros had taken for an altar, but proved to be a small dais or pedestal. It was a contrivance of some sort: when he set foot on it, it was hardly a handspan above the floor, but once he was settled, it rose to set him well above the rest of the gathering.

He looked down upon them, though he could have had no mage-sight. Maybe he perceived them by sound and scent, and by the heat of their bodies. "The rumor is true," he said. "We have come to a wall. We are facing famine. And the source of perpetual Night is willing itself to death."

"Despair is our birthright and oblivion our hope," someone murmured, half in a chant.

"Indeed," the king said, biting off the word. "Still there is the paradox of our existence: that we must feed on what grows in the light to live; that if we are to serve our purpose, we must avoid despair. Oblivion will come for each of us, but if we are to grant its blessing to all that is, we must fight to preserve our strength. We must live so that all else may die."

No one responded to that. Daros sensed the currents in the hall: fear, hostility, a strange exhilaration.

"I have given thought to this," the king said. "Since the days of the first king, the maker of night has been our greatest weapon and our most sacred charge. Now it fails. And yet, this world that halts our war, this nexus, this swallower of Gates, might it not be a power to rival that which we are about to lose?"

"It is filthy with light," said a voice from the conclave. "If it had not trapped us and rendered our Gates useless, we would have made a sacrifice of it and its searing hell of a sun, and mercifully forgotten it."

"Its dark is as strong as its light," the king said. "The slaves of light have polluted it, but once it is cleansed, it will be as potent a weapon as ever the first king found ready to his hand."

"Yet if we are weak," said the other, "where will we find strength to do such a thing?"

"We are strong," the king said. "For a while we were invincible. So shall we be again. Nothing in that pebble of a world can truly stop us, once we discover what it has done to bind our Gates."

"The Gates before it still open on the slave-worlds," said one of the conclave who had not spoken before. "We'll strip them bare—and pray to the Mother that the wall breaks before we starve."

"Strip them," the king said, "but as slowly as you may. No worlds are to be sacrificed until the Gates are free again. See that the lords and commanders are made aware of this. If any disobeys this command, let him be fed to the light."

They bowed to that. None disputed it.

"Go," he said to them. "Harvest the worlds. You, my priests—come to me in the tower at the changing of the guard."

They were all obedient servants. They left to do their duty. He remained, standing still. When the last of them was gone, his head bowed to his breast. He drew a breath that caught like a sob. Then, astonishingly, he laughed. "A war," he said. "An honest war. I will be remembered for it until the last world crumbles into dust."

Daros escaped by the same way he had come in. The kitchens had not noticed his absence; his magelings, the few that were left, were alive and profoundly glad to see him again.

The dark day wound down. Near the end of it, at last, the beacon in the Gate sparked to life. It was brief, hardly more than a tugging at the awareness, but it brought Daros full awake. It was all he could do to move as a slave moved, mute and slow, and to shuffle with the rest out of the kitchens into the dining-hall.

His stomach was an aching knot. He choked down the bread and the hard lump of cheese that had been set in front of him, and drank the oddly astringent water. When the rest of the slaves rose, he rose with them, nigh as mindless as they. He was seeking with his mind for a sign, any sign, that Merian's mages had indeed, at last, passed the Gate.

There was none. When he went walking in dream, he found nothing: not the Mage, not the king in the tower, not twice nine mages of his own world and one Olenyas. He was alone in the dark.

The king's voice echoed in the cavern of his skull, and the voices of the lords in the tower and the conclave. They had found the end of things: a world to which all Gates led. What if . . .

Surely it could not be. His world was no more remarkable than any other. Gates touched it as they touched a myriad worlds—or had done before the dark lords came. All Gates did not lead to his own world, or its mages, either. There had been the Heart of the World, but that was a nexus of powers, like the Mage's prison. It had not been a world in itself.

And yet the lords had seemed most certain. Their advance was halted. They could go no farther. The world that they spoke of, its sun, its moons—it was Daros' world. He was sure of it.

Maybe the war was won after all, or at least frozen in impasse. Maybe—

The power that swallowed stars, that blasted worlds into ash, surely had not been brought to a halt by the simple existence of Daros' world or any other. The raiders only served that power. They were mortal, as he had had occasion to observe. The dark was not.

The raids might end and this human enemy be driven back, but the greater enemy would remain. For a few moments he had indulged in hope, in certainty that a simple war would end it all. But it would not be simple. The great matters never were.

The mages came to the citadel on the third day after they passed the Gate. They came heavily shielded and in battle order, darkmages warding lightmages, and Perel leading them. In his black robes he fit this world rather well.

Daros was aware of them long before they came to the citadel. Khafre and Menkare had found a procession of passages that led to an unguarded postern; he and they and Nefret slipped out together. He almost thought, standing under the sky, that he could sense light beyond the veil of darkness: a sun, stars, moons perhaps.

His magelings drew in closer. They had found a balance in this hideous place; their magery was growing stronger, their spirits less frail, and of that he was proud.

They had steeled themselves to endure the dark world, but the coming of true-born mages—gods, as they thought—drove them close to panic. Daros found himself in the lead and the others behind him, as the mages came up the steep way to the citadel.

Daros advanced a step or two. Perel quickened his pace as his companions slowed. They embraced as brothers, which in the way of war they were. Perel withdrew first, searching Daros's face with mage-sight. His own face was hidden behind Olenyai veils, but his eyes were keen. "Well and well," he said. "The boy's a man. These are your mages?"

"All that are left of them," Daros said.

Perel bowed to them. "Your sacrifice is great," he said, "and your courage greater still. I'm honored to be in your presence."

He had done a great thing, a thing that put Daros in his debt. The magelings stood straighter, and their hearts were firmer. They had begun to remember their strength.

Truly, it was considerable. More than Daros had thought, more than he had hoped for. They all drew together in the lee of the wall, Perel's mages coming in close, murmuring their names and offering greeting with the courtesy of their order. They eyed Daros askance—even yet his reputation ran before him—but he sensed no hostility, merely curiosity.

He hoped that they were gratified. "We've been exploring the citadel," he said. "Khafre and Menkare have found a number of forgotten or unguarded ways, apart from this one. Nefret has learned the guards' patterns. We could break this place."

"Would it make a difference?" asked Perel.

"Very little," Daros said. "This world is like a hive: it's clustered with cities, tunneled with mines. It reaches through Gates to worlds where the sun still shines, so that its lords and its slaves may eat."

"We had thought," one of the mages said, "that these lords drank blood."

"They're mortal," said Daros. "They worship oblivion; they live in the dark. But they're flesh and blood. They eat bread as we do."

"No blood?" The Mage seemed disappointed.

"Nightwalkers live on blood," Nefret said. Her voice wavered at first, but then grew stronger. "The lords use them like hounds, to hunt through Gates, to find new worlds. Then they reward them with the blood of captives."

"How many Gates?" asked Perel. "How many worlds?"

"Many," said Daros. "But there will be no more, they say, until they break a wall that's risen to bar their Gates. From everything we can discover, it seems to be our world that's stopped them. Did you know you'd done that to them?"

Perel's blank look was answer enough. One of the others said, "You're sure it's our world? Our walls?"

"It can't be any other," Daros said. "Maybe it has something to do with the Ring of Fire. Can you speak to your fellows? Did you keep a binding when you came through the Gate?"

"We tried," Perel said. "It broke once the Gate closed. We're alone here. Unless—maybe you . . . ?"

"Not I, either," said Daros. He stiffened his back and drew a breath. "No matter. You are what I prayed for. You'll be enough. Khafre has found an empty barracks. Better yet, it has a passage to the storerooms. You'll have food, water. No one should find you."

"What will we do, then? Simply hide?"

"For a little while," Daros said, "until you have the lie of the land, and until I'm certain of a thing or two. I think I know what we can do, but it may be more than we're capable of."

"Yes?" said Perel.

"Yes," Daros said. It was almost a sigh. "This world is populated with slaves. If they can be freed and persuaded to turn on their masters . . ."

"Indeed," said Perel. "That would be an intriguing solution. But how does it drive back the darkness?"

"That will take more than this one world. It will take ours, too, and the world in which the emperor is, and one other. That one I can reach. The others . . . if we can't come to them, there may be nothing we can do to end this war."

"I prefer hope to despair," Perel said. "Come, bring us in. We'll settle as we can, then see what we can see."

Daros had been in command too long. He welcomed Perel's air of brisk decision, but it stung a little. He had wavered and wobbled and dithered for a long count of days. This Olenyas stood outside a postern gate, not even having seen the inside of the citadel, and knew at once what to do and how to do it.

The Olenyas had training. Daros had experience, though hardly as much as Perel had, and a degree of headlong folly that could pass, in certain quarters, for courage.

And he had knowledge. He was not sure how much he had yet, or how much of it was truly useful, but he would gather more as he could.

He did not say any of that. He simply said, "Come."

Daros saw the mages settled in the forgotten guardroom, and made certain that they could raid the stores of food and water. He left them eating packets of hard cakes that must be a form of journey-bread, and drinking jars of water. They would have liked him to stay, but he had a thought in his mind, and it was best if he continued among the slaves.

Nefret stayed with them. She would serve as messenger if there was need, and she would teach them all that she knew of this place and its people. The others followed Daros back to captivity.

Sometimes slaves died. Their bodies vanished, and nothing more was said of them. It seemed the overseers reckoned Nefret dead; there was no outcry, no inquiry. Her niche that night was as empty as Daros' dreams.

In the morning, when maybe a sun rose beyond the thick wall of shadow, a lord and his following strode into the dining-hall as the slaves broke their fast. He stood with haughty expression and folded arms while his companions passed up and down the hall, running hands over faces, prodding arms and thighs, singling out this slave and that.

Daros gritted his teeth at the touch of those hard hands, and secured his shields as best he might. The man who had examined him thrust him sharply away from the table, toward the wall. A number of slaves stood there already. Menkare was among them, and after a moment, Khafre.

All of those chosen were larger than their fellows, and stronger. The rest stayed where they were, mute and empty of thought. The chosen formed in a line and marched out of the hall. They turned, not down the corridor to their usual day's labor, but up a stair. It led to more barracks, level upon level, but then to the first of the training courts.

It was empty now of men in training, but the lord waited for them there, and with him one who might be a priest. Neither man had any glimmer of magery, but both had eyes, for whatever use they might be in this place. Daros kept his head down and his body slumped in imitation of the slaves around him.

The priest drew from his robe a thing of metal and glass that looked somewhat like the whirring sphere in the tower. This was smaller; it emitted no light. It did not whir, but hummed softly as he held it up, balanced on his palm, spinning and spinning.

A faint sigh ran through the slaves. One by one, then all together, they stood straighter. Their faces were still blank, their eyes still gone, but somehow they seemed more awake. Still slaves, thought Daros, but slaves with a glimmer of conscious will.

His heart beat so hard that he feared the lord could hear it. The feather on his breast was still, but there was awareness in it. It might almost have been an eye, looking out upon this place with cold intensity.

The lord hissed softly. His escort sprang from behind him, scattering through the court. Steel rang as they drew swords. They struck without warning.

Not a choosing after all, Daros thought in despair, but a culling. Except that . . .

They were not striking to kill. The ones chosen, freed of binding on their bodily will, whirled into defense. Some fled. Some leaped on their attackers. Some few stood with the passivity of slaves.

Those who fled and those who stood motionless were cut down. Those who fought were let be. Daros understood this in the flash of an instant, even as a long curved blade slashed at him. He darted in under it and caught the wrist of the man who held it. The speed of his attack carried him fully round, and the swordsman with him, sword and all. He braced, twisted.

Hot blood sprang over his hands. The swordsman wheezed and died. Daros recoiled.

He had never killed a man before. But he could not stand in horror, gaping at the thick wetness on his hands. He was a slave—waked to fight but not to think. With all the strength that he had, he lowered his head and his hands, and calmed the swift gasp of his breathing, and stood as the other slaves stood.

The blood dripped from his fingers, dripped and dripped. He felt rather than saw the lord halt in front of him. One of the lord's men knelt and brushed a hand over the body. "Dead," he said.

The lord did not acknowledge the word. It was much too brief to encompass the whole of it: reek of blood and loosed bowels, sprawl of body stiffening in the lightless cold.

He gripped Daros' chin with a gloved hand. Daros struggled not to resist as the lord wrenched his head up. He turned all his furious resentment toward his shields, to conceal the eyes that he had, and the living will.

The lord could see. His eyes fixed on Daros' face. For an instant, altogether without his willing it, Daros saw into and through those eyes. They did not have sight as he knew it: sight that relied on light. This was . . .

He saw heat. Heat of the body, heat of the air about the body. His world was a pattern of shifting shades of darkness, and about them a deep red cast, like the embers of a dying fire.

He saw Daros in red on red on red: a tall and robust man-shape, its heat faintly concealed by the robe it wore. It seemed he did not see eyes. His lip curled at the stink of cooling blood. "Take it," he said to one of his men. "Clean it. Bring it to me."

The man kicked Daros' feet from under him, then heaved him up and carried him out. He made himself as heavy as he could, a limp, lifeless weight dragging at the guard's hands. The man cursed him but did not drop him.

In the hall, the culling ended; the dead were carried away. Just before he passed out of earshot, he heard the clang of weapons, and the voice of one whom he had taken to thinking of as a sergeant: "Up weapons! On guard!"

But Daros was not to be trained to fight. He suspected that he would not live much longer, either, for the crime of killing a lord. He bided his time, gathered his power, held fear sternly at bay. Fear was the very breath and life of this place. He would not let it conquer him.

THIRTY

THIS CLEANSING WAS MORE THOROUGH THAN WHEN DAROS HAD FIRST COME to this world as a slave. He was stripped of the dark robe—but not of the things he wore about his neck, which were invisible, intangible, imperceptible—and passed through cold fire and cold water and a scalding blast of steam. Then slaves scrubbed him all but raw, and clipped his hair and shaved his beard and scraped every scrap of hair from his body.

When he was as naked as a man could be, they dressed him in a garment as tight as a skin but strangely flexible, binding him from throat to ankle. It covered him, but left nothing to the imagination. He had a brief, thoroughly unworthy thought, of radical fashions and wanton women.

The thought fled as soon as it appeared. In that strange not-nakedness, he was brought to a room in which stood four others likewise clipped and clad. None was of either world that he knew. They were all eyeless, but sharply alert. Their stance, their carriage—they were warriors, honed to a deadly edge: Olenyai of their people.

He did not know what he was doing there. He was quick on his feet and had some little talent for weapons, but he was not a warrior. If it was enough to have killed one of the lords, then the lord's kin would be disappointed. That had been blind luck. Daros could hardly expect to chance upon it again.

Once again they stood in a featureless space and faced attack. This came in the shape of great looming figures, shapes of darkness that sent off waves of icy cold, breathing forth the stench of tombs. They swarmed through more doors than Daros would have imagined such a room could have. Their claws were long and vicious, their fangs as sharp as a serpent's.

These were nightwalkers, drinkers of blood. They felled one of the warriors in that first moment, and stooped over him, rending his throat, draining the blood from his still twitching body.

Daros fought for his life and soul. Concealment be damned; he freed Estarion's knife from its cord. It was a poor enough weapon against such enemies, but it was the best that he had. He set himself with his back to the wall, though that could trap him beyond hope, and built a second wall of cold steel.

Those princes of warrior slaves trusted in their skill, but against enemies faster, stronger, and far more hungry than they, one by one they dropped and died. Only one other withstood the attack. He was quicker than sight, quicker even than the nightwalkers; he seemed to vanish, then to reappear in unexpected places.

One of the nightwalkers fell, gutted by Daros' steel. He braced against the rest, but they drew back. The other surviving warrior had captured a nightwalker from behind, and snapped its neck.

Those who remained bowed their strange elongated heads and folded their clawed hands and retreated. Daros sagged against the wall, but kept his dagger up, trusting nothing in this ghastly place.

A lord entered through the one obvious door. As much as they all resembled one another, Daros marked him for the lord who had been in the training court. He was alone, but not unarmed.

He ignored the living men to examine the dead. Each, once he had touched it, shriveled and crumpled in upon itself, then sank into dust. He wiped his gauntleted hand on his thigh and straightened, and turned toward the ones who had done the killing. The warrior stood motionless in the middle of the room. Daros had had the wits to stand straight, but still with his back to the wall. The knife was about his neck again, hidden if never forgotten.

The lord smiled thinly. "You will come," he said.

The warrior obeyed without hesitation. Daros judged it wise to follow suit. Slaves waited outside to dress them in robes of much better quality than they had worn before.

The lord waited with a remarkable degree of patience, but it was not infinite. As soon as they were seen to, he led them brusquely and at speed up through the levels of the citadel.

They passed the walls and wards of the lord's tower. Daros had what he had hoped for, somewhat after he needed it. In truth he would rather have remained a slave below, free to come and go, and therefore to seek out the mages. A fighting slave was taken through Gates; was a soldier in the war. That was the goal he had aimed for—not to be chosen for this, whatever it was to be.

There was no way out but death. He did not want to die yet. He went where he was led, therefore, and observed as much as he might.

They were near the top of the tower before they stopped. Daros thought that he could hear the humming and whirring of the thing that the king guarded so closely. The air had a throb to it; it pulsed just below the level of perception.

A man was waiting for them in a room full of strangeness: dark shapes that, to Daros, meant nothing. The man was a priest; his face was tired, his expression less than delighted as the lord brought the two slaves to him. "Only two? We need more."

"We need soldiers. Those we have in plenty. These—they'll always be rare." The lord jabbed his chin at Daros. "That one gutted a nightwalker with his bare hands."

"And killed one of your own clan before that," the priest said. "Now you own his life. Would that you had brought me a dozen such."

"Often I bring none at all," the lord said. "Do your work, old man, and be content with what you're given. There's no time for foolishness now."

The priest snarled to himself, but when he turned his back pointedly on the lord, it was to gather a selection of what must be ritual objects and spread them on the table between himself and the others. The warrior slave had not moved since he was brought here; therefore Daros did the same. They stood shoulder to shoulder, almost exactly of a height, though Daros was somewhat broader.

While the lord watched with a show of disdain, the priest built a spidery structure of metal and glass, clicking each part into the next. When it was done, it looked somewhat like the visor of a helmet. He performed no incantation, raised no power, but at a flick of a finger, the thing came to life. He laid it over the warrior slave's face.

The man screamed, brief and piercing. Daros came nigh to leaping out of his skin. The priest betrayed neither shock nor surprise. Even as that terrible cry died away, he lifted the visor of metal.

The warrior slave opened narrow dark eyes—in shape like Daros' own, though his face was different, rounder, smoother, and his skin was like old ivory. He seemed neither glad nor frightened to be given back his eyes. Or perhaps he had not, not exactly. There were no whites to them. They were black from edge to edge, but glistening as eyes were wont to do. They were alive; they were unmistakably present. They were like the lords' eyes; exactly like.

The priest approached Daros. Daros' mind gibbered, shrieking at him to flee. But if he moved, he was betrayed, and therefore dead.

His shields were as strong as he could make them. He steadied himself as the visor came near to his face. It was cold, no warmth in it of the man who had made it or the one who had worn it just before him. It clasped him like icy fingers. In the last possible instant, out of pure instinct, he shut down mage-sight, and squeezed his eyes tight shut.

The pain came without warning. It was exquisite—it was agony. It was like needles thrust into his eyes. A scream ripped itself out of him, leaving a taste of blood in his throat.

The cold metal thing retreated. His eyes were open. He still had them. What he saw . . .

A world in shades of red and black. Patterns of heat and cold. Shapes that he could recognize, but altered immeasurably.

Mage-sight was still there. He could see with that as he had seen before. But his own eyes, the eyes of his body, were no longer as they had been.

Many things that he had done were irrevocable. But this one, somehow, seemed more than that. He should have run; should have made himself invisible, and hidden with the mages. He could have freed slaves, fomented revolt. He might even have found another way to win passage through the lords' Gates.

It was all he could do to stand as if it did not matter. When the lord said, "Follow," he followed, because he had left himself no other choice. He must not despair. Despair was death.

The lord led the two of them to yet another barracks, but much smaller than those that Daros had seen before. It could hold perhaps a hundred men, but at the moment he counted barely three dozen standing at attention beside the bed-niches. All were dressed as he was, with eyes that saw the dark as no dark at all. They were all armed: each with a sword and a knife, and a sheath of a shape that would carry the weapon that flung dark fire. Even here, it seemed, those weapons were kept locked away.

These men had volition. They looked on the newcomers as men of any fighting company might, in a mingling of hope and doubt. If their souls were bound, it seemed their minds, to some extent, were not.

The warrior who had passed the test with Daros was coming to himself. He stumbled somewhat as he walked to the end of the ranked fighters. When he took his place there and turned to face the lord with the rest, his face twitched, then twisted in confusion.

Daros fell in beside him, but he had had enough of playing deception. He looked the lord in the face, level and expressionless. The lord seemed somehow amused. When he spoke, the words were addressed to both of them, but his eyes remained on Daros. "Be glad now, both of you. You are the best of the best, the chosen ones, the strongest of all. You serve at our right hands; when you die, the Night will take you as her own."

Daros' fellow recruit bowed his head in submission. Daros refused.

The lord laughed and saluted him. "Good! We need the strong ones. Serve well, and more rewards may yet await you."

He left then, still laughing, as hard and cold as everything else in this world. In his wake, the company of the chosen eased visibly. Their eyes turned toward the newcomers; some of them smiled. There was no warmth in those smiles, and nothing remotely comforting.

"New meat," one of them said, smacking his lips. "Tender and sweet. Tell us, meat—did you taste nightwalker blood?"

Neither answered. The others closed in, smiling and smiling. Daros found himself pressed shoulder to shoulder with the other, and then back to back as the circle eased them away from the wall and out into the free space of the hall.

"Meat," said the one who seemed to speak for the rest. He was tall and lean, a whipcord man. His skin to mage-sight was as white as new milk, his close-cropped hair pallid gold. His eyes, like the eyes of all those here, were black from rim to rim, but Daros had a fugitive thought that when he had lived in the light, they had been the color of a winter sky.

"Meat," he said again. "Fresh meat. How many did you kill, meat? Did you eat any of them?"

"Was it required?" Daros asked. It was certainly folly, but he could not help himself. "I barely had time to work up an appetite."

The pale man moved in close, crowding him, sniffing like a hound. His teeth were small and even, which was rather surprising; Daros would have expected a direwolf's fangs. "Pretty," he said. "Very, very pretty. Have we destroyed your world yet? Are your women as pretty as you?"

"Almost." Daros bared his own teeth. They were much longer and sharper than this man's; much more truly a predator's. "Did your women geld you themselves or did they trust the dark lords to do it for them?"

The pale man's attack was completely silent, not even a growl of warning. But Daros had provoked it; he was waiting for it. Even with that, the other's weight bore him back and down. He twisted in the air. He half-succeeded: he came down hard, but the other toppled beside him.

For the third time in that brutal day, he fought for his life. He was tired; the other was fresh. He had a weapon, but he must keep it hidden if he could. He had his hands, and his teeth if he would use them. He had the depth of his anger at all of this, at what had been done to the two worlds he had lived in, at what had been done to him.

The pale man was as strong as a snake and lethally fast. They were all fast, these warriors of the dark. Daros defended himself blindly, striking without thought, beating clawed fingers from his eyes, locked and rolling across the hard stone floor. The pale man jabbed a knee up hard, aiming at his privates. He blocked it and thrust it aside, wrenching with all his force, ripping sinew, cracking bone. The pale man howled and lunged, clawing at his throat.

He snapped at the hands and the arms behind them. He tasted blood—rich and iron-sweet. The great vein of it pulsed in the white throat. He sank his teeth in it, his sharp white teeth. He drank deep.

He recoiled in a sudden shock of horror. His mouth was full of blood and worse. He gagged. The pale man convulsed, locked in death-throes. Daros vomited a bellyful of blood, vomited until nothing came but bile.

Hands drew him up, held him. They were surprisingly gentle. The one closest was the warrior who had passed the testing with him, too new to the freedom of his mind, maybe, to be properly afraid.

Daros could not stop retching. If his stomach would only come up, he could die, and it would be over. But it stubbornly refused to leave its place.

Someone held a cup to his lips. He drank perforce. It was water. He kept it down, somewhat to his amazement. It washed the taste of blood from his mouth. It could never cleanse the stain of what he had done.

He had been so sure, so arrogantly sure, that his spirit was free; that this place had no power to corrupt him. Now two men lay dead by his doing, and the blood of one stained his face and hands. He was as dark as any other man in that room, as deeply tainted by the tide of shadow.

He stood straight. The men about him drew back. There was fear in their eyes.

One still held the jar of water. He cleaned himself with it as best he could. They watched him as wolves watch the one who has killed their pack-leader.

"If you are thinking that I will lead you," he said, "stop thinking it now. I have no presence here. I know nothing of what your veterans know."

"The lord who brought you—he leads us," one of the warriors said. "We fight as he bids. Who leads here, that's won by combat. You did win that. Don't tell us you didn't mean it."

Daros bit his tongue. He had meant it—willingly or no. He had known what he did when he locked in combat with the pale man. He must have known in his heart how it must end. How could he not?

"Tell me, then," he said: "what we do here, what we are for. Be sure it is the truth. I will know if you lie."

They blanched—in the strange sight he had been given, their faces darkened as blood, and therefore heat, drained away. One spoke for them all. He marked that one: a warrior from Tanit's world, he would wager, a giant of a man with the full lips and blunt features and the dark gleaming skin of the lands to the south of the black land. He had a deep voice, like stones shifting.

"We are the lords' warriors," he said, "their bodyguards, the commanders of their raiding parties. They give us their eyes, so that we can see as they see, and give us back the great part of our will, so that when we fight in one of the worlds, we may make choices in difficult circumstances, and protect the lesser troops under our command.

"We are not free. You killed a lord in the testing—he was one they could afford to lose, or they would never have given him such duty. You will not be permitted to do such a thing again. If you have dreams of finding your way back to your own world, give them up. You will go back, very likely, if your world exists at all—but you are now of this world and not of that one. Its light will blind you and its sun destroy you. You belong to the dark world now. Never forget that."

"I was exiled from my world," Daros said.

"So were some of us," said the giant. "And some of us were sent to fight the enemy that came out of the night, and were taken into his armies instead. There is no escape from our lords or from the darkness they serve. You are wise not even to dream of it."

"Slave-warriors," Daros said. "My world has had them."

"This world lives by them," the giant said. "Mountains, worlds full of slaves, all bound to the will of the masters. We are the highest of them, the strongest and best. We are the chosen. There is pride in that, if your heart knows any such thing."

"My heart knows the taste of blood," Daros said, "and the lure of oblivion."

"The lords will love you," the giant said, "if you can restrain yourself from killing any more of them. Slaves' blood—you may drink that with fair freedom, if you do it wisely. They'll blame it on the nightwalkers; those will escape and feed, if they can manage it. But lords—never touch those. Lords are our gods. However much you hate them, they hold the cords that bind your soul."

"I shall remember," Daros said.

He turned to face them all. They kept a wary distance. "If I lead you, you do as I bid—barring a lord's command. Yes?"

"Yes," they said in a ragged chorus.

"Good," he said, letting them see the teeth that had ripped the pale man's throat. "Dispose of that carrion. Then come with me. I have weapons to win, and fighting muscles to find again. I was too long below, among the cattle."

They glanced at one another. *Oh, yes,* he thought as he scanned their faces: he was a bold, bad man, and would be bolder and badder when he was strong again. Which had best be soon.

He could feel the worlds shifting, the tides of darkness turning. It was growing stronger. It was inside him, eating away at his heart. If he was to have any hope at all of vanquishing it, he could not tarry much longer.

"Weapons," he said to the men whose command, by sheer blind luck, he had won. "Now."

They leaped to obey him. He sauntered in their wake, as a prince of slaves should do.

THIRTY-ONE

WITH THE SIGHT HE HAD BEEN GIVEN, DAROS COULD AT LAST DISTINGUISH between night and day in this place. Night was cooler, gentler on the eyes. Day was perceptibly brighter. If he turned his eyes toward the sky, he saw the swirling darkness, clouds of heat and cool, and beyond it the furnace of the sun.

On the third day, he was at weapons-practice with the rest of his company. The dark flame was not dark at all; it was red within red within red, a seethe and coil of power that consumed whatever it touched. The weapons that hurled it were simple enough to wield. They needed little precision, only strength to lift them. Swords, bows, spears—those needed art, and of that he had much to learn.

As he practiced his archery in the largest of the courts, he was aware that one of the lords had come to watch, attended by men like those about him: slave-warriors with living eyes and bound souls. It was a great temptation to spin on his heel and aim his arrow into the lord's heart, but he was stronger than that—barely.

Pity, he thought as he lowered his bow and released the arrow from the string, and turned slowly to face the lord. It was the king himself. His dark-on-dark eyes fixed on Daros. "Prepare your men," he said. "You raid tonight."

Daros bowed. The king's lip curled in what might be a dour smile, or might be scorn. "Take many slaves," said the king. "Empty all their storehouses. But leave the fields. We may need them later."

Daros bowed again. The king laid a hand on his shoulder. He tensed, still bent in obeisance, but held his ground.

"You are not like the others," the king said. "Serve me well and there may be more to hope for than the command of a simple company."

Daros lifted his head. "Freedom?"

The king laughed. "Are you not free now? The worlds are yours—in our service. Would you not rather have power? Conquest? Blood in gleaming rivers?"

Daros set his teeth and was silent. The king patted him like a dog and left him to seethe in peace.

No one in this world had a name. That was the first sacrifice to the dark: the sound that embodied a man's spirit. But some of the slave-warriors remembered who they had been before they were taken away. He who had passed the test with Daros was Chenyo; the giant was Mukassi. Others mattered less than those two, but Daros remembered names when he could.

He was not to take most of the slave-warriors in his company. Three, he could take; the rest would be true slaves, fighters from the courts below. He chose Chenyo and Mukassi and a man of his own world, a Shurakani who had been called Janur. Janur seldom spoke; in weapons-practice he was single-minded in his quest to be perfect. Daros suspected that he had kept more of his mind and will than many of the others.

He was not a mage. The lords killed mages wherever they found them, and shattered worlds in which magic was strong. So would they do to Daros' world if they could break the wall that barred the Gates.

It was rather a pity that Janur had no magery, but it mattered little for what Daros had in mind. What mattered more was that there would be no nightwalkers on this raid, and no lords. Those, he had reason to know, were spread dangerously thin. They were mounting a monstrous assault on his world, of which this would be but a testing of the waters.

He knew perfectly well what that made him. He was bait for a trap, he and the dozen other leaders who would raid that same night, some on his own world, others elsewhere. If he came back alive, he would be accorded due honor. If he died, the lords would be rid of him. They could not lose, whichever way the dice fell.

He and his three lieutenants were given armor and mounts. The scaled beasts were not as dangerous as they looked: they were placid in the main, docile and rather sluggish. Still, in armor scaled like the beasts' hides, in tall helms and sweeping cloaks and panoply of weapons, and mounted on the fanged, clawed creatures, they were a vision from a nightmare.

The slave-troops would march afoot, matched in pairs. They shepherded wagons drawn by more of the scaled beasts, and carried the shackles that Daros remembered too well. Those who would fight surrounded them, armed much as Daros was.

Menkare and Khafre were among the fighters. He found them as much by gait and feel as by sight. Their magery was a spark of fierce warmth, burning bright within the ruddy glow of their bodies.

He could not approach them. He was being watched. They must ride out with the rest of the companies, out onto the plain, and there the Gates would open. Their orders were simple: raid, rob, withdraw. They were to fight no more than they must.

They were the third of the companies to ride out. The others were of similar size, with the same orders. They marched in silence broken only by the rattle of cartwheels and the occasional squeal of a beast. No one laughed or spoke or sang. Only the commanders were free to think thoughts that were mostly their own. The rest were altogether enslaved.

They rode down from the citadel and out onto the plain. There where the land rolled to a long level, two pillars stood. They were thrice the height of a tall man, and that same distance apart. The wagons could pass easily between them, or six men abreast with room to spare.

Priests stood on either side, as still as the pillars. They held rods like smaller versions of the flamethrowers. As the first company drew near the Gate, the priests raised their rods. Dark fire arced between them and leaped to the top of the pillars. A lintel shaped itself, so that it was a Gate indeed, and a swirling madness of worlds beyond it.

The priests chose the worlds to which the raiding parties would go, speaking a single word as each party came to the Gate. The word that Daros heard was *Avaryan*. It was well that he was mounted and not afoot, or he would have stumbled. Did they understand how great was the irony, that they should direct the forces of dark with the name of the god of light?

The Gate hummed and throbbed. Magegates did no such thing. This, like the force or device or spell that the king guarded, had a flavor about it of a thing made by hands. A machine, thought Daros, driven by magic.

They made machines in the Nine Cities, automatons that walked and spoke a tinny word or two, or clocks in which they tried to trap time. None of them had ever, that he knew of, trapped a mage and fed his machines with the mage's power.

That was a potent thought, but he had no time to think the whole of it. The Gate caught him and his following, and drew them in.

They came in under a shield of darkness. Yet with this sight he could see beyond it to the glory of the moons and the myriad of stars. He drew in the air of his own world, his body's home. The earth's power surged up and over him, drowning him in blessed strength.

They rode down a long line of headland, with the roar of the sea on their right hands, and sea-grass hissing as they marched through it. They had not so very far to go. A village huddled in a fold of the coast, ripe with the reek of fish. Nets were spread before the houses; boats were drawn up on the shingle. Even in these days, they were prosperous. They had herds of cattle and woolbeasts, and stores of grain and of salt fish—perhaps they traded the one for the other.

There were walls about the village, raw with newness, and wards on the walls. A mage was in the village. Daros thanked the gods for answering his prayer.

Dark fire broke the walls, crumbled them into dust. Raiders ran for the storehouses and the cattle-pens. People surged out of the houses, strong people, armed and ready. They had fire: torches and magefire. The light of them seared into Daros' brain.

Almost too late, he dropped the visor of his helmet. He could see through it—it was like dark glass. He could ride, raid, fight where he must. He did not strike to kill. The terror of his mount held most of them off; they went for the fighters on foot. Those had orders: to defend the wagons and the herds, once they were taken.

The fighting was fierce, the defenders strong. Daros took little notice. The mage's presence was a beacon before him. It was a woman; she wielded bolts of magefire, blasting attackers who came near. He in his armor, shielded with his own force of magery, struck aside a bolt aimed direct at his head. He overran her, heaved her across his mount's saddle, and turned the beast about. It was remarkably agile for so large and cold-blooded an animal; it wheeled with uncanny speed, whipping its head from side to side, scattering and rending fighters who sprang to their mage's defense.

She was winded, briefly shocked out of her senses. In that brief blankness of mind, he set in her the thing that he had prepared. It was memory and a message, and a compulsion laid on it. Just as she came to herself, he let her slip from his hands.

She leaped to the attack. He had not prepared for that. She surged upward toward his face, armed with lightnings, and struck his helm. It spun away, driven by more than mortal strength.

She hung in midair, eyes as wide as they would go, frozen in shock. He was hardly more in command of his wits. That face—he knew—

Mother?

He never spoke the word. She never dealt the deathblow. His mount leaped away from her, roaring and lashing its tail.

The battle was nearly done. With the mage distracted, the village had been easy prey. They had what they had come for: grain, fish, cattle. There were few slaves; the villagers had fought too hard. They did not linger to destroy the village. Raid only, the king had said. Daros would do exactly as the king had commanded.

The Gate was waiting. He gathered his forces, took swift count of the wounded, gritted his teeth while they were flamed to ash. Death had been swift, and merciful. And none of them was a mageling.

It wrenched at his heart to pass through that Gate again, to abandon his own world for the dark land. But he could not stay, even if he could have abandoned his mages. He could no longer abide the light. He was a creature of darkness now. He could only pray that his spirit would not go the way of his eyes, and give him over altogether to the lords of the night.

THIRTY-TWO

L ADY?"

Merian started awake. She had had no intention of falling asleep on this of all days, but the sun was warm and she was exhausted. The attacks had been growing stronger, the raids more numerous. The enemy had broken out of the bounds of Anshan and begun to raid again in random parts of the world.

Last night had been the worst of all: a dozen raids in a dozen places, towns and cities sacked, but for once no people killed—those who were not taken were left to do as they would. Tonight, she feared, would be even worse. And she dozed in the sun in Ki-Oran, weighed down with the burden of the child. It would be born soon, if there was any world for it to be born to.

"Lady!"

She blinked at the young mage who ran errands for her. He was Asanian, and unusually fair-skinned even for one of those gold-and-ivory people. His face was deathly white now. "Lady," he said, "there is a mage here from the northern coast. She will speak to no one but you."

Merian sighed and heaved herself up. Izarel steadied her; she scowled, but stopped herself before she snapped at him. Gods knew, her condition was not *his* fault. As for whose fault it was . . .

He was in the dark world. More than that she did not know.

She should have had the mage brought to her in the kitchen garden in which she had been sunning herself, but she was too stubborn and the sun too full of sleep that she needed badly but should not indulge in. In the cool of the tower, she roused a little more. She sent Izarel ahead to prepare her receiving-room. The word was rather too grand for that cupboard of a place, but it had a window to let in light and air, a small circle of chairs, and a couch on which she could rest her swollen body.

She turned her steps toward the least comfortable of the chairs. Izarel, ahead of her in mind as well as body, steered her deftly toward the couch. She was settled on it before she could raise an objection. He laid a light robe across her knees, set a cup and a jar—full of clean water very lightly laced with wine—on the table beside her, and arranged a bowl of fruit and a platter of bread and cakes to his fastidious satisfaction. Only then would he yield to her will and go to fetch the mage.

It was a woman of Shurakan, somewhat to her surprise: a strong woman, not beautiful, but her face was difficult to forget. Even so, Merian groped for a name to set to the face. It was never one she would have expected to come to her from a fishing village in the north of Anshan.

"Lady," she said. "My lady of Han-Gilen. What—"

The Lady Varani sat where Izarel directed her. She ignored the wine that he poured and the cakes that he offered. She had the look of a woman at the edge of endurance, a bare hair's breadth from breaking. She was pale under the bronze of her skin; her hands shook, though she clasped them tightly as if to still them.

For a brief, wild moment Merian wondered if the lady had discovered who had sired Merian's child. It was generally accepted that, like her mother before her, Merian had bred an heir for herself alone. Easier to let the world think that and be suitably scandalized than to try to explain how the exiled heir of Han-Gilen had begotten a child from the far side of a Worldgate.

But Varani barely took notice of Merian's bloated body. Her eyes were fixed on another thing altogether. "Lady," she said, "last night the dark ones raided us, stole our grain and fish, ran off our cattle; they took half a score of villagers, but left the rest."

"Yes," Merian said. "It has been reported to me. Your village suffered lightly in comparison with others."

"Yes," Varani said. Her eyes lowered. "And yes, lady, well you should wonder why that would require my presence here, away from the people I was assigned to guard."

"I am wondering," said Merian, "what the Lady of Han-Gilen is doing in a fishing village and not in one of the cities of the Hundred Realms."

"I am a Gate-mage," Varani said. "I go where I'm needed. And I asked . . . I asked for a humble place. I felt that it was necessary."

"Atonement?" asked Merian.

"All of us have sins for which we should do penance."

"You did not raise your son badly."

She flung up her head. The pain in her face, in her eyes, made Merian gasp. "Did I not?" she said.

"Tell me," said Merian. Her heart was cold and still.

Varani seized her hands. It happened so fast, was so strong, that Merian could raise no shields. It flooded her power, overwhelmed and drowned it. Even shock, even fear—it swept them away. Only one thought remained, with a glimmer of despair: *I never told him about the child.*

The child who was close to being born; the child who, doubly mageborn, doubly a mage of Gates, lay wide open and defenseless to that flood of power and knowledge.

Merian opened her eyes on sunlight, a broad river, a ripple of reeds. He was there as he had been in dream before, in the semblance and fashion of the world in which for a while he had been trapped.

He smiled, but his eyes were somber. "Beloved," he said, "I beg your forgiveness for what I've had to do. As I stand here in this place, the forces are gathering. The Gates are being prepared. The war is truly beginning. Here in this burst of power, I've given you all I know. I would come to you if I could, but I won't endanger you so. I'll find a mage to bear the message; I'll set it in him as best I can, and pray he takes no harm from it. This is not a thing I've tried before—I don't even know if it can be done. But if it can, it must."

All the while he spoke, so clear and yet so remote, his message unfolded itself in all its enormity. She knew, indeed, what he knew. All of it. And yet . . .

"He is alive," she said, a long breath of thanks to the gods. "He is well. The mages are in place, and doing as they had intended to do. Lady, he's done splendidly!"

"Has he?" Varani was still gripping her hands. "He would let us think that. How not?"

Merian's moment of incredulous joy slipped away before she could grasp it. She wondered when she would know it again, if she ever did. "Tell me," she said.

"You never asked how the message came to me," said Varani. "Because I'm his mother? He didn't even know me. See!"

Merian saw night; black darkness. Raiders broke down the walls of the little town by the sea. Varani fought as a mage could fight, with bolts of light. She had reckoned the number of attackers, and taken note that most of them were afoot; only four were riders, massive shapes in fantastical armor, as scaled and clawed and spined as the beasts they rode.

One of them took no apparent notice of the fight, but rode straight toward her, ignoring any who got in his way. She smote him with power, but the bolt flew wide. His beast reared up. He seized her and flung her with bruising force across the pommel of a high saddle.

As she lay winded, he struck her with a bolt of pure power. It pierced her brain;

it ripped aside her shields, her protections, even her will to resist. It lodged deep and grew roots. Then at last it set her free.

She rose up in rage. She fought with her body, trusting no longer to her tainted power. She struck off the helm that shielded the gods knew what horrors.

She froze, as Merian froze within the memory. That face—oh, gods, that face. His hair was cut close to the skull as it had been when first Merian saw him. He was leaner, almost gaunt. His eyes . . .

They had taken away his eyes and left darkness in their place. He looked on his mother as if he could see her, but there was no recognition in that lightless stare. The dark was in him, was part of him. The son that she had known was gone.

"No," said Merian—quietly, she thought; calmly enough, all things considered. "No. He can't be. He can't—"

"I think there can be no doubt that he is," said Varani. Her voice was flat, bleak. "It was a risk; we all knew that. We gave him no training, taught him no discipline. Our fault; our failing. Now it has destroyed him."

"No," said Merian again. She knew perfectly well that she might be the worst of fools, but she could not, would not, believe that Daros was lost. "He gave us what we need. We know now what we face. He would never have done that if he had turned traitor."

"He well might," said Varani, "if his masters had in mind to fill us with lies and so overwhelm us."

They are not lies. Merian did not speak the words. She called Izarel to wait on the lady, to see that she was given every comfort. Merian, for her part, called a council of the last resort: the most urgent of all. She summoned one who might have both the knowledge and the power to advise her.

The Prince of Han-Gilen resembled his son little except for the bright copper of his hair. He was a tall man and strongly built, but neither as tall nor as broad as Daros; nor did he have his son's beauty. He had a proud and somber face, a face altogether of the plains, and an air of one whose forefathers had been princes since before there were kings in the world.

Merian did not know him well. His kin had been her kin's oldest allies, but this prince kept for the most part to himself—as, before this war, had she. His lady she had known slightly better, since Varani was a Gate-mage, but they had crossed paths seldom. She had not even been certain that he would answer the summons. He was a very great prince, and more like his son than one might think: neither son nor father took orders well or obeyed them easily.

But he had come, nor had he kept her waiting for much longer than it would have taken him to free himself from his duties in his own city. He had paused to put aside court dress, to clothe himself sensibly in well-worn riding clothes; he came through a Gate of his own making, and presented himself at the gate of the fort.

The guards took him for one of the many messengers who came and went on Merian's business. They passed him easily enough, but without the pomp to which he must be accustomed. She thought he might be offended, but his dark eyes were glinting as Izarel admitted him to her receiving-room. He bowed low, and waved away her apologies for neither rising nor offering him proper respect.

"Lady," he said in a much warmer voice than she had expected, "we need not stand on ceremony. Aren't we kin from long ago?"

Much more so than he knew, she thought. She smiled and held out her hand. He took it and kissed it with gallantry that made her laugh. "May I?" he asked, tilting his head toward the swell of her middle.

It was an uncommon request, but among mages a considerable courtesy: to pay tribute to the child, and bless it. The child, as far as she could tell, had survived the flood of magic from Varani's mind, and taken no harm from it. She was aware of the prince's presence: Merian sensed curiosity, but no fear.

This was a mage of great power, of whom Merian had never heard an ill word. He was also, and that decided it for her, the child's grandfather. He was kin; it was his right. She nodded.

He laid his hand where the child was, coiled with her thumb in her mouth, dreaming the long dream of the womb. She roused at his touch. Merian felt a thing both familiar and utterly strange: a tendril of magery uncoiling, reaching out, brushing her mother and her grandfather with a flicker of wonder, a gleam of delight.

Merian gasped. The prince's expression was astonished. "But—this is—"

There was no lying to a mage. Merian looked him steadily in the face. "It is."

"But how?"

"Dreamwalking," Merian said.

His eyes widened slightly. "Indeed? There are ancient texts that speak of dreamwalking in the reality of the flesh, but no mage in this age of the world has succeeded."

"He said," she said somewhat delicately, "that you were a great scholar of magic from long ago. He intimated that we might have done well to consult you before we raced blindly ahead."

"As he did?" the prince said. His voice was cold.

"My lord," said Merian, "I need your wisdom badly. I need your understanding as well. Will you allow me to give you the message that he sent to us last night?"

The prince inclined his head. So, she thought: his lady had not told him. Had there been a quarrel, then, that sent the ruling lady of a great realm to be a village mage on the coast of Anshan? Had their son had something to do with it?

She must trust in her instinct, and the urging of her magery. She took his hands and gave him all that Varani had given.

For a long while after it was done, he sat beside the couch, very still, his eyes as blank as his son's had been. Merian slipped her hands free from his unresisting fingers and took the opportunity to rest a little.

When she opened her eyes again, he had just begun to stir. His face had aged years. "I . . . see why you summoned me," he said. "This is far from mere feckless-ness. This is treason, high and deadly."

"Is it?" Merian asked him. "Do you believe that, my lord?"

"What am I to believe, lady? What he did to his mother was one of the forbid-den arts. It was, in a word, rape. Even if the rest can be true, and he continues to play the game of masks, that is profoundly damning."

"Would he know that it's forbidden? He was never formally a mage."

"My fault," the prince said as his lady had, heavily. "He has so little gift or talent for constraint. I thought that if I left him to find his own way, he would find the right one. His every choice since he became a man has been wrong. Every one."

She rested her hand where the child lay, listening to the echo of their voices within the domed chamber of the womb. "Every choice?" she asked.

"He could have chosen a less difficult time."

"I don't think that was his choice to make," she said gently but with firmness that would remind him, she hoped, of who and what she was. "The gods do as the gods will. I ask you: dare we trust the message that he sent?"

"You ask me, lady? I would have condemned him to death when first he broke the law of Gates. He has done nothing creditable since. Great grief though it costs me, I must face the truth: that my only son is flawed beyond redemption. He was born without the instinct for order that is the mark of a civilized being."

"I ask you to consider," she said, "what you would do if you were in his place. Tell me that, my lord."

She watched him gather his thoughts and turn them away from the bitterness that was his son. "If it were I," he said slowly, "I would play the game of masks to the end. I would do what I could to protect where I was sent to destroy: to slay few or none, and to send word to my people of what I knew."

"That is exactly what he did," she said. "No one died where he raided. I would wager that the slaves he took will not stay slaves long. There was word among the rest, of the mages' freeing slaves and mounting a revolt. He asks us to be ready, to gather our power, to strike when the time comes."

"If he can be trusted," his father said.

"Can we trust you?"

"To the ends of life," he said.

"I believe that he is your son," she said, "and that whatever darkness may have taken him, in the end he will prove his loyalty to his world and his kin."

"And his daughter?"

"He knows nothing of her," she said.

"And you say that you trust him?"

"I do," she said. "Enough not to put him to such a test."

"Then you need me not at all."

"I need you, my lord," she said. "I need the knowledge that is in you. The Mage who drives the darkness is dying. If we can hasten its death, might not the darkness die?"

"The Mage did not create the darkness," the prince said. "The armies of night may weaken once the Mage is dead, but the dark is like a river. It will hardly fade away because the one who opened the floodgates is dead."

"Even so," she said, "with the Mage gone and the slaves freed, we may be able to destroy the men who serve the darkness. Then maybe—if there is knowledge somewhere, some spell, some working, that can conquer the shadow—"

"I will need my library, lady," he said, "and as many scholars as you can spare. They need not be mages, as long as they can read, and remember what they read."

"I will send you scholars," she said, "and instruct them to read quickly. I think there may not be much time left."

"I, too," he said. "May I have your leave to begin?"

"My lord, you may," she said.

THIRTY-THREE

THE PRINCE OF HAN-GILEN RETURNED TO HIS PRINCEDOM AND HIS LIBRARY, to find a dozen keen-witted scholars already exclaiming over the trove of treasure that they had found among the shelves and bins and chests. His lady spoke no word of rebuke for being left to sleep while her lord had come and gone. She asked only that she be allowed to return to her village. "They need me there," she said.

Merian sighed and let her go. If there was to be peace in that family, it would not come tonight.

Already, even before the sun set, she knew that the night would be difficult. It was barely dark before the attacks began. Again they were raids for provisions and slaves; there was little killing and no destruction. Mages and fighters were able to drive back a raid deep in Asanion and another in the north, but the cost of that was high: the enemy would kill if provoked. They swept the defenders with dark fire.

Swords and spears were of no use against that. Arrows had some little effect, and mage-bolts more, but the mages were shackled by their own laws. They could not kill a thinking being with magic. Defend, yes; destroy the dark things that sometimes came with the enemy and fed on blood; but when they faced a raider armed with dark fire, they could strike to wound but not to kill. So were they killed while the enemy escaped.

No word came from Han-Gilen, nor was there another message from the dark world. Mages seeking to pierce through shadow to the world in which Estarion was imprisoned, could not come near him. They could only hold fast, strengthen their armies as they could, and wait.

Greatmoon came to the full five days after Daros raided the village in Anshan. He had not been seen again; if he had been one of the armored and mounted raiders, he had not revealed himself to anyone who fought against him.

Every night Merian dreamed of him. They were honest dreams, not dreamwalking; some were memories, but many were fragments of the message that he had sent. He had left her another key, but it remained as cryptically impenetrable as the bowl that she had bidden Hani bring her from Starios.

She was sitting in her receiving-room that evening, staring fixedly at it by the light of the setting sun. It offered no more answers than it ever had. There was no writing on it, no spell woven in it that she could find. It was only a worn stone bowl with a dark stain inside it.

Water. The thought came from everywhere and nowhere. *Fill it with water.*

They had tried that long before, summoned a mage skilled in scrying and asked that she practice her art on the bowl. She had found nothing. "Worse than nothing," she had said. "This a dead thing. It kills visions."

But the voice in her head was very clear. It was, she realized with a shock, a child's voice. As if to upbraid her for her slowness of wit, the child within rolled and kicked, hard, so that she gasped.

She fetched water from the jar on the table and filled the bowl just to the brim, being very careful to spill none of it. She drew slow breaths to focus, to draw inward to her center. Someone was waiting for her there: a young person with a riot of copper-colored curls, and gold-green eyes with a hint of a tilt to them, and Daros' face carved in dark ivory.

They joined hands and bent over the water. The light of sunset shimmered in it. Then the dark came, much swifter than in the world without.

They looked down into a place Merian had not seen before, yet remembered: it had come to her within Daros' message. The Mage—this was its prison, and the strange angular figure was the Mage itself. It lay bound with cords of metal, yet it also stood upright, wrapped in a shimmer that at first she took for a cloak. After a moment she saw the shimmer of plumes and knew: they were wings.

It was impossibly strange, and weirdly beautiful. It met her stare, gold to gold, and said, "Kill me."

"How?" said Merian.

"Kill me," it said. "Kill me now. Great sorrow comes unless you kill me."

"I see you," said Merian, "but I have no power to come to you."

"Kill me," it said. "Kill me now."

It would say nothing else. She could do nothing. The Worldgates were shut, barred by shadow. The Heart of the World was lost. After a while the Mage's fetch collapsed into its body, withering and vanishing with a long sigh.

She drew back from the water. Both the Mage and the dream-child were gone. She was left with a sense of failure, though what she could have done, or whether she should have done it at all, she could not have said.

Night was falling. Gates were opening, armies advancing. She took up the many threads of duty, the wards, the sendings of mages.

Something thrust a dagger in her belly, and twisted.

She had been sitting at the table, knowing full well that Izarel would object when he came back from running errands and found her. She had a flash of regret for that defiance as she crumpled to the floor.

It was too early. She could not lose this child. She could not—

People were lifting her, carrying her. She saw a blur that might be Izarel's face. There were others: mages, and—Batan?

He did not have the blank, shocked look of many men in the presence of a woman giving birth. The mages twittered, but he waded through them to sit beside her, and took her hand. "You won't be able to claim this one," she said.

He laughed. "But I might claim you after—if this one's father doesn't. Maybe he'll have to fight me for you."

"Do that and I'll feed you both to the sea-drakes," she said.

His grin was broad and insolent and very comforting. "At least then I'll get to see who snatched you out from under my nose."

Pain seized her, rent her asunder, passed. One did not become accustomed to it. She doubted that one forgot it, either, whatever the mothers of many might say. Batan had both her hands in his. The mages had drawn back before the force of his glare. But he smiled at her.

"He'd be jealous if he could see us now," he said.

"Oh, yes," she said, trying to be light, though her breath came in gasps. "He would be furious."

"Good," said Batan.

"Don't you have a holding to defend?"

"Not tonight," he said. "I came here to see you."

She raised her brows.

He did not oblige her with an answer.

There was no midwife in Ki-Oran. She had reckoned it too soon to summon one to a fortress full of warriors. When the baby reached her time, then the chief of the mage-healers in Starios would come, and a small army of midwives and nurses.

The baby was coming. There were mages; Vian was a healer. No one else could come, not at night, not with the enemy infesting every Gate.

They were all more frightened than she. It was too soon—everyone knew that. But the child, for all the shock of the pains that forced her into the world, was unafraid. Her calm flowed into Merian, calming her in turn. This was as it should be, it said. This was the gods' will.

Dream had wrought her. Magic sustained her. She was doubly mageborn, doubly bred of Gates. Was it so astonishing that she should not be born in quite the same way as other children?

She came swiftly, although the pain stretched each moment into endlessness. The mages had raised a wall of light. The child was born in it, wrapped in it as if in sunlight, bearing a Sun in her hand.

Vian the healer laid her on Merian's emptied belly. Merian would not have been surprised at all to see the child of the dream, but this was a newborn infant like any other: tiny, red, bellowing in rage at the shock of the air. Even her supernal calm had been no match for that.

Merian cradled her. Her cries faded to gasps and then to silence. She looked up as her mother looked down, with the clear eyes of a mage in a face so young it hardly had shape yet. She was very small, but perfectly complete: fingers, toes, all tiny but all perfect. The strength of her lungs she had already proved. Her eyes were infant blue, her skin too angry yet from the birth to be sure of its color, but the damp sparse curls that grew on her skull had an unmistakable coppery sheen.

Merian laughed at the splendor of the jest. This was the very image and likeness of her father. Once she began to grow, no one with eyes could fail to know what lineage she had.

Out of that thought, Merian drew her name. "Elian," she said. "Elian Kimerian."

She was too young to smile, but the warmth that came from her was as like to it as made no matter. Yes, that was her name. She was Elian, and Merian-too. Other names would come to her later, but her truename, the name of her spirit, sealed her to the world.

Morning brought the invasion. The princess regent opened a Gate in Merian's very chamber. Her arrival was like a blast of wind. Merian shielded her daughter from it, but Elian was unperturbed; she was nursing, and that took precedence over any distraction.

Daruya stood over them, fists planted on hips, glaring with a ferocity that Merian had not seen in her since she was as young as this child's father. "You could have died," she said.

"But I didn't." Merian folded back the blanket from Elian's face. "Elian," she said, "greet your grandmother."

"And not before time," Daruya said. She held out her hands. Elian turned her face away from the breast; she deigned to let her grandmother lift her.

Daruya's inspection was swift but thorough. She folded back the fingers from the tiny right hand; a sigh escaped her at the spark of gold there. Of the rest, she saw everything that was to be seen. "The young lord or the old?" she asked.

"Do you need to ask that?"

"No," said Daruya. "Nor will I demand an explanation—yet. You truly believe that I can approve of this?"

"Of course you can," Merian said. "This is a twofold heir; and the father's half of her inheritance is one that our line has never been able to claim."

"He knows?"

"The father, no. The grandfather, yes."

Daruya's brows rose. "You will not explain that, either—yet. So that was how you lured him out of his princedom. No one has been able to do that for time out of mind."

"I summoned him," said Merian. "He came. He never knew how close our kinship was until after he had come."

"Perhaps he suspected." Daruya dismissed the thought, and him, with a toss of the head. "Pack up your belongings. I'm bringing you back to Starios."

"No," Merian said.

Her mother ignored her. Izarel had come in, drawn by the scent of magic. Daruya addressed him peremptorily. "Call the servants. Your lady is going home."

"I am home," said Merian.

Izarel hung on his heel.

"I am not leaving," Merian said to him. "Go now. When I need you again, I'll summon you."

He left with palpable relief. Merian faced her mother. She had been lying down long enough. Rising made her dizzy, but that passed quickly. She held out her arms. Rather blindly, Daruya laid Elian in them. In the manner of very young creatures, Elian was deep asleep.

"Mother," Merian said, "it's touching of you to come roaring in here like the wrath of the gods, but I haven't needed setting in order for some while now."

"This is a fortress on the front of battle," Daruya said. "It is no place for a newborn child."

"Is it not my place to be the judge of that?"

"If you fail to see why she should be taken to safety, then your judgment is even more faulty than I feared."

"Nowhere in this world is safe," Merian said. "It will all be gone before this child is weaned, if we don't find a way to win the war first."

"There is one safe place," said Daruya. "Endros Avaryan."

"What, the old royal city? The Tower of the Sun? Shall we go to sleep beside our firstfather, we three, and hope to wake on the other side of oblivion?"

"Don't mock it," Daruya said sharply. "The well of power there is even stronger than it is here."

"It draws from the same source," Merian said. "When the Ring of Fire falls, so will the Tower. The world itself will be blasted into ash."

"And you speak of it so lightly." Daruya sank into the chair that stood beside the bed. She was as tired as they all were, driven to the edge of exhaustion. "Whatever we do, we should do it quickly. I've called out the armies, and armed the lesser Gates. Wherever the enemy appears, our forces will appear to fight him. They have orders to seize whatever weapons they can. Mages will discover if they can be made by magic or by craft. I have also," she said after a pause, "raised an army of picked fighters to turn the tables on the enemy: to pursue him through his own Gates, and take the war to him in the dark world."

Merian should have been outraged. The mages of Gates were hers; they were not her mother's to command. But whether it was the aftermath of the birth taking the edge off her temper, or the inevitability of the logic that informed all her mother had done, she could muster no more than a spark of irritation. "Your army will be welcome," she said, "to fight beside my army of mages. Those whom we sent are doing as they were bidden. When the enemy's slaves are in revolt, we attack."

"My troops will move in the dark of Brightmoon," Daruya said.

Seven days. Merian set her teeth. Now her temper was rising. "My mages in the dark world will send a summons when the time comes."

"How will they do that? Sacrifice another of their own to the dark army?"

That was cruel. "Some of them are already in it," Merian said sweetly. "They will come with word."

"Seven days," her mother said. "Have your mages ready."

"This is mad!" Merian burst out. "You rush in headlong, you know nothing of where you go—"

"We do know," Daruya said. "Your lover gave us all that we need."

"You trust him?"

"Do you?"

"Yes," Merian said. "Damn you, yes."

"I do not," said Daruya. "But last night we captured another of the dark captains, and put him to the question. It seems your fallen prince told the truth."

"It could be a trap."

"So it could," Daruya said, "but no worse than what we face if we continue to do nothing."

That was manifestly true. Merian hissed but said no further word.

Her mother rose, stiff with exhaustion, and kissed her, and then Elian, on the forehead. "Seven days," she said.

It was an ultimatum. Merian set her lips together and held her peace.

THIRTY-FOUR

SIX DAYS.

The Prince of Han-Gilen arrived much as the princess regent had, but he had had the grace to ask leave before he appeared in her receiving-room. It was much changed since he was last there: rather against Merian's will, it had become the nursery. Elian's cradle stood near the wall. There was never a mage far from her.

The rest of the room was crowded with gifts. Mages had brought them, things that they reckoned an infant could use, or bits of tribute, or garlands of flowers from far quarters of the world. Soldiers had come, too, or sent their captains; villagers who dared venture outside their walls; lords from round about, and lords from farther away with mages, and lesser Gates, in their service. One day had passed, and already this room was full; the stream of booty had begun to overflow the door and trickle down the stair.

It was ungracious to refuse anything that was given. After a suitable interval, Merian would give most of it to the poor; it was the custom. But it must be seen in her possession first, and universally admired.

The prince, like the princess regent, arrived empty-handed. He bowed to Merian and bent over the cradle. The child in it was awake, watching the dance of lights that one of the mages had wrought for her. He wove a net of gold and silver fire and set it to dancing with the rest. She was much too young to laugh, but her pleasure was a warmth in Merian's belly.

When he straightened, he was smiling. He looked much more like his son then, however briefly; he was somber soon enough. "She is an ornament to both our houses," he said.

Merian accepted the tribute as her daughter's due.

"I have a gift for you," he said. "One of your scholars found it. If I may?"

That was mage's courtesy. She lowered her wards to accept the gift.

The book in which the scholar had found it was ancient; the tongue was long vanished from the earth. The scholar had not been perfectly certain of every word, but she had rendered it as best she could.

The text was not long at all. Much of it, if the scholar had known it, was embedded within, in the shape of the words. *Sea of worlds, drifts of foam. Darkness into light.*

A bowl of water. A feather in the wind. Winged splendor bound and forced into servitude.

The seed of knowledge would take root and grow. Merian could only pray that there was time for it to bear fruit before her mother's madness overwhelmed them all.

"I don't think she is mad," the prince said, caught still in her thoughts. "There is another thing that we found, raiding through my library. The message declared this world to be a nexus, a core and center of Gates. The enemy must break it in order to go on, but in the breaking, might close their own Gates forever. They can do nothing until they find a way past us. And that did baffle me, lady, because as dearly as I love this world, I never had reckoned it the heart of all that is. Even the Heart of the World, despite its name, was only a way-station of sorts. It, in itself, had no power over Gates.

"We found, buried between household accounts from the reign of the third prince and a grimoire so black it had to be thrice warded before I could touch it, a scroll of tales for children. It told of the mages of Anshan, how they made alliance with a race of gods from the stars. Falcon-gods, they were called. They flew from world to world and from sun to sun, and they trailed streamers of light behind them. But where light is, there must be shadow. As the ages passed, the shadow began to swallow the light.

"The gods begged the mages for aid in reining in the shadow and bringing back the light. The mages had sworn oaths of aid and alliance, and so were bound. Most had no objection; they had gained much from their allies, had learned great arts and powers.

But a few had always whispered that the gods were no gods at all, but beasts with the minds and powers of men. They gathered the young and the foolish and the merely afraid, and convinced them that the false gods were fair prey; that they should be overcome and their power seized. Then the mages would rule the worlds, and be as gods themselves.

"There was one among this faction who nursed a great grievance. He was brother to the ruler of the mages, but his mother had been but a concubine. He was the elder and the stronger and, he reckoned, by far the better fit to rule, but the law was against him. He had to see a foolish stripling, a mage of no more than adequate power, preferred forever above him.

"He was not a darkmage as we would reckon it, but he had long been a student of the darkness that the falcon-gods had created. In time, he became enthralled with it. He began to worship it. He became its priest, and he gathered others of like mind, and founded a cult of oblivion.

"There was a war—one of many, all forgotten now. It ended with the falcon-gods destroyed and the priesthood of the dark vanquished and all their power taken away unto the final generation. Their lord escaped with a number of his followers, after his power was taken but before he could be put to death for the murder of gods. What became of him thereafter, no one knew."

"Not all the gods were destroyed," Merian said. It was enormous, this truth. Too enormous to encompass in these brief moments. "One lived, and was enslaved. The dark enemy—they are our own. Do you think they know?"

"It was a hundred generations ago and more," he said, "and theirs was a cult of forgetfulness. The Forbidden Secrets—I think those might have been theirs, and the order that protected them were their heirs and survivors, escaped to the far side of the world."

"The Gates end here because they began here. The gods found no other world so blessed with magic or so numerous with mages. They built their Gates to pass back and forth." Merian had not known she knew this. It was coming from inside of her, from the place where Daros' message lay, and from the vision in the water. Oh, indeed, she had been given a key, and this was the lock in which it turned. "When they died and the priests' power was taken away, the knowledge of these Gates faded. Their captive would hardly have wished to remind them. Then how—why—"

"Inevitability," he said. "Sooner or later, the dark priests would come back this way, and find the world that they no longer recognized as their own. Their prisoner is weak, and likely dying. It can no longer protect us, if indeed it ever did. Who knows what it remembers? As ancient as it is, and as crazed with confinement, it may not itself know what it knows."

Merian had her doubts of that, but she did not voice them. "Our fault," she said. "In the end, all of this is our fault. We thought we were but one more obstacle on the road to oblivion. Our ancestors—our kin—built that road."

"For myself," said the prince, "I appreciate another irony. The Sunborn devoted his life to battle against the dark. His heir fought against him on behalf of the balance of light and dark. And now, after all, the mad conqueror has been proved right, if not precisely sane. The dark truly was to be feared; truly would come to overwhelm us all."

"Do you think . . . " She could hardly form the words; there was something terrible about them. "Do you think this is the great cause for which he was enchanted into sleep? Is it time for him to wake?"

"No," said the prince, as flat as a door shutting. "You have been in the Tower. Is he sane? Has he dreamed his way out of the rage that would have destroyed this world?"

Merian looked down at her hands, at the golden *Kasar* that had come to her from that first father of her line. It burned perpetually; she was never free of pain. But in the Tower, there had been no pain at all.

She had been very young when her great-grandfather took her there. He had taught her how to use the *Kasar* as a Gate, not quite like the one inside her, but of that kin and kind. He had shown her the chamber in the heart of the black crag above the river of Endros, and brought her before the sleeper on his bed of stone. She had been properly awed, and suitably humbled, by the strength of that son of a god: even enchanted, even in sleep as deep as death.

He had not been sane. Not even slightly. All his being was banked rage. If she woke that, she could only conceive of waking it to do what the dark priests would do: to blast this world to ash.

"We may be as forgotten as the mages of Anshan before that one is ready to wake," the prince said. "No, lady; we have no one to rely on but ourselves. It's fitting, yes? It began with our world. It will end here."

"But," said Merian. "The dark world. I thought it was theirs. How—"

"I would wager," he said, "that it was their refuge after they fled the justice of their kin. They cloaked it in darkness and opened Gates to worlds of light, so that they could be fed and clothed and provided with servants. Women, too, one would suppose, since all the priesthood were men. Their blood may be so far removed from us now that there is little common kinship left."

"They were ours in the beginning," she said. "They remain ours until the end. Ours to burden us with shame; ours to overcome if we can."

He bowed to her. She was the heir of the Sunborn, his expression said. However great a prince he might be, he was and always had been her vassal.

"You have given us a great gift," she said. "We are in your debt."

"You are not, lady," he said. "Are we not kin? Do not kin look after one another? I ask only one thing in payment."

"Ask," she said, "and it is yours."

"Give me leave to visit my granddaughter," he said.

"My lord," said Merian, "that right is yours by blood and bond of kin. You had no need to ask for it in payment."

"I was not done, lady," he said. "Give me leave to do that. And when we both judge that it is time, send her to me. Let me teach her what I know." She would have spoken; his upraised hand silenced her. "Lady, I know I earned no credit in the raising of my son. I would hope to be more proficient in instructing my son's child."

Merian startled herself with the intensity of her resistance. This was her child—*hers*. But she had a little sense left. "When we judge that it is time," she said, "you may foster my daughter."

That time might be never. She left that unspoken. But he was content.

He left her with a great deal to ponder, and little time in which to do it. She had mages to gather, a war to prepare. And there was Elian. Merian had refused a wet-nurse: she would nurse her child herself. Yet that day, after the prince had returned to Han-Gilen, she sent for the robust young woman who had been presented to her when Elian was born. She had been polite in her dismissal; she was glad of that now. If she had flung the woman out bodily, she might have had difficulty in persuading her to take the position after all.

Jadis had nursed three of her own, all weaned now, and half a dozen for ladies in Seahold. She was sensible and calm, and she had no fear of mages. Their comings and goings, the opening and shutting of Gates, roused barely a blink after the first hour. She kept quietly to a corner, she tended Elian when there was need, and she intruded not at all on the business of war.

Well before that day was over, Merian's breasts ached abominably. She bound them tight with bands as Jadis instructed, and schooled herself to ignore them. It was harder by far to watch this stranger nursing her child, but that too she endured.

Batan found her late in the day, creaking through the beginnings of the swords-man's dance. He had been in Seahold; she had heard him ride in with a great clatter of armor and hooves, and a shout of laughter that she could never mistake. Batan was not nor had ever been a quiet man.

Except in the birthing of a child. With that in memory, she smiled as he came into the practice-court. "Welcome, my lord," she said. "All's well in Seahold?"

"As well it can be, lady," he said. "And you? I saw the little one—she's grown already. I could swear she smiled at me."

"I wouldn't be surprised if she had," said Merian.

The pause had given her back her breath, or most of it. She returned to her exercises, cursing her weakness but determined to overcome it.

"You're back to it early, lady," he said. "Is it safe for you to do that?"

"I'm not fragile!"

He blinked. She had startled herself; he recovered more quickly than she. "No, lady, you are not fragile. But you're not even two sunsets out of childbed. Should you be pushing yourself so hard?"

"I can rest after all this is over." He frowned at her. She tried to smile—if she remembered how. "Come now, my friend. I'm a mage, and I'm Sun-blood. I'm as strong as I need to be."

"I do hope so, lady," he said.

She lowered the wooden sword and wiped the sweat from her brow. "Batan, will you do something for me?"

"Anything, lady," he said.

"If this goes as I fear it will, look after my daughter. See that she's safe. And when you can, bring her to the Prince in Han-Gilen."

That only slightly surprised him. Word was out, she could see; there were already rumors enough of a redheaded child and the rare gift of the Red Prince's presence. "Not to the princess in Starios?" he asked.

"Take her to the prince," said Merian, "if it's no longer safe here."

"You're riding with the army."

She had been fool enough to hope that he would not come to that conclusion—at least, not until she was safely gone. She should have known better. "Don't tell my mother," she said.

"She probably will come after me, at that," he mused. "How much of an army will I need to defend myself?"

"None," said Merian. "She has a virtue rare in princes: she only blames those who are worthy to be blamed."

"And I won't be, for letting you go?"

"All of that blame is mine," she said. "Will you promise? Take my daughter to the prince; keep silent to the princess until I'm well gone."

"I will promise," he said, "on one condition."

"I will not give you my firstborn," she said swiftly.

He laughed. "Of course you won't. She's already spoken for. A kiss, lady. That's all I ask. Give me a kiss, and I'll be your servant to the death."

That was so preposterous and so utterly presumptuous that she could think of no better response than to give him what he asked for. He was a man of experience; he was thorough, and he much enjoyed the taking of the gift.

She felt nothing. As soon as she courteously could, she withdrew, and resisted the urge to wipe her mouth. He was flushed; it spoke much in his favor that he had not fallen on her in blind passion.

Many men would have deluded themselves with hope, but he looked into her face and saw the truth. His sigh was full of regret, but she sensed no anger in it. "Lady," he said, "whoever has your heart, I envy him with all that's in me. If you aren't the very world to him, then he's the greatest fool there ever was."

She could find no answer for that. What was she to Daros? Did he even remember her? Or had the darkness faded all memory to oblivion?

Batan did not linger long. People were calling him; there was work to do before dark. Merian had her own lengthy tally of duties, but she evaded them for yet a while. This was the last breathing space she would have, maybe, before her mother took the war to the enemy.

Daruya would not ride into the dark world. The regent could not; her place was in the rear, directing the armies. Lords and generals would lead, men Merian knew well enough, and mages of her own order, the strongest and the most skilled. Merian was not expected to have a part in it. She would stand guard over the Ring of Fire, and nurse her child, and let her soldiers and her mages protect her. She was the heart of the empire: the heir to the regent, the empress who would be.

Indeed it was very wise and prudent. Time was when she would have accepted it without a murmur, nor ever dreamed of running off as Daros had, over and over, headlong and heedless and caring only for the whim of the moment. She knew what that had won him: exile and worse, perhaps even his soul's destruction.

She had a sudden, overwhelming need to see her daughter, to hold her, to draw in the sight and scent and feel of her. Elian was asleep when her mother came to her; she roused, but not into the infant's outraged wail. Although her eyes were still newborn blue, Merian fancied she could see the gold-green beneath.

"Please understand," she said, "and if it is in you, forgive—if I don't come back, it was never because I didn't love you. I'm going to find your father and save him, and maybe, if the gods allow, I'll save the world."

Elian did not tax her with the arrogance of that. She was Sun-blood, too; she knew in her bones what they were born for.

Merian sat with her for a long while, marking every moment and sealing it in memory. When she had gone into the dark, this would sustain her. It would, gods willing, give her victory.

THIRTY-FIVE

THE BLACK LAND WAS UNDER SIEGE. NIGHT AFTER NIGHT, RAIDERS BURST OUT of gates, stripped and pillaged, then vanished with their booty. Estarion had strung a cord of magic from Waset to Sakhra, dispersed the magelings along it, and anchored it with the priest Seti-re. It protected the cities and the greater towns, but the villages had only men with spears and arrows to defend them.

With Daros gone, there was no one to make new mages. Estarion tried with the best that he had: the young priest who, with Seti, was as strong as mages could be here. The headache lasted for days. The priest felt nothing whatever, except alarm when Estarion collapsed ignominiously at his feet.

The humiliation passed. The ache of grief did not. He had come to love that maddening and gifted boy as a son, and the boy was gone.

That was the way of the worlds. His task was to defend this one, but it was all too evident that, even with the half-dozen magelings that Daros had left him, he could not do it.

The next dark of the moon after Daros' departure was harrowing. A score of villages were raided, stripped, and abandoned. For a long while after the raiders stormed back through their Gates, the darkness lingered, obscuring the stars.

The sun vanquished it, but it seemed reluctant to submit. Streamers that might have been cloud, but had the depth of darkness, melted away into the morning light.

Estarion had gone up to the roof of the palace to watch the sun rise. Tanit was there when he came. She had his penchant for high places, and a custom of reassuring herself that the sun indeed had risen and the day was come, and for a while the dark was held at bay.

She smiled at his coming and slid in under his arm, resting comfortably against him. Her sigh was weary, but contentment for the moment overrode exhaustion. "A long night," she said.

"And a welcome morning." He bent to kiss the crown of her head. "Tonight you should sleep. The rest of us will stand guard for you."

"When will the rest of you sleep? Do you even remember the last time you saw your bed?"

"Vaguely," he said. "I slept in council yesterday. Was anyone too terribly offended?"

"Most of them were too deep asleep to notice." She looked up into his face. Her eyes were hollowed, her face worn. She was as beautiful as he had ever known her to be. "We can't go on like this. Sometimes I think, if we simply surrender, can slavery be any worse than what we're suffering now?"

"It is worse," Estarion said. "Much worse."

"How so? Slaves have no minds left. They don't even know they're enslaved."

"Their souls do."

She shook her head. "No. No, I shouldn't talk like this. It's the dark; it gets into all of us. Except you. It can't touch the Sun inside you."

"It does try," he said. He ran his finger down her cheek, and coaxed her into a smile. "Are you hungry? I could eat half an ox."

"And I the other half," she said with a flicker of laughter.

They went down hand in hand, to find the nurse waiting with their son and a grand announcement. "Sun!" he declared. "Sun!"

His father met his mother's glance. It was an omen, that word. It was hope where there had been none, and joy where they had all been sinking into despair.

Estarion swept Menes into his arms and spun him about in the splendor of the morning sun; and sang to him the morning hymn to Avaryan that every priest sang at sunrise of his own world. Menes clapped his hands and crowed, and echoed bits of the hymn, the melody perfect, bright and clear as the song of a bird.

Estarion needed that memory for what he had decided to do. He saw to it that Tanit lay down to rest in the cool of her chamber, tended by maids with fans and watched over by a pair of her own guards. He promised solemnly that he too would sleep, once he had attended to an errand.

She refrained from asking him what it was. Her spies would tell her in any case; Estarion would have found them at fault if they had not.

The temple rested in midmorning quiet. The rites of the morning were over; the priests had dispersed to their daily tasks. There were fewer of them than there had been; some had gone to aid in the defense of towns and villages, some had been killed or taken, and a few had gone home to their kin. Those who remained had much to do to keep the temple in order and to perform all the rites as custom prescribed.

The old priest Seti was sweeping a corridor between the shrine of the god and the priests' houses. He looked like a servant, wizened and frail, but his eyes were as bright as ever.

Estarion deftly extracted the broom from his hands and plied it himself. Seti shook his head. "We're two of a kind, aren't we? Do your keepers fret as much as mine do when you dare set your hand to anything ordinary?"

"Probably more," Estarion said, "though never as much as they did when I was a king of kings. In Asanion especially—in the land of the Lion—it was a great horror to them if I so much as set foot on common earth."

"It is difficult," Seti said, "to be a great lord's servant."

They had reached the end of the passage, and the gate that opened on the court of the priests. Estarion bowed Seti through it and followed with the broom in his hand. Withered and bent though he was, Seti moved briskly enough; Estarion did not have to shorten his stride by much to keep pace.

The old priest led him to one of the houses, not his own; this one was deserted. It was clean, but a little sand had sifted across the floor; the bed was a bare frame. There was a pair of stools by the wall, and a fan hanging limp from a cord.

It was not so warm yet that the fan was a necessity. Seti drew the stools into the center of the room, sat on one, and cocked his head at Estarion.

Estarion sat cross-legged on the floor. Stools here were lower than his long limbs liked, and the floor was comfortable enough, spread with a reed mat over the trodden earth.

"Tell me what you're thinking of," Seti said.

Estarion's lips twitched. "Mischief," he said, "of a particularly dreadful kind. Will you aid and abet me?"

"Need you ask?"

Estarion laughed. "You were a hellion when you were a boy. Weren't you?"

"Not at all," said Seti. "I was disgustingly dutiful and frightfully censorious. Thank the gods, I grew out of it. Tell me, then: what are we going to do?"

"I am going to sit here," Estarion said, "and you are going to watch over me. Don't be alarmed by anything I do, unless I stop breathing. If I do that, rouse me at once. If I vanish, go to my queen and stay with her. Bid her strengthen all the defenses that she can; if it's necessary to abandon the villages, then she must do so. Then pray, because nothing else will save this world."

Seti heard him out calmly. "I understand," he said.

That was Seti: no nonsense about him. Estarion drew long steadying breaths, settling more comfortably, drawing his awareness in toward his center. Seti watched in silence. His presence was a focus, an anchor to this world.

He cast his consciousness outward and upward, into the sun. Without Sun-blood he would never have dared such a thing. Even with it, the roaring blaze of heat and light nigh seared his spirit-self to ash. But the dark could not come near it. He spread wings of flame and flew like a falcon through that living furnace.

It buffeted and battered him. It burned the wits out of him. But he had a purpose, and that purpose was woven into the fabric of his being: to find the other—flesh of his flesh, scion of his blood and bone.

The worldwinds blew him hither and yon. The dark groped for him. But the sun shot him like an arrow from the bow, direct to the target.

He opened his eyes on simple mortal light. His sight was blurred, uncertain. He could not seem to focus. His body yielded to his will, but reluctantly; limbs flailed when he would have stretched out his hand, and a sound escaped him that sounded exactly like an infant's cry.

Dear gods. What—how—

A giant loomed above him. These eyes would not come altogether clear, but the ivory oval of face and the riot of hot-gold curls sparked recognition. Her voice was loud and its timbre stranger; he struggled to make sense of the words. "Hush, baby. Hush."

The body only howled the louder. He was as confused as the eyes he wore; only after a long moment did he remember that he did not need a mortal voice to speak.

Merian, he said in his mind. *Merian! Look within.*

She started visibly. "Great-grandfather? Where—"

Here!

Thank the gods, she was not as fuddled as he was. She bent closer, peering; her breath hissed—not in astonishment but in anger. "Get out of there! You madman— she's but a few days old. You'll burn out her mind!"

He would not. The mind he was in was much more elegant and complex a structure than the body it inhabited. Yet for Merian's sake, and out of courtesy to the young mage into whose body his working had cast him, he slipped free of it and stood in more or less his own shape. It wavered; it was transparent. He could not sustain it for as long as if he had had a body to inhabit. He prayed it would be enough.

He looked down at the body that had drawn him to this world, then up at the one who was incontestably her mother. "Great joy to you," he said, "and to this heir of the Sun."

"So there will be," she said sharply, "now that she has slightly more hope of living to inherit. But you didn't know, did you? You were aiming for me."

"Yes," he said. "Would it be possible . . . ?"

He never finished. Her shields had dropped, her power enfolded him. Her body was grown and trained in its magery. It set him in a place of safety, in the outer reaches of awareness. There he could stand as if in the green pasture on the slope of Mount Uveryen, dressed as a shepherd of the north, and she faced him in the mingled grey and violet robes of a mage of Gates.

Her temper had cooled considerably. She embraced him, holding tight for a long moment. He hated to let her go. But time was short.

He took from her, with her consent, the knowledge of the child, her birth and parentage, and all that had happened since he left this world. There was so much of it, so strong and some of it so strange, that he could not absorb it all at once. Yet three things he saw clearly. What Daruya intended, and what Daros had become, and last and least expected, the knowledge that the Red Prince had brought from Han-Gilen.

To take the war into the dark world, that was sense enough in this mad age. Daros . . . His heart mourned, but his head was clear and cold. "That is not well," he said, "for I'd hoped to make use of his presence there. I have a thing in mind, child, but it needs a mage of great power."

"There are over a score of mages there," she said. "Surely one or more of them—"

"Don't be a fool. You know what he is."

"I know what he's been turned into."

"Are you sure of that?" he asked her.

"His own mother saw him. He took her mind by force, and never knew her at all."

"That's grievous," he said, "and in many more ways than one. For what I have in mind, I need mages who can match me, or near enough. One in your world. One in the heart of the dark. And I here, on the other side of the night."

"Why, that's simple," she said. "I'll be the mage in the dark world. My mother will stand here. That's Sun-blood threefold."

"Your mother?" Estarion made no effort to keep the disbelief from his voice. "Even if she would let you do so profoundly irresponsible a thing, what makes you think that she would have anything to do with this?"

"I'll convince her," Merian said.

"How long will it take you? Time is running out, child. We have but days left. Then it will end—one way or another."

"Yes," she said, as intractable as Sun-blood could be. "Tell me what you would do. How mad is it?"

"That depends," he said. "It cost me high to come here, because the dark is so strong between. If we forge a Great Binding, each of us, in the dark and in the light, we may bring light to the dark world. I think, if we do that, we may cleave the darkness itself."

"For that you need Sun-blood," she said: "Sun's fire. Magery alone isn't enough—even as potent as his."

"He knows the dark world," said Estarion, "and the Mage who created it."

"Therefore the darkness is in him," she said.

But your mother—"

"When did you stop trusting her?" Merian asked him. "Or did you ever trust her at all?"

That stung, though he reckoned himself strong enough to keep his temper. "I gave her my empire."

"Certainly," she said: "when you were tired of it and no longer cared who ruled it. I was too young. Who else could it be?"

"Why, did you want it?"

"No!" He had startled the word out of her. She glared at him—if she had known it, exactly like Daruya in her youth. "What are we quarreling for? Do we have that much time to waste?"

"No," he said. "No, we don't. If you can prevail on you mother, then do so. You have until tomorrow's sunset. If it's only the two of us and what power the mages in the dark world can give us, then so be it. I doubt it will be enough, but better any effort than none at all."

"I will persuade her," she said. From the sound of it, her teeth were clenched.

He brushed her forehead with a kiss, startling her. "Fight well," he said, "but don't take too long."

He let go the bonds that held him to this world. It was like falling through infinite space, spinning weightlessly in a night of stars and darkness. The dark opened below and swallowed him.

He opened his eyes. He was still sitting in the priest's house in the temple. Seti watched him with quiet eyes. The angle of the sun had scarcely changed. Yet within, he was profoundly different. He had learned things that harrowed his heart. It would be a long while before the grief passed.

But what he could use, he would. "Seti," he said. "The war ends soon. If we all die, will you forgive my failure?"

"Do gods need forgiveness?"

"Maybe not," said Estarion, "but mages do."

"Then I forgive you," said Seti, "if forgiveness should be necessary."

His words comforted Estarion immoderately. They were also the last thing he heard for some considerable time. He had felt nothing, no weariness, no weakness, until he toppled bonelessly to the floor. He had no strength left, no power to drive back the dark. So much dark. So little light. For every sun, an infinity of night.

THIRTY-SIX

DAROS HAD LOST HIMSELF IN NIGHT. HE RETURNED TO THE DARK WORLD from the raid in such a state that only the force of habit kept him from dropping every shield and betraying himself. He had done a thing that was as sternly forbidden as the heedless passage of Gates: he had forced a mage's mind. And that mage, by the humor of the dark gods, had proved to be his mother.

He was doomed, he had known that already. He had hoped against hope that he was not damned. Now that hope was gone. He had become what he feigned to be: a slave to the lords of the dark.

After his return from his own lost world, as the sun of this place rose beyond its shields of darkness, he escaped from the lords' tower and went hunting mages. He would not so endanger them as to enter their hiding place, but he sent out a lure, a thread of magic. The one whom it had caught took his time in coming, but after some while, Daros heard his step and saw the blood-red glow that was his body.

Daros drew his hood down over his eyes. When Perel came round the corner in the deserted passage, even to mage-sight Daros would be no more than a shape of shadow.

The Olenyas understood veils and robes. His curiosity had a sting to it, but Daros resisted the temptation to fling off his hood. Perel would learn the truth soon enough. Now, still, he trusted Daros. Daros needed that—the worlds needed it.

"It's done," he said to Perel. "I've sent the message to your lady. Pray your thousand gods that she believes it, and acts on it."

"She will," Perel said. Then after a pause: "My lord, are you well?"

"Well enough," said Daros. "It doesn't matter. You—are you strong? Are you succeeding?"

Perel nodded. "The binding on the slaves is a remarkably simple thing, stamped like a sack of coins from the same mint. Once we free one, the rest of the slaves bound with that one begin to work their way free as well. It's rather wonderful. One working, one man roused to awareness of what was done to him, and twenty more rise up beside him."

"There's no murmur of it above," Daros said. "No one there knows of it."

"Everyone below is sworn to silence," said Perel. "When the time comes, the signal will go out; the slaves will rise. All over this world, they'll raise the revolt."

Daros took a dark pleasure in the news. "Good," he said. "Splendid. The gods must be with us. Who knew that so many people could be so adept at pretending to be enslaved?"

"Well," said Perel with a touch of discomfort. "There is a small binding within the oath, to hold their tongues for them until they're all set free."

Daros' lips stretched in a mirthless smile. "Ah well," he said. "What's virtue in a war such as this? We're none of us innocent, in the end. Only let us win back the light; then we'll remember the laws again."

"My lord," Perel said, drawing closer, peering into the darkness of the hood. "What is it? Have they harmed you?"

Daros wanted to laugh like a mad thing, but he had a little sense left. "They've done nothing that I can't undo." And now he was lying to a friend as he had lied to the dark lords.

It was in a good cause. He lightened his voice as much as he could and said, "I've breathed the air of home again. It's made me remember why I fight."

"Ah," said Perel. "It's been years for you. Why did you even come back?"

"I had to," Daros said.

Footsteps sounded; voices. Daros would not have said that he fled, but he retreated quickly, in what order he could. Maybe Perel tried to call him back; maybe not. He was long gone before the Olenyas might have found words to say.

The mages were safe. The war was proceeding apace. Daros returned to his prison, walking slowly once he had escaped the mage's too-clear perception. His wards were armed; he had not far to go before he walked where slaves of his kind were permitted to walk. His hunger for light was approaching desperation—even knowing that the touch of it would burn out his eyes.

There was no light left inside him. He could remember stars, but when he sought the sun, there was only pain. His fingers clawed, itching to tear out the eyes that had been forced upon him. With an effort that wrenched a gasp from him, he knotted them together within the sleeves of his robe.

They were waiting by the stair that led upward to the lords' tower. The wards that he had set were undisturbed. They had not crossed the line; they stood just behind it: a dozen warrior slaves and the king himself. A priest stood behind the king as if to use him for a shield.

Daros halted. Another dozen men closed in behind. He had not sensed them at all. To magery they were still invisible, warded in a way that he had not seen before.

The priest advanced warily from his hiding place. He had a thing of metal in his hands, round like a ball, made of wire and glass. It looked very like the thing that the king guarded in his tower. Something stirred inside it, something that Daros' eye did not want to fix upon.

The priest trembled as he drew nearer. The warrior slaves closed in behind Daros, barring his retreat. The thing in the priest's hand whirred and hummed. Then, to the priest's manifest astonishment, it began to spin, throwing off sparks of dark light. Completely without conscious will, Daros struck it with a slap of power. It burst asunder.

The priest shrieked and collapsed. But the king was smiling. There was nothing reassuring whatsoever in that curve of thin lips in the black beard. He cocked his head at the warrior slaves who surrounded Daros—none of them from his own barracks; these were all strangers. They got a grip on him; something slipped over his head from behind and snapped tight.

He could breathe, just. It felt like steel cord digging into his windpipe. But worse was the constraint upon his magery. Breath was mere fleshly necessity. Magery was the essence of what he was.

The king's smile widened. He turned and began to climb the stair.

Daros stood alone in a bare cell of a room. They had stripped him of everything but the cord about his neck. Estarion's knife, the Mage's feather, Seti-re's stone—gone. All gone. His arms were drawn up over his head and bound by a rope to a ring in the ceiling. His feet touched the cold stone floor, just.

Warrior slaves had hung him like a newly slaughtered ox and withdrawn.

Without magic to warm him, the chill of this sunless place was sinking into his bones. His feet and hands were numb. It would be a great irony if, having survived all this while in the dark world, he died of simple cold.

He had nowhere to go but inside himself. That was not the most pleasant of places, but it was better than the world without. There was light in it after all: sunlight caught in the gold of Merian's hair. She never had been able to tame it; even when she was most severe and queenly, curls of it persisted in escaping any bonds she set on them. He loved to tangle his fingers in it, covering her face with kisses, until she laughed and protested, then retaliated in kind.

In this dream or memory, she was not laughing. She sat in a circle of mages and hard-bitten personages who could only be warriors and generals. Somewhat incongruously, she cradled an infant in her arms. The child was too young to look like anything in particular, but there was no mistaking the color of its hair.

The council was settling the affairs of a great war: matters of armies and weapons, attack and invasion. The child was asleep with its fist in its mouth. He could not focus on the war; his eyes and mind kept returning to those tiny and perfect fingers, and those copper-bright curls.

What he felt, he did not know. Joy. Incredulity. Wistfulness: that such a thing could not be in any world but that of dream.

Something was nagging at him. After a long and reluctant while, he gave it a name: pain. A mailed fist was striking him again and again, with beautifully calculated precision. It broke nothing, but it hurt a very great deal.

He opened eyes on a world altogether alien to that of sunlight and a child's face. Red and black: blood and darkness. One of the lords had the honor of striking him even after he had groaned and come to himself. The king watched, arms folded, dispassionate. After a stretching while, he said, "Enough."

The lord lowered his arm. He was breathing quickly; he flexed the arm as if he were glad of the respite.

The king looked Daros up and down, then walked in a circle, examining him fore and aft. His finger brushed points of particular pain: elbows, knees, back and buttocks, ribs. Daros' breath hissed between his teeth. Perhaps in spite of the lord's care, one rib was cracked.

Last of all, the king laid a hand on his genitals. He held them lightly as they did their best to crawl into Daros' belly. One twist of the fingers would crush them.

With what might have been regret, the king's hand withdrew. "It seems human," he said to the priest who had been hiding behind him. "Can you be sure it has what we need?"

"As sure as I can be, lord," the priest said.

"It seems perfectly powerless now."

"It is bound, lord," said the priest. "Its humanity serves our purpose well: it requires fewer strictures than the other."

"It will be docile? It will serve our purpose?"

"It is bound," the priest said again.

"Do bear in mind," the king said rather too gently, "where we found it, and what it had risen to before we understood that our devices were going mad because of something among the slaves, not some rebellion from the thing in its prison. This slave should have been bound beyond resistance; and yet it was spying in passages forbidden to it."

"This binding will hold," the priest said.

Daros had had enough. "I am not an it," he said. "I am human—at least as human as you. Will you do me the courtesy of killing me quickly, and get it over?"

He more than half expected to be ignored, but the king turned those lightless eyes on him and raised a brow. "But," he said, "we have no intention of killing you. Not at all. You are much more useful alive than dead."

"As what? A hostage? You know or even care who I am?"

"Who," said the king, "no. What you are—yes, that matters. Your kind are an offense before the gods. But my priests assure me that you are more than the usual run of magical vermin. A great deal more, they insist. So much more that we can make actual use of you."

Daros had begun to see where this was leading. "No," he said. "Oh, no. You can't make me—"

"It is fortunate that intelligence is not a requirement of this captivity," the king said. "Only power. And power you have, power like a sun. Light casts shadow, the ancients teach us. The greater the light, the deeper the shadow. Your light will feed our darkness. Your power will make us strong."

"No," said Daros. Desperately he beat against the binding that held his magery. To kill with power was forbidden—not only because it was murder, but because it killed the power itself. Estarion had done it. It had driven him mad.

In the end he had gained back both his magic and his sanity: he was Sun-blood, after all. Daros was mortal. If he killed with power, he killed that power. Then the lords would destroy his body, and it would be over, done with. He would be gone. The Mage would die. And—

Agony rent him to his center. He hung gagging, retching, no strength in him to curl about the focus of the pain.

They had not gutted him, nor gelded him, either, though he could almost wish they had. The lord with the iron fist lowered it and stepped back. Very slowly the agony faded.

"I am not to be ignored," the king said mildly. And to the lord: "Cut him down."

The lord looked as if he might protest, but he did as he was bidden. Daros dropped bonelessly to the floor. His hands, his neck, his power were still bound. He lay on his face, trying not to count the number of his hurts. His magic hammered still against the bindings. Were they a little weaker?

A foot hooked beneath him and flung him onto his back. The king stood over him. "If you submit," he said, "and consent to serve us, your servitude will be much lighter and your lot less difficult. But whether you will or no, you will be the most potent of all our slaves."

Daros bit his tongue until it bled. He could cry like a child; he could beg for mercy. He could be defiant or rebellious. It would not matter. There was no escape from this but death.

He lay limp, as if he had been defeated. Warrior slaves heaved him up. He was glad to require three of them; his dead weight was considerable. He only regretted that neither the lord nor the king could be troubled to assist their servants.

They grunted as they hauled him out of the cell and up a narrow stair. They were not above dragging him, catching bruises on every step, until they had come to the top of the tower. A door slid open. Priests waited beyond, and a structure such as Daros had seen before; but those had been small enough to hold in the hand. This was nigh as broad as the room, and as high as a tall man. Set in it was the device that the king had guarded, or its near twin.

They caged him in it. It closed upon him, encasing him like armor, holding him immobile. No fortress between the worlds, this; no prison for an inhuman Mage. He would endure his slavery within this world.

The bond about his neck had let go when the cage enclosed him. It made no difference. Each cold metal band ate a little more of his will, sapped a little more of his strength to resist. It opened him to the whirring, humming thing set in the cage, and tempted his power; it lured it out, into the trap.

So had they captured the Mage long ages ago, and bound him to their will. For all Daros' struggle to shut down his mind and suppress his power, he could not stop the trickle through the cracks in his shields.

This was the thrice ninth hell of the Asanian priests. As before when he was simply taken prisoner, he had no useful choice but to retreat into his own mind. It was a capacious place, crackling with lightnings, most of them dark.

The Mage waited in one of the deep halls. It wore a semblance of life and vigor, but its voice was faint, its shape not quite substantial.

"You," Daros said with no love at all. "You did this."

"The fault is mine," the Mage said, "but this was not my will."

"They know what I am. Who else could have told them?"

"You," said the Mage. "You told them. Your presence in their tower, your hunting and spying—their machines saw you. Be glad, youngling. If the roar of your magic had not overwhelmed the piping and twittering of theirs, your little mages would have been betrayed."

"Would it have made a difference?" said Daros bitterly. "I'm trapped now as you were. Are. Will be—but not for much longer, no? Now that you have a successor."

"Not much longer, no," the Mage said. "Youngling, listen. The gift I gave you, the feather of my wing—"

"Gone," Daros said. "They took it with the rest."

"No," said the Mage.

It gestured with its chin. Daros looked down. The feather hung as it had for so long, secure on its cord. He closed his hand about it. It felt real—as it would; he was dreaming.

"No dream," the Mage said. "Use the gift. Build with it."

It had been speaking sensibly until then—human sense. For that, Daros had doubted that it was real. But this strange twist of thought, that was indeed the Mage. Did it seem a little more substantial?

"Build," said the Mage. "Hold and guard. Then later, fight."

It melted to mist before Daros could demand that it explain. He could not call it back, even in memory. But its feather remained, solid and real in his hand.

For lack of greater inspiration, he slipped it from its cord and wielded it like a pen. When he drew it through the air, it left behind a glimmering line. He shaped the letters of his name, a little stiffly for it had been a long while since he held a pen. They hung before him, gleaming. With swift strokes he drew walls about it and surmounted them with towers. Then he drew a gate, but locked and barred it.

He paused. He was breathing hard as if he had lifted each stone of a living wall and set it upon another. Yet he moved more freely. The trickle of magic through the wards had stopped.

The Mage's voice whispered through the feather in his hand. "Build strength, youngling. Build resistance. Hold fast."

He fancied that he could hear sadness in that voice, a touch of wistfulness. It had never had that strength, even as great as its power was. Once trapped, it had had no power to free itself, nor to refuse the use that was made of it. It had lacked even the courage to seek the death that would free it.

Daros had little that the Mage had not given him. It had served him poorly enough. He was as trapped as the Mage had ever been. His magery was protected, yes, but for how long? The dark lords needed it. They would find a way to take it. That was inevitable.

Or he could die. He had thought that he was ready. Yet, enclosed within his wards, he could not find the determination to do the necessary. The mages might succeed; the war might end. Even the darkness—it might yield to light.

Not if the dark lords had his power, enslaved, to do with as they would. He must die. He must not give them even the hope of turning him against all that lived and walked in the light.

THIRTY-SEVEN

NOW. IT MUST BE NOW.

Merian started awake. She had snatched a few moments' rest between the long day's preparations and the night's incessant attacks; but it had not been overly restful. Her dreams were dark, full of madness and pain. And then, sudden and piercingly clear, came that voice like a hawk's cry.

You must move now. There is no time to waste!

It was two days still to the muster. They were nearly ready, but she had yet to speak to her mother of Estarion's message. It was not cowardice, she told herself. The less time she gave Daruya to ponder objections, the easier it might be to win her over.

But the urgency in that voice, the desperation beneath, set her heart to pounding. She knew the voice. It was the Mage, the creature whose power the dark lords had enslaved. She reached to the place where it had been, hoping to catch it, hold it, learn more of it, but it was gone.

Quickly, before she lost courage, she touched her mother's mind, away in Starios. She had good hope of finding Daruya too preoccupied to trouble with her, but Daruya happened to be resting as well. She basked in the sun as all of their blood were wont to do, in the innermost of her chambers, where even her husband must ask leave to enter.

She admitted Merian to her mind with remarkably little testiness. "Trouble?" she asked.

"Maybe," Merian said. "I had a sending. The dark ones' Mage—it summoned us all. Now, it said. We must attack now."

"Did it?" Daruya frowned. "How could it know what we intend?"

"The mages know," Merian said. "It is a mage. Maybe—"

"Maybe we've been betrayed."

Merian's heart constricted. "No. He would never—"

"Is the Mage a he?" Daruya inquired.

"Mother," said Merian, scrambling her wits together. "This is a true sending. Whatever the cause, I believe we should obey it. All is ready, or as ready as it can be. And there is something . . . "

When Merian did not immediately go on, Daruya raised a brow. "Something that rives you with guilt?"

"Something that you may find objectionable, but it comes from the emperor."

"The emperor is lost on the other side of the dark."

"He found his way to me," Merian said: "in strict truth, to Elian; he was hunting the youngest heir of the line. He has a plan that may scatter the darkness."

"A plan," said Daruya, "that you think I may not like."

"I know you will not," Merian said. "It requires one of us in this world, and one of us in his—and one between, in the dark world."

There was a pause. Daruya's understanding was swift. "He was going to rely on the Gileni. Yes?"

"The Gileni is lost," Merian said, though the words knotted her belly with grief, "and in any case it should be Sun-blood. We were born in and of the light; the light is alive in us. It fills us. Who better to break this thing that shatters worlds?"

"Who better to rescue the father of your child?"

"That supposes that he needs rescuing," Merian said with a hint of sharpness. "Mother, we need you to hold this world as he holds the other. I'm the youngest, the mage of Gates. My place is in the dark world."

"Your place is here, as my heir."

"There is a newer heir," Merian said. "If I don't come back, I trust you to see that she lives to inherit."

"You're sending her to me after all?"

"No," said Merian. "She's going to Han-Gilen. But—"

Daruya rose. Merian braced for the blast, but her mind-voice was soft and dangerously mild. "You would send my granddaughter there, and not to me?"

"Elian is the prince's granddaughter, too. And," said Merian, "he, unlike you, is not in the vanguard of the war. He can keep her safe until all of it is over—for good or for ill."

Daruya liked that little, but she had ruled an empire long enough to recognize sense when she heard it. "Were you planning to tell me any of this?"

"I'm telling you now."

"Yes—and telling me to mount the attack without delay. What were you afraid of, that if I had time to think about it, I'd find a way to stop you?"

"Something of the sort," Merian admitted. "But, Mother, there really isn't—"

"I see no other way," said Daruya. The taste of the words must have been bitter. "Tell me what the emperor would have us do."

Merian was almost too startled to reply. "Swear you won't stop me before I pass the Gate."

"I will not stop you," Daruya said. "I will hate every moment that you are gone, and dread every outcome until you come back. But when have I ever stopped you from doing as you pleased?"

That, for her, was tenderness. It tightened Merian's throat. "I will come back. We will win this war."

"You do that," said Daruya.

"You will call the muster tonight?"

"Today," said Daruya.

"Then you trust—"

"I trust you. Now go, or we leave you behind."

Merian went. Even as she retreated into her own body again, the call thrummed through her. It was the Great Summons, that she had not heard in all her years: calling every mage of this world to the muster. Mages passed the summons to mortal lords and commanders. The armies of the Sun began to move.

Almost without willing it, Merian sent the summons winging outward through the darkness, toward Estarion on the far side of the night. She did not know whether it came to him; she could only hope.

Men were stirring in the fortress. Half would stay to guard it; half would go. So too with the mages who had come to her here. Some must ward the world, but some would take the war to the enemy.

She would go in armor, and armed. Her greatest weapon was her magery, but she would fight if she must. Her mail was shimmering steel, the surcoat over it the violet and grey of her order. Gold shimmered through it; Sun-brooches clasped the shoulders. It was rather too splendid for her taste, but the army needed to see that Sun-blood marched with it. It was a price she paid for the rank she had been born to.

Elian's nurse was ready, in a guard of strong mages. She surrendered the child into Merian's arms, for a little while. Merian clasped her close to breasts that still ached in their bindings, and breathed the sweet infant scent of her. It was more than difficult to relinquish her into Jadis' care again, to open the lesser Gate, to send them to the prince in Han-Gilen. When they were gone, Merian's heart was as empty as her womb.

She straightened with an effort, and steeled herself. She would come back; she made it a vow, sworn on the searing pain in her hand. She pressed that hand to her heart. "May the gods witness it," she said.

The sun was still high as the last of the armies gathered and waited. Mages linked mind to mind across the face of the world. Merian gathered their power together within the Ring of Fire, in the heart of Ki-Oran. She forged of it a key, and set it to the Gate within her.

Darkness resisted, surging against the Gate like a tide. She set all their con-joined strength against it, to break its power, to open the Gate.

It was too strong. Without the Heart of the World to bolster the rest, all the mages, even with Merian, were not enough. If she had been Estarion—or Daros—

Despair was the darkness' weapon. She countered it with the Sun within her. It shrank away—then roared back like a wave of the sea.

Just before it would have drowned her, it broke. It frayed and shredded and melted into mist. Astonishment froze her in the last act of defense.

Now! cried the Mage's voice. Desperation sharpened it, and yet it sounded faint and growing fainter. *Go now!*

There was no time to waste. Before the dark could come back like the swing of the tide, she thrust open the Gate. The armies of the Sun poured into the dark world.

Estarion sat bolt upright in the queen's council. Her chamberlain told the tally of cattle and fodder, barley and storehouses. Those were vital matters, matters of the people's survival, but they were deadly dull; and the news was all bad. The enemy was stripping them bare.

The Great Summons rang in Estarion's skull. It was so strong, so compelling, that it was all he could do not to leap to his feet and run to a muster on the other side of the sky. Even some of those in the council sensed it, however dimly. Tanit sat as stiff as he, eyes wide, staring into the blank and singing air.

He rose. "It's time," he said.

Lord Bes droned on, but the rest welcomed the distraction. The more warlike rose to face him. He addressed them through the buzz of the chamberlain's voice. "The battle has come. Arm and prepare your men. Tonight, we fight."

Some of them were pale, some flushed with excitement. They were all firm in their courage. They were not a warrior people, but they had learned to fight. Daros had taught them. His legacy in this world, Estarion thought fleetingly. There was no time for sentiment.

He bowed over Tanit's hand and kissed it. It was steady, strong. Only a mage would know how hard her heart was beating. "One stroke," she said to him. "One hard blow. That's all we have in us. Guide it well, my lord."

He should go, but he lingered. He had every intention of surviving this as he had so much else, and yet he could not leave before he had impressed in memory every line of her face. He ran his finger down her cheek, and kissed her softly on the lips. "Until morning," he said.

"Until morning," said Tanit.

The defenses of the city and the string of cities from Waset to Sakhra were as strong as mages and cats, priests and warriors, could make them. Estarion tightened the weaving of the wards and saw that the mortal guards were armed and ready. When that was done, and the land of the river was as well protected as it could be, he turned his steps toward the temple of the sun-god.

Seti was waiting for him. The old priest had summoned a handful of priests whom he trusted, and instructed them in their duties. They had prepared the room for him in the house in which he had met Seti before. The bed was moved to the center and hung with clean linen. Lamps stood at head and foot, ready to be lit when the night came.

There was a light meal waiting, as Estarion had requested: bread, cheese, clean water. He ate and drank carefully. Fasting was no part of this: he needed to be strong. When he had had his fill, he suffered the priests to surround him with their chants and incense. It did nothing for his magic, but it consoled them greatly. It comforted him, too, in its way. He had left his priesthood with his empire, laid it all aside to become a shepherd in the Fells. Yet when all was done and said, he was still what he had been born to be: mage, priest, lord, and king.

As the last chant died away, he lay on the bed, which had been made long enough for him. Seti sat in a chair beside him. The others divided: half to retreat to the inner room, to rest; half to take station about him. They would guard him while he journeyed to the heart of his magic.

He settled as comfortably as he might, and steadied himself with long, deep breaths. Each brought him closer to his center, drew him deeper into his power. He was aware of the priests watching over him, of Seti's blind eyes that saw clearly to the soul. The world beyond them, the people, the river flowing forever to the sea, all that had become a part of him since he fell through the Gate, wrapped him about and made him strong. Strongest of all was the queen in her hall of audience, and their son in his nursery, playing contentedly in a patch of sunlight. He gurgled at the touch of his father's mind, and laughed, teasing it with flickers and flashes of power.

Strong young mage. The joy of that rode with him into the heart of this world, and so outward through the memory of Gates. He bore with him the light and power of the sun, and the splendor of stars, and the cold glory of the moon that ruled the night in this world.

The dark had retreated somewhat. It had not faded or died; it hung like a wave about to break. But some strong blow had weakened it.

He sought the Mage in its prison, passing swiftly through the paths of the night. He found the chamber, the many Gates pulsing uncontrolled, and the long strange shape limp and lifeless in its bonds. It was not dead, not quite, but its power had broken, and all the structures of its making had collapsed. The dark world swirled with confusion. Slaves rose up; lords who had never dreamed of such a thing were fighting for their lives.

The Mage's power mustered one last feeble flicker. It touched Estarion's and held, gripping like a soft hand. *Time is short. Be swift. He cannot fight forever.*

"He?"

The Mage slipped free. *Swift,* it said. *Be swift.*

The last of it was no word at all, but a vision as the Mage sank down into death: a shape of shadow caged in steel. Another mage. Another captive. Fighting—resisting.

Estarion did not want to set a face to that shadow. Yet there was no escaping it. No other mage anywhere had that particular strength, that core of bright recklessness.

His long cry of grief and rage echoed through the worlds. Did Daros hear it?

There was no telling. He was bound beyond escaping: from without by the dark lords, and from within by the bitter battle to destroy his magic before the dark lords seized it.

There was no time for mourning. Estarion must find the sun in the dark world, and through it bind the sun on the world in which he was born. Threefold power, threefold strength. Sun-blood to Sun-blood.

Merian passed the Gate into the dark world. In the same instant, his power leaped through her to Daruya in the world of his birth. It was remarkably like the skein of mages along the river: each one reaching to the next, and binding all the rest together. They wove and bound and locked. Without pausing to ask leave, he made himself their master. This binding was his. He ruled it as he had ruled empires, with no more effort than it took to draw breath.

THIRTY-EIGHT

MERIAN PASSED THROUGH THE GATE INTO THE DARK WORLD. ARMIES crossed with her, armed with light. They brought a dawn that this world had not seen in ages beyond reckoning.

Battle raged on the barren plains, in the fortresses and the slave-cities, and across the beds of the dry seas. Slaves had risen against their masters. Mages urged them on. For weapons they had whatever they could find: stolen knives and spears, miners' picks, cooks' knives, even bricks and stones. Anything that could be lifted to strike or hurl, they had. And if that failed, they had their teeth and fists and feet, the power of their bodies, and the sheer weight of numbers.

Merian's forces came through the Gate in the heart of that world, before the king's citadel. The battle was fiercest here, the dark lords most numerous, and not all their slaves had joined the revolt. The warrior slaves fought, many of them, for their lords. Their weapons were strong and their anger terrible. They blasted the lesser slaves with dark fire, mowing them down like grain.

Light alone was not enough against those. Too many wore helms without eyes, shielding them from the searing pain. Freed slaves, who had no such protection, burned and died, but those whom they fought, fought on unharmed.

Merian was aware of Estarion within her, his grip on her power, his enslavement of its will. But she had expected it; she knew him, and she had had the same thought.

She had divided herself; her power held its own deep realm, but her body's will kept its freedom. She led the assault on the citadel, mounted on a senel that, being blind, had no fear of the dark.

But she had not come to command these armies. The chief of the Olenyai had that honor here, and at his back the commander of the imperial armies—great lords and generals both, and far better versed than she in the arts of war. Her art was another altogether. She had come for that. The rest, little as the armies might have liked to know it, was diversion.

As the rams rolled through the Gate, driving toward the gate of the citadel, she took a handful of mages and went in search of the postern that Daros' message had promised. She damped the light about them, dimming it to nothing, calling up mage-sight to make her way through the dark. Glimmers of light from the battle cast a fitful glow on the sky, and limned in deeper shadow the curves and corners of the walls.

There was war in heaven. The darkness overhead roiled and surged. The earth rumbled underfoot. The fabric of creation had begun to fray.

Merian thrust down fear. Her companions had enough of their own; she must have courage for all of them. She pressed to the fore. The wall of the citadel stretched endless before her. It was wrought without mortar, stone fitted to stone with no gap between. There seemed to be no gate, either, but that which the armies beset, now far behind her.

The way grew impossibly steep. They had to leave the seneldi; even afoot, they struggled on sheer slopes. Merian began to despair. If there was no way in but the one gate, even an assault of magery might not win them through soon enough. The dark was not yielding to the threefold attack upon it. Something, some force, had risen against them.

She must come to the heart of the citadel. The heart of it all was there—and hope, if any at all was to be had.

She halted on the narrow track, turning to face the rest, taking their measure one by one. If any could not bear the force of dark and fear, she would send him back now.

They were all strong, all firm in resolve. Strongest and firmest of all was one who hung back, almost invisible even to mage-sight. Even as Merian's eye fell on her, she raised power to blur it. Merian struck aside the working with a fierce slap of temper. "My lady!"

The Lady Varani sighed, perhaps in relief, perhaps in resignation, and lowered the hood that had concealed her face. "Lady," she said coolly.

"I never summoned you here," Merian said through set teeth, "nor would I have allowed it if you had asked. What possessed you to—"

"My son is here," Varani said. "Is there time to debate this, lady? If my ears tell me true, the enemy is holding all too well against your armies. His walls are strong and something else rises within. Something that—I fear—"

Merian would not let her go on. "Go back. Now. Urziad, look after her. Don't let her—"

"With all due respect," Varani said, "you need me here. There is a gate ahead. It's well hidden, but I can sense it: there's the dying glimmer of a beacon on it. Let Urziad and the rest go, if you must, but let me lead you. This art is mine, to find what I look for. Would you lose it out of folly?"

"Out of policy," said Merian. "Your rank forbids—"

"As yours does?"

"Lady," Kalyi said before Merian could erupt, "time's passing. The enemy is not growing weaker. If we have to fight our way in, we'd best do it quickly, or we lose all element of surprise."

If indeed there had ever been any, Merian thought grimly. "Very well," she said. "But if your death incites a civil war in the empire, I refuse to accept the blame."

"My lord will cast no blame on you," Varani said. "That will be entirely mine."

"I do hope so," said Merian.

Varani had the grace not to be excessively satisfied with herself. She turned and led the way, surefooted in the dark, on that sheer track. The others, none mountain-born as she was, followed more cautiously. Merian elected to take the rear. Her heart was full of doubt: dangerous in a mage at war, deadly in a commander. If she had erred in giving the lead to Varani, she would lose it all, war and world both.

The postern was indeed well hidden. Merian would have passed it by. But Varani halted, questing like a hound after a scent, and ran her hand along the bend of the wall. It yielded with a sound like a sigh, sank inward and froze.

"Your key," Varani said to Merian. "Here."

"What—"

"You have that which opens all doors. Will you use it?"

A riddle. Merian's wits were thick and slow. Her power was not her own; nor, it seemed, was much of her intelligence. Much too sluggishly, she remembered the thing that burned incessantly in her hand. She set the *Kasar* to the door. The flare of white heat left her blind, dizzy, and stunned.

The door slid open. The passage within was black dark. Kalyi kindled a spark of magelight, a dim blue glow to light their feet. Sparks echoed it, a track laid by mages: vast relief to them all, and a glimmer of hope. Perel and his mages had prepared the way for them.

Varani led. The others were there to shield and ward, and to keep watch for the enemy. Merian had nothing to do but follow and keep silent, and try not to stumble.

This she had not foreseen. Nor the length of the hunt, the darkness, the weight of lightless stone. The diversion had succeeded: these passages were deserted, their defenders drawn off toward the beleaguered gate.

Urziad went in search of the mages, if any were left here; most or all of them would be abroad, leading slaves against their masters. Varani was still on the scent, following the track upward and inward. Merian knew where she must be going. The compulsion of it reached even through her own fogs and confusions.

Estarion was weakening. Daruya, with the Sun's power to draw on, had risen to match him. Merian, trapped in the dark, was no more than a link in the chain, without strength or volition of her own.

She must break free; must find her will, wield her power. Two alone could not fight this fight. She was the center, the key. This heaviness of spirit, this darkness within her, was the enemy—far more so than men fighting men under the starless sky.

One mage remained in the citadel after all, waiting for them. It was a darkmage, hardly more than a child, but strong in her power. The track ended in the passage in which she waited, up against a long stair. There was a strange scent in that place, somewhat like thunder and somewhat like blood. It raised Merian's hackles.

The others seemed not to notice it. The darkmage, whose name was Gaiya, greeted them with rigid composure and a spark of gladness that she could not quite conceal. She spoke in a whisper. "They have the prince," she said. "They caught him here. The Mage is dead; they've bound the prince and will compel him to work their magics for them, unless he dies first. We didn't know until we'd scattered to wage the war. If our mages should have come back and tried to free him—"

"No," Merian said. "The war needs them more. Can you guide us to him?"

"He's in the lords' tower. That's warded. We haven't been able to break the wards, and he forbade us to force them. Then he was taken, and there was the war, and—"

As strong as she was determined to be, she was near tears. This had been a cruel duty. That none of the mages had broken was a tribute to their strength and the clarity of their power.

"Go to Perel," Merian said, "and serve him as you may. We'll find our way upward."

"But—" said Gaiya.

"Go," said Merian. "Give him this message for me: 'Fight until it all ends, or until I myself bid you stop.'"

"Until it ends," Gaiya repeated, "or you command it to end."

"Yes," Merian said. And for the third time. "Go."

The child fled with relief that almost cleansed the air of the memory that haunted it. The others would have been glad to follow, but they had a war to fight.

Merian had some of her wits back. It was Varani now who seemed fuddled, who stood slack with despair. "If they have him," she said, "there is no hope for any of us."

"He'll die before he surrenders," Merian said.

No one gave voice to doubt, which was a kindness. Time was running out; but now she had a focus, and knowledge. "Upward," she said. "Those who would come, come. The rest of you, go where Gaiya went. I'll have no deadweight in this."

They all stood watching her. None retreated. She nodded briskly and began to ascend the stair.

There had been wards. They left a memory behind, like the scent of blood and terror below. The Mage's death had broken them. They would rise again if Daros surrendered his will to his captors.

Merian's heart was keening, nor would it desist for any will she set on it. Yet her mind was very clear. She had left confusion down below. The mortal war, the war in heaven, had shrunk to insignificance. It was all coming to this single point, this stair, this tower and its captive.

Varani walked close behind her. The others trailed somewhat, weaving wards as they went. Kaliya, in the rear, climbed with drawn sword.

Merian's weapons remained in their sheaths. This fight would have little to do with steel. The quiet grated on her nerves. No sound of fighting came through the walls. Her legs ached. Her breasts ached. She was weary to the bone.

They were near the top of the stair. Varani's hand gripped her shoulder. She halted. After a moment she heard it: a sound below the threshold of mortal hearing, like the pounding of waves on a distant shore.

Wards, beleaguered by a force such as she had not seen before. It had nothing in it of living spirit. It made her think, somehow, of the automatons that craftsmen made in the Nine Cities to amuse the Syndics' children. Metal and glass; power without soul. Magic trapped and twisted to mortal will.

That was the secret—the key. Stripped of magery, the dark mages of Anshan had found another way. It was darker than dark magic, and cruel beyond conceiving.

If she had harbored any faintest glimmer of pity for those mages so long bereft of their power, it vanished in that moment of understanding. She broke the door at the top of the stair, and blasted the guards beyond it with the Sun's fire.

They went up like torches. Even in her rage, she was taken aback. Altogether without intending it, she had taken all that was in her, Sun-power threefold, and wielded it as if it had been hers to command. Estarion's startlement, her mother's shock, sparked in her awareness.

The light of the working lingered, plain light of day in any mortal world, but unbearably, searingly brilliant here. Those defenders who had not fallen to the blast of fire were felled by the light. They lay writhing, screaming soundlessly. She stepped over them. Behind her, Kaliya did the merciful thing: a swift stroke of the blade to each throat.

Merian was beyond mercy. She followed the path of fallen defenders. The end of it was a door, and a barren room, and a cage of metal about a shape of shadow.

The defenders there wore shielded helms and carried the weapons that spat dark fire. She left them to Kaliya and the other mages. Estarion was broad awake inside her, and Daruya in a rage that nearly matched her own. They confronted the last of the defenders, the tall man who stood in front of the cage. Royal blood knew royal blood.

The dark king had shielded his eyes with a band of metal and black glass. In his pale face with its black beard, Merian saw a distant echo of Batan and his people, the warrior folk of Anshan.

He had no power to see what she was, and perhaps no spirit for it, either. He had courage; that, she could not doubt. His men fell before they could even lift their weapons, but he neither wavered nor flinched. "Whatever becomes of us," he said, "the dark will rule."

"That might be true," she said, "or it might not. Either way, you will be dead. You were condemned long ages ago for crimes beyond the reach of mercy. Your crimes have only grown worse since you fled that sentence. If there could ever have been hope of appeal, that is altogether gone."

"Indeed?" said the dark king. "And who are you to stand in judgment?"

"I am everything you ever feared or fought against. I am the destroyer of darkness, the bringer of light. The Sun begot me. The light reared me. I rule in the Sun's name."

He flung back his head and laughed. "Brave little maidchild! When ours are so puny, we drown them. How were you let live? Pity? Scorn? Weakness of spirit?"

"Only the weak resort to mockery." She raised her hand. The Sun in it roared and flamed.

Just as she gathered power to blast him, a shadow darted past her toward the shape in the cage. The bolt of light flew wide. The king sprang. Merian stumbled aside, warrior skills forgotten, fixed on Varani, who had flung herself at the cage, and at the thing that whirred and spun on top of it.

The king howled and leaped toward Varani. Merian clutched wildly at his arm and spun him about. He slashed at her with a steel claw.

Merian's arm and side burned. She snatched her sword from its sheath, stabbing with all the strength she had. The blade struck armor, turned, and snapped. The king spat in contempt. She slashed her second blade, the long sharp dagger, across his throat. The hot spray of blood spattered her face and drenched her armor.

She gagged in disgust, but she had already forgotten him. Varani tore at the cage with bleeding fingers. Merian caught her hands and held them, though she struggled, cursing.

"Lady," Merian said. "Lady, stop."

After a stretching while, Varani yielded. Merian kept a grip on her until she had eased completely, then let her go, but warily. The cage showed no sign of her efforts. The thing of metal spun faster, that was all. The shape within the cage was visible as if through dark glass. The width of the shoulders, the copper brightness of the hair, were unmistakable, though the rest was lost in shadow.

He was alive—just. The king and his guard were dead, the rulers of this world gone away to the war, but the soulless thing that held him cared nothing for that.

It ate at his mind and power, sustaining the life in him when he would have let it go, and bleeding away his magery like a slow wound.

The *Kasar* was a white agony in Merian's hand. She raised it to unlock the bonds of the cage, but hesitated. If he was deeply enslaved, wholly bound to the dark, she would unleash a horror that would put the Sunborn's madness to shame.

Varani read it in her eyes. Merian braced for recrimination, but in some deep corner of her spirit, the lady had found both strength and sanity. "If he must be killed," she said steadily, "I beg your leave to do it. I gave him life. Let me take it away."

"Not yet," said Merian. She could barely speak. The tide of the dark was rising. The magery in her, doubled and trebled, strained to hold together. The effort of sustaining it across the worlds, against the force of the dark, had begun to wear on both the powers within.

The dark, like the cage, had neither mind nor soul. It simply and inexorably was. A mage, even a god, one could fight. But how could any fleshly being stand against the universe itself?

"Light," said Estarion within her. "Fight darkness with light."

"Darkness so vast?" she demanded of him. "Oblivion so absolute?"

"Can you see any other way?" asked Daruya.

"No," said Merian. "But—"

"Tides of light," said Estarion. "If all the mages could be gathered—if he could be freed, and persuaded to lend his power—"

"He is dead or corrupted," said Daruya. "The other mages must be enough."

"The other mages are fighting a war across the face of a world," Merian said.

"Call them in," said Estarion.

"There's no time." Merian swayed as she spoke, buffeted by the force of the dark. It smote the bond that joined the three of them, and battered the edges of the light. The war was a bloody confusion; the lords had rallied, and the armies of freed slaves were flagging, their numbers terribly depleted, their makeshift weapons broken or lost. She could feel their despair in her skin, in the outer reaches of her magery.

With no though at all, she set the *Kasar* to the cage. Its cold metal resisted, but Sun's fire was stronger than any work of hands. The whirring thing spun faster, faster, until it was a blur. It burst asunder in a flash of blinding light. In the sudden and enormous silence, the bars of the cage drew in upon themselves. The shell of glass crumbled into the sand from which it was made.

The captive lay on a bier within, robed in darkness. No breath stirred. His eyes were open, empty of light. His flesh was cold.

His mother breathed warmth upon him. She gave him light; she poured out her own life to feed his. Merian laid her hands over Varani's, not to stop her, but to give her what strength there was to spare.

It might be madness. She could find no light in him. They had taken his eyes, his life, his spirit. There might be nothing left of him at all. But she could not stop herself. She was corrupted, maybe; enspelled. It mattered nothing. There was no hope. The light could not win this war. Not without all the power that they could bring to bear.

THIRTY-NINE

DAROS SWAM UP OUT OF DEEP WATER. HE LEFT THE ARMS OF MOTHER NIGHT and drifted through stars, drawn inexorably upward.

The thing that he had fled, the ceaseless, whispering temptation, had faded greatly, but it was not gone. It had set in his bones. It murmured through his walls and barriers; it thrummed in the stones of the dark world.

Darkness and corruption. Doom and damnation. He dived back into oblivion, but strong hands held him up. He struggled; he fought. They would not let go. They were too many, too strong.

They wrenched him out of darkness and into searing, agonizing light. He twisted, gasping, biting back the cry. The taste of blood filled his mouth: he had bitten his tongue.

Something hard and cold clasped his face. He lay in blessed dimness. His eyes were shielded. He looked into faces recognizable even to what his sight had become. Mages: Kalyi, Urziad, a stranger or two. Merian. And—

He could flee, but there was nowhere to run. He could not hide. She had seen— she knew—

"Later," his mother said. Her voice was taut with pain. "Help us. The dark—"

The dark was rising. A great hunger was in it, a craving for the blood and bones of living worlds. It beckoned to him, whispering, tempting. He would be its greatest servant, its most dearly beloved. The light was bitter pain. Darkness was sweet; was blessed. It would embrace him and make him its own. He would be the great lord, the emperor of the night. All worlds would bow before him.

"Indaros!"

The light of the Sun's child was bitter beyond endurance. She was made of light; filled with it, brimming over. She touched him with it; he gasped. She, merciless, gripped tighter. "Remember," Merian said fiercely. "Remember what you are!"

Doomed. Damned. Lost to darkness.

"Indaros."

Foolish child. Did she imagine that she could bind him with that name? In the darkness, all names were taken away.

"Indaros!"

It struck like a scorpion whip. It seared him with light and filled his veins with fire. It shot him like an arrow, full into the heart of the dark.

He laughed. Death, had he yearned for? Here was the death of the shooting star: pure glory. He was a conflagration across the firmament, a stream of fire in the face of the night.

The dark fought back, thrusting again and again into his heart. Its whisper rose to a roar. Death, oblivion, annihilation—the surcease of purest nothingness.

Estarion could not hold. It was too far, the dark too deep. The weight of flesh dragged at him. If he could but cast it off, he would be free. He could fight untrammeled.

There was the answer to every riddle, the key to every door. Cast off the flesh; be pure light. Be magic bare, untainted by mortal substance. Become the light, and so embrace the dark, and swallow it as it had swallowed light.

The flesh disliked that thought intensely. Foolish flesh.

"Great-grandfather." Merian was in his thoughts as he was in hers, interwoven with them. "I'm in the center. Your heir behind me, my heir before me—I'm unnecessary. I stand in the heart of the dark world. If I let go—if I loose the fire—all of it will end."

"And you," he said. "You will end, too."

"I don't matter. I'll be in the light."

"No," said Estarion. The truth unfolded in him, in glory and splendor. What he was; what he was meant for. Why the gods had brought him to the land of the river and set him on the far side of the dark. He understood at last why he had been moved to surrender the key of his life to Seti-re. If he had not so divided his soul, the flesh would have bound him too tightly; he could not have escaped, whole and free. That surrender, that bit of folly, would save them all.

He was not afraid. There was a strange, aching joy in it.

Tanit—Menes—

If he did not do this thing, there would be no world for them to live in, no sun to warm them, no life to live to its fulfillment. The dark would rule. The worlds would crumble into ash.

Merian was still rebelling, still insistent, and Daruya beyond her, for once remembering her headlong youth. "Empress," he said to them, "and empress who will be. Rule well. Remember me."

They babbled in protest. He took no notice. The dark gaped to swallow them all.

Someone stood at the gate of it, a lone still figure, eyes full of darkness but heart blooming suddenly with light. Daros had lit the spark. Estarion fanned it into flame.

The young fool tried to thrust him aside; to take the glory for himself. But Estarion was too strong for that. He eased the boy gently out of the gate. The fire was in him now, consuming him. The pain of it was exquisite. It seared away the flesh; let go the constraints of living existence.

Great blazing wings unfurled. He was a bird of flame, soaring up into the darkness. Song poured out of him: the morning hymn to the Sun that every priest in his empire sang at the coming of every morning; that he had sung to his son in the land of the river, and so consecrated him to the god his forefather.

It was pure adoration; pure light. Pure joy. Freedom beyond imagining—glory, splendor. Beauty unveiled.

Dawn broke over the dark world: true dawn, the rising of the sun above the king's citadel. The last slaves of the darkness burned and died. The armies of the Sun stood blinking in the light, bloodied, battered, but victorious.

FORTY

NO LIGHT CAME THROUGH WINDOWLESS STONE, AND YET MERIAN FELT IT like a wash of warmth over her skin. The threefold power that had been within her was gone. She was herself again, separate. Her mother blessed her with startling sweetness before slipping away out of this world. Estarion . . .

The name called forth a vision of singing light: a bird of flame soaring up to heaven. In that death was no oblivion. He was gone from all the worlds—and yet a part of every one, embodied in the suns that shone upon them, and the stars that brought beauty to the night. There was no grief, no loss. Only joy.

She laughed, there in that dark place, even though she wept. How like Estarion to find a way out of the world that none had ever ventured.

She came back to herself to find her mages staring at her, standing half-stunned amid the slain. Only Varani had forgotten her existence. She knelt beside her son. He was conscious, but barely. Flickers of flame ran over his body, tongues of fire born of the power that was in him. It fed on the darkness inside him, burning deep, searing all of it away.

Merian knelt across from Varani. "He did it," she said. "He opened the gate of the light."

Varani's eyes were burning dry. "Yes, he redeemed himself. Now he'll die. May I have your leave to go, to take his body back to Han-Gilen?"

"He won't die," Merian said. "I won't let him."

"Do you have that power? Even you, Sunlady?"

"No," said Merian. "But he does." She laid her hand over his heart. At her touch, the garment that had covered him shredded and frayed, falling away. It was woven of the dark; it could not bear the touch of the Sun.

His skin felt strange: now burning cold, now searing hot. His heart was beating too fast almost to sense, fluttering like a bird's. It could not go on: man's heart was not meant for such a thing. A little longer, and it would burst asunder.

Light was her substance. The Sun was in her blood. Yet she was not purely a lightmage. The dark was in her, soft and deep—not the dark that had devoured the stars, but the softness of a summer night, the sweet coolness of evening after the heat of the day, the blessing of clean water on flesh burned by the sun.

She gave him that blessing. She cooled the fire that consumed him; she softened the dark with light, and made the light gentle, easing the torment of body and spirit. His heart slowed. He drew a long deep breath, and then another.

She slipped the shield from his eyes. They had squeezed tight shut, in horror of the light. She brushed her fingers across them. "Look at me," she said.

With an effort that was almost a convulsion, he opened his eyes. Darkness coiled in them, writhed and melted and was gone. He looked into her face, and saw as a mortal man could see, by the plain light of day.

She looked up herself, in astonishment. The roof of the tower was gone, vanished like the darkness in him. Clear sky arched overhead; a sun shone in it, undimmed by cloud. Her eyes returned to Daros. He lay in the light, bathing in it. With no thought at all, she kissed him, tasting on his cheeks the salt of tears.

"I'm dreaming you," he said. "I must be. The emperor, the dark, this light—it can't be real."

"It's very real," she said.

She helped him to sit up. She would have reckoned that enough, but he insisted on trying to rise, though he did it in a drunken stagger. She braced him with her shoulder. His mother, to both their surprise, bolstered him on the other side.

Little by little he steadied. When he essayed a step, his knees did not buckle too badly.

By the time they reached the door, he was almost supporting his own weight. Merian contemplated the long stair in something like despair. She could not lift him down it: her power was too weak. It would come back, but not soon enough.

But one power was always hers, no matter how weak she was. The Gate inside her was free again, with no darkness to bind it. She could not pass from world to world, not yet; but from citadel to plain, that she could do. The others linked their magery with hers and followed, a skein of Gatemages dropping out of air at Perel's feet.

The battle was over. Mages and soldiers of the Sun moved among the slain. Parties of soldiers and freed slaves had begun to clear the field. Tents were up, and the wounded limping or being carried to them.

Perel stood with the commander of the Olenyai and the general of the armies, looking out from a hilltop over the field. Merian and the rest emerged from the Gate just below them.

Perel was in motion almost before they touched the ground, leaping toward Merian, catching her as she fell. She beat him off with fierce impatience, thrusting him toward Daros. "Forget me! Help him!"

But Daros alone of them all was solid on his feet, oblivious to any of them, staring at the aftermath of battle. He did not seem aware that he was naked, or that the air, though sunlit, was chill. She began to wonder, with sinking heart, if the light had taken more of him than the dark that had lodged in his soul; if his mind was gone, too, burned away by the cleansing fire.

He took no notice of Perel at all. But Merian he did see as she scrambled herself up and came round to face him, gripping his arms, shaking him. It was like shaking a stone pillar: he never shifted.

His eyes were clear. He recognized her, though he frowned slightly, as if even yet he did not believe that she was real.

She wrapped her cloak about them both. That woke memory; he started slightly, and stared harder. "I remember . . ."

"We're not dreamwalking," she said. "Not any longer. This is true. It's over. The dark is gone. The war has ended. We can go home again."

"Home." A gust of laughter escaped him, almost like a gasp of pain. "Where is that, for me?"

"With me," she said. "Wherever I go."

"You don't want me. After what I did—"

"You were the key to the gate," she said. "Every world should honor you."

He shook his head, but he was wiser than to keep protesting. She turned in his arms. Everyone was watching them: the lords and mages on the hilltop, the soldiers and slaves below. "This is my lord," she said to them, "my prince and consort. But for him, this victory would never have been."

There was a long pause. Just before she would have burst out in anger at their discourtesy, first Varani, then Perel and the lord of the Olenyai, and after them the rest, went down in homage. All of them: every living being on that field.

It was no more than his due, though he hardly knew where to look. For a prince, he had precious little sense of his own importance.

"You'll learn," she said.

"Is that a command, my lady?"

"It is, my lord," said Merian.

A smile touched the corner of his mouth. It was a frail shadow of his old insouciant grin, but it would do, for the moment. "I have no gift for obedience."

"But love—you have a great gift for that."

"Ah: I'm an infamous libertine. Are you sure you want that beside you for the rest of your days?"

"How many women have you lain with since you met me?"

He had lost the stain of the sun that had so darkened him in the land of the river: a blush was clear to see, turning his cheeks to ruddy bronze. "None," he said indistinctly; then clearer: "None at all. But, lady, while I dreamed of you, I never—"

"Our daughter is in your father's care," she said.

She felt the shock in his body. "Our—"

"It was real," she said. "Every moment of it. The proof is in Han-Gilen."

"Han-Gilen? Not Starios?"

She nodded.

"Why—" He shook himself. "Questions later. And answers—many of them. But now, the war. There are still dark lords alive. If you would have me find them—"

"You need do nothing but go home and rest," she said.

"Not until it's over," he said. "All of it. My lords, if someone could find clothes for me, and boots—boots would be welcome—I'll begin the hunt."

"You will hunt nothing but sleep," Merian said firmly.

But he was equally firm in resistance. "I belonged to them. They're in my bones. Give me men, mages, a mount—I'll find them all and bring them back to you."

She searched his face, and the mind behind it, which he made no effort to conceal from her. The anger in him was deep and abiding; but he was sane. He was not wild with vengeance.

"Bring them to me," she said, "and I will sentence them. My lords, you will obey him as you would obey me. Whatever he asks for, see that he has it."

There were no objections, spoken or unspoken, save one. "You do insist on this?" his mother asked him.

He would not meet her gaze. He had shrunk, all at once, into a sulky child.

She gripped his arms. One could see, watching them, whence came his height and breadth of shoulder; she was a strong woman, in body as in mind. Her eyes burned on his face. "Do as you must," she said, "and do it well. You are worthy of your lineage. Though perhaps," she said, "your parents are not worthy of you."

That astonished him. He stared at her, his sulkiness forgotten. "How can you say that? I have never been—"

"You have redeemed yourself many times over. Whereas we have acquitted ourselves poorly in every respect. If you can find it in you to pardon us—"

He silenced her with a finger to her lips. "Mother, don't. Don't talk like that.

Let's forgive each other; let's forget if we can. There's a long stretch of darkness behind us, and, one hopes, a long stretch of light ahead. Maybe we can learn to be proper kin to one another."

"I can hope for that," she said.

He smiled, bowed and kissed her hands. "Then may I have your blessing?"

"You may have it," she said. Her voice was steady, but her eyes were brimming. She drew his head down and set a kiss on his forehead, then let him go. "You honor us all, my child. You give us great pride."

As long as the fight had been and as weary as they all were, the sheer number of those who came to Daros' muster was astonishing. He had his pick of warriors and of mages; and among them two whom he had thought never to see again.

Neither Menkare nor Nefret had taken physical harm from the battle. Their power was intact, indeed stronger than ever. They had been tempered like steel: forged in fire. They looked long and hard at him, as everyone did now; but like the others, they eased visibly after a while.

"You look," said Nefret, "as if you've been burned clean."

"That is precisely how it feels," said Daros.

She clasped him tight, squeezing the breath out of him, but there were no words left in her. It was Menkare who said, "We mourned you for dead. Thank the greater gods that we grieved too soon."

"I am rather grateful myself," Daros said. "And you? Are you of a mind to go hunting with me?"

"Rats or lions?" Menkare asked.

"Rats in the barley," said Daros.

"I'm in the mood to hunt rats," said Nefret.

"And I," Menkare said. "Pity we have no cats here; they're the best hunters of all."

"You are my cats," Daros said, "my mages of the river. Come, hunt with me."

They grinned at that; Nefret's pointed face and small white teeth were not at all unlike a cat's. With a much lighter heart, Daros turned to the task of choosing the rest of his hunters.

The hunt was not long, as rat-hunts went. Those lords whose slaves had not turned on them and rent them in pieces had gone to ground, away from hunters and the horror of the sun and, come the night, the stars and the dance of a dozen little moons about this barren and stony world.

Daros tracked them by the shudder under his skin. Nefret with her gift of prescience was even better at it than he, and Menkare was blindingly quick in the capture. It grieved them somewhat that they could not kill what they hunted, as it would have grieved the little fierce cats of their own world, but they submitted to the will of the gods—and most especially the goddess of gold, as they called Merian.

They were enthralled with her. It gave them no end of pleasure to discover—and not from Daros—that their lord was her consort; that there was an heir, a child so like her father that no one in the world of the gods could deny her parentage.

That was a thought so strange, so patently impossible, that Daros could hardly think it at all. That Merian loved him, that she wanted him, was shock enough; he doubted it more often than he believed it. But that their dreamwalking had brought forth a child—he could not make himself believe it. He kept his mind on his hunt instead, and left the rest for when the hunt was over.

He hunted through a chain of lesser Gates. Merian and her mages had closed the Worldgates to prevent an escape, but the Gates within this world were open. There were many; most had the soullessness of the dark lords' devices. Those he broke as he found them, scattered them into the elements from which they were made. After the first three or four or five, mages ran ahead of him, seeking out these false Gates and destroying them, while he hunted through Gates that had no need of forged metal or trapped magic.

The lords were barred from both. Their power was broken. The Mage was dead, its prison destroyed in the blaze of light that had overcome the dark. Their devices of metal were only metal now; the lords had no magic with which to bring them to life.

Daros still could not think too much on these matters. The memory of the cage was too strong, the horror of it too close to his spirit. The hunt was his release, the cleansing of his mind and soul.

The last nest was the worst. They had come full circle, back to the citadel and the deep halls beneath, dungeons that descended into the bowels of the earth. There the last of the lords had barricaded themselves with walls of stone and steel. And there, at last, were the women: blind, gravid things locked in cells like the children of bees. Whether they were born or made so, he did not know or care to know. But it made him all the more grimly determined to expunge this race from the worlds.

Daros had to go down into the dark from which he had so barely escaped. The mages and the warriors of the Sun brought light with them, but Menkare and Nefret knew the same horror that he knew: the horror of return to endless night.

They did not flinch from the long descent. He could hardly be less brave than the mages whom he had made. He steadied his mind and firmed his steps and led them all into the darkness.

One weapon he had which he had not been able to use during his long deception: the flame of his power, which was born of the sun. He clothed himself in it, and sent it before him, a wall of light. He struck their wall of stone and steel and shattered it.

They came out fighting. Desperation made them vicious; they laughed at wounds, and courted death. They would take Daros and his hunters with them if they could.

Daros had had enough of fighting. He struck them down with a mighty blow of power, laid them low without ever drawing his sword. It was yet another broken law, he supposed; mages had so many. But he was long past caring. He gathered them up and bound them, and flung them through the Gate within him, on their faces before the princess-heir where she sat in judgment.

FORTY-ONE

MERIAN HAD LONG SINCE LEARNED TO BE SURPRISED BY NOTHING DAROS did. Daros was a law unto himself; there would never be any changing it.

Even so, the arrival of a score of dark lords, beaten unconscious by a stroke of power, was more than slightly startling. Outrageous, some of her mother's generals declared. They were not mages, but they were most careful of mages' laws—both those which they understood and those which they did not.

It happened that she was judging captives whom Daros had brought in in the days before. They would not use the citadel; that would come down, she had decided, and the slave-cities would be razed, and new cities built for and by the slaves who still wished to live on this world. Her place of judgment was the plain on which the battle for the citadel had been fought, just outside the camp that her armies had made. Many of them were present even so late in the judging, watching and listening as she heard such defenses as could be offered.

There were not many, but she heard them all, over and over again. She was putting off the decision, and avoiding the sentence that must be levied. There truly was no choice. Death for them all, every one. Nothing that they had said had persuaded her to let them live.

And now they were all captured, all brought before her, and Daros standing above the last of them in borrowed armor. She still was not accustomed to the changes that this world had wrought in him. He was thinner but no narrower: he had grown into a man since she first saw him, an idle drunken princeling in the ridiculous height of fashion. His face had lost its prettiness but gained in beauty. Time and pain had drawn it fine; the smile was never so quick as it had been, and the expression into which it had settled was somber—a prince's face, lordly and stern.

He was distracting her now with his presence. She made herself focus on the prisoners, all of them, conscious and unconscious. Those who were awake were sour with scorn, looking with contempt on the beasts that had conquered them. To them, all not of their blood kin were no more than animals; slaves, bred for servitude.

She rose from the seat of judgment. "These are all of them?" she asked Daros.

He nodded. He had a tight-drawn look, as if he had snapped, but somehow put himself together again. "All but the women," he said, "but those are no more threat to us than a nest of maggots."

She raised a brow at the thickness of disgust in his voice, but left it until she had dealt with the men of that nation. "Wake them," she said to him.

He bared his teeth. It was not a smile. His power lashed out, sharp as the crack of a whip. Every one of his newest captives snapped erect.

The emotion with which all of them regarded him was not entirely or even mostly contempt. It was hate. He basked in it; courted it. He dared them to turn against him.

"I have heard all that I have need to hear," she said through that fog of loathing. "My judgment is made. My sentence is—"

"Lady," said Daros. He did not speak loudly, but his voice carried without effort across the field of the judging. "Lady, may I speak?"

Can I prevent you?

She did not say it aloud, but with him she had no need. The twitch of his smile, though slight, was genuine.

"Lady, you choose death. I can well see why: it would seem to be inevitable. And yet, will you give them what they long for above all else? Will you offer them free passage into oblivion?"

"You would have me keep them alive?" she asked him. "Are you so eager to fight this war again?"

"Not at all," said Daros. "But, lady, death is a reward. Shouldn't your sentence be a punishment?"

"There is no punishment great enough for what they have done."

"Maybe not," Daros said, "but I can think of one that they would find rather painful."

She raised a brow. "And that is?"

"Some of their slaves—born here, or bred of worlds that were destroyed after their capture—have expressed a desire to stay here. Yes? Give the lords to them— men, women, children born and not yet born. Let them be slaves to their own slaves."

"I had thought of that," Merian said. "But if they rise again, if they find a way to restore their rule—who knows what devices might be hidden here, or what powers they might call on? They escaped our world once, and even stripped of magic, still succeeded in destroying a myriad worlds before they could be stopped. I will not risk such a thing. Not again."

"Wise," he said. "Merciful, in its way. Even just. But I am not in a merciful mood. I would rather they live, and live in suffering, than find relief in death. Unless . . ."

She waited. All of them did, even the fallen lords: and that was tribute to the power he had over them.

"Give them to healer-mages," he said. "Let them be made new—the women and children most of all, but the men, too. Set the seeds of light in them, nurture it, and let it grow. Teach them to be truly human: to know love as well as hate, awe as well as scorn, humility as well as arrogance. Give them hearts, and let them know the fullness of what they have done. Give them guilt and shame—even redemption, if such is possible."

The silence was absolute. Even the wind had ceased to blow. It was a terrible, a wonderful solution, but there was no mercy in it whatsoever.

"And if they can't be made new?" Merian asked, since no one else seemed to have power to speak.

"Then do as you will," said Daros.

She nodded slowly. "I will grant you this," she said, "as a gift to you. On one condition."

He stiffened ever so slightly, but his voice was as calm as ever. "And that is?"

"That you oversee the healing and dispose of those who have been healed, if any of them can be. Likewise those who cannot—their deaths must be at your command."

He bowed low. It was a prince's bow, and a prince's face that he raised to her. "As you will, my lady."

"You will not leave this world until it is done," she said. "It will be years; it might be a lifetime. Can you bear that?"

"I understand," he said, "and I accept it."

"Then let it be done," she said.

The camp's servants had pitched a tent for Daros among the rest of his hunters, between the edge of the camp and the camp in which the captives remained under guard. He did not indulge in disappointment. He had no right, after all, to expect anything of Merian, still less to be housed in her own tent—especially after he had undercut her judgment. It was generous enough of her to let him lay sentence on the dark lords; he could hardly ask her to admit him to her bed as well. He had the rank and the authority of a consort, and that, as useful as it was, was more than he deserved.

The tent was luxurious, for a tent; it was suited to his newly royal rank. It even had a pair of attendants: Menkare and Nefret, who greeted him with expressions that made him ask, "What did you do to the servants?"

"We let them live," Nefret said, even as Menkare said, "We bribed them to find other masters."

They stopped and glared at each other. Nefret won the silent fight; she said, "We belong with you."

"Your people," said Daros, "the slaves whom you freed—they need you. Whereas I—"

They've been seen to," Nefret said. "While we were hunting, they were sent home, all of them—they all wanted to go. There's none left here."

"Then you can go home," Daros said. "There's no need to stay with me. These are my people who are here; my kin, my own kind."

Her brows drew together. "Are you telling us that you don't want us any more? That we're not gods, and not worthy to be seen in your presence?"

"No!" He had almost shouted the word. Menkare winced, but she gazed at him steadily.

"Don't you want to go home?" he demanded of her. "Don't you want to see the river again, and go fishing in the reeds, and live among your own people?"

"My people are dead," she said. "Raiders killed them all. You are my people now. My god, if it pleases you better."

"You know I am not a god," he said.

"Close enough," she said.

"Nefret," he said. "You honor me, and greatly. But I won't have you stay just because you have nowhere else to go. Waset would take you, and give you great rank and worship, after what you have done for your world. So would any city along the river, and many a king. You're a god in your own right. You don't need me to give you a place in the worlds."

"I know that," she said. "I want to stay. Your lady, the golden one—she is even more wonderful than you. I want to see the worlds, and walk under strange suns, and know other rivers than the river of the black land."

"We can go back, you know," said Menkare. "Even if we serve you, if you give us leave—we can go home to visit, and if we're needed. There's no dark any longer. The Gates are open. The worlds are free again."

Daros blinked. He honestly had not thought of that. He had been too intent on the fact of their exile; but they did not see it as such at all.

"And your people?" he asked them. "What if they need you to stay?"

"Then we'll stay," said Menkare. "But we got on rather well without magic before the dark came. Now that the dark is gone, I expect the world will go on as it always has. Magic is for gods, my lord. Mortals do well enough without."

"And you? Are you god or mortal?"

"Why, neither, my lord. I'm something between." Menkare smiled suddenly, and patted Daros on the shoulder. "There—don't look so stunned. Do I look as if I'm suffering? It's glorious, this gift you've given—even at the price you laid on it. I've no desire to give it back."

Daros, who had been about to ask that precise question, shut his mouth with a click.

"My lord," said Nefret, reading him as effortlessly as she ever had, "we stay with you because we love you—and because you so clearly need looking after. Would you even know where to find dinner, let alone remember to eat it?"

He bridled at that. "I'm not that helpless! I've fended for myself before. What makes you think I can't do it now?"

"Princes can't," she said with calm conviction. "It's not allowed. You are a prince of princes. You must have attendants—it's required. Wouldn't you rather have us than a flock of strangers?"

"I'm not so sure," he muttered.

She laughed, which was cruel, but bracing, too. "Of course you would. Now stop your nonsense and let us get this armor off you. Has it even *been* off since you put it on?"

"I don't—"

Her nose wrinkled. "Obviously it hasn't. Menkare, find someone who can put together a bath for him."

Menkare was already on his way. Daros sighed and submitted. That was a prince's lot, always: to suffer the tyranny of servants. And these—yes, he would admit it to himself: he was glad that they had stayed. They were more than servants. They were friends.

Still, he said, "If you ever grow homesick, even for a moment, I'm sending you back. Is that understood?"

"Perfectly," Nefret said without a spark of honest submission—and no glimmer of expectation that he would do as he threatened, either.

Daros lay in his soft and princely bed, scrubbed until he stung. The borrowed armor had not fit as well as it might; there were galls and bruises and a boil or two, at which Nefret had been suitably outraged. It was all gone now, and a light warm coverlet over him, sparing his hurts as much as it might.

He should have been dead asleep, but his stubborn mind persisted in keeping him awake. Even closing out all that he had done and would do, he still could not force himself to sleep.

A warm presence fitted itself to his back. Light hands stroked him where it did not hurt overmuch; kisses brushed his nape and shoulders and wandered round to the freshly shaven curve of his jaw. Fingers ran through his cropped hair, ruffling such of it as there was.

"This will not be allowed to endure," Merian's voice said in his ear.

He turned in her arms. She was both smiling and frowning—smiling at him, frowning at what the lords had done to him. "What, I'm not pretty any longer?" he asked her.

"You aren't," she said. "That's all gone. But beauty—you have more of that than ever. Will you promise to grow your hair again?"

"If you'll let me cut it now and then."

"Now and then," she said, "I'll consider it."

"You do mean it, then. What you said. That I'm your consort."

"You doubted it?"

"I don't know what I thought," he said. "This tent—it's not—"

"I need a place to hold councils and be royal. You need a place to rest. As do I. Would you object too strongly if I did my sleeping here with you?"

His heart swelled. He could barely speak. "I would be somewhat . . . dismayed . . . if you did not."

She smiled. The pure golden warmth of that smile nearly reduced him to tears. But those were all burned out of him; he did not know when they would come back.

"This match is approved of," she said. "My mother has no objections. You know that yours does not. The breeding, as they both say, is impeccable."

"My father? *He* approves?" Daros shook his head. "Ah, but he would. Whatever he thinks of me—"

"He loves you," she said. "He grieves for you. He's glad beyond measure that you are alive and well and proving your worth in the worlds."

"And even if he were not, he would still be enormously pleased. Once again at last, Han-Gilen and the Sunborn's line unite in marriage."

"He is not as cold as that," Merian said, "and I am not in the mood for a quarrel. You will have to face him eventually: I gave our daughter into his care until the war was over."

His breath hissed between his teeth. "Our— Tell me. Tell me how it happened. Why you never told me."

"You know how it happened," she said. "You were there, dreamwalking with me. I never told you because there was never time. You were lost to the dark not long after I knew it myself. I didn't believe it, either, not until there was no escaping the truth."

"Is that why?" he asked. "Did you name me your consort because it was the honorable thing? Because a child needs a father?"

"Among other reasons," she said, "yes. But when I chose you, there was no such constraint. I wanted you long before I could admit it to myself. When I understood what our dreamwalking had done, I had already decided that if you came back, if you were alive and still had your wits, I would take you as my lover."

"But not—"

"I'm Sun-blood," she said. "My first lover would inevitably be the father of my heir. You know that, surely."

"Yes, but—"

"If you don't want the rank or the marriage," she said, "I won't force it on you. You will always be Elian's father. I will not—"

"Elian? Her name is Elian?"

"It seemed appropriate," she said.

He did not know whether to bellow at her or kiss her. Elian had been a princess of Han-Gilen long ago; she had loved and in time married the Sunborn, and borne his heir. She was Merian's foremother and his own kinswoman. It was a name of great honor in both their houses.

"Let me see her," he said: peremptorily, he supposed, but he could not help it.

She took no offense. She opened her mind and showed them the child whom he had seen in dream: the child with his face, whose ancestry none could mistake.

"It was true," he said in wonder. "All of it—all true."

"As true as life itself," she said. "Still, if you don't want the marriage, the child is still yours. I'll not forbid you your share in her raising."

"You'd trust *me* to raise a child?"

Her smile grew wicked. "There's no preceptor so strict as a rake reformed, and none so stern as a father who spent his youth in debauching other men's daughters."

"*Ai!*" It was a cry of pure pain, but laughter broke through it. "Lady, you wound me to the heart."

"Good," she said: "you have a heart to wound."

"After all, it seems I do." He paused. She made excellent use of the silence, but he was not ready yet to give himself up to it. "What you've sentenced me to, this task here—it may be long. Are you telling me that when it's done, my exile is ended? I can go home?"

"You can return to the service to which I swore you," she said. "Have you forgotten that? I never have."

"This is all part of—"

She nodded.

"Lady," he said. "You've no need to bind me. I will belong to you if you will it or no, with oaths or without them, wed or unwed, sworn or unsworn, for as long as there is breath in my body."

"That's an oath," she said. "That's a binding."

"Yes," he said. "So it is."

"Forever and ever?"

She slapped him hard. It struck the breath out of him. "No evasions," she said. "And no grinning at me, either. This is a true binding. Once it's made, you'll not be escaping it."

"Should I want to?"

"Not while I live," she said.

"Even though I am hopelessly disobedient, reckless, feckless, headstrong, and impossibly insolent?"

"Even so," she said.

FORTY-TWO

THE LORD SERAMON WAS DEAD.

Tanit had known in her heart when he bade her farewell that it was not a simple battle he went to, nor a plain rite of the temple. She had her duties, her people to protect, her armies to muster and send forth; that night was most terrible of all, the worst since the shadow came to the black land. Yet the raids stopped abruptly toward midnight. The darkness lingered, but the enemy turned their backs even where they were winning the battle, left captives and carts of grain from the storehouses, and vanished into the air.

It was not over then. Not for her lord, though the world was almost frighteningly quiet. She endured it as long as she could; saw to the wounded and the merely terrified; set her house in order, and last of all before she left it, lingered in the nursery where Menes lay asleep.

He was breathing—she assured herself of that. He dreamed: his brows knit, his lips pursed, his fists clenched and unclenched. Almost she fancied that she could see a play of delicate flame over his skin, but when she peered closer, there was nothing.

She kissed his brow, smoothed his thick dark curls, and left him with tearing reluctance. He was safe: he had his nurse, his guards, the young godling whom the Lord Re-Horus had made before he vanished into the dark. All prayers and protections were laid on him, and the gods' power, and guardian spells wrought by both of the gods who had come from beyond the horizon to tarry in Waset.

The one who remained lay in the temple. She needed no guide to find him. Her heart knew always where he was.

They had laid him on a bier, surrounded by priests and chanting and the scent of incense. He was alive then, but the spirit in him was far away, lost on the roads of dream.

She knelt beside him. The priests rolled their eyes at her, but none was bold enough to send her away. She made no effort to touch him. It was enough to rest her eyes on the alien beauty of him. Nothing like him was in this world.

How long she knelt there, she did not know. The sun sank slowly toward the western horizon; toward the land of the dead. He never moved, never changed, and yet it seemed to her heart that he sank with the sun: drifted farther and farther away, more and more distant from the flesh that had contained him.

At long last the sun passed out of sight from within the temple. In a little while it would touch the jagged line of cliffs across the river. It was already dark in this room, but a soft glow shone out of the body on the bier, even before the priests lit the lamps at its head and foot.

The glow faded so imperceptibly that she hardly believed it could have existed. But when it was gone, she knew. He was gone. He had flown beyond the horizon, and left his body behind.

She could not find it in her to grieve, not properly, as a wife should when her husband was dead. She laid her hand on his cheek. It was cooling slowly in the heat. She found herself thinking, not of death, but of a nest from which the bird has flown: a bird of light, spreading wings that stretched from horizon to horizon, soaring into the night.

"I told you," she said. "You would leave, and I would be left behind. You never believed me. But I knew."

The priests stared uncomprehending; all but Seti, who though blind had clearer sight than anyone she knew. He was gazing into his private dark, smiling, but as she glanced at him, a slow tear ran down his cheek. "The gods are gone out of the world," he said.

"They live forever beyond the horizon," she said.

"So they do," said Seti, as if he humored a child.

From him she would accept it. She kissed him on the cheek, softly, and said to the priests, "Summon the servants of the dead."

One or two looked as if he would protest, but she was the queen. Under her steady stare, they all bowed and left, all but Seti. He was an untroubling presence; he comforted her with his silence.

She returned to her lord's side. Not even the semblance of life was left in him. She took his hand in hers. It was still supple, but its swift strength was gone. She stroked the long fingers, committing to memory the feel of his skin. It would have to last her for long years, until she saw him again.

She had every intention of doing that. It might be impossible; she did not care. This was the half of her self. She would get it back.

She stayed with him until the servants of the dead came. They wrapped him in white linen, folding it close about his long limbs, and carried him away to their houses on the far side of the river.

Seti left when they left, leaning on the arm of a strong young priest. She sat alone in the flickering lamplight. Slowly it dawned on her: the night was clean. No shadow tainted it. No armies came riding across the river to raid the villages.

There had been respite before, a year and more of it. But this was different. There was no darkness behind the stars; only the night, pure and unsullied. Something about it made her think of her lord: dark beauty with the splendor of a sun in its heart.

She wept then, a little, because she was mortal and she was weak and she yearned for his arms about her and his warm rich voice in her ear. She yearned so strongly that almost—almost—she could have sworn—

"Beloved."

That was his very voice. It lived still inside her. Yet it seemed so real, as if indeed, impossibly, he could be there.

She turned slowly.

He was standing behind her. The light within him was clearly visible. She could not meet his eyes at all, any more than she could stare straight into the sun.

"Dear heart," he said. "What did I promise you?"

"That you would never leave me," she heard herself say. "But—"

"I couldn't keep my body," he said. "There are rules and prices, and that is one of them. But nothing could forbid me to come back to you. That oath I swore, and oaths are sacred. They bind even the gods."

"Even you?"

He seemed bemused. "I suppose I am a god now—truly; not simply a mage from beyond a Gate. I wasn't thinking of that when I did it. There was no other way to kill the dark, except to overwhelm it with light. But to do that, I had to give up whatever mortal substance I had."

His words were profoundly strange, but that was nothing new or remarkable. She reached carefully and touched him.

He was not flesh, no; it felt like holding her hand in sunlight, yet sunlight given shape and form. He moved under her hand. He seemed to breathe, though that might only be habit from his earthly self. She could wrap her arms about him and hold him, and he could complete the embrace. The warmth of it, the sheer white joy, was almost more than she could bear.

A good part of it was his. He had likened his magery once to living with one's skin off. Now his skin was lost altogether.

"I can't stay long," he said. "I can't be with you as I am now, not often; I'm scattered through the worlds, among the chains of Gates. I hold back the dark from all of them. But part of me is always here. It will never leave you. If you need me, or simply want to be with me, look in your heart. You'll find me."

"Always?"

"Always," he said.

"And when I leave this flesh behind? Will I be as you are?"

He ran his finger down her cheek as he had done so often before, a gesture so tender and so familiar that her eyes filled anew with tears. "The greater gods have promised, beloved. When your body has lived out its span, you will come to me. We will never again be parted."

The question that rose in her was inevitable, but far from wise. She did not ask it. The gods knew when she would die. It was not right or proper that she should know. She said instead, "I shall live every day in gladness, and sleep every night in peace, with that before me."

"O marvel among women." He kissed her, long and slow and ineffably sweet. He said no word of farewell, but then he had not left her. Only this semblance was gone. The truth of him, the living essence, lay folded in her heart.

The dawn was coming, bright and free of fear. She wiped away her tears and composed herself. Her son was waking: she felt him within her, close by his father.

She would tarry with him until the day came. Then she would go out, and put on her mask of paint and royal pride, and be queen of her people. They would mourn because the gods had left them, and rejoice because the darkness was gone. She would give them what comfort they needed, and rule them as best she could.

After a while they would forget their grief. Hers was already passing. She must not seem too glad, not yet; none of them would understand. But in her heart, where he was, she could rest in his warmth and be deeply content.

ABOUT THE AUTHOR

Judith Tarr is the author of more than two dozen acclaimed novels, including *Lord of the Two Lands, Throne of Isis, Pillar of Fire,* and *King and Goddess.* A graduate of Yale and Cambridge Universities, she holds degrees in ancient and medieval history, and breeds Lipizzan horses at Dancing Horse Farm, her home in Vail, Arizona.